Frank G. Slaughter

FOUR COMPLETE NOVELS

Frank G. Slaughter

FOUR COMPLETE NOVELS

Doctors' Wives

Surgeon's Choice

Women in White

Sword and Scalpel

AVENEL BOOKS · NEW YORK

Copyright © 1980 by Frank G. Slaughter.

Doctors' Wives copyright © MCMLXVII by Frank G. Slaughter.
Lines from The Jerusalem Bible copyright © MCMLXVI by
Darton, Longman & Todd, Ltd., and Doubleday & Company,
Inc., reprinted by permission of the publisher.
Surgeon's Choice copyright © MCMLXIX by Frank G. Slaughter.
Women in White copyright © MCMLXXIV by Frank G. Slaughter.
Sword and Scalpel copyright © MCMLVII by Frank G. Slaughter.
All rights reserved.

This edition is published by Avenel Books,
distributed by Crown Publishers, Inc.,
by arrangement with Doubleday & Company, Inc.

a b c d e f g h

AVENEL 1980 EDITION

Manufactured in the United States of America

Library of Congress Cataloging in Publication Data

Slaughter, Frank Gill, 1908–
    Four complete novels.

    CONTENTS: Doctors' wives.—Surgeon's choice—
Women in white.—Sword and scalpel.
    I. Title.
PZ3.S63165Fi   [PR3537.L38] 813'.52   80-17743
ISBN: 0-517-322153

CONTENTS

Doctors' Wives

AUTHOR'S NOTE

Quotations identified as "from a medical journal" in the text are from "Psychiatric Illness in the Physician's Wife," American Journal of Pyschiatry, *Vol. 122, pp. 159-163, August 1965, Copyright 1966, American Psychiatric Association. They are used with the kind permission of the editor of the* Journal *and the author of the article, Dr. James L. Evans.*

I first learned of the "iron sludge" technique for treating intracranial aneurysms from an article in the September 26, 1966, issue of Newsweek, *describing the work at the University of California at Los Angeles of Drs. John F. Alksne, Robert Rand and Aaron G. Fingerhut. The brain operation described in the latter part of this novel is a modification of their technique.*

Frank G. Slaughter, M.D.
January 15, 1967

CHAPTER ONE

I

It was shortly after four, when Mabel, the blonde and buxom waitress on the afternoon shift in the Snack Bar across the street from the hospital, went out to sweep the parking space in front of the shop. She'd come on at three and the change from the late summer heat to the air-conditioned interior always made her arthritis painful, so she was glad of an excuse to get out in the warm September air for a few minutes before the five o'clock rush began. The shop, all glass, stainless steel, red-cushioned stools at the counter and booths against the wall, occupied one corner of the Faculty Apartments parking lot. Across the street, above the ambulance unloading ramp, blue neon lights spelled out EMERGENCY ENTRANCE.

Weston University Hospital occupied the entire opposite side of the long block across from the Snack Bar, a mass of buildings with connecting walkways, built of cinder blocks painted white and tall columns of steel-framed windows. On the lunchroom side of North Avenue one end of the block was taken up with the towering building that housed the Faculty Clinic, a privately operated medical group to which much of the medical school faculty belonged. Only about five years old, the clinic had already been enlarged several times and, during the daylight hours, a constant stream of people flowed through its marquee-covered portico at the far corner of the block.

The Faculty Apartments, owned by the university, occupied the entire end of the block, facing west on Weston Boulevard. Diagonally across the street from it, in front of the main entrance to the hospital, stood the housing facilities for married residents, interns and students, consisting of four apartment complexes with an enclosed playground. The main classroom buildings for the medical school were on the opposite corner of Weston Boulevard and North Avenue from married student housing, convenient to the hospital and all parts of the group of buildings that made up Weston University Medical School.

"Where'd you go on your day off yesterday, Mabel?" Abe Fescue, the short-order cook, lounged in the open door of the empty lunchroom, smoking a cigarette that was forbidden inside. A small transistor radio atop the counter, also forbidden when customers were in the shop, filled the air with a rock-and-roll tune.

"On the Parkway," said Mabel. "I like to drive up there this time of the year."

Located in the foothills east of the Great Smoky Mountains, Weston was primarily a manufacturing city. It had become a major medical center when the medical school had opened some fifteen years earlier, quickly outstripping in importance and stature the small, older university of which it was a part. Rogue River curved around the city, with a dam some ten miles to the south forming a lake and a source of hydroelectric power that had made the town a natural location for a major textile operation.

"Fall's comin' early this year," Mabel added. "The leaves are already turnin' up towards the Knob."

"Won't bother me none," said Abe. "Come Thanksgiving, I'll be heading south for Miami."

"You short-order cooks are like birds, always flying north or south. I suppose you'll lose all your money at the tracks again this winter and come borrowin' from me next spring like always, so you can pay your rent the first month."

"This is going to be my best winter." Abe was a thin man of indeterminate age. His face was scarred by acne from childhood, and the inevitable tattos, relic of Navy service, almost covered his upper arms.

"Why d'you stay around here winters anyway, Mabel? You could make twice as much in tips working in South Florida and still get your old job back in the spring, when the weather turns warm again. Good waitresses are like short-order cooks; they can get a job anywhere."

"I like it here." Mabel looked with affection at the neon lights of the emergency entrance and the towering walls of the main hospital. "When I was a little girl, I had my heart set on bein' a nurse; then I married a louse and by the time I got rid of him, it was too late. I've got a lot of friends in the hospital, and workin' here, I keep track of most everything that's goin' on over there. Makes me feel like I'm part of it."

"You own some of it, too, from all those checks you've picked up for students that couldn't pay," said Abe. "Don't be a sucker all your life, Mabel."

The waitress took no offense. She didn't expect anyone to understand that the hospital and medical school staff were just like a family she'd never had. Coming and going through the years with their waffles, hamburgers, steaks, hashed browns, scrambled eggs, and coffee, she had heard all their troubles and their joys. Sometimes, when a student was broke and hungry, she paid for the food checks herself, and maybe she did lose a little that way—she'd never stopped to figure it up and wasn't going to. Helping them gave her the feeling of being a part of the exciting world of medicine, a sense of being needed she had never found until she'd come to the Snack Bar when it had opened nearly ten years before.

The sweeping finished, Mabel lit a cigarette of her own, tossing the match into the gutter. It was only the first of September and still warm, but there was a faint touch of fall in the air. Up on the Parkway, where she'd driven for a few miles the afternoon before, it had been a lot cooler, a tangible promise of what was soon to come.

In the haze of the late afternoon sunlight, the mountains were a bluish-tinted backdrop for the green-clad foothills to the east and the valleys between, with the fields of corn brown and sere as they waited for the harvesters. Later, when winter finally came, the mountains would take on a mantle of snow and the students would be driving up on weekends for skiing and fraternity house parties.

Down here in the valleys, though, it was still warm enough for water skiing—by the hardy. As Mabel smoked, she saw a girl skier in a bright yellow bikini flash across the lower end of North Avenue, where it dead-ended into Riverfront Drive, a block below the intersection of Weston Boulevard.

"Looks mighty quiet over there." Abe nodded toward the hospital. "You can hardly believe all hell could break loose any minute in that emergency room."

"Won't be much goin' on today, a lot of the doctors take Wednesday off to play golf. Besides, only the first-year students are in school yet. The rest won't come in for another week."

"Maybe business will pick up then and we'll have a chance to get a bonus on weekends." Abe tossed his cigarette butt into the gutter with a flip of his thumb. "Guess I better get some tomatoes sliced for the five o'clock rush. You coming in?"

"Not yet. I want to enjoy the fresh air awhile longer. Hope Jeff Long and that little Monroe girl come by tonight when she goes off duty. She's had enough trouble—with that skunk of a husband leaving her as soon as he was able to support himself and now her little boy havin' trouble. Janet deserves somebody nice like Dr. Long."

"There you go with another of them soap operas you're always dreaming up."

"What's wrong with soap operas?" Mabel's Irish temper had been stirred at last. "Some of the best people listen to 'em. The last time I was through the clinic, I was talking to Mrs. Weston—"

"The D.A.'s wife?"

"Yeah. She listens all the time. I could name you a lot of other important people who do, too."

"Give me a ball game any day—or a horse race."

"Go on inside and slice your tomatoes. You got no feelin' for the real things of life."

"And me married four times?" Abe grinned. "I could write a book about what you call the real things of life—nagging, bitching, sleeping around, having abortions. Who wants 'em?"

The door closed behind him as he went inside and Mabel could see him moving toward the end of the counter, where a door gave access to the cooking area behind it. The charcoal grill was already hot, waiting for the procession of hamburgers, chopped sirloins and tenderloins that would pass across it during the next five or six hours. The round metal rings in which the hashed browns were cooked on the flat metal grill with the gas flames beneath were stacked neatly at one side, a package of eggs occupied the shelf above, and the drawer beneath was filled with loaves of bread and packages of rolls sprinkled with sesame seeds.

A brief lull would occur around ten, if they were lucky, giving them time to clean up before they were swamped again by a flood of nurses going off duty at eleven, meeting interns and residents there for a brief rendezvous before checking in at the Nurses' Home on the other side of the hospital block.

Halfway around the end of the counter, Mabel saw Abe stop suddenly and turn quickly to push open the outer door. "Hey Mabel!" he called. "Some doctor just shot his wife."

"Who was it?" The waitress covered the distance to the door at a trot.

"Didn't get the name. The announcer broke into the music and I knew you'd want to hear it."

"I hope it's nobody at the hospital. Quick! Turn the radio up!"

The cook grabbed the small radio and twisted the volume knob.

"Now see what you did!" Mabel cried, when it came off in his hand, ending the broadcast in a squawk. "How are we going to know who it was?"

"Watch the emergency entrance of the hospital while I try to get this damn thing going again," Abe said. "Of all the times for . . ."

II

Amy Brennan was driving home from the District Six meeting of the state medical auxiliary, tooling along the new four-lane interstate highway through the foothills at seventy-five miles an hour. The air conditioner of her new Eldorado was purring and the FM radio was playing a Brahms concerto softly, soothing her thoughts, after the cat-scratch battle with the representative of the downstate faction who had invited herself to the meeting.

Everybody had known the visitor was there to curry support in favor of her own candidate for president-elect when the auxiliary met during the convention of the state medical association next month. But Amy had played it cool—she could say that much for herself. And it hadn't been easy, especially the way her temper had been on a hair trigger lately, since her campaign to become president-elect had taken her on a tour of the state, visiting each of the districts.

"Cool Amy," Pete had sometimes called her in the early days of their marriage, but lately they'd hardly seen each other enough for him to call her anything. Ostensibly, the purpose of the tour of the state auxiliaries had been to talk about the role of doctors' wives in preventing the further spread of Medicare, but its real purpose had been to line up votes for Amy. Since she was a little girl, she hadn't left anything to chance, if she could help it, and as a result, her carefully planned campaign was now rolling like a juggernaut. The representative of the downstate faction had soon seen the handwriting on the wall, as far as her own candidate was concerned, and when she'd been forced to fly home without an endorsement from the members of District Six, it had been the same as conceding Amy's election.

The campaign had been a tough and exciting one, for District Six was no pushover. A lot of doctors in the area had no love for the medical school at Weston and even less for the Faculty Clinic that had taken away some of their most prosperous patients. With so many four-lane highways crisscrossing the landscape it was easier for a patient to drive to Weston for one of the fast but complete diagnostic studies for which the clinic had become famous than to wait in the office of a hometown doctor for an examination that couldn't touch the clinic's for thoroughness. Doctors' wives usually echoed their husband's prejudices, however, and with Pete Brennan president of the Faculty Clinic Corporation, as well as the leading neurosurgeon in the state, Amy had been forced to work especially hard to get their approval.

She had enjoyed it all, though, particularly the political maneuvering and infighting that had brought her, at thirty-nine, to the top of the heap in the women's side of state medical politics. And she couldn't help chuckling now at the thought of how she had maneuvered the downstate faction's representative into admitting her candidate's liberal sentiments, even to the point of apparently favoring Medicare—the next thing to labeling her a communist and the kiss of death among the conservative-minded wives of District Six.

Still, she decided as the sleek car flowed along the new highway, it would be just as well to play down the tactics she'd used against the other candidate when she talked to Pete. He was sometimes a bit sticky about her political maneuvers and they'd even quarreled about it once or twice. But her brother Roy would love to hear about them. As District Attorney for Weston County, Roy was moving into a wider sphere of political operations, and wanted Amy to take charge of women's activities in the race for state attorney general he was planning to make next year against the incumbent, Abner Townsend. But Amy was too busy right now with her own plans to think of anything beyond the convention next month, so she'd made no commitment.

Everybody had come through when she'd called on them, she remembered with satisfaction. Roy's wife, Alice, didn't go in for organizational activities as a rule, but she'd made an exception for her sister-in-law and helped Amy entertain visiting doctors and their wives. Lorrie Dellman, Maggie McCloskey, Della Rogan, Grace Hanscombe and Elaine McGill had been loyal, too: but then they had all stuck together pretty closely since Amy had organized them into what Pete liked to call the "Dissection Society."

Pete claimed that all the women did at their monthly sewing-circle get-togethers was to dissect the characters of people they knew—mainly other women. What he didn't know was that Amy had been carrying out a plan in organizing the group from among the wives of the six men who had formed the nucleus of the faculty for the new Weston University Medical School which had been organized at the end of the Korean war. That plan had even then been concerned with promoting Pete's own future, both in the medical school and in state and national medical politics, for which she was already setting her sights.

Pete Brennan, Paul McGill, George Hanscombe, Joe McCloskey, Dave Rogan and Mort Dellman had all been together in Korea, where Roy Weston had been working in the Inspector General's office. Roy had persuaded the six of them to join the faculty of the new medical school when they got out of the Army after the armistice. And none of them, Amy was sure, had ever regretted the move. Relaxing now as the big car sped homeward, she turned her thoughts to the first time she'd met Pete.

It had been at the Weston Country Club, the Saturday night dance everybody who was anybody in the city attended. He'd been in a group around the piano where Lorrie Porter was playing while the orchestra was taking a break, improvising jazz with the lazy competence Lorrie brought to everything she did.

Tall and a bit florid, Pete was then—and now—a solidly built man with the map of Ireland written on his face and in his blue eyes. He had caught Amy's attention at once. Being tall for a woman, she was naturally attracted to big men. Two years out of Vassar and four years post-debutante, with reddish blonde hair that needed no rinse and a good figure, she could have had her choice of a half-dozen men in Weston and elsewhere, but she'd always been particular. Not for her was just an average husband; the man she married, she had long since decided, must be a leader and a professional man—which meant most likely a lawyer or a doctor.

Amy had come to the club that night with Roy and Alice. As her brother crossed the crowded ballroom with a drink for her, he'd seen the direction of her gaze and grinned. "You look like a bird dog at point, Sis. Want to meet him?"

"Who is he?"

"Major—Dr. Pete Brennan. Just out of the Army and signed up with a half-dozen others of my friends from Korea for the faculty of the new medical school."

"What's his specialty?"

Roy looked startled. "What difference does that make?"

"Surgeons and internists are the aristocrats of the medical profession. You ought to know that, Roy."

"Never thought about it, but Pete qualifies. He's a neurosurgeon and surgical chief of the 319th General Hospital in Korea."

"Is he married?"

"No."

"Attached?"

Roy grinned. "Would that make any difference?"

"No. But it's simpler if he isn't involved."

"Far as I know he's a rover, which ought to make him feel at home in Weston—before marriage or after. The seven of us spent a lot of time together in Seoul, playing poker, drinking a bit, the usual things. All of 'em are top-notch men and Pete's the pick, a fine surgeon and an excellent administrator. Women are attracted to him like flies to a sugar bowl, though. What makes you think you have a chance to nail him?"

"I'm the kind of wife an ambitious doctor needs, for one thing. And I'm not exactly hideous."

"Come to think of it, you aren't," Roy grinned. "But since he's my friend, maybe I should warn him against a conniving female—"

"You do and I'll kill you," said Amy. "If he does his part, I can make Dr. Peter Brennan the most popular surgeon in town and the richest—maybe even the biggest doctor in the state. What more could he ask for?"

"To be loved for himself."

"He'll have all that he needs, too."

"If Pete goes for you, Sis, it isn't going to be something you can just turn on and off," Roy warned. "The woman who marries him will know she's married to quite a man. And she'd better be a real woman, not just somebody who's scheming to get ahead."

"For that I ought to punch you in the nose." Amy's temper had always been quick. "Go to hell! I'll introduce myself to him."

"I just wanted to make sure you knew the score. Come on."

They had been married less than six months later in the biggest wedding Weston had ever seen. One by one the other members of Pete's group had been married, too: Mort Dellman—actually not an M.D. but a Ph.D. biochemist who was also a laboratory whiz—to Lorrie; Dave Rogan, the psychiatrist, to Della; Joe McCloskey, the urologist, to Maggie; and Paul McGill, whose specialty was dermatology, the skin, to Elaine. All had been snapped up by local girls or—as was always happening with doctors—by girls working at the hospital. George Hanscombe, the internist of the group, had been married since the end of World War II to an Englishwoman named Grace Barrett.

The five doctors' wives—plus Lorrie Dellman and Alice Weston—had been the nucleus around which Amy had begun to build her own clique long before she'd become interested in the medical auxiliary. With her instinctive flare for organization, she'd known the group would be of help to her someday—and to Pete. Besides they were all congenial and Alice and Lorrie were distant cousins.

As a starter, she'd invited them to a luncheon at the old Weston place, with its tall columns, spacious grounds and faithful retainers. At a time when most of the others had been living in apartments while their husbands got started again after Korea, the possibility that they might one day enjoy the sort of luxury Amy accepted as a matter of course, had been a magnet— to all except Lorrie and Alice, of course. Daughter of Old Jake Porter, Lorrie, too, was to the manner born—and didn't give a damn—while Alice had grown up in Jake Porter's home as his ward. Being a Weston carried with it a lot of advantages, too—of which Amy was quite cognizant. Even though her father had not been a ranking member of the management of Weston Mills when he died, he'd still owned a considerable amount of stock. And thanks to the business acumen of Jake Porter in negotiating the deal by which Tropical Fabrics had taken over the mills, Amy had become financially independent.

Not that she and Pete had needed her money long. As Roy had said that first night at the club, Pete Brennan was a born leader of men, with enough Irish charm thrown in to talk any woman out of her inhibitions—as Elaine McGill had once reminded Amy somewhat maliciously. But then Elaine's husband, Paul, was a dermatologist and, while nearly everyone had skin trouble at one time or another, even if they escaped acne as teenagers, doctors in that specialty didn't draw down the big fees surgeons got. So she could hardly blame Elaine—who'd been a schoolteacher—for being envious.

Amy sometimes suspected Elaine and the others of secretly yearning to share some of Pete's vigor, too. And sometimes she would almost have been willing to divide it with them—until he'd begun to taper off after those frequent evening faculty conferences had started about a year ago.

Pete had risen fast in the medical world; Amy had to hand him that. He'd had more than one offer from larger and more important medical schools to join their faculties. But since the Faculty Clinic had become a veritable bonanza almost overnight, his salary as a Clinical Professor of Surgery at Weston University Medical School was now the least part of his income.

Pete was very popular with his fellow doctors, and with practically no effort had been elected second vice-president of the state medical association last year. At the next convention he was sure to be raised to first vice-president, the next year to president-elect, and the next to president. But thanks to a year of intense politicking Amy would be president of the auxiliary at least a year before Pete picked up the gavel of the state association.

The thought of reaching her immediate goal before Pete was able to achieve a similar status at the state level brought a warm feeling of satisfaction—succeeded almost instantly by a stab of fear. Until just then, she hadn't stopped to wonder how Pete would react to her reaching the top in women's medical politics before he attained a similar position in the state society. And at the thought that she might have let her ambition endanger her marriage, Amy's right hand moved from the wheel to touch the spot on her left temple where the familiar throbbing pain of migraine had just appeared.

"Damn!" she said aloud. A migraine attack now could mess up everything. With the all-important district meeting successfully concluded, she'd planned to be particularly nice to Pete tonight and had hurried home, although originally she hadn't expected to get back to Weston until tomorrow. As soon as she got home, she had planned to call him at the clinic and suggest that they meet at the club for dinner. First they'd have a few drinks at the bar where several of the Dissection Society girls were sure to be. Some of them spent as many evenings at the club as they did at home and in the ladies' lounge she could give them a quick account of her triumph.

When dinner was over, she and Pete would return to the big house with the white columns on the knoll overlooking the river. Like most of the other university children, Jenny and Michael were still away at summer camp. They wouldn't be back until after Labor Day, and she'd given Ethel, the live-in maid she'd inherited along with the house, the night off by telephone—just after buying the new nightgown before leaving for Weston. From there on, she knew she could trust Pete to pick up the cues.

Mentally adding the times Pete hadn't been home to those she'd been away for the vitally important district auxiliary meetings, Amy was startled to discover how little they had really been alone together in the past year. All of which made tonight particularly important—if she could just stop the damn migraine that was now like a spike being driven into her skull.

Glancing at her watch—an Omega with a diamond-studded band given her by Pete after he'd collected a five-thousand-dollar fee for a disk operation on the wife of Sam Portola, who headed the syndicate that now owned Weston Mills—Amy saw that she could just make George Hanscombe's office before five for a hypo of ergotamine tartrate and Demerol to relieve the pain—if the lights were right coming off the interstate. It was just then that the soothing tone of the Brahms concerto was broken by the voice of the radio announcer: "We interrupt 'Music for Midafternoon' to give you a special news bulletin."

Amy reached for the radio switch, wanting no news of a new backset for the U.S. forces somewhere in the world, or another race riot, to heighten the steady throb of the migraine. With her hand halfway to the controls of the radio her muscles suddenly went rigid, however, and the Cadillac swerved dangerously as the fingers of her left hand tightened on the wheel.

"Tragedy struck this afternoon in Weston's fashionable Sherwood Ravine district," the radio announcer continued. "According to a report just phoned from an observer on the scene, a prominent Weston physician, Dr. Mortimer Dellman, shot to death a few moments ago his attractive wife Loretta. Details of the tragedy have not yet appeared on the news tickers but a man with Mrs. Dellman at the time, said to be a prominent physician, was also seriously wounded."

Amy leaned forward to hear the broadcast over the rush of wind around the car.

"Police have thrown a cordon around the home of Dr. Dellman but one ambulance was seen to leave for University Hospital and another has just arrived. Stay tuned for further developments in this fast-breaking marital tragedy of high society."

CHAPTER TWO

I

The clock on the dresser said four when Elaine McGill eased herself out of bed. Crossing the bedroom of the small lakefront cottage to the dresser for a cigarette, she lit it with the gold-plated lighter Paul had given her for their tenth anniversary. Two hours, she thought, should be ample time for the sperm deposited around her cervix to find their way into the uterus. In fact, one of them should already have joined up with her own ovum, if she'd figured the time right and interpreted correctly the rise in temperature she had so carefully noted with an accurate thermometer record every day for the last six months. That rise, according to the textbook she'd studied at the hospital library, was supposed to indicate ovulation—and the best time to achieve pregnancy.

Elaine had spent a lot of time studying the reproductive function these past several years when she had been trying so desperately to become pregnant. The more she studied, the more she marveled that something so vitally important to the preservation of the human race had seemingly been left largely to chance. Everything about it, in fact, violated her innate sense of logic, of an orderly and divine planned motion of the spheres and the smaller units of the cosmos.

Before marrying Paul McGill, Elaine had been a mathematics teacher in

Weston High School. She had been working on her doctorate when the handsome dermatologist had joined the faculty of the new medical school along with Pete Brennan and the others.

Not that Elaine had orbited anywhere near Amy Brennan's sphere before her marriage. She'd grown up in North Carolina, gone to N.C.C.W.—now the University of North Carolina at Greensboro—and taken her Master's degree in mathematics at Columbia before coming to Weston. But since Paul McGill had been one of the Five Horsemen of the Apocrypha—Dave Rogan had cooked up the absurd designation while they were in that Army hospital in Korea—she'd naturally joined Amy Brennan's Dissection Society.

Serious-minded as she was and something of an intellectual, the fact that Paul was ten years older than she had only intensified his attraction for Elaine. They had been married about four months after he joined the medical school faculty but for a while having children hadn't seemed financially advisable. With the opening of the Faculty Clinic, however, Paul's financial prospects had changed almost overnight and Elaine had immediately stopped all use of contraceptives—except for a few months' use of "the pill" when it had first come out and reports said women who used it were more likely to get pregnant after they stopped than before.

Elaine had been happy in Weston until her apparent sterility had begun to trouble her. Now, after nearly fifteen years of marriage, she sometimes found herself wondering resentfully why she had to be barren when a substantial part of the human endeavor, it seemed, was directed at bringing about the union of two cells, the sperm and the ovum, at just the right moment in the menstrual cycle of a woman.

Everything that went before was actually window dressing to that simple microscopic event, the ultimate *climax coitum*, so to speak, that kept a large part of the world's business running at a profit. The girl in the bikini on the billboard smoking KOOLS; the baseball player in the shower shampooing with PRELL, spraying himself with LIFEGUARD after toweling, and slicking his hair down with BRYLCREEM, if he was "man enough to try it"; the exotic perfume guaranteed to draw men like flies because its "secret" ingredient was really musk, the stink of animal sex lure; dinner by soft candlelight with gypsy violins playing; the view of Los Angeles from Mulholland Drive at midnight—all were designed to bring about, almost as an anticlimax, the gutsy business of thrust and parry, until the *coup de grâce* was delivered by the explosive force of mutual ecstasy and languor immediately seized spent bodies to bring on sleep, so the final microscopic stages of the union could be accomplished.

All of it—the whole elaborate mechanism that kept hundreds of industries humming to promote human sexual union while pharmaceutical houses were equally busy manufacturing "the pill" that prevented its full completion and accounted for a sizable slice of the G.N.P.—had one purpose, one driving force more powerful than the hydrogen bomb, or even a great earthquake. The force that united a male and a female during a few brief moments for the purpose of preserving the species.

That same force made the chromosomes and the far smaller genes of the human sex cell march together with relentless tread to become one. In this new being were joined all the characteristics of both parents: the gene for hemophilia that, carried only by the female, would one day destroy the offspring with uncontrollable hemorrhage; the genes for the male parent's blue eyes or the web toes handed down from great-grandfather Albert; the *acrus axillaris*, a tiny muscle that crossed the armpits of perhaps one individual in a million for generation after generation with no perceptible purpose, except that eons ago some primate ancestor had needed it; the short legs and long body from the father's side combined with the large buttocks from the mother's—all these and a million more characteristics distributed by chance, or by divine pattern from a heritage of incalculable years, came together in the chromosomes of two people who met, cohabited and, because they wanted to or because in the heat of passion someone forgot to take a pill beforehand or inject a household cleanser afterward, produced a new being.

Perhaps the final penetration through the cell membrane of the ovum by the head of the single spermatozoon that made impregnation possible was fully as ecstatic as the union of the bodies preceding it. Who could say, when not even Sigmund Freud had been able to dredge up a memory of that climactic moment from the formless plasma of the unconscious? Certainly there was no ecstasy for the tail of the gobbled-up male cell; once its function of moving the sperm through the female generative tract to penetrate the cell membrane of the ovum had been accomplished, it died unheralded and was absorbed, very much as the black widow spider eats its mate after the latter fulfills its single purpose, reproduction.

It was all too hit-or-miss for logic to play much of a part in it, Elaine McGill had long since decided, but she had made one final try anyway. That try had brought her this Wednesday afternoon in September to a lake cottage the Hiltons had lent her and Paul while they were in Europe on a sabbatical, brought her here with a man she hardly knew and whom, she told herself firmly, she had no desire to know after today.

One thing she didn't have to worry about—detection. Paul always played golf on Wednesday afternoon and stopped at the Nineteenth Hole of the Weston Country Club for a drink after his shower. He rarely got home before six and long before that she would be back in Sherwood Ravine, preparing dinner while the memory of what had happened here this afternoon rapidly faded—forever.

The sensible thing, she knew, would be to dress and leave now, while Mike Traynor was still asleep. She could call him from a service station on the way back to town and make sure he was awake; he'd said he had to take over for one of the interns in the emergency room of the hospital at five o'clock. But something held her back, something she wasn't quite ready to admit into conscious thought, but which nevertheless stirred her pulse to a swifter beat.

Pausing before the mirror on the bathroom door, Elaine admired her own naked image there, knowing she was even more lovely today at thirty-nine than she'd been fifteen years ago when Paul, newly appointed Assistant Professor of Dermatology in the medical school, had married her. Her body had filled out during those years; a woman who knew she was loved always gained weight. Her dark hair was wound about her head now in a coil of coppery braids; Paul liked it tumbled about her shoulders when they made love, so it had seemed somehow unfaithful to him to let it down this afternoon.

Her breasts were just full enough, she thought, though she had felt the demanding mouth of an infant upon them only once. She'd been especially despondent over her inability to conceive last year and Paul had sent her on a visit to her sister in Philadelphia, who had just had a baby. One afternoon when Sally had been out, Elaine had taken the bottle from the infant and given it her own breast instead.

Even now, she could remember with a shiver of pleasure the feel of the small mouth upon her breast, the rasp of the baby's tongue upon her nipple. But she'd been dry, of course, and the baby had soon set up a howl, so she'd hurried to put the rubber nipple back into his mouth—after which he promptly fell asleep.

Her waist, reflected in the mirror, was still sweetly curved, the hips just full enough to make men turn to look at her when she walked across a public room. The legs, she knew, were superb. She'd won a "perfect leg" contest at a summer resort at the end of her third year in college and had been besieged the rest of the summer every time she appeared on the beach by college boys on the make.

Both she and Paul had superb bodies and good minds, even though at fifty, he was a good eleven years older than she and seven or eight more than Pete Brennan and the others, who made up the ruling hierarchy of the medical school—except George Hanscombe who was the oldest of the group. So why had the children they wanted so passionately been denied her and Paul, when someone like Lorrie Dellman, who really didn't give a damn, was like a brood sow—until Mort had put his foot down and had her tubes tied off after the last Caesarean.

It wasn't that she and Paul hadn't tried hard to start a family. God knows she'd run the poor man ragged the four or five nights of each month, when her carefully determined ovulation cycle had indicated she was able to become pregnant. Jack Hagen, the gynecologist at the Faculty Clinic, had tried every test known to man on her, too, and all the treatments. Hormone injections, tubal insufflation—pumping air up through the uterus and tubes until your belly felt like a balloon—she had undergone the whole gamut but with nothing to show for it.

Finally, she had persuaded Paul to have his sperm examined but they'd drawn a blank there, too. Mort Dellman in the medical school laboratory said he'd never seen wrigglier sperm than Paul's. But they still didn't seem able to propel themselves up the short distance of maybe five inches to her Fallopian tubes and penetrate the ovum she broke out of its follicle every month as regularly as clockwork—if the evidence of her thermometer was to be taken as valid, which Jack Hagen assured her it could.

At first, Elaine had thought the reason she didn't get pregnant might be because Paul was so hasty that he hardly ever managed to get inside her before he lost his seed. But when she'd finally gotten up the courage to ask Jack Hagen about that, he'd assured her it probably didn't make any difference. Only two things were really needed for pregnancy, he'd said: a viable ovum, which a healthy woman like her produced regularly about every twenty-eight days, and the presence of sperm—capable of fertilizing it—in the entrance to the generative tract within twenty-four hours or so of the monthly ovulation. Paul always got that far—though usually not much farther.

"Premature ejaculation," Jack Hagen had labeled Paul's trouble. He had further volunteered that a lot of men, even young ones, suffered from it—mostly because of nervousness or some defect in their psychological sexual development. Elaine had toyed for a while with the idea of suggesting that Paul see Dave Rogan, who was a close friend as well as a psychiatrist, but had given it up, knowing Paul didn't like to talk about his trouble.

In time, Elaine had learned to take care of the fact that Paul was rarely able to bring her to a climax, but way back in her mind there was always the nagging wonder whether she wasn't being denied something. Lorrie could have told her, she was sure. God knows Lorrie seemed to enjoy sex, judging by the number of times she'd put horns on Mort. Even a louse like him deserved better and once or twice, when she'd seen Mort undressing her with that feverish look he got in his eyes after a few drinks, Elaine had even considered encouraging him a little. Mort was certainly fertile; he—or somebody—had kept Lorrie pregnant most of the time, until her tubes had been tied.

Paul had put his foot down on any question of artificial insemination, when Jack Hagen had advocated it. In fact it was the only question on which he and Elaine had really quarreled since their marriage. What was to be gained—he wanted to know—by injecting another man's sperm into her cervix, when Mort Dellman had labeled his own O.K.? The trouble, he insisted, had to be connected with the acid-base balance of Elaine's own generative tract, a condition that must be destroying the sperm before they could reach the ovum. Besides, he said, the whole thing was immoral—Paul was very strait-laced about sex. And since no doctor would inseminate her without the written permission of her husband, she had been forced to resort to an older, if less honored, method this afternoon.

It ought to work, too, she thought, looking at the tousled dark head on the pillow. Mike Traynor was as perfect a specimen as she was—and she'd been careful to pick a lover, even if for only a single appearance, with Paul's coloring and general features. Working the whole thing out and finding the right donor—it assuaged her own moral scruples a little to label Mike thus—had taken a long time. Logic told her it would have been more scientific to use the computer, nerve center of the new data-processing system Mort Dellman had devised to speed up examination procedures in the Faculty Clinic. That of course had been impossible but, as a mathematician, Elaine was sure she had worked it all out logically anyway.

Once she'd found Mike Traynor, she'd been forced to play a role she had never played before, that of a strumpet. But it had all been justified by the need for a child, she reminded herself again—though hardly by the fact that she had found herself enjoying the role. Or that the sight of Mike Traynor's dark head on the pillow now should stir an answering warmth within her body.

In the end though, sex hadn't really been any different with Mike Traynor from what it was with Paul—only a little longer. Fearful of destroying the acid-base balance, or whatever it was Paul had been talking about, she had lain upon the bed afterward, tense and unfulfilled, waiting for the new seed which had just been implanted in her generative tract to reach her ovum; Mike Traynor, on the other hand, had gone to sleep.

The bell on a nearby church steeple tolling four reminded Elaine that Mike had said he had a class at five; he was a senior medical student at the university substituting as an intern on medicine for the summer. The cottage by the lake in the foothills of the Smokies where so many of the medical faculty had summer places was a good half hour from Weston, so she decided to wake him. Going to the closet, she put a wrapper about her naked body and tied the sash. Then, with the half-smoked cigarette between her lips, she went over to shake Mike awake.

He rolled over and looked up at her, his eyes foggy with sleep. Then he grinned and reached up to take the cigarette from her lips and put it between his own.

"Well, aren't you the eager one?" he said. "And you so shy before."

"Wh—what do you mean?"

"Did you think I didn't realize you never crossed the wire?"

"Wire?"

"This kind of a race should be a photo finish. But when I get going, I can't always slow down—at least not the first time. Now the second—"

"It's four o'clock—you said you had a class at five." She knew she didn't sound convincing.

"I can get to class in twenty minutes. Anybody liable to come here before five—like a husband?"

"Nobody knows I'm here. He's playing golf."

"Then what are we waiting for?" With a movement so casual that it was completely disarming, he sat up to loosen the sash holding the wrapper around her waist and push it off her shoulders. Startled by the action, she made no move as the garment fell to the floor in a pool about her feet.

"Man! O man!" His admiration, she knew, wasn't feigned. "Imagine all this being wasted on Old Dermatographia."

"Who?" she asked—a little breathlessly. Things were moving very fast, but she was far from sure she wanted to slow them down.

"That's the name the students have for your husband. He's got his pet theory that a person's nervous make-up can be determined by the way the skin reacts to being marked with a finernail. Dermatographia means writing on skin—you know—like writing on a blackboard."

"I remember hearing him speak of it."

"He's always stroking the patients' backs; if they've got a quick nervous reaction, the mark turns red. You'd be amazed how often he can spot people with psychosomatic ailments, just by writing on their skin."

"Does he do that to women patients?"

Mike grinned. "It's bad enough to put horns on a guy without revealing his secrets. I've got principles, baby." He touched her breast and whistled softly when the nipple became erect, straining at the touch until the dark skin of the areola took on a pigskin-like appearance. "Come here, beautiful."

The first time she had merely accepted him, shutting her mind and her emotions off from what was, for her, purely a mechanical act carried out to ensure creation of the child she hoped to bear. This time he took her and the difference was so great that just before the explosive moment of orgasm she was sure she would faint dead away. Then it was over and this time she knew—with some deep primeval instinct granted occasionally to women—that the sperm would reach the waiting ovum.

"Now that was a photo finish if there ever was one." Mike Traynor exhaled a sigh and reached for the cigarette he'd put into the ash tray by the bed. "And what a race!"

As he left the bed and started putting on his clothes, Elaine pulled up the sheet to cover her naked body. With the movement she shut him out of her life as casually as he had come into it, sternly repressing any thought of the explosive moment of pleasure she'd just experienced in his arms. Now that she was going to bear Paul a child, her mind had already erased even the thought that another man's seed had made it possible.

"See you later, baby." Mike Traynor waved good-bye from the door but Elaine didn't bother to acknowledge the farewell. She was lying with her knees drawn up as Jack Hagen had told her to do. Fifteen minutes, he'd said, should be long enough but she decided to take a little nap just to be sure. There'd be plenty of time to get home before Paul finished his golf game and his drink at the club.

She heard Mike Traynor's old car sputter into life but didn't hear the radio that came on when the switch was turned. Only the last words of the news broadcast reached Mike's ears, but they were enough to make him gun the car and head for the hospital.

"Christ!" he thought. *"If this was last Wednesday, the guy being taken to the emergency room from Dellman's house could be me!"*

II

"Well, that's that." Police Lieutenant Eric Vosges watched the ambulance with its sheet-covered occupant move down the curving driveway into the street. "The cream of Weston society, and she winds up in the meat wagon with a bullet through her, as dead as any whore on Houston Street that held out on her pimp. What was she anyway—a nymphomaniac?"

"Unh-unh!" Sergeant Jim O'Brien pushed the battered hat back from his forehead and spoke without taking from his mouth the pipe that was always there when he was awake. "Nymphos sleep around hunting for a man who can satisfy them. Lorrie Porter—that was her maiden name—really liked it. I can remember the first time she got into trouble, couldn't have been more than sixteen when Amy Weston's brother knocked her up—"

"The D.A.?" Vosges' tone was only slightly shocked. Brought in from outside to put beef into Weston's police force after some students at the university had staged a panty raid on one of the girls' dormitories that had turned into a riot, he had quickly discovered that Weston wasn't much different from any other university city of a hundred-odd thousand people.

"Roy wasn't the first," said O'Brien. "Jake Porter—he was the real power in Weston Mills then—knew Lorrie had round heels even at that age, but he didn't do anything about it. Guess Jake figured it was in the blood. After all, he's still chasing girls at seventy-five—and able to do something about it, with a little help, when they let him catch them."

"But Mrs. Dellman had everything!"

"Everything except what she wanted, I guess." Sergeant O'Brien scratched his head. "Don't ask me what that was."

"You were speaking of the D.A."

"That's done and over with a long time ago. Roy wanted to marry Lorrie, but the old man would have none of it. He knew his daughter well enough by then to know she'd wreck Roy's future. The abortion was done by a madam down on Houston Street and everything was okay, until the girl started hemorrhaging and had to be brought to the hospital. It took some doing but we managed to cover it up."

"Was that wise?"

"It was if you wanted to stay a cop here in those days—and probably still is. The town was owned then by the Westons and Jake Porter. You played the game their way or you struck out."

"Do enough of the old ways remain to get him off?" Vosges nodded to where Mort Dellman was being ushered into the back seat of a police cruiser.

"Probably. What I can't figure out is why he did it. It's no secret that Dellman married Loretta Porter for her money. He isn't an M.D. like the others that started the Faculty Clinic; I think he's a chemist or something. But he's a born administrator; runs that place like a machine. Nobody around here likes him much, though, and he wouldn't have gotten into the country club if he hadn't been married to the daughter of the man who built it."

"He's done all right for himself—until now." Vosges eyed the obviously expensive house with the large kidney-shaped swimming pool at the back under the pines.

"Marrying Lorrie helped," Sergeant O'Brien agreed. "But ever since he organized that medical production line they've got at the Faculty Clinic, Dellman's had a firm hold on part of a gold mine."

"Do the doctors there do good work?"

"You've got to go clear to the Mayo Clinic for anything better."

Vosges shook his head. "And he wrecked it all today with one shot."

"That's what bugs me. Why would he do it?"

"The unwritten law still holds good in most parts of the country."

The grizzled policeman shook his head. "You can't tell me that in the twelve years or so he's been married to Loretta Porter, Dellman didn't know that practically every guy in town with hot pants was shacked up with his wife at one time or another. He must have had dozens of opportunities to shoot some of our most prominent citizens, if he'd wanted to. So why did he pick on this particular one?"

"Who knows?" The police lieutenant shrugged. "Think the guy he shot will make it? He looked pretty rocky to me when the ambulance took him away."

"Ten years ago a bullet in the middle of the chest would have been curtains, but they've got some pretty hot doctors at the University Hospital these days—especially that refugee fellow Dieter. Patched a hole in my nephew's heart a year ago, right after he first came here. The boy had been an invalid since he was a baby, now he's out for the swimming team at the university." O'Brien knocked out his pipe and started filling it again. "I still say there's something screwy about this setup."

"Maybe it was her he intended to kill."

"That don't fit either. Old Jake Porter is the richest man in these parts and Lorrie would have inherited a sizable chunk of his dough. I don't see anybody as smart as Dellman deliberately cutting himself off from that. Besides, he's done his share of tomcatting around town, so what right does he have to feel so virtuous?"

"What's the answer then?"

"That's what's bugging me. I can understand him plugging the guy—if it was somebody he didn't like. But he's known the poor devil for years. They were all in the army together in Korea, came here when the med school opened, and worked together every day. I tell you, Eric, there's something about this thing that doesn't gee."

"Don't strain," Eric Vosges advised. "If this town's like most, it will come out in the wash."

CHAPTER THREE

I

It was a quarter past four when Della Rogan and Grace Hanscombe parked the golf cart they had been using in the space reserved for the vehicles beside the caddy house.

"Eighteen holes is too much at my age, Della," Grace said with a groan as she got out of the cart. She wore light beige Bermuda shorts, a yellow blouse and a yellow bandeau to hold her blonde hair away from her face while playing. At forty-eight, Grace was still well-preserved, with the fresh outdoor look many Englishwomen seem to be able to retain through life.

"I'm glad I'm not a champion," she added. "The work of staying in shape would kill me."

"You're champion unofficially," said Della, as she lifted her clubs from the cart.

"Today was a fluke. I don't know what put you off your game, Della, but it must have been something earthshaking for me to beat you. Come to think of it, you haven't been yourself since you came back from that tournament in Augus—"

"Forget it, Grace!" Della's voice was sharp.

"Look here! I was only—" More angry than hurt, Grace stopped as Della shouldered the clubs and started toward the driving range. Then raising her voice she called: "If you decide to be friends again, stop by the house for a cup of coffee in the morning. I've been feeling so damned lousy the past few mornings, it'll be a relief to have even a grouch to talk to."

When Della didn't answer, Grace turned toward the clubhouse, leaving her clubs for one of the caddies to take to the locker room, where they would be put away by the maid. It was one of the prerogatives of being the wife of an officer in the club, as well as chairman of its most important women's committee—after golf, which Della Rogan headed. Being the wife of the city's leading internal medicine specialist did have some advantages—along with the disadvantages—she thought, as she headed for the bar and a tall drink, besides representing quite a jump from being a barmaid.

II

Walking across the grounds toward the driving range, Della Rogan was surprised by the weight of her clubs. It was the first time in weeks she remembered carrying them herself. The caddies always did that, and there was always a golf cart to transport her from green to green so she could save all her energy for the vitally important strokes themselves.

Crossing the putting green adjoining the swimming pool, where a group of young people were squealing happily in the late afternoon sunlight, she approached the driving range, and putting her bag into the rack beside one of the driving slots, took out her favorite driver.

"Leroy," she called. "Bring me a bucket of balls, please."

A grizzled colored man looked out of the adjoining caddy house. "Yes'm, Mrs. Rogan," he said, and disappeared momentarily, before reappearing from another door carrying a bucket of golf balls. "Want me to tee 'em up for you?"

"No, thank you, I just want to practice my drive a little."

Della picked a wooden tee from one of the side pockets of her golf bag, an elaborate one of tooled leather—and very expensive. Dave had given it to her as an anniversary present just before she'd left for the Southeastern Women's Open Championship at Augusta. Remembering the tournament—and what happened afterward—she shoved the tee into the ground with suddenly shaking fingers, placed the ball upon it and took her stance, the driver gripped tight in her sun-browned hands.

Whack! She drove the ball hard, watching it soar far down the range, straight as an arrow, before dropping to the ground.

Could a guilty conscience have had anything to do with Dave giving her the bag? she wondered. It was very expensive, but she'd casually mentioned seeing it in the pro shop so he'd known she wanted it.

Whack! The second ball started true, then began to veer in a perceptible slice, striking the ground well to the left of the first one.

She'd been away an awful lot this year playing in tournaments. Dave hadn't accompanied her, of course; a psychiatrist couldn't just pick up and go traipsing off whenever his wife played golf. They'd quarreled bitterly over his not being able to attend the Southeastern Women's Open at Augusta, but he'd insisted that, with several patients at a crucial point in their therapy and testimony in a court case coming up, he just couldn't interrupt it. Besides, she knew, he didn't mind staying home and was fond of the kids—both away at camp now like most all faculty children. And there was always Mattie, the live-in maid, to take care of them when Della was away.

Not many wives of doctors on the medical school faculty had a live-in maid, but with Della gone so much of the time playing golf, it had seemed the thing to do. In fact, she remembered now, Dave himself had suggested it. At the time it had only seemed an act of consideration on his part, but maybe there had been another reason why he'd been willing for her to be away so much, a reason she might not even know of until it was too late. Just that had happened to others—even to some of her friends.

Teeing up again, Della stroked the ball almost viciously, but this one sliced even more than had the others and she put down the club quickly because her hands were trembling so much that she was afraid she would drop it. Unconsciously the cause of her sudden doubt of Dave was the knowledge of her own guilt, but she refused to allow that thought access to consciousness, knowing its capacity to blast into bits her snug little world of club life, golf tournaments and the row of trophies on her mantel. It was simpler to suspect Dave and transfer the guilt to him; the trouble was that her love for him and her knowledge of his love for her made it practically impossible to convince herself.

If Dave wasn't so damned considerate of her, she thought with a flash of anger, maybe nothing would have happened at Augusta. He never objected to her playing in tournaments, even when it meant leaving him and the children for several days, and lately he hadn't even been making many sexual demands on her. Which had seemed just as well at the time; after eighteen holes of golf, plus an hour or so of practice shots, she was usually too tired for that sort of thing. Come to think of it, they hadn't made love in six weeks. With the Southeastern Championship at Augusta and now getting ready for the club championship here at Weston, she'd been away nearly half the nights and exhausted the others, but Dave hadn't seemed to mind.

Or had he? she wondered, as she swung on the ball.

Whack! She stared at the spot where the ball should have been with unseeing eyes.

Could he possibly have heard of what had happened at Augusta—after she'd won the Women's Southeastern?

"You all right, Mrs. Rogan?" Leroy's soft-voiced question startled her.

"Of course I'm all right. Don't be impertinent!"

She was breaking the club rule that frowned upon any tongue-lashing of its employees, for caddies and attendants were harder to find every year. Dave was vice-president of the club in charge of personnel and she'd often heard him say that, with the government changing the wage-and-hour laws every session of Congress, nobody knew where they'd be able to get help any more.

"Why did you ask, Leroy?" She forced herself to be conciliatory.

"You just topped your drive, Miz Rogan. Ain't seen you do that in ten years."

Della looked down the driving range and, seeing nothing where the ball should have landed, let her eyes drop slowly. It seemed an eternity before they found the small white object hardly a dozen feet from where she was standing.

"Take my clubs to the locker room please, Leroy," she said in choked tones. "I've got to have a drink."

III

Alice Weston never looked at TV in the afternoon, once the last soap opera was finished. By that time, she was so emotionally spent that she had to lie down for a while before taking her bath and dressing for dinner. Having never known real unhappiness, Alice found the tribulations of the sad people inhabiting the dream world of the afternoon soap operas almost more than she could bear. She never listened to the news: real-life misery always left her depressed for a long time. But she bore the soap operas bravely, out of a sense of duty. After all, it didn't seem right for one person to have everything and not suffer a little for the troubled world—if only through the proxy of a TV screen.

A half-hour in bed in the afternoon with the blinds drawn was like a cathartic, however, flushing away the troubles of the soap opera world and leaving Alice ready for her bath in preparation for the ritual before-dinner martini she and Roy always shared—when he was home. Vanessa, the full-time cook-maid, prepared the dinner, did the cleaning and even the grocery shopping, so Alice had little responsibility as far as running the house was concerned. But Roy did like for her to prepare his martini with her own hands, the vermouth barely flavoring the gin, the olive bruised just enough for a hint of the bitter oil in its skin to seep into the drink itself.

They'd been married almost twenty years, since she was eighteen. Yet not once had Alice ever confessed to Roy that she always diluted her own drink with water while she was making it. The stimulation of alcohol whenever she allowed herself to drink that much, which was almost never, always made her a little unsure. She knew people did awful things when they had too much to drink. There was always a lot of that sort of thing in the soap operas and she was afraid of what alcohol might do to her own tidy little world.

Then she remembered that Roy had said he wouldn't be home for dinner—some sort of a pretrial conference would make him late. Maybe she'd call Corinne Marchant to come and stay awhile with her, she thought, and the idea made her feel happy, driving away the sadness left over from the afternoon TV serials.

Alice had just taken off her dress and was stretched out on the bed in her slip in semidarkness with the window air conditioner purring softly—even with the mountains only fifty miles away, Weston got pretty warm in early September—when the phone at the bedside rang. Drowsily she lifted it from the cradle; like the rest of the room and herself, the phone was pink and white.

"Alice?" She recognized the high-pitched, somewhat querulous voice of Jake Porter.

"What is it, Uncle Jacob?" The tough old man had taken Alice and her widowed mother in after her father's death and practically raised her as his own daughter, so she always felt about him like she felt about one of the Biblical patriarchs. For that reason, she'd never been able to bring herself to call him Uncle Jake, as Roy did—though everybody knew Jake Porter bore no resemblance to a Biblical character, except perhaps King David in his Bathsheba days.

"Where's Roy?" the old man demanded.

"I don't know. At his office, I suppose."

"I've called there. They don't know where he is."

"He said he wouldn't be home until late. Do you want me to have him call you when he gets here, Uncle Jacob?"

"I can't wait that long; I need him now. Roy's got to clamp the lid on before this town erupts like a volcano."

"We couldn't be having a race riot in Weston." One of the characters in "Edge of Day" was a beatnik who was always bragging about how he had been in the march to Selma. Just seeing him on the TV screen upset Alice so much that she almost had to turn off the rest of the story, as soon as he appeared. Almost—but not quite.

"Hell, no!" said Jake Porter. "You mean you don't know what's happened?"

"Know what, Uncle Jacob?"

"The news. It's all over the TV."

"I never watch the news. It upsets me."

"Lorrie's been shot—killed by that son-of-a-bitch she married. A man with her was shot, too."

"Oh!" As the room started revolving slowly, Alice clung desperately to the receiver, the only solid thing immediately at hand. She knew she was going to faint. Mother always said her nervous system was too delicate to stand shocks and had carefully shielded her from them.

"Don't you faint, Alice!" The old man's squawk in the receiver was like a cold douche, reviving her a little. "I've got to find Roy."

"Who?" From some deep reservoir of courage she'd never been called upon before to tap, Alice found strength to ask the question. "Who was the man with Lorrie?"

"The radio broadcast didn't give his name. I think they said he was a physician but I was so upset when I heard it that I can't be sure. I called the hospital but they won't tell me a damn thing either."

"Why the hospital?"

"Damn it, Alice! Haven't you heard what I've been saying? Mort Dellman caught a man in bed with Lorrie this afternoon and shot them both. Lorrie's dead and the man's seriously wounded. He could be Roy."

The telephone dropped from Alice's fingers as the familiar cramping pain just to the left of her navel doubled her up in sudden agony.

"Alice!" The old man's voice came from the phone. "Alice! Are you there?"

Clutching her abdomen with her left hand, she managed to pick up the phone again. "I've got to go, Uncle Jacob."

"Go?"

"To the bathroom. I'm having a colon attack."

The explosive cramping agony came again and she dropped the phone. Rolling over on her side, she slid from the bed and started to crawl toward the bathroom on hands and knees, gasping with agony when every move brought on the terrible cramping pain.

"Hell, Alice! Don't you have anything better to do at a time like this than—" Her own cry of pain blotted out the pungent word but from the door of the bathroom she heard, as if from a great distance, the final exasperated splutter of the old man over the phone hanging from the bedside table by its cord.

"If your mind was half as active as your gut, Alice, you'd be the smartest woman in the world."

IV

Maggie McCloskey was sitting in the small bar across from the ladies' lounge when Della Rogan came in and ordered a gin and tonic. The men still pre-empted the Nineteenth Hole, but the club had turned what was once storage space back of the main bar into a small, intimate room where the women could have a drink in shorts after the game.

Maggie was on her third or fourth, judging by the rather glazed look in her eyes, but Della didn't want to speak to her until she had swallowed the first drink and ordered another. She didn't want to be reminded that, of all the members of the Dissection Society, Maggie was the only one who had gone so far as to get a divorce—yet.

Born Margaret Smith, Maggie had been a secretary in the psychiatric department of the medical school before her marriage to Joe McCloskey, and Della an X-ray technician. They had both come from the same town in eastern Tennessee, but Della had lost track of Maggie until they'd met again at the new hospital and medical school of Weston University some fifteen years earlier.

Back in Tennessee Maggie had grown up on the other side of the tracks from Della and, though Della never reminded her of it, or even thought about it, Maggie had seemed determined to run herself down, even after Joe McCloskey married her. Actually, as Della very well knew, Maggie had no reason to feel inferior to anyone. She had been an extremely capable secretary to Dave Rogan and had been instrumental in bringing Della and Dave together, when they had double-dated once with Maggie and Joe.

Just what was the trouble between Joe and Maggie, no one could ever be sure. Joe was a small, somewhat prematurely bald man, with courtly manners and a degree of kindness and tolerance somewhat unusual in a urologist, whose work brought him in contact with some of the seamiest aspects of human behavior. Della had always suspected that the main trouble was Maggie's feeling of inferiority, which again didn't make sense. For Maggie had been very pretty when she and Joe were married and was still a handsome woman, though the marks of dissipation had begun to mar her beauty, particularly since the divorce, when she had been drinking more heavily than before.

For whatever reason, liquor only seemed to exaggerate Maggie's increasingly frequent lapses into the customs and language of her early upbringing. In fact, Della sometimes thought she was deliberately flogging herself by making people disgusted with her and her behavior. And being naturally kind and genuinely fond of both Maggie and Joe, she felt sorry for Maggie and tried to help her, often at the expense of her own feelings, when Maggie lashed out blindly, striking at anything within reach.

Physically, two women could hardly have been more different than Maggie McCloskey and Della Rogan. Where Maggie was rounded almost to the point of plumpness, Della was wiry. Where Maggie was dark-haired, Della had started out as a sandy redhead and had gradually bleached out from the sun of the golf course, where she spent at least half of her time, to a yellowish blonde. And where Maggie was highly emotional, Della was quietly capable, holding herself in check lest Dave who, as a psychiatrist, dealt with emotionally disturbed people all day, come home to the same sort of atmosphere at night.

It was Joe McCloskey Della really felt sorry for, kind, unfailingly courteous, quietly unprepossessing Joe. He'd tried desperately to avoid the divorce, she knew. But Maggie had seemed to take pleasure in flagellating both herself and him, until in the end there had seemed to be no other answer. Since then, Della and Dave had tried to have Joe over for dinner several times to cheer him up. But with her gone so much playing in out-of-town golf tournaments even that hadn't worked out very well. Besides, she was sure Maggie had heard about the invitations and had been all the more unpleasant because of them.

"Hear about Lorrie?" Maggie's voice was already a little slurred.

"Who is it this time?"

"The angel Gabriel—unless he's the flying faggot I think he is."

"Stop clowning, Maggie." Tired as she was and with the alcohol from the drinks not quite into her bloodstream yet, Della's tone was short. "What's with Lorrie?"

"She's kaput. Morte."

"You mean she's dead?"

"That's the general idea."

Startled, Della strangled on her drink and Maggie gleefully gave her a crack on the shoulder blades that jarred her teeth.

"Don't gulp your whiskey, Della girl; it'll last longer if you take it slow. Believe me," she added bitterly, "when you have to live on the lousy pittance Joe McCloskey gives me as alimony, you need to make every drink count."

"What about Lorrie?"

"Mort shot her a few minutes ago—according to the radio and TV. Right through the heart, the man said, though believe me it would have been more appropriate if he'd aimed somewhat lower."

Della Rogan felt a cold chill start somewhere in the region of her heart. "Was she. . . ?"

"Alone? I thought you'd ask that." Maggie was getting all the enjoyment she could out of her friend's shock. "Is she ever?"

"For God's sake, Maggie. What do you know?"

"The broadcast said a 'prominent physician' was with Lorrie when Mort drilled her. Whoever he was, he got shot, too—what the lawyers call *flagrante delicto.*"

"Who was it?" Cold sweat was breaking out on Della's forehead, though minutes before she had been hot and thirsty. It couldn't be Dave, of course. Or could it?

"That's what nobody's been able to find out yet. But you can bet a lot of faculty wives have been telephoning each other frantically ever since it happened, wondering whether the man in the case is her husband."

"How do I know you're not making all this up?" Della emptied her glass and shoved it across the bar to the bartender for a refill.

"Threw the fear of God into you, didn't I?" Maggie cackled. "Most of us have been sleeping with each other's husbands for years. Somebody had to get caught sometime."

"Knock it off, Maggie! The bartender's listening."

"Manuel's heard all this before—or he will in the next few days."

"Then it's really true?"

"Ask Manuel, if you don't believe me," Maggie said indignantly. "He heard it too."

Della glanced at the bartender and the cold chill within her deepened when he nodded. "All I know is what was on the radio, Mrs. Rogan," he said. "You see, I keep this little transistor set on when nobody's here."

"Turn it on now!" Della's voice was harsh.

"The manager doesn't like—"

"Turn the damn thing on, Manuel," said Maggie McCloskey. "The male victim could very well be on the board of directors, you know."

"If you ladies say so." Manuel switched on the transistor set just as Grace Hanscombe appeared in the door of the small bar.

"They've got the gory details on the TV set in the Nineteenth Hole—in color," she said, and there was a concerted rush from the small bar to the larger one, where a group of men and women were gathered around the TV set.

"There goes Mort!" Arthur Painter was a lawyer who specialized in estates; he pointed to the screen, on which a chunky man in his shirt-sleeves was being led by a sheriff's deputy to a waiting prowl car. "I wonder if he took out that new policy on Lorrie long enough ago for the company to have to pay it."

"I wrote the policy and we'll never pay it." At thirty, Earl Bieson was already a Life Underwriter and a member of his company's Million Dollar

Club—plus suffering from high blood pressure and failing kidneys.

"Don't you two ever think of anything except wills and insurance?" said Della.

"Hello, Della," said Arthur Painter. "Where's Dave?"

A dead silence followed the question, until Maggie said, "A lot of wives are wondering where their husbands are right now, Arthur. I'm glad I don't have—"

"Shut up, Maggie!" Della was straining to get a good look at the TV screen. "Don't forget what will happen to your precious alimony if Joe's been shot."

"The bastard couldn't do that to me." Maggie blanched and gulped the remainder of the drink she carried in her hand. "Could he, Arthur?"

"What are you talking about, Maggie?" The lawyer reluctantly took his attention away from the screen.

"You drew up my divorce settlement—and got enough out of it for yourself. If Joe was knocked off by Mort Dellman, do I lose my alimony?"

"You lose it." At the words Maggie looked as if she was going to be ill. "But Joe's insurance is made out in a trust for you."

"Then I'll get double indemnity—for the accident?" Maggie's color started to come back as she turned to the insurance man. "You wrote the policy, Earl. Don't I get double?"

"If Joe's the one that was shot and he dies, his estate would collect double indemnity." Even the thought seemed to cause Bieson pain. "They haven't given the name of the man yet but the last I heard he was alive and on the way to the University Hospital."

"It could be Joe," said Maggie. "He was always after Lorrie just like the rest of you—and a lot who aren't here."

A scene familiar to all of them had just come on the TV screen, a house set back among the trees with a curving driveway in front. In Sherwood Ravine, lots had to be an acre in size and the houses a minimum of a hundred feet from the street, so most were set back as much as a hundred and fifty feet.

"Keep the peasants from seeing what goes on among the nobility," had been the motto of old Bob Bieson—Earl's father—when he had built the development. Originally intending to provide space for rich men's houses, the area had now become largely populated with doctors, dentists and lawyers, the new-rich aristocracy of the profession that the postwar world had created so quickly.

On the TV screen, ambulance attendants were wheeling out a stretcher on which lay a still form, covered with a sheet.

"That must be Lorrie," said Della as they lifted the stretcher into the ambulance.

"She's certainly dead," said Maggie. "Or she'd somehow have managed to get rid of that sheet before now."

"You're drunk, Maggie," said Grace Hanscombe." Come on. I'll take you home."

"Not me. I'm going to stay here until they name the prominent physician who was with Lorrie when Mort gunned him down."

"I'll go with you, Grace," said Della Rogan. "It's almost time for Dave to come home." She stopped suddenly, knowing the hell she saw in the Englishwoman's eyes was mirrored in her own.

"Let's get another drink," said Della. "We both know we're afraid to go home."

"One thing's certain." There was a rough burr of cockney in Grace's voice, an accent she usually managed to keep hidden. "This will be the first night in a long time the husbands—and wives—in Sherwood Ravine will all be sleeping in their own beds."

CHAPTER FOUR

I

Marisa Feldman was passing through the emergency room from her quarters in the Faculty Apartments across the street, on the way to an early dinner in the hospital cafeteria, when an ambulance, its siren still going, stopped at the ramp outside. As a stretcher was wheeled in hurriedly, she gave a quick glance at the man lying upon it, noting the apparent absence of breathing, the pallor of shock—or death.

"What is this?" she asked, for something about the victim's appearance had rung a warning bell in her brain.

"D.O.A., ma'am—Doctor," said the ambulance attendant, noting the long-skirted white coat she wore because she planned on making ward rounds after dinner.

"Why didn't you take him to the hospital morgue?"

"Nobody's pronounced him, Doctor." Only rarely did hospitals have enough interns to ride ambulances since the impact of Medicare, so she knew the ambulance driver's medical training would have been limited to the brief course in first aid required by law in most states.

"When we put him into the ambulance he was as alive as anybody can be with a bullet in the middle of the chest," the second attendant volunteered. "But he has no pulse now."

"A bullet wound!" Marisa Feldman's mind clicked into action like a computer. "Get him into that cubicle over there! Fast!"

As she spoke, she was reaching for the phone. Dialing the hospital operator, she said urgently, "This is Dr. Feldman, call 'Cardiac Alert' on the paging system, please—emergency room."

When she turned to the cubicle, an orderly was already helping the ambulance attendants lift the wounded man onto an examining-treatment table. And over the loudspeaker she heard the voice of the paging operator, crisp and distinct: "CARDIAC ALERT! ALL STAFF PERSONNEL TO THEIR STATIONS! CARDIAC ALERT—EMERGENCY ROOM."

This was only her second day on the hospital staff, so Marisa Feldman had met only a few of the medical school faculty. But she had learned about the procedure for handling serious cardiac cases—like cessation of the heartbeat—at a briefing session Dr. Hanchmann, Chief of the Medical Services, had given her yesterday. And she approved thoroughly of the routine used here for handling such emergencies.

The two words "Cardiac Alert!" would bring a trained resuscitation team to the emergency room at once, alert the Special Intensive Care Unit to be ready for a new patient, and send to the scene the most experienced doctors in the hospital in every field that might be involved in a cardiac emergency. Marisa wasted no time waiting for them, however, but took immediate command.

"Did you use a respirator?" she asked one of the ambulance men.

"There wasn't time, Doctor."

The words told her only a short period had elapsed since cessation of breathing so there might be some hope that brain damage of any serious degree had not yet occurred. The immediate problem therefore was twofold:

first to get the heart started and second to get the patient breathing again, thereby increasing the oxygen level in his blood as rapidly as possible to overcome any temporary damage that might have been done to the brain cells by its brief absence.

"Get an airway in and start the resuscitator," she told the duty intern who, sweating and red-faced, had appeared beside her at the strident summons of the loudspeaker. From where it hung on the wall, Marisa Feldman plucked an obstetrical stethoscope. Its bell was attached to the headband and, with the tips of the soft rubber tubes attached to it in her ears, she was able to lean over and listen to the heart while leaving both hands free for closed-chest resuscitation.

The first step in this new and dramatic method of restarting stopped hearts, which had lessened so sharply the need for the sort of dramatic surgery involved in opening the chest itself and massaging the heart directly, was the determination that cessation of the heartbeat had actually occurred. The precaution was necessary lest the organ be damaged by the somewhat rough treatment given it during the heavy pressure made directly upon the chest in the maneuver of squeezing the heart between the spine and the sternum, or breastbone, just as a surgeon operating under direct view would squeeze it in his hands to stimulate the stopped organ and restore the beat.

Marisa saw the wound when she pulled down the sheet covering the injured man's chest; small and neat, it was just over the cardiac area and a little to the right. Her expert appraising glance also took in the distention of the veins in his neck and the mottled cyanosis over his upper chest, neck and face completing the visible clinical picture.

At her side, she heard the intern's voice, shrill with surprise and horror, exclaim: "My God, it's Dr. ———." But the name he spoke was lost to her as she leaned forward to press the stethoscope against the wounded man's chest, shutting away all sound except what came by way of the column of air trapped between the metal bell of the stethoscope, the tubes connecting it to the plastic tips in her ears, and her own auditory canals closed off by her eardrums. Nor would the name necessarily have meant anything to her, since this was only her second day on the faculty of the school.

In the stethoscope, the air column was like an amplifier magnifying every sound within the chest. At first Marisa heard nothing—the sign of death. Then, when her eardrums had adjusted somewhat to the slight change of air pressure, as the metal bell was pressed hard against the pallid skin of the victim's chest wall, she detected a faint rippling sound, like water heard from a great distance as it flowed across a stretch of rocks.

The ripple was without rhythm or pattern but the mere fact that it was audible at all provided the last bit of data needed by the marvelously complex system of memories, impressions and observations that made the human brain a far more complicated and efficient machine than any data-processing system devised by man.

As the ripples of sound had set each of her eardrums into delicately vibrant motion, the first of the three bones of the middle ear, the *malleus*, or hammer, lying against the drum also began to vibrate faintly. This movement was transmitted by mechanical force through two adjoining tiny bones, the anvil and stirrup—medically the *incus* and *stapes*—to a small opening known as the "oval window," separating the middle from the inner ear. Vibrating against the membrane covering of the oval window, the stapes had set up its own faint mechanical ripple in the fluid that filled the semicircular canals of the inner ear.

In rapid sequence, the air wave vibrations of sound falling upon the eardrum from outside the body had been changed to mechanical motion in the middle ear, then back to fluid waves in the semicircular canals of the inner ear. Moving through those canals, the tiny impulses of wave motion stirred delicate hairlike nerve endings in the organs of Corti, sensory terminals for the auditory—hearing—nerve itself, just as the skin of the fingertips forms the organs of sensation for touch, temperature and pain.

In the organ of Corti, the mechanical energy of the fluid wave was once again transformed—in a marvelous and intricate way which even now men were not able entirely to understand—into infinitely small electric impulses traveling along the nerve channels to the center of hearing in the brain cortex. There they were simultaneously interpreted as sound and a picture of this sound sent, through other connecting nerve fibers of the brain, to the centers of memory in the frontal lobes.

Digested, analyzed and compared with other information stored away during years of study in medical school and in hospitals, the whole picture had been subjected in an instant of time and completely without conscious thought to an analysis far more intricate than was possible by any man-made system of electric circuits. Somewhere in the memory and judgment areas of the brain, a complete pattern suddenly formed, like a jigsaw puzzle when the final piece is dropped into position. And once formed, the pattern was flashed to the centers of conscious—rather than unconscious—thought, where it became a concept ready to be voiced.

"*Cardiac tamponade!*" Marisa Feldman spoke the diagnosis aloud quite unconsciously, so sudden and explosive was the concept that had taken form in her mind, produced from the stream of data pouring into her brain from every sense.

When she looked up, the shocked look still visible in the eyes of the intern, fumbling with the plastic airway he was sliding between the teeth of the injured man, plus its counterpart upon the face of the graying nurse supervisor, who had appeared at her elbow, told Marisa they had recognized the victim, but that was of no importance to her.

Her first casual glance at the sheeted form on the stretcher had told her something was wrong with the picture, inconsistency in the clinical pattern of death summed up by the ambulance attendant's casual description of D.O.A.—dead on arrival. The tiny rippling sound heard in the stethoscope had revealed that the dying man's heart, struggling instinctively to preserve life, still fought against the constricting pressure of the blood accumulated in the confined space of its own protective membrane by its desperate attempts to maintain life.

But the tiny and already almost imperceptible movement of the heart would cease, she knew, unless that pressure was relieved in a matter of seconds. And wasting no time, she moved resolutely to do just that.

II

It was not quite five o'clock when Janet Monroe stepped out upon the small terrace adjoining the cafeteria atop the new surgical wing of the University Hospital, only a few steps away, via an enclosed passage, from the Special Intensive Care Unit where she was nurse-in-charge. She had chosen to have only a quick sandwich and coffee at the snack counter for dinner, rather than the full meal allowed nursing staff members during each eight-hour shift under their contract. That way she had been able to use fifteen of the thirty minutes allowed for dinner to make a quick visit to the Surgical Pediatrics ward several floors below where Jerry was a patient. The way her son's small face had lit up at the sight of her had tugged at her heart. The terms of the divorce from Cliff Monroe hadn't allowed her much in the way of alimony; he'd still had two years of his residency to go and you couldn't get blood from a turnip. Janet had been left with no choice except to go on working after the divorce, leaving Jerry after three each afternoon in the cooperative nursery maintained by the hospital and medical school in a basement room of the married student housing building for the benefit of working mothers. Most of them were putting their husbands through medical school or residencies or, like herself, working as nurses to support themselves, and often children, after the divorce that ended so many medical student marriages.

What had depressed her wasn't Jerry's appearance; he was bouncingly healthy and obviously the pet of the ward. It was the fact that the hospital staff hadn't yet been able to pin down the cause of the sudden convulsive attack he had suffered two afternoons ago.

Janet had been dressing on her evening off in the small apartment she and Jerry shared—except from 3 to 11 P.M. six days a week—for a date to go with Jeff Long to the pops concert in the new Municipal Amphitheater. Jerry had been playing in the yard and she'd been surprised to see him open the door of the apartment and cross the living room to the bedroom door. Usually he insisted on staying outside in the play yard with the other children until dark, since her day off was the only time he had a chance to play with them in the afternoon.

Turning from the mirror to watch him cross the bedroom toward her, she had thought how sturdy and fine he was with his blue eyes, red cheeks and thick mop of dark hair. Boys usually took after their fathers but Jerry leaned toward her family in the genes he had inherited and there was little of Cliff in him to remind her of the past. He was a happy and contented little boy, even though she had to waken him shortly after eleven each evening and carry him the half block between the nursery and her apartment.

Jerry had been halfway across the bedroom when Janet realized that something seemed to be wrong with him. Normally he ran everywhere he went, but today his steps were slow. Once he seemed to stagger, as if his foot had caught in the rug and he was very tired, and when she reached out for him, he stumbled into her arms and put his head against her breast.

"My head hurts." The solidity of his strong little body reassured her somewhat, calming the moment of panic she'd experienced when he appeared to stumble.

"Mommie will get you a baby aspirin." Half-strength and flavored to taste like candy, the tablets were so attractive that she had to keep the bottle high up on the medicine shelf to keep them away from him. Carrying him— she was still in her slip—Janet went to the bathroom, found the tablets and gave the little boy one.

It was nothing, she had told herself, as he started chewing happily on the tablet. When she gave him a cup of water to wash it down, he seemed to choke a little but that could come from trying to swallow the slightly chalky tablet, she was sure. In fact, this whole performance could easily be explained by his wanting her to stay with him, rather than go to the concert. It wouldn't be the first time a slight stomach-ache or even a sniffly nose had suddenly developed when Jerry knew the sitter was coming on her evening off.

"Want to lie down for a little while, darling?" Janet had pressed her cheek against his soft one. "Mrs. Bodey can give you your dinner later." A widow whose small pension was supplemented by baby-sitting chores at night in the neighborhood, Mrs. Bodey lived several doors down the street.

"Aw right, Mommie."

She had carried him over to the crib and placed him in it, then pulled up a chair and sat beside him, crooning a lullaby as she stroked his warm cheek. For a moment she considered calling Jeff Long and canceling their date. After the divorce from Cliff, she hadn't gone out for a whole year, until Jeff had convinced her that she needed to get away occasionally for her own emotional health.

He'd been right, of course, as he was about almost everything. An anesthesiology resident couldn't afford to fail, he'd told her once with the familiar, and by now beloved, grin; in the white glare of the operating-room lights there was no way to cover up his mistake.

She was going to have to make a decision about Jeff soon, Janet had told herself for at least the hundredth time as she sat beside the crib. She'd put it off again and again because she knew only one decision was really fair to Jeff—and she didn't want to make it for purely selfish reasons. However much she'd come to depend on him and love him, it wasn't fair to saddle Jeff with another man's child, even though Jerry adored him. And it was equally unfair to let Jeff go on loving her without any hope of marriage.

It wasn't that her own unhappy experience had really prejudiced her against marriage; God knew Cliff had never really contributed anything, except the seed that had given Jerry life. Actually the marriage had been a fiasco from the start and Janet had often wondered whether Cliff hadn't married her because she was about to receive her degree in nursing and could support him through medical school, only to be abandoned with a child and a divorce, after he had received his M.D. and was able to earn a living for himself.

Janet had thought Jerry was asleep when the first convulsion came, a seizure that made the little boy jerk spasmodically and his eyes roll upward until almost nothing showed except the whites.

It wasn't the first time she had seen the baby in a convulsion; when he'd been about a year old, he'd once had a high fever and a spasm. Even in her natural concern over what was happening, Janet didn't allow herself to panic. Instead she held him close until the jerking stopped, and even had the presence of mind to note that one side of his body seemed to be jerking more than the other. But when the spasm ceased and she saw his eyes rolled back and heard no sound of breathing, her heart seemed to stop.

Fortunately, she'd known exactly what to do. Nothing was to be gained by calling a doctor, with the inevitable delay. The hospital emergency room was only a few blocks away and skilled help was always available there, especially Jeff Long and big, capable Ed Harrison, who was not only the resident on Pediatrics but a friend, too.

Jerry had suddenly started breathing again while she held him in her arms after the convulsion, a stertorous sound like an old person snoring. Placing him in the crib from which she had lifted him during the convulsion, Janet had run to the closet, seized a cotton print dress and pulled it down over her head. Zipping it up she had picked up the keys to the Volvo that was her single extravagance during the two years since the divorce.

Jerry was breathing more normally and his body was relaxed when she lifted him from the crib. He even opened his eyes drowsily and one chubby hand reached up toward her cheek as she moved downstairs with him in her arms.

The Volvo had been parked in the driveway and she had placed the little boy upon the seat, closed the door, and gone around to the side and got in. Even in her anxiety, Janet had retained enough of her normal faculties to realize that this convulsion wasn't like the one Jerry had suffered several years before. For one thing it was more severe; for another, it seemed to be somewhat limited to one side. She didn't have time to think much about that, however, for in less than ten minutes, she was parked at the emergency-room ambulance unloading ramp. She was carrying Jerry into the hospital, when his body began to jerk in her arms with another convulsion.

The rest of that evening seemed almost like a dream now—after seeing Jerry apparently completely his normal self a few minutes ago. The nursing supervisor in the emergency room had put in an immediate call for both Ed Harrison and Jeff Long. And as the competent assured routine of the hospital swiftly meshed into action around her and Jerry, Janet had felt the blind panic she'd experienced at the start of the second convulsion begin to subside.

It had ended as swiftly as the first, even before Ed Harrison could reach the emergency room. Once again the little body had gone through the agonizing period when respiration was arrested by the spasm of the chest muscles and lips and ear lobes started turning blue with the cyanosis of oxygen lack. Then as explosively as with the first spasm, Jerry suddenly began to breathe again and a few moments later looked up to smile at Janet.

That had been two days ago, but Dr. Deemster, Professor of Pediatrics, had decided to wait for a brief period of observation. Ed had explained the reason: "Cases like this are often due to a small hemorrhage into the subarachnoid space around the brain, Janet. If we do a spinal puncture now, we might disturb the pressure relationships and increase the bleeding."

"Isn't there anything you can do?"

"I'll give him some elixir phenobarbital to quiet him down a bit. We'll do a spinal puncture in a couple of days and see what we find. Meanwhile we can make some other tests and have some consultations."

Today was the day; the ward nurse had told her Dr. Rogan was seeing Jerry for a neurological consultation about six and the puncture would probably be done then. Ed had promised to let her know, for on its outcome might well hinge Jerry's future.

Deliberately Janet forced the problems she faced from her mind and looked westward toward the dark range of the Smokies. She'd taught herself to make her mind blank like this every now and then since that day, two years ago, when she'd come home from duty to the small apartment and found Cliff's belongings gone—else she was sure she would have lost her mind. A note on the dresser had said that Jerry was with Mrs. Bodey but Cliff had never come back. Shortly afterward Janet had filed for the divorce he wanted.

Actually, she admitted now as she stubbed out her cigarette preparatory to going back to the Special Intensive Care Unit, Cliff's going had been something of a relief. Certainly her financial status hadn't been any worse, perhaps even better, with the necessity of paying for his tuition, food and cigarettes now removed. To be abandoned by her husband was still a blow to a woman's ego, however, no matter how much of a louse the man was. And for a while she had been numb, until Jeff Long had practically dragged her back into a life outside her work, the apartment and Jerry. Now Jerry's convulsions, with their ominous portent of something serious, threatened to push her back into the state of self-pity and despondency from which she had been only beginning to emerge.

A glance at her watch told her it was five and she stood up, just as the loudspeaker in the cafeteria outside which she had been sitting crackled into its dramatic—and chilling—announcement: "CARDIAC ALERT! ALL STAFF PERSONNEL TO THEIR STATIONS!"

Janet stiffened at the first words of the announcement. Her first thought was of little Jerry, his breathing mechanism stopped by the muscle spasm of another convulsion, his lips and ear lobes dusky with the dread blue tint of cyanosis. Her place of duty was in the Special Intensive Care Unit, according to the standard operating procedure for the most urgent emergency a hospital had to face, the immediacy of a stopped heart. But if it were Jerry whose heart had been stopped by another convulsion, she needed to be at his side, regardless of duty. Torn by indecision and horror, Janet couldn't move one way or the other, until the second part of the announcement released her: "CARDIAC ALERT—EMERGENCY ROOM."

Once more able to breathe, she turned on a run for her station.

III

It could be Pete, was Amy Brennan's first thought as the numbing news poured from the radio in the announcer's excited voice. Lorrie was completely amoral and had made a play for anything male whenever she felt like it—which was often. Pete was about as male as you could get, she reminded herself, while his wife—busy with her own little plans for personal glory—had been neglecting him shamefully. The thought made her step down hard on the accelerator and the big car leaped forward, while the radio chattered on with more details about the tragedy—except the name she wanted—and was afraid—to hear.

She was turning off the interstate when she noticed the red warning light on the gas gauge and the pointer at "Empty." Disturbed as she was, she had no way of knowing how long it had been there, so she decided not to take a chance on running out of gas before she could get to the hospital. Two service stations were located at the foot of the exit ramp and, pulling into the first one, she drew to a stop beside the pumps.

Two men came from inside the station. One was young and red-haired; the other, gray-haired and stooped.

"Fill it up please—high test," said Amy. "And don't bother with the oil."

While the old man put the nozzle into the tank and started the pump, the younger one began to clean the windshield. He usually chose that job; with the short dresses now in vogue, the view from his position was often spectacular.

Amy's eyes roved restlessly, until she saw the wall pay phone inside the station. Opening the door and stepping out, she fumbled in her purse for a dime but found none, so took out a quarter and handed it to the younger man.

"Some change please—for the phone."

He took the quarter, clicked two dimes and a nickel out of the change counter he wore on his belt and gave them to her. "Charge or cash ma'm?"

"What?"

"For the gas. Do you want me to charge it?"

"Yes." She reached in her purse and handed him her charge card, then moved to the telephone almost on a run. Trembling fingers dialed the hospital number but when the hospital operator answered, she almost hung up, afraid of what she would hear.

"This is Mrs. Brennan," she managed to say. "Would you ring my husband's office?"

"There's a Cardiac Alert on, Mrs. Brennan. We can't ring any phones inside the hospital for outside calls."

"What's a Cardiac Alert?"

"A serious heart case just arrived. The lines have to be kept open until the alert goes off."

"Is—is it one of the staff doctors?"

"I believe so, yes."

"Can you tell—"

"Here's a call now for X-ray. I'll have to handle it."

Numbly, Amy hung up the phone and left the booth. When the younger attendant brought her the small blue plate on which lay the charge slip and her card, she scribbled her name automatically on the slip and dropped the card in her wallet.

"You all right, Mrs. Brennan?" the younger man asked.

"Y-yes. Why?"

"You look like you've seen a ghost."

Amy stared at him, her pupils dilating. Then, with a gasp of horror, she ran to the car, got in and started the engine. Her hands were trembling so much that she could hardly hold the wheel, however, and she put her head down upon it while she fought for control.

"Dear God," she whispered. "Don't let it be Pete."

The act of praying restored her composure enough to drive out of the station and into the street leading to University Hospital. Watching her, the younger of the two attendants scratched his head thoughtfully.

"You know I'd swear she was prayin' just before she left here," he said.

"Prayin'?" The older man shook his head. "You're imagining things again, Ed."

"Yeah, guess I am at that. I used to service her car when I worked at the big company station downtown. That's Dr. Brennan's wife; he's a big-shot surgeon at the university and she's got everything already. So what would she be prayin' for?"

IV

Maggie McCloskey didn't get to see the rest of the newscast out—neither did Grace Hanscombe. The ambulance on the TV screen had barely disappeared down the street when Maggie suddenly turned green and staggered toward the door leading across the hall to the ladies' lounge. Obviously, she wasn't going to make it without help, and remembering that she was the chairman of the decorating committee for the club and would have to find a cleaner for the carpet in the hall in case of an accident, Grace grabbed Maggie by the shoulder and the belt of her skirt.

Propelling her charge expertly through the door of the Nineteenth Hole, Grace crossed the hall and shot through the lavatory section of the ladies' lounge, kicked open a door and managed to shove Maggie into one of the toilet stalls an instant before the deluge came. She grimaced at the sound of retching from the stall but didn't leave. Even though she was getting pretty disgusted with Maggie McCloskey, Grace wouldn't desert a dog at a time like this.

"Water!" When Maggie's anguished cry came from the stall, Grace took a glass from the shelf over the lavatory basin and filled it from the tap.

"If you feel yourself passing out, dunk your head in the can," she advised as she handed in the glass.

"God damn you, Grace!" Maggie gasped when she finally staggered out of the toilet cubicle and leaned over a basin to splash water on her face. "Do you have to treat me like a pig?"

"You are a pig!" Grace's own fears erupted in a geyser of angry words. "Eating pizza and then swilling down all that liquor."

"It wouldn't have happened if I hadn't gotten upset. I was worried—"

"About Joe?"

"Why not?"

"A little late, aren't you?" Grace's laugh was a bark of anger and disgust. "You aren't worrying about whether or not he's the one that was shot, only whether you can collect double indemnity. And you had to crucify him in a divorce court, just because you weren't able to give him what a man's got a right to expect from the woman he marries."

"You English bitch!" Maggie squalled. "Don't think I didn't know you and Joe slept together at that medical convention the time George and I both passed out. But I bet it wasn't any good."

"For your information, Joe's quite a man—not that it's any of your business, you frigid bitch."

"I'll kill him—telling another woman a thing like that. It's not my fault he was never able to arouse me."

"No?" Grace raised her eyebrows. "Well, he aroused me—and I know something about men."

"I'll bet you do! Everybody says George found you in a barroom but I never believed it. The place he found you in was a London whorehouse."

Grace started for the door, but turned with her hand on the knob. "I was a barmaid in London in '45, Maggie," she said with considerable dignity. "Times were hard then and it's a respectable occupation. But I've made George a good wife and, if you so much as hint at what I just told you, so help me I'll strip the flesh from your body with my bare fingernails layer by layer."

"You can't threaten—"

"Go dry yourself out somewhere before you get the D.T.'s. Then get down on your knees and ask Joe to take you back and teach you how to be a real woman. I don't know why, but he still loves you."

"H-how do you know that?"

"A man usually tells the truth when he's drunk—or making love." Grace grinned crookedly. "Maybe that's why psychoanalysts always have a couch in their offices. Just take my word for it—Joe loves you. If he wasn't the one Mort shot this afternoon—or if he was and gets over it—pray God it isn't too late to go back to him."

She went out, slamming the door behind her. Across the corridor she could see a knot of men and women still gathered around the TV set in the Nineteenth Hole but she was afraid to look. Instead, she examined the carpet in the corridor and was pleased to see that, thanks to her forthright action, Maggie hadn't spilled a drop on it after all.

God what a mess it would have been cleaning up that pizza, she thought as she turned into the women's bar, which was empty now—except for the bartender.

"Double Scotch and soda, Manuel." She took a seat on one of the stools and when the dark eyebrows rose as he reached for the bottle, added, "I'm English, you know. And it's after five o'clock."

As it turned out, though, Grace didn't have time to enjoy her drink. She was barely half finished when Maggie McCloskey came in from the ladies' lounge. She'd washed her face and combed her hair but she still looked green about the gills and held on to one of the chairs grouped around a table to steady herself.

"Any more news?" she asked.

Grace shook her head. "The radio says they've taken the man in the case to the hospital but they haven't told who he is yet. I heard Arthur Painter tell somebody he'd tried to call the hospital but they've got some sort of an emergency on there and won't accept calls from the outside. Have a drink, Maggie. You look like the wrath of God."

"I'm going to the hospital." Maggie started for the door. "Joe may not have needed me before, but if he was the one with Lorrie, he'll be needing my blood now. We're both B-Rh negative and they're not easy to find."

"Wait for me, you're in no shape to drive." Grace swallowed the rest of her drink in a single gulp. She'd been trying to drum up her own courage to the point of going to the hospital and was happy to find an excuse. As they came out of the small bar, they saw Della Rogan in the door of the Nineteenth Hole.

"Hey, Della!" Grace called. "Want to go with us to the hospital?"

Della hesitated only momentarily. "I'll follow you," she said. "If you get there first, wait for me so we can all go in together."

"We'll wait for each other," Grace agreed. "God knows we all need somebody to lean on."

It couldn't have been Dave with Lorrie, Della assured herself as she hurried across the parking lot to her station wagon. He couldn't do that to her when she was getting ready for the Southern Women's Championship at White Sulphur next month. A scandal would put her so on edge she'd never be able to play her best.

But even as she started the engine, Della Rogan knew in her heart that the man who had been shot could very easily be Dave. Or Pete Brennan. Or Joe McCloskey. Or Paul McGill. Or George Hanscombe. Or Roy Weston.

It could be almost any man in town, for Lorrie had never been caste-conscious in her amours.

CHAPTER FIVE

I

By the time the paging operator's voice finished the announcement, Janet Monroe had run across the passageway connecting the Special Intensive Care Unit with the new surgical wing. Her first move was to glance quickly at the bank of cathode-ray tubes on the wall above the chart desk; the action was a reflex, part of the training participated in by the entire hospital staff through dry runs, until everyone's response was automatic, once the warning was sounded that a human life was in delicate balance due to the failure of the heart to maintain its function.

The Special Care Unit was used mainly in the treatment of serious coronary heart attacks. Through electrodes taped to the body of each patient in the twelve rooms making up the section, a constant flow of tiny electrical impulses—in reality action currents pulsing through cardiac muscle with every component of the heartbeat—was fed to each of the cathode-ray monitor tubes, where a wavy line traced the pattern of the patient's heart action across its face. Beneath each tube was a second glass screen, part of the closed-circuit television system whereby each patient was kept under constant surveillance, even though no one else was in the room.

All twelve rooms of the unit equipped with closed TV, continual E.K.G., and piped-in oxygen were in use that afternoon. There never were enough beds available, for the cost of equipping and operating a setup like this was fantastic and only those who needed that kind of constant care were put upon it. Under the standard operating procedure of the hospital for Cardiac Alert, however, one of these beds must be made available immediately, even though it meant moving someone to another room at once.

"I got the call on the beeper." Dr. Stirling Kent pushed his head in the doorway of the chart room. A little breathless, he still held in his hand a small apparatus about the size of a cheap transistor radio. Ordinarily carried in the breast pocket of a house officer's white uniform, or the long-skirted coat worn by the teaching staff, this device enabled doctors to be reached at any time—like the men from U.N.C.L.E. When the small monitor beeped out its signal, the bearer went immediately to the nearest telephone to receive the call waiting for him.

"Ran all the way from the soda fountain," he panted. "What's up?"

"I don't know." Janet liked young Kent, for unlike many of the house officers, he wasn't always talking about getting out into practice and starting to rake in the dough. Cliff had talked of little else and even now, nearly two years after the divorce, she couldn't think of him without a twinge of pain and anger. It wasn't just that Cliff had used her, living off what she made nursing while he finished medical school and then dropping her as soon as he was able to support himself and start looking for greener pastures. Rather her anger was directed at herself for falling in love with someone who was unworthy and cheapening herself in her own eyes because of it.

"Help me decide who to move," she said to young Kent. "We'll have to get at it right away."

His eyes went to the bank of TV and cathode-ray monitoring tubes, scanning them as Janet had done when the call first came. The heart patterns portrayed there were about as varied as anything so basically similar could be, lines made up of jagged peaks and valleys as the strength of the electric impulses generated in each heart rose and fell.

"Mrs. Taylor's still fibrillating, so that lets her out," said Kent. "Dignan's P-R interval is twice what it should be and he could go into a ventricular rhythm any time."

"Mrs. Sanborn's still not compensated." Janet took up the account. "And Mr. O'Toole had another small coronary this morning. They all need the kind of close watching we give them with the monitors but the S.O.P. says we've got to clear a room pronto. Dr. Hanscombe will raise hell if he brings an acute coronary up here and we're not ready."

"It's most likely the guy Dellman shot," said Stirling Kent.

"What did you say?"

"I was looking at it on the tube just now in the soda fountain. Dr. Dellman caught a prominent physician with his wife and shot him a few minutes ago. The wife's dead and the man he shot is in the E.R."

"Loretta Dellman? I can't believe it."

"That's what the newscast said."

"I specialed her once, when I was a senior in training. It's hard to think of her as being dead; she loved life so much."

Stirling Kent grinned. "According to the hospital grapevine, she loved a lot of other things, too—even interns and students."

"You know how gossip is." Janet flushed, remembering very well the wild rumors just before her divorce and how true some of them had turned out to be. While he was living on what she had made nursing, Cliff had played the field—she'd learned after the divorce. He'd been another Mike Traynor; there was always one or more in every medical school class. They usually had no trouble finding partners for their amours either—which didn't make her much better than they, Janet thought bitterly, even though she'd had a marriage license.

"If a prominent physician was with Lorrie Dellman, it could be any one of a dozen of the high brass around here," said Kent. "Wonder who's the unlucky one?"

"Mrs. Tatum has the least to lose of anybody here if anything goes wrong." Janet ignored the last remark. "After all, she has an advanced malignancy in addition to the heart."

"Maybe we'll be doing her a favor by taking her off the monitors," said Kent. "I'll explain to her what's up while you get an orderly to help push the bed. I can't wait to see who that prominent physician turns out to be."

II

Two operations, one of them minor, were in progress in the main operating suite when the call sounded over the muted loudspeaker in the workroom, where two student nurses were putting up treatment trays to be sterilized later in the giant autoclaves. There were no loudspeakers in the operating theaters themselves; surgeons at work needed to concentrate on the job at hand without the continual stream of summons that poured from the paging system all day.

"I'd better tell Miss Straughn," said Millie Cash, the senior student on O.R. duty.

"What does it mean?" asked a second-year student.

"Usually a case of cardiac arrest—stoppage of the heart. We have to get an operating room ready in case they need to open the chest and massage the heart. But with the Pacemaker and this new closed-chest resuscitation thing, they don't do that much any more."

"I bet it's exciting."

"Not so you'd notice it." Millie spoke from the wisdom of two additional years of experience. "The doctors are always on edge with those cases. If they don't get the heart started again within a few minutes, the patient will turn into a vegetable from brain damage due to lack of oxygen. I'd better get in there, or they'll have a patient up here for a thoracotomy before Miss Straughn knows it and I'll catch hell."

Like all the nurses working in the O.R. section, Millie wore a pale green scrub suit. Though unlovely in cut, the sleeveless suits were still much liked by the O.R. nurses. Tied at the waist with a cord, they were comfortable and no slip was needed under them, a fact than an intern or student could quickly recognize. Which was fine, for the less a man figured a girl had on the more likely he was to overlook more visible faults.

Pulling the mask she wore hanging from her neck by its strings over her nose and mouth, Millie stepped through the swinging doors into the adjacent operating theater. A middle-aged surgeon; the surgical resident, Carl Hagstrom; an instrument nurse; a sponge nurse; and the anesthetist, Jeff Long, were grouped around the table upon which the patient lay.

Helen Straughn looked up sharply at the creak of the swinging doors and frowned at Millie Cash. It was bad surgical technique for people to be coming in and out of the O.R. any more than was absolutely necessary. Even though she ran the suite like a military unit, somebody was always breaking technique, forgetting to put covers over their shoes before they came in or a dozen other things that could bring in wayward bacteria. Then days later a wound would pop up infected on one of the wards and the O.R. staff would catch the devil because of it. Helen's years of experience with student nurses had taught her they would seize any opportunity to parade before a group of doctors; when she saw Jeff Long look up and grin at Millie, she moved quickly to where the girl was standing.

"Cardiac Alert, Miss Straughn." Millie spoke before the supervisor could start to bawl her out. "The paging operator just announced it."

Helen Straughn's manner changed at once. "Circulate here while I open the emergency thoracotomy pack in O.R. Four," she directed. "We'll take the sponge nurse off here, if one is needed in a hurry." Lowering her voice to a bare whisper, she added, "Watch Dr. Whetstone's forehead. It's a tough case and he's beginning to sweat."

Millie nodded and took the folded cloth pad Helen Straughn handed her. As she moved close to the table, Dr. Whetstone looked up with a frown. Although the suite was always at the same temperature summer and winter, his face was red and sweat had begun to pop out on his forehead, a sure sign that he was having some difficulty.

"Where's Miss Straughn?" An attending surgeon who operated only occasionally at University Hospital, Whetstone was jealous of the treatment he received there and always insisted upon having the resident assist him and Helen Straughn circulate.

"Cardiac Alert, Doctor," said Millie Cash. "Miss Straughn is opening the thoracotomy pack in O.R. Four."

"We've got a new S.O.P. on cardiac arrest cases since Dr. Dieter came, sir," explained Carl Hagstrom. "It's designed to make sure someone familiar with the closed-chest resuscitation procedure will be on the scene at once. But just in case it's necessary to go in and massage the heart, we also prepare an O.R. for thoracotomy."

"Which rarely happens any more, thank God." Jeff Long spoke from behind the wire frame that held the draperies off the patient's face and also marked the barrier between the sterile operative field and the potentially contaminated world just outside it. "It's amazing how often a good hard sock on the chest can bring a dead man back to life."

"Just be sure we don't have to sock this patient, Doctor," said Whetstone testily as Millie stepped in close behind him. Reaching up swiftly with the pad in her hand, she wiped his forehead before he bent over the wound again.

"She's fine, Doctor," Jeff Long said amiably. "Not a bit tired—yet."

Millie Cash almost laughed but choked it back in time and when Jeff Long winked at her, winked back. He was a brash young man and said to be gone on Janet Monroe, but he was also the most capable anesthesiologist the hospital had developed in a long time, with a great future before him.

Even Dr. Dieter preferred Jeff to Dr. Macready, the department head who was getting a bit old for the sort of excitement open-heart surgery always generated. If Monroe didn't have the good sense to nail Jeff, he was fair game. Everybody knew that when he finished his residency next year, he could step into a twenty-thousand-dollar-a-year job without even trying. Which would have made him extremely eligible, even if he hadn't been ruggedly handsome into the bargain.

Busy again in the depths of the incision, the surgeon missed the barb Jeff Long had thrown him but nobody else in the O.R. did. With the surgical team now relaxed, the operation began to go more smoothly and a few minutes later Dr. Whetstone stepped back from the table.

"Finish the closure, please, Dr. Hagstrom," he directed. "Chromic for the fascia and interrupted silk for the skin."

"Yes, Doctor." Anyone less pontifical than Whetstone would have detected the satirical note in Carl Hagstrom's voice. Telling a man with five years of surgical training since graduation and several hundred operations of his own how to close an incision was a bit like instructing an expert watchmaker about the kind of spring to use in one's watch.

Helen Straughn came back into the O.R. just as the scrub-room door was closing behind Dr. Whetstone. "There's a bullet wound of the heart in the emergency room," she said. "Dr. Dieter's on his way there now. He'll want you for the anesthetic, if he operates, Dr. Long. I've put in a call for a nurse-anesthetist to take over for you.

"As soon as Dr. Hagstrom finishes here, you can change and handle sponges in O.R. Four if we do the thoracotomy, Miss Tyndall," Helen Straughn told the sponge nurse. "An intern will be scrubbing on instruments."

"Who shot who?" Jeff Long asked. With Whetstone out of the room and the incision being closed swiftly and skillfully by Carl Hagstrom, the atmosphere had become normally informal.

"I don't know the last who," said Helen Straughn. "But the first was Dr. Dellman—I hear he found a man with his wife."

"Wow!" Jeff Long whistled. "Anybody we know?"

Which was exactly what Helen Straughn was wondering, too. It could be Pete Brennan—and the thought made her feel cold inside.

III

As the strident call of the loudspeaker penetrated to every corner of the hospital, those assigned duties in the emergency procedures to be set in motion as part of a Cardiac Alert dropped whatever they were doing and went immediately to their positions.

At the blood bank, located in the basement adjoining the morgue and the pathology laboratory, a technician who had been preparing a batch of the plastic bags, in which blood was stored, for a donor drive among the newly arrived first-year students, dropped her work and moved to the record section. Plucking a stack of punched cards from the drawers of a tall steel filing cabinet, she stacked them into the rack of an IBM machine and, at the touch of a switch, the machine began sorting them into groups and subgroups. Thus almost the instant the blood type of the patient whose life was in danger became known—and a sample for typing would be taken at the earliest moment in the emergency room, to be whisked via pneumatic tube to the blood bank—she would be able to report the number of units of blood available if needed. At the same time she would communicate with the blood bank of Weston's other hospital, St. Michael's, drawing upon them if needed.

Another technician started setting up a preparation of typing serum, ready for the blood sample that might arrive at any moment, while the first now moved to prepare a half-dozen plastic containers of Type O blood and send it to the operating-room suite where it would be ready to charge the so-called heart-lung pump, in case open-heart surgery was necessary. Type O blood had the advantage that in an emergency it could be given to anyone without serious complications, tiding them over until blood of their own type was available.

With the new closed-chest resuscitation technique, in which the heart was rhythmically squeezed between the breastbone and the spine by external pressure on the chest, driving blood into both the lungs and the vitally important blood channels to the brain cells, it was theoretically possible to keep a person alive, even with no spontaneous heart contraction, long enough to open the chest, insert tubes into the heart chambers and let the pump take over. And however unlikely this possibility might be in a single case, it was still a part of the standard procedure to prepare for it when the Cardiac Alert was sounded.

As Janet Monroe and young Kent started to move the bed, with a patient still upon it, out of the room they had selected, an operating-room orderly appeared on the run. Seizing a wheeled cart upon which stood the bulky apparatus of the Cardiac Pacemaker, plus everything necessary to make a small incision in the chest, should the emergency demand direct massage of the heart, he pushed it out of the Special Care Unit toward the nearest elevator bank. There, under another provision of the Alert, an operator was waiting with an empty elevator, ready to carry the cart to the level where it was needed, in this case the ground floor.

Even in the gleaming stainless-steel kitchens preparations for the staff's evening meal had hurriedly to be adjusted, since a considerable portion of the hospital personnel would be locked into their present duties until the Alert was off, disturbing meal schedules. Secretaries preparing to go off duty at five thirty waited in the offices where they worked, as well as doctors whose presence might conceivably be needed before the emergency was concluded. Teams of house officers trained especially in the chest-heart pressure technique, also moved toward the emergency room, ready to take over if the first team on the scene became exhausted by the strenuous procedure.

In the clinical laboratory that was the heart of the great hospital, technicians moved rapidly to clear the apparatus for evaluating blood gases—oxygen and carbon dioxide—in case the heart-lung machine was utilized. And an electronics technician, whose job it was to keep the delicate monitoring instruments used in many places besides the Special Intensive Care Unit, as well as the Cardiac Pacemaker, in repair, left his shop on the run with his special tool kit bound for the center upon which all activities of the great hospital were now concentrated, the single stretcher table in the emergency room where Marisa Feldman was working swiftly and surely.

IV

The human heart is at once the most protected and most vulnerable part of the body, the very nature of its protection creating its vulnerability. Encased in a tough, fibrous and relatively unyielding sac called the pericardium, the vital pump begins to contract rhythmically when the body is little more than a single cell, with no blood to circulate and no arteries and veins yet in existence through which it can flow.

For centuries, men have argued the question of whether death is a cessation of function in some center of the brain where the soul is concealed, with all body functions slowing to a halt, once the end of man as a person and a personality has occurred. Or whether death occurs only when the heart ceases to function and the blood supply to the brain is cut off, causing the death of the brain cells themselves.

Whatever the mechanism of death, it often occurs when the slender blade of a knife or a tiny leaden bullet, slipping through the soft tissues between the ribs, penetrates the tough muscular wall of the heart, leaving an opening that acts like a valve. With every beat, blood is then pushed through the tiny opening in the heart muscle to accumulate in the pericardial sac, its return being prevented when the pressure in the chambers of the heart falls to minus as they fill for the next beat. Then, with the muscular wall contracting once again, another spurt of blood is forced through the opening into the unyielding sac outside. With no means of escape, it, too, accumulates in the pericardium, increasing in amount with each beat of the heart.

Physical law states that two objects cannot occupy the same space at the same time. One therefore has to yield and this can only be the softer heart which, pumping on in an attempt to maintain the vital circulation, gradually finds itself with less space in which to operate. Thus the blood escaping from its chambers through the small wound with each beat gradually squeezes the heart down, just as it might be constricted by the hand of a deliberate murderer. Finally it can operate no more and comes to a halt—the condition known as *cardiac tamponade*.

Marisa Feldman had recognized the clinical pattern of tamponade at the instant when the evidence accumulating in her brain since she had first glanced down at the still figure upon the stretcher told her what was happening inside the chest of an apparently dead man. The soft murmuring sound she'd heard in the stethoscope could only mean to her trained ears and mind that, clinically, death had not yet occurred. Therefore the intrinsic control mechanism of the heart, the muscle, the Purkinje fibers, the bundle of His making up a special nervous tissue system of communication within the heart itself to insure that it would continue to beat even though shut away from all nervous control by the brain—all were still trying to keep the pump in action, even though the cardiac muscle had no room now to relax and fill the chamber with blood after contraction.

"Tamponade?" The intern fumbling with the valves of the resuscitator echoed the dread words as Marisa removed the stethoscope from her ears. She met his gaze and read his thoughts, as his brain searched for some bit of information from his studies which for the moment eluded him, but she wasted no time on explanation. More important work must be done at once, if that faint heart action was to be preserved, nurtured and given strength. And it must be done within a matter of seconds before the brain centers were damaged beyond repair from lack of the vital flow of oxygen by way of the bloodstream.

"Fifty cc. syringe! Eighteen-gauge needle!" Marisa's words galvanized the emergency-room staff into purposeful movement. The supervisor, a gray-haired wintry nurse whose years of watching men and women at their worst had accustomed her to immediate action, moved swiftly. From a shelf beside the table, she took down a sterile package and opened it quickly.

Without troubling to scrub—infection was the least of the wounded man's troubles today—Marisa picked up the syringe and attached the needle to it. With a single skilled movement, she thrust the point through the skin just to the left of the breastbone—the sternum—about three rib spaces below the collarbone. Guiding the shaft of the needle between the tough cartilages attaching the rib ends to the sternum, she thrust deeper until she felt a click against her hand, as the needle penetrated the tough, tightly distended pericardial sac.

"Aah!" A murmur went up from the small knot of spectators grouped around the entrance to the cubicle, as blood spurted into the barrel of the syringe when the needle broke into the cavity around the heart. Nobody understood exactly how the hospital grapevine worked, but a dramatic case in the emergency room almost a block away from the interns' quarters could bring a half-dozen interested spectators in a matter of moments.

At the head of the table, the intern on emergency-room duty had finished slipping an airway into the wounded man's mouth and throat. A curved plastic tube flattened to make insertion easier, it was designed to hold the tongue forward and provide an open channel to the trachea, the windpipe whereby air entered the lungs. Over the flanged outer end of the airway, he now pressed a mask connected by its flexible tubing to a respirator.

A lifesaving machine of tremendous intricacy, the latter consisted of a tank of oxygen and special valves that allowed pressure to be built up high enough to inflate the lungs thoroughly, then shut themselves off from the tank and simultaneously opened another outlet by which the gas could escape from the lungs as they deflated. By thus alternately filling the lungs with oxygen and then expelling it, the device achieved, far better than any other method was able to do, a very effective simulation of respiration.

While the syringe in Marisa Feldman's hands filled rapidly, the E.R. nurse was opening another. When Marisa separated the needle from the full syringe, the nurse took it from her with one hand and handed her the empty syringe with another. As Marisa was attaching the empty syringe to the needle, the nurse expelled the dark blood from the full one into a sterile basin she had quickly unwrapped, retaining a small amount which she transferred to a test tube, to be whisked to the blood bank for typing.

"Better mix some citrate with that—he may need it for a transfusion." Marisa spoke without taking her eyes off the second syringe, which was now filling rapidly as she maintained the steady pull upon the plunger.

"Tamponade, Dr. Feldman?" The voice was somewhat harsh, with a definite Teutonic accent and, in spite of her intense concentration on the vital job of removing blood from the pericardial sac, Marisa stiffened involuntarily. A solidly built man had moved up to the table as those around it shuffled back respectfully to give him room.

Having heard the voice at the staff conference the evening before, she recognized it as belonging to Dr. Anton Dieter, the brilliant heart and chest surgeon, but the accent still brought memories Marisa had thought exorcised from her mind during the years in England and at Harvard. A refugee from East Germany, Dieter had made a reputation in those fields long before he had been lured to Weston and the University Hospital to beef up the medical school teaching staff.

"I happened to be passing through and recognized the symptoms," she explained.

"*Gut!* You have already injected adrenalin into the heart?"

"Not yet. It seemed more important to remove blood from the pericardium at once."

"Quite right. I will inject the adrenalin. A syringe and long needle please, nurse. And bring the cardiac cart with the Pacemaker."

A smaller syringe with a long slender needle was in Dieter's hand almost before he finished speaking. At the same moment, the nurse placed upon the sterile towel in which it had been wrapped an ampule of adrenalin from a supply kept in alcohol in a jar, so it would be sterile and ready for any emergency. With a small file—also from the jar—Dieter swiftly nicked the neck of the ampule, broke it off with a gauze sponge to prevent possible laceration of his own fingers from the fragments of glass, and began to draw its contents up into the syringe.

"Pardon *Fräulei*—Doctor." Dieter's hands moved into the space beside Marisa's, carrying the small syringe filled with the clear adrenalin. The hands, as they plunged the slender needle directly through the chest wall about an inch below where Marisa had placed the first needle, were slender and very facile, the wrists a little stocky and perhaps more hairy than those of most men. They didn't touch Marisa's hands, but she had to fight against recoiling a little, as she carefully disconnected the syringe from the larger needle and handed it to the nurse again, receiving an empty one in its place.

"How much have you aspirated, Doctor?" Dieter said.

"A hundred and fifty cc."

"We should see some effect soon." Again Dieter's faint Teutonic accent struck Marisa's ears like the clanging of the bell in the prison at Frondheim. "Keep on, please. I shall work around you."

Fully two inches of the smaller needle attached to the syringe in Dieter's hands had now been thrust through the chest wall, quite enough to penetrate into the muscular part of the heart. When he pulled back the plunger of the syringe, no blood spurted into the syringe, showing that the point was in the muscle. Injecting half the contents of the syringe, he pushed the needle on in until the metal shank dimpled the skin and injected the remainder into the chamber of the heart he had penetrated, then removed both needle and syringe with a swift movement.

No one could doubt who was in charge now, as the hospital resident who had accompanied Dieter pushed the wheeled cart loaded with monitoring devices and the electrical stimulator called the Pacemaker close to the table. Marisa experienced an instinctive moment of resentment at having been shoved, so to speak, into the background; after all, it had been she who had recognized that the patient might be saved—even though the ambulance diagnosis was D.O.A.—and had acted accordingly. But the call of "Cardiac Alert" on the hospital loudspeaker had made every available doctor part of the emergency, so she knew she couldn't blame Dieter for appearing. Besides, cardiac surgery was the field in which he was internationally known and if an operation were necessary, it was extremely important that the need should be recognized immediately because of the time element involved.

The deft hands with the tufts of hair on the wrists appeared once again within Marisa's field of vision, this time holding the insulated handles of a pair of electrodes connected to the Cardiac Pacemaker. At the end of each handle was a disk of metal—the electrode itself—from which a wire led to the machine. Taking care not to get in her way, Dieter placed the metal electrodes on the skin of the wounded man's chest, one on either side of the needle Marisa had inserted.

"I think the heart is fibrillating," she said. "I was able to hear a faint sound in the stethoscope but it wasn't rhythmic."

"So? Then we'll give it an extra jolt." Dieter gave rapid-fire instructions for setting the controls of the Pacemaker to the resident who accompanied him. In cases of fibrillation, where the normal rhythmic action of the heart muscle had been lost and a completely disorganized pattern of contraction substituted instead, the sudden sharp jolt of a powerful electric current often literally shocked the muscle back into a normal rhythmic pattern once more.

"Push the button, please," Dieter instructed and the machine hummed momentarily, then as quickly stopped. In that instant, however, an electric current had flowed from the coils, tubes and diodes of the Pacemaker through the wire to one of the electrodes, thence into the heart which lay almost quiescent beneath the chest wall, through the heart muscle and back to the second electrode in the machine, completing the circuit.

In response to the jolting pulse of electricity, the heart leaped like a suddenly roweled horse and Marisa felt it strike the point of the needle penetrating into the pericardial sac, causing a perceptible jolt against her hand as she held the syringe.

"Gut!" Dieter's explosive grunt of approval when he saw the syringe move in her hand was pure German, but he lapsed immediately into his slightly accented English. "Switch the Pacemaker to normal rhythm please."

The dials clicked again as the adjustments were made and the machine began to hum, less lively now that the amount of current used was smaller, but nevertheless enough to flow in a steadily rhythmic pulsation.

"I can feel a pulse at the temple," the intern handling the resuscitator reported.

"It means only that we are pumping blood through the circulation," said Dieter. "The heart must take up a rhythm of its own before we can say he is alive."

The issue remained in doubt only a few seconds longer, however. As the artificial Pacemaker stimulated the heart to contract in a steady rhythm, a dramatic change began to take place in the wounded man.

The distention of the neck vessels which had first warned Marisa of what was happening quickly disappeared as the heart, with much of the blood which had literally throttled it in its own pericardial sac now removed, found room to do its work again and the circulation took up its normal activities. And with an adequate supply of oxygen now being pumped into the lungs, where the normal interchange with the blood took place, the mottled blue color of the upper chest, neck and face began to change to the pinker hue of normal oxygenation.

"It's a miracle!" one of the interns who was watching exclaimed.

"Not yet," Dieter corrected him. "His heart contracts; his lungs are inflated and deflated; oxygen even goes into his blood—but we may only be making a corpse go through the movements of liv—"

He broke off speaking when the rhythm of the resuscitator valve suddenly changed. Ever since the intern had started the machine, the steady click-click of the valve, alternately inflating the wounded man's lungs and allowing the air to escape, had not changed. Suddenly now, the interval between the clicks shortened and became irregular, a sure sign that the patient was beginning to breathe of his own accord, the force of his own respiration against the machine changing the rhythm of the valves.

"He breathes! He lives!" Dieter exclaimed. "Congratulations, Dr. Feldman! You have brought about a resurrection!"

CHAPTER SIX

I

Hurrying through the door of the emergency room just as the clock on the wall marked five when he was due to be on duty, Mike Traynor came upon a dramatic scene: the slender woman doctor with the dark hair cut short and the arresting, if somewhat angular, features withdrawing blood from the pericardial sac; the stocky figure of Anton Dieter, holding the electrodes upon the chest of the wounded man; the intern with the mask of the resuscitator over the patient's face, hiding completely the features that would have identified him.

Well, he thought. *For once we're having some excitement around here.*

He didn't doubt for a moment that the patient on the table was the "prominent physician" mentioned in the radio broadcast, and craned his neck over the shoulder of one of the interns to try and see who it was. But the mask of the respirator hid the wounded man's features and Mike was afraid to ask anyone his name. Like many top-notch surgeons Dieter was known to have a quick temper and Mike didn't want to risk incurring his anger.

That newest faculty member wasn't bad, Mike decided when he turned his attention to Marisa Feldman. Of course she could hardly be considered at her best, sweating over the aspiration of blood from the chest of the poor guy on the table. She'd only been on the faculty for two days, but everyone in the school knew that in her field she was considered to be almost as skilled as Dieter was in his. A refugee educated in England, the scuttlebutt said she'd gone into East Germany to help relatives but had been caught there and put in some sort of a concentration camp. Jews weren't liked in that section, even then, and the Russians hated them. But she'd somehow managed to make her escape, finish her education in England, and put in a couple of years as an instructor at Harvard, before coming to Weston with the rank of assistant professor.

The fact that Marisa Feldman was close to thirty didn't bother Mike Traynor at all—or that she was a Jew. He'd always heard Jewish women were passionate and the older any woman was, the more grateful she was likely to be to a younger man who took an interest in her.

Yes, he decided, Dr. Marisa Feldman was definitely worth investigating. The fact that he was a student and she was on the faculty might make things a bit difficult, of course, but it also made the problem more interesting. As a specialist in seduction, Mike liked a challenge and this one looked worthy of his skill.

Just then, the intern handling the resuscitator removed the face mask to adjust the airway and Mike Traynor had a brief glimpse of the wounded man's face that was enough to send him scurrying out of the cubicle. At the door of the emergency room, he met Lew Saunders, his roommate in the interns' quarters.

"Cover for me ten minutes, Lew," he said, seizing the other student by the arm. "I've got to make a telephone call."

"Always chiseling, aren't you, Mike?"

"This is really important. Besides you'll want to see what they're going to do with the heart case over there."

"You're right at that," said Saunders. "But be sure and get back in twenty minutes. I've got a date."

"I promise." Mike was already headed for the locker room, where he'd hung up his coat and put on a white jacket before coming on duty. Thrusting the white coat into the closet space reserved for the students, he grabbed his own jacket and ran down the ramp up which the stretchers were wheeled from the ambulances.

A row of telephone booths was located along the wall directly across from the Snack Bar and he dived into one of them. Fortunately he remembered seeing the name Hilton on the road leading to the cottage where he'd left Elaine McGill about a half hour ago. A quick look in the directory told him there were two numbers listed under Hilton, the second a county exchange which almost certainly meant the cottage. Dropping a dime into the phone, he dialed the second number.

The horny old bastard, he thought as he waited for the phone to ring. Then he began to laugh because it was a rare joke after all.

While he'd been shacked up at the lake cottage with Old Dermatographia's wife, the skin writer had been laying the hottest thing in town.

II

Elaine McGill was awakened by the sound of the telephone. Still half drugged from the explosive release of long pent-up emotions she'd found in the arms of Mike Traynor the second time, she came groggily from sleep and picked up the phone.

"Mrs. McGill! Elaine!" It sounded like Mike's voice.

"Yes?"

"It's me. Mike Traynor. Have you heard yet?"

"Heard what? I've been asleep."

"You haven't had the TV or the radio on?"

"No. What's this all about?"

"Just the biggest scandal that's ever hit this town. The hospital's trying to get you."

"Why?"

"Your husband was with Mrs. Dellman this afternoon. Dr. Dellman shot them both."

"That's impossible," she said quickly. "Paul couldn't—"

"I saw him in the emergency room with my own eyes, he took a bullet in the chest."

Elaine held on to the bedpost for support. "Will they have to operate?"

"Dieter hadn't decided when I came to call you. Dr. McGill was practically dead with a wound in the heart but a new woman doctor over at the hospital realized what it was in time to save him. Don't worry. In Dieter's hands he should be okay. That guy's a genius when it comes to anything involving the chest or the heart."

"I'll be there as quickly as I can. Tell them that for me."

"I don't think that would be wise—considering. Do you?"

"No, I suppose not." More than anything else she wanted to get him off the phone.

"I just thought you ought to know," he said. "And don't worry. This Dieter is a whiz."

Elaine slammed down the phone and began to dress in frantic haste. Paul and Lorrie! It was the last thing she would have suspected. With the others, yes. Once at the Dissection Society, Maggie McCloskey had said they all had one thing in common—their husbands had slept with Lorrie Dellman.

But if Paul had made it with Lorrie, why did he have so much trouble with her?

III

"You can switch to simple oxygen administration now," Dieter told the intern handling the resuscitator. The resident who had accompanied the surgeon took the handles of the Pacemaker electrodes and Dieter picked up the patient's wrist, counting the pulse by the sweep hand of his watch.

"One-twenty but regular and pretty strong for a man who was dead a few minutes ago," he reported. "Somebody see what the blood pressure is."

"That was quick thinking, Dr. Feldman." He turned to Marisa while the blood pressure cuff was being applied to Paul McGill's arm. "I'm not quite sure I would have made the diagnosis that quickly." Coming from Dieter, she knew it was high praise—and resisted the impulse to be grateful to him for it. "I heard faint heart sounds with the stethoscope," she explained. "Shall I remove the aspiration needle now? The flow seems to have stopped."

"For the time being, yes," said Dieter. "But stay close by, if you will. When his blood pressure rises, he may start pumping blood out through that bullet hole in his ventricle again before we're able to close it with a few sutures. The wound of entry is pretty obvious there at the front of the chest. Did anybody examine his back for a wound of exit?"

"There was hardly time. The ambulance attendants had labeled him a D.O.A. when I happened to see them bringing him into the emergency room and noticed that the veins of his neck were congested."

Dieter's bushy eyebrows rose again. "Then you really did raise him from the dead, Dr. Feldman."

The graying emergency-room supervisor looked from one of them to the other, as she cleared away the syringe and needles from the small table. What could there possibly be between those two? she wondered. The Jewish woman doctor had only been there two days but, looking at them, you could fairly see the sparks of animal magnetism flying.

"He seems to be breathing all right," Dieter observed. "Let's see if he has established a heart rhythm of his own yet."

The resident lifted the electrodes from the chest wall as the nurse clicked off the switch. Dieter kept his fingers upon the pulse for a full minute, while he studied the sweep hand of his watch.

"The beat is pretty fair—and regular," he reported. "I think we can turn him on his side gently to look for a wound of exit."

No sign of any exit wound showed anywhere, and Dieter's expression was grave as they eased the patient back once again.

"Now we'll have to remove the bullet like they do on television," he said. "Wheel him into the X-ray and let's see what we can find. And nurse—"

"Yes, Doctor."

"Bring along the respirator and the Pacemaker just in case we need it. Coming, Dr. Feldman?"

Marisa hesitated only a moment. "I was on the way to dinner—but it can wait."

"Thank you," said Dieter as he pushed the examining table out of the cubicle. "I would like for you to stand by, in case the pericardium starts filling up again."

Some fifteen minutes later, Dieter stood across the X-ray table from Dr. Sam Penfield, the hospital roentgenologist, studying the fluoroscopic screen illuminated by the X-rays flooding up through the chest of the patient from the tube beneath the table. A small spot, quite dark, showed against the lighter background of the lungs and the soft tissues of the chest wall. It was located in the shadow of the heart, which could be seen beating regularly.

"*Mein Gott!*" In moments of excitement, Dieter still lapsed into his native tongue. There was good reason for him to be excited now, for the bullet was tumbling slowly within a small restricted area.

"The damn thing's inside the heart!" said the roentgenologist in an awed voice. "Right in the middle of a ventricle, would be my guess."

"No chance that it's outside the chamber—in the pericardium or muscle?" Dieter asked.

"Not the way it's moving," said Penfield. "If it were in the pericardium or the muscle, the shadow would move in rhythm with the heart. But you can see that it seems to be tumbling about in the stream of blood passing through the ventricle, which means it has to be free."

"Take a look at this, Dr. Feldman." Dieter moved aside so Marisa could approach the screen. "You may not ever see anything like this again."

"I never saw anything like it," Penfield volunteered.

"What is his condition?" Dieter asked the intern who was standing at one end of the table, his finger on the temple pulse used by anesthetists to count the heartbeat during operations. A blood pressure cuff had been placed on the patient's arm and a stethoscope strapped against the front of his forearm, so the blood pressure could be taken while he was on the table.

"Very good, sir," said the intern. "Pulse one hundred. Respiration twenty-four. Blood pressure one hundred over seventy."

"The heart seems to have a good stroke," Marisa Feldman observed, watching the beat on the fluoroscopic screen. "There must not be much blood within the pericardium."

"And no more being pumped out through the wound, from the looks of the heart shadow," Penfield agreed.

"What do you say, Dr. Feldman, to lowering the head of the table and dropping the bullet through the aortic valve into the aorta, so it can be pumped out into one of the arteries of the legs?" Dieter asked casually. "All we would need to do then would be to make a short incision over the vessel, open it up and take out the bullet."

"Your reasoning would be sound, Doctor—if the bullet is in the left ventricle." Marisa Feldman's English accent became more clipped. "But if it's in the right, you will be pumping the bullet out into the arterial tree of the lungs, where the vessel caliber gets smaller all the time. Before you knew it, you'd cause a pulmonary embolus and probably death."

"So?" Anton Dieter's tone was slightly amused. "You are logical as well as beautiful, Dr. Feldman."

She stiffened slightly when she realized he'd only been testing her with the question, then relaxed. "I didn't know you were making a joke, Doctor."

"It was no joke; I merely wanted to confirm my own thinking." Dieter turned to the intern. "As Dr. Feldman has pointed out, if the bullet is in the right ventricle and if it accidentally slips out into the pulmonary circulation, we could have a very grave situation on our hands. See that the patient is moved very carefully to the operating room. We don't want that little bullet to start traveling."

"The front office hasn't been able to locate his wife yet, Doctor." The emergency-room nurse had come into the X-ray room. "They've been trying her home but nobody answers and no one else knows where she is."

"Then we'll have to operate without her," said Dieter crisply. "We can't afford to wait any longer."

"A couple of police officers are outside, Dr. Dieter," said the nurse. "Will you have time to speak to them before you go upstairs?"

"Only for a moment. Call Dr. Long please and ask him to order the preoperative medication. If you would accompany the patient to the operating room, Dr. Feldman, I should be very grateful."

IV

Lieutenent Vosges and Sergeant O'Brien rose from the visitor's bench of the emergency room as Anton Dieter approached.

"I have to be in the operating room in a few minutes, gentlemen," the surgeon said briskly. "The nurse said you wanted to see me."

"Does Dr. McGill have a chance, Doctor?" Eric Vosges asked.

"An excellent one—considering that there's a bullet inside his heart."

"Inside his heart?" O'Brien exclaimed. "That's one for the book, isn't it?"

"It's not exactly an everyday occurrence," Dieter agreed. "I haven't had time to get any details of this unfortunate happening. How many shots were fired?"

"Only one." O'Brien grinned. "The bullet went through Mrs. Dellman's heart first, but they were pretty close together at the time, so it wasn't particularly difficult."

"So?" Anton Dieter's eyebrows rose. "Is that all, gentlemen?"

"We may want a supplementary report after you finish the operation," Vosges told him.

"Of course." Dieter clicked his heels. "Good day."

Lieutenant Vosges and Sergeant O'Brien had left their car in the parking lot across the street. As they crossed toward it now, they saw four women converging on the emergency-room door from different parts of the lot. All looked worried and one stumbled as she walked between two of the others. None noticed O'Brien, although he lifted his hat politely to them.

"Friends of yours?" Vosges asked with a grin.

"I know them all, but I could hardly blame them for not noticing me at a time like this. My guess is that each of them has heard the broadcast and is hurrying to the hospital to see whether it's her husband who has an acute case of lead poisoning."

He looked back to where the four had come together at the emergency-room door. They appeared to hesitate, waiting for one to be the first to enter. Then Amy Brennan stepped through the door and the others followed.

"There go the wives of four of the most prominent doctors in town," O'Brien added. "All close friends of Lorrie Porter's, too. The things I've heard about some of the parties they have would curl your hair."

"I guess they've got a right to be scared," said Vosges. "Right now each one probably sees her own little world starting to crumble about her."

"Half the time Amy Weston—she's the tall one that came in the white Cadillac—wouldn't give you the time of day," said O'Brien. "Now she's scurrying like the rest to find out who's the loser. Come to think of it, I guess they all are."

"How do you figure that?"

"That group and two or three others pretty much run the society end of town—chairman of this and that fund-raising project, the symphony, Festival of Arts—the whole bit. Amy Brennan is high up in the state medical auxiliary, too, from what I read in the papers. If I know Dellman, he's going to turn heaven and earth to beat this rap, and that means those women and their husbands, plus a few others, will have to help him whether they like it or not." He grinned. "If you ask me this is just about the craziest caper Lorrie Porter ever pulled."

"Why do you say that?"

"When Lorrie was a girl, she was always getting into scrapes. I worked as a security guard in the old Weston Mills before joining the police force, so I had to get her out of a lot of them. Nothing really ornery, mind you—just her idea of fun. When I see all those women scuttling into the hospital to find out which one of them will have to hide her head until this thing blows over, I could almost believe Lorrie planned it that way."

"Can it blow over?"

"Of course."

"You can't just sweep murder under the rug."

"You forget that Weston Mills makes some of the biggest rugs in the world; they'll find one to hide even this particular pile of dirt under. Come on, Eric. We've got to locate this guy's wife and break the news to her."

Lieutenant Vosges saw the car flash through a red light as they were approaching an intersection some ten minutes later. He made a quick left turn to follow, switching on his siren at the same moment, and soon passed the car ahead. But, when he started to swing over toward the curb to slow it down, Sergeant O'Brien said quickly, "Keep ahead of her, Eric, with the siren going."

"What the dev—"

"That's McGill's wife. The one we're looking for."

Vosges stepped on the throttle again as O'Brien leaned out and waved for Elaine McGill to follow them. When she nodded her understanding and fell in behind the police cruiser O'Brien leaned back in his seat.

"You know what would be ironic?" he said.

"This whole damn thing's ironic, if you ask me."

"Suppose the reason nobody could find her was that she was out two-timing the doc with another guy?"

"That would be a switch all right."

O'Brien sat up suddenly. "That's it."

"What?"

"I told you something about this whole thing didn't gee."

"I still don't get it."

"Lorrie Dellman was shot *through* the heart and Dr. McGill has a bullet in his, from the front. What does that mean?"

"You tell me."

"Unless Dellman was shooting from under the bed, the positions were switched so when he shot what he thought was a man seducing his wife, it really was his wife seducing a man. Oh I'll bet Lorrie is really cackling over this one—wherever she is."

CHAPTER SEVEN

I

It was half after five when Dr. David Rogan, psychiatrist for the Faculty Clinic and head of that department in Weston University Medical School, finished dictating a note on the final patient of the day and shut off the Dictaphone. Like everyone in both the clinic and in the hospital, he had been cognizant of the drama being played out across the street in the emergency room. But since he had no assigned duties during a Cardiac Alert, he had resisted the temptation to cross over to the hospital to see what was happening, increasing the press of people who could only hinder the resuscitation team in its work.

That strange communication network called the hospital grapevine had informed him, via his secretary, that Paul McGill had been shot by Mort Dellman "in the very act," to use her phrase. Remembering that he had not yet been able to examine Janet Monroe's little boy in the consultation requested that morning by Dr. Deemster, the Professor of Pediatrics, Dave decided to stop by before going home and took the elevator to the ground floor of the clinic.

Of medium height, he was almost half bald at forty-five, the sparse remaining hair at his temples already two-thirds gray. Golf and yard work over weekends kept his body trim, although he had to watch his weight, both for cholesterol and to avoid what George Hanscombe, the clinic heart and circulation expert, called "creeping inflation of the waistline." Which wasn't easy with Della away so much of the time playing in golf tournaments, and a colored housekeeper whose forte was that gastronomic atom bomb known as "Southern cooking."

Like most psychiatrists, Dave Rogan had the slightly withdrawn look that comes from observing human foibles and peccadillos with an understanding eye, in his case through rimless glasses without which he couldn't read a street sign at ten feet. But right now his normal psychiatrist's calm was diminished by a problem not unusual in husbands—his inability to understand his own wife. It had been two weeks now since Della had gone to Augusta for the Southeastern Women's Open Championship in a huff because he couldn't go with her, but so far he hadn't been able to make any perceptible progress toward arranging a peace.

No quarrel of theirs had ever lasted half this long, he thought as he stepped out of the elevator in the lobby of the clinic, almost deserted now that the tide of ailing humanity surging through the doors every morning at eight had receded for another twenty-four hours. Usually family quarrels in the Rogan household followed the same pattern as with most married couples. There would be a spat, after which Della gave him the silent treatment for a day or two; or if it were a real quarrel, she usually slept in the spare room for one or two nights as a pointed reminder of her displeasure. In the end, though, they'd always made up without the threat of divorce.

This quarrel had started much the same way, but somewhere along the line, particularly after Della had returned from Augusta, the pattern of recovery had failed to develop normally—in fact not at all. He'd made the usual overtures that were expected of him as evidence of his repentance for sins committed—or attributed—but they had accomplished nothing. Each morning, Della marched off to golf, and each evening they sat home in stony silence after dinner until it was time to go to bed. Fortunately, the children were still away at camp; as a psychiatrist he knew very well that marital discord, even the small amount of it that happened between him and Della, could have a shattering effect on developing personalities if long continued.

So there was nothing to do but wait until Della decided to reveal the as yet unnamed sin of which he had been judged guilty through that strange and tortuous process of reasoning—or unreasoning—called feminine logic. But he was a peace-loving man; after dealing with emotional storms, it had always been a relief to come home to someone who, perhaps largely because she was physically exhausted from playing eighteen holes of golf or more, didn't meet him at the door with a chip on her shoulder. And he wanted nothing so much right now as a cessation of hostilities, however accomplished.

Leaving the clinic, Dave crossed the street and entered the hospital by way of the emergency entrance, a short cut to the Pediatrics ward where he was going to examine little Jerry Monroe. As he passed through the small waiting area outside the white tiled emergency room, he was surprised to see Della, Grace Hanscombe, Maggie McCloskey and Amy Brennan waiting at the desk and looking uncertain, as people always did when not sure where they should go. The sudden look of relief in Della's eyes when she spied him came as a surprise, after the icebox treatment she'd been giving him for over a week.

"Hello, girls," he said. "If you've come about Paul—"

"Paul!" Amy Brennan gasped. "Then he was the one?"

Dave's eyes moved from one of the women to another, noting the same look of relief Della had shown at the sight of him.

"None of you knew who the man was, did you?" he exclaimed.

"The radio broadcast didn't give the name," Della explained. "We all decided to come and help each other."

"Is Paul going to be all right?" Grace Hanscombe asked.

"I don't know anything except what came over the hospital grapevine," he said. "But I'll talk to the E.R. supervisor and see what I can find out."

He came back in a few moments. "Paul has a bullet in his heart, but seems to have been in good shape when he left here. Dieter has taken him up to the operating room."

"I need a drink." Maggie McCloskey sat down suddenly on a nearby bench.

"I'll get you some water." Going to the cooler in the corner of the waiting room, Grace Hanscombe took down a paper cup from the dispenser and filled it with water. Maggie's hands were trembling so much that she couldn't hold the cup still, so Grace steadied them while she drank.

"Are you going to the operating room, Dave?" Della was hoping he'd be free to go home with her; she was beginning to feel a little shaky herself in reaction to the tension under which they'd all been laboring since the first broadcast had gone on the air.

"I have to see Janet Monroe's little boy in consultation," he explained. "I'm on my way now."

"Is Elaine here?" Grace asked.

"The nurse I talked to said they've been calling her at home but there's no answer."

"Elaine and Paul have been using the Hilton cottage at Lake Tabitha this summer," said Grace. "George and I were out there to supper with them last week."

"I'll tell the operator to try the cottage," he said. "Paul always plays golf on Wednesday and Elaine may have taken someone out to the lake for a swim."

Just then the outside door opened and Elaine McGill came in. She looked at the women, then at Dave. Knowing the question that was on her lips and sensing that she couldn't bring herself to speak the words, he said quickly: "They've taken Paul to the operating room, Elaine. Dr. Dieter thinks he'll be all right but they couldn't wait for you."

"I was at the lake."

"The bullet's in the heart. Dieter is going to go in and take it out." It was a measure of Anton Dieter's reputation and the rapid advance of surgical knowledge that none of them were shocked by the extent or nature of the operative procedure. Open-heart surgery had become so much a part of the hospital's operation since Dieter's coming to Weston that it was almost taken as a matter of course.

"Can I go to Paul?" Elaine asked.

"He's already gone to surgery," said Dave, "but they'll bring him back to the Special Intensive Care Unit afterward. I've got to go to Pediatrics Four for a consultation but it's on my way and I can drop you there."

"Do you want any of us to stay, Elaine?" Grace Hanscombe asked. "I can, if you like."

"So can I," said Della.

"I've got a migraine," said Amy. "But I'll be glad—"

"Please don't." Elaine's tone was grateful. "It will be a long operation, won't it, Dave?"

"Probably. Takes quite a while to get ready for one of these jobs, and after it starts, things can't be rushed."

"I'll be all right," Elaine assured the four women. "Thank you all for coming."

"If there ever was a time to be honest this is it," said Grace. "We really came because we didn't know who the man was and we were all scared stiff."

Dave found himself wishing it had been Della who had spoken, even though the words would have been an admission that she suspected he might have been unfaithful to her. Whatever it was that had shattered the quiet understanding and trust which had been so important a part of their marriage through the years, had apparently come to a climax during that last golf tournament Della had played in at Augusta, the Southeastern Women's Open. He'd been waiting for her to tell him about it, knowing she must unburden her mind of her own accord, if what had been between them was to be restored. But she didn't seem ready yet and he was too good a psychiatrist—and too understanding a husband—to push her.

"You'll be late for dinner, won't you Dave?" Della asked.

"Probably; Ed Harrison is going to do a spinal puncture on Janet Monroe's little boy and I really should stay and see what it shows, if I'm going to make an intelligent diagnosis. You look bushed, hon. Why not go home and lie down until I get there? Then we'll go out to a drive-in or some place and have a bite."

"All right." Della's tone was dull; the animation she'd shown at the sight of him seemed to have vanished.

"I'll try not to be too long," he promised. "Come on, Elaine, I'll drop you off at the Intensive Care Unit."

"How could Elaine be so calm?" Maggie McCloskey said as they were leaving the waiting room. "Our husbands weren't even involved and we were all scared stiff."

"I guess she was numb," said Della.

"If you ask me we're all pretty numb," said Grace. "Where did you hear the news, Amy?"

"What?" So sharp had been Amy's relief at discovering the man in the case wasn't Pete, that she'd been half in a daze while Dave Rogan was speaking to them, listening but barely hearing. Even the migraine had been numbed a little momentarily by her worry over Pete; now it began to throb again.

"I asked where you were when you heard the news," Grace repeated.

"Fifteen or twenty miles west of town on the interstate, coming back from the District Six meeting."

"I'd forgotten about that. How did you come out?"

"I have the pledge of their votes."

"Congratulations! That cinches the election, doesn't it?"

"I think so."

It must be the migraine that made her feel so little satisfaction in announcing her triumph, Amy thought. In fact whatever triumph she remembered feeling had been blasted by the sound of the announcer's excited voice on the radio.

"I wonder what Act Two will be," said Maggie McCloskey.

"What do you mean?" Della's voice was sharp.

"None of us are fools enough to think we've seen the end of the play. This afternoon each of you had to face up to the fact that your marriage might be shot—just as mine already is. I ought to feel triumphant; God knows you all had enough to say about my getting a divorce from Joe. But right now all I can feel is sorrow, for you and even more for myself."

"Let's get the hell out of here," said Grace. "Three of us, at least, have husbands who'll be coming home tonight. We'd better be there to give them hell, just in case they've been thinking about doing a little tomcatting, too."

II

The Special Intensive Care Unit was located on the top floor of the Medical Building, part of the old section of the hospital. Through the door of the small waiting room, to which Dave Rogan had taken Elaine McGill, she could see the nurses' station, with its banks of electronic monitor tubes and the desk where Janet Monroe was working on charts in the spill of light over the desk, leaving the bank of tubes above in shadow. Elaine hadn't realized she was hungry, until Janet brought her a tray of coffee and buttered toast. Now she was eating mechanically while her mind slowly recovered, in part, from the shock of what Mike Traynor had said when he called her at the cottage on the lake, the still hardly believable fact that Paul had been with Lorrie that afternoon and had been shot by Mort Dellman.

Through the large window of the waiting room, Elaine could see the corner of the new Surgical Building and a bank of windows, one quite large and very brightly lit. She knew enough about the hospital to realize the window marked the location of the main operating suite, but it was still hard to believe that all this wasn't really a nightmare and that, in the room behind it, Paul's life still hung in the balance.

Did she have the right to pray—she wondered—when hardly three hours before she had been in the arms of another man—and as guilty as Paul?

In her favor was the fact that the desperate measure she had adopted was motivated by the purely unselfish desire to bear Paul a child, even though the seed that let it come into being might not be his. At the time, that need had seemed ample justification for the first joining of her body with Mike Traynor's and she had no regrets. But what justification could she possibly find for the second—except Mike's unabashed lust and her own desire for him?

She could have dressed and left the cottage when she awakened; there was no denying that. Instead, she had wakened him earlier than she needed to do in order for him to make his five o'clock assignment at the hospital. Awakened him, she admitted now in a moment of complete honesty, because deep inside her there had been an unanswered question, a doubt whether she was really the woman she thought herself to be, with a woman's ability to respond fully in the physical act of love-making that was such an important part of real marriage.

No, she couldn't blame Paul, when she herself was as guilty as he was. Nor could she really blame Lorrie Dellman, for Lorrie had given them all fair warning at Amy Weston's house over a year ago—during a meeting of the Dissection Society.

They had been playing bridge after Amy's cook, Ethel, had served the peaches flambeau. Lorrie had made a small slam in spades; she was a wild bidder, but surprisingly often made the bids anyway. While Amy dealt, Lorrie had begun to make the cards, riffling the deck expertly. . . .

III

"God, but I'm horny," Lorrie had said, as casually as if she was discussing the weather.

"Contain yourself," said Maggie McCloskey. "Mort's not around."

"Why Mort? Any old port in a storm, you know."

"Don't talk foolishness, Lorrie," Amy said severely.

"With me it isn't foolishness." Lorrie put the made deck beside her on the table and picked up the hand that had been dealt her. "Or maybe one of you gals would like to go upstairs for a little while. I can promise you an interesting—"

"Lorrie!" Amy snapped. "That's going too far—even for you."

"Don't tell me none of you ever thought about it—or tried it."

"Some things you don't talk about," said Maggie. "I bid two hearts."

"Two spades," said Lorrie. "This is the twentieth century, girls. A hundred years ago a woman wasn't supposed to have any erotic feelings, except when her husband turned her on."

"Like putting a key into a lock," said Grace.

"And only one key was supposed to fit," Maggie added.

"When he got through, she was supposed to be turned off," Elaine had said and remembered again how she had blushed at having inadvertently revealed the truth about her intimate life with Paul. "What I mean is—"

"We all know what you mean, Elaine," Grace Hanscombe said. "It's happened to all of us, I imagine—and more than once."

"Girls!" said Amy. "Let's get back to a pleasant subject."

"I maintain there isn't a more pleasant subject," Lorrie insisted. "The reason a lot of women don't talk about it is because they don't want to admit publicly that they occasionally have the urge to go to bed with some man other than their husband. The truth is, you're all afraid to let yourself go because you think a man gets some sort of power over you for a couple of minutes—at the climax—when you've got to keep going, whether you want to or not."

"Did you ever want not to?" Grace Hanscombe asked.

"What would be the use of getting started in the first place?" said Lorrie. "What you forget is that the man doesn't even have as much control as you—and that makes you the victor."

"Hunh!" Della Rogan exclaimed. "Two minutes of victory and nine months of penance."

"What you have to settle for is a negotiated peace, Della," Grace Hanscombe said with a grin.

"How'd you spell that last word?" Lorrie asked and there'd been a round of laughter.

It was two hands later that Lorrie had dropped the bombshell.

"You know what might be fun," she said.

"Here we go again," said Maggie. "What is it this time?"

"Let's swap husbands."

There was a startled silence, then a burst of laughter—most of it forced.

"Nobody but you would think of such a thing, Lorrie," said Elaine.

"Don't tell me that. You've all thought of it more than once. Come clean now and let your hair down."

A dead silence—a guilty silence—greeted the thrust. Then Amy said harshly, "We're all romantic, else we wouldn't be married, Lorrie. Of course we sometimes dream of being carried off by a Prince Charming. Who hasn't?"

"Only he always turned out to be a dud," said Maggie.

"It takes two, you know, Maggie," said Lorrie.

"Do you know something about Joe?" Maggie had demanded suspiciously.

"No. But since you brought it up, it's not a bad idea. Small men are usually powerful lovers."

"You stay away from him!" Maggie squalled.

"Don't get excited," said Lorrie. "Joe's a urologist and women have more bladder and kidney trouble than anything else. I'll bet a day doesn't pass that a dozen female bottoms aren't turned up for him—"

"If Joe so much as . . . ." Maggie had lapsed into incoherence.

"We get together every month anyway, so why not make these sessions more interesting?" said Lorrie. "Think what fun it would be to take on someone else's husband in the interim and report on it every month."

"Lorrie!" It was a chorus of virtuous—and not entirely honest—reproof.

"I mean it. You're all suffering from sexual malnutrition because you have too much of the same diet."

"What do *you* do?" Maggie asked. "Take vitamins?"

"You might call it that. At least I sample an occasional new dish to help me stay young."

"I'll say one thing," Grace Hanscombe volunteered. "Fornication seems to agree with you. I never saw anybody look so damn healthy."

"You can all be the same way," Lorrie assured them. "Now take us: we're seven couples—counting Alice and Roy—and there are seven nights a week, so we can make rounds at least once a month."

"Suppose you're married to a once-a-week man?" Grace asked.

"Maybe the vitamins I prescribe will help him. Who knows?"

"From what I hear, you've got a good start already on this husband-swapping business," said Maggie.

Lorrie grinned. "Wouldn't you like to know?" Waiting for Maggie to splutter into angry incoherence, she continued, "But this time, we'll all start even. What do you say?"

"If this is a joke, Lorrie, it's gone far enough," Amy snapped.

"It isn't a joke and it's going farther."

"What do you mean by that?"

"Our husbands are medical men—at least Mort's practically an M.D. and Roy's the clinic lawyer. When they want to try out a new drug, they run a clinical test, so there's no reason why we can't do the same. Afterward, we'll have a clinic with case histories, like our husbands do when they're discussing whether or not they've made a mistake in treating something."

"You mean a clinical pathological conference, don't you?" said Della.

"What's that?" Since Roy Weston was a lawyer, Alice wasn't familiar with medical terminology.

"It's when the patient's already dead and you're trying to find out what killed him," Della explained.

"We have a few of those, too," Grace agreed.

"I'm betting I can wake up even the dead ones," Lorrie offered.

"Forget it, Lorrie," Amy said sharply.

"Who elected you spokesman, Amy?" Maggie demanded.

"You mean you—?"

"No. But I'm not going to have other people making decisions for me. I say put it to a vote."

Amy shrugged. "Whatever the decision, I'll not have any part of it."

"Maybe Pete will have different ideas, Amy." Lorrie's grin was taunting. "After all, a man who's been chained to an iceberg can't be blamed for getting excited when he sees a palm tree on the horizon."

Amy stiffened, and for a moment Elaine thought she was going to explode.

"Hit you where it hurt, didn't I?" Lorrie chuckled. "Personally I could never see why a full-blooded handsome Irishman like Pete ever married a prude like you anyway."

"Lay off it, Lorrie," said Della Rogan. "Our husbands are close friends and we've all got to live together. It won't help any for us to start scratching each other."

"What about you, Grace?" Lorrie asked. "Aren't you in favor of a little variety?"

"I was seduced by an Irish lance corporal before most of you were wearing bras," said Grace wearily. "When you've had one you've had them all."

"What a terrible thing to say!" Elaine remembered protesting.

"My experience doesn't match Lorrie's, of course," said Maggie Mc-Closkey, "but—"

"Are we going to play bridge or musical chairs?" Grace demanded.

"It sounds more like musical beds to me," said Della.

"Let's take a vote on Lorrie's proposal," said Maggie.

"I vote Yes," Lorrie said promptly.

"No!" Amy said firmly.

"Me, too," said Della.

"I'll abstain," said Grace. "After all, I'm a foreigner."

"I vote No," said Maggie. "So you lose, Lorrie."

"I didn't think you'd have the guts to take me up." Lorrie shrugged. "But I thought I should give you a chance before I put Plan B into effect."

"What's Plan B?"

"Since all of you refuse to be honest, I'm going to make the experiment for you myself. I'll have each of your husbands and if you want any pointers afterward, I'll give them to you."

"At least it would be an expert opinion," said Grace.

"I'm not going to listen to this drivel any more." Amy pushed her cards into the center of the table and got to her feet. "This is my house and I think this party is over."

"You're overlooking a good thing, Amy," Lorrie warned her. "All of us admit to being bored, which means we're tired of our husbands' love-making. I'm willing to do all of you a favor by examining each case thoroughly, making a diagnosis, and recommending a course of treatment— unless the case is beyond hope. Nobody could be a better friend than that."

"You've got a point there," Grace admitted. "But I think my case is beyond hope."

"Maybe you're not using all your ammunition," said Lorrie.

"What does that mean?"

"I don't know how you English manage it, but you age a lot better than we Americans do. I know you're past forty-five, Grace, but you could pass for forty any day—except maybe early in the morning, or when you've gone to bed loaded the night before. Fixed up, you look fine, and so do the rest of us. We just need to work a little harder at being lovers than we're doing at being wives."

"Thanks—for nothing," said Maggie bitterly.

"We're all married to reasonably handsome men—even if some of them are beginning to get a little potbellied. In other words, we're normal lower upper-class prosperous professional American couples. We've got every reason in the world to be happy except one: we're bored stiff with each other and with our husbands—which puts us at the dangerous age."

"That's only supposed to apply to men," said Grace.

"It applies to women, too," said Della Rogan. "Dave sees cases all the time. Lorrie's got us pegged all right. At first we were needed by our husbands and later by our children, so we were kept busy and productive. Now we send the children to camp in summer, and in another five years or so most of them will be going off to boarding school or even to college. We're cut out of our husbands' professional lives and they don't want to play golf or poker with us. Our children don't need us much any more and the maid looks after the house. We're bored at home, so we start having various symptoms."

"I have colitis," said Alice proudly.

"That's a common one—along with a lot of others," said Della.

"But it doesn't have to be," Lorrie interposed. "A woman who's having an exciting love affair isn't bored. She's alive and eager. Her glands are working full speed and she's in high gear."

"Until she runs out of gas," said Grace. "Let's face it, girls. Nothing spoils a love affair like marriage—especially to a good provider."

"Grace!" Amy protested.

"We're all living examples of it—except maybe Lorrie."

"The pill is supposed to keep women young and eager," Maggie protested. "You don't even have to go through the menopause any more."

"Dave still sees cases of involutional melancholia in women at the menopause every day," said Della.

"For God's sake," Maggie groaned. "Can't we talk about something cheerful?"

"I'm cheerful," Lorrie said brightly. "In fact I'm downright excited."

Elaine remembered looking at her and feeling a sudden cold fear clutch her heart as she thought that it would be hard for any man to resist Lorrie when she was like this. In fact, looking back on it now, Elaine didn't doubt that Lorrie had already decided to go through with Plan B, whether the rest of them liked it or not.

But why did she have to begin with Paul? Or had he really been the first?

CHAPTER EIGHT

I

Ed Harrison was ready to do the spinal puncture on Jerry Monroe by the time Dave Rogan finished his neurological examination. Dave always welcomed neurological consultations though he would have chosen a different patient if he could, for he was genuinely fond of Janet, who had come down from the ward when the pediatric resident called her, to be with Jerry. Jeff Long would have been there, too, if he hadn't been occupied with preparing for the operation on Paul McGill.

Originally—and often still—neurology and psychiatry were one specialty, termed naturally neuropsychiatry. And reasonably so, since one dealt with the anatomy of the nervous system and with pathological changes in the tissue, while the other was concerned with disturbances of function which were rarely traceable to an anatomical abnormality, except when rarely— now that penicillin cured it—the end results of a syphilitic infection produced insanity. More recently, the two fields had been splitting apart, however, with neurology coming more into the province of medicine, as opposed to surgery; and psychiatry, which occupied practically all of Dave's working time, assuming a category of its own separate from the other two.

Which was absurd, Dave always told his students at the beginning of the course he taught in basic psychiatric principles during the third year of medical school. The mind was a most integral part of the body, and so was the nervous system; how else explain the way a purely emotionally engendered fear or uncertainty could create nervous energy in the form of measurable electrical impulses, which could then travel along the vagus nerve to the stomach and disturb its function so markedly that the organ proceeded to digest itself and form an ulcer. This, in turn, might respond to medication but some cases required the skill of a surgeon, either to close the opening when it digested its way entirely through the stomach wall, spilling highly irritating digestive juices out into the abdominal cavity and creating a grave emergency, or to remove the acid-bearing portion of the stomach in order to save the rest from eating itself up.

"Do you know anything more about Dr. McGill, sir?" Ed Harrison asked Dave as he scrubbed his hands at the tap in the corner of the treatment room of the Pediatrics ward. The little boy was still half asleep from the preliminary medication; the psychiatrist had been forced to awaken him in order to test the reaction of the pupils and the movements of the eyes.

"Dr. Dieter said he was going to have the heart-lung pump ready in case they needed it. That means it will take at least an hour to get ready in the operating room. I hope to look in on the operating room before I leave the hospital."

"Did you find anything positive here, Dr. Rogan?" Janet asked.

"Not much. The reflexes may be a little more active on the right side, but you know how hard it is to evaluate something like that in a child."

"Did you think the neck muscles were at all rigid?" Ed Harrison asked.

"I couldn't be sure. He's pretty relaxed now."

Harrison bent over Jerry, who was lying on the treatment table with the ward nurse supervisor beside him, ready to place him in a position for the spinal tap. "Wake up, young man," he said. "You gonna sleep all day?"

The little boy opened his eyes. "Hello, Dr. Ed," he said and, seeing Janet, smiled, "Hi Mommie."

"Hi, darling," she said. "Just do what Dr. Ed tells you and everything will be all right."

"I know, Mommie."

"I want you to lie on your side and the nurse is going to hold you," the resident told the little boy. "You may feel a pin prick in your back, Jerry, but don't move and I'll try not to hurt you. Okay?"

"Okay, Dr. Ed." The long lashes drooped again and Harrison nodded to the nurse, who swung the little body over expertly until the boy was lying on his side, with his head tucked down and his knees up. She put one arm below his knees and the other around his neck so if he tried to straighten out, she could prevent him.

The purpose of the bowed-out position was to separate the vertebrae and widen the spaces between them through which Ed Harrison planned to insert a needle. Penetrating into the spinal canal, the membrane-lined space around the vital nerve cord inside the vertebral column, the needle would allow him to obtain a sample of the fluid that circulated there in communication with a similar space around the brain and also inside it.

Spinal puncture was a vital diagnostic adjunct in any condition involving either the brain, the spinal cord, or the meninges that formed the continuous lining of both. The presence of pus would indicate a fulminating meningitis. Too many lymphocytes usually signified an inflammatory condition of the brain itself known as encephalitis. The appearance of blood in the fluid could have a multitude of causes, ranging from head injury to the brain damage of an apoplectic stroke in older patients.

Putting on sterile gloves, Ed Harrison painted the child's back with a crimson antiseptic in a circle about six inches in diameter, then draped over it a small sheet with a window some two by four inches in size cut into it. Feeling through the cloth for the spinous processes of the vertebrae, the projecting bony points that formed the visible portion of the backbone, he located the first and second lumbar spines and moved the window to expose them. Then with a tiny needle and syringe, he raised a small wheal of novocaine so skillfully that the boy didn't even waken.

From the tray on the table beside him, Ed Harrison now took a flexible needle, through whose center ran a metal wire called a stylette. Centering the point of the long needle in the middle of the small wheal he had made with the novocaine, he pushed it through the skin and deeper into the tissues, continuing until his fingers detected the barely perceptible click inside the spinal canal itself, where the needle penetrated the meningeal layer forming its outer covering.

Carefully, he withdrew the metal stylette from the center of the needle, holding it ready to be replaced should there be any noticeable increase in the fluid pressure. If the spinal fluid pressure was markedly increased, usually from injury or brain tumor, a sudden release of pressure in the lower part of the spinal canal could cause the brain itself to be jammed down against the base of the skull, with serious effects and sometimes death.

No increase in pressure showed, however, only a steady drip-drip from the end of the needle. The fluid was of almost its usual state of clearness but, when Ed Harrison filled a small test tube half full and held it up to the light, the red tinge of blood was distinctly visible.

"Bleeding," he said. "But from where?"

"That's what we've got to find out," said Dave Rogan. "I expect this is about as much as we had better disturb him tonight. You can ask for consultations in the morning with both Neurosurgery and Vascular Surgery."

Ed Harrison nodded. "I'll see to it. Let's hope he doesn't hemorrhage again before we can locate the source of the bleeding."

"Is that likely to happen, Dr. Rogan?" Janet Monroe asked quickly.

"No more than before the puncture," he assured her. "Only a small amount of fluid was removed so the pressure relationships couldn't have been disturbed much."

Ed Harrison plucked out the needle and stuck a small dressing over the spot where it had gone through the skin.

"Is it possible that this may be the end of the trouble?" Janet asked, and the younger doctor looked at Dave Rogan, waiting for him to answer.

"It's possible, yes," the psychiatrist admitted. "But experience with hemorrhage around or in the brain shows that half of them will recur, unless the cause is located and removed."

"But that can be dangerous?"

"There is some danger, I wouldn't try to deceive you. But every time the bleeding recurs, it roughly doubles the difficulty of both finding the cause and removing it. That's why we need to go on with some diagnostic studies, even though Jerry seems to be all right now."

"I understand," she said. "What's the next step?"

"Dr. Brennan and Dr. Dieter will have to decide that. My guess would be a radioactive brain scan and possibly a cerebral arteriogram." Dave Rogan picked up the small case in which he kept the instruments for neurological examinations—an ophthalmoscope for studying the eye grounds, a reflex hammer, a small brush for testing skin sensation, a needle for evaluating the response to pain, a tuning fork for testing the vibratory sense, and other similar tools. "But try not to worry; just be glad we discovered the hemorrhage before it becomes really severe."

Dave Rogan left the ward on that note. Angiography, the injection of a chemical that was opaque to X-rays directly into the arteries going to the brain, so they could be visualized, was a valuable tool, but not without danger. More important: If an X-ray of the cerebral arterial tree, the multiple network of branches by which blood was carried to every part of the brain, confirmed the diagnosis that was beginning to take form in his mind, the outlook for the life of little Jerry Monroe was no better than 50 per cent. There was no point in telling Janet that just now, however. She was troubled enough already as it was.

Crossing from the old building to the new, where the operating rooms were located, Dave took the elevator up to the floor above the main surgical theater level. Halfway down the corridor, he opened the rear door of the glass-fronted observation gallery, where operations could be watched by as many as a dozen people, both through the glass and also by means of a closed-circuit television camera pointed directly at the surgical incision. Thus even though the surgeons were working in the depths of a wound in the skull or the heart, the closest details could be brought directly into the visual range of those watching in the observation gallery.

The brightly lit operating theater was the scene of bustling activity as preparations went on for the major drama that would be played out shortly on the tiled stage below. The technicians had not yet finished charging the heart pump with blood, Dave saw, so the actual surgery might not start for another half hour or even longer. Knowing he could be of no help to Paul McGill as long as he was in the expert hands of Anton Dieter, Dave left the gallery and took the elevator down to the ground floor and the door leading outside.

I hope Mort doesn't plead temporary insanity, he thought as he entered the door of the Faculty Clinic on the way to his office. Decisions like that were always hard for a psychiatrist to make and, knowing Mort, he doubted whether the biochemist had ever done anything without a clearly thought-out purpose and procedure.

All of which made it difficult to understand why Mort had almost killed a friend that afternoon, when he could have had ample opportunities on other occasions to select someone else as a target.

II

"Damn Joe McCloskey!" Maggie fumed as she and Della Rogan were leaving the hospital.

"What are you so mad at Joe for?" Della was so relieved to discover the man Mort Dellman had shot wasn't Dave, she couldn't even be short with Maggie.

"Why couldn't it have been Joe instead of Paul McGill? After I knocked myself out getting here to give him blood."

"Just now you were mourning about losing your alimony if it were Joe; now you wish it had been. What sort of woman are you, Maggie?"

"I didn't mean I wanted him shot. But Joe could at least be grateful for me wanting to give him blood."

"Why don't you go tell him?"

"And let him know—"

"What?"

"Nothing," she said sullenly.

"That you still love him?"

"For Christ's sake. Just because Dave's a psychiatrist, do you always have to be psychoanalyzing people, Della? Before you start running other people's lives, take a hard look at your own."

"What are you talking about?" Della stopped short at the entrance to the parking lot.

"I drink—you play golf. What's the difference?"

"I play golf because I like it."

"Yeah? And I drink because I love the stuff. Besides, don't think Dave stays home every night while you're off playing in tournaments."

"I don't expect him to."

"Must be nice having so much confidence in your husband. All those stories you hear about golf widows—you can't tell me the same thing doesn't apply to golf widowers."

"What do you know?" Della demanded.

"Nothing at all." Maggie shrugged. "But I bet you won't be quite as comfortable the next time you go away to play in a tournament."

Della didn't answer, for Maggie's random shot had hit her where it hurt—badly. But it all wouldn't have happened, she reminded herself, if Dave hadn't been tied up with that court case and unable—or unwilling—to go with her to the Southeastern Women's Open at Augusta two weeks ago.

It was the first time they hadn't been together on their wedding anniversary since they were married. The tournament couldn't be changed because of that, of course, but why did Dave have to be so damned honest that he couldn't claim he wasn't able to testify at that particular time? Roy Weston would have postponed the trial. After all Roy was a friend and a member of the Faculty Clinic Corporation, too.

They'd quarreled bitterly over Dave's not being able to go, though. And even though just before she left for Augusta he had given her the golf bag she'd wanted so badly as an anniversary present she'd gone off in a huff, not even letting him drive her to the airport but taking her station wagon and parking it there in the lot.

Her anger hadn't kept her from playing well, though. She'd come in three strokes ahead of the field and within one stroke of the course record for that particular tournament. Naturally the victory had excited her and she'd called Dave to tell him, but hadn't been able to reach him. When she'd gotten back, he'd said he'd gone to see Elizabeth Taylor and Richard Burton in *Who's Afraid of Virginia Woolf?* that night—Della didn't particularly like movies and, knowing Dave did, she had no real reason to think he wasn't telling the truth.

That night in Augusta, she hadn't been moved by love for Dave, however, or by the consideration that he, too, might have been lonesome, with the children away at school and her at Augusta. And when her night flight home had been canceled because of bad weather, she'd even blamed him for that too, irrational though she'd known it to be even then.

She'd been crossing the lobby from the hotel transportation desk, after learning she couldn't get a flight back to Weston before early morning, when Eve Post, the girl she'd beaten that afternoon for the Women's Southeastern, had corralled her. Della liked Eve; they'd been opponents before. And when Eve insisted that, since she wasn't leaving, she join a celebration party with the rest of the tournament crowd in one of the hotel suites, she'd been just irritated enough with Dave for not being at home and for everything else, to accept.

It wasn't as if she hadn't known what champagne did to her either; at home she never drank it except with Dave. But the congratulations on her victory had called for several toasts and there hadn't seemed to be any harm in having dinner with a half-dozen people she knew from professional tournaments, particularly the handsome professional from Pebble Beach, who had been her dinner date. What she hadn't figured on was the way the effect of the champagne and the rest of the drinks she'd had would hit her all at once. Or that there really was something to the old belief that, if you drank a glass of water after taking on considerable champagne, you'd get high all over again.

It had been an exciting evening—as much of it as she was able to remember. But there hadn't been much doubt about the broad picture of what had really happened, not when you woke up at dawn in bed with a man you'd just met the night before—who wasn't your husband.

The whole thing, she told herself now for the dozenth time, had been Dave's fault. If he'd gone with her to Augusta, as he should have done with such an important tournament—and on her anniversary, too—none of it would have happened. Or if he'd been home when, bubbling over with the excitement of winning and nearly equaling the course record for women, she'd called to tell him of her victory, she would have gone on to bed and her conscience wouldn't be driving her crazy now.

What had happened this afternoon piled on top of everything, had been too much. And even though Dave had extended the olive branch just now and she had tentatively accepted it, she wasn't going to let him off that easy. The thing to do was break the damn thing and throw it in his face to show him what happened to husbands who neglected their wives.

"So that's what goes on at a golf tournament." Maggie's voice snapped Della out of her reverie.

"What d'you mean?" Feeling her cheeks burn, Della knew she'd never fool Maggie.

"You're no good at hiding your sins, Della. Your eyes give you away and you're blushing like a schoolgirl caught in the hay. What was he like?"

"Don't be absurd."

"I won't tell Dave, if that's what is worrying you. After all, we women have to stick together where those things are concerned."

"Where do you want me to drop you?" Della's voice was sharp as she started across the lot.

"If you're going to be so damn high and mighty," said Maggie, "I'll get a cab back to the club. Thanks—for nothing."

When Maggie headed for one of the telephone booths against the wall of the hospital, Della started to call her back and apologize. Then she shrugged and went on to where she had left her own car in the lot.

Why couldn't Dave have come home with her? she thought resentfully. It was after five o'clock already and the clinic was closed. Besides he wasn't a pediatrician and Ed Harrison was perfectly capable of looking after that nurse's child. Dave's big fault was that he always thought of other people before he did his own family—like now, when he was more concerned over a patient than over the fact that his wife was upset. He was a psychiatrist, so he should have seen how disturbed she was in the waiting room and come on home with her when she asked him.

By the time she got home, Della was thoroughly angry with Dave and sorry for herself into the bargain. Pouring a glass of milk and making a sandwich, she ate morosely at the kitchen table. Then, after scribbling a note telling him there was sandwich meat, bread and mayonnaise in the refrigerator and that she was going to bed with a headache, she climbed the stairs to the children's room and closed the door, a pointed reminder that she didn't want to be bothered.

III

In front of the clubhouse, Maggie McCloskey paid the driver and got out of the cab. Her own car was still in the lot and for a moment she considered getting it and driving away from the city, away from everything that reminded her of the happiness she'd known in Weston, before her whole life had started coming apart.

When she and Joe had been courting, they'd driven along the river on many an evening like this to a restaurant located high up on the side of the mountain that marked the western border of the valley in which the city lay on the banks of Rogue River and the lake formed by the dam downstream. Right now, she would have given anything she possessed to recapture, if only briefly, just one of the moments when they'd parked the car at the edge of an overlook in the summer twilight to watch the pattern of the lights take form in the lowlands spread out below them.

But something had gone wrong along the way. And though in this moment of self-analysis brought on by her depressed spirits, the absence of alcohol, and the tragedy of Lorrie's death, Maggie faced the fact that the fault was largely hers, she wasn't able to pin down the point at which her marriage had actually begun to fall apart.

Certainly it hadn't been in those first several years when she'd kept on working as Dave Rogan's secretary, while Joe was busy organizing the Urology Department of the medical school. They'd had only his salary then and the house in Sherwood Ravine. They'd bought it before they could really afford the payments, but it had been so perfect, sitting there at the head of the glen looking down the wooded ravine to the slope of the highest hill in Weston, perhaps a half-mile away, that they hadn't been able to resist it.

With the monthly payments on the house so large, Maggie had done the decorating herself after finishing work each day at the clinic. She'd always loved that sort of thing and had wanted to go to Pace Institute in New York to take up decorating at the end of her second year of college. But her father had died suddenly that summer and she'd barely had enough money left after the funeral to finance a year at the Katherine Gibbs School, preparing herself for a job as a medical secretary.

Assigned one day from the secretarial pool shortly after she came to Weston to fill in for Joe McCloskey's regular secretary, she'd found the innate courtliness and obvious gentility of the bantam-sized urologist infinitely attractive. The two of them had hit it off from the start and they'd been supremely happy, even on Joe's salary, for a while. Then Mort Dellman and Pete Brennan had come up with the idea of an automated diagnostic clinic staffed by faculty members of Weston Medical School, with a substantial part of the professional fees collected there going to the staff of the clinic.

Fearing that the quality of teaching in the school would suffer, the trustees of the medical school hadn't been in favor of the change. In the end, they'd had no choice, unless the school was to lose their best teachers. For with the income of doctors in private practice beginning to skyrocket in the fifties, making an extra source of income available to much of the faculty had been the only way to keep from losing most of them to other schools, where the rules about outside private practice were somewhat less strict. And as it had turned out, the quality of teaching had not suffered at all. Instead it had improved, for Weston had been able to lure important men in many fields to the staff because the phenomenally increasing reputation of the Faculty Clinic drew them there.

The clinic setup had worked out especially well for the six who had come there together from Korea—Joe McCloskey, Dave Rogan, Pete Brennan, Paul McGill, George Hanscombe, and Mort Dellman who, as Director of Laboratories, had ridden herd on what envious doctors in the surrounding area called a "medical production line." Patients loved the clinic, too, because it could accomplish in two days at most what would take a week of running from one specialist to another. Of course the doctors had been forced to work harder than before and their home life had been sharply curtailed. But the prosperity that went with being on the clinic staff more than made up for that.

Or had it? Maggie wondered now.

Take herself—she'd been busy and happy as a secretary. Even after they'd moved to Sherwood Ravine, she'd done much of her own housework, decorating the home, digging in the garden, hiking with Joe in the early evenings before dinner along the trails that circled the ravine or watching the trout dart in the rocky pools of the brook that tumbled down through the gorge below the house in a succession of small waterfalls. But soon the demands of both teaching and the clinic had begun to keep Joe from getting home in time for the afternoon walks—though he'd still found time, she remembered with a flash of resentment, for the weekly golf game with some of the others and the twice-monthly poker games.

At first Maggie hadn't resented that part of Joe's life, for having been together in Korea before they came to Weston and working together during the day, the six men—plus Roy Weston—were a close-knit group. But time, and a mounting discontent, had changed her viewpoint.

She hadn't really needed a full-time maid, particularly after she stopped work at the clinic; after all, she'd done all the housework herself in the early years, except for a woman to clean one day and iron another. But Joe's income had doubled almost overnight, and when Della, Grace and Elaine had gotten theirs—Amy Weston of course had live-in servants she'd inherited from her mother and so did Lorrie and Alice—Maggie couldn't very well go on doing her own housework and hold up her head in the level of society that successful doctors moved into from the very beginning. With almost nothing to do at home and no real purpose any more, there'd been more time to spend at the club—and the bar.

The story of my life, she thought bitterly. *And what do I have before me? Nothing.*

Getting out of the car she slammed the door, and started across to the pro shop entrance, the shortest way to the Ladies' Bar, where soft-voiced Manuel would listen to her—if nobody else would.

CHAPTER NINE

I

On Wednesday afternoons Pete Brennan usually played golf with Paul McGill, Joe McCloskey and whoever they could find to make out the foursome. Sometimes it was Arthur Painter, who did most of the legal work for the Faculty Clinic Corporation. Roy Weston was a member of the corporation, since it was he who had persuaded the doctors to come to Weston, but he was also district attorney for the county and aiming for the job of attorney general of the state the next year, so it hadn't seemed best for him to handle the clinic's legal affairs.

That particular Wednesday, Pete had begged off from the golf game. Taking his Porsche from the parking lot, he'd driven along River Road until he came to the Rogue River dam, about ten miles downstream from Weston. He'd left the car in the parking area of a marina near the dam and descended the slope to the boat sheds and dock to the edge of the lake.

Rogue Lake being a power project, boating was allowed, and the whole area had become aquatic-minded, with water skiing a major sport in summer and fishing in the dozen of coves created when the river valley filled, attracting people the year around. Pete kept an eighteen-foot outboard at the marina for pulling the kids on skis, for overnight camping and for fishing trips, whenever he was able to take them.

At the boat sheds near the water level, he had his outboard runabout put into the water from dry storage where it was kept, except when Michael and Terry were home in summer and using it every day. Filling the tank with gasoline at the marina pump and adding the necessary oil, he pushed the button to start the motor and was pleased when it roared into life on the second turnover, even though he hadn't used it more than a half-dozen times all summer.

With the clinic running full blast, plus his duties as president of the Faculty Clinic Corporation, Pete didn't get much time off any more, missing at least half of the Wednesday afternoon golf sessions. This afternoon he had been moved by more than just the urge to feel the wind in his face and the surge of the motor at the stern of the boat when he opened the throttle. More than ever before he needed time alone to think. And since he wasn't expecting Amy back until tomorrow, this had seemed the best time to do it.

There wasn't any use denying it any longer, he admitted as he put the engine in reverse and backed away from the marina dock—things just weren't going right between him and Amy. Lately, this business of getting to the top in the state medical auxiliary had become an obsession with her, until it was almost as if the two of them were engaged in a battle to the death for supremacy.

Actually, Pete felt no overpowering urge to become president of the state medical association. The position would come to him in time and meanwhile there was plenty to occupy him besides medical politics. The clinic was growing so fast that they were going to have to consider putting up a new building before long, one somewhat better adapted to the production-line type of diagnostic study, for which the organization was already becoming famous far beyond its normal patient drawing area.

At the last meeting of the A.M.A., Pete had seen one of the twelve-channel sequential multiple analyzers that could make thirty different laboratory blood analyses an hour. Such an apparatus would be fine for the clinic, he had realized at once, but they would need more room to accommodate it and the increased stream of patients that would be pouring through when the laboratory test rate was stepped up. X-ray, too, needed more space, as did the radiation laboratory, the record room with its new data-processing equipment, the insurance office that was twice as busy now with Medicare, as well as new offices for additional clinic doctors.

Pete could handle all that with the help of Mort Dellman's undeniable genius in that field, even though Mort had been more surly than usual lately and more insistent on building up clinic income sometimes to the detriment of professional efficiency. Dave Rogan and Joe McCloskey had both spoken to Pete about that recently, and he knew that, with the pressure of discontent building up, there was bound to be a showdown at one of the corporation meetings soon. Being a biochemist, not a physician, Mort's point of view was bound to be different from theirs, but his obvious commercialism was beginning to get on Pete's nerves, too—as if he didn't already have enough to worry about with Amy and his rapidly disintegrating marriage.

Putting the gear lever into "Forward" Pete opened the throttle and steadied the wheel as the boat began to plane over the smooth surface of the lake. The vibration of the motor settled into his muscles and his nerves, acting as something of a cathartic and washing away the petty troubles that had accumulated since his last golf game had given him the much needed weekly release of tension.

Clinic problems, as well as the purely professional decisions arising in his own practice of neurosurgery, were something he knew how to handle. But when it came to doing something about what was happening between him and Amy, he felt himself baffled.

Looking back on it now, it was almost as though she had been seized by a fever, a disease that had slowly changed her in the past several years into a driving, relentlessly ambitious woman who was completely different from the girl with whom he had fallen in love that night at Weston Country Club when Roy had introduced them. That night—and for a long time afterward—Amy had seemed to be the wife he'd always dreamed he would have one day—tall, assured, handsome rather than delicately lovely, the bearing of her New England heritage apparent in her face and in her carriage. She had stirred a fire within him that night which still continued to glow, but lately she seemed to be intent upon destroying it, for reasons he could not understand.

He'd recognized the aggressive streak in her even before they were married, but then it had only seemed to complement his own capacity to work hard for what he wanted. She'd been disappointed, he knew, by his decision not to become Professor of Surgery, when the post had been vacant some five years ago. Having always had money and accepted it as a matter of course, Amy hadn't been able to understand how Pete could turn down the prestige that went with the full-time professorship and what it would have meant to her for a mere clinical teaching position, even with the opportunity for money-making afforded by the clinic. The task of getting the clinic organized and into successful operation had been a real challenge at the time and now that it had become an undoubted success, his judgment had been proved correct. But he sometimes thought Amy still considered the clinic itself as an enemy.

At first, he had been pleased when she had turned her tremendous energy to medical auxiliary work, but that, too, had quickly become a tooth-and-claw affair. Now she literally ate, slept and dreamed political maneuvering. And while she seemed completely oblivious of it, he knew that even her own circle of friends—represented most closely by the members of the Dissection Society—had begun to draw away from her.

Guiding the boat into a secluded cove, he broke out a spinning rod and some lures, and began to cast into the edge of the weeds, not so much hoping to catch anything as to give his hands something to do while his thoughts ranged and he sought to grapple with his dilemma.

The trouble wasn't sex, he was sure; actually that had almost disappeared from their relationship these past eight to twelve months while Amy had been engaged in her relentless campaign to become state president of the auxiliary. Sex was always in plentiful supply around a hospital, the major part of whose personnel was composed of women, and he'd had no trouble finding all the release he needed there.

Perhaps the simplest thing would have been to establish a completely outside relationship—as Roy Weston had done. At least Alice seemed content. But deep inside him somewhere, Pete's Irish ancestry carried with it a streak of conformity, perhaps due to the Catholic teachings of his childhood, although when he'd married Amy, he'd joined the Episcopal Church, to which her family had belonged for generations. In any event his conscience wouldn't let him be satisfied with the sort of unresponsive wife and passionate mistress setup the French seemed to accept as a matter of course and which existed to a high degree in the levels of Weston society where all of them moved.

A divorce would rock their small world but not destroy it, although it might well destroy Amy by cutting away at one stroke her connection with medical politics and wounding her fierce New England pride. Lots of doctors got divorces at his age, it was true; he could name a half dozen on the medical school faculty. Most of them soon married younger women—the secretaries, nurses, technicians with whom they were thrown in daily contact. And the new wives often brought to these second marriages an understanding and love that had largely disappeared from the old.

But Pete loved his children and he loved the girl he had married, if there were only some way to bring her back and spare her the shame of the sort of scandal that had happened many times in even so small a city as Weston, when husbands started looking abroad for the easily found solace they no longer found with their wives.

It was almost six o'clock when Pete Brennan finally nudged the outboard runabout to a berth at the marina dock and tied it up. The attendants would take care of hoisting it from the water with the giant hydraulic cradle and putting it on a wheeled dolly for dry storage. As he was passing the office, the manager came to the door.

"All hell's broke loose in town, Dr. Brennan," he said. "It's been all over the radio and TV."

"What's that?"

"A doctor—Dellman, I think it is—shot his wife and another doctor who was with her this afternoon. The woman was killed and the man's in the hospital—not expected to live."

Mort Dellman and Lorrie! It was hard to believe, not that Mort wasn't capable of it; there was a hard, vicious, cold, calculating streak in him that Pete had recognized long ago and avoided in his contacts with the brilliant biochemist. But Mort must have known of Lorrie's penchant for hopping in and out of beds; she'd certainly made no secret of it. And knowing it, Mort should have had better sense than to destroy the gold mine represented by his marriage to Jake Porter's heir.

"Who was the man?" he asked.

"They didn't give his name for a while, but it was announced just now," said the manager. "It's Dr. McGill. He's got a boat out here and a nicer quieter fellow you couldn't find anywhere. Who would have thought—?"

Pete was already on the way to his car. His first thought was that with Amy still away at the auxiliary meeting, Elaine would need all the help he could give her—Paul, too, poor devil. And God only knew what it would do to the Faculty Clinic.

II

George Hanscombe came through the front door of the clinic just as Dave Rogan started inside to put away his neurological kit and get his hat before leaving for home. Older than the psychiatrist by some ten years, Hanscombe was tall, with the well-clipped and groomed look of the upper-echelon executive or professional man, even to the small brush of mustache on his upper lip. His hair was still dark—rumor said by courtesy of a masculine rinse that had zoomed into popularity recently. Nobody kidded him about it, however; almost completely devoid of humor, George Hanscombe was the epitome of brisk efficiency and expected everyone else to be the same.

"Thought you were playing golf, George," said Dave, standing aside for the internist to come through.

"I was on the way to the club when a call came from Sam Portola's wife. She thought she was having a heart attack, so what could I do?"

"Nothing—except go," Dave agreed. Portola was the head of the syndicate that now owned Weston Mills, a millionaire and, with his family, among the most important patients of the Faculty Clinic group. "Was it a coronary?"

George Hanscombe shook his head; since he wore his hair rather long, the effect was somewhat that of a slightly peeved lion. "Nothing but gas. She insists on eating all that rich Italian food. I had to spend the afternoon working with her until she could erupt in a good solid belch."

"The old Five-F syndrome?"

"What's that?"

"Have you forgotten your medical school days? Fair, fat, forty and full of flatus." Then Dave's face grew serious. "You heard about Paul and Lorrie, didn't you?"

"Yes. I came by the hospital just now." The internist grew even more sour than before. "They tell me Paul's in the hands of the Great God Dieter, so I guess the kraut will pull off another of his miracles—or at least claim one."

"Anton's got plenty of evidence to back up his claims," said Dave. "Too bad about Lorrie."

"And Mort. After all he only did what any red-blooded—"

"Come off it, George. Mort's a louse and we all know it, but Lorrie was one of the most completely normal people I ever knew."

"Normal!" George Hanscombe exploded. "I suppose that's some of your Freudian business?"

"I think Freud would have approved of her. Most of the troubles we psychiatrists see come from people butting their more primitive instincts against the stone walls of their inhibitions. Lorrie just let hers go."

"Adultery is adultery."

"You sound like Gertrude Stein," Dave said with a grin. "With that sort of reasoning, all of us would be guilty—including you. It isn't as if Lorrie hadn't given us all fair warning of what she was going to do, either."

"What do you mean by that?"

"Don't you remember what she told us that night at the club, when she came into the game room during the orchestra intermission?"

"I'm not sure."

"You, Joe, Paul, Roy and I were playing poker."

"Got no time to remember anything now," said George. "Grace will be home from the club by the time I get home and dinner will be ready. She's been so damned irritable lately, I never know when she's going to take my head off."

"Go on then. Glad to see I'm not the only one who's in the doghouse."

At the newsrack in front of the clinic, Dave dropped in a dime and took out a copy of the final edition, rushed on the streets with news of the afternoon's events. A picture of Lorrie Dellman occupied the center of the front page, with the story in black type all around it. . . . Seeing her smiling at him from the newspaper, Dave found himself remembering even more clearly the incident he had mentioned to George. In fact the dress she was wearing in the newspaper picture was the same one she'd worn the night of the dance, as usual cut rather daringly low to emphasize the fact that she was well endowed by nature.

"Mind if I sit in?" Lorrie had asked when she came into the game room where they were playing, a half-filled glass in her hand. Mort Dellman had been away that night, inspecting some new automation equipment they planned to buy for the clinic and so had Pete Brennan. Lorrie had come by with Roy and Alice Weston and, like most everybody at the dance, she was already a little high.

"This is a man's game." George Hanscombe was losing and that always made his temper even shorter than usual. "Go play with the women, Lorrie."

"They're afraid of me," she said with that gamin grin of hers that always preceded some salty observation.

"Why?" Roy had asked.

"I had a heart-to-heart talk with all of your wives at Amy's house yesterday," Lorrie informed them. "I made them a proposition and now they're worried that I really meant what I said."

"Did you?" Dave asked.

"Of course. I don't lie—not even to myself."

"That's asking a lot of anybody," Dave remembered saying.

"Stop gabbing." George had lost again. "Let's get on with the game."

"By the way, George," said Lorrie. "How long has it been since you put on a tuxedo and took Grace to a fine restaurant or a night club?"

"A couple of years ago—at the convention."

"I'm not talking about conventions," she said. "A lot of people get drunk and wind up in somebody else's room then. I mean how long has it been since you made a date with Grace and took her out for an evening of wining, dining and dancing?"

"What the hell does that have to do with playing poker?"

"Maybe if you paid more attention to Grace and less to poker and golf—the stock market too—she wouldn't always be talking about going back to England." Lorrie's voice had suddenly taken on a cutting edge.

"That's going too far, even for you, Lorrie," Roy Weston had protested.

"Let her talk," Dave remembered saying. "Maybe she's saying something we all need to hear. Go on, Lorrie."

"I'm not going to listen to such drivel." George threw down his cards and stood up. "After a man has worked all day to make enough money so his wife can drive a Cadillac, have a full-time maid, play golf and get drunk at the club, he shouldn't have to play gigolo just because she doesn't have enough to do to keep her happy."

"Hear! Hear!" said Lorrie and this time there had been a real cutting edge to her voice. "Spoken like a true American husband—the dullest guys in the world."

"What's this proposition you were talking about?" Roy asked with a grin, as George Hanscombe left for the bar in a dudgeon.

"Now that I see you together, I'm not sure you aren't all beyond help," said Lorrie. "But I'm willing to do whatever I can."

"Which is?"

"The other day I told your wives I'd go to bed with each of you, then report back on your particular cases and prescribe treat—"

"Good God, Lorrie!" Paul McGill exclaimed. "Do you realize what you're saying?"

"Sure." Lorrie grinned impudently. "I'm offering to make a legitimate experiment out of something we've all been experimenting with illegitimately anyway. One thing's sure: you're all lousy lovers, or your wives wouldn't be so dissatisfied with the status quo. Because you're all my friends, I'm willing to put my years of experience on the line to help you out."

"Just how do you propose to institute treatment?" Dave asked.

"At first I thought it would be enough to report back to your wives, like in a clinic," said Lorrie. "But now I've decided both husband and wife should be given the diagnosis together and treatment discussed. You see it would really be a purely clinical procedure."

"Maybe clinical," Dave remembered interjecting. "But hardly pure—by most people's standards."

"I'm not using most people's standards, just my own," said Lorrie. "Do any of you doubt my credentials for carrying out the experiment? I don't have to remind you that most of you have good reason to know."

Nobody had answered until Paul McGill said: "Really, Lorrie. If this is your idea of a joke."

"Who's joking?" She looked from one to the other but got no answer. "Come on; who's going to be the first test case?"

Still nobody answered.

"Then I'll just have to sneak up on each of you," she said. "Good night, boys."

They hadn't felt much like playing poker after that, for none of them had been sure whether or not Lorrie was joking.

Now it appeared that she wasn't.

III

Mike Traynor was working in the emergency room, sewing up a kid who had fallen while on skates, when Pete Brennan came in from the parking lot.

"Know anything about Dr. McGill?" Pete asked him.

"He's in surgery, Dr. Brennan. Dr. Dieter's getting ready to take a bullet out of his heart."

"What about Mrs. McGill?"

"I saw her talking to Dr. Rogan and several doctors' wives in the waiting room a little while ago," said the E.R. nurse supervisor, who had come over when she saw Pete. "I think they said Dr. McGill would be taken to the Special Intensive Care Unit after surgery. That's probably where she is now."

"Mrs. Brennan was with them, but I believe she's left already," the nurse added as Pete was going out the door.

Pete wheeled at the door. "My wife?"

"Yes sir."

"But that's impossible. She's out of town."

"I saw her, Dr. Brennan. She must have gotten back early."

It didn't make sense, Pete told himself as he headed for the elevator. Amy had said she would spend the night so her enemies—that had been her own word—couldn't work behind the scenes after the meeting to gain an advantage.

Janet Monroe looked up from the desk of the Special Intensive Care Unit when Pete Brennan came in. "Dr. McGill's still in surgery, Dr. Brennan," she said. "Mrs. McGill is in the waiting room."

"How's she taking it?"

"Very well, sir."

Elaine managed to smile when Pete sat down beside her and took her hands in his. "Everything will be all right," he assured her. "Dieter is a whiz."

"Dave came by just now. He says Paul's chances are good."

"Have they started the operation yet?"

"He said they're getting the heart-lung machine—whatever you call it—ready."

"That takes time. I'll go up and watch."

"You'd better go home to Amy, Pete."

"Then she really was here?"

"She heard the broadcast like the others—and didn't know who the man was. The girls all came together but Amy still looked upset when I left them downstairs. She needs you more than Paul does, Pete."

The idea of Amy needing him seemed so unlikely that Pete found himself wondering. Still it must have been something of a shock to Amy to think he might have been the man with Lorrie. And that could certainly account for her being upset.

"Sure you don't want me to stay with you?" he asked Elaine.

"I'm all right now, Mrs. Monroe is looking after me."

"Be sure to call me if you want me."

"I will—and thanks for coming, Pete."

"I was out on my boat on the lake all afternoon. Only learned what happened a few minutes ago."

As a clinical professor, Pete had a small office in the hospital, as well as his more elaborate suite across the street in the Faculty Clinic. Going directly to his hospital office, he dialed his home telephone number.

IV

Amy was halfway home, driving mechanically and still half in shock from the headlong race there and the sudden rush of relief at discovering Pete hadn't been in danger after all, when the pounding agony of the migraine reminded her forcibly of what she had been going to the hospital for when she'd heard the first broadcast. Briefly she considered turning back, until she saw by the dashboard clock that George Hanscombe's office would have closed half an hour ago. She could always go to the emergency room for an injection, of course, but that would mean an explanation to the intern on duty, who would naturally be suspicious of anyone asking for a hypodermic that included a narcotic.

Pete wasn't in the hospital; she'd learned that from the operator when she stopped by the switchboard on the way out. Rather than turn back now she decided to go on home, hoping he might be there by now and could give her something out of the emergency medical case he kept at home for night calls. Her plans for the evening had been shot away, first by Lorrie's death and now by the migraine. But there was certain to be something in the refrigerator she could use to make Pete a sandwich for his dinner. As for herself, right now food was the farthest thing from her mind.

At the house, Amy fumbled a little with the key; the pounding of the migraine was already blurring her vision, as it always did until she got relief. Finally, she managed to open the door and make her way into the kitchen. Grasping at the first thing that might help relieve the pain, she took a bottle of bourbon from the store of liquor in the small cabinet behind the built-in bar that opened to the family room. Pouring some into a glass without stopping to measure it out carefully, she filled the rest of the glass with ginger ale from a bottle in the refrigerator and drank down half of it in one shuddering swallow.

Carrying the glass, she climbed the stairs to the master bedroom and finished the drink. Since her stomach was empty, the alcohol was absorbed almost immediately and she could feel its warmth begin to pervade her body, though the throbbing pain of the migraine still continued. Just then the phone rang and, putting down the empty glass, she picked it up.

"Amy?" It was Pete's voice.

"Yes."

"I was out in the boat and got to the hospital just after you left. Elaine said you seemed to be upset. Are you all right?"

"It's a headache." The whiskey was already slurring her voice a little.

"I'm getting ready to leave for home. Do you want me to bring anything?"

"Ethel's off and I don't feel like making dinner."

"I'll stop by that fried chicken place and bring a couple of boxes. Anything else?"

"No. That will be fine."

"See you in about half an hour then."

"'Bye." She hung up the phone, half blind still from the migraine, in spite of the powerful jolt of whiskey she had drunk. Stumbling toward the bed, she started to lie down, until her eyes fell on Pete's small medicine case. He sometimes made calls at night, when a close friend became ill and worried, and to save trouble, kept a small kit ready with drugs and some dressings that might come in handy in an emergency.

There ought to be something in that bag she could take for the migraine, Amy thought, perhaps an ampule or two of Demerol. Of course she couldn't inject it without a sterile syringe but even taken by mouth it still might be effective if she took two ampules at once.

Going to the closet, she took down the small case and opened it but saw no Demerol, the drug she had been looking for. In a small pocket inside the case, however, she discovered about a dozen tiny tubes, each with a needle covered by a plastic guard attached.

"Morphine sulphate one-fourth grain," she read, and recognized at once what the small tubes were. Called syrettes, each contained a quarter-grain dose of morphine in a tiny collapsible tube, like the little toothpaste samples the kids sometimes brought home from school, though smaller.

Having taken a first-aid course given by the PTA as part of the civil defense disaster training program, Amy knew how to use them. Sponging off her arm with cotton and alcohol from the medicine cabinet, she took one of the syrettes, removed the small plastic cover from the needle and, jamming it into her flesh, squeezed the small tube empty, forcing the drug solution under her skin.

As she massaged the skin where she'd made the injection with the cotton pledget to hasten the absorption of the drug by the blood vessels in the tissue beneath it, she felt the powerful dose of morphine begin to take effect in a feeling of languor that seemed to spread outward from the site of the injection. The throbbing in her temple soon lessened, too, and the effect of the drug, combined with the drink she'd already had, was somewhat like that of floating on a cloud. She resisted the desire to lie down and fall asleep, however, determined to enjoy to the fullest this marvelous state of nirvana into which she had literally injected herself by squeezing the tiny tube of the morphine syrette.

As she started to undress for her bath, Amy noticed the small case from which she'd taken the morphine still lying on the bed where she'd left it when she'd gone into the bathroom to get alcohol and cotton from the medicine cabinet. She started to close the case but, moved by a sudden impulse, took out nine of the tiny syrette tubes and put them into a drawer of her dressing table beneath the lining paper. Then, closing the small case, she put it back where it had been on the closet shelf.

The migraine attacks, she knew from experience, could come on at any time and the relief she had already obtained from the morphine was far greater than from the piddling injections of Demerol and ergotamine George Hanscombe always gave her. This way, she could take care of herself without being a bother to George when the attacks came.

By the time Amy finished undressing and stepped into the shower the pain was entirely gone and she was all but walking on air. She showered quickly, and then, hoping to wash away some of the drowsiness, turned the needle spray on "Cold" for a moment, so her body was all rosy when she stepped out of the shower and began to dry herself with a nubby towel. She was admiring the glow of her skin in the pier glass mirror on the door of her bathroom when Pete came into the bedroom.

"Well!" He gave a whistle of appreciation. "This is a pleasant surprise."

Amy's first impulse was to hide behind the towel. An instinctive prudery had always kept her from letting Pete see her nude, if she could help it; even when they made love, she'd always insisted that the room be dark. But the combination of morphine and whiskey had removed most of these inhibitions, so she made no move to cover her naked loveliness.

"I didn't hear you come in," she said as she went on drying herself with the towel.

"Maybe I should try coming home like this more often," he said with a grin.

Amy walked over to the closet, warmly conscious that Pete's eyes were following her every movement and thankful that she'd kept her figure. Riffling through the hangers, she started to take down a gown and robe combination, such as she usually wore at night, then removed from another hanger a somewhat filmy negligee instead. Wrapping it about her, she went over to her dressing table and began to brush her hair, quite conscious that every movement of her arm with the brush accentuated the fullness of her breasts under the thin fabric.

In the mirror, she saw Pete come up behind her before she felt his hands on her shoulders. The contact sent a tingling feeling through her, somewhat like the way she remembered feeling when he'd first taken her in his arms on their honeymoon, but also a bit like the sensation she'd experienced when the hypodermic began to take effect just now. Dropping the brush, she reached up to take his hands and leaned backward as he lowered his head to kiss her throat, turning her head so he could find her lips.

It had been a long time since they had kissed like that and, when his hands slipped down to push the robe from her shoulders and bare her breasts, she didn't resist. Instead, her hands moved along his temples, holding his head between her palms as she kissed him eagerly. When his hands caressed her breasts and the warm flesh beneath them, she stood up and turned in his arms, freeing the thin robe from her shoulders and letting it fall to her feet.

Lying on the bed, watching Pete as he undressed quickly, Amy suddenly began to laugh.

"I'm not that funny-looking," he said in mock anger. "What's the joke?"

"The chicken will get cold—and I don't give a damn."

CHAPTER TEN

I

Looking down from the glass-walled observation gallery, Marisa Feldman found herself less than ten feet away from the operating table occupying the center of the theater. Upon it lay Paul McGill, his entire chest and abdomen bare, as well as the right groin. The two concave lights above the operating table, focus of all the activity in the room, were so placed that those working there did not cast a shadow. When the body of one of them came between the light and the operative area, the other lamp would still flood it with illumination. Sterilized handles were attached to the center of the lights so the surgeon could reach up and adjust either or both of them to his exact requirements during the operation without contaminating his sterile gloves.

Anton Dieter had not yet appeared, but the scene below was a beehive of activity. At one side, three technicians worked over a machine of shining metal, glass and tubing. Its central portion consisted of a large plastic tube about three feet long and perhaps four to five inches in diameter containing more than a dozen metal disks attached to a central spindle by which they could be rotated.

Now motionless, the complex of disks and spindle, the very heart of the apparatus that could take over the function of both heart and lungs, would begin to revolve at the flick of a switch. Each rotation would expose to an atmosphere of pure oxygen in the long tube a thin film of the blood mixture filling the lower part of the horizontal cylinder as it was picked up by the revolving disks. The mixture itself, called the perfusate, was composed of roughly three-fourths blood from the hospital blood bank and one fourth a solution of saline, plus a small amount of heparin to keep it from clotting.

The observation gallery was almost filled with students and interns. They discussed the scene below in muted tones, though no sound from the gallery itself could reach the operating room.

"That long gadget is called the oxygenator," an intern was explaining to several first-year students. "As the blood is picked up in the form of a film on those metal disks, the oxygen that fills the tube is absorbed by the hemoglobin in the red blood cells, and the carbon dioxide is given off into the space there at the same time."

"Why is that?" a student asked.

"The atmosphere in the tube is practically pure O_2. With a high O_2 in the tube and a low concentration in the red cells, oxygen is absorbed by the hemoglobin and carried to the rest of the body. At the same time, with a high CO_2 in the blood and a low concentration in the top part of the tube, where the O_2 is, the blood gives off its CO_2."

"Just like in the lungs?"

"Except that the machine—it's really called a pump-oxygenator—takes the place of both the heart and the lungs. That way the surgeon can open the heart, if he has to, and work inside it, replacing valves or patching abnormal openings while the circulation goes on without the heart or lungs being involved at all."

"How long can he do that?" the student asked.

"The longest I ever saw a patient on bypass—the whole procedure is called a cardiopulmonary bypass—was three hours. But Dieter's a slick operator; he rarely keeps one on it more than an hour and a half."

"What happens to the heart during that time?" another student asked. "Doesn't it move at all?"

"If Dr. Dieter uses the bypass tonight, you'll see that Dr. McGill's heart will contract only slightly. With nothing much to do, it sort of lays down on the job."

"Gee!" said another student. "This is just like Ben Casey, isn't it?"

"Actually, the blood is cooled and the patient's temperature lowered at the same time," the intern explained. "Once they've cooled, the tissues don't need much oxygen so everything operates at a low tempo. The heart doesn't have to do much work and it's protected that way, along with the brain."

The students filling the front row had left a little space on either side of Marisa Feldman. Now a dark-haired and brashly handsome fellow in a white coat came in and pushed himself to the front, taking the space next to her and forcing her to slide over a little.

"My name's Traynor, Dr. Feldman," he said. "Mike Traynor. I saw that job you did down there in the dispensary with the tamponade. It was great! Just great!"

"Nothing so spectacular as that." Marisa had been in America long enough to recognize what the students called a "brown-nose" job.

"Is this the first operation you've seen Dr. Dieter do?"

"Yes. I was on a month's vacation before I arrived here yesterday."

"From Harvard?"

"I've been on a fellowship there for two years since finishing my clerkship in England." She gave it the English pronunciation, as if the word were spelled "clark" instead of "clerk."

"That's like an internship over here, isn't it? Or a residency?"

"Roughly, yes."

In the center of the operating theater below, an assistant had begun to paint the patient's abdomen with a brilliant-colored antiseptic solution. Almost at the same moment, a somewhat stocky figure in the usual green scrub suit, cap and mask appeared from the door leading to the scrub room.

"That's Dieter!" The intern who spoke uttered his name in much the same tone he might have used for a visiting king. "Now you'll really see something."

II

The appearance of the surgeon galvanized both the observation gallery and the theater itself into a state of stepped-up tension. Those in the gallery leaned forward to watch, even though Dieter was only putting on his gown and gloves. Marisa found herself tensing with the rest, not even noticing that Mike Traynor's shoulder pressed against hers rather more than was justified by even the packed state of the gallery. A beautiful woman got used to that sort of thing, particularly when she lived in a world populated largely by men, as the medical one was.

On the floor below, Dieter had finished putting on his gown and gloves. He looked up to the glass-walled gallery and his eyes moved along the row of students and interns until they found Marisa's in the very center of the group. With the contact, she felt the impact of his personality across the space, even through the plate glass of the viewing window, just as she'd felt it downstairs in the emergency room something over an hour ago.

Being a realist, she didn't deny the attraction she had felt the first time she'd come in contact with Dieter. Yet at the same time, something deep inside her was strongly urged to resist that attraction, an inner antagonism triggered by the rough burr of his German accent, when he'd spoken to her downstairs.

That Anton Dieter would seek to enlarge upon their initial meeting, Marisa did not doubt, just as she knew from the feel of Mike Traynor's shoulder against her own that he would like nothing better than an invitation to her apartment. That, too, was part of the sixth sense any woman possessed, the instinctive knowledge that a man was interested in her, moved by the animal urge to sexual contact which was, after all, the vital force underlying all relationships between men and women, no matter what the circumstances of their meeting.

As to what she would do about Mike Traynor's bumptious aggressiveness and a distinctly subtle pass, when his hand slid off his own knee and touched her leg, she had no doubts. Romantic relations between faculty and students could never cause anything except trouble; and besides, for all his dark handsomeness and pure animal energy, she felt no attraction toward Mike Traynor.

Anton Dieter was another matter altogether, she admitted, as she watched him going purposefully about the business of preparing for an important surgical procedure. What had sprung into being between them downstairs was a complicated force of attraction and repulsion, a force that could go much deeper than any casual sexual encounter and indeed could probably not be kept at such a level, if she wished. Yet, as she watched the somewhat stocky figure that had taken over the center stage below, just as he'd taken it over in the emergency room earlier, she no more doubted that she would be faced with such a choice than that Anton Dieter would shortly perform another of the surgical miracles which had sent his reputation zooming upward like a rocket in flight.

What troubled her most was that the decision might be forced upon her before she was ready for it, either emotionally or—most important of all—physically.

At the latter thought, Marisa was gripped by the old fear, the horror she had hoped was shut behind her by the gates of Frondheim prison, but which, she knew, she must shortly battle once more. Moved by a sudden urge to flee, to postpone for a little while at least the start of the ultimate conflict, with its now familiar and traumatic ending, she half started to rise in her seat and leave the observation gallery. But just then, one of the circulating nurses on the operating-theater floor below plugged the microphone cord trailing from beneath Dieter's gown into a receptacle in the floor and his voice, booming out of the loud speakers at each end of the gallery, rooted her to her seat.

"Dr. Hagstrom, resident surgeon, is assisting me," Dieter announced. "Dr. Jeff Long, resident in anesthesiology, has charge of that most important part of our activities. The apparatus you see beside the operating table is a disk-oxygenator, commonly referred to in the lay press as a heart-lung pump. We hope we shall not have to use it but we must be ready in case we do."

"A Weston-Dieter Production," an intern in the back of the gallery intoned in a remarkably close imitation of the surgeon's voice. "Photographed in gorgeous Medicolor."

Marisa found herself relaxing as a wave of laughter swept through the gallery. Dieter's manner was a bit theatrical, it was true, but she knew that many great teachers deliberately dramatized in order to seize the attention of their students.

The first assistant had now finished painting the entire exposed portion of the patient's abdomen and groin with a reddish-brown antiseptic. As he finished one area the intern acting as second assistant painted on a second coat of the solution designed to kill the skin bacteria that were always present. The painting completed, both men stepped back and Helen Straughn approached the table with an aerosol spray can in her hand. Moving up and down in even strokes, she covered the whole exposed area of skin with a liberal coating of spray from the can.

"Miss Straughn is applying an adhesive compound," Dieter explained through the microphone resting against his chest beneath his gown. "In a moment, we will cover the entire field with a transparent plastic sheet, cutting down the number of draperies that will be needed and expediting our work."

Jeff Long had been busy while Dieter was speaking, skillfully inserting a laryngoscope into the patient's mouth and throat. A metal tube with a light at the end, the instrument enabled him to slide a rubber tube with a small balloon rubber cuff at the end directly down through the patient's larynx into the trachea, or windpipe. Removing the laryngoscope and leaving the tube in place, he quickly inflated the small cuff around the end of it—now located deep in the patient's trachea—to form an airtight seal. In this way air could only enter and leave the lungs through the intratracheal tube and pressure could be maintained inside the chest after it had been opened surgically.

Dieter now moved up to the table to take one side of a sheet of thin plastic from the sponge nurse. Carl Hagstrom took the other and they unrolled it, laying it upon the brilliantly painted skin of the wounded man and smoothing it over the abdomen and the groin where it was held in place by the adhesive Helen Straughn had sprayed upon it. Around the plastic-covered area, they now draped sterile towels and sheets, tinted a pale green like the scrub suits of the doctors and nurses, the draperies and gowns, in order to ease the strain upon the eyes from the bright lights of the operating room.

"This is a case of a bullet wound of the heart." Dieter looked up to the observation gallery once again. "X-ray shows the bullet still inside the heart; judging from the position of the wound of entry it would appear to be in the right ventricle." Here he pointed to a reddish spot on Paul McGill's chest, a little to the right of the midline and almost on a line with the nipple of his right breast.

On the wall of the operating room across from the observation gallery, a window of frosted glass was illuminated when Helen Straughn tripped a small switch. Drawn there in bold strokes with a black wax pencil were the outlines of a human heart with the various chambers clearly marked. Beside it, another ground-glass window containing the X-rays also glowed, the white image of the bullet clearly distinguishable within the somewhat dimmer shadow of the heart and the much lighter pattern of the lungs surrounding it.

"As best we are able to re-create the path of the bullet, it came somewhat from the right," Anton Dieter continued. "Such a path would take it into the right side of the heart but the fact that it passed through another body first and therefore may have been deflected makes it possible that the bullet could have entered from almost any angle."

"Two with one shot," said a student admiringly. "Where I come from that's some shooting."

A burst of laughter, unheard below, rocketed through the observation gallery, but subsided when Dieter continued: "We hope the use of the disk-oxygenator will not be necessary, but we will first expose the femoral artery so it may be opened and cannulated, allowing it to be connected to the oxygenator and afford a return of arterial blood to the body, should we have to resort to its use."

He was working as he talked, his hands moving swiftly like—Marisa Feldman thought—those of a master pianist. The operating team, too, functioned smoothly as a small incision was made in the right groin and hemostatic clamps caught small bleeding vessels which were quickly tied off. It was much easier to see what was going on than would have been the case if the incision had been surrounded by towels, as in older operative techniques. Besides, the plastic sheet glued to the skin not only removed the possibility of contamination of the wound itself from bacteria on the surface but materially increased visibility of the operative area, both for the surgeons and for the observers.

From where she sat, Marisa Feldman could watch Dieter's hands probing swiftly with a curved pair of blunt-ended scissors in the depths of the small groin wound. After a few moments, he put down the scissors and picked up curved forceps which he slid under the femoral artery, a whitish-looking tube perhaps the size of one's little finger, visible now as it pulsated in the depths of the wound. An assistant slipped the end of a piece of cotton tape between the jaws of the clamp and Dieter closed them shut, pulling the tape beneath the artery and isolating it where it could be reached quickly. A few more quick strokes exposed a vein, thin-walled and blue, nearby. This, too, he isolated with a piece of tape and, leaving the intern who was handling instruments to cover the groin wound with a moist cotton pad, Dieter and Carl Hagstrom moved up to the chest.

"We will expose the heart through a median sternotomy incision by splitting the breastbone," the surgeon explained into the microphone, using the lay term for the flat, thin bone forming the front of the chest cage in deference to the presence of first-year students in the gallery, who had not yet begun the study of anatomy. "This incision gives free access to the heart itself and allows us to investigate both the right and left sides."

Dieter's hands were moving as he spoke, laying open with the scalpel that seemed an extension of his living flesh the skin in the midline directly over the sternum. The knife went down to the bone in one swift stroke and for a moment the wound itself was hidden as Dieter and the assistants moved swiftly, clamping off bleeding vessels and tying them with fine catgut ligatures drawn from metal spools. The upper end of the incision had halted some two or three inches short of the hollow of the neck; now he extended it both to the right and the left for several inches, giving the appearance of a Y.

"The major drawback to a median sternotomy incision is that thick scars called keloids tend to form when it heals," Dieter explained as he worked. "For this reason, we form a Y at the upper end so the scar will not show above the collar."

He moved now to the lower end of the sternum and extended the incision a short distance downward through the outer layers of the abdominal wall there. "The entire sternum must be exposed, too, else we should not be able to split it widely and thus gain the exposure we need."

"That Dieter's an artist," Mike Traynor said but Marisa Feldman hardly heard him, so engrossed was she in the rhythmic movements of the surgeon that were like a stylized ballet. For a moment she was even able to forget that the chief player in the drama was a German, from the race that had destroyed her parents and forced her to undergo the ultimate degradation.

Dieter was now splitting the outer covering of the sternum, the periosteum, with a single scalpel stroke down its center. Picking up a chisel-like instrument bent at a right angle near its lower end—known as a periosteal elevator—he began to scrape the periosteum back from the midline on either side, exposing the bare bone for the entire length of the sternum.

"Oscillating saw, please." The intern handling instruments gave him a heavy object covered with a sterile sleeve. At its end, a metal spindle projected through an opening closed with a drawstring at the end of the sleeve. Bolted to the spindle projecting from the body of the motor hidden by the protecting sterile cover was an oddly shaped sawblade, the toothed edge being an arc of about an eighth of a circle, like a wedge cut out of a completely circular saw.

"We shall use the oscillating saw to cut almost all the way through the sternum." Dieter stepped upon a switch placed close to his right foot beside the operating table and the cutting section of the saw began to vibrate with a high-pitched whine. When he lowered it to touch the sternum, a fine spray of bone dust was sent in either direction as the saw bit into the bone. On the other side of the table, Carl Hagstrom was directing a steady stream of sterile water from a syringe upon the blade to keep it cool.

As cleanly as if it were cutting a board, the saw cut into the breastbone for its entire length. Handing it to a waiting nurse, Dieter next accepted an oddly shaped tool which the instrument nurse was holding ready for him. It had a small blunt foot with a blade just above it about two inches long but sharp on only one side. Just above the blade the shank of the instrument was thick for a short distance, thinning out again for perhaps a foot to end with a cross-handle upon the top.

"It is possible to cut completely through the sternum with the oscillating saw—at the risk of sawing into the heart," the surgeon told the observers. "In order to be absolutely safe we will cut the inner part of the sternum with the Lebsche knife."

With the words, he slid the foot of the knife over the top end of the sternum, setting the cutting edge firmly into the slot cut by the saw. Carl Hagstrom picked up a metal mallet and at Dieter's nod began to tap upon the thickened portion of the knife just above the cutting edge, moving the blade down along the course already charted by the saw to split the sternum neatly for its entire length.

Behind the blade of the Lebsche knife, the intern and the sponge nurse worked rapidly, smearing the cut edges of the bone with wax to close off the spongy marrow forming its middle and stop the ooze of blood from it. When Dieter removed the instrument from the incision at its lower end, he, and the assistant also, took wax and worked upward until the entire exposed surface of the marrow was closed off and all bleeding stopped.

Using two retractors, rake-like instruments with handles about a foot long, the intern now held the cut edges of the sternum separate so Dieter could examine the posterior, or inner, layer of periosteum covering the back of the sternum, searching for bleeding vessels which might interfere later with the operation.

The heart itself was already visible within its pericardial sac through the opening in the bone, beating steadily and strongly.

Using a gauze sponge held between the jaws of forceps, Dieter gently pushed away the tissues beneath the upper end of the now divided sternum, exposing a tough fibrous band extending across the space thus opened. When he slipped a curved forceps underneath the band and cut it through, the split in the breastbone widened suddenly.

"I have just cut the interclavicular ligament," he explained. Using his gloved finger, he was pushing the pericardium away from the underside of the sternum as he spoke, moving down on either side until it was well separated away.

"Rib spreader, please."

An instrument with heavy blunt prongs was now inserted between the cut surfaces of the bone. A ratchet drive on the instrument enabled the jaws to be separated. And, as the space between the cut halves of the sternum widened appreciably, the heart in its enveloping pericardial membrane was more fully exposed. A blood-tinged fluid could be seen within the pericardium and a small amount of it leaked out into the space through the opening made by the bullet.

"Another advantage of the median sternotomy incision," Dieter said, as he finished twisting the ratcheted screw of the rib spreader, "is that in most cases the pleural cavities surrounding the lungs need not be opened. However, should we open either cavity intentionally or inadvertently, no lung collapse would result because Dr. Long has prudently put in an intratracheal tube and the patient is now receiving positive pressure anesthesia."

From the instrument table, he picked up a slender pair of thumb forceps, toothed at the end. With them, he was able to tent up a section of the pericardium and, when the resident caught it on his side with forceps, nick the membrane with a knife. Placing a small clamp on each side of the marrow opening, so the whole thing could be lifted well away from the heart, Dieter slit the pericardium widely, exposing the heart muscle beneath it.

"You will note, Dr. Feldman, that there has been no further leak from the ventricle wall since you released the heart from strangulation by tamponade." Dieter looked up to meet her eyes through the glass wall of the observation gallery and, realizing that the all-male audience in the observation gallery had transferred its attention from the operation to her, Marisa blushed. "Heart wounds often close themselves, once enough blood is accumulated in the pericardial cavity to decrease the movement of the heart markedly. The danger is that the accumulation will throttle the heart and kill the patient. Only Dr. Feldman's prompt action prevented this from happening to Dr. McGill.

"Here is the wound of entry." His eyes on the operative field once more, Dieter indicated a dark spot on the heart surface where a small amount of hemorrhage into the muscle had occurred. "Presumably the bullet is in the right ventricle but we cannot be sure with the wound of entry where it is; the bullet could have gone through the septum between the ventricles and now be located on the left side. Before we make any attempt to find out where it is, therefore, we must expose the pulmonary artery so we can block it and prevent the bullet from escaping into the lung circulation where—as Dr. Feldman pointed out in the X-ray room—it could cause a fatal embolism by blocking the blood supply to a large portion of the lung."

Using a slender thumb forceps and a curved pair of dissecting scissors, the surgeon began to separate the tissues at the upper part of the heart between the pulmonary artery supplying the lungs and the aorta, the giant channel that carried blood to the rest of the body. A hush fell over the observation gallery as he worked, for even the greenest student there knew a false step could lead to a hemorrhage which might be uncontrollable. Dieter, however, acted as if he had no knowledge of the dreadful consequences of even a slight misstep, working as calmly as if he were separating a toenail from its bed.

"That guy must have ice water in his veins," one of the students in the gallery said in awed tones.

"Brennan's just as good when it comes to the brain," said an intern.

"Or McCloskey in the bladder," another agreed. "This place is lousy with good surgeons—internists, too."

Dieter was working curved forceps behind the pulmonary artery. When it appeared on the other side, he seized the end of a piece of tape between the metal jaws and drew it back through, clamping the two ends together and lifting the artery up so the students could see where it took its origin from the right ventricle.

"Since we can now prevent the bullet from being accidentally dislodged into the lung circulation, we are ready to explore," Dieter announced. "Purse-string suture, please."

Just to the right of the visible portion of the ventricle could be seen the thin-walled upper chamber for that side of the heart, called the atrium, with the giant veins, the superior and inferior vena cavae, bringing blood to it from the entire body, except the lungs. On the thin wall of the atrium, Dieter began to sew a circular pattern, roughly an inch and a half in diameter, thrusting the needle completely through the wall of the chamber with each stitch.

"The purse-string I am placing can serve two purposes," he explained to the gallery. "First it will enable me to insert a finger into the right side of the heart and determine whether or not the bullet is there."

Putting down the needle and its holder, with which he had been placing the suture pattern, Dieter pointed toward the diagram on the ground-glass view box against the wall.

"On the other hand, if the bullet went through to the left side, we shall have to put the patient on the oxygenator, allowing us to open the heart widely, remove it and repair the wound where it penetrated the septum between the ventricles so as to prevent an abnormal communication from forming there later on. Fortunately, if we have to use the cardiopulmonary bypass, we will be able to insert plastic tubes directly into both the inferior and superior vena cavae through this purse-string area and thus provide a route by which blood from the entire body will pass through to the oxygenator."

The purse-string suture was now in place, ready to be drawn together in much the same way an old-fashioned tobacco or powder pouch was drawn shut, to close the opening he would make in the center of the circle encompassed by its stitches. Carl Hagstrom held up the two ends of the suture, lifting the wall of the atrium as Dieter picked up a sharp pointed knife with his left hand, holding his right index finger ready.

With a swift movement, he stabbed the blade into the center of the circular pattern he had sewn in the wall of the atrium. Blood spurted out as the knife blade entered the heart, but an instant later his finger had plunged into the opening. As Carl Hagstrom tightened the purse-string, the wall of the atrium was drawn snugly about the surgeon's finger, shutting off the flow of blood around it.

"I am able to feel the inside of the atrium and the tricuspid valve between it and the ventricle." Dieter described his findings as he moved his exploring finger about within the heart itself. "The valve does not seem to be damaged."

As he pushed deeper into the heart, the thin wall of the atrium, held snugly around his finger with the purse-string, was carried along with it, much as one might push in the side of a paper bag.

"Now my finger is in the ventricle touching the bullet," he said, and the air in the operating-theater room was suddenly filled with a tension that could be felt even in the gallery.

"The bullet is loose in the ventricle as we suspected. Tighten the tape around the pulmonary artery please, Dr. Hagstrom."

The resident lifted the ends of the tape beneath the vessel and crossed them so as to prevent any flow of blood through it. "It's tight, sir," he reported.

"We can block the circulation to the lungs for only a few seconds without severe danger," Dieter said, and Marisa Feldman found herself leaning forward, waiting tensely, her heart pulsing in her throat. "I hope to work the bullet back through the wound of entry."

"Christ A'mighty!" one of the students said hoarsely. "My heart won't stand much more of this."

"I have the bullet against the wall of the ventricle now." With the fingers of his left hand, Dieter supported the spot on the outside where it had gone through into the heart, separating his fingers so as to leave the wound itself free. "The nose of the bullet is entering the wound from inside the ventricle and I am now pushing it through the wall."

Another "Aah" went up from the gallery when a glint of metal appeared suddenly on the surface of the heart, growing larger as Dieter's finger pushed it through from the inside. Gingerly, Carl Hagstrom seized the steel-jacketed bullet with forceps whose jaws contained a number of delicate teeth interlocking together. When he drew the projectile out, a spurt of blood gushed up from the reopened wound, but stopped at once when Dieter plugged it with his left index finger.

"Release the pulmonary artery, please, Dr. Hagstrom." Even in the gallery, the onlookers could sense the exultation in the German surgeon's voice over a truly remarkable surgical maneuver. "Then please to place some sutures in the ventricle around my finger in order to close the wound of entry."

The sutures were quickly placed, biting into the muscular wall of the heart on either side of the tiny opening through which the bullet had both entered and been withdrawn. When Carl Hagstrom drew the strands snug, Dieter removed his finger. Only a faint drop of blood appeared between the two sutures.

"One more should do it," he said, and separated the long ends of the two sutures which had already been put in place so Hagstrom could place another between them. With three sutures tied, no blood oozed from the ventricle.

"We were very fortunate," Dieter said to the gallery. "Since it was not necessary to open the heart, except to explore it through the soft wall of the atrium, it will not be necessary to place the patient upon the disk-oxygenator after all. If you will hold the purse-string please, Dr. Hagstrom, I shall remove my finger from the atrium."

Only a small gush of blood occurred before Carl Hagstrom could draw the purse-string tight, after Dieter withdrew his right index finger from within the heart. With that suture tied and several others reinforcing it, the small wound in the atrium was also closed.

"What is his condition, Dr. Long?" Dieter asked.

"Fine, Doctor. Pressure one hundred ten over seventy. Pulse one hundred."

"No sign of shock?"

"None."

"Good. We will not transfuse; no need to expose him to the hepatitis virus. And since the wound is dry, it should not be necessary to drain."

The closure went rapidly. Marisa Feldman left the gallery as the wires designed to pull the two halves of the sternum back together and hold them in place were being put in by means of a stout awl pushed through the outer layer of the flat bone. A glance at the clock on the wall at the back of the gallery told her the operation had taken an hour and a half, but caught up in the tense scene, it had hardly seemed half that long.

It was hard to believe now that only a little over two hours ago, she had looked down at the still form on the ambulance stretcher and heard the attendant dismiss Dr. Paul McGill as a D.O.A.

CHAPTER ELEVEN

I

It was almost six o'clock before Alice Weston began to recover from the bout of gripping agony that had seized her when Jake Porter had called her, looking for Roy. There was an extension phone in the bathroom, so she had managed to call George Hanscombe's office at the clinic. By then it was closed, but the staff doctor on night duty was familiar with her condition and ordered a refill of the prescription she took from time to time when she was having colon trouble, delivered to the house from a nearby pharmacy. Since her last checkup had been more than a year before, he also suggested that she come to the clinic early the next morning.

When the medicine came—a green solution with what looked like ground-up leaves in the bottom—Alice took a double dose. By the time the pain began to subside, she had listened to the six o'clock local TV broadcast—breaking her rule never to listen to the news—and knew that Paul McGill had been shot by Mort Dellman. Shortly afterward, Roy's office called to say he would be tied up with business connected with the arrest of Dr. Dellman and wouldn't be home for dinner.

Alice had already prepared Roy's martini and her own before the call. She drank hers and ate a bowl of soup she warmed up on the stove, fumbling with the controls, for it was the first time in months she had touched the stove. On Wednesdays, when the maid was off, she and Roy usually went to the club for dinner after the ritual martinis.

In her disturbed emotional condition, Alice had forgotten to dilute her own drink. When the hot soup stirred up the circulation in her upper digestive tract, the alcohol was quickly absorbed, filling her with a warm glow she hadn't dared to let herself feel for a long time—not since she was a senior in high school and Lorrie had come home from college that first Christmas.

Jake Porter had been away on business the night Lorrie arrived. When Lorrie dared Alice, they started drinking before dinner and took the bottle upstairs when they went to bed. Lorrie had talked Alice into taking a last drink at bedtime and, by the time she'd finished undressing, the younger girl was half drunk.

When Lorrie came into her room from the connecting bath they shared, rubbing her hair dry with a towel after her shower, Alice was already in her somewhat prim muslin gown. Brushing her hair at the dressing table, she hadn't been able to turn her eyes from the reflection of Lorrie's nude body in the mirror as the other girl crossed the room to sit on the bed.

"You ever been with a boy, Al?" Lorrie had asked.

Alice shook her head, blushing, her eyes still on Lorrie's golden body. "H-how did you get the tan all over?"

"I use a sunlamp in winter."

"N-naked?"

"Sure. Why not?" Lorrie's eyes had a bright gleam in them that made Alice feel all funny inside. "Stand up, Al."

When Alice obeyed, Lorrie stooped and, taking the hem of the muslin gown, lifted it over the younger girl's head, leaving her standing naked on the rug beside the bed, her skin all pink and white, in the reflection of herself in the mirror, where Lorrie was brown—and blonde where Lorrie was dark.

"You've grown up, Al." Lorrie's voice had taken on a new note, a tension that hadn't been there before. "You've filled out here." She touched the already full breasts. "And here."

Alice had felt a hot flush all over when Lorrie's hand rested casually on her waist, just above the swell of her hips, then moved down across her smooth round belly. She knew she should turn away, but she had no strength—or desire—to do so.

With one swift movement, Lorrie had crossed the room then, turned the key in the lock, and reached up to flip the light switch beside it, leaving only the light over the dressing table burning. She was back in an instant and, with one sweep of her hand, pulled down the sheet on the bed.

"Want another drink, Al?" she asked.

Alice shook her head; already the room was going around in a dizzy circle, like one of those swings at the county fair.

"What are we waiting for then?"

Alice had gone to sleep in Lorrie's arms afterward, warm and surfeited with love. When she'd awakened in the middle of the night to feel Lorrie's hand caressing her warm flesh, the now familiar excitement had risen again, demanding the satisfaction Lorrie was so expert in giving—and receiving at Alice's own grateful, loving hands.

That Christmas had been the happiest in Alice's memory—until Lorrie went back to Sweet Briar. The following summer, Lorrie had gone to Europe and, when she'd come home at Christmas a year later, she'd had a crush on a French count who had followed her to the States. She'd had no time for Alice, and right after that, Alice had started going with Roy, who'd cut a dashing figure in his uniform of an officer in the R.O.T.C. at college.

Seized with a desperate loneliness now, Alice stumbled to the phone and dialed a number. "Corinne?" she asked when a woman's voice answered in a deep contralto.

"Yes, dear." Corinne Marchant often sat with the children during the school year, whenever Alice and Roy were going out. She also stayed with Alice during Roy's increasingly frequent absences on political matters.

"Roy's tied up at the office and I've had a colon attack, Corinne," said Alice. "I've taken some medicine for it, but could you possibly come by and stay with me until I get to sleep?"

"Of course, dear. You say he'll be late?"

"His secretary phoned to say he wouldn't be home until midnight or maybe afterward. Something about that Mort Dellman business. I'll leave the door on the latch, Corinne."

"I'll be there in ten minutes."

As Alice was putting the butter dish she'd used for her crackers back in the refrigerator, she noticed Roy's martini on the shelf. Picking it up she drank it down before she could have a second thought. Then, leaving the door on the latch, as she'd promised Corinne, she went upstairs to put on her filmiest nightgown, the martini already heightening the feeling of anticipation stirring within her.

II

"You've been drinking too much again, Grace," were George Hanscombe's first words when he came into the living room after his ritual evening visit to the bathroom following dinner. Located on a lane leading off Sherwood Ravine, the lot was spacious and the house comfortable and large, like all houses in this area.

Crossing to the family room, where a small bar occupied one corner, he poured a generous measure of Scotch, his favorite drink, splashed soda into it and stirred it with a glass rod. He had formed the habit of taking his drinks without ice while in England, one of the few English customs of which he approved.

"Why shouldn't I drink? You do." Grace was tired and cross. Coping with Maggie McCloskey at the club and bringing her to the hospital, plus the worry about whether or not George had been shot, was more than any woman should have to put up with in a single afternoon.

"Now Grace, you know you have diabetes." George's calm tone infuriated her even more than the words, which she'd heard him speak in exactly that same reproving tone a thousand times. She didn't have a severe case; in fact she hadn't shown sugar now for at least a year.

"Does that mean I have to be a zombie?" she demanded angrily. "I might as well be dead."

"Now Grace." Still the same tolerant note. "You have a lovely home here, with the club and your service work to keep you busy."

Twice weekly, she put on a slate blue uniform and cap to push a cart containing magazines, candy and immediate necessities like writing paper, envelopes and ball-point pens from ward to ward, selling them to patients. It was part of the activities of the Hospitality Shop located on the first floor of the hospital. The proceeds went toward scholarships for student nurses at the university.

"I'd rather be a barmaid again," she flared, knowing she could always strike a nerve that way. Whenever she got high enough to mention it in public, George always corrected her by saying she had been hostess in a restaurant, which was actually a bit closer to the truth. What she'd really done was entertain guests in a very high-class London pub, helping out when the regular bar girls were too busy to serve everybody quickly.

"You were never a barmaid, Grace," George said—just as she'd known he would. Picking up a magazine, he crossed to the lounge chair before the TV. Fifteen minutes after the first program began, he would be asleep snoring softly, with his mouth open.

"Would you be ashamed of me if I had been one?" Grace demanded.

"I don't know." He opened the magazine. "I've never considered the idea."

"You weren't ashamed before we were married," she snapped. "I remember how anxious you were to get me in the hay—"

George went on reading his magazine as if he hadn't heard.

"Tell me the truth, George. Were you ever with Lorrie Dellman?"

He looked up. "Did you say something, dear?"

"I asked whether you ever slept with Lorrie Dellman."

"Of course not. Whatever gave you that idea?"

"All your friends did. Why not you, George?"

"Don't speak disrespectfully of the dead, Grace," he said severely.

"I'm not disrespectful; I even admire Lorrie. After all she did what she wanted to—whenever she wanted to do it."

He shrugged and went on reading without answering.

"You're about the same age as Paul McGill, but he's a better man than you are, George," said Grace.

"Why do you say that?"

"Paul made it on a Wednesday. You're no good except Saturday night—and not much then."

"Don't be vulgar, Grace. What the hell's gotten into you?"

She had reached him at last, she thought with a vast satisfaction. Men didn't relish being told they were less anything than others, particularly when it came to sex.

"I'm tired of the same thing day after day and night after night, that's what." The words broke through at last and surged up in an uncontrollable flood. "I'm tired of being only a mild diabetic; why can't I have the real thing or nothing? I'm tired of sitting home nights waiting for you to come home from medical meetings. And still sitting home nights when you're here, not even getting a word through to you because you're snoring in front of that damn TV set. I'm tired of playing golf and bridge at the club, tired of the same old faces, the same old affairs."

He'd gone back to the magazine, so she let him have a shot amidships.

"Why couldn't it have been you with Lorrie this afternoon, George?" she demanded.

"What?"

"Was it because it's Wednesday instead of Saturday? Do your testicles only function for an hour every Saturday night?"

"For God's sake, Grace. What's gotten into you?"

"You and I are getting old, George. Life is passing us by. What happened to all those promises you made in England? The ones you used to get me into bed with you."

"As I remember it, you didn't need much persuasion," he snapped.

"We don't have much time left, George." She was half crying now. "Why can't we spend some of our money, go on a cruise, take a trip to Eng—?"

"Now Grace. We've been into that."

"To Rio then? The International Congress of Cardiology is meeting there next month. A travel agent sent us a folder about it."

"You know I have responsibilities, Grace—and classes."

"The others go to a lot of medical meetings. You've got some men on your staff who could teach your classes. They'd be glad to get the chance."

"That's out of the question," he said shortly.

"That's why you never take a vacation, isn't it—except to play golf and bridge in the summertime at some place like Deerslayer Lodge when classes aren't on? You're afraid one of those bright young men will turn out to be a better doctor than you, George. Everybody in the hospital knows you don't give them a fair shake."

"Grace," he said stiffly. "I refuse to listen to such drivel."

"You've got to listen, George. We're married for better or for worse—and God knows it couldn't get much worse." She had really begun to cry now. But when, not knowing what to do, he tried patting her on the shoulder, she threw his hand off.

"Why don't you talk to Dave Rogan, dear?" he suggested, but when her shoulders stiffened, added hastily, "or Jack Hagen. After all, the meno—"

"Women don't have the menopause any more. You're a hell of a doctor if you don't know that. Gynecologists give them hormones and they grow old gracefully—no hot flashes, no thin bones, nothing. It's the Fountain of Youth, George. Women can stay young forever. Only men get old."

"Now you're talking foolishness again."

"I read about it in a column by a doctor. He says there's no male menopause either, that it's all in your mind. So why can't you make it Wednesday, like Paul McGill did? Oh God, how I envy Elaine." She jumped from the sofa and ran to the stairs leading up to the bedrooms. "Good night— No, damn it! There's nothing good about it."

She was asleep when he came up, exactly at ten as always. Nor did she waken when he got in on the other side of the double bed.

III

Pete and Amy Brennan were lying in bed smoking and watching TV about eight thirty, when the telephone rang.

"Don't answer," Amy said quickly. "I—I'm still in the mood."

"How can I make it a second time with that damn thing ringing?"

"Take it off the hook."

"And have the operator hear us panting. She'd figure it was an emergency and send the cops."

"Answer it then—but don't go 'way."

He picked up the phone and put the receiver to his ear. "Dr. Brennan."

"Pete!" It was Roy Weston.

"What is it, Roy?"

"You'd better come down here to the jail. Mort Dellman wants you—and so do I."

"What good can I do Mort? He needs a lawyer."

"Mort doesn't want a lawyer—at least not right now. He insists on talking to you."

"Can't it wait 'til morning?"

"If you don't get down here and quiet Mort down, he's going to spill his guts to the newspapers. You know what that will do to the clinic—and half the men in town."

"All right," said Pete resignedly. "I'll see what I can do to cool him down."

"Hurry, Pete. I can't keep the lid on this thing much longer."

Pete looked across the bed at Amy, naked as an houri under the pale blue sheet. What a time to have to be thinking about a louse like Mort when, after ten years of perfunctory love-making, your wife suddenly sheds all her inhibitions.

"All right, Roy," he said into the phone. "I'll be there right away."

"What's wrong with Roy?" Amy asked as he hung up.

"Mort Dellman wants to see me. Roy says I'd better come or Mort's going to blow the whole story of Lorrie's affairs—starting with Roy himself, I gather—to the newspapers."

"But that was a long time ago."

"It could still ruin Roy's chances in the election. Abner Townsend is always lecturing on morality. Think what he could make of this in the campaign, when Roy runs against him."

"I don't want to think about Mort, or Roy, or Lorrie right now. I want to think about us." Amy's voice was slurred a little from the morphine but Pete was too disturbed by what Mort Dellman could do to the clinic to notice.

"Take a nap while I'm gone, darling." He kissed her, then slid out of the bed and began to dress. "It will help you gain strength—for when I get back."

"You're the one who'll need the strength, lover." Amy giggled. "Better put the chicken in the refrigerator as you go through the kitchen. We can have it for breakfast."

IV

From where she was sitting in the small waiting room just off the Special Intensive Care Unit, Elaine McGill saw the stretcher move past. Jeff Long walked at the head of it and smiled encouragingly at her but Paul was surrounded with so much apparatus—the tubing and bottles of two intravenous sets being carried by the operating-room nurses who had come with the stretcher, the connections for the electrocardiograph, the blankets covering his body—that she couldn't see his face at all. It was almost as frightening as the waiting had been, but she didn't try to go to his room, knowing everyone was much too busy there to be bothered with her. A few minutes later, Anton Dieter stopped at the door of the waiting room.

"I'm Dr. Dieter, Mrs. McGill," he said. "We met last year during a reception at Dr. Hanscombe's."

"I remember. It was shortly after you came to Weston."

"Your husband is fine. We were able to remove the bullet fairly easily." From his pocket he took the shiny, steel-jacketed missile and held it in his palm for her to see. "Of course, the authorities will want it."

"I certainly don't." Elaine shivered. "How soon will Paul be awake?"

"That depends on several things. Your husband was clinically dead for a period of time, Mrs. McGill—without respiration or a perceptible pulse. We don't know how long that period was, but there is no doubt that the brain cells were without oxygen for a while."

"Then he could still—?" She stopped as a case she'd read about came into her mind, a patient whose heart had ceased to beat, during an operation. Though finally revived, he had never regained consciousness and had lived on for years in a state of stupor. "Then he could still have trouble?"

"After Dr. Feldman recognized the condition and instituted emergency treatment, your husband came back remarkably quickly, so there is every reason to believe he may recover completely," Dieter assured her.

"But you can't be sure?"

"I'm afraid not."

When Dieter left, Elaine groped her way to a chair in the small waiting room. Until now, everything had centered about the dramatic operation and she hadn't even thought of the possibility that the greatest damage might have been done before the surgery was even started, damage which might well be irreparable, in spite of all the medical facilities of a great hospital which had been marshaled to save Paul's life. No one could tell just how long it would be before they knew whether his brain was damaged because they had no way of knowing themselves, until he either regained consciousness or continued in a state of stupor.

Until then, she could only wait—and pray.

She was still sitting in the small waiting room when Jeff Long came out of Paul's room. From her chair, she could see the closed-TV picture of the room on one of the monitor tubes, and beneath it, the flashing line marking the picture of Paul's heart action as recorded by the electrocardiograph. Janet Monroe had explained to her how the system worked and that it was better for her not to remain in Paul's room, where the nurses and interns would be busy watching his postoperative condition, but that she could see him anytime she wished by glancing at the monitor tube.

Jeff Long had been introduced to her as the anesthesiologist. He paused briefly at the nursing station, then came over and sat down beside Elaine.

"Jan—Mrs. Monroe—tells me you're worried about Dr. McGill," he said. "You needn't be; he's doing fine, though he may not become conscious for several hours."

"Dr. Dieter says you won't know until then whether—whether he'll have all of his faculties."

"Why not cross that bridge when we get to it—if we have to?" he said cheerfully. "The important thing now is that he's come through the operation safely."

"Why are they giving him oxygen and doing all those other things, if Dr. Dieter successfully removed the bullet?"

"They're only protective measures," he explained. "The bullet went into the right side of the heart—perhaps you could understand better if I made a diagram."

"I'm sure I could."

He went to the chart desk and returned with a blank sheet of paper and one of the metal chart clipboards. With swift strokes, he drew a rough diagram of the heart, the four chambers separated by the central partition called the septum.

"Fortunately the bullet didn't hit anything solid in its course, like a rib or even a metal button," he explained. "Otherwise it might have mushroomed and made a much worse wound than it did. Actually the hole where the bullet entered the heart was very small and only a few sutures were required to close it."

"Wasn't that hard to do?"

Jeff Long smiled. "Not for Dr. Dieter. He operates on hearts like most surgeons do on the appendix, but we still leave as little as we can to chance. We're injecting heparin into Dr. McGill's bloodstream to keep clots from forming where the wound in the muscle was closed. And we're also watching to make sure the communication system in the heart isn't interrupted by swelling or hemorrhage."

"I'm afraid I don't understand."

On the diagram he'd made of the heart chambers, Jeff Long outlined with a pencil what looked like the branches of a tree, spreading out through the muscle of the four heart chambers. A central trunk ran through the septum, of which he had spoken, separating the right side from the left.

"These might be called the telephone circuits of the heart," he explained, pointing to the treelike pattern he had drawn in. "Each beat originates in a center located up here in the right auricle—the small upper chamber. It spreads through these branches I've drawn and causes both auricles to contract, filling the ventricles with blood during the first half of the heartbeat. At the same time, the electrical impulse of the heartbeat has been traveling along this trunk of tissue I've drawn through the septum"—here he indicated the single trunk—"before spreading out through the ventricles and causing them to beat."

"It's all pretty complicated, isn't it?"

"The first time you see it, yes. Actually it's really no more complicated than your telephone—maybe not as much." He turned back to the drawing. "Because the main channel for the nerve impulse of the heartbeat to the ventricles passes through the septum, it's a pretty vulnerable area and swelling or hemorrhage in such a narrow space can press on the nervous tissue carrying the impulse and shut off the message."

"Causing death?" she asked quickly.

"Possibly—if we aren't prepared for it. Usually the ventricles immediately take up a separate rhythm of their own, though one that's slower than the impulses sent out from the auricles for the normal heartbeat. But in case they don't start doing their own work immediately, everyone who works in the Intensive Unit knows how to operate the Pacemaker."

"Pacemaker?" She frowned.

"It's a device to stimulate the heart from outside by passing a small electric current through the muscle. Dr. Dieter used it in the emergency room when your husband was brought in—"

"I thought the woman doctor took care of him there."

"Dr. Feldman no doubt saved your husband's life by withdrawing blood from the space around his heart. Dr. Dieter arrived shortly afterward and got the heart started functioning again with the Pacemaker."

"Is this liable to happen—this swelling you spoke of?"

"We think not. Certainly there's no sign of it now and, as I said, we take no chances. The oxygen he's getting will take a load off his heart, the heparin will prevent clotting, and we're ready in case there's a block."

"I guess you anticipate everything."

"Most everything. Dr. McGill is in excellent condition now and there's no reason why you should stay here—though you're free to if you wish."

"You'd rather I didn't, wouldn't you?" Elaine hadn't missed the brief pause or its significance.

"That depends on how you feel about what happened this afternoon."

"What do you mean?"

"My concern is for your husband, Mrs. McGill; he's my responsibility until he recovers completely from the effects of the anesthetic. So far everything is going well, but the balance in cases like this can be weighted easily against the patient by something so apparently trivial as an emotional disturbance."

"Are you worried about my making a scene?"

"I want to be sure you don't—at least not until there's no likelihood of its crippling his heart."

"All I want is for my husband to be well again, Dr. Long. I'd like to be here to tell him so when he regains consciousness."

"Then we both have the same goal." Jeff Long smiled. "There's a couch in the small room at the end of the corridor; the intern on duty sleeps there when we have a critical case. Why don't you lie down and get some rest?"

"Could I ask you one more question?"

"Of course."

"I've heard that the students call my husband Old Dermatographia. Could you tell me why?"

"It's a term of affection. Dr. McGill is an unusually perceptive and wise physician. He teaches us that the skin reflects the whole state of the body, including the emotional balance. If I hadn't wanted more than anything else to become an anesthesiologist, I'm sure I would have applied for a residency on his service."

"Thank you, Dr. Long. I guess that's about the highest compliment you could pay him, isn't it?"

"It certainly is. Now you'd better get some rest so you'll be ready to see him when he becomes conscious."

"I don't think I could sleep. Not after so much has happened."

"I can take care of that, too," he assured her. "Mrs. Monroe will give you a Nembutal."

"If you're sure it will be all right."

"It's just what this doctor ordered," he said cheerfully. "Leave everything to us. We're professionals at this business, you know."

If she only could really leave it to them, Elaine thought as she lay on the narrow cot in the small room, waiting for the yellow capsule to take effect. Until this afternoon, she had left almost every major decision up to Paul, as he preferred. But now she had not only to think of her own life, and his, but also the child who was still only the single cell formed less than five hours ago within her body.

Briefly she wondered whether she should tell Paul about that afternoon, but put the thought away at once. Paul was a proud man and nothing could break a man's pride more quickly or more effectively than the knowledge that his wife had been unfaithful to him. She felt no actual guilt herself; what she'd done had been merely part of her own biological need to bear a child without which no woman was really fulfilled. But she knew she couldn't expect Paul to see it that way.

Nor did the fact that Paul had been caught *flagrante delicto* with Lorrie Dellman and the scandal his action would make for them both really make any difference. Man, though monogamous by custom and even by law, was not really a monogamous creature and nature had obviously not intended for him to be—else why were there more females in the human species than males.

Knowing Lorrie, and remembering the bet she had tried to make with them all that afternoon at Amy's, Elaine was not at all certain that Paul had even been the aggressor this afternoon. To Lorrie, he'd no doubt represented a conquest she'd never been able to make before; Elaine herself had seen to that by keeping him away from the others at medical conventions and avoiding the pattern of heavy drinking that characterized so many in their own circle. Somehow, she was certain, Lorrie had managed to inveigle Paul into coming to her house that afternoon and from that point on he'd been a sitting duck.

It was too bad that Mort had chosen that particular time to go hunting.

CHAPTER TWELVE

I

The Weston County jail was the most modern in the state, occupying the top floor of the new courthouse. Pete Brennan was taken up in a special elevator by an armed guard.

"Mr. Weston's down the hall in the interrogation—I mean the conference room," the officer said.

The door to the big room was open and Pete went inside. A number of offices opened out from it, somewhat like the setup of a newspaper city room. Roy Weston, his collar open, his face red with anger and irritation, was pacing the floor in one of them, tongue-lashing a younger man whom Pete recognized as Jimmy Lastfogel, the assistant district attorney for Weston County. When he saw Pete, Roy came out and motioned for the surgeon to follow him into another office.

"Thank God you were home when I called, Pete," he said. "The reporters have been badgering me for the last two hours. I've been able to stave them off so far with a lot of malarkey about the dangers of pretrial publicity and the need to guard the prisoner's rights against self-incrimination."

"It sounded like an open and shut case from the radio broadcast," said Pete. "I was out on the lake in my boat this afternoon, but when I got back to the dock and heard about it, I rushed back to the hospital. I called Uncle Jake, but he said he'd already made funeral arrangements and wanted as little fanfare about the whole thing as possible."

"That's what we all want—but that bird-brained assistant of mine had to gum the works."

"How?"

"I wasn't available when Mort was brought in and Jim O'Brien was busy looking for Elaine. Seems like she was at the Hiltons' lake cottage this afternoon and didn't hear anything about all this until somebody thought to call her there."

"The same thing happened to me out on the lake."

"A lot of us were too busy to listen this afternoon, it seems. Jim O'Brien and Eric Vosges sent Mort to jail in a prowl car when they finished investigating the case on the ground at Mort's house. They went to the hospital to see about Paul and talked to Dieter briefly just before he took Paul up to the operating room, then went out to look for Elaine. But instead of letting things wait until I was available, Jimmy Lastfogel started quizzing Mort—you know, the enterprising TV prosecutor grilling the suspect and getting him to confess the crime." He banged the desk with his fist. "You'd think any first-year law student would know better, since the Supreme Court decided the Escobedo case the way it did. Confessions aren't allowed as evidence any more."

"What did Mort say?"

"What didn't he say? First he insisted that Jimmy get a court reporter in. Then he proceeded to tell the whole story—for the record. So what do I have?—a confession covering everything about this case I might have been able to dig up for myself and use as evidence. Now all I can do with it is shove it."

"It's still open and shut, isn't it?"

"Not when it gives Abner Townsend just what he needs to torpedo my candidacy for state attorney general."

"Maybe I'm a little dumb about legal matters, but—"

"If I don't go after Mort hammer and tongs and try to get a conviction, Abner will claim I'm protecting him because I'm a member of the clinic corporation. Personally, I'd like to see Mort burn for killing Lorrie. She may have liked sex—but who doesn't? And she never hurt anybody. Now this damn confession has nullified all the evidence I might introduce."

Roy sat on the desk and lit a cigarette with fingers that still shook from anger. "I think Mort planned it this way, knowing damn well that if he confessed to everything I might use against him, then repudiated the confession, I wouldn't be able to introduce any of it in evidence if I brought him to trial. He's smart enough—and unprincipled enough—to do it."

"How did you happen to get wind of it?" Pete asked.

"Jim O'Brien knew where to find me; he knows everything that goes on in this town. When he came back to headquarters after locating Elaine McGill and discovered what was going on, he called me. But by the time I got here, the whole thing was in the reporter's stenotype machine. And you know what a scandal there'd be if I tried to bribe a court reporter to tear up her notes."

"Did Mort repudiate his confession?"

"That's why I called you. Mort sent for me just now and, cool as you please, said he'd been interrogated without being warned of his rights while he was under a great emotional strain because of the death of his wife. He claims he doesn't know what he told Jimmy Lastfogel and the reporter but that whatever it was, he now denies everything."

"Did he sign the statement?"

"No. But that wouldn't make any difference under the Escobedo ruling. The confession would be thrown out if he wanted it to be, even if he'd sworn to it on a stack of Bibles."

"Mind telling me what he confessed to? Or is that forbidden, too?"

"I don't see why not. As soon as Mort beats the rap, he'll probably sell the whole story to a magazine for a fortune. I SHOT MY WIFE AND HER LOVER—believe me it would make a story to beat anything on the best-seller list. According to Mort, as long as Lorrie kept her amours in the family, so to speak, he didn't particularly mind. The way he looked at it— and he's pretty close to the truth there—a lot of us have been sleeping with each other's wives for years, probably providing the variety that's kept several marriages from breaking up."

"I don't imagine many marriage counselors would agree with that kind of therapy," Pete said with a grin. "But you may have a point."

"Anyway Mort admitted that Lorrie was too much for him, so he didn't mind her extracurricular activities, as long as she confined them to members of the club. Lately though she'd been putting out to a student."

"A medical student?"

"A curly-haired and curly-tailed senior named Mike Traynor—"

"I know him—got a nurse in trouble a couple of years ago. We almost booted him out."

"Too bad you didn't."

"Turned out the nurse was almost as bad as he was."

"Anyway, Mort suspected what was happening—or Lorrie may have even told him. It would have been her idea of a good joke. Mort's had her watched for some time now and his watchdog discovered that the guy was coming around on Wednesday afternoons, when most of you play golf."

"He couldn't have chosen a better time."

"Mort decided to use this Traynor as an object lesson to scare the hell out of Lorrie and make her go back to the club. I guess he also planned to put the fear of God into some others we could name, too, but the main purpose apparently was to scare Lorrie into laying off medical students."

"It was a clever plan."

"Just the sort of thing Mort would think up—and go through with," Roy agreed. "The trouble was, it was pretty dark in the bedroom they were in. Mort's a crack shot but apparently he didn't figure on Lorrie being on top."

"What?"

"Jim O'Brien and Eric Vosges checked the angles and directions the bullet must have taken. They both say it couldn't have been any other way. But who would have thought Paul McGill would be the one that was with her?"

"I would have bet Paul was a virgin when he married Elaine—and hadn't looked at another woman since," Pete agreed.

"Chances are, Lorrie lured Paul out to the house this afternoon some way—maybe it was connected with that crazy bet she made with the girls."

"Wait a minute. What's this about a bet?"

"You mean Amy didn't tell you?"

"Not a word."

"It was over a year ago. They were all at a meeting of that sewing circle they have—"

"The Dissection Society?"

"Yeah. Alice told me about it then. It seems that Lorrie started analyzing our marriages. I gather she told the girls they weren't getting what they were entitled to. She offered to make a study of each of us men in bed—and report on her findings."

"You don't mean they took her up?"

"Of course not—that's probably why Amy never mentioned it to you. As for Alice, she couldn't care less; half the time when I board her she's asleep before I get through. Anyway, none of them would take Lorrie up, so she told them she'd do it anyway—and apparently did."

"So that's why Lorrie tried to get me out in a car with her at the club dance last year," said Pete.

"You mean you didn't go?"

"I happen to love your sister, with all her faults—though I don't know how I can stand them much longer."

"I've been wondering about that, too," said Roy. "Ever since she was a little girl, Amy's always had to be boss. I guess it was because Mama was always running over Dad. The only way I could ever get the best of Amy when we were kids was to knock the daylights out of her, so it looks like you'd better start doing the same thing. But getting back to Mort. After he repudiated his confession, he demanded to see you, so I called you."

"Guess I'd better talk to him then."

"Do me a favor, Pete. See if you can get him to plead temporary insanity."

"Will that get you off the hook with Abner Townsend?"

"It's my only chance. And maybe Mort's too."

"Do you think he'll do it?"

"It's either that or take his chances with the so-called unwritten law—

and you can never tell how a jury is going to react to that."

"If Mort's figured this thing out the way you think he has, he's probably covered that angle, too."

"Then make him understand that it's the closest to a sure-fire bet he can have for acquittal. A man comes home and finds his wife in bed with another guy and shoots him in a fit of rage—that makes him not responsible for his actions, as far as most people are concerned. No jury in this part of the country would convict him if he claims he went mentally berserk. In fact I might even keep it from coming to trial at all, if Mort will cooperate."

"How?"

"We've got a grand jury sitting now. If I can get this case before them and have a psychiatrist—"

"Not Dave Rogan!" Pete exclaimed.

"Dave's the last one I would want," said Roy. "In the first place he probably wouldn't certify Mort as insane. And, whether he did or not, Abner Townsend could still claim it was all rigged. I'll get a psychiatrist from Atlanta or Asheville. With the right kind of testimony, we can sweep this whole thing under a rug and Abner Townsend won't be able to do a damn thing about it."

"What happens to Mort? I've got to know that before I can advise him."

"He'll have to leave town in any event—this way it won't be in a coffin."

"Have you suggested this to him?"

"I'm the district attorney, Pete! I'm supposed to do my best to hang Mort and I would try if he hadn't beaten me to the draw. Now we've got to get out of it the best way we can."

"I still don't see how you can keep the lid on this scandal, if Mort insists on making news out of it."

"We can't—if he insists. If we can get him to let me bring the case before the grand jury with a plea of temporary insanity, the proceedings will be secret and we can probably keep them that way. But we've got to move fast."

"Can I talk to Mort privately now?"

"Of course. I'll have him brought down here. Tell him not to worry about the place being bugged. The last thing we want right now is another confession."

II

Pete Brennan had never particularly liked Mort Dellman, and under other circumstances would hardly have chosen the stocky clinical pathologist as an intimate associate. Like the others of the small group of doctors forming the nucleus of the Faculty Clinic, he'd been thrown with Mort for two years in the Army general hospital in Korea where they'd all been working. When the rest had applied for faculty positions in the new Weston University Medical School fifteen years before, at Roy's suggestion, Mort had applied, too—on his own.

Mort's credentials as a biochemist and a skilled laboratory director were beyond reproach, whether any of them liked him or not. All of them, plus the Board of Trustees of the medical school, had recognized his genius in his field so he'd won a faculty position. When they decided to open the Faculty Clinic for their private practice—outside their teaching work—Mort had made valuable suggestions for automation and increased efficiency, so they'd naturally made him director of the clinical laboratories. Busy primarily with medical work, too, they'd been happy to hand him the job of setting up the administrative organization of the clinic—all of which he had done exceptionally well.

It had been Mort who had developed the automated techniques that let the Faculty Clinic process twice as many patients a day as any other group of the same size in the country, except perhaps several in California that were using the same techniques. In fact, Pete suspected that the Faculty Clinic was patterned very closely after some of those California organizations, since Mort had been working for one of them when his reserve commission had suddenly dragged him into the army and the Korean war.

When computers first came into prominence, Mort had seen their possibilities for storing and retrieving medical data rapidly and had scored a clean beat on most medical groups in the country by persuading the others to invest in a computer. Recognizing the potentialities of the clinic as far as publicity was concerned, he had also invited magazine writers to witness its methods of operation and write them up in the sort of pseudoscientific general reports that were fully acceptable ethically, yet managed to be a very effective form of medical advertising.

Roy had left the door to the small office open. When Pete saw a turnkey ushering Mort Dellman through it, he came around the desk and shook hands. "Have they been giving you a bad time, Mort?" he asked.

The biochemist dropped into a chair and accepted the cigarette and light Pete gave him. He was of medium height with a somewhat beefy face, deep-set shrewd eyes, and a shock of graying hair. His clothes were rather rumpled and his eyes somewhat bloodshot.

"I've been giving myself a bad time, but I'm all right now," he said. "Lorrie's dead and I can't help her, so I've got to get out of this thing the best way I can."

"Maybe you'd better not talk until you get a lawyer—"

"I'm building my own defense right now. You know how Lorrie was, Pete. If you didn't get your share like the rest, it was your own fault. I'm sure you had plenty of opportunities."

Pete made no comment, since none seemed to be indicated.

"As long as Lorrie kept her activities in the family, I didn't particularly mind. A man gets tired even of a special dish, if it's put before him too often. I don't mind admitting she was too much for me alone and letting my professional confreres dally with my wife occasionally gave me a hold over them I might not have had otherwise. I don't flatter myself that many of the people around here like me and frankly I don't give a damn—except where you're concerned."

"Why me?" Pete asked, startled.

"I admire you more than any of the others, though Dave Rogan has always treated me squarely, too. Maybe it's because of that Irish charm of yours." He grinned wolfishly. "Or I could be a latent homosexual—like one or two I could name."

"Get on with your story."

"Roy probably told you about that confession his eager-beaver assistant trapped me into making," Mort said with a knowing grin, and Pete was sure now that Roy Weston's surmise about the purpose of the confession had been correct. "I could forgive Lorrie most anything except shaming me by having an affair with a medical student. Can you imagine what sort of a story that would make in the intern's lounge?"

"Not a very pretty one, I'm sure."

"This guy had been coming around on Wednesday afternoons so I figured to use him to scare the hell out of Lorrie and maybe put the fear of God into some other people."

"Are you saying you went out there this afternoon planning to shoot this—what's his name?"

"Traynor? Hell no! I only intended to wing him a little. But who would have thought Paul McGill would have been there instead?"

"He'd never been with Lorrie before?"

"Not that I know of—and the man I hired kept pretty good records. How is Paul, by the way?"

"He'll live. Anton Dieter took your bullet out of his heart."

"Good! I always thought Paul was a fuddy-duddy, but I wouldn't want to hurt him."

"Do you have any idea how Paul got mixed up with Lorrie?"

"All he had to do was to go to the house. You know that."

"But why would he go?"

"Lorrie must have asked him to stop by; I remember her saying something about a skin irritation when I left this morning. Or was it yesterday morning? Anyway our house is right on Paul's way to the club where he usually plays golf on Wednesday afternoons, so he wouldn't suspect anything. Or maybe Lorrie was expecting the medical student and he didn't show up, so she settled for Paul. Anyway you couldn't expect him to resist much, with her jaybirding around."

"Jaybirding?"

"She read about it in a magazine; I think it may have been *Time*. It seems that a lot of nutty women have started doing their housework at home in the altogether. They call it jaybirding—I suppose because they're naked as jaybirds."

"You must be kidding."

"Get the article for yourself, if you don't believe me. The weather's been hot and the children were at camp, so Lorrie took it up this summer. She says it's wonderful and I'll say one thing, she certainly had me going home to lunch for a while."

"Too bad you didn't go home today," Pete said dryly.

"Wasn't it? The way I figure it, once Lorrie got Paul in the house, he was caught in a situation where even a stone statue wouldn't have been able to resist. It was just his luck that I decided to make an example of that damn medical student today."

"Roy can chew you up in court, if you admit that you deliberately went home this afternoon to shoot Traynor. Particularly when you knew he'd been with Lorrie before."

"You don't think I'm that dumb, do you? My defense is going to be the unwritten law. I shot defending my home and my marriage; no jury would convict a man for that."

"What about temporary insanity? It would fit into that defense and strengthen it a lot."

"Not a chance! With a rap like that pinned on me, I might escape the electric chair. But they'd sure as hell send me to a state hospital for maybe a couple of years—until some dumb bunny of a hack psychiatrist decided I was normal. And even then they could try me again. No, I'm going to beat this rap all the way—my way."

"Why did you send for me then?"

"I'm going to need a lawyer—maybe somebody like Percy Foreman. It's up to you and the rest of the boys to pay for him."

Pete gave him a startled look. "How do you figure that?"

"You've got to save me to preserve the standing of the Faculty Clinic and the reputation of the ones Lorrie had already gotten to with that crazy bet—"

"You knew about that?"

"She thought it was a good joke. I guess the joke's on her now."

"Would you believe I never heard of the bet until Roy told me about it just now?"

"I'd believe anything you tell me, Pete. That's why I sent for you—that and because you're president of the clinic corporation."

"What does the corporation have to do with it?"

"I'll have to get off the faculty—which means the clinic, too—so I'm willing to sell out to the rest of you for money to finance my defense."

"Under the unwritten law?"

"Yeah. I'll take the chance that a jury may convict me of manslaughter or unpremeditated murder—with maybe two to ten years in prison. Even if they do, I'll still walk out in a year or so with a hundred thousand dollars in the bank."

"How do you figure that?"

"I'm asking a hundred thousand for my share of the clinic—and its future."

"You're dreaming!"

"If I am, it's a nightmare—for the rest of you, not me."

"But we don't have a hundred grand, Mort."

"Maybe not in cash—but your credit's good. Each of you takes better than fifty thousand a year out of the clinic, plus your university salary. If you, George Hanscombe, Dave Rogan, Joe McCloskey, and Paul McGill each take ten thousand a year out of that fifty, you can pay back a hundred-thousand-dollar loan in two years—with maybe another year to take care of the interest."

"You seem to have it all figured out," said Pete.

"I'm not exactly stupid; you ought to know that. A hundred thousand dollars isn't nearly as much as I would make from the clinic in the next few years, but I'm getting sort of tired of the place anyway. With Lorrie gone, I can take that hundred thousand and enjoy myself."

"Where?"

"They're crying for medical personnel in South Africa and a lot of other places. Biochemists trained as clinical pathologists aren't a dime a dozen either."

"But a hundred thousand—"

"Think about it and you'll find it's a cheap price to pay. After all I automated the clinic and made more than that for the rest of you in the past five years."

"None of us would deny that," Pete admitted.

"What do you say then?"

"I can't say anything until I talk to the others—and Paul McGill isn't in shape to decide anything right now. Give me a week."

"Too long. I don't like jails. If Roy doesn't spring me in a day or two, I'm going to throw a *habeus corpus* at him."

"Five days?"

"Three. If Paul's in as good shape as you say, you can talk to him by day after tomorrow. But you'd better be persuasive, Pete. It's my neck I'm risking and I won't give an inch."

III

Roy Weston came into the small office after Mort Dellman had been ushered out by the turnkey. "You look like you've seen a ghost, Pete," he said.

"I have. Is there anything to drink around here?"

"In a jail?" Roy grinned and opened a desk drawer, taking out a bottle of bourbon. Pete took a stiff jolt and lit a cigarette with fingers that shook a little.

"He's a cheeky bastard," said Roy. "I'd really like to sink my teeth into him in a courtroom."

"Forget it. Any good that might do you in gaining votes would be more than lost because of the way the newspapers would handle the scandal."

"That's why I wanted you to talk him into pleading temporary insanity."

"He won't buy it, Roy."

"Why?"

"The way Mort figures it, he'd be shoved into a state hospital; and he doesn't have any more confidence in the staffs of most of those places than I do. He thinks he might not get out for a couple of years."

"It's better than the rope."

"Mort doesn't figure to get the rope. Just to be sure, he's gonna get a high-powered lawyer—somebody like Percy Foreman."

Roy Weston whistled. "They come high."

"Mort isn't worrying about that. He intends for George, Dave, Joe, Paul and myself to pay the bill. We're to buy him out of the clinic for a hundred thousand."

"A hundred thousand dollars!"

"His share's worth that. I can't argue with him about it."

"So?"

"I'm going to talk to the others tomorrow and make arrangements for the money."

"Don't forget that I'm a member of the clinic corporation. I'll pay my share."

"Not on your life. This is our baby and we're stuck with it. Besides, think what Abner Townsend could do with that information in the next campaign."

Amy was asleep when Pete got home. She'd pulled the pale blue top sheet up under her chin and was sprawled out on the bed like a child. The light over the bed was still on and she looked lovelier in the spill of the light than he'd remembered seeing her for a long time.

How could he have ever considered divorce, he wondered? But then he had to admit that for more than five years now there hadn't been anything between them like the brief period tonight, when they had once again been two young lovers finding new rapture in each other.

Where does it go?—that youthful rapture—he wondered as he undressed. What happens to two people who love each other? What invisible wall rises between them over the years—for no real reason?

In their own case, he'd put most of the blame on Amy's ambition. But in all fairness to her he had to admit that he'd known about that before they were married. The clinic had occupied much of his time these past five years but the real trouble, he decided now, must have been his own desire for money—money he'd made with his own hands and not the fortune that was Amy's, most of it safely invested in high-yield bonds with the interest going into a trust for the children.

He had been a fool, he admitted as he faced the possibility of all he'd worked for being blasted into nothingness by the scandal Mort Dellman could create. A fool to let anything threaten what he and Amy'd had together in the beginning. If they'd only spent a little more time working at their marriage, each giving in a little to the other's weaknesses and recognizing the other's strengths without resenting them, the years when they'd gradually drifted apart could have been an entirely different story altogether.

Amy didn't move when he got into bed and switched off the light. Her face was against the pillow, so he didn't notice the pupils of her eyes. Had he done so, the tight constriction from the dose of morphine she'd given herself just before his arrival earlier that evening might have told him something was wrong, something so dreadful that he'd never even considered it a possibility.

But then, some other things he'd never considered possible had happened today, too. It was a long time before he finally got to sleep.

IV

It was after nine o'clock and Maggie was alone in the small Ladies' Bar, nursing a bourbon and ginger ale morosely, when Manuel, the bartender, touched her elbow.

"We're about to close up, Mrs. McCloskey," he said in his soft Cuban accent. "You want me to call you a taxi?"

"Taxi?" Maggie shook her head to clear her vision but his features remained blurred. "My car's in the lot."

"A taxi would be better, Mrs. McCloskey. You can leave your car in the lot."

"All right. Call one for me, while I finish this."

"Wouldn't you rather have a cup of coffee? I've made some for myself."

"Okay." Maggie was too tired and depressed to argue. With Manuel's coaxing, she managed to get down two cups of coffee by the time the taxi came. He helped her from the now deserted club into the cab and closed the door.

"3501 Sherwood Ravine Drive," she murmured and sank back against the cushions. At her home, she got out of the taxi and paid the driver.

"You all by yourself ma'm?" he asked.

Maggie swayed and held on to the cab for support. "Do I look like twins?"

"I'll just keep the lights on the door until you get inside," he suggested.

"Thank you." Maggie stumbled up the drive and, after some fumbling, managed to fit the key into the keyhole. She opened the door and, reaching inside, brought her hand down across the bank of light switches beside the door, flooding not only the house itself—a rambling one-story structure of old brick with wide eaves to which floodlights were attached at the corners—but also the yard.

The coffee had stimulated her enough to lessen somewhat the torpor induced by the alcohol, though not enough to clear her foggy mental processes. More than anything else at the moment, she wanted to escape from the reality of her own blank future into the nirvana of sleep, but she'd had just enough coffee to make it elude her.

The master bedroom with its empty twin to her own bed depressed her even more, as she stripped off her clothes, letting them fall where they dropped, and put on a nightgown. In the bathroom, she opened the door to the medicine closet, not knowing exactly what she was looking for—until she saw the bottle half filled with small yellow capsules. Unscrewing the top from the bottle, she dribbled four of them into her palm and, turning on the tap, filled the plastic cup from the toothbrush rack at one side with water.

With the capsules halfway to her mouth, she stopped and frowned in concentration, trying to remember something Joe had told her about them. But the memory refused to come, so she swallowed the capsules, washing them down with water. She'd taken four before—that much she could remember—so there was no reason why she couldn't now.

Back in the bedroom, she started to turn down the covers of her bed but the emptiness of the second one and the feeling of loneliness it always gave her was enough to make her turn to the adjoining room and throw herself down upon the spotless counterpane.

There, tears finally came and with them, at last, oblivion.

CHAPTER THIRTEEN

I

The operation on Paul McGill had been almost finished and only the closure remained, when Marisa Feldman left the glassed-in observation gallery, with its dramatic view of the brilliantly lit scene encompassing the operating table with the patient upon it, the team of surgeons and assistants gathered around it and, in the penumbra of lesser illumination, the circulating nurses, the electronic monitors that kept watch upon heart action, blood pressure, respiration and other vital functions and, ready as always while heart surgery was going on, the pump that could take over completely the function of both circulation and breathing in an emergency.

The hospital cafeteria was closed at this time of night, she knew, although it opened briefly after ten o'clock to provide coffee and sandwiches for the nurses who came on duty for the night shift at eleven and for members of the medical house staff working late with emergencies. Conscious of being quite hungry—it was eight hours now since she'd had lunch—Marisa left the hospital and crossed the street to the brightly lit Snack Bar.

The small gleaming restaurant was only half filled and she selected a red-cushioned booth in the corner. The menu in the rack beside the napkin dispenser was apparently for children; the dishes offered were pictured in gleaming color.

Mabel, the buxom blonde waitress, put a glass of water before her and waited for the order.

"Everything looks so good," Marisa said with a smile. "Just bring me what's best."

"Tender-medium, Abe. Easy on the oil for the hash browns, French for the salad." Mabel ticked off the order as she inscribed it upon a small check pad, circling the abbreviations for the various items. "Coffee now, Dr. Feldman?"

"How did you know my name?" Marisa wasn't wearing the uniform that subtly distinguished different classes of hospital personnel: long-skirted white coat for the teaching staff, white duck jackets and pants for the house officers, rumpled whites for the orderlies, and nylon for the nurses, maids and attendants—with their distinctive caps setting the nurses apart.

"Being new here you wouldn't know about the hospital grapevine, but it knows about you, Dr. Feldman," Mabel said with a smile. "We've got a special connection over here with the hospital, the medical school and the Faculty Clinic. Want to hear a sample of what's come over the grapevine about you?"

"Y-yes. If it isn't too critical."

"You get a good report." Mabel went to the big gleaming urn with its three glass tubes, one clear for hot water and two dark brown with coffee. She drew a cup, and leaning over the narrow lower counter in the booth section, placed it on the table before Marisa.

"You're Dr. Marisa Feldman—lovely name, Marisa, by the way—and you're an Assistant Professor of Medicine." Mabel had been working expertly at the big refrigerator while she talked over her shoulder. Now she set a brown plastic bowl of salad before Marisa and expertly arranged a knife and fork on a napkin beside it. The spoon had arrived on the saucer with the cup of coffee. "They tell me you're real good."

"Who tells you?"

"The grapevine. A secretary in the personnel office says one thing, a technician in the laboratory, another. Two interns were discussing you last night at supper. Put it all together and before you know it, there's a full dossi—what's the word? I heard it once on 'The Man from U.N.C.L.E.'"

"Dossier?"

"That's it. Pretty soon you've got a full dossier."

The coffee was delicious, so was the salad. Marisa was enjoying them both when the door behind her opened, letting in a blast of warm air from outside to dilute the air-conditioned coolness of the interior. From the corner of her eye she saw Mike Traynor come in. When he saw her at the booth, he took a step in her direction; the booths were all occupied. Marisa looked away quickly, so as to give him no encouragement. And, after hesitating a moment, he shrugged and moved down the row of booths to the end, where a rangy blonde girl was sitting alone, reading a paperback.

"Mind if I sit here?" Marisa heard him ask, and when the blonde smiled and put her book aside, spoke a silent prayer of thanksgiving that she had been spared the chore of being rude. The last thing she wanted tonight was to joust with an amorous young male.

"Dr. Dieter!" Marisa heard Mabel exclaim warmly when the door opened a second time, letting in another gust of humid air from outside. She stiffened involuntarily at the name, but forced herself to relax, lest he notice the effect it had upon her.

"They tell me you saved Dr. McGill," Mabel was saying to Dieter. "He's such a nice man."

"How do you do it, Mabel?" The surgeon and the waitress seemed to be on the best of terms, an American characteristic which Marisa, even after two years in the United States, found somewhat hard to accept. "I just finished the operation, yet you know all about it already."

Mabel laughed. "This is the crossroads of Weston, Doctor—like that place at Times Square and 42nd Street they used to call the Crossroads of the World."

"I bet you know everything that goes on across the street."

"Just about."

"Then you already know Dr. McGill was really saved by Dr. Feldman here." Marisa looked up from her salad as Dieter paused before her booth.

"May I join you, Doctor?" he asked. "Everything else seems to be filled."

"Of course." By then she'd had time to control her instinctive reaction to the Teutonic burr in his voice, and the unpleasant memories it brought. "R.H.I.P."

Dieter looked blank. "I'm afraid I don't—"

"An Americanism I picked up at Harvard." Having shown her superior knowledge, at least in the sphere of slang, Marisa decided to be gracious. "Rank has its privileges, you know."

"I'm not pulling rank, as the Americans say," he assured her. "If you'd rather—?"

"Please sit down. I was just trying to be funny and not succeeding very well, I'm afraid. It's my English background."

"What are you having?" Anton Dieter asked as he slid onto the other side of the booth facing her.

"A tender-medium—whatever that is."

"An excellent choice. I'll have the same, Mabel. That other fine dressing of yours—the remoulade—for the salad, please. And light on the croutons."

"I know just how you like it, Doctor." Mabel obviously adored him.

"I had hoped you wouldn't leave the operating suite before I could thank you properly for saving Dr. McGill's life this afternoon," Dieter said to Marisa. "He's a very fine person."

Prepared to dislike the surgeon, Marisa found herself warming under his praise instead—and steeled herself against it.

"I couldn't have taken the bullet out of his heart," she reminded him.

"I'm not so sure of that." Dieter stirred sugar into his coffee. "I suspect that you are a very resourceful person. But since there will be no fee, suppose we share the credit."

"The approach is certainly original," Marisa said a bit tartly, but Dieter only grinned. Apparently he wasn't easy to insult.

"And the purpose?" he inquired. "Have you decided that?"

"The usual, I imagine."

He shook his head. "I have a feeling that nothing about you is quite what you call the usual, Dr. Feldman—and I hope the same can be said of me. Then we understand each other?"

"Perfectly."

"Good. That saves a lot of trouble—and time."

"Don't be too sure of that."

"We avoid two words in medicine—always and never. I maintain the same rule in my personal life."

Marisa's steak had come by then. It was small but thick and tender, with the potatoes beautifully browned and a toasted bun spread with butter.

"Please eat your dinner," Dieter urged her. "Your food will get cold."

Like the salad and coffee, the steak, potatoes and bun were delicious—and cooked perfectly. "It's a lot better than the English food I grew up on," Marisa admitted.

"The same goes for German sauerbraten or *bigos.*" He saw the sudden pain in her eyes at the mention of a favorite Polish dish and said quickly, "Forgive me if I have offended."

"My family were Polish Jews; they're all dead now."

"I didn't know."

"My older brother was a lieutenant in the Polish army. The Nazis executed him."

"So that's why you were antagonistic to me?"

"Were, Doctor?"

"Perhaps I did take too much for granted, particularly on such short acquaintance. Mabel finds me irresistible and I was hoping you would, too. Anyway we have plenty of time, since we're to be professional colleagues. How do you like Weston?"

"Very much—so far."

"I am a very direct man, perhaps too direct." He hadn't missed the inflection in her voice. "But I suspect you are direct, too, so we shall get along, I am sure."

Dieter's food arrived and he started wolfing it down, then forced himself to eat more slowly. "You must pardon my table manners," he said. "We were so long with too little food in East Germany that even now in America, where there is plenty, I cannot help eating like an animal."

The word struck Marisa's senses like a warning bell, reminding her of human animals who spoke the same language this man had learned to speak as a child.

"My father was a professor in the university at Frankfurt, but we were never Nazis," he continued. "I was not old enough to be taken into the army when the war began and because I wanted to become a doctor, the Nazis let me attend the gymnasium and the university. When the Russians took over East Germany, my father was lucky enough to find among the officers in the occupying Russian troops, a friend who had been a professor before the war. He saw to it that I was allowed to finish my medical education and was given a chance to work in the vascular surgery clinic of Moscow University."

He emptied his coffee cup, but Mabel was there immediately to refill them both. "Would you care for dessert? They have a delicacy here called Black Bottom Pie."

"I shouldn't, but—"

"Surely you don't need to worry about calories—or cholesterol. Two orders please, Mabel."

The pie was everything he'd said it was, rich, delicious and filled with chocolate. Comfortably fed, Marisa found that she needed all her will to resist Dieter's powerful masculine charm and remind herself that he was a German. Or to remember the reasons why she hated them as a race.

"You know, I'm sure," he said, "that the Russians were performing all kinds of far-advanced experimental surgical procedures in the laboratories of Pavlov during the reign of the czars."

"I studied about Pavlov's experiments in England."

"Recently they developed a wonderful machine for suturing blood vessels together during vascular surgery. I managed to smuggle one out when I escaped."

"If you were doing what you wanted to do in Russia, why did you leave?" she asked. "I thought the Russians gave considerable freedom to scientists."

"I was relatively free—for Russia. But we occasionally saw American medical journals and, when I realized they were moving much faster over here in my field than the Russians were, I decided to escape to West Germany and come to America. It was relatively easy before the Berlin Wall was built."

"I remember very well what it was like in East Germany," Marisa said, making no attempt to hide the bitterness in her voice.

"Your accent is English. How did you happen to be there?"

"I was a little girl in Poland when the Ger— the Nazis came. My brother was killed but my mother and I escaped to England with the Polish freedom forces. She died there but my father remained in Germany in prison." Marisa's voice became bitter in spite of her resolve to try to be pleasant. "You were safe in school, so you can't have any idea what it was like for a girl in those concentration camps—a Jewish girl."

"In a hospital in Russia I saw some of those who were freed by the Russians when they invaded Germany. Please don't talk about it, if it causes you pain."

"The hate that has been bottled up inside me for so long makes it difficult even now to speak of it," she admitted.

"Especially to a German."

"Yes."

"But we're both Americans now. That's behind us."

"All but the memories."

"With happiness they will fade in time. You're doing what you want to do—as I am. That's the most important thing."

"I'm afraid you don't have as much to forget." She couldn't have told why she was speaking to him of things she hadn't put into words for a long, long time. But somehow she felt that she had to—and that he would understand.

"At first, I didn't know my father was alive," she continued. "When I learned that he was—after I'd studied medicine in England—I went back to East Germany to try to bring him out, but they took me prisoner. Father had an advanced case of angina pectoris and the Germans wouldn't give him nitroglycerin to relieve it—so I bought the drug myself."

"In prison?" His eyes didn't leave hers.

"Yes—with the only currency available to me then."

Intent upon their conversation, neither of them noticed the gasp from Mabel, who had managed to listen even while moving briskly back and forth behind the counter, serving the few customers in the sandwich shop now.

"No wonder you hate Germans," he said softly.

"I had no right to cry on your shoulder. Excuse me, please." Marisa rose suddenly in her seat.

"It's there—any time you need it." He stood up, too, and when she fumbled in her purse, said quickly, "Please let me—"

"No." Her voice was taut. "I'm perfectly capable of looking after myself."

He stood back to let her pass him to the cash register, where Mabel was adding up the check. "Of course, you are," he said gently. "Good night, Dr. Feldman, I'm sorry if I upset you."

"Good night." She paid the check and almost ran from the lighted interior of the Snack Bar into the darkness of the street outside.

It had been a long time since she had cried—not since the night she'd stumbled back to the dormitory of the prison after her first visit to the quarters of the commandant.

"She's a very lovely girl," Mabel said as she made Dieter's change.

"Very lovely—and very troubled." Dieter moved back to the booth and left a liberal tip. "Troubled by things you here in America can't even conceive of. But I think she may be groping her way back."

"With your help?"

"With my help—if she will let me. Good night, Mabel."

II

"Don't believe I've seen you around here before," Mike Traynor had said as he eased himself into the other side of the booth from the blonde at the end of the Snack Bar. "My name's Mike Traynor. I'm a senior over there"—he nodded toward the building across the street—"substituting this summer as an intern."

"Sibyl Carter," said the blonde. "My roommate and I took an apartment down the street a week ago. She's a private duty nurse, but she's on duty now, and I didn't want to eat alone."

Whether the blonde had intended to or not—and being world-wise, he suspected that she did—she'd told him a lot.

"Are you a nurse, too?" Mike asked.

"I'm a graduate student in sociology at the university; finished at Vassar last June. I work part-time with the social service department of the hospital, so it's more convenient to live in this section of town."

"Sociology, eh? That should be interesting."

"I'm working on a research project, interviewing unmarried mothers in the O.B. clinic and putting their stories on tape."

"Bet you get some real ones."

"You should hear some of them." When the girl accepted the gambit, Mike was sure he was home safe.

"I'd like to." He glanced at the booth where Dieter and Marisa Feldman were engaged in earnest conversation and felt a deep burn of resentment surge within him. The damned Jewish bitch! Snubbing him one minute and making up to Dieter the next like a teenager on her first date. It was disgusting.

Mable put Mike's hamburger before him and he bit into it savagely before turning back to the blonde. "How about tonight?" he asked.

"I don't know. My roommate's on three-to-eleven."

"We've got two hours. Unless you have other plans."

"Oh, no."

"Give me a minute to eat this and we'll be on our way." He finished wolfing his hamburger and drank his coffee, while the blonde was paying her own check. Paying his, he followed her out.

She had a white Mustang and, as he got into it, he saw Marisa Feldman walking toward the Faculty Apartments. When she passed under the street light, he got a glimpse of her face and was sure that she had been crying.

So she and Dieter had quarreled. When he got around to it, he'd try that Feldman again. One of the most exciting things about women was that you never knew when they would change their minds.

When Mike came in shortly before midnight, Lew Saunders, his roommate, was looking at television in the room they shared in the interns' quarters, where Mike was living while substituting that summer.

"You cut it close as usual." Saunders looked at his watch. "You're supposed to be on emergency call after midnight, you know."

"I'm here—with time to get a quick shower," said Mike. "And believe me, I need it."

"Who was it this time?"

"A graduate student in sociology—with her own apartment."

Lew Saunders gave a low whistle. "And a roommate?"

"A graduate nurse—on three-to-eleven. I saw her picture in the apartment and she might interest you, when she changes shifts next week."

"Aren't graduate students in sociology a bit intellectual for you, Mike?"

"This baby was—at the start." Mike grinned as he started to the shower. "She's got a tape recorder and puts everything on the record."

"Everything?" Lew Saunders raised his eyebrows.

"Damnedest thing you ever heard. How would you like to be trying to make the grade while this New England accent was dictating through her nose: 'Erogenous zones responding to stimulation. Clitoridal erection becoming marked. Introitus now receptive to phallus. Penetration maximal. Pre-orgasmic excitement beginning. Increasing rapidly. O-o-orgasm!'"

"Sounds exciting!" Lew Saunders bellowed with laughter.

"Strangely enough, it was. We had a playback right afterward but she got so worked up, she forgot to turn on the recorder that time. I left her moaning because she didn't have a complete record."

"I don't see how you do it, Mike. How many times does that make today?"

"Four. And you'd never guess who I was with this afternoon."

"The waitress across the street in the Snack Bar?"

"For God's sake, Lew! Mabel's old enough to be my mother. Besides she doesn't like me. Would you believe Old Dermatographia's wife?"

"No."

"Take it or leave it." Mike shrugged as he stepped through the bathroom door and reached in to turn on the shower. "I can tell you this much—Old Dermo was writing on the wrong skin this afternoon. He's been neglecting his homework."

III

A great hospital at night is like a sleeping city, its resident population safely tucked away well before the change of shifts at eleven. Yet a continuous bustle of rubber-soled activity, a constant, though muted, obbligato hums always just underneath the hush that lies over the buildings, the corridors, the dimly lit wards, the brightly illuminated chart rooms, utility areas and ward diet kitchens, where a coffeepot always boils after midnight to help those on duty keep awake during the long, lonely hours until dawn.

Backs, irritated from the day's stay in bed, have long since been rubbed with fragrant, stimulating alcohol and glycerine. Evening medications have been given: a narcotic for pain, a mild barbiturate for sleeping. All necessary treatments for the day are finished—unless the patient's condition necessitates continuous medication—to be resumed with the bustle of awakening at 6 A.M.

Here a white-coated intern or resident, dressed in rumpled white duck, heads for the house staff's quarters, shoulders drooping with weariness after a day of work that may have been all of eighteen hours or even longer. On the way, he exchanges hurried greetings with an assistant resident in obstetrics, coat freshly starched, on his way up to an emergency delivery.

In the basement of the hospital, the night work shift is busy preparing for the activities of the day. Rubber-wheeled trucks piled high with treatment trays, dressings, green-tinted linen for the operating rooms, and hundreds of other supplies requiring sterilization, move through the silent corridors below ground toward the giant autoclaves.

In the power plant at one corner of the hospital quadrangle, connected to the main building by a maze of subterranean conduits carrying water, heat, steam, electricity—the very lifeblood that must continue to course through the arteries of the hospital, whether day or night—an engineer is always on duty, a boiler is always stoked and fired, producing steam for the autoclaves, scalding hot water for sterilizing utensils in the utility rooms and the diet kitchen sinks.

Through the almost silent corridors connecting the wards, an electrician, tools hanging from his belt, hurries to repair an overloaded circuit breaker, turning his eyes away when he meets a silently moving stretcher upon which lies what was only a few moments before a living human, the face now covered with a sheet as the body is wheeled to the morgue. There it will be placed in one of the compartments of a huge refrigerator, to await the revealing knife of the pathologist in the morning.

In one of the obstetrical delivery rooms, the first cry of a newborn is like the notes of a flute in the midst of the symphony of life that forms the musical theme of a hospital. In one of the Intensive Care rooms the steady click-click of a respirator, inflating and deflating lungs which, for one reason or another, no longer function of their own accord, sets the rhythm for the drums, while the clang of a falling metal pan occasionally adds the touch of the cymbals' clash. The hum of a suction machine, removing life-threatening mucus fluid from a severely decompensated heart case, is like the throaty note of a cello.

The grunting motor of a milk truck leaving the main kitchen delivery area after unloading its cargo of milk, provides the deep vibrato of the tuba. An ambulance, approaching the emergency-room entrance, sounds a high-pitched note like a trumpet's wail. And the sound of cars, impatient to be on their way after being stopped by the traffic light at the corner, floats through open windows like the melodious tones of French horns and the deeper blast of trombones. Even the violins are there in the plaintive cry of a schizophrenic in the locked psychiatric ward, endlessly repeated like some mad motif that seizes hold of the melody and will not be silenced.

Ordinarily, the symphony of the sleeping hospital was a music Janet Monroe loved to hear; often as she traversed the corridors on the way off duty, she would stop to listen, entranced by some hitherto unheard note and seeking to learn its source. Tonight, however, she had hurriedly given her report to the night supervisor of the Special Intensive Care Unit and was on her way to take a look at Jerry before going home for the night. Troubled by the implications of the reddish tinge in the small tube of spinal fluid Ed Harrison had drawn from Jerry's body, Janet heard none of the hospital's symphony tonight.

The small light burning beneath Jerry's crib gave just enough light for her to see that he was sleeping quietly. She did not wake him but leaned over to kiss him lightly, before turning back to the chart room. A glance at his chart told her there had been no change since she'd been with him earlier when Ed Harrison had done the spinal puncture and Dave Rogan the neurological examination. Pulse, respiration and temperature were all normal and, looking at the chart alone—or even at Jerry sleeping in the crib—it was hard to believe anything was threatening his life.

But threat there was in Ed Harrison's terse note about the color of the spinal fluid; in Dave Rogan's request for neurosurgical and vascular consultation; as well as the order for a radioisotope scan that had proved so valuable in revealing hard-to-identify conditions.

Janet was putting Jerry's chart back on the rack when Jeff Long came into the chart room. "Just missed you on Intensive," he said. "Figured I'd find you here."

"I wanted to look in on Jerry before I went home."

"I came down after we brought Dr. McGill from the O.R. but Jerry was already asleep by then."

"He still is, but I'm worried, Jeff. What does it all mean?"

"I missed my dinner." He took her arm. "Come on. I'll walk you as far as the Snack Bar."

"I couldn't eat—"

"You'll feel differently with one of Mabel's waffles under your belt and a cup of coffee. Come on before I drop dead of starvation at your feet."

In the Snack Bar, Mabel greeted them with a smile and ushered them into one of the red-cushioned booths. "How's your little boy, Mrs. Monroe?" she asked.

"Not so good," said Janet. "I brought him into the hospital two days ago with convulsions."

"Is that nice Dr. Harrison taking care of him?"

"Yes—and Dr. Rogan."

"He couldn't be in better hands." Mabel's confidence in Weston University Hospital and the Faculty Clinic was sublime. "Let me get you some coffee while you're deciding what you'll have. It will perk you both up."

When Mabel had taken their orders, Janet reached blindly across the table to Jeff and he covered her slender hand with his strong one, knowing she needed the support of his own strength. "That blood in Jerry's spinal fluid, Jeff. It means something really bad, doesn't it?"

"Not necessarily." He knew his voice wasn't convincing—but then he wasn't convincing himself.

"Just what does it mean?"

"I'm out of my field there."

"Tell me the truth, Jeff. Anything is better than this uncertainty."

"I talked to Ed about it when I came to see Jerry earlier," Jeff admitted. "All anybody can tell at the moment is that it probably means something congenital."

"Something I gave him?" It was a cry of guilt.

"You're mixing hereditary conditions with congenital ones, Jan. People inherit a defect, probably because it's been handed down in the family from generation to generation—like color blindness, or hemophilia. Congenital only means something you're born with, it has nothing whatever to do with the parents."

"But it's still bad?"

"They won't know until all the reports are in. Right now the bleeding seems to have stopped, or Jerry would be having more convulsions."

"But it can start again?"

Mabel came just then with their food, but Janet didn't touch hers at once. "It could, couldn't it?" she insisted.

"That's what is bothering us all," Jeff Long admitted. "But you mustn't look at only the worst that could happen. The chances are Jerry was born with some little defect in the circulation around the brain, or the meninges covering it. What we've got to find out now is just where that defect is and cure it."

"But can they cure it? Is he going to be like—like one of those spastic children Dr. Rogan examines sometimes?"

"Spastics usually have brain damage when they're born," he explained. "Except for the small amount of bleeding in the spinal fluid when Ed did the tap just now, both he and Dr. Rogan said they could find very little abnormal."

"Maybe if I'd stayed at home and not worked when I was carrying him things would have been different," said Janet. "But we always needed money for Cliff's tuition and other expenses."

"Your working or not working wouldn't have made a minute's difference, darling," he assured her. "Eat your waffle and stop blaming yourself for something you couldn't possibly have had anything to do with."

"They're a nice young couple," Mabel said to Abe Fescue as she was clearing away the dishes after Jeff and Janet left. "Too bad about her little boy."

"Didn't I hear her tell you the headshrinker is looking after the child?"

"If you mean Dr. Rogan, yes. He's a fine doctor."

"You been to him yet?"

"Of course not. There's nothing wrong with my brain."

"You never can tell." Abe grinned. "I had a wife once had asthma. One of them headshrinkers claimed it was due to nerves but I always figured she was born with ice water in her veins instead of blood. Coldest-natured woman I ever saw; wouldn't let me get in bed with her until I'd taken a hot bath that left me limp as a dishrag. I tell you that woman was always either wheezing or freezing."

"Oh you!" Mabel leaned on the counter and looked across the street at the new Surgical Building. "I sure wish I could have seen Dr. Dieter take that bullet out of Dr. McGill's heart."

"Yeah," said Abe. "It must have been exciting—but not half as much as having the husband come in with a gun just when you're—"

"Don't be crude! Dr. McGill's a very nice gentleman."

"Gentleman, shentleman! He was still bangin' another guy's wife. Why don't you feel sorry for this guy Dellman?"

"Because nobody likes him. Everybody knows he only married Lorrie Porter for her money."

"So now he's got it?"

"Unh-unh! She wouldn't have gotten it until Mr. Jake Porter died—and he's still very much alive."

"It looks like Dellman killed the goose before she could lay the golden egg," said Abe. "With all the money old man Porter's got, Dellman could have had himself a ball in this town."

"The way I hear it he did anyway. So what right has he got to shoot his wife and that nice Dr. McGill?"

"Better ask the D.A. the next time he comes in here," Abe advised. "You claim to know his wife so well; maybe you and Mrs. Weston could get together and figure it all out from those soap operas you both look at on TV."

IV

Grace Hanscombe awakened a little after four in the morning with a headache—as she often did. George was heavier than he should be and his weight caused his side of the bed to sink. As a result she slept on an incline and had to prop herself with a pillow to keep from rolling down against him. During the night, the pillow usually gave way, though. And since she didn't always wake up, the unconscious attempt to stay on her side of the bed created a tension that kept her from sleeping well and gave her the headache.

It was not that she was repulsed by George. In her way she supposed she loved him as much as the average wife loved her husband after fifteen years of marriage—which wasn't necessarily very much. She'd always had a healthy interest in love-making too, and enjoyed it still, even after seventeen years of marriage and what had gone before. But when it was over, she was feminine enough to like her privacy, without being forced to sleep jammed up against a man who had been sweating for ten or fifteen minutes and whose skin, whenever she happened to touch it—which she tried not to do— felt sticky.

Grace had suggested a long time ago that they have separate beds instead of the old-fashioned double one George liked. She would even have settled for one of the new-type twins that could be jammed together to form a king-size double bed, letting her have her own springs and mattress. But George liked for her to be where he could reach over and pat her when he came back to bed, after getting up in the middle of the night.

One of these days Joe McCloskey was going to have to take out George's prostate and she shuddered to think what that would do to his ego. Maggie had told her Joe said a lot of men lost their potency altogether after a prostate operation and she knew George well enough to know what a blow that would be to his self-esteem.

Not that his loss would trouble her much. After all, she was older than Amy and the others and had already begun to experience some of the sudden flashes of heat that threatened to suffocate her, even in winter. She'd had to give up sweets, too, when the semiannual checkup at the Faculty Clinic had shown a low sugar tolerance, indicating a mild case of diabetes. Having grown up in England where there were plenty of puddings and other rich foods, Grace didn't think giving up sex could be much worse than the rigorous limitation of sugar George had insisted upon when the mild diabetes was discovered. And even if George wasn't able to make it very often, she was still attractive to men, as had been proved several times at medical conventions and elsewhere.

Grace knew she shouldn't have gotten so upset with George last evening. He was really very sweet—except about a few things, like that business of patting her fanny and waking her up in the middle of the night. Surely a doctor ought to know a man had no business doing things like that unless he had ideas—which George never had at that time of night.

The memory of yesterday afternoon and the terrible hour until they'd reached the hospital and learned the truth brought on one of the hot flashes and, slipping from beneath the covers, Grace went to the open window. The cool night air quickly brought relief but she made a mental note to talk to Jack Hagen about stepping up the dose of hormones. Jack said a woman really didn't need to have any symptoms of the menopause, if she didn't want to, but deep in her heart, Grace knew her trouble wasn't just hormones. She was bored, bored to the very marrow of her bones—with George, with the club, with her friends, with Amy Brennan's constant pushing in that medical auxiliary business, with Weston.

God but she'd like to be in England again. Back in an English pub, where you could joke over a pint of ale with a costermonger or an earl, and pitch your skill with darts against the men. No need to worry about sugar there; if you got diabetes the National Health Service took care of you.

George had even refused to consider going back to England, however. Nearly five years of it during the war, he'd said, was enough to last him the rest of his life. Actually Grace had felt much the same way when they'd left England, all torn and bruised from the war. She knew it wouldn't ever again be as she remembered it from her childhood; time had a way of dulling memories—even of love. But she needed something badly and England was far enough away to offer a change from the deadening monotony of her life in Weston, perhaps even a chance to find a meaning she hadn't found here.

The mornings were cool in early September here close to the Great Smokies and, suddenly starting to shiver, Grace crept back into bed. She didn't prop herself with a pillow but moved close to George, seeking comfort in her moment of deep depression. His body was warm and she felt a sudden rush of affection for him when he reached over and patted her bare thigh where her nightgown had slipped up. His hand lingered against her skin, causing her pulse to quicken for a moment in the old way. But then it slid off and he gave a gentle puffing snore, telling her he'd actually been asleep all the time and the movement only a reflex.

Oh God! she thought. *I'm married to an old man. And I'm getting old myself, while any sort of meaningful life is passing me by.*

CHAPTER FOURTEEN

I

Elaine McGill was awakened by a gentle tug at her elbow. She sat up quickly on the narrow couch, where she'd slept soundly since taking the capsule Janet Monroe had given her last night on Jeff Long's orders.

"Is my husband—?"

"Dr. McGill's fine." The nurse who had awakened her was smiling and she saw now that the room was illuminated by daylight. "It's six o'clock and he's asking for you."

Elaine's hand went instinctively to her hair. "Give me a minute."

"Of course. The lavatory is down the hall. Do you have everything you need, Mrs. McGill? Lipstick? Comb?"

"They're in my handbag. You're sure he's all right?"

"We've discontinued the oxygen. His pulse rate and E.K.G. tracing are normal."

Paul was propped up slightly in bed when Elaine came in about fifteen minutes later. He was pale but managed to smile and she was glad she'd taken time to wash her face in cold water, comb her hair, put on lipstick and rouge and freshen up her dress as much as she could.

Before he could speak, she moved quickly across the room and kissed him warmly on the mouth. "I'm so glad you're all right, darling," she said.

"You mean you don't blame—?"

"Of course not."

"But the scandal?"

"We'll weather that together."

"Then you do forgive me?"

"Don't say any more." She put her finger across his lips. "I love you; that's the only important thing."

"What a relief!" He took a deep breath and she knew she'd handled it exactly right. "I was afraid I'd lose you."

"If you ever two-time me again, you might," she said lightly. "But not this time."

"I really didn't intend to—"

"Hush." She put her finger to his lips again. "It's done and over with. The important thing is that you're all right."

"The nurse said Anton Dieter took a bullet out of my heart."

"Yes. I saw it."

"It's too bad about Lorrie."

"She's dead, Paul. The whole thing's over and done with. We don't even have to speak of it again ever."

"Everything all right in here?" The nurse had poked her head into the door. "Your E.K.G. wave just kicked up a storm for a beat or two."

"That was from relief." Paul managed to laugh. "Everything's fine!"

"I'd probably better not stay any longer," said Elaine. "You need your rest, Paul."

"And you need sleep," he agreed. "Thank you again, darling—for being an understanding wife. And most of all for being you."

Outside the hospital, the city was already beginning its daytime life with the movement of early traffic along the streets. The Snack Bar was almost empty, when Elaine crossed to it and went inside. Taking a stool at the counter, she ordered scrambled eggs, toast and coffee.

While the cook was preparing them skillfully at the grill, she was conscious of admiring glances from a couple of truck drivers having coffee at the other end of the counter. The knowledge that men she didn't know found her attractive at this time of the morning, after what she'd been through in the past twelve hours, was almost as stimulating as the strong black coffee the counterman served her before starting to cook her breakfast, and she ate slowly, enjoying the food.

Elaine was crossing the parking lot to her car when she saw Mike Traynor come out of the emergency entrance of the hospital and head for the Snack Bar. He saw her at the same moment and changed direction so as to intercept her. She tried to ignore him, but when he called to her she turned slowly.

"Were you speaking to me?" she asked.

"How is Dr. McGill?"

"Fine, thank you. I left him a few minutes ago."

"Surely you're not going to take him back."

"That doesn't happen to be any of your business, Mr. Traynor."

She had kept her voice low but he couldn't fail to hear. And when she saw him flush angrily, she knew he understood her meaning.

"Look here! If you think you can use me—"

"Mr. Traynor!" The icy coldness with which she pronounced his name cut off the flow of angry words. "You have another year of medical school, I believe?"

"Yes. But what's that got to do—?"

"My husband is a member of the faculty. If I mention to him that you accosted me here, I doubt if you would be allowed to finish and get your degree."

He started to speak again as she got into the car, then thought better of it. From her tone he didn't doubt that she would do just what she had threatened to do. And after that business with the nurse—who hadn't had the good sense to take the pill or even carry a suppository—he certainly couldn't afford any trouble over the wife of a faculty member.

Women! He'd never understand them—which maybe was just as well. Most of the time it wasn't worth the effort—in Mike Traynor's world.

II

It was six thirty when Della Rogan woke up in the children's bedroom of her home in Sherwood Ravine. She'd taken a Nembutal after shutting herself up in the bedroom and had almost immediately gone to sleep, not even hearing Dave when he came in. Going to the window, she saw that the sun was already up and the weather looked fine for golf. The idea really didn't generate much enthusiasm within her; she would much rather have gone back to bed. But the way her game had been falling apart since she'd come back from Augusta, she needed the practice, if she were going to make any sort of showing at all for the club championship next week.

Her clothes were in her closet and dressing room off the master bedroom, where Dave would be asleep. Tiptoeing along the hall, she looked in and saw that he was lying on his right side, facing away from her, with the pillow bunched up under his head.

For a moment she was tempted to wake him and apologize for making him get his own dinner last night, then decided against it. He'd refused to come home with her from the hospital, even though he couldn't have helped seeing how disturbed she'd been, so he deserved to be punished a while longer. She would just slip out of the house to the club for an early round of golf before it got hot, leaving him to get his breakfast at the hospital; he often did that anyway when he had scheduled early morning ward rounds.

Moving as softly as she could, Della took fresh lingerie from her dresser drawer and went into the bathroom to sponge and dress. The brassiere she'd picked out of the drawer had a broken strap and she came out of the bathroom to get another, wearing only a pair of sheer nylon briefs. Dave turned over and yawned hugely.

"Hello, honey." Reaching for the pillow she would have used had she

slept in the same bed, he shoved it under his head to prop himself up.
"What're you doing up so early?"

"My game's off. Thought I'd get in an early round."

"Alone?"

"Got some shots I need to work out." She was fumbling in the drawer,
looking for a bra. "Somebody else will be out early and I can probably get
in eighteen holes before lunch. Then if I take a nap afterward, maybe Grace
or one of the girls will go round with me in the afternoon."

She slid her arms through the straps of a fresh brassiere and reached
around for the hook, but had trouble locating it.

"Come over here and I'll do it for you," Dave offered.

She couldn't very well refuse, for she'd been grateful for the quick warmth
that had come into his eyes when he awakened to see her, nude for all the
covering afforded by the sheer nylon briefs he liked for her to wear. Crossing
the room, she moved over to the bed and waited for him to hook the bra.
But when his hands lingered on her bare back, she moved away quickly and
began to look for her skirt and blouse in the closet.

"Do you really need all that much practice?" he asked.

"Of course. The club championship tournament starts next week."

"You could use a little practice in some other things," he said casually.
"As a psychiatrist, I usually see the worst side of women, but this morning I
can certainly see the best side of you. What we need is a second
honeymoon."

"We played golf on our honeymoon."

"So you remember?"

"Of course I remember!" Della snapped. "It wasn't that long ago."

"Only fifteen years, close to a fifth of the three score and ten allowed to
us. Anyway you look at it, we've got nearly four of those decades behind us,
Della."

"You're the one who's getting fat and old—not me." She was laving her
face with protective cream; the sun could be very bright in September and
Paul McGill was always warning her against too much exposure to it.
Already she was troubled with little places of thickened skin which he had to
treat with the liquid nitrogen that didn't leave a scar like the electric needle
did.

"You've still got a great shape on you, honey," Dave said with a grin.
"Maybe what we need is another child."

"Two are enough. We agreed on that years ago."

"That was when the kids were small, but in a few years they'll be gone off
to prep school and college. It would be pretty wonderful to have somebody
little around the house then."

"Is that another way of saying I don't stay home enough?" she demanded
angrily. Since Augusta, her nagging conscience had kept reminding her that
she ought to spend more time at home. Now, with one of the perverse quirks
that so often characterize feminine logic, she found reason to shift the blame
to him. For if he had gone with her to Augusta, as he should have done,
none of it would have happened and her guilty conscience wouldn't be
driving her mad.

"I've never objected to your being away." Dave hadn't missed her
immediate reaction, and being familiar with most of the many faces of guilt,
was troubled by it. "It's just that I've seen so many marriages where people
began to drift apart after the children left for coll—"

"Ours are still far from that."

"Not as far as we want to think. Or from marriage either, considering the
way college students are marrying these days. Maybe I'm selfish but I'm
thinking of the time when I may be alone a lot while you're away winning

those national golf championships. It would be pretty wonderful to have
somebody little to tuck into the crib that's up in the attic."

He'd struck the nerve again, and her reaction was instinctive, the same
sort of lashing out that makes a child who feels itself shamed strike even
those who would help it.

"You don't want me to excel at anything," she stormed. "You sit up there
in that office of yours at the clinic and think you're managing everybody's
lives, when the truth is, you can't even manage ours."

"You may be right at that," he admitted. "Everybody knows doctors'
families get the poorest medical care of any group."

"So you admit you can't fix everything?"

He grinned. "If you'll tell me what I'm guilty of, dear, I'll know how to
plead."

"There you go, making jokes! You never take me seriously, Mr. God."

Dave's face sobered. "There's where you're wrong, Della. Maybe I
neglect some of your emotional needs; even a psychiatrist has a hard time
understanding women, and most doctors don't understand their wives. It's
a price we have to pay for being so closely involved in the lives of others all
day long. If you'll just tell me what I've done wrong this time, I'll try to
make it up to you."

She turned away quickly, but not before he saw the sudden hell in her
eyes and the flush of guilt in her cheeks. Something had happened in
Augusta, he was sure now, something he was completely powerless to do
anything about, unless she broke down and told him about it. And he was
pretty sure now that she wasn't going to do that.

The realization brought a sense of futility and an even greater sense of
pain. Della, he knew, was an unusually level-headed woman. She'd been a
rock throughout the years when he came home at night, exhausted from
coping with the emotional problems and crises of his patients—until golf
had started taking her away so much.

A natural instinct told him another man was involved. He was enough of
a realist to know, too, that occasional sexual infidelity was in no sense an
absolute barrier to the successful continuation of a marriage. In fact, as a
psychiatrist he could have made a convincing case for the negative, if he'd
cared to debate the question. But it still hurt to think that Della had given
herself to another man. What was worse, whenever she was away for any
time playing in a tournament from now on, he wouldn't be able to help
wondering just what might be happening.

At the door she turned and lashed out at him again. "You're just like the
rest of the men; you want a wife always at your heel like a dog." Then, with
one of those sudden switches of mood that make women the delightful
creatures they are, she said: "Can you get your breakfast at the hospital?"

"Sure. I've got to see Janet Monroe's little boy before office hours
anyway."

"The one you stayed to see last night?"

"Yes."

"Was anything wrong with him?"

"I'm afraid so. He's had convulsions and there's blood in the spinal
fluid."

Della remembered enough from her days as an X-ray technician to know
something of the significance of the finding. But she was too tense right now
to feel anything except irritation that Dave had mentioned it and caused her
to feel guilty about the way she had reacted to his staying at the hospital
yesterday afternoon to examine the child.

"It's probably just something temporary," she said.

"I hope so. I didn't wake you up when I went to the hospital last night, did I?"

"You went to the hospital?" She turned in the doorway, startled by the question.

"About one o'clock. Maggie McCloskey tried to commit suicide."

Della leaned against the doorframe when her legs suddenly felt as if they were turning to water. "How . . . how did it happen?"

"The usual—barbiturate and alcohol. Lucky for Maggie Jeff Long was there. He kept her going with a respirator until they could wash the drug out of her system with intravenous fluid. She's on my private ward."

"Maggie's not crazy."

"You could get two opinions about that this morning—one, I suspect, from Maggie herself. Actually she's on my service because all attempted suicides go there." He gave her a keen look. "You all right, hon? You're as white as a sheet."

"It's just the shock. Tell Maggie I'll do anything I can to help."

"She's the only one who can help now. If she's finally willing to admit that, maybe we can get somewhere. Have a good game."

Della didn't answer but plunged through the door. Why does he always have to be so damned understanding with everyone else and never understand me? she thought resentfully as she went down the stairs. He could forbid me to play and ask me to stay home more. That was the trouble with being married to a psychiatrist, they understood you too well.

Or did they?

If Dave understood her, why didn't he know that if he put his foot down about her golf, she wouldn't be able to play so much and she'd have an alibi when she started losing tournaments. Instead, he let her go on knocking herself out trying to beat everybody else, when all she really wanted to do was enjoy the game a little. Enjoy it the way she and Dave had done before he'd got too busy with the clinic making his fifty thousand a year to play with her and she'd been left with a feeling of having no real part in his life any more.

It would almost be better, she thought, to have a mild case of diabetes like Grace; and, remembering that George Hanscombe usually left early for the hospital, she turned into the Hanscombe driveway, when she came to it about a quarter mile down the ravine. Sure enough, George's car was already out of the garage, so Della parked hers in the driveway and went around to the back door.

Inside she could see Grace wearing a housecoat and drinking coffee, while she watched the "Today" show on television. When Della rang the doorbell, Grace came to the window and looked out, then went to open the door.

"Come in and have a cup of coffee," she said. "I need cheering up this morning—I feel like a walking corpse."

"I don't feel so hot myself." Della dropped into a chair at the kitchen table while Grace poured the coffee. "Dave was helping me dress to play golf."

"That can hold things up," Grace said with a grin. "But why play golf if that sort of exercise is available at home—without having to bother about dressing?"

"In the morning?"

"Take my advice, dear, and strike whenever the iron is hot. There'll come a day—and all too soon—when it doesn't get hot very often and even then you usually have to settle for lukewarm."

"Can't you talk of anything but sex, Grace? You're as bad as the men—or Lorrie."

"Poor Lorrie. I'm going to miss her," said Grace. "She was in a class all by herself—a completely honest woman. Why did that bastard have to shoot her anyway? He's done worse than she ever did."

"Dave wants me to have another baby," Della changed the subject.

"You've still got the figure for it and you're still young enough. Why don't you?"

"A lot of right you've got to talk," Della said furiously. "Why don't you have one yourself?"

Grace looked away quickly so Della wouldn't see the pain in her eyes. She and George didn't have any children and she knew the reason—though George didn't. Jack Hagen had laid it on the line; that attack of what was called appendicitis she'd had in the early months of the war hadn't really been appendicitis at all, he'd told her. Salpingitis—an inflammation of the tubes leading from the uterus to the ovaries that often left those vital channels sealed off beyond any repair by surgery—had been the real diagnosis.

In the early days of the war when the boys, so handsome and young, had been marching off to battle, it had been the patriotic thing to do. Only how was she to know that one of those gallant brave young men would leave her a sinister legacy that would keep her from bearing children ever after?

"Did I say something wrong, Grace?" Della was really fond of the Englishwoman.

Grace smiled crookedly. "Just an old skeleton walking over my grave."

"How about some golf this morning?"

"Not today. I bawled George out last night because it wasn't him with Lorrie. Now I've got the willies. Can you remember back when you were poor, Della?"

"Of course. Why?"

"Weren't we all happier then?"

"I . . . I guess so."

"What happened to all of us, Della? You're miserable; I'm miserable; Amy's killing her marriage to Pete trying to keep ahead of him. Elaine had to go through hell last night wondering whether Paul was going to die; Lorrie's already dead. The only one of the group I know that's really happy is Alice—with her soap operas. Maybe she's got more sense than any of us."

III

Pete Brennan was still asleep when Amy woke up and was startled to find that she had slept all night nude, something she hadn't even done on her honeymoon. As she groped her way back through the fog that still hung over her brain, she began to remember something of what had happened before Pete had been called away and she'd fallen asleep.

She wished now he'd awakened her when he'd come back to bed; perhaps if he had, they could have held on a little while longer to the precious rapture they'd shared with such abandon and such delight. But it was lost this morning, lost with the waning effects of the morphine, as her body went about the business of destroying the drug, just as it did any alien substance.

For a moment, she considered injecting another of the tiny syrettes, seeking to escape from the reality of the day, but put the thought from her. She was strong enough not to need any crutch, she reminded herself firmly, except when the sickening throb of the migraine began.

Slipping from the bed, she went into the bathroom to take a shower and try to wash away some of the fuzziness that still clung to her brain. She came out of the shower wrapped in a voluminous terry-cloth robe; the way she felt this morning, the last thing she wanted was to stimulate Pete into a repetition of last night. But he was in the shower in his own bathroom, singing his college alma mater as he'd done practically every morning since they'd been married.

While Pete was bathing, Amy dressed quickly in tailored slacks and a blouse; she'd made it a rule at the beginning of their marriage never to pad about the house mornings in an old bathrobe with curlers on her head and cream on her face like so many women did. Briefly she debated telling Pete about her success at the District Six meeting, but discarded the idea. There would be other—and better—times, now that she'd discovered the magic key that opened the world she'd almost forgotten existed since the days of their courtship and honeymoon.

"Good morning, dear." Pete came out of the shower, a towel wrapped around his middle like a skirt. He smelled of shaving lotion and hair tonic as he bent over to kiss her. Though he was forty-two, his body was only a little heavier than it had been in his college days—thanks to golf and regular workouts in the small gymnasium and swimming pool in the basement of the Faculty Apartments. His hair was dark and curly with only a faint sprinkling of gray at the temples. And his eyes could still dance, as they did now when he rested his hands upon her shoulders.

"We had us quite a time last night, Shug." How long had it been, she wondered, since he'd called her by that pet name? "We should do that more often."

"Maybe we will," she forced herself to say.

"What got into you anyway?"

"I remember pouring a drink downstairs—the migraine was pretty bad by the time I got home from the hospital. I guess by the time you got here I was loaded."

"Whatever it was, I'm for it." He went over to the chest of drawers and took out a pair of shorts, dropping the towel and stepping into them. Amy felt a sudden moment of panic at the thought of what he would say if he knew what really had loosened the normally tight hold she maintained upon her impulses.

Last night had been an isolated incident, she assured herself. If she'd been able to reach George Hanscombe's office yesterday afternoon and had gotten the injection for migraine, she wouldn't have had to take the morphine. And even while one part of her body was busy remembering how much more relief she'd gotten from the tiny syrette than from her usual injection, another and sterner part was telling her she mustn't ever do it again.

"What was it you had to go out for last night?" she asked as Pete was putting on his pants.

"Something important, you can bet on that. Wild horses couldn't have dragged me away from you otherwise." He grinned. "If you were loaded, you may not remember, but you were really something—the sort of thing only Mohammedans are supposed to dream about."

"Was it an emergency?"

"Of a sort. Roy called to say Mort Dellman wanted to see me."

"What did he want?"

"I'll tell you about it at breakfast." He'd finished dressing now and put his arm around her waist as they crossed the room to the door. "Ethel must have it about ready; I smell bacon from downstairs. I've got to see Arthur Painter this morning, so I'll have to eat in a hurry."

"Is . . . is Mort going to make trouble?" she asked, as he pulled out her chair at the table. It was only set for two, since the children were still at camp.

"No." He took the coffee cup she filled for him from the silver urn. "But he'll have to go away when he gets out of this trouble—"

"Can he—get out, I mean?"

"He thinks so—and Roy does, too. Being in the position he's in, though, Roy can't say so in words. Mort wants to sell the rest of us his share in the clinic—for a hundred thousand dollars."

"It's worth that much, isn't it?" Having always had plenty of money, the amount didn't startle Amy.

"More, in fact. I'm calling a meeting with the others today at lunch. Some of 'em will squawk, of course, until they realize they don't have a choice."

Amy's fingers had just closed about the handle of her coffee cup but, at his words, the cup began to rattle so much in the saucer that part of the coffee spilled over on the snowy white tablecloth.

"What's the matter?" Pete's tone was concerned.

"Nervous, I guess." She tried to smile and knew she wasn't doing a very convincing job of it.

"That's not like you."

"Too much unaccustomed activity last night, maybe." She forced a laugh which sounded equally hollow.

"You'd better start getting accustomed to it again."

"What did you mean by not having any choice?"

"Let's face it. Mort could tell some pretty tall tales if he got started—most of 'em true."

"But not about you—and Lorrie?"

"You know better than that. Oh, I sampled her once or twice, before we were married—every new man who came to town did. But not since."

Amy breathed more easily. It didn't occur to her to doubt him. Pete had never failed to tell her the truth.

"We'll have to buy Mort out and it's up to me to find some way to raise the money," he continued. "Not many of us have that kind of dough lying around."

"I could lend it to you." She knew better by now than to say "give."

"Thanks." He was busy eating. "But all the members of the Faculty Clinic Corporation will have to be in on this deal, except maybe Paul McGill. I don't think there'll be any difficulty in getting the loan, but you can do me a favor, if you will."

"Whatever you want."

"I called Uncle Jake last night from the hospital but he just wanted to be left alone then. Would you go over and see him this morning and find out what we can do for him—about Lorrie?"

"Of course." Amy was glad of the opportunity to be doing something for Pete, postponing for a while, at least, the time when she would have to tell him she was going to be president of the state medical auxiliary a year before he became head of the medical association.

IV

Grace Hanscombe had saved a morning urine specimen, as she'd done ever since her blood sugar test had shown a high curve a year ago. After Della left, she tested it automatically, hardly noticing what she was doing, until the color of the solution suddenly changed to a deep orange.

Shocked—it was the first time she'd ever seen any change at all—she repeated the test, but the result was the same. Going to the phone, she dialed the clinic number with trembling fingers and asked for George's office, knowing he always went there to dictate letters and reports before starting morning rounds in the hospital. Recognizing the urgency in Grace's voice the secretary put her through to him at once.

"I have only a minute, Grace," he said.

"I showed sugar this morning, George."

"What color?" His voice changed and became crisp and incisive.

"Orange. It's quite a lot, George."

"You've had breakfast, haven't you?"

"Yes—with you, George."

"Of course. Come to the clinic as soon as you can get dressed. Go directly to the lab. I'll phone them before I start rounds."

"Wh-what will you do?"

"We'll start with a sugar tolerance curve. You were upset last night over Lorrie and that could give you the sugar. And Grace—"

"Yes, George."

"I may not know much about women, but I do know a lot about diabetes." She knew it was his way of apologizing and reassuring her and was grateful for it.

"I'm sorry about last night, George," she said. "I was upset about Lorrie and I'd had trouble at the club with Maggie McCloskey. She was drunk."

"Maggie was brought to the emergency room last night about midnight, Grace. Tried to commit suicide."

For a moment, Grace couldn't believe what she heard. "Did you say tried?" she asked finally.

"She didn't quite make it. They pumped her out and Dave Rogan has her on one of his wards. Take your time coming down to the clinic, dear; there's no need to drive fast. You can wait in my office after the tests are finished. They'll phone me the results."

Grace hung up the phone and went upstairs to dress. How many more, she wondered, would Mort Dellman's single bullet bring down? It had killed Lorrie, almost killed Paul McGill, and from what George said had come almost as near getting Maggie McCloskey. It had thrown her into a severe diabetic attack and certainly Della hadn't been herself this morning, when she'd stopped by the house.

As for Elaine McGill, she remembered now the strange way Elaine had reacted yesterday, when she had offered to stay at the hospital. She'd always been pretty fond of Elaine and Paul; since Paul was about George's age, the two of them had been somewhat closer than the rest of the boys. Elaine had been strangely calm yesterday afternoon, for someone whose husband might be dying. Perhaps it had been with relief at learning that Paul wasn't dead. At least she hadn't seemed to blame him at all.

Which was pretty logical, Grace decided as she started to dress. After all, Lorrie had taken on all their husbands at one time or another anyway.

As she finished dressing and went out to the Mercedes George had given her for Christmas, Grace decided that Alice Weston was the only one of the Dissection Society who hadn't been affected by Lorrie's sudden death. They were cousins of a sort but Lorrie had always been pretty contemptuous of Alice, so there couldn't have been much love lost between them.

As she was parking the Mercedes at the hospital parking lot, Grace saw Alice hurrying into the clinic, bent over a little as if her stomach was hurting her. And she knew then that Mort Dellman's bullet had gotten Alice, too.

CHAPTER FIFTEEN

I

Alice Weston was going through the Faculty Clinic, as the duty officer had suggested when he'd phoned the prescription to the drugstore for her the night before. Since more than a year had elapsed since her last checkup, she was following what was called the "routine medical check."

At the desk where she registered, she was given a clipboard to which was attached a digest of her previous record in the clinic, condensed and abbreviated so it could be punched on IBM cards. With it was a blank sheet on which to write her present symptoms and a sheaf of cards for the examinations to be done that day. As she was entering the long corridor behind the appointment desk she saw Grace cross the reception room to register but there was no opportunity for them to speak to each other.

In a small cubicle at one side of the corridor, Alice removed her clothing, except shoes and briefs, putting on one of the disposable paper examining gowns that turned clinic patients into duplicates of each other whose very souls, it seemed, could be punched into the proper spaces on the IBM cards of the clinic record. The paper gowns were much better than the old cloth ones, though. The nurses made some attempt to select one that was nearly your size so you, at least, didn't look as if you were walking around inside a tent.

Alice had come to the clinic without breakfast, so she went first to the laboratory. Built under Mort Dellman's personal direction, this heart of any large clinic was constructed to attain the highest possible degree of efficiency and mobility in carrying out the necessary examinations. On both sides of the central corridor were small cubicles, barely large enough for the patient to sit erect in a chair with an arm board attached and for the technician to stand beside her while drawing blood.

Alice always dreaded the needle, but the girl in the crisp white uniform this morning was very skillful and the pain was hardly more than the prick of a brier. From a rack on the wall of the cubicle, the technician drew a tiny strip of adhesive which she fastened expertly over the small red spot on Alice's arm where the needle had penetrated the skin and vein in one quick single thrust. The specimen of blood she had drawn in the syringe would be divided up for all the various examinations to be made in the laboratory.

Outside in the hall the technician pulled a paper cup from a dispenser on the wall and drew it full of a yellowish liquid from an adjacent container. "Drink it all," she commanded. "It prepares you for—but you've been here before, haven't you, Mrs. Weston?"

Alice nodded and emptied the cup. The liquid had the familiar sweet taste, a little tart with lemon flavoring. The combination of glucose and carbonated water would be absorbed from her empty stomach into her blood rather quickly; about an hour later, at a station farther along the examining line, another blood sample would be drawn.

Just exactly what all this meant, Alice didn't understand, except that somehow the information from the first blood test and the second, fed into a data-processing machine to be compared with her previous examinations, would come out with a diagnosis of a normal blood sugar or diabetes. When the technician stamped the time on one of the half-dozen data-processing cards clipped to the board Alice was carrying, she saw that the blood-test part of the examination had taken exactly four minutes.

A few yards farther along the corridor, Alice stepped into Station 6, stamped in red on her routing card, and lay down on a table. Another faceless figure in white—to Alice they all looked alike—expertly strapped a battery of metal electrodes to her wrist and ankles, connecting them by rubber insulated wires to a panel of knobs and dials on the wall. She dozed while the machine buzzed away, recording an electric tracing of her heartbeat on sensitized paper, until the technician put one of the electrodes over her breast and she shivered at the contact with the cool metal.

"We're almost through, Mrs. Weston," the girl said. "I just have to do this lead, and then record the heart sounds."

"Doesn't a doctor do that?"

"You haven't been through the clinic lately, have you?"

"Not for over a year."

"We use a phonocardiograph now and make a tape recording of your heart sounds." She showed Alice a small metal box which could be slid into another apparatus standing in the corner of the room. "The tape is in this box, and after we make the recording, it is sent along with your electrocardiogram. When the cardiologist reads the E.K.G. he can also listen to the tape and study a six-foot X-ray film of your chest that tells him the size of your heart. This way, the doctor can do a complete heart examination and never lay a hand on you. Next year, they hope to do the whole thing by computer and maybe we can do away with doctors altogether."

Alice laughed dutifully at the joke. But remembering what examinations had been like in the old days, before the Faculty Clinic had been automated, the technician's attempt at humor began to sound more and more like a prediction of the future.

Another of the cards on the clipboard was punched as she left Station 6, and she saw that she had been inside that cubicle exactly eight minutes. As she went out, a door opened across the hall and she recognized Grace Hanscombe getting on another table over there, an exact duplicate of the one she had just vacated.

At the next station, Alice's pulse and blood pressure were recorded by another technician—she still hadn't seen a doctor and knew she wouldn't until the end of the examination. One step farther along drops were put into one of her eyes, dilating the pupil so the inside of the eyeball—the eye grounds, it was called in medical terminology—could be photographed in color on TV videotape, where it could be studied later by an ophthalmologist. The tension of her eyeballs was also tested for glaucoma, an insidious disease which, if undetected, could cause blindness before the victim knew what was happening.

At another station, the capacity of her lungs to contain air was measured. A lessening of ventilation, as it was called, would indicate emphysema, another insidious killer that needed to be recognized early. At the next, her chest was X-rayed almost as rapidly as she could pass in front of the machine. And at another, her weight and height were recorded, along with a lot of other measurements, of whose significance she had no idea.

The next stop was for the smear of the Pap test, which helped to discover cancer of the female reproductive organs. All of this, Alice knew from hearing the doctors talk shop at cocktail parties, combined to give as complete a picture of the whole patient as it was possible to get by every mechanical device which could be used to lessen the need for expert medical personnel—the hardest quantity to find, she knew, in the whole clinic setup.

At the last stop before she was to see a doctor, a technician drew a second blood sample from Alice's arm. A glance at her watch told her exactly an hour had elapsed since she'd drunk the flavored glucose mixture after the first blood sample had been taken. Here, she was also directed to void a specimen of urine into a numbered container, completing the laboratory examinations.

Alice was tired by the time she was ushered into a somewhat sparsely furnished office. An X-ray view box was on the wall and the examining room next door contained the familiar table which could be put into a dozen positions for internal examinations. She had just finished writing an account of last night's attack on the blank white sheet of the clipboard—she'd been so busy earlier that she hadn't had a chance to make those notations—when the door opened and a young woman came in wearing the long white coat of a doctor.

"Good morning, Mrs. Weston." The faint English accent was pleasing. "I'm Dr. Feldman."

"The new woman doctor?"

Marisa Feldman smiled. "I'm a woman, I'm a doctor, and this is my third day in Weston—so I suppose you're right."

"I didn't mean to be rude," Alice said quickly, feeling an instinctive liking for the slender young woman doctor with the high cheekbones and the brilliant arresting eyes.

"I'm sure you didn't." Marisa Feldman took the chair behind the desk. "I may be new here, but I'm not new at treating conditions such as you have, Mrs. Weston. Dr. Hanscombe spoke to me about you this morning."

Marisa didn't tell Alice that George Hanscombe's words had been: "Alice Weston's got her gut in a spasm again. Please see her for me and try to get her relaxed."

"May I have your record, please?" Marisa asked.

Alice handed over the clipboard and Marisa Feldman began to study it. After a moment she reached over to a small console with numbered keys and punched a few of them. After a brief interval during which she seemed absorbed in what Alice had written about her most recent attack, the machine began to click and several of the familiar punched cards dropped out of a slot.

Alice knew this was a part of her previous record, as well as a report on the examinations which had already been finished. Marisa Feldman glanced at them, stacked them beside the blotter pad on her desk and continued reading.

"You seem to have had a pretty rough time last night," she said finally.

"It was terrible—until I took the green medicine the clinic duty officer prescribed. I've taken it before but my bottle was empty and I'd been doing so well that I hadn't had it refilled. Last night I had to take a second dose before I could get relief."

"The green medicine—as you call it—is an old-fashioned but still very effective remedy, belladonna, phenobarbital and peppermint water. We used a lot of it in Boston; up there we called it the 'Magic Elixir.' Do you feel better this morning?"

"Much better, thank you."

"Suppose we finish the examination then. Will you go into the next room and lie down on the table?"

Marisa Feldman's hands were gentle and knowing. They found the tender spot, low down on the left side of the abdomen, but there was none of the sudden pain that always occurred when George Hanscombe pressed there. As the gently probing fingers kneaded the spot, Alice could feel herself relaxing.

"There, that's better," said Marisa Feldman. "You had quite a spastic area here but it's relaxing now."

Even the instrument examination, which Alice had always dreaded, was almost pleasant in the hands of this handsome woman doctor with the facile fingers and pleasant manner. It was finished almost before Alice realized it had started.

"You still have some spasm and a mild infection of the lining membrane of the colon," Marisa told Alice as she was wrapping the paper gown about herself once more. "Did anything occur recently that might have caused the attack last night?"

"My cousin was killed."

"Mrs. Dellman?"

"Yes. We grew up together and were very close." It wasn't the truth, for she and Lorrie hadn't gotten along at all well lately, but Alice didn't want the new doctor to think she was neurotic. George Hanscombe had called her that once and she'd never entirely forgiven him for it.

"The shock could easily have caused the attack," Marisa assured her. "I think you should be a little careful of your diet for perhaps a week, Mrs. Weston. Stick to bland foods; you've been on a low-residue diet before, so you know what is allowed. And take the eli—the mixture as before. If you have any more trouble just call me. Dr. Hanscombe feels that I should have charge of your case from now on. I hope you don't mind."

"Oh no." Alice blushed. "I'm glad."

"I would like to see you in about three weeks—just for a visit. You're in excellent condition except for this little trouble and I think we can control that."

"Thank you, Dr. Feldman," Alice said gratefully. "My husband is a member of the clinic corporation, so we'll probably be seeing you socially."

"I hope so. Good-bye."

Alice departed in a warm glow, her abdominal discomfort quite forgotten. The new doctor was wonderful; she could hardly wait to tell the girls about her at the next meeting. But then she wondered whether there would be a next meeting of the Dissection Society—with Lorrie dead.

She wasn't going to feel sad about Lorrie, though. After all it was Lorrie's fault for running after men—when Alice herself had longed to give her all the love anybody could desire.

In her office, Marisa Feldman jotted down a few notes on a slip of paper and attached it to one of the IBM cards with Alice's record. The salient facts would be punched in later by the punch-card operators, so they could be retrieved quickly by the computer when needed in the future.

One note Marisa didn't make, but her face was thoughtful as she put the record into the slot where it would be carried by a continuous belt to the central record storage section. It had taken her only a few moments to realize that Alice Weston was a Lesbian; there'd been too many of them in the prison at Frondheim for the telltale signs to be missed by a trained observer. Knowing this, she couldn't help wondering what Alice's husband was like, and what sort of married life they could possibly have together.

II

After Pete left for the hospital, Amy changed into a linen dress—slacks hardly seemed appropriate for visiting a father who had just lost his only daughter. The Weston house—it was still called that in the town, although Amy had occupied it as Mrs. Peter Brennan for some fifteen years now—

was located on a knoll overlooking the river several miles from the newer development in Sherwood Ravine where most of the other doctors' wives lived. Jake Porter's home was about a half mile away from Amy's on another rise, with a shallow ravine between them.

The Westons had moved south from New England after the Civil War when land could be bought for a song and labor was almost as cheap as it had been under the slave system. By applying New England thrift and know-how to rug and fabric weaving, Amy's grandfather had made a fortune and established himself as the leading citizen in that part of the state. Jake Porter had been younger, a foreman at first in Weston Mills, but with a genius for management that had shortly put him into a position of authority and eventually part ownership.

Amy's own father hadn't been the businessman her grandfather had been, but Jake Porter was managing the mill by then and building his own fortune with massive investments in timberland and industrial property. It had been Jake who had negotiated the sale of Weston Mills to the Portola interests at the time of the second New England textile migration from the union-dominated, high-cost labor markets of the North to the huge unorganized pool of cheap and largely ignorant labor in the South.

As a result, though actually no relation, Amy and Roy had grown up thinking of Jake Porter as their uncle. When Roy married Alice, Jake's ward, the ties had been cemented even more closely. Amy, Alice and Lorrie had grown up almost like sisters, until finishing school and college had separated them for a while. Then marriage had brought them all back together again, when Mort Dellman and Pete Brennan had come with Roy and the others from Korea to become members of the faculty of Weston University Medical School. Now everything was in danger of being blasted by the single shot from Mort Dellman's pistol—unless Pete could find the hundred thousand dollars Mort demanded for his share of the clinic.

Amy didn't doubt that Pete would be able to arrange a loan to buy out Mort, however. The real danger was that, if Roy put pressure on Mort because of his own political ambitions, their tight little world would be blown apart by a scandal that could force the trustees of the medical school—who were not too happy about the success of the Faculty Clinic anyway—to take action and demand the resignations of those involved from the faculty. That, of course, would be very bad for the clinic, necessitating a change of name and perhaps endangering the solid reputation it had built as one of the finest organizations of its kind in the entire Southeast.

Amy had decided to walk to Jake Porter's rambling, cypress-shingled home, where she'd spent so many happy hours when she was a little girl. She was hoping to recapture, if only for a little while, that now almost forgotten period when Weston had been small and she, as daughter of the most important man in town, the most envied and eligible girl in it. Halfway to the house, she was sorry she hadn't taken her air-conditioned Cadillac out of the garage, for the day was hot and she could feel the thin summer dress beginning to stick to her perspiration-wet skin across the shoulders.

High up on the slope of the mountain to the west, she saw the sun glint off metal and knew the source was the antenna at the top of the system of microwave relay towers that carried telephone conversations and TV images across the crest of the mountain range. The tower stood beside a road leading down to a pocket in the mountains where Deerslayer Lodge was located, and she wondered whether—once the nightmare of yesterday and the next few days was over—she might be able to talk Pete into going up there for a week. They'd spent their honeymoon at Deerslayer Lodge and, with the help of the tiny syrettes she had cached in her dresser drawer, they might find again some of the bliss they'd shared there—but which they had seemed to have lost until last night.

Jake Porter was sitting on the porch in a rocking chair when Amy came up the steps. He occupied the big old house alone, cared for by a pair of colored servants who lived in an apartment over the garage.

"Good morning, Uncle Jake." Amy leaned down to kiss the old man's leathery cheek. "I guess you know how sorry we all are about what happened."

"Sit down, Amy." The old man sounded tired. "It was nice of you to come."

"Pete wondered whether there's anything we can do to help with the funeral arrangements."

"It's all taken care of, Amy. I called the funeral parlor and told them to give her a decent burial. Dr. Potter's out of town, but the canon from the cathedral across town will hold a graveside service." Potter was the minister of the largest Episcopalian church in Weston, to which most of those among the higher levels of society in town belonged.

"Lorrie wouldn't want anything elaborate," Amy agreed. "Will the children be here?"

"I sent Jasper to bring them from the camp they're in up near Asheville," said Jake Porter. "They would have been coming home Tuesday anyway to start school."

Jasper was the colored chauffeur-houseman who helped look after Jake Porter. Amy's children were in the same camp.

"Lorrie always had her own mind," the old man added. "I hope the man she was with lives."

"Dr. Dieter took the bullet out of Paul McGill's heart last night," Amy told him. "Pete says he should be all right."

"What about Dellman?"

"They've got him in jail. He's offered to sell his share of the clinic to the others in the corporation."

"For how much?"

"A hundred thousand dollars."

"That means he expects to get off—probably on the unwritten law. I'll be glad to see the last of him, too. Don't see why he had to kill her, though—unless he thought Lorrie had something to do with my changing my will."

Amy had been listening with only half her mind. "What did you say, Uncle Jake?" she asked.

"I couldn't stand the idea of Dellman getting hold of my money after I died, so I changed my will about a month ago. Left everything in trust for Lorrie's kids, with the bank as trustee. Good thing I did, too, the way things turned out."

"Lorrie loved the children. She'll be glad they're going to be taken care of."

"They will be—you can count on that." There was an odd intensity in the old man's voice but half bemused as she was, Amy didn't notice it. "Dellman isn't going to make any trouble for your husband and the others, is he, Amy?"

"What do you mean, Uncle Jake?"

"You know what I'm talking about."

"Pete says Mort's going to leave Weston as soon as the court decides what to do with him."

"It will be good riddance—for everybody. Lorrie wasn't really bad. She loved the children and she may even have loved Dellman—at first. But she couldn't do without men any more than a wino can leave the bottle. I guess you could call it a disease with her and now it's killed her, just like any other disease. Maybe it's my fault for letting her run loose so much when she was young. Or maybe she got her ways from me; I haven't exactly been a monk, you know."

Not knowing what to say, Amy said nothing.

"Not that I regret what I've done any more than Lorrie did; it's just the way we were made. Tell that fine husband of yours to come to see me. I want to talk to him about this whole thing."

"Maybe he can come over this evening."

"You've got a good man there, Amy, a fine human sort of a man. Sometimes he's going to do things you don't like; after all, you take a lot after that rock-bound New England branch of your family. But go easy, girl. A good marriage is about the most precious thing in the world. Lorrie's mother and I had it, so I know what I'm talking about."

"Pete and I are doing fine, Uncle Jake."

"I hope so—but there's been talk. Some people even say they think he won't be able to stand your driving much longer and you'll end up with a divorce."

The words hit Amy between the eyes like a blow with a cudgel. Pete divorce her? It was unthinkable.

"You're smart, Amy, and you're ambitious like any other woman." Jake Porter had apparently not noticed the effect of his words upon her. "Just don't let your own ambitions wreck your marriage."

"I won't, Uncle Jake." She got up quickly and moved down the steps, stumbling a little from the shock of what she had just heard.

"Thank you for stopping by," he called after her, but she didn't even hear.

By the time she reached the corner, Amy was able to regain some control of herself. When she looked back, Jake Porter was still sitting in the rocking chair on the porch of the house, with his chin dropped forward on his chest as if he were dozing. It was hard to believe he had just rocked Amy Brennan's snug little world to its very foundations.

III

The worst thing about drinking was waking from the stupor brought on by alcohol, but this time it was different. Maggie McCloskey floated for a long time between consciousness and unconsciousness, trying to sleep while, it seemed, the whole world was seeking to keep her awake. Somewhere in between, there was a torturer who choked her, burned her throat with a hot rod, and pricked her with needles, like the drawings of Dante's Inferno she remembered studying in college. Finally, she awoke, to find herself in unfamiliar surroundings, the antiseptic whiteness of a hospital room.

Her head throbbed, her throat was sore, and her face felt as if someone had been beating her. Her arm hurt, too, but when she tried to move it, she saw that it was strapped to a bandage-covered board, from which a small plastic tube dangled. And when she turned her head to follow the course of the tube, she could see that it was connected to a flask hanging from a stand, a flask half-filled with a yellowish-colored liquid.

The movement of her head brought a window within her range of vision. When she saw the distant slope of the mountains through it, she knew she was still in Weston, probably at the University Hospital. The outside, too, was bright with midday sunlight, which meant that she must have been out for a long time.

"Awake?" a fresh young voice asked and a student nurse with short red hair and freckles moved into her range of vision.

"Wh-what time is it?"

"Almost noon. You're having lunch."

"How long have I been here?" It was an effort to talk, partly from the languor that still beckoned to her and partly from the strange soreness in her throat.

"You were admitted to the emergency room around midnight, but they didn't bring you to this ward until nearly five o'clock this morning."

Maggie tried to make sense out of the figures. She'd gone home about ten—that much she remembered. Midnight was two hours later, so she must have passed out. What about the period from midnight to 5 A.M.? The effort was too much, however, and finally she gave up and went back to sleep.

When she woke again, her head was much clearer. The bottle of fluid hanging from the stand had been changed; it was now a brilliant red color and the shadows upon the mountain visible through the window told her it must be afternoon.

"Lunch was yellow." The hoarseness of her own voice startled her. "Dinner's red."

She began to laugh, but the laughter soon changed to sobs, sobs she wasn't able to control for a long time. When finally they stopped, she lay staring blankly at the white ceiling of the new private wing—the old ceilings were fly-specked—staring at the nothing that was her life.

CHAPTER SIXTEEN

I

Pete Brennan had called a meeting of the Executive Committee of the Faculty Clinic for lunch, in a small private dining room off the staff lounge on the top floor of the clinic. Most of the staff ate the noonday meal across the street at the hospital cafeteria. In order to save time, however, the small dining room had been placed adjacent to the lounge for the convenience of the medical staff in holding lunchtime conferences. Everybody was there except Mort Dellman and Paul McGill, neither of whom, under the circumstances, could have been expected to participate.

"Lock the door please, Dave," Pete said to the psychiatrist, when the food had been served and the waitress had left. "You're the nearest to it."

Dave Rogan locked the door and sat down again. Nobody asked the reason for the secrecy; more than enough had happened in the past twenty-four hours to justify it.

In a few succinct words, Pete told of his conversation last night with Mort Dellman. When he finished, the stricken looks on the faces of most of the men gathered at the table reflected his own feelings after leaving the jail last night. Since then, however, he'd had time to do some thinking and to make at least some preliminary plans for salvaging what they could out of the difficulty in which they found themselves.

"Mort hasn't got anything on me," George Hanscombe blustered. "I never—"

"He's had a detective watching Lorrie for a long time, George," Pete warned. "Better be sure you're pure."

"Sure you're pure!" Dave Rogan laughed mirthlessly. "If it wasn't so darn true, Pete, that would be funny. It must have been a Freudian slip."

George Hanscombe opened his mouth to speak, then shut it without saying any more.

"It would take a louse like Mort to put a private eye on his wife." Joe McCloskey was chubby and his hair was thinning, but he was one of the most solid and dependable members of the group, as well as a highly skilled specialist in his field, and everybody in the clinic respected him. "What I can't understand is why he did it. After all, he must have known Lorrie had been sleeping around for years."

"Shooting Lorrie was an accident," Pete explained. "She'd been laying this medical student and Mort planned to make an example of him."

"Mort knew Lorrie was bound to get herself mixed up in a scandal someday," said Dave Rogan. "My guess is that he put the detective on her so he'd have a stick to hold over Jake Porter's head, if it came to a divorce. Jake worships those grandchildren and would have put up a pretty large settlement to keep his daughter's sex life from becoming known to them."

"It looks like Mort has us dead to rights," Joe McCloskey admitted.

"But why would he do that to us?" George Hanscombe protested. "After all, we cut him in on this clinic when we didn't have to do it."

"Mort cut himself in by becoming a member of the medical school faculty originally," Pete reminded them all. "Let's not kid ourselves that a lot of the Faculty Clinic's success hasn't been due to him."

"Actually, Mort stole the automation idea from those clinics out in California that started it," Dave Rogan pointed out. "Though I doubt that the rest of us would have realized its possibilities, if he hadn't sold us on the computer."

"So we buy him off?" Joe McCloskey asked.

"At a hundred thousand?" George Hanscombe's voice was a little shrill. "Are you crazy, Joe?"

"I didn't ask you here just to scream because you've been hit," Pete said sharply. "How many of you would sell out today for a hundred thousand?"

There was no answer.

"Then what we need to do now is to decide how to go about arranging the deal."

"I don't have that kind of money," George Hanscombe protested.

"You've got your stocks with Merrill Lynch," Joe McCloskey reminded him.

"You're crazy if you think I'm going to tie them up."

"You make as much as the rest of us, George," Pete said pointedly.

"But you've got Amy's—"

"Shut up, George," Dave Rogan said wearily. "You know Pete has paid his own way ever since he came here."

"Thanks, Dave," said Pete. "My guess is that, counting lawyer's fees and the like, it will cost us maybe from twenty-five to thirty thousand apiece—including the interest."

George Hanscombe opened his mouth to protest again, then apparently thought better of it.

"One thing worries me," said Joe McCloskey. "How can we be sure Mort won't take our money and then sell us out? For the kind of story he'd build up out of what's been going on in a town like Weston, some magazine would probably give him another fifty grand. Or he could always write one of those 'as told to' books."

"What's been happening here goes on in practically any town this size—even without a university," said Dave Rogan. "We're a very close-knit community within a larger one and things sort of build up."

"Until they explode—like now," said Pete.

"We're still in a jam," Joe McCloskey insisted. "All your psychoanalyzing isn't going to change that, Dave."

"It can still make us take a long look at our own lives to see how we got into this mess," said the psychiatrist. "Maybe twenty-five thousand is a cheap price to pay for a little self-analysis."

George Hanscombe's snort was an explosive comment. "You can talk, Dave. You're not on a big margin in the stock market, with the Dow Jones touching bottom."

"But look at all you made when it was touching top, George."

Pete Brennan held up his hand for silence. "We all have excellent financial statements and good prospects, so we're A-1 credit risks. I say we borrow what we need, paying it back to the bank just like we would any other loan. It may cramp some of us, but like Dave said, it might be worth it in the end."

"You still haven't answered my question about how we can be sure Mort won't double-cross us," Joe McCloskey reminded him.

"I'm not sure he doesn't have something like that in mind," Pete admitted. "Last night he told me what really happened yesterday afternoon. You see he expected to find this medical student with Lorrie and planned to crease him, as a warning. This morning I wrote down all Mort told me—"

"Not to your secretary, I hope," said Joe McCloskey.

"I'm not that big a fool, Joe. It would have been all over the clinic in half an hour and across town by noon. I wrote it down by hand and the document's right here." He took a long envelope from his pocket. "I'm going to mail it to myself by registered mail this afternoon and leave it in my safe-deposit box unopened when it's delivered. That will establish the time it was written."

"That's damn clever, Pete," said George Hanscombe.

"Writers do it all the time to protect manuscripts; a patient told me about it once. By sending themselves a carbon copy of whatever they want to protect, they automatically have proof that it was written before a certain date."

"Then Mort can only double-cross us by putting the noose around his own neck with the admission that he actually went out there intending to shoot the student," said Dave Rogan. "That should hold him."

"What about Paul McGill?" Joe McCloskey asked. "Where does he come in on this?"

"Paul's got nothing to gain by making any deal with Mort, so I think he should be left out," said Pete. "I take it we're all agreed that we should form a group and borrow the hundred thousand we need. Mort sells us his share of the clinic legally for that amount and, if I know Arthur Painter, he'll figure out some way to make it all a business expense. Give me a show of hands."

Three hands went up at once; George Hanscombe finally raised his, making it unanimous.

"I'll have Arthur get the papers and consult the bank," said Pete. "Is there anything else?"

Nobody broached a new subject, so the meeting broke up. Dave Rogan stayed behind after the others had gone.

"I've been thinking about this mess we've got ourselves into, Pete," he said. "Got a minute to talk about it?"

"Sure. Let's have another cup of coffee and a cigarette."

The waitress had left a glass Silex container bubbling on a hot-plate in the corner. Pete filled two fresh coffee cups and brought them over to the table where Dave Rogan was sitting. He was very fond of the psychiatrist, and in the beginning of their association they'd spent many pleasant hours in bull sessions. Lately, though, they'd both been too busy with teaching duties and the demands of the clinic to leave much time for anything else.

"I guess you know I've got Maggie McCloskey on one of my wards, Pete."

"Joe told me. Will she be all right?"

"She's safe this time, but maybe not the next."

"Why would she do it?"

"Maggie still loves Joe. She was at the club yesterday afternoon when the news came that Mort had shot Lorrie. The first reports didn't mention Paul's name, only that a prominent physician was also involved. Maggie, Della, and Grace Hanscombe came tearing over here—each wondering whether her husband was the man in the case."

"Amy was here, too. And last night—" Pete stopped suddenly as a possible explanation of Amy's behavior came to him.

"You were going to say?"

"Amy was—you might say—more affectionate than usual, when I got home."

"That early broadcast put the fear of God into all of them," said the psychiatrist. "George told me just before lunch that Grace showed a heavy spilling of sugar this morning for the first time in a year. Her glucose tolerance curve is all shot to hell, so he's put her into the hospital because he's afraid she might go into a diabetic coma."

"That must have been what was eating George just now. He's not usually as stubborn as he was this morning."

"I guess any one of us would be shaken up, if his wife spilled sugar into the urine to prove she still loved him. Grace's diabetes will quiet down in time; she was only a mild case before. It's Maggie and Joe I'm worried about. Did you know he's been paying the bartender at the club to persuade her not to drive home when she'd stoned—which is practically every night?"

"No."

"After she left the hospital yesterday, Maggie went back to the club and stayed there until the bartender sent her home in a taxi. Evidently she was too much disturbed to go to sleep, so she took some barbiturate capsules that were in the medicine chest. Joe's been driving by the house late every night to see whether she was all right. Fortunately, he suspected something was wrong when he saw the whole place lit up last night and took her to the hospital. Jeff Long was on duty and put an intratracheal catheter into her windpipe, so he could pump oxygen into her. Then he gave her an intravenous drip with a psychic energizer to jolt her brain and she began to come around early this morning."

"Sounds like it was close."

"Too close. When Maggie wakes up, I'm going to try and scare her into taking the cure."

"Most alcoholics don't, do they?"

"No. But I think I've got something I can hold over Maggie this time. Her rushing to the hospital yesterday afternoon proves she still loves Joe, and we both know he's been eating his heart out for her ever since the divorce. Maybe I can parlay those facts into getting her straightened out."

Pete Brennan stared at the white tablecloth and the smudge of ashes that had fallen on it from his cigarette. He was remembering Amy's relatively wanton—for her—actions last night, and seeing them now as a symptom of something disturbing. Because no matter how much it had pleased him at the time, that kind of behavior wasn't typical of Amy.

"What's happened to all of us, Dave?" he asked. "Where did we go wrong?"

"A psychiatrist doesn't have any hard and fast rules for distinguishing right from wrong, Pete."

"I mean how did we get our lives into such turmoil? Most of us have been sleeping around for years—Lorrie was . . . just honest about hers. But what did it get us?"

"Pleasure?"

"Maybe at the moment. But how long does it last? And how much is it worth?"

"It lasts only a moment—and it isn't worth a damn thing."

"Then why do we do it? Surely that kind of behavior can't be considered normal."

"That's another term psychiatrists try not to use, but I know what you mean. Maggie drinks too much. Grace Hanscombe has a sudden flare-up in what was a mild diabetes. My Della plays too much golf. Amy has migraine. Alice Weston has spactic colitis. I guess Elaine McGill is the only real balanced one in the crowd, but she's sterile and can't find a reason for it."

"Who's to blame—or what?"

"We husbands aren't quite what you'd call normal either. We work too hard for our own good, and our wives don't get the understanding they should from us. Take George Hanscombe for example. He's darn near paranoiac in many ways, like a lot of so-called normal people. Voted for Goldwater, belongs to the John Birch Society, may even be a Klansman for all I know—he's certainly rabid enough on the subject of segregation. Grace is a warm, fairly intelligent English girl who would have been supremely happy married to the owner of a middle-class English pub. She really was a barmaid, you know. Instead she marries George, tries to be worthy of him, and does a fine job—with damn little help from him. The wonder is that she hasn't had diabetes—or something else—before."

"I'm not going to ask you to analyze me." Pete managed to grin. "You're too penetrating this morning for comfort."

"All of this is really elementary," Dave Rogan assured him. "Actually, I'm no better able to cope with my own wife's problems than the rest of you are. You don't think Della's a golf champion only because she loves the game, do you?"

"But—"

"Because I'm a psychiatrist, Della's got the conviction that she's intellectually inferior to me—which doesn't happen to be true. As long as she was busy with the children, she didn't have time to brood on it; nothing builds a woman's ego like having handsome children who need her. But the thought of them going away to prep school and college has already started eating away at her self-esteem. So she becomes a golf champion to prove she's physically superior to me—which she is."

"What are you going to do?"

Dave grinned. "Get her pregnant again, if I can ever pin her down that long. But it looks like I'll have to substitute lactose tablets for those birth control pills she takes; the damn things don't leave anything to chance."

"What I still don't understand is how we all got so mixed up, when none of us is really very far from what's ordinarily considered normal," Pete insisted. "There are maybe a hundred members of the medical school faculty and we must have thirty of them on the staff of the clinic. Are we the only abnormal ones?"

"Watch out for that word 'abnormal,'" Dave Rogan warned. "The main trouble is that we're very much alike in income, social level, the way we live—which makes us a pretty inbred group by any standard you could imagine."

"Inbred?"

"You, Joe, George, Paul, Mort, myself—and Roy—sort of drifted together in Korea, but not just by chance. In many ways, we're very much alike. We're intelligent, ambitious, with lots of drive. We're go-getters, the kind of men who succeed, no matter what field they're in. In Korea we came together out of the whole hospital staff by a process of natural selection. An accident of fate—the opening of the medical school here—threw us all together after the war in Korea was over. We married women from different walks of life but the pressure of circumstances started squeezing them into the same mold."

"Like what?"

"The pattern of conformity—for one thing. We all live in the same sort of house. We belong to the same club. We drink the same liquor. Pretty soon we were all leading more or less the same sex life. So who cares if we change about a little?"

"You make us sound like guinea pigs in some sort of a diabolic experiment."

"Maybe that's what life really is—the devil testing us out to see whether we're eligible for hell."

"I don't buy that," Pete protested. "It would mean being in hell twice."

"Most people are."

"What's the answer then?"

"For men it's the sort of friendly competition we have here in the clinic every day. We're so busy we don't have time to build aggressions that might be channeled into physical symptoms or emotional disturbances. With the women we marry, though, it's different. At first they have jobs to do—helping us get started, making a home, raising small children, the things a woman knows she's better at than any man could ever hope to be."

"Having a nice home, a beautiful wife and children have always been pretty attractive to me," Pete protested.

"They are to all of us—until we start taking them for granted. Happiness—in marriage, in your work, in your living—isn't just something you can drift along with. If you do, you'll find pretty soon that you've lost it. Happiness has to be worked at, making a house, raising children—"

"Maggie and Grace don't have any kids," Pete protested. "That doesn't stack up very well with this theory of yours."

"Why do you suppose they're more seriously ill than the others?"

"And Amy?"

"Sure you want my opinion?" Dave asked.

"I would appreciate it."

"I'm not sure Amy isn't in more danger than the others, Pete. That's one reason why I wanted to talk to you today."

"Surely she hasn't consulted you."

"Neither have the others—except Maggie who was automatically put on my service because she's a potential suicide. Amy's ambition worries me. Surely you've noticed it—particularly lately."

Pete nodded soberly. "At first it wasn't so intense. She already had a position here, she was independently rich, and she could help a doctor-husband get started. She did, too, I don't deny that. We had some battles in the beginning, mainly because I insisted that we live on my salary. But then the clinic got going and I suddenly began to earn as good an income on my own as her father ever had."

"Think clearly now," Dave Rogan interrupted. "Was that when she began to be interested in the medical auxiliary?"

"About the same time, yes. I think it was just after I turned down the post of Professor of Surgery across the street."

"Didn't she have her first migraine attack then?"

"Come to think of it, yes."

"Ever wonder why?"

"Are you saying that was when Amy began to think I didn't need her any more?"

"At least the unconscious doubt must have been there," said Dave. "Amy's always been independent and ambitious. She's been a leader in every community activity a woman can get into in Weston, and now she's spreading her sphere to include the state. But she's paying a price for it already—though so far only in migraine."

"Are you implying that it could get worse?"

"Who can tell? For one thing, Amy's no longer sure of you. None of our wives are, or they wouldn't have been so upset when they heard on the radio that a doctor was with Lorrie yesterday afternoon."

Pete filled his coffee cup again and lit another cigarette. He wasn't surprised to discover that his hand was shaking so much he had difficulty controlling the lighter.

Had it been fear that had changed Amy so much, he wondered? Or relief at learning he wasn't hurt? Somehow neither answer fitted the picture, yet he had no other clue. And you could hardly ask even a close friend like Dave why your wife—who had become almost frigid these past several years—would suddenly start behaving like a wanton.

"Like I said before"—Dave's voice brought him back to the present—"I think the trouble with our little group is what I call inbreeding. We men are together here all day at work and our wives are together at the golf course, the club bar, or with that group of Amy's you named the Dissection Society. Even when we socialize, it's mainly together, and we usually attend the state medical conventions in a body. It's a case of familiarity breeding something more than contempt, a sort of letting down of barriers that's like a game of musical chairs."

"Maybe it would be more appropriate to call it musical beds," said Pete. "Do you think we'll change—after what's just happened?"

Dave Rogan shook his head. "We're all forty or thereabouts—and some beyond that—so the damage is already done. What we've got to do now is learn to live with ourselves and make the best of what we've got." He squashed out his cigarette in the saucer of his coffee cup and stood up. "I've spent all the time philosophizing I can afford to right now. Have you had a chance to see Janet Monroe's little boy?"

"Not yet," said Pete. "I was planning to do it after we finished here but I've got to talk to Arthur Painter on the phone and start him to work on the deal with Mort—and the loan. Got any idea of what may be the trouble with the kid?"

"My guess would be a congenital aneurysm in the Circle of Willis that's been leaking a little. Anton Dieter is going to see the child this afternoon and Ed Harrison is setting up a radioscan for tomorrow morning."

Radioscanning was a relatively new method of locating tumors within the body through the tendency of malignant tissue to absorb certain radioactive isotopes—in this case usually a mercury salt. Using a sensitive instrument related to a Geiger counter that reacted to the presence of radioactivity, it was often possible to outline the presence, and even the shape, of a growth deep within the body by recording on an X-ray film the increased degree of radiation emanating from the tumor cells.

"That's about all you can do at the moment," Pete Brennan agreed. "I'll see the boy before I leave this afternoon. Janet's a fine girl who's had a tough break. She deserves some good fortune—like getting the kid well and marrying Jeff Long. I hope we can bring it off."

But as he took the elevator upstairs to his office and for the talk with

Arthur Painter about the loan, the neurosurgeon knew that if Dave's tentative diagnosis was correct, the odds against success were very great indeed.

II

"Why did you do it?"

The question startled Maggie McCloskey into answering without stopping to think—as Dave Rogan had intended it to do—an eruption of truth from the preconscious portion of her mind, where it had no chance to be colored by emotion.

"I wanted to give Joe my blood—but he didn't need it." Her eyes filled with tears. "He used to need me—but he doesn't any more. Nobody does."

Suddenly Maggie realized what she was saying, the truth she hadn't admitted previously to anyone—hardly even to herself.

"Damn you, Dave Rogan!" she exploded as the psychiatrist came into view. "How did you get in this room without me hearing you?"

"You were too busy feeling sorry for yourself. Besides, I wanted to startle you into giving me an honest answer."

"How can you be so sure?" She was already beginning to recover a little of her old composure.

"Because it was the answer I expected. The feeling of not being needed is a basic cause, as well as a symptom, of the Doctor's Wife syndrome."

"Doctor's wife what?"

"It's a well-known condition—Doctor's Wife disease, if you don't remember the meaning of syndrome. That's a collection of symptoms by the way, denoting a specific disease pattern."

"You're kidding."

"I was never more serious. Della has it—only her symptom is golf, not suicide."

Maggie stared at him, her eyes dilating slowly with horror. "You think I tried to—?"

"Didn't you?"

"Christ no! Why would I want to do that?"

"Because you think you're no longer needed. You just admitted it."

"You caught me with my pants—my defenses—down."

"You told me the truth, the first time. Now you're covering up." Dave took a seat at the foot of the bed and began to fill his pipe. "Exactly what did happen last night, Maggie?"

"Della and Grace and I were at the club having some drinks when the news about Mort shooting Lorrie came over the TV. How is Paul?"

"He'll live. Keep on about yourself."

"Why should I?"

"You're my patient. This is my service."

"Psychiatry?"

"The same. Tell me your story! I haven't got all day. Some other doctors' wives—and a lot of people in general—have the same disease you have."

"I still don't believe it."

"My time is valuable and you're getting it free," he told her bluntly. "Get on with your story."

"I was sick yesterday afternoon at the club after I first heard the broadcast. Then I remembered Joe's a Type B-Rh negative like me and they're hard to find, so I started for the hospital."

"Were you still sick?"

"Was I?" Maggie blanched a little at the memory. "Grace drove me and Della followed us."

"So even though you were sick, you still started for the hospital to help Joe? What's next?"

"You know. It was Paul that was shot—not Joe."

"So?"

"After we saw you downstairs, I had an argument with Della in the parking lot. Did you really mean that about golf being her symptom?"

"Yes. But we're talking about you."

"I took a taxi back to the club and got drunk as usual. Manuel got me a taxi when they closed the bar a little before ten o'clock. I left my car in the lot." A spasm of pain crossed her face. "I've gone home that way before—lots of times."

"Why were the lights all on at the house?"

"I guess I must have hit the bank of switches by the door with my hand when I turned the front lights on. I remember the driver kept his headlights on until I could find the keyhole." She started to laugh, with a touch of hysteria.

"None of that," Dave Rogan said sharply. "Keep on with your story."

"I was drunk but not sleepy—Manuel had given me some coffee at the club. I guess it was the sight of the bed that really upset me."

"What bed?"

"Joe's—the other twin; it's empty. I found some capsules in the medicine chest, so I took some of 'em."

"How many?"

"Three or four. I've taken that many before."

"But not when you were already drunk."

Her eyes opened wide. "I was trying to remember something about those capsules before I took 'em, something Joe once told me. He said you don't ever take 'em when you've been drinking. Was that what put me out?"

"The combination of pentobarbital and whiskey can be lethal," he told her. "You weren't even breathing when you were brought to the emergency room. Fortunately a very smart young doctor happened to be on duty and recognized the condition at once."

"Did they wash out my stomach? Is that why my throat's sore?"

"You'd had the pentobarbital for two hours, long enough for most of it to be absorbed. The first thing Jeff Long did was to put an intratracheal tube down your windpipe, so he could attach you to a respirator and pump oxygen into you. He also put a small nasal catheter into your stomach, but there wasn't much there."

Maggie shivered. "Do you have to talk about me like I was an animal—something you were using for an experiment?"

"Animals don't try to kill themselves, Maggie. They've got better sense."

"I told you it was an accident," she flared.

"And I don't believe you." Dave took a lighter from his pocket and lit the pipe again.

"Why?"

"You've been trying to destroy yourself ever since you started drinking so heavily, long before you and Joe broke up. Alcoholism is a form of suicide, Maggie. When you add barbiturate poisoning—"

"I told you that was an accident."

"And I say it wasn't. Just now you had no trouble remembering that Joe had told you never to mix the drug with alcohol. Yet you claim that last night you couldn't remember."

"I was drunk," she said sullenly.

"But not drunk enough to go to sleep without help. And not drunk enough so you couldn't find the capsules and count them out."

"I just wanted to sleep."

"I'm sure you did—permanently. Hollywood actresses who take barbiturates in so-called suicide attempts usually manage to telephone a friend or somebody at the last moment. But you made no attempt to call."

"How do you know?"

"The phone was still on the hook when they found you. You'd undressed, put on a nightgown, and were lying on the bed in the next room. I wondered about that, until you told me just now about the twin bed."

She turned her face away from him. "I couldn't bear the thought of Joe knowing."

"Now we're beginning to get somewhere," Dave said briskly and moved from his seat at the foot of the bed to knock out his pipe in the ash tray on the bedside table.

"I don't see how."

"You've finally admitted that you tried to kill yourself because you feel Joe doesn't need you any more. You wouldn't finish the job in the room you'd shared with him because you were ashamed of what you were doing. And you're afraid now that you may get to the point where you'll try it again—and succeed."

"Who are you? God—or somebody?"

"I could have told you all those things when I came in here just now. I see this pattern often—and not just in doctors' wives. It's also fairly common where men rise rapidly in a profession like law, insurance or even in business and their wives aren't able to keep up with them—or think they can't. The important thing was for you to admit all this to yourself."

"Then you've only been leading me on?"

"That's what a psychiatrist really does, Maggie—lead people on until they see the truth about themselves. Fortunately you're not too far gone to face the facts and you're intelligent. That puts us halfway on the road back."

She wondered if she dared believe him, or if he were only saying it to encourage her. "How do you figure that?"

"The most important force in any woman's life is the knowledge that she's wanted and needed. Her whole physical and emotional make-up is geared to that one drive and losing that knowledge can be as crippling physically as a severe heart attack, or ulcer. Or if she's lucky, the kind of mild colitis or cystitis that sends so many women to doctors. Mentally, the mildest reaction is psychoneurosis; the most severe is some form of real mental disease."

"Or suicide?"

"Yes."

Maggie took a deep breath. She was almost afraid to ask the question that was on the tip of her tongue, yet it had to be asked—and answered. "Just now you said I was halfway back. But to what?"

"Joe needs you, whether you know it or not."

"If he does, why did he shack up with that slut in Greenville?"

"Do you really want the answer? I'll have to be brutal."

"Y-yes."

"Because he wasn't getting what he had a right to get at home."

"I never denied him," she flared. "He lied if he told you that."

"Joe didn't tell me anything; I've seen too many cases like yours not to know the pattern by heart. Besides, what right do you have to be so damn virtuous, after that convention of the Southern Medical in New Orleans?"

The impact of his words struck her like a punch in the solar plexus. When her stomach suddenly tied up in a knot, she groped for an enameled basin beside the bed, but Dave Rogan beat her to it.

"Don't start puking on me because you can't face your own guilt," he snapped. "A lot of husbands and wives didn't sleep in their own beds that night—or a lot of nights before and since. When a man isn't able to satisfy his wife, even though he seems to be potent, he begins to wonder whether it's his fault. There's only one way to find out—another woman."

"Was he all right—with her?"

"How in the hell would I know? Intelligent and educated people don't go around talking about things like that. There's one way you can reassure him though—and don't ask me to draw a diagram for you." He picked up her chart folder from the foot of the bed. "I've got to go now. Feel like some real food?"

"I could use a bowl of soup with some crackers. And a cup of coffee."

"Good girl. I'll order the intravenous discontinued and see you in the morning. We'll talk some more."

He was at the door when she called, "Dave."

"Yes."

"You said just now that Joe needs me. How do you know, if he hasn't talked to you about us?"

"Because of Joe you're here and able to ask for soup and coffee, instead of being on a slab beside Lorrie Dellman. Since the divorce, he's been driving up to the turnaround in front of your house every night about midnight, to see if you're all right. Last night when he saw all the lights on he went inside.

"It was Joe that brought you to the hospital, Maggie. And if you've got half the sense I think you have, you'll thank God for him in your prayers tonight. I'll have my secretary send up an article on the Doctor's Wife disease. Since you were once a medical secretary yourself, you'll be able to understand the terms. I think you'll find it very interesting reading."

CHAPTER SEVENTEEN

I

Janet Monroe got up at eight, stopped by the Snack Bar for breakfast, and came to Jerry's ward a little after nine. The chart said he had slept all night, and when she came into the room he stood up in the crib and held out his arms to her.

"You have to stay in bed, darling," she told him. "Dr. Ed wants you to."

"Can we go home today, Mommie?"

"I don't think so. We'll have to wait and see what Dr. Ed says."

"But you'll stay with me, won't you?"

"Until lunch. Then I'll have to go home and put on my uniform. Some sick people upstairs need me."

Dave Rogan and Ed Harrison came by about a half-hour later making rounds. The older doctor made a quick neurological examination, then put the instruments he had used back into the pocket of his long-skirted white coat.

"Everything's normal this morning," he reported. "Have you remembered anything else about the convulsions that might help us, Janet?"

"I'm not sure—it all happened so suddenly. The muscles of the right side may have been more involved than the left." When she saw a quick glance pass between the two doctors, she added quickly, "Does that mean anything?"

"It could help us localize the cause," Dave Rogan told her. "We need all the information we can get."

Ed Harrison stayed in the room after the psychiatrist left. "We're going to be doing a few things today, Janet," he said. "I thought I'd warn you so you wouldn't be disturbed."

"Like what?"

"There'll be a neurosurgical consultation with Dr. Brennan. And I've asked Dr. Dieter to see Jerry, too. We don't know yet but Dr. Dieter will probably want to do a cerebral angiogram."

Janet was familiar with the procedure—and its significance.

"You still think it's something serious, don't you?" she asked.

"I'm afraid so. The fact that Jerry hasn't had any more convulsions is in his favor, of course. The bleeding we discovered with the puncture last night seems to have stopped—for the time being at least. But we want to stay ahead of it by finding the cause before another flare-up of hemorrhage can complicate the picture." At the door, he stopped with his hand on the knob. "Have you seen Jeff this morning?"

"No. The nurses say he hasn't been around."

"Mrs. McCloskey tried to commit suicide last night. Jeff was up until five, keeping her alive."

"How awful!" Janet exclaimed. "What did she take?"

"Alcohol and sleeping pills. Fortunately Dr. McCloskey found her in time."

"They—they're divorced, aren't they?"

"Yes. But he's still carrying a torch for her."

"At least she has that much. I came pretty near it once or twice myself, so I know what she must have felt."

Ed Harrison glanced at the little boy, who was standing in the crib with his elbows on the rail and his thumb in his mouth. If the presumptive diagnosis proves correct, he thought, Janet was in for something even worse than her divorce from Cliff Monroe—at least a 50 per cent chance that her baby wouldn't survive. Only the need to care for little Jerry had kept her from a serious emotional breakdown when Cliff Monroe had moved out, he knew. And if something happened to Jerry now, it would be even worse for her than before.

Janet came back to the hospital about two o'clock, this time in uniform, planning to spend a half-hour or so with Jerry before she went on duty at three in the Special Intensive Care Unit. As she came into the ward, one of the nurses was putting Jerry into a wheelchair.

"He's going up to Dr. Dieter's office for examination," she said. "I believe Dr. Brennan is going to see him up there, too."

"I'll take him up," Janet offered. "If they don't finish before I go on duty at three, I'll ask Dr. Dieter's nurse to call you when he's ready to come back."

Jerry enjoyed the ride through the busy corridors and up in the elevator to the office suite in the new surgical wing. There Janet turned him over to Dr. Dieter's nurse who put him on the examining table. Dieter came in just then and shook hands.

"This is a fine young lad you have here, Mrs. Monroe," he said with his faint Teutonic burr. "Dr. Brennan is coming over from the clinic, so I'll go ahead with my own examination while he's getting here."

Watching the way the vascular surgeon went about the examination and his gentleness with Jerry, Janet felt a little better. As for the little boy, he took to Dieter from the start, laughing uproariously as the doctor stroked his belly to test the reflexes of the abdominal muscles. Maybe there won't be any more bleeding or convulsions, Janet told herself. Things like that did clear up sometimes of their own accord, with no one ever discovering the cause.

At least the thought was something to hang on to, something far better than the diagnosis of brain tumor that had been her first thought, when she'd seen Jerry's body start to jerk with the initial convulsion.

II

Pete Brennan came into Dieter's examining room just as the vascular surgeon finished examining Jerry Monroe's eyes with an ophthalmoscope.

"I have just finished, Doctor, if you would like to make your own examination." Dieter still used some of the Old World formalities. "The eye grounds seem to be normal."

Pete made a quick neurological examination; he'd already seen a summary of Dave Rogan's tests on the consultation sheet sent to him from Pediatrics.

"You can take him back to the room, Mrs. Monroe," he told Janet when he finished. "Dr. Dieter and I will discuss the case and let you know our recommendations later."

In Dieter's office, Pete sank gratefully into a comfortable chair and lit a cigarette. "I've really been running today," he said.

"The business of Dr. Dellman?"

"That—plus a lot of other things. Mort's offered to sell his share of the Faculty Clinic for a rather large sum, which he needs quickly. A lot of details are involved and, as president of the corporation, most of them wind up in my lap."

"Will the authorities release him?"

"Nobody knows—until he's brought before the grand jury."

"In Europe such cases are recognized as being in a special category," said Dieter. "The French call it a *crime passionnel*—which is as good a description as any."

"What do you think of Mort Dellman, Anton?"

If he was surprised by the question, Dieter didn't show it. "I would say that he is a very smart man, an excellent technician and administrator. But he would never make a good doctor."

"Why?"

"A doctor must have a greatness of heart, if he is to be a real physician. Dellman doesn't have it. I think it may be best for your clinic that he is getting out before he becomes—how do you say it over here?—the rotten apple that spoiled the barrel."

It was an apt description of Mort Dellman, one of the best Pete had ever heard. "What do you think of the child?" he asked.

"Convulsions are more in your field," Dieter demurred. "Perhaps you should make your guess first."

"It can't be much more than an educated guess at this stage," Pete Brennan admitted. "The skull X-rays showed nothing, but I wouldn't expect them to. Last night Dave Rogan thought perhaps the reflexes might be more active on the right side, which certainly fits in with the right-sided convulsion the mother described, but she was undoubtedly excited at the time and could have been wrong. As of now I see nothing to suggest a brain tumor. We should know definitely tomorrow when the brain scan is finished, but I think it will be negative."

Dieter nodded. "Those are my conclusions, too. Which leaves the most likely possibility an aneurysm in the region of the Circle of Willis, with an intermittent leak of blood."

"Can you do the angiogram tomorrow, after the scan is finished?" Pete asked. "I have to go to Lorrie Dellman's funeral in the morning, but I should be back by lunch."

"I will schedule it in the morning." With a skilled vascular surgeon on the staff, the tricky job of injecting a dye that was opaque to the X-ray and would therefore show the pattern of the brain's blood vessels had been turned over to Dieter. Cerebral angiography—literally photographing the blood vessels of the brain—was an important technical advance that was yielding valuable dividends in evaluating and treating strokes and other conditions affecting the brain circulation, offering the possibility of help to many cases for which there had been no treatment before.

"Are you thinking what I am thinking?" Pete asked.

"That this may be a case for using the California technique of aneurysm thrombosis with iron sludge?"

"Yes."

"We shall see after the angiogram is done tomorrow. If the technique proves suitable for this case and we succeed, it will be a fine thing for the mother and the child."

Pete heaved himself reluctantly out of the chair. "I've got to look in on Paul McGill. He's a good man and a friend; thanks for saving him for us."

"It was Dr. Feldman who saved him." Dieter's eyes twinkled. "I expect to see her soon and will give her your thanks."

So that's the way the wind blows, Pete thought as he took the elevator to the Special Intensive Care Unit. Only in America could a Polish Jew and an East German strike up a romantic attachment in the three short days since Marisa Feldman had joined the staff.

III

Paul McGill was out of bed in a chair when Pete Brennan stopped by his room after leaving Dieter's office. Pete had always liked the dermatologist, even though their personalities were completely different. Where Pete was extroverted, with a typical Irish enthusiasm for life and living, Paul was more introspective and reserved. Both were intelligent and skilled in their field of work, however, and each respected the other.

"How's it going, Paul?" Pete asked.

"Not bad as long as I don't cough," said the dermatologist. "Then it feels like the place where Dieter split my sternum is going to come apart. But I'm so glad to be alive, I can stand that."

"Anton Dieter says if that new Jewish girl from Harvard hadn't recognized what was happening, you would have been another mortality statistic. How's Elaine taking it?"

"Like a trouper." Paul McGill's eyes warmed. "She came to the hospital as soon as she heard about the shooting and stayed here last night."

"Elaine's a fine girl. Amy's very fond of her, and so am I."

"I guess none of us know what our wives are really like until something like this comes along. I was scared to death that Elaine would leave me."

"I hope you asked her to forgive you."

"I did have that much sense." Paul's face was sober. "But I'm not so sure about the members of the corporation. Have I damaged the clinic, Pete?"

"If you have it will get over it." Pete grinned. "My guess is that whatever patients we might lose for various reasons, will be more than compensated for by the women who will want to see you."

"I'm really not a Don Juan, you know."

"Neither are the men these women are married to. I think they'll be tolerant."

"I've been trying to decide all day whether to submit my resignation."

"You can be sure we wouldn't accept it if you did. We had a meeting today at lunch but that didn't even come up so you can be sure the others feel as I do. Mort Dellman has offered to sell us his share of the corporation stock—for a hundred thousand dollars."

"That's quite a profit—considering that he only put in ten thousand at the start like the rest of us. What did you decide?"

"We're going to buy. I've asked Arthur Painter to make the arrangements—and borrow the hundred thousand from the bank. We agreed that you shouldn't be liable for this extra debt, Paul."

"But I insist on it."

"You've suffered enough in this business already. Nobody thinks you should be penalized any more."

"I'm responsible for the whole thing," the dermatologist protested. "Actually I'm the one who should pay the hundred thousand and give the stock to the rest of you."

"We wouldn't hear of that." Pete debated briefly whether to tell Paul that his being the object of Mort Dellman's marksmanship had been wholly accidental, but decided against it. Not only did he feel an obligation not to reveal what Mort had told him in confidence, but he was male enough to sense that the revelation might depress the wounded man at a time when he still needed his strength to recover as rapidly as possible.

"I still insist on being responsible for my share of the debt like the rest of you," Paul said.

"All right—if you want it that way."

"I do, and I'm sure Elaine will, too. Anyway I'll speak for her."

"When the papers are ready, I'll bring them by for you to sign," Pete promised. "Anything else I can do for you?"

"No. I just thank God that you had the foresight to lure Anton Dieter here—and Dr. Feldman."

When Pete Brennan had left, Paul pressed the call button beside the bed. "Please ask Dr. Rogan to come by whenver he has a chance," he told the nurse who answered on the small speaker at the head of the bed. "There's no rush."

His conversation with Pete had settled one thing that had been troubling him, but another question still needed answering. Only Dave could do that—if anybody could.

IV

It was after four o'clock that afternoon when Marisa Feldman stopped in to see Grace Hanscombe. The day had been something of a blur for Grace since George, looking more disturbed than she'd ever seen him, had plucked her out of the clinic line, shortly after the first blood sugar specimen had been taken, and hustled her into the hospital without even giving her time to go home for her clothes. She hadn't realized how rotten she felt, until she was settled into bed in Marfield, the exclusive private ward section reserved for staff members, their families, and V.I.P.'s. Since then nurses and interns had been poking needles into her until she felt like a pin cushion.

"I'm Dr. Feldman," Marisa said with a smile. "Dr. Hanscombe is tied up with a heart case and asked me to come by on my way to dinner and check up on you."

"Is it that late?" Grace asked.

"Hospital dinner hours are earlier than others. How do you feel?"

"Lousy. But just hearing your English accent has made me feel better."

"You're English, too?"

"Was. Dr. Hanscombe and I were married during the war. I've been over here nearly twenty years. How about you?"

"I was born and grew up in Poland, but we managed to escape when war broke out—that is my mother and I did. I went to school in England but was in prison in East Germany for a while afterward. Later I came over here and took a fellowship at Harvard. But I still love England."

"So do I—what I remember of it. I'm going back as soon as I can get straightened out from this." It was the first time Grace had put in words the decision that had come to her sometime during the night, perhaps when she'd tried to get close to George for warmth and he'd remained asleep.

Marisa opened the chart folder she carried in her left hand and glanced at the laboratory report sheet. "You're coming around nicely," she said. "Your last blood sugar was almost normal."

"Could this possibly have happened the way it has? I mean, could my whole system suddenly go blooey just like that?"

"It has probably been happening gradually over several days," said Marisa. "Have you been testing your urine every day?"

"Yes. No. I didn't test it yesterday, I remember—or the day before." She grinned. "I was mad with my husband."

"And since he was making you test it, you got back at him by not doing it?"

"You don't happen to be a psychiatrist, by any chance?"

"No. But I treat a lot of digestive-tract disturbances and they're closely related to emotional tension. Do you have any idea what might have set you off this time?"

"I *know* what it was," said Grace. "I was mad at Geor—at Dr. Hanscombe—because he wasn't the one Mort Dellman shot."

"I'm afraid I don't understand."

"You have to have been married for twenty years to a man who thinks God created sex on Saturday night to understand. I take it you've never been married?"

"No."

"Take my advice and don't. Stay single and play hard to get—but not too hard, mind you."

Marisa Feldman smiled. "I understand that part."

"Make the men in your life want you because you're an attractive woman and they know damn well somebody else will get you if they don't. Not just because you run a comfortable house, see that their clothes are washed, their food is properly cooked and served, and because you're there between the sheets whenever they're ready."

Marisa changed the subject somewhat abruptly. "I saw a friend of yours in the clinic this morning—Mrs. Weston."

"Alice?"

"Yes."

"I suppose her gut is in a gripe again—probably over this Mort Dellman business like the rest of us. But I wouldn't have guessed it made that much difference to Alice whether Roy shacked up with Lorrie or not. God knows he's had enough women in this town over the past fifteen years, but this was pretty close to home so I guess Alice was afraid of having her nice warm little world disturbed. When you know her better, you'll find that she lives in a world of her own that's largely make-believe, like a little girl playing dolls."

"Your world is certainly real enough."

Grace looked at her sharply. "Why do you say that?"

"Only that you have a very realistic attitude toward it, Mrs. Hanscombe. After all, Mrs. Weston had a mild colon spasm, but you almost went into diabetic coma."

Grace looked away, her face suddenly drawn. "It's not so much that my world is realistic, Dr. Feldman, but that most of it has long since passed me by. And what little I do have is all shot to hell."

"You'll feel better tomorrow, when your blood sugar gets back to normal," Marisa assured her.

"Do you think it will by morning?"

"I'm sure of it. Why?"

"I may not see my husband this evening; he'll probably forget I'm here and go home. Will you tell him I'd like to get away from the hospital long enough in the morning to go to Lor—, to Mrs. Dellman's funeral? She was one of the few people I know who was completely honest and I always liked her."

"I shall leave the order for a pass myself," Marisa promised. "And I'm sure you're more honest than you give yourself credit for being."

Grace looked startled, then grinned. "You're nobody's fool, are you?" She held out her hand and Marisa took it. "We might become friends at that— even though you're young and pretty and you'll be working closely with my husband. After all, we English ought to stick together."

V

Paul McGill was back in bed when Dave Rogan came in and pulled a chair up beside him.

"What a day," the psychiatrist said. "From the way you look, Paul, I think Mort's bullet wounded a lot of people worse than it did you."

"Why do you say that?"

"Grace Hanscombe's in the hospital one jump ahead of diabetic coma, though she didn't even have to take insulin before. Maggie McCloskey mixed alcohol and barbiturate last night and we barely got her pumped out in time."

"I guess I caused a lot of trouble."

"It had to come someday. When a group of people get their lives as intertwined as most of ours have been for years, you wind up with a powder keg that eventually has to blow itself up, and everything else around it."

"Will the parts ever settle back together?"

"Not in the same pattern, I hope. But that happens more often than you'd think, too. People's lives start repeating themselves as soon as they take off diapers; the way they behave under stress is pretty well determined in childhood. Given a similar situation later on, they'll usually repeat the same reaction."

"Not me," Paul McGill said firmly. "This was my first and last slip."

"I had an idea it was the first," Dave said. "Did you send for me to get that off your chest?"

"Not entirely. Something's troubling me."

Dave Rogan leaned back in the chair and lit his pipe. "Let's have it then."

"I . . . I don't even talk to Elaine about intimate things," Paul admitted. "Does that mean I'm repressed?"

"In the true sense of the word, perhaps yes," said the psychiatrist. "Freud made the word popular—or maybe I should say unpopular—but few people really understand what he meant. Freud saw repression as an unconscious mechanism whereby an individual denies certain impulses access to conscious thought, leaving their emotional energy—perhaps that's as simple a term as any—to appear later in the form of physical disease, the various mental symptom patterns of neuroses, or even the more serious illness that we call psychosis. But most of us still have a lot of repressions that never bother us."

Paul McGill started to speak, then hesitated, obviously embarrassed.

"What happened to you could have happened to anybody, Paul," said Dave, hoping to get him started on what he had to say without too much delay. "The musical beds game is being played around this town often enough for almost anybody to have been in the position you were in the other afternoon, and the same could be said for practically any other town regardless of size. People behave according to the same basic drives, whether they're rich or poor and whether they're in Terre Haute or Timbuktu. The pattern of human behavior hasn't changed appreciably that I've been able to see since the time of Pithecanthropus erectus."

"Maybe so, but I still can't figure out how I got into this mess. I love Elaine and she loves me. Neither of us have had anything to do with the hanky-panky that goes on around town."

Dave Rogan grinned. "You just dated yourself, Paul."

"How?"

"With that expression 'hanky-panky.' They're calling it by its real name now—and not only in books."

"I'm afraid I don't even know the words," the dermatologist confessed.

Dave Rogan glanced covertly at his watch. Paul McGill was his friend and he wanted to help him if he could. But Della would be starting dinner soon; they'd long ago formed the habit of making the evening meal with the children a discussion period in which everyone was free to have his say. And even though the children were in camp, he was still hoping to have a quiet talk with Della during the meal. She liked to have it on schedule, though, and so did he. An early dinner made for a long evening and he loved the quiet period after the children had gone to bed, when he and Della could read or talk together without interruption—except that lately their lines of communication seemed to have been breaking down.

"You sent for me, Paul," he reminded the dermatologist. "Was there anything in particular you wanted to talk about?"

"It . . . it's pretty personal."

"A man shouldn't have any secrets from his confessor—or his psychiatrist."

"I guess you're wondering how I happened to be at Mort Dellman's house the other afternoon."

"I figured that was your business—and Lorrie's."

"I was getting ready to play golf; you know I always play on Wednesday afternoon. Lorrie had been having a skin eruption that she said was bothering her. I'd given her some drug samples when she was in the clinic last week and she called me Wednesday afternoon early to say she was out of the samples and asked me to drop some more by the house on my way to the club. I didn't think anything about it, so I took the samples with me and went by there."

"I suppose she was alone when you arrived."

"You're not implying that—"

"You were snared by one of the oldest ploys in the world, Paul."

"Why me?"

"I suspect you were the only one in our particular group that Lorrie hadn't gone to bed with. I remember Della saying once that Lorrie had bragged during a bridge game about how she could seduce any one of us, if she really tried."

"But I never—"

"I'll take your word for that. What happened when you got to the house?"

"She wanted me to take a look at a place on her back. She was wearing some sort of a negligee—pretty thin."

"And nothing under it, I suppose."

"Well, no."

"Quite a lot of women have taken up what they call jaybirding lately, particularly in hot weather. During the day when they're alone in the house, they like to pad around the house naked. They claim it makes them feel free, but I've got a hunch it's another form of the latent tendency to exhibitionism that underlies the psychology of most women."

"Elaine's not like that."

"She likes to wear low-cut evening dresses when she goes out formal, doesn't she?"

"Yes."

"Then she's the same as every other woman. Before the new styles came around they'd make a fetish of keeping their knees covered when they sat down, yet think nothing of wearing a bikini on the beach that was even smaller than the briefs and bra they wear as undergarments. What happened next?"

Paul McGill blushed. "It was so fast after that, I'm not real sure myself."

"My guess is that you sort of got raped. Did you resist?"

The other man's flush deepened. "No."

"Good for you. Your repressions aren't as deep as I was afraid they might be. So you and Lorrie were pretty busy when Mort came in and fired the shot."

"Well . . . yes."

"I'm sorry to tell you, Paul, but under the circumstances you didn't have any more chance of resisting than Mark Antony had when Cleopatra went after him. You can at least satisfy your conscience with that assurance—if it needs any satisfying."

"That's not what I wanted to talk to you about," Paul protested. "I've already confessed the whole thing to Elaine and she forgives me, so there's no need for it to be on my conscience."

"Are you bothered because you enjoyed it?"

"No."

"Then what's the beef?"

"I . . . I'm what you might call hasty with Elaine."

"Premature ejaculation?"

"Yes—but I wasn't with Lorrie. The thing that bothers me is how can I love my wife as much as I do and not be a real man with her, when I was able to be with another woman?"

"Lorrie wasn't just another woman; you were seduced by an expert." Dave Rogan got to his feet. "I think I know the answer to your question, but it will take a little more time than I've got this afternoon to make it clear to you. Think about the problem tonight; I'll drop by tomorrow and we'll talk about it some more. I may be able to show you the answer and help you into the bargain."

VI

Della Rogan came into the Ladies' Grill at the club and went up to the bar for a drink. She was tired to her very bones and, worst of all, she'd played a lousy game all day.

"Gin and tonic, Manuel," she said. "Where's everybody?"

"I heard some of the ladies saying Mrs. McCloskey and Mrs. Hanscombe are in the hospital, Mrs. Rogan. Didn't you know?"

"I knew about Mrs. McCloskey but I've been on the course all day. Did Mrs. Hanscombe have an accident?"

"Not that I know of. There wasn't anything about it in the news."

Della sipped her drink, wondering why it tasted like the quinine her mother used to dose her with in the springtime down in southern Georgia to keep off malaria. Grace had complained of feeling lousy that morning but she hadn't seemed to be really sick so it must have been something sudden. Right now she'd be almost willing to have something sudden herself, Della admitted, rather than face the thought of a golf ball sitting nice and quiet on its tee tomorrow, waiting for her to slice it into the rough the way she'd been doing all day.

Leaving her glass half-emptied, she went to the telephone and rang the hospital, asking for Dave.

"Dr. Rogan's office thinks he's with Dr. McGill, but the line to Intensive Care is busy," the clinic operator told her. "Is it something urgent, Mrs. Rogan?"

"No. It can wait until he comes home."

"If I hear anything from him, I'll tell him you called."

"No, please don't," Della said quickly. "I wouldn't want to bother him."

If Janet Monroe's child and Paul McGill were more important to Dave than his own wife, Della thought resentfully as she went back for another drink, he deserved to eat a TV dinner when he got home. And to see the Thursday Night Movie, no matter how old it was.

Then a happy thought struck her. Tomorrow was Lorrie's funeral and she had a perfectly good excuse not to play golf.

CHAPTER EIGHTEEN

I

It was after five o'clock Thursday evening before Marisa Feldman finished seeing the patients George Hanscombe had asked her to visit on the private wards. It had been a long day and she was tired, so she decided to have an early dinner at the hospital cafeteria and go to her apartment for a quiet evening of reading and television.

As she was placing her tray on a table in the corner of the cafeteria, Janet Monroe stopped beside it. Janet, too, had been planning to eat alone, but when she saw the slender woman doctor with the arresting features and the lovely dark hair, some impulse she could not have named made her take her tray to Marisa's table.

"Dr. Feldman?" she asked.

"Yes." Marisa looked up from the table where she was arranging the dishes she had chosen.

"My name is Janet Monroe. I'm the nursing supervisor on the Special Intensive Care Unit."

"Oh yes. Dr. McGill is your patient."

"He doesn't need much nursing any more. Dr. Dieter says he'll be able to go home early next week."

Marisa hoped the warmth that rose in her cheeks at the mention of Anton Dieter's name wasn't apparent to the nurse.

"Do you mind if I share your table?" Janet asked. "I'd like to talk to you about something."

"Of course not." Marisa gestured toward the empty chair. "I'm afraid I have a lot of dishes. I was in prison in East Germany for a while and when I see all this food, I almost go berserk."

Janet arranged the salad, pie and coffee she'd chosen on the table and transferred both their trays to a nearby cart.

"I read in the hospital bulletin that you had come here from Harvard," she said, as she pulled out the chair across from Marisa and sat down. "I was wondering whether medical school and hospital life is different there from what it is here in the South."

"In what way?"

"I mean about medical school marriages. I've been divorced about two years—from a student who graduated that spring."

Marisa didn't miss the sudden bitterness in the nurse's voice as she continued: "It was one of those meal-ticket marriages. I worked and put my husband through medical school, then he left me for another woman—with money."

"I'm sorry. Actually though, you may be better off."

"How can you say that?"

"Forgive me. I have no right to tell you what is good—or not good—for you. This is a very personal thing."

"I'd still like to know what you meant."

"A friend of mine at Harvard recently published a paper on medical school marriages," Marisa explained. "The divorce rate among them is very high."

"Who knows that better than I do? But why?"

"For one thing there's never been a time when young doctors could make so much money right after they finish their residencies. In most cities, too, their income puts them immediately into a social—how do you say it over here?"

"Bracket?"

"Yes. A social bracket considerably higher than they would normally reach for many years. Many of them married young, often in college. The girl sacrificed her own education to help her husband complete his residency, then children came and the wife was left behind. Divorce—or worse—resulted."

"Worse?" She saw the shocked look in the young girl's eyes. "What could be worse?"

"Alcoholism, drug addiction, mental illness. It's not a pretty picture."

"Maybe I'm better off than I think," Janet admitted. "I was very bitter at first. But when I look back on everything, I can see that part of what caused the break with Cliff was my fault."

"My friend who wrote the study found there was usually reason to blame both partners in the marriages that failed," Marisa agreed.

"I'm sure of that—now."

When she saw Janet Monroe's eyes suddenly fill with tears, Marisa knew she had suddenly stumbled upon the real reason why the nurse had joined her for dinner.

"I've never had a child, Mrs. Monroe, but I'm a doctor and a woman," she said. "Do you want to tell me about it?"

The girl hesitated momentarily, then the words began to tumble out: "Soon after our marriage, I realized that Cliff had only wanted me because I could work and put him through medical school. He—he started staying away from home and running after other women. I was hurt and angry—I guess I wasn't thinking straight."

"Women in love rarely do."

"I decided to get back at him and make him settle down—with me—by having a baby. Only it didn't work. When he found out I was pregnant, he beat and kicked me. I almost had a miscarriage." She stopped suddenly, then hurried on: "Now my little boy has some sort of congenital condition that's causing convulsions."

"And you blame yourself?"

"Y-yes."

"How could you possibly feel guilty about what happened?"

"When Cliff beat me, couldn't that have caused the cells in the embryo not to develop properly?"

"That's possible, of course. But even if prenatal trauma was a factor in causing your son's condition, it was your husband that was to blame, not you."

"No, the fault was really mine."

"How can you say that?"

"Before we married, I agreed that I wasn't to get pregnant until after he was out in practice and we could afford children."

Marisa smiled. "Pregnancy can't always be prevented that easily."

"With the pill it can—almost a hundred per cent. But I deliberately stopped taking it, so Cliff had a right to be angry."

"And you blame yourself?"

"It's been driving me crazy. You see, I tricked Cliff, thinking that if I had a child I could hold him. I thought the breakup of my marriage was punishment enough. But now my baby might die, too."

"Are you a religious person, Mrs. Monroe?"

"I was—I guess I still am."

"Then you believe in God?"

"Oh, yes."

"Do you honestly believe God would punish you for your misdeeds—even if you were guilty—by crippling your child?"

"I—I don't know."

"He wouldn't be much of a god if he did, would he? Not the sort you could respect and love."

"When you put it that way, I suppose not."

"Even in the Old Testament, the Shema we Jews recite at our services instructs us to love God."

"I never thought of it that way." Janet felt a great load suddenly lift from her shoulders. "I guess I've been pretty much of a fool, Dr. Feldman. Jeff—Dr. Long—told me the same thing, but he wants me to marry him, so I thought he was only rationalizing."

"Dr. Long is a fine young man; I've heard nothing but good about him. Are you going to marry him?"

"I don't think so—at least not for a while, if ever. One experience with marriage was enough for me."

"Forgive me, but is Dr. Long pressing you?"

"Not really. He has to give two years to the Army, after he finishes this last year of residency. If we do marry, both of us want to start with at least an even chance of making a success of it. And we don't think being separated right at the start would be good for our marriage."

"I'm sure it wouldn't," Marisa agreed.

"You're so lovely—and capable. I'm surprised you've never married," Janet said as she stood up to go. "Or maybe you haven't met Mr. Right—as they say in a teen-age romantic magazine?"

"I've never read one of those, but it could be true. Good night, Mrs. Monroe."

"Good night, Doctor. And thank you for being so helpful."

As she watched the girl in the crisp white uniform move across the cafeteria to the door leading to the walkway connecting it with the building where the Special Intensive Care Unit was located, Marisa felt a surge of the old melancholy begin to oppress her.

She was beginning to be at least half certain that she might at last have found Mr. Right—as Janet had called him. The trouble was that she was wrong—wrong in a way she had long since decided could never be corrected.

II

Pete Brennan had finished up for the day a little after five, when Arthur Painter called.

"I've got to go to Atlanta in the morning, Pete," the lawyer said. "But I've made a rough draft of the Dellman papers and if you want to go over them with me tonight, I'll stay here at the office until we finish. Then my secretary can type them first thing in the morning and you can get them signed tomorrow."

"I was just going home to dinner," said Pete. "Let me call Amy and see what the situation is."

"Arthur Painter wants me to work with him on the sale of Mort's share of the clinic tonight," Pete said, when Amy answered the telephone. "What are your plans?"

"I have to go to the medical auxiliary fashion show at the YWCA," she said. "Didn't I tell you about it this morning?"

"You may have, but I've had trouble remembering things since last night."

"I don't even remember much of that. Next time I'll watch how much I pour into a glass before I add the ginger ale."

"I'll sneak a bigger shot glass into the bar cabinet if you do," he told her. "Since you're tied up this evening, I'll go work with Arthur. Okay?"

"Of course, darling. See you later."

"Sounds fine."

When she hung up, Amy stood looking at the telephone thoughtfully for a long moment. Her innate honesty and sense of fairness made her hesitate to do what her mind was urging her to do. She'd never checked up on Pete before, not even during the past year, when he'd spent more and more evenings at the hospital for staff conferences—or so he had said. But her conversation with Jake Porter that morning had shaken her more than she would admit to anyone except herself. And faced with the bleak future of a life without Pete, she was willing to do anything that needed to be done to hold him.

Picking up the phone, she rang Arthur Painter's office. The lawyer himself answered. "Is Pete there yet, Arthur?" she asked.

"He called just now to say he was grabbing a sandwich and would be right over," the lawyer told her. "We've got a lot of work to do tonight, if we're to put the Mort Dellman deal through in the three days Pete's given me to do it. Did you want him to call you?"

"No. Just give him a message, please." Amy felt a little giddy with relief at discovering that Pete had been telling the truth about spending the evening with the lawyer. "I have to go to a fashion show that's being put on at the YWCA by the medical auxiliary and I forgot to tell Pete I'll probably be as late as ten thirty getting home."

"I'll give him the message, Amy. Anything else?"

"About the loan for buying out Mort, Arthur. Are you likely to have any trouble raising the money?"

"Not a bit," he assured her. "Any bank in town would lend your husband a hundred thousand tomorrow on his personal note—without endorsement. That's how much the businessmen of Weston respect him."

"Don't tell him I asked, please."

"Of course. I understand your position, Amy. After all, I'm your lawyer, too. Good night."

"Good night, Arthur."

Amy was singing as she went to take her shower before dressing for the fashion show. Uncle Jake Porter had been disturbed this morning, or he never would have relayed what was obviously a baseless piece of gossip.

Pete couldn't possibly be considering divorcing her. After all, she was the perfect doctor's wife.

III

Arthur Painter looked at Pete Brennan over the tops of his unifocals and drummed his fingers on the blue cover of the topmost of a sheaf of legal documents lying on the blotter of his desk.

"You sure you want to do this, Pete?" he asked once again.

"Yes." Pete tried to keep impatience out of his voice. Arthur was a good lawyer and a friend, as well as a trustee of the indenture by which a large part of Amy's fortune was tied up in trust for the kids. The income tax on the returns was thus paid at the children's lower rate, so Amy's income wouldn't be added to the top of his already substantial one, putting them into a ruinously high income tax bracket.

"What about the others?"

"As members of the corporation, they'll have to sign it, too. But I told you we all agreed to it."

"The papers are all here," Painter told him. "You read the carbon copy and I'll make the notes for my secretary on the originals."

"Good. Mort wants this thing settled before Roy takes the case to the grand jury."

"That shouldn't be for a couple of days at least. Lorrie's funeral isn't until tomorrow morning."

"It's still the way Mort wants it, Arthur. How soon can we close the whole deal?"

"As soon as all of you—and Dellman—sign. Two sets of documents will be necessary; one is a straight sale and purchase agreement between the members of the Faculty Clinic Corporation and Mort Dellman, whereby he sells you his share in the clinic for a hundred thousand dollars. The other is a note for the hundred thousand to the First National Bank of Weston."

"The bank didn't quibble?"

The lawyer permitted himself a wintry smile. "Roy Weston is a director and so is George Hanscombe. Your wives will sign, too, of course."

"I take it there's no way out of that?"

"State law requires it. Surely you don't think Amy would object?"

"No. She offered to lend us the whole amount herself."

"You were wise not to accept, both as an individual and as her husband. What about Paul McGill?"

"He and Elaine insist on being a part of this. I gave him a chance not to be in it, but he refused."

"How about the insurance policies?" Pete asked when they'd finished going over the documents.

"Earl Bieson is working on that but there shouldn't be any trouble," the lawyer told him. "Twenty thousand additional on each of your lives under the clinic's group policy, assigned to the bank until the note is paid off, is all that's needed. The whole thing's ironclad."

"Then I'll see that the others and their wives sign these papers tomorrow and get them back to you." Pete got to his feet. "Anything else?"

"Mort Dellman is still getting the best end of this deal. I could almost believe he planned it that way. He gets rid of an unfaithful wife and makes three hundred thousand for himself—"

"One hundred thousand, Arthur."

"A hundred thousand." The lawyer corrected himself hastily. "Plus a chance to leave a community where nobody likes him much anyway—all with one bullet. I'd say that was an exceptional day's shooting."

"Not if his neck is stretched."

"It won't be. I heard this afternoon that Douglas Turner is going to defend him, if the grand jury returns an indictment."

Pete looked startled. "When did all this happen?" Turner was the most successful defense lawyer in a dozen states, a flamboyant old-school type who boasted that no client of his had ever been executed.

"This morning, apparently."

"I don't see Mort putting out that kind of money—even to save his neck."

"Mort isn't paying it. Jake Porter is."

"But Jake hates Mort's guts."

"So do a lot of other people. But Jake loves those grandchildren and he isn't going to see them have the knowledge that their father was hung left as a black mark against them for the rest of their lives."

A bell rang in Pete Brennan's mind. "Just now you said three hundred thousand—"

"A slip of the tongue," Painter said quickly.

"Was it? Tell me the truth, Arthur."

Painter shrugged. "This is in strict confidence—especially as far as the others in the clinic organization are concerned."

"Of course."

"If they knew, they might squawk about signing your agreement. They aren't as well off as you are, Pete."

"I agreed that it was confidential." Pete was beginning to be irritated by the lawyer's fussiness.

"His interest in the clinic isn't all your friend Dellman is selling." Painter picked up the blue-folded legal documents. "Jake's giving Mort two hundred thousand to leave the country and never communicate with his children again—payable to him by deposit in a Swiss bank he's been sticking money into for several years."

So that had been at the back of Mort's mind last night, Pete thought. With three hundred thousand dollars as a nest egg and the sort of salary a man of his undeniable ability in the clinical laboratory and medical administrative field could demand in a dozen parts of the world besides South Africa, which he had mentioned, Mort would be far better off than he'd been in Weston. And he'd be rid of the embarrassment of Lorrie's amours into the bargain.

Pete wondered whether he should tell Roy Weston about what Arthur Painter had said. The story Mort had told him the other night about only wanting to crease the backside of that medical student—whatever his name was—could have been something Mort had dreamed up as part of an elaborate scheme to get rid of Lorrie and fatten his own pockets at the same time. And knowing Mort as he did, Pete didn't put it beyond him.

"Like I said"—Arthur Painter seemed to be reading Pete's thoughts— "you could almost believe Mort Dellman planned it all this way. He's certainly smart enough—and unscrupulous enough. But I guess we're all lucky to be getting rid of him as cheaply as we are."

Outside the lawyer's office, Pete got into his Porsche. The dashboard clock told him it was only eight thirty, which meant that Amy probably wouldn't be home for another couple of hours according to the message Arthur Painter had given him. He toyed with the idea of killing time in a movie but couldn't remember the name of anything decent playing in town, so he finally turned the car southward along River Road. In front of an apartment house set back from the river, he parked and got out.

The elevator took him to the sixth floor. Halfway down the corridor, he stopped and punched a bell. He could hear the staccato sounds of guns firing in a television Western inside, but they softened immediately and moments later the door opened.

Helen Straughn stood in the doorway, looking quite different—in mint green slacks and a yellow blouse, with a matching green band about her flaming red hair—from the way she did as supervisor of the operating-room suite at the University Hospital.

"Come in, stranger," she said. "I was beginning to think Mort Dellman had got you, too—with that famous bullet of his."

IV

George Hanscombe met Joe McCloskey at the front door of the clinic as they were both leaving for the day. Being taller, George pushed the door open for Joe to go through first. Outside, they stood somewhat awkwardly under the marquee, each hesitating to ask the other the question that was on his mind.

"Where are you eating, George?" Joe asked.

"I don't know. I didn't want to eat at home alone so I phoned the maid to go on."

"How about the Snack Bar then?"

George glanced toward the gleaming chrome and glass structure at the corner of the parking lot. "I suppose it will do as well as anywhere else. I'm going to see Grace later."

"Let's give it a try then."

When the two men came through the door, Mabel looked up from the counter and smiled warmly. "Good evening, Dr. McCloskey. Dr. Hanscombe," she said. "Take the booth at the corner; the air conditioning doesn't blow right on you there. I'll bring you some coffee."

The two men slid into the red-cushioned seats, facing each other. The restaurant hadn't yet begun to fill with the six o'clock crowd, so there were only a few customers. They ordered and George Hanscombe took his saccharine bottle from his pocket and put it on the table between them.

"What's it like, being alone, Joe?" he asked.

"Hell!" said the urologist. "Pure hell! But why should that bother you? Grace is out of danger, isn't she?"

"She didn't go into coma, but she probably would have in another twenty-four hours if she hadn't discovered the sugar this morning."

"That's something to be thankful for, at least."

"Grace isn't a severe diabetic, Joe. Why would her blood sugar control system suddenly go haywire?"

"Didn't you test your urine for sugar and albumin when you were taking final exams as a medical student?"

"Sure. That's routine."

"How many in the class showed sugar—or albumin?"

"About half, as I remember it. Are you saying this sudden flare-up was psychosomatic?"

"What does Dave Rogan say?"

"I haven't asked him. He's been pretty busy—"

"I know."

"Joe." The internist's face was suddenly concerned. "I didn't mean—"

"Let's face it, George," said the pudgy urologist. "Mort Dellman might as well have shot all of us, when he got Lorrie and Paul. That bullet blew our nice orderly little world apart—not that mine wasn't shot to hell already."

"Maggie came through last night O.K., didn't she?"

"Yes. Dave Rogan even thinks he may be able to make some progress with her now—unless she gets mad with him and takes herself out of the hospital."

Their food came just then and they gave their attention to it, so there was a hiatus in the conversation. Over the second cup of coffee, George Hanscombe said: "Our wives have everything a woman could desire: plenty of money, time to enjoy themselves, servants, nice homes, charge accounts, a position in the community. Good God! What else do they want?"

"Maggie seems to want to drink herself to death."

"And Grace keeps harping on going back to England."

"Think she'll go?"

"After today it looks like that—or a severe case of diabetes."

"Let her go, George. That way at least you'll have some chance of getting her back—if you want her."

"Of course I want her."

"Have you told her so lately?"

"I tell her every night. With this prostate of mine, I can't last more than four hours before getting up. A thing like that is a constant reminder that you're getting old, and after I get back in bed I usually reach over and touch Grace. She's always warm and soft—you know how a woman feels in the dark. Just knowing she's there used to give me the assurance that I'd have somebody to grow old with, somebody I love. I've never admitted this to anybody before, Joe, but the reason I've always refused to let Grace go back to England was because I wasn't sure she would ever come back."

"I know how that is," Joe McCloskey agreed. "Last night when I went in the house and found Maggie stretched out on the bed, barely breathing, I thought she'd be gone for good before I could get her to the emergency room. The worst hour I ever spent in my life was that one—until Jeff Long got her breathing again."

"You've been divorced for six months. Surely that makes a difference."

"It only makes things worse. How do you think I feel while I'm driving by the house every half hour after ten o'clock, when they close the bar at the club, until I'm sure Maggie's safe at home? Since last night I've been saying a prayer of thanksgiving that she's still alive for me to be that close to her."

"Do you have any idea what's behind the whole thing? Her drinking, I mean—and last night?"

"No more than you have."

"That's none at all."

"Dave Rogan insists that it's all mixed up with Maggie's childhood, with her feeling that she came from the wrong side of the tracks. But why should that make any difference?"

"I don't know," George Hanscombe admitted. "I grew up on a tobacco farm in North Carolina and worked my way through college and medical school. None of my ancestors ever owned a slave and I was the first in my entire family even to go to college. Grace's family have been solid Welsh tavern-keepers for generations, so she's got no reason to feel inferior to me. Yet she's always throwing that business of having been a barmaid at me."

"Dave Rogan's got a theory about practically everything and half the time I don't agree with him, but he may be right about the Doctor's Wife disease. Dave claims that the trouble with doctors' wives as a group is that so many of them come from middle-class people, the kind who study nursing, or learn to become technicians or secretaries."

"Why in the hell would that make any difference? My family weren't even middle-class; during the Depression we were as poor as Job's turkey."

"Apparently that isn't where the sore spot develops. No matter what a doctor's background is, he still has to go to college in order to get into medical school. A lot of people think that having gone through both places automatically makes him an intellectual."

"Doesn't it?"

"Hell no, George. Taken as a group, doctors are about the narrowest-minded educated people you could think of. We've fought against every major social advance since Herbert Hoover was President."

"But socialism must be stamped—"

"That's a bunch of crap, George, and you'd know it if you ever stopped to really think. The world's changing every day and the social order with it. This country is never going back to all that States' rights guff and the sacred cow of purest private enterprise you so-called conservatives worship. This is a changing world and you've got to change with it—or be left behind."

"I don't quite agree," George said stiffly.

"I'm not asking you to. I'm just pointing out a few of the forces that make so many doctors' wives crack up—mentally, physically, or both—about the time their husbands reach the peak of their success. Take your own case. You came from a dirt-farmer family, but you're as highly regarded in this town as anybody I know because you're the best internist. You're on the board of the largest bank. You're a Senior Warden in the Episcopal church. And you're on the board of the Weston Country Club. You can look Amy Brennan in the eye any day and nobody would know you started at the bottom while she was born at the top. But how did you get there?"

"Mainly by hard work—and sacrifice."

"That's only part of it—maybe not even the most important part. You got where you are because the M.D. after your name automatically makes you the social equal of a Weston—or anybody else. Look at Sam Portola. He's got money enough to buy the whole town, but socially he never made it to where you are right now—and he never will."

"You make it sound logical," George admitted. "But—"

"Take my own case," said the urologist. "My family came to eastern

North Carolina in the days of the lord proprietors. We've even produced a couple of Episcopal bishops—which is about as good proof of a deep-seated case of dry rot in a family as you can possibly get. But if it hadn't been for the sulfa drugs and penicillin, I'd be nothing but a high-class clap doctor, like urologists were in the old days, and you'd be looking down on me."

"You're exaggerating, Joe."

"Only to prove my point that a doctor who's worth his salt not only gets rich—unless he's a complete dope—but also winds up at the top of the social ladder, too—if he wants to be there. The trouble is that lots of times the women we marry aren't ready to go up that fast. Or they tell themselves they aren't—which is even worse."

"You may have a point there," George Hanscombe admitted. "We spend most of our time making decisions people live or die by, so we've got to be right a good portion of the time. It's the women who have time to be uncertain."

"Uncertainty can drain away a person's self-esteem faster than almost anything else," Joe McCloskey agreed. "I don't have to tell you that feeling sorry for yourself can get you in the heart, the stomach, or the bladder. Why do you think I see so many women with cystitis?"

"The glucose regulatory function of the liver and pancreas are just as vulnerable," George Hanscombe agreed glumly. "To say nothing of Alice Weston's colon. Sometimes I wonder why it is that when women get psychosomatic complaints, an excretory function is so often involved."

"Because that's the way they're made. Why else?"

George Hanscombe laughed, and absorbed in their conversation, neither of them heard Mabel's gasp of indignation. The Snack Bar was still almost empty and she'd been plying them with fresh coffee all through the conversation, so she'd hardly missed a word.

"I guess the Lord must have had doctors in mind when he made women," George agreed; then he sobered. "So what do we do about Grace and Maggie?"

"Dave doesn't want me to see Maggie for a while so I'm playing it his way. I have a lot of respect for Dave, and besides, I don't know anything else to do."

George Hanscombe slid out of the booth and reached into his pocket for his wallet. "I guess I'll have to let Grace go back to England—and hope it will be only for a visit. Sometimes lately, when she was giving me hell more than usual, I even envied you, Joe. But I guess we're really in the same boat."

"Up the creek without a paddle," the urologist agreed.

"You certainly got an earful that time, Mabel," said Abe Fescue, when the two doctors had paid their bills and left the restaurant. "But you know there's a lot in what the little fellow said."

"Aw go race your horses!" Mabel said in disgust and began to clear off the table.

Abe grinned. "From the way it riled you, I'd say they must have come pretty close to the truth."

"Truth!" Mabel snapped. "They were so busy feeling sorry for themselves, they didn't even leave a tip. A couple of big shots they are. Better I should serve interns—or even students."

CHAPTER NINETEEN

I

Twilight was beginning to fall when Marisa Feldman crossed the street to the Faculty Apartments and took the elevator up to her one-bedroom corner apartment. She didn't pause in the tastefully furnished living room but walked through it to the small balcony that opened upon it. Pulling up an aluminum porch lounge, she stretched out on it and lit a cigarette, smoking it slowly while she watched darkness settle over the city.

The apartment was located high up in the central tower of the building, so she had a good view of nearly half the city from the balcony. Southward, the rolling terrain was mostly green pineland, with here and there the regular geometric pattern of a cornfield, the stalks, fodder, and ears already turning brown with the approach of autumn.

To the west, the hills rose steadily toward the dark line of the mountain range, some fifty miles away at this point, she had been told. When she looked toward the river, she could see that the water was already taking on the darker hues of approaching night. And though she could hear the staccato roar of a motorboat, she was barely able to distinguish the curving V of its wake in the swiftly falling darkness.

It was the part of the day Marisa had always liked best. In Cambridge, where she'd had an apartment close to the Harvard Yard, she had often gone walking through the center of the great university in the early evening, absorbing the peace that seemed to characterize the pursuit of learning. When she had first come to Weston, she'd thought that much the same quiet atmosphere prevailed here—and it still might on the university campus at the end of town for all she knew, since she hadn't had a chance to go there yet. But here at Weston Boulevard and North Avenue, where the medical school and hospital were located, the lavalike turbulence of emotional conflict boiled continually, just as it did wherever any group of humans, be they only two in number, came together.

Somehow, it reminded Marisa of a scene she'd witnessed in Yellowstone National Park, when she'd taken a three week's bus trip westward from Boston the first summer after her arrival there from England two years ago. The Devil's Garden—she remembered the guide calling the area that came to mind—was a place where the fires of volcanic energy kept popping to the surface from deep within the earth, roiling the thin outer crust until a particularly violent burst of energy sent a towering spurt of steam and scalding water hurtling upward, losing its energy before subsiding to leave the area once again smooth and peaceful—until another geyser broke through.

She had heard enough of hospital gossip in the brief period since she'd arrived at Weston to know that more than one geyser had already erupted here in connection with the shooting of Dr. Mortimer Dellman's wife yesterday. And she had gained the impression that much of the hospital and medical school personnel were waiting to see where the next explosion would occur—hoping to be there to watch it.

Below her, in the faculty parking lot, the floodlights suddenly flared into brilliance, turned on by an automatic clock. The sudden burst of light bathing the rectangle of concrete, caught Marisa with her defenses against memory down, thrusting her backward some six years—into another place and another time.

II

The prison compound at Frondheim had been bathed in just such a brilliance that night, when she had started across the open quadrangle from the long dormitory building in which she and the other women prisoners slept, packed closely together like sardines in a can, toward the hospital building on the opposite side. Marisa hadn't been able to keep from shivering with dread at the tangible menace in the rifle barrels of the guards aimed down at the compound from sentry booths along the top of the wall.

This was the moment for which she had taken the chance of crossing over into East Germany and risking the arrest which had occurred almost as soon as she set foot on the border. But even though she'd been warned by British authorities of what would happen if she tried to find her father in an East German prison and bring him out to freedom, she could not control a sense of satisfaction that at last she was near to him.

This was the first time she'd been allowed to visit her father since she was brought to the prison, although she had made application for visiting privileges as soon as she had been transferred to Frondheim, where Elijah Feldman had been in prison for some time. When she'd come into the prison ward he was only a frail body lying upon a cot, his eyes closed, the hands upon the blanket that covered him almost transparent, so thin and pale had he become.

"Papa! Papa!" Marisa had cried out with the pain of seeing her once strong and laughing father reduced to a creature in whom life itself seemed barely present.

"Marisa! *Liebchen!*" The old man opened his eyes at the sound of her voice. Seeing her and realizing that she was actually there, he tried to rise upon his elbows, but gasped suddenly with the effort, his face contorted with pain as he fell back upon the pillow.

"What is it, Papa?" she cried.

"Der Schmerz!"

"Wo ist es?"

"In das Herz, und der Arm." A gasp of pain broke off the words but Marisa understood their meaning. "Pain in the heart and in the arm" could be only one thing—angina pectoris.

"Nurse!" she had called out although she had seen no nurse since she had come into the ward, only the single balding orderly, who had leered at her when he took the pass she gave him. Receiving no answer to her call, she ran back to the small room at the end of the ward where the attendant had been when she'd come in. He was still there, sitting in a chair reading a lurid-covered magazine, and had grinned up at her with the same look in his eyes.

"My father is having an anginal attack!" she cried. "An attack!" she repeated when he showed no sign of comprehension. "He needs medicine—nitroglycerin—at once."

"There is no nurse here, *gnädige Fräulein.*"

"Then let me get it from the medicine cabinet. I am a doctor."

"A woman doctor?"

"Yes! Where are the medicines?"

"Up there." He nodded toward a cupboard above his head. But when she reached up to open the closed wooden doors he seized her around the waist.

"Not so fast, *Fräulein Doktor*. You are still a prisoner, are you not?"

"Of course."

His little eyes gleamed. "If I let you have the medicine, what will you pay?"

"I have no money."

"Money? Who has money? Now for a kiss, I might not look when you get the medicine you want."

She hesitated only a moment. "All right. But the medicine first."

He shook his head. "First the kiss, then the medicine." His hands slipped up along her body as he rose from the chair with an agility rather surprising for one of his bulk. His fingers squeezed her breasts, as he bent to kiss her, and the smell of sauerkraut and cheap wine on his breath almost nauseated her.

Steeling herself against the almost overwhelming impulse to flee, she let him kiss her, his thick lips slobbering over her face and down her neck. Nor did she resist when his fingers began to unbutton the neck of the cheap cotton uniform she wore and started fumbling for her breasts, since her own hands were busy opening the cabinet above his head and searching frantically there for the nitroglycerin bottle.

She saw it just as the orderly broke the left shoulder strap of her brassiere and, with a cry of triumph, scooped her left breast from the cotton fabric cup. By then, she had managed to seize the nitroglycerin bottle and, when he bent his head to thrust the nipple into his mouth, buried her elbow into his right eye socket, bringing a cry of pain.

As he staggered back, clutching his face in his hands, she darted from the room and ran down the space between the row of beds, hiding her half-exposed breast as best she could with her left arm. Beside her father's bed, she hastily opened the bottle, shook out one of the tablets, and gave it to him. Elijah Feldman needed no instruction to place it beneath his tongue. And, as the nitroglycerin—absorbed into the body as rapidly from that spot as it might have been had it been given by hypodermic—began to exert its dilating effect upon the coronary arteries of the heart, the pain started to fade and his tortured features relaxed.

Quickly, Marisa slid the bottle, with perhaps a dozen tablets still in it, beneath his pillow. Then hurriedly she did what she could to repair the damage to her uniform and her person caused by the guard's pawing so her father wouldn't see it and realize how she had managed to get the nitroglycerin.

"*Gott sei dank!*" The sick man opened his eyes again. "Until a week ago they let me have the tablets whenever there was pain but since then they have given me no more. I have prayed for death to free me from the agony, but even that has been denied me."

"I hid the bottle under your pillow," she told him. "Keep it there and use it whenever you need it."

"But how did you—?"

She put her fingers over his lips, for the orderly was only a few steps away, his face red with anger. "Tell no one you have it," she warned her father. "I will come to see you again when I can."

"*Fräulein Doktor!*" The orderly's eye was already beginning to swell. "Your visiting pass has expired. You must leave at once."

Marisa made no objection. Getting up quickly, she was through a nearby door and out into the brightly lit compound before the orderly could stop her. Stifling the impulse to flee to the haven of the women's quarters, as poor as that was, she walked slowly lest one of the guards in the sentry towers along the walls think she was escaping and shoot her down, even though she had gone to the hospital with an official pass signed by the commandant, Colonel Wilhelm Geitz. Such things, she knew, had happened, so little value did her captors place upon the lives of those they guarded.

A woman warden with a flashlight directed Marisa to her pallet in the long dormitory. She saw the woman's eyes on the disarray at the neck of her uniform where the orderly had torn two of the buttonholes in his eagerness. But when she gave no explanation, the warden went back to her post at the end of the long room.

Lying on her pallet in the darkness, Marisa sobbed silently in desperation, not only for herself, but for her father. Her training in medicine—she had already graduated from medical school in England—had taught her how agonizing the pain of angina could be without the relief of nitroglycerin, to say nothing of the feeling of impending death that accompanied it, a sensation that some sufferers described as being even worse than the pain.

The medicine she'd managed to obtain would relieve Elijah Feldman for a while, if the hospital orderly hadn't found it and taken it away. But in her father's condition, it couldn't last very long—about a week at most. And once the tablets were used up, there seemed to be no way she could get more for him.

As it had happened, however, her problem was soon solved; Zelda, the girl who occupied the pallet next to her, revealed the way as they were working in the prison factory the next day. Under the other girl's prodding questions, Marisa recounted what had happened the night before and her fear for her father, when the agonizing pain came once again and there was no relief.

"Why don't you buy the tablets for him?" Zelda asked.

"I have no money."

"You're rich," said Zelda.

"With what?"

"You're pretty. You have a figure like Sophia Loren. And you're Jewish."

"What's that got to do with it?"

"German men think Jewish women are passionate. Make a deal with them."

"Who do you mean?"

"How about the orderly to start with—the one who tried to rape you in the hospital ward?"

"Not him." Marisa shuddered. "I couldn't go through with that."

"You'll be surprised what you can go through with after you've been in one of these places for a while," said Zelda. "But I guess you're right. With what you've got, you might as well aim for the top."

"Colonel Geitz?"

"No less. Some of the girls have been getting extra food and cigarettes for visiting him occasionally. You ought to be able to write your own ticket—as the Americans say."

Marisa hadn't taken Zelda's suggestion seriously until, on the third day after her visit to her father, the hospital orderly from the ward had fallen into step beside her as the women were marching to their dormitory from the mess hall.

"We found the tablets you gave your father the other night, *Fräulein Doktor,*" he said. "The old man has been having a lot of pain, but I could fix it so he could get more medicine, if you'd cooperate."

"How?"

"One of the women attendants is paid to let some of the girls out of the barracks at night, so they can visit the guards' quarters and enjoy themselves. After all, it isn't right for so much beauty to go to waste. You could be one of them." Seeing her hesitation, he added, "With such pain as your father has been having, I don't think he will live very long without the medicine."

The next morning, Marisa made formal application to see the commandant—on personal business. The word "personal" seemed to be the open-sesame to his presence, for she was pulled out of the work line that afternoon and sent to the administrative offices of the prison, where she shortly found herself in the presence of the commandant himself.

Looking at Colonel Geitz, sitting in a reclining chair behind his desk, Marisa wasn't sure he was much to be preferred to the orderly, except that he was probably clean. About fifty, she judged, he was somewhat portly, red-faced and wheezed a little.

"What did you wish to see me about, *Fräulein?*" he asked.

"I'm ready to make a bargain with you, Colonel."

"You're hardly in a position to bargain."

"On the contrary, I'm in an excellent position." Unbuttoning her uniform, she stepped out of it. Beneath it she wore only the brassiere and shorts that were undergarments for the women prisoners; when the rate and intensity of Colonel Geitz's wheezing began to increase, she knew she was winning.

"The rest, please." His voice was hoarse. "I'm not yet convinced."

As calmly as if she were preparing to take a shower in the dormitory washroom, Marisa unbuttoned her brassiere and took it off, then stepped out of the shorts, holding both garments in her hand. The Colonel's face was twice as red now as it had been when she'd come in and he seemed to be having trouble getting his breath.

"Turn around, please," he ordered, and she turned, like a statue upon a pedestal, until she faced him again.

"As you say, your bargaining position is excellent, *Fräulein,*" he admitted. "Perhaps after a demonstration of your capabilities—"

Without answering, Marisa stepped into her shorts, put on her brassiere and buttoned it, then donned the uniform and buttoned it, too—all the way to the top.

"What are your terms, *Fräulein?*" It was capitulation, complete and absolute, but she felt no elation. After all, she had never doubted the outcome.

"I'm a doctor, Colonel Geitz. My father is a patient in the prison hospital with a serious case of angina pectoris. He needs nitroglycerin tablets from time to time because of agonizing pain, but you have chosen not to make them available to him. Appoint me medical supervisor of my father's ward, with free access to whatever medication he needs, and I will spend one night a week in your quarters."

"Two."

Marisa shrugged. "It doesn't matter. Is it a bargain?"

"I accept. You will come to my quarters tonight."

"Only after I've made sure my father has an ample supply of nitroglycerin."

"Agreed." He scribbled an order on a piece of paper and handed it to her. "This will assign you as nursing supervisor of your father's ward."

"Good day, Colonel."

"Until tonight, *Fräulein Doktor.*"

Outside the building, Marisa leaned against the post until she stopped trembling. But when she came to Colonel Geitz's quarters that night, she had been able to prove a conviction for which there was perhaps no true medical explanation, namely that, with a sufficient exercise of will, a woman could so control her body that no feeling existed in her generative tract, not even pain, and no nerve impulses at all would reach the brain to involve the emotions.

Elijah Feldman lived nearly six months in comfort. By that time, Marisa was physician for the entire prison hospital and most of the staff had forgotten she was actually a prisoner. Thus one day when she was sent to East Berlin to vaccinate a new group of prisoners about to be transferred to Frondheim, she had managed to slip across the border into West Berlin.

The British consul there had arranged for her return to England, where she had obtained a clinical clerkship in internal medicine without difficulty. Even then, young British doctors were fleeing in droves from the country rather than submit to the steady encroachment of the National Health Service upon their cherished professional freedom. Several years later, Marisa had followed the same course, by way of a two-year clinical teaching fellowship at Harvard Medical School.

There she had learned a distressing physiological fact: her success in divorcing herself of all feeling during the time she'd spent with Colonel Geitz had been too complete. In doing so, it seemed, she had succeeded in depriving her reproductive tract of all feeling—presumably forever.

III

Janet Monroe was leaving the Pediatrics ward where Jerry was a patient when the telephone rang in the chart room. The charge nurse answered, then handed the receiver to her.

"Janet?" It was Jeff's voice.

"Yes."

"I was trying to get there before you went off duty, but got stuck with a pentothal in the emergency room for a shoulder reduction and just finished it. Can you meet me across the street at the Snack Bar?"

"I think so—yes. Jerry's already asleep."

"Good. See you in a few minutes."

He was waiting for her, tall and ruggedly handsome in his crisp white ducks, when she crossed the street. The restaurant was almost filled with the eleven o'clock rush of interns, nurses and students, but they found a booth in the corner.

"What's so important?" Janet asked, when Mabel had taken their order and brought them coffee.

"A proposal."

It would be so easy—for both her and Jerry—to say yes, Janet thought. Jeff Long was everything a girl in her right mind could want; handsome, talented, kind, Jerry adored him and he was even independent financially, since he came from a wealthy Georgia family. But then she'd thought many of the same things about Cliff—and how wrong she had been. In her heart, she knew it wasn't really fair to compare Cliff and Jeff; and she was fond of him in a way she'd never felt about her former husband. But something she couldn't put into words at the moment still held her back.

"Please, Jeff," she said. "I need to be free for a while—especially with Jerry sick."

"You've been brooding too much," he protested. "Marriage doesn't have to be like what you had with Cliff."

"What about Mrs. Dellman? And the others—Dr. Hanscombe's wife and Mrs. McCloskey? Their husbands are at the top, but look what it got them. One's dead and another would be, if you hadn't been there when she was brought in last night. They tell me Mrs. Hanscombe almost went into coma, too."

"We're not like them," he protested.

"I'm not so sure, Jeff. I imagine all those couples loved each other, maybe they still do. I've been divorced, so I know something of what Mrs. McCloskey must have felt to bring her to—"

"That could have been an accident. Not many people know how dangerous it is to mix alcohol and barbiturates."

"Does Dr. Rogan think it was?"

"No," he admitted.

"See what I mean? A lot of medical marriages—particularly when the doctor is very successful, as you're bound to be—suffer from some sort of a sickness later on. I was talking to Dr. Feldman about it at dinner."

"She's an old maid!"

"What an awful thing to say about somebody so lovely and nice!" Janet cried indignantly. "She was telling me about a study of student marriages a friend of hers made at Harvard. A lot of them cracked up, just like mine did."

"We've been over all this before," he reminded her.

"What happened yesterday to Mrs. Dellman only makes what I'm saying more true." She reached across the table to squeeze his long, skillful fingers in a gesture of trust and affection. "Please, Jeff, I'm very fond of you and so is Jerry. Can't we just be good friends?"

"I hope we'll always be friends—but there's another alternative."

She gave him a startled look. "Are you suggesting—"

"Of course not. You know me better than that, Janet."

"I thought I did. What's this mysterious alternative you're talking about?"

"Lately I've been doing a lot of thinking about us—and the future. Dr. McCready is going to retire in another five years or so and Dieter practically came right out the other day and said he would boost me for the job of head of the Anesthesiology Department."

"That would be wonderful for you, Jeff."

"I'm not so sure—if it means your turning me down because you're afraid of what success could do to our marriage."

"That's not fair," she protested. "You're trying to put the burden of knowing I had cut you out of the chance here on my conscience."

"Not so fast," he said with a grin. "I didn't say I wanted to take the job."

"But—"

"I asked you over here tonight and let you make all your old arguments first, just so I could cut the ground from under your feet."

"What in the world are you talking about?"

"After I finish my residency next July, I've got to give two years to the Army. With my training, I'm sure to be sent to a big general hospital like Walter Reed or Brooke, which wouldn't really be much different from working right here."

"That's what you want, isn't it?"

"I had been thinking a lot about what I really want—even before this Dellman business came up. It wasn't any secret around here that a lot of top-brass marriages were in trouble—Brennan's for one. And the Mc-Closkeys already had their divorce."

"That's what scares me."

"About a month ago I saw a squib in the *A.M.A. Journal* about a project one of the big foundations is working on to start a top-flight medical school at Saigon in South Vietnam. It was intimated that young doctors willing to teach there would have the time they spent credited on their military service."

"Something like the Peace Corps?"

"I guess so. As I understand it, the whole thing is a private venture in partnership with government. Anyway I wrote them several weeks ago and today I had an answer. If I want it, the job will be mine next July when I finish here—chief anesthesiologist for the hospital and Professor of Anesthesiology in the medical school."

"That's wonderful, Jeff."

"It's a real challenge, but don't get the idea that this is some grandiose project. They're starting small and it will be an uphill fight to train really competent doctors. One thing's sure; there's not much money in it. I won't even make as much as if I were in the Army, but fortunately that doesn't make an awful lot of difference."

"Think of the good you'll do. And the satisfaction you'll get out of doing it. You're going to take the job, aren't you?"

"I wired them my acceptance this afternoon. This thing's been cooking for several weeks, but I haven't mentioned it to you because I figured it wasn't fair to tell you about it until I was definitely committed."

"Why?"

"Just now you accused me of putting pressure on your conscience," he reminded her. "No matter what happens, I'm going to Vietnam for two years, Janet, maybe longer. They're going to need teachers badly in their School of Nursing. I hope you'll decide to go, too—as my wife. And we shouldn't have any trouble finding a native amah—or whatever it is they call them—for Jerry."

"Suppose Jerry doesn't come through this trouble he has?" She finally put into words the fear that was tormenting her. "Or is left an invalid?"

"You'll need me more than ever." He didn't try to minimize the gravity of Jerry's condition. She was too intelligent—and too good a nurse—for that.

Janet felt her defenses crumbling. As Jeff had said, her own arguments had been largely destroyed before she could make them. In fact the only reason to refuse him now would be that she didn't love him enough.

"You don't have to decide right away," he said. "I've already committed myself, but you could sign up at any time. I think we could do important work out there, Janet. Most important of all we'd be happy."

Looking at him across the table of the small booth, Janet was tempted strongly to say yes—and fought against it, knowing that this time she had to be absolutely sure. If she married Jeff and the marriage failed, she would never be given another chance at real happiness—of that she was convinced. Once the pattern of marriage and divorce was established, it was easier to make the break each time and tell yourself you could start again, when in actual fact the odds against success went higher with every failure.

Deep in her heart something told her the affection she felt for Jeff Long, built upon a solid foundation of mutual interest, warm admiration, and the satisfaction of work shared, was a far more solid basis for a successful marriage than had been the largely physical passion that had brought her and Cliff together—and later torn them apart. But she needed time to be sure, to think out her fears and recognize them for the groundless worries she was already half convinced they really were. And particularly to see what happened to Jerry.

"For a start, why don't you get assigned to seven-to-three duty," Jeff suggested. "That way we can spend a lot of time together this winter taking a night French course I'm signing up for at the university."

"Do they speak French in Vietnam?"

"Educated people do. The medical school classes will be conducted in French; they once ruled the country, you know. There will be a lot of concerts and things we can go to this winter here in Weston, too. I'm off three evenings a week and every other weekend."

"I've been thinking about making the duty change, anyway," said Janet. When she'd come back to work after the divorce, she'd been forced to take the three-to-eleven shift because nothing else was available at the salary she needed to support herself and Jerry. A seven-to-three shift was opening soon and she could have it if she wished, but she'd held off, thinking of the long evenings in the apartment, after Jerry was asleep.

"You don't need to work any more, just so you'll be occupied evenings," said Jeff.

"How did you know that?"

"I was in love with you before you married Cliff—remember? And I probably know nearly as much about what makes you tick as you do yourself."

"How could I ever have any mystery for you, if you know me so well?"

"There'll always be the mystery of how anything as nice as you could happen to me," he assured her.

"I'll make a bargain with you, Jeff," she said impulsively.

"Name it."

"I'll change duty hours to seven-to-three. And I'll take the French lessons with you; I always loved the language anyway and Mrs. Bodey can sit with Jerry."

"That sounds like capitulation to me. What's the catch?"

"You must promise not to ask me to marry you for six months."

"Accepted." He held out his hand with a grin. "As long as you don't try to limit my thoughts. And when the six months are over?"

"If I can't make up my mind by then, you wouldn't want me anyway."

As they shook hands, Janet glanced at her watch. "Goodness! It's almost midnight. Do you know what Jerry's program is for tomorrow? I didn't get to see Ed Harrison tonight."

"Dieter has tentatively scheduled a cerebral angiography on him for eleven, if the radioscan is negative." He didn't add "for brain tumor"; there was no point in troubling Janet any more than she was troubled already.

CHAPTER TWENTY

I

The medical journal Dave Rogan had promised to send Maggie McCloskey arrived Friday morning. The article he had marked was a paper presented at a meeting of the American Psychiatric Association. After she finished her breakfast, Maggie started to read; before she'd gone very far, however, she began to be acutely uncomfortable.

"Frequent admissions of physicians' wives to a private psychiatric hospital raised the question of a possible relationship between the husband's occupation and the occurrence and manifestation of illnesses in the wives," said the opening paragraph.

The study, she saw, was of fifty cases, carried out in a prestigious private psychiatric hospital. Seven of the wives in the report had participated actively in the husband's practice early in marriage, as Maggie herself had done in the work of the Faculty Clinic during the years when she had been Dave Rogan's secretary. But when their husbands took on other nursing and office help, they had soon begun to feel left out and unneeded, an almost exact statement of Maggie's own state of mind for nearly a decade.

She'd been busy and happy during the first five years after she and Joe had first been married, even though she had continued to work as Dave's secretary most of that time. After they bought the house in Sherwood Ravine, she had been busy decorating and landscaping it, but once the clinic was operating freely, it hadn't seemed right for the wife of a doctor making over $25,000 a year to be without a full-time maid.

Maggie was intelligent enough to know the breakup of a marriage couldn't be blamed simply on the fact that the wife had a maid and therefore little to do. Her own trouble went deeper than that; in fact warning signs—if she had only known how to recognize them—had appeared during the first weeks of her marriage to Joe.

In only nine of the fifty couples, the article said, had "frequent and mutually satisfying sexual relations" existed throughout the marriage. The rest listed much variation while, in thirteen, sex as a meaningful part of their lives was "very infrequent or mutually unsatisfactory."

On the honeymoon Maggie had attributed her lack of response to Joe's love-making to physical discomfort during the act; later she'd blamed it on him. When she continued not to reach a climax, except on rare occasions when she'd been drinking heavily at parties or conventions—she'd gone to Jack Hagen on the pretext of having a Pap test. But Jack had pronounced her perfectly normal and she'd been ashamed to confess to him the real reason for her visit.

She should have consulted Dave Rogan then, she realized now. But she'd been brought up by her mother to be very reticent about such things; in fact, she was sure her parents had stopped sleeping together long before her father died, for they'd had separate rooms as far back as she could remember. Now she found herself wondering whether that could have had anything to do with her frigidity. The word itself repelled her, however, and she turned back to the medical journal.

"A family history of emotional disturbance was present in thirty-one of the wives' families," the article said. "In eighteen of these families, there was a history in parents or siblings of psychiatric hospitalization, suicide, or psychotic illness."

So that had been the real nature of her mother's "nervous breakdown." Mother had blamed Father for it, railing against him for being ineffectual and afraid to ask for a raise or a more important job. Maggie had accepted her mother's accusations at face value, too, knowing her father to be easygoing and not inclined to argue back. But Joe was very much like that, too, yet she knew Pete Brennan and the other doctors in the Faculty Clinic had a tremendous respect for him. And the students had twice voted him their favorite teacher.

The most frequently cited characteristics of the mothers of the doctors' wives who had required institutional psychiatric care, she read on, were "domineering," "distant," "rejecting attitude toward the patient," "moody," "demanding," and "rigid."

That was Mother, Maggie admitted wryly, then sobered when she remembered the same thing could be said about her own attitude toward Joe much of these past ten years.

"Fathers were most often seen as having a close relationship with the patient, as being shy or retiring, easygoing, strict and dependent," she read, but by now the tabulation of symptoms and facts had begun to depress her. For the first time since she'd finally regained complete consciousness yesterday afternoon, she felt the need for a drink. But there was no chance of getting one in the hospital, and after the night before last, she was afraid to ask for a barbiturate.

Maggie was intelligent enough to realize that most of the rising sense of anxiety she felt came from the almost uncanny similarity of the symptoms enumerated in the psychiatric article to those which had characterized her own family life as a child—plus the undeniable fact that in her own marriage, she had tended to imitate almost exactly the story of her parents' difficulties. It was no wonder, she thought, that her father had died early of a heart attack and her mother had been a querulous, demanding invalid for so much of her life.

The next paragraph in the report was labeled "Symptomatology." Maggie hesitated a moment before going on, sensing what she would find: "anxiety and muscle spasms"; "depression and excessive drinking"; "overuse of drugs or alcohol"; "suspiciousness"; "suicidal attempt"; "persistent pain"; "hostility"; "agitation"; "feelings of rejection"—they were all there, like ghosts come to haunt her.

Most chilling of all was a paragraph that said: "Seven patients had sufficiently long-standing histories of overconsumption of alcohol to warrant a secondary diagnosis of alcoholism. A secondary diagnosis of drug addiction was made in the case of eleven patients, while eleven others had histories of using addictive drugs to the point of psychological and physiological dependence."

That she was physiologically dependent on alcohol—the real test of an alcoholic—Maggie was already convinced; by now her nerves were fairly screaming for the solace of a drink. She almost put the article aside at that point, but the morbid fascination of looking at herself, as it were, through a microscope, made her go on.

In discussing the fifty cases, the reporting psychiatrist said of some four-fifths of the women: "Nevertheless, prior to illness, they had been quite successful. They were well educated and pursued a variety of intellectual and cultural activities in their leisure moments. They were able to marry men with high sociocultural standing. As a group they had successfully weathered the difficult years of their husbands' medical and specialty training and the early years of practice. Only after an average of almost thirteen years of marriage was an overt illness manifested.

"By the time of admission, these women had raised families averaging almost three children, and participated in community activities and had furthered their social aims. Most patients in this group possessed enough ego strength prior to illness to achieve a superior level of social adaptation."

Maggie laid down the article and turned her eyes to the smooth white blankness of the ceiling. She hadn't really started going to the club very often until she'd gotten a full-time maid and was no longer responsible for any real duties about the house. Like many others she knew—and not all of them doctors' wives—she'd become at about that same time what the psychiatrist making the report had characterized as "overly dependent upon the environment for reinforcement of her self concept."

"With a mean age spread between husband and wife of 5.6 years," the report continued, "the peak age for onset of illness [early 30's] occurred at the time when most physicians, including the husbands of these women, were established and in their peak years [late 30's] of active practice. Underscoring the possibility of a relationship here is the prevalence of complaints about the increasing absence of the husband at the time when the wife's personal involvement in her husband's work is decreasing."

"Sexual incompatibilty," she noted, had existed "in at least seventy-five per cent of the cases."

"Marriage to an older man, whose vocation may have been unconsciously associated with omnipotent, understanding, protective attributes," the article said, "may be interpreted as an attempt by many of the patients to resolve persisting Oedipal conflicts. Illness developed when the equilibrium of the adjustment was disrupted by such reality factors as the increasing involvement of the doctor in his work, or a conflict between his personality characteristics and the idealized expectations of his wife.

"Despite the broad variety of diagnostic categories, three symptomatic themes recur: depression, drug addiction and somatization [physical complaints]. As the doctor became increasingly involved in his work, depression was precipitated by the physiological loss, which intensified the wife's ambivalent feelings. In addition, the wife, previously an active participant in her husband's career, was faced with the loss of this role. The secondary symptomatic theme, the use of drugs, is specifically related to the husband's profession by virtue of ready accessibility of medications. Thus the patient unconsciously symbolized her dependency needs through the use of one of the most fundamental and gratifying resources the physician has to offer—drugs used to relieve pain.

"The third theme, frequently interwoven with the previous two, appears in the history of somatic [physical] symptomatology, particularly of pain. This symptom also points to the hostile-dependent aspects of the husband-wife relationship. Pain brings a patient to the attention of the physician, who, in turn, directs his energy to the alleviation of that pain. Nothing can be more frustrating, confusing or embarrassing to the physician than pain of undiagnosed etiology which he cannot relieve. It is a symptom which professionally cannot be ignored or left unattended; it must receive that attention which, in his wife's view, the doctor devotes to his patients, perhaps to the exclusion of his wife's needs.

"The recorded comments of family, patients and therapists gave a number of indications that the husbands had contributed to some extent to the illnesses of their wives, a participation which extended beyond the doctor's preoccupation with his work. The physician, secure in his omnipotent roles with patients who are frankly dependent upon his professional capabilities, rejected his wife's dependency strivings except when they were expressed as demands for medical attention. He then, without apparent cognizance of their emotional basis, gratified these needs by resorting to his professional role. A number of patients, for example, who were addicted to drugs, continued to have ready access to them even after the addiction was evident, and in several cases the drugs were furnished by the husbands. Furthermore, of seventeen patients who left the hospital prematurely, that is against the recommendation of their therapists, six were withdrawn by the husband; the other twelve patients did not have any pronounced difficulty in persuading their husbands to condone this action. In many incidences, the husband was unwilling or unable to set limits on his wife's behavior. This passivity, or even cooperation, in his wife's psychopathology suggests that those doctors felt guilty about their own inability to meet the emotional needs of their wives."

Maggie put down the medical journal when the freckled nurse came into the room.

"Would you like something to drink?" the girl asked.

"Yes. A double Scotch—on the rocks."

"The best we can do is Seven-Up—or Coca-Cola."

"Make it a Coke then." As the nurse was leaving the room, Maggie called to her: "This journal belongs in Dr. Rogan's office. Would you see that someone sends it down to him?"

"Of course, Mrs. McCloskey." The girl took the journal and Maggie felt better almost immediately. During the last few moments, the damned thing had seemed like a snake lying there on the table waiting to strike her.

"Nurse," she called, as the girl was at the door.

"Yes, Mrs. McCloskey."

"Will you shut the door, please? I want to be alone with my superego."

II

Lorrie Dellman's funeral was set for eleven o'clock, in the cemetery back of the old Episcopal church. Only the older families in Weston had lots there; the town had long since been built up around the church and it was no longer fashionable to have a cemetery almost in the center of the city. As a result, new ones had been laid out in the suburbs, complete with perpetual care, fountains, and recorded music played from hidden loudspeakers among the trees.

Della Rogan had gone by the hospital for Grace, who had telephoned that she'd been given a pass to attend the funeral. Elaine McGill came along. Amy brought Alice Weston with her; living as close together as they did, there didn't seem to be any reason for bringing two cars.

Maggie McCloskey was still in the hospital; Dave Rogan had ordered her not to go to the funeral, knowing that, even though he'd already made considerably more progress toward showing her the path she must follow in the future than he'd expected to make by now, the emotional shock of seeing Lorrie's coffin and knowing that, but for Joe's love and Jeff Long's skill, her body could be inside one just like it, might be too much for her.

As for the others, Lorrie had been their friend and the thought of anyone so alive and vital being shut away beneath the surface of the earth was sad enough to make anybody weep. Besides, all of them felt a little guilty, knowing that under slightly different circumstances any one of them could have been inside the coffin.

Jake Porter had decided on a simple graveside service. Even so, Amy Brennan was surprised by the large number of flowers.

"Uncle Jacob talked to me this morning on the phone," said Alice. "He said flowers came from people all over town. It's surprising how many people knew and liked Lorrie."

"I met one of her college classmates a few years ago at a medical auxiliary meeting," said Amy. "She said Lorrie was the most popular girl in the class—and not just with boys."

"She wasn't always kind to me." Alice wiped her eyes with a tiny handkerchief. "But I loved her."

Mort Dellman was there with Sergeant Jim O'Brien. Amy saw no sign of handcuffs but, from what Pete had told her, Mort was counting on the grand jury to let him off and would have no reason to try to escape. Pete had told her Mort had asked him to make arrangements for a reservation on a plane for South Africa, where he planned to start a new life. Which was probably just as well; they had only tolerated him before because he was married to Lorrie and because of his place in the clinic.

Lorrie's children were with Jake Porter, sitting at one end of two rows of chairs arranged for the family at the graveside under the canopy. Della and Grace stood at the back of the crowd. When Dave and Pete Brennan arrived, Dave made his way across the grass, dodging gravestones, to stand beside Della. He gave her arm an affectionate squeeze and, when she groped for his hand with hers, took it and held it during the rest of the service. Neither spoke, but both knew that her silent reaching out to him had removed in an instant much of the stiffness that had been between them for the past couple of weeks.

The canon of the new cathedral across town was a young and very earnest priest who was causing raised eyebrows among the several Episcopal congregations in the city, particularly the older ones, by spending much of his time with factory workers and their families and Negroes in the slum area called Brooklyn, something no minister in Weston had ever dared to do.

The canon was tall, very young-looking and serious in his vestments. At the stroke of eleven, he stepped up to the head of the coffin and waited for those who had been standing a little outside the immediate area, reluctant to get near the coffin, to move closer.

"It has been requested that I read from the gospel of St. John, chapter eight," he announced. Opening the Bible, he began to read in a clear voice that carried to the edges of the crowd:

> Jesus went unto the Mount of Olives and early in the morning he came again into the temple and all the people came unto him and he sat down and taught them. And the scribes and Pharisees brought unto him a woman taken in adultery.

The word shattered the placid scene at the graveside like a bombshell. The young canon ignored the gasps from the women and the disapproving frowns of the men as he continued to read:

> And when they had set her in the midst, they said unto him, "Master, this woman was taken in adultery, in the very act. Now Moses and the law commanded us that such should be stoned; but what do you say?"

> This they said, tempting him that they might have to accuse him. But Jesus stooped down and with his finger wrote on the ground, as though he heard them not. So when they continued asking him, he lifted up himself and said unto them, "He that is without sin among you, let him first cast a stone at her."

> And again he stooped down and wrote on the ground, and they who heard it, being convicted by their own conscience, went out one by one, beginning at the eldest, even unto the last. And Jesus was left alone and the woman standing in the midst.

> When Jesus had lifted himself and saw none but the woman, he said unto her: "Woman, where are those thine accusers? Has no man condemned you?"

> She said, "No man, Lord." And Jesus said to her, "Neither do I condemn thee. Go and sin no more."

With no change in his manner to indicate his realization of the effect the passage had caused, the young canon turned the pages of the Bible and began to read the ritual litany for the burial of the dead.

The service was quickly over. Moving along the line of relatives sitting in the chairs beside the grave, the priest came to Mort Dellman and held out his hand to him as he had the others. Dellman hesitated, then shook hands before he moved away with Sergeant Jim O'Brien at his side without attempting to speak to either Jake Porter or the children.

As the crowd began to disperse, the buzz of conversation filled the air. It would be a long time before Weston stopped talking about the effrontery of the young canon in coming right out and mentioning the word "adultery" at the funeral. Things like that just weren't spoken of publicly in an upright moral community, especially during a High-Church Episcopalian service.

"The very idea of him reading that passage," Alice said indignantly as she and Amy were walking toward the car, stepping around the graves in the old cemetery. "Why, it's almost like he was condoning what Lorrie did. And did you see him shake hands with Mort?"

Amy didn't answer. She had seen Pete Brennan with Roy Weston at the edge of the cemetery. And as they moved toward their own cars, she hurried Alice along to intercept them.

"I was just telling Amy it's really sacrilegious, what that priest said," Alice fumed when they caught up with Pete and Roy. "I'll bet the bishop will give him what for, when word of it gets to him."

"He was only reading the words of Jesus," Pete said.

"I don't care. Some things shouldn't be spoken of—and this was one of them."

"Are you throwing stones?" he asked, and Alice stiffened.

"Pete Brennan!" she cried. "I hate you!"

"I'm sorry, Alice," he said. "I guess what the minister said sort of upset most of us. After all, who are we to—?"

"I don't know about you," Alice began angrily.

"Shut up, Alice!" Roy Weston said wearily.

"I won't—"

"Shut up, Alice!" he repeated and Alice lapsed into a hurt silence.

"Uncle Jake told me he had asked the canon to read a special passage." Amy hadn't spoken before during the entire interchange. "Do you suppose that could have been his idea?"

"It must have been." Pete Brennan looked back to where the old man was being ushered to his limousine. "I don't think the canon would have dared to do it without a request from the family. As Alice just said, the bishop would certainly give him hell if he had."

"But why would Uncle Jacob do a thing like that?" Alice said.

"I expect because he knows a lot of us have been critical of Lorrie," Amy said, and Pete gave her a startled look.

"Critical because of what she did—or because she was caught?" Roy asked.

"A little of both, I guess." Amy turned to touch Pete's arm, almost apologetically. "Will you be home for dinner, darling?"

"I may have to operate on the Monroe child and I've got a staff conference at the hospital," he told her. "It might be late, but I'll get there as soon as I can."

"I'll let Mary fix dinner and go on home," she said. "We'll pile the dishes in the sink and she can do them in the morning."

He knew what she meant and his pulse quickened as he turned to his own car.

III

"There's something you hardly ever see nowadays," Grace Hanscombe said as she and Della Rogan were getting into Della's station wagon after the funeral service.

"What's that?"

"An honest preacher—with guts!"

"He only read the words of Jesus himself."

"Jake Porter's the largest contributor to the church, trying to buy himself a little burn salve, I guess, for the hereafter. From what I hear, he can use it."

"But Jesus forgave the adulteress."

"Would you have forgiven Lorrie—if it had been Dave instead of Paul McGill?"

"I don't suppose so."

"And what about Dave—if you were to stray."

"Maybe after a little while; he's more tolerant than I am."

"How do you suppose Elaine felt? She was standing near us."

"She's always been pretty religious, you know," said Della. "I guess that Bible passage would mean something to her."

"If she's got good sense, she won't let this break up her marriage," said Grace. "Sometimes I think I'd love George more, if he would tomcat around a little—at least enough to prove he could still do it. I can't even make him mad any more. When it gets that bad, I guess a marriage is pretty well shot."

"You're talking foolishness, Grace," Della said as she started the car.

"No, I'm not. With me it's die with George—or live without him. I don't mind telling you this diabetes episode scared the living hell out of me."

"You're crazy, Grace." Della stopped the station wagon and let another car go ahead. "George isn't Cary Grant, neither is Dave. But he's still a good provider."

"A woman needs more than that. The truth is, I don't think he really loves me any more."

"Why would you say that?"

"Before all this happened I'd been pestering him to let me go back to England—not because I really wanted to go, mind you, but mainly because he didn't want me to. Last night he came to see me in the hospital and suggested that I go to England for a visit."

"Are you going?"

"Sure. But now he's taken all the pleasure out of it, because I won't be making him mad by going."

"How long are you going to stay?"

"I don't know. Maybe for good unless I get to the point where it will feel good to be waked up in the middle of the night by a man patting you on the behind—even if that's all he's going to do."

"I guess Lorrie Dellman getting killed has changed a lot of our lives. I've decided to give up golf tournaments." Della put into words a decision she hadn't known she'd made until that moment.

"I can't believe it."

"Golf's fine when you're playing for the exercise—and the fun of it. But when you've got to stay in training like an athlete, and ride around in one of those damned little carts because you have to save up your energy for the strokes, it's time to quit."

"But you're near the top, Della."

"There isn't any top. Tournament play is something like an alcoholic taking the first drink of the day; you can't stop with the first or the second or the third. There's always another tournament ahead that you've got to try and win."

"You almost sound happy about it."

"I guess I am, in a way. Dave wants us to have another child."

"Do you love him enough to go through that again?"

"Yes. I just decided it—out there in the cemetery."

"I saw you holding hands," said Grace. "As for me, I've gotten so used to having George around, I can't tell whether I still love him or not."

"Maybe that's what married love is, being happy to have someone around."

"I didn't say I was *happy* to have him around," said Grace. "I said I was *used* to having him around. Most of the time he irritates the hell out of me."

"Obviously he cares a lot for you or he wouldn't have agreed for you to go to England."

"George is a good doctor, Della; he's always concerned for his patients. He's discovered at last that I'm sick, so he'll do whatever he thinks is best for me. I guess one reason why so many doctors' wives crack up is because the husbands are so busy being concerned for their patients they don't have much time left to be concerned about their wives. I've often heard George say doctors' families are neglected medically."

"He certainly isn't neglecting you. You admitted that yourself."

"Whose side are you on anyway?"

"Both. I'm fond of you and I'm fond of George. I'd hate to see either of you unhappy."

"George won't even know I'm gone—until Saturday night," Grace said with a shrug. "If I do say so myself, I'm pretty good in the hay. I'll give George this much, too. Once he gets out of the starting gate, he can gallop home at a pretty respectable pace."

"Then why are you thinking of leaving him?"

"I guess because the strain of keeping up has finally got to me."

"What does that mean?"

"In England I can grow fat and get a lot of joy out of life—even if I have to take insulin. Here I've got to wear a girdle to keep my fanny from spreading. George is still handsome with that clipped mustache of his and that distinguished little pot, so I have to dress smartly and not look bad compared to the other faculty wives. I drink a lot of liquor I don't particularly care for, because everybody in our group does. Over here I'm fairly smothered in respectability, but basically I guess I'm too much of a slut to enjoy it."

CHAPTER TWENTY-ONE

I

Paul McGill was out of bed when Dave Rogan came by on the way to the hospital cafeteria for lunch after the funeral. The dermatologist was sitting in a chair by the window, with the distant panorama of the Great Smokies looking like a movie backdrop on the western horizon.

"I saw Elaine at the funeral, Paul," said Dave. "She'll be by to see you after lunch."

"I don't know what I ever did to deserve something as wonderful as she is," said the dermatologist.

"I don't have to ask how it's going with you." Dave stretched out in the one easy chair the room afforded and stuffed his pipe with Rough Cut. "Imagine having your heart opened up day before yesterday and being out of bed already. When I was an intern we used to keep appendix cases down longer than that."

"Dieter says there's no sign of any accumulation of fluid in the pericardium or the pleurae. He thinks I'll be able to go home the first of the week. It's a funny thing," Paul McGill added with a wry smile, "but I can even detect a change in the way people treat me since all this happened."

"What kind of a change?"

"I guess I must have been pretty much of a clod medically—and maybe socially; after all, dermatology isn't the most exciting specialty in the world. You can get to be pretty much of an old maid, doling out ointments and freezing hyperkeratoses all day. But now, it's suddenly like I was a hero or something."

"They say every man has a secret ambition to live to be ninety and be indicted for rape," said Dave. "You've made the leap from what you call an old maid to the role of Don Juan. Naturally, a lot of people whose lives are pretty humdrum envy you. Come to think of it, maybe I do myself."

"It's still a strange thing."

"Not as much as you think. A writer friend of mine has made a fortune out of novels based on real-life heroines who were wicked women—people like Jezebel, Rahab the harlot of Jericho, Cleopatra and the like. He believes the books are popular with women because they want to see how much the hussies of history were able to get away with. And men like them because every man secretly wonders what it would be like to have one of those females around the house."

"I guess there's a lot in what he says."

"Not that Lorrie was basically wicked. Psychiatrically she was more normal than most of us, because she had less inhibitions and gave free rein to the instincts most of us refuse to admit, because we're afraid they might bust open the nice little water-tight compartments we squeeze our lives into."

"When I look back on it now, I can see that I've been pretty well boxed in ever since I was a child," Paul admitted.

"How old were you when your father died?"

"Four." The dermatologist gave him a startled look. "But how did you know that? Oh, I remember now. The intern who took the history the day after the operation asked me about my family history."

"I didn't look at it."

"Then how did you know?"

"Your whole symptom pattern fits that of a boy who was reared by his mother in the absence of a father."

"Father didn't really die until ten years ago. When I was about four he walked out of the house and never came back."

"That makes you an even more typical case. I suppose your mother was pretty bitter about the whole thing."

"Once I asked her what Father was like and she wouldn't even speak to me for two days. Just put food on the table before me, and didn't answer when I begged her to tell me what was wrong. After that, I never made the mistake of mentioning his name again."

"Did you ever find out what really happened between them?"

"An uncle—my father's brother—came to see me in college and I asked him about it. It was the old story—another woman. They ran off together but weren't married and after a while she left him. Father tried to come back to Mother but she wouldn't let him. She was pretty stiff-necked about such things."

"Count yourself lucky you didn't turn out to be a homosexual," Dave Rogan said. "The family pattern you describe is pretty common among them. I suppose your mother tried to bring you up as Lord Fauntleroy?"

"She did her best, until I rebelled. When I insisted on playing football at school, she kept hammering at me that I mustn't let myself grow up to be like other men, treating the nice women they married like animals."

"Is that why you waited so late to marry?"

"I suppose so. I didn't marry until after she died and I suppose I might have remained a bachelor, even then, but Elaine came along. She's so sweet and gentle—"

"And physically like your mother too?"

"Why, yes." The dermatologist's eyes opened wide. "Are you saying that had anything to do with my falling in love with Elaine?"

"It almost certainly made you single her out from other women. Men who've been close to their mothers in childhood often marry women who are very much like them."

Paul McGill didn't speak for a long moment and Dave Rogan smoked on without prodding him. One of the most important assets of a successful psychiatrist was patience; the willingness to wait while the patient searched his soul and finally saw the motive for his own acts.

"Elaine is like mother in many ways," Paul said at last. "Could that have anything to do with . . . my trouble?"

"It probably has everything to do with it. I suppose Joe McCloskey has checked you out for physical defects?"

"Joe says there's nothing wrong with me and Jack Hagen gave Elaine a clean bill of health, too. Surely you don't claim my seed aren't able to join with hers because of some psychological factor."

"There are investigators who go that far, but not me; I think the union of sperm and egg is too elemental an affair to have been left to anything except mathematical probability. Even there, the odds are weighted so heavily in favor of conception that it's a miracle it doesn't occur every time."

"Jack did a viability test on my sperm and nothing's wrong there either," said Paul. "My personal belief is that Elaine has some kind of hyperacidity in her generative tract that kills them before they reach the ovum."

"Are they ever really deposited there—inside her generative tract, I mean?"

Paul McGill flushed. "I get that far—but not much farther."

"What about Elaine?"

"What do you mean?"

"Does she achieve orgasm regularly?"

"I don't know. She's never complained."

"Most women don't until they turn up with something psychosomatic, or a real neurosis. Then we psychiatrists have the devil of a time working out the real cause of the trouble."

"You mean this sort of thing is common?"

"Most of the married patients I see give a history of disturbed sexual functions. I'm downright ashamed of you, Paul. The students call you Old Dermatographia because you're always stroking patients' skins to show their nervous make-up and how it affects their symptoms. Yet here you have a prima facie case on your own hands and you don't even recognize it."

"You mean Elaine?"

"She seems somehow to have escaped the Doctor's Wife syndrome so far, in spite of the fact that less than twenty per cent of women suffering from that trouble report a normal sex life. In this case, I'm talking about you."

Paul flushed with obvious irritation. "Maybe you'd better explain."

"You already know the answer, but you're too stubborn to admit it. Your mother raised you to believe most men mistreat their wives, especially in connection with the sexual function. I don't know whether she told you that in so many words, but she managed to imply it. The act of deserting her was enough mistreatment in her eyes to condemn your father, though I suspect he was justified in leaving her."

"That's a strong statement, Dave. I'm not sure I like it."

"I didn't expect you to. This kind of truth is rarely pleasant."

"What next?"

"You marry Elaine, who's a lively girl and perfectly normal—except that she looks like your mother and reminds you of her. Naturally you love your wife, but when it comes to going to bed with her, your overdeveloped superego keeps getting in the way."

"Why?"

"A lot of things influence that sort of a mechanism. Offhand I'd say the main thing is fear of incest."

"Good God!" The other man's face was a mask of horror.

"There speaks the overzealous conscience. One part of your emotional system has a perfectly normal desire to make love to your wife, Paul, but another part keeps insisting it's too much like making love to your mother. So you get part of the way but can't go the rest—before there's no need and no capability to go any farther."

"But Lorrie?"

"Lorrie was nothing like your mother—or Elaine. In fact, I'd be willing to bet you had wondered more than once what being with her would really be like."

"I wouldn't have admitted it an hour ago," Paul McGill confessed. "But lately that idea had driven me almost nuts."

"I guess all of us had it at one time or another—unless we found out. Most any attractive woman can make a man wonder just that if she wants to. And you can be damn sure they know it, or they wouldn't dress the way they do—to say nothing of advertisements.

"But getting back to your case, Paul. You don't fool the old unconscious mind very long. Down deep inside your mind, you suspected what was holding you back with Elaine, but you needed to be sure and about the only way was to try someone else. You're a pretty moral sort of a guy, like me, though, and you love your wife too much to go philandering. That's why you jumped at the chance to take those samples to Lorrie."

"But—"

"The clinic pharmacy could have delivered them," Dave reminded him. "The truth is you were as ready to be seduced Wednesday afternoon as a Vassar girl on a Yale weekend. But don't tell Elaine that. Let her keep on thinking Lorrie caught you in a moment of weakness."

"You're not going to put any of this on my record, are you?"

"And make you lose the Don Juan reputation?" Dave Rogan grinned. "Just be sure you don't go running after my wife, you lecherous old bastard."

II

As he was leaving the Intensive Care Unit where he had been talking to Paul McGill, Dave Rogan met Jeff Long in the corridor.

"The brain scan on Jerry Monroe was negative for tumor, Dr. Rogan," said the anesthesiologist. "I just came from the radioisotope lab."

"Thank God for that. Is Dr. Dieter going to do the angiogram?"

"It's set up for three o'clock. Before I start the pentothal I thought the kid ought to rest a bit and get some fluids to wash out the radioactive mercury salt they gave him for the scan."

"I'll try to get up to X-ray for the angiogram, but tell them not to wait for me," said Dave. "How's Janet taking it?"

"She'd made her own diagnosis of brain tumor. Now she's so happy it isn't that she hasn't started worrying about the rest."

"We won't mention the other possibilities until we're sure then," said the psychiatrist. "Statistically, the chances with a congenital arterial condition are a lot better than with a brain tumor anyway." He glanced at his watch. "I've just got time to see Mrs. McCloskey before lunch."

A glance at Maggie McCloskey's chart told Dave the psychiatric journal article had precipitated some of the effect he'd been hoping to obtain. At midmorning she'd had an attack of hysteria and the resident on the Psychiatric ward had given her a sedative. When Dave came into the room, he was carrying the medical journal she'd sent out to the desk under his arm.

"What's the trouble?" he said. "Couldn't you take it?"

"None of your business," Maggie said, sullenly.

"Did you read the article?"

"Yes."

"The nurse told me you asked her to take it out of the room. Why?"

"It was like a snake, waiting there to strike me."

He grinned. "The article—or your conscience?"

"Then she told you about that superego crack?"

"Of course. We keep full records on this ward. I didn't know you were *au courant* with Freudian terminology."

"I went to college, you know—even if I did have to leave in the middle of it."

"Is that why you feel yourself inferior mentally to Joe?"

"Inferior? To that clunk?" Maggie lapsed into incoherent rage, and Dave Rogan took time to light his pipe again.

"Why can't I go home?" she demanded after a while.

"You can—if you really want to."

"Do you mean that?"

"Of course. This isn't a closed ward and you haven't been committed."

"I should hope not."

"But if you're worth salvaging, as I think you are, Maggie, you'll stay here for a while."

"So you can go digging into my unconscious mind and see what dirt you can dig up? Didn't you read the article yourself? I've got an Oedipus conflict; I want to go to bed with my father."

"I didn't know your father. How much is Joe like him?"

Her eyes suddenly filled with tears. "Damn you, Dave Rogan! Do you have to know so much about people? It's . . . it's indecent."

"You've got me wrong, Maggie," he said cheerfully. "I'm a run-of-the-mill psychiatrist whose wife has got the Doctor's Wife disease just like you have."

"Why don't you cure her then? If you know so damn much."

"I don't want to cure her. Golf is a lot easier on her psyche—and on me—than alcoholism or drug addiction would be. Or even lower back pain."

"What about Grace Hanscombe? Is she a patient of yours, too?"

"Not of mine—Dr. Feldman's. You know she has diabetes, don't you?"

"It's only a mild case. She doesn't even take insulin."

"Grace isn't a mild case any more. Her blood sugar shot up all at once yesterday. If she hadn't been testing her urine regularly, she might have missed it and gone into coma."

"You can't put diabetes down to the Doctor's Wife syndrome."

"Grace's diabetes was mild and fully under control; it only went haywire yesterday morning."

"And Mort killed Lorrie the afternoon before. I guess that was the shot heard around this little world of ours, wasn't it?"

"It may turn out to have blown a lot of lives apart," said Dave soberly. "I'm praying it will blow a few together, or at least leave the pieces where we can get at them."

"How's Paul?"

"Fine. Dieter is letting him up."

"And Elaine?"

"She's the picture of health—and happiness, too. Even a psychiatrist doesn't always understand women, Maggie. Can you tell me why Elaine would be proud of Paul, even though he was shot making love to another woman?"

"That's simple," Maggie said with a shrug. "Every wife likes to think her husband is attractive to other women; it builds up her ego to know he chose her over them. Elaine has just had proof that Paul isn't the clod he seems to be, and with Lorrie dead, she doesn't have to worry about his trying to do it again."

"If you can be that analytical," Dave said with a grin, "I don't need to be giving you any psychotherapy."

"Then you really think it's safe for me to go home?"

"No."

"Why?"

"There's a part of that article you apparently didn't read—at the end." He opened the journal he was carrying and leafed through its pages until he found what he was seeking. "Listen to this: 'A number of factors should be considered in the therapeutic approach to this type of patient. First, symptomatic relief of depression and the fulfillment of dependency needs inherent in the hospital situation often enable such patients to return rapidly to a high level of social functioning, without necessarily effecting a change in the underlying psychopathology. The patient and her family may then conclude that she is well and ready to return home. Second, the natural desire to maintain a good relationship with the professional colleague may cause the therapist to acquiesce consciously or unconsciously to the patient's neurotic demands, for instance to requests for intensive investigation of physical symptoms.

"'Third, the transference feelings of patients with a high index of hysterical fixation may be complicated and difficult to treat. They carry many of their feelings toward their physician-husband into their relationship with the physician-psychiatrist.

"'Fourth, because of the likelihood that the husband will continue to be absorbed in his professional commitments and can no longer serve as the principal source of gratification for his wife's dependency needs, the patient must be encouraged to establish a separate and personally meaningful role for herself.'"

"Is that what you're trying to do for me?" Maggie asked. "Establish a separate and personally meaningful role?"

"No, Maggie. I want to do exactly what the article says, encourage you to establish a separate and personally meaningful role for yourself. The trouble is, you haven't been willing to let anybody help you—not even Joe."

"But he—"

"I know you've got that 'born across the tracks' complex where Joe's concerned, but you couldn't be more wrong. You were my secretary, remember? I know your intelligence and your capabilities—if you'd only stop running yourself down."

"Why don't you straighten me out without leaving everything to me?" she flared. "You're the psychiatrist. You're supposed to know what makes me tick."

"I've got a pretty good idea, but I don't think you're so far gone that we have to start digging so deeply into your unconscious."

"Not even after what I tried to do?"

"I'm counting on your having sense enough to realize that's no way to treat the mind God gave you," he said bluntly. "Believe me, talking to you like this is a lot better than having to give you electric shock."

He'd fired the shot deliberately, counting on the fact that she had seen some shock being given, when she'd worked as his secretary, to help him appeal to the intelligence he knew she possessed. And when she suddenly paled a little, he knew the missile had found its mark.

"What is it you want me to do?" she asked.

"There's an A.A. meeting scheduled for Saturday night not far from here. I want you to go to it."

"Alcoholics Anonymous!" Her voice rose sharply on a note of near hysteria. "Are you crazy?"

"It's the only thing that's going to help you, Maggie. Once you try suicide, you've stepped over the line. Nobody can tell when you'll follow the same pattern again—and Joe may not be there the next time to bail you out."

The thrust shook her up, as he had intended.

"Do you really want to die?" he demanded, following up the advantage it had given him.

"I want—things back like they were when we all started here," she wailed.

"You can't go back. Nobody can do that. But you can change the future, so it's even better than the past, if you're willing to work and help yourself. The question is, are you ready to admit you've got to have help—or you'll die?"

"You and your damned medical journals," she wailed, and he knew he had won the first skirmish. From here on it was going to be up to her—and to Joe.

CHAPTER TWENTY-TWO

I

Pete Brennan came into the X-ray room a little after three thirty. Little Jerry Monroe lay on the table on his right side, his head still strapped to the flat surface with adhesive in order to hold it still. Jeff Long was sitting beside the child, his finger on the pulse at the temple. On the tray beside him were the syringe and needle with which he had given a small dose of sodium pentothal intravenously to keep Jerry from moving during the injection and the taking of X-rays.

On another table were the syringe and needle with which Anton Dieter had skillfully sent a probing point deep into the tissues of the small neck, searching for the carotid artery pulsing there. Finding it, he had swiftly injected a solution of sodium diatrizoate that had filled the arteries of the brain for a brief period, allowing them to be visualized with the X-rays.

Now the films were coming from the automatic developer. Six of them had been taken in rapid succession following the injection, with the tube exactly thirty-six inches above to capture the pattern of the brain's arteries as the dye coursed through them. A technician took the finished films from the dryer and placed them against the ground-glass fronts of a battery of view boxes fixed to the wall.

"There you are," said Dr. Sam Penfield, the hospital roentgenologist. "A small aneurysm of the anterior communicating artery—as pretty as you please."

There was no doubting the evidence. The pattern of blood channels at the base of the child's brain was outlined by the opaque dye and the X-ray as clearly as if drawn there in an anatomical diagram, the arteries white against the darker background, where the rays had gone through the soft tissues of the brain without being impeded, photographing themselves upon the sensitive chemicals of the film. Where the dye had filled the vessels, the rays had been held back by the metallic salt that was its main constituent, forming a sharply contrasting pattern of white against the dark background.

Pete Brennan moved close to the bank of viewers, studying each of the films carefully. Anton Dieter had made the injection, but the condition it revealed was now within Pete's own field of neurosurgery, a tiny sac connected to a blood vessel lying at the base of the brain where branches of the carotid artery formed a pattern called the Circle of Willis.

Suddenly he gave an exclamation of surprise and looked closely at the fourth in the series of films, the one showing the aneurysmal sac at its greatest degree of filling by the injected dye.

"Take a look here, Sam," he said to the roentgenologist. "Isn't that a leak of dye through the wall of the aneurysm?"

Penfield came closer with Anton Dieter at his elbow and examined the film a moment. Calling for one of the technicians to bring him a magnifying glass, he studied the part of the film in question once again, then stepped back and handed the magnifier to Pete Brennan.

With the area enlarged several times, it was obvious that some of the dye had indeed leaked out from the sac, proof of a rupture which at any moment might become a massive hemorrhage. Handing the glass to Anton Dieter, Pete went into the other room, where Jeff Long was watching Jerry, who lay on the table sleeping.

"Any sign of convulsive movements, Jeff?" he asked.

"No, sir. What's the trouble, Dr. Brennan?"

"We can see a small aneurysm on the anterior communicating artery, but there's a slight leak into the surrounding tissues. We can detect the shadow of the dye outside the aneurysmal sac."

"That must be where the original hemorrhage occurred. Doesn't leave you much choice, does it?"

"We'll have to go in," Pete agreed. "What sort of shape is he in?"

"Fine, sir. I put him pretty well out with a sodium luminal injection before he left the room so it took very little pentothal for the angiogram— just enough to keep him from squirming at the needle prick."

"I'm going to use a stereotactic approach so it will take several hours to get ready," said Pete. "Will your basal anesthesia hold out that long?"

"I'm sure it will."

"Good; then you might as well take him back to the room now. Dr. Dieter and I will have a talk with his mother."

Anton Dieter was still studying the X-rays when Pete came back into the viewing room. "It sure looks to me like a good case for the injection of iron sludge," said the neurosurgeon. "Do you agree?"

"Perfectly."

"I would appreciate your working with me, Anton, if you have the time."

"For this, I would make the time," said Dieter promptly.

"I'm going to try a stereotactic approach through a burr hole, so we'll need a lot of films," Pete told the roentgenologist. "Do you think there's a chance of overradiation?"

"Not of the skull area," said Penfield. "We'll put a lead shield over the lower half of his body while he's on the operating table, to protect the reproductive organs." More and more, careful X-ray specialists were using such protection for young boys, lest they accidentally be made sterile by X-rays while the other parts of the body were being studied.

Janet Monroe had been sitting in the waiting room of the X-ray department; she was in uniform, ready to go on duty. "Your son's doing fine," Pete Brennan told her when a technician brought her into the viewing room. "Jeff Long is taking him back to the room."

"Then it's nothing—" Janet stopped. "Excuse me, please, Dr. Brennan. I guess I'm pretty jittery."

"Something would be wrong with you, if you weren't," he assured her. "We've located the trouble. It's just what we thought."

"Not a tumor?" she asked quickly.

"No. There's a small aneurysm of one of the arteries beneath the brain. Come closer and you can see it here." He took a pointer and indicated on an X-ray film the location of the trouble.

"It—it's very distinct, isn't it?"

"That makes our job a lot easier," Pete assured her.

"You'll have to operate, won't you?" Janet was too good a nurse not to know the significance of the aneurysm.

"Yes."

"When?"

"This afternoon."

"But why the hurry?"

"Ordinarily we might be able to wait a few days," Pete explained. "But there's a complication. When Dr. Harrison found blood in Jerry's spinal fluid yesterday, we knew something had been leaking. Obviously, in the light of these X-rays, it was the aneurysm."

"But it stopped."

"Only for a little while. These films show that it's leaking again, which is what we would expect. About half the cases of hemorrhage from an aneurysm inside the skull have another episode of bleeding within six months. Half of these occur within ten days."

He didn't tell her that with those who rebled, the mortality was often as high as 75 per cent, knowing how that information would make him feel if Michael or Terry was involved.

"A year ago the outlook for your son would have been very grave," he continued. "Fortunately a new procedure was described recently by some West Coast surgeons. The risk with their operation is much less than with the old way of going in and tying off the vessel the aneurysm is connected to."

"A new operation?"

"For us, yes. But those who have used it report excellent results. Dr. Dieter and I have been waiting for a suitable case. Jerry seems to fulfill all the requirements."

"What—what is this new procedure like?" Janet asked.

"It's amazingly simple. A small amount of what is called a sludge containing very fine iron filings is injected into the aneurysm itself and held there by means of a small magnet until a clot can form and obliterate the sac."

"But how can you locate something so small deep inside the brain?"

"That problem was solved a number of years ago by what we now call the stereotactic technique," he explained. "By taking measurements on X-ray films shot from several angles, we can calculate just how deep the aneurysm lies and the exact angles the magnetic probe must take to reach it. Then, using the stereotactic frame, we need only make a small opening to insert the magnet and inject the sludge."

He didn't amplify the description of the operation further. There was no point in worrying her with the knowledge that placing the magnetic probe—upon which the whole success of the procedure depended—exactly so it would touch the wall of the aneurysm involved an extremely delicate technique in so small a patient.

"When will you operate?" Janet asked.

"It will take a couple of hours to get the stereotactic setup ready in the O.R." Pete Brennan glanced at his watch and saw that it was already past four o'clock. "If we all have an early dinner, we should get started around six thirty."

II

Amy had attended a luncheon meeting of the Symphony Guild after leaving the cemetery following Lorrie's funeral. There'd been an executive committee meeting afterward and she hadn't gotten home until after five.

All through the afternoon, she'd been conscious of a nagging feeling of unease whose cause she refused to admit to herself. As she came up the steps to the portico of the majestic house, with its tall fluted columns located on the knoll overlooking the river, she was debating in her mind whether or not to ask Pete about the thing that was troubling her.

"Dr. Brennan just phoned, ma'm." The maid had come from the kitchen when she heard the front door opening. "He said he's got to operate on Mrs. Monroe's child around seven o'clock so he'll be late getting home."

"I'll have dinner alone, then, Ethel." Being the wife of a neurosurgeon, Amy had long since learned that such operations could frequently run to five and even eight hours. "Dr. Brennan will probably get a sandwich on the way home, if he's very late. Or I can fix him one."

"Yes'm. You want your dinner now?"

"Might as well."

Amy barely touched the food. The feeling of uneasiness she'd had almost all day was still with her, like a lump in her throat she couldn't swallow. When she finished, she went up to the bedroom she shared with Pete and, picking up the telephone, dialed the number she'd been trying to decide to call all afternoon.

"Uncle Jake?" she asked when the old man's voice sounded in her ear. "Are you all right?"

"Sure, Amy. What's the trouble?"

"Pete has an emergency operation, so I thought I'd see whether you needed anything."

"The children are here; they're all I need. You troubled about something, Amy?"

"No. Y-yes."

"What's bothering you, girl?"

"The passage of Scripture the minister read this morning—about the woman taken in adultery. You asked him to read it, didn't you?"

"Yes." The old man chuckled. "He balked a little at first. But he knows I'm the biggest contributor in the diocese, so he finally gave in."

"Why did you do it, Uncle Jake?"

"I thought some people around here needed reminding about the virtues of forgiveness and tolerance—one person in particular."

"Was . . . am I the one?"

"Yes, Amy."

"Something you said this morning made me think I was."

"If you thought in your heart that it applied to you, then it must have," the old man said.

"But why, Uncle Jake?"

"Like I told you this morning, Amy, I'm very fond of you and that husband of yours. But a woman never was meant to be the boss of any household; that's a man's job. Whenever somebody takes it from him there's bound to be trouble."

"What do you know that I don't know, Uncle Jake?"

"Nothing—but if I had a wife that seemed hell-bent on being a bigger man than me, I'd either tan her behind or leave her. You've got a fine man, Amy; all the man any woman could want. Don't run him away. Good night."

She felt the first throb of pain in her temple as the receiver clicked in her ear and knew the tension which had been building up inside her all day was finally ready to explode into the agony of migraine. Hurrying to her dresser, she opened the drawer and searched beneath the lining paper for her small cache of morphine syrettes. Finding one, she unsheathed the tiny needle, swabbed off the skin of her arm with alcohol, and thrust the point through the skin, pushing it into the tissues beneath where the injection would be absorbed quickly. Squeezing the small tube, she rolled it up carefully until it was empty and the last precious drop of the narcotic solution had been injected.

As it had done two nights ago, the warm sense of relaxation began to spread through her body at once, fanning out from the tiny needle prick in an ever widening circle. She didn't yield immediately to the languor of sleep, however, wanting her body to be fresh and sweet with the perfume Pete liked when he came home. Taking a quick shower, she dried her skin, powdered her body and dabbed the perfume here and there. Then, putting on the nightgown she'd bought before leaving the District Six meeting place—could it only be two days ago?—she stretched out on the bed with a magazine to wait for him.

Her eyes soon began to droop, however. After a while, the magazine dropped from her fingers as she drifted off to sleep.

III

Roy Weston was about ready to call it a day at five thirty on Friday afternoon, when the telephone rang in the outer office.

"The jailor says Dr. Dellman wants to see you," his secretary called to him through the open door.

"Tell him I've already left for the day."

He saw her speak into the telephone; then she turned to call through the door again: "They say upstairs he's pretty insistent. Claims he's going to demand a habeas corpus or something."

"All right, I'll see him. Tell the turnkey to have him brought to the interview room."

The snotty bastard! Roy thought as he rode up in the special elevator from his office in the courthouse to the jail above. It was bad enough for Mort Dellman to torpedo any chance he might have of running for state attorney general; now he had to go throwing his weight around, just because he knew he had the screws on a lot of people who were close to Roy himself.

The more he thought of Lorrie, vital, warm, fun-loving—and his first love long ago—lying in that coffin under six feet of earth, the more Roy relished the idea of prosecuting Mort Dellman for shooting her—and the devil take the consequences. When the biochemist was ushered into one of the small offices around the central interview room shortly after Roy arrived, the attorney was ready to chew him out. Mort, however, looked cocky and Roy felt his hackles rise even higher at his manner.

"All right," he said shortly. "What is it?"

"I want out of this place."

"You're a prisoner. It's not for you to say when you can come and go."

"It will be—unless you take action to get me out of here."

"What kind of action?"

"You can bring me before the grand jury whenever you want to, Roy—I want it to be now. Your damned jail isn't exactly the Waldorf, you know."

"I'll take it under advisement."

"You'll damned well be advised to get at it now," said the biochemist. "The law says you can't hold me without some sort of charge—and that means a hearing."

"All right," said Roy. "Tomorrow's Saturday and Monday's Labor Day. I'll arrange for you to be brought before the grand jury on Tuesday."

"No go. I want the hearing tomorrow."

"On Saturday?"

"I don't give a damn whether it's Saturday or not. Either you order the hearing or I'll institute habeas corpus proceedings."

"Since when have you been reading law?"

"I know my rights." Mort Dellman grinned wolfishly. "You ought to know that from the way I foxed you on that confession."

"Suppose I don't buy your request?"

"Like I said, it will be habeas corpus. And you can bet I'll reveal some facts that will make newspaper headlines over the weekend."

Roy was tempted to let Mort Dellman do just what he'd threatened and start talking, on the chance that when he talked in court, the prisoner would admit that he'd gone to the house on Wednesday afternoon planning to shoot Lorrie and the medical student, thus hanging a noose around his neck. But he put the thought away, tempting though it was.

It was true that Roy's own chances of going on with the campaign against Abner Townsend next year for the attorney general post in the state seemed hardly worth anything now. But if Mort accused him in court of prejudice because of that puppy-love affair with Lorrie years ago, the newspapers would blow it up into a *cause célèbre*. Then any small chance he might still have of going to the state capitol in the future would have been destroyed.

"All right, Mort," he said. "I'll call the grand jury together tomorrow."

"What time?"

"Elmer Hill's the foreman, but he's out of town and won't be back until tomorrow afternoon. I'll have the rest of the panel called for seven o'clock tomorrow evening; Elmer ought to be here by then."

"That will have to do, if you can't make it any earlier. Will Paul McGill be able to testify?"

"I wouldn't think so; he was only operated on forty-eight hours ago. Why?"

"I want a deposition from him stating clearly what he was doing at my house that afternoon with my wife. Will you have it taken, or shall I get my lawyer to do it?"

"Who is your lawyer, by the way?"

"I haven't fully decided yet but I can get one in a hurry if I need him."

"I'll take Paul's deposition in the morning," Roy promised. He didn't think the dermatologist would be able to give any testimony that would be damaging to Mort Dellman's case but if there were any such possibility, he could take advantage of it by taking the deposition himself and asking the questions. "Anybody else you want called?"

"No. Once Paul admits what he was doing with Lorrie, that should be all the evidence I need. Just be damned sure you ask him the right questions."

"I'm as interested in justice as you are," Roy said shortly. "If the jury can't meet tomorrow evening for any reason I'll notify you."

"You'd better damn well see that they do meet," Mort Dellman told him. "See you at the trial, Roy."

Watching the prisoner leave the office, Roy decided he'd much rather see Mort Dellman in hell. But the way things were going, that possibility seemed remote indeed.

IV

The chief nurse of the hospital had found someone to relieve Janet Monroe for the three-to-eleven shift and Janet was sitting beside Jerry's crib on the Pediatrics ward when Jeff Long came down with the stretcher about twenty minutes to six to take him up to the operating suite. The child had been sleeping quietly since he'd been brought back from the X-ray department after the angiograms had been taken.

Jeff gave Janet a keen look, noting the droop of her shoulders beneath the white uniform, the drawn lines about her mouth, and the redness of her eyes from weeping. "Don't take this so hard," he told her. "It could be a lot worse, you know."

"I don't see how."

"There's only been a small leak of blood this second time. It could have been a massive hemorrhage that would have made using the new operation impossible."

She put out her hand to touch his arm with an instinctive, pleading gesture that tore at his heart. "Tell me the truth, Jeff. What chance does Jerry have?"

"Every chance in the world; that's the beauty of the iron sludge technique. Dr. Brennan described it at a staff meeting right after he first saw it used in California. Believe me, the results are miraculous."

"I could see the aneurysm in the X-ray," she said, still doubtful. "But finding something that small inside the skull must be like looking for a needle in a haystack."

"You're wrong, darling." The orderly had lifted Jerry to the stretcher and was waiting for Jeff outside the door. "With the aneurysm demonstrated so well in the films, Dr. Brennan can tell exactly where to place the stereotactic frame. With that to guide him, placing the probe is only a matter of determining two mathematically exact angles. Where they intersect is the path the probe will take."

"I . . . I guess I'm too worried to comprehend," she admitted.

"Of course you are. Tomorrow, when it's all over and Jerry is fine, I'll take you up to the O.R. and get out the stereotactic frame so you can see exactly how it's done. Now cheer up and don't start worrying if we're up there a long time. This sort of thing takes a lot of measuring and figuring to get the exact angles. Most of the time Jerry won't even be under anesthesia at all, but I'll be right there with him every minute."

"What have I ever done to deserve somebody like you?" she said impulsively and Jeff Long grinned.

"You're yourself, and you're Jerry's mother. We three are going to have a lot of fun together when this is all over."

V

More than an hour had passed since Jeff Long had given Jerry Monroe a light preliminary anesthesia and passed a tube into his trachea through which the anesthetic had been given during the first stage of the operation. The stereotactic frame, a circular ring of metal, so calibrated that measurements could be read off it in millimeters, had been placed on the small shaven head and locked into place exactly by means of adjustments fixing it to the ear openings, the orbital rims above the eyes and the hard palate inside the mouth. With the frame thus fixed, two basic planes from which to measure and construct angles had been set up: the horizontal one running from the upper eye-socket rims through the ear openings, and the vertical perpendicular to it at a point exactly dividing the between-ears distance and thus at the exact center of the skull.

Using extensions attached to the basic ring of the frame, Pete Brennan had located exactly a point at the back of the skull. There he had made a small incision, barely an inch long, and through it had drilled a small opening into the skull with a burr-shaped trephine. Introduced through this opening, a slender, flexible tube, smaller in diameter than a grain of rice, had been pushed easily through the brain tissue into one of the cavities of the brain—the ventricles, as they were called in medical terminology.

A small amount of a chemical like the one used to visualize the arteries and the aneurysm in the X-ray had then been introduced into the brain cavity through the small tube and, by moving the patient's head, allowed to flow forward into the front portion of the third of the four brain ventricles. It was visible now on the X-rays taken immediately afterward as a blob of white opacity, establishing the location of what was called the anterior commissure, the main point of departure as far as the brain itself was concerned for calculating the distance and the angles necessary to reach the aneurysm that was threatening little Jerry's life.

"That angle should do it," Pete Brennan announced with satisfaction as he looked up from the table at one side of the X-ray room, where he and Anton Dieter had been making calculations and measurements on the films taken of the anterior commissure with the metal stereotactic ring in place. "I take it that we are all in agreement concerning the angles and the distance?"

Dr. Sam Penfield, the radiologist, had also been watching the measurements and calculations being made from the X-ray films. When he nodded agreement, Pete Brennan said, "Shall we get to work, Anton?"

Jeff Long looked up quickly when the surgeons came back into the operating theater, which they had left at the end of the first stage of the surgical procedure in order to study the X-rays. "We've got it all worked out as neat as a pin—I hope," Pete Brennan said in answer to the younger doctor's unspoken question. "Is he all right?"

"Fine," said Jeff. "The basal is holding him nicely."

"I'll make the second incision under local then," said the neurosurgeon. "It's better to have him as near conscious as possible, so we can detect any untoward effects as the probe goes through the brain tissue."

Concentrating on the delicate task of making the final angle adjustments and locking in place the metal sleeve through which the magnetic probe would be inserted, Pete Brennan felt all of the troublesome details that had taken so much of his time since he'd reached the marina dock two afternoons before and heard the shocking news of Lorrie Dellman's death, fade into the background. His entire world at the moment had shrunken to only the brightly lit operating room, the table, and the drapings, beneath which Jerry Monroe's little body was completely hidden now except for the shiny metal ring of the stereotactic frame, its several attachments, and a small circle of bare scalp beneath it, painted a brilliant scarlet with the antiseptic used in preparing the operative field.

The years of education and technical training which had prepared him for his profession, and the minutely exact measurements of angles and distances he had just finished making from the preliminary X-ray studies—all of these were as much instruments of use as the metallic bridge he now attached to the circular frame and the calibrations upon the smaller attachment affixed to it, by which the predetermined angle of entry was exactly reproduced.

Using a blunt probe exactly similar to the grooved magnet which would be inserted later, he located on the small patient's scalp the spot where the second burr-opening would be made through the skull to expose the brain beneath. A small wheal of novocaine at that point removed any possibility of causing pain, since both the bone and the brain beneath were quite impervious to it. The small scalp incision was carried down to the bony outer layer of the skull and a burr-shaped trephine quickly made the opening through it. Then, using a sharp-pointed scalpel, Pete nicked the outermost of the meningeal layers covering the brain, allowing the vital tissue of the very heart of the nervous system to be visualized in the depths of the small skull opening.

For the blunt probe he had used to locate the skin and skull incisions, Pete now substituted the magnetic probe, with a slot down its side through which the needle for injecting the iron preparation would be passed, once the instrument was in place and its position verified by X-ray. As Dr. Sam Penfield read off the angle settings for the slender permanent magnet, Pete Brennan once again checked the angulation of the sleeve through which the magnet would be inserted. When the two sets of figures agreed exactly, he began to push the probe gently into the brain tissues.

"Watch him closely, Jeff," Pete told the anesthesiologist. "If there's any change tell me right away."

The warning of encroachment upon some vital center of the brain might come in a dozen ways—a sudden change in the pupil of one of the eyes, a slight convulsive movement, alteration in the vital functions of respiration or pulse.

No change occurred, however, as the probe was pushed ever deeper into the brain tissue. Only a short portion of the metal shaft remained outside the skull, when the surgeon reached the mark he'd nicked on the outer surface of the magnet with a file, indicating that it had penetrated to the exact distance the earlier measurements had predicted mathematically would be necessary to reach the small aneurysm located at the base of the brain itself.

"It's in place, Sam," Pete Brennan told the roentgenologist, and the waiting X-ray technicians quickly took films in two planes, the vertical or anteroposterior—known in hospital jargon as A-P—and the lateral, directly from the side. Developed rapidly, they were returned to the operating room and the view boxes on the wall, where the surgeons studied them with the roentgenologist.

"That small leak we noted in the angiogram is right at the end of the probe." Everyone in the operating room could feel the pride and pleasure in

Pete Brennan's voice. "I'd say the probe's against the wall, wouldn't you, Sam?"

"Right on the nose," Dr. Penfield agreed. "You had your sights on it all the time, Pete."

Since the probe had been introduced through a fixed metal sleeve whose angle was locked into place on the stereotactic frame, the task of inserting a slender needle along the groove in its side without disturbing the magnet was simple. Holding the needle—without a syringe attached—between his right thumb and forefinger and steadying the probe with his left hand, Pete Brennan slid the needle slowly along the groove in the probe. He had previously marked off on the shaft of the needle the length of the magnet, so he could tell when the point, probing deep within the brain, had reached the aneurysm.

When the tiny file mark on the shaft of the needle was opposite the outer end of the probe, indicating that the point was now just touching the wall of the aneurysm, he paused a moment. When he began to push a little farther, perhaps it was only his imagination that made him feel an increased resistance to the needle point as it pressed against the wall of the aneurysm sac. In any event, he was sure he felt a faint snap or click inside the brain, tangible if not audible, as the aneurysm wall was penetrated.

A deep indrawn sigh went up from the tensely watching spectators when a tiny stream of blood suddenly spurted from the open end of the needle. Pulsing with the heartbeat in an arc of crimson to spatter upon the green draperies, it told them they had hit their target deep inside the brain.

"*Ach Himmel!*" Anton Dieter's explosive grunt of elation punctuated the scene.

"Ditto!" Pete Brennan grinned. "The sludge, please."

The scrub nurse had been waiting with a small amount of the viscous iron mixture in a syringe. She handed it to him now and, shifting the fingers of his left hand to the shank of the needle, he attached the syringe to it carefully, stopping the arching pulse of blood. When he drew back gently on the plunger of the syringe, a drop of red spurted into the syringe, telling him the point was still inside the aneurysm, and he began to inject slowly, forcing the somewhat resistant iron mixture down through the needle and into the aneurysm sac. He continued the injection until the entire amount he had calculated would be necessary to fill the sac by measuring its diameter on the X-ray films of the angiogram Anton Dieter had taken earlier that afternoon was injected. Then steadying both needle and probe, he stood back so the X-ray technicians could snap confirming films.

While the latter were being developed, the tiny skin wound was closed around the probe with several silk sutures to prevent the entrance of infection over the several days it would be left in place. During that time, if all went well, the powerful magnetic field around the end of the probe would hold the iron particles fixed inside the aneurysm and promote the formation of a tough metallic clot. This in turn would gradually be replaced by fibrous tissue growing in from the aneurysm wall, thus closing it forever.

The final films showed a small blob of sharply outlined metallic particles exactly where the aneurysm had been, the effect for which they had been striving. Pete Brennan felt a surge of satisfaction as he carefully placed a small doughnut of cotton and gauze over the projecting outer end of the probe to keep it from being jarred out of place, then covered that with a voluminous dressing to further protect the vital magnet. When the draperies that had hidden the anesthesiologist were removed, Jeff Long looked up and grinned.

"Not a quiver, Dr. Brennan," he reported. "You were right on target all the way."

From the watchers in the gallery, there came a sudden spatter of applause, audible even through the thick glass of the observation window.

VI

Marisa Feldman had been half-expecting a call from Anton Dieter that evening. When it didn't come by eight o'clock, she decided to take a shower and get into bed to look at television. She was just stepping out of the shower when the telephone rang. Wrapping a towel about herself, she went into the bedroom and picked up the phone.

"Marisa?" She recognized his voice at once and was startled by the sudden feeling of warmth it engendered within her.

"Yes—Anton."

"I tried to call you earlier, around six."

"I was with Mrs. Hanscombe, working out her diet and insulin dosages. She plans to leave for England on Monday."

"I went into the operating room a little before seven," he explained. "Dr. Brennan wanted me to work with him on the Monroe child."

"Did the operation go all right?"

"Perfectly. I'll tell you all about it, if you will have a drink with me."

"Now?"

"There's a cocktail lounge in the next block, a nice quiet place."

"But I just stepped out of the shower."

He chuckled. "In that case, I'd better come up there."

"No." She found that she was laughing, a pleasant feeling she didn't remember experiencing for a long time. "I'll dress quickly. Will slacks and a blouse do?"

"With you in them, they'll be sensational. I'll meet you at the front of the Faculty Apartments in fifteen minutes."

Marisa's excitement mounted steadily as she dressed. She was almost like a schoolgirl, she thought, on her first date. When she came down the steps at the front of the Faculty Apartments, wearing silver slacks, a loose white silk blouse, and with her dark hair tied with a silver ribbon, Anton Dieter gave a low whistle of appreciation.

"Would you like to walk awhile?" he asked as he took her arm.

"I'd love it."

The night was warm and the stoops of the houses along the street were alive with people. The older among them were just talking or sitting quietly, enjoying the evening, while here and there in the shadows, the younger could be seen in close embrace.

"You'll love this town when you've had a chance to get accustomed to it," he assured her. "This area around the hospital houses a lot of people who work in the rug mill. Some of their forebears came here from New England, when the mills moved a long time ago."

"Parts of Boston are like this, especially such older neighborhoods as Cambridge," she said. "I love it already."

They soon reached the cocktail lounge he had spoken of. Instead of going in, however, Anton Dieter said, "There's a little park about a block away overlooking the river. Would you just as soon sit there for a while? We can have the nightcap later."

"I'd much rather stay outside."

At the end of the street they came to a small park with benches scattered among the trees. It occupied a slight elevation overlooking the river that wound its course around much of Weston's outskirts before widening out markedly downstream nearer the dam. One of the benches in the shadows at the far end of the park next to the riverbank was vacant and Anton Dieter guided her to it.

"When I first came to Weston I used to walk down here at night and sit by the river, thinking how lucky I was to be here," he said. "Now that you've come, I'm sure I have even more reason to feel lucky."

Things were moving a bit fast for Marisa. To gain time, she asked, "How did you happen to come to Weston—after New York?"

"The main attraction was the offer they made of my own research institute in experimental surgery, with no politically appointed board to tell me what I can do and not do. After my years at the Institute of Experimental Medicine in Russia, this sort of setup looked like paradise."

"Has it proved to be?"

"That and more. If I were in private practice, I would have to devote at least a third of my time to the business side of medicine, cultivating good will among other doctors, so they would send me patients—and sending patients to them. Here at Weston, the medical school pays my salary—with help from the Porter Foundation—and finances my experimental laboratory. I hold operative clinics for the students and make teaching ward rounds, all of which I love. But the major part of my time is spent in experimental studies, without having to worry about whether or not they will ever bring in a cent of income."

"You promised to tell me about the aneurysm operation," she reminded him.

"Are you familiar with the case?"

"Yes. I didn't see the X-rays though."

"They showed a definite aneurysm at the base of the brain. We decided to use that iron sludge technique."

"The one that was described in a news magazine some time ago—I think it was *Newsweek?*"

"Very much like it. Pete Brennan is a very fine neurosurgeon and has added some touches of his own. He knows of my interest in these blood vessel disturbances, so he asked me to scrub with him."

"It must have been exciting."

"The most exciting thing is the possible future applications of this process. Take apoplexy, for example; the one thing a stroke patient dreads more than anything else is a repetition of what happened to him the first time. With this technique, it may eventually be possible to close off the section of vessel that ruptures in a stroke and prevent a second hemorrhage. Besides, if we can prevent the slow leak from a ruptured artery that continues in so many stroke cases, we can prevent extensive brain damage and give the injured parts a chance to heal."

"Listening to you makes internal medicine seem pretty humdrum."

"Don't you believe it," Dieter laughed. "I had an ulcer while I was planning to escape from East Germany. It almost perforated before I could get out of there."

"How did you manage it—the escape."

"The Russians thought they were doing me a favor by making me a surgical fellow at the Institute of Experimental Medicine—and they did. Some of the most advanced vascular work in the world has been done there, but I didn't like the idea of spending my life working with a political commissar looking over my shoulder. So, when they let me attend a medical meeting in Yugoslavia, I sneaked over the Italian border. How about you?"

"They kept me in prison in East Germany for two years." She couldn't keep the pain of the memory out of her voice and, sensitive to her every mood, he said quickly, "Don't speak of it if it causes you pain. I saw some of those prisons and I know what they are like."

"Talking about it always disturbed me before," she admitted. "But strangely enough, it doesn't seem to bother me with you."

"That is the nicest thing you could have said to me, *Liebchen.*"

They had been sitting close together on the park bench, drawn by the sense of comradeship that had developed between them. When he felt her suddenly stiffen and draw away, he said quickly, "Forgive me if I am presumptive."

"It's just that my father used to call me *Liebchen,*" she explained, and he saw that her eyes were troubled and afraid.

"There's something you should know about me, Anton—if we're to be friends."

"I hope we will be more than that. But don't speak of it unless you're sure you want to tell it."

"I do. It wouldn't be fair to you not to."

He listened in silence while she told the story of her stay in prison, the months when she'd spent two nights a week in Colonel Geitz's quarters, so her father wouldn't be tortured with the pain of angina. And particularly the way she had been able to endure it all by shutting away all feeling from the most intimate parts of her body.

"How can you be sure this anesthesia you speak of will persist?" he asked, when she had finished the account.

"There was an instructor at Harvard; I was fond of him."

"He made love to you?"

"You could hardly call it that. I felt nothing—just as it was with Colonel Geitz."

"And you think that means it will always be the same?"

"I'm trying to tell you I'm not really a woman at all, Anton." It was a cry of pain—and desperation. "The woman in me was killed in the prison at Frondheim."

"I refuse to believe that, *Lieb—*"

"Please don't call me that."

"Surely you know how I feel," he said gently. "How I've felt since I first saw you that afternoon in the emergency room."

"But it cannot be." She was close to tears. "Don't you understand? You're fine and decent and honorable. How could I ever love you as you deserve to be loved, when my body would feel nothing?"

When he put his arm about her, she stiffened instinctively against the contact, then leaned wearily against his shoulder, drawing solace from his strength.

"You are wrong about many things, Marisa. First about your lack of response."

"But—"

"I heard it in your voice when I called you tonight. And I can feel it in your body now."

Remembering the warmth that had flooded her when she'd recognized his voice over the phone earlier that evening, Marisa dared to hope he was right. But she was afraid to let herself believe it, lest the old sense of disappointment and frustration seize her again.

"At Frondheim you initiated a conditioned reflex," he explained. "The Institute of Experimental Medicine, where I studied, was once headed by Pavlov, and much of his work was done there. Pavlov first conditioned a dog to produce saliva by ringing a bell and giving it food immediately afterward. Later, he found that saliva would flow when only the bell was rung, even though food was not given."

"I know about those experiments. That really may be the mechanism in my case, but—"

"What you have forgotten is that Pavlov was also able to decondition the same reflexes he created."

"But how can an entire organ system of my body be taught to live again, when it hasn't responded for almost four years?"

"The response began tonight, *Liebchen*—and you didn't have to teach it," he reminded her. "You tell me you taught yourself to shut off all nerve impulses that would naturally respond to the touch of a man. Yet I am touching you now."

He turned her face up to him and kissed her gently. In spite of wanting desperately not to resist, Marisa felt her lips close tightly. But when he started to draw away, she suddenly put her arms about his neck and pressed her mouth against his, holding it there until she felt the tension of the muscles relax and her lips soften and yield beneath his, as she responded to his kiss.

"So!" He was a little breathless—as was she—when finally they drew apart; and she could feel his heart beating rapidly against her breast. "We have begun successfully with what the anatomy book calls the *musculus orbicularis oris*. Already, *Liebchen*, the deconditioning has started."

When she found herself laughing as she settled once more into his embrace, Marisa could at last dare to hope her cure had indeed begun.

CHAPTER TWENTY-THREE

I

It was after nine o'clock before Pete Brennan finished talking to Janet Monroe about the operation. Figuring that Amy would have had her dinner before Ethel left, he stopped at the Snack Bar for a quick hamburger and a cup of coffee, but it was still not ten when he let himself into the house.

Downstairs was dark, but he could see a spill of light from their bedroom at the top of the stairs and decided that Amy must be reading there or looking at TV on the bedroom set. Moving quietly, in case she had fallen asleep, he climbed the stairs and came into the bedroom.

The bedlamp was still burning and the magazine Amy had been reading when the narcotic had taken full hold was lying beside her. She looked young, defenseless and very lovely, lying there in the filmy nightgown that allowed the flesh tints of her skin to show through. Her cheeks were somewhat flushed from the effects of the drug and her breathing was slow and even. Nor did she respond when he touched her bare shoulder gently.

Puzzled by her failure to awaken, he did what any other doctor would have done automatically; placing his hand on her forehead, he lifted her left eyelid with his thumb, and what he saw there sent a shock wave of alarm through his senses.

The pupil of Amy's left eye was almost pinpoint in size, nor did it contract with the light as it should normally have done, although he lowered the lid and raised it again twice so the light could strike the eye. The right eye was the same and a sense of horror and apprehension began to grip him as he fumbled for her pulse. It was slow and steady, with a rate of eighty, which was normal, but her respirations, when he counted them with the sweephand of his wrist watch, were only fourteen to the minute.

Almost dreading what he would find, Pete went to the closet and opened the small medicine case he kept there for emergency calls. Only two of the dozen morphine syrettes he usually carried remained and he racked his memory, trying to recall the last time he'd used the case, or had examined it. When he did remember, he closed the case and put it back on the shelf. There'd been twelve of the syrettes in the case when he'd last opened it—of that he was sure. Now there were two.

Amy showed no sign of wakening while he searched the room. Nor did it take him long to find what he was seeking, for in her haste she'd neglected to hide the evidence of what was causing the stupor in which he'd found her. At the bottom of the wastebasket under a pile of tissues, he discovered the small flattened-out syrette tube, with the needle attached. Just how long she'd been taking morphine, he had no way of knowing. Only Amy could tell him that and she was still sleeping under the influence of the powerful opiate.

His steps dragging, Pete left the bedroom and went downstairs to the kitchen. He dialed George Hanscombe's home telephone number and when there was no answer, tried to calm his racing thoughts long enough to figure out where George might be. Other than his work, his home and the club, the internist had no interests Pete could think of. He wouldn't be at work this late at night, for the clinic was always covered by one of the younger staff men as night duty officer. And he wasn't at home—so only the club was left as a likely choice.

"Dr. Hanscombe's in the bar, Dr. Brennan," the attendant who answered the telephone said. "Shall I get him for you?"

"Please."

George came on the phone a few moments later.

"Since when have you hung around the club at night?" Pete asked.

"Grace is leaving for England Monday, Pete. I'm accustoming myself to being alone—by getting soused."

"She'll be coming back."

"I wouldn't count on it and I'm not even sure it's the best thing for her. I guess I've been getting on her nerves; the diabetes almost slipped up on us yesterday."

"I'm sorry, George. With the troubles you've got, I don't feel like saddling you with mine."

"What's wrong?"

"Amy's having one of her migraine attacks. I know you've treated her for it and I was wondering what you were giving her."

"I haven't seen Amy for migraine in quite a while," said the internist. "Thought she'd stopped having the attacks. Did this business about Mort Dellman upset her?"

"Could be."

"I was giving her an injection of ergotamine tartrate to reduce the spasm of the internal carotid artery and Demerol to relieve the pain. I can call the hospital and have the night nurse in the emergency room fix up the injection for you."

"Don't bother," Pete told him. "I've got some quarter-grain morphine syrettes in my case—"

"I wouldn't do that." The other doctor's voice was suddenly crisp.

"Not in this one instance?"

"Migraines are recurrent affairs, Pete. A strong neurotic element often triggers the attacks, if it doesn't actually cause them. Morphine's bad for it, especially in doctors' wives."

"Why them?"

"There's an article on the troubles doctors' wives have in the *American Journal of Psychiatry*. I wouldn't have seen it myself, if Dave Rogan hadn't called my attention to it."

"I always thought the Doctor's Wife disease was a joke."

"Being a neurosurgeon, you wouldn't see many cases, except maybe the disklike syndromes of lower back and neck pain," said George Hanscombe. "But believe me, it's no joke. A lot of women who develop it wind up eventually with narcotic addiction. And they usually get started with morphine from the husband's medical bag."

Pete stared mutely at the phone, until George Hanscombe's voice in his ear caught his attention again. "You there, Pete?"

"Yes."

"I thought we were disconnected for a moment."

"Thanks, George. I'll give Amy some aspirin and codeine. If that doesn't relieve it, I'll call the emergency room and have them fix a hypo of ergotamine tartrate. We're close to the hospital so I can easily run over and get it."

"If Amy's having that much trouble, I ought to see her again," said the internist. "I hadn't felt she needed to be kept on preventive medication because her attacks were infrequent. It could be that the situation has changed now."

"Is there a preventive medication?"

"A new drug called methysergide maleate seems to work very well in preventing migraine attacks. But it's still closely connected with emotional tension, so maybe Dave Rogan ought to see her, too."

"I'll talk to her about it. Thanks, George."

When he hung up the phone, Pete realized he was still hungry. Opening the icebox, he took out a can of beer, some bread and a package of sliced ham. While he made a sandwich and ate it slowly, he went over again in his mind the implications of what George had said. Any way he added up the facts, they gave a troubling answer.

Amy had apparently not been subject to migraine attacks for quite some time, since she hadn't consulted George Hanscombe. Yet tonight she'd had one that was apparently so severe, she'd filched a morphine syrette from his case and given it to herself. What was more, nine additional syrettes were missing from his bag besides the one he'd found in the wastebasket in the bathroom.

Had she been taking them long? he wondered. Or was tonight the first attack? And if so, had Lorrie's funeral brought it on?

He remembered speaking to Amy at the cemetery but she'd seemed to be her usual self, so that didn't seem likely. Then he did remember something. The night Lorrie had been killed and he'd come home late, Amy had mentioned that she'd had a migraine attack but had taken something for it and the pain had been relieved.

Her behavior that night certainly hadn't been normal for Amy, but he'd put it down to her being emotionally excited about what had happened that afternoon and to the stiff drink she had said she'd taken. Now he wondered whether she had taken an injection, too, an injection which, combined with alcohol, would have swept away the inhibitions that were a part of her normal make-up.

The more he thought about it, the more certain he became that this must have been the sequence of events that evening. There was one possible way to find out, if he were lucky; finishing the sandwich and the can of beer, he went upstairs to the bedroom.

Amy was still asleep but had turned over on her side, so he could be sure she was not dangerously affected by the drug. A quarter-grain of morphine wasn't really a very large dose for an average-sized individual and, judging by the effect it had had upon her, he was fairly sure she hadn't been taking the drug very long. If she had been, a larger dose would have been required, since the body quickly became accustomed to it.

Looking around the room, he asked himself where she might have secreted the other morphine syrettes and his eye lit upon the dressing table beside the bed. Pulling out the drawers one by one, he looked through them, searching particularly under the lining paper, where anyone hiding something would be most likely to place it.

He found what he was looking for in the third drawer he opened—eight of the morphine syrettes. And he was filled with a great sense of relief, for whether or not Amy planned to continue taking the drug—and her having hidden eight of the syrettes seemed to indicate that she did—he could be reasonably sure now that she had only taken two lately, probably one the night after Lorrie was shot and another tonight. Which meant, fortunately, that if his assumptions were true, the danger of addiction was not yet very great. And Amy was intelligent enough, he knew, to understand the danger, once he pointed it out to her.

But what had made her take the drug in the first place? he asked himself as he undressed slowly and got into bed—unless she'd heard about him and Helen Straughn. The likely answer seemed to be No, for Amy was not one to avoid facing up to facts, even the truth that her own marriage might be in danger.

Was she troubled by some pain that might have meant a serious illness then? Or something like a fear of cancer so great that she was afraid to seek medical advice?

Lots of women did avoid going to doctors on just that account, he knew, but that answer didn't seem logical as far as Amy was concerned for she was an intelligent and highly sensible woman.

As for a love affair with another man, he didn't even consider it, certain that Amy's stern conscience wouldn't let her engage in the sort of bed-hopping that was so frequent at their level of Weston society.

One by one he canvassed the possible things that might have disturbed her deeply enough to bring on two severe migraine attacks in four days and lead her to filch morphine from his case in order to get relief. And one by one he discarded them until he came to a final possibility—her ambition.

Amy had survived one major disappointment some five years ago, when he'd chosen a clinical professorship and the lucrative clinic practice over the position of Professor of Surgery. She had actively promoted him for the professorship, but she'd seemed to adjust, after he'd explained that organizing the Faculty Clinic would forbid his taking the full-time teaching job. And when the clinic had proved a bonanza from the start—only partly because their streamlined diagnostic setup, the first really automated clinic in the country, had received a lot of publicity—his position in the university community had quickly risen at least as high as it would have if he were Professor of Surgery.

It was about then, he remembered now, that Amy had set her sights on promoting herself into a high position in the state medical auxiliary. And though after their one major quarrel over the professorship, she had appeared to sublimate her own desires to his—at least he had thought so at the time—he wondered now whether the nagging unfulfilled wish to see him professor could have been there all the while. And whether it might have had something to do with her present difficulty.

When he considered that question seriously, however, he didn't think it was the answer either. For with his decision to go ahead in medical politics and seek actively the office of president of the state association, Amy had been assured of a position in the medical hierarchy that was actually considerably higher than would have been hers if he were simply Professor of Surgery at Weston University Medical School.

All of which got him nowhere in deciding what had happened to Amy, and finally, his brain wearied from thinking, he drifted off to sleep.

II

When the taxi stopped in front of the house where the Alcoholics Anonymous meeting was to be held that night, Maggie McCloskey almost told the driver to take her back to the hospital. It wasn't that there was anything about the house, or the neighborhood, to disturb her. It sat back from the street on the west side of town looking toward the mountains, the neatly clipped lawn, the bright-colored drapes at the window, and the warm light shining through from the inside giving it a welcoming touch.

What troubled her most about the place—and this whole venture that Dave Rogan had practically strong-armed her into—was the obvious normalcy of the house, its frank wholesomeness and the air of neighborly invitation that practically oozed from it.

"You won't be called on to say or do anything; in fact, you don't even have to give your name, if you don't want to," Dave had promised. And so she'd come, clutching at straws because she knew that the next time she came home drunk and took sleeping pills, she might not be rational enough to regulate the dose and could easily wind up like poor Lorrie, down there in the cold ground of the churchyard.

The thought made her shiver, as if she were already walking over her own grave, but it also made her more and more doubtful of finding anything here that might help her. For this was obviously a normal house, inhabited by normal and probably happy people, judging from the warmth of the drapes and the light, people who had never come near to suicide—or wished for death.

While she was waiting, a man and a woman walked up the driveway from a car that had parked farther down the street. They were welcomed at the door by a rather dark-skinned woman with a coil of dark braids piled upon her head. When the door opened, a gust of human voices engaged in pleasant social conversation had momentarily escaped from the house and Maggie looked once again at the slip of paper Dave had given her, to make sure the address on it and the number on the door were the same.

"You're going in, ma'm?" the driver asked and she wondered if he had sensed the sudden fear that had gripped her. Or if he knew what this place was.

But that seemed ridiculous, for it was just like a dozen houses on the same street, except for slight differences in construction.

"Yes." Maggie fumbled in her purse, took out two one-dollar bills and gave them to him. "Keep the change."

"Thanks, Mrs. McCloskey." Maggie knew now why the driver's face had seemed familiar when he had picked her up in front of the hospital. Weston's taxi drivers had taken her home drunk so many times from the club that most of them knew her well by now.

Until that moment, she'd been telling herself she had nothing in common with the people she could see moving about inside the bright warm home. Now she knew she wasn't any better than they—or even than the wino bums who cadged handouts along Main Street downtown. And that knowledge gave her the strength to follow the gravel walk to the front door and push the bell.

"I'm Eve Santo." The woman with the dark braids greeted Maggie at the door. She was comfortably plump and her eyes were warm with welcome. "Come in and meet the bunch. You're Margaret McCloskey, aren't you? I've seen your picture on the society page."

"Not lately. I've been busy—with other things."

"All of us have been through that, too," said Eve Santo. "You're among friends here, Mrs. McCloskey."

"Please call me Maggie." It was impossible not to like the other woman.

"Of course. This is my husband Harry."

Harry Santo was as thin as his wife was plump and Maggie found herself reminded of Jack Spratt who, not eating fat, was as thin as a rail. As a child she'd always felt sorry for the poor man. But now, with cholesterol out of practically everybody's diet and fat long since indicted as a killer, he was revealed as one who had only been following a healthful course.

Eve Santo took her around the two rooms that were filled with people, drinking coffee and eating little sandwiches and cookies. Most of them were completely at ease and Maggie could see no difference between this party and hundreds she had attended on the other side of town—except that there was no bar and no liquor.

Strangely enough, though, they seemed to be having as good a time with each other as people had in the groups of which she had been a part. There was much good-natured raillery but, though Eve Santo introduced her to everyone and she participated briefly in conversation with a few, Maggie soon began to experience a sense of withdrawal, a feeling of standing aloof that made her responses to the friendly conversation of those in the house grow less and less warm, until suddenly she decided that she had to leave.

"Can I use your phone to call a taxi, Mrs. Santo?" she asked.

"Of course. Some of those here tonight live near you, though. They'll be happy to drop you by your home a little later."

"I'd rather go now, if you don't mind." She didn't want to admit that she had come from the hospital and was going back there.

"I'll call you a taxi right away." Eve Santo dialed the phone and gave the order, then turned back to Maggie.

"Please don't be depressed," she said. "These first meetings are always difficult; that's why we try to make them social occasions, if we can. But you're still with new people and it disturbs you because you feel they know your troubles and are feeling sorry for you. A.A. doesn't work on that principle, Maggie."

She opened the drawer of a small table in the hall where they were standing and took out a booklet. "Take this with you and read it later. The information it contains will clear up a lot of misunderstanding you may have about us."

Maggie dropped the booklet into her bag, trying to hide the trembling of her fingers.

"Here's your taxi." The lights of a moving car had just appeared in front of the house. "Good night, Maggie. And good luck."

"Good night, Eve. And thanks."

Maggie almost ran down the walkway to the car, not even noticing in her haste that it wasn't a taxi after all—until she recognized a familiar figure holding open the right front door.

"Hello, Maggie," said Joe McCloskey. "Will I do instead of a taxi?"

"Joe!" She went into his arms and he held her for a long moment standing there by the car, while she wept.

"How did you happen to be here?" she asked as he was backing out of the driveway.

"When Dave told me he'd talked you into coming to an A.A. meeting here, I figured this wasn't for you. Dave's like most psychiatrists; he figures he can pull strings and make people behave like puppets, but he wasn't married to you for fifteen years. If he had been, he'd have known you've got too much sense to be a real alcoholic. I've been parked across the street ever since before you came. When the taxi you ordered just now stopped down the street looking for the house, I figured you must have called it, so I gave the driver five dollars and sent him on his way."

"Oh Joe! It was awful in there!" She sat close to him, seeking to gain strength from him. "Everybody was so nice."

Joe grinned. "Obviously lower middle class."

"I could just see them feeling sorry for me and that was the worst of all. I need a drink, Joe. Let's go get a drink."

"Sure, darling."

She'd expected him to object. When he didn't she lay back against the cushion of the seat, closing her eyes and letting the rush of cool air from the car's air-conditioning system soothe her flushed face. Only when the car drew to a stop, did she open them—and was startled by the bright glare of fluorescent lights and neon tubing spelling out in flashing letters:

BURGER HEAVEN

"I said I needed a drink!" She caught the angry note in her voice before it could rise to a screech, and bit back any further words.

"The thick milkshakes they have here are the best you ever tasted," Joe said cheerfully. "I've been having one every night before I went to bed."

"After you'd seen that I got back to the house?" She was suddenly quiet.

"Y-yes."

"Oh Joe!" Her irritation at him, even the craving for a drink, was washed away by a surge of tenderness. "Can't we start over?"

"Sure, darling. That's what this is all about."

Minutes later they were startled by the voice of the carhop girl standing beside the car: "You'd better order something, mister. The boss don't like people sittin' here just neckin'."

III

Mabel was cleaning up in the Snack Bar, getting ready for the eleven o'clock rush, when Marisa and Anton Dieter came in. They were holding hands and the girl was flushed and happy, like a college girl on a date with her steady.

They ordered coffee and drank it almost in silence, obviously still a little stunned by what had happened to them. When they finished, they went out and across the parking lot toward the entrance to the Faculty Apartments, still holding hands.

"I told you they'd make it, Abe," Mabel said triumphantly. "Did you see the look in her eyes?"

"A Jew and an ex-Nazi." The short-order cook shook his head. "It just don't make sense."

"The trouble with you is you don't have any faith," Mabel said loftily. "If you'd been at Mrs. Dellman's funeral this morning like I was, you'd have seen that these people over there"—she nodded toward the hospital across

the street—"are just like everybody else. When folks're in love, it don't make
no difference who they are—or where they come from."

"But a good-lookin' Jewish gal like that Doctor Feldman. Why does she
want to waste herself on a German like Dieter?"

"You ought to read the Bible more," Mabel reproved him. "Don't you
know it says that the lion and the lamb shall lay down together?"

"I guess you're right." Abe grinned. "From the way them two were
looking at each other, there's sure going to be some layin'—"

"Oh you!" Mabel exclaimed in disgust. "Go fry an egg!"

CHAPTER TWENTY-FOUR

I

In the living room of Helen Straughn's apartment, across town from
University Hospital, she and Pete Brennan were watching the Saturday
afternoon football game on the television screen—without seeing it at all.
Wearing golden sandals, gold-colored slacks and a white blouse, with her
red bronze hair—almost hidden in the operating room by the helmetlike
caps the scrub nurses wore—tumbled about her shoulders, Helen was an
extraordinarily beautiful woman. None of the look of stern discipline she
wore during her working hours was in her eyes as she looked across at Pete,
then leaned over to kiss him.

"I'll get you a beer," she said. "Poor darling, you look like you need it."

"This business of buying Mort Dellman's share of the clinic has run me
ragged." He raised his voice so he could be heard in the small kitchen where
she was opening the beer. "To say nothing of the trouble he caused by
shooting Paul McGill."

"That's not what's troubling you." She brought the tray with the beer on
it and put it down before him. "You might as well face the truth; I have
already."

"What truth?" He took one of the cans of beer and began to fill a glass,
pouring it expertly down the side so it wouldn't foam over.

"Ever since night before last, you've had all the symptoms of a man who's
having second thoughts about leaving his wife." She reached over and
switched off the TV. "I haven't exactly lived like a nun, you know. By now I
can recognize a guilt-stricken husband when I see one."

Pete shook his head in a bewilderment that might have been comic if it
hadn't been so troubled. "Before Mort shot Lorrie, I was certain that I
wanted to divorce Amy and marry you."

"And now?"

"I'm not sure it would be best for any of us."

"At least you're honest," she said. "I guess that's what really made me
fall for you in the first place."

"What do you mean?"

"You've got something, Pete—integrity I suppose is the best word for it.
Anyway it appeals to an orderly sort of person like me."

"It could be that I've got cold feet because I'm afraid what happened to
Lorrie could happen to you or me."

"That never crossed my mind. Your wife has the strait-laced New
England conscience her ancestors handed her. She would never go gunning
for the woman who broke up her home."

"Don't put it that way."

"If you'd divorced her and married me, what other way could it be put?"

"It's not your fault or mine—that we fell in love."

"That argument won't hold water either—it never does. I've had other affairs and I don't claim to be anything but what I am, a rather passionate woman who attracts men—and needs them."

"Don't make yourself sound like a Jezebel."

"I'm rather like her, you know. Jezebel was a determined woman—with principles. She thought the worship of Baal and Ashtoreth was best for her husband's people and almost succeeded in convincing them—until she ran up against Elijah."

"Where did you learn all that?"

"The Bible. I'm also religious—which may strike you as sort of odd. The fact of the matter is, your wife and I are alike in some ways; we're both very determined."

"Are you determined to give me up?"

"I thought you settled that just now."

"I said I wasn't sure. Now you seem to be."

"I haven't been certain from the first that it was best for you to divorce Amy and marry me. Now I know it isn't. Until this Dellman business came along, I kidded myself that the community you and I live in by day over at the hospital and the medical school was sophisticated enough for our marriage to work. Of course, people would have done their best to make me feel like a pariah for a little while, but I told myself they'd forget, after I'd proved myself to be the proper wife."

"They still might."

"Unh-unh! Three days ago, a husband caught his wife and another man together in adultery. In a fit of righteous indignation, he killed her and wounded the man, which makes Weston just like any other community, with everybody conforming to what's expected of them. The Bohemian period is over—if it ever really existed. Every husband is going back to his own wife—at least for a while—and the grand jury will set the killer free, because there's an unwritten law that a man has to protect his home."

"You think Weston's going to change that much?"

"The town isn't changing, just going back to what it originally was. One thing's sure, it will never be the same again."

"And you think that's what happened to me—this conformity idea of yours."

"I know what happened to you," she said. "You've fallen out of love with me and back in love with your wife. I can't tell you how it happened or why—only you can do that. But it did happen, so somebody had to lose you. And now that my dream of respectability is over, I'm glad I was the one and not her."

"You're pretty philosophical about all this."

"What do you want me to do?" she said with a shrug. "Go on a crying jag and beg you to marry me?"

"Of course not. But what will you do?"

"What I've done before. You don't own me, Pete Brennan; I've never even let you give me jewelry, remember? We'll break clean, like the honest fighters we are. You go back to Amy and I'll take that Mediterranean cruise I've been wanting to take. You're not going to suggest that we keep on with this affair, are you?"

"No."

"It wouldn't be good for you to come around here anyway." She grinned crookedly. "One day you'd find another man here and that would be a real blow to your ego."

"There's no reason we still can't be friends."

"No reason at all. We're adults. We respect and like each other. But our relationship must end there."

He couldn't help feeling a sense of relief and also guilt, but it seemed best not to mention either.

"You'd better go back to Amy now," Helen Straughn told him. "Don't make the mistake of believing she's as strong as she appears to be—no woman is. That's only a front we put up to keep the men we love from walking over us. My guess is *L'affaire Dellman* has shaken her up as much as it has the rest of us. If she cracks, be sure you're there for her to lean on."

II

"What I don't understand is why all this secrecy, just to examine a couple of slides," said Lew Saunders, as he took his student-days microscope out of its case in the room he shared with Mike Traynor in the intern quarters of University Hospital and set it on the table. "Or why you're so concerned. You've been hopping around like grease on a hot griddle."

"Just examine the slides." Mike's eyes were feverish and his hands shook as he took a cigarette from a crumpled pack and lit it.

Methodically, Lew Saunders set up the microscope, placed the slide Mike had prepared and stained under the objective, put a drop of cedar oil on it and lowered the oil-immersion lens until it just touched the globule of oil.

"This is a lousy light," he grumbled as he adjusted the goose-neck reading lamp until it was centered on the reflecting mirror beneath the microscope, sending a concentrated beam of light up through the slide and the lens system of the instrument.

With his eyes glued to the twin oculars of the microscope, Saunders began to turn the adjustments: first the gross, until the cells on the slide came into rough focus; then the fine, sharpening the picture until it stood out in the field of the instrument, with the colors and structure of the material sharply defined.

"Jesus Christ!" he exclaimed.

"What is it?" Mike Traynor demanded. "What do you see?"

"The finest preparation of intracellular, biscuit-shaped diplococci you ever saw."

"Oh my God!"

"Whoever you got this smear from has got the hottest dose of—"

"G.C.?"

"No doubt about it. Take a look." When Mike turned away from the microscope, Lew Saunders saw the stricken look on his roommate's face and realization hit him.

"You, Mike! It's yours!"

Mike Traynor nodded; at the moment, he was beyond speech.

"Man, you've really got yourself a dose. I never saw pus cells more crowded with the old Neisseria gonorrhoeae." Suddenly Lew began to laugh.

"It's nothing to laugh about," Mike Traynor said furiously.

"Don't you see?" Saunders went into another fit of laughter. "This is poetic justice, if there ever was such a thing. Mike Traynor, the Casanova of Weston Medical School, has got the clap! Ohh! This is priceless!"

"Shut up," Mike snarled. "Do you want to broadcast it all over the place?"

"Who gave it to you?"

"That bitch from Vassar. The one with the tape recorder."

"It's a hot case all right; three days after exposure is about the shortest time I ever heard of symptoms occurring. Man, when this gets out—"

"You wouldn't do that to me, Lew." Mike Traynor looked as if he were going to faint. "I'd be ruined."

"Your supply of women around here would certainly dry up, that's for sure. But when you're admitted to the hospital, it's bound to be on the record. And you know the grapevine."

"I'm not going to be admitted."

"You may not know it, boy, but by this time tomorrow you're going to be sick as hell."

"By this time tomorrow, I'm going to be practically well. Penicillin still cures G.C., doesn't it?"

"Sure—unless that babe was treated before and got herself a penicillin-resistant bug."

"I'll have to chance that. What's the biggest-size ampule made for injecting penicillin?"

"I saw some in the emergency room with five million units."

"If I inject one of them today and one day after tomorrow, I ought to be cured in forty-eight hours."

"Probably. Unless the bug turns out to be resistant."

"Can you get the ampules for me, Lew?"

"I don't know. A thing like this could be pretty sticky, if you have to be admitted later and it comes out that I knew. Besides, if I inject you and next week you start shedding your hide with a drug reaction—"

"Just get me the penicillin and I'll inject it myself. If there's any trouble, I'll swear I diagnosed myself and tried to treat it."

"Well, all right."

"You're a real friend, Lew. I'll get you a girl sometimes."

"Oh no," said the other intern. "You're jinxed." He began to laugh again. "Talk about poetic justice."

"You already said that," Mike Traynor told him. "Get the penicillin."

"I'm going." Lew Saunders reached for his white coat. "But while I'm gone, be thinking about what a hell of a fix you'd be in if Dr. Fleming hadn't discovered the notatum mold that makes penicillin one day about thirty years ago. And thank God for him."

III

Dave Rogan had been been making rounds on the psychiatric wards; whenever he was in the city on the weekends, he always paid a quick visit to his department of the hospital before dinner on Saturday. As he was leaving, he saw Elaine McGill pull into the parking lot, and crossed the street to where she was locking the doors of her station wagon.

"Got a minute, Elaine?" he asked.

"Sure," she said with a smile. "I'm on my way to see Paul."

"He's fine. They moved him from Intensive Care last night to make a room available for Janet Monroe's little boy."

"I hope the child's all right. Paul was talking about the operation last night."

"Pete Brennan did a brilliant job. The only trouble now is keeping the kid still with that magnetic probe in his brain but they've got enough personnel on Intensive Care to look after him."

"That's the second miracle in three days. The first was what Dr. Dieter did for Paul."

"You could call it that. If Pete had been forced to go after that aneurysm the old way, the chances of saving Jerry wouldn't have been much better than fifty per cent. Now, it looks like he's going to come through beautifully." He glanced toward the Snack Bar and saw that it was almost filled. "I'd buy you a cup of coffee, but what I have to say is sort of private."

"We're private enough right here," said Elaine. "I'd invite you to sit in my car but the way things have been around here lately, I'm afraid it might cause talk."

"Maybe we'd better not tempt fate." Dave grinned. "Tell me, do you have a picture of Paul's mother in your house?"

"Of course. You know the kind of retouched enlargements that used to be fashionable thirty years ago."

"Ever look at her? And then at yourself in the mirror?"

"Paul has told me more than once how much I resemble his mother. At first it made me mad; I guess I even hated her for a while. But I've gotten used to it now."

"I'm going to ask you a pretty intimate question, Elaine. But only because I'm very fond of you and Paul and want to see both of you happy."

"I know that, Dave."

"You say you used to hate Paul's mother sometimes. Was it after you and Paul had made love?"

When she didn't answer right away, he knew he was on the right track.

"How did you know?" she asked finally.

"Paul sent for me the day after the shooting. Something was troubling him."

"Then he *was* potent with Lorrie?"

"Yes."

"I've wondered. But Paul never talks about intimate things and I hesitated to ask."

"He was worried because he was potent with her and isn't very often with you."

"I guess that would be a normal male worry, wouldn't it?" She laughed, but not very convincingly.

"It wasn't himself Paul was worried about, Elaine. I think he realized for the first time the part a woman who really enjoys sex can play in it."

"And how a man can fail his partner?" Remembering what had happened earlier that fateful Wednesday afternoon, Elaine looked away lest Dave notice the warmth that the memory of it brought to her cheeks.

"The important thing," he said, "is what are you going to do about it?"

"Me? How can I keep Paul from remembering his mother?"

"By not being like her."

Elaine caught her breath. "Are you saying I should be like Lorrie?"

"Only where Paul is concerned. If you try, I think you can give a pretty good imitation of her." He grinned. "Maybe I'm older than I thought, or I would know already. But isn't there a pretty interesting pair of knees under that too-long dress Paul makes you wear?"

Her eyes twinkled. "It's a little public here, but if you really want to find out, I can always get back into the car."

"I'll take your word for it; after all, Della's been away a lot lately. But if you have an entirely new—and a lot smarter—wardrobe when Paul comes home, I don't think he'll mind paying the bill."

"I'll be a hussy." Elaine's eyes were shining. "But if Paul doesn't deliver, warn Della she's going to have competition. Don't forget Pygmalion and Galatea."

IV

The weather had been worsening to the south toward Atlanta since morning, and Elmer Hill, foreman of the Weston County Grand Jury, was delayed in his flight home. It was after seven Saturday evening before the jury was finally assembled in the courthouse and the hearing on Mort Dellman could begin.

When the prisoner was brought into the locked room where the jury was sitting, Roy was surprised to see that he was accompanied only by the bailiff, who had brought him downstairs from the jail.

"It was my understanding that the accused had engaged counsel," he said to the foreman.

"I plan to be my own counsel," Mort Dellman interposed blandly. "Since I have done nothing that any normal man wouldn't do to defend the sanctity of his home and his marriage, I don't need anyone to twist the law in my behalf."

It was a clever move, the sort of thing Roy should have expected, particularly after Mort's slick ploy with the confession on the afternoon of the killing. But Roy wasn't at all sure he had a case anyway, so he hesitated only a moment before turning to the court reporter, who was taking down the proceedings word by word on a shorthand machine.

"Let the record show the prisoner was warned of his constitutional right not to give testimony and to be represented by counsel," he directed.

"I waive both rights and throw myself upon the mercy of the gentlemen of the grand jury," Mort Dellman added.

"That should be sufficient, shouldn't it, Mr. Weston?" the foreman asked.

"Yes—so long as it is a matter of record that the prisoner was warned of his rights and that he is not required to testify."

"Are you ready to proceed with the hearing then, Mr. Weston?"

"Yes, sir. I shall read first a deposition given under oath this morning by Dr. Paul McGill, a patient in the University Hospital who is unable physically to attend the hearing and testify himself."

"Any objection?" the foreman asked Mort Dellman.

"None whatever, sir."

"Proceed then, Mr. Weston."

The reading proceeded briskly.

Q.—Your name?
A.—Paul McGill.
Q.—Occupation?
A.—Physician. I am a specialist in dermatology—diseases of the skin.
Q.—Where do you reside?
A.—At 2625 Sherwood Ravine Road.
Q.—Where were you about 4:30 P.M. on the afternoon of July 1?
A.—At 5051 Sherwood Ravine Road.
Q.—What were you doing at the time?
A.—I was engaged in sexual intercourse.

Roy had tried to get Paul to avoid the word, knowing the effect it would have on the jury in Mort Dellman's favor. But Paul had insisted, for the same reason.

"I'll be damned," one of the jurors said in an awed voice. "He's a regular studhorse, ain't he?"

Roy ignored the interruption and continued with the reading:

Q.—With whom were you having intercourse?
A.—With Lor—Mrs. Mortimer Dellman.
Q.—What happened then?
A.—I'm not sure.
Q.—Did you see Dr. Dellman come into the room?
A.—No. Suddenly I heard a shot and at the same moment I . . . I blacked out.
Q.—When did you next regain consciousness?
A.—Around midnight, I guess it was.
Q.—Where?
A.—In the Special Intensive Care Unit at University Hospital.
Q.—And you knew nothing of what happened in between?
A.—Nothing
Q.—Did you see Dr. Dellman at any time that afternoon?
A.—No.
Q.—Did you know who shot you?
A.—No. When I first became conscious at the hospital I didn't know what had actually happened. In fact my first thought was that I must have had a heart attack.
Q.—One other question, Dr. McGill? How long had you been engaged in sexual intercourse with Mrs. Dellman when you heard the sound and blacked out?
A.—Maybe five minutes.

"Didn't even get to finish," said the juror who had spoken before. "What a shame."

"This is the end of Dr. McGill's deposition." Roy Weston ignored the interruption.

"Call your first witness, please, Mr. Weston," said the foreman.

"Bailiff, call Dr. Sylvester Short, Medical Examiner for Weston County."

Dr. Short, a portly man of some sixty years, who was also Professor of Pathology at the medical school, gave the usual background information for the record concerning his training and qualifications.

"Dr. Short," Roy said. "Did you on September 1, examine the body of Mrs. Loretta Porter Dellman, deceased?"

"I did."

"Would you tell us your findings, please?"

"Death came from a wound in the left side of the heart, damaging both the cardiac muscle and the left coronary artery."

"The coronary artery? Would you explain, please?"

"The coronary arteries are two in number and supply blood to each side of the heart muscle. The bullet destroyed at least a half inch of the left coronary artery, thus depriving a large portion of the heart of vitally needed blood. The effect was the same as massive coronary thrombosis."

"And that was?"

"Instant death."

"Did you find the bullet that caused this extensive damage?"

"No, sir. The bullet passed entirely through the body of the deceased. The wound of entry was in the back of the chest on the left side. The wound of exit was in the front of the left chest."

"And death was instantaneous?"

"No question about it."

"No more questions."

There were none from the jury and Dr. Short was allowed to leave.

"Call Sergeant Jim O'Brien," Roy directed.

Sergeant O'Brien settled into the witness chair, nodded to several members of the jury, and was sworn. He was obviously an experienced witness.

"Sergeant, were you called on September 1, to the home of Dr. Mortimer Dellman at 5051 Sherwood Ravine Road at about four thirty in the afternoon?"

"I was."

"By whom?"

"By Dr. Dellman. He called the police station and reported that he had killed a man who was with his wife."

"Did he identify the man at the time, Sergeant?"

"No sir."

"Did he say he had killed his wife?"

"No sir."

"What did you find when you reached the house?"

"Mrs. Dellman was dead, shot through the chest. Dr. McGill was seriously wounded. I didn't think he would live to get to the hospital."

"Where was Dr. Dellman?"

"In the adjoining room. He gave us the weapon when we came in."

"We, Sergeant?"

"Lt. Vosges was with me."

"What kind of a weapon was it?"

"A twenty-two-caliber target pistol."

"How many shots had been fired?"

"One."

Taking a small box from his pocket and opening it to show a bullet lying on a piece of cotton, Roy held it close enough for the sergeant to examine it. "This one?"

"Yes sir. I scratched an identifying mark on it."

"Are you sure the bullet came from the pistol Dr. Dellman handed you?"

"Yes. I fired another bullet from the weapon later and had them compared ballistically by the FBI. Dr. Dellman's pistol unquestionably fired the shot that killed Mrs. Dellman and wounded Dr. McGill."

There were no more questions and the sergeant was dismissed.

"Call Dr. Anton Dieter, please," Roy Weston directed.

Dieter came in, was sworn and gave the usual background information.

"Dr. Dieter," said Roy. "Did you, on September 1, operate upon Dr. Paul McGill?"

"I did."

"And what did you find?"

"A bullet, twenty-two caliber, steel-jacketed, located inside the right ventricle of the heart."

"Did you remove the bullet?"

"I did."

"Can you tell us its approximate course?"

"The bullet entered Dr. McGill's chest about a half inch to the right of the sternum—"

"The breastbone?"

"Yes. It penetrated the chest wall and also the wall of the right ventricle, one of the four chambers of the heart, landing inside the ventricle."

Roy Weston took the small box from his pocket, opened it and once again showed the jury and the witness the bullet lying on a piece of cotton at the bottom of the box.

"Is this the bullet you removed, Doctor?"

"Is it the one I turned over to Sergeant O'Brien at his request following the operation, Mr. Weston?"

"It is the same bullet."

"Then it is the one I removed."

"I have no more questions of the witness," Roy Weston told the foreman of the jury.

"You may step down, Dr. Diet—"

"One minute." It was the rather garrulous juror. "Did you say the bullet entered the front of Dr. McGill's chest?"

"I did."

"Wasn't he something?" the man said, with obvious admiration. "Not only takes a man's wife but makes her do the work." When a titter of amusement passed like a wave over the faces of the jurors, he added, "Lazy bastard, ain't he?"

"We will present no more evidence at this time," Roy Weston announced. "It seems proved beyond question that the prisoner killed his wife and wounded Dr. McGill. I ask therefore that he be bound over to Circuit Court on a charge of manslaughter."

"Just a moment!" It was Mort Dellman. "Don't I have the right to testify?"

"In my opinion, your testimony is neither necessary nor advisable at this time, Dr. Dellman," Roy Weston said coldly. He didn't know exactly what Mort was up to, but he preferred to have as little of the sordid affair brought out as possible, even in the relative secrecy of the jury room.

"I think the jury is entitled to know the facts before they consider whether or not to bring an indictment against me," Mort Dellman insisted. "Both my life and my professional reputation are at stake here."

"It is my duty to warn you, both for yourself and for the record," Roy said formally, "that since you have been apprised of your rights and have chosen to be without counsel, any statement you make can be introduced in evidence as part of your trial, if an indictment is returned."

"The truth never hurt anyone," Mort Dellman said in a tone of pious righteousness.

"You may make a statement, Doctor, if you believe it will assist us in arriving at a decision in your case," said the jury foreman.

"I do believe that, sir," Mort Dellman assured him.

"Proceed then. But please remember that you may stop at any time and refuse to answer any questions put to you without in any way prejudicing yourself."

"I understand." Mort Dellman turned to face the entire jury. "On the afternoon of September 1 of this year, gentlemen, I came home earlier than usual. It had been brought to my attention previously that a Buick Wildcat automobile had been seen parked in front of my house on several afternoons, but a number of people I know own such a car, so I merely thought some woman friend might be visiting my wife. She grew up in this community and had a large number of friends.

"When I entered the house, I found no one downstairs—our children are all away at a summer camp and the maid was off on Wednesdays. I climbed the stairs and approached the bedroom my wife and I share, but when I was about six feet from the door, I heard voices inside the room. The room was somewhat dark but the door was partly open. When I heard a man's laugh,

I guess I sort of lost control of myself. There is a small study on that floor where I keep a pistol since a rash of burglaries occurred in our neighborhood lately."

He paused and, pouring a glass of water for himself from a pitcher on a small table nearby, drank it down before continuing.

"As I have said, I was laboring under a very strong emotion. I think any of you would feel the same if you heard a man's laugh and your wife's voice from a darkened bedroom in your home at four thirty in the afternoon. I remember throwing open the door of the bedroom and seeing my wife in the arms of another man. As to what happened then I can't be sure. I remember raising the gun but I don't remember firing it. When I regained control of my senses, I found that my wife was dead and her lover was unconscious. I called the police at once and you know the rest of the story."

The foreman looked at the rest of the jury. "Any questions?" he asked.

Watching them, Roy Weston saw that the man who had spoken several times before was frowning. "How good a shot are you, Doctor?" he asked.

"I qualified with a pistol as an army officer in Korea. And I also shoot sometimes in local contests at the pistol range."

"How far away were you when you fired?"

"As I said, I'm not sure exactly what happened. I may even have taken several steps into the room; the venetian blinds were drawn and it was rather dark."

"Any further questions?" the foreman asked and the juror shook his head. "Any questions from you, Mr. Weston?"

"No," said Roy. "I have no more witnesses to bring in at this time either."

"The bailiff will take Dr. Dellman into custody," said the foreman of the grand jury. "I would appreciate your waiting outside the jury room until we reach a decision, Mr. Weston, in case we need to call you back to explain any points of the law."

"Of course." Roy followed the court reporter outside and offered her a cigarette. She was a pert young woman, an experienced reporter and, he knew, very sharp.

"What do you think the verdict will be, Mr. Weston?" she asked, as she accepted a light.

"An indictment for manslaughter—what else?"

"They're going to turn him loose."

"Why do you say that?"

"Only one guy on the jury saw that this whole thing smells to high heaven."

"What do you mean?" Roy asked warily.

"Loretta Dellman was no saint; that's common knowledge. But Dr. Dellman also makes a play for anything wearing skirts whenever he can. My roommate's a secretary at the Faculty Clinic and gives me all the dirt."

"Like what?"

"Mrs. Dellman was playing cozy with a curly-tailed wolf of a medical student. I had a few dates with him, until I found out I'd have to learn judo. My guess is that Dellman couldn't stand the idea of knowing the students were talking about him being cuckolded by one of them and went there that afternoon to get the guy. But Dr. McGill was there instead and got the bullet intended for somebody else."

"Do you have any proof of this?"

"All I know is what I read off the stenotype." The girl grinned. "These high-society shenanigans are not for the likes of me."

The door to the jury room opened and the foreman looked out.

"Please come in, Mr. Weston—also the reporter," he said. "We have reached a decision."

Inside, the reporter took her place at the stenographic machine and the foreman put on his glasses before taking up a piece of paper on which something had been written with a ball-point pen.

"We, the Grand Jury of Weston County," he read, "sitting on the fourth day of September, find that Mrs. Loretta Dellman came to her death by the accidental discharge of a weapon in the hands of Dr. Mortimer Dellman, her husband. We therefore find no cause to bind Dr. Dellman over for trial and he is hereby ordered released from custody."

CHAPTER TWENTY-FIVE

I

Dave and Della Rogan were sitting on the sofa in the cypress-paneled family room watching TV, when the broadcast was interrupted by a local news bulletin that the grand jury had freed Mort Dellman with a verdict of accidental death.

"How could they figure that?" Della asked.

"Mort undoubtedly claimed the unwritten law, as far as shooting Paul was concerned, and the jury must have figured that Lorrie got in the way of the bullet. It's a screwy sort of verdict, but I guess it's the best for all concerned. Now everything can go back to normal again."

"Except that Mort's a hundred thousand dollars richer."

"He's more than that. The rumor is that Jake Porter gave him two hundred thousand not to claim custody of the children and let the old man adopt them."

"So Mort came out better than anybody else?"

"I guess you could say that, though getting Joe and Maggie back together means a lot to me—and more to them. They're going on a world cruise the first of October; Maggie told me when I saw her this afternoon. The one I really feel sorry for is George Hanscombe."

"Why? If he'd ask Grace to stay here, I think she would."

"Maybe. But George is a good enough doctor to know that wouldn't be best for Grace, after the diabetes almost got away from them a few days ago. He's letting her go to England because he loves her enough to see that it's best for her."

"She can always come back."

"George is gambling on that but my guess is she won't. Grace never consulted me and I probably couldn't have helped her if she had. There are too many points of frustration between her and George and they're both too old by twenty-five or thirty years to really make any basic changes in their approach to life and each other. Grace can adjust; after all, she'll have enough to live on comfortably and she'll be in England where she has relatives. But George's life has been arranged in pretty watertight compartments for so long, it's going to be hard on him."

"Do you think Pete and that nurse will go on?"

"That nurse, as you call her, happens to be an extremely capable and fine woman, hon. Like George, Helen probably loves Pete enough to give him up. I've always figured that in the end, Pete would go back to Amy anyway, once he realizes how brittle Amy's defenses really are."

"And us? What about us, Dave?"

He moved his arm to draw her more closely to him. "I'm pretty sure Mort's bullet missed us." He yawned. "It's about bedtime. What say we go to church in the morning, then drive down along the lake for dinner? The kids will be back Tuesday and things will be pretty lively around here—for a while."

At the foot of the stairs, Della turned back to where he was checking the latch on the front door.

"I stopped taking the pill a couple of days ago, Dave," she said casually.

"Hmm." He grinned and the look in his eyes set her heart beating a little faster. "What day would this be in your cycle, by the way?"

"The thirteenth or fourteenth. I haven't paid much attention to it for quite a while."

"We may be too late this month, but it's still worth a try. Next month we ought to hit that old ovulation date right on the head. You go on up; I'll fix us a drink and bring it with me."

It was going to be fun painting the crib that had been stored up in the attic more than ten years now, he thought as he mixed bourbon with ginger ale. Almost as much fun as having a little fellow toddling around the house again.

II

It was nearly eleven o'clock before Roy Weston finished preparing and signing the documents connected with Mort Dellman's release from jail, following the decision of the grand jury. Mort had insisted on their being prepared tonight. And though Roy knew what was in Mort's mind—the possibility that one of the county judges might become disturbed over the rather summary action of the grand jury in freeing him and order his re-arrest—Roy was anxious to get the whole thing off his mind, too, so he'd stayed at the courthouse to prepare them.

By encouraging the jury to sweep the whole affair under the rug, so to speak, Roy had the satisfaction of knowing he had saved many of his friends—and himself—from the scandal of epic proportions that could have resulted if Mort had been brought to trial. But he also knew he had removed any possibility of running for the job of attorney general of the state in the forthcoming election, since Abner Townsend would certainly seize upon Mort Dellman's release as a major campaign issue if he did.

It didn't really matter any more, Roy tried to tell himself, but without much success. Weary and discouraged, he took a bottle from the lower drawer of his desk and poured a glass half full, drinking it down without even noticing the sting of liquor upon his throat. In the parking lot outside, he got into his Cadillac, but when he reached the street, didn't turn toward his home. Instead, he headed westward toward the new apartment complex the Biesons were building on a hillside around a small lake.

The apartment he sought was on the third floor, but the window was dark. Ordinarily, she never went to bed until after midnight, he knew. But on the chance that she might have decided to go earlier tonight, since she wasn't expecting him, he took the elevator up and rang the bell. When no one answered after a few moments, he went back to his car and headed toward home.

The clouds had been lowering all afternoon and now it had begun to rain. Usually, when he was out late Roy called Alice before starting home; even though they slept in different rooms and she was often asleep when he got home, she didn't like for him to come into the house at night without her knowing it. But tonight, he was too depressed and tired to stop on the way and, putting the car in the garage when he reached the house, let himself in with his own key.

A small light burned downstairs, since Alice sometimes had to go down in the middle of the night for the green medicine, if her colon started acting up. Stepping out of his loafers so as not to disturb her on the landing upstairs, Roy stopped at the downstairs bar off the family room for another quick drink, then climbed the stairway in his sock feet.

The entire upper floor was dark but he didn't turn on the light in the hall. He'd come home so many times late at night that he knew the way to his own room by instinct now. As he was passing the door to Alice's room, he heard what sounded like voices and, thinking that perhaps she had forgotten to turn off the small television set in her room, he moved to the door. Before he could open it, the sounds came again and, startled by their nature, he put his ear to the wooden panel.

In much the way a stethoscope magnified the hidden sounds of breathing and the heartbeat inside the body, the wooden panel of the door and his eardrums magnified the sound within the room. He heard Alice's gurgling laugh and then the throaty tones of another woman's voice, a voice that sounded familiar, but which he could not place at the moment.

Shocked by the implication of what he was hearing, Roy considered for a moment going on to his own room and leaving Alice and whoever was in there with her alone. But the whiskey he'd drunk before leaving the office and downstairs just now was beginning to heat up his brain and with it another, headier excitement started to rise. Turning the knob of the door carefully so as not to warn those inside, he pushed it open with his right hand and reached inside quickly, flipping the light switch with his left.

As the room was flooded with light, a shriek of surprise came from Alice. She rolled over, scrambling desperately for a sheet to cover her naked body, but the other woman made no move to cover herself. Instead she raised herself on her elbows and looked up at Roy with a mocking light in her eyes.

"Don't stare, Roy," said Corinne Marchant. "You've seen us both naked before."

As Roy gaped at her and at Alice, now sitting up in bed, with the sheet drawn up under her chin, watching both him and Corinne warily, the Frenchwoman added: "You've got what we French call a ménage à trois, darling, so why not make the best of it? I can assure you that you'll find it interesting."

Roy stared at them while the liquor rose in his brain and the pounding of his pulse accelerated steadily. The contrast between the two women was remarkable: Alice all soft, pink and very feminine, with her rather full breasts and rounded hips; Corinne, slim and tanned, like the athlete she was. The more he looked and the more his pulse pounded in his ears, the more he could see that Corinne's suggestion made sense. What decided him, however, was the sudden avid look in Alice's eyes and the way she let the sheet fall and shoved it away from her body with a casual movement.

Beginning to loosen his tie and unbutton his shirt, Roy started to laugh, and, after a startled moment, the two women joined him.

"Two for the price of one!" he chuckled. "By God, Corinne, I think you're right."

III

It was shortly after midnight when Mort Dellman reached Weston County Airport. A single attendant was at the counter of the only airline serving the city with night flights.

"Is the 1 A.M. flight to Atlanta on time?" he asked.

"We're socked in, sir."

"What d'ya mean, socked in?"

"The flight's been canceled out of here on account of bad weather."

"When's the next one?"

"Nine o'clock tomorrow morning."

"Nine o'clock?"

"We can't be too sure of that one either, sir. The weatherman says this front is going to hang around for a while. As long as it does, there won't be any planes landing here."

Nine o'clock! He couldn't chance it!

The morning papers were already off the press. He'd picked one up outside when he'd come into the airport, and the first thing everyone would see in the morning would be the bold headlines:

GRAND JURY FREES DOCTOR

Roy Weston had been a fool not to prosecute him, Mort knew, but the state attorney general was far too astute a politician to overlook the chance to torpedo Roy's chances of running for the post. An hour after Abner Townsend saw the morning papers, he would be dragging a judge in the capital from his Sunday paper, asking for another warrant. Which meant that Mort Dellman had to be out of Weston and across the state line—preferably out of the country, too—before that could happen.

His escape plan was foolproof and he could have made it, too, if the rain hadn't socked in the flight to Atlanta. The reservation he'd had Pete Brennan make for South Africa had been only a feint. His real destination was Brazil, where there was no extradition treaty with the United States. With a hundred thousand for his share of the Faculty Clinic and another two hundred from old man Porter in the kitty—plus what he had been stashing away through the years in Switzerland and the lever the accidental death verdict of the grand jury would give him when he had a lawyer claim the benefits for the accident policy he'd taken out on Lorrie a year ago, he could have lived high in Brazil, while he decided what to do next—until this damned weather had upset his plans.

There was only one answer—a rental car. Even then he'd never make it to Atlanta before nine o'clock, which meant the people he rented the car from would certainly recognize him and the police would know almost immediately where he had gone. He'd have to take that chance though, and try to sneak across the state line by taking a back road.

The car rental booth was across the foyer of the airport and he was striding toward it when his eye was caught by a sign over an empty booth:

CHARTER FLYING SERVICE

And underneath it the promise:

WE FLY YOU ANYWHERE AT ANY TIME
IF BOOTH IS UNATTENDED, DIAL 389-7677

Stepping into a telephone booth, Mort dropped a dime into the slot and dialed the number. It rang several times before a sleepy feminine voice answered.

"Charter Flying Service?" he asked.

"Just a minute, please."

"This is Charter," a man's voice said.

"I want you to fly me to Atlanta."

"The weather's too bad, sir. Nothing's coming into Weston Airport tonight."

"That doesn't mean nothing can leave it," Mort Dellman said. "How does a thousand dollars sound to you for flying me to Atlanta. Or fifteen hundred to New Orleans?"

"It's still pretty risky."

"I'm paying you well."

"Who is this?"

"My name's Richards. I'm at the airport now and I'm ready to go whenever you are."

"Why do you have to get to Atlanta in such a hurry, Mr. Richards?"

"A member of my family is dying in Dallas. It's important that I get there as quickly as possible."

"You said fifteen hundred to New Orleans, didn't you?"

"Yes. If you hurry."

"I'll be at the airport in twenty minutes. You'll know I'm there when you see the lights go on in my hangar. It's close to the airport building."

"I'll come over to the hangar when they go on."

It was a little over fifteen minutes before the lights went on. Picking up his bag, Mort crossed over to the hangar in the rain. A man was busy working on a light plane, filling the wing tanks with gasoline.

"I'm Mr. Richards," Mort called to him. "How soon can we take off?"

"Right away, sir—as soon as I finish filling the tanks and file a flight plan with the tower." He looked more closely at Mort. "You say your name's Richards?"

"That's right. You want me to pay you in advance?"

The man hesitated only momentarily. "Yes."

Mort counted out the money and put it into the pilot's hands when he finished filling the tank.

"This is a helluva night for flying, Mr. Richards," the man said. "But I can't afford to turn down fifteen hundred bucks."

And I can't afford not to get out of the country, Mort Dellman thought as he swung his bags up into the plane. From New Orleans, he was pretty sure he could get a plane for Mexico City before Abner Townsend could stop him. And once there, it would be a simple matter to go on to Brazil.

IV

After leaving Helen Straughn's apartment Saturday afternoon, Pete Brennan had driven home and taken Amy to dinner at the club. It hadn't been a very festive occasion, however. Amy seemed depressed and several times he thought she was going to tell him something, but each time she'd turned the conversation along another line. Around nine o'clock, they returned home and, after the ten o'clock news broadcast announced the action of the grand jury in freeing Mort Dellman, they went to bed.

It was just before dawn when Pete awakened. A glance at the other side of the king-sized bed told him it was empty. The door to Amy's bathroom was closed but a line of light showed beneath it, telling him where she was. While he was debating knocking upon it, the sound of retching made the decision for him.

When he opened the door, Amy was standing in front of the washbasin, her head held tightly between her hands and a look of agony on her face. When he took her in his arms, she clung to him like a child. Reaching for a washcloth, he moistened it beneath the tap and gently wiped her face and her mouth with a cool cloth.

"Migraine?" he asked.

"Woke up with it," she gasped. "Nauseated."

He drew a bath towel from the rack and threw it over his shoulder, in case she had another fit of vomiting. Guiding her back to the bed, he helped her lie down. Then, placing the folded-up towel beside her where she could reach it, he moistened the washcloth again and put it on her forehead.

"Lie as quietly as you can," he told her. "I'll call the emergency room for a hypodermic."

Using the extension in the next room, Pete rang the hospital and got the night emergency-room nurse immediately. "I need a hypodermic of ergotamine tartrate and Demerol, Miss Tabor," he told her. "Mrs. Brennan's having a severe migraine attack. I'll run over and get it."

"We're not busy, Doctor," said the nurse. "The night orderly can bring it over to you in my car."

"That'll be fine. I'll meet him at the front door."

"He should be there in ten minutes."

When he came back into the bedroom, Pete saw at once that Amy had moved while he was away. The dresser drawer where she had hidden the morphine was not quite completely closed, though he remembered closing it tightly after he'd found and removed the drug. She was lying upon the bed again, however, with the washcloth pulled down over her eyes.

"The night orderly is bringing over the injection George Hanscombe always gives you, dear," he said. "Do you need anything else?"

"Some ginger ale over ice might help my stomach."

"I'll get it while I'm waiting for the hypo," he said, although he was pretty sure the request was only a device to get him out of the room. By the time he'd found the ginger ale and poured it into a glass filled with ice in the kitchen, the grizzled night orderly was at the door, with the sterile syringe and needle wrapped in a sterile towel.

When he came back upstairs, Pete saw at once that Amy had been up again—as he had expected. This time the door to his closet was not quite shut and he was sure she had been looking there for the medicine case, which he had removed after finding the syrettes and put in the glove compartment of his car.

"This will straighten you out in no time," he told her as he made the injection with the plastic disposal syringe most hospitals used to prevent the possibility of carrying the deadly virus of serum hepatitis from one patient to another.

"Hold me, Pete." It was a whisper of entreaty and, slipping into bed on his side, he took her in his arms. Her body was tense at first but as the medicine began to take effect, he felt the tension gradually lessen.

"Head feel better?" he asked after a while.

"The pain's almost gone now."

"You might feel better if you drank some of the ginger ale. I'll get it for you."

"No. Don't leave me. I'll get it." She turned over and, taking the glass from the bedside table, drank it through a straw he'd put into it in the kitchen. Turning back, she nestled against him once more, and after a little while moved even closer. When her lips sought his, he kissed her and found her mouth soft and labile beneath his own. Her arm tightened about his neck and when his hand touched the warm skin of her back, where her nightgown was rolled up, she shivered a little and pressed herself against him.

He made love to her gently then, filled with a great tenderness he'd never remembered experiencing before. Amy had always seemed so self-sufficient she'd never aroused that sort of a feeling within him. When it was over and she was close against him, warm and relaxed, he said, "Is there anything you want to tell me, dear?"

She'd been lying with her eyes closed, utterly relaxed from the drug and from the love-making. Now she opened them and looked up at him, as he propped himself up on his elbow so he could look down upon her face. There was no tension now and no apprehension in her eyes.

"It all seems sort of foolish," she said.

"What does?"

"Worrying about what I had to tell you."

He grinned. "Maybe if more husbands and wives prepared for serious discussions as we just did, there wouldn't be any need for the discussions after all."

"There's need for this one. You found the little tubes?"

"The syrettes? Yes. I still don't understand why you used them."

"It was Wednesday night, after Lorrie was shot. I got a severe migraine on the way home from the District Six meeting, even before I heard the news on the radio. The presidency was cinched. I had enough votes to win but—"

"Was? Had? Isn't the present tense appropriate?"

"Not any more. When I saw myself in the mirror while you were downstairs just now, scrabbling around hunting for that morphine because I couldn't face what I had to do, I realized I'm no better than Maggie McCloskey, or any other alcoholic or addict. Being president of the auxiliary before you became head of the state medical association didn't seem important to me any more."

"Was that what brought on the attack when you were on the way home?"

"I'm sure it must have been. I'd been under a lot of tension over there but what really worried me was my selfishness in wanting to get ahead of you."

"You're wrong."

"How?"

"What really troubled you was the fear that you might hurt me. But you couldn't be afraid of that, unless you love me even more than being auxiliary president."

"I know that now, but for a while I was in danger of letting it become too important. Driving home from the meeting, I began to realize that, and something inside me triggered the attack. I was on my way to George Hanscombe's office to get an injection when the radio broadcast told me about the shooting. After that I was so concerned that you might have been hurt—"

"Didn't you call the hospital?"

"Yes. But the Cardiac Alert was on."

"The clinic operator could have told you it was Paul."

"By that time I was too upset to think clearly. When I left the hospital after we talked to Dave Rogan, the clinic was closed and by the time I got home the pain was so bad I was almost blind. I was undressing up here, when I happened to see that little case of yours. I don't know what made me do it, Pete. I guess I was upset about so many things—worrying about losing you because of my ambition, worrying about your being shot, disturbed about Lorrie and troubled for Elaine and Paul—that it all sort of piled up on me. When I saw the little tube, it seemed to offer a way to relieve the pain."

"As I remember that night, it did a lot more than that."

"If I didn't feel so wonderful now, I'd feel ashamed of the way I acted then."

"But you're not?"

"No."

"You don't need to—not ever again. A husband and wife who really love each other shouldn't be ashamed of anything that expresses their love and makes them happy."

"From now on I'm going to spend my time trying to be what you want me to be, not what I thought I wanted to be," she promised. "I'll start by calling up the delegates today and releasing them."

"I don't want you to do that."

"Why?"

"You're a person, Amy, an individual in your own right—with a lot of drive. When a woman like you marries, she almost always uses that drive to make her husband over into whatever she decides she wants him to be. Five years or so ago, you were hell-bent for me to be Professor of Surgery. When you failed, your ego felt slapped down and resented it, so you went on the auxiliary kick to get ahead of me."

"I don't want to get ahead of you any more."

"You don't now—because you've just been made love to. You're enjoying what the sexologists call postcoital lassitude."

"Hurrah for postcoital lass—whatever it is."

"I couldn't agree more. A few hours from now, you'll be Amy Weston Brennan again, with all your energy intact. And believe me, I'd rather have that energy directed toward making you president of the national medical auxiliary than making me over. I happen to be a stubborn Irishman who's perfectly satisfied with the way he is."

"I'm satisfied with the way you are, too." She took his face between her hands and pulled his head down to kiss him. "Right now, I want to be made love to again."

"Not unless you've got an ampule of testosterone propionate hidden somewhere that I can give myself with that syringe," he told her with a grin. "I'm almost forty-five years old, you shameless wench, so what you have in mind is physically impossible for another couple of hours at least. Let's go to sleep."

CHAPTER TWENTY-SIX

I

Alice was already at the breakfast table when Roy came down shortly before eight Sunday morning. Sitting across from him while the maid served them, she was as demure and composed as if nothing that had happened last night had actually transpired.

Women! he thought. I'll never understand them.

But why try when they were far more interesting and exciting if you took them as they were. He had been taking Alice for granted all these years. And looking at her now, with every hair intact, the epitome of the successful professional man's wife in the upper social level, you would never think she could—

"The paper says the grand jury turned Mort Dellman loose." Alice looked up from the headlines, which were all she read—except the funnies.

"I guess I was too busy after I came home last night to mention it."

"I've been wondering why he shot Lorrie. But I guess it must have been because Uncle Jacob changed his will."

"What?" Roy looked up from his section of the paper, startled by what he thought he'd heard—and couldn't believe.

"Uncle Jacob changed his will several weeks ago—put everything in trust for the children, with the bank as trustee."

"How do you know this?"

"Uncle Jacob told Amy about it day before yesterday, when she went to see whether he needed any help about the funeral. Amy told me yesterday at the funeral but I was so upset about Lorrie being bur—I guess I just forgot it."

"The conniving bastard!" Roy exploded. "I knew something about that statement of Mort's before the jury didn't jibe with Paul McGill's deposition, but I couldn't figure out what it was. Mort said the room was dark but Paul didn't, so Mort actually knew who he was shooting all the time. This was a chance to get back at Lorrie over the medical student and clean up on his own account with the hundred thousand he'd get for his share in the clinic, plus the two hundred thousand he planned to stick Uncle Jake for letting the children stay here, and the insurance. I've got him."

"But the jury set Mort free."

"I can always reopen the case with new evidence and I'm going to do it, no matter what the consequences. This establishes a clear case of premeditated murder." He reached for the telephone book, and finding the number he wanted, dialed it rapidly.

"Jim," he said when Sergeant O'Brien answered his phone, "I want you to haul Mort Dellman in wherever you can find him. I've got new evidence and I'll get the warrants—"

"You're too late."

"You mean he's already skipped town?"

"He skipped all right. The eight o'clock news is just coming on. Turn on your radio and you'll get the details."

Roy switched over to the sidetable and switched on the small radio they used sometimes for listening to the early morning news. When the first words of the broadcast struck his ears, he hung up the telephone and sat listening closely:

The identity of two men killed in the crash of a private plane just north of Birmingham early this morning has now been definitely established. One was Percy Damon, owner of Weston's Charter Flying Service and pilot of the plane. The other was Dr. Mortimer Dellman, freed only last night by the Weston County Grand Jury in the killing of his wife, the socially prominent former debutante, Loretta Porter, daughter of Jacob Porter, a leading industrialist.

According to the tower at Weston County Airport, the plane took off in very bad flying weather shortly after midnight, the pilot having filed a flight plan showing New Orleans as its destination. Police authorities who found the plane several hours ago reported that Dr. Dellman was carrying a large amount of money on his person.

"So that's that." Roy reached over and shut off the radio when the announcer turned to national news. "Abner Townsend won't be able to make anything out of the case now."

He looked across the table and grinned at Alice. "You look mighty pretty this morning, sweet. I think you're going to enjoy being the wife of the next state attorney general."

II

Sunday mornings, Mabel always went to early Mass, then came by the Snack Bar for breakfast. The terms of her employment allowed her one free meal a day, in addition to the one she ate while on duty in the evening—usually on the run.

"Everybody at church was talking about Dr. Dellman getting off and then being killed in a plane," she said to Geraldine, the morning-shift cook, as they were enjoying coffee and cigarettes together in the almost deserted restaurant.

"In here, too." Geraldine was inclined to be phlegmatic.

"It's funny." Mabel looked across the almost deserted street to the emergency entrance of the hospital. "To look over there now, you'd hardly believe all hell could break loose before you could say boo—like it did last Wednesday afternoon."

"That was something," Geraldine agreed.

"I guess Dr. Dellman getting killed sort of wraps the whole thing up. From what I've been hearing across this counter the past few days, a lot of people have had their lives changed since last Wednesday. It was pretty exciting while it lasted, though."

"Yeah," said Geraldine. "I guess it was."

"It's sorta like the passage the priest read from the Bible this morning. I think I still remember it:

A generation goes, a generation comes, yet the earth stands firm forever. The sun rises, the sun sets; and then to its place it speeds and there it rises . . .

"That reminds me," Mabel sighed. "Monday morning you'd better tell the assistant manager to take that other waffle iron and have it fixed. The upper-class medical students will be coming back to school next week. They sure do like our waffles."

Surgeon's Choice

CHAPTER ONE

I

Greg Alexander was perspiring freely by the time the red warning light went off in the small air lock of the hyperbaric chamber, indicating that, with the pressures now equal, he could open the main door between them without danger of lowering the vital concentration of air in the larger compartment. Through the small glass port, or window, set into the steel wall of the air lock, he could see one of the group of ex-Navy divers who operated the chamber from outside. And when the technician held up his hand with thumb and forefinger joined in the circle that was a universal sign of approval, Greg turned the latch opening the inner door and stepped into the brightly lit main compartment.

A highly sophisticated adaptation of the old-style pressure tank used to prevent—or treat—the "bends," which had so often crippled caisson workers years ago, the hyperbaric—literally "high pressure"—chamber had been devised for medical use, where the high oxygen concentrations it made possible were of considerable value in many special surgical procedures, as well as in diseases where air pressure was important.

Compressing air into the metal cylinder—not much larger than the buried tanks of large service stations—also concentrated the heat inside that air, so the temperature always rose rapidly during the initial period of pressure rise. Greg had undergone just such a rapid compression inside the cramped space of the air lock, hence the fine layer of perspiration that now covered his body and his sudden shiver when he encountered the cooler air inside the chamber itself.

Essentially a steel tank with glass ports through which the technicians outside could maintain a constant watch on those inside and pumps for controlling the pressure of air inside the chamber, as well as gauges reading constantly the temperature, humidity and other important factors, the chamber was a self-contained unit, with its own power source, in case of an electrical failure. Set into the side was a smaller air lock for the insertion of necessary instruments and medications, or the removal of tissue specimens for immediate pathological study, without disturbing the pressure level within the main part of the chamber. At one end stood a small compact laboratory cabinet and sink, allowing immediate emergency chemical procedures to be carried on inside the chamber.

The scene that met Greg Alexander's eyes was a familiar one: he might almost have been looking into a mirror, for, in hundreds of operations, he had himself occupied the central position at the narrow operating table. Hans Werner, the grizzled caretaker-technician for the Laboratory of Experimental Surgery, was in his usual place at the table's head but Dr. Jack Smith, professor of veterinary medicine at the nearby university veterinary school, occupied Greg's usual position beside it, holding up his rubber-gloved hands so their sterility would not be lost. The star of this little tableau, upon whose staging was centered tonight the entire life-preserving facilities of one of the two or three finest clinics in the world, was a brown and white spaniel lying quietly in the cone of brilliant light cast by a lamp in the ceiling.

Like everything else inside the hyperbaric chamber, the lamp was elaborately protected from any possibility of a short circuit or spark, which, because of the high concentrations of oxygen often used in hyperbaric medicine, could convert the entire inside of the tank into an inferno. Even the pumps that activated the suction apparatus for surgery and the drills, saw and other mechanical tools were all operated by air pressure through metal tubes brought in from outside—designed to remove any danger of spark.

The old Austrian technician was crooning a lullaby to the dog as she breathed oxygen through a special mask. Trained to tolerate the mask without struggling, she was breathing easily as she lay there, her belly swollen with pregnancy and the long white scar of a healed surgical incision across her chest in sharp contrast under the bright light to the sleek brown of her coat. The dog's eyes were bright with interest—and with trust—for she had lain on this same table several times before.

"No action yet?" Greg asked.

"Not so far, but the contractions are rhythmic, so it could come at any time," said the veterinarian. "Sorry I had to keep you from the symphony, but you did ask to be called when things got going and Hans said you would want to be here."

"Hans knows I skip the symphony whenever I can find an excuse." Greg smiled as he moved up to the table and reached across the old technician's shoulder to scratch the dog's ear, while her tail thumped against the cushion of the operating table in an acknowledgment of the gesture of friendship. "Maybe Letty does, too, and chose tonight just to help me."

"You must learn to enjoy music, Dr. Alexander." Hans Werner's voice still had a guttural accent even after more than twenty years in the United States, all spent in the animal house and experimental laboratory. "Ach! If you could only have been in Vienna in the old days, you would have heard music that was music."

"I'll go there when I retire, Hans," Greg promised.

"On a stretcher that will be," said the Austrian. "Or a bier."

When he'd stepped into the chamber from the air lock, Greg Alexander's swift glance had noted that the preparations he had ordered for Letty's accouchement were all made, as he'd been sure they would be. The large sterile tray at the far end, covered with a greenish tinted sterile sheet from the main operating room suite, was ready in case an emergency Caesarean section became necessary. Everything seemed well under control, however, so he allowed himself to relax.

Hans was Greg's right hand in the laboratory, where he spent as much of his time as could be taken from his duties as chief surgeon of The Clinic: he depended on the old Austrian, not only during the experimental surgery, from which had come the most advanced operative procedures in heart and lung transplant in in the world, but for the care of the animals, which, like Letty, became quite as much individuals as any human patients—with the added ingredient of love. The animals early learned to love and trust their keepers and so the element of fear, so often a deciding factor in the outcome of delicate and dangerous surgery, was absent with them, making animal surgery usually more successful than operations on humans.

"Letty's enjoying this." Conscious for the first time in a long and busy day of being bone tired, Greg pulled up a stool beside Hans. "She knows she's the prima donna tonight."

"How long ago is it since she was your first successful heart-lung transplant case?" Dr. Smith asked.

"About seven months. Now she's racking up another first by having pups."

Letty whimpered softly as a contraction gripped her uterus, then relaxed again.

"She's about to go into high gear," said the veterinarian. "We could give her Nembutal but I'd rather not. Sometimes the puppies are so sleepy afterwards you have trouble making them breathe."

"Dogs knew about natural childbirth long before people did," said Hans Werner. "Don't vorry. Letty will take care of herself when the time comes."

"While we're waiting," the veterinarian said to Greg Alexander, "would you mind cluing me in on this hyperbaric technique? We horse doctors don't have such modern equipment in our business."

"A lot of clinics wouldn't call this rusty old tank very modern," Greg admitted wryly. "Down at Duke they've got a triple chamber that makes ours look like the one-horse shay."

"Still it vorks," said Hans Werner. "What you have accomplished in the old laboratory, Dr. Alexander, a lot of new schools, with all that steel and glass, will never do so well."

"We're now under only two atmospheres of pressure, and that's just a precautionary measure for Letty's safety, to take all the load we can off her heart during delivery," said Greg, going back to Dr. Smith's question. "I don't imagine you've noticed much of an effect from it at all."

"Nothing except an acute exacerbation of my normal claustrophobia, and a sudden sweat right after they closed the outside doors."

"We all have that experience," said Greg. "When you pump a lot of air into a small space, you pump a lot of heat in with it. This is a small chamber and the air conditioning isn't very effective. I had a larger chamber in the new laboratory I planned two years ago."

"The one the Board of Trustees wouldn't approve?"

"Yes. Just between us, I'm glad they didn't, because it wouldn't have been adequate for our needs. Hospital construction is changing so fast that what I wanted to build two years ago would have been antiquated by now. This time I'm going to shoot for twin chambers, with an air lock between, maybe even one of those wet tanks like they have at Duke for simulating deep-sea dives."

"I don't see how you're going to be able to anticipate future developments if medicine is changing as fast as you say it is," Dr. Smith observed.

"We can't anticipate everything. But since the National Institute of Health gave me the funds to build this small chamber, we've—at least learned what we'll really need later on."

"I still don't understand completely how it works," the veterinarian said.

"Fundamentally, all we have here is a tank and a pump for compressing air into it," said Greg. "The air inside the chamber now is under twice the pressure we normally breathe outside, but you're not conscious of it because it's both inside and outside our bodies. The only reason for using pressure with Letty is to put more oxygen into her blood and thus ease the load on her heart—or rather the one we gave her at operation seven months ago."

"That's the part that really bugs me," Dr. Smith admitted. "When I studied physiology, we were taught that the hemoglobin in the red blood cells is saturated with O-two in the lungs and can't carry any more."

"That's true."

"Then how can raising the pressure in the chamber or breathing pure oxygen—or even both, as Letty's doing now—get more oxygen into the body?"

"The fluid part of the blood—the plasma—carries the extra oxygen to the tissues," Greg explained. "With normal breathing at atmospheric pressure, the red cell hemoglobin carries roughly nineteen or twenty cubic centimeters of oxygen for every hundred cc. of blood, but only three tenths of a cc. is dissolved in every hundred of plasma."

"That would have a negligible effect as far as the supply of oxygen to the body cells is concerned."

"Exactly. Even breathing pure O-two at atmospheric pressure only puts about two cc. of oxygen into each hundred cc. of plasma. But raise the pressure to three atmospheres while breathing pure oxygen and the amount dissolved in the plasma jumps three times."

"That's quite a change."

"At five times atmospheric pressure, we've been able to keep dogs alive in this chamber with no real blood in their circulations at all, using only a substitute that contains no red cells or hemoglobin. You can see what that would mean with a severe case of hemorrhage, for example."

"What about other uses?"

"We're in pretty much new territory there, although new work is being published all the time," Greg admitted. "The main argument I used to get the grant for this chamber from the National Institute of Health was that with it we can keep an organ we're going to transplant into another body alive and healthy a lot longer than we'd ordinarily be able to do. Hyperbaric oxygen is also pretty effective in early anerobic infections, but we've had only a few opportunities to treat those yet."

"For transplanting in humans, I can see that you could use the double chamber you mentioned," said Dr. Smith. "Think you can convince the board of that?"

The dog whined into the oxygen mask before Greg could answer. "I think they come now," said Hans Werner, and Greg looked quickly at the electronic monitor tube at the end of the chamber. The pattern of Letty's heartbeat was being shown there in a steady progression of moving lines across the face of the tube, and was also being recorded permanently by a sensitive stylus upon a moving strip of electrocardiographic tracing paper.

"The beat is steady and regular, with no sign of fibrillation," he said on a note of quiet satisfaction. "I think we're going to make it O.K." He leaned over to scratch the dog's ear again. "Stay with it, Letty, you're the only one of your kind in the world tonight."

Four puppies were shortly delivered in rapid succession. Afterward the veterinarian kneaded the dog's belly gently until the placenta was expelled.

"I don't believe her pulse varied a beat during the entire delivery." Greg's voice was quietly exultant. "This should be the final proof, Hans."

"For me," the old Austrian said with a shrug, "it was proved already."

"Any idea when you'll do your first human heart-lung transplant?" Dr. Smith asked as he and Greg paused in the air lock for the very brief period of decompression necessary after an exposure of two atmospheres.

"That's in the lap of the gods. We've had a number of successful transplants of the heart alone, but for both the heart and the lungs, even closer selection is required. It might be next week—or next year."

"I'm flattered that I could play a small part in tonight's triumph." Dr. Smith shivered as the temperature in the air lock rapidly declined with the loss of pressure, the reverse of what had happened when the huge steel tank had been inflated. "How long will it take us to decompress?"

"Actually, you and I could step out now with no danger of getting the bends," said Greg. "But it's just as well not to rush things."

"I've done a little scuba diving and this high oxygen pressure business intrigues me," said the veterinarian. "Do you mind if I look in on your experimental work from time to time?"

"I'll be disappointed if you don't," Greg assured him. "If we're lucky enough to get approval from the trustees for a set of chambers like they have at Duke, we hope to study what happens to skindivers who keep going down, even after they pass the point of safe return."

Outside the building, Greg turned up the collar of his tweed jacket. The February wind was whipping up from the harbor, as only that of a Baltimore winter could do, and there was a threat of snow in the lowering sky.

"You can see how much the board thinks of the Laboratory of Experimental Surgery," he said wryly as they crossed to the main enclosed corridor of the hospital by way of an open walkway. "They didn't even give us a covered passage to it."

"It doesn't seem right," said the veterinarian. "Some of the most important work on organ transplant has been done here—but only because you persevered in spite of all the handicaps."

"Many of medicine's most valuable discoveries have been made under similar conditions," said Greg, "so I suppose I've got no real cause to complain. Doctors are lousy money raisers, so we need a few millionaires on our boards—"

"As stubborn ones as Sam Hunter?"

"Don't forget that he's got as much money as the rest of them put together."

"I'm not forgetting it," said Dr. Smith. "But is he likely to let you forget it? If I had anything to do with it, the board would vote you a medal when it meets Saturday morning. Instead, they'll probably kick your teeth in, if the way they've treated the most important department of the whole clinic in the past is any example."

II

Just off the rotunda of the central building that alone had housed the original clinic, a doctors' call-board was set against the back wall of the main corridor. The light behind Greg's name was still on, showing that he was in the hospital, and he pushed the button beside it, turning off the light behind his name there and also on a similar board before the telephone operators in an alcove off the hospital foyer.

Above the call-board was a bronze plaque with the raised letter across the top: "THE CLINIC FOUNDATION AND HOSPITAL IN THE CITY OF BALTIMORE." Beneath it, a group of other letters, smaller in size, spelled out: "An Institution for the Care of the Sick, Operated Not for Profit by a Board of Trustees Elected by the Members of The Clinic."

Conceived and brilliantly executed in a day when group medical practice was almost unheard of, The Clinic—as its founder had insisted upon calling it—had been the dream of one man, Dr. Henry Anders. Fifty years later on this February afternoon, the soul of Henry Anders was still a vigorous current flowing through every part of the great institution. Moreover, the "Members of The Clinic," composed not only of its staff but also of those who, as Fellows, had honed their medical and surgical skills to a fine point during two years devoted to postgraduate study here, contained within its ranks more famous medical and surgical names throughout the world than any other institution could boast.

In the rotunda, Greg Alexander paused in the shadows beside the marble figure of Christ, which, two stories high, dominated the entire entrance foyer. It had been a long day for The Clinic's chief surgeon, beginning with morning rounds in the surgical building, then a clinical demonstration in the old surgical lecture room with its steeply rising rows of seats filled with students and Fellows, followed by a quick lunch in the hospital cafeteria before the usual afternoon of work in the Laboratory of Experimental Surgery.

Finally had come the conference, lasting far longer than planned, with Keith Jackson, the brilliant Harvard-trained architect who was in the final stage of planning a projected new hospital and diagnostic clinic building complex to replace the old, and long since outgrown, brownstone buildings of the original clinic and hospital.

Although a continuous tide of humanity ebbed and flowed through the hospital foyer only yards away from the statue, it was quiet here in the shadows behind it, and Greg felt an almost physical force holding him back from stepping out into the flow, which would, in a sense, rejoin him to the rest of the world.

The conference with Keith Jackson plus Letty's delivery had made him late again in getting home, a fact which, he knew, would only increase the wall of tension that had been growing between him and Jeanne these past months.

Or was it years?

The change had been so gradual that, coming home dead tired each night from his work as executive head of The Clinic—although Dr. Henry Anders II, son of the founder, held the nominal title of director—he could not tell when it had actually begun.

Twenty years ago, when Greg had first come to The Clinic as a young Fellow in Surgery, with four years of medical school at Johns Hopkins and a two-year internship there behind him, he had met Jeanne for their first date "at the feet of Jesus," in the parlance of the young doctors and nurses. For an instant now, as he stood in the shadows, he was startled to see her appear—as she had then—from the other side of the great statue, the fluted cap of a senior student nurse upon her golden hair and the blue cape hanging from shoulders, which, after all these years, were just as proud and lovely as they had been then.

Then the girl said, "Good evening, Dr. Alexander," and he realized that his imagination had been playing him tricks again, obeying a deep inner wish that he and Jeanne could both go back to that long lost first meeting here and recapture some of the years of happiness and loving companionship which had followed.

The spell broken, Greg came out of the shadows into the brighter light of the foyer and the ebb and flow of the human tide through it. As he was pulling up the collar of his jacket again, preparing for the cold outside the double doors, a tall young doctor in a white coat came through and stopped at the sight of him.

"I guess you could shoot me, Dr. Alexander." Bob Johnson's tone was rueful. "I went out to the delicatessen to get some salami and while I was gone the call came from Hans. Did you have to go into the chamber?"

"It was no trouble at all, Bob." Greg was very fond of the Senior Fellow in Vascular Surgery, who was his right hand. "Your friend Keith Jackson kept me over here until nearly eight anyway and all I had to do was stop by and congratulate Letty."

"She came through all right then?"

"Not so much as an extrasystole. Four puppies and all beauties. Maybe Hans will let you have one of them for your boy."

"Were you pleased—with what Keith showed you—sir?"

"More than pleased. Have you seen it?"

Bob Johnson shook his head. "Keith's been acting very mysterious lately and Mary's hardly been able to get him out of his drawing room for meals. Well, good night, sir. I promise that you won't be disturbed any more tonight. You must be worn out."

"I'm a little but a drink and some food will take care of that. Going home?"

"Not just yet. I want to recheck everything for the heart-lung transplant demonstration we're doing for the convocation. We can't have anything go wrong with all that medical brass watching. See you in the morning, sir."

On the steps outside, looking down the curving driveway to the broad street in front called The Parkway, Greg paused while a delivery truck passed. A couple of inches less than six feet, he was of medium build and, at forty-five, beginning to thicken a little around the middle because he rarely had time for any physical exercise except his work. His iron-gray hair was thinning a bit at the front but he still refused to wear a hat, even in winter, largely because he knew he'd never be able to remember where he'd left it last. The eyes beneath slightly bushy brows had lost none of their keenness, or kindliness, during the years, though some of the merriment that had twinkled at their corners, when he was younger, had been erased since he'd begun to worry so much about Jeanne.

When he'd been a Senior Fellow like Bob Johnson nearly twenty years ago, Greg and Jeanne had moved as newlyweds into an apartment in one of the brownstone-front, common-walled houses that had lined the other side of The Parkway then. Now they occupied an apartment in almost the same spot, one of several penthouse units that made up the top floor of the tall building which, with the adjoining Clinic Inn, more than a decade ago had replaced the older houses with their white marble steps that had once lined the south of the thoroughfare. Buildings housing married Fellows and residents and the Nursing Home for the hospital completed a two-block front now. And compared to these modern structures, the brownstone of the rotunda which had housed the original clinic, and the two hospital wings on either side, only a few years less aged, were now relics of the past.

"Paper, Doctor?" When a newsboy thrust a copy of the evening paper before Greg Alexander's eyes, he saw across the top the heavy black headline:

MURDERER THOUGHT TO BE IN BALTIMORE AREA

From his pocket he fished out a dime and shoved the paper beneath his arm as he started down the walkway past the sundial in the center of the grassplot bounded by the curving drive. As he paused at the booth by the gate to acknowledge the greeting of the guard—part of whose aorta he had replaced with a tube of nylon mesh five years before—he could see a line of expensive-looking automobiles lined up under the marquee of the Clinic Inn next door to his apartment house.

Friends and former Fellows would be gathering in the Falstaff Room already for drinks and rehashing of old times, he knew, and it would be pleasant to sip a tall drink with them but he resolutely put temptation aside. Things had become strained between him and Jeanne since that day two years ago, when he had come from the trustees' meeting that was always held at the end of a Convocation of the Members of The Clinic with the news that his plan for a new building complex had been summarily defeated. But he was loyal enough to her, and to what they'd had together,

not to take the easy way out and avoid facing her anger at his being late by
stopping for a more pleasant hour at the inn.

Thinking of Jeanne, Greg glanced up to one of the two balconies fronting
upon the street atop the Clinic Apartments, marking the location of the two
penthouses. In summer, she'd often waved to him from the height, as he
crossed The Parkway, but tonight the balcony was empty. He didn't notice
the quick movement back into the shadows of the man who had been
leaning over the rail of the adjoining balcony to watch him. But when Dr.
Henry Anders II, director of The Clinic and only son of its founder, opened
the door leading into the adjoining penthouse to Greg's, there was a smile of
vast satisfaction on his somewhat overly handsome face.

III

On another—and smaller—terrace, well below the penthouse level, Keith
Jackson lit a cigarette as he studied, for perhaps the hundredth time, the
buildings sprawled upon rising ground across The Parkway. He wasn't
seeing the ugliness of the brownstone front, the windows filmed with
pollutants that fouled the atmosphere or the rounded dome of the rotunda,
however. Instead, his mind's eye had captured a vision, a soaring tower of
twenty stories with two more underground, a temple of healing epitomizing
the vastly complicated medical science of tomorrow, with, flanking it at half
that height, two hospital wings that would provide adjunct service and
double the capacity of the institution.

Inside the tower itself would be concentrated facilities for several hundred
patients, postoperative, cardiac, severe infections—any conditions requiring
constant watching and intensive treatment. With no patient more than fifty
feet from centrally located nursing stations upon each floor and each room
under constant watch by means of monitor tubes fed by closed-circuit TV
cameras anchored near the ceiling, a patient need never feel that he was
alone.

With a wealth of information about pulse, temperature, respiration, the
electrocardiographic tracing—shortened in hospital shorthand to ECG—the
oxygen level of the blood and a dozen other factors which could strongly
influence the often delicate balance between living and dying continually
being watched by sensors developed for monitoring astronauts in orbit
hundreds of miles above the earth, and programmed through a master
computer to sound a strident warning of any deviation from normal, the sick
patient could be far more closely watched than if a skilled nurse were
actually standing by the bedside. Most important of all, the double load of
patients the Intensive Care Tower allowed would require little additional
hospital personnel, an extremely important factor in a day when the supply
of highly trained nurses did not even equal half the demand.

It was a magnificent dream, one that had been forming slowly in Keith
Jackson's creative mind ever since Greg Alexander had invited him two
years earlier to submit preliminary drawings for new clinic and hospital
buildings to replace the now thoroughly antiquated ones across the street.
The limitations imposed then by the trustees—and carefully detailed for
him several months before by Greg Alexander, when Keith had asked about
submitting plans again—had been like a blanket upon any creative action,
however, and he hadn't even considered submitting sketches—until Henry
Anders had brought the magazine article to him hardly a week ago. Nothing
else had been needed to release the creative flow after that, and, working all
night at the drawing boards he kept in the apartment, Keith had captured

in the lines, angles and shadows of preliminary sketches, the essential substance of the dream before it could flit away.

When he'd showed the sketches to Greg Alexander for the first time earlier that afternoon, he'd been ready to do battle for his concept and for its execution in place of the more humdrum, conventional sort of building complex which a staid architectural firm downtown had already designed and which awaited only the approval of the trustees to begin its execution in steel, brick, mortar and stone.

The eyes of The Clinic's surgeon-in-chief had lit up the moment he saw that soaring tower and the graceful wings supporting it, and he'd nodded approval again and again while Keith pointed out the many advantages of the design.

Later Greg Alexander had added suggestions here and there, filling out from his vast experience the picture the architect was sketching. The surgeon himself had suggested a more full use of the master computer to marshal the flow of information from patients to the central storage center and also to execute the tremendously complex orders which were so important in the modern-day treatment of the desperately ill. The first frown had come to Greg Alexander's brow when Keith had mentioned an estimated cost of twenty-eight million dollars.

"The plans we already have would cost barely two thirds of that," he protested. "Fifteen to eighteen million according to the architect's estimate."

"But look at the difference in efficency and the number of patients you could handle, Doctor," Keith had protested. "Your skilled nursing staff need not be any larger than with the first plant, perhaps even smaller, yet you can care for half again as many acutely ill patients as you do now. And by utilizing the somewhat newer buildings behind the original structure for ambulatory and convalescing patients, as well as those being examined for pre-admission studies, the capacity of the diagnostic clinic can easily be doubled, as well as the number of patients in the hospital itself."

"Would you be able to run a time-study analysis before the trustees' meeting Saturday morning?" Greg Alexander asked.

"It may take some doing," said Keith. "But a friend of mine is an assistant analyst for TRW. I've already talked to him about this project and the company has been pioneering medical automation, so it may be that he can run a few studies for us between now and then."

"I'll need that when the Board of Trustees meets on Saturday after the convocation, along with as detailed preliminary sketches as you're able to give me."

"You'll have them," Keith had promised, and only now, when he thought of the work he had to get done before Saturday, did the young architect become a little scared.

After he left Greg's office, Keith had remembered his brief talk with Dr. Henry Anders II and wondered whether he should mention it. But there had been no reason not to believe Dr. Anders' explanation of his visit to the architect's office a week earlier, for who could have a greater interest than the son of the founder in seeing a monument to his father's genius rise above the old clinic.

A tapping sounded on the door behind him and through the glass Keith Jackson saw his wife, Mary, beckoning him inside to dinner. The apartment was one of the smaller ones in the building, with two bedrooms, a den which he used as an at-home office, a living room with a dining area, kitchen and bath.

"I met Dr. Alexander just now as I was going out to the delicatessen at the corner," she told him when he came inside. "He said your preliminary sketches are truly inspiring."

"The sketches are fine; I'm a good enough architect to know that without Dr. Alexander's approval." Keith pulled out a chair for Mary at the small table. "But I still don't understand why Dr. Anders brought the idea to me."

"Perhaps he remembered your plans from two years ago!"

"Not when he was a leader in the faction that torpedoed Dr. Alexander's ideas. By the way," he added, "I saw Dr. Anders come into the building as I was parking my car in the garage. Do you suppose Dr. Alexander called him about the project?"

"Really, darling," said Mary. "Don't you ever see anything but a drawing board?"

"What have I done now?"

"Dr. Anders has been sneaking into the apartment house through the garage for more than six months now."

"Why?"

"He's sleeping with Dr. Helen Foucald. No, I guess sleeping is the wrong word. He never stays more than a couple of hours."

"Two hours! What is he? Superman?"

"Just about that—from what I hear."

"Where do you get all this stuff?"

"Don't forget that I was a nurse across the street. Everybody over there knows Dr. Anders will make a pass at anything in skirts that looks promising—and go even farther when he finds one with enough curiosity."

"Curiosity about what?"

"Really, darling." Mary had the grace to blush. "Don't you ever listen to gossip?"

"Why should I—when you'll tell me eventually?"

"Let's just say that Dr. Henry Anders II is said to be bigger than life."

"But Dr. Foucald's such a prim thing—more like an old-maid school-teacher."

Mary learned over and kissed him.

"Thanks," he said. "What was that for?"

"For not really seeing Dr. Foucald. She makes a pregnant wife look like something the cat dragged in—with those Paris clothes of hers and that figure. But what makes you think there's any funny business about Dr. Anders wanting you to do the new plan?"

"I don't know—except that it's no secret how he and some others on the board fought Dr. Alexander to a standstill when he wanted to build a modern hospital two years ago. The main reason I wasn't even going to submit a plan this time was because the conditions were too rigid. Now suddenly, the sky's the limit."

"Don't look the gift horse too deep in the mouth. Have you figured what six per cent commission is on twenty-eight million dollars?"

"I still can't help wondering if Dr. Anders is trying to steal a march on Dr. Alexander."

"You mean like claiming he thought of the new plan first?"

"Maybe. He made me promise not to tell Dr. Alexander about his part in it, but he also insisted that I show the sketches to Dr. Alexander no later than today."

"Did he say why?"

"Only that if Dr. Alexander knew about his part in it he might be prejudiced against the plan."

"Dr. Alexander's not that sort of person," said Mary. "Besides, he's responsible for the whole convocation—"

"I thought they only had those at universities for graduations. Or when they give an honorary degree to a big shot who might donate a lot of money."

"Old Dr. Anders called the first meeting a convocation and the name stuck," Mary explained. "Former Fellows who have made some spectacular accomplishment through research or a new discovery are asked to present their findings before the group. If it's a new operation, the surgeon who worked it out usually does one as a demonstration, like the heart-lung transplant Dr. Alexander's going to do Thursday afternoon on a dog."

"How did you know about that?"

"Bob Johnson's the Senior Fellow in Vascular Surgery and Dr. Alexander's assistant, remember? Harriet was telling me about it in the laundromat this morning."

"That reminds me," said Keith. "The clinical laboratory is a pretty important part of an automated setup like the one I'm planning. Maybe I ought to spend some time with Dr. Foucald discussing the details."

"See that you spend that time in the lab then," Mary warned darkly. "With plenty of people around you."

CHAPTER TWO

I

Standing beside Ted as they waited for their entrance cue for the evening performance, Vivian Tarentino Hunter was a pocket Venus in her white nylon tights. The youngest daughter of an Italian circus family, born in Sarasota and reared there, Vivian had gone on the road at twelve with the one-ring Tarentino Circus her father had inherited from his father. Leaving the sawdust ring to go to college, she had met Ted at Florida State University, where he was already a member of the famed college circus troupe, and quickly earned a berth for herself with the flying trapeze act of which Ted was already a part.

The second son of Sam Hunter, the multimillionaire oil man and corporation stealer, Ted had gone to Tallahssee instead of following the traditional Hunter course of a B.A. degree at Austin, a year in Europe and an M.B.A. at the Harvard Business School. Actually, old Sam hadn't looked with particular favor upon his son being a circus performer, but since it was a college affair and Ted's grades were excellent, his bellow of protest had been somewhat muted. But when Ted announced just before graduation that he and Vivian had been married for three months, old Sam had hit the ceiling and disinherited his second son, refusing even to meet his daughter-in-law or see Ted receive his diploma at Tallahassee.

Ted and Vivian had been a double act during his last year at F.S.U., so it had been natural for them to take their talents to the ailing Tarentino Circus, traveling by truck from small town to small town, playing in large high-school auditoriums or whatever they could find. But with cataracts and retinal degeneration slowly cutting off his vision, Papa Gus Tarentino was about ready to throw in the towel at the end of the present season. Vivian had been taking a correspondence school business course so she could work as a secretary when Ted went to graduate school in the fall to get the M.B.A. his father had wanted him to get in the first place—but with the difference that if he won the coveted Harvard degree now, he'd be under no obligation to anyone.

Ted's left arm was around Vivian as they waited beside the exit from the auditorium floor for the elephant act which preceded their own to clear the ring. When he saw the line of elephants suddenly veer toward them, he quickly swept Vivian to safety behind him and, in the same movement, seized a stick lying on the ground close beside him. As he whacked the lead elephant on the snout, driving it back into the line, he could see the cause of the elephant's sudden fright, a mouse that had scampered across its path. And swinging the stick like a golf club, he knocked the tiny rodent out of the path of the other animals, saving the whole herd from stampeding.

"Quick thinking, fellow," said Joe Califino, the swarthy roustabout and elephant handler, as he passed them at the end of the animal queue. "Another minute and this lousy circus would have been spread all over the walls."

"You hurt your hand, Ted." Vivian's cry of concern directed his attention to a drop of blood on his right hand where a splinter from the stick he'd picked up protruded perhaps a quarter of an inch from the skin. Just then, however, the calliope—in the Tarentino Circus it took the place of a band—sounded the opening bars of the music introducing their act. So, reaching across with his left hand, he seized the end of the splinter between thumb and forefinger and jerked it out before falling into step behind Vivian for the march into the ring.

"Nothing but a splinter," he told her. "I pulled it out."

The "Ahhh" of admiration that went up from the audience when Vivian poised at the edge of the ring in the glare of the spotlight always gave Ted a thrill of appreciation, even though muted by the small size of the small-town crowd tonight. Once or twice, as he climbed hand over hand up to the trapeze while Vivian was being hauled up by the roustabout who watched their ropes, Ted felt a slight pricking in the web between the forefinger and thumb of his right hand where the splinter had gone in when he'd whacked the elephant a few moments before. But he had forgotten about it by the time he reached the trapeze bar to stand beside Vivian.

As the music of the calliope changed to a rock-and-roll rhythm, they swung into the routine they had worked out during their final year at F.S.U. and had taken on the annual tour of the college circus, including a swing through Europe that summer. In time with the throbbing beat, the two of them performed like a single being, going through the inricate evolutions of their act without a net, high above the heads of the spectators, while Papa Gus and Joe Califino watched from below, ready to throw their own bodies into the path of a fall, should either of the performers slip.

In preparation for the climax of the act, Ted gripped between his teeth a rubber guard to which a shorter trapeze bar was attached by means of a carefully looped nylon rope. Swinging down into the catching position of the trapeze performer, he anchored himself firmly while Vivian stood upon the bar above him, swinging in an arc.

When Ted was securely fixed in the catching position, she unhooked the short bar attached by the looped rope to the rubber guard he held with his teeth. For three swings she balanced without support upon the longer bar, then suddenly pitched forward in a somersault at the end of an arc, diving into the semi-darkness while the spot followed her progress. A gasp came from the audience as she flew through the air like a lovely white bird, plunging for a distance of more than two thirds of the space between the trapeze and the floor of the arena, while the carefully looped nylon rope attaching her to the rubber guard held between Ted's teeth uncoiled itself. Ted had seized the rope between his hands to take some of the shock of impact from his teeth. When he felt the slight jerk at the end of her fall, he gave the rope a twisting motion and removed his hands to leave her body spinning below him at the end of a tether, supported only by the rubber guard he held in his teeth and the nylon rope.

For three full swings across the ring, Vivian spun like a top at the end of a string. Then the watching roustabout flipped the ascent rope across her path so she could catch it with her leg and release her grip upon the trapeze. Ted, too, seized the rope above her and, clamping his legs about it, slid to the floor to stand beside Vivian, bowing to the applause of the audience before they stepped into the clogs they had left at the edge of the ring and started to their quarters.

"Your old man's picture's in the afternoon paper, Ted." The roustabout thrust a newspaper at him as they passed the area where the trucks were being loaded for tonight's move to another small Maryland town. "Send him a ticket to the show tomorrow night and maybe he'll buy the circus."

"Fat chance of his coming." Ted managed to smile, but more and more lately he'd felt sad at the long separation from the proud old man; and the sight of Sam Hunter's face in the newspaper picture only made it more acute now.

The Tarentino Circus traveled upon trucks, several of which had been converted into mobile homes for the performers and crew. Ted and Vivian had their own tiny compact compartment at the back of a truck driven by Joe, the elephant handler. It was parked on the lot behind the auditorium now, ready to move as soon as the performance ended and the rest of the equipment had been loaded aboard. Inside their mobile apartment, Ted lifted Vivian's short blond pony tail to kiss the back of her neck.

"They loved you tonight, hon," he said.

"What there was of them," said Vivian. "What did Joe say to you outside just now?"

"Dad's picture is in the paper." He opened the afternoon edition to reveal a four-column cut of Sam Hunter stepping down from his private jet.

"Why would he come to Baltimore now?"

"Dad's been a trustee of The Clinic ever since old Dr. Anders operated on mother over ten years ago and saved her life. Every two years they have a convention there toward the end of February. The trustees meet right afterwards and dad always comes up to Baltimore then to have his checkup before the meeting."

"He looks a lot older than the last picture I saw of him. Do you suppose he knows you're this close by?"

"He knows all right."

"Then maybe he'll—"

"Not yet," said Ted. "If either of us goes to the other now, it would look like giving in. I guess we're both a little stiff-necked; we're that much alike. But when I can hand him a diploma from the Harvard Business School, I'm sure we'll all be together again."

II

The sixth sense that tells a performer the temper of an audience, even through the closed doors of a dressing room, warned Georgia Merchant when the change came in the club itself. The first catcall was in the middle of Guy's favorite song, the imitation he did of Harry Richmond, complete with top hat and cane, and Georgia was on her feet at the raucous sound, heading for the door. By the time she reached the wings of the small stage of the sleazy Baltimore Street nightclub, however, almost the entire audience was beginning to boo.

Both the scene and the sound were all too familiar and Georgia was glad she had taken the precaution of getting dressed a little early, unconsciously, she realized now, as a precaution against just such an eventuality as this. With a quick glance, she checked the zippers on the several layers of fabric that covered her final costume, iridescent pasties over each of her nipples, and the briefest of G-strings, made of the same material. A second glance at the mirror beside the wing exit told her that, at forty-five, she was still as lush of form as she had been at thirty, when she and Guy were married. Only the face had begun to show the ravages of worry about him and the strain of the nightly grinds in smoky bottle clubs. Fortunately those lines could still be covered by the expertise she'd developed in makeup as the toll of years had left deeper and deeper marks.

True to the tradition into which he had been born, Guy was still trying to go on with the song, but when he turned toward the wings, the look in his face warned Georgia that something far deeper was wrong than the displeasure of a largely drunken audience at a failing comic. The grayness of his cheeks and the look of pain—physical, not mental—in his eyes, even as he sought to carry on his act and keep up the front, told her he was having another of his now periodic attacks.

"Get him off, Georgia!" Aaron Schwartz, the pudgy nightclub manager, was chewing nervously on the stump of his cigar. "A Teamster local's out there on a binge. They'll start tearing the place apart any minute now."

"My music, Gus," Georgia called to the piano player who led the four-piece band. "Loud and fast."

The drummer caught the words and stamped down hard on the pedal that pounded the bass drum. Guy looked startled, but, when he saw Georgia strutting out from the wings with the slinky stride of a stripper, as only she could do, the look of relief on his face almost made her cry.

"Go lie down, honey." She spoke out of the corner of her mouth as she passed him, and the light man mercifully darkened the stage, leaving only a bright spot on Georgia and giving Guy time to slink off without being conspicuous.

"Take it off, baby!" A voice shouted good-naturedly from the back of the crowd, and, when laughter swept the room Georgia knew the immediate emergency was over. Over, that was, as far as the club's being torn apart by the patrons was concerned, but probably far from over for Guy, if this attack followed the pattern set by the others.

Anxious to finish her act and get back to Guy, Georgia signaled to the drummer to step up the tempo of the bumps and grinds for which she was famous, and the rest of the band had no choice except to follow the lead of the pounding beat. Being the featured performer, she normally didn't start the real strip until the act was half finished, dragging it out with flip asides to the audience, while she slowly peeled off long gloves and toyed with a feather boa, a technique she'd perfected long ago on the burlesque stage in a happier and more prosperous era. But now she wasted no time and the layers began to come off in fairly rapid succession.

At first the audience loved it, but, as the flimsy draperies that made up her outer costume followed each other to the floor, she sensed that they had begun to realize they were being cheated of the full measure.

"For God's sake, take it easy, Georgia," the manager pleaded when she paused in the wings after stripping down to the net bra that covered the pasties and the outer—and larger—of her two G-strings.

"How's Guy?" she asked as the audience began to shout for her return.

"He's having pain; we sent for a doc."

The roar of the audience was an animal sound now and heavy feet had begun to stamp in rhythm with the music. As Georgia hesitated, torn between the need to go to Guy and the knowledge of what would happen if the audience got any uglier, the manager gave her a shove that sent her stumbling back onto the stage and into the spotlight.

Baffled and angry, she stood stock-still for a moment, glaring at the impatient drinkers. Then, as the drummer began the beat, she deliberately put her hands behind her head and, squatting almost upon her heels in the classic pose, began a slow and sinuous rise to her full height, ending with a thunderous bump, as the drummer hit both cymbals at once with a mighty crash.

The audience roared its approval once again and she went into a fast routine that was one of her specialties, crossing the stage rapidly from one side to the other until, on the final round, she tossed the net bra and the outer G-string at the audience.

She was running through the wings toward her dressing room when the manager barred her way, forcing her to stop as the roar from the crowd followed her, a tangible force demanding that she return.

"For God's sake, give them another round, Georgia," he begged. "They'll tear the place apart if you don't."

"But, Aaron—"

"The doc's on his way and Guy's better now. Get out there, please."

"I'll stop them this time." Her lips set on a tight line. "Get me a wrapper for when I come off, Aaron."

At the first beat of the drum, she seized each of the flimsy pasties, half-dollar-sized bits of fabric covering her nipples, and tore them off to the thunderous approval of the audience. Lifting her arms and clenching her fists so her breasts stood out, she began a rhythmic march across the floor, while the men stood on their chairs and shouted approval. The music was rising to a crescendo now, repeating the climax of the act, for, in tearing off the pasties, she had already passed the legally allowed limit in that particular area.

The spotlight man was following her every movement but even he was caught off guard when, desperate to stop the applause somehow and let herself reach Guy, she suddenly bent at the corner of the stage, seized the flimsy G-string that was now her only garment and, ripping it loose, tossed it to the audience.

The operator reacted quickly and killed the light, throwing the stage into darkness as Georgia ran into the wings and seized the wrapper from the hands of the manager. A thunderous roar of approval followed her from the audience, but she was already in the dressing room and on her knees beside the couch where Guy lay.

"How are you, darling?" she asked.

"Fine—" He grimaced. "Can't fool you, Georgia. The pain's pretty bad, even after a nitro tablet."

"Where?"

"Same as always, in here." He touched his chest over his heart, then ran his fingers out along his left arm.

"Here's the doctor," someone said from the back of the room and a short, plump man carrying a medical bag pushed his way to the couch. He felt Guy's pulse, took his blood pressure, listened to his heart, asked a few questions and requested a telephone.

"It's outside, doc," said the manager.

"What are you going to do, Doctor?" Georgia followed him from the dressing room.

"Send him to a hospital. Any preference?"

"The Clinic," Georgia said automatically, naming the only hospital she knew of in Baltimore.

"Good place. He's probably having a coronary attack." The doctor dialed the telephone and spoke a few quick words, then turned to her.

"Ambulance will be here in a few minutes," he said. "I'll phone the emergency room to be ready for him."

"Will he—?" Georgia couldn't go any further.

"Can't tell," the plump doctor said cryptically. "Is this the first attack?"

"He's had others. Each time it's worse."

"You're sending him to the finest heart clinic in the world, ma'am." The doctor's tone was less brusque now. "They'll do what has to be done."

"How can I ever repay you?"

"Don't bother. I've seen you perform many times; in fact, I was out front just now when someone called me in who recognized me." The roly-poly doctor's eyes twinkled and he bowed with an oddly courtly gesture. "My pleasure."

And for the first time in many years, Georgia found herself blushing.

III

Frank Lawson hadn't planned to start casing the parking lot of the tavern at the edge of the city quite that early. But his mind had been changed by the steady stream of police reports pouring in on the motel radio, describiing the five-state manhunt in progress since he had been identified as the bank robber who'd gunned down a teller two days before some five hundred miles away.

It wasn't his fault that he'd had to murder a second time, when a traveling salesman had picked him up on the road, he thought resentfully; the damned fool shouldn't have tried to wrest the gun from him. But he'd been lucky at that, for the salesman had been his size; after changing clothes with the corpse and driving the station wagon to the nearest airport, he'd gotten a jet start, so to speak, on his escape.

He would have made it, too, if a nosy airline clerk hadn't seen his picture in the paper hours after his plane left and notified the police. By that time, he was off the plane in Baltimore and holed up here in this lousy motel. But with the information the clerk had given them the police had been able to narrow the scope of their hunt to the Baltimore area.

The bank robbery had failed when the teller sounded the alarm and, with the salesman's money all gone and his nerves screaming for a fix, Frank Lawson hadn't been able to wait any later to make his move. The two joints he'd smoked an hour ago hadn't even taken the edge off the craving for heroin that was torturing his body. But with dollars in his pocket and an automobile, he knew where he could find a pusher on Baltimore Street to supply what he needed. And fifteen minutes later he'd be floating on Cloud Nine.

Tuesday wasn't a good business night for a tavern like this one, he knew, so he couldn't expect the cash register to be exactly running over. But there was sure to be enough to get the fix and get away before the cops could find him. And somewhere in the next city there'd be a savings and loan office in the suburbs waiting to be robbed, another motel and a cheap broad, until the time came to rob, and kill, again, if anyone tried to get in his way.

The sixth car in the row he was casing proved to be everything he was looking for, a maroon Mustang like thousands of others on the road at all hours, with the keys hanging in the lock, where a kid had left them when he'd rushed his girl inside to get her properly high before renting a room in the motel. Lifting the keys, Frank Lawson put them in the side pocket of his jacket and settled his hand over the pistol already there.

Crossing the lot, he entered the tavern, noting in one quick glance that it was like a thousand others he had visited, many of them for the same purpose as tonight. Along one wall of the small entryway was a glass-fronted cabinet containing cigarettes, candy and cigars. The cash register was opposite the door, with rows of package goods on shelves at the back. To the right was an archway giving access to the usual dim-lit smoke-filled room, its walls lined with booths.

A small platform occupied one corner of the room, with a postage-stamp dance floor where a young couple—probably the very one who'd been in the Mustang—was swaying in a close embrace. Two men were on the stools before the bar nursing glasses of beer while they talked to the bartender, but less than half of the booths were filled.

"Can I help you, sir?" He hand't seen the blonde in the short skirt and long black sheer stockings, who appeared to be doubling as waitress and cashier, until she appeared from the other room. He saw now that tables were in there, too—for those, he presumed, who weren't interested in the music—which meant that the take might be better than he'd hoped.

"I need some change for the cigarette machine, please," he told her.

"Certainly, sir." She went behind the counter and rang up "No Sale" on the cash register. As the drawer opened, she reached out to him for the bill but, when Frank Lawson's hand came out of his pocket, the pistol was in it instead.

"Keep quiet and you won't get hurt, sister," he said in a low voice. "Understand?"

The blonde nodded, just as they always did. Even if she'd tried to yell, he knew nothing would come out but maybe a squeak that wouldn't have been heard above the blare of the music.

"Hand me the bills," he directed, and she scrambled nervously in the slotted money tray for a small handful of money, most of it in lower-denomination notes.

"Now the bigger ones—under the tray," he ordered, but her hands trembled so that she could hardly lift out the tray, and, reaching over, he grabbed the pile of tens and twenties, shoving them into his pocket. Luck was with him tonight; the manager must have been too lazy to go to the bank that morning.

"Now walk out with me," he directed the girl. "And be quick."

She was shaking and so pale he thought she was going to faint. But she managed to emerge from behind the cash register and made no resistance when he seized her arm with his left hand and propelled her through the door. She shivered when the cold outside struck her in her skimpy costume. But it also seemed to stimulate her, for she walked on steadier legs as he guided her along the side of the building in the shadows. When he came to a niche where several garbage cans stood, he stopped her and lifted the gun in his right hand.

"No, please," she whimpered, but he didn't let the plea deter him from expertly bludgeoning her back of the ear with the butt of the pistol. As she started to crumple like a rag doll, he gave her body a shove, causing it to fall into the dark niche behind the cans. It would be awhile before she was found there, and, with the combo drowning out the voice of anyone who called for her inside, he might gain an extra fifteen minutes, if he were lucky, before someone discovered what had happened and called the police.

Moving swiftly to the Mustang, he got in, slipped the ignition key into the lock and started the motor. It was one of the high-powered ones, he noted with satisfaction, and felt a momentary regret that he would have to ditch it so soon to throw the cops off his trail. Driving out of the parking lot at the usual rate of speed, he turned into the street outside and stepped on the gas gradually, feeling the powerful motor seize the small car and move it forward.

Two blocks ahead, he saw an expressway overpass and, when a ramp appeared on the right, turned up it, for the expressway could get him across town in a few minutes to the fix he needed so badly. Still thinking about the way his body would start to float in the air once the needle entered the vein and the plunger of the syringe was driven home, he failed to notice the DO NOT ENTER sign at the foot of the ramp. And by the time he got to the top and realized he'd come up a "Down" ramp by mistake, it was too late to stop the car before it was out on the expressway itself.

As he wrestled frantically with the four-in-the-floor gearshift, trying to put it into reverse and send the car back down the ramp, Frank Lawson's eyes suddenly dilated with horror at the sight of the heavy truck bearing down upon him. An instant later the little car was scooped up by the behemoth and sent hurtling off the overpass bridge to the street below.

But long before it struck, Frank Lawson was unconscious.

CHAPTER THREE

I

"What did you see out there?" Helen Foucald spoke from the sofa, where she was pouring martinis from a silver shaker, already frosted from the ice inside, into two glasses of exquisitely cut crystal.

"What do you mean?" Doctor Henry Anders II, at forty-five, had the build of an athlete, from tennis and golf, and the aristocratically handsome features bequeathed to him by his father—though little of that great surgeon's understanding and compassion for the people who came to him for help.

"You look like the cat who's just lapped up the cream, but there's nothing out there except a Baltimore February night. And nobody could be very happy about one of them."

Helen Foucald had taken off the tailored skirt and blouse which, with a long-skirted laboratory coat, was her daily uniform in The Clinic. As chief of the clinical laboratories and a highly skilled biochemist and hematologist, with a Ph.D. in her own right, she was severely businesslike by day. But now, in a long hostess gown belted about her slender waist, and with her surprisingly full breasts unbrassiered, she was softly feminine. The change even involved her face, softening her features and making them seem a little more full. But her eyes had lost none of their directness and the long-fingered hands were as skillfully efficient pouring the martinis as they were twisting the fine-focusing controls of a binocular microscope.

"It never ceases to amaze me how you change like a chameleon merely by crossing the street." Henry Anders leaned back comfortably upon the sofa and enjoyed his martini.

"Of late it's getting harder and harder to change back," Helen admitted. "Those damned estrogen pills I have to take so you can have your way with me—as the Victorians used to put it—must be responsible. Five years ago I looked like a boy and had to fight off more than one loving female, but lately I've had to take some of the padding out of my bra."

She swallowed half the martini in a single luxurious gulp, flicked her tongue voluptuously into the glass and skillfully transferred the olive to a position between her teeth, crunching it as she reached for the shaker to fill her glass again. The action never failed to excite Henry, which she very well knew, as well as annoy him.

"How many times have I told you it's plebian to eat the olive?" he demanded.

"But I *am* plebian," she insisted. "My ancestors were treading grapes in France to make wine when yours were holed up in New York with General Howe while Washington and his men were starving at Valley Forge."

"I still say America would have been better off if England had won."

"Don't forget that if my ancestors hadn't helped Washington, England probably would have." She looked at him reflectively. "You're something of a prig, Henry. I often wonder how anybody with so many inhibitions manages to shed most of them with his pants."

"Don't be vulgar, Helen. It doesn't become you."

"Why can't you understand that I'm two people who live on different sides of the street, Henry? If the Southside-of-The-Parkway me ever took my place on the Northside, my laboratory would be so full of young males breaking beakers and test tubes, there'd never be any work done." She finished her martini and put down the glass. "Where will you be seen with the charming Mrs. Claire Anders tonight?"

"At the symphony. We're patrons, you know."

Helen glanced at her watch. "Patrons are supposed to be late, I know. But if you're going to make your usual entrance just before intermission, you'd better get along with your chores."

II

Jeanne Alexander was in the living room of the apartment, nursing a highball glass morosely, when Greg let himself in. One look at her flushed face and glittering eyes told him it was not her first drink, and probably not her second.

"Hello, darling." He leaned down to kiss her but she turned her head and his lips touched only her hair. "I'm sorry I was late."

"It's nothing new," she said dully.

"After the meeting of the board on Saturday, I should be able to let up a little. We could run down to White Sulphur or the Homestead for a few days. Or we might even go to Florida; it's been too long since we've had a weekend away to ourselves."

She only nursed her drink without answering, and he felt a twinge of pain at the memory of the gay and laughing person she had been only a few years ago. The slender figure hadn't changed it was true. She could still wear the same size she'd worn when they were married nearly twenty years ago, too, and her face was unlined, although, with all its customary animation gone now, her features were almost like a mask.

She had never drunk much before the past year, usually a dilute bourbon highball nursed all evening whenever they went to a cocktail party. But he'd come home many an evening lately to find her like this, and the small bar off the living room was always well stocked, although he rarely had time for a purchase. Going to it now, he poured himself a generous measure of bourbon, splashed soda into it and dropped in two ice cubes.

"Did you fix yourself a sandwich?" he asked.

"I don't want anything. There's ham and salad dressing in the refrigerator; and bread in the breadbox with potato chips."

"Want me to make one for you?"

"I said I don't want anything."

He took his time about making the sandwich and sat eating it at the small table in the kitchen where they'd always had breakfast—until lately. The more he thought about the changes in Jeanne this past year, the more frustrated and utterly baffled he felt. Nothing he could say seemed to reach her any more. The small endearments that had once made them so close, hands touched in passing, a light kiss on her hair, still golden and soft like an aureole about her head, her small hand groping for his as they waited in line at the theater, the warmth of her body as she leaned against him, the casual exploring touch of their tongues as they kissed, promising a greater intimacy later—all these were gone, and missing them brought again the feeling of a band constricting his heart, a band that must be burst asunder before it was too late.

Or was it already too late?

Jeanne's footsteps behind him made him turn his head. She was standing in the kitchen doorway, holding an open medical journal in her hand, and the fire of anger in her eyes brought at least a little animation to her features.

"The new issue of *Surgeon* came today," she said. "Why did you let Henry Anders steal credit for your work?"

He didn't need to look at the journal to know what she meant; The Clinic librarian had placed a copy on his desk earlier that day with a bookmark between the pages where the article began. He could recall the heading once again without effort—but not without a sense of shame.

"Experimental Transplantation of the Canine Heart and Lungs, by Henry Anders II, M.D., Gregory Alexander, M.D., and Robert Johnson, M.D.; Report of Ten Successful Cases." Jeanne read the title, her voice hot with anger, and closed the journal.

"Did Henry do any of the work?" she demanded.

"No."

"Did he do the operations you described in the article?"

"He took out the heart and lungs in the first few cases."

"The ones that failed?"

"Y—yes."

"Then why—?" She choked on her anger and couldn't go on, but even then, he was thankful. For the fact of her being angry could only mean that the interest she'd always had in his work and his career wasn't entirely gone. And as long as even a spark remained, there was still hope that she would regain the zest for life which had always been her most notable characteristic.

"Henry's director of The Clinic," he said.

"While you do all the work."

"He does routine surgery, leaving me time for work in the experimental laboratory."

"Like this heart-lung transplant operation you devised."

"That—and others."

"If you had stood up for your rights when Henry's father died, you'd be director, not Henry."

"This is the way old Dr. Anders wanted it—so does Henry."

"You mean he asked you to let him share the credit?"

"Well—yes."

"And you were spineless enough to do it?"

Greg flushed at the accusation and wondered whether there was really any point in trying to explain—when he couldn't even think about the article himself without a twinge of guilt and shame.

"Don't bother to answer." The contempt in her voice lashed him like a whip. "It's written in your face."

"You don't understand," Greg protested. "Henry made it plain that putting his name on the article was the price of his support, when I present the new hospital plans to the trustees at the end of the week."

"And you sold your finest piece of work for that?" She threw the journal at him and he was forced to dodge in order to keep from being hit in the face. "You've been under Henry Anders' heel so long, it's the only place you deserve to be—like any other worm."

"Jeanne, I—" But she had gone back into the living room, leaving him with his mouth open and his protest unvoiced. After a moment, he began to eat his sandwich again, but he might as well have been chewing on a piece of soggy paper towel.

How to explain that the elder Dr. Anders had been the only real father he'd ever known? And what that had meant to a boy who had grown up in a Carolina orphanage, working half the day and going to school the other half, earning a scholarship to Chapel Hill by being valedictorian of his high-school graduating class when he was fifteen years old, managing a fraternity boarding house dining room at Johns Hopkins and working summers as a substitute intern at the Baltimore City Hospital to earn pin money. Even then, he probably wouldn't have been able to finish medical school for lack of money if Dr. Henry Anders hadn't taken an interest in him when he had accurately diagnosed a rare case in the junior year surgical clinic, and lent him money enough for tuition and the precious books that cost almost as much.

The new buildings were to be a monument to the memory of The Clinic's founder on its fiftieth anniversary, now only a few days away. If he had to buy the support of the founder's son by giving him credit for work he hadn't done, who was hurt save himself? He could bear that hurt, as he had borne the rejection of his plans two years ago, but he was beginning to wonder whether he could bear what it was doing to Jeanne, and his marriage.

Greg finished his sandwich, drank a glass of milk, rinsed the dishes and put them into the dishwasher. When he went back into the living room, Jeanne and her glass had vanished, but the closed door of the bedroom into which she had moved almost six months ago was mute testimony that nothing between them had changed. In fact, it had only become worse.

Beset by the sense of loneliness the closed door of the bedroom always caused. Greg went into their bathroom and brushed his teeth. Jeanne's wet bathing suit hung on the towel rod, for she still swam daily in the indoor pool that served both the apartment house and the adjacent motor hotel, owned by the same firm. It was almost the only activity, except the reflex ones of living, eating and sleeping, she hadn't given up, however, and he had come to dread the time when he would find the black nylon bathing suit dry. Remembering her slim loveliness in the brief black suit, he reached up to press the damp fabric to his cheek, then used it to wipe away the moisture that had come into his eyes.

"Jeanne!" He knocked on the closed door of the bedroom. "Please listen to me at least."

But there was no answer, and, after knocking and calling again, he gave up—as he had done so many times before—oppressed by the invisible wall that separated them even more than did the closed door, a wall he could neither penetrate with his love nor climb by force.

III

Helen Foucald was taking a TV dinner out of the oven when the telephone rang. She answered it on the kitchen extension and was startled to hear Claire Anders' New England twang.

"Helen, darling," said Henry Anders' wife. "Is Henry still there?"

"What makes you think he would be?" Helen asked guardedly.

"Henry hates the symphony, so I was sure he would stop by your apartment to salvage at least some pleasure from the evening."

"You have an almost uncanny way of knowing what's going on, Claire. Could it be that you have ESP? Or do you bribe the doorman of my apartment house?"

"Perhaps the ESP—certainly not the doorman. Actually, I don't know anybody I'd rather have my husband fornicating with than you."

"I'm glad you're so broad-minded, Claire."

"Really, darling, I'm only being practical." Claire blithely ignored the thrust. "Half of Henry is quite enough for me—at the moment." Helen didn't miss the implications of the words—or the threat. "Really it's a pity so few men are as potent as they think they are, isn't it?" Claire continued. "If Henry keeps slipping the way he has been lately, he soon won't be enough for two women any longer."

"Why don't we have lunch together one day and flip a coin for him?" said Helen.

"What a perfectly exciting suggestion! And how civilized! But I'm afraid Henry wouldn't like that; his ego is really so fragile. Give the dear boy his dues though; nothing's small about him except his mind. Well, the symphony is about to begin; I'm calling from a booth in the lobby. Thanks for sending Henry home. I imagine he'll make it just before intermission as usual."

"You're welcome, Claire."

"By the way, darling. Have you noticed that he's been behaving a bit oddly the last week?"

"What do you mean?"

"He's been acting like my brothers used to do when they'd hidden a dead mouse in my bed—as if he's put something over on somebody."

"Come to think of it, he has been a little smug," Helen admitted. "Are you worried that he may be seeing another woman?"

"Oh, nothing like that; between us, we're quite able to keep him in line. After all, what man of Henry's potency has a wife *and* a mistress who can stay with him all the way?"

"If that's a compliment—"

"But it is, darling. It is. I'm sure Henry knows how lucky he is. Oh well, I imagine he's up to some sort of skullduggery in connection with The Clinic. He's always playing politics over there, you know."

"That must be it," Helen agreed. "Good night, Claire."

"Good night, Helen. We really must get together sometime and exchange experiences. It should be exciting, and, you being French and all, maybe I can learn something."

"I doubt that," said Helen. "No offense, of course."

"But of course." The click of the phone sounded in Helen's ear as Claire hung up, but her face was thoughtful as she replaced the receiver on the hook. Come to think of it, Henry had been acting rather differently lately, as if excited about something he was keeping secret. But that sort of excitement always made him an even more prodigious lover than was ordinarily the case, so she'd not bothered to examine its sources, knowing he couldn't resist very long the urge to boast of whatever small triumph he had accomplished.

Removing the TV dinner from the oven, Helen put it on a tray with a glass and bottle of *vin rouge* and carried it to her bed. Arranging herself comfortably among the pillows, she flicked on the TV set with the remote control; it was attached to the wall some six feet above the floor at just the right height for viewing from bed without having to crane one's neck forward in order to bring the screen into view. When the usual situation comedy with its carefully spaced inanities and periodic spattering of canned applause came on, she began to eat slowly and reflectively. But after a moment the screen and its words faded from both vision and hearing, although her other senses were quite alert.

Only the demanding urgency in her loins had been soothed by Henry Anders' expert love-making; in spite of what marriage manuals called "postcoital lassitude," Helen's mind was operating as accurately as the small computer in her laboratory across the street. Henry was slowing up; there was no question about it. If Claire had noticed it, perhaps it was more than Helen herself had realized, and that, she admitted, could pose a serious problem for her.

In spite of their idle persiflage about tossing a coin for Henry, Helen knew perfectly well that Henry Anders' wife had no intention of sharing him if the time came when there was really not enough to share any more. The son of The Clinic's founder was about as hidebound an individual as Helen had ever known, except in the one particular of his sexual prowess. And with that beginning to wane, Henry Anders II, Symphony Patron, Senior Warden of the Episcopal Cathedral, Rotary District Governor, member of this and that board and supporter of this and that charity, would become what he really was, a dull and boring man who would grow more so as he grew older.

Understanding her own passionate nature, as well as its source—a drive to excel in all she did, not only by outperforming the men with whom she worked by day but also bringing them to heel, so to speak, at night—Helen realized fully how difficult it would be to find a satisfactory substitute for Henry Anders. The fact that under other circumstances she could hardly have stood him at all was in itself a protection against a love that might leave her defenseless by shattering, in its demands for giving rather than taking, the protective shield she'd built around the one weakness that could destroy all she had accomplished through the years—the fact that sometimes the demands of her body were stronger than her will.

IV

It had taken Georgia Merchant only a few minutes to dress and get the old car from the parking lot behind the dingy downtown hotel where she and Guy were living during the Baltimore engagement. She didn't even take time to remove her makeup but drove rapidly to the hospital. Even so, when she inquired at the nursing desk of the emergency room at The Clinic, she was told that Guy had been taken directly to the intensive care unit for immediate admission.

It was somewhat of a shock to see how old and bedraggled looking the buildings of the hospital were and for a moment she was troubled by the thought that the medical care here might be on a par with them. But then

she remembered that this was actually one of the most famous medical
institutions in the country, perhaps even the world, and took what small
comfort she could from the thought.

The intensive care unit—the ICU in hospital shorthand—was in a
remodeled portion of one floor, a dozen rooms partitioned off from what had
been obviously a large waiting room at one time. The nurse's desk was in
the center, where, merely by turning in her chair, she could scan the
electronic monitor tubes grouped in banks on either side of her. But this
arrangement, too, was far more antiquated—in appearance at least—than
had been the hospitals in St. Louis, Detroit and Chicago to which Georgia
had rushed Guy after attacks similar to the one tonight.

But now she knew what the monitor tubes in the nursing station were for.
The bottom row gave a continuous visual record of the heartbeat, the blood
pressure, the respiration and other functions, while the one just above it was
connected to a closed-circuit TV camera inside each room. As she
approached the nursing station, Georgia could see Guy on one of the
monitor tubes; a doctor in a white coat was listening to his heart while a
nurse adjusted the flow of oxygen through a nasal catheter into his lungs.

"I'm Mrs. Merchant," she told the nurse at the station. "My husband
was just brought in."

"The doctor who phoned said Mr. Merchant was a coronary case, so he
was brought directly up here," said the girl. "Dr. McNeal is examining him
now but you can give me some information for the admitting office."

"You move quickly here, don't you?" said Georgia.

"We're not quite so antiquated as we look, Mrs. Merchant," the nurse
said with a smile. "Besides, the cardiology service is one of the most active
in the hospital."

By the time Georgia had finished giving the nurse the information she
needed for the records, a black-haired young doctor in a white coat came out
of Guy's room, carrying a chart in his hand. He spoke briefly to the nurse,
wrote some orders, then came over to a small lounge overlooking the street,
where Georgia was sitting. If he noticed anything odd in the fact that she
was still heavily made up for her performance, he didn't mention it.

"Your husband's feeling much better, Mrs. Merchant," he said. "I gave
him another hypodermic when he arrived."

"Thank you, Doctor."

"He tells me that he has been admitted to several other hospitals for a
similar condition."

"The first time was in St. Louis nearly two years ago," said Georgia.
"We're in show business, so we travel around a lot."

"Do you know what the diagnosis was there?"

"Coronary thrombosis. He was in the hospital a month and wasn't able
to work for another three months."

"What kind of work does your husband do?" the young doctor asked.

"He's a song and dance man, though he hasn't done much dancing lately.
I guess you wouldn't even remember vaudeville?"

"Only what I see on the tube," he said with a smile.

"Guy was a headliner in his day. You know—songs, dances and nifty
patter. But lately—" she didn't finish the sentence.

"Did he have much pain before the first coronary attack?"

"He complained of feeling uncomfortable at times for maybe six months,
but he thought it was indigestion. The doctor who sent him in tonight
thought this might be another coronary."

"We can't be absolutely sure," said Dr. McNeal. "But from the looks of
the electrocardiographic tracing on the monitor, it doesn't appear that he
has an actual thrombosis. Do you understand the difference?

"I'm not sure."

The young heart specialist turned over a sheet on the clipboard he was carrying and quickly sketched in the outline of a human heart. Upon it he drew heavier lines in two branching patterns, very much like trees with the trunks beginning near the top of the heart and gradually spreading out to cover its whole structure with an interlacing pattern of branches.

"The dark pattern I've drawn in here represents the coronary arteries," he explained. "They come off the aorta—the large artery that carries blood to much of the body—just after it leaves the heart. The coronaries supply blood to the heart muscle itself but, as people grow older, they often tend to thicken—"

"They told me in Detroit that Guy had hardening of the arteries."

"I could see the changes in the vessels inside his eyes with the ophthalmoscope," said Dr. McNeal. "In this case, the major cause of the trouble is a gradual thickening of the inner lining of the coronary arteries. Sometimes a clot—what we call a thrombus—blocks a major branch of one artery. If the block is large enough, the blood is cut off to a considerable section of the heart muscle and death is often instantaneous. But if the area involved is smaller, the damaged muscle heals slowly and a scar forms. That's probably what happened with your husband's first attack in St. Louis."

"And you think this one is less severe?"

"From present appearances, yes. The fact that he was subject to anginal pain from time to time shows that the lining of his coronary vessels has gradually thickened, decreasing the amount of blood reaching the heart muscle. The pain of angina is actually a warning of an insufficient blood supply to the heart but the pain causes spasm, too, and that makes the condition worse, unless medication like nitroglycerin is given immediately to dilate the arteries. This attack apparently started out as angina pectoris—the medical term is coronary insufficiency—and doesn't seem to have gone beyond that yet."

"Does that make any difference—as far as Guy is concerned?"

"My guess is that recovery should be fairly rapid," he told her. "That is, if there has been no real blocking of the coronary arteries."

"How soon will you know?"

"Possibly in no more than twelve to twenty-four hours—but only as far as this attack is concerned. You understand that, don't you?"

"We've been living with this for over two years now, Doctor," said Georgia. "It worries Guy that he can't carry his share of the load any longer and I guess that doesn't help his heart either."

"Emotional tension always makes heart disease worse."

"There are less and less bookings for men in the kind of show business we're in; most shows don't have comics any more, so Guy can't even get work as a straight man feeding lines to them. He's a proud man, Dr. McNeal. You might not think it now, but he really was good once; played the top English music halls when he was hardly out of his teens." Georgia's shoulders had drooped momentarily but she was past feeling sorry for herself long, or for Guy, and faced up to reality. "So what's to be done?"

"Until a few years ago—nothing."

"And now?" She wondered whether she dared grasp at the hope his words seemed to imply.

"Various operations have been devised in recent years to increase the blood flow to damaged hearts, though not all of them are as successful as we would like them to be," said the young doctor. "Lately, Dr. Gregory Alexander here at The Clinic has been removing the thickened lining of the coronary vessels from some cases with very good results."

"You mean he can actually go inside the arteries?"

"The technique is rather difficult to explain. Actually, a small jet of gas is used to strip out the inner layer of the vessel wall."

"Could that get Guy back on his feet?"

"I don't want to raise false hopes, Mrs. Merchant. Even if Dr. Alexander accepts your husband for surgery, I must warn you that it is not without considerable danger and only selected cases are helped at all."

"I've learned enough about heart disease these past few years to know that what's happening to Guy almost every day now isn't without considerable danger either," said Georgia. "So any way you look at it, we don't have much to lose."

"That's the sensible attitude to take," Dr. McNeal agreed. "I'll ask Dr. Alexander to see your husband in the morning but it will probably be several days before we can tell you just what to expect."

"You've given me hope, Doctor," Georgia said gratefully. "For folks like me and Guy, that's been in short supply for a long time."

CHAPTER FOUR

I

Dr. Herbert Partridge, Senior Fellow in Neurosurgery, looked up when Bob Johnson came into Operating Room 16.

"Sorry I had to call you, Bob," he said. "This fellow—what's his name, Lew?" He spoke to the anesthesiologist, who was partly hidden behind the tent of draperies separating him from the operating field where Partridge was working, assisted by the resident on the neurosurgical service.

"Frank Lawson—at least that's the name the police gave us."

"He's got some broken ribs but they don't seem to have caused any air leak into his chest," said the neurosurgeon. "We've put in a tracheostomy tube to keep a clear airway and the chest X-ray is over there on the viewbox. See if you think anything needs to be done about those ribs, Bob."

Bob Johnson went over to the bank of ground-glass viewboxes attached to the wall of the operating theater and flipped the small switch at the bottom of the nearest box. The outline of a man's chest came into view, the rib fractures plainly visible. They were clean, however, without the bone splinters which could have penetrated the lung and caused an air leak into the chest cavity, squeezing down the softer lung tissue with its accumulated pressure and decreasing the respiratory function until death by suffocation occurred.

"Looks clean enough to me, Herb," he said. "I don't see any sign of pneumothorax."

"Take a look at the other pictures; you won't see anything like this very often."

The films on the two adjoining viewboxes were of the upper vertebral column and skull; when he saw the neck vertebrae, Bob Johnson whistled softly in amazement. Two of the lowermost cervical vertebrae, as the neck section of the spine was called, looked as if they had been crushed by a hammer. Bone fragments were scattered in the surrounding tissues and the bones themselves were fragmented badly.

"Looks like somebody tried to guillotine him with a dull blade—and quit half through," said the chest surgeon.

"It was almost that," Partridge agreed. "Lawson held up a tavern tonight and was escaping in a stolen Mustang when he took the wrong ramp and came up on the expressway facing the traffic. A big truck tossed that Mustang over the guard rail of an overpass like I'd kick aside one of my kid's March Box trucks he's always leaving on the living room floor. With two vertebrae crushed and the spinal cord severed in the lower cervical region, the poor devil might as well be one of those frogs we used to pith in physiology class in medical school to study reflexes. Anything below his neck that doesn't operate mechanically by reflex action is just about out of the picture now."

"How about the respiration?"

"He wasn't breathing when they got him to the emergency room," said the anesthesiologist. "But the duty intern was on the ball and put him on a Mark IV respirator before he did anything else. I'm carrying him on the respirator now through the tracheostomy tube."

"Do me a favor and stop by the emergency room on your way out, Bob," said Herbert Patridge. "I promised to send a preliminary report down to a couple of policemen who are waiting there."

"What do you expect to be able to do?"

"Nothing but clean up the wound and put on some kind of a support to keep Lawson's head from wobbling like a rag doll. He sure doesn't have anything else to hold it up."

"How long do you think he'll last?"

"Maybe an hour, maybe a week. He might as well be dead either way. Even if he recovers consciousness, which I doubt, he'll have to be in an iron lung or on a Mark IV for the rest of his life."

Downstairs, Bob Johnson found two policemen drinking coffee in the small automatic canteen off the corridor leading from the emergency room into the main part of the hospital. There was a small lounge there with a telephone for the convenience of the police and reporters.

"Dr. Partridge is going to be tied up in surgery for another hour at least," he told the officers. "He asked me to give you a preliminary report for him."

"What's Lawson's condition, Doctor?" The older of the police officers took out a notebook. "The intern in the emergency room doesn't seem to think he has much to go on."

"The spinal cord was severed in the lower neck region, which means he'll be a paraplegic for the rest of his life—if he lives," said Bob. "He'll probably be an iron lung case, too. Have you notified his family?"

"Don't even know whether he has one yet," said the second officer. "We only managed to identify him from some cards that were in his wallet. He's Frank Lawson, bank robber, ex-con, murderer and heroin addict. Stuck up a bank a few days ago and shot a teller, then killed a salesman who gave him a lift. I'd like to see him get out of the hospital, so he can at least walk to the electric chair."

"If Lawson had gone a little farther across the expressway, the truck that hit him would have been forced to swerve down that ramp," said the first policeman. "With a rig that size coming down out of control, God only knows how many homes would have been smashed—and the people inside them. Do the state a favor, Doctor, and let Lawson die."

"We're not allowed to make that decision yet," Bob Johnson said. "His relatives still have to be notified. Will you take care of it?"

"Lawson's got a police record a mile long; if anybody ever admitted they were kin to him, it will be in the FBI files," said the older officer. "We'll wire Washington first thing in the morning to notify the relatives—if any. But either way, he has to be a case for the medical examiner."

At the big call-board off the main lobby, Bob Johnson punched the button that clicked off the light behind his name. As he was turning away from the call-board, Dr. James McNeal came up and pushed the button, turning off the light behind his name.

"What's got you out so late tonight, Jim?" Bob asked as they started through the foyer toward the front door.

"Just admitted a severe case of coronary insufficiency on ICU," said the Senior Fellow in Cardiology. "He may be a candidate for one of those gas-jet jobs."

"So?" Bob Johnson's eyes brightened. "Just let us get this heart-lung transplant demonstration Dr. Alexander's going to do for the convocation Wednesday afternoon out of the way, and we'll be ready for him."

"It'll take a day or two to evaluate his condition," said the cardiologist. "Got time for a beer in the Falstaff Room across the street?"

"Sure. What's the occasion?"

"A lot of the old boys will be over there bragging tonight, and it might be nice to sit around and listen to them. Give you some idea of the plush life that could be waiting for us when we leave these hallowed—if somewhat dingy—halls."

"You wouldn't be looking for some prospective employer, would you?"

The cardiologist shook his head. "You'll never get me to practice outside a university hospital, or at least a large clinic like this!"

"In spite of the poor pay?"

"The pay'll be good enough—as long as you're not greedy. The private clinic setups most medical schools have now for their faculties takes the financial sting out of teaching. You still headed for Walter Reed?"

"The first of July. Dr. Alexander's already lined me up as assistant chief of the thoracic and vascular section over there. When my two years with the Army are over, I hope to come back and work with him here."

"More power to you," said Jim McNeal. "I'm going to head farther south; these Baltimore winters are beginning to get me down."

II

Since midafternoon, expensive cars had been stopping under the marquee of the Clinic Inn across The Parkway from the hospital and diagnostic clinic complex. Cadillacs, Continentals, Eldorados, Mercedes, Jaguars, Porsches, a couple of Rolls-Royces—all exhibited the traditional M.D. emblem with the staff and serpent of the caduceus upon it.

The bar and adjoining dining room of the Falstaff Tavern were now swarming with prosperous-looking men and their expensively dressed women having dinner. The scientific program of the biennial Convocation of the Members of The Clinic would not start until Wednesday afternoon, but the evening before and the morning preceding its beginning gave the Members an opportunity to renew old acquaintances and enjoy the social atmosphere, which was even more important than the professional side of the alternate-year get-togethers.

Since a full-dress meeting of the Board of Trustees that governed Clinic and hospital administration was also held on Saturday following a convocation, political currents sometimes ran so swiftly that they swept everything else aside. Medical politics was the subject under discussion by a group at a table in a corner of the lounge, when Bill Remick, a roentgenologist from Washington who was also on the building committee of the board came into the tavern.

"Hey, Bill," he was hailed by Joe Palentino, a New York internist sitting with two other Members at one of the tables. "Over here."

Remick gave his order to a passing waitress and made his way across the room, stopping to shake hands with a half dozen friends on the way.

"You know Abe Lantz from Cincinnati and Jim Paynter from Miami, don't you, Bill?" Joe Palentino said as the X-ray man took the empty chair at the table.

"Sure," said Remick, shaking hands with the others.

"Where's Amy?" Abe Lantz asked.

"She couldn't make it; a new grandchild takes precedence over a convocation any day."

"Makes you feel old though," said Lantz. "I thought my wife would have a fit when she heard we were to be grandparents but now she's as doting as they all are."

"You're close to Greg Alexander, Bill," said Joe Palentino. "How about a preview of his plans for the new hospital and clinic buildings to replace the old monstrosity?" He nodded toward the window where the lights of the dark massif of The Clinic across the street were visible. "We've been hearing some strange rumors."

"Don't write off what you call a monstrosity yet, Joe," said Bill Remick. "Fifty years ago, when that was built, it was the last word in hospital architecture."

"And anybody who has lived in one of those cells up there on the second floor off that rotunda won't ever get over feeling a little nostalgia at the thought of its passing," said Abe Lantz.

"Yet it's got to go," said Jim Paynter, putting into words what they had all been thinking.

"Not if Sam Hunter has his say," said Joe Palentino. "I hear he's just as stubborn about any change as he was two years ago, when he led the stampede that destroyed Greg's plans for a really modern hospital and diagnostic clinic."

"What I don't understand is why Greg took it lying down," said Abe Lantz. "A dozen medical schools would be glad to have him as professor of surgery. He could pick up and leave here any time he wants to at probably twice the money."

"It happens that The Clinic is Greg's life," said Remick. "He's never told me—and I wouldn't ask him—but I'd be willing to bet that, before he died, Dr. Anders made him swear to stay on here and keep the place going the way the old doc intended for it to go."

"But Greg wasn't even kin to old Dr. Anders," said Abe Lantz. "Why has the mantle passed on to him?"

"Because there wasn't anybody else to pass it to," said Joe Palentino. "Not many sons turn out the way their fathers would like them to—and Henry II, least of all."

"Do you think Greg has come up this time with a compromise plan Sam Hunter is liable to accept?" Jim Paynter asked the X-ray man. "Old Sam has quite a faction of die-hards behind him on the board. If Greg doesn't knuckle under, he'll get steamrolled again."

"Don't ask me," Bill Remick said. "You all know how I tried to get Greg to stand up and fight Sam Hunter two years ago."

"And maybe lose everything?" Jim Paynter asked.

"The Clinic is something very special," said the roentgenologist. "It's been an example to doctors all over the world for fifty years and I don't see us settling for second-rate buildings just because Sam Hunter has half the oil wells and money in the world besides being a stubborn old goat."

"What would be your idea then?" Joe Palentino asked.

"Personally, I'd like to see the new hospital begin where the one that's just been built at the Georgetown Medical Center in Washington leaves off as far as automation is concerned."

"Automation's a dirty word in the vocabulary of a lot of doctors, Bill," said Abe Lantz. "You and I know what it promises for the future because we've seen it at work. But the average doctor sees himself as possibly one day being replaced by a data processing machine."

"That's absurd!"

"Of course it is, but there's the bogey-man just the same."

"Look what's happened since the sulfonamides and Penicillin were discovered nearly forty years ago," said Bill Remick. "A lot of people said then that doctors would soon be doing nothing but writing presciptions for pills, but look what happened. The drugs quickly became tools that let us broaden the scope of our work and the same thing will be true in an automated setup. I say anything a computer can do for me, let it do it; that way, I'll have more time to study real problems without wasting so much time on routine matters."

"Besides getting a couple of extra afternoons off a week for golf," said Jim Paynter. "One thing is for sure: the young men coming out of medical schools now are looking for positions with group clinics; most of 'em aren't even interested in slogging to build an individual reputation for themselves the way we did."

"More power to them if they can see two patients in the time it used to take us to see one," said Bill Remick. "God knows there aren't enough doctors to go around now, and even with automation things are bound to get a lot worse before they get better—if ever."

III

In O.R. 16, Herbert Partridge finished applying the plaster cast that would hold Frank Lawson's head in an arched or hyperextended position and pulled off his gloves. The respirator clicked on with mathematical regularity; it was adjusted to send a pulse of oxygen through the tube in the patient's windpipe approximately sixteen times a minute, inflating the lungs and simulating breathing. So sensitive were the control valves of the machine that even the slightest attempt at spontaneous breathing would trigger the pressure control mechanism of the respirator, changing the rhythm of the softly clicking valves.

"Any sign of respiratory movement, Lew?" Herb Partridge asked the anesthesiologist.

"Nothing," said Dr. Gann. "He'll never breathe again without help."

"How about his heart?"

"As strong as yours or mine and the blood pressure's been well maintained all the way, too. If he ever wakes up, he'll be able to think—but for the rest of it, he might as well be a zombie."

"Sort of gets you, doesn't it?"

"No matter how many of these you see, you always have a feeling of helplessness with a paraplegic." Dr. Lewis Gann was an experienced older man who had seen most of the ills to which humans were subject. "Sever the spinal cord in the lower back and a man has at least half a body that functions; with arms that work, he can drag the other half around. But cut the upper cord—"

"This poor devil was a loser before he ever started," the young neurosurgeon agreed. "One of the cops who followed the ambulance told me he's spent more of his life in prison than he has out of it."

"He's still a human being—and entitled to live as long as we can keep his heart and brain functioning," said the anesthesiologist. "Which means a Mark IV or an iron lung."

Herb Partridge's eyes went to the monitor tube on the wall, where, picked up by the marvelously sensitive devices used to watch astronauts in flight thousands of miles away, the electronic pattern of the heartbeat was being registered in a flashing picture of rising and falling lines.

"Let's get a cup of coffee," he said. "This case is giving me the willies."

"Stay with him about an hour after you get to ICU," Dr. Gann told the nurse-anesthetist who had been assisting him. "The nurses up there ought to be able to take over then."

A small, brightly lit section of the staff dining room was half filled with nurses and house staff on night duty when they drew cups of coffee from an urn that bubbled constantly at one end of the serving counter. The younger doctor picked up two doughnuts from a tray nearby, but the older man passed it up.

"My cholesterol was up when I had my check last month," he said. "Maybe it's from too much animal fat like Dave Connor claims, but my guess is the real culprit's what I go through every time we take a patient off the heart-lung pump after Greg Alexander finishes one of those long jobs inside the heart. I tell you, Herb, if surgery gets any more complicated, it will soon be completely beyond the ability of ordinary men like me to stand the strain."

"Maybe somebody will build a robot to give the anesthetic." Herb Partridge was beginning to unwind after the tense two hours in the operating room.

"Years ago, about the time you were playing cops and robbers, people got all excited about what they called technocracy," said Dr. Gann. "A lot of 'em even convinced themselves that the machines were going to take over the world."

"Now it's computers."

"As long as it takes men to make the gadgets, I think we're safe." The older doctor dripped saccharin into his coffee cup from a plastic bottle, then carefully screwed the top back on and placed it in the pocket of his coat. "It's when the machines start making other machines on their own that we'll really have to worry."

"That may not be too far off. I was reading the other day that they've got computers programmed now to study the results of other computers and report on them."

"Maybe if the studiers find enough errors," said Dr. Gann, "they'll all get mad with each other and destroy themselves."

A nurse popped into the dining room, her eyes bright with excitement.

"Letty's had pups!" she announced, and a sudden spattering of applause swept the room. "Four of them!"

"Makes me feel good to know you can't keep an old dog down," said the anesthesiologist. "I guess it's a new day for medicine, too—when a dog with another dog's heart and lungs can still have pups."

IV

"Unhook me, Henry." Claire Anders dropped her mink coat upon a chair in their large bedroom. "I'm dying to hear what you're up to that's so mysterious."

"What do you mean?"

"When you came to the concert tonight at your usual time—just before intermission—you looked like a cat that's been lapping up the forbidden cream. That look always means you're up to some skulduggery."

Henry unhooked her dress at the top and ran the zipper down her back so she could shrug it off her shoulders and let it drop in a pile at her feet. She wore only the briefest of lingerie and a strapless support bra, which she unhooked with a deft motion before bending to loosen the garter belt that held up her stockings. Kicking off her shoes, she peeled them off, then unhooked the garter belt and stripped off both it and the briefs.

"I bet Helen doesn't look a bit better naked than I do," she said as she removed diamond clips from her ears.

"You're well preserved, Claire." Henry started taking the studs from his dress shirt. "For your age, of course."

Claire made a face at him and raised both hands to loosen the diamond beret in her hair, a movement that caused Henry to miss one of the studs, although he'd seen her thus many thousands of times.

"Helen's only thirty-five but she hasn't had you all these years to keep her young, Henry," she said. "After all, there's nothing like a loving husband to keep a woman's endocrines functioning properly."

Claire walked over to her closet, passing close to him, and picked out a sheer negligee, which she slipped on. "You still haven't told me what you were so mysterious about," she reminded him as she went back to the dressing table.

"I've laid a trap for Greg." Henry stepped out of his pants and hung them over the chair. "He won't get out of this one."

"What is it?"

"When he presented the plans for a new clinic and hospital complex to the trustees two years ago, they sent them back to be modified into something less expensive. He's supposed to present that at the next meeting."

"The one on Saturday?" Claire was brushing her hair.

"Yes. I saw the plans of a new, way-out hotel in a magazine recently and remembered that a young architect named Keith Jackson had submitted a very original design for the hospital and clinic two years ago. When I took the magazine to Jackson and suggested that he draw something like it for The Clinic and show it to Greg, he took off like a rocket."

"Wasn't that rather obvious, dear?"

"I made Jackson promise not to tell Greg I had anything to do with it."

"Is it that good?"

"It's out of this world, Claire, but nobody could build it around that statue of Christ in the lobby. You remember the clause in father's will, don't you?"

"The one that said the statue must always be central and any changes in the existing buildings must be made on the same site?"

"Else the whole property reverts to me." Stepping out of his shorts, Henry scratched his hairy chest luxuriously. "Jackson's plan would cost so much that the board would never build it here on the old site. And if The Clinic is moved out on the Beltway, where a lot of the board already want it, the present property will revert to me and I'll be rich."

Claire had been removing her makeup with cleansing tissue; she had the sort of soft peaches-and-cream complexion that showed little sign of age. When she turned on the bench, her eyes suddenly widened and a pleased smile came over her face.

"Why, you're all excited about this, aren't you, darling?" Getting up, she dropped the negligee. "For goodness sake! Come to bed before you burst a blood vessel—or something."

CHAPTER FIVE

I

The illuminated dial of the travel clock on the bedside table showed 5 A.M. when Sam Hunter awakened in one of the VIP suites of the Clinic Inn. His checkup at the laboratory was to begin with blood examinations at eight and the instruction sheet sent him in Dallas several days earlier had warned him neither to eat nor drink anything after midnight. His mouth felt dry and the headache that always lasted until after he'd had his morning coffee was in full throb now, but there was no point in waking Moto, his valet and chauffeur, who was sleeping in the other room.

Even ten years after Evelyn's death, old Sam still felt lonely when he waked in the morning and saw the other half of the bed empty. Young Sam hadn't produced a grandchild yet to comfort an old man during his declining years and with Ted gone, there really wasn't much left in life, even for one of the richest men in the world. Except to make more money—and lately that had even begun to lose its thrill for him.

If only Ted hadn't married that wop girl and run off with a circus, he thought, but even the old sense of resentment no longer burned with the same fire; there just wasn't enough energy left in him to ignite it fully. It wasn't that Sam Hunter particularly blamed his younger son for wanting a fling; God knows he'd had his at about the same age as Ted—and his father and grandfather before him. Ted's particular crime had been in bringing foreign blood into a line that went back to the Revolution, when the original Theodore Hunter had come over like many another Scotch-Irish adventurer to help the Colonies fight their battle for freedom and see what he could get out of it for himself.

The first Ted had recognized a good thing when he saw it; when the war was over, he'd moved with the tide of expansion southwestward, first into the Yazoo region, where he cannily bought land and sold it weeks before the bubble burst, then on to Louisiana and eventually to Texas. Texas land had been the real basis of the Hunter fortune, especially when it began to spout the black gold of oil. But now that Ted had spurned his overtures to drop the girl and once again resume the course his father had charted for him, clinging instead to the daughter of a man whose fleabag of a circus was barely able to keep moving, and with young Sam seemingly incapable of producing an heir, all the Hunters had striven to gain and hold through nearly two centuries must, it appeared, eventually go into a foundation. And that meant being doled out to hospitals and schools by trustees who had no appreciation for the fact that the largesse they handed over to others represented the blood, the guts and the sweat of a line of empire builders.

It was a depressing thought, a prospect that made Sam Hunter feel old beyond his sixty-eight years. But he knew he had to go on, if for no other reason than to keep alive the hope that one day Ted would admit his mistake, divorce his wife and come home to his rightful place.

Why does the damn clock have to run so slow? old Sam thought savagely when he saw that the long hand had moved only a quarter of the distance around the dial since he'd awakened.

Throwing the covers back, he padded to the bathroom in his bare feet and took his teeth out of the container where Moto had put them to soak in Polident. Rinsing them off, he stuck them in his mouth and clamped them down on the cigar without which he was hardly ever seen in public. But even the smoke of the expensive tobacco tasted like burning rope, and, after a few puffs, he ground it out in an ashtray and switched on the television set.

Only a farm program was on at this time of the morning, telling how to grow an early vegetable crop in Maryland. Which didn't mean a thing to an oil and cattle man from Texas, especially when he didn't believe half of what so-called agricultural experts tried to tell him anyway. Going to the window, Sam Hunter pulled back the heavy drapes and looked out across The Parkway to the lights of The Clinic, for dawn had not yet begun to break.

He wasn't such a fool as not to realize the various pressures that were being applied to members of the Board of Trustees, or the maneuvering going on in preparation for the meeting at the end of the week. The old Clinic building had been good enough for Dr. Anders when he'd operated on Evelyn, so why did it have to be any different now? he asked himself. There was an assurance of stability, of permanence about the old brownstone buildings, a conviction that there was good in the past which needed to be preserved. And with old Dr. Anders dead, Sam Hunter felt that the trust of seeing that things were not changed had passed to him.

At almost that same moment, Ted Hunter awakened in the snug apartment located in the back of one of the circus trucks, which provided living quarters for him and Vivian. He felt a slight sticking pain in his right hand between the thumb and forefinger, where the splinter had gone in when he'd seized the stake to whack the elephant on the snout and prevent a stampede. But when he sucked on the spot for a moment, the pain went away.

Through the thin partition, he could hear Joe Califino snoring in the driver's cubbyhole just back of the cab, so he knew they had already reached their destination for tonight's performance, under the sponsorship of the inevitable local charity, and were parked somewhere, probably near the auditorium. Miraculously, the advance agent for the circus still seemed able to find bookings, even in a day when the big shows played for the most part in coliseums or large auditoriums and drew the lion's share of the customers. But a breakdown or a spell of bad weather could wreck a small show like this, so the number of circuses like the Tarentino outfit was growing smaller every year.

Feeling chilly, Ted reached down to the foot of the bed and pulled up a blanket, being careful not to disturb Vivian, who was sleeping like a lovely blond baby beside him. Unable to get to sleep again immediately, he lay with the blanket pulled up to his chin, still feeling the shivery sensation between his shoulder blades and dreading the cold outside, which he must face in a few hours when they began to move the circus equipment into the inevitable small-town auditorium. Everybody had to help in an outfit as small as the Tarentino Circus, but Ted would have worked beside the roustabouts anyway, for he was very fond of Papa Gus and knew well on what a narrow profit margin the outfit operated.

Down on the Rio Grande, where the Hunter family had large holdings, a rambling cottage stood on a rise overlooking the river. The sun was a warm there even in winter and the oranges hung heavy on the trees, like the golden apples his mother had read about to him when he was a small boy. Ted felt a wave of nostalgia and his throat tightened at the memory of the days when he and Sam, Jr., had ridden over the rolling pasture lands, stopping to peel off their clothes and frolic in a waist-deep pool, where the languid flow of the creek had been halted for a time by a makeshift dam of fallen tree trunks from last year's hurricane.

Then, as if sensing his mood even in his sleep, Vivian moved against him and the reality of her loveliness, warm and fragrant in his arms, dispelled any other thought.

II

At first, Guy Merchant wasn't sure what had awakened him, until it came again, the odd skipping beat of his heart he'd noticed many times before. Usually, it presaged the start of the pain and the terrible sense of impending disaster that accompanied a severe attack of angina. The pain could usually be assuaged—if he didn't wait too long—by slipping beneath his tongue one of the tiny tablets of nitroglycerin he always carried with him. He knew he could get the tablet now merely by pressing the bell beside his hand on the bed to call the nurse from her station just outside the door, but he held back.

More than once in the past year, knowing the burden he had become to Georgia, Guy had tried to keep her from realizing that one of the attacks of anginal pain was coming on, hoping he could hold off taking the nitroglycerin until the slow shutdown of blood to the heart could cause death and free her from the burden of him and his illness. But each time, the agony in his chest and left arm, plus the fear of impending death that went with it, had become so severe that his resolve had broken down and, driven by a compulsion beyond resistance, he'd reached for the blessed tablet.

As yet he felt no pain, however, and he lay there waiting, dreading it, yet hoping he'd have the strength to keep from pressing the call bell when the fire of agony lanced through his chest. When the odd little pause in the heartbeat came again, reaching consciousness only because it was like a familiar sound no longer heard and therefore noticed, he reached across with his right hand, and felt the pulse beating in his left wrist. The rhythm of the beat was somewhat irregular but that was nothing new; he'd noticed it many times, especially in the past three months, when he'd felt his pulse surreptitiously so as not to disturb Georgia with the knowledge of his concern.

It came once more, the pause that seemed endless, and for an instant Guy knew some of the apprehension that accompanied an anginal attack, though none of the pain, before he felt the throbbing pulse once again through the artery beneath his finger.

Perhaps ten beats followed in steady progression, then the pause began once more—but this time without an end. And realizing that his heart had stopped, Guy Merchant only had time before blackness engulfed him to pray that it would never beat again.

III

Peter Carewe wasn't surprised when the tall stewardess with the red hair dropped into the vacant aisle seat beside him as the early morning plane from New York to Baltimore was taking off from La Guardia. He'd seen her eyeing him when he came aboard a few minutes earlier and had recognized the look; it was one he saw in one form or another in the eyes of more than half the women he met, the appraising glance, the unanswered question— although later he managed to answer quite a few of them.

The girl was worth considering, though he couldn't muster much enthusiasm this early in the morning. If it hadn't been for a UN secretary from Sweden, he would have been in Baltimore last night, instead of having to get up before dawn and whistle down a taxi in the almost deserted canyon of First Avenue, where the mammoth towers of the United Nations Plaza Apartments shot skyward on the bank of the East River.

"You're the doctor from WHO, aren't you?" the stewardess asked as she buckled her seat belt. The plane was nearly full and the aisle seat beside him had been one of the only empty ones in the front of the plane.

"Dr. Peter Carewe. Yes."

"I saw the TV special about you last week. Your work must be very exciting." The special had featured him as an example of the corps of doctors from the World Health Organization who ranged about the globe, fighting disease wherever they found it.

"Swatting flies isn't exactly the most glamorous occupation in the world." He relaxed and admired the redhead's legs in the short tunic that had become the uniform of the stewardess on almost every airline in the world.

"You're just being modest, Doctor. According to the TV special, you're 00-7 with an M.D. And *he* certainly got around."

"The trouble is you don't meet many glamorous women in the jungles I've been slogging through, hunting tsetse flies and the mites that carry strange fevers," he assured her. "I usually have better luck on airplanes."

The redhead accepted the ploy for what it was, just as he'd accepted her taking the seat beside him instead of the narrow bench back of the forward door provided for the stewardesses during takeoff and landing when all of the seats were filled.

"Are you on the way to The Clinic Convocation?" she asked.

"How did you guess?"

"The TV special said you were once a Fellow there. I took a year of nurse training at The Clinic, until the glamour wore off and I decided I wanted to live a little instead of marrying an intern and putting him through his residency."

"You may have turned down a good bet. Doctors who finish a fellowship at The Clinic go up pretty fast when they go out into practice."

"Unh unh!" said the stewardess. "I saw too many girls left behind with a divorce and a couple of kids to look after, while her ex married some gal from the Junior League who could help him build up a society practice. That's not for me."

"What is for you?"

"A chance to live a little and meet interesting people—like you."

As the plane moved down the runway at a rapidly increasing rate of speed, preparatory to becoming airborne, Peter Carewe took another look at the stewardess' legs and decided to stake out at least a tentative claim. If he took the professorship in the School of Public Health which had been offered him in Baltimore he would be doing a lot of traveling out of there and it might not be a bad idea to have a few irons in the fire. The girl appeared to be in her late twenties and although this would be a good twelve years less than his own age, he prided himself on being as fit—and as lusty—as he had been in his twenties.

"Are you based in Baltimore?" he asked casually.

"New York. Baltimore's a pretty dull town."

"I keep an apartment in the United Nations Plaza." The plane was airborne now and the stewardess had started to loosen her belt. "I'm in the telephone book and I'll be back in New York at the end of the week," he added. "Give me a ring and perhaps we can have a drink together."

"That will be nice." She stood up and smoothed down the white tunic. "Coffee, Doctor?"

"Please."

"We don't have time to serve breakfast between New York and Baltimore, but I can get you a sweet roll or a danish."

"Danish for me. I haven't started worrying yet about cholesterol."

The plane was banking now and through the oval window beside him Peter Carewe could see the sprawl of the United Nations buildings stretching along the East River, with the tower where his apartment was located nearby. Yesterday he'd sat in the office of the courtly Danish physician—himself a world authority in the field of public health—who directed the Western division of the network of men, women and facilities known as the World Health Organization, or, for short, WHO.

"We've had a protest from the office of the Russian delegate about that TV special NBC did on you last week, Peter," Dr. Nordstrom had said.

"On what grounds?"

"Our Soviet friends don't need grounds for their protests; they seem to have some sort of a machine that grinds them out merely by pressing a button."

"They must have cooked up something."

"On the program you implied that whenever a problem happens to lie in territory behind the Iron Curtain, WHO people are sometimes denied freedom of access to facilities we need in our work."

"Aren't we?"

"Of course. I just had to pass the protest on to you as a matter of record."

"You can tell the Russians where to shove it," Peter said bluntly. "Anything else I should know?"

"We may have another detection job for you. A batch of oral polio vaccine being used in California has been causing some rather severe reactions. It may be simply a contaminant, but I've sent a culture team from Los Angeles to look into it. How long will your meeting last in Baltimore?"

"I'm addressing the banquet on Thursday night and could leave right after that, if the matter became urgent."

"It isn't likely to develop that fast, so enjoy yourself," said the director. "But we can't let this thing out in California go too long without trying to find out what happened. If people start being afraid of the oral vaccine, we shall lose our most effective weapon against polio."

"I'm going to tell about the way we isolated and identified the monkey kidney virus in my address Thursday night," said Peter.

"Let's hope we can run this one down as quickly as you did that difficulty," said the director. "Confidentially, I'm going to recommend you for a Nobel prize in health for that job."

"It wasn't that important," Peter protested.

"It was—and other people besides myself know it." The director picked up a letter on his desk and held it between his fingers. "Is there any truth to this rumor that the School of Public Health in Baltimore has offered you a professorship?"

"It's true; John Teague and I had dinner together a few nights ago. But I'm not sure I should accept."

"May I ask why?"

"Maybe I'm not ready to settle down yet."

"You'd be turning down one of the most prestigious chairs in the field."

"I still don't understand why it was offered to me."

The director smiled. "I think you're being unduly modest, Peter. After all, you're the nearest thing there is today to the sort of death detective Paul De Kruif used to write about. As dean of the School of Public Health in Baltimore, Dr. Teague might want to add some glamour to his faculty."

"You make me feel like a Hollywood movie idol," Peter protested.

"After that television special the other night, you could be just that."

"Actually, I've been approached. One of those Oxford gray rabbits who inhabit the warrens of Madison Avenue called the day after the broadcast and suggested that I consider a series on TV with the same title, 'The Doctor from WHO.'"

"It might be good public relations for our profession."

"Maybe. But I wouldn't want to be tied down to a weekly job."

"Then you've turned down the Baltimore offer?"

"Not finally. I promised John Teague to come by and talk to him about it while I'm down there. But there's a thrill to running down something like that monkey kidney virus, a feeling of adventure and accomplishment I'm afraid I wouldn't find as a professor. Maybe in another ten years I'll be ready for it—when I'm fifty and beginning to slow down a little."

IV

Flight 216 had been four hours late leaving Atlanta, having encountered bad weather. Fortunately for Dr. Ed McDougal, one of the airport bars stayed open all night to accommodate the nocturnal flow of travelers, so by the time the big four-engined jet was airborne shortly before dawn, he was pleasantly lubricated and quite ready to forgive the airline for the delay.

Not so Hannah McDougal, however. She had matched Ed drink for drink while they waited, but the liquor only made her more than normally quarrelsome. When the trim stewardess set a breakfast tray before her, she eyed the food disdainfully—but not Ed.

"Boy! This looks good!" He tucked the corner of his napkin into his shirt front just beneath the collar and tore off the end of a small envelope package of sugar, letting it trickle into the steaming cup of coffee a second stewardess had just poured from a vacuum flask.

"Do you have to eat like a farmhand?" Forced to fight continually a tendency to accumulate weight around the hips, seeing anyone else enjoy food always irritated Hannah.

"That's what I started out as." Ed was feeling too good to let Hannah and her chronically bad temper spoil his day. "Might go back to it, too— after I make my pile."

"Don't count on my being with you."

"Suit yourself." The big surgeon with the shock of graying red hair buttered a piece of toast and popped it whole into his mouth.

"You wouldn't miss me at all." Hannah's tone was petulant.

"Oh, I'd miss your bitchin.'" He tackled the scrambled eggs and sausage. "Nothing makes a man work harder than knowin' his wife will give him hell when he gets home. That way he's got a good reason to stay at the office and make money."

"Then at least I'm worth something to you."

"Just admitted it, didn't I? Of course, you used to be good in the hay—"

"Do you have to broadcast it to the world?" she hissed.

"Lettin' a thing like that get around never hurts a woman, hon. You were really something before we were married. Remember that time we went to the house party on the Severn? Man oh man!"

The memory was pleasant—and poignant—enough to silence even Hannah McDougal's acid tongue for the moment.

"Champagne?" A stewardess stood beside them, a bottle poised.

"Champagne for breakfast! This is the life!" Ed picked up Hannah's empty glass with his own and held them while the girl filled them both, then handed Hannah's to her.

"To the old days, dear." He touched his glass to hers and emptied it in one swallow, holding it out for the stewardess to refill when she turned from serving those on the opposite side of the aisle.

"Do you have to be such a pig?" Hannah said furiously under her breath as the girl moved down the aisle. "The way you embarrass me."

"Don't mean to, hon. Don't mean to. It's just my way."

Hannah nibbled at the breakfast resentfully, unwilling to dull the remaining glow of the whiskey and the added one from the champagne with food. Most of the time she felt dead inside; only the stimulus of alcohol or Benzedrine could bring her to life for a while. And even then, the letdown afterward was worst of all.

"Bet when I asked you for a date that day at the stenographic pool, you never dreamed you'd wind up the wife of one of the most successful surgeons in Texas." As usual, Ed was talking with his mouth full, chewing vigorously between the words. "We've come a long way from those days, hon; never had a chance to really think how far, until Greg invited me to talk on pancreatic surgery at the convocation."

"Just be sure you're sober enough to do it right."

"I never mix alcohol and surgery. You ought to know that."

Proof of what Ed had said about his success was hanging in the clothing rack at the front of the airplane, a full-length ermine coat that had cost close to $10,000 at Neiman-Marcus.

He'd never been niggardly with her, once he'd begun to make some money, Hannah admitted to herself as she lay back in the seat and closed her eyes. The big diamond on her finger was ten times the carats of the one he'd given her when they were married. And the matching wedding ring was a far cry from the dime-store band he'd slipped on her finger before the Bowling Green justice of the peace who had married them one summer night.

They'd barely had enough money between them to pay for the motel near Annapolis, where they'd spent their honeymoon, and the bottle of whiskey Ed had bought, along with crackers and cheese for the wedding feast. But it had been as close to paradise as Hannah had ever come—before or since.

Dear God. What has happened in the years between? she asked silently, without realizing that this was the first time she had prayed in years.

How could Ed have been a big, boisterously happy Fellow in Surgery in those long-ago days, charming every woman he met with his Texas drawl and his red-headed, handsome exuberance, a catch any girl would have been proud of—and then turn into a pig who smacked his lips over a glass of free champagne, ate with his napkin tucked in his shirt and talked like a rustic.

What did I do to deserve this? Could the Lord possibly be punishing me for deliberately trapping Ed into marriage?

She'd known he wanted her for a long time before the house party on the Severn that summer. Just as she'd known she had to yield soon or see him lured away by some of the other girls, who were willing to go with him anywhere he wanted—and as far as he wished. But in yielding she had to make sure of marriage, and that had taken some planning.

The opportunity she'd been waiting for had come several months after their first date. Four girls from the secretarial pool had rented the cottage that summer and word of it had quickly spread through The Clinic. Invited by one of the four to a weekend house party, Hannah had asked Ed and they had driven down in his old Buick on Saturday afternoon.

The festivities were already in full swing when they arrived. Everybody was frolicking in the lazy tidal river, an arm of the Chesapeake, sailing the small catboats that went with the cottage or just drinking up the

considerable supply of liquor brought by the male guests. After a couple of
drinks to catch up, Ed and Hannah had danced awhile to the music of the
portable record player that was blaring out in one corner of the big living
room, then had gone swimming with the rest.

When someone challenged Ed as a Texan to take care of cooking the
steaks on an outdoor fireplace in the late afternoon, he'd agreed enthusi-
astically and Hannah had been given no opportunity to protest, though she
would much rather have spent the rest of the afternoon playing the game of
amatory hide-and-seek she had planned in preparation for the evening.

She had been sitting alone on the dock after supper in the warm August
darkness, morosely watching the play of lights from the cottages along the
river on the surface of the slow tidal stream and the bright glow of the moon
just beginning to rise in the east where the river emptied into the
Chesapeake Bay, when Ed plumped himself down beside her and handed
her a filled glass.

"Been hunting for you for ten minutes, sweetie," he said. "Nobody
seemed to know where you were."

"You were busy," she said a little acidly. "So I came out here."

"Had to take charge of the steaks or somebody would have messed 'em all
up. I guess nobody 'cept a Texan really knows how to cook steaks out of
doors. Drink up. We've got us some lovin' to do."

"Suppose I don't want to."

"You were hot enough a couple of hours ago. Man, I'm still panting from
that kiss you gave me when I came down from putting on my trunks in the
boathouse."

She'd taken a long drink from the glass before answering deliberately,
"Maybe that's as far as you're going to get."

"Now, don't say that, sugar," he protested. "If I thought you'd gone to
all the trouble of bringing me here to this nice romantic spot just for a little
pettin', I'd be downright disappointed."

She couldn't help laughing at his tone, but her pulse had already begun to
beat faster from the warmth of the alcohol in her veins. To hide her reaction
from him, she drank another third of the potent mixture in her glass, adding
further fuel to the fire.

"What made you think there'd be anything else?"

"Oh, a guy can tell." His arm slipped about her and she had to fight
against yielding immediately to the fierce, demanding possessiveness of his
kiss. Finally, she pushed herself away, for it wasn't part of her careful plan
to let him think she was quite the pushover she fully intended to be—in
time.

"Let's finish our drinks," she said a little breathlessly.

"Sure." Ed emptied his glass. "All the time I was cooking the steaks I
was thinking about how warm and loving you can be. The hotter the steaks
got, the hotter I got."

"You certainly didn't show it."

"Depends on where you were looking." He handed her glass to her.
"Finish this and let's take ourselves a little swim."

"My suit's wet."

"Who said anything about suits?" He was unbuttoning his sport shirt as
he spoke and pulling it over his head. "We're going to take us a swim Texas
style."

"Not right here," she gasped. "Everybody can see with the moon coming
up."

"Me, I don't care." He was stripping off his slacks as he spoke and she
looked away instinctively. "If you insist on being modest, step inside the
boathouse. I'll swim in there in a minute and hang my clothes on a nail."

Inside the boathouse, it had taken her only a moment to step out of the playsuit she was wearing and the briefs and bra under it. There wasn't any use kidding herself about what was going to happen—or that she didn't want it to happen and hadn't intended for it to happen.

For perhaps the dozenth time since her friends had invited her down to the Severn for the weekend, Hannah had made a quick mental calculation—with the same answer. She was as regular as a clock and this was the fourteenth day of her cycle, probably the very day of ovulation, so the odds in favor of pregnancy were higher than at any other day of the month.

She had lowered herself into the warm water by the time Ed came swimming into the boathouse, lying on his back and holding his clothing up in a compact bundle while he propelled himself by kicking. He found a ladder that extended down into the water from the boathouse above and climbed it, looking like a dripping Greek god in the pale gleam of the moonlight as he hung his clothing on a nail and then, with a barely audible splash, slid under the surface and disappeared.

The water inside the boathouse barely came to her shoulders as Hannah searched it for the phosphorescence that would betray Ed's presence. But he had turned to swim behind her and, when his head broke water, his hands went around her body to cup her breasts in his palms. With a gasp of pleasure, she leaned back against him and reached up to take his head between her hands, turning her face so he could reach her lips as he stood holding her body against his.

She felt the proudness of him thrusting against her as his mouth opened to her kiss, then his hands sliding down over her hips to the cleft in her loins, parting the soft flesh so she could settle upon him with a deep shuddering sigh. For a single moment she lost consciousness at the height of her own release until his voice brought her back to the present.

"Do you need to do anything?" he asked. "I mean, to keep from getting pregnant. The Clinic doesn't look with favor on its Fellows knocking up secretaries."

"I don't think this is the right time," she lied.

"Good. There's a room upstairs over this boathouse. When I changed up there this afternoon, I figured we could use it later."

"Suppose somebody finds us."

"Everybody came here tonight with the same idea in mind. We just happened to get started earlier than the rest, which puts us one up on them."

She giggled. "You can say that again."

Hours later, as they lay in each other's arms with all passion sated, he'd said: "One of these days we've got to get ourselves married, sugar—when I get a weekend off."

"Do you really want to?"

"How could anybody not want something like you around every night when he gets home. You're the most, baby."

And she did love him, she'd told herself as she responded to his skilled caresses. Besides, he'd mentioned marriage himself, so she hadn't really conned him into it or anything.

When the stewardess took their trays away, Hannah moved a little closer to Ed in the comfortable first-class seat, letting her shoulder touch his. He was relaxed and happy, smoking one of the thin cigars he'd taken up instead of cigarettes after removing the first lung from a patient for cancer over ten years ago.

Almost twenty years had made a difference—in both of them—but the toll on Ed had been remarkably light. A sprinkle of gray showed in his red hair, but the salt and pepper effect made him look distinguished, where before he had been merely handsome. He kept himself fit, too; but not with the lazy games of golf most doctors favored, riding from green to green in an electric cart. Four days at noon he played a fast game of handball in the YMCA near his office, and he was still club champion in his class. His waistline was the same as it had been when they were married and he had the same zest for life and for love.

Not that she'd let her own figure go either, Hannah assured herself. Tennis at the club several afternoons a week still kept the muscles in tone, even if two quick scotch and sodas were needed afterward to recapture the momentary zest of competing and winning.

What had happened between her and Ed wasn't physical, though inevitably it had its physical side. The trouble was that somewhere along the line, especially since the boys had grown up and gone to Yale, the zest and ardor which some older people—and a precious few, when she thought about it—seemed to find in life had somehow escaped her.

It hadn't seemed to escape Ed though; he was as affectionate as ever, in spite of what he called her bitching. For a moment she experienced a surge of affection for him, something she'd felt only rarely for a long time. But when a gentle snore escaped from his lips, her own tightened with annoyance and the old feeling of futility and depression seized her once again.

V

For the convocation, the regular staff of The Clinic had been assigned to various committees. In addition to the building committee, where Helen Foucald had asked to be placed in order to safeguard the interests of her laboratory, Greg had put her on the welcoming committee, charged with meeting various dignitaries and their wives and making certain that they were transported to the Clinic Inn, where rooms had been reserved for them. She was still in bed, though awake, when Greg Alexander telephoned.

"I hope you weren't asleep, Helen," he said.

"I was just waking. I like to take a while at it."

"Could you shorten the process a bit this morning?"

"Of course, Greg. Is anything wrong?"

"Almost everything's right, as a matter of fact. Letty had pups during the night."

"That's wonderful."

"I want to see her before I start making final preparations for the heart-lung transplant I'm doing tomorrow for the convocation, but I'd also planned to meet Peter Carewe's plane this morning. Could you do that for me?"

"When does he arrive?"

"There's an early jet out of La Guardia. He wired me last night that he'd been held over in New York and would take that flight."

"I sometimes take it myself when I go to New York for the weekend," she said. "I'll have plenty of time to meet the plane."

"Thanks. Since Peter's our dinner speaker, I thought we ought to give him a little VIP treatment."

"Especially when he's an authentic VIP. Congratulate Letty for me; she certainly made history last night."

The morning traffic made the trip to the airport somewhat longer than Helen had counted on. As she hurred into the terminal, the announcement of Flight 26's arrival was just coming over the loudspeakers and she had only time for a reassuring glance into her compact mirror before she spied the tall form of Dr. Peter Carewe coming off the plane.

She had no trouble recognizing him; he was just as handsome as he had been on TV a week before. She saw his eyes scanning the crowd and knew he was looking for Greg Alexander. But when they reached her, they stopped dead center and a warm glow came into them. Conscious that she must be blushing at the uninhibited admiration in his gaze, she stepped forward.

"Dr. Carewe?" she asked—quite unnecessarily.

"Yes." He came over to her in three quick strides. "You saved my life."

"H—how?"

"When I saw you standing there, I said to myself, 'Peter, my boy, you're not going to leave this airport until you know who that beautiful woman is.' You saved me the risk of getting slapped for speaking to you—or maybe getting punched in the nose by an irate husband."

She laughed. "Not many I see around here would dare try that. I'm Dr. Helen Foucald. Greg Alexander sent me to meet you."

"Good old Greg," he said. "I hope you haven't had breakfast."

"N—no, I haven't."

"The best I could get on the plane was a cup of coffee and a danish and I'm starved." He signaled a passing skycap and handed him a baggage check and a dollar. "Claim this for me, will you," he said. "I'll pick it up outside after breakfast."

"I hope Greg didn't break a leg or anything," Peter said when they were seated in the airport restaurant.

"Oh no. Letty had pups during the night."

"That's what I always liked most about Greg. He'd pay as much attention to a sick dog in the experimental lab as he would to the chairman of the Board of Trustees."

"Letty's something special," Helen explained. "Greg did a heart-lung transplant on her over six months ago; and for her to have pups just in time to be reported at the convocation is more than any of us hoped for."

"I take it you're on Greg's side in this battle I've been hearing about for a new clinic."

"I certainly am," she said. "If you could see how antiquated my department is—"

"Your department?"

"I've been chief of laboratories for three years now."

"That's why I haven't seen you before. It's been over five years since I've been back for one of the convocations."

"I came here from the Lahey Clinic in Boston," she explained. "I was a Fellow there for two years after I got my degree from the Sorbonne."

"I did some work at the Sorbonne before I went out to Japan to study tsutsugamushi fever," he said. "It's even more antiquated than The Clinic."

"I read your report on that work," she told him. "It's too bad they couldn't go into it in more detail on 'The Doctor from WHO' the other night on TV."

"That program was mainly a public relations ploy for the World Health Organization. I just happened to be chosen for it."

"For the very good reason that you're the most glamorous man in the entire organization."

"Glamour doesn't count for much when you're trying to drain a malaria swamp in Kenya, or spraying for tsetse flies in the Congo." The waiter came and he ordered for them. "But enough about me. Tell me about yourself."

"Mainly I'm a hematologist, but I'd had some experience running a laboratory in Paris and Dr. Anders selected me for the job here."

"Is Henry still the same conniving bastard he always was?"

"I—I don't know what you mean," she said, startled by his amazingly accurate description of Henry Anders.

"You must have been steering clear of him then. How do he and Greg get along?"

"All right, I suppose. Why?"

"Henry has hated Greg Alexander ever since the old doc practically disinherited Henry by making The Clinic a foundation so Greg could keep it going the way the old man intended for it to go."

"They seem to get along all right." If Peter Carewe noticed anything wrong in her voice, he didn't make it known, but attacked the ham, eggs and coffee, which had just arrived, with the same vigor he'd put into a campaign to control an epidemic of cholera.

"Henry knows Greg is the real genius behind The Clinic's continued success, so he wouldn't let it come to a showdown between them and risk being slapped down by the trustees," he said over the second cup of coffee. "Henry's way would be to try to discredit Greg somehow so he'd resign. The thing I can't understand is how Greg has managed to stand it this long—or Jeanne."

"I don't know her too well."

"Jeanne's brother, George, was a classmate of mine at Hopkins. We used to have dinner with Greg and Jeanne every now and then when Greg was still a Fellow." He sat back in his chair and wiped his mouth with a napkin. "Nothing's better than ham and eggs for breakfast—with a beautiful woman across the table."

The implication in his voice made Helen blush again and she wondered whether he would think her an inexperienced old maid. "It's a wonder you haven't married then," she said.

"Never found a woman who could improve on room service—for the ham and eggs. I didn't see a wedding ring on your finger, perchance did I?"

"No. I'm too busy running a laboratory."

"Not too busy to have dinner with me tonight, I hope."

"Do you always move this fast?" she asked with a smile.

"Only in special situations. Actually, I may not have but two days here; some trouble is brewing in a batch of oral polio vaccine on the West Coast. If the people we have working on it don't run down the culprit soon, I'll have to fly out there and start looking into it."

"Since you're off to the wars, so to speak, I couldn't well refuse you, could I?" said Helen. "I live in the Clinic Apartments."

"Good," he said. "Anybody as beautiful as you are this early in the morning must be a real knockout by candlelight around midnight."

"You might be disappointed."

"I picked you out of the crowd just now."

"But I was looking for you then—and that attracted your attention."

"You would have attracted my attention if you'd been facing the wall," he assured her, and Helen decided it was time to change the subject.

"Is there any truth to the rumor that you may settle down and become a professor?" she asked.

"Now that I have seen you, maybe yes. Tell me, can you cook ham and eggs?"

"I once took a course in cooking at the Cordon Bleu." Then her eyes twinkled. "But I thought you preferred room service."

CHAPTER SIX

I

The clock in the lobby of the hospital read eight when Greg Alexander crossed it and took a right-hand corridor that joined the diagnostic section of The Clinic to the surgical building. Just off the corridor was a self-service canteen for the convenience of the staff and visitors, with banks of machines that dispensed food and drinks merely by dropping a coin into waiting slots.

He hadn't awakened Jeanne when he'd left the apartment that morning; in fact, he could hardly remember when they'd had breakfast together. She'd been sleeping poorly in the early part of the night, he knew, because he had often heard her small TV set after midnight.

He was stirring a steaming cup of coffee from one of the vending machines when Dr. David Connor, the staff cardiologist, came in and went to the coffee machine. As he turned with a cup in his hand, the somewhat pudgy heart specialist saw the surgeon and came over to sit with him.

"You look sort of peaked, Dave," said Greg. "Everything all right?"

"I went to the symphony last night."

"We missed it; I was late getting home."

"You didn't miss anything. Pozl was waving his arms and his hair as usual. Haven't seen you eating here often. Thought you preferred the staff dining room to this kind of food."

"I do. Letty had pups during the night and I'm going by to see her."

"Heard about it already," said the cardiologist. "Congratulations."

"Thanks—for Letty. What brings you out so early, Dave?"

"Jim McNeal admitted a heart case last night, a broken-down vaudeville hoofer named Guy Merchant."

A bell rang somewhere deep down in Greg Alexander's brain. "Gentleman Guy?"

"Could be. Friend of yours?"

"I saw him in a show downtown when I was a student at Hopkins. He was the headliner then."

"Not any more, I imagine. Jim said he was brought in from one of those joints down on Baltimore Street."

"I guess hoofing is on the skids these days, along with vaudeville and burlesque."

"Merchant almost skidded out this morning," said the cardiologist. "He had a cessation a couple of hours ago but the nurse on ICU was watching the monitor tube and saw the heart pattern flatten out. She had the Pacemaker on him in less than a minute and by the time Jim got there he was ticking again."

"You've got that resuscitation routine worked out well."

"Provided it happens in the intensive care unit. If this fellow had been on one of the regular floors, we might never have gotten his heart started again in time to save him from being a vegetable the rest of his life because of brain damage due to lack of oxygen."

A thought raced through Greg Alexnader's brain. Dave Connor was the hospital gossip, a bachelor who loved nothing better than feeding information into the grapevine that connected every department without wires or other means of transmission, an invisible network over which a rumor could travel from the furnace room to the superintendent's office in less time than it took to walk the distance. This might just be the place to launch a trial balloon in preparation for the showdown with the trustees later on in the week, he decided, knowing the information about his plans would be sped faster by Dave than in any other way.

"There's a way of making certain that it does," he said casually.

"Does what?" Dave Connor was munching on a danish pastry.

"You were talking about cessation of the heart—in the intensive care unit. There's a way of concentrating patients who are likely to have that sort of a thing happen to them where facilities for resuscitation will always be available. I was talking to Keith Jackson—"

"Seems like I've heard that name before. Who's he?"

"A young architect who lives in one of the apartments below me. You probably remember the sketches he submitted for the new building two years ago."

"That could be it. They were way out, weren't they?"

"For then, I guess some people might say they were, but not today. Anyway, Keith has an idea for a new approach to building what we need."

"I thought you fought that out two years ago, when the trustees turned down your first proposal."

"I wasn't thinking far enough ahead then, so maybe it's just as well they did turn me down," the surgeon admitted. "Keith has come up with an idea for what will probably be the most highly automated hospital in the world—and also the most advanced."

"As I remember it, that was the trouble with your first plan—particularly where Sam Hunter was concerned," Dave Connor demurred. "He claimed that the impersonal care such a hospital would generate wasn't in keeping with what Henry Anders intended when he founded this place."

"Sam Hunter's wrong, Dave. The more I look into this question, the more I'm convinced that the future of medical care lies in a high degree of automation. You knew Dr. Anders well, so you know this is exactly the sort of a thing he would like to see here on The Clinic site today."

"Maybe. But you don't expect to change Sam Hunter, do you?"

"As well try to put a smile on one of those faces on Mount Rushmore," Greg Alexander said. "But he's not the only trustee."

"He's the only one worth five hundred million dollars," said the cardiologist. "Which means that when the chips are down, whatever Sam Hunter wants built is what will be built—and it'll be put where he wants it. Don't go butting your head against a wall again, Greg. You got squashed once—"

"Perhaps because in my heart I knew what I was proposing wasn't what The Clinic really needed. This time, I'm convinced we've got the answer."

"Powerful forces are against you this time, too, maybe more powerful than before, from all I hear. I'd hate to see Henry Anders get you into a position where you'd have no choice except to leave—and wreck whatever future this place does have."

II

Henry Anders II smiled when he saw the systems analyst with his clipboard and pocket calculator checking the traffic through the main corridor of the diagnostic building as he came in shortly before nine o'clock. It proved that the bee he had planted in Keith Jackson's bonnet a few days earlier was already buzzing, in ample time to stir up enough talk in the hospital for some of it to spill over to the Board of Trustees well in advance of the Saturday meeting.

The Clinic's director was feeling a little fagged, but pleased—with everything. Not only was his plan moving smoothly but the latter part of the evening with Claire had been quite rewarding. She was quite a woman when she wanted to be, and last night she had wanted to be. The thought that he was doubly blessed in this respect perked him up a little, particularly when he saw Helen Foucald hurrying through the lobby after dropping Peter Carewe off at the Clinic Inn.

"Why so fast?" he asked as he fell into step with her.

"I'm late. Greg asked me to run out to the airport and pick up Dr. Peter Carewe."

"The boy wonder of the mosquitoes? I could never stand him when we were students."

"I found him rather charming. We had breakfast together at the airport."

"Watch out for that fellow, Helen. He's up to no good where women are concerned."

"What are you up to, Henry?" She was surprised at her instant reaction to his criticism of Peter Carewe.

"What do you mean?"

"Claire called me last night—before you got home."

"She told me about that. It wasn't my idea."

"I suggested that we have lunch together some day—to compare notes on your prowess as a lover."

"For God's sake, Helen! Do you have to speak of me as if I were a stud?"

"That's what you really are, aren't you, Henry? I suppose all your women eventually learn they have to pay some sort of a fee."

"This is no place for public discussion of such a subject," Henry said stiffly. "We can talk about it tonight."

"I can't see you tonight. Peter Carewe invited me to have dinner with him."

"Maybe he wouldn't be so anxious if I told him—" He broke off at the sudden look of contempt in her eyes.

"You'd do it, too, wouldn't you?" she said icily.

"Of course not. I was just—"

"If I become interested enough in Peter Carewe, I'll tell him about us and a few others, Henry. But *I'll* do the talking."

She was at the door of the lab now and paused with her hand upon the knob. "Do you understand?"

"Well, I—"

"Do you understand, Henry?"

"You can depend on me, Helen."

"I hope so." She turned the knob and opened the door.

"Wait a minute," he protested. "How about tomorrow—?"

"I'll see you at the first session of the convocation this afternoon, Doctor." She was suddenly brisk for the benefit of the technicians in the busy laboratory visible through the open door. "Perhaps we can discuss that case in more detail then."

III

"Miss Jeanne!" The heavy knocking on the bedroom door and the sound of her own name finally brought Jeanne Alexander from the drugged sleep she had achieved by taking a Nembutal sometime after midnight. At first, she thought it was Greg calling to her as he had done after she had shut herself up last night and locked the door. But then she recognized the voice of Ethel, the maid, and went to unlock it.

"Miss Jeanne, you ought not to lock yourself in like that," Ethel said indignantly. She had been with them for many years and had her own key to the apartment.

"I'm sorry, Ethel. What time is it?"

"Pretty near nine o'clock." The maid's tone indicated her diapproval of anyone's sleeping that late. "I've been here 'bout an hour but, when I didn't hear no breathin' from your room, I got worried. S'pose somethin' happened to you in there. We'd have to break the door down."

"I'm sorry, Ethel."

"You orta be, Miss Jeanne. I met the doctor leavin' as I was comin' in, and tried to get him to let me fix him some breakfast. Imagine an important man like him not havin' nothin' but coffee and them stale danish pastries they sell at the canteen."

"He usually eats in the hospital cafeteria," Jeanne protested.

"Lately I've been findin' them cellophane wrappers off the pastries in his coat pockets, when I go through 'em before sending 'em to the cleaners. The way he's been workin' I bet he don't even take time to go to no cafeteria. I tell you, Miss Jeanne, that man's killin' hisself for sure."

"Was he—did he seem to be all right?"

"He was in a hurry—and all excited 'bout a dog named Letty havin' pups last night. But it don't make no sense."

The maid broke off when Jeanne laughed on a note of hysteria. "You all right, Miss Jeanne?"

"Yes, Ethel, I wasn't laughing at you."

"You can fire me for sayin' so if you want to, Miss Jeanne, but it ain't nothin' to laugh about when a fine man like the doctor has to sleep by hisself every night. I been noticin' the way things are in this house and it just ain't right. Seems to me you should be thankful you ain't got no worse competition than a dog."

"I think you're right, Ethel," Jeanne said, suddenly sober. "Thank you for reminding me."

"What do you want for breakfast?"

"I'll step across to the motel coffee shop." A rooftop passageway connected the two buildings. "A lot of people I know will probably be over there."

"Do you good to get out," the maid approved. "You been staying too much to yourself lately."

In her bedroom, Jeanne pulled the nightgown over her head in front of the full-length mirror on the bathroom door and studied her body in the glass. She could find little fault with it, even at forty. Daily swimming in the enclosed pool atop the motel next-door had kept her slim and her weight was within ounces of what it had been when she and Greg were married almost twenty years ago. She could still wear a size twelve dress, too, without alterations.

The trouble couldn't be the menopause, she told herself as she stepped into the shower and turned it on; she was still as regular as a clock. Or the Doctor's Wife Syndrome that was being talked about so much nowadays. Until two years ago, she had considered herself a vital part of Greg's life, sharing his troubles and triumphs, with no feeling of being shut away from anything that concerned him.

The shutting away had been her own action, she admitted now, and, at the sudden wave of depression that swept over her, she deliberately turned the shower control to "Cold" and stood gasping in the needle-sharp stream, hoping the shock would drive it away.

It did help and before depression could grip her again, she dressed hurriedly and took the elevator down to the sixth-floor level, where the enclosed crosswalk connected the apartment house and the adjoining inn. She had intended having breakfast at the coffee shop on the first floor, but the rooftop dining room was half full because of the convocation, so she turned in there instead.

"Good morning, Mrs. Alexander," the hostess greeted her warmly. "Any place you'd prefer to eat?"

Jeanne's first impulse was to choose a corner away from the crowd that partially filled the dining room, many of them former Fellows and their wives back for the convocation. But she deliberately put down the urge to hide and answered the hostess' greeting with a smile.

"Over near the window will do, thank you."

A glass wall of sliding doors, closed now, separated the restaurant from the patio and pool. The hostess pulled out a chair at a table where the sun shone through a window and placed a menu before her. Almost instantly, a smiling young waitress brought ice water and filled a cup beside her place with coffee.

"I'll take soft scrambled eggs, sausage and wheat toast buttered," she told the girl, and leaned back in her chair. Recognizing several former students of Greg's she acknowledged their greetings with a nod and a smile but was glad when no one came to the table. Then, across the restaurant she saw a woman in an ermine coat enter and stand beside the hostess, obviously surveying the room to see whether or not she knew anyone there. In the instant that Jeanne recognized Hannah McDougal, Hannah saw her too, and started across the room, followed by the hostess.

"Jeanne, darling!" Hannah bent to kiss her cheek. "Mind if I have a cup of coffee and something with you?"

"Of course not, Hannah. Sit down."

Jeanne had never been really close to the other woman, but their husbands had been in the same class of Fellows at The Clinic and she had seen Hannah a number of times at medical conventions. Ed McDougal was known to be quite a comer, she knew, both in practice and in medical politics in Texas, and Hannah's coat further testified to his success.

"Did you just get in?" Jeanne asked.

"A few minutes ago—almost twelve hours late." Hannah dropped her coat across a chair and took a seat at Jeanne's elbow. "The plane was late and the food was lousy—as usual. The only thing good was the liquor."

"Where's Ed?"

"Across the street. Sam Hunter's having a checkup this morning and Ed wanted to see him between examinations. Confidentially, Ed's afraid Greg may con Sam out of a lot of money for The Clinic here and get him to cut down on what we're supposed to get for the university medical school down in our town."

"I thought that battle was fought out a couple of years ago at the trustee's meeting—when Greg lost."

"Ed refuses to believe Greg will give up that easy." Hannah reached for a saccharin pack from the sugar bowl. "Now that Sam Hunter has disinherited his younger son, Ted, there'll be an even larger bequest when the old man dies, and it doesn't make sense for him to leave it here. Really, Jeanne, you don't spend millions of dollars on a new hospital in a place like this. How do you stand living around here anyway?"

Jeanne had asked herself that same question more than once during the past year. Now she felt called upon to defend The Clinic, if only because she had never particularly liked Hannah McDougal.

"The Clinic Apartments are very nice," she said. "And it's convenient to Greg's work."

"I guess it does come in handy for your husband to be able to get his breakfast at the hospital dining room—particularly when there's been a party the night before and you don't feel like getting up," Hannah conceded. "Thank God we've got a good housekeeper. She's been with us more than ten years and I just leave the running of the house to her."

Jeanne's breakfast arrived and Hannah's eyebrows lifted at the sight of the plate and the pile of toast beside it on the saucer.

"How do you manage to say so trim and eat like that?" she demanded. "I eat practically nothing and still have to keep my behind girdled up until I feel like I'm wearing armor. Fortunately, Ed likes me a little plump; he's the bouncing kind."

"Just bring me some eggs without any toast," Hannah said to the waitress who poured her coffee, and turned back to Jeanne. "You still didn't tell me how you stay so slim."

"I don't eat like this every morning," Jeanne admitted. "Almost every day I swim in the pool here on the rooftop, too."

"Our pool's back of the house but we can't use it in winter. I think I'll get Ed to enclose it." Hannah looked around the room, nodded to several people, then turned back to Jeanne. "Well, what's the dirt?"

"Dirt?"

"You know—the dope about the old crowd. Whose wife has left him since the last convocation and who's sleeping with whom."

"Really, Hannah. I don't keep up with things like that. Greg works late most of the time, so we don't see much of the old crowd."

"Not having children, you wouldn't and maybe you're better off at that," said Hannah. "Ed, Junior, knocked up a Mexican girl a few months ago and we had a hell of a time paying her off. The price these abortionists get nowadays is terrible."

Hannah's eggs arrived and she attacked them as if she were famished. "I saw Peter Carewe across the airport when we came off the plane," she said when her plate was clean. "He was with a woman, so we didn't get to speak to him."

"Peter and my brother George were good friends," said Jeanne. "We used to see a lot of him when they were students."

"I sure would like a romp in the hay with him," Hannah confided. "Did you see him on the Doctor from WHO program?"

"I'm afraid not."

"You missed something. They tell me women practically mob him everywhere he goes, like a movie star."

"That must be a new experience for a doctor."

"Don't kid yourself, dear. Women are always after 'em." Hannah started to light a cigarette, but her hand shook so much that she had to steady the lighter with the other one.

"Are you all right?" Jeanne asked.

"Of course I'm all right. Why?"

"You seem nervous."

"Show me a woman forty-two years old married to a handsome and lusty man who makes a hundred thousand dollars a year that isn't nervous."

"But why?"

"When he's surrounded all day long by young women in white uniforms, or else naked under an examining sheet? Don't tell me you don't worry."

"I never have."

"Maybe you don't need to, being married to Greg."

"What does that mean?"

"Only that he's one in a million. Out in practice, all the doctors are busy climbing over the others to get ahead and kicking the other fellow in the face for good measure while they're going up."

"That's Greg's only weakness," said Jeanne. "He's so married to his work he lets other people take advantage of him."

"Believe me, having a husband who's married to his work is a lot better than having one whose eye's always roving. Ed McDougal will lay anything that wears a skirt, if he gets a chance."

"Then why do you put up with him?"

"The biggest reason I suppose is habit; you get to expect certain things when you're married to a go-getter—like this coat. When I come into a restaurant wearing it, every woman in there envies me. Me"—she gave a short bark of a laugh—"Hannah Shultz who was a thirty-five-dollar-a-week secretary until I managed to snag Ed. Now I get a new Continental every two years and my clothes come from Neiman-Marcus or Bergdorf Goodman."

"They're certainly smart."

"The best always are. Besides, Ed's still pretty vigorous and if you've got to have a man panting over you several times a week, it might as well be somebody who can make you pant a little, too."

Jeanne suddenly realized that she couldn't remember when she and Greg had last made love. He'd been staying at the hospital a lot these last few months but it had never occurred to her even to suspect another woman— nor did she now.

"I always liked you, Jeanne. You're not like that bitch Claire." Hannah's voice brought Jeanne out of her reverie. "Persuade Greg to play ball with Ed and Henry on this deal to move The Clinic, and he can get rich enough overnight to buy you a coat like mine."

Somewhere in Jeanne's brain a warning bell suddenly rang. "Why would anybody want to move it?" she asked.

"To get out of this lousy neighborhood, for one thing," said Hannah, and leaned closer, dropping her voice to a more confidential tone. "Ed and Henry have got a way all worked out to develop the property across the street after The Clinic is moved to the new location that's been proposed on the Beltway at the edge of town. If Greg gave up his opposition to it, they'd let him have a piece of the syndicate cheap."

"Syndicate?"

"That's as much as I can tell you now." The other woman's manner was suddenly guarded, as if she realized she had said too much. "But you always treated me nice and I'd like to see both you and Greg get ahead. If he plays ball with Ed and Henry, he can get enough of old Sam's money to build a new clinic and still line his own pockets." Hannah stood up and reached for the coat.

"I'm going upstairs and get me some sleep," she said. "That damn plane had the most uncomfortable seats I was ever in and Ed snored all the way— when he wasn't watching the stewardess' legs. I tell you, if they get those uniforms any shorter, they can just let the girls take the place of in-flight movies as far as the men are concerned."

When Hannah was gone, Jeanne sat looking out the window, but not really seeing the dull February day outside, while she rehearsed the conversation again in her mind. She didn't consider for a moment suggesting to Greg that he take up Hannah's idea of joining Henry Anders and Ed McDougal in whatever it was they were planning. What did concern her was how she might find out more about it and possibly help Greg, as the first step toward curing the illness of her own marriage and keeping it from becoming like that of Hannah and Ed. For, in spite of the ermine coat and the diamonds, Hannah McDougal was obviously a desperately unhappy woman.

The trouble between her and Greg dated back, she decided, to the night two years ago when he had come home from the post-convocation meeting of the Board of Trustees, dejected after the plan he'd worked on so hard had been turned down summarily, following a savage attack by Sam Hunter. Easygoing though Greg was, compromise where a principle was concerned wasn't part of his nature; which, she realized now, was probably why his agreeing to develop another set of plans had both surprised and disappointed her.

Disappointment—that was the key, she was sure. Since the day when she'd first seen him in the hospital, she had put her whole life into Greg and his career. And his agreeing to the sort of pedestrian structure the board seemed to have in mind, instead of the real hospital of the future she knew he wanted to build, had caused a wave of bitterness to sweep over her, bitterness at him for seeming to yield on a matter of principle, where he had never yielded before.

Now she suspected that his apparent yielding had been merely a regrouping of his energies to approach the problem from another point of view. But disappointed as she had been then, she had treated him unfairly at a time when he was carrying more burdens than any man should be required to carry.

The experimental work in heart-lung transplantation had been his main concern even then, for without new facilities to carry it on, the whole thing was certain to be crippled. Yet in her disturbed condition, she realized now that she'd seen even it as a rival, a place where he buried himself because he couldn't face her scorn at his having failed her. But if Greg had been willing to share credit for his pioneering work with Henry Anders—who deserved no credit—then he must have wanted the additional facilities a new clinic and hospital would give him more desperately than he had ever wanted anything else in his life.

It was sobering to realize how much her failure to understand and to help must have hurt him. And how the hurt must have increased almost from day to day, as she had shut him ever more completely out of her life. She felt a moment of sudden panic now, a touch of the fear she had experienced momentarily less than an hour ago, when Ethel had told her how excited Greg had been when he left for the hospital that morning. But with it went a sudden rush of gratitude that there was still time—as long as her only competition was a dog. Somehow she had to help Greg, and, in the process, save her marriage and regain her own self-respect.

But where to begin?

Then a name came into her mind, a name he'd mentioned last night when he'd come home all excited about some new plan, but which she'd ignored in her anger over the surgical journal article. Now she got up and went to the cashier's desk, paid her bill and returned to the apartment building. In the elevator, however, she didn't punch the button for the penthouse floor, but descended to the lobby. Searching the rows of mailboxes, she finally came upon a name that rang a bell in her mind, and, noting the apartment number 8-A above the mailbox, returned to the elevator and pressed the button for that floor.

IV

Georgia Merchant had been asleep just before dawn, when the sudden stoppage of Guy's heartbeat had created the greatest emergency a hospital can face. The ensuing swift and purposeful action by the hospital staff had awakened her, but Guy's room was filled with people, so she could no longer follow closely what was happening upon the closed-circuit television monitor tube above the nurse's desk. From long hours spent in similar ICUs about the country, however, she knew where to look for what medical people called the "vital signs."

Watching the monitor tube where Guy's heartbeat had been registered, she had seen the flashing beam of the electrocardiograph reappear after a few moments, indicating that his heart had begun to function again. And as she watched the tenuous flicker of motion upon the glass front of the monitor, she found herself praying silently that these capable people would fail in their endeavors and that the existence which had become practically intolerable for him might cease without causing him any more pain.

Her prayer was not answered, however. And watching Dr. McNeal approach the waiting room some ten minutes later, she had felt a surge of anger against the efficient hospital staff, a reaction to her own guilt at having allowed herself to wish even for a moment that Guy's heart would not start again.

"Your husband's heart is beating again, Mrs. Merchant." The young doctor sat down in a chair across the small coffee table from her, with its pile of old and dog-eared magazines. "I'm sorry I couldn't take time to tell you what was happening, but we had only minutes to get it started again before his brain would have been damaged from lack of oxygen."

"I think he would rather you hadn't started it, Doctor."

"Patients with anginal pain often feel that way."

"And I think I agree with him."

"That's understandable, too, Mrs. Merchant. But we have no choice."

"Why not, when you know there's no hope?" she burst out. "Why couldn't you just let him die in peace?"

Dr. McNeal looked at her with eyes that were tolerant and understanding. "You love your husband, so in the final analysis you, next to him, are best equipped to decide whether he lives or dies. Are you prepared to take that responsibility upon yourself?"

Faced with the question, Georgia could only shake her head; there was no evading his logic.

"Can you tell what happened yet?" she asked.

"The heart rhythm is only just now being established, but from the look of the ECG pattern on the monitor he must have had a massive thrombosis, probably involving a major branch of one of the coronary arteries."

"That's very bad, isn't it?"

"Unless there's another cessation—the term we use to describe a stoppage of the heart—the next forty-eight hours should tell us whether the immediate damage from the thrombosis will be more than his heart is able to cope with."

"And if it is?"

"Then he will no longer be able to maintain enough circulation to keep vital functions such as kidney action going and the blood will start backing up in the lungs, causing congestion along with other symptoms—the picture we call heart failure."

"Do you think that's likely to happen, Doctor?"

Dr. McNeal nodded slowly. "His heart was barely maintaining the circulation before the last attack, so I don't expect it to be able to cope with a large thrombosis like this one. But you can never be sure in these cases."

"Last night you spoke of a possible operation," she reminded him.

"That was before this new crisis. I have asked Dr. Connor, The Clinic's cardiologist, to see your husband this morning and Dr. Alexander, the surgeon, will see him, too, for consultation. By that time we may be able to give you a more definite prognosis."

Dr. Connor, whom Dr. McNeal introduced to Georgia as the heart specialist, gave her no encouragement, however, when he saw Guy later. One of the nurses showed her the location of the hospital canteen, where she obtained coffee, but, when she returned to the ICU and again began to watch the pattern of Guy's heartbeat being recorded by the flashing point of light that moved steadily across the glass front of the tube to the opposite side, then was resumed again on the left, even she could see that the peaks and valleys of the ECG record were gradually contracting.

Which could only mean that Guy's heart was failing, as Dr. McNeal had implied that it almost certainly would.

CHAPTER SEVEN

I

Sam Hunter was finishing his glucose tolerance test when Helen Foucald came into her office. Through the door leading to the main laboratory, she could see that a blood specimen was being taken from his veins by one of the technicians and was shocked at the change that had come over the old man in the nearly two years since the last convocation.

At that time, old Sam had been full of vigor, dominating the trustees' meeting and riding roughshod over Greg's plan, until in the end the matter had been deferred to give him and his committee a chance to plan another building that might fulfill the provision in the will of The Clinic's founder that the statue of Christ in the administration rotunda must always be a central feature and at the same time would be within the cost limits Sam Hunter himself had insisted upon.

Helen went into the main laboratory while the technician was placing a small dressing over the puncture wound in Sam Hunter's arm where she had withdrawn the blood. Picking up his routing sheet, she noted that this was the last test requiring fasting that morning.

"Would you like to come into my office, Mr. Hunter?" she asked. "I'll have someone bring you coffee and toast there."

The idea of food perked the old man up somewhat. As he followed her into the office, he pulled one of his stogies from his pocket and bit off the tip before lighting it with a match from an old-fashioned matchbox.

"When you're used to ham and eggs at seven o'clock, you can get pretty hungry by ten," he grumbled.

"Sorry I can't find the ham and eggs." Helen took the seat behind the desk while the old man sprawled in a chair beside it. "But I'm beginning to understand your preference for them."

"Don't tell me the French have taken up that American habit."

"I just had breakfast at the airport. Dr. Alexander asked me to meet the banquet speaker for the convocation."

"The fellow from the World Health Organization?"

"Yes, Dr. Peter Carewe."

"That UN business is another waste of money. Spending it on people that don't have the gumption to try and help themselves is like pouring dollars down a rathole."

"Part of what is spent for the WHO is for your own protection, Mr. Hunter." Having defended Peter against Henry, Helen now found herself playing the same role against the Texas multimillionaire. "If we keep down disease in other countries, we'll have less of it coming in here—including a disease called communism."

"The money could be better used in Red-hunting and quarantine measures."

"Like keeping Mexicans from crossing the border?" Helen asked innocently, and the old man gave her a' sharp look.

"As smart as you're good-looking, aren't you?" He sighed. "Wish I were forty years younger."

"That's the nicest compliment I've had in a long time. What are you going to do about a new clinic and hospital at the trustees' meeting on Saturday, Mr. Hunter?"

"Don't see any reason to change my mind from what we voted for two years ago," he said. "What's the sense of pouring out all the money Dr. Alexander wants to put into this location when people are living like pigs all around it?"

"They are the ones who need help the most, Mr. Hunter."

"You mean they're the ones that need to help themselves. When Henry Anders built the Clinic, this section was populated with working people. Women got out every morning to scrub the stone steps until they shone and it was a pleasure just to walk down The Parkway. Now what do you have? Slop and filth everywhere, bringing disease."

"Poverty's at the base of it, Mr. Hunter. Don't forget that."

"Haven't you heard? The government's outlawed that. All they're doing is throwing good money after bad and that's what I'm trying to keep from happening to this hospital. Rebuild it here and you'll have the same people flocking in for free medical care who've been putting the place in the red lately. Relocate it out in the suburbs and it will attract people that can help support it, the kind it ought to attract."

"The finest doctors in the country still apply for fellowships here," Helen reminded him. "Because they know they'll get the best training and experience in what you call a rathole that they can get anywhere."

"Maybe. But if the work here didn't have to be cluttered up with taking care of so many people from the slums, it would be more efficient."

"I've been told that the first Dr. Anders decided to build here because he wanted to provide a place where poor people could come without too much hardship."

"That was when the people in the neighborhood were honest working folks who took pride in what they were doing, not a bunch of loafers." The toast and coffee arrived just then and Sam Hunter tackled it with some of his vigor. "That's the trouble now, Doctor, people want everything handed to them on a silver platter without working to get it. Anything worth having is worth working for."

"But sometimes disease doesn't wait."

"Oh, some soft-hearted do-gooder is always around to bleed over people. Most of those who live around here could work if they were willing to get a little dirt on their hands. What has all the money the poverty program's been dumping into places like this done anyway? Paying high-school dropouts sixty-five dollars a week to finish school so they can become typists that don't even know how to spell cat? Or training waitresses to spill soup and leave tables dirty?"

"The slum dwellers could be taught new technical skills."

"Taught! You can't teach them anything."

"Perhaps nobody has tried hard enough."

"It's not the place of The Clinic Foundation to do that. How can I go to my business friends and tell them I want money to build a new hospital in the middle of a neighborhood that's practically a pigsty? They'd laugh in my face."

"Slums can be changed. I could show you where it's already beginning to happen, Mr. Hunter, if you'll take the time to go with me."

"To some block where OEO—if that's what you call it—has poured in a million to create a showplace?"

"The OEO financed several health centers but the people have done the rest themselves—the people and the landlords."

"I read about that, too."

When Sam Hunter jumped from his chair and went to the window, Helen wondered for a moment if she had baited him too far. Not only might his opposition to Greg Alexander be heightened by her arguments, but he could have a stroke, too, judging by the angry pulsing of the torturous artery in his left temple.

"What's that building down there?" he asked suddenly, and Helen came over to the window to join him.

"Where?"

"What looks like a new addition to the experimental laboratory. We haven't authorized building anything here since the last trustees' meeting."

"That's the new hyperbaric chamber—part of the setup for experimental surgery."

"Hyperbaric?" The old man frowned. "Isn't that some foolishness about pumping up an operating room like a tire?"

"The word means 'high pressure,' Mr. Hunter. Dr. Alexander is very—"

"Did he have that building put up when we already turned down a plan of his that included one of those things two years ago?"

"The building was erected last year; I believe it was financed by a grant from the National Institute of Health."

"The government?"

"Yes. But I understand that Greg—Dr. Alexander—paid for much of the equipment himself."

"I'm going to call a special meeting of the board Friday afternoon to look into his actions," the old man snapped. "If he wants to remain an employee of The Clinic—"

"I'm sure Greg Alexander does want to remain an employee—as you so quaintly put it—of The Clinic, Mr. Hunter." Helen's voice was biting. "But if he knuckles under, don't think it's because he's afraid of you or the board. It will only be because he wants to keep a top-flight medical institution where the people who need it most live. If you had known the first Dr. Anders as well as you claim to, you'd know that was his dream, too."

II

Dr. David Connor did his job well. By ten o'clock bets were being taken in the quarters of the resident house staff on Greg Alexander's chances of selling his new plan for an automated hospital and clinic to the trustees at the end of the week. Odds on Greg dropped sharply when the grapevine also carried the news that Sam Hunter, looking more dour than ever while having his annual regular checkup, had stormed angrily out of Helen Foucald's office earlier that morning, and was demanding a special meeting of the Board of Trustees to censure Greg.

As for the subject of the wagers, Greg was showing Peter Carewe, who had come over to the hospital to say hello, the effects in experimental animals of the high concentrations of oxygen achieved in the hyperbaric chamber, after experimental infection with anerobic—oxygen-hating—bacteria, as opposed to ordinary organisms which thrived in an atmosphere of oxygen. Earlier experiments had given striking results but he had insisted on running a second series to verify the first.

In the Laboratory of Experimental Surgery adjoining the old surgical building, Greg looked across the small table where Bob Johnson was autopsying a rabbit which had been used in the experiment. The animal had been killed moments before, painlessly with an injection of Sodium Pentothal.

"You can see that hyperventilation with oxygen under pressure inhibits bacterial growth *in vivo* as well as it does *in vitro*," he told Peter Carewe. *In vivo* meant inside the living body, while *in vitro* meant in laboratory cultures or in chemical experiments.

"A series of one case?" The doctor from WHO raised his eyebrows slightly; it was a standing joke in medical schools that students often came to weighty conclusions on insufficient evidence.

"An omen perhaps. Naturally, we'll repeat the experiment until we know for sure."

"Helen was telling me about your heart-lung transplant case having pups," said Peter. "Congratulations, Greg."

"We got in that murderer who was almost killed on the expressway last night, Dr. Alexander," said Bob Johnson. "Herb Partridge asked me to see him about an hour or so after Letty had her pups, but there was nothing vascular or thoracic involved."

"I didn't even see the papers or hear the news this morning," said Greg. "What happened?"

"This guy had already killed a couple of times and was making his getaway after holding up a tavern when he took the wrong ramp. The police say he's been in prison most of his life and was headed for the gas chamber before he escaped."

"Was he badly injured?" There was a sudden intensity in Greg's voice.

"Almost decapitated, according to the paper," said Peter Carewe.

"Herb Partridge did a laminectomy last night," Bob Johnson added. "Two cervical vertebrae were destroyed and the spinal cord was severed. About the only things functioning in him are the brain and the heart, but they're pretty well cut off from any nerve connection to the rest of the body."

"Did you say the cervical cord was severed?" Both of the men noticed the excitement in Greg's voice now.

"Cut clean in two in the lower cervical region," said the younger surgeon. "He's on a Mark IV respirator and Herb doesn't know whether or not he'll regain consciousness. But his heart is pumping away just like nothing had happened—" Bob dropped the scissors he was holding as the full import of what he was saying struck him.

"If he's going to die one way or another, he may be just what we're looking for," said Greg.

"What do you mean, Greg?" Peter asked.

"As a donor—for a transplant."

"But can you possibly find anyone in the time we have who's far enough gone to be the recipient?" said Bob.

"An ideal case may be in the hospital already," said Greg. "Dave Connor was telling me about him at breakfast, a man who's had several coronaries and almost went out with cessation early this morning."

"That must be the one Jim McNeal was talking about for a gas-jet dissection last night," said Bob. "But Jim told me at breakfast that he'd had a cessation and if the nurse on ICU hadn't happened to be watching his monitor when the ECG curve flattened out and got a Pacemaker on him in time, he'd have been gone for sure. Jim says he's real rocky still and his heart's failing."

"Which makes him all the more urgently in need of a new one," said Greg.

"If he lives as long as this spinal case does," Bob agreed. "But from what Jim said, it will be touch and go."

"As soon as you finish here, Bob, have the heart-lung pump checked out." Greg spoke from the doorway of the laboratory and Peter Carewe was close behind him.

"What about the heart-lung transplant you'd scheduled for tomorrow?" he asked. "I've been looking forward to that."

"Wouldn't you rather see a human transplant instead?"

"Of course."

"Maybe we can arrange that but we've got to work fast. I'm going to see Dave Connor; he's got to be convinced first."

III

The door of apartment 8-A was opened by a pregnant young woman in a smock.

"I'm Mrs. Alexander from upstairs," said Jeanne. "May I come in for a moment, Mrs. Jackson?"

"Oh yes, Mrs. Alexander." The girl's smile was warm. "Please call me Mary—and don't look at this apartment. Little Keith is walking, so everything's topsy-turvy. My husband worships your—but then I guess almost everybody does."

Everybody except me, Jeanne thought. *I only pray I'm not too late!*

The small living room was tastefully, though sparsely, furnished, as was the dining room visible through an archway.

"Keith's too much of a visionary for us ever to be rich," Mary Jackson apologized. "But I do try to buy nice things."

"I imagine vision is worth a lot to a creative person."

"Oh yes. I wouldn't want him anyway else—just as I'm sure you wouldn't want Dr. Alexander to change. All the nurses worship him."

"You were a nurse?"

"A supervisor across the street—until I got too big to get between the beds and the walls. Harriet and Bob Johnson talk about Dr. Alexander all the time. Bob says he's the finest surgeon in the world and Keith is just overjoyed to be working with him on the new Clinic plans."

"My husband has been busy and I haven't wanted to bother him, so I haven't seen them," said Jeanne. "Do you suppose your husband has a sketch around here?"

"They've been all over the place for a week—ever since Dr. Anders suggested the idea to him."

"Dr. Anders?" Jeanne asked, startled.

"Oh, my goodness!" Mary Jackson put her hand over her mouth. "That's supposed to be a secret, particularly from your husband."

"I'll keep the secret," Jeanne promised. "It's just that I didn't know Henry Anders was involved in this particular project."

"Dr. Anders saw this article about a new hotel in Atlanta; there's been a lot about it in some of the news magazines. They say it's all glass and just like outdoors, except that it's still closed in. Anyway, he thought something like that in the new Clinic would be a fine monument to his father and remembered that Keith had submitted some sketches two years ago." She smiled deprecatingly. "I'm afraid those were pretty far out, though; Keith was in a sort of avant-garde phase then. But when Dr. Anders brought the article to him, along with some other material about new trends in hospital construction, Keith took off like a rocket."

"Did Dr. Anders give any reason why he brought the sketches to your husband, instead of going through the building committee?" Jeanne asked.

"He said there was some tension between him and Dr. Alexander about the new hospital and he wasn't sure Dr. Alexander would look with favor on it if he knew the idea had been suggested by him." She gave Jeanne a quick look. "Is anything wrong, Mrs. Alexander?"

"I don't know. Did you say you have some sketches here in the apartment?"

"They're in the den; Keith uses it as a sort of studio here at home." She led Jeanne down a short hall to the door at the end. It opened into a smaller room containing a drawing table; sheets of drawing paper were scattered all over the place.

"This place is a mess, but I don't dare touch anything," Mary Jackson said. "Keith calls these fragmentary sketches his seeds."

The ideas represented by what had been called "fragmentary sketches" were brilliantly conceived, even daring, Jeanne saw; yet, for all their soaring grace, there was a practicality about them, too. Mary leafed through a pile of larger drawings on the table by the window and pulled one out. Placing it on the table, she switched on the overhead light to bathe it in brilliance.

What Jeanne saw there almost took her breath away.

Where others had sought to enclose the giant statue of Christ that was the central figure in the rotunda, Keith Jackson had somehow managed to create the illusion of separating it from all earthly attachments. Massive steel pillars at the corners supported the entire structure of a central tower composing the very heart of the building. The intensive care floors were arranged in the form of a U, with the open end facing The Parkway. Inside the U stood the statue, with floodlights bathing it from below and above, a visible symbol of everything The Clinic had stood for since its founder first conceived it.

"The central section, where the statue is located, has a glass roof three stories high," Mary Jackson explained. "The operating theaters, the admitting areas where the patients are brought in the night before surgery and the main laboratories are all underground. There are two floors of them, with the emergency entrance by way of a tunnel at the back."

"It's beautiful!" Jeanne cried. "Simply beautiful."

"Keith says Dr. Alexander flipped the first time he saw it. You can't see the floor detail too well in these sketches, but each wing is a separate unit with its own nursing station on every floor. That way, all sixteen rooms in each unit are visible from the nursing station, besides having their own closed-circuit television and the monitors that are used now for watching the vital functions. Being a nurse, I guess I'm more enthusiastic about this than some other people might be."

"I was a nurse, too," said Jeanne, "though it's been quite a while ago."

"Then you can see how efficient this arrangement is compared to most hospitals. Keith says it's ten years ahead of the times."

"It may be more than that."

"The hospital wings where patients go after they leave the ICU tower are structured to give them the greatest freedom in looking after themselves, so much less personnel will be needed," Mary explained. "Keith hasn't worked out the details of that part yet, but they'll be very simple—actually, more like hotels. The central ICU tower is the one that caught his fancy."

"And mine," Jeanne agreed. "I've never seen anything like it."

"There's never been anything like it, Mrs. Alexander—at least not in hospital construction. Keith thinks that when it's finished, it's bound to upgrade the character of the whole neighborhood. He says even a slum landlord won't be able to look at that tower without wanting to make his own buildings better places for people to live."

"When you see it there in the sketch, you can believe he's right. Is this the drawing my husband saw?"

"It's the basic plan, but more of the details are drawn in on the sketch Dr. Alexander has in his office. He was so enthusiastic about it that he asked Keith to get a friend of his to run some traffic study patterns, so a few changes may have to be made later on. But this is so close to being final that whatever changes have to be made won't make any real difference in the eventual appearance of the structure."

"Then this plan is the one my husband will show to the trustees on Saturday?"

"We certainly hope so; Keith's been working night and day to get the drawings ready. He's even hired two extra draftsmen and he'll be a walking zombie himself by then from lack of sleep, but the whole thing should be in a form that will capture even a trustee's imagination."

"I hope so," Jeanne said fervently. "Thank you for showing it to me, Mary. You've been very kind."

"Surely Dr. Alexander must have spoken to you about it," said the architect's wife. "Keith says he never saw such a look of awe on a man's face as was on your husband's when he saw the sketches for the first time."

"I can understand that, now that I've seen it myself. Good-by."

"You won't mention Dr. Anders' connection with it?"

"I promise."

But as she was walking back to the elevator, Jeanne decided that nothing in her promise to Mary Jackson prevented her from finding out, from whatever source she could, just what mischief Henry Anders was up to now.

CHAPTER EIGHT

I

"You're out of your mind, Greg," said Dave Connor when the surgeon told him what he hoped to do for Guy Merchant.

"We've done more than a hundred dogs, Dave, most of them both heart and lungs. As Hans has said more than once, what difference is there between transplanting organs into dogs and putting new ones into human beings?"

"There's a helluva lot of difference." The cardiologist's voice always rose when he got excited. "A man's got a soul and a dog hasn't."

"Got any proof of that?"

"For Christ's sake, Greg, this is no place for theological discussions. I just don't think it's right to kill this poor devil before his time comes."

"How long will that be, the way he is now?"

Dave Connor shrugged. "A few days at most. He was already on the ragged edge when he had the attack of angina while he was doing his act last night in that joint where he and his wife were working."

"What does she do?"

"She's a stripper and still somewhat of a looker. Used to play the top houses in burlesque before they degenerated into the sort of grind houses they are today."

"She stayed with him then?"

"You never saw two more devoted people."

"And, therefore, more worth saving as two, not one."

"Don't try to sway me with sentiment!" Dave Connor snapped irritably. "I'm looking at the thing from the viewpoint of what's best for you."

"That's what I want you to forget, Dave."

"Have you even considered what undertaking a heart-lung transplant in an unsuitable case can do to your chances of getting the kind of new clinic and hospital you want out of that bunch of hard-headed businessmen who control the trustees?"

"Frankly, no."

"They'll say you only did it to impress them and that, if you don't have any better sense than to accept a poor risk and give The Clinic a bad name, you've got no business being in charge at all."

"I'm not in charge, you know."

"I don't know any such damned thing! Henry's only a front; without you, this place would fall apart. And right now a spectacular failure by you might be all that's needed."

"The Clinic survived old Dr. Anders' death."

"Only because you were here to carry on what he started."

"You're forgetting something important, Dave."

"What?"

"We all took an oath in our last year of medical school. Part of it says: '*So far as power and discernment shall be mine, I will carry out regimen for the benefit of the sick and will keep them from harm and wrong.*'"

Dave Connor flushed. "How many doctors today live strictly by those precepts?"

"You and I do. That's why you can't deny this man the chance to live that I may be able to give him, just because you're afraid I'm going to be blamed if I fail."

"But does it have to be now? When so many of your enemies are here at one time?"

"Lots of my friends are here, too. Don't forget that."

The cardiologist shrugged. "All right—as long as you understand what you're risking. What do you need to know in order to evaluate him for surgery?"

"Everything."

"Guy Merchant has had at least four coronary attacks and God knows how many episodes of anginal pain. Which means that his heart circulation hasn't been keeping up for probably more than a year and a lot of the muscle has been replaced by scar tissue. Last night he had a severe anginal attack but fortunately there was a doctor in the audience, with a medical bag in his car parked close to the theater. He gave Merchant Demerol and a vasodilator, so he escaped an actual block of the coronary vessels that time. But to show you what a ragged edge he travels on, this morning he had a real coronary."

"With the cessation?"

"Yes; even the monitor shows it now. Merchant's heart is in early failure, his liver is already starting to enlarge and we can hear some moisture at his lung bases. We're giving him the works, of course, to help his heart keep up the circulation. But our measures aren't taking hold, which means there just isn't much reserve left."

"Making him an ideal case for a transplant."

"Except for one thing."

"What's that?"

"He's got an advanced case of emphysema, too; been a heavy smoker practically all of his life. Right now we can hardly get enough oxygen into his lungs to keep him alive, because his vital capacity is curtailed from the emphysema. Maybe you can give him a new heart, if you can find one—"

"We may have one; that's what gave me the idea."

"Who?"

"The convict who was injured last night. He's a perfect physical specimen below his neck and all we need are his heart and lungs."

"But are you ready for an operation of that magnitude on a human being? There have been plenty of heart transplants, and a lot of failures. But the heart and the lungs—"

"I've got ten living dogs whose heart and lungs came from others in one piece, Dave. One had pups last night and we've even swapped from one dog to another and back again. Actually, the technique of heart-lung transplant is simpler than putting in the heart alone, because you have less blood vessels to suture."

"It's going to be a hell of a job explaining to Merchant's wife what you propose to do."

"We can't just stop with the wife; both of them have to know," said Greg. "Can Merchant stand it?"

"I guess so; he's sedated, but conscious. Do you want to talk to them now?"

"There's no point in arousing their hopes before I have permission to use the convict's organs when he dies. Will you go to them with me after I get the legal details straightened out?"

"Can't you just get permission from this convict?"

"Herb Partridge doesn't think Lawson will ever regain consciousness and the police still haven't been able to find any family. Which means I've got to go to court first."

"You're going way out on a limb, Greg," Dave Connor said doubtfully. "I wonder if Im not a fool for going out there with you."

"Answer me one question: would you want me out on that limb if you were in Merchant's place?"

"Hell yes!"

"Then it's settled. I'll be in touch."

II

Ed McDougal was sitting in Henry Anders' office when he came back from making rounds on his private patients about eleven o'clock. Henry didn't bother to see those on the open wards oftener than a couple of times a week. Bob Johnson and the other Senior Fellows on surgery could be counted on to take care of any patient who got in trouble. And by putting in an appearance on the wards two or three times a week, Henry could defend himself, if he had to, at the monthly review of cases during the regular staff meetings.

"Henry, old boy!" Ed pumped his hand. "How the hell are you?"

"Fine, Ed. How are things in Texas?"

"Couldn't be better."

"Getting rich, I suppose?"

"I'm getting my share—and not complaining. Who was that looker in the white coat I saw you talking to in the corridor just a bit ago?"

"You must mean Helen Foucald. She's head of our clinical laboratory."

"Been doing some experiments with her lately, Henry?"

"You know we've always been heavy on research here, Ed." Henry Anders smiled knowingly as he reached for a cigar.

"You're a dog, Henry! I don't know how you do it." Ed McDougal's voice became businesslike. "I was planning to get here last night and see Sam Hunter before he started his checkup, but the plane was late. Have you seen him yet?"

"No. I was planning to drop in on him at the Inn before I go home tonight."

"We'd better not let all that dough be going around without a guard," said the Texas surgeon. "Sam's not himself these days. Ted's marrying that wop girl from the circus shook him up."

"Did he really disinherit the boy?"

"Threw him out in the cold, I hear. Swears he's leaving every dime of Ted's inheritance to our new medical school down home and your Clinic. Now's the time for us to make our play, boy."

"What good will it do me? Dad's will expressly stated that I get the property, but only if The Clinic moves to another location."

"Then we'll move it. You still want my help with that little deal you were telling me about at the Southern Medical, don't you?"

"Of course."

"Well, I've been doing my part. You'll be surprised how many of the board I've talked to since then—and how many I've convinced that the new Clinic needs to be out on the Beltway." Ed leaned forward and jabbed his finger at the other surgeon. "What have you been doing, Henry?"

"I've got some pretty important people lined up for the syndicate to develop the property." Henry took a paper from his pocket and handed it to the Texas surgeon. "Take a look at this."

Ed McDougal read the list and nodded approval. "Between us, we'll put this thing through, Henry—and make ourselves rich into the bargain."

"We haven't settled how Sam Hunter's money is to be divided yet," said Henry Anders, and Ed McDougal gave the other surgeon a quick, suspicious glance.

"You wouldn't double-cross old Ed, would you, Henry? Maybe with some ploy of your own?"

"I've already got the ploy. The only question is how we divide what we can wangle out of Sam Hunter now."

"Building a new medical school costs a lot of money."

"So does building a new Clinic."

"How about a third for you and two thirds for my school?"

"That sounds fair." Henry had been hoping for a fourth.

"So what is this plan of yours?"

Henry Anders quickly sketched the stratagem upon which he had embarked by showing the hotel pictures to Keith Jackson. When he finished, Ed's eyes gleamed with frank admiration.

"It's perfect, Henry boy," he said. "Old Sam will be against the new plan simply because Greg wants it and that should be enough to torpedo the whole project by convincing the board that it can never be built without Sam's money. By the way, how much would the one Greg's planning now cost?"

"Keith Jackson's rough estimate is about twenty-eight million."

Ed McDougal whistled softly. "Built here, of course?"

"Yes."

"Out on the Beltway, where the land has already been offered, you wouldn't have the expense of tearing down the present buildings, or building around any of them to keep operating. That could lop off a couple of million, I would imagine."

"Nearly three, I've been told."

"Then old Sam's got plenty for both of us and some to spare." Ed held out his hand. "Check, partner, we're in business."

Henry Anders withheld his hand. "With one provision."

"What's that?"

"Greg Alexander is out."

"That may not be easy," Ed McDougal warned. "Greg's got a fine reputation—not just here but in the country at large."

"So make him professor of surgery in your new school."

"I've got that job sewed up for myself. Besides, you know as well as I do that he's turned down a half dozen professorships already."

"Then give him an endowed department of experimental surgery. You must have some millionaire friend in Texas who would like to have his name on such an institute."

"I could arrange that." Ed McDougal nodded slowly. "And Greg might bite—after he's slapped down hard by the trustees on Saturday."

"Make him bite," Henry Anders said bluntly. "Make him bite, or it's no deal."

"Why are you so anxious to get rid of Greg?"

"He robbed me of my birthright by persuading my father to leave The Clinic to a charitable foundation and I swore then to get even with him some day. This is my opportunity."

"It's a deal, but you'd better talk to that architect and make sure he doesn't get cold feet and compromise on his plan if Greg suggests cutting costs. Somewhere along the line, Greg's bound to realize he might have a chance to put the plan through by decreasing the cost, especially if it's as good as your description."

"I've got Jackson so sold on the idea of the new buildings as a monument to my dad that I don't think he'll accept any sort of compromise, even if Greg suggests it," Henry Anders assured the other surgeon. "Architects are creative people, like artists and writers. Jackson will fight for his brain child."

"We're both going to have to depend on that." Ed McDougal stood up. "I'll go out and find old Sam and see how he feels. What about his checkup?"

"It was due to begin here this morning, a couple of hours or so ago."

"That means he didn't have any breakfast."

"What difference does that make?"

"About all the pleasure left in life for Sam comes from eating. Just about now he should be fit to be tied, so I'll go drop a few hints that Greg is giving him the run-around. That should have about the same effect as a small atomic bomb."

III

Jeanne Alexander and Claire Anders had agreed to have lunch in the motel coffee shop at noon to make final plans for the luncheon on Thursday for the wives of the Members attending the convocation. A leading dress shop was putting on a fashion show for the affair, fully cognizant that the wives of prosperous doctors were always a lucrative market for their merchandise.

"I've snagged something else that ought to interest these girls," Claire said over a salad and coffee.

"What's that?"

"A clinic on how to be a widow."

Jeanne started to laugh, then saw that Claire was serious. "Whatever gave you that idea?"

"A lot of 'em are going to be widows before many more years. Let's face it, my dear: our husbands have one of the highest death rates as a group in the male population."

"It still seems sort of disloyal to be anticipating it."

"Not disloyal, realistic. Most of these gals have a considerable vested interest in their husbands' careers. After all, a lot of them supported their men through residencies and fellowships."

"I did—they were some of the happiest years of our marriage."

"You're entitled to more than memories now and so are two thirds of those who'll be at the luncheon," said Claire. "Do you know that successful doctors and their wives have one of the highest divorce rates of any upper income group?"

"Maybe a divorce lawyer would be more appropriate for your clinic then."

"You've got a point there; the only trouble is that it's the husbands who jump over the traces. Did you hear about the Smiths?"

"No."

"A few months ago, Ed took up with this filly who's only nineteen—and him fifty-five if he's a day. He divorced Millicent and is shacked up with this child in an apartment, but one of these days he's going to get a hell of a shock when they're in bed together and she looks at him half asleep and says 'Daddy!'"

"Why, that's incestuous."

"Whatever that means, I guess it is—but getting back to this widow business, I've asked the trust officer of a bank I've got some stock in to give a clinic on widows. He's a handsome fellow and puts on a good show. Most of these women are going to outlive their husbands by ten years or so, if they escape a divorce, so they might as well go first class either way."

"You have a point there," Jeanne admitted.

"Think of all the medical marriages we know. How many women are suffering from the Doctor's Wife Syndrome?"

"You don't have to look far," said Jeanne soberly. "I've been a victim of it myself for some time now."

"Was that the trouble? I thought it might be the menopause."

"The pill would have taken care of that."

"But what do you have to feel unwanted about, Jeanne? Greg's the nicest man I know and everybody knows he's never looked at another woman. While Henry—well, surely you must have seen him coming and going from Helen Foucald's apartment."

"Well—"

"It's a very satisfactory arrangement—as I was telling Helen last night."

"You talked to her about it?" Jeanne was horrified.

"Why not? You'd better be glad you didn't marry Henry that time he was so hot after you."

"We only had a few dates," Jeanne protested. "Henry introduced me to Greg on one of them and after that I couldn't see anybody else."

"I guess that's another reason why Henry hates Greg so; I thought it was all because the old man liked Greg so much."

"You really think he hates Greg?"

"My husband is an easy hater," said Claire. "I talked to Henry's old nurse once and she said that even as a child he'd never let anyone else play with his marbles."

"Aren't you being hard on him?"

"I know Henry better than anybody else could. You see, Dr. Anders wanted more out of his son than Henry could provide, things like intelligence and the sort of dedication that drove him to establish The Clinic. Greg has all of that, so Henry has to hate him."

"You ought to be a psychiatrist."

"Oh, Henry's not hard to figure out. He even hates me, because I've got things he knows he'll never have—money, breeding and class. But he likes having a woman with all those things, so he'll hang on to me."

"Did you know he's trying to drive Greg out of The Clinic?"

The startled look in Claire's eyes told Jeanne she had no part in whatever Henry Anders was plotting. "Even Henry wouldn't be dumb enough to try that," said Claire. "Whatever gave you that idea?"

"I think he hopes to get the trustees to vote down Greg's plans for The Clinic a second time on Saturday. After that sort of a slap in the face, even Greg would have to react, probably by leaving The Clinic."

"That would be almost the only way Henry could attack him," Claire said thoughtfully. "What I can't understand is why Henry would be such a fool. He always was a little paranoiac, it's true, but this could really be serious. If he drives Greg out, The Clinic will begin to fall apart. Half the staff would resign in less than six months."

"Maybe that's what he wants. Then the property will be his under the terms of his father's will."

"The conniving bastard!" said Claire. "He started to tell me something last night about Greg, but he was all excited and something else came up." She lowered her voice. "But if this new plan is everything you say it is, the trustees might just be as taken with Keith Jackson's sketches as Greg and you apparently are, which would solve the problem."

"Sam Hunter's apparently the key to the whole thing," Jeanne explained. "Ed McDougal's up here to keep Sam Hunter's money for his medical school. He's joined forces with Henry."

"How did you learn all this?"

"Hannah and I had breakfast together this morning—accidentally."

"How is Neiman-Marcus' favorite customer?"

"Jittery, if you ask me. I think she's afraid Ed may divorce her for another woman; at least she talked about it almost all the time we were together."

"The Doctor's Wife Phobia," said Claire. "As I remember Ed, Hannah's got good reason to worry. He always was a woman-chaser and, with those black Irish good looks of his, plenty of them are willing to be caught."

"I don't think it's Ed that Hannah's worried about. It's losing the income and position he's given her. I gather that he lets her spend money like water."

"Hannah's a fine-looking broad and a man like Ed McDougal would get

a lot of satisfaction out of seeing his wife in the best. But how did she happen
to let on about the Sam Hunter business?"

"Apparently she thinks Greg has lost already and felt sorry for me. My
guess is she thought I might warn him in time to accept defeat gracefully."

"Which he'd never do, so Henry thinks he'll win either way." Claire was
dead serious now. "If the trustees decide to move The Clinic at Saturday's
meeting, Henry will be rich and independent of me. And if they leave it here
and turn down Greg's plan, he'll be rid of your husband. Either way, we've
got to stop him."

"You really don't have to get involved, Claire."

"I'm involved already. Once Henry's rich, I could be replaced by a young
filly. It isn't a very pleasant thought, Jeanne."

"I'm sorry to be the one who gave it to you."

"You did me a favor," Claire said briskly. "If Henry and I were divorced,
I would have to find myself a younger man and that's never satisfactory for
very long. Henry would be in the same fix, though you couldn't get him to
admit it. One woman isn't enough for him yet, so he'd take a young girl
right away. But once his age starts to catch up with him—and it's already
beginning—she'd probably shed him, too, and take him to the cleaners in
the process."

Claire got to her feet and began to gather up purse and gloves. "Henry
and I are good for each other and I guess, at that, we're more honest than a
lot of married couples, who just go on hating until one of them gets enough
worked up to have a fatal heart attack. Thank God it's usually the man."

IV

It was past noon when Greg Alexander and Dr. Philip Dennison, the
county medical examiner, were ushered by a secretary into the chambers of
Judge Paul Sutler, The judge was a handsome man in his sixties, and an old
friend of Greg's.

"You gentlemen are making me have a sandwich and a glass of milk for
lunch during the noon recess of court." He gestured to the tray the secretary
had just put down on his desk. "What is so important that you want me to
get indigestion?"

"Dr. Alexander came to me this morning with a request, sir," said the
medical examiner. "I don't feel that I can honor it without an order from
you."

"What is the request, Greg?" the judge asked.

"I want your authority to remove the heart and lungs from a dead man."

"Couldn't Phil do that at autopsy? I take it that this is a coroner's case."

"It's Frank Lawson, the man injured in the expressway accident last
night."

"The escaped prisoner who murdered the salesman during his getaway?"

"Yes."

"Then he's dead?"

"Not yet—but none of us at the hospital think he can last very long with a
severe head injury and the spinal cord severed in the lower neck region."

"I suppose you want to do a transplant?"

"Yes—a double one."

"What's that?" the judge asked with a frown.

"The heart and lungs in one operation."

"Sounds like a large order. Who's the patient?"

"His name is Guy Merchant. He's had a number of coronary attacks, the last one this morning, and his heart is slowly failing. Dave Connor doesn't think he can live more than a few days longer—"

"Without a new heart and lungs?"

"Yes."

"This is a tricky legal problem." Judge Sutler rubbed his chin thoughtfully. "Have you tried to get permission from Lawson?"

"He hasn't regained consciousness and our neurosurgeons don't believe he will."

"What about relatives?"

"The police haven't been able to locate any," said Dr. Dennison. "Apparently Lawson was a loner."

"And a condemned criminal who has been identified twice as a murderer," Greg said.

"That's the trickiest point of all," said the judge. "Undoubtedly, the state would put Lawson in the gas chamber, if he could ever be brought to trial."

"I'm afraid that's never going to happen," said Greg.

"I'm dealing only in hypothesis now," Judge Sutler explained. "Until Lawson's in prison and a death order has been signed, we have no right to become his executioner."

"This isn't an execution," Greg protested. "I fully intend to take measures to keep him alive as long as possible."

"Won't that defeat your purpose, if the patient you're trying to help is going downhill?"

"It's a risk we shall have to take," said Greg. "In organ transplantation there are two major problems: first, preserving the donor organs until they can be connected up to the circulation of the recipient. And second, overcoming the tendency of the body to reject any tissue that isn't its own."

"Can you be sure this won't happen with Lawson's heart?"

"Not entirely," Greg admitted. "But his blood type is O—the universal donor—which is in our favor. We're running some other tests now and should have at least preliminary results by the latter part of the afternoon, but we also have ways of combating the rejection phenomenon, if it does occur."

"How about the technical difficulties of the operation?"

"My assistant and I have already done more than a hundred transplants in dogs, nearly half of them involving both heart and lungs. Most of them are doing well. One of our first cases had pups last night."

"It's an impressive record."

"We're not worrying about the surgical technique," Greg assured him. "All we ask is that the heart and lungs we use are in the best possible condition, which seems to be true with Lawson."

"Greg and I have discussed the question of what standards to use in determining death, sir," said the medical examiner. "We both agree that the three usual criteria—absence of heartbeat, absence of respiration and absence of brain activity, must be observed."

"I wonder if they're enough from the moral viewpoint," said Judge Sutler. "What worries me is that, if you can take Lawson's heart out of his body, put it into someone else, and start it to beating again, it couldn't possibly have been dead in the first place."

"We know that tissues die at different rates," said the medical examiner. "But with the heart no longer functioning, death of all tissue is inevitable. Greg and I agree that absence of any evidence of brain activity, as determined by the electroencephalograph, should be the ultimate test in this case."

"Suppose the heart stops first? Won't you lose valuable time while you wait for the electroencephalograph to tell you the brain is dead?"

"We can get around that by connecting a pump-oxygenator, such as we use to maintain circulation during open-heart operations, to Lawson's heart immediately after it stops beating," Greg explained. "That way, we can keep the blood flowing and maintain an adequate supply to the heart through the coronary arteries."

"In other words, you would be keeping a part of a dead man alive until you could transfer that part to another person?"

"That's it exactly," said Greg.

"And even though Lawson will be legally dead before you remove his heart and lungs, you will take every measure to see that those particular organs still live?"

"Yes."

"That's what I mean by a moral question," said the judge. "If you can take a living vital organ from a man's body, aren't you in essence committing murder?"

"Not when the organ you remove is the only part of him that could be considered alive," Greg argued. "Actually, though, I believe the moral question solves itself."

"How?"

"My obligation as a physician is to keep a human being alive as long as my abilities and the resources at my disposal will allow. In this case, I shall be going one step farther than is ordinarily the case by keeping Lawson's heart alive even after the rest of his body is dead."

"There's a nice point of something there," the judge admitted wryly, "but I'm not quite sure what it is."

"As a criminal, Lawson's life belongs to the state," said Greg. "Surely, if the state has a right to *take* his life, it also has a right to *give* part of it to save another life."

"You've got an eloquent argument there. Let me think about this for an hour or two and telephone you my decision. Can you wait that long?"

"I think so."

"Call me earlier if things start moving too fast."

V

It was past one o'clock when Greg Alexander came to the intensive care unit following his meeting with Judge Sutler and Dr. Dennison. He examined Guy Merchant carefully, studied the chart for some time, then came over to where Georgia Merchant was sitting. She had seen him briefly that morning when he had first examined Guy, but he had not talked to her then. Now he sat down beside her.

"I'm Dr. Alexander, Mrs. Merchant," he said.

"The heart surgeon?"

"I do the cardiac surgery here—as well as other things."

"There's no hope for Guy, is there, Dr. Alexander? I mean, he's beyond being helped by an operation?"

"On the contrary," said Greg. "If you'll take a walk with me, I think I can show you something you'll be interested in seeing."

Outside the building, he guided her to the Laboratory of Experimental Surgery and the animal house in its attached building beside the newly built hyperbaric chamber. It was feeding time when they entered, and the barking of dogs anticipating the meal greeted them.

"They sound happy," said Georgia doubtfully.

"Contrary to what you might have heard, they are treated very well."

"Is this where—you experiment?"

"This is the Laboratory of Experimental Surgery. I want you to see a special case over here in the corner."

Letty lay quietly with her puppies nestling against her, nursing happily. "This is our prima donna, Letty," he said. "Last night she gave birth to these puppies."

"They're adorable."

"Would you believe that six months ago Letty received a transplant of both a new heart and a new set of lungs?"

Georgia caught her breath suddenly, for his purpose in bringing her here had become apparent. "But the operation has never—"

"Half the dogs here have had successful heart-lung transplants—some more than once—Mrs. Merchant. You can see for yourself how healthy they are."

"But that's different from humans."

"Not as far as the technique of the operation is concerned. We worked it out here on dogs and our rate of success is surprisingly high."

"I—" Georgia suddenly felt a little faint. "I think we'd better go outside."

"Of course," he said. "I had no wish to upset you, but I thought it might help you to see Letty."

Outside the building, Georgia took a cigarette from her bag. When her hand trembled so she couldn't get the lighter to work, Greg held it for her and after a few moments, she was composed again.

"Are you asking my permission to experiment on my husband, Dr. Alexander?" she asked.

"We're no longer experimenting, Mrs. Merchant." Greg opened the door to the corridor and the elevator leading to the intensive care unit. "My assistants and I have been doing heart-lung transplants successfully for more than two years now."

"But only on dogs."

"The technician who looks after our laboratory animals says the *real* pioneering was with dogs. When we operate on our first human, we will merely be repeating a procedure we have done many times before."

"But it still wouldn't be the same."

"I'm not going to tell you that operating upon a human being will not be more of a strain than upon an animal, even an animal for whom you have a great deal of affection, as we have for Letty and the others. But the actual technique of the operation is the same; the only difference is that in dogs we have been able to work out and solve many of the problems that caused some of the earlier heart transplants to fail."

"But operating on a dog must be simpler than on a human."

"Actually, it's more difficult. The organs of a dog are much smaller and its tissues, much thinner."

"Has the rejection problem really been solved, Doctor?"

"Not completely, but we've come a long way with that, too, in the past several years."

"Surely transplanting both the heart and the lungs is much more difficult than the heart alone."

"Strangely enough, it isn't," he said. "You see, the lungs have a circulation of their own: a large artery carries blood from the right side of the heart to the lungs and a similar vein brings it back to the left side of the heart. In a heart transplant, we connect the heart to the body circulation and also to the lungs, but when transplanting both heart and lungs, we don't disturb the circulation of the lungs at all. This cuts the actual suturing almost in half."

"I suppose you have a donor, or you wouldn't even consider surgery for Guy."

"We do have—an ideal one in fact."

"May I ask who it is?"

"An accident case that was admitted last night. He was seriously injured when a truck struck his car on the expressway."

"Has he given permission?"

"This patient is expected to remain unconscious; that's why I couldn't talk to you earlier. An hour ago, I made application to Judge Sutler for permission to use his organs. The judge has promised to give me his decision this afternoon."

"Why from a judge?"

"The man is Frank Lawson."

"The murderer?" Her eyes filled with horror.

"He's a fine physical specimen—and young."

"You're very sure of yourself, aren't you, Dr. Alexander?" Georgia's voice was not without a tinge of bitterness. "Arranging for the transplant before you consulted me."

"I was considering your feelings and those of your husband, Mrs. Merchant. If I had told you when I was here earlier that I was ready to transplant as soon as a suitable donor was found—and you had agreed—the period of waiting could have been very hard on you. Especially since your husband's condition has already begun to deteriorate."

Georgia drew a deep breath; it was hard to believe this whole thing wasn't really a nightmare. "This decision is a heavy responsibility for me, Doctor."

"Nobody knows that better than I do," said Greg. "I make decisions almost like it nearly every day."

"But not for the person who is dearest to you in the world."

"No. That would make a considerable difference."

"If Guy is deteriorating already, how do you know he will live until the operation can be performed?"

"We don't know," he admitted. "But when the time comes to act, there will be no time for indecision, so I must have all the details arranged beforehand."

Georgia turned to look out the window, but saw nothing of the chill February sky outside. Every instinct urged her to leave matters entirely in the hands of this quiet surgeon, who was so courteous, considerate and confidence-inspiring. Her indecision came not so much from any doubt of his ability or his evaluation of Guy's condition, as from her own guilt over the feeling she had experienced that morning, when, even while the desperate battle for Guy's life had been going on in the room, her prayer had been that those efforts might fail.

If she gave her permission and the operation succeeded, she knew she could never forget that, had her prayer been answered, she would have condemned Guy to his death. Then it suddenly occurred to her that Greg Alexander himself might be the answer to her prayer for, in a way, he possessed in his skilled fingers the power to turn death into life. Turning to face him, she asked, "What chance does Guy really have of your operation being a success? Fifty-fifty?"

"With luck, more than that. Our mortality with dogs is now down to around twenty-five per cent."

"And without the operation?"

"Dr. Connor and Dr. McNeil tell me death is certain in a few days, perhaps sooner. But even if it wasn't, the emphysema in your husband's lungs wouldn't allow him to live very much longer. The time would come soon when he would need oxygen continuously."

"I don't have the right to decide!" she cried. "You'll have to ask Guy."

"I was going to do that in any event."

"Don't try to high-pressure him, please, Dr. Alexander. Just tell him what the situation is and let him make the decision for himself."

"Why don't you come into the room with me? Then your conscience can't hurt you, no matter what happens."

"I might break down and upset Guy," she said doubtfully.

"I'm a pretty good judge of character, Mrs. Merchant. Shall we go in?"

"Hello, ducks!" Guy greeted her with the English term of endearment that had meant so much to them through the years. "Are you all right?"

"I'm fine, darling," said Georgia. "Dr. Alexander has something to talk to you about."

Guy Merchant listened silently while Greg summarized in a few words the procedure he proposed to follow with the heart-lung transplant.

"I've known ever since I felt my pulse stop this morning that only a miracle would help me, Doctor," he said when Greg finished. "Perhaps you're that miracle."

"I can't guarantee it," Greg warned.

"It's an all-or-none shot, so I've got nothing to lose. Georgia will sign the permit."

"We shall move you to the operating room sometime before the surgery actually begins," Greg told him. "So don't be alarmed when they come for you."

Guy smiled. "I already know what it is to die, Dr. Alexander. And it's not half as bad as you might think."

VI

Ed McDougal caught Sam Hunter as the oilman was having his last X-ray around one o'clock. The two picked up Henry Anders at his office and were lunching at a corner table in the motel restaurant across the street from The Clinic.

"Why didn't you let me know Dr. Alexander had built that new building, Henry?" Sam Hunter demanded.

"It didn't cost us anything." Henry Anders flushed, for the older man's tone was that of a parent reprimanding a child.

"What building is this?" Ed McDougal asked.

"Greg managed to wheedle enough funds out of the National Institute of Health to build a hyperbaric chamber," Henry explained.

"Without permission from the board?" Ed was quick to recognize a possible break.

"No outlay from Clinic funds was required," said Henry. "Apparently Greg didn't seem to think it was necessary to get permission."

"I never could see any use in wasting money operating on dogs anyway," said Sam Hunter. "Isn't the budget for the laboratory going to rise with all that new equipment in operation?"

Henry Anders tried to remember some details of the budget but couldn't; he'd always left such things to Greg. Sensing that Henry didn't know the answer to the question, Ed McDougal stepped into the breach.

"Operating a hyperbaric chamber is bound to cost money," he assured the oilman.

"Do you have one at your hospital down home, Ed?"

"We looked into it some time ago and decided against it."

"Why?"

"Cost, mainly." It wasn't the truth, but he couldn't let the opportunity go by to prejudice Sam Hunter further against Greg. "Besides, oxygen under pressure hasn't turned out to be the panacea a lot of people predicted it would be when they first started using it abroad."

"You mean Dr. Alexander has been experimenting with something that's not accepted medically—something foreign?" Sam Hunter rose to the bait, just as Ed had hoped he would.

'It's not exactly that," he temporized.

"What is it then?"

"In some experiments"—he was careful to emphasize the word—"enough good results have been shown to justify the expense."

"What percentage?" Sam Hunter insisted.

"I can't give you the exact figures, sir, but I do know the results have been disappointing in many cases."

"You should have stopped Alexander before he spent all that money, Henry," said Sam Hunter.

"But it was government funds, sir."

"And whose pockets did they come from?" The old man pushed his coffee cup aside and bit off the end of a cigar. "That's the trouble with the country now: everybody wants a handout from the federal government. And the damned fools we send to Congress are always ready to give it to them to get votes."

"It's got to stop somewhere; you're right about that, sir." Ed McDougal carefully fueled Sam Hunter's anger.

"It's going to stop here, as far as this particular thing is concerned," the old man snapped. "Do either of you have any idea how much it takes each year to run that experimental laboratory?"

"I don't remember the exact cost, but it's considerable," said Henry Anders.

"Enough to put The Clinic in the black if it was out of the budget?"

"Possibly." Following the lead Ed had given him, Henry wasn't letting a chance slip by to prejudice Sam Hunter further against Greg.

"We'll have to stop that waste, too!" The old man banged his fist on the table so hard that a cup bounced off to the floor. "You can bet the trustees will have something to say about it."

Bill Remick, the Washington roentgenologist, had been watching the three from a table not far away. And since Sam Hunter made no particular attempt to lower his voice, a good portion of their conversation had come to his ears.

"From what I can hear, Ed and Henry are doing a hatchet job on Greg over there," he said to Abe Lantz, who was with him.

"It's no secret that Ed wants to corral a lot of old Sam's dough to build a medical school in his own hometown, where there's a small university," said the internist. "And of course Henry opposes Greg whenever he gets a chance—for a lot of reasons."

"Don't the damn fools know this place would fall apart without Greg?"

"Henry would probably like to see that happen. Then The Clinic property would go to him under the old man's will and there are rumors of a new condominium project that would make Henry a millionaire."

"Where did you hear all this?"

"The rumors have been floating around for some time. You can't pin anybody down, but I'd be willing to bet that a lot of our brother Aesculapians here in Baltimore are in on the deal."

"Trustees, too?"

"Could be. They're as hungry as anybody else for a fast buck."

"Then it's time somebody defended Greg." Bill Remick got to his feet. "Pay the check when it comes, Abe. I'll fix it with you later."

"What are you going to do?"

"Ed and Henry have been working old Sam over from one side. It looks to me that it's time to give him a little going over from the other."

"He'll slap you down—hard."

"Sam Hunter may have a billion dollars, but his colon's as full of diverticula as everybody else's," said the roetngenologist. "When you see them in the fluoroscope the way I do, you can't tell a millionaire from a pauper."

"Hello, Mr. Hunter," Bill Remick said cordially as he approached the other table. "Couldn't help hearing you discussing the fine work Greg Alexander has been doing here with the hyperbaric chamber."

"What are you talking about, Bill?" Ed McDougal demanded.

"You must know how valuable oxygen under pressure is, Ed," said the X-ray man. "Or Henry should, if you don't. Some of the major work in that field has been done right here by Greg Alexander."

"I let the section heads run their services pretty much by themselves, as long as everything is satisfactory," said Henry.

"Glad to hear you approve of Greg's results then," said Remich blandly. "I really didn't believe the rumors I've been hearing of friction between you two."

Remick turned to the oilman. "I don't imagine you read medical journals, Mr. Hunter, so you wouldn't realize that Greg Alexander has made The Clinic the most important center for research in heart and lung transplantation in the country. I happen to know he has less trouble getting National Institute of Health grants for his work than any other clinic in the country."

"From what I hear, he's wasting money," Sam Hunter growled.

"Then you haven't been listening to people who are knowledgeable in the field of heart surgery." Remick's voice was suddenly sharp.

"What do you know about it, Bill?" Ed McDougal demanded. "Your field is X-ray."

"As it happens, I've been working with the National Institute of Health on cineradiography," said the roentgenologist. "That's X-ray motion pictures, mainly of the circulation, Mr. Hunter. And I know that nobody is more respected at NIH than Greg Alexander, especially considering the difficulties he works under."

"What do you mean—difficulties?" Sam Hunter asked.

"Surely Henry told you Greg runs the experimental laboratory with the smallest budget of any department in the hospital. Most of the money for his work actually comes from federal grants and private gifts from people who realize how important it is."

"What about this new building?"

"The hyperbaric chamber?"

"Yes."

"I helped get National Institute of Health funds for that—after the Board of Trustees was so short-sighted as to vote down the plans for the new buildings including it two years ago."

"But it's no good."

"Who told you that?" Bill Remick asked.

"Henry here—and Ed."

"Really, Henry." Bill Remick's eyebrows were raised in mock surprise. "Do you mean to tell me you let Mr. Hunter believe Greg's managing to build the hyperbaric chamber isn't the most important thing that's happened at The Clinic lately? Even you"—Remick's voice suddenly cut like a surgeon's scalpel—"must know how important it can be in transplant operations to have the donor organ saturated with oxygen. Some people believe this technique alone is going to open up an entirely new field of surgery."

"He still didn't get the approval of the trustees," Sam Hunter said doggedly.

"Board action isn't required for expenditures where other sources of funds are available—and they were here," said Bill Remick. "I think you're being sold a bill of goods, Mr. Hunter. If you ran your business this way, you wouldn't have those millions of yours very long."

CHAPTER NINE

I

Greg was scheduled to open the program of the first professional meeting of the Convocation of the Members of The Clinic at three o'clock Wednesday afternoon with a paper on hospital automation. At fifteen minutes before the hour, he, Bob Johnson, Herb Partridge, the neurosurgeon, and Dave Connor stopped by the room in the intensive care unit where Frank Lawson had been taken from the operating suite the night before. The respirator was clicking along steadily, inflating the wounded man's lungs sixteem times a minute with oxygen from a large tank beside the bed.

"His pulse is ninety to a hundred," the nurse who had been sitting beside the bed reported. "Blood pressure's one hundred over sixty."

"No spontaneous respiratory movements?" Greg asked.

"None at all, Dr. Alexander."

Dave Connor listened to the unconscious man's heart, then took the tips of the stethoscope from his ears, folded up the tubing and stuck it in the side pocket of his long white coat.

"The heart's functioning well," he said. "Probably too well for your purposes, Greg."

"Especially with Merchant going into heart failure."

"What do you think will cause death here eventually, Dr. Connor?" Bob Johnson asked.

"There's no reason for his heart to stop beating, unless something outside the heart itself makes it stop," said the cardiologist. "That's all I can tell you."

"I think death will come from the brain," said Herb Partridge. "It must have been pretty badly damaged for him to remain unconscious so long. Besides, I had to ligate both vertebral arteries, so the cerebral blood supply is lessened. And with spinal fluid leaking from the neck wound, there's always the probability of an ascending infection around the upper cord to the brain itself."

"Merchant can't last very long, either," said the cardiologist. "His liver is enlarging steadily and the moisture at the bases of his lungs is increasing, which means that his heart is waging a losing battle in spite of all the help we're giving it with digitalis and oxygen. He could use a new heart right now, Greg. Too bad you can't give him this one."

A high-pitched beep came from the small pocket sentinel which, like all of the hospital staff, Greg carried in the breast pocket of his long-skirted white coat. He moved at once to the nurse's desk and picked up the telephone.

"There's an outside call for you, Dr. Alexander," said the operator. "Just a moment, please."

Judge Sutler's voice came on the line. "You can go ahead in the Lawson case, Greg," he said, "but I must insist that the medical examiner be present to certify death."

"I'll call Dr. Dennison as soon as we take Merchant to the operating room," Greg promised. "Thank you for your promptness, sir."

"I'm dictating an official order for your protection. We'll mail it to you tonight. How is your patient?"

"He's losing ground, sir. I don't know whether he will outlast Lawson or not."

"I hope he does. Good luck with the operation."

"The judge has given his permission for us to use Lawson's organs," Greg told Bob Johnson and the others when he came back into Frank Lawson's room. "It's almost three o'clock, so I'd better get down to the lecture hall to open the convocation. Have you got the slides, Bob?"

"Right in my pocket, sir," said the younger surgeon. "I'll go down and check out the projector before the convocation officially begins."

II

A stream of doctors was pouring across The Parkway from the motel to the hospital entrance for the opening session of the convocation when Bill Remick spotted Peter Carewe's tall form among them. He called to the public health man to wait for him; the two had been friends during the fellowship days but had rarely seen each other since.

"How do you stand on this question of moving The Clinic, Bill?" Peter asked.

"I'm agin it," said the roentgenologist. "Who's been propagandizing you?"

"John Teague mentioned it when I had dinner with him in New York last week and I spoke to Jeanne Alexander on the phone for a few minutes before I left the motel. She thinks a movement is underway to dump Greg at the same time, but that's hard to believe."

"I've been telling Greg that ever since the trustees' meeting two years ago." Bill Remick's voice was grim. "But you know how hard it is for Greg to think ill of anybody."

As they were entering the hospital, Peter Carewe glanced up at the massive statue in the rotunda. "I guess if you had to pass that statue twice a day going and coming, it might influence your thinking."

"Particularly if you thought that way in the beginning," Bill Remick agreed as they turned into the corridor leading to the surgical lecture hall.

When the surgical section of the hospital had been built originally, some fifty years earlier, the main lecture room had been placed between two of the largest operating theaters for a definite reason. According to the custom prevalent at that time, cases presented to students at clinical sessions in the lecture room were then wheeled directly into one of the operating theaters. Merely by filing from the lecture hall into rows of seats arranged on one side of the operating theater, the students were then able to watch the actual operative procedure and witness the verification of the diagnosis made during the lecture presentation just preceding, or enjoy the discomfiture of the surgeon when his predictions turned out to be wrong.

The evolution of more sterile techniques, and particularly the rise in hospital infections, had completely changed the pattern of procedure, but had not changed the arrangement of the lecture room. The south wall still featured the tall windows originally designed to provide a maximum of sunlight for the examining area, a strip of open floor twenty feet wide across the end of the room beneath the windows, with a door on either side, which had originally opened into one of the two main operating theaters.

In the lecture hall itself, the seats rose in a steep incline until the back row was on a level with the third floor of the surgical building, enabling the occupants to look down directly upon the lecture area with only the limitations of their vision affecting their ability to observe the cases under discussion. Doors at the top of the incline gave access from above to the upper tiers of seats, while two passageways on either side led to the first-floor corridor.

More recently, the doors opening directly into the operating theaters had been blocked off and closed in order to prevent traffic through the area. But the doctors' lounge and scrub rooms for each of the main theaters still occupied the space underneath the incline where the seats were located.

In order to make the activities going on in the operating rooms visible to observers, small enclosed observation galleries had been built at the second-floor level in each of the two main operating theaters. But since they could contain only a few observers, closed-circuit television cameras had been installed more recently, at Greg's insistence, looking down upon the center of each of the two theaters. The activities there during surgery could thus be photographed by the cameras and carried to screens set well up on the walls on either side of the center podium. And merely by switching on the closed-circuit cameras, those in the lecture hall could watch closely the surgery being performed in either or both of the main operating theaters with no danger of contaminating the patients.

The lecture hall was almost filled with Members of The Clinic and staff, plus a few students, when Peter Carewe and Bill Remick came in and found seats. Around them the buzz of voices filled the room but, as yet, the space on the ground level contained only a podium with a microphone for the speakers and a desk and chair for the presiding officer. Above the desk and against the wall, was a screen so arranged that it could be raised or lowered by means of a switch beside the projector set into the middle of the second row of seats.

About five minutes before three, Henry Anders and Ed McDougal came in from one of the lower floors. Since he was going to preside at the opening session of the convocation, Henry went to the desk at the front while Ed climbed to a spot high up, calling greetings to friends as he sought a seat.

"Those two are working hand and glove," said Peter Carewe to Bill Remick. "And from the looks on their faces, they must think the world's their oyster."

"This particular oyster may not have the pearl they're expecting to find in it." Bill Remick surveyed the now almost packed rows with a swift glance before settling back in his seat. "A lot of the most famous names in American medicine are here and between them they can influence people with considerable amounts of money. If Greg can come up with the right sort of a structure to replace these old buildings and preserve the spirit of The Clinic, most Members will support him. It might just be that Ed McDougal and Henry Anders are betting on the wrong horse with Sam Hunter."

III

At two minutes before three, Hans Werner pushed a wheeled cart into the open space at one side of the lecture room. On the cart, the brown and white spaniel named Letty lay upon a blanket; beside her was a carton loosely covered with a towel. Bob Johnson was checking out the projector, and, as he flipped the switch beside it, the screen slowly descended upon the wall behind the podium.

The clock on the back wall said one minute to three when Greg Alexander came in and took a seat near where Hans Werner was standing patiently beside the cart, soothing the dog lying upon it by scratching her head at the base of her ears. When the hands of the clock showed three, Henry Anders banged on the table sharply with a gavel and the room became silent.

"It is my pleasant task to welcome the Members of The Clinic to the twentieth biennial convocation," he announced. "I want to tell you how pleasant it is to see so many familiar faces once again. If my father were alive, I know it would have given him great pleasure to greet each of you personally, as I hope to do before the convocation ends at noon on Friday.

"I have been asked to invite all of you and your wives, sweethearts—or secretaries"—he waited for a guffaw of laughter to sweep the room—"to a cocktail party being given by Claire and myself with Hannah and Ed McDougal in the Falstaff Room at the Clinic Inn from five to seven this evening."

A wave of applause greeted the announcement.

"Believing that all work and no play may make jack, but also makes Jack a dull boy"—he paused briefly for the titter of appreciation—"we have scheduled no night sessions for the convocation, allowing each of you to entertain himself in whatever manner he chooses."

"Got any good telephone numbers, Henry?" somebody asked, and there was another round of laughter.

"I am pleased to announce that registration for the twentieth convocation has already exceeded any previous one, with more undoubtedly still to come," Henry continued. "Members of the Board of Trustees are reminded of our regular meeting on Saturday morning. Also, one member of the board has requested that the trustees meet on Friday at four P.M. to consider a special matter which will be placed before them by this trustee."

"So the battle begins," said Bill Remick to Peter Carewe. "They're not wasting any time."

Henry Anders paused, apparently waiting for some reaction to the announcement. When none came, he glanced at Greg, as if he expected an objection from him, but Greg was looking at his notes. Flushing angrily Henry whacked his gavel on the table to still the stir of conversation.

"The first paper on the program is by Dr. Gregory Alexander," he announced. "The subject is hospital and clinic automation."

Greg moved to the podium and, placing a folder he was carrying upon it, faced the audience.

"Before I start discussing the topic assigned to me," he said, "I wish to announce a change in the printed program sent to each of you in advance. Originally, we had scheduled an operative clinic tomorrow afternoon in which my assistant and I planned to transplant the heart and both lungs from one dog to another. In our hands, this procedure has now been successful a number of times, and one of our patients has been alive for more than a year. She shows every sign of good health, as I think you can see."

At his words, Hans Werner gently lifted the leash around Letty's neck and the spaniel stood up, wagging her tail.

"Actually," Greg added, "Letty went what might be called the second mile last night and produced even more convincing evidence that the heart and lungs we transplanted into her chest over a year ago are now functioning well." Reaching into the carton, he lifted two of the puppies in his hands and held them up, while Hans Werner took out two more as a ground swell of applause swept the room.

"Last night, two human patients were admitted to the hospital whose presence has caused me to change the program somewhat from that which had been announced." Greg handed the puppies to Hans, who put them into the carton and wheeled the cart from the room. "One is now in progressive heart failure from a severely damaged heart; the other is unconscious with a lacerated cervical cord and a severe brain injury. All of us are agreed that he cannot live, and, since he has no known relatives and is an habitual criminal known to have murdered a man during a recent robbery, I petitioned the court this morning for permission to remove his heart and lungs immediately after death and transplant them into the body of the coronary patient I mentioned—if he lives long enough for this to be possible. Until the decision is made one way or another, however, I must keep two operating teams in a constant state of readiness, so I have been forced to cancel the operative clinic previously scheduled for tomorrow afternoon."

The room was silent now, gripped by the drama in his words, as he continued: "We cannot, of course, tell just when, or if, it will be possible for us to perform this transplant. However, should it become possible, we have made arrangements to notify all of you at the Inn who might be interested in watching the procedure, which will be presented on closed-circuit television in this same room."

As calmly as if he had not just made the most dramatic announcement of the entire convocation, Greg opened the folder that held his paper. He did not notice when, high up near the top row of seats, a tall man with graying hair and heavy horn-rimmed glasses, who had been rapidly making notes on a stenographic pad, hurriedly left the room and headed for a booth outside the emergency room containing a phone marked: "Reserved for Police and Press."

IV

"My discussion of hospital and clinic automation will of necessity be rather brief," Greg began. "Most of the information was accumulated while preparing plans for a possible new set of clinic and hospital buildings as chairman of the building committee of the Board of Trustees. Two of the most advanced hospital plants being built today are undoubtedly those at the Georgetown University Medical Center in Washington and the University of Alberta in Canada. Together they represent a distillation of what is known about automation in hospital and clinic procedure throughout the world, at the moment. The subject is widening so rapidly, however, that what is new today may already be superseded tomorrow, so I shall therefore give you only a brief sketch of some of the salient points."

His audience was fully attentive, for not one among them was not conscious of his own stake in the course medicine took in the future, or that automation would largely determine that course.

"The problem can be stated very quickly," said Greg. "The cost of medical services, according to authentic reports, is now rising at about three times the rate of other living costs, judged by the consumer index. In nineteen sixty-seven, the cost of an average hospital room was fifty-five dollars per day; it will reach one hundred by nineteen seventy-five, while the total national health bill will rise from fifty-four billion dollars, representing six per cent of the GNP for nineteen sixty-seven, to one hundred billion and eight per cent in the same period. Health as an industry will likewise rise to where one and a half million doctors and nurses and four and a half million hospital workers will be needed by nineteen seventy-five.

"Remember that I said 'needed.'" He pointed to the screen where Bob Johnson had projected the stark figures by means of the slide projector. "None of us, of course, is obtuse enough to believe that the number of people required will be found, which means that something else must take the place of human hands. That something can only be machines, medical robots, if you please.

"The statistics I have given you represent what is needed merely to maintain the status quo, but just what is that status quo actually worth? Books could be written, and have been, about the dismal failure of what we like to consider the finest medical system in the world to provide an adequate level of health to the American people. I shall give you only a few examples of just how dismal that failure really is:

"The United States now ranks thirteenth among nations in infant mortality, with countries like Japan and Finland well ahead of us, although their standards of living cannot compare with ours. During the most prosperous twenty years in United States history, when we sent rockets soaring into space toward the moon and other planets, we actually dropped seven places in such a vital statistic as the infant mortality rate.

"Our low quality of health cannot be blamed on poverty when we are the richest nation in the world's history, for even when the sick man gets to a hospital today he has no assurance that the care he receives will be comparable in any way to the wealth of the nation. Not long ago, the Columbia University School of Public Health reported that forty-three per cent of the nation's five thousand, two hundred general hospitals gave care that can only be called 'poor to fair.' In fact, a recent study of general practitioners in a southern state suggested that the average patient who consulted them might be almost as well off if he had gone to a witch doctor."

There was a murmur of indignation among the listeners, but he ignored it as he continued: "These are facts we must not only face but correct. With the United States dropping to ninth place among nations in the standard indices of health, we of the medical profession can no longer face the public in our practices and claim to be guardians of their welfare, when we have failed in our task. It is true that the greatest cause of cost increase in medical care is the rising expense of hospital operation, an expense which can largely be charged to inefficiency. But although the medical profession rarely supervises the day-to-day operation of a hospital, the fact remains that we are deeply concerned with its administration because its failure reflects on us in the minds of the public. If we only use it, our influence upon hospital planners and administrators can be very great, and we must not hesitate to do so in the future.

"Since labor is the greatest problem, doctors must take the lead in insisting that labor-saving procedures be introduced into hospital and clinic care. When a single machine now being manufactured in Sweden can process three thousand blood samples an hour, while performing eighteen different tests on each sample, the individual laboratory technician is already largely outmoded, except as supervisor of the machine. What is more, such machines can be connected to computers which will print out the result faster than human hands can possibly write, without the one error in every six determinations that now results from human laboratory operations.

"Diagnosis, too, can be computerized and automated to a great extent, as is being demonstrated by research in many parts of the country and by the number of papers on medical automation appearing in such a widely circulated medical publication as the *Journal of the American Medical Association*. Merely by having a patient sit in a special chair, it is now possible to determine and record simultaneously heart action, pulse, respiratory rate, blood pressure and even the emotional state, printing the results on computer tape and sounding a warning when abnormal findings are discovered. What is popularly called an 'electronic nurse' can give the doctor in his hospital office at any moment the temperature, heart rate, blood pressure, electrocardiographic tracing and respiration of a patient in a distant part of the hospital or even in another building. Our sensitive monitors in the operating room, many of them developed for watching astronauts far out in space, now tell us the condition of the patient at every stage of the operation merely at a glance. The same can be done in the intensive care units, which are a central feature in every really modern hospital being constructed today.

"Even in the business office, automation can cut costs remarkably," he continued. "Doctors' orders, pharmacy requests, X-ray requisitions and many other items can be handled automatically by a computer, cutting down the same three hundred out of every thousand dollars of hospital expense, as determined by a recent study, chargeable to handling costs and records, a really inexcusable expense when methods are readily available to prevent them.

"Two years ago I was charged by the Board of Trustees with the task of planning a modern hospital and diagnostic clinic to replace this outmoded structure which we all love, but which is now unprofitable and even dangerous to operate. On Saturday, I shall present to the board a complete plan for the most highly computerized hospital in the world today, as well as the most beautiful. Fifty years ago the present Clinic was in a modestly prosperous district of middle-class homes; today it is the center of a slum whose inhabitants rarely earn enough to be classed above the accepted guidelines for the determination of poverty. When this hospital and clinic were built, Dr. Anders wished to show how they could serve a community, as well as the world; the fact that the community has deteriorated along with the physical plant of the hospital does not change, in my opinion, the purpose for which it was built. With a modern plant, we can still render a service to people who need it much more now than did those in this area fifty years ago. On Saturday, I shall present to the Board of Trustees for their consideration, the preliminary architectural drawings for such a modern hospital-clinic complex, one that will be a truly fitting tribute to the man whose vision made possible the founding of this clinic a half century ago."

Greg closed his folder and stepped back from the podium as a wave of applause spread through the audience. Before anyone could ask a question, Henry Anders hurriedly announced: "Because of the shortness of time, there will be no discussion of this paper. None of you, I am sure, want to be late for the party, so we will go on to the next speaker, Dr. Abraham Lantz. His topic: 'The Early Diagnosis of Pulmonary Embolism.'"

V

Bob Johnson joined Greg outside the lecture hall. "Did you see Jud Templeton there this afternoon?" he asked.

"Are you sure?" Greg understood at once the significance of the name, since Jud Templeton was a roving reporter for both the morning and afternoon newspapers, and a legendary figure in Baltimore journalism.

"No doubt about it. I recognized him from the emergency room. He was at the back of the hall, taking notes like mad. When you announced your plans for the transplant, he fairly bolted from the room."

Greg glanced at his watch. "That means he'll make the final editions of the afternoon paper. Now the fat's really in the fire."

"Why, sir? It seems to me that the publicity will help the cause."

"The other side is sure to claim I released the story to the press."

"Who do you suppose did invite Templeton here?" Bob asked. "A big shot like him wouldn't ordinarily cover just a medical meeting. The paper would send a stringer."

"I don't know."

"Do you suppose *they* did it?" Greg didn't pretend not to understand whom Bob meant by *they*.

"My guess is that I was expected to object to the announcement of the special meeting of the board," he said. "If I had, the reason would have been made public, putting me in a bad light early in the session."

"Then you know the reason for the special meeting?"

"Dr. Foucald told me this morning that Mr. Hunter is going to demand an investigation of my building the hyperbaric chamber."

"But it was constructed with government funds."

"That doesn't make any difference to Sam Hunter. He's got a feud going with the government, too."

"Do you plan to put Lawson in the chamber when the time comes for the transplant?"

"I don't think so," said Greg. "We'd have to raise the pressure to at least three atmospheres and we might lose more than we gain, because of the time it would take to decompress. Besides, I suspect our greatest problem is going to be keeping Merchant alive until Frank Lawson dies."

"It would be nice if we had two chambers connected together."

"Keith Jackson has included them in the new plans, with a connecting air lock so we can use each chamber separately, or move freely from one to another without decompression," said Greg. "I asked him to do it when he started to make up the detail drawings."

"But if they're already squawking about the chamber we have—"

"Sometimes a man has to 'dream the impossible dream' as the songwriters put it. We might as well give them something to really squawk about."

CHAPTER TEN

I

Taking advantage of the momentary stir while Abe Lantz came forward to start presenting his paper, Helen Foucald slipped out of the lecture hall. Peter Carewe had been watching her and followed; in the corridor outside, he overtook her easily with his longer stride.

"Where are you going in such a hurry?" he asked.

"Back to the laboratory to check on some tests we're running."

"I was hoping we could have a cup of coffee together somewhere."

"There's a small coffee shop off the corridor just outside the laboratory if you don't mind stopping by there with me first to see how the tests are going."

"What's so important in the lab at this time of day?"

"Greg asked me to run some cell compatibility tests between Mr. Merchant, the heart case he mentioned, and the donor."

"I'm not familiar with the technique," he said. "You can bring me up to date on it."

"The original tests were devised by some French investigators," she explained as they entered the laboratory and went over to where a technician was working at a table by the window. From the rack in front of the technician Helen took a small tube containing a bottom sediment of a dark red solid, a middle section that was yellowish in color and a short column of whiter material floating on top.

"This is heparinized blood from the donor," she said. "The dark sediment at the bottom is composed mainly of red cells, the clear section in the center is serum and a pedicle of white cells is floating at the top."

Putting that tube back into the rack, she moved on to another one. "After sedimentation, the pedicle was strained off through a nylon filter and a suspension made containing several dilutions. As near as we could, we divided it into concentrations of one, two and four million cells. The part that came to the surface was then separated after being put through the centrifuge to get as pure a preparation of lymphocytes as possible."

"Ingenious."

"Has Dr. Johnson made the intradermal injections?" Helen asked the technician.

"We gave him the preparations from both Merchant and Lawson," said the girl. "He injected them about an hour ago."

"Isn't this like a test for allergens?" Peter asked.

"It's very much the same," Helen agreed. "By injecting several dilutions of a preparation of the donor's lymphocytes into the skin of the recipient, and vice versa, we should be able to tell by the skin reaction around the injection within twenty-four hours just how much each will react to the other."

"I wonder if there'll be that much time. Greg said just now that the recipient is already in heart failure."

"We're running a second set of tests for that very reason, checking for lymphocyte agglutination. The results won't be ready for another hour, though."

"Meanwhile, we can be having that cup of coffee," said Peter, and they left the laboratory for the vending area nearby.

"In a way I feel responsible for the special meeting Henry announced just now," Helen said when Peter set two cups of coffee down upon the small table she had selected in the busy shop.

"Why?"

"Sam Hunter didn't know about the hyperbaric laboratory until he saw it through a window of my office this morning. I guess I spilled the beans."

"Are you sure that's the reason he called the session?"

"It must be; he was furious. I warned Greg right away, but there doesn't seem to be anything he can do."

"Surely Greg couldn't have expected to hide anything as huge as a building."

"Since it was financed with an NIH grant, and Bill Remick helped arrange it, I guess Greg just forgot to notify the other members of the board. Mr. Hunter got very angry when I tried to defend Greg and I'm afraid I only made things worse by arguing with him."

"After hearing Greg speak this afternoon, I've got an idea he will land on his feet. By the way, what are you wearing for dinner tonight?"

"A pale blue dress. Why?"

"An orchid should go well with that, worn in your hair."

"Why there?"

"In the South Seas, a girl wears a flower behind her ear, signifying whether she's willing to be courted—according to the color of the flower."

"The trouble is, I don't know what color indicates what."

"Red's my favorite," he said promptly. "It stands for—"

"Availability?"

"Something like that."

"Do you want me to wear red?"

"I'm not quite sure yet." The bantering note had gone out of his voice. "Are you?"

She shook her head, wondering how many more hours would pass before someone told him she was known throughout the hospital grapevine system to be the mistress of Henry Anders.

"Promise me one thing," she said quickly. "However it ends, there must be no regrets."

"I'm the one who's supposed to say that," he protested. "You've got our roles reversed."

II

Guy Merchant was asleep when Greg came into his room with Bob Johnson and Dr. James McNeal, Senior Fellow in Cardiology. Folding back the sheet over the sick man's feet, Greg pressed his finger into the puffy skin over his right ankle and studied the pit in the waterlogged tissue left when he removed it.

"The edema's increasing," he said softly, so as not to awaken the sleeping man.

"We've stepped up the oxygen to ten." The heart specialist nodded toward the bottle attached to the large oxygen tank beside the bed. Through it, the gas was bubbling rapidly, churning into a froth the water that half filled the bottle. "He's breathing practically pure oxygen but his ear lobes are still dusty from cyanosis."

"Obviously the vital capacity is very low," said Greg.

The amount of air the lungs could contain between full inspiration and full expiration was a fairly accurate index of those organs' efficiency. But in the type of emphysema caused by smoking, where the lungs largely lost their capacity to expand and contract with breathing, the vital capacity was always sharply limited.

"Even without the damage to his heart, he would have gotten into trouble soon from emphysema," said Dr. McNeal. "Now the congestion from cardiac insufficiency has curtailed his breathing capacity even more."

"How much longer?" Greg asked as they moved on to Frank Lawson's room.

"My guess would be no more than twelve hours," said the cardiologist, but they both knew that no actual limit could be set, for entirely too many factors were involved.

The click-click of the respirator attached to the tube in Frank Lawson's windpipe greeted them when they opened the door of his room. Greg leafed through the top pages of the chart handed him by the nurse who had been watching to see that the tracheostomy tube didn't become clogged.

"His temperature has been rising slightly for the past several hours," she reported. "Dr. Partridge ordered chloramphenicol intramuscularly."

Bob Johnson raised his eyebrows; a powerful antibiotic, the drug would tend to combat any infection that might shorten Frank Lawson's life.

"Herb has no alternative," Greg reminded the younger surgeon. "Lawson's his patient and he has to keep him alive as long as he can."

"X-ray did a portable film of the lungs right after lunch," said the nurse. "The report may already be at the desk outside."

"See if it is, please." While she was gone, Greg moved closer to the bed to study Frank Lawson's face, which was puffed and swollen from the trauma that had almost sliced off his head. When he lifted one of the injured man's eyelids, he saw that the pupils were dilated and did not contract from the light that entered them, a sure sign of brain damage.

"The lung X-ray is clear, Doctor," the nurse reported.

"Thank you," said Greg. "How does his condition appear to you, Miss Strong?"

"He's losing ground," she said without hesitation. "Dr. Partridge thinks the rise in temperature may be from an ascending infection around the temperature center of a slowly spreading hemorrhage."

The temperature center was located in a small, but vital, area of the brain that controlled most of the body functions absolutely necessary for life. If either hemorrhage or an infection were approaching it, Frank Lawson's hours of life might be shortened considerably, but with no way to look inside the brain and see, they could only wait.

When the doctors came into the small waiting room, Georgia Merchant looked up from the magazine she had been staring at for the last half hour without really seeing either the words or the photographs in it.

"Guy's worse, isn't he, Dr. Alexander?" she asked.

"I'm afraid so."

"Maybe it's better this way. He wants to die and you'll be saved the loss of a patient."

"I would hope not to lose him, Mrs. Merchant."

"We both appreciate your being willing to gamble your own reputation on a case as far advanced as Guy's," she said. "I think he might have kept that attack from coming on this morning if he'd called for nitroglycerin."

"Are you saying he deliberately tried to bring about his own death?" Bob Johnson asked.

"He's tried before by holding off the medicine," said Georgia. "This time he might have made it if the nurse hadn't been so quick. That's why, when

Dr. Alexander offered him the operation, he jumped at it as a way of doing what he wasn't able to do for himself."

Surprised at how quickly Guy Merchant had agreed to such drastic and dangerous surgery, Greg, too, had come to much the same conclusion.

"What about you?" he asked her. "Can we do anything to help you?"

"Everybody is more than kind," she assured him. "I've been praying that, if you can't save him the way you'd like to do, he doesn't come out from under the anesthetic at all. But he's going so fast now, you're not likely to even be able to operate, are you?"

"The situation doesn't look promising."

"It's strange the way things work out. Anybody in show business will tell you that Guy's been a decent and honorable man all his life, while Lawson's been a criminal since he was a boy. The one way Lawson might be able to atone for some of his sins before he dies would be to make it possible for Guy to go on living, at least for a while. Maybe if he were conscious and knew the sort of future he would have, not being able to use his arms and legs and living in a respirator in prison, he would want Guy to have his heart."

"Not many people have the generosity and the courage to die for others," Greg reminded her.

"I suppose so," she said. "I don't even feel exactly right about praying for Guy to get well, when I'm really praying for somebody else to die."

III

In his office, Greg asked his secretary to get Jud Templeton on the phone at the newspaper office downtown but she reported that he was still at the hospital.

"Try that telephone off the emergency room where reporters sometimes phone in their stories," he said. "If Mr. Templeton is there, please ask him to come up."

It was no more than ten minutes before the newspaperman was ushered into Greg's office by the secretary. "Thank you for coming up, Mr. Templeton," he said. "I'm pretty busy or I would have come down to see you."

"This is *your* castle, Doctor. What can I do for you?"

"I'm more concerned about what you can do *to* me. If I'd known you were in the lecture hall this afternoon, I would have asked you to leave before I made the announcement about the transplant."

"Your front office invited us to send a reporter to cover the convocation proceedings, Doctor."

"I'm still surprised that it would be a reporter of your caliber, Mr. Templeton."

"I'm here by special invitation. Didn't you know?"

"I'm afraid not."

"A special press card was sent to the office about noon by messenger, admitting me to all sessions of the convocation."

"By whose authority?"

Jud Templeton took a press card from his pocket and put it on Greg's desk blotter. It was made out in the reporter's name—and signed by Henry Anders II.

"You seem surprised," he said when Greg handed him back the card. "Is anything wrong?"

Greg shook his head. "Your invitation is in good order. But I still think it would have been better not to publicize the transplant so early."

"If you're hinting that you would like to have the story killed, it's already in the presses for the Wall Street Final."

"You didn't lose any time."

"The public has a right to know you're on the verge of making medical history, Dr. Alexander."

"There have been other transplants."

"But not from a murderer to a burlesque straight man. There's a particular name for that kind of story—it's 'human interest.'"

"Did it occur to you that your premature publicity may have jeopardized my chances of being able to operate at all?"

"Georgia Merchant's not going to object and neither is Guy. They're the Lunt and Fontanne of the burlesque world and too attached to each other for either one of them to deprive the other of a chance to live."

"You seem to know them well."

"I used to be a candy butcher in the old Gayety Theater back in the thirties. I don't know anybody I'd rather give a break to than Georgia and Guy. Whichever way this operation ends, Doctor, I'm going to do a feature on her that ought to put her back in the big time."

"Don't you realize that as soon as your story comes out, thousands of people will be pulling for Frank Lawson to die?"

"It couldn't happen to a lousier guy—and the sooner the better."

"The medical examiner and I have to determine when Lawson is legally dead, Mr. Templeton. And with all this publicity, I might unconsciously be more careful to be sure he's dead before I start to remove his heart and lungs, than I would ordinarily be. That could jeopardize the success of the operation."

"The Doctor's Dilemma? That's an angle I hadn't thought of."

"I'm sorry I mentioned it."

"Oh, I would have thought of it eventually, you can be sure of that. But the more I do think of it, the better this story is turning out to be. When do you think you'll operate?"

"Maybe not at all—after Judge Sutler reads your story."

"You don't have to worry on that score."

"Why?"

"Along with the routine request for reporters to cover the convocation, we also got a tip that something dramatic would be announced."

"When was this?"

"Before noon—when my card came."

Greg frowned. "Do you have any idea why?"

"My guess is somebody wanted us to report the special meeting of the Board of Trustees that was announced in the lecture room. I heard some whispering down there that you're about to be given the shaft."

"That wasn't worth a visit from the star reporter for both papers."

"You're a more important man than you think, Doctor, but this time you're right," said Templeton. "We also had a tip from the judge's office and a copy of his order releasing Frank Lawson's body to you as soon as the medical examiner pronounces him dead. Judge Sutler knows a good story when he sees it, even if you don't."

"You could at least have asked me about it first."

"And have you killed the story?"

"There isn't any story yet, Mr. Templeton. Nothing has actually been done except to make the decision to operate, if circumstances work out so I can."

"Right after the six o'clock news goes on the air tonight, thousands of people will be rooting for Guy Merchant and praying for Frank Lawson to die. You doctors have been worrying about where you can get a supply of hearts and other organs for transplant. Why not from condemned criminals like Frank Lawson?''

"That's a ghoulish idea.''

"But still a good one. Judge Sutler told me on the telephone not an hour ago that he was finally persuaded to let you have Lawson's body because you said that, if the state assumed the right to *take* a man's life, it should also assume the right to *give* that life to another.''

"That's another time I should have kept my mouth shut,'' Greg said wryly.

"Why—when you spoke a profound truth? Before you take Frank Lawson's heart out, you're going to have to put him on a heart-lung pump, aren't you?''

"Possibly—for a few minutes at least.''

"And when you've taken his heart and lungs out, you'll shut off the pump, won't you?''

"Yes.''

"What's the difference between sending five thousand volts of electricity through a man's body and simply throwing the switch on the heart-lung pump so it will stop? That's certainly a lot less barbarous way to execute somebody than with the electric chair or the gas chamber, to say nothing of that civilized custom we call hanging.''

The newspaper man pointed to a painting on the wall, a reproduction of Rembrandt's famous *Anatomy Lesson*. "Didn't the early anatomists learn a lot about the body by dissecting living criminals?''

"That's what the medical histories say.''

"Why not let some of these punks who start riots and kill innocent bystanders know they'll be taken apart alive with forceps and scalpel if they get caught. It might even make them have second thoughts.''

"Really, Mr. Templeton, I'm sincere.''

"Believe me, I couldn't be more serious about anything, Doctor. I got mugged one night last year when I was on an assignment. This is a sore subject with me.''

"What I'm trying to tell you is that a matter of ethics is involved in your printing the story of my announcement to the convocation.''

"You mean there's not supposed to be any cult of the personality among doctors?''

"That's one way of putting it—yes.''

"You'd better tell that to the headline-grabbers of your profession. We reporters know better.''

"Such publicity wouldn't do The Clinic any good either.''

"That's where you're wrong, Dr. Alexander.'' Jud Templeton's voice was entirely serious now. "I grew up in this town and I know how proud it has always been of The Clinic. But there still has to be a man at the top, a captain of the team, and he's the guy the public wants to know about. That's been lacking here since old Dr. Anders died.''

"We wanted it that way.''

"Maybe you did; I'll give you credit for really believing the guff about ethics that so few doctors practice any more. But publicity is damned important for The Clinic right now, if not for you. Every time you pick up a magazine these days there's an article in it about the high cost of medical care or the mistakes doctors and hospitals make. Hardly a week passes without another book attacking the medical profession, and the way you're all getting rich.''

"I'm a teacher. Don't put me in that class.''

"I'm familiar with the setup here and with your work, Doctor. In fact, I could come pretty close to naming your salary. The public needs to know at least one clinic in the country doesn't worry about whether or not you can put up a dime when you're sick."

"There are a lot of others like ours."

"They're not the ones you read about in the books and articles that try to run down American medicine. Put a new heart and lungs into Guy Merchant even for a week, Doctor, and you'll have a line of people a mile long waiting to get into the hospital."

"That's partly what I'm afraid of," Greg admitted. "We already have more than we can handle."

"But not more than you *could* handle, if the facilities and money were available. I know all about the battle that's going on over whether to move The Clinic. I had my appendix out ten years ago in your private ward and it was antiquated even then, so something's got to be done. Once this story breaks, a howl of objection to moving it will go up; in fact, I might just be able to help you get the money you need to rebuild this beloved monstrosity."

"Are you saying we should work together?"

"We could both do worse, Doctor. Maybe I was a bit underhanded today in breaking the Merchant-Lawson story without telling you, but you wouldn't have given it to me otherwise, so I didn't have any choice. From now on, though, we can both profit by co-operation."

"How?"

"You see that I'm kept informed as the Merchant-Lawson story breaks and I'll see that The Clinic gets the full benefit of the publicity."

"I'll have to think about that."

The newspaperman smiled. "Just getting you to admit that much means I'm ahead of where I was when I came in this afternoon and you had planned to chew me out. Believe me, Doctor, we both have the same goals. I'm sure we can do a lot more working together than pulling separately."

IV

A few moments after Jud Templeton left, the telephone in Greg's office rang. It was Helen Foucald.

"I've got the results on those agglutination tests you asked me to run, Greg," she said. "Do you have time to come down to the lab and look at them?"

"I'll be right there."

At the laboratory he found Helen and a technician in one corner, jotting down the results from a bank of test tubes which had been set up in front of a strong light. "Here on the left is the normal lymphocyte transfer test," she explained. "As you can see, there's no agglutination."

"That's even more than we had hoped for," said Greg.

"Over here we have the leuko-agglutination test, which is also negative. The irradiated hamster test and the histocompatibility tests can hardly be read accurately before tomorrow noon."

"I've got an idea that won't do us much good. Merchant's failing rapidly."

"What about Lawson?"

"He's showing a change, but as yet we're not sure exactly what's happening."

"Can I do anything else?" she asked.

"No, you've helped me a lot, Helen. I see you found Peter Carewe all right this morning?"

"I didn't find him, he found me." Greg didn't miss her blush.

"I'm sure Peter was much happier having you meet him than he would have been with me."

"He didn't seem to be displeased." Helen smiled. "We had breakfast together at the airport restaurant."

"Peter's quite a boy," said Greg. "And he's doing a wonderful job in his field."

"We're having dinner tonight—unless you're liable to need me."

"Could you make it at the Inn, where I can reach you? If we operate, we'll need a lot of blood-gas determinations in a hurry."

"Of course," she said. "We'll be going to the cocktail party first, anyway, so it will be simple to stay on."

When he returned to his office, Greg was surprised to see Jeanne sitting in the chair beside his desk. Her smile was a bit tremulous until he closed the door and pulled her out of the chair into his arms for a long kiss.

"I know doctors' wives should stay out of their husbands' offices," she said, "but I need to talk to you."

"No more than I needed your being here. Is anything wrong?"

"Not with me any more—I hope."

"That's the best news I could possibly have, darling."

"I visited Mary Jackson in her apartment this morning and she showed me some of Keith's preliminary sketches for the new Clinic. I understand now how you feel about them."

"They're breath-taking, aren't they?"

"Yes. I—Greg, can you ever forgive me?"

"There's nothing to forgive."

"But the way I've acted lately—and last night. Throwing that medical journal at you was unforgivable."

"I had time to think about that afterward, and you were entirely right," he told her. "I should never have tried to compromise with Henry and the faction that's fighting me. It's only made them stronger and lost me some support."

"Are they strong enough to defeat your new plan?"

"Possibly, but I'm not giving in. If the trustees don't want the kind of Clinic I'm going to offer them, they can do without it—and me."

"You can take that chair in experimental surgery at California any time you wish," she reminded him.

"If it comes to that, we will," he said. "I'm not going to let my work be hampered any longer by inadequate facilities, but we'll cross that bridge when we come to it. Right now, I'm too happy to have you back from that far country you've been living in to care about anything else. Do I dare ask what brought you back?"

"I'll tell you later," she said. "Will you be able to go to Ed and Hannah McDougal's cocktail party?"

"I'm afraid not, darling. Bob Johnson and I hope to do a human heart-lung transplant sometime tonight."

"Is this the time for that?" she asked quickly, and he knew what was worrying her—the same thing that had made Dave Connor reluctant to approve the transplant.

"You don't choose the time," he said. "It just happens, like the conjunction of two planets that produced the Star of Bethlehem. But it's the man who's waiting for a new heart and lungs I'm worried about—not the effect my failure might have on the board."

"I didn't mean that."

"I know. You're right, of course; whatever happens, it's bound to influence them one way or another."

"When do you think you can come home?"

"Certainly not until this operation is settled, which means probably tomorrow morning. Bob and I have two operating rooms set up and waiting now."

"I don't think what I have to tell you can wait that long," she said. "Hannah McDougal and I had breakfast together."

"I didn't know you liked Hannah that much."

"I don't. But when I saw in her what I was in danger of becoming, I knew she'd done me a great favor. Did you know Ed is trying to get Sam Hunter's money for a new medical school in Texas?"

"Yes."

"He's up here doing everything he can to keep The Clinic from getting more than a small amount of it."

"That makes sense from Ed's viewpoint. After all, Mr. Hunter's a Texan, too."

"That isn't all. He and Henry Anders are working to drive you out of The Clinic."

"Did Hannah tell you that?"

"No—Claire. We had lunch together."

"Claire's a smart girl, but why would she go against Henry?"

"She has the money in the family now, so she can hold the reins on him. I think she believes a triumphant Henry would be insufferable."

Greg chuckled. "When did you become such a psychiatrist?"

"Since this morning—when I realized Ed McDougal was trying to sabotage you and your work. Is there any way to fight them, Greg?"

"The only way I know is to make the transplant succeed. You can do one thing for me, though."

"Anything I can do—you know that."

"Go on to the cocktail party this evening without me and see what you can learn."

"If you want me to."

"I do. And darling—"

"Yes?"

"As soon as this case is finished and the board meeting's out of the way, we're really going to have that trip I've been promising you—a sort of second honeymoon."

"Aren't we a bit old for that?"

"We'll give it the old college try just the same. By the way, take a look at the final edition of the afternoon paper before you go to the party. I didn't intend it this way, but I think we'll be exploding a small bomb under Ed and Henry just about the time the party starts. Excuse me, my phone's ringing." He picked up the receiver as the light started flicking upon the base of the telephone.

"I'm up in intensive care, Greg." Dave Connor's voice on the telephone was urgent. "You'd better come up here right away."

CHAPTER ELEVEN

I

When he stepped off the elevator at the ICU floor, Greg realized at once
what was happening, for Guy Merchant's labored breathing could be heard
yards away, along with the ominous rattle in his chest. Taken together, they
could only mean his failing heart had almost reached the point of no return.
Because it was no longer able to pump blood satisfactorily into the rest of
the body, fluid was now seeping through the walls of the lung air sacs,
causing a congestion that could quickly result in the critical state called
pulmonary edema.

"We've put in a catheter and I've just injected fifty milligrams of
ethacrynic acid intravenously." Dave Connor was completing an injection
when Greg came in. "Unless his kidney function is shot, too, we ought to
start extracting fluid from the bloodstream and the lungs within fifteen
minutes or less and take some of the load off his heart."

"Don't you think a tracheostomy is indicated?" Greg asked. "He needs as
clear an airway as he can get."

"That's why I called," said the cardiologist. "Do you want to do it up
here?"

"We can work better in one of the anesthetic rooms, where Lew Gann can
watch him and use suction to remove fluid from the airway," said Greg. He
didn't add that Guy Merchant would be ready then for the transplant, for it
didn't seem likely that there would be one.

"He's all yours," said Dave Connor. "Good luck."

Greg rang the operating room supervisor from the nurse's station on the
ICU. "Please set up for a tracheostomy right away, Miss White, and call
Dr. Johnson," he said. "I'm bringing down Mr. Merchant; we can do it in
the anesthetic room for O.R. 2."

II

It was nearly an hour before Greg returned to his office on the top floor of
the surgical building. Somewhere during that time he remembered the
beeper in his pocket giving its strident summons, and, when he asked the
operating room supervisor to take the message, her report that Dr. Edward
McDougal was waiting to see him. But too much had to be done at the
moment for him to take time out to see the Texan.

The tracheostomy had been skillfully performed by Bob Johnson. A small
operation carried out through an incision in the neck and the wall of the
windpipe just below the Adam's apple, it allowed a curved tube to be
inserted and left in place, giving a direct airway to the lungs and making
breathing much easier for patients with congestion and moisture in the
respiratory passage. After that, he had talked briefly to Georgia Merchant,
explaining why the small surgery had been necessary, and had then visited
Frank Lawson, confirming the fact that he, too, was going downhill, though,
unless the treatment being given Guy Merchant was far more effective than

they could expect it to be, not fast enough to allow completion of the transplant.

Greg found Ed McDougal pacing up and down in his office. The beefy surgeon's face was flushed with anger and annoyance.

"Where the hell have you been?" he demanded. "I called for you an hour ago."

"I've been supervising a tracheostomy."

"On the heart patient?"

"Yes." Greg dropped into the chair behind his desk, suddenly conscious of a weariness that extended into his very bones. "What's bothering you, Ed?"

"That grandstand play you pulled downstairs at the convocation this afternoon. What else?"

"It was just a simple announcement."

"You know damn well you can't transplant the heart and lungs successfully from one human being to another who's so far gone in heart failure that you have to do a tracheostomy."

"I've done it enough times experimentally to prove you're wrong, Ed."

"But dogs aren't people. The problems aren't the same."

"I didn't know you were doing experimental surgery."

"Me experiment?" The other surgeon gave a bark of a laugh. "Hell, man! There's no money in that."

"I wasn't working for money."

"I know what you're doing. You're trying to make a big splash to impress the board." The Texas surgeon thrust his head forward belligerently. "Do you deny that your patient's dying?"

"I wouldn't plan to operate on him if he weren't. What is it you want from me, Ed? I've got work to do."

"Call this grandstand play off. You can always say the patient's too far gone to stand the operation, and this time you'd be telling the truth."

"Merchant has improved considerably since we did the tracheostomy," said Greg.

"Dave Connor says he's still failing."

"How do you know that?"

"Henry called Dave."

"You didn't worry about ethics, did you?" Greg's voice was like a whip and the other surgeon flushed.

"Henry's director of The Clinic. He can go wherever he likes."

"But *you* can't come here telling me what I can and cannot do. If Henry wants to forbid me to operate, let him do it himself."

"You know Henry." The Texas surgeon threw up his hands in disgust.

"I know his way is to work underhandedly. What's your way, Ed—a knife in the back?"

The other man flushed. "You don't have to be insulting."

"What else are you when you come in here and try to browbeat me? Or when you rushed to the hospital as soon as you got here this morning and corralled Sam Hunter to influence him against the plans I have for the new hospital?"

"How did you know that?"

"Jeanne and Hannah had breakfast together."

"That loud-mouthed bitch! If she—"

"Hannah didn't tell Jeanne anything I didn't already know, so don't blame her. Just blame yourself for conniving—"

"But—"

"And don't think I don't know you and Henry have joined forces to try and force me out of The Clinic."

The statement brought Ed McDougal up short. "Believe me, Greg, that wasn't my idea," he protested.

"But you agreed to join forces with Henry just the same. You've got your nerve, Ed, coming up here and giving me the devil when you and Henry are busy doing everything you can to destroy me. For your information, I plan to operate on Guy Merchant, if organs become available in time. And nothing you or Henry can do will dissuade me."

"We'll ruin you in the board meeting—"

"Go ahead and try. I'm through with compromise; it wasn't worth the trouble anyway."

"What do you mean?"

"I had worked out a plan for rebuilding that was so conservative even someone as blind to what's really needed here as Sam Hunter and his followers are, would get behind it. But I'm not even going to present it now."

"Then the rumors are true that you've got a way-out plan under wraps?"

"I told the Members this afternoon that I'm going to present such a plan to the board."

"We don't have to be enemies, Greg." Ed McDougal's tone was suddenly conciliatory and Greg gave him a suspicious look.

"Why the milk and honey?" he demanded. "You want Sam Hunter's money for your new medical school and I want it for The Clinic. Right now, I'll admit your chances look a lot better than mine, but a lot can happen between now and Saturday."

"If neither of us asks for too much, we might both come out ahead," the Texan suggested.

"What about your agreement with Henry?"

"I told you I wasn't for that."

"Maybe you're telling the truth, Ed; I don't know. But when Henry joined forces with you, I'll bet he stipulated that I must be a casualty of whatever finally emerges. Now you come offering to make a deal behind Henry's back, so how do either of us know you won't double-cross us both when the time comes?"

The Texan shot up out of his chair, his face fiery red with anger. "I came here to give you a chance because I didn't really want to go along with Henry's plan to force you out," he snapped. "But now I feel no obligation to help you keep your job."

"I'd like to think you have enough love for The Clinic's welfare not to leave us out in the cold when it comes to Sam Hunter's money, Ed." Greg went to the door and opened it. "And because I give you that much credit, I'm going to tell you something you don't know—though you will in a little while anyway. There was a reporter at the opening session of the convocation this afternoon."

"Why you son of a—!"

"I didn't have anything to do with his being there."

"The hell you didn't!"

"I think you'd better leave, Ed."

"I'm not going until I tell you what I think of you."

"You've already done that, so why waste your breath? Henry invited Jud Templeton, the newspaperman I was talking about."

"How do you know that?"

"Templeton told me after he'd filed the story. I saw his press card— signed by Henry."

"Why would Henry do that?"

"You mean he didn't confide in you?"

"The last thing any of us want is for this controversy to get into the newspapers. You should know that."

"Well it's there already. Henry did it deliberately."

"But why?"

"He's working with you, not me; why don't you ask him? My guess is he wanted the announcement of the special session of the board be made public, figuring that I'd demand to know why. Then he could reveal that Sam Hunter wants to censure me for building the hyperbaric laboratory. Anything Sam Hunter does is news, so it would have worked—if I'd been fool enough to ask why the meeting was being called."

"Of all the damn fools—"

"That's our Henry, but you should have expected something like it when you teamed up with him to knife me in the back." Greg shook his head. "I've had about all of you and Henry I can take for one day, Ed. Better go, or you'll be late for your party."

When the Texas surgeon was gone, Greg dropped into the chair behind his desk and began to shuffle through some papers upon it. But the words printed there faded into black scrawls on the white paper and presently he pushed the sheets aside and picked up the phone.

"Can you ring the telephone the reporters and the police use just outside the emergency room?" he asked the operator.

"Yes, Doctor. It's a pay station but I have the number."

"Please ask Mr. Jud Templeton to come to my office."

"Of course, Dr. Alexander. I'll do it right away."

When he put down the phone, Greg sat back in the chair and studied the medical school diploma framed on the wall. The words were in Latin, but he could remember as well as if it had been only yesterday the voice of the commencement speaker long ago quoting Robert Louis Stevenson's famous tribute to physicians in general:

"There are men and classes of men that stand above the common herd: the soldier, the sailor, and the shepherd not infrequently; the artist rarely, rarelier still, the clergyman; the physician almost as a rule . . . Generosity he has, such as is possible to those who practice an art, never to those who drive a trade; discretion, tested by a hundred secrets; tact, tried in a thousand embarrassments; and what are more important, Heraclean cheerfulness and courage."

Courage, he had, Greg decided; it had certainly taken that to tackle one of the last frontiers of surgery, replacing failing organs with strong ones from those who could not use them any more. And, most of all, to confine his work to those most complicated, yet most important of organs, the heart and the lungs.

Generosity, he was sure he had shown in trying to win over those who opposed him, seeking to understand their unwillingness to take a step which they were afraid might damage The Clinic, whose welfare they were sworn to guard as trustees. Actually he'd been generous to a fault—and almost lost Jeanne in the process, but there was a limit to which generosity could go. And when a man carried the spirit of compromise so far as almost to alienate his wife, when he saw his enemies working to blemish his reputation publicly and, what was more important, sabotage the work by which he hoped to save lives that were otherwise doomed, it was time to fight those who fought him with their own weapons.

III

"Come in, please, Mr. Templeton," Greg said when the secretary opened the door for the newspaperman.

"I must say, I wasn't expecting a call this soon, Doctor."

"I've been thinking about your offer to help me."

"You could certainly use it," said Templeton. "A lot of people are after Sam Hunter's money and each one is willing to cut the other's throat to get it. It doesn't speak well for the quality of charity St. Paul wrote about, does it?"

"Most authorities translate charity there as love."

"Or that either. The Hippocratic oath is undoubtedly one of the purest ethical statements ever propounded, but, like almost everything else in the way of ideals in times like these, it's honored in the breach as much as in fulfillment. Where do we start, Doctor?"

"Perhaps here." Greg took a small key from his pocket and unlocked the center drawer of his desk. From inside it, he removed a sheet of draftman's tracing paper, which he handed to Jud Templeton.

The journalist studied the soaring lines and angles, the shadows and sharply etched dramatic highlights for a long moment.

"Are you releasing this now?" A note of awe was in his voice.

Greg shook his head. "Hardly anybody except myself and the architect has seen it. This drawing will not be released publicly until after the trustees meet on Saturday."

"When it may be as dead as a doornail! This could be your biggest gun, Doctor. Let me run a cut of it in tomorrow afternoon's paper and people will be bombarding your Board of Trustees with thousands of calls and letters demanding that it be built as a fitting monument to old Dr. Anders and to that statue over there in the rotunda."

"I promised to present plans to the trustees."

"These aren't your first, are they? I remember hearing something about another set being drawn by a firm of architects downtown."

"I first saw that sketch less than a week ago," Greg told him. "Keith Jackson's been working night and day since then to make the preliminary drawings for me to show to the board."

"Do you think an ossified mind like Sam Hunter's can appreciate the beauty of a structure like this? I've seen that office building of his in Dallas and a more thoroughly uninspired piece of architecture was never built."

"Mr. Hunter's not the only member of the board."

"Let's not kid ourselves, Doctor. Most of the members expect him to put up the money for the new building, whether The Clinic is built here or out on the Beltway, so they'll vote with him."

"Where would you rather see it go?"

"I live just off the Beltway, so I'd like to have it where my daughter-in-law can rush my grandchildren to it if they get the bellyache. What's more important, she can be sure some knife-happy surgeon isn't going to operate for appendicitis when all the kid has is that thing where the lymph glands in the belly become swollen because of a respiratory infection."

"Acute mesenteric lymphadenitis."

"A family I know of had three kids operated on for appendix in as many days—until the father got suspicious and demanded a consultation with a young professor of pediatrics from the university medical school. Three kids operated on for appendicitis in forty-eight hours! Do you know what the odds are against that happening?"

"It would take a computer to figure it."

"But only a cheap adding machine to calculate what it cost that couple in surgeon's fees and hospital bills. So however much I'd like to have The Clinic in my own backyard, I can see that it's needed more right here in the worst slum in the city."

"Will you help me keep it here?"

"I can damn sure try," said Templeton. "I've got an interview set up tomorrow morning with Dr. Peter Carewe. He impresses me as being the kind of a guy who won't weasel on anything I ask him, and if I use the right kind of questions, he'll probably come through with the right answers. Ever since that TV program the other night, people would listen if he recited 'Gunga Din' through his nose." He picked up the sketch again. "This must be the plan Dr. Anders spoke about when he called me this morning and invited me to sit in on the first session of the convocation."

"You didn't say anything about that before," Greg said quickly.

"I only thought of it after I left here, and you've been tied up ever since."

"Just what did Henry Anders tell you?"

"He said some sort of dramatic announcement would be made. And he also said a new plan is in the offing and implied that there would be a hell of a fight in the board over it."

"Of which he would furnish you with the details?"

"That was the size of it." Jud Templeton's gray eyes studied him quizzically. "You seemed surprised, Doctor. Wasn't Dr. Anders in on the secret?"

"Frankly, no."

"That sort of puts a different aspect on things, doesn't it?"

"Quite different."

"Do you suppose somebody could be setting you up, Doctor?"

"Setting me up?"

"As a patsy, to be knocked off at the right time. Keith Jackson's got the reputation around town of being brilliant but sort of way out—you know, almost avant-garde. And with all that conservative element on the board, it might just be that someone is trying to give you and Jackson enough rope to hang yourselves."

"That sounds rather far-fetched."

"Maybe yes and maybe no. Let's not forget that Dr. Anders knew all about this plan when he called me this morning, in spite of the fact that you say only you and Jackson have seen it. Did Keith Jackson even mention him to you?"

"No."

"You're sure?"

"Absolutely."

"What shape were these sketches in when Jackson first showed them to you?"

"That's one of them you have now."

Jud Templeton picked up the sketch and held it up to the light once again. "Notice how much detail he has here; this is hardly the sort of rough sketch an architect would knock out just because he was struck by an idea in the middle of the night."

"I can see that now," said Greg. "But you can't deny that it's inspired."

"No doubt about that, but men are inspired by a lot of things. Just because there may have been an ulterior motive behind the original inspiration doesn't alter the fact that a work of art often comes out of it."

Greg Alexander ran his fingers down the row of tabs on a telephone-number index beside the phone on his desk. When he came to J, he pressed down a tab and the top flew up, revealing Keith Jackson's office and house numbers, along with others. Picking up the phone, he dialed nine for the outside connection and then the number; Keith himself answered the second ring.

"This is Dr. Alexander," said Greg. "How's everything going?"

"Fine, Doctor—except for sleep."

"One of the trustees has requested a special meeting Friday afternoon at four o'clock and I have an idea there'll be a demand then for the preliminary plans. Could you possibly make it?"

"There goes *another* night's sleep—but we'll have something ready for you."

"I'm going to ask you a question, Keith," said Greg. "And I need a frank answer."

"What is it, Doctor?"

"When you first brought your sketches to my attention a couple of weeks ago, had anyone else suggested the idea to you?"

There was a moment's pause, then the architect said, "I think I told you the idea originally came from an article—I believe it was in *Life* or *Look*—about that new hotel in Atlanta. It showed a possible way to handle the problem of the statue."

"Do you remember who brought the article to your attention?"

"I promised not to mention it."

"This is pretty important, Keith. The success of the whole project may hinge on your answer."

"It was Dr. Henry Anders, sir. He said he thought something like the Atlanta hotel theme would be a fitting memorial to his father, but he didn't want me to mention his part in it to you."

"Did he say why?"

"He was afraid you might be prejudiced against the idea because it came from him. I didn't know you very well then, Doctor, so I accepted his explanation. Lately, though, it's been troubling me and I'm really glad you asked about it."

"Thanks, Keith."

"Is anything wrong, Dr. Alexander?"

"No. I think everything is going to work out all right."

"Then I'd better get back to my work. Good-by."

"You were right, I've been booby-trapped," Greg told Templeton when he hung up the phone. "Those who don't want The Clinic rebuilt here suggested that idea to Keith Jackson, figuring I might fall for it and present the trustees with a radical design most of them wouldn't go along with."

He picked up the sketch again and studied it for a moment, then handed it to the newspaperman. "Take another look and tell me what you think?"

"I've already made up my mind," said Jud Templeton. "Whoever's behind all this—and I think I could name names if I had to—has outsmarted himself. When do I get a chance to run the sketch in the newspaper?"

"How about the Friday afternoon edition?"

"Fine. But I'll need it well before that. Making a cut takes time."

"Take it with you now. I'm trusting you that the newspaper piece won't come out until Friday afternoon."

Greg handed Jud Templton the sketch and he put it in his writing case, handling it as carefully as if it had been a precious jewel. "I'll do my piece at home telling about the heroic struggle to keep greedy profiteers from destroying the greatest medical institution in the world," he promised. "And I'll have an engraver friend make the cut outside the paper so nobody will have an inkling of it until I hand the whole thing to the city editor Friday morning."

"You're being very helpful," said Greg. "I'm indebted to you."

"There was a price involved, don't forget that. You're to keep me up to date on the progress of the Merchant-Lawson operation." Jud Templeton glanced at his watch. "The paper owns a TV and radio station; we've got the six o'clock spot covered already but I'll need two or three lines on the case for the eleven o'clock news."

"I've an idea the whole thing will be settled by then—probably against us. We almost lost Merchant less than two hours ago in an acute heart failure."

"What about Lawson?"

"He's losing ground."

"But not fast enough?"

"That's about it."

"How's Georgia taking it?"

"Very well."

"She's a trouper," said Templeton. "Do you mind if I talk to her? She's always good for a feature and the slant of a wife on this sort of a situation might be very interesting right now."

"Not if she doesn't object."

"One other thing. Can I do a feature about you?"

"NO!"

"I knew you'd say that, but what a story it would make. Imagine thumbing your nose at one of the richest men in the world to further the dream of a man who wasn't even related to you."

CHAPTER TWELVE

I

The afternoon session of the convocation was almost over when Greg looked in through a door that gave access to the upper row of seats in the lecture room. Henry Anders was no longer presiding and Greg was not able to see Ed McDougal anywhere. A change of speakers was taking place just then and a number of doctors were leaving, among them, Helen Foucald.

"If you're looking for Henry," she said, "he gave the task of presiding to Dr. Remick as soon as that Texan came back at the end of the coffee break. I imagine they're out plotting against you."

"Well, at least it's nice to know they're consistent."

"Greg."

"Yes."

"There's something you ought to know. I learned it accidentally."

"You don't have to betray any confidences, Helen."

"Maybe the time has come to burn a few bridges."

"It might turn out that you backed the losing team. We're playing in a very fast league."

"That's why I want my part of the game to be on the level," she said. "Henry's cooking up some sort of a scheme to get you out on a limb so he can saw you off at the right moment. I don't know the details but—"

"I know them already, Helen, so don't burn your bridges yet."

"But how?"

Greg looked at his watch. "Just about now the Wall Street Final editions of the afternoon paper will be hitting the newsstands. Henry invited a reporter at the opening session so he and Ed McDougal could publicize the fact that the Board of Trustees will probably try to censure me Friday afternoon. But they didn't figure on my announcing the transplant and it's such startling news that their little plan got pushed out of the way."

"Henry must be fit to be tied."

"Ed McDougal came to my office during the coffee break this afternoon. He offered to back me—up to a limit—and split Sam Hunter's money with me."

"Poor old man, so narrow-minded and so convinced that he's right."

"Paranoia in a mild form is an occupational disease of both age and big business," said Greg. "Old Sam is no worse than a lot of others; when he sees the facts, he usually does what's right."

"I take it that you didn't accept Dr. McDougal's offer."

"No."

"Could you have still built The Clinic here if you had?"

"Possibly. But if I had taken the bait, the first chance Ed got he'd double-cross me, just as he was willing to double-cross Henry."

"Poor Henry," she said. "He does so much want to be a really big man but he never is, except when he's making love. I guess you could call him a human phallic symbol."

II

When Greg came back to where Guy Merchant lay upon a table in one of the anesthetic rooms, he found a nurse-anesthetist watching the patient while Dr. Lewis Gann smoked his pipe in the adjoining lounge and dressing room for the surgical staff.

"What do you think of Merchant's condition now, Lew?" the surgeon asked.

"He's still losing ground, but a lot more slowly than before Bob did the tracheostomy. How about Lawson?"

"Herb Partridge thinks there's a slow hemorrhage into the deep centers of the brain. We'll have to wait and see."

"I heard your announcement about the new automated hospital," said the anesthesiologist. "What is my department going to be like?"

"You'll be working underground most of the time. I can tell you that much."

"Then your setup will be somewhat like the one at Georgetown?"

"Keith Jackson hasn't worked out the details yet, but the principle will be the same. Patients for surgery will be admitted to the operative section the night before and go directly from their own rooms on the lower levels to the O.R. by the shortest possible route the next morning. Every precaution will be taken to avoid any possibility of contamination and cut down the incidence of postoperative infection."

"No interns scurrying in and out at the last minute taking histories and doing preoperative physicals?"

"All of that will be done in the diagnostic clinic—except for acute emergencies. The patient's record will be stored in the data processing system and printed out as it is needed by the computer."

"Do you have in mind letting a computer take the history—like they're experimenting with out in Minnesota and some other places?"

"If we can get the money for it—yes."

"You're thinking big, boy." Dr. Gann shook his head admiringly. "Real big."

"The heart of the whole project is a twelve-story high-rise ICU built where the present rotunda stands, with the statue of Christ at its base surrounded by glass. And we'll have full-sized twin hyperbaric chambers underground, placed so we can go from one to the other for transplantations without having to be decompressed."

"Still not interested in artificial hearts?"

"Other people are working on that," said Greg. "My job is to make heart-lung transplants feasible, and, with the surgical technique worked out, we can concentrate on problems of rejection. The only way to do that is to perform transplant operations as often as we can and then fight the rejection battle as it arises, using what we've already learned from dogs and from the patients we operate on as the basis for future progress."

"Suppose Ed McDougal and his crowd succeed in blocking you? I've got some money on you in the hospital pool."

"If I can't have what I need here, I'll go somewhere else. Maybe you'd better go out and hedge that bet, Lew."

"If you can lay a career on the line, I guess I can risk five bucks," said the anesthesiologist.

One of the Junior Fellows in surgery burst into the lounge, carrying a newspaper in his hand. "This just hit the newsstands," he said excitedly. "You're all over the front page, Dr. Alexander."

Jud Templeton had been as good as his word, Greg saw. Blazing across the top of the front page was a headline in bold black type:

CLINIC SURGEON TO PERFORM HEART-LUNG TRANSPLANT

Beneath it, under Jud Templeton's by-line and with a two-column cut of Greg was the story:

> A startled Convocation of former Fellows of The Clinic and staff doctors today heard one of their number, Dr. Gregory Alexander, announce at the opening session of their biennial convocation his intention to make surgical history. Probably while the group is still in session for their meeting, Dr. Alexander plans to transplant the heart and lungs of a convicted murderer into the body of a patient dying of heart failure. Guy Merchant, the prospective recipient, is a well-known musical comedy figure of former years. The proposed donor, Frank Lawson, is a four-time loser who may have a chance before the day is over to fulfill the well-known Shakespearean adage that *"Nothing in his life became him like the leaving of it."*

There was more: brief summaries of Greg's experimental work, as described in previous newspaper accounts, and a biographical sketch of him, Guy Merchant and Frank Lawson. Greg handed the newspaper back to the excited young doctor, who left immediately to spread the news throughout the hospital.

"Somehow I don't get the impression that you were surprised by those headlines," said Dr. Gann.

"Jud Templeton warned me this afternoon after he'd sent the story to the copy room."

"I was hoping you'd stolen a march on Henry and his motley crew by getting in touch with Templeton yourself."

"Hen did that for me," said Greg. "He invited Templeton to cover the convocation, thinking I would object to the Friday special sesion of the board and sentiment would build up against me when it was learned that I will probably be censured. But I accidentally stole a march on him by announcing that I had canceled the dog transplant operation scheduled for tomorrow in order to keep the operating teams free for the one we hope to do this afternoon or evening. As it turned out, nobody paid much attention to the special board meeting; I didn't even see any reference to it in the newspaper."

"So Henry and Ed got the shaft—on their own petards? It couldn't happen to a more deserving pair. Can you stay here for ten minutes or so, in case the nurse watching Merchant needs help?"

"Sure. What's your hurry?"

"I want to get some more money down on you before news of this gets out and the odds start changing."

III

The final edition of the afternoon newspaper hit The Clinic and its environs like an exploding bomb. Those who had been attending the convocation first saw it when the afternoon session broke up for the McDougal-Anders cocktail party, shortly before five o'clock. Even before the party started in the Falstaff Room of the Clinic Inn, however, it was a major topic of conversation for the Members.

Henry Anders and Ed McDougal saw the newspaper as they were crossing The Parkway for a conference of war. Henry turned a little pale at the sight of the bold black headlines and poured himself a drink as soon as they reached the suite Ed had rented as headquarters for his political maneuvering. Only after a gin and tonic, did Henry's normally florid face regain some of its color.

"A lot of Members aren't going to like this publicity," he ventured. "I guess Greg hung himself with the rope we gave him by having that reporter there."

"Don't be a fool!" said Ed McDougal. "Greg would never have allowed premature publicity about the transplant if he'd had anything to say about it. This is the best break he possibly could have had—and you gave it to him."

"But you said he talked to Templeton."

"Only after the story was written. Templeton didn't want to risk having Greg use whatever influence he had with the publisher to call off the story."

"I still don't see—"

"Then you'd damn sure better start looking," the Texan said savagely. "You and I know the experimental work that will make this transplant succeed—if it does—was done with a budget of peanuts. Much of that came out of Greg's own pockets too, so now he can argue to the board that, if he's able to do what he's doing with so little money, he could accomplish a lot more if he really had some funds."

"He'll never convince Sam Hunter of that."

"Sam's not the only one on the board, remember? For five years or so The Clinic's been coasting on the reputation it built up during your father's lifetime and what Greg has been able to do. This transplant business could be just the shot in the arm it needs to be back on top professionally, and, if that happens, Greg can thumb his nose at Sam Hunter and the rest of us with a campaign to raise funds and rebuild the way he wants to do. But it would be Greg's clinic then—don't forget that it doesn't even have your father's name on it—and you'd be out on your fat behind."

Henry Anders poured a second gin and tonic and drank half of it in one gulp. He was sweating, although the room was not excessively warm.

"Wh—what do we do?"

"First we'll try to undo the mess you made by tipping off that reporter, starting with Sam Hunter," said the Texas surgeon. "But let me do the talking. I know how to handle the old man; all you'll do is put your foot in your mouth again."

Moto, Sam Hunter's valet, let them into the millionaire's suite. "Mr. Hunter has been sleeping, Dr. McDougal," he said. "He was very tired when he finished the examinations this morning and he has more tests tomorrow."

"We won't be long, Moto," Ed promised. "Just a couple of things we wanted to ask Mr. Hunter about." He looked around the sitting room of the suite. "You don't have the afternoon paper yet?"

"Mr. Hunter reads only the morning Dallas *News* and, of course, the *Wall Street Journal.*"

"Moto!" Sam Hunter called from the bedroom. "Who's out there?"

"Dr. McDougal and Dr. Anders, sir."

"Tell them I'll be out in a minute."

"Make yourselves comfortable, gentlemen," said the valet, and vanished into the bedroom. Sam Hunter came out a few minutes later, wearing a silk dressing gown.

"I was getting ready for that party," he said. "Why aren't both of you downstairs being hosts?"

"We thought you should see something first." Ed McDougal handed him the newspaper, folded so the bold headlines were the first thing he saw. The old man skimmed through the story, the half glasses he usually wore, perched low on his nose, then gave it back.

"I thought doctors were supposed to avoid publicity," he said. "Isn't there something about that in your code of ethics?"

"This is certainly a breach of ethics, sir." Ed seized the opening gambit the old man seemed to have given him. "From what I learned in the hospital this afternoon, there's no chance of the man who's supposed to receive the new heart even living long enough to be operated on."

"Alexander's no fool," said the oil baron. "If I were losing, I guess I'd try some sort of a grandstand play like this, too."

"It does appear to be an act of desperation, sir," said Ed. "But it's also deceitful, don't you think, to imply that you plan to save a man's life when you know perfectly well you've got no chance of doing it?"

"I'd call it smart. Didn't know Alexander was that good a poker player."

"Are you going to let him get by with it, sir? Surely this grandstand play won't change your mind."

"Nothing changes my mind until I get ready to change it. You ought to know, Ed, since you're so determined to get a lot of money out of me for that medical school of yours down in Texas."

"But, sir—"

"You're a good poker player, too. I'm surprised that you'd try to put over something as obvious as this scheme of yours to discredit Dr. Alexander," the old man added. "As far as I'm concerned, this business about avoiding publicity you doctors make so much fuss about is a lot of hokum. You criticize other doctors who make the headlines, but you still grab every chance to make them yourselves."

"I don't think you're being quite fair, Mr. Hunter." Ed McDougal had lost some of his assurance. Like Henry Anders, he was beginning to sweat.

"I used to own some movie theaters down in Texas before the war," said Sam Hunter. "As a courtesy to doctors, we would accept messages for them while they were in the theater, flash telephone numbers for them to call on the screen. I got sort of suspicious after some of the managers reported the same doctors seemed to be getting calls all the time. When we checked at the box office to see who came through, we discovered that most of the ones who were always being paged in our theaters weren't even there, so we stopped the free advertising."

"That sort of thing is frowned on by the medical societies," Ed protested.

"But doctors still go on doing it just the same. I had a chance to think things over while I was trying to go to sleep this afternoon. It seems to me like some of you fellows are pushing me sort of hard on this Clinic thing." He turned to Henry Anders. "That's a right smart woman doctor you have there in the laboratory, Henry. She's lock, stock and barrel for Dr. Alexander, so maybe there's more to him than I thought. Anyway, I'm going to talk to her some more and maybe to him, too, before I make up my mind about what I'll do at the board meeting. What chance does he have with the heart transplant idea of his, by the way?"

"None at all, sir," Ed McDougal said quickly.

"I didn't ask you, Ed. You've been so busy getting rich down in Texas, you wouldn't know anything about it anyway. What do you say, Henry?"

"He's never done the operation on a human being, sir."

"How about dogs? Dr. Foucald said something about that and so did that X-ray fellow."

Henry Anders took a deep breath. He didn't want to admit Greg Alexander's success, yet he knew he couldn't fool the old man very long.

"Speak up!" Sam Hunter barked. "Or don't you know what's going on in your own clinic—like Dr. Remick said today?"

"Greg—Dr. Alexander has transplanted both heart and lungs in a number of dogs, sir. I don't know how many are alive but one of them did have pups last night."

"It looks like somebody's been trying to make a fool of Old Sam." The millionaire nodded slowly. "I don't know anything about medicine, but the last man that tried it with oil down in Texas wound up in the poorhouse. Now get out of here and let me get ready for the party. Is that handsome wife of yours going to be there, Henry?"

"Oh yes, sir. Claire's looking forward to seeing you again."

"She's a better man than you are," said Sam Hunter bluntly. "See you downstairs, gentlemen."

Outside, Henry Anders took a handkerchief from his pocket and wiped the sweat from his face. "The old coot is on to us, Ed," he said. "What are you going to do?"

"I'm going to drop a few hints among the trustees that this newspaper article was planted by Greg," the Texas surgeon told him. "How well do you know Dr. Foucald?"

"Rather well." Henry began to perk up somewhat.

"Been layin' her regularly?"

"Well—yes."

"I thought so, from the look on your face when I saw you together in the hospital this morning. How is she in the hay?"

"Neither of us have complained." Henry was regaining some of the assurance he'd lost under Sam Hunter's lashing tongue.

"Wish I had time to try a little jousting there myself, but that dough of

Sam Hunter's is too important to my plans. Does she live in the apartment building next-door?"

"Yes. In one of the penthouses."

"Why don't you go up there and lay down the law to her, so she'll know what to say if the old man talks to her again?"

"That's a good idea." Henry Anders brightened perceptibly. "Tell Claire I've been delayed at the hospital for a little while."

"Make it a quick one; we need to talk to a lot of people. This is the only chance we'll have to get them all together, except the dinner Thursday night, and it may be too late by then."

IV

Peter Carewe hadn't noticed Helen leave the lecture room during the afternoon session. When it was over, he looked for her among the departing crowd, and, not finding her, went to the laboratory. There he was told by her secretary that she had left early to dress for the cocktail party.

"Do you know her home telephone number?" he asked.

"I'll get her on the phone for you, Dr. Carewe. You can take it in her office." When the phone rang, Helen was on the line.

"My secretary said that gorgeous doctor from the WHO wanted to speak to me." At the lilt in her voice he felt a sense of happiness peruse his entire body. "Most of my technicians are women, so be careful how you wander around there or the laboratory results for the rest of the afternoon will all be in error."

"I looked for you at the end of the clinical session," he said. "Thought we might have a quick drink before the cocktail party."

"I'm afraid I'm not dressed."

"In that case, I'd better come up there."

"That will be nice," she said. "I'll leave the door on the latch."

He was there in less than ten minutes. As she had said, the door was unlatched and he let himself in, closing it behind him.

"That you, Peter?" Helen called from the bedroom.

"It had better be."

"I'll be out in a minute. Make yourself comfortable."

When she came out of the bedroom, she was flushed from the bath, and from his presence—like a schoolgirl, she thought, on her first date. Her dress was deceptively simple, of yellow linen, with a gored skirt that flared out as she turned for his inspection.

"You're the one who's gorgeous." He took her hands, leading her toward the sofa, but she deftly guided him to a love seat on the other side of the room instead. The sofa was a reminder of too many things she'd just as soon forget at the moment.

"Ever since we had coffee together I've been thinking about when I'd see you again," he said. "I wanted to tell you about the dinner I'm going to order—"

"It will have to be at the Inn. Greg wants me to stay in touch, in case he does the transplant."

"This is the first time I ever hated Greg in my life," he said. "But maybe we can find a corner to ourselves. We'll take hours eating and more hours afterward over brandy in my suite, enjoying the miracle of digestion."

"You must have had a French ancestor. Only a Frenchman could appreciate that sort of an evening."

"My mother was French."

"And mine, American."

"No wonder you have so little accent. We're really two citizens of the world, aren't we?"

"Oh, my experience can't begin to equal yours. Father was a correspondent for the old Paris edition of the *Herald Tribune* and my mother was a fashion editor. We lived in a village outside the city, until they sent me to an American preparatory school inside Paris."

"Are they there now?"

"My parents were killed in an airplane crash in the Alps just as I was getting ready to go to college."

"That's the best way to go—together."

"The insurance they left took me through the Sorbonne and a Ph.D. I was embarked on a career in hematology until I decided to come to the United States instead."

"To Boston—you told me about it this morning."

She laughed. "You swept me off my feet so completely, I can't even remember what I did or said."

"Neither can I, except that when I saw you there in the airport this morning, I knew I'd found my heart's desire. Doesn't that sound corny?"

"Not if it isn't what you call a line."

"Would I use a phrase like that as part of a line?" He threw up his hands in mock horror. "It could only come from the heart."

"Really, Peter, you're delightful." She leaned forward to kiss him, but when he put his arm about her and crushed her mouth beneath his own, what she had intended to be a light caress turned into the almost blinding heat of desire. Suddenly helpless before the hot tide of passion that swept over her, and feeling the swift stirrings of his own surging desire, she knew that in another instant he would lift her and carry her to the bedroom—and willed with all the surge of passion flowing through her that he would.

Perhaps no sound could have intruded so completely into the fierce rush of desire that gripped them both as the grate of a key in the lock. Helen heard it first and, pushing Peter away, was halfway to the door of the apartment when it opened to reveal Henry Anders standing there gaping at them.

"Why, Henry!" Helen's voice was a little shrill and the intruder could not have been such a fool as not to have realized the nature of the scene he had interrupted. "Did I forget to lock my door? I must be more careful."

"I guess I must have pushed it open when I was getting ready to knock," Henry Anders mumbled.

Peter Carewe's glance went quickly to the lovely flushed woman standing between him and Henry's bulk, then to Henry's embarrassed face. He didn't miss the shrillness in Helen's tones, or Henry's bumbling embarrassment—and both sent a chill through him.

"Thought you'd be at the party, Henry," he said to help cover up the awkwardness of the situation. "You're one of the hosts, aren't you?"

"Claire sent me up to tell Helen she won't need the"— Henry's eyes raced quickly around the apartment until they lit upon a lovely antique silver coffee service in a glass-fronted cabinet—"the coffee service. Turns out that the Inn has one, so there's no need for you to bring yours, Helen."

"Thank you, Henry." Helen's voice was calm now. "Peter and I are coming down in a few moments."

"I'll see you there then." Henry backed out of the room, closing the door.

For a moment after the latch clicked, there was a silence; then Helen said, a little too brightly: "Where were we?"

"I was about to sweep you off your feet, I believe is the cliché that expresses the situation," said Peter, and her heart contracted at the note of pain in his voice. "But that would be a little anticlimactic now, wouldn't it?"

"I'll get a wrap," she said. "You're the celebrity of this occasion, so I shouldn't be monopolizing you."

CHAPTER THIRTEEN

I

"Back so soon, darling?" Claire asked when Henry, looking baffled and angry, appeared in the Falstaff Room, where the Members of The Clinic and their wives had begun to gather for the cocktail party. "I gather Helen wasn't in the mood."

"Didn't Ed tell you I had to see a patient in the hospital?" he demanded shortly.

"Come now, darling. It's your loyal and devoted wife you're talking to, somebody who knows you never let duty interfere with pleasure."

"Can you say anything but the same about yourself?" he snapped, but Claire had already turned to greet a doctor from Minneapolis and his somewhat dumpy wife.

"How nice to see you," she said warmly to the guests. "Do have a drink. Hannah and Ed McDougal are a little late."

"Where the hell are our co-hosts, anyway?" Claire spoke to Henry again as the couple from Minneapolis moved on. "Ed came in here, told me you'd be late and ran away. And Hannah hasn't shown up at all."

"All hell has broken loose." Henry plucked a glass from the tray of a passing waiter. "Haven't you seen the afternoon paper?"

"I've been busy here, seeing that everything was ready for the party."

"Jud Templeton was at the convocation this afternoon when Greg announced that he expects to do a human heart-lung transplant before morning. It's all over the front page."

"So?" Claire's eyebrows lifted. "It would seem that Greg stole a march on you two."

Henry exploded into an oath that startled some of those nearby and emptied his glass hurriedly. "On top of that, Sam Hunter is acting up."

"You should have better sense than to get into these situations without consulting me, darling," Claire told him sweetly. "And to tie yourself up with Ed McDougal of all people; he'll double-cross you the moment your back is turned. Ah! Here come our co-hosts now. Looks like they're having a snit."

Ed McDougal and Hannah had come into the room and Claire moved over to greet them. "I was beginning to be afraid you two had forgotten your own party, darlings," she said.

"Sorry we're late, Claire," said the Texas surgeon. "I had to change clothes."

"You're so efficient, Claire," said Hannah. "And since the guests are almost all men, I knew you'd have everything under control."

"Now that you're here, I'm sure we can handle them," said Claire. "You always do things on such a big scale down in Texas, darlings. I feel like we ought to barbecue a bull or something, so you'll feel at home."

"Break it up, Claire," said Henry. "Sam Hunter just came in."

"Aren't you afraid to let all that money go unprotected, Ed?" Claire asked. "I thought you and Henry would be guarding him on either side, like the men from Brinks—with Hannah bringing up the rear. After all, somebody might talk Mr. Hunter into giving a buck or two to their favorite charity." She left the others and moved across the room to greet the old financier, who was standing alone in the door, looking over the people there.

"Mr. Hunter!" she said warmly. "How nice to see you!" Leaning forward, she let the old man kiss her cheek.

"You're about the only one here who could say that and really make me believe it, Claire," he said. "You're wearing well."

"That's because I vary my diet. Wouldn't you like a drink?"

"Some bourbon and branch water, if you have such things here."

"Of course we do." Claire signaled a waiter. "Bourbon and water for the gentleman—I'll have the same."

"You're quite a woman, Claire," the old millionaire said admiringly. "If I were thirty years younger, I'd do my best to put horns on Henry."

"Confidentially, you'd do it, too," Claire assured him. "You must have been quite a rounder in your day—and I'll bet that day isn't far behind you."

"I'm complimented, Claire, but it's a lost cause." Sam Hunter took the glass the waiter handed him and stared at the pale amber contents morosely. "Nothing much to live for any more except making money and browbeating everybody I can. And that's a damn poor excuse for anybody's existence."

"Are you going to let them move The Clinic outside the city?" Claire lowered her voice as she guided him toward a corner table.

"I don't know yet." The old man studied her over his glass. "You know Henry will be rich if I do, don't you?"

"I'm not sure I want him rich."

"Why not?"

"We're an ideal couple as it is. I've got money and Henry's got—shall we say—an unusual capability of pleasing a woman."

"So these rumors I've been hearing about him are true?"

"They're true, Mr. Hunter. Remarkably so, in fact."

"I knew there must be some reason besides his charming personality why women seem to like him so much," said the old man. "I gather you think that if Henry had money, you might have to share him with others."

"I already share him; right now he's more than one woman has a right to expect. But things will change. And as long as I have the money, I can keep him from roving."

Sam Hunter smiled. "They call us Texans wheelers and dealers but a smart woman can put it over us any day. I'll think about what you've been saying, Claire. Go on now and entertain your other guests."

"Are you sure I can't do anything to make your stay here more pleasant?" she asked.

"Not any longer, my dear," said Sam Hunter sadly. "Not any longer."

II

There was a stir of interest when Peter Carewe came in with Helen Foucald. Helen saw Claire and Sam Hunter together and deftly guided Peter across the room to where the two were standing.

"Hello, Claire," she said. "You look ravishing tonight."

"It's mutual," said Claire.

"Good evening, Mr. Hunter," said Helen.

The old magnate bowed gallantly and Claire said, "I presume this is Dr. Carewe. I'm Claire Anders."

"Our hostess!" said Peter warmly.

"One of them. The other one is conferring with my husband and her husband over there in the corner of the room, planning some sort of skulduggery. She's the one flaunting the ermine collar and the deep V."

"I want to apologize for my behavior in my office this morning, Mr. Hunter," said Helen. "I'm afraid I was very rude to you."

"You held up your end of it very well, Doctor. I always admire anybody who puts up a good fight—even against me."

"There's Jeanne Alexander and the Pucketts," said Claire. "Excuse me while I go and speak to them. Why don't you three take one of the tables?"

"You seem to have an exciting life, young man," said Sam Hunter when they had seated themselves and a waiter brought drinks for Helen and Peter.

"I stay busy."

"Spending American money on naked savages who go back to eating each other as soon as they use up what you give them?"

"You've got the WHO mixed up with UNESCO, Mr. Hunter. I'm busy making the world safe for capitalism by stamping out disease so industry can move into undeveloped lands and exploit native labor."

"Humph!" said the old man, but there was a gleam of amusement in his eyes. Sam Hunter could respect a worthy antagonist; in fact, one reason he'd come to Baltimore prepared to face down Greg Alexander and the plan for a new Clinic was because Greg had given in at the board meeting two years ago and agreed to accept a compromise. The surgeon had, however, risen sharply in the old man's opinion since he'd learned of the newspaper article that afternoon.

"I saved one of your own drilling outfits from having to shut down in the Persian Gulf just last year, Mr. Hunter," said Peter.

"How's that?"

"Some *Anopheles gambiae* mosquitos—the kind that carry malignant malaria—had been brought into the area on company planes. We found them in baggage loaded in Ghana and for a few months the whole operation was about to be stalled by malignant malaria—"

"So you went about swatting mosquitoes?"

"No." Peter grinned. "We used the human approach—killed them with sex."

"What a happy way to die." Claire Anders had just joined the group again with Jeanne. "I'd like you to meet Jeanne Alexander, Sam. I'm trying to convince her you're not an ogre at all but a very nice man."

Sam Hunter greeted Jeanne with courtly grace and Peter Carewe kissed her. "It's been too long since I've had one of those dinners you used to cook when I was a senior medical student, Jeanne."

"None of us had any money," he explained to the others, "so Jeanne would make a big pot of sauerkraut and wieners and ask us over. Where's Greg?"

"I talked to him a little while ago on the phone," she said. "He has to stay close to the operating room until the question of the transplant is decided."

"Nobody's talking about anything else, and Ed and Henry are fit to be tied," said Claire. "Confidentially, they planned this whole affair to impress you, Sam, and now Greg's stolen their thunder. But don't let me interrupt whatever you were discussing."

"I was telling Mr. Hunter how we stopped an epidemic of malignant malaria in the Persian Gulf last year, when Anopheles gambiae mosquitoes carrying the disease, were brought in by plane," said Peter. "You see, we'd learned how to record the mating call of the female mosquito on a tape recorder, so all we had to do was to play the tapes close to open flames from a kerosene burner. Then when the males came flying in, they were incinerated."

"That's cruel," said Claire in mock horror. "Did the females incinerate themselves too, like the Indian wives used to do—what do they call that?"

"Suttee!" said Sam Hunter. "I saw it happen once in India when I was traveling there a long time ago."

"How terribly romantic," said Claire. "Like something the Bronte sisters might have written."

"Life doesn't happen that way," said Peter. "In the Persian Gulf, the female gambiae soon took up with other mosquitoes, but fortunately they didn't breed true. Pretty soon all the carriers of malignant malaria died off and so did the epidemic."

"The eternal adaptability of the female," said Helen. "Sometimes I think it's the only thing that has kept the human race alive."

"Are you a philosopher, Doctor?" Sam Hunter asked.

"My work usually deals with the smallest unit of the human body, the single cell," she explained. "When you study life in a microcosm, everything boils down to simple principles of growth and survival."

"Monotonous, isn't it?" said Claire. "I'm glad humans vary the pattern."

"As I watch a culture of cells, every now and then one of them begins to vary beyond the ordinary limits established by genetics, as we know it," said Helen. "When that happens, a predator is loosed upon the rest of the growth and the destruction is almost beyond belief."

"Are you implying that those of us who succeed in business are predators who prey upon ordinary little people?" Sam Hunter asked.

"Not necessarily," she said. "But do you deny that strong men usually succeed because of the failure of many weak ones?"

"If all were of the same strength, no one would get ahead."

"I still say that orderliness is admirable," she insisted. "That way the entire life cycle of a single cell is predictable, along with the nature of its offspring."

"It's a lot more fun to have a little variety," said Claire. "Fortunately, the pill has taken care of that situation."

"With everybody so busy enjoying themselves, they'll stop bothering to raise children," Jeanne objected. "Then the birth rate will fall off even more sharply than it already has and we'll be overrun by more fertile races. I think it was Will Durant who said in one of his lectures that the final determining factor in the rise and fall of any civilization is the birth rate. As it becomes more and more highly developed, the rate tends to fall—"

"The American birth rate has been dropping steadily, except for the brief period of upsurge produced by the war babies," said Helen.

"Exactly," Jeanne agreed. "While at the same time, the population of the less highly civilized areas—according to our standards—is increasing faster than the food supply. Eventually they'll overrun the more highly developed nations and then the cycle will start all over again."

"What the more highly civilized nations need to realize," said Peter, "is that by helping others to learn to look after themselves through measures like birth control and raising more food, they're actually protecting their own cultures. What really destroys an advanced civilization is selfishness, their refusal to share with others the bounty their own intelligence produces."

"You're leaving out one important factor, Doctor," said Sam Hunter.
"What's that, sir?"

"Hard work. If the 'have nots' you're so busy bleeding about would get
out and work, they'd pretty soon rise out of their own ruts into the higher
level of the 'haves.'"

"You can't work very hard when the tapeworms, hookworms, or filariae
in your body use up your food faster than you do, Mr. Hunter," said Peter.
"And it's hard to be energetic when your blood's so pale from anemia that it
doesn't even look like blood at all. As a doctor, the world is my practice and
I can't see much sense in the American government paying farmers not to
plant wheat and corn when everybody concerned would be a lot better off if
they were allowed to plant all they could and sell it for use abroad. The only
countries I've seen where communism has made any real inroads lately are
those where the people were so hungry and sick they'd turn to anything.
That's why we in the UN are working so hard to find cheap sources of food,
like wheat and rice strains that produce twice as much grain as the ones we
have now."

"The answer may be somewhere else," said Helen. "In our laboratory,
we've managed to create a few mutations by exposing algae to X-ray. Some
of them have bred true for many generations."

"What do you mean, Doctor?" Sam Hunter asked.

"A mutation is a new individual that doesn't follow the pattern of the
parent cell or, with more complicated growths, the pattern of the species,"
she explained. "We're studying the green growths called algae that
accumulate in water everywhere, hoping to find a mutation that will grow so
rapidly it piles up cells and eventually forms a source of food."

"But algae need food, too, don't they?" Jeanne asked.

"They *do*," said Helen, "but there's an almost inexhaustible supply in
organic waste that's now thrown away or destroyed. By growing algae
selectively, so to speak, we hope to fine a food source whose proportions of
protein, carbohydrates and even fats can be regulated by controlling the
area in which they grow. A highly concentrated protein food material that's
cheap to produce is the one thing most hungry people in the world need
more than anything else."

"So you'll feed them up to where they're strong enough to destroy us, eh,
Doctor?" said Sam Hunter.

"I don't think that's a valid argument, Mr. Hunter," she protested. "The
course of history has been that, as a people become better fed and more
civilized, they tend to lose many of their more aggressive characteristics."

"Fat and lazy?"

"Which would you rather have, Mr. Hunter?" Peter Carewe asked. "Fat
and lazy Chinamen enjoying the good things of life, or a hungry horde
waiting to pour down into the rice bowl of Asia and seize control of half the
world?"

"There's a weakness in your theory, Dr. Foucald," said the oilman. "The
Germans are one of the most highly industrialized civilizations in the world
and have been for a long time. They eat well and heavily, yet they've started
two wars in my lifetime."

"I think the danger is that people who are prosperous can get so fat and
lazy they don't bother to control the few individuals who turn into predators
in order to achieve positions of power for themselves," said Jeanne
Alexander. "That's what happened in Germany, but I still think a nation
hungry for food is more of a danger in the world than a few individuals
hungry for power."

"Especially if the rest of the world watches out for the development of
such megalomaniacs, and controls them," said Peter Carewe.

"And how do you propose to do that, Doctor?" the oilman asked.

"That's the function of the United Nations, sir."

"Humph!" The old man expressed his opinion of the world organization in the single expletive. "What have they done? A lot of talk and nothing else."

"Perhaps that's just where the UN has actually accomplished most," Peter Carewe insisted. "It's true that there has been a lot of talk, but with our modern means of communication, the whole world has been able to hear, and many of them see, who's really trying to keep peace and who's doing everything they can to set men against each other. If it hadn't accomplished anything else except that, I think the United Nations would have amply justified itself, but the really important work of the United Nations is being done in health centers throughout the world, trying to relieve disease, improve health, decrease suffering and cut down birth rates that keep people so poor they can't provide for the children they're so busy producing."

"Hear! Hear!" said Claire Anders. "Now, why don't you beautiful and intelligent people stop monopolizing each other and start mingling with the guests. This is supposed to be a social get-together and not a forum for deciding the problems of the world."

III

"You do have a way of corralling the most handsome men, Claire," Hannah McDougal said when Claire came over to where she was standing in the corner with a glass in her hand, talking to Henry. Hannah's face was flushed and a slight slurring of words betrayed the fact that she had been drinking steadily since she had come into the room—to say nothing of before.

"I wouldn't say that, darling," said Claire. "Where's Ed?"

"Off somewhere having a council of war."

"Why aren't you with him, Henry?" Claire asked. "Or have they excluded you from the highest councils?"

"Damn it, Claire—"

"Please—no profanity before our guests. Excuse me, Hannah, I quite forgot that you're a hostess."

"You're welcome to forget it when the time comes to pay the bar bill," Hannah told her. "The way these people are swilling down expensive liquor is enough to make you shudder."

"I still think we should have had a barbecue," said Claire as she moved away to speak to other guests.

Hannah gave Henry an appraising look and, conscious of it, he preened himself a little. "This party's getting pretty dull," she said. "What say we cut and run?"

He looked around to see if anyone could have heard, but they were alone at the moment. "What about Ed?"

"Oh, he'll be gabbing with those cronies of his until the small hours. It always happens this way when we go to a convention, so I've learned to look after myself." The implication was obvious enough even for Henry Anders to understand.

"Ed deserves anything that happens for running off and leaving us alone." Hannah moved a little closer so her body casually touched Henry's. "Why don't we have a drink together in my suite upstairs. The liquor's better and I'm sure there are a lot of things we need to talk about."

"How soon?" Henry wet his lips with his tongue.

"Maybe half an hour. People will be drifting out to dinner by then."

"Henry's about to make his play," Claire observed *sotto voce* to Jeanne Alexander when she saw Hannah McDougal drift casually toward the door, stopping to speak to several people on the way.

"Don't you even mind?"

"If it wasn't Hannah, it would be Helen Foucald, though I have an idea that arrangement is due for a shake-up, judging by the look of those two yonder in the bar." Claire nodded toward where Helen and Peter had been joined by the dean of the School of Public Health. "It would take a lot stronger woman than Helen—or me—to resist a man like that Peter Carewe. I think she's gone off the deep end for him."

"I still can't help being a little shocked by all this," Jeanne confessed. "Maybe I'm too old-fashioned for today."

"Stay the way you are and shelter what you already have in the love of a good man," Claire advised. "You'd be surprised to know how infrequently that happens."

CHAPTER FOURTEEN

I

Dr. Herbert Partridge was halfway down the corridor to the lobby, intending to cross The Parkway to the Inn, in case the party was still in progress, when the pager in the pocket of his white coat beeped sharply. He turned aside immediately to the nearest telephone—in the office of the pediatric section.

"Dr. Partridge."

"Intensive care wants you, Doctor. The nurse said right away."

"Tell Dr. Johnson and Dr. Alexander I'm going there and will report as soon as I find out the situation." The neurosurgeon knew Frank Lawson's heart was still beating, for, if it had stopped, the Code One alert would have been flashed on the entire hospital paging system.

Code One automatically sent teams trained in all phases of cardiac resuscitation to the area of emergency, including those specially skilled in using the new closed-chest method, where the heart was literally massaged between the breastbone and the spine by pressure upon the chest. It also alerted a team for open-chest surgery, if that became necessary, but between the new closed-chest method and the cardiac Pacemaker that could jolt a stopped heart into action with repeated minute currents of electricity, open-chest surgery was rarely ever used any more for this greatest of complications.

Herbert Partridge found the intern assigned to intensive care beside Frank Lawson's bed. Across from him was a nurse who had also been watching the slowly dying man; no patient with a tracheostomy tube in place was ever left unwatched, because of the possibility that the tube might be blocked by coughed-up secretions and cause immediate suffocation.

One look at Frank Lawson's face explained why the neurosurgeon had been called. As if amused by some macabre joke hidden deep within his brain, his features were twisted in a maniacal grin.

"He started doing that about five minutes ago," the nurse said with a shudder. "It's almost like he was laughing inside at something."

"Risus sardonicus." Herb Partridge spoke the words that popped into his conscious mind from some deep store of memory, put away long ago in medical school and rarely used since.

"Doesn't that have something to do with poisoning?" the young intern asked.

"Strychnine causes convulsive spasms of the face and neck at first before it involves the whole body," said the neurosurgeon. "So does tetanus."

"He couldn't possibly have developed tetanus this early, I'm sure." The intern leafed through the chart quickly. "Besides, they gave him toxoid when he was brought in."

Herbert Partridge's trained mind was working like the computer it actually was, sorting wheat from chaff as it considered the possibilities represented by the symptom complex he was watching and seeking to reach one diagnosis that fitted the entire picture. Suddenly the whole pattern fell into place.

"He's gone into a convulsive state," he told the intern.

"But why?"

"The hemorrhage must have reached some of the vital centers of the brain. We had a warning of it earlier, when his temperature started to rise."

"Why is the convulsion limited to the upper neck and the face?"

"Actually, it isn't. If the rest of his body hadn't been disconnected from the brain when his spinal cord was severed, this would be a generalized spasm. And if that tracheostomy tube wasn't giving him a clear airway through the windpipe, we'd be fighting right now to keep his breathing from being shut off entirely by the contraction of his throat and chest muscles."

"I've never seen anything like this," said the intern in an awed voice.

"The only muscles actually receiving impulses from the brain and going into spasm are those connected to that part of the nervous system which is still intact," Herb Partridge explained. "That means the cranial nerves connected to the brain itself and those coming off the first few segments of the spinal cord above the point where it's severed. Everything below the spinal cord wound is disconnected and, therefore, cannot respond, so the rest of his body doesn't convulse."

"I'm glad of it," said the nurse. "This is scary enough."

The pocket pager in Herb Partridge's coat beeped again and he went to the phone at the nurses' station; it was Greg Alexander.

"Frank Lawson's in an almost continuous convulsive state," the neurosurgeon reported in answer to Greg's query. "It's the damnedest thing you ever saw. Only the face and upper neck muscles still connected to the nervous system are in spasm."

"How about the heart?"

"The rate has increased sharply, so the brain control by way of the autonomic nervous system is undoubtedly involved, too. Do you want me to bring him down to the O.R. suite so you'll be ready?"

"I'd appreciate it," said Greg. "Lew Gann and Bob Johnson went to get an early dinner in the cafeteria and I can't leave the area. You don't think Lawson's in any immediate danger of a heart stoppage, do you?"

"No. His pulse is still strong. What about Merchant?"

"The tracheostomy helped his breathing but his heart's weakening fast. I think this is going to be close, Herb—very close."

"I'll bring Lawson down to one of the anesthetic rooms and attach electroencephalographic terminals to his scalp so we can monitor the brain waves. From the looks of his condition right now, they should be skittering all over the tube."

"Is Mrs. Merchant still up there?" Greg asked.

"I think so. She was in the waiting room when I came up."

"Ask someone to show her down to the corridor outside the O.R. I think I'd better bring her up to date on what's happening."

A sofa had been placed at the end of the corridor beyond the line, plainly marked upon floor, walls and ceiling, where only authorized operating room personnel were allowed to go—and then only when wearing special shoes.

"What's happening, Doctor?" Georgia asked when Greg came down the first-floor corridor to where she waited. "Dr. Partridge said they're taking Frank Lawson to the operating room."

"He's begun to have convulsions and we want him where we can be ready in case there's any sudden change," he explained.

"What about Guy?"

"Putting the tube into his windpipe and giving him the special injection has helped some," said Greg. "But his lungs are beginning to fill up again, showing that his heart is still having trouble keeping up the circulation."

"Can you give him something else to remove the fluid?"

"We don't want to use the drug too often. It hits the kidneys pretty hard to make them remove extra fluid and we could damage them."

"Maybe it would be better to just let him go on and die."

"I couldn't do that, Mrs. Merchant, even if you asked me."

"I know," she said. "This morning when they were trying to start Guy's heart, I prayed for him to die. My conscience has been troubling me ever since."

"It shouldn't," he assured her. "You had no way of knowing then that we might have a chance to save him."

"The newspaperman who talked to me this afternoon said you're risking your own position here to give Guy a chance. Is that true?"

"What I'm risking isn't important, compared to being able to save a life that's doomed otherwise."

"But if you *should* fail, couldn't things be bad for you?"

"Doctors always hate to lose a patient—in spite of the jokes you hear about us."

"I got a glimpse of Frank Lawson's face as they were taking him to the operating room." She shuddered at the memory. "He's dying, isn't he?"

"Yes."

"And the sooner you operate on Guy, the better off he'll be?"

"No question about that."

"Then can't you hurry Lawson's going a little?"

"Even the court can't name me his executioner, Mrs. Merchant."

"Would you accept the responsibility if it did—in order to save the life of another?"

Greg shook his head. "Chronic hospital wards are filled with people dying from cancer and other incurable diseases. If we perfect the heart-lung transplant operation to where it's rather uniformly successful, there will be a lot of pressure from people doomed by heart disease to take the hearts of those who can't be saved and give them to those who can. But doctors shouldn't be forced to make the final decision."

"Why?"

"Taking another man's life is still murder, unless the state orders it; I'm not at all sure it still isn't murder, even then. My own conscience would make me wait until Frank Lawson is pronounced dead, even if the state gave permission to end his life earlier."

"It's all so complicated," she said. "I want to have Guy well and I know that's what you want, too. Just go ahead and do what you think needs to be done, Dr. Alexander. I'd rather not even know what's happening until it's over—one way or the other."

"That's the better way, I'm sure," he agreed. "Once we start operating, we won't be able to keep you posted on the course of events anyway. Don't you want me to order a sedative for you so you can get a little rest?"

"No, thank you. Guy and I always bore our share of the load, until he got to where he couldn't carry his any longer. It would be sort of disloyal to him if I let down now."

On his way back to the operating suite, Greg met Jud Templeton outside one of the first-floor doors leading to the surgical lecture room. "I'm keeping a weather eye on those closed-circuit TV screens in there," he said. "The emergency room intern says that, when you operate, the whole thing can be seen there."

"We do televise important operations," said Greg, and added pointedly—"For doctors."

Jud Templeton grinned. "I've got a special invitation—remember? Are you going to revoke it?"

"No."

"They tell me that Lawson's gone into a convulsive state. Is this the end?"

"The beginning of it."

"Couldn't happen to a more deserving fellow. Any repercussions on my story?"

"Not yet. I think it threw the enemy into a state of confusion, but they'll counterattack before long."

"If Lawson hurries up his dying, you may be able to deal them another blow with a successful transplant. It's like an old-time Western—the beleaguered garrison, the Indians outside the wall and the relief column racing to the rescue. Only, this time, I guess the Indians are ahead."

"We haven't given up the fort," said Greg with a smile. "There may still be quite a battle."

II

The announcement via the TV screen that both Guy Merchant and Frank Lawson were now in surgery exploded in the midst of the Anders-McDougal cocktail party in the Falstaff Room at the Clinic Inn. Peter Carewe and Helen Foucald saw it first in the bar, where they were having a drink before dinner.

"I'll have to be in the lab when the operation on Guy Merchant really starts," she said. "Sometimes emergency proceedings are needed in a hurry to determine blood gases and things like that."

"But we can still have dinner here while you're waiting."

"Why not?" She opened her bag and took out the small, cigarette-case-size pager. "When the time comes, the hospital operator can call me."

A general exodus from the room had followed the TV announcement. "Call me when the real action starts, will you, Bill?" Peter told Bill Remick, who was just leaving. "We'll be here in the dining room."

"Well, that ends the party." Claire Anders took a fresh drink for herself and moved over to where Sam Hunter was talking to Jeanne Alexander.

"Nothing's duller than the end of a dull party, when you have to stay on feet that already hurt, waiting for the last straggler to leave," she said. "Jeanne, why don't you and I take Mr. Hunter to dinner in the restaurant?"

"I wouldn't be able to eat anything until the transplant operation is settled," said Jeanne. "You and Mr. Hunter go on, Claire. I'll have milk and crackers or something in our apartment, where I can watch the TV screen. Good night, Mr. Hunter. I enjoyed talking to you."

"Good night, Mrs. Alexander," the old man said. "Your husband and I haven't always seen eye to eye lately, but I can still wish him well with his surgery."

"That's more than a lot of people are doing right now," said Claire. "Don't worry about the luncheon tomorrow, Jeanne. Everything's under control."

"Where's Henry?" Sam Hunter asked as he and Claire moved toward the dining room, where the head waiter greeted them obsequiously.

"Oh, he's occupied somewhere," Claire said airily. "Probably deep in the heart of Texas—to make a lousy pun."

"You're a very remarkable woman, Claire," said the old man as they were being seated at the table. "I've never known but one like you."

"Don't tell me she was a saloon keeper on the frontier. You know—the one with the heart of gold who's a pushover for the handsome gambler."

"She was a countess in Italy—Salerno, to place it exactly."

"I remember Salerno well." Claire's tone was suddenly faraway. "Henry and I went there on our honeymoon. What was she like—this *contessa* of yours?"

"Very lovely and very blue-blood—like you."

"But not gone to seed, like my family."

"You certainly haven't gone to seed, my dear," he said gallantly.

"Only because I'm what you Texans call a maverick. Even as a little girl, I wouldn't let mother put me in starched dresses and do my hair in pigtails. Instead, I played baseball with the rest of the boys, until I was around fourteen."

"What happened then?"

"The groceryman's son and I were wrestling one day and he accidentally found out I wasn't a boy. I discovered the same thing a few minutes later—and I've never been the same since."

Sam Hunter smiled. "How much of this sort of talk is a shell to hide your disappointment at being married to a windbag?"

"You're not supposed to know that," she protested. "Ed McDougal and his cronies are somewhere upstairs right now, planning how they're going to pull the strings to make you jump."

"What if I don't jump the way they want me to?"

Claire studied him for a moment—then smiled. "My guess is they're much more liable to jump the way *you* want them to. I'm sure you didn't get to be one of the richest men in the world by letting people like Ed and Henry run over you."

"I owed ten years of additional happiness with my wife to your husband's father," the old man said soberly. "If I go on now and let Dr. Alexander build this new hospital he's planning behind my back—"

"Greg Alexander never did a really underhanded thing in his life," said Claire. "My guess is that he's got an idea and thinks you'll buy it, if you see it in a really understandable form and not just as a fragment."

"If I go along with that idea, it would be a blow to Henry."

"And to Ed McDougal?"

"I've dealt with Ed's kind all my life, but I don't want to slap Henry down, even though right now I suspect I should take him across my knee and give him a good hiding."

"Do what you think is best according to your conscience; I'll take care of Henry," said Claire. "Now, tell me about this Italian contessa of yours. She sounds like somebody I'd like."

"She was very sophisticated and I was anything but—still am, for that matter. But when you've got half a billion, you can do as you damn please and the worst people will say about you is that you're eccentric. The contessa taught me that the relationship between a man and a woman who don't intend to marry can still be—I don't exactly know the word."

"Something more than tumbling a Mexican maid in the barn when your parents weren't looking."

"Why, yes. How did you know?"

"Women have their moments, too, but if they've got any sense, they soon realize that romantic love eventually burns itself out like a fever. So most of 'em end up marrying the boy their family approves of and living moderately happily ever after—on their memories. Dessert every meal can get pretty tiresome; you need some meat and potatoes for regular fare—until your hips start spreading and you have to cut them out. You'd be surprised how many of my friends spend most of their time going from doctor to doctor or knocking themselves out with tranquilizers because they're not willing to accept reality and make the best of it. What every woman really needs is a perfect husband and a perfect lover; it's too bad they're rarely ever found in the same person."

"The contessa said almost the same thing."

"It must be a wonderful fulfillment for a woman to know she will live on as a romantic image in the heart and mind of a man she was happy with, however briefly." Claire's tone was wistful. "I imagine it's little like being immortalized in a painting, the way Goya did the Duchess of Alba."

"Aren't you happy with Henry, Claire?"

"Who's happy?" she said with a shrug. "Henry is a lousy husband but a superb lover. When he finishes love-making, he goes to sleep; and when he gets up in the morning, he goes to the hospital." Her smile was overly brilliant, her tone brittle, like a piece of fine china. "I have the best of Henry when I want it and only a little of the worst, so I'm very fortunate, wouldn't you say?"

"And yet you're afraid."

Claire Anders gave the old millionaire a startled look and for a moment the hard bright façade she presented to the world crumpled, like the false front of a Western movie set in a high wind. But it was only for an instant, then everything was in place again.

"Why do you say that?"

"Once in Salerno, I saw the contessa looking at a workman who was repairing a wall. There was the same sort of hunger in her eyes, just for an instant, that I'd seen in the eyes of a coyote caught in a fence on the range and starving. I knew then that it was time for me to go back to the States, while I still had some memories I wanted to keep."

He reached across the table and put his hand over Claire's in a gesture that was extraordinarily tender for a man who had broken powerful opponents on many occasions, ruthlessly and without compunction. "Whatever happens on Saturday, I won't let it be anything that would cause you pain."

"Thank you, Sam." She squeezed his hand. "But what about Greg's new building?"

"I'll cross that bridge when I come to it. To have earned the loyalty of so many people, I suspect Dr. Alexander is strong enough to take another disappointment—if he has to."

CHAPTER FIFTEEN

I

"I wonder what Claire and Sam Hunter are so busy talking about," Peter Carewe said as he and Helen were waiting for the steaks he had selected to be cooked. "I wouldn't have thought they had much in common."

"Claire's a rare sort of bird—and so, I imagine, is Mr. Hunter."

"I don't know her very well."

"That's a condition she would have remedied by now—if I hadn't seen you first."

"I'm glad you did," he told her. "Now, tell me something about your work. I want to learn all about you between now and Friday."

Dear God, not everything, Helen thought, but deep in her heart she knew the prayer would be of no avail. She'd seen Peter's eyes when Henry Anders had burst into the apartment that evening; while he might not have jumped to any conclusions then, he was no fool and Henry's every action, when he found them together, had spoken the truth far louder than any words could have done.

"I've been working with Greg Alexander on the problems of automating the laboratory," she said.

"I enjoyed his paper this afternoon—but I was envious, too," said Peter. "In the jungle, we're lucky to have a microscope and enough material to do an elementary job of culturing bacteria."

"I've seen some of the machines Greg spoke about," she said. "They've even got one now that can take mass survey electrocardiograms, and sound a warning when the test shows something abnormal."

"A lot of mossbacks in the AMA aren't going to like anything that looks like production-line medicine," he warned. "They've been fighting it since the thirties."

"They'll have to accept automation. Progress is already passing them by."

"Shape up or ship out, eh?"

"Why not, when doctors are digging their own graves by sticking to the horse and buggy approach to medical care represented by the individual physician practicing alone in his own office? A whole new medical generation is coming out of the hospitals now. They know nothing except partially automated clinic medicine and that's enough to make them realize the handwriting's on the wall for the old ways. When they get out into practice and see patients running all over town from doctor to doctor, spending days getting a complete examination and laboratory checkup that could be done in one place in a tenth of the time and at half the cost, things are going to change—fast."

"There will still be opposition by the conservative wing," he warned. "Look what's happening here this week—in a clinic that's been one of the most advanced medical centers in the world for the past fifty years."

"If Greg wins out on the new building, we'll prove we're right."

"Whatever happens, you're safe," he assured her. "You could be a success in any field if you bring to it the same energy you put into your profession."

"The same is true of you."

"Oh no. I'm the doctor from WHO—medical playboy."

"I'll never believe that, not after the way you put Sam Hunter in his place when he started belittling your work tonight."

"It could cost me my job. That old man is powerful."

"Not as powerful as the Russians—and you coped with them."

"That was a labor of love. Speaking of love, I've know you about nine hours now and I'm more strongly attracted to you than I've been to any woman I've ever met."

"I guess it's entirely unmaidenly of me, but that goes for me, too."

"Then what stands between us?"

"In the first place, love at first sight doesn't happen—except in popular novels and in the movies."

"It happened to us—at least to me."

"But your feeling is physiological."

"What's wrong with physiology? We couldn't get along without it."

"It's all right for an affair—the more physiology and less real love you have then, the better off both parties are. But I'm not sure I want to have an affair with you, Peter."

"Surely you're not afraid?"

She shook her head. "I'm thirty-five years old and not exactly repulsive, so it stands to reason that I've slept in other beds than my own—and not alone."

"Spare me the details."

"That's one reason why I'm not sure I want an affair with you," she said. "Already, you aren't certain you could keep it at just that level, else it wouldn't make any difference to you how many men I've slept with. In fact, you'd hope, subconsciously at least, that the number was large."

"Wherever did you discover that kind of reasoning?"

"It's really rather elementary psychology. If I've had a lot of lovers, it stands to reason I'm pretty good in bed."

"We're talking about *you,*" he said with a show of anger. "Not some streetwalker."

"I may not be far above those, either. You have no way of knowing."

"If I have good taste in anything, it's in women," he protested. "That's why I singled you out this morning the very first time I saw you."

"Your picking me out was a real compliment—and I appreciate it," she said. "You have quite a reputation as a connoisseur and practically every woman here tonight was wondering what it would be like to go to bed with you. A woman can make love with a man she doesn't respect and even enjoy herself—we're perverse creatures, you know. But to live with a man and be happy, she's got to respect him."

"Do I have to perform some feat of arms to convince you I'm sincere, like a knight of old vying for his lady fair?"

"Lancelot won Guinevere's love simply by being *le bel knight sans reproche* if I remember the French correctly."

"I'm not perfect enough for that." His tone was serious now. "I'll even admit to being a little vain and really enjoying the adulation that goes with my job."

"Plus the opportunities for—shall we say—amorous dalliance?"

"That too. After all, I'm a normal male animal."

"The phrase Claire Anders used was 'gorgeous male animal.'"

"But not gorgeous enough to sweep you off your feet?"

"I'm trying to tell you I'm not like those girls who've been throwing themselves at you. I have a career of my own, to which I am very dedicated."

"That needn't—"

"Two careers rarely fit into a marriage. Look what happens so often in the movie colony."

"As well compare hothouse orchids to cabbages."

"Nevertheless, the symptoms can be diagnosed," she insisted. "I'm a very competent woman who's been holding her own successfully for some time in a masculine world. Which means that I'm essentially masculine myself."

"Nobody could guess it to look at you."

"I'm talking about my essential drives, the forces that made me chief of laboratories here at The Clinic."

"Any woman who's active in spheres outside her home has the same drives you have, but that doesn't necessarily mean she has to leave home because of them. Claire Anders is a good example."

"Claire feeds her ego with her intellectual superiority over Henry—plus the fact that she's wealthy in her own right."

"What do you feed on?"

"My ability to hold my own in my field against all comers."

"Was that the reason you left France? Because French women are expected to stay at home and not play a large part in men's affairs?"

"That—and marriage."

"I wondered about that," he said. "Did you love him very much?"

"I thought I did. He was older, a professor, and I considered myself his intellectual inferior."

"I'll give odds that you learned better."

"It's no bet. I saw him at an international medical convention in Boston several years later. He'd turned into a little pouter pigeon of a man, all bombast and no substance."

"Do you really think he was any different then than when you thought he was your ideal?"

"I'm sure he hadn't changed a bit. But I had, and I wondered then what I had ever seen in him."

"Did you ever decide what it was?"

She nodded. "You may not like to hear this, but I'm being very honest with you. I suppose it's no accident that the great lovers of history are so often small men; they make up in other ways for their lack of height. He taught me not to be afraid of drives—the essential id, I suppose it should be called in Freudian terminology. I'd known they were there but I'd been suppressing them through fear."

"You know why you really broke off that affair, don't you?"

"I told you—"

"You were rationalizing then—to avoid admitting the real reason for your flight from France. Your relationship with this pouter pigeon was purely physical and, being a woman of strong urges, you were afraid his attraction for you might put your mind into servitude to him."

She didn't answer, but instead lifted her glass and looked at the amber liquid as if searching within it for some portent of the future. "Here we are, trying to be very modern, even flippant, about what's happened to us in the last nine hours," she said at last. "And neither of us succeeding very well, because I suspect that deep down inside us, we're both pretty old-fashioned."

"Don't let it get around. You'll ruin my reputation as a playboy."

"Would that be so bad?"

"That's what I'm trying to decide. I haven't had a chance to talk to you about it but John Teague has offered me something of a roving professorship, with two purposes. One is to use the glamour that has latched on to me to induce more young doctors to enter the public health field."

"I don't know anybody who could do it better."

"I wouldn't take the job for that reason alone, but John also wants me to help him sell a much larger concept."

"To whom?"

"This city, to start off with; then, using it as an example, to the rest of the country and perhaps the world—though that's too big a task at the moment. He calls it the 'Whole Man Concept.'"

"I heard him talk on it at one of the staff meetings," she said.

"Do you agree?"

"Absolutely. Greg is fighting for the same thing in trying to keep The Clinic where it's always been, instead of letting it be moved out on the Beltway."

"Until this morning, I didn't think much about John's offer. But since I met you, the idea of staying here has become pretty attractive."

"You mustn't be guided by that," she said quickly.

"Suppose I left the decision to you—what would it be?"

She looked away and he saw her fingers tighten on the stem of the wine glass until he wondered whether it might not snap.

"Don't rush the decision," he said, wanting to help her and conscious, too, that he needed to gain time for himself. "We'll talk about it again—at breakfast."

II

As Herb Partridge had predicted, the pattern of Frank Lawson's electroencephalogram on the monitor appeared to have gone crazy. Through electrodes attached to his scalp, the tiny action currents of electricity accompanying all brain activity were led to the delicate machine, where they were amplified to enable them to be studied carefully. Small and large waves appeared helter-skelter on the tube of the monitor with practically no relationship to the pattern of wave motion characterizing normal brain action.

"I never saw anything like this before," said the neurosurgeon when Greg Alexander came in with Dr. Philip Dennison, the medical examiner. "His brain has practically gone wild."

"The blood pressure's beginning to fall a little, too," reported the nurse-anesthetist who was watching the patient. "It's one hundred now over seventy."

"As the pressure falls, the rate of hemorrhage into the brain itself will probably decrease," said Herb Partridge. "Which means dragging the whole thing out even farther."

"How do you plan to handle the organs for transplantation?" the medical examiner asked.

"My assistant, Bob Johnson, is standing by in the other operating room," Greg explained. "Merchant has been in there for the last several hours so we could have him near the main pump-oxygenator. When the time comes here, I'll make a quick incision and remove the heart and lungs. Meanwhile, Bob will be getting ready in the other room."

"Do you plan to attach Lawson's heart to a pump to maintain the coronary circulation?" Dr. Dennison asked.

"I think not—unless we have trouble preparing Merchant for the transplant," said Greg. "We discovered with our dogs that the time you take connecting the donor organs to the pump-oxygenator can be better spent in getting the transplant into place in the recipient and the blood vessels connected up so its circulation can function. Fortunately, we'll be transplanting both heart and lungs, so the problem of making the necessary blood vessel connections is not nearly so great."

"How's that?"

"By making a temporary coupling to the aorta first, we can circulate the recipient's blood through the donor's coronary arteries immediately," Greg explained. "That way, we can keep the heart alive while we're completing the other connections."

"Don't you still have the problem of keeping it alive during the transfer period?"

"If things work out as we hope they will, we should have ample time for that," said Greg. "While we're putting Merchant on the heart-lung pump we will be cooling his body rapidly to reduce the need for oxygen by the brain cells. As soon as we remove the donor's heart and lungs, we will place them in a container of Tyrode's solution and cool them rapidly, too. Once the tissues are cooled, their need for oxygen is reduced markedly, giving us more time to connect them to the body of the recipient. Of course, it would be better if we were able to place the donor in a hyperbaric chamber and saturate his heart and lungs with oxygen before removing them. But our chamber is located beside the Laboratory of Experimental Surgery, so the disadvantages in carrying the organs to the operating theater and the time involved more than outweigh anything we'd gain."

"Wouldn't it be better if you had both patient and donor side by side in adjacent pressure chambers?"

"When the new hospital is built, that's the way it's going to be."

"When? Not if?"

"It will be built someday—even if I have to move on somewhere else to make it possible."

"Has it come to that?" Dr. Dennison asked.

"I hope not," said Greg. "But there are plenty of other places with laboratories where I can go on with my work."

"I watched an open-heart operation once," the medical examiner said. "Just seeing a patient lying on the table without the heart and lungs functioning, while a pump made of metal, plastic and rubber took over, gave me the willies. And when they started warming the heart at the end of the operation and it went crazy, that was too much for me."

"Ninety-five over sixty," the nurse-anesthetist reported. "The pulse is definitely weaker, too."

"Maybe Lawson will do one decent thing in his life and not waste time dying," said Herbert Partridge.

"Move him into the operating theater, Herb, and get things ready," Greg said quietly. "I'd appreciate your prepping him while I check on Merchant."

"Sure," said the neurosurgeon, and moved immediately through an adjoining door to the scrub room between the two main operating theaters, with its row of basins and, above each, a container of sterilized brushes.

"Those currents still look pretty strong to me." The medical examiner glanced at the monitor tube with the crazy pattern of brain waves registered there and shook his head doubtfully. "It could be quite a while yet."

"With the pressure dropping like it is, we can't afford to take any chances," said Greg. "If the hemorrhage in Lawson's brain hits a really vital center, he could die before we're ready."

"Dr. Alexander." The operating room supervisor spoke from the door, her voice urgent. "Dr. Johnson would like you to come to O.R. 2 right away, please. The patient's pulse is very weak."

III

"It happened so quickly, I hardly had time to call you, sir," Bob Johnson said when Greg came into the adjoining theater. "He was knocking along just like he's been doing for the past several hours, when suddenly he gave a gasp and his pulse started fading."

Where before Guy Merchant's breathing had been regular, though shallow, the rate was varied. The valve of the respirator would click rhythmically three or four times in a row, showing that the sick man was making no effort to breathe at all; then it would click rapidly as faint respiratory movements tripped the delicate controls and allowed breathing directly into the oxygen-filled breathing bag.

"Looks like he's had a pulmonary embolism," said Greg. "I should have anticipated it."

"Shall I start prepping him, sir?" Bob Johnson still wore the gown and gloves he'd worn while performing the tracheostomy and so did not need to scrub again. At Greg's nod, he changed swiftly into fresh sterile gown and gloves while the entire operating room staff moved into action like a well-kept machine.

"Make an incision over the femoral artery so we can get a cannula in there as quickly as possible," Greg directed as he moved to the scrub room. "Unless his condition improves in the next few minutes, I'm going to open his chest and put him on the pump-oxygenator."

It was a daring move, but the only choice if Guy Merchant were to be kept alive until the organs from Frank Lawson's body became available. In a case of severe coronary thrombosis, the danger was always present that clots would form inside the heart, where the blood supply to a portion of muscle had been shut down. Obviously this had happened and one of the clots had broken loose as an embolus floating in the bloodstream. Traveling through the pulmonary circulation from the right side of the heart, it had entered ever smaller arteries in the branching treelike pattern of the vessels in the lung, until finally one was reached through which it could not pass.

Trained to anticipate and cope with even the direst emergencies, the operating team went into action without panic or any lost motion. The fact that nobody knew just how long a patient could safely be carried on the pump-oxygenator with his heart and lungs practically stilled and his body in a state of what might be called suspended animation from cooling, was a problem they would face when it arose.

That the heart-lung pump could take over safely from the vital organs for which it substituted during the several hours often necessary to replace vital parts of the heart, such as valves, or to repair abnormal openings from faulty development, was well known. What Greg planned to do now, however, was to substitute the pump for Guy Merchant's heart and lungs while they waited for the substitute organs to become available. Thus every second Frank Lawson lived longer than the perhaps hundred and eighty minutes that it was known to be safe to keep the heart stilled, would take them that much farther into the unknown. And should Lawson's heart continue to beat for hours, the point might well come at which Greg would simply have to remove the pump connections, let Guy Merchant die and face the accusation that he had tried to keep him alive when death was inevitable so he could claim to be the first to transplant both heart and lungs, even in a hopeless case.

CHAPTER SIXTEEN

I

The announcement at the Anders-McDougal cocktail party that the main actors in the critical heart-lung transplant were being taken to the operating theaters had quickly emptied the Falstaff Room in favor of the surgical lecture room. But when the closed-circuit television screens at either side of the lecture hall remained blank and no immediate word came of just when actual surgery would begin, beyond the fact that both patients were ready, many of the doctors who had rushed there with the first announcement began to drift away.

When the screen on the left was suddenly illuminated with a picture of the hurried preparations being made to put Guy Merchant on the heart-lung machine, the room was less than half filled. Jud Templeton had been sitting on one of the back rows of seats, catnapping while he waited for some action to begin. At the sudden stir among the onlookers when the screen was illuminated, he came wide awake and moved quickly a dozen rows nearer the screen so he would be able to see better. At the same time, he took from his pocket a small notebook and a ball-point pen.

Jud had witnessed enough operations to be reasonably familiar with what was going on, but some of the equipment was new. A small plump man with a pince-nez was sitting two seats away from him and, when he recognized Dr. Timothy Puckett, a pediatrician who was also chairman of the Board of Trustees, he moved to the seat beside him.

"Where is the heart-lung pump?" he asked.

The small doctor looked at him over the rim of his glasses. "The pump-oxygenator is that machine you see at one side of the operating room, where the technicians are working," he said somewhat prissily. "First time you've ever seen open-heart surgery?"

Jud Templeton nodded, figuring that by remaining silent he was less likely to betray his lack of professional status. As he had hoped, Dr. Puckett seemed to have mistaken him for another doctor.

"The heart of the pump actually consists of those stainless steel discs inside the long plastic cylinder in the center; the one that's about a third filled with blood." Dr. Puckett evidently enjoyed showing off his knowledge. "A constant stream of oxygen pours through the long cylinder, and, when the metal discs revolve, they pick up a thin film of blood, exposing it to oxygen in the upper part of the tube, where it is absorbed by the hemoglobin of the blood. Carbon dioxide leaves the blood at the same time and is removed chemically before the oxygen is used again."

"It's certainly ingenious."

"And very efficient," said Dr. Puckett. "It takes the place of both the heart and the lungs by not only pumping blood through the body but supplying it with oxygen and removing the carbon dioxide at the same time."

"It hasn't been connected yet, has it?"

Dr. Puckett looked at him pityingly, as at one whose ignorance was beyond belief, but still did not appear to be suspicious.

"The patient's body is being cooled rapidly now to decrease the need for oxygen. At low temperatures, the metabolism of the body cells is slowed remarkably and they need very little oxygen in order to live, so the pump is able to supply it."

"Remarkable."

"When I was a Fellow here twenty years ago, none of this was even dreamed of."

"Isn't Dr. Alexander taking quite a chance?" Jud Templeton asked. "I mean, with a procedure that's still not fully established and all?"

"Working in a large clinic like this with a big charity population to draw from, Greg Alexander is able to do things that those of us in individual practice wouldn't dare to do," Dr. Puckett admitted.

"I guess a lot of doctors try to cut men like Alexander down because they don't have as much on the ball as he does," Jud Templeton observed. "Take this business about automating the hospital that he reported on this afternoon. Not many men would have the foresight or the courage to look that far ahead."

"There are arguments on both sides." The smaller man pursed his lips. "I've always believed in the biblical advice not to put new wine in old bottles."

"That was a practical matter a few thousand years ago; the bottles were made of skin, and, if the new wine hadn't finished fermenting, the gas might burst them." When Dr. Puckett looked disconcerted, he added, "I guess you use penicillin, don't you?"

"Of course."

"If you follow the same line of reasoning in your practice, you ought to feed your patients moldy bread instead."

"The inference seems rather far-fetched," Dr. Puckett said stiffly.

"That new wine-old bottle idea is like a lot of other adages," said the newspaperman. "Originally there was a very simple explanation for them, but people kept repeating them with an air of wisdom until finally they got so hoary with tradition that everybody lost sight of why they came about in the first place."

"You may be right. I never thought about it."

"You said just now that Dr. Alexander's a pioneer because, with such a large charity population in the area, he can do things other people might be afraid to do. Isn't that an argument against moving The Clinic?"

"Well—perhaps. But there are even stronger arguments in favor of it."

"Like what?"

Again Dr. Puckett shot him a suspicious look but seemed satisfied that the questioner was simply naïve. "There's the matter of access, for one thing. On the Beltway, paying patients from out of town could reach The Clinic much more easily."

"Dragging a sick kid a two-hour bus ride each way just so a few private patients can be comfortable doesn't sound like what old Dr. Anders had in mind when he built this hospital." Jud Templeton made no attempt to keep the contempt out of his voice. "I'll bet if the trustees decide to move it, the newspapers in this town will start raising hell. Poor people wouldn't be able to get to The Clinic any longer the way they do now, so nobody would gain, because then pioneers like Dr. Gregory Alexander wouldn't have the clinical material for important research and what The Clinic has meant to medicine for the last fifty years would be lost."

As the small doctor suddenly rose and started for the door, Jud Templeton grinned. Unless he was mistaken, Dr. Timothy Puckett would be busy preaching a new gospel to his fellow trustees between now and Friday's meeting.

II

"How is he, Lew?" Greg asked the anesthesiologist as he reached for a sponge to push back the rubber fingers of his glove so they would fit snugly over the tips and not interfere with the sensitivity of his touch. Having prepped and draped both the chest and groin of the patient, Bob Johnson was now making an incision in the latter area.

"Blood pressure's barely perceptible," Dr. Gann said. "If you had decided to do this ten minutes later, you'd be operating on a man who's clinically dead."

"Finish getting the femoral cannula in, Bob, then cannulate the inferior vena cava," Greg directed. "I'm going to do a median sternotomy so I can compress the heart while you connect the pump."

Beside the operating table, the pump technicians were working swiftly and skillfully, completing the task of charging the vital machine with pooled blood of Guy Merchant's type from the hospital blood bank. The surface area of his body had been calculated that morning and the fact determined that he would need just less than four liters—each a thousand cubic centimeters on the metric scale and just over a quart—of blood circulating per minute to maintain life when the pump took over. Now the machine stood waiting.

The long cylinder where the shining steel discs would shortly start turning to expose the blood to oxygen, just as was normally done in the lungs, was closed. The sterile plastic tubes that would connect it to Guy Merchant's body were filled and the ends were double-wrapped in bags of polyethylene to maintain sterility.

A resident surgeon was working on Guy Merchant's extended arm, exposing a small artery and vein in order to insert flexible plastic tubes called cannulae into them so the venous and arterial blood pressures could be constantly reported by lines moving across the face of the monitor that faithfully recorded all vital functions where they were instantly visible to the watching technicians, the surgeon and the anesthesiologist. Through a needle in Guy Merchant's foot vein, an anesthetic solution containing a muscle relaxant was slowly dripping into his body, while the respirator connected to his lungs by way of the tracheostomy tube and windpipe inflated them rhythmically sixteen times a minute.

Taking the scalpel handed him by the instrument nurse when he moved up to the table, Greg drew the blade the full length of Guy Merchant's breastbone, or sternum, splitting the skin and the tissues beneath it down to the bone in a single stroke. Inside a rubber bag beneath his body, an icy slush was being circulated meanwhile, rapidly lowering his body temperature.

"Oscillating saw," Greg said, and the instrument, protected by a sterile cover, came into his hands. The motor that drove the wedge-like blade, with its arc-shaped outer edge covered with teeth, began to whine and, as the blade vibrated rapidly back and forth, he lowered it to touch the whitish bone revealed in the depths of the incision.

The whine of the saw deepened as it bit into the bone and a spray of dust rose, to be dampened down as the resident, who had moved up to assist Greg now, sprayed sterile water upon the saw to keep it cool. Moving carefully so as to cut almost, but not quite, through the breastbone, because of possible damage to vital structures beneath it, Greg quickly sawed the length of the sternum. Then, with a heavy blade called a Lebsche knife, whose blunt, hoe-shaped foot protected anything beneath it from injury, he finished splitting the bone. Severing ligaments at its upper and lower end, he quickly spread the sternum apart, freeing the underside of the bone from the pericardial sac covering the heart.

"No perceptible pulse or spontaneous respiration," Dr. Lewis Gann reported.

"No pulsation in the radial cannula," the technician watching the electric monitor echoed.

As coolly as if he had not heard the reports indicating that Guy Merchant's heart action had ceased and he was now technically dead, Greg reached into the chest cavity through the narrow opening provided by the split breastbone and took the heart itself in his hand. At the same moment, Dr. Gann switched the respirator to a more strongly positive pressure in order to inflate the lungs and counteract the failure of Guy Merchant's respiration, which had occurred even before the heart had ceased to beat.

The heart was visible in Greg's hand now, lying immobile, with a wedge-shaped area of almost black muscle tissue indicating where the coronary artery had been blocked that morning by a thrombus, when Guy Merchant's first heart cessation of the day had occurred. Still keeping every movement deliberate and purposeful, for haste here could tear delicate structures and destroy any chance of success, Greg began to squeeze and release the heart rhythmically, simulating, with externally applied pressure by his own hand, the pumping effect normally achieved by each contraction of the heart.

The change in the patient's general condition from this maneuver was startling. With blood now being forced into the lungs and the rest of the body, the color of the tissues visible in the open wound improved remarkably as the normal exchange of oxygen in the lungs was resumed. The instrument nurse breathed an audible sigh at the success of this first step, but there was no relaxation of attention, for yet another critical action remained, the change from the pumping action of Greg's hand upon the exposed heart to that of the far more complicated pump-oxygenator.

"You're a pretty good heart substitute, Greg," said Dr. Lewis Gann. "If you can hold out."

For the first time, through a throat microphone beneath the collar of his gown connected to a jack in the floor, Greg spoke directly to the audience watching in the surgical lecture room by means of closed-circuit television.

"This patient went into *extremis* rather rapidly," he said, "so we had to act quickly in order to restore cardiac function until we are able to place him upon the pump-oxygenator. You can't see the change in the tissues without color, but we are maintaining a fairly adequate respiratory interchange by manual pressure alone."

While he was speaking, the resident assisting him had inserted a rib spreader, an instrument with blunt jaws which could be opened to any degree desired by means of its ratchet drive, into the incision. When the younger man turned the screw, the jaws of the instrument separated widely, opening the divided breastbone and giving Greg more room in which to continue his manipulation of the heart, as well as affording a complete view of the operative field for the onlookers.

Turning his head, Greg glanced at the small monitor screen back of Dr. Gann, where the TV picture being reproduced on a larger scale in the lecture room could be seen.

"I think you can see the area of darkened muscle here on the surface of the heart." With a blunt forceps from the instrument table, he traced the outline of the wedge-shaped area of damage with his free hand. "This is where the blood supply of the heart muscle was blocked early this morning due to an acute coronary thrombosis. When added to the chronic heart damage already present from hardened coronary arteries and previous episodes of thrombosis, this new insult brought on a state of heart failure which has progressed in spite of all measures to support the heart. The sudden emergency of the last few minutes, however, we believe to have been caused by an embolus to the lungs."

"Don't forget to remind them that you just brought a dead man back to life," Dr. Gann said *sotto voce*.

"As you know," Greg continued, "I propose at the earliest possible moment to transplant the heart and lungs of a healthy individual who is dying from an injury to the brain. Unfortunately, the progressively deteriorating condition of this patient made it necessary to intervene before the organs to be transplanted became available.

"My assistant, Dr. Robert Johnson, has just finished placing a cannula in the femoral artery through the small incision you may be able to see on your television screen in the right groin and upper thigh," he continued. "This will allow a return of arterial blood to the body after it has passed through the pump-oxygenator. He is now threading a perforated tube upward through the common femoral vein into the inferior vena cava to carry blood from the lower two thirds of the body to the pump before it can reach the heart.

"The pump, of course, is designed to maintain a steady flow of blood throughout the body, while at the same time supplying oxygen to this blood and removing carbon dioxide from it. The patient is also being cooled and I can already detect a marked lowering of temperature in the tissues around my hand. Once we are able to connect him to the heart-lung pump and inject previously cooled blood into his circulation, the rate of body cooling should increase very rapidly until we obtain a general temperature of about seventy-seven degrees Fahrenheit, the optimum for this sort of procedure."

Bob Johnson had finished placing the cannulas and two plastic tubes now led from the small wound in Guy Merchant's upper thigh to the heart-lung pump, with clamps in place to prevent circulation through them yet. Quickly, Bob changed gown and gloves and, slipping into the position Greg had been occupying, placed his hand around the heart and took up the rhythmic squeezing of the muscle without a beat being missed.

"We are now ready to connect the venous system of the patient to the pump-oxygenator, after which it will no longer be necessary to compress the heart or to operate the respirator," said Greg. "Fortunately, we shall not need to place special cannulas into the coronary arteries to maintain the heart's own circulation, as would be the case if we were repairing or replacing a valve or closing a defect."

While speaking, he had taken a forceps and gently picked up a portion of the thin-walled upper chamber, or atrium, on the right side of the heart. Using a needle threaded with tough black silk, he now began to sew a circular pattern called a purse-string suture around a portion of the wall about the size of a half dollar.

"If you remember your anatomy," Greg spoke into the microphone again for the benefit of the audience beyond the wall in the lecture room while he was placing the suture, working around Bob Johnson's hand, which still rhythmically squeezed the more muscular part of the heart comprising the ventricles, "the superior vena cava collects blood from the upper part of the body and the inferior vena cava does the same for the lower part. Both of them empty into the right upper chamber of the heart, the atrium, where I am now placing a purse-string suture preparatory to opening it. Early heart transplants were extremely difficult until a technique was developed for leaving a cuff of the atrium around the point where the two large veins enter it, making it necessary to suture only atrium to atrium, a far simpler and shorter method of reconnecting the right side of the heart."

He had finished placing the purse-string now, forming a pattern that looked very much like the mouth of an old-fashioned bag of Bull Durham tobacco used for rolling cigarettes.

"Since we plan to leave the larger portion of the right atrium in place when suturing the donor heart to it," he continued, "I shall put a tube into the superior vena cava through this opening. Dr. Johnson has already cannulated the inferior vena cava through the comon femoral vein."

As he spoke, he cut through the thin wall of the atrium with a pointed scalpel, controlled the spurt of blood by tightening the purse-string immediately and closing the opening. "Thus, we can leave the tubes in place while we suture the right side of Lawson's heart to Merchant's and keep the heart-lung pump running."

"Pump ready, Doctor." One of the pump technicians answered his unspoken question.

Skillfully, Greg placed loose snares of cotton tape around both the superior and the inferior vena cava outside the heart. Handing them to the resident, who was still acting as first assistant while Bob Johnson maintained the rhythmic pressure upon the heart itself, he picked up a plastic tube with a bulb-shaped end handed him by the instrument nurse. Loosening the purse-string suture momentarily, he pushed the tube gently through the atrium and into the opening of the superior vena cava, where the assistant immediately tightened the snare, forming a tight connection around the tube so no blood could leak by it. The second snare insured that no blood flowed through the lower vein and the entire volume of blood that normally returned to the right side of the heart could now be diverted to the pump.

The pump technicians had been watching Greg closely. As soon as the venous flow was under control, one of them threw the switch that started the metal discs spinning in their bath of blood inside the long plastic cylinder at the center of the machine. At the same moment, Greg reached down to remove the clamp closing the tube connected to the femoral artery in the thigh.

"Body clamps off," he said, warning the technicians that there was no block now between the heart-lung pump and Guy Merchant's circulatory system, save the valves of the machine itself.

"Line pressure, one hundred." The technician spoke as he watched the gauge, with one eye on the second hand of his watch.

Ordinarily, no longer than forty-five seconds was necessary to build up enough pressure to maintain the circulation. Having quickly reached the desired rate of revolution the pump was humming softly and already the reservoir of blood in the long cylinder was starting to turn a brighter red as oxygen was absorbed by the continuous film covering the upper part of the moving steel discs.

"Blood temperature ninety degrees," the second pump technician reported.

Since no blood was now flowing into the heart it lay flaccid and empty in Bob Johnson's hand.

"Respirator off," said Dr. Gann, and the sudden cessation of its rhythmic click-click—no longer needed with no blood flowing through the lungs—was louder *in absentia* than it had been while audible.

When the pump technician opened the valves connecting Guy Merchant's circulation with the machine itself, the line pressure dropped at once as blood flowed into his body. But the pump quickly raised it again to the needed level of about one hundred and eighty millimeters of mercury, corresponding roughly to a normal blood pressure.

Blood collected by way of the great veins and the two tubes inside them was now being carried to the pump, where, through the medium of the spinning discs, its oxygen supply was replenished and the waste carbon dioxide removed. A little higher concentration of the latter than normal was maintained in the blood being circulated by the pump, however, because the concentration of carbon dioxide regulated the flow of blood through the arteries of the brain, a flow which must be maintained at all costs, lest damage to that extremely sensitive organ occur during the period of shift from circulation by heart to circulation by pump. Leaving the pump, the blood now flowed under increased pressure into the groin artery, where Bob Johnson had placed the cannula at the beginning of the operation, back-flooding the entire arterial system of the body with freshly oxygenated blood.

Physiologically, every part of Guy Merchant's body, save the heart and lungs, was now functioning, though at considerably less than the normal rate because of the sharp lowering of all body processes by the steadily increasing cold. Not until the blood temperature reached thirty-five degrees on the Centigrade scale used in scientific work (roughly eighty-five on the more familiar Fahrenheit scale), would the pump technicians open the heat inlet on the pump heat exchanger and rewarm the blood slightly to make certain that it fell no lower than that level.

"Urine output one cc. per minute," reported a technician whose duty it was to watch that function. To the untrained observer, urinary flow might seem of little importance but actually it was a sensitive indicator of the adequacy of the arterial pressure, and therefore of the blood flow to the kidneys.

"The patient is now on the pump-oxygenator," Greg announced by way of the microphone. "His heart and lungs are no longer needed and all other body organs are functioning normally."

III

"I've been in practice twenty-five years, but this sort of thing scares the hell out of me," said one of the older doctors watching the TV screen in the lecture room. "Imagine somebody just lying there, not breathing, his heart not beating, while a machine keeps him alive. It's enough to make you believe in robots."

"If you ask me, this automation business has already gone too far," another doctor said. "A little more of it and we'll be done away with altogether."

Neither noticed Jud Templeton quietly taking notes on a pad with a stubby pencil while they were talking.

"For my money," the first doctor said, "we ought to stop fighting Medicare and fight automation."

"I wouldn't want it to get around but I haven't done half had at all with Medicare," a third man chimed in. "Take most of the old people who come into my office. I used to give them a quick glance and a prescription for a tranquilizer so I could get them out fast, knowing I was losing money every minute I wasted on them—"

"But not any more," the second doctor agreed. "I'm doing twice as much surgery on people over sixty-five as I did before Medicare—and getting paid for it. A lot of 'em have chronic gall bladders or diaphragmatic hernias that can be demonstrated in the X-ray. Before Medicare came along, I didn't want to X-ray them because I couldn't be sure I'd even get paid for that. Now I'm doing routine gall bladders and G.I. series and finding a lot of operable conditions."

"Why don't you vultures start treating the whole patient instead of some organ you can operate on and take the government for a big fee?" A stocky red-haired man who had been sitting in the second row smoking a pipe spoke in tone of disgust. "If you'd take a decent history before ordering a gall bladder X-ray and finding a low-grade chronic condition that isn't causing any real trouble, you'd know a lot of these old people are just lonely because their children have left home and don't have time to bother with them any more. Nine times out of ten those digestive symptoms you use as an excuse for surgery are nothing but spasm of the G.I. tract a visit from the kids at Christmas could cure. Take a knife to them and they've got something physical to center their complaints on, which makes it twice as hard for us psychiatrists to get anywhere with them."

There was a moment of indignant silence, then the three who had been so busy with Medicare moved away, ignoring the red-headed doctor, who didn't seem troubled at all by their attitude. Nothing was happening on the TV screen that looked exciting now, so Jud Templeton moved into a seat beside the psychiatrist.

"You certainly put them in their place," he said. "I couldn't help overhearing—and admiring."

"Who are you?"

"My name's Templeton."

"Jud Templeton?"

"Yes."

"Thought I recognized you. Who let you in?"

"I'm here by invitation." Jud handed him the press card. "Courtesy of the director."

"You just used a dirty word." The psychiatrist handed him back the card and held out his hand. "I'm Dr. Jake Stafford, a maverick from the psychiatric service. I was hoping Greg Alexander had finally realized Henry Anders is getting ready to take him to the cleaners and hired himself a press agent."

"I'm for free," said Templeton.

"Except the headlines you can get out of it?"

Jud shrugged. "You just heard what your friends had to say about Medicare, so what right has the medical profession to look down on newspapermen any more?"

"You've got a good point there," Stafford admitted. "As you may have guessed, I don't have a very high opinion of a lot of my medical confreres."

"Care to elucidate?"

"Not for publication—yet. I'm writing a book on what's happened to the medical profession in the twenty-five years since I finished school. We've gained more in knowledge and lost more in respect from the public than in any previous century in history."

"What's your diagnosis, Doctor?"

"Money—what else?"

"Everybody's got a right to make money."

"Nothing's wrong with making money—so long as it doesn't become your whole aim in life."

"I can see now why you named yourself a maverick," said Jud Templeton. "Were you always that way?"

"Maybe," said Stafford. "When I joined the Army in 'forty-two, medicine was still a calling. But when I came out in 'forty-six, it had become a trade."

"Would you care to risk a guess why?"

"I *know* why. Those of us who were in the service were thoroughly disgusted with the brown-nosing that got eagles for men who put the desire for power and position above the kind of service Hippocrates wrote about. We longed to get back in civilian practice the way the Israelites yearned for the Promised Land; the pastures were greener and there was plenty of water in the streams, so we came out expecting to find things the way they were before—only better."

"And they weren't?"

"Hell no. The minute we got out, we discovered that the guys who'd been smart enough to stay behind had gotten rich. While we'd been serving our glorious country in uniform, they'd been collecting ten-dollar bills for house calls and sticking them in the side pockets of their coats, until they could bury them somewhere so the Internal Revenue wouldn't know they'd ever collected them. Between calls, they'd been buying up property that was bound to zoom in value as soon as the war ended, taking advantage of every investment opportunity that came along for somebody who had a pocketful of money. Meanwhile, what was happening to us in uniform?"

"If you were as broke as I was, you were damn lucky to get enough to eat and pay your bar bill at the officers' club!"

"That's just about the size of it," said the psychiatrist. "A lot of us had to borrow money to pay our insurance so we could afford to be in uniform. When we got out, those debts came due pretty fast and who could blame us for trying to catch up to the ones who'd stayed behind and got rich?"

"Which made you as bad as they were."

"Maybe worse," Stafford admitted. "At least we had a choice of the way we would go, while, with patients flooding the doctors back home with money, they could hardly go but one way. The trouble is that, while we were getting rich in the years right after the war, we lost something pretty precious—our professional dedication. And when we no longer had that, we could hardly expect the next medical generation to find it suddenly."

Dr. Stafford examined his pipe and saw that it had indeed gone out while he was talking, then stuck it in the pocket of his tweed jacket. "Whenever I can, I come down here and watch Greg Alexander at work, but not because I particularly admire what he's trying to do," he continued. "Take that fellow he's carrying on the pump"—he gestured toward the screen—"while he frees the organs he hopes to remove and waits for the call from the operating room on the other side telling him this murderer—what's his name?"

"Frank Lawson."

"Telling him Frank Lawson is about to do the decent thing and die early. But what good is it all going to do?"

"A life may be saved."

"For what?"

"In his time, Guy Merchant had a lot to be proud of."

"His name was up in lights, yes, but you know how show business is. I doubt very seriously if Merchant even has the sixteen quarters of coverage he'll need to get more than the minimum under Social Security. So even if Greg Alexander does give him a new heart and lungs, what's it going to mean to him?"

"Life, for one thing."

"You can't cut out one man's heart and put it into another man without detaching the nervous control from the brain. The new heart has got to function on its own, which means it can't respond to the sight of a pretty girl walking down the street in a mini-skirt by stepping up its beat, whether the acceleration is going to be needed or not. If Merchant happens to exert a bit too much, his heart won't be able to respond to that either and the moment the amount of blood being pumped to his brain is less than what his brain needs, he'll keel over in a faint."

The psychiatrist shook his head vigorously. "I meant what I said to those three medical vultures just now, Mr. Templeton. One of the greatest tragedies in life is to be old and alone. I see the flotsam and jetsam of that tide floating up in my geriatric clinic every day and there's nothing I can do to make them feel wanted again. You can find foster parents for a cute little child with the certainty that it will be loved and wanted for itself. But who's going to adopt an old man who doesn't always make it to the bathroom before he wets his pants and goes to sleep before the TV set snoring so loud that nobody else can hear the program? The tyranny of the aged feeds on the guilt complexes of their children. When you're young, you hate your parents because of the authority they have over you. But when you're older, you're afraid to put them away—like Indians did the oldsters back in their days—because you know your own kids might do the same thing to you."

"Wouldn't you say it would be worthwhile to save the brain of an Einstein by giving him a new heart?" Jud Templeton asked.

"Of course, but Einsteins are few and far apart. And who's to say what brains are worth saving and what shall be let die? There's a moral question here, too, you know."

"Would you have Dr. Alexander stop his work just because the moral side of it hasn't been solved yet?"

"Of course not." Dr. Jake Stafford grinned. "Who knows? I may want one of those transplants myself, when he gets so he can really make it work most of the time. Greg Alexander is so devoted to his work that he never lets other considerations trouble him and, whenever I get disgusted with my money-grabbing colleagues, the way I was with those three just now, I look to him to restore my spirits—and my faith. As long as men like him are around in medicine, I can believe that the sort of dedication we had twenty-five years ago still exists."

"Do you think Dr. Alexander will win out in his battle with the trustees for an automated hospital and diagnostic clinic?"

The psychiatrist looked at him quizzically. "You for or against?"

"For—all the way. Are you?"

"For, naturally, but I've got nothing to lose. They can't teach robots head-shrinking, and half the time we psychiatrists don't know what the hell we're doing ourselves." Then his voice took on a more sober note. "Just the same, I wish Greg Alexander hadn't spoken on automation today. It scares the daylights out of a lot of doctors—and with some reason."

"I don't see why."

"A doctor spends four years of college, four years of medical school, and maybe fifty thousand or so of his old man's money for the M.D.—plus five more years in hospital residencies if he wants to be certified. Naturally, the thought that he may be largely replaced by a diagnostic machine can tie his gut up in knots."

"So what's the answer?"

"The same one that coped with the Industrial Revolution in England a few hundred years ago. Making more goods available to people always creates more jobs and more need for what those jobs produce. With machines taking over the diagnostic chores and some of the treatment ones, too, doctors can give their patients a better grade of medical care. Which means more people living into old age to provide more work for more doctors. We're the only profession in the world, Mr. Templeton, whose idealism always pays off in dollars. And don't tell me that isn't the best of all rewards—doing good and getting paid for it, too."

"Please, Dr. Stafford." Jud Templeton held up his hand in mock protest. "You'll have me starting all over—in your field—when I've got a story to write."

"What's your lead?"

"The old tried and true, of course," said the newspaperman. "Today a man in white held back the angel of death with gloved hands. . . ."

CHAPTER SEVENTEEN

I

Peter Carewe and Helen Foucald were just finishing their dessert when the beeper on the table beside them emitted its high-pitched, compelling sound. "Here's the end of a perfect evening," she said. "I've got to call the hospital operator."

"Greg has put the heart patient on the pump," she reported when she came back to the table. "We have to do frequent blood-gas determinations while the pump is operating to make sure the CO-two level doesn't get too low and cut down the blood flow to the brain, as well as watching the electrolyte balance."

"Can't somebody else in the lab do it?"

"Some of these determinations are a little intricate, so I usually have to read the instruments. We only have a couple of technicians on duty at night and they'll need help."

"Any idea how long you'll be?"

"The laboratory assistant I talked to said Frank Lawson is still alive, so it could go on for quite a while."

"I'll walk across with you," he offered.

"Please don't. Let's end the evening as it is now, with soft lights and brandy."

"You talk as if there won't be others."

"That's up to you. Tonight will give you a chance to think a little—and back out if you like."

"How about breakfast together?"

"I'd love it, but you may not want to get up as early as I do. I have to be in the laboratory by nine."

"In the bush, the day is half gone by nine o'clock," he told her as they walked to the door.

"I'll meet you in the restaurant here at eight-fifteen then?"

"No room service?"

"Let's not push our luck," she said quickly. "It's a long time till morning and I'll understand if you change your mind."

He stood watching her until she disappeared through the door of the restaurant and his expression was thoughtful as he moved to the long bar and took one of the stools there.

"Bourbon," he told the bartender, but when the glass was set before him, he sat looking at it for a long time without tasting it.

II

"Keep watch on things here, Bob; I'm going across and take a look at Lawson." Greg stepped back from the operating table, where he had been carrying out some of the preliminary dissections preparing Guy Merchant for the time when he would remove the organs which were to be replaced. "How is he, Lew?" he asked.

Dr. Lewis Gann looked up from behind a tent of draperies. "Knocking along. I'm just marking time with a slow drip of succinylcholine and enough Pentothal to keep him quiet."

Greg glanced at the lines racing across the monitor tube and the chart on the small table beside Dr. Gann. "Everything seems to be holding up O.K."

"Physiologically, you're correct, but we could have a real philosophical bull session over that statement," said the anesthesiologist. "The patient is cold, his heart doesn't beat, he doesn't breathe. In fact, you could make a good argument that the only thing alive about him is that gadget there." He nodded toward the pump-oxygenator. "And a burnt-out fuse could snuff out what life is left in that."

"His brain is still working." Greg pointed toward the wavy line on the bottom of the monitor, where almost alone among the body indicators, the even slow pattern of the electrical waves collected by terminals strapped to Guy Merchant's skull showed life as they moved across the cathode ray tube in a rhythmic progression.

"Reminds me of when I visited the cave paintings of Trois Frères in France," said Dr. Gann. "They were made over twenty thousand years ago, but when the artist wanted to depict motion in a herd of deer being hunted by Stone Age men, all he had to do was show a wave passing through a line of antlers. Maybe we haven't come as far as we think, in spite of all our fancy gadgets."

One of the nurses laughed and as the operating team relaxed visibly, Greg gave the gray-haired anesthesiologist an affectionate punch on the shoulder.

"If we didn't have a screwball philosopher like you in the operating room at a time like this, Lew, I guess we'd all explode with tension," he said. "Just at the right moment, you always come up with some sort of an oddball observation that takes off the heat."

"I have to be worth something," said Dr. Gann. "With this automation movement you're making yourself the apostle of, anesthesia will soon be nothing but a couple of bottles dripping solutions into a patient's veins and an electronic monitor watching over him to turn them on and off. Still, if the heart and lungs can be replaced by a machine, I suppose I shouldn't squawk."

"Were you able to get most of Merchant's blood out before you started using the perfusate?" Greg asked the head technician. Perfusate was the term used to describe the blood mixture used to charge the heart-lung pump before the metal discs began to spin.

"I'd say three quarters of it at least, Doctor," said the technician. "We couldn't risk taking any more for fear the circulation wouldn't hold up."

"That should help a great deal."

"Just what do you hope to gain by not using Merchant's own blood, Greg?" Dr. Gann asked.

"It's an idea of Helen Foucald's. She thinks that replacing Merchant's blood with another makes a severe rejection less likely soon after the transplant. Our work with dogs seems to support the theory."

"We'll save as much of Lawson's blood as we can and use that for transfusion later. That way, we'll theoretically be supplying the heart with a considerable percentage of the blood to which it was accustomed, and thus further decrease the possibility of a rejection."

"It's a clever idea," said the anesthesiologist. "But I never heard of it before."

"I wouldn't have thought of it myself if Helen hadn't suggested it," Greg admitted. "She works with cells all the time and thinks having a different set of lymphocytes circulating in the bloodstream from those of the person who's receiving the transplant might decrease the probability of rejection."

"You're going to use ALG, too, aren't you?"

"As much as we can get. I've ordered a fresh supply flown from Munich."

The newest—and potentially most valuable—weapon against the tendency of the human body to reject tissues other than its own, anti-lymphocytic globulin—ALG for short—was made by injecting human lymphocytes into animals, much as was done in producing tetanus antitoxin and other serums. When the animal reacted by producing antibodies in the blood capable of paralyzing and even destroying human white blood cells, it was then bled and the antibody-rich factor called globulin extracted. This in turn could be used to help prevent the white blood cells of the transplant recipient from attacking the new organ received from the donor—the physiological process called rejection, which had caused so much trouble in earlier transplant cases.

Still wearing his gown and gloves so it wouldn't be necessary for him to scrub again when he changed to resume surgery, Greg took a shortcut through the scrub room and the doctors' lounge beneath the surgical lecture room to enter the other operating theater and the adjoining anesthetic room. There, Herbert Partridge, the medical examiner and a nurse-anesthetist were watching the monitor that recorded Frank Lawson's brain waves, as well as his temperature, blood pressure and heart action.

Greg noted with approval, as he passed through the operating theater itself, that the tables against the walls had been covered with sterile sheets by the scrub nurses. Beneath them, he knew, everything was ready for the rapid opening of Lawson's chest in order to remove the heart and lungs; two nurses, scrubbed and ready, sat on stools at one side, their gloved hands protected by sterile towels.

"How's Merchant?" Herbert Partridge looked up when Greg came in.

"He almost went out on us, but I got him on the pump in time."

"How long can you carry him?" The medical examiner asked the question that was uppermost in all their minds.

"The most we've ever had a patient on bypass during surgery was a little over three hours," said Greg. "Beyond that—we're in unknown territory."

"Any reason why it couldn't be longer?"

"Prolonged cooling seems to decrease the chances of obtaining a satisfactory function of the heart afterward," said Greg. "In Merchant's case, though, we're not going to use it, so that factor doesn't hold. The thing we need to be concerned about most is the effect of cooling on the brain."

"It's getting an adequate oxygen supply with the pump, isn't it?"

"Yes. And as long as cooling keeps the need of the cells for oxygen down to a minimum while enough blood actually reaches it to maintain that small degree of vital function, I suppose theoretically a brain could be cooled indefinitely," Greg said as he moved over beside the table and stood looking down at Frank Lawson. "But that's only in theory, nobody actually knows."

The respirator still clicked away with its steady rhythm, inflating and deflating the injured man's lungs. The wavy lines registering the various components of the heart action upon the cathode tube of the monitor were as strong and regular as ever, too. Only the tracings of the brain waves showed any significant deviation from normal. Here the pattern was still as disorderly as before, and the height of the waves was distinctly less, hardly half of what it had been when Greg had last visited the room.

"His brain is dying fairly rapidly," said Herb Partridge. "It's been particularly noticeable in the last half hour."

"Suppose the heart keeps on beating spontaneously, even after the brain registers death?" Dr. Dennison asked. "What then, Greg.?"

"The A.M.A. recommends that two doctors certify death in potential transplants and neither of them can be the operating surgeon, so that lets me out and leaves the actual decision to you and Dr. Partridge."

"Judge Sutler's order says death must be established unquestionably," said the medical examiner. "I have no choice except to wait until all indicators have ceased to function before letting you go ahead."

"We understand that," Greg assured him.

"A while ago it was a race between Merchant's heart and Lawson's but Merchant faulted in the stretch," said Herb Partridge. "Now the race is between a machine and Lawson's heart."

"One thing is certain," said Dr. Dennison. "No race like this was ever run before."

III

Ed McDougal poured a stiff drink for Dr. Timothy Puckett and handed it to the potbellied pediatrician. "Calm yourself, Tim, and tell me just what this guy said."

"He isn't just a guy. His face looked familiar to me in the lecture room but I thought it was because he'd been a Fellow here at one time. It wasn't until I saw him later at that telephone the reporters use outside the emergency room that I realized who he is."

"So it was a reporter. What did he say?"

"I think he's suspicious about the business of moving The Clinic." They were sitting in the extra suite Ed had rented to serve as headquarters during the campaign and to give him a base of operations away from Hannah and her querulous demands. Ed had been busy all evening entertaining a steady stream of influential doctors among the Members and trustees, lining up support for the campaign upon which he and Henry Anders had embarked.

Dr. Tim Puckett's news of his encounter with Jud Templeton was the first adverse happening of the evening, but Ed wasn't particularly worried about it. The smell of scandal could hardly be wafted as far as Texas, and, by that time, the whole thing would be locked up so tight that nothing could change it. Under other conditions, Ed wouldn't even have bothered about Tim Puckett's fears, but, since the small man was chairman of the Board of Trustees, he had to keep him reassured and in line.

"Just how much do you think this fellow knows?" he asked. "You couldn't have been such a fool as to blab to him about this syndicate?"

"Of course not." The gulp of almost pure bourbon he'd taken when the glass was put into his hand was warming the little man's stomach and stirring his courage. "This guy's got extrasensory perception or something."

"Don't be a damn fool, Tim. How far had Greg gone with the operation when you left?"

"He's got the patient on the heart-lung pump."

"And the other one—the donor?"

"I don't know. He's in the anesthetic room outside the other operating theater, so they didn't have the TV cameras on him."

"Merchant's heart must have gone bad even faster than Greg expected. He can't carry him but so long on the pump and, if Merchant dies before the transplant can be done, this publicity gimmick could backfire. We can always claim Greg has given The Clinic a bad name and demand his resignation."

"Resignation?" Dr. Puckett looked horrified. "Who said anything about resigning?"

"Henry Anders insists on it. Don't tell me you didn't know that?"

"Of course I didn't know it! Greg and Jeanne are among our best friends." The whiskey was shoring up Puckett's self-confidence. "Do you think I want to preside as chairman of the board over the death of The Clinic?"

"The funeral—if it comes to that—won't happen during your term of office, Tim." Ed reached over to pour more bourbon into Puckett's glass and drop in some ice. "Besides, it doesn't have to happen just because Greg Alexander's not around any more."

"But—"

"Look at this thing sensibly, Tim. I know it sounds big to be a Member of The Clinic, when you're running for an office in the state medical association—I use it myself whenever it will do me any good. But have you ever stopped to think how much the doctors practicing here in town lose by having an institution close by that leaves it up to the patient to say how much of a fee he can pay—or none at all? Old Dr. Anders got a lot of free publicity out of that gimmick and it meant something in the old days, when so many people were poor. But with the average income per capita going up all the time, to say nothing of what it costs a doctor to maintain an office, what's the sense of letting a lot of people get the kind of medical care they can get across the street without paying a dime for it?"

"I—I never thought of that."

"Then it's time you did—along with the rest of the doctors around here. The Clinic has been able to get by without changing its financial requirements because people like Sam Hunter and a lot of other patients of old Dr. Anders have been willing to ante up at the end of the year to cover its deficit. But that can't last forever with taxes the way they are."

"Greg's kept up The Clinic's reputation."

"Maybe he has; I never did say Greg didn't have ability. But he hasn't shown much sense by staying here at twenty thousand a year when he could have made a hundred in private practice. With Greg gone, The Clinic will lose a lot of its drawing power for people who can pay their way, which means more patients for you fellows who are right here on the ground and don't believe that idealistic crap Greg and old Dr. Anders were always handing out."

"But if this fellow Templeton is on to the syndicate—"

"He's not on to it—unless you told him."

"I said I didn't," Dr. Puckett squawked indignantly.

"Then all he's doing is putting two and two together. Maybe he did come up with the right answer, but you can be damn certain he won't print it in a newspaper without proof."

"Are you sure?"

"Of course I'm sure. Some pretty important people are in on this deal and one of them ought to be able to shut off Mr. Jud Templeton when the time comes. Right now, it's to our interest to let him keep on writing about the transplant operation. Obviously, Greg is feeding information to him, hoping to profit from the publicity, so we'll just let him go ahead and print it. If Greg had to put his patient on a heart-lung pump before he could even get Lawson's heart, this whole stunt is going to fail and we can use that against him at the trustees' meeting. Things are breaking just the way we want them, Tim. The first time Greg fumbles, we'll just pick up the ball and run with it for a touchdown."

"Shouldn't we cancel that meeting Friday afternoon?"

"Sam Hunter demanded it to look into the question of Greg's building the hyperbaric chamber without consulting the board and we can't do anything to make Sam mad, so we'll have to go through with it."

"Suppose Greg succeeds with this operation? Won't that be proof that building the chamber was justified?"

"If the patient lives, Sam Hunter will have the rug pulled out from under him, but that's his hard luck. What we've got to do is make Greg show these new plans there's so much talk about so we can get a crack at them before the regular meeting of the board on Saturday morning."

"How?"

"By going ahead with the Friday afternoon meeting, without any fixed agenda."

"Suppose Greg has already shown the plans to this fellow Templeton."

"He can hardly do that before the board sees them, and he thinks that will be Saturday morning. Once the board has nixed the plan, they won't do Greg or anybody any good."

"You may be right," said Tim Puckett. "I don't know."

"Stop worrying," Ed McDougal told him. "That automation speech of Greg's scared the hell out of a lot of doctors and we're gaining support steadily. By the time the banquet comes off tomorrow night, I'm pretty sure we'll have enough votes to squelch anything he tries to do. Right now, we want Greg to have all the publicity he can get on the actual operation; that's the rope we're going to hang him with."

When Dr. Puckett left, Ed McDougal switched off the lights in the suite and left it, locking the door. At the bank of elevators, he punched the "Up" button and, when the elevator came, rode up two floors to where his and Hannah's suite was located.

He always felt keyed up after one of these wire-pulling deals and was ready for a celebration. Besides, he owed Hannah something for not being able to take an active part in the cocktail party earlier that evening, and the best way to celebrate—as well as keep her happy—was for them to hang one on.

Hannah's belongings were scattered through the living room of the suite; her purse was on the chair, her shoes in the doorway leading to the bedroom—which meant she'd come in loaded. Hannah herself, in her slip, lay sprawled across the bed asleep, snoring gently. When he took her by the shoulder and turned her over, she didn't rouse and, leaving her there, he went to the bathroom and examined the shelf under the mirror.

The bottle of red capsules she carried with her everywhere was there, with the top off. But when he counted them and found only two missing from the two dozen that had been in the bottle when they'd left home last night, he was sure she hadn't taken enough to form the lethal combination with alcohol favored by declining movie actresses and fading members of the jet set.

Leaning over the bed, he straightened out Hannah's legs and turned her on her side so she couldn't swallow her tongue. Taking the bottle of amphetamine tablets she always carried with her out of her bag, he set it down on the bedside table along with a glass of water, knowing that, when she finally roused in the morning, she would need them to get herself wide enough awake to order coffee from room service. Then, locking the door behind him, he returned to the suite he had left a few minutes before and picked up the phone.

"Bell captain," he told the operator and, when a man's voice answered, said: "This is Dr. McDougal in suite four-forty. Any chance of obtaining some entertainment tonight?"

"It can be arranged, sir." The bell captain's voice was discreetly low. "But there's quite a demand and the cost may be high, say fifty for a top-quality performer?"

"Send her up," Ed said, and poured himself another drink. After all, entertainment at a medical convention was deductible.

IV

In Sam Hunter's suite, the financier sat in pajamas, robe and slippers, watching the TV screen but paying little attention to what was happening there. The afternoon paper lay on the table beside him, with Jud Templeton's story on the front page. Moto, the valet, had left a glass of warm milk and some crackers in a cellophane packet on the table; the old man opened one of the packets now and took out a cracker, crunching it between his teeth before washing it down with the milk.

He'd been having heartburn a lot at night lately and made a mental note to tell Dr. Connor about it when he had his physical tomorrow. Even the milk didn't help much, though, particularly since the break with Ted. He'd had to get up early every night and take a couple of antacid tablets to relieve the discomfort before he could get back to sleep.

Ever since his talk that evening with Peter Carewe and Helen Foucald, and later with Claire Anders, Sam Hunter had been filled with a vague discontent, whose source he couldn't immediately identify. However pragmatic his own point of view might be in his business, he could appreciate dedication and loyalty when he saw it and had recognized those qualities in both Helen and the doctor from the World Health Organization. He knew enough, too, about the worldwide operations of his companies to recognize that what Peter had told him about the Persian Gulf incident was true.

Whatever he might think about the United Nations as a whole, he could admire a man like Carewe. And there, he faced the truth at last, was the source of his discontent. In Peter Carewe, he'd seen many of the qualities Ted possessed, qualities of dedication and devotion to ideals, which, he recognized now, had been the source of most of the friction between them and had finally resulted in the break, when Ted had married the Italian girl and gone off with the circus.

Perhaps because the memory of the old is far more vivid for the distant than the recent past, Sam Hunter found himself recalling those carefree days in Italy when, for a few months, he'd even considered giving up the place waiting for him in his father's growing business back home. He had long since destroyed the few dabs he'd made at painting then, but now he felt once again, as if excavated from the remains of that long-distant but happy period, some of the pride of accomplishment he'd felt in them.

Obeying an impulse he had rigidly resisted until now, Sam Hunter went to the telephone and picking up the receiver, dialed the long-distance operator and gave her the number of his telephone charge card, followed by a number in Texas. When Mike Hawkins, chief of the security detail that guarded his properties and operations all over the world, answered, he said: "Mike, do you know where Ted is?"

"The weekly report from the people that check on him for us came over my desk only yesterday, Mr. Hunter. Just a minute and I'll get it from my file."

After a brief period, the security chief spoke again in the telephone. "Ted's not far from you, sir."

"I know that from the reports before I left. But what town?"

"Let's see. Tonight the circus is playing in Reistertown, Maryland. Tomorrow they'll be in a small town not far from there." Sam Hunter copied down the name. "I'll have next week's itinerary in a few days, want me to call you?"

"Never mind. What about business?"

"The agency reports pretty small crowds at the circus. Are you going to see the boy while you're up there, sir?" Mike had been with Sam Hunter since before young Sam's birth and had often taken the boys on hunting and fishing trips when they were growing up.

"I don't know, Mike."

"I hope you will, sir. The agency says Ted and the girl have a real good act. They turned down a chance to audition for Ringling a few months ago."

"Then he's making a go of it?"

"You didn't think he wouldn't, did you?"

"No, I suppose not."

"The circus may not last out the season," said Mike Hawkins, "but I guess Ted and the girl plan to stay with the old man to the end."

"Thanks, Mike. Everything all right down there?"

"Fine, sir. Your checkup going okay?"

"They're ramming a tube in one end or the other every few minutes," Sam Hunter chuckled. "I guess it's when they start ramming it in both ends at the same time that you really have to worry. Good night, Mike."

"Good night, sir. Give Ted my regards, if you see him."

Sam Hunter was thoughtful as he went back to the table and finished his milk and crackers. Then he went into the bathroom, removed his teeth and put them in a cup of water into which he dropped a tablet that fizzed. Rinsing his mouth out with water, he turned the light out and went back to the bed, where he removed his robe and lay down, pulling up the covers.

For a few moments, he lay staring up at the ceiling, then, with a purposeful movement, reached up and switched off the light, turned over on his side and was almost instantly asleep.

CHAPTER EIGHTEEN

I

The audience in the lecture room had dwindled to no more than twenty-five people when Greg Alexander opened the door from the operating theater just outside which Frank Lawson lay. He was still wearing the gown and gloves he'd worn while making the incision into Guy Merchant's chest and attaching his circulation to the heart-lung pump. As he moved to the podium in the center of the room, there was a stir among those sitting upon the seats and a few who had fallen asleep were roused by the others. Jud Templeton came wide awake at the sound of Greg's voice but was careful to remain slumped down so as not to call the surgeon's attention to his presence.

"I'm not going to apologize for this procedure having taken so long, because it is beyond my power to shorten it," Greg told the waiting group. "I *can* report to you that Mr. Merchant is holding up well, now that his respiration and circulation have been taken over by the pump-oxygenator. We've not lost hope of being able to carry out a successful transplant, but I would be less than truthful if I didn't admit that the odds against success are increasing with every passing moment. That's about all I can say at this time."

"What about Lawson?" one of the watchers asked.

"His brain picture is growing steadily more chaotic, proving that the damage from hemorrhage is progressive. I wish it were possible to connect a monitor in here so you could see the electroencephalogram, but we didn't exactly anticipate this sort of situation."

"Wouldn't it be better just to let Merchant die?" one man asked. "This seems only to be prolonging the agony."

"Would you want me to make that decision, if you were in his place, Doctor?" Greg asked.

"Well, no. But—"

"Actually, I can't even use what I would want done in my own case as a standard by which to make such a decision," said Greg. "Life is life and as long as I can preserve it, I have no choice. Are you familiar with the case of Dr. Smirnov in Russia?"

"No," the questioner admitted.

"Smirnov is regarded as one of the world's leading mathematicians. He was injured in an accident not long ago while on his way to an important scientific meeting and was rushed to a hospital, apparently dead. In the next twenty-four to thirty-six hours, he was clinically dead several times, yet, each time, he was revived by the same technique we use in this hospital for resuscitation when the heart has stopped. Today Smirnov is alive and at work."

"With no damage to his brain?" one of the onlookers asked.

"There has been some slight impairment of his faculties. But merely preserving most of such a brain is of incalculable value to science."

"How can you stand the strain yourself, Greg?" Abe Lantz asked. "Just watching it makes me want to go out and get a stiff drink."

"I'm sorry we can't serve it to you here, Abe. I don't mind admitting that once or twice tonight I could have used one myself."

The door to the operating room Greg had just left opened, and Herb Partridge spoke through it. "We need you in here, Dr. Alexander. Pronto!"

II

Greg's first glance was not at Frank Lawson but at the monitor tube. The change he saw there warned him, far more accurately than any examination of Lawson could have done, that the critical moment was fast approaching. The heart picture still followed its regular pattern but the amplitude of the beat had markedly diminished, even since he'd left the room a few moments before. As for the electroencephalographic pattern, it was difficult to distinguish any movement there at all; only rarely did the flicker of an electric wave show upon the screen.

"There was a sudden change," said Herb Partridge. "I think we will have brain death at any moment."

"Get him into the O.R. and uncover the instrument tables." Greg was pulling off his gown over his gloves as he spoke. As he stripped off the gloves themselves and dropped them into a waste container, a scrub nurse was already holding up a fresh sterile gown before him. And while one of the two circulating nurses tied the strings of his gown, he thrust his hands into fresh gloves being held out for him by the scrub nurse.

"I'm going to prep him, Phil," he told the medical examiner. "But I'll not make an incision until you and Herb give the word."

Dr. Dennison nodded without removing his eyes from the monitor, where the rapidly dwindling pattern of heart and brain action were being portrayed. Moving swiftly, Greg painted Frank Lawson's chest with an antiseptic solution and, with the help of a resident who had been waiting, scrubbed and ready with the nurses, covered it with a broad sheet of transparent plastic. A second large sheet with a window covered the whole table, leaving exposed only the front of the chest. He did not look at the monitors while he worked, for the task of establishing death now legally belonged to the medical examiner, according to the order Judge Sutler had issued that afternoon, and to Herb Partridge.

"Test the temperature of the Tyrode's solution," he told the circulating nurse.

"It's four degrees Centigrade, Doctor."

"Bone cutters ready?"

"Yes, Doctor."

"Get ready, Greg." Dr. Dennison was studying the sweep-second hand of his watch as it crept around the dial. Upon the cardiac monitor, the heart wave had now flattened out to a straight line and there were no more waves on the brain monitor.

"One minute without heartbeat," the medical examiner said and Greg picked up the scalpel, ready to make the incision. "Frank Lawson is dead."

"I agree," said Herb Patridge and his words still echoed in the room as Greg's scalpel moved in a wide arc across the dead man's chest below the collarbones, cutting through muscle and down to ribs and breastbone in one stroke. It was the cut used by pathologists in the autopsy room, allowing maximum exposure of the organs in the chest. At the center of the arc, he made a downward stroke, splitting both skin and tissues beneath down to the breastbone.

"Dissect the flap outward on the right side, exposing the upper chest," he instructed the house officer who was assisting him, handing him the scalpel he had used and picking up a fresh one, with which he began to separate the muscles from the chest wall. In a matter of moments, sufficient exposure had been obtained to reveal the upper two thirds of the rib cage. And when a heavy bone-cutting forceps came into his hand, Greg inserted it beneath the ribs and began to cut rapidly across them, lifting up a flaplike window from the chest itself to expose the heart and the lungs beneath.

So swift were his movements, perfected by long practice to almost a stylized grace, that less than five minute elapsed between the beginning of the incision and the complete exposure of the heart and lungs within the chest cavity. At what he saw there, Greg didn't break the rapid movement of his work; but he felt a sudden sense of impending disaster, nevertheless. For, where the ribs had been broken when Frank Lawson had crashed to the street below the underpass, the outer surface of the pleural covering over the lungs was dark with hemorrhage. And although the original X-rays had not shown any involvement of the lungs themselves, he had no way of knowing whether the hemorrhage had extended into vital lung tissue since the night of Lawson's accident, jeopardizing seriously the chances of success with the transplant.

No time could be wasted in conjecture now, however. In rapid succession, he clamped the great vessels connected to the heart: the aorta, from which blood was carried to the body other than the lungs, which had their own private circulation; the superior and inferior vena cava that brought blood back to the heart from the upper and lower part of the body, respectively; the bronchial arteries supplying the tissue of the lung itself with the blood necessary for life, as distinguished from the main lung circulation, whose function it was to expose the blood to oxygen.

He did not put clamps on the heart side of the major vessels, lest the walls be crushed by the instruments and thus interfere with the new connections, medically termed anastomoses, which would have to be made to place Frank Lawson's heart in Guy Merchant's circulation. And he left a section of the large artery called the aorta, perhaps two inches long, attached to the heart in order to facilitate its connection to Guy Merchant's own artery system.

Less than ten minutes had passed before Greg lifted the heart and lungs together from Frank Lawson's body and immersed them gently in a large basin filled with the solution called Tyrode's, cooled to four degrees Centigrade. A gasp went up from the instrument nurse holding the basin when the heart muscle contracted strongly from the stimulus of the cold solution, and Greg experienced the first spurt of hope he'd allowed himself to feel since he'd opened the chest and seen the dark stain of hemorrhage across Frank Lawson's right lung.

Carrying the basin with its precious contents, he moved by way of the adjoining scrub rooms to the other operating theater. There, warned of what was happening, Bob Johnson was working swiftly, removing Guy Merchant's useless heart and lungs from his body.

III

Like magic, so rapidly does word of an extraordinary event spread through the corridors of a great hospital, the surgical lecture room had begun to fill with people. They clustered mainly in the lower right-hand seats, where the screen had suddenly become active after the brief scene on the left screen, when the closed-circuit TV tube had faithfully recorded the medical examiner's dramatic announcement and Greg's immediate action.

When Greg lifted Frank Lawson's heart and lungs from his body, Jud Templeton glanced at his watch, made a quick mental calculation and bolted for the corridor and the telephone. "How long can you hold the presses, Casey?" he asked when the voice of the city editor came on the line.

"An hour if we have to, maybe longer. What's up?"

"Dr. Alexander is starting the transplant. Give me a rewrite man and I'll dictate the first part of the story. Then I can keep feeding it to you in batches, until the deadline."

"Sounds like you're watching over his shoulder," said the city editor.

"It's almost that. Damnedest sensation I ever had, looking right down into an incision with a television camera."

"Any chance of pictures?"

"I'll try to snap the TV screen with a Minox and fast film, if I don't get caught, but they probably won't turn out. Anyway, we couldn't run them until tomorrow."

"O.K. Here's rewrite."

"I just watched a great surgeon carrying a living heart in his hands," Jud Templeton dictated tersely into the phone as soon as the rewrite man's voice spoke in his ear. "The heart had to be living, although the former occupant was legally dead, because the surgeon is now putting it into the chest of another man . . ."

IV

When word had come from the other operating theater that Frank Lawson was dead, Bob Johnson started at once on the final stages of preparing Guy Merchant to receive the new heart and lungs he needed so badly. He was busily at work when Greg came in carrying the basin of Tyrode's solution with its precious contents. Changing gown and gloves quickly, Greg stepped up to the table in Bob's place, surveyed the situation in one quick glance, and gave it an approving nod.

"You can start warming now," he told the anesthesiologist and the pump technicians.

Immediately, Dr. Gann stopped the circulation through the pad beneath Guy Merchant's body of the icy slush which had been helping to keep his temperature at a low level, while the pump technicians opened the heat exchanger to start warming the blood flowing through the heart-lung pump into Guy Merchant's body.

Working swiftly, Greg finished removing the now useless organs and dropped them into a basin held by the instrument nurse. Almost in the same motion, he reached down into the basin of cold Tyrode's solution he had placed upon a stand beside the table and lifted out the heart and lungs which moments before had been inside Frank Lawson's body.

The most critical stage of the technique Greg had worked out in experimental operations on dogs involved breaking off the actual circulation of blood to the heart itself through the coronary vessels for the briefest possible period. To make that time lapse even shorter, he had devised a temporary coupling composed of a circular clamp and a Teflon gasket, with which to connect quickly the cut end of the recipient's aorta to that of the donor. In this way, blood under the force of the pump was allowed to surge through the arterial system of the body immediately and enter the small openings of the coronary arteries. Lying just at the beginning of the aorta itself, they could thus serve to maintain the vital circulation to the heart muscle while he rapidly completed the rest of the connections necessary before the new heart could begin to function.

While Bob Johnson applied the aortic coupling, Greg was using a very fine needle to place a row of sutures joining the right side of Frank Lawson's heart to the remaining cuff of Guy Merchant's atrium outside the mouths of the great veins and the tubes which still connected them to the heart-lung pump. So practiced was the entire team that no words were actually necessary as the step-by-step procedure moved through the familiar routine. When he finished the aortic coupling, Bob moved to connect the bronchial arteries and veins, using nylon mesh tubing which Greg had also developed for this purpose. And, by that time, Greg had finished his first row of sutures on the right side of the heart.

"Body temperature rising steadily," Dr. Lewis Gann reported as Greg started the second row of sutures to make the right-sided connection tight. More important, with the adequate supply of oxygen now in the blood surging into the coronary arteries, the muscle of the new heart had once again resumed its normal pink color.

It took a little while longer for Greg to place a row of sutures connecting the aorta and replacing the temporary connection made by means of the special clamp and the Teflon cuff. When that was completed, he made another incision in the notch just above Guy Merchant's breastbone and opened a space through which he drew the trachea from Frank Lawson's lungs, attaching the cut end to the skin with several sutures. He slipped a tracheostomy tube into this opening and, when Dr. Lewis Gann shifted the respirator connection to it, the new lungs were now ready for expansion.

When he heard a sudden gasp from the instrument nurse and looked at the chest incision, Greg saw that Frank Lawson's heart, now connected entirely to Guy Merchant's body, had already begun to contract of its own accord. The motion was not the rhythmic contraction of a normal heart, however, but the helter-skelter, purposeless sort of contraction known as "fibrillation," the usual response of a heart after chilling. On the cardiac monitor tube, the flat line indicating no heart activity had suddenly been seized by a crazy profusion of waves, somewhat similar to those that existed in Frank Lawson's brain just before death.

"You've done it, Greg!" Dr. Lewis Gann exclaimed from behind his tent of draperies. "Congratulations!"

"We've gone this far many times before," Greg warned quietly, but even those watching on the screen in the surgical lecture room some distance away could hear the note of quiet satisfaction in his voice as it came to them by way of the auditory part of the system.

"Ready to defibrillate," he said quietly, and the instrument nurse handed him two sterilized plastic rods to which were attached round platelike metal electrodes. From each of the rods, a rubber-coated wire ran to the Pacemaker defibrillator, standing close by the table where the supervisor stood ready to press the switch that would automatically send a measured single jolt of electricity through the heart.

Working very carefully, Greg slid one of the electrodes into place beneath the heart. Then, while Bob Johnson held it, he placed a second one in front, with the organ itself between the two platelike connections.

"Contact, please!"

The supervisor pressed the button upon the machine and Frank Lawson's heart jerked in a powerful contraction as the momentary current went from one metal electrode to the other, passing through the muscle of the heart itself on the way. Except for a sudden sharp rise in the wave pattern with the introduction of the electric current from outside the heart, however, there was no change in the wild jumble of contractions. Tension rose perceptibly in the room, but Greg ignored it, intent upon what he was doing.

"Once again, please," he said, and the nurse pressed the button, sending a second charge of electricity through Frank Lawson's heart.

The sudden complete cessation of movement in the monitor pattern following the leap upward with completion of the circuit between machine-heart-machine was startling compared to the squirming "bag-of-worms" action the heart had been exhibiting before. Almost hesitantly, as if reluctant to begin, a faint single contraction occurred, then another, then another, in a steady rhythm that indicated a resumption of the normal beat. As it grew stronger with each contraction a cheer broke out from those in the operating room and from the crowd which now half filled the surgical lecture room watching the television screen.

"We're not out of the woods yet." Greg's eyes were on the monitor screen as he spoke. The heart pattern portrayed there was obviously growing stronger all the while, but only when the peaks marking the electrical impulses that initiated each contraction approached normal, did he turn back to the operative field to complete the closure that marked the end of the dramatic operative procedure.

"Do you want to try inflation, Lew?" he asked the anesthesiologist. If the connection between respirator and the new airway was not tight, now was the time to correct it, but, when Dr. Gann turned a valve on the respirator, inflating the lungs, the pressure held and the exhale valve tripped automatically, allowing them to deflate.

"We're ready to come off the pump," said Greg and tension gripped the operating room again at his words.

Actually, this stage was even more critical than had been the task of putting Guy Merchant on the heart-lung pump at the beginning of the operation. Any failure correctly to adjust pressures here could interfere easily with the rhythmic action of the heart, beating quietly now but not pumping blood, bringing it to a halt. Then another jolt of the elctric current would be needed to start it, with possible damage to the delicate control network inside the heart itself, through which the nerve impulses controlling the beat were transmitted. Just as dangerous, a failure during the crucial moments of transfer from mechanical to physiological action could interfere with the vital circulation to the brain, leaving Guy Merchant a vegetable, even if the new heart and lungs function perfectly.

"I'm clamping the venous cannulae," Greg warned the techhnicians as he slowly began to close down the tubes which had been feeding blood from the body veins into the spinning heart-lung pump. One technician called out the steadily rising venous pressures indicated on the pump, while another read the arterial pressures as reported on the electronic monitor from the tiny tube of nylon inserted into an artery of the hand at the beginning of the operation.

"Loosen the snares," Greg directed.

Bob Johnson reached behind the heart to where the tapes that surrounded the inferior and the superior vena cava, with the cannulae still inside them, maintained a snug fit around the plastic tubes. With the snares loosened, blood flowed past the tubes into the right side of the heart, but at the same moment Greg loosened the purse-string in the wall of the atrium, which he had placed long ago, it seemed, when Guy Merchant had been put upon the pump. A faint froth of blood and air escaped around the tube, removing the small amount of air which had entered the heart while the connections to Guy Merchant's circulatory system were being made. When no more froth escaped, he slid the cannula quickly out of the superior vena cava, allowed the atrium to fill with blood and spill out through the purse-string opening, then closed it by tightening the ends of the suture. The tube in the lower of the great veins would be removed later through the common femoral vein, into which it had been inserted.

The pump-oxygenator, its steel discs still spinning, was now forcing blood into Guy Merchant's body through the tube in the artery of his upper thigh but was taking none from it. As the pressure in the right side of the heart rose from the blood now pouring into the atrium from the great veins, the valve that controlled its emptying opened and filled the adjoining muscular chamber on the right side, called the ventricle. Stimulated by the change in pressure, the ventricle began to pump blood through the lungs, from which it was returned to the left side of the heart, where the same sequence of events occurred.

Seconds ticked away while the vital pressure gradients recorded on the monitors and the gauges of the heart-lung pump rose steadily. Blood being forced into Guy Merchant's circulation was now passing through the tiny capillary vessels connecting veins to arteries in even the most distant parts of his body and pouring into the heart from the right side, while the surging force of the pump still filled the aorta and the rest of the arterial system. When the pressure grudients reached the desired level, the pump technician at the valves began to shut off the flow into the body. And as the pressure inside the now vigorously pumping left ventricle overcame the back pressure in the arterial system from the pump, the valve between ventricle and aorta opened and blood surged through.

"Femoral cannula closed, Dr. Alexander," said the pump technician as he turned the valve through which blood had been flowing to Guy Merchant's body from the machine. "He's on his own."

Greg was watching the monitors. When the arterial pressure recorded there continued to show a level that was obviously able to maintain the vital brain circulation, he began to tie the ends of the purse-string suture, closing finally the opening through which the cannula in the superior vena cava had carried blood from Guy Merchant's body to the pump. Only the click-click of the respirator filled the room now as the whirr of the pump ceased, and Greg reached for the wire sutures used to pull the two halves of the split breastbone together.

"The patient is now maintaining his own circulation without assistance," he announced to the watching audience and everyone there could easily hear the note of pride in his voice. When he looked up at the clock over the door, he was startled to see that barely an hour had elapsed since the medical examiner had given him the go-ahead to begin the epochal transplant.

V

In the adjoining lecture room, Jud Templeton blinked as he turned his eyes from the television screen. He looked at his watch, then sprinted for the telephone. When the rewrite man to whom he had been feeding elements of the story intermittently over the past hour came on, he said jubilantly:

"Pull out all the stops, Jeff! He's made it!"

"Give me a lead, Jud. The city editor's having a fit."

"How about this? *'Tonight a murderer atoned for his sins as no other man has ever done in history, when Dr. Gregory Alexander, a quiet, self-effacing surgeon at Baltimore's world-famous Clinic, successfully transplanted the murderer's heart and lungs to the body of a dying man.'"*

CHAPTER NINETEEN

I

It was nearly midnight before Greg was finally able to telephone Jeanne. "Congratulations, darling!" she cried.

"How did you know?"

"You're all over the television. Half the eleven o'clock news was devoted to you."

"I can't leave the hospital tonight, but I would love to see you at least for a few minutes," he told her. "Could you meet me at the feet of Jesus?"

"I'll be there—in five minutes."

"Take longer if you need it."

"No. That will be enough."

She was waiting at the foot of the great statue when he came into the lobby after reporting the successful conclusion of the operation to Georgia Merchant. Visiting hours were long over and the rotunda was empty, save for an intern and a nurse whispering in the shadows and the telephone operators behind their grille.

"You look worn, darling," she said. "Was the operation so difficult?"

"Not the operation—but the waiting. We almost didn't make it."

"Then Merchant will live?"

"Everything's functioning well but we still have to watch for infection— mostly of the lungs—and rejection."

"After tonight, how could the trustees turn you down?"

"I'm afraid the operation won't really change things. It might even have the opposite effect."

"Why?"

"There's a great deal of jealousy among doctors. Some will want to cut me down just because I had the courage to do something they wouldn't tackle."

"But it's they who should beg you to stay. You're still going to push your plan for The Clinic, aren't you? It's too beautiful to be lost."

Greg looked up into the dimness of the rotunda. The marble features of the Christ somehow seemed different. He thought his eyes were playing tricks on him, until Jeanne, whose gaze had followed his, suddenly cried, "He's smiling! It's a good omen, Greg! I know it is!"

"What you're seeing is most likely the effect of the shadows there under the dome," he said. But somehow he wasn't surprised at the feeling of assurance and peace that had suddenly come over him, as if perhaps He, too, had seen Keith Jackson's sketches and wanted to come out of the shadows into the sunlight.

"When can you come home?" Jeanne asked.

"Perhaps tomorrow night. I'm going to send Bob Johnson home. Lew Gann and I will take turns watching over Merchant." He glanced at his watch. "It's time for me to let Bob go off duty now. Thanks for coming over, darling."

"I—I'm glad you wanted me after—"

"That's all over now," he said quickly. "Forever."

"Go back to your patient," she told him. "I think I'll sit here at the foot of the statue for a while."

"Ask the night watchman at the guard post by the entrance to see that you get across to the apartment safely. There's been some mugging in this area." He bent to kiss her. "Good night."

"Good night, dear."

When he was gone, she remained standing at the foot of the great statue, recalling the times she'd met Greg there for a few stolen moments when he had been a Fellow and she a nurse. She didn't notice the presence of another person, until Georgia Merchant said, "Mrs. Alexander?"

"Yes." Jeanne turned to face her.

"I saw you talking to Dr. Alexander just now and the receptionist told me you're his wife. I'm Mrs. Merchant."

"I'm so glad your husband came through the operation safely, Mrs. Merchant," said Jeanne warmly. "It must be a great relief to have it over with."

"To tell the truth, I don't know whether to be happy or guilty."

"But why?"

"I let my faith weaken for a while," Georgia confessed. "When it seemed that Guy had gone so far there could be no bringing him back, even with the operation, I kept asking myself whether I loved him enough to let him die and wasn't selfish in wanting him to live."

"I think that's a very natural way to feel."

"I'll always be grateful to your husband for taking the burden of decision off my shoulders."

"You must be exhausted," said Jeanne. "We have an extra room and I'll be happy for you to use it."

"Thank you, Mrs. Alexander, but I couldn't." Georgia's smile was wry with the pain of many years of rebuffs. "You see, I'm a stripper—a striptease dancer."

Jeanne Alexander looked up at the features of the statue, then back at the woman before her.

"I seem to remember reading that the leader of the women who followed Him was a dancer. If He didn't hold that against her, I'd be pretty small to hold your occupation against you, wouldn't I?"

Georgia Merchant's shoulders straightened and her chin lifted. "I *was* beginning to feel sorry for myself and Guy wouldn't want that. Your husband is one of the gentlest men I've ever known, Mrs. Alexander, as gentle even as my Guy. I guess we're two of the luckiest women alive; thank you for helping me not to forget."

"I'm glad I could help," Jeanne said quietly. "You see, I once came very close to forgetting myself."

"I'll be all right now," said Georgia. "Guy might wake up and want to know I was nearby. Thanks for being so kind."

As Jeanne was leaving the hospital, a newspaper truck pulled up the driveway and stopped at the entrance. The driver got down from the cab and lifted a package of morning papers from it. Going to a coin-operated rack beside the entrance, he unlocked it, shoved in a stack of papers, placed one in front and locked it back in a swift succession of movements, before leaping upon his truck and starting down the driveway again.

Across the top of the copy he'd slid into place in the front of the vending machine, Jeanne could see the bold headlines:

CLINIC SURGEON MAKES MEDICAL HISTORY
Performs Surgical Miracle

II

Guy Merchant regained consciousness—if it could be called that—shortly after dawn. At first, he wondered whether he were alive and not simply a soul in transit, for he seemed to be floating between earth and sky. When his eyes were able to focus, however, he recognized the same dull white ceiling of the room where he had been taken, a long time ago it seemed now, when his breathing had become so difficult. And when he moved his shoulders, seeking a more comfortable position, the pain in his chest confirmed the fact that he was alive and in the flesh, instead of a random spirit on the way to whatever was its final destination.

"Mr. Merchant?" The face floating above him slowly cleared like a color slide being focused on a screen, and he saw that the speaker was a nurse. She was wearing a gown and mask but he could see enough hair escaping around her cap to determine that she was red-haired, reminding him that he hadn't seen Georgia for a long, long time. He tried to speak and ask for Georgia, but wasn't able to force air through his voice box, which seemed strange, for he could feel the rhythmic expansion and contraction of his chest with breathing, and the pain that went with it.

"Your wife's outside," said the nurse. "You're in isolation, so she can't come in for a while."

He tried to speak again and ask if the operation was over, but gave up because there simply wasn't any air to form the words.

"We're trying to keep infection away from you." Strange that he could see the nurse perfectly now and hear her, yet the words that formed in his brain wouldn't come from his larynx. "I'll send word to your wife that you're awake, and perhaps she can see you later today. You were operated on nearly ten hours ago, Mr. Merchant."

Another face appeared beside that of the nurse and he recognized the young surgeon who was usually with Dr. Alexander.

"You're doing fine," Bob Johnson assured him. "We gave you a new heart and lungs and they're working very well."

The younger man reached toward something that was out of Guy's sight beside the bed and the rhythmic clicking stopped. "Try to take a breath for me, please."

Guy concentrated on the act of breathing but nothing happened. Before he could suffer any apprehension, however, the clicking started again, and, with it, the regular filling and emptying of his lungs.

"Dr. Alexander was up most of the night watching over you, Mr. Merchant," Bob Johnson explained. "He's getting some sleep now and you'd better get some more, too. The nurse is going to give you a hypo."

Guy could feel the sting of the needle as the drug was injected; then almost immediately he was floating downward again into the familiar pleasant void.

III

Helen was wondering whether she would find Peter waiting when she came into the motel dining room shortly after eight. He was standing by the cashier's booth, however, and moved at once to guide her to a secluded table distinguished from the rest by a magnificent arrangement of red roses.

"How did you know they're my favorite flower?" Her eyes were warm as he pulled out her chair.

"They had to be. Roses are independent, yet beautiful—like you."

"No wonder women can't resist you. The charm stays on, like a light left burning."

"Let's talk more about this idea that women can't resist me," he said. "Are you speaking from experience?"

"Didn't you make me eat ham and eggs yesterday morning, when a protein cereal and orange juice is my regular menu?"

"I've already ordered for both of us. Want to know today's menu?"

"Ham and eggs?"

"Eventually—first we'll have a fresh honeydew melon, brought here from Florida especially for you."

"Don't tell me you had that flown in since yesterday—like the roses?"

"I would have, if the restaurant hadn't had them in stock."

"Is this part of the famous Carewe technique of whirlwind courtship?"

"You can't blame me if I work fast. I only have a few days."

"Has something new come up?" she asked quickly, and he nodded.

"A night letter from Lars Nordstrom, my chief at the UN section in New York. He wants me in Los Angeles no later than Monday afternoon to take charge of the search for that polio vaccine contaminant I was telling you about."

Both of them were subdued a little by the thought that their time together would be so short. Only when the waitress had poured a second cup of coffee for them did Peter suddenly ask, "Have I told you I'm in love with you?"

"Please, Peter." Helen put down her coffee cup with a hand that had suddenly started to tremble. "You mustn't."

"Why not?"

"Let's just keep this light and pleasant—the way it's been so far."

"That's only a front we've been using to cover the way we've really felt about each other since the moment I saw you at the airport yesterday. Don't deny it."

"I can't," she confessed. "But there are reasons why we mustn't be serious."

"Are you in love with someone else?"

"Oh no!"

"And are you in love with me?"

"I think I am." The moment of truth had come, she could no longer evade it. "Yes, I know I am."

"Is it Henry Anders then?"

"Why do you say that?"

"The way he acted last night toward you—like he owned you. I never liked the bastard anyway, but even in medical school he had a formidable reputation with women." He took both her hands in his across the table. "Don't tell me you love him?"

"Oh no. You see I—"

"No details—please."

"I was going to tell you before this—this went too far. But then I was afraid of losing you and thought we could just enjoy the time you're going to be here together."

"What's happened to us isn't something you can just enjoy for a while and forget, Helen. I've had plenty of casual affairs and this is different."

"So what do we do—get married?"

"Are you sure enough of yourself for that?"

"Not yet—but I don't think I'm far from it."

"I'm nearer than that," he said. "Say the word and we'll head for Elkton this morning. Years ago you could get married there at any time of the day or night."

"I couldn't do that to you, darling." Her voice was sober. "You see, I know myself—and my needs."

"I figured that's what's been troubling you," he said. "And sometime around midnight I came up with what may be the answer."

"What is it?"

"Something like a physiologic test to distinguish between love and simply sex attraction, plus finding out just how well we're suited to each other physically."

"Room service?"

"Something more appropriate, I think, for us."

"I'm not the kind of woman who jumps into the bed of any man who asks me—no matter how attractive he is."

"We're both scientists, so why not a scientific experiment?"

"Experiment? That's a new name for an affair."

"We both know this wouldn't be just another affair. What we need is a chance to get to know each other and find out some things for ourselves. For instance, it's quite possible that with your—" He fumbled for a word and she supplied it—somewhat bitterly.

"Experience?"

"I didn't plan to put it so bluntly. The truth is, you might not find me quite the lover I seem to have the reputation of being."

"And vice versa."

"Since we're using such starkly realistic phraseology—yes. But however that part of it turns out, we could have a pleasantly comfortable weekend together, with no strings attached. Then Monday morning, I'll fly away for a while and you'll have time to think things out."

"You still haven't named the place for this—experiment. Shall it be my apartment or your suite?"

"Neither. Did you ever hear of the Chalet Julienne?"

"No."

"It's a typical Swiss-type inn located in the Catoctin Mountains not far from Frederick, only a couple of hours or so drive from here. Two old friends of mine, Carl and Julia Koenig, run it. They don't have many guests in winter and we'll be treated like royalty."

"It's an attractive prospect," she admitted.

"Nobody else need know," he assured her. "I have to leave for California Sunday afternoon, so you can drive your car to the airport Friday afternoon and I'll meet you there. We'll leave your car in the parking lot and I'll rent one. That way, I can abduct you, and shut you away somewhere—like Rumpelstiltskin."

CHAPTER TWENTY

I

Jeanne Alexander had been up an hour when Greg called at eight. She hadn't eaten breakfast, however, hoping he might have time to join her.

"Just thought you'd like to know Merchant seems to be doing well," he said. "Mainly, I called to tell you I love you."

"I couldn't blame you if you didn't."

"And I couldn't stop if I tried. I wish I could come over for breakfast, but I've called a conference for nine o'clock to evaluate Merchant's condition and I have to get all the information I can for it."

"I thought you said he's doing all right."

"He is—so far."

"You're worried about rejection, aren't you?"

"That's the next hurdle. Even with ALG, it can still happen, though that's our best weapon. I've got to run now—"

"Greg!"

"Yes, dear."

"Isn't there some way I can help?"

"You've helped already. Just knowing we're together again has made all the difference in the world."

"Will you be able to go to the banquet tonight?"

"I'm going to try. I'll have to call you later about that."

When he hung up the phone, Jeanne put on the percolator and made some coffee, while she poured cereal in a bowl and sat down at the kitchen table. She was eating when Ethel came in.

"The doctor sure has been making a name for hisself," the maid said proudly. "He's all over the newspapers, the television, everywhere. When's he coming home?"

"I went over to the hospital to see him last night," Jeanne told her. "He hopes to get home tonight. We're supposed to go to a banquet."

"Do you good to get out—with him. Just bein' yourself again is what he needs most."

The maid's wisdom, Jeanne thought wryly, was greater than her own. But she still needed to do something tangible to allay her feeling of guilt for having let Greg down at a time when he had been more troubled than during the whole period of their marriage—if only she could find a way.

Pulling on a heavy sweater, she stepped out upon the balcony that surrounded two sides of the penthouse. From this lofty viewpoint, she could see the whole of The Clinic, squat and ugly across the street in its brownstone dress.

California would be bright and cheerful, the sun warm most of the year. She had seen the medical school in which Greg would work there; it was all steel and glass while here everything was dingy and drab. Yet, however drab and uninspiring it might look now, she knew the complex of buildings across the busy Parkway was as much a part of Greg as his own heart—and something no surgeon could replace. More than twenty years of his life had gone into another man's dream, and now, with Keith Jackson's plan for a soaring tower of healing in place of the drab and the brown, he hoped to turn that dream into a flame brighter even than old Dr. Anders had ever conceived.

She didn't for a moment really believe he was as unconcerned as he claimed to be about the outcome of the controversy which would reach its climax Saturday morning. The Clinic was Greg's life and to give up the dream now of what it could be, would be nothing less than heartbreaking for him. There had to be something she could do and somehow she had to find it. The trouble was that time was so short; only two more days until the convocation would be over and the crucial session of the Board of Trustees would begin.

Then, when her spirits were at their lowest, she suddenly remembered something that sent her inside to ring Claire Anders on the telephone.

"Sorry I had to leave you to entertain all the men last night, when Greg started the operation, Claire," she said. "But I couldn't think of anything except what he was going through."

"You did me a favor, darling," said Claire. "Helen went to the laboratory and I had Peter Carewe to myself for a drink—but nothing else, worse luck."

"Did you mean what you said yesterday at lunch about our working together to keep The Clinic from being moved, Claire?"

"Of course, but things look bleak. Henry is sure Greg has overstepped himself in operating on Merchant and that they have him where they want him."

"I'm worried about the same thing," Jeanne admitted. "Greg claims the idea of going somewhere else doesn't bother him any more but I know better."

"The Clinic would never be the same without Greg," Claire agreed. "Lord knows I've tried to keep Henry from making a fool of himself, but he's hell bent on it this time. So where does that leave us?"

"There may be a chance of blocking Henry and Ed, if you'll help me."

"Say the word."

"Yesterday morning, when Hannah barged in while I was having breakfast, she let drop something about a syndicate being formed to develop The Clinic property when it goes to Henry after the move to the Beltway. She hinted that if Greg stopped opposing the move, they'd cut him in. Do you know anything about it?"

"Henry knows I don't approve of moving The Clinic, so he's pretty secretive about his plans," said Claire. "What did you have in mind?"

"From what Hannah said before she clammed up on me, some other people besides Henry and Ed must be involved in this syndicate. I was thinking that if we could possibly get a list of them, it might be useful."

"A little judicious blackmail?"

"Well—yes."

"Henry's got a desk upstairs in his study that he always keeps locked. If he's got a list of people in the syndicate, it will be there."

"But can you get it?"

"I learned to pick the lock a long time ago, hunting for *billets-doux* from Henry's girl friends, before he settled down with Helen. I think I still know how to do it. Give me a little while and I'll call you back."

"I'll be waiting," Jeanne promised.

The call came in less than half an hour. "We hit pay dirt, Jeanne," said Claire. "I found the list tucked away in Henry's desk. What do you have in mind doing with it?"

"Jud Templeton has been treating Greg well—"

"Jud's just the man. Get your pencil and write these names down. They're dynamite."

When Jeanne finished copying the list Claire read to her over the telephone, she sat studying the names written there for a long moment. It was an impressive array of men prominent in medical, political and business affairs, a truly formidable barrier for one woman to buck alone. Yet she knew Greg wouldn't use it if she showed it to him, so the job was hers. Finally, she leafed through the directory, found a number and dialed it.

"Mr. Jud Templeton, please," she said when the operator at the newspaper offices downtown answered.

II

The conference Greg had called to evaluate Guy Merchant's condition was being held before the Thursday-morning session of the convocation began. At his request, Dave Connor listened to the patient's heart and lungs and studied the laboratory reports, while Bob Johnson brought up the portable X-ray films of the chest taken that morning. The three of them, with Dr. Gann, gathered after the examination in the doctor's lounge between the two main operating theaters of the surgical building.

"Dr. Zenoff's busy with a fluoroscopic examination," Bob Johnson said as he flicked on the switch of a portable X-ray viewbox. "But I got an off-the-cuff reading on the film from the Senior Fellow in X-ray. All he sees is cloudiness at the bases of the lungs and he says that may be only a pleural reaction."

"You can't take out the heart and lungs and connect up another pair without roughing up the inside of the chest cage a little, so some cloudiness can be expected," said Greg. "What do you think from your examination, Dave?"

"He's in remarkably good condition," said the cardiologist. "Frankly, when I saw you putting him on the pump while the donor was still alive, I was sure you were way out on a limb that was half sawed off already."

"I felt a little that way, too," Greg admitted. "Do you agree that haziness at the lung bases may not have any real significance?"

"There's some moisture in the lower lobes of the lungs, too; I could hear râles in the stethoscope," said the cardiologist. "But there was a lot more of it yesterday before we gave him the diuretic."

"This is a new pair of lungs," Bob Johnson reminded him.

"I'm not forgetting that—and it worries me a little," said Dr. Connor.

"Do you think we should give him another injection of ethacrynic acid?" Greg asked, but the cardiologist shook his head.

"There doesn't seem to be enough moisture to justify hitting him with anything that strong at the moment, particularly since the kidneys seem to be functioning very well," he said. "I think the best procedure is to watch and wait."

"Meanwhile, we'll give him one or two transfusions with Lawson's blood," said Greg, "just in case the moisture in the lungs is the beginning of a rejection phenomenon. The transfusion should provide him with some fresh white blood cells, too, in case his infection-resisting powers have been knocked down by this six-mercaptopurine and methylprednisolone we're giving him to keep down the rejection, along with ALG."

"Do you see any suggestion of rejection in the cardiogram, sir?" Bob Johnson asked Dr. Connor.

"Not at the moment. The first thing we'd expect, if his body tried to get rid of the transplant, would be a fall in the ECG voltage. But the R-wave of limb lead two"—he pointed to a wavy line on the electrocardiographic tracing—"seems to be as high as it has been at any time."

"What do you think about moving him to intensive care?" Greg asked. "We can watch the ECG a little better on the monitors there than we're able to do in the O.R. And we won't have quite so many people moving in and out with the possibility of bringing in outside infection."

"It sounds like a good idea," said Dave Connor.

"I'll vote for that," said Dr. Gann. "The chances of any virulent bacteria getting to him while his immunity is knocked down so severely by the drugs you're giving to prevent rejection will be considerably less on ICU than down here."

"Bob will help you move him, Lew," said Greg. "I promised to make a report at the opening of the convocation this morning on Merchant's progress."

From the lounge, he went into the surgical lecture room, which was gradually filling with Members of The Clinic in preparation for the morning presentations. Minutes before the cluck struck ten and Dr. Timoty Puckett gaveled for attention, Ed McDougal and several others of his faction came in.

Ed looked a little hung over, Greg thought, but that wasn't unusual for him at medical conventions. He seemed to have lost none of this assurance, however, by which Greg judged that Ed and his cronies had been successfully lining up support on the Board of Trustees for themselves while he was busy last night with the transplant operation. Jud Templeton was lounging, as usual, at the back of the room.

"Dr. Alexander has requested a few minutes at the beginning of the session," Dr. Puckett announced. "Go ahead, Greg."

"Some of you have asked for a report on the heart-lung transplant patient we operated on last night," said Greg. "Dr. Connor has just examined him with me and finds his general condition very good. The only possible adverse sign we see now is a little moisture at the bases of the lungs and we're not sure this is significant under the circumstances."

"Is he breathing without the respirator?" Ed McDougal asked.

"Not yet," Greg admitted.

"Then it sounds like your operation was a failure."

"Not necessarily." Greg contained his temper, recognizing the purpose of the question. "In some of our experimental transplants, respiration hasn't actually begun for several days following operation. In a few others, we've had to stimulate the phrenic nerves electrically to produce contraction of the diaphragm for some time before spontaneous breathing was resumed."

"What about rejection?" another man asked.

"That's our major concern," said Greg. "We're deliberately holding off using heavy doses of immuno-suppressive drugs, as was done in some of the early heart transplant cases, so as not to knock down his defenses against bacteria. Usually, this sort of an infection begins in the lungs, which is another reason why the presence of the moisture there this morning gives us some concern. We are, of course, giving him antibiotics to prevent infection and keeping him isolated."

"What are the chances of his living now?" Ed McDougal asked.

"I think it's too early to evaluate them yet," said Greg. "The fact that he came through surgery in satisfactory condition is a considerable plus value in his favor. The deciding factor in survival will no doubt be whether his body accepts the transplant or rejects it."

When there seemed to be no more questions, he started toward the door leading to the lounge, but Ed McDougal's voice stopped him before he left the room.

"There's been some pretty sharp criticism of your action in subjecting this patient to an operation whose results are so uncertain," he said. "What do you have to say about that?"

Realizing that the purpose of the question was to crystallize the opposition to him, Greg's immediate reaction was one of anger, but he controlled it.

"Anyone who dares to break through a new frontier is liable to get a few arrows stuck in him." He spoke directly to the questioner. "Usually from the rear, by people who are afraid to explore unmarked territory."

There was a wave of laughter and Ed McDougal reddened at the thrust.

"I've always considered that my major obligation to a patient is to keep him alive as long as possible," Greg continued. "This man was clinically dead by the time we were able to get the heart-lung pump in operation and bypass a heart that had failed—yet this morning he's alive. If you can figure out how that makes me guilty of negligence toward him, you're welcome to do so."

Turning on his heel, Greg left the room, but not before it was swept by a spatter of applause. At the podium, Dr. Timothy Puckett gaveled hurriedly for order and began to introduce the first scheduled speaker of the morning session.

III

Jud Templeton was waiting in the corridor outside the lecture room when Greg came out. "You've won rounds one and two, Doctor," he said. "If you can keep up the pace, you'll get a TKO at the very least."

"You skipped one round."

"The smoke-filled room?"

"Yes."

"Maybe we ought to print that sketch sooner than we intended. The cut of it turned out beautifully."

"Not yet," said Greg. "We may not even get to use it Friday if the question of hospital plans doesn't come up at the afternoon meeting—"

"I wouldn't be too sure they won't."

"Why?"

"If Guy Merchant is still living Friday afternoon when the special meeting comes to order, any attempt to censure you because of your work in experimental surgery is liable to fall pretty flat, with the world applauding you for being a pioneer."

"I think we should stick to schedule. If we detonate our only bomb too soon, the effect may subside before Saturday. By the way, that was a nice piece you did on Mrs. Merchant."

"Georgia deserves all the kudos she can get. Her world might seem to be a pretty scurvy one to you, but it's a very human one nevertheless. And in it, she's a great lady."

Greg smiled. "I'm not quite so square as my predilection for work might make you believe, Jud. I've seen her perform and agree wholly."

"Do you happen to know where she is?"

"She told me earlier she was going back to her hotel for a few minutes to get a shower and a change of clothes. She ought to be back soon."

"A few telegrams came for her in care of me," said Jud Templeton. "Seems like a lot of other people aren't square either, Doctor. Where do we go from here?"

"Watch and wait is all we can do. Are you going to stick around?"

"I think I'll go back to the shop and write a follow-up, then get some sleep."

"I envy you," said Greg as he took the elevator to his office. "I've still got work to do."

"Mr. Templeton!" It was the emergency room nursing supervisor with a slip of paper in her hand. Since the play the newspaperman had given The Clinic's favorite surgeon, he was very popular with the staff. "That phone you've been using outside the emergency room was ringing just now, so I answered it. You're to call Mrs. Alexander at this number."

"Dr. Alexander's wife?"

"Yes. I recognized the number."

"Thanks," he said, and headed for the telephone, wondering why Greg Alexander's wife would call him here.

IV

Helen Foucald was busy at her desk Thursday morning, clearing it so she could attend the morning session of the convocation when her secretary ushered Sam Hunter into the inner office.

"Did they send you down for some more special examinations, Mr. Hunter?" she asked. "We finished up the routine things yesterday."

"I've just finished in otolaryngology." Sam looked at the green routing sheet in his hand. "And I'm on my way to proctology. Reminds me of a book I read a long time ago, called *Through the Alimentary Canal with Gun and Camera*."

Helen Foucald laughed. "It's not so bad, as long as you can still smile. Can we do something for you here in the laboratory?"

"It's you I came to see. Can you have dinner with me tonight and go to a circus?"

"I had planned to go to the banquet," she said doubtfully.

"Your friend Carewe is going to be pretty busy with the banquet and I thought you might not mind helping cheer up a lonely old man." The odd intensity in his voice told her this was not a casual invitation, particularly when he added, "Besides, we'll probably be back by the time he finishes with the speech and the autograph hunters after it."

"That doesn't matter at all," Helen said quickly, sensing how anxious he was for her to accept. "I shall be happy to go. Did you say the circus?"

"It's only a small one that will probably play in a Shrine auditorium—if there's such a thing in the town we're going to."

"I'll wear something warm. Those places can get pretty drafty."

"How about six o'clock? The town isn't far away and we can have dinner somewhere along the road."

"Six o'clock will be fine," she assured him. "Shall I meet you in the lobby of the Inn? I live next door."

"If that suits you?"

"It suits me fine. I'll see you at six."

"I shall be desolate," Peter said when she told him of Sam Hunter's odd request as they were going in for the morning session of the convocation. "You'll be basking in the limelight and enjoying it, with admiring women all around you. I'd be jealous if I were there."

"How about a nightcap when you get back?"

"I'd love it—provided some amazon hasn't abducted you by then."

V

"This is Jud Templeton," a male voice said when Jeanne answered her telephone shortly after ten o'clock.

"Oh yes, Mr. Templeton. I appreciate your calling so quickly."

"I would have made it sooner, but I'm at the hospital and the paper had to call me there. Just finished listening to your husband give a report to the convocation on that operation he did last night. It was a spectacular job."

"I need your help, Mr. Templeton—for my husband."

"Any favor I can do either of you is a pleasure, Mrs. Alexander."

"I suppose you've heard rumors that The Clinic may be moved."

"I've heard—and I don't like it any more than Dr. Alexander does."

"Did you know that a syndicate has been formed to develop the property if the trustees decide to move it?"

"I've heard a rumor, but I've seen no real proof."

"Would you consider a list of those in the syndicate real proof?"

"If some of the names on that list are vulnerable, Mrs. Alexander"—she sensed the rising excitement in his voice—"we may not need proof."

"They're vulnerable, Mr. Templeton. More vulnerable than you would believe."

Jud Templeton chuckled. "Newspapermen are like doctors, Mrs. Alexander. They see human nature at its worst more often than they do at its best, so I'm always ready to believe the worst of my fellow-men. When can I see the list?"

"I'm free right now."

"It may be just as well if we're not seen together near The Clinic," he said. "Where would you suggest that we meet?"

"I'll walk north several blocks along The Parkway," she said. "I'll be wearing a dark London Fog coat and a matching hat."

"Give me five minutes."

Jeanne often walked the central pavement strip of The Parkway, even in cold weather, so she was sure no one who knew her would think it odd for her to be there. Four blocks beyond the hospital, she turned back and almost immediately saw Jud Templeton approaching.

"You didn't waste any time," he said with a smile.

"I'm trying to help my husband, Mr. Templeton, and there isn't much time."

"Maybe we can gain some—if this list is all you say it is."

Jeanne handed him the sheet of paper and he ran his eyes down its length, pursing his lips once or twice in a soundless whistle.

"I never cease to be amazed at the avariceness of human nature," he said finally. "Every one of these men is rich by any standard you name, yet they all succumbed to the possibility of making a fast buck. Who's the leader?"

"Dr. Ed McDougal—from Texas."

"He would be—this is a Texas-style operation. But I need to fire a round or two at targets nearer home. Believe me, it's going to be a pleasure to scare the daylights out of a few of our leading medical citizens."

"You're not going to publish the list in the paper, are you?"

"As a bunch of names, it means nothing, but if I bear down hard enough on some of these characters, one of them may just blurt out the whole scheme. Then I'll have something I can put headlines on and we'll blow this whole thing to smithereens."

"Where are you going to start?" she asked.

"Dr. Timothy Puckett seems to be the one who's got most to lose, I'd say. As chairman of the Board of Trustees, he's supposed to be like Caesar's wife, so I'll give him the first chance to repent of his sins."

"Promise you won't tell my husband about this."

"Your husband is the finest surgeon I know, Mrs. Alexander—but he'd probably be the worst conniver. You and I will handle this little hatchet job ourselves."

VI

Seen by day, the sleazy environs of the nightclub area were even shabbier-looking than Georgia remembered. After two days at the hospital with crisp-uniformed doctors and nurses everywhere, she shivered at the thought of going back into the world it represented. Yet she had good friends there, people who had stood by her and Guy before in times of trouble and would stand by her again, she was sure.

In the club where she had been working, the chairs were still turned upside down atop the tables as the early morning cleaners had left them after doing their work. A single bartender was polishing glasses behind the long bar and a lonely drinker sat at one end, nursing a beer.

"Hi, Georgia," said the bartender. "How's Guy?"

"He came through the operation O.K. The doctors say he's doing well."

"Must have been pretty exciting. You and him have been all over the newspapers."

"I've been too busy to read them," said Georgia. "Is Aaron in?"

"Sure. He's working on the books in his office."

The office door was open and she saw Aaron Schwartz bent over the desk. He was a rumpled bear of a man, so near-sighted that he had to wear thick lenses. He looked up when Georgia tapped on the door, then got up with surprising agility for his size and came around the end of the desk to take both her hands.

"Georgia!" He greeted her warmly, leading her to a chair by the desk. "You and Guy are famous! Have you seen *Variety*?"

Georgia shook her head. "I've hardly been out of the intensive care unit at The Clinic since the other night."

"*Variety* picked up Jud Templeton's piece about you." He handed her the newspaper that was the bible of show business. There in the middle of the second page, in a box where it could hardly be missed, was the article Jud Templeton had written. It was illustrated with a photograph of her, not as she was now, but as she had been as a burlesque headliner.

"I couldn't be more glad if it had happened to me," Aaron Schwartz assured her. "The booking agents will be on your trail any minute."

"I'm a little old for another career now, Aaron."

"Don't you believe it," he said. "You're too high-class for a rat race like this." The wave of his cigar took in the shabby surroundings of the nightclub.

"Are you firing me, Aaron?"

"Firing?" He looked at her with honest pain in his eyes, and she reached out to squeeze his hand.

"Forgive me. I've been under a terrible strain."

"Of course you have. I was going to wait until later to talk to you about this." Georgia understood what "later" meant—until she no longer had Guy hanging around her neck, like the millstone he had considered himself to be.

"I've got to face the future sometime, Aaron. What do you have in mind?"

"Traveling burlesque is coming back. Not the kind we have now with a bunch of young broads who don't know enough to even draw down a zipper without stumbling over themselves, taking off their clothes to canned music. In the old days, burlesque was an art, and the humor a lot better than the stuff you hear coming in on television these days. I've been thinking about putting together a traveling show, not to play the old burlesque houses, but regular theaters on one-, two- or maybe three-night stands, with a whole week whenever we hit a city that's large enough. A show like that will need class and that's something you've always had."

"What about Guy—if he lives?"

"If I put the package together, I'll need somebody I can trust to watch over it, a sort of traveling manager. Guy could handle that in his sleep."

"It might be the answer to our problems, Aaron—after I get me a new face." Georgia's eyes fell to the newspaper and the picture. "The rest of me still stacks up pretty will with what it was fifteen years ago, but you could check the bags under my eyes in any railroad station."

"Don't give that part a thought. It will take a while to put this package together and there's a surgeon out at The Clinic who's remodeled some of the most famous faces in show business. How about it?"

"Don't ask me to make a decision now, Aaron, but you're a sweet guy to think of it. I just came by to say hello and pick up my check."

"I made it out last night and was going to send it over to the hotel this morning." He handed her the check and, when she saw the amount, tears suddenly came into her eyes.

"It's too much, Aaron," she managed to say.

"The check? It's your regular salary."

"That—and everything." She blew her nose with her handkerchief and dabbed her eyes. "You don't owe me all this—the week wasn't half finished when I had to stop the other night."

"Call it an advance, then, until we can get started on this new project. Besides, you kept those Teamsters from wrecking this joint."

"It may be a long time—months even—before Guy's back in shape."

"You won't have to be at the hospital all that time, will you?"

"I wouldn't think so, why?"

"I'm going to need some expert help in putting this package together and nobody's more of an expert in this business than you are. You can help me find some of the old burlesque comics, the real greats, and a couple of young strippers with class that you can train as you go along. That'll be the toughest part of all, and where I'll need the most help from you."

"It sounds interesting. And I could certainly use the weekly pay check."

"Whatever happens to Guy, he'd want you to go on working, Georgia. You're one of the few aristocrats in this business—"

"A gone-to-seed aristocrat."

"Not on your life. You're still better than ninety-nine per cent of the others and with the right kind of show, you'll be back on top again in a few months. That would be the best present you could give Guy, wherever he'd be."

"Thanks, Aaron—for the check and the vote of confidence."

"Don't worry about anything except Guy. You're on the payroll right along, and, when he gets to where you aren't worried about him all the time, start remembering some of the old routines. You know: Cleopatra and the Asp, the new patient in the hospital—skits like that. You're still the best straight woman in the business."

When she left the club, Georgia went to the hotel nearby where she and Guy had been living. The clerk put down the copy of *Variety* he was reading and gave her a big smile.

"Good morning, Mrs. Merchant," he said. "How's your husband?"

"He's holding his own, Mike." Georgia handed him Aaron Schwartz's check and he counted out part of the money, shoving it beneath the grilled cashier's window.

"Take out the rest, Mike, we owe it to you," she said, but he shook his head.

"We'll put that on the cuff until Mr. Merchant is so you can work again," he said. "About the only class this joint has any more is from people like you two. Judging by the piece in *Variety*, though, you won't be staying here much longer."

"That picture was taken over ten years ago, Mike. Better take your money while I've got it."

"I'm betting on you, Mrs. Merchant; so's the boss. He told me to tell you not to worry about the rent. The fact is, we ought to pay you to stay in a dump like this."

CHAPTER TWENTY-ONE

I

"That son of a bitch!" Ed McDougal was pacing the living room of the suite where he'd spent the night, a half-filled glass of bourbon and water in his hand and his beefy face still suffused with anger. "He'll find out what it means to cross me."

"Greg did more than cross you, Ed," said a doctor from Boston who was pouring himself a drink before lunch from the array of bottles on a nearby table. "He spitted you right through the gizzard this morning—before everybody."

"He'll regret it before I get through with him," the Texan snapped. "Until then, I was willing to work out some sort of a compromise that would let Greg at least retreat with honor. Now it's dog eat dog."

"I told you that was the way it had to be in the beginning," said Henry Anders.

"Where the hell were you last night when I was lining up support, Henry?" The Texan finished the contents of his glass in a gulp. "Seducing somebody's wife who'd heard what a great lover you are?"

"Of course not." Henry Anders looked away quickly lest his guilty flush betray him.

"We've got to change strategy," Ed said suddenly.

"What do you mean?" squeaked Dr. Timothy Puckett, who had been talking to the Boston doctor in one corner of the room.

"All along we've figured that this transplant patient would die and we could nail Greg with a vote of censure in the board Friday afternoon on two counts: building the hyperbaric laboratory without approval and tarnishing the reputation of The Clinic by a bad choice of patients in operating on Merchant. But since it looks like the fellow's going to live for a while, those arguments may not hold water."

"When did you decide that?" Dr. Puckett's face was now creased with anxiety.

"Just now, when I realized that Greg wouldn't have torn into me like he did this morning at the convocation if he wasn't pretty sure he's in the driver's seat."

"That makes sense," said the Boston doctor. "So what do we do now?"

"For Christ's sake, do I have to spell out everything for you fellows?" Ed threw up his hands in disgust. "We let old Sam press his charge against Greg and maybe be voted down. Then we drop a bomb by demanding that Greg produce the secret plans we've been hearing about." He turned to Henry Anders. "Will Keith Jackson have them ready by then?"

"I imagine so. When he phoned me right after Greg first saw them, Jackson said Greg flipped over them and wanted him to get out as detailed a set as he could in a hurry."

"Any way you can check up?"

"Jackson and Greg are working pretty closely on this thing and everybody knows I'm against Greg," said Henry doubtfully. "It might tip them off if I asked about the plans now."

"Guess you're right," Ed McDougal agreed. "If we raise enough of a squawk at the special meeting, he'll have to produce something. And if this thing is as far out as you say it is, old Sam will hit the ceiling."

"The plan's far out, all right," said Henry. "It's not like anything you ever saw in the way of a hospital."

"Guess that's all we can do at the moment then," said the Texan.

"And no more of this retreat with honor business for Greg," Henry Anders insisted.

"He's your meat, Henry," said Ed. "I'll even help hold him while you carve him up."

II

Georgia Merchant woke from a nightmare in which she'd watched Guy's slowly beating heart pressing down upon her until it had seemed that it would smother her. She remembered lying down in the room for a moment to rest after taking a shower, before going back to the hospital. Her watch told her now that it was after one o'clock, which meant she'd been asleep about two hours.

She knew the meaning of the dream: some rebellious part of her mind, which she had denied access to consciousness, had taken advantage of her sleep to remind her that Guy's living might well mean the failure of the plan Aaron Schwartz had outlined to her a few hours ago. And the vision of Guy's beating heart pressing down upon her and threatening to kill her had been a symbol from her unconscious mind of its rebellion against what his living could mean. Overcome with guilt that such a thought had somehow managed to reach consciousness, even through the back door, so to speak, of a dream, she reached for the telephone and dialed the hospital. When the operator answered, she gave her the extension number of the operating room suite.

"This is Mrs. Merchant," she told the nurse who answered. "Is my husband—"

"Dr. Alexander had him moved back to the ICU about two hours ago, Mrs. Merchant."

"Are you sure he was all right?"

"He's doing fine, Mrs. Merchant. I went with the stretcher up to intensive care. Dr. Alexander wanted him where they could watch him a little more closely with the monitors and where so many people wouldn't be going in and out as they do here."

Georgia dressed quickly and drove to the hospital. When she came to the small intensive care waiting room she saw Bob Johnson talking to the charge nurse. While she waited for him to finish, her eyes moved along the banks of cathode ray tubes above the desk of the nurses' station until they found the one upon which was flashed the closed-circuit TV picture of the room Guy was in.

She could see his chest rise and fall with the forced respiration, but the bandage about his neck, where the tracheostomy tube had been put in, made it impossible for her to see his face. And when her eyes dropped to the monitor tube just below the picture of the room, she saw that the flashing pattern of his heart was strong and regular, far different from the irregular pattern that had characterized it before he had been taken to the operating room yesterday afternoon.

"I hope you got some rest." Bob Johnson had finished writing an order and came over to where she was sitting. "We looked for you to tell you we were bringing him back here, but someone said you'd gone back to the hotel to change clothes."

"I took a shower and fell asleep."

"It was the best thing you could have done. You must be thoroughly bushed."

"Is Guy all right?"

"There are some signs that he may be developing a slight rejection reaction, but we're taking measures to combat it." They had warned Georgia about this most dangerous of complications, so she knew what he meant.

"Is there something I can do—give blood or anything?"

"We're taking care of that. Why don't you come down to the cafeteria and have something to eat with me? The nurse will call me on the beeper if there's any change."

"I think I will," said Georgia. "I can't even remember when I've had anything except coffee and danish pastry."

"Those mechanized waitresses off the main corridor don't have much imagination," he agreed. "Some real food will do you good for a change."

When they were eating in a corner of the big cafeteria, Georgia asked: "If my husband comes through, Doctor, what shape will his heart be in?"

"Excellent—from our experience."

"I seem to remember reading somewhere that cutting all the nerves makes a change."

"A lot of investigators worried about that in the beginning and so did Dr. Alexander," he said. "You see, the heart is normally controlled by two sets of nerves belonging to what is called the automatic, or autonomic, nervous system, enabling it to respond immediately to demands upon it from exercise, emotional tension and the like by speeding up the rate. Naturally, those nerves are cut during a transplant operation and, since they're very small, we make no attempt to bring them back together."

"Would they grow back if you did?"

"We think they do grow back to a certain extent, but we can't be sure, because the heart also responds to the amount of adrenaline and other hormones in the blood. In fact, we're putting a small amount of a drug resembling Adrenalin into your husband's bloodstream in order to step up the heart rate, since it tends to be a little slow immediately after these operations. In our dogs, we find that after a few weeks to a month— sometimes a little longer—this hormonal control is able to make a transplanted heart respond to change almost as quickly as the normal one would do."

"So he should be able to live a normal life?"

"Except for strenuous activity—although I wouldn't promise that he'll ever dance again."

"We may have a chance to form our own traveling troupe and Guy would be the stage manager."

"A heart as strong as Frank Lawson's should be able to stand that."

They ate in silence for a while. When he brought a second cup of coffee to the table for each of them, she asked: "Isn't there a famous plastic surgeon here at The Clinic?"

"Dr. Pinzon?"

"I don't know his name."

"Dr. Pinzon is probably the most famous cosmetic surgeon in the world."

"Face lifting and that sort of thing."

"Much more than simply that sort of thing," he assured her. "He's a real artist."

"When Guy is all right, do you think he would see me?"

"You have only to make an appointment, but I think you're worrying unduly."

"In show business a woman needs to look at least ten years younger than her age, Doctor."

"Dr. Pinzon can do better than that easily," he assured her. "Just speak to me when you're ready and I'll take care of the appointment for you."

"You're very kind."

"Nice people deserve nice treatment. Besides, when I tell my wife I had lunch with Georgia Merchant, she'll flip her lid."

III

Jud Templeton timed his arrival at the Clinic Inn to coincide with the exodus of the Members of The Clinic from the afternoon session of the convocation. Most, he knew, headed straight for the bar, so he wangled a table for two near the door and sat sipping a gin and tonic while he watched the stream of prosperous looking men pouring into the bar and the adjoining lounge. He hadn't been waiting long when he saw what he was looking for—

the plump form of Dr. Timothy Puckett. Fortunately for Jud's purposes, the chairman of the board was alone.

"How about my buying you a drink, Dr. Puckett?" he called. When the pediatrician came over and sat down, he signaled a waitress, who took his order.

"You've certainly been faithful at the convocation, Doctor," said Jud. "I saw you there this morning."

"I'm Chairman of the Board of Trustees, so I feel that I ought to help out as much as I can." Puckett's eyes were searching the crowd.

"That's a pretty responsible position," said Jud. "Especially with the new hospital being built and everything."

"We haven't decided on a new hospital." Puckett spoke with some severity.

"I understand that it's not definitely settled. But there are rumors all over the place."

"Rumors?" Jud didn't miss the sudden flash of anxiety in the little man's eyes.

"Everybody seems to have his own ideas about what should be done. Some want to keep The Clinic here and just renovate the old buildings, but I understand that would cost as much as building a new one."

"It's a very expensive process."

"Another faction's behind Dr. Alexander and his plans for the highly automated hospital and clinic on the present site he spoke about at the opening session yesterday. You know—one of those places where they have computers doing everything but sticking you in the tail."

"You seem to be well informed on the subject, Mr. Templeton." Puckett's voice was a little frosty now.

"I make it a point to keep abreast of what's going on around town, Doctor. Confidentially, though, I hear the third faction has the upper hand right now."

"Third faction?"

"You know, the one that wants a brand-new hospital and clinic built out on the Beltway."

"There's something to be said for all the proposals," said Dr. Puckett cautiously.

"Naturally, as chairman you have to stay uncommitted," said Jud. "The most interesting thing I've come across yet involves what use will be made of the present property if The Clinic is moved to the new location."

"It goes to Dr. Henry Anders II under his father's will," said the pediatrician. "I thought everybody knew that."

"I mean afterwards," said Jud. "There's a rumor going around that a syndicate has already been formed to develop this section into a whole new city, with high-rise apartment houses, shopping centers—the whole works. If that goes through, the men in the syndicate will certainly make a killing."

"It's legal, isn't it?" The plump doctor was beginning to sweat a little.

"Oh, I guess it's legal. But from what I hear, a number of doctors are in that syndicate and, if it should come out that some of them are members of the board and voted to have the hospital moved, it would make one of the hottest scandals this town has ever seen."

"I'm sure there's no truth to that rumor, Mr. Templeton." Puckett was a little pale now.

"I'm thinking of doing a piece on it, just the same." Jud calmly removed from his pocket the list Jeanne Alexander had given him shortly before noon. Spreading the sheet out on the table as if he were going to use it for notepaper, he searched in his pocket for a pencil while, from the corner of his eye, he watched Dr. Puckett's eyes freeze upon the list, like a bird dog pointing a covey of quail.

"Wha—what's that?" he whispered.

"Just a list of names somebody gave me. Men who might be in the syndicate to develop The Clinic property."

"Who—who gave it to you?"

"A woman. I'm always getting suggestions from anonymous sources, but it sometimes turns out that they're quite valuable. I've only had a chance to glance at this one," he added, pretending to study the list. "Good Lord, Dr. Puckett! Your name's here, too."

The pediatrician started to push back his chair. His hands were shaking and, in his agitation, he knocked over his glass. But before he could rise, Jud Templeton's left hand closed about a flabby wrist, muscling him back into his chair.

"A lot of people are going to be pretty indignant if the trustees vote to move The Clinic and I decide to publish this little list, Doctor," he said.

"This is b—blackmail."

"Call it whatever you will. It's still not as bad as the deal you and your friends are planning to pull Saturday."

"But I—"

Your Texas friend won't give a damn when the scandal breaks because he'll be safely away from the stink. But can *you* ignore what people will say to a headline like this?" With a pencil he printed in bold block letters across the top of the list:

LEADING DOCTORS IN ON CLINICAL STEAL

"For God's sake, keep that covered," said Puckett.

"Even if you don't go to jail, you're a little old to start practicing again somewhere else after your license is taken away, Doctor." Jud released Puckett's wrist and the little man shot from his chair. As if propelled by a rocket he fairly raced for the elevator.

"What did you say to him?" Peter Carewe dropped into the empty chair across from Jud. "I never saw Rabbit move so fast before in all my life."

"Was that what you called him in medical school?"

"That—and worse. He went into pediatrics because grown people couldn't stand him."

"I'm looking forward to your speech tonight, Doctor," said the newspaperman. "The paper's even buying my dinner."

"I still want to know what you said to scare old Puck like that. Maybe I could use some of it on African witch doctors when they get into my hair."

Jud Templeton took his hand off the list he had covered when Peter Carewe sat down at the table. "Know any of these? Besides Dr. Puckett, I mean?"

The doctor from WHO studied the list for a moment, then shoved it back to Jud. "I know most of the doctors on there."

"Several of them are on the Board of Trustees. If things go to suit them Saturday morning, they'll vote to move The Clinic. Then, one fine day, when everybody's forgotten about that, plans will be announced for a big project here. And lo, the gentlemen on the list will profit much by being silent stockholders in said corporation."

"Verily a scheme worthy of Mephistopheles himself." Peter Carewe whistled softly. "Where do I enlist?"

"Here and now," said Jud Templeton. "Just make a point of seeing as many of those men as you can and casually mentioning a rumor you've heard that a newspaperman is busy running down a story about a group of doctors belonging to a syndicate. You won't have to include Dr. Puckett;

I'm not sure his heart would stand a second scare."

Peter Carewe stood up and looked around the room. "I can see three of them here now," he said. "Good hunting."

Jud Templeton raised his glass. "Tally ho!"

IV

In Ed McDougal's suite, the Texan was trying to calm Tim Puckett down and not succeeding very well.

"I tell you, Ed, Jud Templeton knows everything," the little pediatrician babbled. "He's going to blow the whole story in the papers."

"What can he blow, when we haven't even incorporated yet? The guy's playing you for a sucker, Tim. Twice he's fished for a story and this time you may have given it to him."

"I didn't say a thing—not a thing."

"Go dry yourself, Puck. You're wetting your pants."

"We've got to call this thing off, Ed. Scandal won't bother you down in Texas, but I'm right here in the middle of it."

"Did this fellow remind you of that?"

"We—ll, yes."

"Like I said, the guy's playing you for a sucker. And you fell for it all the way."

"You really think so?" Puckett quavered.

"I know so."

"But where did he get that list?"

"Somebody talked, probably when he was drunk—or with a woman. If I find out who it was, I'll break him with my own hands."

The door to the suite opened and Dr. Jake Geiger came in. Like Puckett, his practice was in Baltimore and he was sweating, though the room was cool.

"Ed," he said. "I've got to see you privately."

"Not now, Jake. Puck here is upset."

"I'm upset, too. Did you know that a newspaperman downstairs has got the syndicate list?"

"Who told you that?"

"Peter Carewe."

"You see," Timothy Pucket squalled. "They're spreading the word around already."

"Who told you?" Jake Geiger demanded.

"Templeton, the newspaperman."

Ed McDougal started for the door, with Timothy Puckett close behind him. "Where you going, Ed?" he demanded.

"To throw that son of a bitch out of the motel. I'll teach him to threaten honest people."

"That's what he wants," Puckett squeaked. "You say he's got no proof of what that list means, so he can't print anything about us. But if you go down there and beat him up, the publisher of those papers is going to want to know why. Then they can print anything they like."

"You may be right at that, Puck." Ed McDougal stopped with his hand on the doorknob. "Down in Texas, we'd do it different, but up here I guess we have to play it close to our chests."

"What can we do?"

"One thing I can do is go see Greg Alexander. He let this man in on the operation yesterday, so he must be working hand and glove with Templeton."

"I don't see Greg doing a thing like that," Jake Geiger objected.

"By now Greg knows he's fighting for his professional life," said Ed. "When the chips are down, a man will use any weapon he can get."

"What are you going to do?" Timothy Puckett asked.

"Ask for an armistice, what else?" Ed said with a grin.

"Why an armistice?"

"Were you in Korea, Puck?"

"No."

"If you had been, you'd know that an armistice is a time when you persuade the enemy to lower his guard so you can stick a knife in his back."

V

Greg was in his office dictating answers to the morning mail into a Dictaphone when Ed McDougal came in. It was a few minutes after five o'clock, so his secretary had already left, but his days were so filled that he usually had to handle his correspondence at odd times.

He had hoped to take Jeanne to the banquet that night to hear Peter Carewe but was wondering now whether he shouldn't call and tell her to go on without him, for he was worried by a gradual change in Guy Merchant's condition during the day. When the door of his waiting room slammed shut and he saw Ed McDougal coming through the office suite, he put the Dictaphone back on its cradle.

"You look upset, Ed," he said.

"I am upset. This is a hell of a crummy trick you're playing, Greg."

"Like what?"

"Setting that bastard Templeton to blackmailing trustees."

"I don't know what you're talking about."

"Don't give me that!"

"This is my office, Ed." Greg's voice was cold. "Suppose you leave now before this goes any farther."

The Texan controlled himself with an effort. "All right," he said. "Let's talk it over."

"That's better. Now what is Jud Templeton doing?"

"He's helping you by spreading rumors."

"A lot of people happen to think what you and Henry are trying to pull is a lousy deal, but I don't know many who would go out on a limb for me. Whatever Templeton's doing, he's doing on his own."

"He's got a list and claims it's the names of members of a syndicate that will develop the property here after we move The Clinic."

"So you're the brains behind that scheme?" said Greg. "I couldn't see Henry thinking it up by himself. When did you work it out? Last year, when he went down to the Southern Medical in Dallas?"

"Of course not," Ed McDougal blustered, but the sudden flash of guilt in his eyes betrayed him.

"I'm disappointed in you, Ed." Greg made no attempt to hide the contempt he felt for the other man. "All the time, I thought it was Sam Hunter's money you were after, so you could build a new medical school in your hometown and be the big shot professor of surgery. But you were just looking to make a killing for yourself by gypping poor Henry out of his inheritance, weren't you? I'm ashamed of you Ed, really ashamed."

"I don't need your shame!" Stung by Greg's tone, the Texan came out of his chair. "I'm telling you now. Call off your dog before he gets hurt."

"I haven't any dog. I told you that."

"Then telephone this fellow Templeton and tell him to stop meddling in things that are none of his business."

"Is Templeton at the Inn?"

"He was a few minutes ago."

Greg dialed nine for outside and then the number of the Clinic Inn. "Please call Mr. Jud Templeton to the phone," he asked the operator. "You'll probably find him in the bar. It's urgent."

"This is Dr. Alexander," he said when Jud answered. "I'm told that you've been threatening people over there in the mistaken belief that you were helping me."

"So that's where the big bull went," Templeton said. "I saw him go out of the door here just now like a Sherman tank."

"Have I got your promise not to continue what you're doing?"

"You've got it, Doctor. If the leader's that scared, I've already done all I can do."

"Thank you, Mr. Templeton." Greg hung up and turned to Ed McDougal. "He won't bother you any more, Ed."

"Why don't we call an armistice, Greg?" Ed's tone was ingratiating now. "After all, we both want what's best for The Clinic."

"How can I call an armistice when I'm not fighting? The board asked me to prepare a plan for a new clinic and hospital and that's what I'm going to do."

"All right—if you don't want to meet us halfway."

"I've slept about four hours in the past thirty-six and I've got a patient who needs help, Ed. My only concern right now is to find out how I can help him."

"I gave you the choice," said the Texan. "Don't say I didn't."

"What happened to you, Ed?" Greg's voice halted him at the door, not so much by what he was saying but by the note of genuine concern in it.

"What do you mean?"

"You were a better than average surgeon when you were here at The Clinic. I know you have a big practice at home and you probably give your patients their money's worth. That should be enough for any doctor, but you had to sell your soul for money. Tell me why, Ed."

"Because money's important. Why else? Maybe I am just another surgeon in a middle-sized Texas town like you say, but my wife wears an ermine coat. What does Jeanne wear?"

"A rather old mink stole, I believe."

"How much have you got stashed away? A hundred thousand?"

"Rather less than that the last time I looked."

"I've got my first million behind me and enough oil leases to bring in a couple more."

"And yet you have to plan crooked schemes with people like Henry Anders to make more." Greg shook his head. "I really feel sorry for you, Ed."

You feel sorry for me!" For a moment the balloon was pricked and Greg looked away so as not to see its collapse. But it lasted only for an instant and Ed was his old blustering self again when he swaggered out of the office.

For a long moment, Greg sat immobile. In the moment of the big man's deflation, he'd had a glimpse of the small shriveled soul inside him. And no matter what Ed McDougal had said about him, done to him, or might yet do, he could find no pleasure in it.

Finally, he picked up the telephone and, when he was connected with Dave Connor, said: "Could you join me on the ICU, Dave? I don't like the way things are going with Merchant and I think we might profit from another council of war."

The examination didn't take long. The portable film of Guy Merchant's chest, taken late in the afternoon, plus the fully kept hospital records and laboratory reports, told them everything they needed to know that was not revealed by Dave Connor's careful stethoscopic examination of the air being forced in and out of the sick man's lungs.

"It's the rising fever you're worried about most, isn't it?" the cardiologist asked while they were studying the hospital record at the nursing station.

Greg nodded. "Lawson's lungs were damaged from the accident when his chest was crushed; I didn't realize how much until I removed them. They're the weakest part of the whole picture here, but I had to use them or Merchant would have died of emphysema before long—even with a new heart."

"Nothing here definitely indicates pneumonia—yet," said the heart specialist. "The X-ray film does show some deeper shadows at the bases of the lungs than it did this morning, which could mean a spreading infectious process—or congestion."

"Any idea which?"

"I doubt if it's congestion; the heart is functioning well, the output is excellent and the T-wave complex in the ECG doesn't suggest any major rejection symptoms as yet."

"So it all boils down to keeping infection from developing in the lungs—or controlling it if it has already developed," said Greg. "As I see it, we've got to cut down on the anti-rejection treatment and hope his normal immune response plus the antibiotic he's getting will keep down whatever infection is already there."

"The two-pronged attack is probably best," Dave Connor agreed. "I wish I could help more, Greg."

"You confirmed my own thinking, Dave. Thanks for your trouble."

"You and Jeanne going to the banquet tonight?"

"I promised her I would. You get around; how's the sentiment on the new hospital running among the Members?"

"I haven't exactly taken a poll but I'd say it's pretty close to fifty-fifty. There's a lot of interest in this bold new plan of yours, whatever it is. I think you've got the opposition worried."

"That's what I want them to be."

"Still going to keep it under wraps until Saturday?"

"My guess is that somebody's going to demand to see the plans at the special meeting Friday afternoon. I hope to have at least the sketches ready by then."

"Don't underestimate Ed McDougal and his crowd, Greg. That could be disastrous." Dave Connor looked across the narrow corridor to the glass-fronted room where Guy Merchant lay. "And losing him just when the board is about to meet could be an even worse catastrophe."

"Whether or not I lose a patient shouldn't affect the future of The Clinic."

"Nevertheless, it will. If Merchant dies, they'll use his death as proof that you jumped the gun and operated, hoping to impress the board. That's bound to go against you, even if it isn't true."

"I'm not trying to impress anybody," Greg said wearily. "Five minutes before I called you, I finished telling Ed McDougal that."

"He came to see you?"

"Yes—and mad as a hornet. Somebody's threatening to expose that little scheme he and Henry have cooked up so Henry will get the property here and they can develop it. He wanted me to call off my dogs."

"Were they your dogs?"

"I haven't had time for that sort of thing, even if I would have tried it."

"Which you wouldn't have," the cardiologist said with a sigh. "Did it ever occur to you that you're your own worst enemy, Greg?"

"Not until lately. Jeanne's been telling me."

"You'd better listen to her."

"I'm too old for conniving, Dave. Being the best surgeon I'm able to be is about all the job I can handle effectively."

When the other man had gone, Greg wrote new orders on the chart, cutting in half the dosage of the immuno-suppressive drugs being given to lessen the likelihood of rejection of the organ transplant and doubling the dose of the broad-spectrum antibiotic they were giving Guy Merchant to keep down infection. He was taking a calculated risk, but this sort of decision making had become so much a part of his everyday life that it didn't occur to him to doubt his own judgment.

Transferring the hospital beeper to the breast pocket of the sport jacket he hadn't had on for, it seemed, eons, he took the elevator to the street floor and The Clinic lobby. Bob Johnson was on duty and he trusted the younger surgeon's judgment implicitly, so he might as well take Jeanne to the banquet. Besides, if there were an emergency, the beeper in his pocket could reach him across the street in the banquet room as easily as it could in the hospital.

CHAPTER TWENTY-TWO

I

Sam Hunter was standing in the lobby of the motel when Helen Foucald came downstairs from the crossover to the apartment building a few minutes after six. She wore a fur coat and cap to match over her dark auburn hair.

"Glad you're dressed warmly," he told her. "The TV predicts a heavy snow tomorrow but we should be all right tonight."

"Sorry I'm late," she said. "I had to run some last-minute blood chemistry studies in the laboratory."

"On Dr. Alexander's patient?"

"Yes."

"How's he doing?"

"His blood chemistry is definitely improved over what it was before the operation, so the heart seems to be functioning well. Greg's worried now about possible lung complications."

Sam Hunter took her arm and guided her through the door to the marquee-covered driveway outside, where a Continental limousine stood with the engine running to keep the interior warm. The uniformed chauffeur opened the door for them and, when they were inside, guided the car out onto The Parkway.

"The chauffeur tells me there's an excellent restaurant about ten miles out of town," said Sam Hunter. "I usually hire limousines when I'm away from home and the drivers always know the best places to eat.

"Want to take off your coat?" he asked as she settled back in the luxurious car. "When you're as old as I am, cold sort of gets to your bones. The car may be too warm for you."

"The laboratory radiators are pretty old, so it's usually on the cold side there in weather like this," she said. "I'm happy just to relax and be warm."

"That wouldn't be a bit of propaganda for a new hospital, would it?"

Helen smiled. "We have to get in our licks whenever we can. Greg has promised that in the new one I'm to have probably the most advanced laboratory in the country, if not in the world. Naturally, I'm doing everything I can."

"Thank you for passing up the banquet," he said. "I know what a sacrifice it was."

"On the contrary, Mr. Hunter, I think it's time I got away—for a little perspective."

"Not letting yourself be rushed off your feet, eh?"

"At thirty-five, a woman has to be sure. At twenty it's different; there's a long time and a lot of opportunities ahead."

"You've never been married?"

"No. I only came close once—in France."

"That why you ran away?"

"What gave you that idea?"

"You don't employ as many people as I do without getting to be a pretty good judge of character. You're a very intelligent and strong-minded woman who might take a man as a lover that wasn't your equal—except as a lover. But you could only marry a man you respected."

"You're very perceptive—and frank."

"It's as much a tribute to a woman to praise her mind as it is her figure— and you have both."

"I consider that a real compliment."

"You don't have to answer, if you'd rather not," he said. "Is it true that you're having an affair with Henry Anders?"

"It's true. You wouldn't have to ask many people to find that out."

"But neither you nor Claire could possibly respect Henry's intelligence. The man's a pompous fool."

Helen's eyes twinkled. "Henry has, shall we say, other attributes, which Claire and I both appreciate."

"What about Carewe? Or am I asking too much?"

"No. I'm glad of the chance to talk to somebody about the whole thing. Until yesterday morning, my world was pretty orderly. I had my work, which I love—"

"And which you're very good at."

"Have you been checking up on me?"

"I check up on everybody who interests me—both friends and enemies."

"Whatever happens about the hospital, I don't want to be your enemy," she told him. "I was impertinent yesterday in my office and I apologize."

"You were merely looking after your own interests and what you think is right," he corrected her. "I would have less respect for you if you'd done anything else."

"Actually, I wasn't quite myself," she explained. "I had just come from meeting Peter Carewe at the airport, the first time I had ever seen him."

"And he bowled you over?"

"Frankly, yes."

"Did you every stop to think that he's probably bowled over a lot of other women in the same way?"

"I'm sure he has and at first I told myself it's nothing but the sort of physical attraction a strong man has for a woman like me."

"What about Henry?"

"He has no more right to expect faithfulness in me than I do in him. Claire and I understand that perfectly." She smiled wryly. "As you said, Henry isn't the most intelligent person in the world, but I'm a woman of strong needs."

"And you doubt that one man could satisfy both your mind and your body?"

"No one has—yet. But Peter is hard to resist."

"Then why resist?"

She took a deep breath. "I guess because I realize how tragic it would be for both of us if either failed the other."

"You could always exercise a woman's prerogative and leave the whole question undecided, you know." Again she was surprised by his perceptiveness.

"Why do you say that?"

"Even if you thought your world was safe before Carewe came along, it really wasn't. Claire isn't going to give Henry up and you've admitted that you don't want him as a husband, so all you've done is make a temporary arrangement like the one you'd probably made before you left Paris. That can't possibly be the final answer for you, so what most people would call your promiscuity is merely an attempt to rationalize the adjustment you've tried to make, even though you know it can't last."

"You should be a psychoanalyst," she said, a little shakily.

"It's nothing but logic. Is Peter Carewe the first man you ever met that you're willing to admit may be your equal in every respect?"

"Yes."

"Then there's only one answer."

She nodded slowly. "I guess I've been avoiding it because I'm afraid I might discover he has a weakness. But that's the chance I have to take, isn't it?"

"I would call it a calculated risk."

"Peter wants me to go away with him for the weekend. I wasn't sure before, but I am now." She put out her hand and squeezed the wrinkled but still strong one lying on his knee. "Thanks for setting me straight."

"All I can do any more is advise," Sam Hunter said with a sigh. "But I don't mind telling you I'd give half of what I possess to be that young doctor for the next few days."

"You're a dear." Helen leaned over and kissed him on the cheek. "How did you ever get the reputation of being such an ogre?"

"Oh, I can be tough, all right," he said. "And don't think that just because you're buttering me up I'm going to be any softer on your friend Dr. Alexander."

"I'm sure even Greg doesn't want you to do anything except what you decide is best for The Clinic," she said. "After all, you were a close friend of the elder Dr. Anders and Greg was like an adopted son to him, so your feelings about him must be the same."

"That's what troubles me most," Sam Hunter admitted. "I keep asking myself what Henry Anders would want and I can't be sure. The way I see it, the present Clinic is a monument to him. He largely designed it himself and practically built it with his own hands. Whatever is built here could never really be the same, so I can't help feeling that changing the old building may be almost the same as pushing over Henry Anders' gravestone."

II

Jeanne opened the apartment door before Greg could turn the lock with his key. She was wearing a silk dressing gown he'd given her for Christmas so long ago that he couldn't remember when it was and the sight of her slender loveliness made some of his weariness evaporate. She came into his arms and clung to him for a long sweet moment, but when he would have guided her toward the bedroom, she laughed and pushed him away.

"Be good now, darling," she said. "We're supposed to be at the head table and the serving starts promptly at eight."

"I'd much rather stay here."

"You can't have people saying you know you're already licked and are afraid to show your face," she said firmly. "Now, go get your shower while I lay out your dinner jacket."

"A boiled shirt after all I've been through?"

"I bought you a new one; it isn't starched and has ruffles all down the front and at the cuffs." She was guiding him toward the shower. "I'll fix some drinks while you're getting your bath."

The shower was scalding hot and he let it soak away some of the tiredness from his body before turning it to cold for a stinging moment of change, then stepped out and began to dry himself with a big nubby towel.

"Ed McDougal jumped me this afternoon," he called to Jeanne through the partly opened door. "He claims somebody put Jud Templeton up to blackmailing him and his gang."

"I know." Jeanne came over as he came out of the bathroom for him to zip her short evening dress up the back. "I did it."

"You?" he asked, startled. "How did you manage that?"

"Hannah let something drop at breakfast yesterday morning that made me suspicious, so I checked with Claire. She found a list of those in Henry's syndicate in his desk and gave it to me. I was the one who turned it over to Jud Templeton." She turned to face him. "Are you angry?"

"No—but I wish you hadn't."

"Why?"

"I guess I'm male enough to want to fight my own battles."

"And I'm female enough not to want to see my male clobbered by a bunch of skunks that aren't fit to touch the ground he walks on." She returned to her dressing table. "That's your one big fault, darling— probably your only one. You're too easygoing and trusting, so people are always taking advantage of you."

"As long as it doesn't hurt anybody but me, I can stand it," he said.

"But I can't, Greg. I've loved you so long I can't remember when I didn't. And when I see you letting other people run over you just to get their own way, it makes my blood boil—at them and sometimes at you."

"There's always more than one way of accomplishing the same purpose." He came over for her to adjust his tie and she stood on tiptoes to kiss him when she finished.

"That's what I decided this morning," she said. "So I'm taking a hand in your affairs, even if you won't do it."

"What changed you?"

"I think it was Hannah McDougal's ermine coat—and her unhappiness. She rooked Ed in, when we were all here together years ago, by deliberately getting herself pregnant so he'd have to marry her. Everybody in the hospital knew it."

"Except me."

"You were busy being a boy scout even then. I can remember crying myself to sleep a lot of times, so lonely I could hardly stand it, while you were over there working on dog operations and not even remembering you had a wife at home. I guess Hannah did the same—for a while."

"What do you mean—for a while?"

"Every doctor's wife has to learn pretty soon to occupy herself—else she turns into a self-pitying whiner or ends up on the short end of a divorce."

"Surely it isn't as bad as that."

"Even the most undramatic woman likes to think of the man she marries as a Galahad or a Lochinvar. But unless her husband is a Quasimodo, a doctor's wife soon learns that a lot of his women patients are in love with him and a few quite willing to do something about it. If he's out in private practice and has any ability at all, his income begins to zoom about that time, too, and he joins a posh country club, where an even larger percentage of the women are on the make."

"I'm beginning to be sorry for what I've missed," said Greg.

"I'm serious," she insisted. "Lots of times doctors marry secretaries or nurses—like me. They hardly ever have the background most of the women their successful husbands meet have, and pretty soon the wife feels herself suffering in comparison."

"When did you start studying your fellow doctors' wives so closely?" he asked.

"Only recently. If I'd started sooner, I might have been able to diagnose my own symptoms before they almost went beyond the point of no return. A book I'm reading says a woman's personality from day to day is as much a part of her hormone pattern as it is of her early upbringing. I don't have to tell you that there are times each month when I'm morose, easily hurt and quick to resent snubs that aren't really snubs at all."

"Like my working late."

"That—and other things that seem important at the time. When she's feeling sorry for herself, it's pretty easy for a wife to decide she's deserted and from there to go on imagining things her husband may be doing—particularly with other women. A lot of times, she's got good reason to imagine them, too."

"You're not painting a very good picture of my brother physicians."

"They're no worse than any other professional group that goes up rapidly—and neither are the wives. If they can learn to stay with their husbands in maturity and find outlets for their energies after the children start leaving the household, they can make a fine adjustment and get along well. For a lot of them, though, it's easier to start feeling sorry for themselves and nagging when there's no real reason. Then one day the husband starts pursuing a younger woman with the inevitable results in so many cases—a divorce."

"You said just now that Hannah had solved her problem—but she's still with Ed."

"Maybe I should have said she's found a placebo that lulls her into not worrying about it. Ed has affairs with other women, so she has affairs with other men. She's still pretty decorative and Ed likes to boast of his success by hanging jewels and ermine coats and that sort of thing on her, all of which bolsters up her feeling of self-esteem."

"That's twice you spoke about the ermine coat," he reminded her.

"When she came into the restaurant with it yesterday morning, I expected any moment to see her start dragging it across the floor like an old-time Hollywood actress. I'll admit that I felt a little sorry for myself at first, but when I saw what's really happened to Hannah, I got a little scared.

Nothing's more pitiful than a woman whose husband has deserted her for a younger one, leaving her nothing except to stare into the mirror every morning and face the fact that she's a day older—and looks it."

"At least you know there's never been another woman as far as I'm concerned."

"Maybe not one you would take to bed with you—but she's there just the same."

"Who?"

"Why do you think health is always depicted as a female goddess called Hygeia? She's always there in the form of a doctor's dedication to his profession, competing with his wife for his affections."

"Where is that drink you promised me?" he asked. "You'll have me crying into it any minute."

She went to the small bar just off the living room and brought back two glasses of bourbon and ginger ale, which she knew was all he ever drank.

"You can't escape the facts of life, darling." She sipped her drink while he finished dressing. "After I saw Hannah, I decided that I'm not going to be a victim of the Doctor's Wife Disease. That's why I got the list from Claire and gave it to Jud Templeton."

"What I don't understand is why Claire would give it to you."

"She wants things as they are—like any other wife who's satisfied with the status quo."

"The status quo in that household wouldn't seem to be very satisfactory from what I hear."

"On the contrary, Claire is perfectly happy with it as it is. Henry's no Lochinvar and never will be, but Claire can easily find a substitute every now and then. Meanwhile, her own ego is amply fed by the knowledge that she's a lot smarter than Henry can ever hope to be."

"After what I've been hearing for the last ten minutes," Greg conceded as he put on his dinner jacket and straightened the cummerbund, "you'll never have any reason to lack for self-esteem. I guess the happiest marriages are where the wife is a lot smarter than the husband and right now I'll admit to being even more of a clod than Henry."

"In some ways—yes." Her eyes were dancing now. "But you're a loveable clod, even if something of a clod as a lover."

"Have you been taking hormones?"

"Hannah advised it this morning, but I'm not quite ready for the pasture yet. Come on or we'll be late for the banquet."

"After that last crack of yours, I'd be willing to be late. One superiority of the male at least is at stake here."

"Maybe you'll feel more superior after the banquet."

"Why?"

"I prepared the menu. You're starting off with bluepoints on the half shell as an appetizer."

III

The auditorium where the Tarentino Circus was performing in a benefit for the local P.T.A. was, appropriately enough, the high-school gymnasium. Chairs had been arranged along either side to serve as box seats, but, to Helen's surprise, Sam Hunter purchased seats in the bleachers, scaffold-like rows of planking that rose in a staircase pattern.

"We can see better up here," he explained as they made their way to seats not far from the top row in the center, the only part of the bleachers that was in any way crowded. Actually, hardly half the seats were filled, a mute commentary on the financial status of the struggling circus. It was obviously a small outfit, too, for Helen had seen only a few trucks parked outside the building, one of them a large red van that, judging from its curtained windows, also served as living quarters for some of the performers.

"I'd think you were pinching pennies if I hadn't just finished one of the best dinners I ever ate," she said. "I like small circuses. We had a lot of them in Europe when I was a little girl."

"I doubt if this one will come up to the standard of those you saw there," said Sam Hunter.

Looking at the shabby equipment, the frayed costumes of the two clowns who were warming up the audience before the show began, Helen could believe he spoke the truth. All of which made her wonder once again why he had gone to the trouble of bringing her here, but she made no attempt to draw him out, sensing that something intensely personal was involved.

The performance began with a parade around the single ring by the clowns, a small herd of elephants, a few performers and the calliope. As the wheezing strains of the old music machine shook the rafters of the high-school gymnasium, Helen relaxed in her seat and let memory carry her back to the days of her childhood in France and the small circus that had played once a year in the village where she had grown up before going to school in Paris. Lost in memory, she hardly noticed the opening acts of the performance, until the calliope burst into a rock-and-roll tune and the pudgy little ringmaster in the high silk hat announced:

"Introducing the Flying Tarentinos!"

The spotlight silhouetted a lovely small girl in white tights at the ringside. Then a lithe six-footer with dark hair appeared beside the girl and they started across to where the ropes for ascent to the trapeze, anchored high up among the trusses supporting the roof of the gymnasium, were being held by a roustabout.

Sam Hunter's sudden intake of breath beside her made Helen glance at him. Startled by what she saw, she looked again at the male member of the acrobatic pair and realized suddenly that she might have been seeing a younger version of Sam Hunter himself. Understanding now why they were there and why the old man had avoided calling attention to himself, she gave all her attention to the two young performers.

The music took up its blaring beat again as the two moved to the center of the ring. The girl was hoisted up to the trapeze with the spotlight following her. But when the young man started to climb up hand over hand, Helen thought she detected a slight hesitancy every time his right hand closed upon the rope, very much like a pulse skipping a beat. It was barely noticeable, however, and as the two young acrobats went into their routine, she saw that they were very good.

Once, as they neared the climax of their act high in the air, the boy's right hand appeared to slip, and, for an instant, the lovely figure of the girl hung by one arm. It could have been deliberate, but, noticing how the ringmaster and the roustabout handling the rope suddenly tensed themselves, Helen wasn't sure and felt a vague sense of apprehension—and puzzlement.

At the climax of the act, when the girl went flying out like a lovely white bird, Helen found herself gasping like the rest of the crowd, until the nylon rope checked her fall and she swung like a pendulum spinning at its end, before seizing the climb rope and sliding to the floor of the ring.

The boy came down much more slowly than the girl had, and, as he stood beside her with the spotlight upon them, taking their bows, Helen thought once that he seemed to stagger. But the girl put her arm protectively

through his and they walked from the ring while the spotlight swung to the
next performer.

"Do you mind if we don't see any more?" Sam Hunter asked.

"Of course not."

At the foot of the row of seats before they were leaving the auditorium, she
put her hand upon his arm and asked: "Don't you want to speak to him?"

"Who?"

"Your son. They're really very good and both of them are beautiful." For
a moment, she thought he would deny the relationship and added quickly,
"They're married, aren't they?"

He nodded but still did not speak.

"Without your permission?"

"I'd rather not talk about it." His voice was harsh for the first time that
evening. "If you don't mind."

"I didn't mean to pry. But he's such a fine-looking young man that I'm
sure you must be very proud of him—and of such a lovely daughter-in-law."

Sam Hunter didn't speak until they were in the car again and headed
back toward Baltimore. When he did, it was not about the circus or his son.

IV

"That hand's bothering you again." Vivian's face was concerned as she
and Ted slipped their feet into the clogs they'd left at the edge of the ring
and started toward the large red van where they had their quarters. "I saw
you hesitate as you went up the rope. And when you almost dropped me, I
knew it was hurting more than you've been admitting."

"I couldn't let the audience think I'm a weakling." Ted managed to smile
although the pain that had been throbbing in his hand for the past twenty-
four hours had now begun to extend up the arm. "Don't you know the
women come to admire your handsome husband as much as the men come
to see you in tights?"

"Be serious, darling. It's really more painful, isn't it?"

"A little. Maybe I used it too much getting the equipment into the
auditorium."

"We're going to see a doctor about it tonight," she said firmly.

"It can wait until tomorrow when we get to Frederick."

"You've been putting off doing anything too long already." Vivian closed
the door of their mobile apartment behind them and, stripping off her tights,
pulled on slacks and a jersey. "I noticed a public phone in the hall across
from the principal's office. Get dressed while I see if I can locate a doctor."

"You'd never find one at this time of night."

"All towns have hospitals these days. Somebody has to be on emergency
duty."

"My husband has an infected hand," she told the woman who answered
the telephone call to the hospital. "Do you have a doctor on duty who can
see him tonight?"

"The resident physician is here. When can you come over?"

"Right away. Ask him to wait for Mr. and Mrs. Hunter."

"Drive out Main Street until you see the neon sign," the woman directed
her. "You can't miss it."

"I've located a doctor," Vivian said when she returned to the truck.
"We'll take the jeep."

They found the hospital without trouble and followed a neon-lit arrow to the emergency entrance. Inside, a small dark-skinned man in a white uniform was bandaging the head of a child.

"Dr. Fernandez will be with you in a minute," a nurse told them. "Just have a seat."

"A Filipino?" Vivian said doubtfully under her breath.

"They have them in a lot of hospitals now," Ted told her. "Most American interns are used up by teaching hospitals or by Army service, so Filipinos have been coming over in large numbers to serve as resident physicians."

Dr. Fernandez was pleasant and spoke fairly good English. "You have a beginning infection here," he said when he finished examining the swollen hand. "Is this a wound perhaps?" He pointed to the red spot where the splinter had entered.

"A splinter several days ago," Ted explained. "But I pulled it out."

Ted couldn't help flinching from pain as the dark-skinned doctor squeezed the loose tissue between his thumb and forefinger, tense now from the swelling. "There seems to be some accumulation of pus here," he said. "We must open it wider and afterward I shall give you an injection of penicillin."

"Do you think some of the splinter might still be in there?" Vivian asked.

"It is possible; we will see when we open it." Dr. Fernandez turned to the nurse. "I shall need a tray with a hemostat, a sharp-pointed scalpel and some ethyl chloride, please."

It took a few minutes to prepare the tray. The ethyl chloride was in a container with a spray nozzle somewhat like the tubes containing dessert topping, but with a much finer and quickly evaporating spray. When the doctor directed a stream of it upon the skin of Ted's hand between the thumb and forefinger, frost formed upon the skin almost immediately as the tissues beneath it were frozen in an area perhaps as large as a quarter.

"This will prevent most of the pain when I open the wound," he explained and Ted felt very little discomfort even when he used the sharp-pointed scalpel to widen the tiny wound where the splinter had gone in. But when he thrust the forceps deep into the tissues and spread its jaws apart, Ted almost came off the stool where he was sitting. Dr. Fernandez probed the wound briefly for a depth of perhaps half an inch but found no sign of a splinter, and only a small amount of thin red purulent fluid escaped.

"I shall put in a drain to keep the wound open," he said, and pushed a small bit of gauze into the wound, again causing Ted considerable pain. It lasted only a moment, however, and afterward the doctor covered the area with several squares of gauze and bandaged it into place. Only a few minutes longer were required to inject the penicillin and give him a dozen brownish tablets for pain.

"I feel a lot better," said Vivian as they returned to the jeep after paying the bill. "How about you?"

"My tail hurts where he shot that penicillin," said Ted. "What's worrying me now is that I won't be able to go on tomorrow night."

"I can do the solo bit I did at F.S.U. before I fell in love with you," said Vivian. "Of course, the women in the audience won't get to admire your manly beauty, but we'll make out somehow."

"The doctor seemed to think this would take care of everything, so I shouldn't be out but a few nights."

"If that hand needs any more treatment," said Vivian, "I'm going to take you to Baltimore to The Clinic."

"I can have it dressed day after tomorrow in Cumberland," said Ted. "Do you think Papa Gus will be able to get us any farther than that? We had a mighty thin audience tonight and with snow expected in Frederick tomorrow, it could be even worse."

But Vivian couldn't answer that question any more than he could.

V

Peter Carewe was sitting at a table in the Falstaff Tavern having a drink with several Members when Helen came to the door after saying good night to Sam Hunter at the front of the elevators. Peter came to her at once and she felt a warm tide of happiness flood through her at this proof that he had been watching for her.

"Back so soon?" he asked, taking her arm and guiding her to a secluded table in the corner.

"We left before the circus performance was over. He went there to see his son."

"Sam Hunter's son in a circus?"

"He's an acrobat or an aerialist—and married to a lovely young girl. They have a very good act."

"Imagine turning down all that money to become the daring young man on the flying trapeze. No wonder the old man was burned up."

"He was very sad tonight. I'd heard something about his disinheriting one of his sons; but I think he realized for the first time tonight that the boy and the girl he married are very, very good, even if the circus is almost on its last leg."

"The kid probably inherited enough of the old man's tenacity to succeed."

"Probably. But I've got the strangest feeling that something is wrong with him."

"What?"

"I can't put my finger on it, maybe because I don't practice clinical medicine. But I'm sure it's something physical."

"Did old Sam say anything about it?"

"No. I didn't mention it to him, either."

"What's the kid like?"

"Sam insisted on leaving as soon as the act was finished. I wish I could have persuaded him to talk to them but he wouldn't hear of it."

"How was your dinner?"

"Wonderful."

"You'll fare even better at the Chalet Julienne. The weather report on the six o'clock news forecasted a heavy snow tomorrow afternoon. We might just be snowed in up there for a week or two with no way to reach the world outside."

"What if I say no?"

"I'd only find a reason to come back to Baltimore and ask you again, after I finish tracking down that vaccine contaminant in California."

"Would you give up going to California if I promised the weekend as a reward?"

"You'd be driving a hard bargain."

"But would you?"

"I'm afraid not. If a few more batches of that virus go bad, half the oral polio vaccine scheduled for next year's immunization program will be no good. That means maybe a thousand kids will have polio who wouldn't otherwise have it, and some of them will walk with braces the rest of their lives, if they manage to walk at all."

"But why is it so important that *you* work on that particular project?"

"I've had more experience with this sort of detective work than any other doctor in the world," he explained. "It's my job."

"Then you'd turn me down if I attached that condition?"

He nodded. "What was it some poet said about that? '*I could not love thee dear so much,/loved I not honor more.*' By now you know I'm not really the hard-hearted sophisticate I pretend to be. Beneath this hairy chest beats a heart of purest gold."

"Don't start waving the flag." Helen reached out to take his hands. "I intended to go with you all the time; Sam Hunter convinced me."

"And you deliberately put me on the griddle? I ought to withdraw my invitation just to punish you."

"You still can."

"And lose what I've been looking for all my life—a woman with a brain *and* beauty. The airport at noon?"

"All right."

"Better bring along a few extra things. I just might get so attached to you that I'll drag you off to California with me on Monday—like young Lochinvar."

CHAPTER TWENTY-THREE

I

Greg awoke sometime after midnight, troubled by a vague uneasiness he had experienced more than once when he had a seriously ill patient in the hospital. It would have been logical to attribute the feeling to extrasensory perception, but on at least half the occasions when he'd felt it before, there had been nothing to worry about, so he'd put it down as a by-product of the concern that was always uppermost in his mind whenever a life hung in the balance.

Jeanne was asleep beside him, the first night she'd been there in many weeks. It had been a long time since they'd known the rapture they'd experienced after their return to the apartment, following an excellent dinner and Peter Carewe's humorous account of his adventures and misadventures as a roving knight fighting against disease.

Greg sat up, being careful not to disturb Jeanne, and swung his feet to the floor. Although there was a telephone extension beside the bed, he moved quietly to the den so as not to awaken her. Dialing the hospital, he asked for the ICU extension. To his surprise, Bob Johnson answered.

"Oh, it's you, sir." The younger surgeon's relief was apparent in his voice. "I've been debating calling you for the past hour."

"What's happening?"

"I think the lung involvement is spreading, sir. Merchant's temperature has been rising steadily since around midnight."

"I'll be there in ten minutes."

Pulling a sheet of paper from the desk, Greg scribbled:

"Gone to the hospital. Merchant worse.
All my love."

Then, putting the note on the bedside table, where Jeanne would see it immediately when she awoke in the morning, he dressed quickly and took the elevator down to the ground level.

It was cold outside with gray clouds hiding the sky and the wind whipping up from the harbor sent a chill into his bones even through a heavy coat. The weather report, he remembered now from the bedside radio on the eleven o'clock news, had predicted snow for the entire area beginning sometime that day. Looking at the sky now, he could well believe the forecast would be correct and the snowfall early.

The hospital lobby was deserted except for the night operator and the cleaning women who were mopping the tiled floor around the foot of the great statue. The corridors, too, were empty as he made his way to the intensive care unit on the third floor of the surgical building next-door to the experimental surgery laboratory.

In a few more hours, the place would teem with life when the shifts changed at seven, and even before that the wards would be busy with morning care. At this hour, though, a stillness gripped the great hospital, a healing stillness of pain- and disease-racked bodies at rest.

Georgia Merchant was asleep, curled up on the single couch in the waiting room of the intensive care unit. He didn't disturb her but went directly to Guy Merchant's room, where he could see Bob Johnson standing beside the bed, adjusting the rubber tube connecting the respirator to the tracheostomy.

Greg listened briefly to the back of the sick man's chest, since the adhesive strappings holding the dressings on the incision where his sternum had been split made it impossible to listen from the front. Afterward, the two doctors went to the nurses' station, where the banked monitor tubes continued to register their graphic patterns of life.

"We taped an ECG reading from the monitor right after I talked to you just now, sir." Bob handed him the strip of paper with the record. "The pulse volume remains constant and so does the blood pressure. There's no appreciable change in the T-wave segment either, but his temperature has been rising steadily."

"That means he's absorbing toxic products from an inflammation in the lungs," said Greg.

"Do you think it's spreading?"

Greg nodded. "Maybe half of each lower lobe is involved now on both sides."

"The antibiotic doesn't seem to be touching it either. And we're giving him the maximum dose."

"As long as he continues to get plenty of oxygen into the blood through the lungs, we're in fairly good shape," said Greg. "But if this inflammation continues to spread and restrict the amount of lung available for respiration, we could be in trouble. How much of Lawson's blood do you think we still have in storage?"

"I'll find out." Bob Johnson dialed the hospital blood bank extension and spoke to the night technician. "About two thousand cc., sir," he reported.

"I'm going to discontinue both the Imuran and methylprednisolone," said Greg.

"How about ALG?"

"We'll stop that, too, for the time being at least; right now he's in more danger from a spreading lung infection than he is from rejection. If we start a slow transfusion with Lawson's blood, the new white blood cells might help fight the lung infection."

Bob Johnson gave the order to the blood bank and hung up the telephone. "How fast do you want it given, sir?"

"Set the drip to inject the first five hundred cc. in an hour, then have the nurse cut it down until we run out of Lawson's blood or it looks like Merchant's circulation is getting overloaded. If this inflammation isn't stopped in the next few hours, it may get out of control."

"I'll get things going right away," Bob Johnson promised.

"You might as well go home then," Greg told him. "I'll be in my office and can get here in a minute."

"I'll be happy to stay, sir."

"I couldn't sleep any more anyway. I'll see you in the morning."

"Good night, sir. Do you think we should tell Mrs. Merchant?"

"There's no need yet. She already knows what the situation is and his condition isn't liable to change that rapidly."

In his office, Greg surveyed the shelves of books against the back wall on either side of the window, seeking something to read. They contained only technical medical books or journals, however, and finding nothing that promised calm to his restlessness, he went to the desk, unlocked the center drawer and took from it one of Keith Jackson's sketches for the hospital central tower.

The drawing was on thin tracing paper, and, obeying a sudden hunch, he took it to the X-ray viewbox that stood on a table at one side of the office, fixed the sheet before the ground glass and switched on the light. Immediately, as he had thought it might, the sketch took on a three-dimensional quality, giving it a fullness and a grandeur that was literally breathtaking. With the outlines of the statue sketched in lightly, he was sure the whole effect would be that of seeing the structure as it would actually exist, if built, with the massive statue dominating the glass-walled center section. He couldn't risk ruining the sketch by trying to pencil in the statue himself, however—that would have to wait until he could call Keith Jackson about seven before the architect went to his office.

Keith, he was sure, would be able to see, as he had, the potentiality in such a presentation when he faced the Board of Trustees that afternoon and a preview of the new plan was demanded by Ed McDougal and his followers—as he had every reason to anticipate that it would be.

About the meeting itself, Greg felt no apprehension. With the technical difficulties of transplanting a human heart and lungs successfully behind him, and with Jeanne so close to him once again, even Sam Hunter's threat of censure was only a minor irritation. The undeniable fact that he had done something no one else had done before and, through it, opened up new vistas for surgical progress, made his position in the rapidly expanding field of organ transplantation more than secure. A half dozen medical schools, he knew, would welcome him warmly and supply everything he would need in his work.

He would hate to leave The Clinic, it was true, just as he had hated to leave his childhood home every September for four years to board the hot and dirty train for Baltimore. But a few days after he registered for classes again each year and became occupied with the engrossing subjects of the medical curriculum, his loneliness had departed. And as far back as he could remember, he had been able to shut out the world outside and bury himself in his work, so he had no doubt that this surcease would be available to him again.

Not that he had any intention of giving up without a fight before the board. He was convinced that the new plan was the logical answer to the future role of The Clinic and its ever-expanding field of influence upon the people here, as well as what it had always been, one of the finest training institutions in the world for young medical men. No matter what might happen to him personally, he still felt too much of a sense of loyalty to old

Dr. Anders to let what The Clinic's founder had worked so hard to build—and in which a considerable part of Greg's own life was invested—be destroyed until every possibility for preserving it had been exhausted.

A glance at his watch told Greg it was only six o'clock, although he could hear the manifold sounds of the hospital's early morning activities meshing into gear. Keith Jackson had been getting precious little sleep lately and Greg hated to see him awaken before seven at the earliest, so leaving the office, he visited Guy Merchant's room to be sure the blood was flowing satisfactorily and that there had been no major change in his condition, then stopped in the lobby, where the night telephone operators worked behind a grilled partition.

"I'm going over to my apartment for about an hour," he told the operator on duty there. "I'm not going back to bed, so you can get me on the beeper if they need me on intensive care."

"Don't worry, Doctor," the operator said. "If I have to, I'll send an orderly over there to ring the doorbell of your apartment."

Jeanne was still asleep, looking like a lovely little girl sprawled out on the bed under a sheet. She'd always taken two thirds of the bed but he'd been happy to have her where he could touch her when he woke up in the night or press a foot against hers and feel the reflex response, even though she didn't awaken.

Pulling up a chair beside the bed, he sat engrossed in the sheer joy of having her back in the big bed and the memory of her arms about him last night. He had been sitting there for perhaps half an hour when she opened her eyes and, seeing him, sat up in bed clutching the sheet about her breasts.

"What are you doing up, and already dressed, darling?" she asked.

"I went to see Guy Merchant about four this morning. Came back only a few minutes ago."

"Why didn't you wake me to get you some breakfast?"

"I was just sitting here looking at you and wondering how I could have neglected you the way I've done the past two years."

"No woman is neglected who knows she's loved." She leaned over to kiss him. "I just forgot it for a while, but all that's behind us now. Hand me my robe, will you? I feel like a hussy with nothing on but a sheet."

"For a while last night you didn't even have that on, but you certainly didn't look like a hussy—or act like one."

"How would you know? Or were those only lies you used to tell me about my being the only girl you ever loved?"

"They're the truth. I guess I'm just hopelessly square."

"Believe me, I wouldn't want you any other way. When I look at Ed McDougal—" She shivered. "Men like that give me the creeps. He really doesn't have any chance of beating you, does he?"

"He may. When it comes to money, most men react according to a predictable pattern, and there's a lot involved. But when the heart I took from Frank Lawson started beating in Guy Merchant's body the other night, I knew I had reached a height from which no man could drag me down."

"It can be lonely up there. You need people to help you."

"That's the main reason why I came home—besides seeing you. I'm going down to Keith Jackson's apartment, as soon as I'm sure he and Mary are awake. The hospital sketch needs one final touch. When that's done, I'll be ready to face the trustees."

II

For a while Friday morning, it seemed that the measures Greg had taken during the night would give Guy Merchant enough weapons—mainly in the form of fresh white blood cells from the man who had also furnished him with a new heart and lungs—to fight a winning battle against the infection that was filling his lungs with the swelling of inflammation, slowly shutting off the rhythmic expansion and contraction of the tiny air sacs, called alveoli, whose thin lining membrane allowed oxygen to pass freely into the bloodstream and carbon dioxide out of it.

Shortly after eleven, Helen Foucald came into Greg's office. He was staring morosely at the desk blotter while he racked his brain for some new way to attack the deadly process.

"Can I bother you for a moment, Greg?" she asked.

"Of course. What's troubling you?"

"I'm planning to go away for the weekend, leaving about noon, but if you think you'll need me here, I'll stay."

"Your idea about using Lawson's blood helped a lot, but we've done everything we can, so there's nothing to do now but wait it out." He glanced out of the window, where skiffs of snow had already begun to fall. "Are you driving?"

"Yes."

"Then you'd better get going. The view out there doesn't look very promising."

"We're only going a little beyond Frederick. Peter knows—" She stopped, then shrugged. "I don't imagine you would approve."

"I'm as fond of you and Peter Carewe as I am of anybody I know, Helen. Nothing would please me more than to see you happy—together." He hesitated, then added, "Does Peter know about Henry?"

"Yes."

"And you're going away together to see whether or not it might still work out?"

"You think it's hopeless, don't you?"

"I think you're both adults and entitled to the sort of happiness Jeanne and I had—have together."

"I'm glad you found it again, Greg."

"So am I," he said. "Now, whatever happens with The Clinic and with Merchant, I'll come out ahead, even if Sam Hunter does manage to conk me this afternoon."

"Don't be too angry with him, Greg," she begged. "Last night I went with him to a performance of the circus his son Ted and his wife are with. Sam Hunter is really a lonely old man."

"Why does he have to take his loneliness out on me?"

"It's not you personally; it's what you represent, what you're making him face."

"How do you figure that?"

"The old have an instinctive fear of tomorrow, knowing that every passing day increases the odds in favor of the next one bringing death. Because of that, Sam would naturally be suspicious of anything that represents a sharp change from the status quo."

"Sir William Osler once said everybody over sixty should be chloroformed—or something like that, but I'm getting too close to that age myself to be much in favor of it."

"There's another side to Sam Hunter's opposition to you, I'm sure," she said. "He really worshiped Henry's father."

"We're kindred spirits there."

"And he sees you as a threat to the image he holds of Dr. Anders."

"Nothing could be farther from the truth," Greg protested. "Dr. Anders was a visionary—ahead of the time. I only want to make The Clinic what he would make it himself, if he were alive today."

"I tried to tell Sam that, but I don't think I succeeded very well. Good luck, Greg—with the trustees."

"Give my regards to Peter. I'm sorry we got to see so little of each other this time, but I've been a bit busy."

"Nobody could deny that," she agreed.

When Helen was gone, Greg went to the intensive care unit and looked in on Guy Merchant, but there was no change for the better. The brief period of improvement with the transfusions had only been temporary; now his temperature was slowly climbing once again. His color was good, however, indicating that enough of the lungs were still functioning to provide an adequate supply of oxygen for the red blood cells to carry to the rest of the body. But how much longer the balance would be in his favor, with the amount of functioning lung tissues being gradually encroached on by the progress of the infection, was problematic.

Greg ordered another portable X-ray of the chest for noon and went to the surgical lecture room, where the last paper of the morning session was being given. Seeing Bill Remick there, he nodded to the Washington roentgenologist and fellow trustee to follow and left the room. Remick joined him moments later in the corridor and they went into the doctors' lounge between the two main operating theaters.

"Why the cloak-and-dagger atmosphere?" the X-ray man asked.

"I need to talk to you about the strategy for this afternoon's meeting."

"That's the best news I've heard yet."

"What?"

"That you're hitting back at last and not letting people push you around."

"You sound just like my wife," said Greg.

"It's true. You're my friend, Greg, but I've got to tell you just the same."

"What you don't realize, Bill, is that when people appear to be pushing me around, it's usually because I've already decided the course I will follow. In the end, things usually work out the way I want them to."

"This thing is too important to take a chance on," the X-ray man insisted. "If it's moved somewhere else, The Clinic will never be the same."

"I agree with you there. That's why I've decided on a little nudging."

"It may take more than a little."

"Perhaps, but I think I can manage that, too—with your help. What do you think will be the opposition's plan of attack?"

"They know I'm behind you, so they don't confide in me."

"How do you see the situation then?"

"If I were Ed McDougal, I would play down this attempt of Sam Hunter's to censure you. The old man called the special meeting this afternoon to press the charge, so they'll have to go through with that to humor him, but your success with the transplant has pretty well spiked their guns. I'm sure Ed recognizes that, even if Sam Hunter might not."

"Any chance that Ed will persuade Sam not to insist on the special meeting?"

"Not the way I see it. By letting a vote to censure be taken, they can see who's wavering and who needs to be worked on before tomorrow, so it will help them, even if they lose. The most important goal they have right now is to make you reveal your hospital plans prematurely, so they'll have time to plan ways to combat it before the final meeting tomorrow morning. I've tried to figure out some way to forestall a demand for the plans at this afternoon's meeting, but so far I've had no luck. No specific agenda has been announced—"

"That's why I came to see you," said Greg. "If you'll help me, I think I can steal a march on them."

"How?"

"Jud Templeton has a copy of the main drawing I'm going to show the board and his piece on it is already written, ready to be published in this afternoon's final editions, after the special meeting. Jud also has a list of the people who will join with Henry and Ed to develop this property after The Clinic is moved, but he can't publish it because they haven't actually started yet."

"Suppose Ed and his crowd become wary and don't demand to see the plan."

"Then I want you to do it."

"How?"

"Even if they don't ask to see it, I'm going to show the sketches anyway," said Greg. "As soon as I start the presentation, I want you to call Jud Templeton." He handed the roentgenologist a slip of paper. "Here's his telephone number. All you have to say is that you're calling for me and that he's to turn loose his dogs."

"It's a smart trick. Ed and his crowd will be fit to be tied."

"That's the idea," said Greg. "I figure that, by showing the new plan before anyone from the opposition has a chance to demand to see it, we'll be sowing confusion in their ranks."

"It couldn't happen to a more deserving crew of scoundrels."

III

Peter Carewe was waiting at one of the car-rental booths at the airport when Helen came in, carrying a small overnight case.

"The weather man says the snow's pretty heavy toward the Catoctins," he said, taking her arm. "If we're going to get through we'd better get started right away. They're putting up some sandwiches and a thermos of coffee for us in the lunch room."

It was barely one o'clock when they pulled away from the front of Friendship Airport and took a country road that connected with U.S. 40 near Ellicott City.

"I'm more accustomed to driving a jeep in the tropics," said Peter. "But my work takes me into some pretty rough country, so I hope I can still cope with a snowstorm. How about breaking out the sandwiches and coffee?"

They ate on the move, for the snow was already pelting down. The going became steadily more difficult on the narrow back road and it took them almost two hours to reach the four-lane arterial highway westward. When they did, visibility was almost nil and ahead they saw a line of blinking red lights marking a highway patrol barricade.

"We're only letting emergencies through westward," said the patrolman who stopped them. "How far were you going?"

"We have reservations at Chalet Julienne in the Catoctins."

"They've been snowed in since midnight. Frederick is pretty well blocked, too, unless it's a very grave emergency. My advice to you is to go back to

Baltimore while you can still make it and wait until we can get snowplows
through."

"When is that liable to be?" Peter asked.

"The forecast says the snow will end before midnight and we'll have
plows going immediately."

Peter looked questioningly at Helen. "What do you think?"

"Let's go back," she said. "There's no point in risking our lives."

He turned the car around and they started back toward Baltimore but the
going was bad even then. An hour had passed when Helen suddenly started
to laugh.

"What's so funny?" Peter asked.

"It looks as if heaven is trying to protect the working girl."

"You'll not escape my clutches that easy, me proud beauty," he said with
a chuckle. "I'm taking you back to my suite."

Helen made no objection; here in the warm car close beside him with the
falling snow a fleecy white curtain outside, Henry and the rest of the world
seemed far away.

"Anyway," she said contentedly, "I'll get to see what this room service
you recommend so highly is really like."

IV

The brown tablets given Vivian and Ted by the Filipino doctor at the
hospital had relieved the pain in his hand and enabled him to get some sleep
while the circus was moving to Frederick that night. But when morning
dawned to a dull and lowering sky with the promise of snow, Vivian could
see that Ted was much worse.

The swelling, which had been confined to the hand itself until the splinter
wound was opened the night before, now extended well up the wrist and was
apparent above the bandage. Ted complained, too, of a severe headache,
which even the tablets didn't entirely relieve, and the feverish look in his
eyes, plus his hot, dry skin, told Vivian their visit to the hospital last night
had not helped control the infection in his hand.

Snow had begun to fall in Frederick well before noon and the half-hourly
weather reports were now predicting an even heavier fall as the front moved
eastward toward Baltimore and the coast. At 3 P.M., the police canceled the
evening performance of the circus to avoid the danger of people being
marooned in the auditorium where it was to be held. When, shortly
afterwards, Ted began to shake with a severe chill and talk wildly in
delirium, Vivian sent for Papa Gus, who was busy preparing the circus for
the full onslaught of the storm.

"Ted's much worse than he was this morning, Papa," she said. "We've
got to take him to a hospital."

"I'll tell Joe Califino to get the jeep. There's certain to be a hospital here
in Frederick."

"Ted's too sick to be treated by just any doctor," she said firmly. "I'm
going to take him to The Clinic and ask his father to see that he has the best
doctors there."

"Mr. Hunter has a right to know Ted is sick," Papa Gus agreed. "It is
the right thing to do."

"We'll use our van," she said. "Joe has driven it through snow before and
that way Ted can lie down all the way."

V

"They're wary, Greg," said Bill Remick as the members of the Board of Trustees began to file into one of the meeting rooms of the Clinic Inn for the Friday-afternoon special session Sam Hunter had demanded. The convocation had officially ended with the final paper at four o'clock and it was now nearly five. Glancing at the large flat package Greg carried, the X-ray man added, "I doubt that they're going to ask for the plans this afternoon."

"Then we'll make them." Greg kept his voice low so only the roentgenologist could hear. "I have everything set up."

He nodded toward a viewbox which had been pushed back against the wall so it wouldn't be noticeable, yet could be seen by everyone in the room once the light was switched on.

"I'll take care of that as we planned," Bill Remick promised.

The tactics the opposition had decided upon were obvious from the first words of Dr. Timothy Puckett, after he gaveled the meeting to order.

"This special meeting has been called for the purpose of taking up a charge made against Dr. Gregory Alexander by Mr. Sam Hunter," he said. "Namely, that he constructed an addition to the present hospital without the authority of the board. No other—"

"Mr. Chairman," Bill Remick interrupted. "Did I understand you to say that this is a special meeting?"

"You know it is, Bill," Timothy Puckett said testily. "The regularly scheduled meeting is tomorrow morning."

"Have you read the bylaws recently, Mr. Chairman?"

"Well, I—"

"Obviously you haven't, so I will read from them in order to bring you up to date." Taking a typed sheet from his pocket, the roentgenologist read:

> When a special meeting is called, the trustees shall be notified
> in writing no less than five days in advance of this meeting
> concerning the matters to be taken up at that time.

"I protest the failure of the chairman to follow the bylaws in calling this meeting," Bill Remick added, "unless you consider this only a part of the regular annual meeting of the Board of Trustees."

"We'll call it that, if you wish." Timothy Puckett missed seeing frantic signals from Ed McDougal. "The regular meeting is now open for business."

"Mr. Chairman." Bill Remick spoke quickly again before anyone else could gain the floor. "I move that Dr. Gregory Alexander, chairman of the building committee for the Board of Trustees, give a preliminary presentation of the plan he has developed for a new building complex to be constructed upon the site of the present one."

Dave Connor seconded the motion, and, stunned by the swift action, Timothy Puckett asked automatically, "Is there any discussion?"

Ed McDougal was rising to his feet when, pretending that the motion had already passed, Greg moved to the corner of the room where he had set up the viewbox.

"Dr. Alexander." Timothy Puckett was groping for some way to stop him. "You are—"

"It was my intention to present plans in some detail to this body at the meeting tomorrow," Greg interrupted firmly, drowning out the chairman's protest. "But since Dr. Remick has made the motion, I shall show you some preliminary sketches."

Ignoring the clamor of voices demanding to be heard, Greg placed the transparent preliminary sketch for the high-rise ICU tower on the viewbox. He and Keith Jackson had spent a busy hour together early that morning and the outline of the statue was now drawn in place in the center of the ground glass front of the viewbox.

"This is a sketch of the proposed new hospital and diagnostic clinic building drawn by architect Keith Jackson at my request." Greg flipped the switch to illuminate the sketch.

A hush fell over the group of shouting men; as if seen in three dimensions, both the statue and the surrounding glass-walled enclosure of the tower stood out in all its startling beauty and grandeur.

"As all of you know," he continued, "one of the provisions of Dr. Anders' will was that, should any alteration in the structure of the present Clinic be necessary, the statue of Christ in the lobby should never lose its position of preeminence. This requirement posed a considerable architectural problem but I am sure you will see, even in this preliminary sketch, that Mr. Jackson has completely fulfilled Dr. Anders' provision."

From the corner of his eye, Greg saw Bill Remick leave the room to call Jud Templeton. As he scanned the faces before him, he could see that the sketch was affecting many of the trustees in the same way that it had affected him when he'd first seen it, with a feeling of awe and reverence far transcending whatever preconceptions they might have had. Only the most prejudiced could fail to see that he and Keith Jackson had brought forth a new creation, a new concept in hospital construction combining beauty and effectiveness in a perfect amalgam.

"Mr. Chairman." Ed McDougal's voice sounded a little stunned.

"Dr. McDougal."

"I move that consideration of this matter be tabled until tomorrow morning at the regular session."

Henry Anders quickly seconded the motion and Dr. Puckett spoke before anyone else could intervene.

"A motion to table cannot be discussed," he announced. "All in favor say 'aye.'"

There was a chorus of "ayes" and, when he called for the "nays," about an equally loud negative vote, but the sweating chairman chose to hear only the former, and announced that the motion had carried.

"Do I hear a motion for adjournment?" he asked, and, when that, too, came quickly, the meeting was over.

CHAPTER TWENTY-FOUR

I

At first, the state police hadn't wanted to let the big red van from the Tarentino Circus move eastward toward Baltimore because of the storm. But when Vivian pleaded that Ted must be taken to The Clinic for treatment immediately, they finally agreed to let it through. Even though the truck was equipped with snow tires and Joe Califino was a skilled driver, the going was slow and more than two hours were required for the some forty-odd miles to Baltimore.

It was six o'clock when they finally reached the emergency entrance to The Clinic and Ted was lifted out and placed on a rolling stretcher. Vivian went inside to make arrangements while Joe parked the truck in the adjacent lot, planning to remain there until Vivian came to give him further orders.

While she was giving the necessary information to the emergency room nursing supervisor, Vivian could see that the hospital routine was meshing smoothly into action, for a young doctor in crisp white ducks began examining Ted immediately.

"Do you have any idea how I could reach Mr. Sam Hunter?" she asked the nurse.

"Is he a relative?"

"Mr. Hunter is my husband's father." Vivian's voice shook a little as she spoke the words that might end her marriage, if Sam Hunter managed to get his way. But saving Ted's life was more important now than either her pride or her love for him.

"Mr. Hunter comes to The Clinic every year at this time," the nurse said. "I believe he's at the Clinic Inn."

"Would you telephone him, please? Tell him Ted is seriously ill and I need help."

"I'll call him right away, Mrs. Hunter. Do you want to speak to him yourself?"

"N—no thanks."

"Dr. Adams is already examining your husband," the nurse told her as she dialed. "You can be sure he'll be well taken care of."

Vivian was sitting on a bench outside the waiting room drinking coffee when the tall old man, whom she had never actually seen but whom she recognized from his picture, came charging out of the elevator followed by Ed McDougal and Henry Anders. He didn't even give her a glance but moved to the door of the emergency room, where Ted was lying on a treatment table, with the young doctor in a white uniform bending over his arm.

"Ted!" The cry of agony penetrated momentarily through the curtain of delirium that threatened to shut away Ted's mind from reality.

"Hello, Dad." The words were slightly slurred. "Where's Vivian?"

"I'm here, darling." Vivian had moved to the doorway, where Ted could see her. "It's all right, you're at The Clinic."

Sam Hunter wheeled upon the small figure. "What have you done to my son?" he demanded angrily.

Vivian stiffened at his tone, but worry about Ted during the long ride from Frederick to Baltimore through the snowstorm had almost used up her strength.

"You turned him out, Mr. Hunter," she said with all the dignity she could muster. "Now I've given him back to you. His life is worth more to me than anything else."

"Dr. Anders," the young doctor said, "this looks like an anerobic infection."

"What?" Henry Anders asked, frowning.

"There's crepitation in the tissues of the hand and lower arm. I'm sure we're dealing with gas"—he broke off, not wanting to speak the dread words "gas gangrene" where Sam Hunter and Vivian could hear—"with a gas bacillus infection."

"Do something, Henry," Sam Hunter demanded, and Henry Anders moved to the table where Ted lay. The dressings had been removed from his hand and the strange odor of the infection, dank and repelling like the air in some freshly opened funeral crypt, reached even into the corridor outside the room. Henry examined the arm briefly, running his fingers along the skin, then turned to Ed McDougal.

"You'd better take a look at this, too, Ed," he said doubtfully. "I don't treat this sort of thing very often."

"What is it, Ed?" Sam Hunter demanded when the Texas surgeon finished a brief examination.

"The prognosis isn't good, Mr. Hunter."

"What does that mean?"

"The boy has a gas bacillus infection of his hand and arm. It appears to be progressive."

"Well, do something about it."

Ed McDougal hesitated, reluctant to speak the words. "Ted's very sick," he said at last. "Unless his arm is amputated quickly, there's little hope of saving him—and not much at that."

Sam Hunter staggered and it was Vivian who took him by the arm and led him to a bench.

"But, Dr. Anders—" the house officer started to say in a tone of shocked protest, only to be cut off by Sam Hunter's strangled cry:

"Amputation? You can't mean it."

"Are you saying the only treatment that can save my husband is to cut off his arm?" Vivian asked incredulously.

"I wish there were some other way except amputation." No one could doubt that Ed McDougal meant what he said. "God knows I wish it."

II

Helen and Peter were crossing the parking lot after depositing their luggage at the Clinic Inn and leaving his rental car at a nearby garage to be picked up. She stopped when she saw the big red van with the letters TARENTINO CIRCUS emblazoned across its sides parked beneath a lamppost so the light would shine into the cab.

"Look, Peter!" she cried. "That truck is from the circus I saw with Sam Hunter last night."

"Are you sure?"

"There would hardly be two Tarentino Circuses in this area at the same time."

"Let's see if anyone's inside."

When Peter tapped on the glass of the door, Joe Califino sat up in his cubicle and swung his legs so he could slide into the seat and run down the glass of the door.

"Are you here with someone from the circus?" Helen asked.

"What's the matter?" said the roustabout. "Ain't I supposed to park here?"

"I don't have anything to do with parking," said Helen. "I saw the circus last night in Frederick and recognized the truck."

"Vivian and Ted—they're inside."

"Those are the names of the young acrobats." Helen gave Peter a quick look and turned back to the roustabout. "Is anything wrong?"

"It's Ted, ma'am. He's got this trouble with his hand."

"I knew something was wrong!" Helen cried. "He almost dropped her last night."

"And scared the daylights out of me and Papa Gus," Joe Califino said.

"Are they in the hospital?" Peter asked.

"Ted got worse last night so Vivian decided to bring him here to his old man," said the roustabout.

"That boy is Sam Hunter's son, Peter," Helen said quickly. "We've got to go in and see about him."

"Of course."

They came into the corridor outside the emergency room in time to hear Ed McDougal's words, and Helen gave a cry of protest as she realized their significance. But it was Peter who spoke.

"What's this, Ed?" he asked.

"Mr. Hunter's son Ted has a gas bacillus infection of the hand and arm."

Peter moved into the emergency room without invitation and touched the skin of Ted's arm above the now puffed and angry wound in his hand. Ted himself had lapsed into delirium again and was muttering incoherently.

"Look here, Carewe," Henry Anders blustered, "you're not on the staff."

"Neither is Ed McDougal, but it looks like he's in charge," Peter said curtly.

"He's in consultation with me."

Ignoring The Clinic director, Peter continued his examination, but a third-year medical student could have diagnosed the nature of the infection and traced its course from the brief history Vivian had given the house officer for the admission record and which he had written on a card.

The germ of gas gangrene, a common inhabitant of the animal—and often the human—digestive tract, had obviously been introduced into Ted's hand by means of the splinter when he'd picked up the stake a few days before to fend off the stampeding elephants. Growing in the body tissue, the virulent organism had been fairly well localized in the hand around the original wound by the body's own defenses, until the incision the night before had broken down the wall of tissue resistance that held it in check. With the wall thus breached, noxious bacteria had been able to break out, like an enemy escaping from a trap, and spread into the surrounding tissues, where they were rapidly overwhelming the body's defenses and would soon become a fatal septicemia. The crinkly feeling beneath Peter's fingers, a certain indicator that gas was being formed there by the rapidly spreading infection, was enough in itself to make the diagnosis.

"Ed's in charge here at my request," Henry Anders started to splutter, but Peter cut him off sharply.

"Did you say amputation, Ed?" he demanded.

"I don't like it, Peter," said the Texan. "But nothing else can save the boy."

"Dr. Adams." Peter spoke to the house officer, who wore a nameplate over the pocket of his duck coat.

"Yes, sir?"

"How would you treat this infection?"

"With hyperbaric oxygen," the younger doctor answered unhesitatingly. "Dr. Alexander's experiments . . ."

"Experiments!" The strangled cry came from Sam Hunter.

"Hyperbaric oxygen treatment for this type of infection is more than an experient, Mr. Hunter," said Helen. "You can't let them amputate."

"You mean there's another treatment that might save Ted's arm?" Vivian spoke for the first time since Peter and Helen had come in.

"His arm and his life," said Peter. "The experimental work done by Dr. Alexander here proves that these infections can be controlled by the special treatment Dr. Adams mentioned."

"Is that true, Henry?" Sam Hunter demanded.

"Well, it is still experi—"

"I had forgotten that The Clinic had a hyperbaric chamber, Mr.

Hunter." Ed McDougal's relief at the avenue of escape opened to him by Peter's words was quite apparent in his voice. "It should certainly be tried first."

"I'll call Dr. Alexander at once," said Helen, seizing the opportunity Ed McDougal's strategic retreat had offered her.

"I'm not sure I can give permission for my son to be experimented on," Sam Hunter objected. "There's been too much of that here already."

"You don't have to give permission, Mr. Hunter," said Peter. "Your son's wife is here and her legal rights come before yours, where Ted is concerned."

Every eye was suddenly upon Vivian, small and still partially frozen with the horror of what had been first proposed for treating Ted. In her need for help and assurance, she turned instinctively to another woman.

"Is what they're saying true?" she asked Helen.

"Yes, Vivian," said Helen. "Amputation might save Ted's life but his arm would be lost. The treatment Dr. Carewe and Dr. Adams suggest has a good chance of saving both."

"Then let him have it," she said firmly. "I give my permission."

"Go call Greg, Helen," said Peter. "I'll stay here."

III

Greg was working in Guy Merchant's room on the ICU when Helen found him. He had slipped a needle between the ribs to the left of the sternum, seeking to enter the pericardial sac surrounding the heart. As he pushed it slowly inward, a reddish fluid suddenly spurted into the syringe attached to the needle.

Busy with what he was doing, Greg hadn't noticed Helen standing in the door of the room and she hesitated to interrupt him in anything so delicate and dangerous as tapping the space around the heart with a needle.

"The fluid doesn't look purulent, Bob." He spoke to the Senior Fellow, whose eyes were also on the syringe. "That means there's no infection in the pericardium and relieving the pressure of the fluid ought to improve heart action."

"It gives us a chance," Bob Johnson agreed. "I guess maybe our last one."

"As soon as I finish removing the rest of the pericardial fluid, I'll tap the pleural cavities to give the lungs all the room we can," said Greg. "Then we can put him in—"

"Greg." Helen spoke from the door, and he looked up in surprise.

"I thought you were out of town, Helen?"

"It's a long story," she said. "Could you possibly see a patient for me in the emergency room right away?"

"Of course," he said. "Bob can finish up here. But what's so urgent?"

"Sam Hunter's son was just brought in with a far-advanced gas gangrene of the arm."

The sudden silence in the room surprised her, but Greg broke it almost immediately. "I'll come right away," he said. "Wait for me."

"Tell me what you can about the case," he said as they were waiting for the elevator to take them to the ground floor. Helen gave him a brief rundown on the events that had transpired since she and Peter had recognized the red circus van in the parking lot outside and had come into the emergency room. Long before she finished, his face was grave.

"You say Ed and Henry have seen him already?" he asked.

"Yes. Ed recommended amputation."

"Most surgeons would—particularly if a hyperbaric chamber wasn't available. We've only realized recently that these anerobic infections can be tackled more successfully with the use of oxygen under high pressure."

"Henry tried to stop Peter from recommending it," she said. "But Ed McDougal was smart enough to see that it got him off the hook."

"And me on it," said Greg soberly. "The first treatment will take at least four hours, including decompression. If it doesn't stop the infection, that's four hours we will have lost when we have to amputate, as a final resort."

"I'm sorry, Greg. The girl trusted Peter and me and refused to let Ed and Henry go ahead. We can't let her down."

"More than that's involved, Helen." At the odd note in his voice, she gave him a quick appraising glance.

"What do you mean?"

"I planned to take Guy Merchant directly to the hyperbaric chamber when we finished taking off the fluid."

"Oh, Greg!" she cried. "I didn't know."

"How could you?"

"Do you think he has a chance outside the chamber?"

"I doubt it—we were hoping the extra oxygen might make the difference—in his favor."

"And now I've robbed you of that."

"You and Peter had no alternative," he assured her. "It looks like we're all having hard choices today."

"How did the special meeting come out this afternoon?" she asked.

"When Ed McDougal and his gang realized how close the vote would be, they managed to table any action until tomorrow morning."

"Did you show the new plan?"

"Yes. I did manage that."

They were just outside the emergency room, and noticing a newspaper vending rack, Greg stopped before it.

"Got a dime?" he asked. "My money's in my wallet in the dressing room."

She fished out a coin and he dropped it into the slot. Taking out a paper, he handed it to her, pointing to the front page, where the sketch of the proposed central section of The Clinic occupied a full half of the space.

"It's beautiful!" she cried. "Truly majestic!"

"Just thought you might want to see what we're risking."

"Oh, Greg. I'm sorry. Truly sorry."

"We aren't licked yet." He held open the door to the emergency room for her to pass through ahead of him. "But wouldn't it be ironic if Sam Hunter succeeds in censuring me tomorrow for building the chamber that saves his son's life?"

IV

The tableau in the emergency room was like a Greek tragedy halted in mid-scene. Peter Carewe stood at one side of the room with Vivian Hunter beside him; ranged against them were Ed McDougal, Henry Anders and Sam Hunter. The girl was pale and looked very small compared to her antagonists and her single protector, but she had obviously not given ground, for the expression on Sam Hunter's face was one of angry bafflement.

"There's a question of ethics involved here, Greg." Henry Anders hadn't yet given up, in spite of Ed McDougal's wish to retreat.

"We can settle the ethical question at once," Greg said mildly and turned to Vivian.

"I'm Dr. Alexander, chief surgeon of The Clinic, Mrs. Hunter," he said. "Did you engage Dr. McDougal and Dr. Anders to treat your husband?"

"I certainly did not." Vivian looked defiantly at Sam Hunter. "Mr. Hunter brought these other doctors and now they say they have to amputate Ted's arm."

"Do you wish me to take charge of your husband's case?" Greg asked her.

"Yes. I certainly do."

"I think that takes care of the ethics question, Henry," said Greg. "Let's see the patient, Mrs. White." He spoke to the nurse who appeared at his elbow, and moved to the cubicle where Ted was lying on a treatment table.

No one spoke during the five-minute examination. When he came out of the cubicle, Greg went directly to a basin at one side of the room and washed his hands carefully, then rinsed them with antiseptic from a bottle on the shelf over the basin.

"Dr. McDougal has already made the diagnosis." He spoke to Vivian. "If what we call hyperbaric oxygen wasn't available, I would recommend immediate amputation, as he did."

"Can you guarantee that this experiment of yours will succeed?" Sam Hunter demanded.

"I can only tell you that in your son's condition even an amputation might very well not save him, Mr. Hunter," Greg said quietly. "Oxygen under pressure is the only thing that offers any hope."

"Please go ahead, Doctor," Vivian begged. "We've lost too much time already, while these others were bickering."

"I'll take him into the chamber immediately," said Greg.

"H—how soon will you know, Doctor?"

"The first exposure to oxygen will take about three hours, all told. We ought to know something when it's over."

"You'll stay with him?"

"Of course. As soon as we obtain the pressure we need in the chamber, I shall open the wound in his hand more widely."

V

At the nurses' desk, Greg rang the experimental laboratory and Hans Werner. "I'm bringing a case of gas gangrene over right now, Hans," he said. "We'll put him into the hyperbaric chamber instead of Mr. Merchant. Please call Dr. Gann and ask the operating room to send over a sterile incision and drainage tray."

"Very goot, Doctor."

"This is a severe case," Greg added. "We'll be in the chamber for two hours at four atmospheres, perhaps longer."

"Do not worry, Doctor," said Hans. "Everything iss ready."

While Ted was being moved by means of a portable stretcher, Greg found Georgia Merchant in the ICU waiting room.

"You have bad news for me, Doctor," she said when she saw his face.

"Not about your husband's immediate condition," he said. "In fact, removing the fluid from the pericardium has improved his heart action."

"What then?"

"I planned to treat him in the pressure chamber after I took off the fluid, but I shall not be able to do it."

"Why not?"

"Another patient has just been admitted who needs oxygen under pressure very badly."

"It's the only treatment with a chance of saving Guy, isn't it?"

"I think so—yes."

"Then how could anyone need it more than he does?"

"This is a young man with a rapidly progressing infection that can be controlled only by means of the chamber."

"Couldn't you treat him later—and give Guy this added chance?"

"We may not be able to save the young man as it is. If we wait, all chance would be lost."

"Are you asking my permission to let the chamber be used for this young man instead of my husband, with the knowledge that not using it for Guy may mean his death?" Georgia asked.

"I've already made the decision but I wanted you to understand why," Greg told her. "We'll do everything we can, of course. Dr. Johnson will be with your husband all the time and I hope things still turn out for the best. I must go now; they're waiting to close the chamber."

CHAPTER TWENTY-FIVE

I

Besides Ted Hunter, muttering and picking at the covering sheet in his delirium, Greg took only Hans Werner, the doyen of the experimental laboratory, and Dr. Lewis Gann into the chamber with him, along with the sterile tray of instruments and dressings he had ordered prepared. Hans had helped with hundreds of operations and was as skilled as any nurse; besides, there was barely room inside the steel-walled tank with its glass-covered ports for the three of them and the cushioned operating table to which Ted was transferred.

The small hyperbaric chamber, which was all Greg had been able to get funds for, was very much like the pressure tanks used for many years in compressing and decompressing divers and caisson workers, whose jobs took them underwater, as well as in treating those who developed what was called "bends" from too rapid decompression. The actual operation of the tank itself was in the hands of specially trained technicians, all of them former Navy diving experts; one or more of these constantly watched the activities going on inside the chamber through one of the glass ports, so as to be ready to take whatever measures might be necessary in an emergency.

Since the air pouring into the tank, as the pump began to raise the pressure, was only one fifth oxygen and the highest possible concentration in the blood was desired, Dr. Gann placed a mask over Ted's face immediately and began to administer pure oxygen, saturating the body tissues quickly as the pressure rose and surrounding the oxygen-hating germs of the infection with a medium in which, hopefully, they would no longer thrive, as they had been doing in the tissues of his hand and arm.

Fortunately unusual, except in wartime, gas bacillus infection did not come into the hands of the average doctor often. Relatively little progress had therefore been made in treatment over amputation, which had been used for centuries, until this method had been devised of putting a high concentration of oxygen, with its powerful dampening effect upon the growth of this particular type of bacteria, into the patient's body through the use of the hyperbaric chamber.

"Think the bug has invaded the bloodstream yet, Greg?" Dr. Gann asked as he added a weak mixture of nitrous oxide to the oxygen flow to achieve the very light anesthesia Greg would need in order to open the wound widely in search of a foreign body and to remove any gangrenous tissue that would encourage the further growth of the invading bacteria.

"I doubt it." Like the others, Greg was sweating profusely as the pressure rose, for the concentration of air into a smaller volume with each stroke of the pump also concentrated its heat and the chamber lacked the elaborate cooling system that marked larger and newer ones. "It's certainly galloping now but I hope we can still get ahead of it."

"Strange the doctor who treated him last night didn't notice the gas. Your nose usually diagnoses these infections."

"There may not have been much last night; it hadn't really started spreading then." Greg had put on sterile gloves and was painting Ted Hunter's hand with an antiseptic, while Hans Werner held it above an arm board extending out from the table. Draping the arm with a sterile sheet, he nodded to Hans, who lowered the hand upon it and held it tightly so Ted would not be able to draw it back if he were able to feel pain through the light gas anesthesia.

Laying another small sterile drape across the arm over Hans Werner's hand, Greg took a scalpel and cut in both directions through the inflamed incision, laying the small wound open widely. Bits of dark, unhealthy-looking tissue he trimmed away, until there was a fresh flow of blood, bright red now from the high concentration of oxygen. And in the depths of the wound, he lifted out with a forceps a broken splinter of wood about a half inch long.

"There's the culprit," he said with a ring of satisfaction in his voice. "We should be able to keep the situation under control now."

It took only a few minutes more to trim away some remaining damaged tissues around where the fragment of splinter had rested. When he finished, Greg put a loose dressing over the wound, allowing it to bleed rather freely in order to wash out as many of the invading bacteria as possible, as well as any remaining bits of damaged tissue, before the bleeding stopped of its own accord through the normal process of clotting.

"Presssure is three atmospheres." Hans Werner was watching a dial set against the wall of the tank. The glass ports had filmed over with moisture with the sudden rise of temperature as the pressure increased. They were beginning to clear now and one of the technicians watching them from outside raised his hand with thumb and forefinger joined to form the letter *O*, indicating that all was well with the chamber mechanism.

"How high are you going, Greg?" Lew Gann asked.

"Four atmospheres for two hours or maybe a bit longer—if you think it's safe."

"That's close to the danger level for oxygen convulsions," said the anesthesiologist. "But I guess you want to hit those bugs as hard as you can the first crack."

"It's the possibility that a few of them may have been seeded into the bloodstream by the treatment last night that I'm worried particularly about," Greg explained. "But we'll hold it at three, if you're worried about him, Lew."

"He's young and strong," said Dr. Gann. "Besides, I can always control an oxygen convulsion, if it comes, by cutting off the O-two and letting him breathe air just as we're doing. Go on to four atmospheres."

"Is the transplant case lost already, Doctor?" Hans Werner asked.

"I'm afraid his lungs are filling," said Greg. "The infection seems to be under control and after removing the pericardial fluid that was cramping the heart we might have carried him with hyperbaric oxygen on the small amount of lung tissue still functioning. But—" He didn't go on.

"Did Georgia Merchant take it hard?" Lew Gann asked.

"She's a trouper, but it hit her, of course. One of the hardest things I ever had to do was tell her we wouldn't be able to use the chamber for her husband as I had planned."

"Life is always a matter of choices," said the old Austrian technician. "If you had not chosen Johns Hopkins, Dr. Alexander. If you had not come to the attention of Dr. Anders when you were a student." He shrugged. "When so much of life depends on chance, you can only believe in a pattern beyond chance, a power that controls even the throw of the dice."

"I wonder if I offended that power by daring to push death back too far," Greg hazarded.

"It's a question to be discussed late at night, over steins of cold beer," Hans said with a smile.

"When the conclusions of the night are to be forgotten in the headache of tomorrow," Dr. Gann agreed.

"Night is the time for doubting," said Hans. "Day is the time for decision—and for work."

"There will be those who say I should not try again," said Greg.

"Will you listen?" Lew Gann asked.

"No."

"Goot!" said Hans. "It works on a dog, so it will work one day with a man. The differences between them are not so great—except in the dog's favor."

"Why do you say that, Hans?"

"A dog is faithful. Can the same be said of all men?"

"No. We're proving that right now in the controversy over the new hospital."

"A dog is also grateful—an emotion that quickly turns to hate in men."

"You're right." Dr. Gann had shut off the anesthetic and Ted Hunter was breathing only oxygen now. "But I could never understand why."

"In Vienna, long ago, I once heard Dr. Freud lecture," said Hans. "I was only a student then and much of what he said I did not understand. But one thing I remember well: he was quoting, I think, from Schiller's play *Wallenstein,* where one actor said of his eyes:

'He has now opened mine
And I see more than pleases me.' "

"Are you saying that gratitude begets hate, Hans, because the grateful one eventually sees his gratitude as an admission of his own inadequacy?" Greg asked.

"I could not have put it so well," the technician admitted.

"If that theory is true," said Dr. Gann, "Henry Anders II has always hated you, Greg, because his father trusted you more than him."

"Not exactly," the old Austrian demurred. "The old doctor learned soon that his son never would be the man he was and turned to Dr. Alexander here to carry on his work. To the junior Dr. Anders, Dr. Alexander is a symbol of his own inadquacy. He sees in the present controversy a chance to remove that symbol, so he works against him."

"I would be willing to be the loser if it would make Henry the doctor his father hoped he would be," said Greg.

"Since that is impossible, it is better to leave him as he is," said Hans.

"How do you think this will all end, Hans?"

"Until this boy came upon the scene, I was prepared to see you defeated, Doctor," said the old man. "I don't know why but somehow I think he may be an omen of the future, though, as always, much will still depend upon the throw of the dice."

"It's a long-shot gamble but the only chance for Ted," Greg agreed.

"Others would be willing to settle for the less hazardous course—and bury their mistake," said Hans. "But take heart; already the oxygen seems to be having an effect."

"That, or removing the splinter," said Dr. Gann. "Upon such a slender thread hangs often a human life."

"Who said that?"

"Me!" said the anesthesiologist with a grin. "Profound, ain't I?"

II

Georgia Merchant was in the intensive care waiting room when the others came there from the emergency room at Helen's suggestion. Now there was nothing for all of them to do but wait: Georgia for Bob Johnson to bring her word that Guy was dead; the others for Greg Alexander to come out of the chamber at the end of the first treatment, and report on Ted's condition.

"Can I get any of you some coffee?" Peter Carewe asked the room. "We have several hours yet to wait before we can get a report on Ted."

No one wanted coffee except Helen and Peter, so he went to the vending machine on the first floor to get it. While he was bringing the coffee, Georgia moved over beside Vivian.

"You did the right thing in letting Dr. Alexander take care of your husband, Mrs. Hunter," she said. "I'm Georgia Merchant."

"Oh!" Helen caught herself immediately and looked at Vivian—but the name meant nothing to the girl.

"We were hoping things would turn out differently from the way they have, Mrs. Merchant," said Helen.

"I guess I was just kidding myself that there was really any hope, Doctor."

"Your husband has already proved that the operation is technically possible with a human being. In the next case—"

"You mean Dr. Alexander would try again?"

"Of course."

"What she's saying"—Sam Hunter's voice was harsh with pain and bitter anger—"is that your husband was another of Dr. Alexander's experiments—just like my son."

"Are you the boy's father?" Georgia asked. "The one who's in the pressure chamber now?"

The old man nodded, but didn't speak.

"I know how concerned you must be, sir, but you're wrong about the experiment part. Dr. Alexander explained to me before Guy was operated upon about the hazards involved, but there was no other chance for my husband—except death. Then tonight—" Her voice broke for a moment. "Tonight he told me he had to remove Guy's last chance of pulling through this so your son could be placed in the chamber. If Dr. Alexander was what you say he is, the last thing he would have done would be to make certain the failure of an operation that could make him world-famous—even to save your son."

III

The two and a half hours Greg decided upon for the first hyperbaric treatment had ended and the occupants of the chamber were waiting for the pressure of air within the steel tank to be reduced gradually to normal. Because of the high pressure Greg had dared to use initially, decompression would take nearly an hour and already the air in the tank was perceptibly cooler as its heat was dissipated, the reverse of what had taken place during compression. Of the effect on the patient, there could hardly be any doubt now; Ted was sleeping quietly and his skin was almost as cool as Greg's own.

"I heard about the meeting of the Board of Trustees this afternoon, Dr. Alexander," said Hans. "What will happen tomorrow morning?"

"We've only postponed the end, I'm afraid," said Greg. "If I had been able to keep Guy Merchant alive even through tomorrow, enough people might have been impressed by the operation and the new plan for the vote to go in favor by a close margin."

"Do you think you could have kept Merchant alive?" Dr. Gann asked.

"I don't know. But at least we had a chance of winning—until this boy turned up with an otherwise fatal anerobic infection."

"I'm glad the decision wasn't mine to make," said the anesthesiologist.

"You would have come up with the same answer, Lew. How could you balance the life of a man more than sixty years old, with advanced arteriosclerosis throughout his body, against that of any young man in his prime?"

IV

Bob Johnson had been at Guy Merchant's bedside ever since Greg had gone to the emergency room to see Ted Hunter. For a while the improvement brought about by removing fluid from around his heart gave some promise of holding, but, as the hours passed, it proved to be only temporary. The respirator continued to pump pure oxygen into Guy Merchant's lungs, but the duskiness of his fingertips, ear lobes and lips slowly deepened, mute proof that not enough oxygen was reaching the tissues through the severely crippled lungs to preserve life.

Knowing that the heart was the heaviest user of oxygen in the body, Bob was surprised that the gift Frank Lawson had given Guy Merchant continued to beat as strongly as it did in the face of the steadily diminishing supply of the vital element. Finally, however, the pulse rate, visible upon the flashing pattern of the electric monitor over the nurses' station, began to increase as the heart strove to answer the call of oxygen lack in its own tissues. Like a fire whose fuel is curtailed, the amplitude of the heartbeat slowly diminished and was barely distinguishable when Bob went to the door of the waiting room and called Georgia Merchant.

"Is it over?" she asked as he led her into the room.

"Not yet, but it can only be a few minutes more. He hasn't been conscious since early this morning."

Gradually the wavy lines on the monitor tube flattened out, then failed altogether and, switching the controls, Bob ran a brief record of the electrocardiogram upon a moving strip of paper. When the delicate pen that normally recorded the tiny electrical current emanating from the heart while functioning failed to move, he reached over and turned off the respirator.

"I'm sorry, Mrs. Merchant," he said. "We almost succeeded."

"Nobody could have done more than Dr. Alexander and the rest of you did," she said. "I'd like to stay long enough to thank him, if I may."

"He should be out of the pressure chamber in about another hour," said Bob. "The way it's snowing outside, you couldn't even get to your hotel before morning anyway, so why don't you just stay here?"

"I think I will, thank you. After all, it has almost become like home."

"Is there anything we can do, Mrs. Merchant?" Peter Carewe asked when she came back into the waiting room, but Georgia shook her head.

"No. Dr. Johnson says I can stay here until morning."

"Of course you can," said Helen, and drew Georgia over to sit beside her. "You and your husband were a team for a long time, weren't you?"

"We were together over twenty-five years. It will be rough without Guy, but I'm still going to do what we were hoping to do together, organize a traveling show of my own. Guy's insurance will help to launch it."

"I'd like to help, too, Mrs. Merchant." Sam Hunter's voice startled the others in the room.

"I appreciate your offer, Mr. Hunter," she said. "But the man whose statue stands in the hospital lobby once said: *'Greater love hath no man than this, that he lay down his life for a friend.'* So I guess Guy played his greatest role tonight. Your helping me now would be like paying Guy for what he did for your son, and I know he wouldn't want that."

No one spoke in the room for a long moment; then Sam Hunter stood up suddenly and went to the telephone at the nursing station. "Do you know the number of the Clinic Inn?" he asked the nurse there.

"Certainly, sir," she said. "Shall I dial it for you?"

"Please."

She dialed quickly, then handed him the phone.

"Ring Dr. Edward McDougal's suite," those in the waiting room heard him say, and, after a brief pause, he spoke again:

"I want you to call off your dogs when the trustees meet in the morning, Ed."

There was another pause, apparently while Ed McDougal tried to argue, but the old man cut him off sharply:

"Never mind why, just give up your opposition to Dr. Alexander's plan or there'll be none of my money in that new medical school you want to build down home. And tell Henry Anders I'll expose that real estate scheme of his, too, if he so much as opens his mouth at the meeting tomorrow."

Sam Hunter hung up before anything else could be said and came back into the waiting room to his chair. After a moment, Helen went over and pulled up a chair beside him.

"I was sure you would do the right thing, when you knew the truth," she said.

"My son may still die."

"At least he's had the only possible chance there could be of saving him. I've been doing the cultures for Greg Alexander's research with this type of infection; it's really miraculous the effect that a hundred per cent oxygen in the pressure chamber has upon them. Greg had everything to lose by not taking the transplant case into the chamber but he took Ted instead, because he knew there was no other way of saving him."

"It seems that I've been wrong about a lot of things lately."

Sam Hunter turned toward where Vivian was sitting near Georgia Merchant and Peter Carewe.

"Young lady," he started to call.

"Her name is Vivian," Helen said quickly and moved to another chair.

"Vivian," he said.

The girl hesitated, then rose and came over to where the old man was sitting.

"You have every reason to hate me," Sam Hunter began, but Vivian interrupted quickly.

"Ted didn't and neither do I, Mr. Hunter; it's just that he wanted to make his own way. He would have, too, if that splinter hadn't caused so much trouble. Did you know he's already enrolled at the Harvard Graduate School of Business in the fall?"

The old man shook his head.

"I've been taking lessons in stenography and typing, too, so I could work to help. He was going to surprise you by sending you an invitation to his graduation."

As he fumbled for her hand, Sam Hunter suddenly looked every day of his sixty-eight years. When Vivian smiled and reached up to take it in hers, he moved his chair closer to her and put his arm about her shoulders. With the old and the young strengthening each other, they waited for whatever was to come.

V

It was almost eleven when the elevator door opened in the corridor outside the waiting room and Greg Alexander stepped out. He glanced once at the monitor which had been recording Guy Merchant's heartbeat and, when he saw that it was dark, needed no other confirmation that his first heart-lung transplant was dead—and with him, his hopes. Straightening his shoulders, he went to the door of the waiting room.

"Ted's going to be fine," he told the small group sitting there.

"Then he's not dying?" Sam Hunter asked.

"The infection is under control. He'll need a few more treatments with oxygen under pressure, of course—"

"But no amputation?" Vivian asked.

"No more surgery. I found the rest of the splinter and removed it."

He turned to Georgia. "I'm sorry, Mrs. Merchant. I hope you see that I had no other choice."

"I understand, Doctor—and so would Guy."

VI

The rotunda of the hospital was empty when Helen and Peter paused in the shadows at the foot of the great statue shortly after midnight.

"I guess Georgia Merchant was right about her husband playing his greatest role tonight," said Peter. "But my plans for this evening certainly went to pieces."

"*'Oh what a tangled web we weave, when first we practice to deceive,'*" said Helen with a smile. "Except this wasn't your first practice, was it?"

"I refuse to answer on the grounds of self-incrimination. But you could end my deceiving by marrying me—now."

"Are you absolutely sure?" Her eyes were shining.

"From this day forward. Will you be my wife, Doctor?"

"This afternoon, I was prepared to go away with you for the weekend and let it end—"

"It couldn't end there," he interposed quickly. "Surely you know that now."

"What I'm trying to tell you, darling, is that being with Vivian—and with Georgia Merchant—has given me a different viewpoint on marriage. If you're willing to risk your freedom, I'll risk my independence."

"Sounds like an even swap," he said, tucking her arm beneath his. "The snow has stopped and it's not far to Elkton; if people can't still get married there at any time of the day or night, we'll sit in an all-night diner drinking coffee and holding hands until the marriage license bureau opens. How would you like to fly with me to California and hunt viruses on your honeymoon?"

"It sounds exciting. But are you sure you want to give up being the Doctor from WHO?"

"I won't call him until tomorrow but Lars Nordstrom will be happy to learn then that he's about to acquire a top-flight laboratory specialist for his staff. From now on, we'll be the Doctors from WHO—the hottest team of bacterial troubleshooters in the field."

VII

Greg had walked with Sam Hunter to the rotunda. They arrived just as Helen and Peter went hand in hand out into the night. "I owe a lot to those two—and to you," the old millionaire said.

"Forget about me," said Greg. "I was only doing my job as a doctor."

"Even if it means I still fight you tomorrow?"

Greg glanced up at the marble features of the statue and was not surprised when it appeared to be smiling again.

"I've got an idea that even you couldn't defeat me in the long run now, Mr. Hunter," he said. "This hospital was built by a man with a dream that's lived on after his death. I suppose it could be called a form of immortality."

"No man ecould wish for greater," Sam Hunter agreed.

"You and I both lost sight of the truth of that dream for a while," said Greg. "You, in the fear that the spirit of the man who conceived it might be lost in the new; I, by not having the courage to let the new dream speak for itself and taking what might be called less honorable measures to advance it."

"The new hospital isn't built yet," Sam Hunter reminded him.

"It will be; I stopped worrying about that yesterday morning at dawn, when I realized that Dr. Anders knew exactly what he was doing when he put the provision in his will that the statue must remain the center point of any new hospital. You see, he knew any surroundings that preserved this"—he put his hand upon the marble and could almost believe it was warm with life—"would also preserve the true spirit of his dream."

"I guess you and I have been concerned about the same thing," Sam Hunter admitted. "We just went about it in different ways."

"Ted's going to be all right, and as a doctor I'd advise you to get some rest," said Greg. "I'll be expecting you to do battle with me tomorrow if I come up with something unworthy of The Clinic and the man who founded it—as I seem to have done two years ago when this controversy first began."

"We may not always be on the same side, Doctor," said the old multimillionaire. "But I've got an idea that we're working for the same goal—and that's what really counts. Good night."

"Good night, sir."

Greg looked at his watch as the spare, erect figure disappeared through the front door. In two more hours he would have to take Ted Hunter back into the hyperbaric chamber, but he'd still come out well before dawn.

And he knew Jeanne would be there, flushed and rosy from sleep, when he came home.

Women in White

CHAPTER ONE

I

June in Miami is much like midsummer farther north, with the difference that the constant sea breeze, sweeping westward across the towering skyline of the famous resort hotels marking the Golden Strand of Miami Beach, plus the sparkling blue waters of Biscayne Bay separating the two cities, tempers both heat and humidity to a pleasant, languorous warmth. The rustle of palm fronds is a constant soft obbligato beneath the more strident theme of automobile motors, the deep staccato roar of motorboat engines, and the higher-pitched whine of jet airplanes beginning the descent to Miami International Airport, one of the busiest in the country.

It was just a quarter to three on a Tuesday afternoon when Helga Sundberg left the rear entrance of Bayside Terrace. The former luxury hotel had been converted to apartments when four blocks of prime bay-front land just north of downtown Miami were turned into the sprawling new Biscayne University Medical Center, with the twenty-story hospital tower its central point. Inhabited largely by the faculty and staff of the center, the old hotel stood in the midst of a tropical garden surrounding the swimming pool where a few of its residents fortunate enough to have the day off were splashing or sunning.

Crossing the putting green beyond the pool, Helga didn't bother to think how nice it would be to swim or lie in the sun; there would be plenty of time for that over the weekend, when she would be off duty from Friday night until Monday afternoon. Immediately ahead was the daily reality of her job as nursing supervisor in the combined medical Intensive Care Units of the great hospital during the eight hours between three and eleven that always brought a succession of small crises, and sometimes larger ones, when the decisions and prompt actions of a highly trained and resourceful ICU nurse could easily make the difference between life and death.

Across the green spread of lawn separating Bayside Terrace from Biscayne General, Helga could see the three-to-eleven shift coming on duty, a brigade of women in white converging upon the towering citadel of the great hospital in a thrice-daily assault. At the concrete marquee over the main entrance, the purring engine of a city bus spilled a barrage of exhaust fumes into the atmosphere as it disgorged a chattering bevy of women in all sizes, shapes, ages, and variety of uniforms. Behind the bus a taxi slid to a stop and five nurses emerged, scrabbling in handbags for change to pay the driver. In the line of cars waiting to approach the marquee a husband, eager to relinquish a white-clad wife and thereby gain eight hours of relative freedom, honked his car horn impatiently. And from the multilevel parking garage across the boulevard, lines of nurses in white nylon, attendants in pink or blue, cafeteria personnel in pale green, and an occasional visiting doctor in summer seersucker converged upon the crossing lines or waited for the light to change.

Reluctant to leave the sunlight for the atmosphere of tension that invariably greeted her when she opened the doors to the main ICU section which, with the adjoining Emergency Department, occupied the rear half of the hospital's ground floor, Helga Sundberg turned away from the main entrance. Following a graveled path, she skirted the bulkhead separating the water from the garden, her goal the Emergency Department entrance at the rear of the hospital.

Tall, blonde, blue-eyed, Helga was vigorously alive with the healthy beauty of her Nordic heritage. Her body, too, in a white orlon pants suit, was as symmetrically proportioned as if her measurements had been calculated by a computer, instead of being the result of a casual encounter between sperm and ovum, each bearing its varied quota of the ultra-microscopic genes that control heredity. What was more, like the healthy human animal she was, she ate what she wanted when she wanted it and had never been sick a day in her twenty-five years of vigorous and uninhibited living.

Pausing for a moment on the bulkhead, the tall nurse watched the joyous leaps of mullet in the bay that stretched here for almost a mile between beach and mainland. No one knew just why a distinctly lower-class fish like mullet—whose major claim to immortality was the fact that, fried in hot fat with a corn-meal-based delicacy called a "hush puppy," it turned into a dish fit for the gods—chose on bright warm days to quit its normal watery environment in ecstatic leaps that often carried it as much as three feet into the air before falling back with a splash. Unless it was from the sheer joy of living or, perhaps more likely, while playing a game of hide-and-seek with some finny predator beneath the surface.

On a solitary concrete piling, barnacle-covered where it jutted from the water as the sole remains of the pier that had served the hotel for a promenade in better days, sat a morose-looking, sleepy-eyed pelican. An almost grotesque gargoyle in repose, it turned into a thing of startling grace and beauty when, with a few flaps of its wings, it rocketed upward, to plunge in an arrow-straight dive into the bay. Seconds later the grayish bird emerged, flapping awkwardly toward its perch upon the crumbling piling, water streaming from its beak around the silvery body of the fish it had captured for its dinner and which, once again perched on the piling, it proceeded to devour with almost obscene relish.

Nearer the bulkhead, where the mud-sand bottom had been laid bare for a few feet by the receding tide, fiddler crabs scurried about, each carrying a single huge claw before it, like a small boy stumbling reluctantly toward his weekly music lesson, bearing his violin case before him. And in the shallows a few snowy egrets stalked majestically on pipestem legs, spearing an unwary minnow or a small scuttling crab every now and then with rapierlike bills.

Where a side path joined the graveled walk that followed the bulkhead, Helga turned reluctantly away from the water, intending to enter the hospital through a door beside the circular drive and ambulance unloading platforms at the entrance to the Emergency Department. The sound of an automobile horn blaring in frantic haste and the anguished squeal of brakes and tires stopped her short, however, as she was opening the side door of the Emergency Room. Turning toward the source of the sound, she saw a station wagon, driven so fast that it barely managed to negotiate the circular drive giving access to the ambulance unloading platforms, come to a screaming stop.

The woman driving the wagon piled out in frantic haste and fell to one knee, only managing to save herself from sprawling full length on the cement by catching the side of the ramp. Helga instinctively started down the ramp to help but the woman waved her back.

"I'm all right, nurse," she said, recognizing Helga's white uniform. "It's my little girl. She's choking to death!"

Moving quickly to the door of the station wagon, Helga pulled it open. The child lying on the front seat appeared to be about four. Her lips and ear lobes were dark from what Helga recognized immediately as the cyanosis of oxygen lack, her skin was dusky from the same cause, and her chest heaved as she tried to suck air into her lungs but without avail, obviously because of an obstruction.

"She was gulping a wiener," the mother started to explain but Helga didn't stop to listen. Picking up the limp burden of the child, she ran up the ramp and through the swinging doors into the Emergency Room itself.

The place was oddly deserted for an area that was usually busy. Helga understood the reason, when she glanced through the door of the small surgery at one side of the Emergency Room and saw the familiar stocky form of Dr. Michael Raburn. The Surgical Fellow, who was also director of Emergency Services, was bending over a wound he was suturing and a spattering line of tiny blood-stains across the front of the surgeon's gown told Helga he was coping with the serious emergency of a cut artery. Dr. Nolan Gaither, the interne on duty in the ER, was also gowned and gloved and stood across from Mike Raburn holding a forceps ready. The seven-to-three nursing supervisor was standing by too, ready to hand the surgeons whatever instruments or dressings might be needed from the sterile reserve table that was always kept set up in anticipation of just such an emergency as they were treating now.

Recognizing that she could expect no immediate help from the ER crew, Helga moved quickly with her burden into the nearest of the half dozen examining-treatment cubicles lining the side of the main Emergency Room. Draping the small form of the child over the examining table, head downward, she gave her a sharp whack between the shoulder blades, hoping to jar loose the bread or meat, which both logic and experience with this not uncommon Emergency Room problem told her was obstructing the opening into the larynx called the glottis and blocking the entrance of air into the lungs by way of the trachea, or windpipe.

When a second whack, even harder than the first, still brought no results, Helga knew more drastic measures must be taken and wasted no time in calling for help. Lifting the child, she stretched her out on the table, this time on her back, with her head hanging over the end in a position designed to facilitate exposing the glottis, if possible, and removing the obstruction.

"Can I do anything, Miss Sundberg?" A student nurse had appeared at the entrance to the cubicle.

"Keep her neck hyperextended," said Helga and, relinquishing the child's head to the nurse, looked for the laryngoscope and tenaculum forceps that should have been on the small table in the corner. They weren't there, but something else was—a sterile needle-catheter setup used for starting continuous intravenous injections, the whole enclosed in a transparent plastic envelope. And with it, Helga saw a chance to save the child, whose feeble attempts at respiration had now all but ceased.

Mike Raburn had lectured briefly only last week on a recently reported method of by-passing the obstruction in cases such as this by means of just such a needle-catheter as lay on the table. And as she started tearing open the plastic protecting it from contamination, Helga's mind was rehearsing the steps he had outlined at the monthly conference of the ICU and Emergency Department staff, comprising the most knowledgeable group of people in dealing with life or death situations at the entire medical center.

While Helga's left hand explored the child's Adam's apple—the cartilage box protecting the larynx and vocal cords—the fingers of her right hand were busy removing the needle-catheter, with its plastic disposable syringe attached and the point of the needle encased within the nylon sheath projecting perhaps half an inch beyond the tip of the catheter. Feeling along the series of cartilage rings of the trachea, she located the cricothyroid membrane just below the Adam's apple. And setting the point of the needle against the now dark blue skin of the unconscious child's neck, she angled it downward about forty-five degrees before thrusting the point through the skin, the lining membrane, and into the trachea.

A quick pull on the plunger of the attached disposable syringe brought air into the barrel, confirming that the needle point had penetrated the respiratory tract itself. Holding the shaft steady, Helga pushed the needle inward about another quarter of an inch, before starting to work the nylon sheath that almost covered it down over the point now resting inside the respiratory passage.

When she withdrew the needle from inside the catheter, leaving the latter in place, air immediately whistled through it. But knowing more would be needed if the near asphyxiated child were to be saved before oxygen lack endangered vital brain tissues, the nurse took down the emergency oxygen tube hanging from a hook attached to the wall panel in each of the cubicles.

The open end of the oxygen tube slipped over the plastic flange at the outer end of the catheter without difficulty. When it was secure, Helga reached for the control valve on the wall beside the oxygen supply and began to turn it slowly. In his lecture, Mike Raburn had emphasized that the valve must be opened carefully, lest the pressure from the main supply of oxygen piped throughout the hospital overinflate the lungs and damage the delicate air sacs.

As Helga listened to the hiss of the gas through the catheter into the little girl's respiratory passage, however, something Mike had failed to mention happened. When the positive pressure built up in lungs straining for air suddenly exceeded the atmospheric pressure forcing the meat fragment against the glottis, the end of the wiener popped from the small throat like a bullet, splattering with catsup and mustard the white uniform of the student nurse who was holding her head. At the same moment the little girl gave a gasping cry, sucking air into her lungs along with the oxygen that was whistling through the catheter. Almost immediately, too, the color of her lips and skin began to improve rapidly as the vital gas passed through the lining membrane of the lung air sacs and into her bloodstream, where it was absorbed by the hemoglobin in oxygen-starved red blood cells.

"Your baby's going to be all right," Helga assured the mother, who had stopped crying and was watching with fascinated eyes the tense drama being enacted in the narrow cubicle.

"Is—is that the piece of meat?" The mother pointed to the section of wiener resting in the lap of the student nurse.

"The cause of all the trouble." Helga picked up the small fragment. "When I gave her oxygen through the small tube, it blew out the obstruction."

"But it's so small. How could anyone choke to death on something as small as that?"

"What happened, Miss Sundberg?" Six feet two, with the broad shoulders of the All-American fullback he'd been at Harvard, Mike Raburn stood in the entrance to the cubicle. He had stripped off the sterile gloves he'd worn during the surgical procedure, but still wore the operating gown, with the line of small bloodstains across the front from the spurting artery he'd been forced to ligate.

"She just saved my daughter's life, that's what," said the mother. "Where were you, Doctor?"

"He was operating," said Helga.

"On a severed artery," Mike added.

"She aspirated part of a hot dog." Helga wondered why the tips of her fingers had started to tingle. "There was no laryngoscope around, so I used that needle-catheter technique you lectured on last week."

"I'm glad to see it works so well. We'll leave the catheter in awhile, but I'll cut down the oxygen." Mike reached up to the control valve on the wall panel and closed it slowly until the hiss of gas through the catheter was barely audible. "Don't want to overinflate her lungs." When he turned to face Helga again, he reached out suddenly, however, and took the flanged connection of the catheter from her hands. "Wait in my office, Miss Sundberg," he said.

"I'm late for—" Helga shook her head to clear it, and didn't succeed. "Yes, Dr. Raburn," she managed to say.

"Take this tube, Miss Stern," she heard him tell the student nurse as she stumbled from the cubicle, but his voice sounded strangely distant. Nor could she understand why her legs felt as if the muscles were gone and why the white tiled walls were swinging slowly in a wide arc. She didn't even realize Mike Raburn was just behind her until she felt his hands beneath her elbows guiding her through a door and easing her into a comfortable chair in his office.

"Don't try to get up," he said firmly. "Back in a second."

When he returned he was carrying a mug of steaming coffee from the urn that stayed hot night and day in the utility room.

"Drink this," he commanded, handing it to her, "all of it."

As Helga obeyed, a wailing cry came from outside the office, followed by the unmistakable sound of vomiting. Mike left and when he came back perhaps five minutes later Helga was finishing the last of the coffee. He took the mug from her hand and put it on the desk.

"Is the little girl okay?" Helga managed to ask but the voice that spoke sounded only faintly like her own.

"Fine. She emptied her stomach and was still yelling, so I removed the catheter. What about you?"

"My fingers still tingle and I feel like I could pass out any minute."

"You realize what a chance you just took, don't you?" His voice was suddenly harsh and accusing. "That procedure's so new it was only reported in the *Journal* of the AMA two weeks ago. You didn't wear sterile gloves either and there was no sign of antiseptic on the skin of her neck."

"What the hell did you expect me to do?" The unjustness of his accusation brought a sudden surge of anger. "That girl was dying."

"I know." His voice had changed again and Helga suddenly realized that her anger had quite washed away the feeling of faintness. When she looked at Mike, too, she saw that he was smiling and wondered how she could ever have thought him ugly.

"Damn you, Mike Raburn," she said.

"That's better," he told her.

"What happened to me anyway?"

"Stress reaction. In order for you to cope with a life or death situation promptly the way you did, a lot of adrenalin had to be pumped into your bloodstream from the suprarenal glands. When the emergency was over, you didn't need the extra adrenalin any longer but it was still there and your body reacted to it."

"Then you deliberately made me mad just now so I would burn it up?"

"Right."

"That was a dirty trick. If you weren't so darned big, I'd sock you."

"Be my guest." He turned his face so his jaw was exposed.

"And break my hand? No, thank you."

When he turned to look at her again, there was an odd look in his eyes, as if he were seeing her for the first time—and liking what he saw.

"How long have we known each other?" he asked.

"Almost two years. Since Carolyn and I came here from Brazil."

"Brazil?" He frowned. "What in the world were you two doing there?"

"Nursing in a mission hospital."

"You—a missionary?"

"I said I was nursing—and no cracks about my being better suited for the role of Sadie Thompson."

"No cracks," he promised. "I was just thinking that for the past two years I've seen you only as a tall, beautiful broad who's also my best friend's girl."

"I'm nobody's girl, except when I choose to be. Besides, Ed Vogel and I broke off two weeks ago."

"He didn't tell me—but then I guess being dropped by you isn't something a man would boast about. What happened—if that's not being too inquisitive?"

"Ed and I had gotten to where we were taking each other for granted. When that happens you either break off or get married—and I'm not ready for that."

"I'd have thought Ed was the sort of doctor a nurse would marry."

"He is, but I've seen too many of these medical center marriages turn sour after the husband finishes a residency, or a fellowship, and goes out into practice."

Mike Raburn frowned. "Maybe I'm dense—but you seem to have left me somewhere."

"Ed is to cardiology what you are to surgery—the hottest young doctor on the staff. Even if he stays here and goes into the Private Diagnostic Clinic—"

"The nearest thing to private practice a faculty member can have," Mike interjected.

"Exactly. Actually it wouldn't make any difference where Ed goes, though. A good doctor in private practice jumps into an income bracket he never even dreamed of being in, with all the fringe benefits."

"Membership in the country club, Wednesday afternoon golf—"

"Plus nurses and technicians, to say nothing of divorcees and debutantes on the make," said Helga. "Of course if his wife has taken care of herself and still makes the right sort of a production out of their love life, she may be able to hold him against that kind of competition. But you've been around the medical scene long enough to know it doesn't usually happen that way."

"We see 'em in here every few days with migraine headaches, colon spasm, or an overdose or morphine snitched from the husband's medical bag," he agreed. "They exhaust themselves at the wheel of a station wagon, taking the kids to speech class and ballet school, or working with the medical auxiliary because they think it will help their husband's practice."

"But when hubby comes home at night, what does he find? A tired wife who doesn't feel like taking a bath and dousing herself with perfume before putting on the sexiest lounging pajamas she can buy, and making like

Cleopatra giving Julius Caesar the hots."

Mike suddenly doubled up with laughter. "You're making Shakespeare turn over in his grave," he protested.

"Old Shakey knew enough about human nature to bring a sexy Mark Antony on the scene just about the time Julius' prostate was making him get up two or three times a night," said Helga. "But the reverse happens in a lot of doctor marriages, when hubby starts watching the women in white who run the average medical community. Unless she's a knockout, a wife in a plaid skirt and loose sweater can't compete with a nurse or technician in tight-fitting nylon, or even a secretary in boots and a mini. Before she even knows it, wifey finds herself on the losing end of a divorce."

"Are you going to be the *femme fatale* who takes him away from his wife?" Mike asked.

"I don't fool around with married men," Helga said indignantly. "I'll go on having my fun until I'm about thirty-five and then I'll pick me a successful doctor of forty-five or fifty whose wife is dead or who's been divorced."

"What about love?"

"Love is for youth—what I'll be looking for is security and affection. I'll be a damned good wife, too, so even if the upkeep is high, he'll be able to afford the sort of bargain he'll be getting. I'll see that we have only upper-echelon friends and in a pinch I might even become president of the medical auxiliary, when he's elected to head the state association. But the most important thing is I'll keep myself so desirable that he'll be eager to come home at night. And when his sexual vigor starts to wane, I know just the sort of hors d'oeuvres that will make his gonads shift into high."

"Stop it!" Mike protested. "You're making me look forward to growing old."

"And I'll be looking for employment if I don't get over to ICU and relieve Carolyn."

"Tell her I kept you. Today you're a heroine, I'm going to nominate you for a Carnegie Medal."

"ICU nurses don't get medals. You ought to know that."

"Or Emergency Room surgeons." His craggy face softened once more into a smile and his dark eyes were warm enough to step up her pulse a beat or two. "It looks like we'll just have to organize a mutual admiration society—and come to think of it, that's not a bad idea."

"Roger." She stood up, swaying a little. But when he reached out to steady her, she pushed his hand away.

"Keep your paws to yourself, Doctor," she said with mock severity. "I never play around on duty."

"For which that little girl out there can be thankful. I guess that makes us two of a kind, Miss Sundberg—and a rare kind at that."

II

In the office of Dr. Jeffry Toler, provost of Biscayne University Medical School and chief administrative officer of the new university medical center, Dr. Rebecca Dalton put down the magazine she had been holding, but not reading, when the door to the outer office opened. Slender, auburn-haired and of medium height, Rebecca was as distinctly feminine, and as forthright, as her biblical namesake. The starched long white coat she wore was emblematic of the medical faculty, and the coiled tubing of the stethoscope peeping from a side pocket indicated that her field was medicine, not surgery. At thirty-two, she was already an associate professor of medicine in the school and a highly respected cardiologist in her own right, as well as a beautiful and highly sensitive woman who was also deeply troubled.

"Forgive me, please, Rebecca." The two doctors were friends of long standing and Jeffry Toler's voice was warm as he came over to where she was sitting and bent to kiss her cheek. "Manning Desmond collared me in the parking garage as I was coming back from Rotary. Your division chief can say less in more words than anyone I know."

Rebecca smiled. "Dr. Desmond taught me more about the human heart than all the doctors I've studied with put together so I can forgive him the verbosity."

"I would be more inclined to call much of it verbiage," Toler said somewhat dryly as he took the tall chair behind his desk and swung it around to face Rebecca. "I imagine you already saw this," he added, opening the afternoon edition so she could see the headline: JURY EXONERATES DR. DALTON IN HEART TRANSPLANT DEATH.

"I missed the radio announcement but it was all over the hospital immediately."

"I'm not surprised. My secretary always knows what's happening around here long before it comes to my attention."

"Dr. Desmond called me before he went to Rotary, Jeffry. I imagine he talked to you about Dr. Barrows' application for retirement."

"The request will be presented to the joint meeting of the Hospital Board of Directors and the Executive Committee this afternoon at five. Manning tells me Jake Barrows has been having angina ever since that coronary three months ago, so there shouldn't be any hitch."

"The medical indications are perfectly clear," she agreed.

"Did Desmond tell you he plans to recommend to the Board this afternoon that you be raised to the rank of full professor and appointed chief of the Cardiology Section?"

"Does it have to come right now?" Rebecca asked quickly. "I'm only thirty-two and you'll be promoting me over several older heart specialists."

"None of whom are as capable as you—or want the job."

"Lately I've been wondering just how capable I really am, Jeffry. It seems—"

"If you're blaming yourself for part of what happened to Ken, don't. Lots of husband-and-wife teams—"

"I was still largely responsible for selecting the cases for those heart transplants. Which makes me equally responsible with Ken for their deaths."

Caught up for perhaps the hundredth time in the past six months by the memory, and the horror, of what had followed, Rebecca turned to stare unseeingly at the large picture window behind the administrator's desk. And recognizing the source of her agony, Jeffry Toler didn't intrude into her thoughts immediately but removed his pipe from his coat pocket and took his time about stuffing and lighting it.

Nobody understood yet, although intensive research was being pursued by dozens of medical schools throughout the world, just why lymphoid cells in the body of a person saved from death by the transplant of a heart or other organ from another so often invaded, and sought to destroy, the very organ that made continued life possible for the recipient. And so no one had really been able to explain why the series of heart transplants Dr. Kenneth Dalton had performed so brilliantly over a period of about a year had suddenly begun to die, one by one, six months ago from the mysterious process called rejection.

As an expert cardiologist, Rebecca Dalton was quite aware that death always watched over the shoulder of a surgeon in the cardiovascular field, where Ken had already achieved a string of brilliant successes even before he started transplanting hearts. One slip, a moment's lessening of the surgeon's confidence in the skill of his own hands, even a minor failure in the complex armamentarium of technical aids that made such surgery possible, and death was always waiting to step in.

Two years ago Ken Dalton had startled the surgical world and the press alike by performing fifteen heart transplants in succession, without a single death on the operating table or in the early postoperative weeks. As head of the Cardiac Research Laboratory and one of the chief heart specialists at Biscayne General, Rebecca Dalton had personally selected the cases for transplant and evaluated the chances of failure. Not from the operation—for Ken Dalton had already honed his skill to a degree of perfection that had earned him a reputation for technical excellence equal to a DeBakey, a Shumway, or a Cooley—but from concomitant disease of the liver or other organs that made success unlikely.

The Emergency Room at Biscayne General and other neighboring hospitals had been the main source of donors and the case from which the court test sprang had seemed typical enough—at the start. Kept breathing mechanically by a resuscitator in the hands of the alert crew manning one of the crack Fire Department Rescue Squad units, a young woman with a massive brain hemorrhage from an automobile accident had been rushed to the Biscayne General Emergency Room from the Golden Glades Expressway.

Her heart was still beating when she was brought into the hospital, proving that it at least was alive. Not so, however, the brain, for the electroencephalogram, taken routinely on all such cases since Ken's spectacular success with heart transplants had created a continual demand for donors, had shown no action currents—the ultimate proof of brain death. While Kevin McCartney, the prospective recipient, waited, his failing heart barely able to maintain enough circulation to keep his brain alive, a frantic search for relatives of the doomed hemorrhage case who might give permission for the transplant had been carried on, with no result.

Three times the respirator had been stopped for five minutes, the period agreed upon in most hospitals as establishing death, but spontaneous respiration had not occurred and the brain waves, too, had remained nonexistent. Yet each time the respirator was reactivated and oxygen once more moved into the red blood cells by way of the lungs, the girl's heart had continued to beat—proof positive that it alone still possessed life. Finally Dr. Adrian Cooper, professor of forensic pathology in the medical school, and county medical examiner, had determined officially that death had occurred and approved opening the otherwise dead body to remove the heart.

It had been one of Ken's most exciting and brilliant operations, Rebecca remembered. An hour after the first incision, Kevin McCartney's new heart was beating strongly in a body revitalized by its presence. The postoperative course had been equally rapid and free from complications, too, and for the past year Kevin had been able to work part time as bartender in the Dolphin Lounge adjoining Bayside Terrace.

His testimony, plus that of the staff and Rebecca, had destroyed the contention of the plaintiff—a brother of the accident victim—that she had been technically alive when her heart was removed. In the face of the barrage of expert testimony brought to bear by the lawyers Jeffry Toler had employed on behalf of both Ken and the hospital, the jury had refused to believe that there had been any life in the body of the dead girl, save only her heart, now beating strongly in the chest of Kevin McCartney and thus saved from death.

Long before the case had even come to trial, however, the gulf developing between Ken and Rebecca had widened when earlier transplant cases, for whose escape from imminent death he had been so highly praised at the time of the original surgery, began to die from rejection.

"Did Ken call you from the courthouse?" Jeffry Toler's question shattered Rebecca's painful reverie.

"I haven't heard from him since I testified at the trial," she admitted.

"I was hoping—" Toler broke off speaking: the look in her eyes had given him the answer.

"The next move is Ken's," she said. "I've done all I can do."

"If he wasn't such a good friend, I'd have tried long ago to knock some sense into that hard head. Or maybe, since I'm a friend to both of you, I should still give it a try."

"You can't help the situation, Jeffry—not while Ken is convinced that I've gone farther in the medical side of heart disease than he has in the surgical."

"Hell!" Toler exploded. "Ken did some of the earliest transplants in this country and at one time was almost as famous as Christiaan Barnard. If you ask me, it's his ego that's to blame."

Rebecca shook her head. "The real trouble between Ken and me isn't ego, Jeffry. It's his conscience."

"How can that be, when he's always given his patients the best he has— and then some?"

"Ken's convinced that fourteen transplant cases died because he let enthusiasm get the better of his surgical judgment. I don't agree, but I'm sure his unconscious mind still blames me for encouraging him to operate on some patients he wasn't sure about."

"All of them lived through the early weeks after surgery."

"Until rejection killed them, yes."

"Then how could he blame you?"

"I'm not much on psychiatry, but I do know that the unconscious isn't always rational."

"I guess the story of your and Ken's marriage isn't so different from some others I've seen in the medical field, at that," Toler conceded. "Both of you were top rank in your fields—until Ken stumbled and decided he was out of the race."

"I've tried to tell him he isn't, but he won't listen."

"In a contest between husband and wife for success in their careers, it's usually the woman who drops out—to have babies."

"We tried, but with no luck."

"Your fault—or his?"

"Neither, according to Jerry Singleton. He says my reproductive system is absolutely normal, and Ken has enough active spermatozoa to impregnate every female in sight—"

"That might just start to happen, you know. This place teems with attractive single women, divorcees, and wives looking to better themselves."

"For God's sake, Jeffry!" Rebecca's voice rose to an almost hysterical note as the rigid control she'd been exercising over her own fears on just that subject suddenly snapped. "What else can I do?"

"You don't have to be letter perfect in everything."

"Suppose I interpret an electrocardiogram wrongly and some poor devil dies of coronary thrombosis, when he could have been saved by pumping heparin into his bloodstream to keep a clot from forming?" Rebecca demanded heatedly. "How long do you think I could live with myself?"

"I guess you're right. But it's hell to stand by and see two of the finest doctors I know of in their fields beat their heads against a stone wall— especially when I know you're eating your heart out into the bargain, Rebecca."

She reached across the desk to squeeze his hand in a gesture of gratitude. "I can at least thank you for caring, Jeffry."

"What do you want me to do about putting you up for promotion this afternoon? If you hold back, people will start jumping to conclusions."

"That I'm trying to save Ken's face?"

"What else? And frankly I don't think that would make the situation between you any better."

"Go ahead, then. Ken's on the Executive Committee, so he'll know about it anyway." She stood up. "I'd better get to work."

"I'll call you as soon as the meeting's over—not that there's any doubt of the decision."

Toler accompanied Rebecca out into the corridor and stood watching her thoughtfully as she walked down the hall, slim, proud, and very lovely, with the afternoon sunlight pouring through the window at the end of the corridor turning her auburn hair into a golden aureole. As the elevator door opened she turned with a parting wave in his direction, before stepping inside.

Back in his office, he turned the afternoon edition over and sourly studied the second-section headline: COUNCIL FINANCE CHAIRMAN ATTACKS HOSPITAL BOARD IN ROTARY SPEECH.

It was bad enough that he would have to watch Ken Dalton's face that afternoon, when Rebecca was promoted to a position in the Medical Department comparable to Ken's own status in Surgery, without having to listen to the fulminations of a politician like Ross McKenzie for an hour.

CHAPTER TWO

I

The clock over the main console of the nursing station said five after three and Carolyn Payson, nursing supervisor of the Consolidated Intensive Care Section, comprising the Medical, Pediatric, and Coronary Intensive Care Units for reasons of efficiency and the most effective use of highly trained personnel, was still on duty. She was considering calling Helga Sundberg at their Bayside Terrace apartment in the unlikely possibility that the other nurse had overslept, when the chime of the Patient Distress Alarm sounded.

One of the world's newest and most sophisticated hospitals—in both construction and function—Biscayne General had been carefully planned to make the maximum of expert care available to the sick or injured. The Emergency Room and adjacent Observation Ward, with the main waiting room and business office, occupied half of the first floor, the rest being devoted to the Intensive Care Units. Concentrated in one section were the expert nursing care, constant physician supervision, and highly sophisticated patient monitoring systems so important in all cases where life was in jeopardy—whether a child in respiratory distress or a heart threatened by the closing of one of its own arteries from coronary thrombosis.

A glance at the flashing red light on the Patient Selector, with its eight numerals and control buttons, told Carolyn the alarm had come from Cubicle Four, occupied by Carmelita Sanchez. And a flick of a switch produced the sharply delineated wave pattern of the electrocardiogram (ECG in correct parlance instead of the more commonly used EKG derived from its original German name) upon the master oscilloscope screen of the large monitor before her.

The select group of ICU nurses were so highly trained in cardiology that they were generally able to interpret an electrocardiogram more quickly and correctly than the average doctor. And as Carolyn watched the moving point of light outlining the ECG pattern upon the sensitized ground-glass screen of the monitor, she saw that, although the patient's pulse rate was somewhat increased, the heart function was still essentially normal—for one who had been in coma three weeks from the often fatal serum hepatitis.

From the elevation of the nurse's station, Carolyn could see all eight cubicles making up Section One of the ICU, a general-purpose medical ward for critically ill patients, as distinguished from the adjoining Coronary Intensive Care Unit, abbreviated naturally to CICU. And through the open glass door of Cubicle Four she could also see that the nurse bending over Carmelita Sanchez showed no sign of alarm.

Pressing the switch of the two-way communication system beside her, Carolyn spoke into the microphone. "Temperature rising, Ella?"

The startled nurse jumped, then leaned over the bed to speak into the grilled front of the internal communications unit on the wall. "Up half a degree, but there's no change otherwise."

"That was enough to set off the PDA. I'll call Dr. Vogel."

Switching the controls of the monitor screen back to their usual function of recording the vital signs, Carolyn reached for the telephone to call the Medical Fellow in charge of the intensive care patients in that category.

"Please ask Dr. Vogel to call the ICU," she told the paging operator.

"Dr. Vogel's out of the hospital for a few minutes, Miss Payson, but Dr. Raburn is taking his calls. Shall I have him call you?"

"Please." Carolyn knew that, although Carmelita Sanchez was technically a patient on the medical service, Mike Raburn had been interested in her ever since he'd performed a liver biopsy shortly after she was admitted to the hospital.

The phone at Carolyn's elbow started blinking moments later. When she picked it up, Mike Raburn's voice sounded in her ear.

"Trouble, Miss Payson?"

"Carmelita's temperature is rising again, Doctor."

"Any of her family there?"

"Only her fiancé, Miguel Quintera."

"Tell Miguel I'll be over to see Carmelita as soon as I'm free; this place has turned into a madhouse again. You'd better put the top half of the cooling blanket on Carmelita, too, but tell Miss Sundberg to watch her temperature closely. It goes down pretty fast with both blanket layers operating."

"Right." Carolyn hung up the phone and passed the order on to the nurse who was specialing Carmelita Sanchez.

Transferred from another hospital in coma two weeks ago, at the insistence of her fiancé upon his arrival in Miami from Spain, where he was a first-year medical student at the University of Madrid Medical School, the lovely Cuban girl was already in an advanced stage of serum hepatitis.

Although the virulent and often fatal liver infection was almost always contracted through transfusion with blood containing the dreaded Australian—shortened to Au—antigen, Carmelita had been inoculated with the virus accidentally. A graduate laboratory technician, she had been taking blood from a patient with the disease when a defective syringe broke, sending a sliver of bloodstained glass into her hand and inoculating her with the deadly Au virus.

Every available weapon had been used in Carmelita's behalf. Large amounts of glucose had been given intravenously to shore up the failing liver and provide much-needed calories to combat those being used up because of the steadily rising temperature. With repeated blood transfusions in large volume, the staff had sought to dilute the deadly virus to a point where the girl's own antibody-producing forces would be able to overcome the life-destroying agent.

But all measures had been to no avail and day after day the young Cuban first-year medical student had sat beside his fiancée or paced the nearby ICU waiting room, his dark eyes wordlessly accusing both doctors and nurses of a failure of which they were already disturbingly conscious, both his presence and the quietly breathing body of the lovely dark-skinned girl a constant reminder of their own helplessness.

"Was that the Patient Distress Alarm again, Miss Payson?" the soft voice of Miguel Quintera, who had been watching TV in the small staff lounge, asked at her elbow.

"Carmelita's temperature rose a little," Carolyn told him. "Dr. Raburn ordered the top of the cooling blanket put on."

"Why does he not come to see her?"

"He's tied up in the Emergency Room but will come up later."

"It doesn't matter." Quintera turned away, his slender shoulders drooping with weariness and loss of hope. "She is dying."

"Something may still happen to save her," said Carolyn. "Don't give up."

But even as she spoke, Carolyn Payson recognized that her voice carried no conviction. For who knew better than she that there were cases where no hope existed, either now or ever, no hope except the blessed relief of death that stubbornly refused to come?

II

"Female coming in," Dr. Valerie LeMoyne called out as she opened the door to the doctors' lounge adjoining the Operating Room Section on the third floor. "Keep decent."

"Be with you in a minute, Val." Dr. Jerry Singleton appeared briefly in the doorway leading to the shower and locker rooms. He wore a towel around his mid-section and his dark wavy hair was damp from the shower. "I want to talk to you."

Moving to the window, Valerie LeMoyne lit a cigarette. Of medium height, she was dark-haired, svelte, and inclined toward somewhat severe fashions bought during an annual vacation on the Continent. Today she was wearing a white nylon pants suit, but with her usual degree of chic.

Val's rise to professor and chief of the Anesthesiology Section at Biscayne General had been meteoric, since she'd come to the United States from Paris and the Sorbonne ten years ago for a residency in her field at Duke.

Jerry Singleton appeared a few minutes later. In double knit blue slacks, a bright blue shirt, maroon sports jacket, and white Italian shoes of soft leather with a crepe sole, he was as fine a specimen of genus *Homo medicus* as one was likely to see—a fact of which Val LeMoyne was physiologically quite aware.

"Without that shapeless hospital gown you insist on wearing at work, you're a very handsome woman, Val." Moving over to where she was standing by the window looking at the street below, he took one of her cigarettes and lit it for himself.

"Since nylon was invented," she said, "women in white have had a distinct advantage over others."

"It does give a better idea of what's beneath while still not removing the excitement of learning for yourself."

"Is that why you and Kay broke up?"

"The divorce was Kay's idea, not mine, but I can't really say I'm sorry; life is harrowing enough for a surgeon without a wife to nag him when he's late for dinner. Besides, Kay had worked enough in a big teaching hospital as a volunteer before we were married to know what goes on in one of the most highly sexed atmospheres existing anywhere—except maybe in a brothel. She refused to believe I wasn't making out on the side."

"Weren't you?" Val's tone held a tinge of mockery.

"Actually, I wasn't. I tried to convince Kay of that, even offered to leave the university and go out into private practice—"

"Where you would have made twice what you make here."

"And more. But I also like teaching, which was something else Kay couldn't understand. I guess because her father's a gynecologist who has made a fortune out of small fibroids."

"To a hysterectomy-minded surgeon they're worth their weight in gold," Val agreed.

"Until a patient drops dead on the day she's leaving the hospital, like the one I lost last week," said the surgeon glumly.

"Nobody can prevent pulmonary embolism, Jerry—just like we still don't know how to prevent the occasional anesthetic death for no reason anyone can find. They're simply hazards both surgeons and anesthesiologists have to face."

"Still, if I hadn't operated on that one, she wouldn't be dead."

"You're not going to let an unavoidable death throw you the way Ken Dalton has let those transplant deaths do him, are you?" she asked sharply.

"No." Jerry Singleton unconsciously straightened his shoulders, which had slumped momentarily. "Like you say, embolism is a normal hazard of even the simplest operation."

"Cheer up," said Val. "You've got a lot to live for, my friend. Just think of all the pleasure you're giving the women you go out with. And when you marry—"

"Oh, no! I'm not putting on the ball and chain again."

"That's what you're saying now. But from what I've seen of divorced men, it takes about a year for them to finish sowing all the wild oats they'd been dreaming about while they were married. Then they settle down and marry again, usually to someone very much like the wife they divorced."

"God forbid! Besides, Kay divorced me—"

"That doesn't make any difference. Still, you might be the exception. Certainly you're much too handsome and sexually attractive for anybody to believe you could really be a family man the second time around, Jerry. And from the hospital scuttlebutt, you've given what was obviously a natural talent for seduction quite a high polish."

Jerry Singleton grinned. "I have to do something in my spare time, and I don't like golf. Come to think of it—and this isn't the first time—why not join me in an exciting and tempestuous affair? I could show you some of the things I've learned."

"I came into the lounge for a cigarette, Jerry, not looking for an invitation to seduction."

"I know you like scuba diving. Why not go to the Keys with me this weekend?"

Valerie LeMoyne stubbed out her cigarette in an ashtray on the window sill before she answered—and hoped he didn't notice the sudden trembling of her hand.

"You're very sweet and very attractive, Jerry," she said on a deliberately casual note. "But I was badly hurt once, there's even a small scar left."

"Scarred hearts thrive on moderate exercise, my dear. All cardiologists recommend it."

"Fair enough," she said. "Will you give me a rain check?"

"Of course."

"I'll let you know Thursday evening." Val looked at her watch. "It's time to start the next case. Good hunting, Jerry."

III

Dr. Karen Fletcher finished her daily thirty laps of the Bayside Terrace swimming pool and climbed the ladder to the rim of the pool. Pulling off the rubber cap that had protected her silver-tinted hair from the water, she shook the silky pile loose until it tumbled about her shoulders. Moving to the beach chair, she picked up a large nubby towel and began to rub her body dry in the nylon tank suit that was almost as revealing as its absence would have been, not at all unconscious of the admiring eyes of a pair of medical students who had been dozing beside the pool until she came out and started swimming.

At thirty, Karen Fletcher had already achieved many of the goals she'd set for herself long ago, when she left the small Midwestern town that was her birthplace for college—and never returned. Already a championship swimmer in high school, she'd been able to parlay an athletic scholarship into a college pre-med course. And the decided flair for bacteriology and pharmacology she'd shown in college courses, plus her emergence as a serious contender for Olympic honors in swimming, had guaranteed her medical school tuition.

From there, Karen Fletcher's rise had been meteoric, for the most part because of a real ability and flair for the fields of pathology and toxicology, but to some extent because a petite beauty, whose pocket Venus proportions were exquisitely perfect, was enough of an anomaly in the musty basements of pathology laboratories to be notably distinctive. Assistant professor of pathology four years out of medical school, she had come to Biscayne University Medical School as an associate professor two years before.

When Karen bent to pick up a comb that had fallen out of the folded towel, one of the watching students gave a shrill whistle of appreciation.

"Cool it, fellows," she said. "The university frowns on faculty-student fraternizing."

"There's nothing fraternal about what I'm thinking right now, Dr. Fletcher." The shorter one, a merry-eyed Cuban, grinned impudently. "Is it true that you won a gold medal in the 1967 Olympics?"

"It was '68, Mendoza, don't make me any older than I am." Karen picked up a short terry robe from the chair and slipped her arms into it, hiding her torso but leaving the superb legs of a championship swimmer fully exposed.

"To me you're the epitome of the eternal female, Dr. Fletcher," said the dark-skinned Mendoza. "It's too bad you're a pathologist and all that loveliness has to be wasted on the dead."

Karen laughed as she picked up the magazine she had brought out with her, in case she felt like reading after her swim. *It has never been wasted yet, my friend,* she thought. *And never will be—not since the day I discovered how really valuable it is.*

Halfway across the stretch of lawn between the pool and the rear entrance to the Terrace, where Karen had an apartment, she came around a jacaranda bush that was a mass of violet-colored flowers and stopped suddenly to keep from running over a small boy of perhaps five. Squatting in the middle of the graveled walk leading from Bayside Arms, the large, less expensive garden apartment complex a good block away, to the old hotel and the hospital, he was panting audibly. But even if she hadn't recognized the boy, the odd ducklike posture and the bluish tint to his lips, ear lobes, and the skin of his torso, exposed by the brief shorts that were his only garment, would have told her medically trained mind that he suffered from congenital heart disease.

"Hello, Dr. Fletcher," said the boy, smiling.

"Are you all right, Dale?" Karen had recognized the small son of Peggy Tyndall, the physician's assistant who was also chief technician in the Cardiac Research Laboratory.

"I'm okay. Just stopped to get my breath."

"Do you have to rest more often lately?"

The tendency to squat suddenly at play and rest long enough to breathe freely again, plus the cyanotic hue of skin and mucous membranes, was characteristic of a heart malformed long before birth and unable to pump enough blood through the lungs to supply the body's need for oxygen.

"Maybe—when I run a lot." Dale jumped to his feet. "'Scuse me, Doctor. I gotta go."

"Where?"

"To see Kevin, he gives me beer."

"To a little boy like you? I can't believe it!"

Dale was gone, running toward the door leading into Bayside Terrace and the Dolphin Lounge, where Kevin McCartney was bartender. After a moment Karen followed but stopped at the door of the dim-lit lounge when she saw Dale climb confidently upon a stool at the end of the bar.

"There's my boy!" Kevin McCartney's rich Irish brogue came to Karen's ears as she watched. "What'll you have?"

"Beer," said Dale. "In a frosted mug—and one for Dr. Fletcher."

"Dr. Fletcher?" Kevin squinted toward the door. "Oh, hello, Doctor. I didn't see you."

"I followed Dale—when he told me you gave him beer."

Kevin laughed. "It's root beer. He likes it in a frosted mug—Western style. Can I get you anything?"

"No, thanks. I've been having my daily swim."

"Bet you could win another gold medal if they were staging the Olympics now. I watched on TV when you won in '68."

"I doubt that I'm in championship form right now, but thanks anyway," said Karen. "You see Dale often?"

"Nearly every day. Why?"

"Would you say he's getting more short of breath lately?"

"I'm okay, Dr. Fletcher," said Dale. "Next year I'm going to school. And when I get older, Dr. Dalton is going to operate on me, so I can play baseball like the other boys."

"I think you're right, Doctor." Kevin spoke softly. "But I didn't want to worry Peggy by mentioning it."

"I'll talk to her," said Karen. "Right now, I'd better go up and get a shower before this air conditioning gives me a cold."

"Any news about Dr. Cooper?" Kevin asked.

Two years away from retirement, Dr. Adrian Cooper, professor of pathology and head of the department, as well as medical examiner for the county, had been felled by a massive stroke, leaving him paralyzed for the past two months. As his second-in-command, so to speak, Karen Fletcher had headed the department with her usual efficiency, though on a temporary basis, ever since.

"I'm afraid it's not very good," she told Kevin.

"Too bad. He's a fine man."

"And a great doctor," Karen agreed. "So long, Dale."

"Good-by, Dr. Fletcher," said the boy as he climbed down from the stool. "Thanks, Kevin."

"Any time, Dale."

"*Madre de Dios!* What a woman!" Mendoza, the Cuban student, had entered the lounge by the side door and taken a stool at the far end of the bar. "Did you look at those gams, my friend—and what goes with 'em?"

"I gave up them games when Dr. Dalton put the new heart inside my chest," said the bartender. "What'll you have?"

"Beer to cool my fevered thoughts. Did you ever see as much woman crammed into such a small package?"

"We Irish don't waste time makin' over women the way you Latins do." Kevin grinned as he slid a tall stein of beer down the polished bar so it stopped directly in front of Mendoza. "We prefer the 'How 'bout it, babe?' approach. You'd be surprised how often it works, too."

"I'm not surprised, we Latins use it too," said Mendoza. "Know what the students call Dr. Fletcher?"

"I can imagine—but what is it?"

"The Black Widow."

"Why? She's certainly not black—"

"And not a widow, either, as far as I know. But something about her tells you, if she'd ever let you make love to her, she'd eat you alive."

"I suppose you'd like to be eaten?"

"You gotta go sometime." Mendoza shrugged. "And what better way?"

"I guess you've got a point there," Kevin admitted. "But she's a good doctor, isn't she?"

"I don't know how she'd be in practice, but as a pathologist she's tops. In fact she's so good as a teacher that for a little while you even forget she's a beautiful woman—and that's saying something. The students have started a pool on whether she'll take Dr. Cooper's place—for good."

"How are you betting?"

"On her, of course. That baby can have anything she wants—including me."

"Even if you're eaten up?"

Mendoza shrugged and drained the stein. "Like we were just saying, what a way to go!"

"Wait a minute," said Kevin, and Mendoza stopped in the doorway. "You're practically a doctor, aren't you?"

"Only one more semester to go. Why?"

"Did you see that boy that was just in here?"

"Sure. I've examined him in the Cardiac Outpatient Clinic, too."

"What's the outlook for him?"

"Not bad—with luck. He's got what's called the tetralogy of Fallot, which means the blood channels inside his heart are pretty well crossed up. Dr. Helen Taussig and Dr. Alfred Blalock in Baltimore worked out an operation years ago that corrects most of the trouble. It isn't very dangerous, either, but most heart surgeons nowadays like to wait 'til the child is around seven or eight, when the heart is large enough for them to use open heart surgery and they can do a better job. The risks aren't much greater than the Blalock-Taussig operation then either.''

"And afterwards Dale will really be practically normal?''

"Almost as if he'd been born that way." The Cuban gave Kevin an appraising look. "How about yourself, friend?''

"I'm fine, just fine," said Kevin heartily. "Going fishing tomorrow, down at Marathon.''

"The boat my family escaped in from Cuba landed at Marathon. I was only a boy but you can bet heaven won't look any better than that place did after five days at sea in an open yawl.''

IV

"Sometimes I wonder whether I'm really cut out for this business," Mike Raburn told Mrs. Faye Connor, three-to-eleven nursing supervisor for the Emergency Department, after talking to Carolyn Payson. "I'm always letting people I can't do anything for make me feel guilty.''

"That's what makes you stand out from the average run of doctors like a diamond in a ten-cent-store ring," said the veteran nurse. "The Cuban girl again?''

"And the medical student she's engaged to. Every time I make rounds and stop to see her, he looks at me like he expects me to pass a miracle and cure her.''

"That's what you get for building up the kind of reputation you have around here. What's happened to Carmelita now?''

"Her temperature just set off the PDA. Second time today.''

"I've never seen anyone as deep in hepatic coma as she is come out of it. Have you?''

Mike shook his head. "Never. I'm getting so I hate to even go by the room. She's so pretty, even through the jaundice, and Miguel's so young—it sort of gets you to look at them.''

"You could pass 'em up, you know. She's really on the medical service.''

"Yeah. But I still go, maybe because I'm nothing but a sloppy sentimentalist at heart.''

"Not at heart—all heart," the nurse corrected him. "Which reminds me—when are you going to get yourself a girl?''

"When I can find somebody who sees the beautiful spirit behind this mug of mine. Not thinking of getting divorced, are you?''

"If I were twenty years younger, I might. Now get out of here so I can do some work.''

A tall interne in rumpled whites appeared at the door of the nursing station. His face was flushed with annoyance. "A Negro woman's out there with a little boy, Mike. She won't let anybody see him but you.''

"Coming, Dr. Gaither." Mike winked at the nursing supervisor. "At least somebody loves me.''

"Don't go fishing for compliments. Everybody at Biscayne General loves you, Dr. Raburn, and you damned well know it.''

In the cubicle to which Dr. Nolan Gaither directed Mike, a tall, striking-looking Negro woman was standing beside the examining table, holding the hand of a boy of perhaps six who lay upon it. The child appeared to be unconscious but every few minutes he cried out and clutched at his abdomen, before lapsing into stupor again.

"Rachel Gates!" Mike Raburn's voice was warm. "What's wrong?"

"Thank God you're here, Dr. Raburn," said the mother. "Joe told me any time we got into trouble and I couldn't get our pediatrician, to come to you."

"This is Big Joe Gates's wife and his son Joey; they're old friends," Mike told the interne. "Dr. Nolan Gaither, Mrs. Rachel Gates."

"I'm sorry if I seemed huffy, Dr. Gaither," said the golden-skinned woman, "but I was worried."

"It's all right, Mrs. Gates. If I'd known your husband was the Snappers' star forward, I'd probably have given you the keys to the hospital."

"What happened, Rachel?" Mike moved into the cubicle and picked up the boy's wrist.

"Joey went to day camp this morning; it's run by our church and the bus picks him up at eight o'clock. The school nurse called me about an hour ago to say he was complaining of pains in his legs and stomach. By the time I got there he was like you see him now—in sort of a stupor."

"Was he all right yesterday?" The surgeon's big hand had been moving gently over the child's abdomen but lingered now just beneath the rib margin on the left side.

"Joey played ball with some neighbor kids after he came home from camp yesterday. We took Big Joe to the airport later; he's in San Francisco helping negotiate the new contract for the players' union. On the way home Joey insisted on stopping for some ice cream, he's crazy about that peppermint stick flavor at Howard Johnson's."

"So am I—and a few million other people."

Taking Dr. Nolan Gaither's hand in a casual gesture, Mike placed it on the upper left side of the boy's abdomen. The sudden alertness in Gaither's eyes told him the interne had detected the enlargement of the spleen beneath the ribs.

"Take a look at the nail beds, too," Mike added before turning back to the mother.

"Anything else you can tell me, Rachel?" He reached for an opthalmo-scope, hanging from a rack on the wall.

"Nothing that I know of. They said at the camp that he didn't fall or anything."

Separating the boy's eyelids, the big doctor flashed the light into the pupil. It contracted immediately, as it should, so he pulled down the eyelid itself and moved the bright spot of illumination about.

"Look at this," he told the interne, and Dr. Gaither transferred his attention from marking out the size of the spleen on the boy's abdomen with a wax pencil to the conjunctiva—the white part—of the eye.

"There was a report in one of the journals the other day about near obliteration of the capillaries in the conjunctiva," Mike said.

"I see that but—"

"Did you order any blood work?"

"The technician has already taken the blood. It should be ready in a few minutes."

"Mrs. Connor," Mike called to the nursing supervisor, "will you watch the patient while Dr. Gaither and I go to the laboratory?"

"Certainly, Doctor."

In the Emergency Department Laboratory, which had its own staff covering the ER itself, the Acute Observation Ward, and the several divisions of the ICU, a technician had just finished staining a blood smear. Taking the slide from her, Mike Raburn placed it beneath the microscope and focused the instrument carefully.

He already knew what to expect from the history, the fact that little Joey

Gates was black, and the near obliteration of tiny blood vessels in the lining of the eyelids—and he was not disappointed. Spread out on the slide in the bright light reflected up through the lens system of the microscope, the normally biscuit-shaped red blood cells showed all sorts of weird configurations instead. By far the larger number were much the shape of an Arab scimitar.

"Take a look," Mike told Nolan Gaither, and slid off the stool.

The interne adjusted the controls of the instrument to fit his own eyes. "My God!" he exclaimed. "Sickle cell anemia."

"What you're seeing is a crisis." Mike reached for the telephone. "Not many that severe get well."

"Get me Dr. Henderson—stat!" he told the operator.

Less than a minute after the operator started paging the pediatric resident, Gus Henderson's voice sounded in Mike Raburn's ear.

"What's up, Mike?" the baby specialist asked.

"Big Joe Gates's son is in the Emergency Room with a sickle cell crisis. His nail beds are already dusky from cyanosis—"

"I'm on my way." The telephone clicked in Mike's ear.

"Alert Pediatric ICU that we'll be bringing them a patient in a few minutes," Mike told the interne crisply. "I'll go talk to Rachel."

"It's a severe crisis, isn't it?" Gaither asked.

"That boy's lung capillaries are so clogged by abnormally shaped red blood cells that he isn't getting the oxygen he needs to keep his brain functioning at full steam. So far, there's only enough oxygen lack to cause semicoma but his pO_2 could drop below the critical level any minute and the brain cells start being damaged beyond repair, along with those in his heart, his kidneys, and a lot of other organs. If we don't reverse that process in the next hour or so, Joey will either die or be a vegetable the rest of his life."

CHAPTER THREE

I

Only occasionally now was Richard Payson able to hold his head still and keep his eyes focused long enough to read the time of day on the clock above the nurses' station controlling the section of the ICU that included the glass-fronted cubicle where he'd lain for nearly a month. But then the time held only one thing for him any more, the five minutes or so before seven in the morning when Carolyn, his daughter, stopped by on her way to her post as morning shift nursing supervisor in the ICU and again during the hour she customarily spent with him at the beginning of the afternoon shift, before leaving the hospital. The flashes of lucidity were farther and farther apart now, too; when they did come, however briefly, his own mental agony and particularly the torture he saw reflected in the face of his lovely daughter were always worse than before.

He'd first realized something was wrong over a year ago, when little things like sudden explosions of temper, of which he was immediately ashamed, had begun to haunt him like specters from the past. He'd not been able to understand the change and only when his signature had started breaking up to a point where the bank began to query him about checks he'd written had he admitted to himself that the strange movements of his fingers, particularly when he was engaged in some activity requiring intense concentration, were more than simply a result of the increasing nervousness that so often gripped him.

The first time he'd really suspected the grave nature of the change within himself was when he'd run to board an airplane and fallen on the dry, non-slippery tarmac. He had experienced real panic then and, on the way back to Atlanta, had consulted Dr. Peter Gross, chief of neurology at Biscayne General and a professor of medicine on the faculty of the medical school. An old friend, Dr. Gross had identified the pattern of progressively rapid deterioration of almost every body function, accompanied by loss of connection with reality at times, as a sinister gift from a forgotten ancestor, the gene of a malignant heritage handed down from person to person.

"Huntington's disease?" Richard Payson had asked when Dr. Gross told him about the diagnosis. "What's that?"

"A progressive deterioration of nerve tissue in the brain, first identified by Dr. George Huntington in 1872 as a strange form of chorea. Did you ever see anyone with St. Vitus' Dance?"

"I had an uncle who was the town ne'er-do-well. Everybody laughed at him because he was always shaking and trembling—except when he got drunk enough to go to sleep. Then he only jerked occasionally."

"How old was he?"

"Maybe forty—or forty-five."

"He probably inherited Huntington's disease—we call it H-D now—like you did."

"But nobody else in my family ever had anything like it."

"H-D usually develops late. How old was your father when he died?"

"Not much over thirty-five, he was killed in an automobile accident—" Richard Payson had stopped, aghast. "Are you saying—?"

"The disease rarely appears before thirty-five or forty."

"Then Father could have developed symptoms—if he'd lived long enough?"

"Quite possibly," Dr. Gross confirmed. "The genes sometimes manage to skip generations but, whenever either parent develops the condition, one or more of the children will have it."

"What are the odds?"

"Fifty-fifty at the very least."

"My God! What have I done to my daughter?"

"You haven't done anything to her," said the neurologist. "After all, you had no way of knowing—"

"Suppose I had? What could I have done?"

"Not having children stops the disease from passing, of course. The main trouble is that people who develop H-D in later life cannot know, while they're young, whether they're going to have it or not—since it usually doesn't appear until after their children are born. And by that time there's no going back."

"How much do you suppose Carolyn knows about this—this Huntington's disease?"

"She probably studied it in her nursing courses at Gainesville. Until a few years ago it was barely mentioned, but there's been a lot of publicity since '67 when Woody Guthrie died of it."

"How long did Guthrie know he had it?"

"The first symptoms appeared about thirteen years before his death."

"You mean I may be a burden on Carolyn for that long?" Richard Payson had asked, his voice taut with horror.

"I can't make a hard and fast prognosis, of course. But—"

"I want the truth, please."

"Considering the rapidity with which your symptoms developed—"

"I probably won't last long?"

"That's a possibility."

"And my only hope?"

"Tranquilizers help sometimes and a lot of other drugs have been tried."

"But none of them actually affect the course of the disease?"

"None that we know of."

"It's incredible that a single one of your chromosomes can determine what will happen to you when you're thirty-five, forty, even fifty years old—and condemn your children to the same fate."

"Not all of them," said Dr. Gross. "There's a fifty-fifty chance because, in the production of sperm and ova for reproduction, each chromosome splits."

"I know almost nothing about heredity, so you'd better start farther back than that."

"Each body cell is composed of a nucleus of dark material known as chromatin and a surrounding zone called cytoplasm that stains very lightly on a microscopic preparation causing the nucleus to stand out," Dr. Gross had explained. "When studied under a high enough magnification, the nucleus can be seen to contain a skein of chromatin with tiny dark spots along the strands that make it up. The dark spots are the genes that carry all hereditary human characteristics. Every normal body cell—except the sex cells which are specialized for reproduction—has forty-six chromosomes divided into two sets of twenty-three each plus innumerable genes. In the offspring, one set comes from the mother's ovum and the other from the father's sperm cell."

"Are you saying that every cell in a person's body carries genes from both the mother and the father?"

"Excluding the sex cells—yes."

"Then how can anyone escape inheriting every trait from both parents?"

"Because the first body cell—formed by the fusion of the sperm and egg—can have only forty-six chromosomes. Which means that, before the two sex cells unite at the time the ovum is fertilized, half of the chromosomes each of them has are discarded in the form of what are called polar bodies to keep the new individual from having ninety-two instead of forty-six chromosomes."

"Reducing the chance of inheriting a trait like H-D to fifty-fifty?"

"Exactly—unless both parents carry it. In that case, transmission of the disease from parent to child is a certainty—"

"God! What an heirloom!"

"There have been some real dillies in history," Dr. Gross confirmed. "Through Queen Victoria, members of royal families all over Europe wound up being bleeders—suffering from hemophilia. It's transmitted through the female but affects only the male."

"So what do I do?"

"Put your affairs in order—and wait."

"For death?"

"We may discover some way to treat the disease—a lot of work is being done on it."

"That's like having cancer and sitting around waiting for someone to discover a cure before you die. It would seem to be about as futile a reason for living as I can think of."

"We used to think the same thing about people who are prone to attacks of apparently senseless violence," said Dr. Gross. "Then a few years ago we learned that many such attacks are caused by epilepsy limited to the temporal lobe of the brain. The whole picture still seemed hopeless, though, until some brain surgeons started removing the part of the temporal lobe that's involved. Or using a much simpler treatment consisting of putting a needle into the area through a small hole drilled in the skull and destroying that part of the brain either with cold or by electric coagulation. Now a lot of these people can be saved to live useful lives."

"How long can we keep the truth from my daughter?"

"I don't advise it, Richard. Carolyn's a brilliant girl, one of the best nurses we have. Besides, she's engaged, I believe, to a fine young pediatrician named Gus Henderson."

"I know him."

"I don't know what their wedding plans are, but neither of them may want to take the chance of bringing a child into the world with a black gene like the one for H-D as a heritage."

"We'll cross that bridge when we get to it," Richard Payson said firmly. "I'm going back to Atlanta—to wait. And don't tell her."

"As you wish, Richard. We've been friends too long for me not to want to help you—even though I think you're making a mistake."

"There's always a way out—for me."

"Some people with H-D take it. But as a doctor I cannot countenance suicide."

"Even when it's the simplest answer?"

Dr. Gross shrugged but gave no answer. And, in the end, Richard Payson had not possessed the courage to take his own life, although he cursed himself many times later because of that failure—now that he was no longer physically able to do so.

II

Gus Henderson's examination of Joey Gates was brief. The clumped red blood cells under the microscope with their bizarre shapes that resembled nothing except sickle cell anemia, plus the urgency demanded by the deepening color of the boy's blood, indicating oxygen lack, made rapid treatment imperative.

"You've got a very sick boy, Mrs. Gates," the tall pediatrician told the mother. "He's in a severe sickle cell crisis and we'll have to put him under intensive care immediately—"

"Aren't there some new drugs, Doctor?"

"We'll use the treatment with intravenous injection of urea that you probably read about, even though we're not as sure of its value as we were at first. Even more important, we'll use potassium cyanate, which seems to have even more promise. Right now, though, the sickled cells are sticking together to form masses that clog the small blood vessels of his lungs and other organs, interfering with his getting the oxygen his brain needs. That's why he became unconscious."

"Can't you give him oxygen?"

"We will, as soon as we can get him to the ICU and start—"

"Gus." Mike Raburn's voice was suddenly urgent. "There's another way—the hyperbaric chamber."

"It's never been tried," said the pediatrician doubtfully. "And we need to get the urea and cyanate started right away."

"He can be getting that intravenously while he's in the chamber."

"What are you talking about, Mike?" Rachel Gates asked.

"We have a large tank here called a hyperbaric chamber," the surgeon explained. "Inside it patients with oxygen lack can breathe the gas under pressure so more of it gets into the blood."

"If the red blood cells can get through the capillaries," Gus Henderson added.

"Obviously we can't increase the number of cells getting through until the drugs have time to exert their effect," Mike said somewhat impatiently. "But we can still double or even triple the amount of oxygen carried by the cells that *do* get through. And that's certainly worth trying."

"Okay," said the pediatrician. "He's critical enough for desperate measures."

"I'll go into the chamber with him," Mike told Rachel. "I've had a lot of experience with hyperbaric oxygen in connection with some geriatric work I've been doing, studying its effect on the deterioration that so often goes with age."

"Big Joe and I appreciate what you're doing, Mike," said Rachel. "Joey likes you a lot, so if he wakes up in there he won't be afraid."

"I'll get things going in the Hyperbaric Laboratory." Mike moved to the wall telephone. But he didn't add that, unless the desperate measures they were taking to save Joey's life were able to turn the tide of crisis in the boy's favor, he might never be conscious enough to be afraid.

The pressure chamber was at the end of the long corridor through the ground floor of the Biscayne General tower that also gave access, by a side door, to the main ICU. As Mike was passing the door, Helga came out of it and the two almost collided.

"This seems to be my lucky day," he said. "Are you okay?"

"Sure. Just because my suprarenals overshot the mark doesn't mean my whole endocrine system is permanently out of balance."

"God forbid!" he said fervently, and Helga laughed.

"I learned one thing today, at least; the superefficient Dr. Raburn is also quite human. Where are you off to in such a hurry?"

"I'm taking a patient into the hyperbaric chamber in a few minutes."

"Will the pressure be very high?"

"As high as we can stand it. Why?"

"I'm beginning to worry—"

"About me?"

"Of course not, you're indestructible." Her voice had taken on a mocking note. "I'm going to put out a sex alert on the grapevine. If all that oxygen you'll be breathing under pressure has the same effect on you that it has on some of those old fellows you've been taking into the chamber, feminine virtue isn't going to be safe around here for the next three or four days."

III

Standing beside her father, after turning the ICU over to Helga Sundberg shortly after three, Carolyn Payson tried hard to keep from crying—and didn't quite succeed. Even someone living in the midst of a constant battle against death, as she did, could hardly fail to be moved by the sight of her own father lying helpless, his body twitching constantly in the purposeless, uncontrollable movements of Huntington's disease.

She had first learned of his illness about a month earlier when, disturbed because she hadn't heard from her father for some time, she had asked a friend in Atlanta to check on him and discovered that he had entered a nursing home of his own volition. Carolyn had gone to Atlanta immediately and brought Richard Payson back to Biscayne General, placing him on the ICU where she could watch him closely herself.

At Carolyn's insistence Dr. Gross had revealed the details of his earlier examination and the marked progression of the disease process since that time. Until now even Richard Payson's eye muscles were beyond control and his eyeballs jerked constantly when he was awake, gripped by the same malignant force that was rapidly destroying the strong, vigorous man of forty-five who had tossed her in the air as a little girl, catching her when she fell, squealing with delight, in arms that could be as gentle as the touch of the mother who had died bringing her into the world.

Sometimes Carolyn thought her father was still able to recognize her. But more often than not these past weeks, as the destruction of a man by his own genes progressed with inexorable determination, she was sure he no longer even knew her. Only rarely did he speak any more either, and even then the words usually tumbled over each other in an unintelligible jargon that was almost always meaningless.

"Let me die! Let me die!"

The three words—the desperate need they signified penetrating even through the grip of the monstrous evil that had risen from the heritage of past generations to destroy him—kept constantly recurring like a desperate prayer. He spoke them again now as Carolyn stood beside his bed, holding a hand that writhed constantly within her grasp. For once the words were amazingly clear, too, considering the meaningless stream that tumbled from his lips except when he was in the grip of strong sedation. And, hearing again those same three words, Carolyn felt her heart twist in an agony of pain and frustration at her own helplessness.

"I've ordered a sedative," a familiar voice said at Carolyn's elbow and she turned to find Dr. Peter Gross standing there.

At the sight of the neurologist's little goatee and soft brown eyes, warm now with compassion for her, she could hold back the tears no longer and buried her face against the white coat of the older doctor.

"Let it come out, child," he said. "He doesn't recognize anyone now."

"But he can still speak."

"Only because the wish to die is more powerful than anything except the life force."

"I'm all right now." Carolyn dried her eyes with the large white handkerchief Dr. Gross gave her. "It's just that everything's happened so fast."

"No faster than your father wanted it to happen, once he knew the truth," the neurologist assured her. "H-D isn't a pleasant fact to face."

"Why must he face it any longer then—when he wants to die so badly?"

"Many sick people say they want to die, Carolyn; you're too experienced a nurse yourself not to know—"

"Surely you don't think he wants to live now?"

"I'm not sure he isn't past knowing what he wants—"

"Let me die! Let me die!" The voice from the bed was a prayer—to God and to those whose hands could play God, at least long enough to deliver a man from torture—and a cry of protest, too, against the crucifixion of the spirit Richard Payson was undergoing.

"Listen to that!" Carolyn seized the lapels of the long white coat Dr. Gross was wearing. "Listen to that and tell me he doesn't know what he wants."

"I've sworn to preserve life, Carolyn—and so for that matter have you. Neither of us has the right—"

"But he was always so strong, so vital. You don't know what it is to see him now."

"We'll make it as easy for him as we can—count on that. It's you I'm worried about."

"I know what's ahead," said the dark-haired nurse quietly. "Quite a lot has been written about Huntington's lately and most of it's in the medical school library. I think I've read it all since I brought Father here."

"Then you realize its place in your own future?"

"It *controls* my future, Dr. Pete. And *has* controlled it, since long before I was born."

IV

Tanks for increasing the pressure under which air was breathed had been used for many years, when deep-sea divers or caisson workers developed complications in their work. The hyperbaric—literally high pressure— chamber at Biscayne General was only a sophisticated version of the older pressure chambers.

Consisting of a double tank with a connecting air lock between, it allowed those involved in treatment or experiments to go from one chamber to the other and had been one of the most expensive single parts of the recently completed hospital. Only a grant from the government, through the Navy, had enabled it to be built at all by the Hospital Board responsible for the giant medical complex on Biscayne Bay.

Occupying a separate room at the back of the squat wing behind the main hospital tower that also housed the Cardiac Research Laboratory, the hyperbaric chamber had thick metal walls interspersed with heavy glass ports. Through them the technicians handling the controls outside, by means of which the pressure was raised and lowered inside the tank, could also watch what was happening inside and carry out immediate measures to release the pressure and enter the chamber, in case of emergency.

The operation of the chamber itself was the province of a specially trained team of technicians, all former Navy diving experts. Two were always on duty whenever the pressure tank was being used. One handled the control panel for the pump that compressed the air inside and the valves by which the pressure could be released; the other technician watched those participating in its use through the main observation port.

Joey Gates, still unconscious, was brought into the Hyperbaric Laboratory on an amazing new stretcher that was practically a portable intensive care unit in itself, developed for handling acute heart conditions. Oxygen from a tank and respirator on the stretcher had also filled Joey's lungs with every breath, while he was being moved from the Pediatric ICU—naturally called PICU by students and staff—to the Hyperbaric Laboratory.

As soon as the boy and Mike Raburn were inside, the metal doors comprising the end of the chamber itself were swung shut and locked into place. Air from the main pump immediately began to rush into the chamber, raising the pressure inside steadily. But since air is only one fifth oxygen and it was vitally important to raise the concentration of the gas in the unconscious child's brain cells as quickly as possible, Mike now removed the mask connected to the oxygen tank on the stretcher, replacing it with a breathing bag and pressure mask drawing from the main oxygen supply of the hospital. Thus, as the pressure inside the hyperbaric chamber was raised, the same effect was exerted upon the breathing bag, increasing the flow of oxygen to Joey Gates's red blood cells and with it the concentration of the vital gas in the body tissues.

"How high do you want us to raise the pressure, Dr. Raburn?"

The voice of the technician from the speaker in the ceiling of the tank was unnaturally loud, shut up as they were in a constricted space. To answer, Mike had only to lift a telephone from its hook on the wall of the tank, within easy reach of the stool on which he was sitting beside the unconscious child.

"Try two atmospheres at first," he directed.

"That should be safe even with him breathing more oxygen."

Mike understood what was troubling the chief technician: the odd fact that the greatest hazard in the use of a hyperbaric chamber was oxygen poisoning, since an overdose of the gas could cause convulsions that were as much of a danger as a lack of the same gas.

"One atmosphere," the voice of the technician reported moments later via the speaker.

"We're okay," said Mike. "You can take it on up."

Gus Henderson had applied a number of delicate sensors to Joey's body, as well as threading a tiny nylon catheter into an arm vein and passing it through ever larger vein channels up the arm and into the chest, where it lay with its tip near the left side of the heart.

Inserting the catheter almost to the heart itself was a precaution taken to prevent irritation of the smaller vein channels leading to it by the urea-cyanate solution being injected to reverse the sickling process in the red blood cells. Flowing slowly from the end of the venous catheter into the large stream of blood being received by the upper chamber of the heart, the atrium, the urea-cyanate solution was less likely to injure the delicate walls of the venous system.

The monitor attached to the special stretcher upon which Joey lay was recording his heart action in a continuous flashing pattern on its small ground-glass screen and at the same time the heart picture was being transmitted by telemetry to a receiver outside the chamber where it could be watched by others. While the pressure inside the tank rose steadily, as evidenced by the manometer on the instrument panel beside the door, Mike carefully checked the intravenous catheter and increased the drip rate in the glass chamber of the IV setup. Still another and larger catheter, placed in the urinary bladder, was showing a steady flow, indicating that Joey's kidney function, a crucial factor in recovery, was holding up satisfactorily.

"Two atmospheres, Dr. Raburn," the technician reported.

"Hold it there for the time being while we give the red blood cells a chance to load up with oxygen," said Mike. "It's hard to estimate the degree of cyanosis with his skin pigment, but I don't think it's getting any deeper."

"Hold on two." The technician moved aside and Gus Henderson's face appeared at the glass port.

"Everything okay, Mike?" he asked.

"It looks that way in here, but he's still unconscious."

"The ECG is coming through fine. How high do you plan to take the pressure?"

"We're at two atmospheres, but it doesn't look as if that's going to do the trick."

"How high can you go before the danger of oxygen convulsion sets in?"

"Probably not much above four atmospheres. Actually, an oxygen convulsion would tell us we're saturating the brain, which is what we want to do, and I could always control it by letting him breathe the air in here and wash the excess O_2 out of his brain cells. But I'd still rather not deliberately throw Joey into a convulsion."

"I just finished talking to Big Joe Gates in California," said Gus. "He was relieved to know the boy is in your hands and said he's coming back as soon as he can get a plane out."

"I think we'll go to three atmospheres now," said Mike. "Can you stick around for a few minutes, Gus?"

"Sure." Then the pediatrician's expression suddenly changed. "Not any more, Mike; they're calling a CODE FIVE for the Emergency Room."

V

Her afternoon interrupted at the start by the arrival of Joey Gates, Mrs. Faye Connor had just finished reading the seven-to-three nursing supervisor's summary of Emergency Department activities during the morning shift, before sending it on to the Nursing Office, when an ambulance whined to a stop at the loading ramp. Seconds later a Rescue Squad stretcher from one of the crack Miami units burst through the double doors leading outside.

"You don't have to knock the doors down, Callahan." The nurse spoke severely to the tall fireman at the head of the stretcher.

"We've got an OD here that's near term, Mrs. Connor. DOA, too, from the looks of it, but I think I heard the fetal heart."

The cryptic abbreviations told a graphic story, one the gray-haired nurse had seen many times during her years in command of the Emergency Department nursing staff. OD meant "overdose," usually of heroin, an all too frequent diagnosis in what had come to be called the Drug Age, and DOA was the universal term for "Dead On Arrival." But it was hearing the fetal heart inside the mother's body that created the real challenge.

"Over here!"

Mrs. Connor led the way to a plywood-walled cubicle that differed markedly from the rest of the dozen examining-treatment areas making up the main Emergency Room. Equipped with the same battery of highly specialized monitoring devices found in the ICU itself, the small room had been designed almost two years earlier in order to provide every facility needed for an immediate evaluation of accident and other cases that might be potential heart donors for Dr. Kenneth Dalton's transplant program.

As the stretcher was pushed into the empty cubicle, the nurse reached for the diaphragm terminal of the phono-cardioscope, a modern-day ultrasophisticated version of the simple stethoscope. Separating the blankets over the patient's abdomen, she pressed the diaphragm against the swollen mound and flipped the switch activating the instrument.

Immediately a faint sound, hurried but rhythmic, came from the loudspeaker on the wall of the cubicle, the unmistakable beat of a baby's heart inside the uterus of its dead mother.

"Hold this, Callahan, if we move fast we may save this baby." As Faye Connor handed the fireman the diaphragm, her mind was working like the computer that was the heart of the hospital's complicated electronic system, considering the alternatives at her disposal and discarding them one by one.

Mike Raburn was in the hyperbaric chamber with the Gates boy and so was not available. Dr. Kenneth Dalton was on call for Emergency, but it would take minutes to reach him, minutes the baby, whose racing heart would soon be slowing to a stop unless something was done to free it from the deadly burden of its own mother's body, couldn't afford to lose. Dr. Nolan Gaither, the interne on duty, was putting on a cast in the plaster room down the corridor some fifty feet away, but reaching him would take time. And even then the nurse had no way of knowing how quickly the still not fully trained reflexes of the young doctor could be galvanized into the action necessary to save the baby's life.

Which left only a single alternative, the one sure way to get expert help quickly and the most urgent call that could be sounded over the hospital loudspeaker system. It would bring a CPR—cardiopulmonary resuscitation—team on the double, ready to tackle a stopped heart or cope with any other emergency.

Only a fraction of a second elapsed between the initiation of her review and the motion of Mrs. Connor's hand toward the red button on the wall of the cubicle. No more than a similar fraction later a high-speed tape recorder activated by the red button was locked into the hospital's public address system, abruptly stopping all other use of it.

"CODE FIVE—EMERGENCY!" The rarely heard summons brought every activity in the hospital for a halt for an instant.

"CODE FIVE—EMERGENCY!" The summons was repeated and, like Sleeping Beauty at the kiss of the Prince, everything suddenly began to move again, but on a new tack, a planned course where everyone knew his or her job perfectly and needed no time-consuming instructions before acting.

CHAPTER FOUR

I

Moments before the alarm sounded, Rebecca Dalton had descended to ground level from the Medical Department located on an upper floor. Emerging from the elevator, she was startled to see Ken step up from an adjoining one and, to avoid meeting him, turned toward the Cardiac Research Laboratory at the back of the building. At the same moment, however, he started toward the lobby, with the result that they collided and he was forced to catch her to keep her from being knocked down. Facing each other with their faces less than a foot apart and his arm around Rebecca's waist, they were like two people frozen in time—until Ken released her and broke the tension of the sudden meeting.

"I heard the operator paging you for the lab a few minutes ago, Reb," he said. "Anything wrong?"

Reb was the pet name he'd given her before they were married. Hearing it now for the first time since they'd separated nearly six months ago twisted Rebecca's heart so sharply that she turned away, lest he see the sudden start of tears in her eyes. And noting her concern, he reached out to touch her, then dropped his hand.

"I'm sorry," he said softly. "Sorry about everything."

"Congratulations on the verdict," said Rebecca but, when she saw his expression suddenly harden, was sorry she had mentioned the subject that had finally caused the break between them.

"At least it took the hospital off the hook." His tone was harsh now. "But nothing will really be changed until—"

Whatever he had been about to say was interrupted by the announcement from the CODE FIVE tape. At the sound both of them turned instinctively toward the door of the Emergency Department, not much more than a dozen feet away, everything except the urgency of the crisis causing the announcement suddenly erased from their minds.

As the husband-and-wife doctor team burst into the white-tiled Emergency Room, Mrs. Connor looked up from where she was following the set routine in apparent DOAs by applying sensors to the chest of the patient.

"The surgical tray's ready," she reported. "The Rescue Squad just brought her in—DOA, and pregnant. You can still hear the fetal heartbeat on the phonocardioscope."

The question of what should be done in such an emergency had been answered by the Emperor Numa Pompilius of Rome more than seven hundred years before the birth of Christ in what had become known as the *Lex Caesaris*—a decree forbidding the burial of a pregnant woman until the child had been removed from her womb, if possible before its heart stopped beating.

A glance at the girl on the stretcher beneath the glaring white ceiling lights told a graphic and tragic story: the features that had once been pretty but were only pathetic now; the frame of lank blonde hair; the enormous abdomen; and most diagnostic of all, the small dark splotches along the course of the veins visible over both arms and legs—all signs identifying the young mother as an addict, most likely on heroin.

Following a routine Ken and Rebecca Dalton had worked out for the special monitor cubicle, Mrs. Connor switched on the ECG connections she had just made—revealing a flat line for heart action on the oscilloscope screen.

"No heartbeat," she said, and moved on, still following the SOP for such cases, to attach electroencephalographic terminals to the girl's scalp, needlelike sensors used to register electric waves denoting brain activity.

The procedure had become routine with all patients brought to the hospital *in extremis*, as a means of determining brain damage—the ultimate cessation of life itself even though the heart might still be beating. In the hectic period when Ken Dalton had performed fifteen heart transplants in one year, the procedure being followed by Mrs. Connor had resulted in the discovery of a number of donor hearts soon enough after legal death to furnish much of the supply needed for the dramatic transplant operations. But for the past six months it had been allowed to lapse.

With only seconds in which to save the child through the age-old procedure of immediate Caesarean section, two things were necessary. One was to determine as certainly as possible, without the electroencephalograph since there was no time for delay, the fact of death by means of the conventional evidence provided by cessation of both heartbeat and respiration. The other was the availability of instruments for the operation and a surgeon capable of performing it.

Fortunately all these requirements were now met by the presence of a surgeon and a cardiologist in the Emergency Room and the failure of the electrocardiograph to reveal heart action in the mother. Ken Dalton pulled on a pair of rubber gloves while quickly surveying the contents of the instrument tray another nurse had already opened upon a table beside the stretcher. Rebecca, meanwhile, was removing the terminal of the phonocardioscope to the patient's chest and placing it over the heart.

"There's no heartbeat," she reported when no sound was heard. "She's clinically dead."

"Somebody call for Gus Henderson and a Pediatric ICU bassinet." Ken was picking up a scalpel from the instrument tray as he spoke. "This baby's going to need all the help we can give it."

With his left hand, he tensed the skin over the mound of the abdomen and, using a long slashing stroke, laid the abdominal wall open from well above the navel to the brush of darkish blonde hair over the patient's pubis.

A second stroke penetrated the peritoneal lining of the abdomen, allowing the distended uterus, its muscle almost black now from the absence of oxygen, to protrude through.

Rebecca did not wait to watch, but moved to a telephone.

"CODE FIVE. DR. HENDERSON," she told the operator. "Emergency Room Three."

As she hung up, the call came from the loudspeaker in the corridor outside, the calm voice of the paging operator saying distinctly and clearly: "CODE FIVE, DR. HENDERSON! Emergency Room Three. CODE FIVE! Pediatric Team! Emergency Room Three."

"She can't have been dead long," said Rebecca as the scalpel in Ken's hand slashed into the thick muscular wall of the uterus. "The blood hasn't started to clot."

Separating with the thumb and forefinger of his left hand the edges of the cut he had made into the wall of the uterus, Ken dissected more carefully now, since too deep a cut could damage the body of the baby within the uterus. A sudden gush of yellowish amniotic fluid from the reservoir in which the child had lain, while developing from the union of two cells to the immensely complicated structure of a separate human being, indicated that the uterine cavity was penetrated. And, slipping his left hand inside the uterus with the back of it protecting the body of the child, Ken opened the incision widely enough in both directions to allow removing the infant with the umbilical cord still attached to the mother by way of the placenta. Dropping the scalpel from his right hand, he searched inside the uterine cavity for a tiny foot.

"The baby's still alive," he reported. "I can feel the fetal heart beating against my hand."

"Thank God!" said Rebecca.

Circling one tiny leg with his fingers, Ken pulled it through the incision he had made into the uterus. In a continuation of the same movement, he found the other foot and extracted it, then gently drew the whole body of the child from the mother's womb.

Holding the baby up with his left hand, he gave it a smack across the soles of its feet with his right. A spasmodic contraction of the tiny chest brought a faint cry with initiation of breathing and, picking up a hemostatic forceps from the instrument table, Ken clamped across the umbilical cord which, until a few moments ago, had connected the circulation of the child with that of the mother, bringing it vital oxygen and sustenance until her own heartbeat had ceased.

Gus Henderson had just arrived and was holding a small blanket across his outstretched arms. When the surgeon placed the baby gently upon it, with the hemostat still dangling from the cut stump of the umbilical cord, Gus moved immediately to the special portable ICU bassinet Helga Sundberg had just brought to the Emergency Room as part of the pediatric emergency routine.

"At least it's breathing and its heart is beating," said Rebecca.

"It couldn't weigh over two and a half pounds, so it's definitely premature," said the tall pediatrician. "And from the looks of the mother's veins, that baby's been an addict ever since it was only one cell. Cold turkey is no fun when you're grown; it must be hell when you only weigh two or three pounds."

They all knew what he meant, "cold turkey" was a graphic description of a method of treating drug addiction by abrupt withdrawal of all narcotics. In the excitement of saving the baby, none of them had noticed that, while Ken Dalton was operating, Mrs. Connor had finished attaching the sensors to the young mother's scalp and switched on the electroencephalograph.

"Dr. Dalton! Look!" Mrs. Connor was staring at the small monitor screen of the EEG where, faintly, but beyond any shadow of a doubt, a familiar pattern was plainly visible.

"She still has brain waves." Rebecca's voice was little more than an incredulous whisper. "Which means she's technically still alive."

II

In the hyperbaric chamber, things were going very well for Joey Gates.

"Three atmospheres, Dr. Raburn," the pressure technician reported. "His pulse is slowing on the monitor out here, too."

"Hold for three for the time being, Matt. I think the cyanosis is less marked."

Once again Mike checked the catheters and found both of them open. The bottle of intravenous fluid was almost empty, however, so he changed it for a fresh one that had been put into the metal tank when they first came in, before the air-tight doors were closed.

"Any idea what the CODE FIVE was about?" Mike asked via the telephone.

"A DOA in the Emergency Room with a live baby according to the grapevine. Dr. Kenneth Dalton's doing a Caesarean, I guess that's why Dr. Henderson got the special call."

"Looks like I missed some excitement."

"You have enough," the technician assured him. "Every time I get on my Honda and start home through the expressway traffic, I pray that I don't get tossed off it and brought to the ER when you're not on duty."

A sudden movement of Joey Gates's arm, the one with the catheter in the vein, caused Mike to reach for it quickly.

"Looks like he's coming around," he said.

"His ECG just took a nose dive, too." The technicians' voice was suddenly tense. Then it relaxed as he added, "But it's back on schedule now."

"The IV catheter must have moved enough to touch the wall of the atrium," said Mike. "I'll pull it back a little before he's completely conscious."

Carefully he adjusted the tiny flexible tube, withdrawing about an inch of it through the small skin wound where it had been inserted. Pulling the stool upon which he had been sitting closer to the low stretcher, Mike kept his hand on Joey's arm now, lest the boy accidentally jerk the vitally important tube from his arm.

For perhaps a quarter of an hour nothing happened except a gradual slowing of Joey's pulse and respiration, both signs that the strain upon his circulation of trying to supply oxygen to his brain and other important tissues was being lessened by the increased amount of the life gas reaching his body cells. Then, just as if awakening from a sound sleep, the boy opened his eyes.

Mike lifted the oxygen mask from Joey's face for a moment. "How do you feel?" he asked.

"Okay—I guess. Where am I, Dr. Mike?"

"In the hospital."

"Where's Mommy?"

"Outside, waiting. I had to give you a special treatment, so we brought you into this room."

"Looks more like a submarine."

"It's actually a tank where you breathe air under pressure—"

The boy's dark eyes brightened. "Like scuba diving?"

"Pretty close."

"Daddy's going to take me scuba diving when I get bigger. We're going to the Penne—" He stumbled over the rest of the word.

"The Pennecamp Coral Reef State Park," said Mike. "You'll see a lot of fish and some of the prettiest coral anywhere. Now let's put the mask back on and breathe some more oxygen so you'll get well in a hurry. Okay?"

The boy nodded and Mike adjusted the mask.

"Breathe deeply, Joey," he said. "You need all of this stuff you can get."

For another half hour the boy breathed the oxygen while his pulse rate continued to drop and his color improved. Then Mike removed the mask and watched him closely for about ten minutes. When he showed no signs of growing drowsy again, and the monitor indicated no change in heart action, Mike shut off the oxygen valve and picked up the telephone again.

"You can lower the pressure, Matt," he told the technician via the telephone. "It looks like everything's going to be all right."

III

As chief anesthesiologist for Biscayne General, Dr. Valerie LeMoyne was in charge of all resuscitation activities in the hospital. Not only had she instituted the training programs and organizational procedures which made a trained CPR—Cardiopulmonary Resuscitation—team available on instant notice to any section of the hospital but she was personally the head of the most important of them, the one always on call for the Emergency Room and the Intensive Care Units. She had arrived in the Emergency Room barely a minute after the CODE FIVE was sounded, along with Dr. Ed Vogel, Research Fellow in Cardiology and second-in-command on the team, who had just returned to the hospital after a brief absence.

For an instant following Rebecca's dramatic announcement that the supposedly dead patient showed at least a faint flicker of life in the nervous system, everyone in the ER was frozen into a tableau. But when Ken Dalton broke the silence everything began to move again.

"Is Dr. LeMoyne here?" he asked.

"Here, Doctor," Val answered.

"Resuscitation is your field. Take over, please."

"Right," said Valerie LeMoyne crisply. "This looks like a straight line arrest. Do you agree, Rebecca?"

"Entirely."

"Then electrical stimulation is out for the moment and we can best stimulate the heart by direct massage through the diaphragm."

"I'll make room." Ken reached for a scalpel from the instrument tray.

"Put on some sterile gloves, Dr. Vogel," Val directed. "You can employ direct massage while Dr. Rebecca Dalton searches for a vein and gets an IV started."

While Ed Vogel was putting on sterile gloves, Ken's scalpel was moving swiftly at the upper end of the incision, extending it upward to make room for the cardiologist to massage the heart through the lax muscular shelf of the diaphragm separating the chest cavity from the abdomen.

As Ed inserted a gloved right hand into the upper part of the incision, Ken began to remove the placenta from inside the uterus. Scooping out the thick, pancake-like organ with the cut umbilical cord dangling from it, he dropped the specimen into the basin Mrs. Connor held out to him and reached for a needle holder with a long strand of suture material attached to the curved needle between its jaws.

Meanwhile, Ed Vogel was feeling for the base of the heart through the thin muscle of the diaphragm. When his fingers closed around it, he began to squeeze the thoracic organ rhythmically, massaging the muscular wall in an attempt to incite a spontaneous contraction and at the same time duplicating artificially its action in pumping blood through the body to preserve life.

At the patient's head, Valerie LeMoyne had pushed down the jaw and inserted a curved plastic airway to hold back the tongue and create a clear airway to the lungs. When she placed a mask over the girl's mouth and nose and switched on the respirator, the breathing bag attached to it began to inflate and deflate in a steady rhythm of artificial respiration. Thus, with blood being pumped through the patient's circulation and oxygen passing into it from the lungs, the inactive life processes were being duplicated artificially in support of the weak evidence of life still apparent from the flickering pattern of the EEG waves on the wall monitor.

"I can feel the lungs being inflated," Ed Vogel reported, "but no cardiac contraction."

"What about the baby, Dr. Henderson?" Val LeMoyne asked.

"It's alive," Gus Henderson reported from the adjoining cubicle, where he and Helga were placing the baby in the special newborn resuscitation chamber they had wheeled directly into the Emergency Room. "But I don't like the way it's breathing."

"Take it to the NICU and let us know if you need any help." NICU was the cryptic designation of the Newborn Intensive Care Unit.

"We're leaving," said Gus.

Rebecca had been working over the patient's right arm meanwhile, probing for a vein with a needle-catheter set.

"Blood's flowing," she announced when a dark stream suddenly spurted back into the barrel of the attached syringe. "Shall I inject a bolus?"

"Please," said Val. "Ten cc. of calcium chloride and a half cc. of Isuprel."

Rebecca busied herself at the outer end of the needle-catheter setup, injecting the medication before removing the needle and attaching the glass adapter of an intravenous tube to the end of the catheter remaining in the vein. Both powerful stimulants, the entire dose of the drugs was being delivered directly into the heart itself.

"Still no heart action," Ed Vogel reported as Ken continued to close the wound in the wall of the flabby uterus with deep running sutures, using his right hand, while massaging the muscular wall of the organ with his left. Blood surged from the cut edges with each squeezing action by Ed Vogel's hand upon the heart, and Ken was hoping by his own massage to make the uterus itself contract and squeeze down the blood spaces opened by the scalpel.

"The EEG waves are very faint." With the respirator automatically duplicating the act of breathing, Val LeMoyne was able to watch the monitor screen, as well as the other orderly activities going on in the room. "There's apparently some life still in the brain but the pupils are widely dilated, which probably means the brain damage would not be reversible, even if we started the heart."

No one there required an explanation; between a dead patient and one that was little more than a vegetable from brain damage, there was really not much choice.

"I just felt a slight heart contraction." Ed Vogel's voice was suddenly tense. "There's another one."

"Display the ECG on the monitor, please," said Val LeMoyne, and Mrs. Connor moved quickly to switch on the sensors she had placed on the patient's chest immediately after sounding CODE FIVE.

A by-product of the sophisticated space research that enables observers in Houston to watch the heartbeats and other vital functions of astronauts a quarter of a million miles away on the moon, the small sensors could pick up even the most minute action currents of the heart muscle and display them in the form of electrocardiographic tracings visible to all on the small ground-glass screen.

For a moment no one spoke, while all eyes were turned to the monitor. The waves being exhibited on the screen were undeniable proof that the heart had indeed begun to beat, but they also graphically described its character, and the periodic and purposeless contraction of individual sections of heart muscle being recorded had no resemblance to either order or continuity of function. Only one diagnosis fitted that picture, ventricular fibrillation, a dangerous complication that could render even a strong heart quite useless.

"You'd better take over from here," Valerie LeMoyne spoke directly to Rebecca, who nodded and moved nearer the monitor to study the pattern.

"It's fibrillation for sure," she said. "Please inject fifty milligrams of xylocaine through the IV needle, Mrs. Connor. Meanwhile we don't seem to have much choice now, except to zap the heart. Do you agree, Ed?"

"Absolutely."

The ICU interne, who was a member of the team, moved the portable pacemaker-defibrillator he had pushed to the room at the sound of the alarm into place beside the patient. At the same time, Val quickly unstrapped the mask of the resuscitator and removed it, cutting off the oxygen. The quickest way to restore a fibrillating heart to a normal rhythm was to shock it—"Zap!" in medical idiom—with a powerful jolt of electricity delivered to the patient's chest over the heart by means of paddle electrodes. Anyone touching the body inadvertently at the time, however, could receive a powerful wallop, so both Ken Dalton and Ed Vogel stepped away from the table.

"Set the controls at four hundred milliwatt seconds." Rebecca was in charge now and there was no hesitation in either decision or action.

The interne set the controls at the figure she had ordered and placed the paddle electrodes over the heart area, so the current could pass from one electrode through the heart muscle and back to the other, completing the circuit. Devised to stop the heart by the powerful jolt of the defibrillating current, in the hope that it would restart itself in a normal rhythm, the machine was an invaluable tool in controlling a condition which, before it became available, had often caused the death of the victim.

At Rebecca's nod, another member of the team pressed the switch on the defibrillator console and the patient's chest muscles jerked sharply from the stimulating current. When the ECG sensors, disconnected during the zapping procedure, were connected once again, the irregular heart action that had turned the surface of the monitor screen into a crazy jumble of lines was gone—but with it all evidence of function by the organ itself.

"Get ready to start massaging again, Ed," said Rebecca quietly. "We're not getting any action."

Ed Vogel had removed his hand from the heart before the current was turned off and stepped back beside Ken Dalton. Now both of them returned to the table and resumed the work on which they had been engaged.

Three times during the next fifteen minutes, faint contractions of the vital cardiac muscles were started by the massaging action of Ed Vogel's gloved hand through the diaphragm, but each time the result was the familiar jumble of lines indicating fibrillation. Twice, after the powerful shocking current had stopped all contractions, the current was switched to the pacemaker, sending rhythmic jolts of considerably less intensity than the zapping procedure through the heart muscle in an attempt to initiate regular contractions. Each time, however, the result was only another flurry of fibrillation, and after the fourth zapping, even the brain waves had ceased, the ultimate criterion of death.

"In my opinion nothing can be gained by any more shocks," said Rebecca quietly.

"I agree," said Val LeMoyne, "but at least the baby was saved."

"For cold turkey?" Ken's tone made Rebecca wish she could take him in her arms and comfort him. "Maybe it would have been better off if I'd let it die with the mother. This place depresses me. Dictate a summary on this case for the record, will you, Reb? I've done all the damage I can do today."

IV

When Carolyn Payson emerged from the elevator into the hospital lobby, after spending the hour at her father's bedside which had become a daily routine for her, she saw the tall figure of Gus Henderson standing beside a bulletin board. Ostensibly he was reading the announcements thumbtacked there but actually, she knew, he was waiting for her. When Gus saw her, his craggy face broke into a smile and he came across the lobby to take her arm.

"I was afraid you'd already left," he said. "Dr. Dalton did a section on a DOA from heroin—"

"Was that the CODE FIVE?"

"Yes." He held open the door of the Coffee Shop occupying a large area just off the lobby beside a covered walkway leading to Bayside Terrace and across from the door connecting the Emergency Department with the lobby itself. The popular restaurant was almost filled with a chattering crowd of students and nurses released from the morning shift but they were able to find an empty booth.

"Anything besides coffee?" Gus asked.

"No, I'm getting too fat."

"On you it looks wonderful. Two coffees—black," he called to Maggie McCloud, the plump, middle-aged waitress behind the counter. "I'll get 'em."

"Two coffees, black, comin' up, Dr. Henderson," said Maggie cheerfully. "How's your father, Miss Payson?"

"About the same, thank you." Carolyn was watching Gus as he maneuvered himself to the counter through the crowd filling the shop. Like many pediatricians, he was a big man but, as she well knew, as gentle as a woman. He came back carrying steaming hot-drink cups.

"I only have a minute, while Peggy Tyndall sets up a tray so I can put some umbilical catheters and an electronic probe into the preemie Dr. Dalton just delivered." Gus slumped comfortably in the booth. "Have I told you I love you lately?"

"Not since last night."

"How about marrying me next week? We could make it this weekend, but I have to work."

Carolyn looked away quickly, but not before Gus had a glimpse of the pain that showed in her eyes.

"What's the matter, darling?" he asked. "Your father worse?"

She nodded wordlessly.

"Anything I can do?"

"No." Carolyn drank from her cup but the coffee was tasteless, like everything lately. Hoping to take her mind off her troubles, Gus said, "According to Mike Raburn, your roommate covered herself with glory this afternoon."

"Helga was late coming on duty, which isn't like her. But she didn't say why."

"Mike said she found a child in the last stages of asphyxiation in the ER and put a needle into the trachea—that new technique he was telling about last week. He was very much impressed."

"Everybody knows Helga's always on the ball. Mike shouldn't have been surprised."

"My guess would be that he's been seeing Helga only as a fine nurse all these months, but for some reason he saw her all at once this afternoon as a woman."

Carolyn smiled. "I remember the day you first saw me as something besides a nursing machine—but then I'd been working on you for a month."

"And think of what I might have missed, if you hadn't."

"I'm not so sure," Carolyn's tone was sober again. "Huntington's disease is hereditary."

"But genetics as a science has made giant strides lately."

"Not with H-D. I've been reading up on it ever since I brought Father from Atlanta."

"It still has to be pretty rare. I don't remember ever seeing another case."

"There may be a thousand in the United States and all of them seem to be traceable back to a small number of immigrants who came over here from Europe nearly three hundred years ago."

"But your father—"

"The gene of H-D is a defective dominant, Gus. It can lie dormant for one or even two generations."

"Then what are you worrying—"

"My father's brother probably died of it, too, which could mean that the gene is growing stronger in my family, so our children would stand a fifty-fifty chance of developing it. Would you want to saddle such a heritage on your sons and daughters?"

"There's a simple way around that—don't have any."

"Something could go wrong and—"

"Not if I were sterilized. Cutting the spermatic cords is a minor procedure."

"A man's entitled to have descendants, darling. With the gene of H-D probably already in every cell of my body, I could very well die by the time I'm thirty-five. You could still marry then and have children of your own—healthy ones."

"Look, Carolyn, I love you and I want you with me all the time. To gain that, I'd be willing to give up anything, including having children of our own."

From the loudspeaker in the corner of the room against the ceiling came the calm voice of the paging operator:

"Dr. Henderson—115. Dr. Augustus Henderson—115. Dr. Henderson—115."

"That's the NICU. Helga must have everything ready," he said. "Will you have dinner with me in the hospital cafeteria this evening? I can't get away, with this preemie going through cold turkey."

"Make it about six, if you can," said Carolyn. "I want to sit with my father for a while afterward."

"See you then." Gus stood up and dropped some change on the table. "And don't go moping because you can't have children, darling. After watching what Baby Hornsby is going through on the first day of its life outside the womb, I'm not at all sure this is the kind of world we want to inject a child into anyway."

Carolyn stayed on in the Coffee Shop for a while after Gus left. And when she did leave, her steps turned toward the small hospital chapel, located just off the corridor leading from the main lobby to the banks of elevators.

Moved by her concern for her father, as well as for herself and her own future, she had returned instinctively to the religious training of her childhood. Slipping into one of the pews, she dropped to her knees on a prayer bench and sought words to voice her plea for divine assistance in what appeared to be an insoluble problem—at least within her own competence.

"Can I help you, Miss Payson?" The soft voice startled her and she turned quickly to see the hospital chaplain standing at the end of the pew where she had been kneeling.

"Father Hagan!" Carolyn remembered the Episcopal priest from the week he'd spent on her ward, when changes in a routine electrocardiogram had suggested the onset of a more serious condition. Thanks to Rebecca Dalton's skill as a cardiologist, plus the care given by Carolyn and the other dedicated nurses operating the CICU of the main Intensive Care Section, the attack had been averted.

"I am pleased that you knew where to come for help." The old minister entered the pew and took a seat beside her as she rose from her knees. "And that it's best sought on your knees."

"I haven't been exactly what you might call a churchgoer, Padre."

"Each of us serves God in his own way, Miss Payson. I suspect yours may be more in accord with His will than most."

"I know my job, at least."

The old chaplain smiled. "I, too, can testify to that."

"I only wish the problem I'm facing now was as easy to answer."

"Your father?"

Carolyn wasn't surprised that Father Hagan knew about Richard Payson. Even a hospital the size of Biscayne General was still a small and almost inbred community. "I didn't see his name on the critical list this morning."

"He's not critical—in the medical sense. But if you had known him before, you would realize what it means to see someone with a brain like his shut off from communication with the rest of the world while he turns into a vegetable."

"Is he conscious?"

"Momentarily at times—long enough to beg us to let him die."

"Is that what's troubling you? The question of whether your father should be allowed to die?"

"That's part of it—the most important part." She drew a deep breath, still not knowing exactly how to put into words the conviction that had been growing in her mind since she had brought Richard Payson into the hospital and Dr. Gross had told her the diagnosis.

"I'm not familiar with your father's condition," said the chaplain. "If you don't mind talking about it—"

"I guess I need to share it with someone. So far I've tried to keep everything to myself, but—"

"I'm here to listen and to help—or to pray."

As she described her father's condition, the gradual disintegration of the mind and the personality until he'd become hardly more than a body torn to pieces by the malignant gene of Huntington's disease in every cell of his body, Carolyn found some of the burden lifted from her shoulders.

"Can nothing be done?" the chaplain asked when she finished.

"Not for my father. But I'm the last in my own family line, so by never bringing children into the world, I can at least stop the gene from being passed on to others."

"You can always adopt a child—"

"That's out too," she said flatly.

"Why?"

"What right do I have to saddle a husband—or the children we might adopt—with a mother who could turn into a gibbering travesty of a human being just when they all probably would need her most?"

"There's an even chance that this won't happen," he reminded her.

"That's still too much of a burden to put on a person you love."

"It's a hard choice—"

"There isn't any choice, Padre. I settled that in my own mind—along with some other things—when I learned the real cause of Dad's illness."

The old chaplain studied her thoughtfully for a moment before he spoke.

"Is there someone you love besides your father?" he asked.

"Yes. Very much indeed."

"Have you told all this to him?"

"Not my resolve to never marry."

"Why?"

She looked up then and he saw that her eyes were wet. But, when she spoke, her voice was well under control.

"I guess I'm enough of a coward not to want to hurt Gus."

"Dr. Henderson?"

"Yes." Then she added defiantly, "Are you going to tell me it's a sin to seize what little happiness I can before it flies out the window?"

"I'm far too frail a vessel to sit in judgment on people who may be serving God much better than I," said the old priest. "But I don't envy you the moment when you must tell Dr. Henderson the truth."

"We've already agreed that we shouldn't have children of our own. Fortunately the rest can wait—as long as the man I love isn't tied to me by marriage."

"What if you should become pregnant?"

"The one-in-two chance of passing a horrible disease like Huntington's to a child would be ample grounds for a legal therapeutic abortion, even if the courts hadn't made abortion in the first three months legal anyway. But I'm taking no chances of that either—"

"You seem to have thought this all out," he conceded.

"And you don't approve?"

The priest smiled and shook his head. "A long time ago, a woman was brought to Jesus by people who sought to have him condemn her. Do you remember his answer?"

"No. But then I've already told you I haven't been the best churchgoer in the world."

"Jesus answered, 'He that is without sin among you, let him first cast a stone at her.'"

"Thank you, Chaplain." Carolyn started to rise, but he put his hand upon hers.

"I suspect that you haven't told me the real reason you came here," he said. "Wouldn't you like to?"

Carolyn hesitated only momentarily. "Remember my telling you that

Father rouses only to beg us to let him die?" she asked.

"Yes."

"I'm sure some part of his brain still knows enough of what's happening, and what will happen, not to want to put any more of a burden upon me. So if the doctors can't let him die, I don't have any choice except . . ."

"There still may be a way—"

She turned quickly. "What is it?"

"Have you read about the 'right to die' controversy?"

"A little—in newspapers and magazines."

"Some hospitals have appointed committees to decide—"

"When a patient's prognosis is hopeless?" she asked eagerly.

"Yes. It's very new here at Biscayne General—and also very secret for good reasons."

"Tell me about it, Chaplain," Carolyn said eagerly. "Tell me, please."

CHAPTER FIVE

I

Helga Sundberg was bending over the bassinet in which Baby Hornsby lay, giving it oxygen by means of a small mask covering its nose and mouth, when Peggy Tyndall pushed the special cardiac catheterization cart into the NICU treatment room. Located just off the eight-bed ward where newborns with any respiratory or other difficulty were given special care twenty-four hours a day, there was never less than one specially trained ICU nurse to every two small patients in the ward.

Peggy was barely five feet, with a blonde pony tail that made her look like a schoolgirl, and a bright warm smile, in spite of having been widowed at twenty with a child destined to be born six months later with congenital heart disease. As a physician's assistant and chief technician in the Cardiac Research Laboratory, she was Rebecca Dalton's and Ed Vogel's right hand, plus being a favorite all over the big hospital.

"Hi, Peg," said Helga. "Dr. Henderson will be here in a minute."

Peggy busied herself in the corner of the room, putting on the gown and mask required for everyone working in the NICU. When she finished, she came over to the bassinet and stood looking down at Baby Hornsby.

"This the post-mortem Caesarean baby?" she asked.

Helga nodded. "Two or three weeks premature and cold turkey into the bargain. That's some handicap to start life with."

"But he'll be okay when the withdrawal symptoms wear off, won't he?" Peggy's tone was a little resentful and Helga understood the reason.

"Maybe. But it's tough sledding for a while—especially starting off your life without a mother."

"I guess I deserved that," Peggy admitted. "But it's hard not to resent a baby that's normal, when you have one who isn't."

"But Dale will be—when Dr. Dalton straightens out his heart."

"*If* Dr. Dalton straightens out his heart. And right now it doesn't seem very likely that he will."

"There are other cardiovascular surgeons—Mike Raburn, for example."

"I know," said Peggy. "When Dale's father was killed in Vietnam, I felt like my own world had come to an end, but I had to go on. When Dale was born and Dr. Rebecca told me he was a Fallot, I even prayed for a while that he would die—"

"Aren't you glad he didn't?"

Peggy nodded. "I guess I'm just tired and depressed. I was busy the two years it took to get my physician's assistant degree. And after that we had a lot of excitement in the lab working on the artificial heart and hoping we could get one going in time to save some of the transplant cases. I didn't have time to feel sorry for myself, but when Dr. Ken and Dr. Rebecca separated, the artificial heart project fell apart, too."

"Dale's still all right, isn't he?"

"As near all right as anybody can be when three fourths of his circulating blood by-passes the lungs, leaving him with barely enough oxygen to get along. Every time I see him squatting to get his breath, I say a prayer that he can keep going until he's eight or so and ready for open heart surgery."

The door of the treatment room opened and Gus Henderson came in.

"Hi, Peg," he said, reaching for cap and mask before starting to scrub at a sink in the corner of the room. "Got the new gold-tipped electrode?"

"It's on the tray, Dr. Henderson." The diminutive technician removed the sterile cover from the tray on top of the cart. "I think I have everything you'll need."

"You always do," said the pediatrician cheerfully. "If I could depend on everybody around here the way I can on you and Miss Sundberg, things would always go smoothly."

"My, aren't we happy today," said Helga. "Love must be wonderful."

"It is. You ought to try it sometime."

"I just might do that," said the ICU nurse.

Lifting the baby from the bassinet, and carrying the rubber tube connecting the mask to the hospital oxygen supply, Helga placed the squirming newborn on the small treatment table in the center of the room, beneath a powerful droplight. Working swiftly and expertly, she strapped the mask in place with a web strap around the head, then wrapped the baby's body below the navel—where the umbilical stump had been clamped by Ken Dalton and covered with a sterile dressing—in a blanket. Moving to the upper half of the small patient, she seated herself on a stool at the head of the table and, sliding her arms down along the baby's sides, took a tiny hand in each of hers and pinned the small torso to the table expertly with a steady pressure.

Gus Henderson had finished scrubbing meanwhile and had put on a sterile gown and gloves. Moving up to the table, he watched as Peggy Tyndall removed the dressing that had covered the navel and the forceps preventing any backflow of blood. After painting the instrument and the skin around the navel with a clear antiseptic, he draped the area with a small windowed sheet. Peggy meanwhile had picked up a pair of sterile ring forceps from a jar almost filled with antiseptic on the reserve table nearby and stood ready to hand him without contamination anything he needed.

Working carefully, Gus removed the hemostatic forceps that had closed off the umbilical cord. The gelatinous strand containing the umbilical artery and vein had functioned as a life channel during the months the baby had been inside its mother's body, receiving oxygen and food through the cord by way of the placenta, plus the sinister gift of heroin, and ridding itself of the waste products of life by the same route. The constant tremor of the baby's muscles, part of the heroin withdrawal pattern, made handling the three-inch umbilical stump a delicate task, even for Gus Henderson's skilled hands.

"We'll put a number 5F catheter into the umbilical artery first," he said.

"You've always used the vein before." Helga was watching closely and trying at the same time to hold the small writhing body as still as possible.

"The gold electrode goes through the 5F," Gus explained. "That way, it can be put directly into the aorta where it can measure the oxygen tension in the main stream of the circulation."

While he was speaking, Gus had been carefully threading the polyethylene catheter into the tiny artery, hardly larger than a matchstick.

"That should do it," he said on a note of considerable satisfaction, when about six inches of the small tube had entered the artery.

Picking up a syringe with a blunt metal tip from the tray, he injected clear saline through the catheter and was rewarded by a few drops of rather dark blood from the open end, when he removed the syringe. From the tray, Peggy used the ring forceps to hand him the electrode. Smaller than the 5F catheter, it was also sheathed in polyethylene, but enlarged at the tip, which shone through the plastic covering with a distinctly golden tint.

"Measuring oxygen tension is simple, if this gadget works the way the journal report I read described it." Gus started to thread the gold-tipped end of the electrode into the hollow interior of the 5F catheter he had already inserted. "Once inside the aorta with arterial blood flowing around it, the electrode will give an immediate reading of the blood oxygen tension on a continuous strip recorder. That way we can tell whether the baby is getting too little or too much."

"Too much?" Peggy frowned. "Is that possible?"

"Very much so," said Gus. "We used to give preemies all the oxygen their blood could absorb, but we know now that a lot of them became blind later because of it."

The electrode had been disappearing into the open end of the umbilical artery catheter while they were talking. Now he ceased threading it in and made the necessary connections to the meter whose readings would be faithfully portrayed on the strip recorder. Immediately, the meter began to register the oxygen tension in Baby Hornsby's blood in millimeters of mercury.

"Fifty!" Gus Henderson's tone was grave. "Looks like we didn't get the electrode in a minute too soon."

Without taking off his gloves, the pediatrician moved to the oxygen control valve and adjusted the flow of the vital gas through its bubble bottle meter to the highest level. Immediately the oxygen tension recorded by the electrode deep inside the small body began to rise. But just then the baby grunted, as if it were having difficulty getting the gas into its lungs, and the tension level dived dramatically, to return quickly when the odd sound could no longer be heard.

"Looks like we're in for a rocky time," said Gus soberly.

"I'd better connect the other sensors," said Helga.

"I asked Dr. McHale to come down as soon as soon as he's free. While we're waiting, I'll start an IV."

Her work finished, Peggy Tyndall left the treatment room with her cart. And by the time Dr. Angus McHale, professor of pediatrics, came into the room with its two rows of four special bassinets arranged against the walls, a constant stream of information was being displayed on the battery of monitors above Baby Hornsby's crib as well as upon the master screen at the nursing station outside, easily visible through the glass half walls of the ward. In addition to the vital oxygen tension pattern revealed on the strip recorder, other sensors reported hydrogen-ion concentration, pulse, respiration, ECG, arterial and venous pressure.

"I've just finished inserting one of those new electronic sensors into the umbilical artery, sir," said Gus. "It appears to be working very well."

The older doctor came over to the bassinet and studied the pattern being printed out on the strip recorder. "I wonder how we ever got along before these gadgets were invented and we had to make it with only our five senses to guide us—"

"Plus the sixth sense every good doctor has to develop," said Gus.

"Of course." The relationship between the tall pediatric resident and the professor was without the tension so many older doctors seemed to feel in the presence of younger ones obviously destined for greatness because of superior ability. As the author of one of the most widely used pediatric textbooks in the world, Dr. McHale's position was secure.

"Being premature is hard enough on a newborn," said the professor, "without adding narcotic addiction to it."

"And maybe HMD into the bargain, judging from the sound of its breathing and that low pO_2," said Gus.

Hyaline membrane disease—identified by the cryptic initials HMD—was a killer that annually destroyed some twenty-five thousand newborns in the United States alone, including a son of a former President some years earlier. The combined product of infant lungs failing to expand fully after being thrust prematurely into an alien world, plus the formation within those air sacs of a proteinlike layer of material that seemed to act as a physical barrier, keeping oxygen from reaching the bloodstream and subsequently the body tissues, HMD was the most serious threat to life in these very small patients.

"How much did this fellow weigh?" Dr. McHale asked.

"Three and a half pounds, sir," said Helga.

"We figure it's maybe four weeks from term," Gus added.

"In that case, it may make it. I just saw some interesting figures from New York on the birth rate of these heroin babies—five hundred of them there last year."

"Too many of them die," Gus agreed. "But even so, the mortality has dropped off sharply from thirty-five per cent or more several years ago. Fortunately this one's not having convulsions like some of them do."

"I understand the mother lived only a little while after she reached the Emergency Room," said the older doctor.

"It's questionable whether she was really alive," said Helga. "If Dr. Dalton hadn't been where he could answer the CODE FIVE immediately, this little man would be down in the morgue too."

"I wonder if Baby Hornsby will ever thank Dr. Dalton for it," said McHale.

The baby sneezed and the small blinking light on the monitor marking the respiratory rate suddenly quickened for a dozen or more breaths and the pO_2 level sagged sharply before settling down. About the same time, the rapidly moving line on the monitor screen marking changes in heart function by way of the ECG suddenly skittered almost off the screen.

"Put an extra dose of chlorpromazine into the IV, Miss Sundberg." Gus Henderson spoke quickly. "This could be the beginning of a convulsive state."

As the nurse moved to a cabinet in the corner of the room and took a glass syringe from it, the tall young pediatrician turned to his chief.

"I think we should intubate and put the baby on CPAP before it gets beyond help, sir."

"It's the quickest way to get oxygen into the body," the older man agreed. "That should lessen the withdrawal symptoms, too."

To the uninitiated, the hospital jargon of diseases and procedures labeled by initials would have seemed as untranslatable as Egyptian temple and pyramid hieroglyphics had appeared to archaeologists prior to the discovery of the Rosetta Stone. But to those in the room, CPAP meant Continuous

Positive Airway Pressure, a method of artificial respiration almost as new as last week's *Journal* of the American Medical Association.

Devised by the director of a pediatric intensive care unit in San Francisco only a few years earlier, CPAP was a method of keeping the lungs inflated between respirations in babies whose breathing mechanism was crippled by hyaline membrane disease. Keeping the air sacs inflated with oxygen and simultaneously removing most of the waste carbon dioxide allowed the greatest possible amount of lung surface to be exposed to the maximum concentration of breathable oxygen, a vital factor in saving these often otherwise doomed newborns.

Gus Henderson's first act in initiating the somewhat difficult procedure was to put in a call for the chief anesthetist, Dr. Valerie LeMoyne. She arrived a few minutes later, carrying a case containing the tools needed for the difficult job of inserting a tube into the tiny trachea, or windpipe.

"Not another cold turkey, Gus," she said. "Getting a tube into a trachea the size of a pencil is hard enough without all that twitching."

"If I could put a gold electrode into the umbilical artery, you can do this," Gus assured her. "And Baby Hornsby needs it badly."

"We'll give it the old college try," said the anesthetist. "Can you bring the baby's head to the end of the table, Miss Sundberg?"

"Certainly, Doctor." Helga loosened the oxygen mask and removed it. Then, exchanging her position at the head of the table for one at the side, she slid the tiny body, still wrapped in blankets, along the table until the anesthesiologist could draw its head off the end into the best possible position for the extremely delicate procedure. Opening the instrument case, Valerie LeMoyne took out the smallest laryngoscope it contained and checked the battery current to the tiny bulb at its very end that produced the light necessary for visualizing the larynx.

"Watch those parameters, Gus," said the anesthesiologist. "We may be in for a few bad moments while I'm getting a tube through the larynx. And hold the baby steady, Miss Sundberg."

Expertly Val slid the laryngoscope across Baby Hornsby's tongue past the soft palate. When she pulled the handle downward the entire area could be visualized through the metal barrel of the scope. Illuminated brightly by the rice-sized bulb at the far end, the tiny larynx came into full view, with the vocal cords separating as the baby tried to cry.

"Talk about a camel going through the eye of a needle," said Gus as Val reached for the small rubber tube to insert into the windpipe. "After one of these jobs I can almost believe it."

"How about the readings, Gus?" Val asked.

"Everything's skittering all over the place, but we expected that."

With a quick, skillful movement, the anesthesiologist slid the rubber tube through the laryngoscope into the opening between the vocal cords, past them through the larynx and into the trachea. Then, steadying the tube, she removed the metal barrel of the laryngoscope through which she had inserted it.

"Neat! Like always!" said Gus admiringly.

"That was the slickest intubation I ever saw, Dr. LeMoyne," Helga echoed.

It took about fifteen minutes to move Baby Hornsby back to the NICU ward and reconnect the sensors that fed vital information to the monitoring screens and meters at the main control station. When he finished adjusting the somewhat complicated pressure apparatus that controlled CPAP, Gus Henderson stopped in the small doctors' office adjoining the main nursing station to dictate a summary of what had been done for insertion into Baby Hornsby's record.

"Did you know Mike Raburn's been singing your praises all over the place?" he asked when he finished dictating.

Helga looked up quickly from the medication chart upon which she had been noting the orders he'd left for the small patient. "What about?"

"He seems to think you saved a child's life in the ER this afternoon."

"I guess I did. She had stopped breathing."

"Mike doesn't hand out compliments that aren't deserved."

Helga laughed. "At least he noticed me."

"He'd have to be blind not to. And Mike's not blind."

"Did he tell you I almost passed out on him?"

"No, and I don't believe it either. For my money, you're unflappable."

"The Unflappable Helga Sundberg. Somehow the title doesn't appeal to me."

"It must have to Mike. I've never heard him rave over any woman before."

Gus left the ward but Helga remained where she was, staring at the master screen of the monitor before her and seeing the face of Mike Raburn when he'd said, "It looks like we'll just have to organize a mutual admiration society—and come to think of it, that's not a bad idea."

And the more she thought of it, the more it appealed to Helga too.

II

Mike Raburn pushed the special stretcher upon which Joey Gates lay, conscious and bright-eyed with interest in the complicated control panel, out of the hyperbaric chamber—to be greeted with popping flash bulbs and TV cameras.

"What the hell's going on?" he demanded, half blinded by the lights.

"You're a hero," said Gus Henderson. "I've been telling the press how you saved Joey's life by putting him in the chamber."

"And going in with him. That took courage, Dr. Raburn." Mike recognized the decorative woman reporter from the local CBS outlet, Marcia Weston, when she shoved a hand microphone in front of him.

"About as much as scuba diving in the Keys, Miss Weston. I still don't know what this is all about."

"You saved Joey, Doctor." Someone had pushed Rachel Gates from the crowd to stand beside him. "Big Joe and I won't ever forget it."

"Do you mind telling us just how this new treatment works, Dr. Raburn?" Marcia Weston asked.

"Joey here was in a sickle cell crisis, which means his red blood cells had become crescent-shaped instead of looking like biscuits. We think sickling is related to the shape of a hemoglobin-S molecule in the cells themselves, and once they've sickled, they tend to get hung up on each other. Eventually the piled-up abnormal cells block small blood vessels and interfere with the absorption of oxygen in the body."

"Endangering his life?" Marcia Weston asked.

"In time. Joey's cells weren't carrying enough oxygen, so we let him breathe it under pressure in the hyperbaric chamber to increase the degree of oxygen saturation in his blood. It's really just an emergency measure, though; the real treatment is being given by fluid from that intravenous flask you see hanging beside the stretcher."

"What's that—a new medicine?"

"A new use for something the body manufactures all the time—urea. We don't fully understand the process involved yet but injection of large amounts of a urea solution seems to change the shape of most of the sickled red blood cells back to normal so they no longer get hung up on each other. Adding a cyanate compound appears to help even more."

"Cyanate?" The woman reporter frowned. "Isn't that poisonous?"

"What you're probably thinking of is cyanide, a deadly poison, but this is a somewhat different compound. The important thing is that cyanate plus urea—or maybe just cyanate alone, we don't know yet—not only seems to reverse the sickling but, when given in small doses continuously, may keep these crises from occurring at all."

"Then they're actually a cure?"

"To cure means getting rid of the disease, Miss Weston. Keeping up a maintenance dose of the drugs merely cuts down sharply the likelihood of further crises like the one Joey had this afternoon."

"One other question, Doctor," said a reporter at the back of the small crowd. "Isn't sickle cell anemia inherited?"

"The tendency toward sickling of red blood cells under certain circumstances seems to be in the group of inherited conditions," said Mike. "Along with blue eyes, webbed toes, a high-bridged nose—and the Mongolian spot."

"What's that?" the TV reporter asked.

"We Americans have a diverse ancestry and occasionally a remnant of it pops up in what you might call a wild gene. When the Mongols invaded Hungary and Austria in the thirteenth century, they apparently exercised a conqueror's right upon at least some of the female population—with or without their active co-operation. As a result, a few Mongolian genes were left behind and one of them crops up every now and then in the form of a pigmented area at the lower end of the spine—"

"You're pulling my leg," Marcia Weston protested.

"The idea is attractive, Miss Weston," Mike said with a grin. "But the Mongolian spot is a true genetic oddity. You'll find it in any good text on heredity."

Marcia Weston smiled warmly. "I wouldn't think of arguing with a Harvard All-American, Dr. Raburn."

III

As the rest of the press contingent was leaving the Hyperbaric Laboratory, the woman TV reporter stayed behind.

"I occasionally do mood pieces for the Sunday magazine section besides my TV work," she told Mike. "You know, sketches and impressions."

"I've read some of your pieces, they're very good."

"Thank you. I've been planning one on the role of women in a busy medical center."

"Sort of a *Women in White*, like the old Sidney Kingsley play?"

"Something like that, but right now I'm more interested in you." She smiled, a bit archly. "As the subject of a profile, of course."

"Women still run the show around here. We men are only puppets."

"That was to be the tone of my piece but, after meeting you, I'm not so sure. Anyway, how about sitting for my tape recorder sometime?"

"It's okay with me," said Mike. "But you'll have to clear it with Administration."

"Dr. Toler's office called and told us you were taking a desperate measure to save Big Joe Gates's son."

"Are you sure?"

"Absolutely. They even told us to get here on the double, if we wanted to photograph you bringing Joey out of the hyperbaric chamber."

Gus Henderson had been walking ahead of them; now he dropped back to say: "The staff also got word straight from the top to co-operate in every way with the press, Mike."

"I wonder why?"

"After that blast by Ross McKenzie to the Rotary Club at noon today about the hospital budget, maybe Dr. Toler has decided to strike back," Marcia Weston suggested. "Big Joe Gates is a name to conjure with in Miami and the black vote is getting larger all the time."

"Toler's smarter than I realized, when it comes to publicity," said Mike.

"Does that mean I can tag along sometimes?" Marcia Weston asked.

"You should have been here an hour earlier," Gus Henderson told her. "Dr. Kenneth Dalton had to do an emergency Caesarean on a woman who was practically dead from an overdose of heroin, to save the child."

"Did he—save it, I mean?"

"Yes. I've got the baby on CPAP." When the reporter looked blank, he added, "Continuous Positive Airway Pressure. It's a new way of treating hyaline membrane disease."

"Didn't that kill the Kennedy baby?"

"That was years ago. We know a lot more about treating it now."

"Could I see this baby?" Marcia Weston asked eagerly.

"Why not?" said Gus. "Dr. Toler seems to have given the press carte blanche and the ICU is just off this corridor."

"I'd like to see the baby myself, since it was delivered in my department," said Mike.

Helga Sundberg joined them when they came into the main ICU and Gus introduced the two women. "Could Miss Weston see Baby Hornsby?" he said.

"Of course," said Helga. "Mrs. Alvarez is specialing the case."

"Are you in charge of the ICU, Miss Sundberg?" Marcia Weston asked.

"I'm the three-to-eleven nursing supervisor."

"And also a heroine in her own right," said Mike.

"So?" Marcia Weston was interested immediately.

"She saved a little girl from asphyxiation this afternoon," he explained, "using a method we'd never used here before."

"But which Dr. Raburn had described so well in class that I could hardly have failed. He's a wonderful teacher." There was a faintly mocking note in Helga's voice and the willowy TV reporter recognized it.

"You'll have to tell me more about that, when we have our interview, Dr. Raburn," she said. "Sounds interesting."

Mike grinned as Helga's eyebrows shot up. "I'll be happy to tell you the whole story," he said. "Then I'm sure you'll want to go on with your piece on women in white."

"If very many of them are as stunning as Miss Sundberg, I'm sure I will," said the reporter. "I didn't know doctors got to work in such pleasant surroundings—except on television programs."

They were at the door of the NICU and Helga opened it for them to enter the small utility nook where gowns and masks were kept, then followed them in. She helped Marcia Weston put on the required coverings and stood in the doorway, as the three of them moved across the eight-bassinet ward to the newborn resuscitator, where a plump nurse with dark skin and hair was watching the latest addition to the nursery.

"Cold turkey is hard enough to take when you're seeing it for the first time—and CPAP is worse," said Mike. "If you feel like passing out, slump my way, Miss Weston. Dr. Henderson is already spoken for, I'm not."

"Do they all look like this?" she asked. "I mean more like a rat than a human?"

"Most overdose cases do," said Gus. "HMDs usually have a peculiar grunting respiration, too, that's almost diagnostic. But with an intubation tube already in its trachea—windpipe to you, Miss Weston—this fellow doesn't make much sound."

"But the baby isn't breathing! I can hardly see its chest move."

"That's because the CPAP keeps the lungs inflated most of the time," Gus explained. "The blood oxygen level is registered on that printer you see by the bassinet."

Mike moved nearer to study the pattern being registered on the moving paper strip of the recorder.

"Looks like close to eighty millimeters of mercury," he said. "What did you start with, Gus?"

"Fifty."

"Hmm! Nice work."

"Credit Val LeMoyne."

"Do you mind explaining?" the reporter asked.

"By keeping the lungs inflated all the time, we raise the blood oxygen level and improve the baby's general condition to the point where it can breathe for itself," the pediatrician explained.

"What will happen to this one after it leaves the hospital?"

"On the basis of statistics, it will probably become an addict."

"Surely that isn't hereditary too."

"No, but the Welfare Department is required by law to offer the baby to the mother or to the mother's family. In the average case it's lucky if it isn't taken—"

"Why do you say that?"

"Any child is better off growing up in foster homes or an orphanage than in a family of heroin addicts. Most of the time the mother doesn't want the baby but too often a grandmother or an aunt does take it. In that case it grows up with the same heritage that produced addiction in the mother and winds up addicted early in childhood."

"How terrible!" exclaimed the TV reporter.

"I guess one thing is worse," said Mike. "Being dead."

At the nursing station, Mike stayed behind while Gus Henderson showed Marcia Weston out.

"I asked Miss Payson to tell Miguel Quintera I'd be up to see Carmelita in a little while, but that was an hour ago at least," he said to Helga. "Did adding the top half of the refrigerating blanket have any effect?"

"Her temperature is down a degree."

"The blanket would do that, but at least it will help Miguel's morale a little."

When Mike and the tall blonde nurse entered the cubicle where Carmelita Sanchez lay, her dark hair spread out on the pillow like a fan, Mike put a restraining hand on the shoulder of the slender Cuban as he started to rise from the chair in which he had been sitting beside the narrow hospital bed.

"Don't get up, please, Miguel," he said. "I just stopped by to check on the refrigerating blanket."

"Her temperature has dropped a degree, Dr. Raburn. Couldn't that be a good sign?"

"As long as her body is capable of any physiological response, we can always hope," Mike assured the girl's fiancé.

"You're a surgeon and Carmelita's Dr. Vogel's patient on the medical service," said Helga as they were walking back to the nursing station. "Yet you spend a lot more time with her than he does."

"Ed's not neglecting the girl—"

"I didn't mean that, we both know he's as good in his field as you are in yours. But we know doctors don't like to spend time on hopelessly ill patients either."

"Nobody likes to be reminded of his failures."

"But you keep coming back and I can't help wondering why."

"I notice that you're always kind and considerate to Miguel, even though it must get in your hair to have him always there in the way," he said.

"My answer is simple. If anybody loved me the way Miguel loves Carmelita, I'd want him to be with me when I was dying."

"Even though you didn't know he was there?"

"I'd know," she said confidently. "There's a special sort of ESP connected with that sort of love."

He looked at her in surprise. "That doesn't exactly agree with what you were telling me not much more than an hour ago about your philosophy of love and marriage."

"I was talking about the future—not the past."

"Then you've experienced this sort of ESP?"

"Two years ago—in Brazil." She studied him for a moment, as if searching his mind and his emotions through the steady dark eyes, then nodded, as if she had learned something from them.

"Carolyn and I went to the mission hospital I told you about just after we got our nursing degrees from the University of Florida," she continued. "We were part of a hospital team from the university, but we stayed on awhile after the others came back. The laboratory chief at the hospital was a very attractive man and I guess what you could call a chemistry developed between us from the start."

"Was he from Gainesville too?"

"No. He'd come to Brazil six months before we arrived, from a position as head biochemist for a firm in the Midwest. I learned later that he had absconded with a lot of the firm's money—Brazil has no extradition treaty with the United States, so it's a paradise for absconders." She smiled, albeit a little crookedly. "By that time, I'd gone off the deep end: paroxysmal tachycardia at the sound of his voice, swooning in his embrace—the whole bit."

"Why didn't you marry him?"

"He finally told me he had a wife back home and three kids. Whatever else I may be, I'm no home wrecker, so Carolyn and I took the next Varig flight out of there for Miami—and landed here at Biscayne General."

"No regrets?"

Helga shook her head. "One thing I don't waste time on is regrets. And now that you've heard the story of my love life, Doctor, you can answer my question about why you keep coming back to see Carmelita."

"I guess it's mostly because I hate defeat but, way back somewhere in my mind, I can't help feeling I've overlooked something that still might pull the girl back."

"Time's getting awfully short," she reminded him.

"That's the hell of it. Suppose she dies and the next day, or the next week, I suddenly remember what it was that escapes me at the moment. If that one thing could have saved her, I'm going to feel guilty for her death the rest of my life."

"So you keep torturing yourself by coming back, hoping that seeing her will blast whatever memory you've lost to the surface?"

"Something like that. I know it sounds foolish—"

"It's not foolish. I'd feel exactly the same way under the circumstances."

"Thanks for understanding. I guess we're beginning to develop some of that ESP you were just talking about."

"What about Joey Gates?" Helga changed the subject abruptly. "How much of a chance would he have had of coming through this crisis if you hadn't thought of taking him into the hyperbaric chamber?"

"Who knows?"

"Obviously his prognosis has been increased considerably because you did, so why not chalk that up as your good deed for the present?"

"You know damned well that doctors don't set quotas—and neither do ICU nurses. Besides, Gus ordered the urea and cyanate."

"Isn't there some doubt—about the urea?"

He looked at her quickly. "Why do you ask that?"

"I read the *American Journal of Nursing,* Doctor, the same as you read the *JAMA.*"

"There *is* a question about urea, but cyanate seems to have real promise. And if Joey should go into coma again, I can always take him back into the chamber."

"You never give up, do you?"

"Not until they carry me off the field. By the way, will you leave an order for the lab to do a red cell check on Joey's blood about 7:00 P.M. for abnormal cells." He glanced at his watch as Helga picked up the small portable hand keyboard by which she could communicate with the central data storage computer bank. "Four-thirty already? The Emergency Room will soon start jumping with the five o'clock traffic rush casualties. See you later."

"Can I depend on that?" Helga's voice was mocking as she started pressing the keys of the communications instrument.

Mike grinned. "Unless the computer decides to stun you with an electric shock and gather you into its embrace."

"In that case," said Helga, "be sure to hurry to my rescue—so I can slump your way."

CHAPTER SIX

I

"Here at Biscayne General we call it the Moriturus Committee for obvious reasons," Father Hagan told Carolyn Payson. "But medical humor is pretty caustic, so the students already have another name for it—the God Committee. And a more appropriate one, I'm sure."

"Why do you say that?"

"According to our belief, only God can give life, so logically only God should decide when to end it."

"But circumstances alter situations, Father."

"And they're considerably different in the medical field than even five years ago," the chaplain conceded. "Every day you and your staff in the Intensive Care Units keep people living who would otherwise be dead. All of which has given rise to a lot of controversy over the technical question of whether a person with no hope of life should be kept alive against his will."

"I don't see how there could be more than one answer."

"Suppose you were old, yet clinging to life, and your relatives should decide you were too much of a burden upon them?"

"I never thought of it that way."

"Few people do," said the chaplain. "None of us like to be reminded of just how mortal we really are, and the idea of accomplishing one's own death, even at the hands of another, smacks too much of suicide."

"But is letting someone else decide when you shall die—and how—really different from suicide?"

"If the dying person makes the final decision, no—but it *is* still legal," said Father Hagan. "The courts have ruled here in Florida that a person may refuse medical treatment and choose death, when life means only pain and suffering."

"That's exactly what my father does when he begs to die."

"Certainly life can hold out no hope—or pleasure—for him," Father Hagan agreed. "But Huntington's disease is often characterized by severe mental symptoms, even psychosis, so a court might rule that he isn't sane enough to make a choice."

"That would be cruel."

"The so-called 'right to die' controversy arose over that very point. The committee makes the decision for patients who are unable to make them for themselves."

"At the request of the relatives?"

"Usually, but first the committee hears competent medical opinion on whether the patient is actually hopelessly incurable. You work every day within the parameters of living and dying, Carolyn, so I'm sure you can appreciate how difficult that sort of decision can sometimes be."

Carolyn nodded. "When heart transplants were first being done, people doomed by chronic heart disease; some of them hardly able to take a deep breath without severe anginal pain from the effort, were suddenly made whole again—as if by a miracle. But then the whole thing blew up when the transplanted hearts started being rejected by the bodies of the people who received them."

"And the career of a very fine surgeon may have been wrecked because he found himself regarded as an executioner when, a few short months before, he'd been hailed everywhere as a savior. If the newspapers were to start mentioning even the existence of a Moriturus Committee at Biscayne General, we soon wouldn't be able to get people to serve."

"In spite of the fact that you're actually being merciful in allowing a hopeless case to die?"

"Who is to say what is hopeless? Dr. Rebecca Dalton told me once that her husband was very near to developing a practical version of the artificial heart, until he started brooding over the number of cases that were dying and stopped his research. Right now I would hesitate to recommend that a patient with advanced heart disease be allowed to die, when tomorrow a mechanical pump may be invented that can take the place of the heart. Such pumps have already worked for months in calves and other animals, you know."

"If you cannot make a decision then, what's the use of having a committee at all?"

"I've asked myself the same question and haven't come up yet with an entirely suitable answer," the chaplain admitted. "But in some degenerative diseases and in many cases of severe brain injury, the patient may be little more than a vegetable, with no hope of improvement."

"You're describing my father exactly." Carolyn put her hand on the old priest's arm in a pleading gesture. "Will you bring his case before the committee, Father Hagan?"

"If you're absolutely certain that is what you want."

"I am," said Carolyn firmly.

"Very well. I'll transmit your request for a hearing to the chairman and you'll be notified when to appear."

"Shall I prepare a plea?"

"We have what you might call a 'devil's advocate'—a lawyer or a doctor—to do that for you."

"What about Dr. Rebecca Dalton, if I can persuade her to plead for me?"

"You couldn't have made a better choice. But let the chairman ask her, it will be best that way."

II

Hospital morgues are generally gloomy places located in the basement of the oldest building connected with the institution. But because Biscayne General was brand new, its basement was brightly lit, well ventilated with year-round air conditioning, and generally cheerful. When Ken Dalton came into Karen Fletcher's office in the Pathology Department at four-thirty, he found her bending over a binocular microscope.

"May I come in?" he asked.

She looked up with a smile. "Of course. You got my message?"

"My secretary said you have information I might want on the Hornsby case."

"I think I have something." Karen's silver-colored hair was gathered into a discreet bun at the back of her neck and she wore flat oxfords, giving her an oddly small and fragile appearance in the freshly starched long laboratory coat she wore.

"I've been running some preliminary tests on the blood of the dead woman in the private laboratory," she added as they moved into the adjoining small room, where a dark liquid was bubbling in a retort. "For heroin or rather morphine, since heroin is changed to that in the body."

"You haven't autopsied her already, have you?"

"Sam Toyota just finished. Anthony Broadhurst called as soon as the hospital notified his office that the mother had died."

"Why would the State's Attorney be interested in a routine OD? Mike Raburn sees them almost every day in the Emergency Room."

"The police have arrested the pimp and pusher she had been living with. He admitted belting her a few times and, if Mr. Broadhurst can prove that the girl actually died from the injuries and not from an overdose of heroin, it will be murder, not just drug peddling." Karen was working expertly while she talked, decanting a small portion of the fluid in the retort from its spout into a test tube.

"What did Sam find?" Ken asked.

"A couple of cracked ribs, but they weren't splintered and there was no air in her chest, so a punctured lung is out. There were plenty of bruises, too, but none of the abdominal organs. With that pregnant uterus sticking out in front of her, it would have been hard for an attacker to rupture a liver, kidney, or spleen the way assassins kill by rupturing the spleens of chronic malaria sufferers in the Far East, unless he knew just where to strike."

Pouring an equal amount of amyl alcohol into the tube, Karen shook it vigorously, then put it into a rack while she fitted a fluted circle of filter paper into a small funnel.

"I'm extracting some of the alkaloid with amyl alcohol, so I can make the final definitive test," she explained.

"The one *you* reported?"

"I didn't know surgeons read laboratory journals." Her tone was warm and, for the first time he could remember, Ken Dalton realized that, beneath the starched white coat and the horn-rimmed glasses, there was a very beautiful and desirable woman.

The knowledge made him feel a little guilty, and he moved a step farther away. Karen didn't miss the unconscious admission, either, and a faint smile appeared on her face as she turned to lift the test tube, with the alkaloid-alcohol mixture, from the rack and pour its contents into the funnel, beneath which she had placed another empty tube.

"I accidentally discovered the short test for morphine while I was still a medical student," she said casually as she removed the tube of filtrate and, picking a bottle from the rack before her, poured a few drops into the brownish solution.

"Fletcher's solution, my sole claim to immortality," she added on a wry note when the mixture in the tube suddenly took on a deep violet tint. "*Voilà*, as Val LeMoyne would say."

"Of course this isn't a quantitative test," she continued, "but if I'd used exact amounts and put that solution into a colorimeter, I'm sure it would register enough heroin to kill her easily."

Ken had turned and was studying her more closely. "Why did you go to all the trouble of telling me this, Karen, when you could have sent a copy of the report to my office tomorrow, or the next day? And it's your afternoon off, too, isn't it?"

"I changed days when Dr. Toler asked me to take Dr. Cooper's place on the Executive Committee this afternoon," she explained. "And I had to do the tests as quickly as possible, so the State's Attorney's office would know whether to arrest the man who beat up the Hornsby girl."

"But you didn't have to go to so much trouble on my account."

"Mrs. Connor brought the body down and told me what happened. I knew you were disturbed—about everything that's happened, Ken, so I thought I could at least assure you that you couldn't have saved the patient."

"The EEG was positive. What if I had concentrated upon resuscitation instead of drama?"

"Could it really have made any difference?"

"Rebecca was there and could easily have slid a catheter-electrode through the mother's external jugular vein into her right atrium while I was doing the Caesarean. We could have stimulated her heart directly."

"Did she suggest it?"

"No," he admitted. "But neither did I."

"The girl died of respiratory paralysis from an overdose of heroin, Ken; I've just proved that to you. So even if you had kept her heart beating artificially long enough to wash some of the heroin out of her system and allow resuscitation, the damage to the brain cells was already irreversible. All you would have produced would have been a human vegetable the county government would have to take care of from now on, at a time when Ross McKenzie and a lot of other people are raising hell about the cost of operating this hospital."

"We still might have saved two lives instead of maybe saving one."

"Did you read the ambulance attendant's report?"

"No."

"They weren't able to get a pulse in the mother for at least five or six minutes before she arrived at the Emergency Room, and after four minutes of anoxia, the brain cells are usually damaged beyond repair. You're not God to decide who's going to live and who's going to die, Ken. You did what you thought was indicated and you saved a life. What else do you want?"

"Maybe you're right," he admitted. "There was a time when I kidded myself for a while that I *was* God—and look how many people I killed while doing it."

"Down here we live with death every day," said Karen with a shrug. "For my own information as a pathologist, I studied all those hearts you took out when you were doing transplants. Not one of them had more than a year or so to live, even as cardiac invalids, and for most of them it couldn't have been more than a few months. You and Rebecca both thought you were doing the best thing for all of them and your operative mortality was the lowest in the country, so you brought them a skill they could never have found anywhere else."

"Except in Houston—or San Francisco."

"Your operative mortality was lower than it would have been in either place."

"They still died," he said doggedly.

"Because their own bodies fought against the healthy hearts you substituted for diseased ones. You didn't kill those patients, Ken; they killed themselves."

"I tried telling myself that, Karen—and it doesn't work."

"For God's sake, why not—when it's the truth?"

"But not the *whole* truth. When the first transplant cases started dying, Rebecca suspected what was happening and warned me, but I had to play my role as the giver of life and keep on operating. After you've been God for a while, it's hard to step down and become an ordinary man again."

"Was Rebecca's warning about rejection the start of the domestic troubles between you?" Karen asked.

"I suppose so; it takes a lot of ego to do any kind of major surgery, particularly on the heart. And it's particularly hard not to resent being shot down by your own wife, especially when you have to stand by helplessly and see people die one by one, after you were warned that it was going to happen and kept on operating."

"Has Rebecca ever thrown it up to you?"

"Reb's not that kind of a wife, but things might have gone better if she had. Then we could have had a shouting match and maybe saved our marriage."

Karen glanced at her watch. "It's almost five. Mind if I go up to the Executive Committee meeting with you?"

"Not at all."

"I know most of the people there will be friendly," she added, "but from what I've heard about Mr. McKenzie's prejudices, he'll probably try to eat me alive."

"Jeffry Toler will protect you," Ken assured her. Then, obeying an impulse he couldn't have explained, but which Karen quite understood, he added, "and so will I."

At the elevator Karen said casually, "Have you seen Dale Tyndall recently?"

"No. Why?"

"He was going to the Dolphin Lounge when I came out of the pool about a half hour ago. Kevin gives him root beer and both of us are pretty sure he's a little more cyanotic and short of breath lately. You may want to suggest that Rebecca check him over soon."

"I'll speak to her about it," Ken promised. "Thanks for bringing it to our attention, Karen. We're very fond of Dale."

"So am I," she said. "I'd hate to see him get into trouble because we didn't watch him closely enough."

III

In the Board Room located on the twelfth floor of the hospital tower, the other members of the Executive Committee of the Board of Directors, governing body of the medical center, were already gathered around a long polished mahogany table when Ken Dalton and Karen Fletcher came in. A coffee urn occupied a small table in the corner, with a stack of insulated paper cups beside it, several of which in various degrees of emptiness were beside the board members.

Outside, visible through a large plate-glass window, was a beautiful scene. Sport-fishing boats plowed the bay southward from the ocean-access small-boat channel at Haulover Island toward their berths along the mainland bay front downtown, while water skiers crisscrossed their wakes. A great white ship was putting out of the new Miami harbor, dredged so the procession of cruise vessels that regularly left for the Caribbean and other ports could berth in the heart of downtown instead of the more utilitarian Port Everglades a few miles to the north between Miami and Fort Lauderdale. The new port of Miami had greatly increased shipping in and out of Miami itself, making it one of the busiest cruise ports in the world.

The chair at the head of the table was occupied by Andrew Graves, a local banker who was chairman of the medical center Board of Directors, functioning essentially as a hospital commission for the county. At Graves's left was Ross McKenzie, veteran county political boss. One of Miami's wealthiest citizens, McKenzie owned extensive groves, as well as a large packing house in the surrounding county area. He had been a long-time member of the governing County Commission and chairman of the Commission Finance Committee.

The chair to the right of Andrew Graves belonged to Jeffry Toler, chief administrative officer of the center, his deceptively guileless blue eyes behind steel-rimmed glasses masking a brain that operated like the central computer in the basement of the hospital tower. At his elbow was the secretary of the Board, Helen Gaynor, with a stenotype machine before her, ready to record the business transacted by the governmental unit supervising the vast medical center.

The medical staff of the hospital and faculty were well represented. Dr. Manning Desmond, a florid and rather pompous physician, was professor of medicine in the medical school. Ken Dalton represented surgery. Dr. Adrian Cooper, whose place Karen Fletcher was taking that afternoon, had been, in his capacity as county medical examiner, something of a liaison between the hospital-medical school complex, the county government, and the myriad conglomeration of municipalities that made up the metropolis that was Miami.

Karen looked deceptively small and defenseless when she occupied Dr. Cooper's chair as the at-large member of the small group making up the Executive Committee of the considerably larger Board, now in recess during the hot summer months. Jeffry Toler introduced her to Ross McKenzie, who grudgingly acknowledged her presence with a grunt. And when Andrew Graves whacked the gavel beside him on a polished wooden block, silence fell over the room.

"The June meeting of the Executive Committee, substituting for the

Board of Directors, is called to order," he said. "All of you received a Xerox copy of the minutes of last month's meeting. If there are no corrections, I declare them approved as recorded. Mr. McKenzie has asked to be heard first." He turned to the grower. "The floor is yours, Ross."

Ross McKenzie was a sturdy man of sixty-five, with the dour expression of his Scots ancestry as much in evidence as the burr he'd retained, even though brought to the United States when he was only ten. He looked around the table as if daring the others to dispute his right to speak first.

"Gentlemen," he said, ignoring Karen's presence, "I am sure you know that, judging from the budget you have submitted to the commission for the fiscal year starting July 1, this hospital is approaching a severe financial crisis."

"Show me one that isn't," said Manning Desmond. "With labor costs skyrocketing since the Civil Service Commission allowed hospital employees to be unionized and Congress raised the minimum wage, how could the situation be otherwise?"

"That's not the point, Doctor," said McKenzie. "All of you know I was against building this medical center in the first place. Now that it has turned out to be the white elephant I warned you it would be, don't expect the city government to bail you out."

"Would you rather have a cockroach-infested medical slum, Mr. McKenzie?" Jeffry Toler demanded bluntly.

"My daughter was born in an old hospital and both she and my wife got along all right."

"Twenty years ago all you needed for an obstetric department was a delivery room, a dozen bassinets, and beds for the mothers," said Toler. "The whole thing cost maybe twenty dollars per patient day then but at this moment it's costing over a hundred dollars a day to keep one premature alive in the Pediatric Intensive Care Unit, after Dr. Dalton managed to get it out of the mother's body before it died too."

"Maybe it isn't worth the trouble," McKenzie growled.

"Which would you rather see, Ross?" Andrew Graves asked. "A few dollars saved or babies lost that could have lived? I dare say you'd sing a different tune if your daughter and your grandchild were involved."

"What did the mother die of?" McKenzie asked.

"An overdose of heroin," said Ken.

"Just as I thought," said the politician. "Saving people who will only wind up costing the county thousands of dollars in welfare payments is a waste of time and money."

"Doctors don't equate human lives with dollars," Karen said quietly, and Ross McKenzie looked startled, then shook his head, as he might have done at a vagrant gnat, and continued his diatribe.

"From the looks of this room, none of you have any idea what a dollar is worth—spending a hundred thousand dollars so the doctors who use it can look out over the bay? And that Intensive Care Unit you've got down on the first floor, the equipment alone cost nearly a million dollars."

"Concentrating all emergency and intensive care functions in one area not only makes a lot of sense, Mr. McKenzie, it has also made Biscayne General the most modern hospital in the world," said Ken. "Most hospitals have small intensive care units scattered all over the place, all needing specialized personnel and very expensive instrumentation. By putting everything having to do with intensive care on one floor, we enable personnel to be shifted to fit the greatest need and avoid duplication of monitors and other electronic equipment. And by having highly trained people only seconds away in the Emergency Department, less time is lost when treating life or death situations."

"Why does Biscayne General have to get so many emergency cases, Doctor? They never have paid their way and never will."

"We built this center where it is because it can be reached in minutes by expressways," said Andrew Graves. "One of the attractions this area has for older people is immediate access to expert medical care, and a lot of the older bay-front hotels over on the beach side are full of them, sitting in the sun and waiting to die—"

"What the hell has that got to do with waste in this hospital?" McKenzie demanded acidly.

"If people in those retirement hotels just dropped dead when their time came, it wouldn't be necessary to have a hospital to look after them that's operating in the red—and our students would lose one of the best sources we have for clinical material," Ken interposed. "But old people don't oblige the city fathers by dying that easy, Mr. McKenzie. They have strokes, heart attacks, inflamed gall bladders, and enlarged prostates. Even with Medicare most of them don't have the financial resources to stand a long siege of illness, so it's up to the local government to provide it for them the same way we provide the whole cost to welfare recipients and also make that care easy to reach from all parts of the county."

"Give me one good reason why taxpayers who don't use charity have to provide for those who do?" Ross McKenzie growled.

"I can give you more than one reason, Ross," said Andrew Graves. "When the occupancy rate in Miami area hotels started falling off because tourists would rather go to gambling casinos in the Bahamas or the Caribbean to say nothing of Disney World and all those amusement complexes being built in Central Florida—the municipal governments in the county were all for turning those hotels into retirement homes and luring old people down here."

"And what can you give them besides the climate that they couldn't have gotten in their home states—without putting a burden on Florida taxpayers?"

"For one thing, we have one of the finest geriatric research programs in the country—financed by the federal government," said Ken. "One of our Surgical Fellows, Dr. Michael Raburn, has been treating a group of older people suffering from a general decline of all body functions because of age and arteriosclerosis until they're almost vegetables with oxygen under pressure in the hyperbaric chamber."

"Another million dollars wasted," McKenzie observed.

"The Navy gave us the chamber and also subsidizes its operation," said Jeffry Toler. "You can't charge that to the taxpayers of the county."

"It all comes out of the same pocket," said McKenzie. "Go on, Doctor."

"As I was saying, Dr. Raburn exposes the patients to the highest pressure of oxygen they can stand without convulsions."

"Experimenting, Doctor?"

"Yes, but for their own good. Men and women who shuffle into the chamber like zombies, rarely speaking or showing interest in anything and having to be fed like babies, walk out seemingly rejuvenated, reasonably alert, and even able to communicate and look after themselves. What is more, the effects aren't just temporary but sometimes last for weeks. And when they do start to wear off, another hyperbaric treatment produces a repeat effect."

"Better not force us to discontinue that program, Ross," said Andrew Graves dryly. "We both may be needing it one of these days."

"Speak for yourself," said McKenzie. "I must say I'm pleased to see that one department, at least, is doing something to keep the old and arteriosclerotic alive, Dr. Dalton. You've certainly done your share personally to reduce hospital overcrowding by senior citizens."

The politician's acid comment was like a stiletto thrust in the body; Ken Dalton stiffened and turned white while Karen Fletcher gasped at the bald implication of McKenzie's cutting words. But nobody spoke as Ken rose to his feet, his chair tumbling backward at the sudden movement. Nor did anyone make a move to stop him when he left the room, walking like a man in a trance.

"Well, Ross." Andrew Graves broke the tense silence as the door closed behind the surgeon's back. "With apologies to Dr. Fletcher, I must say that you have just qualified for the title of All-American son of a bitch. Congratulations!"

"I only spoke the truth and everybody knows it." McKenzie showed no sign of either sorrow or resentment. "Dalton's killed so many people that, if they were all women, he could be called a modern Bluebeard."

"Dr. Kenneth Dalton is one of the truly great surgeons this country has produced in modern times," said Jeffry Toler. "I shall make it a point to apologize to him as soon as this meeting is over."

"You won't be apologizing for me," said McKenzie. "If he wasn't guilty, why did he turn tail and run?"

"Probably to keep from killing you," Dr. Desmond observed dryly. "It's a good thing I wasn't in his place. I'm nearer your age, McKenzie, and I certainly would have given myself the satisfaction of slugging you."

"All right, gentlemen," said the politician. "I came here to listen to some concrete proposals for handling the financial crisis this hospital faces—and so far I haven't heard any."

"We gave you our budget for the fiscal year starting in July," Graves reminded him. "What are your suggestions?"

"Cut your operating costs in half by not admitting any non-paying patients except life or death emergencies. And stop teaching a lot of young punks to be specialists, so they can get rich instead of settling in small towns and practicing the sort of medicine that's needed there."

"That makes about as much sense as cutting off your head to spite your face," Andrew Graves snapped. "If you politicians can't come up with a better solution to medical care costs than that, the full medical center Board of Directors will have to request that a referendum be put on the ballot this fall. We'll let the people decide whether they want Biscayne General to stay open and make up our deficits out of tax dollars, or close it and let a lot of people die because they can't get medical care."

"I guess you know what the answer of the voters will be to that question, Mr. McKenzie," said Manning Desmond. "People are proud of this medical center and what it means to the community as a whole. Well over half of our patients are old enough to vote and the rest have parents."

"Is that a threat, Doctor?" McKenzie inquired in a tone of contempt he might have used toward a yapping poodle. "Or a bluff?"

The older doctor shrugged. "Take it whatever way you prefer. But if we're forced to cut down our teaching functions by lack of patients and funds, we'll lose thousands of dollars in research money from government grants."

"Maybe the public would be better off without what you call research," said McKenzie. "I understand that Dr. Dalton learned to transplant hearts by operating on dogs. And I don't have to remind you that at least fourteen people would be alive today, if he hadn't learned so much."

"The patients Dr. Dalton operated on had only a few months or a year at most to live," said Karen Fletcher. "In fact several of them had been a burden on the city for years because of severe heart disease."

"And in the course of performing heart transplants," Toler added, "Dr.

Dalton and Dr. LeMoyne were able to work out some important advances in anesthesia for open heart surgery and heart-lung pump operation that will help save many children otherwise doomed by congenital heart disease, as well as older people who will need artificial heart valves and the like."

"Both of the Daltons have learned a lot from studying the problem of organ rejection that will make kidney and other organ transplants more successful," said Karen.

"I'm not here to argue medical questions with doctors; you're supposed to know what you're doing in that field, at least," McKenzie snapped. "I'm just warning you that the Finance Committee will okay the same budget you had this year and not a cent more."

"But you know it takes considerably more to operate this hospital than it did the old one," Jeffry Toler protested.

"You wanted this white elephant and you've got it, Dr. Toler. We aren't going to give you any more money to run it than you had for the old plant, so if you find yourself short before the end of the fiscal year, you'd better buy some padlocks before you run out of money, so you can lock up the place."

"But—"

"What's the next order of business, Andrew?" said McKenzie. "I can't stay here all night."

Andrew Graves looked down at the agenda before him. "The only other item of importance is to approve the retirement of Dr. Jake Barrows for disability—"

"What's wrong with him?"

"Dr. Barrows suffered a severe coronary thrombosis recently," said Manning Desmond. "He has continued to have attacks of angina and in our opinion can no longer function efficiently as chief of the Cardiology Section. I have recommended that Dr. Rebecca Dalton take his place as section chief, with elevation to the rank of full professor."

"Kenneth Dalton's wife?" McKenzie's tone suggested that he couldn't believe what he was hearing.

"Yes."

"How old is she?"

"Thirty-two, I believe."

"You mean you're willing to make a woman that young head of the most important section of the hospital?"

"The medical faculty is willing," said Manning Desmond.

"What is it you object to, Mr. McKenzie?" Karen Fletcher's tone was deceptively mild. "Her age—or the fact that she's a woman?"

"Both. Plus the fact that she's Dr. Kenneth Dalton's wife." He wheeled upon Manning Desmond. "Didn't she help decide whether those transplant cases would be operated on?"

"Yes."

"For God's sake what are you trying to do? First you want to promote a woman to a man's job, and then you admit that she's incompetent."

"I have personally examined the hearts that were removed before the new ones were put in, Mr. McKenzie," said Karen. "They were all badly diseased and none of those patients could have lived much longer than six months—if that long."

"And now they're all dead?"

"All but one."

"Your prejudices are well known, Ross," said Andrew Graves severely. "If you would spend a few days observing the work of this hospital closely instead of criticizing it all the time because you didn't want us to build it, you'd know that Dr. Rebecca Dalton is one of the foremost heart specialists in the country."

"While you're airing your prejudices, Mr. McKenzie," said Karen, "I think you ought to know that my assistant, Dr. Sam Toyota, is a Japanese."

"And the chief technician in the Nephrosis Research Laboratory is a Negro, Ross," said Andrew Graves. "I know because he does tests on my grandson."

"You can run a melting pot and a women's lib movement in your school if you want to." McKenzie was closing his briefcase. "But just don't ask me to wheedle any more tax dollars out of the budget than I've told you the commission will give you. Vote me 'No!' on Dr. Dalton's promotion, Andrew. I have another appointment this evening and I'm not going to waste time arguing with you."

Before anyone could protest—and no one made a move to—he stalked from the room.

"Well, that's that," said Andrew Graves. "I guess we have only one choice. I'll initiate a petition tomorrow, asking for medical center financing to be put under a special millage and out of Ross McKenzie's hands."

"The county machine can deliver a lot of votes," said Manning Desmond doubtfully. "And all will be against the proposition."

"We'll just have to deliver more," said Dr. Toler.

"How, Jeffry?"

"Mike Raburn saved the life of Big Joe Gates's little boy this afternoon. The whole thing will be on the six o'clock TV news, as well as in the papers tomorrow."

"And Big Joe is the star black forward of the Miami Snappers." Andrew Graves whistled softly. "Elections have been won with less."

CHAPTER SEVEN

I

"You look tired, darling." Carolyn Payson and Gus Henderson had finished dinner and were sitting at a small table in one corner of the half-empty hospital cafeteria.

"It's been one of those days," said the pediatrician wearily. "Did you see Mike Raburn on the six o'clock news—with Joe Gates's boy?"

"It was on the color TV in the waiting room when I came through. But why Mike instead of you? A sickle cell crisis is a pediatric condition."

"Mike's had more experience than anybody else here with the hyperbaric chamber. Besides, it was his idea to use it and I've got everything I want, except you."

"I thought you'd already had all of me. Or is this some new technique you've learned from Ed Vogel?"

"I'm talking about marriage, darling. The first of July I'll become an assistant professor of pediatrics, with a chance to get in on the income from the Private Diagnostic Clinic. I can pay off everything I owe in my education in a few months and we can start in the black. You won't even have to work—"

"I'd want to."

"Then why don't we get married tomorrow?"

"I couldn't saddle anyone with the burden of my father, Gus. Caring for him since he's been here has already used up almost all the money he has, and I've been putting away everything I can against the time when I'll have to start paying it myself."

"I just finished telling you I'll be in the black soon after the first of July. And my credit's good right now."

"I couldn't let you do that. It wouldn't be fair."

"Not if I'm willing?"

"I'd still feel guilty. Why can't we go on like we have been?"

"That isn't fair to you."

"Have I ever complained?" Carolyn asked.

"No, but—"

"It's settled then."

"I ought to warn you that after July 1 I'll be free almost every night."

"And I'll still get off duty at three o'clock every afternoon," she reminded him with a smile. "In plenty of time to cook your dinner."

Gus glanced at his watch, then reached for the trays they had pushed to one side of the table when they finished eating. "I'd better make rounds—"

"Wait a minute, darling. I want to ask you something."

"Fire away."

"What do you know about the Moriturus Committee?"

"The what?" Then his face suddenly cleared. "You mean the God Committee."

"It's called that too, I believe."

"Don't do it, Carolyn." Gus's face was etched with concern as he reached across the table and covered her hand with his own.

"How do you know . . ."

"You could have only one reason to ask about that committee—your father."

"Then you do know something about it?"

"The whole thing's supersecret, as much as anything in a hospital is ever secret."

"You're not on the committee, are you?"

"No. Who told you about it?"

"Father Hagan. I asked him to call a meeting to consider what to do with my father."

"I still wish you hadn't, Carolyn."

"Why? When Father wants to die?"

"I don't deny him the right to wish for death—or even to take his own life. But—"

"No one else can make the decision for him," she protested. "He can't do it himself and the only words he ever speaks are 'Let me die.'"

"It's you I'm thinking of, darling. I've presented two cases to the committee for Dr. McHale, both of them mongoloid newborns with meningoceles and spina bifida—and both hopeless. You know a lot of those are born with pyloric stenosis, too, keeping anything from getting out of the stomach."

"I've seen several mongoloids in the Surgical ICU after their stomachs were operated on to relieve the obstruction."

"Those didn't have open spinal columns. They're easy enough to save but the worst cases are still practically brainless. The families of the two I presented didn't think it was fair to their other children to try to bring them up and they couldn't afford the cost of an institution. The God Committee approved not doing surgery on them."

"I guess that's why we didn't see them in the ICU."

"There was another reason," said Gus. "The personnel in your department are trained to preserve life, and having to watch a human being die by inches because no food or fluid can enter the body is a very traumatic experience. We just put those two in a separate room on the Pediatric Ward and tried to see as little of them as we could, but it took them a long time to starve to death and more than once I was tempted to put them out of their misery with a syringe full of air injected into a vein. Believe me, it would be doubly hard on you where your father is concerned."

"I can't stand watching him lie there, Gus," Carolyn protested. "Torn apart by something nobody can do anything about."

"Did you say Father Hagan has requested a hearing before the committee?"

"It's already settled."

"All I can do is hope you won't feel guilty afterward and blame yourself."

"I'd blame myself more if I let him live."

"I guess you would at that," he admitted. "It's a hell of a choice to watch someone you love forced to make. I only wish I could help."

"You can," said Carolyn. "By continuing to love me—"

Gus lifted the hand he was holding and gave it a quick kiss. "There's about as much chance of that not happening as for hell to freeze over—in Miami of all places."

II

Jeffry Toler got Rebecca Dalton on the phone, in the hospital cafeteria. "Where are you, Reb?" he asked.

"Just finished eating chicken and dumplings, which I can't resist, even though I have to starve tomorrow."

"Can you wait for me? I'm just leaving for home."

"I'll meet you in the lobby. I have to run over to the Terrace for a minute anyway."

"Have you seen Ken lately?" Toler asked when he stopped beside her a few minutes later in the first-floor lobby.

"Not for several hours, since he did the Caesarean in the Emergency Room and saved the baby."

"I heard about that, it took quick thinking."

"Quick surgery, too. I doubt that anybody except Ken, or maybe Mike Raburn, could have moved that fast. But wasn't Ken at the meeting of the Executive Committee this afternoon?"

"He was for a while. But things didn't go well and he left—rather suddenly."

"Do you mean he blew his top over my appointment as professor and chief of the Cardiology Section?" she asked quickly.

"He left before that came up for consideration."

"So he may not know about it yet?"

"He'll learn soon enough, probably has already," said Toler. "This all happened because Ross McKenzie went into one of his tirades. Incidentally, McKenzie also tried to torpedo your promotion—seems to think a woman's place is in the home."

"He may be nearer right than I've ever been prepared to admit, Jeff. At least where my husband's love is concerned."

"I don't think Ken would agree with that, Reb. I'm on my way now to apologize, if I can find him—on behalf of the Board."

"Would it be cricket to tell me just what Mr. McKenzie said?" Rebecca asked, and Jeffry Toler gave her a quick résumé of the events of the afternoon meeting. When he finished, her expression was grave.

"With Ken already depressed over those transplant patients that died, something like this coming right after losing the OD this afternoon could be the nudge to topple him over the brink—"

"You don't mean . . . ?"

"There are other ways of committing suicide, both professionally and physically, than putting a gun to one's temple. I'll have to try and find Ken."

"He's not in the hospital, I had him paged."

"I've got a hunch where he may be." She put her hand on the administrator's sleeve in a pleading gesture. "Let me handle this, please, Jeff. After all, I've got the most to lose."

III

The Dolphin Lounge had been almost deserted when Ken Dalton came in, just before seven. The pre-dinner drinkers had already moved on and it was too early for after-dinner drinking to really get under way. Ken glanced at the bar with a look that was almost furtive, then visibly relaxed when he saw the familiar stocky torso, broad shoulders, and battered Irish mug of Kevin McCartney above the polished mahogany surface.

"Still here, Doc." Kevin's brogue was straight out of County Cork. "I'm too ornery to die for a long time yet."

"Let's hope so," said Ken, taking a stool at the bar.

Kevin had been his third heart transplant and was now the only living one. He'd been the most difficult one, too, for the only available heart had been considerably smaller than the battered and failing organ removed from Kevin's chest in order to make room for a new central pump. But the delicate job of suturing required to adapt the smaller heart to far larger blood vessels had given Ken the confidence in his own skill that had led to the next dozen operations, with no deaths at the time of surgery or shortly afterward.

Kevin had been visiting in Miami when his third heart attack crippled an already weakened organ beyond repair by the natural healing forces of the body, leaving him the choice of either a transplant or death. Following the successful surgery, he'd stayed on and taken the bartender's job in the Dolphin Lounge so as to be near the doctors and the hospital that had given him life again. In a way, the burly Irishman haunted Ken, however, reminding him of the fact—all too certain since he and Rebecca had pulled Kevin through four rejection crises, each more severe than the previous one—that the Irishman was living on borrowed time.

"Everybody that came in here for a drink before dinner was talking about the baby you saved this afternoon, Doc." Kevin filled a frosted stein with draft beer and slid it across the bar to the surgeon. "It must've been a fast job."

"Did they tell you I might have saved the mother, if I hadn't been so centered on getting to the baby?"

"I didn't hear it that way and I don't think many people will see it that way either. How's the kid by the way?"

"Cold turkey, which means about as near having no reason to live as you can get."

"Except one—it's alive."

"That may be small comfort considering what it has to look forward to."

"Don't you believe it. Between livin' and not livin', there ain't no question, Doc. No question at all."

"I didn't know you were a philosopher." Ken took a drink from the stein.

"All the philosophy I need is wrapped up in just bein' alive. The way I figure it, I'm not only keepin' myself alive, I'm also keepin' that girl's heart alive. That makes you responsible for both of us, too. So no matter what anybody says, Doc, you can't do no wrong."

"*Nolle nocere*—do no harm—is the first principle a doctor learns in treating a patient, particularly a sick one," said Ken soberly. "But you're only one out of fifteen, Kevin, and the last one at that. I wonder how many of the others would subscribe to your philosophy."

"You have to look death in the face all the time the way we did to know what it means not to see it staring at you even for one day," the bartender assured him. "Everybody you operated on was lookin' the Grim Reaper right in the eye and, believe me, we were all scared stiff. That's why you've got to go on with that experimental work of yours. Young Mike Raburn tells me you and the missus—"

"Ex-Mrs."

"I don't accept that either. I've cooled too many bottles of Cold Duck for you and Dr. Reb not to know you two make a team. So the sooner you get back together and start your work goin' again, the better it'll be for both of us—and a lot of other people, whose hearts are beginnin' to wear out."

"Got any pretzels?" Ken's tone was almost curt and Kevin recognized that he had touched a sensitive spot—as he had intended.

"Sure, Doc—and the evenin' paper. Why don't you take that booth in the corner? I'll bring 'em to you with another stein of beer."

IV

It was nearly eight-thirty when Rebecca came into the Dolphin Lounge and took a stool at the bar. She waited patiently for Kevin McCartney to finish serving a man drinking beer at the other end of the bar and about a dozen students and house staff members, who had grouped several tables together in one corner of the room near the jukebox and were dancing to the jarring beat of a rock tune.

"That stuff sounds worse than bagpipes." Kevin finally moved along the bar to where Rebecca was sitting. "I left Ireland to escape all that wailin' and it's followed me here. What'll you have, Dr. Reb?"

"I'll try an Angel's Tip."

"Your husband was in here about an hour ago," said the bartender casually, as he poured crème de cacao into a tiny glass, floated about a teaspoon of heavy cream above it, and then balanced a maraschino cherry pierced with a toothpick atop the whole. "He had a couple of beers and some pretzels."

Knowing quite well why Rebecca had come to the lounge, Kevin had given her the information she wanted without making her undergo the embarrassment of asking whether Ken was drinking heavily, as he had on one or two occasions lately.

"I think Doc comes in here to check up on me, and make sure I'm behavin' myself," Kevin volunteered.

"Are you?"

"Sure." Knowing Kevin as well as she did, Rebecca sensed the overheartiness in his voice and felt a sudden sense of alarm.

"I don't remember seeing you in the Cardiac Research Laboratory last month."

"You know how it is, Dr. Reb." The bartender looked embarrassed. "When you feel as good as I do, you forget them things."

"Forget? Or avoid reporting?"

"Why would I do that, Doctor?"

"If you didn't want to remind us that you still need to be careful, you might just not come in for your checkup, fearing there could be some reason for us to really start worrying about you."

"Can't fool you, can I?" Kevin admitted sheepishly.

"Not after what we've been through together."

"How could I forget when you were the one that persuaded me to have the transplant—and Dr. Ken to do the operation—after I'd been given up as a hopeless case by everybody else?"

"I want you to report to the Cardiac Research Laboratory at nine o'clock tomorrow," Rebecca said firmly. "Peggy Tyndall will do an electrocardiogram and some other special tests. I'll probably see you around eleven, when we'll have most of the reports we need."

"Could you make it day after tomorrow?" Kevin asked. "I planned to leave real early in the morning for the Keys and a day of fishing out of Marathon. A guy that keeps a boat down there wants me to go with him."

"All right," said Rebecca. "But no fudging this time."

"I'll be there, Doc."

Rebecca finished the liqueur and pushed the glass and a dollar across the bar. "If you aren't in the lab day after tomorrow, I'll come looking for you," she said in parting.

"Who was that?" the man at the other end asked when Kevin set another stein of beer before him.

"Dr. Rebecca Dalton. She's the chief heart specialist for the medical center and married to the best surgeon in the world."

"Some people have all the luck. But if I owned a looker like that, I sure wouldn't be letting her drink alone in bars."

V

The breeze from the bay had died with the coming of darkness, stilled by the black shadow of a thunderstorm making up to the west over the vast river of grass called the Everglades. The air was hot and muggy when Rebecca came out of the Dolphin Lounge, and particularly oppressive after the air conditioning inside.

The pool between the apartment hotel and the bay front was brightly lighted but only a medical student and his girl were swimming, so she decided to take a dip to cool off before settling down to a couple of hours of reading in the penthouse apartment where she lived alone, since Ken had moved to a lower floor almost six months ago.

In her bedroom she undressed quickly and, noticing a trim blue maillot on a hanger in one of the large zipper bags used to protect clothing from mildew in the damp warm climate of South Florida, took it down. The smell of moth crystals in the fabric was strong, reminding her that she hadn't worn it in a long, long time.

Could it really be the same one she'd bought ten years ago in preparation for that week of happiness they'd spent poking around the island-studded expanse of Florida Bay aboard a houseboat Ken had rented for their honeymoon? They were married the day after receiving their medical diplomas, and with low-paid interneships at the old Biscayne General coming up a few weeks away for both of them, the houseboat had been all they could afford, and all they needed, besides themselves.

Looking back on it now, Rebecca was sure she'd fallen in love with Ken their first day in the medical school Anatomy Laboratory, when he'd offered to help her with the dissection. Pride and the determination to carry her own weight had made her refuse the offer then and she still prided herself that she'd maintained her own personal and professional independence, through ten years of marriage.

Ken had called her "Rebel" that morning but his smile had taken any sting out of the words. And although they had been academic competitors all through the four years of medical school, with now one, now the other leading in the grade averages posted at the end of each year, Ken had beaten her out by half a point in the final months.

During the small amount of free time their studies allowed, they'd been inseparable almost from that first day in the Anatomy Laboratory. The excellence of their class averages had assured both of them a free choice of interneship appointments, jointly, or separately. But, loving South Florida and each other, they'd chosen Biscayne General where they could keep on being together, this time as man and wife—until six months ago.

Nor had either of them changed very much physically, she was sure. Ken worked out daily in the small gym of the medical center Rehabilitation Department and he was still as leanly handsome as he'd been ever since Rebecca had known him. His blue eyes were troubled most of the time now, it was true. And sometimes, when she watched him crossing the stretch of green lawn between the hospital tower and Bayside Terrace, Rebecca could see that his shoulders drooped a little from the burden of guilt he'd taken upon himself, when the list of living transplant recipients had grown shorter almost every week. But when they happened to meet in the course of their daily duties, his smile was still there, even though just seeing it sent a stab of pain through her at the loss of what they'd had for so long together.

Nor had she changed physically, Rebecca assured herself, holding the blue maillot up in front of her body. The breasts were just as high and as proud, although they had felt no lover's touch during the lonely months since she and Ken had started drifting apart. The waist was fully as slender, the hips as sveltely rounded, the thighs and calves as slim as ever. True, she wore her sandy auburn hair short, where before it had touched her shoulders when she let it down at night for bed. But it curled naturally, retaining the same lustrous sheen, even with the passage of the years. And although she had started wearing glasses for reading, the gray eyes were, she was sure, as direct as ever and as capable of warmth.

In a gesture of reassurance, Rebecca stepped into the blue maillot and, reaching back, tried to slide the zipper upward. It resisted, not, she told herself, because she'd put on weight but from rust, but after a moment of fiddling with the fastener, the metal teeth locked smoothly and she slid it upward. Turning before the mirror, she told herself she could easily pass for the same twenty-two-year-old girl whose entire body had tanned to a golden tint during that week among the unnamed Keys and hidden waterways dotting Florida Bay.

Caught up in memory, Rebecca had almost forgotten for a moment the realities of the present. But a second look in the mirror reminded her that in other than purely physical ways the image reflected there was not the same. The reality of present unhappiness did indeed threaten more than ever now to destroy memories which, with evidence mounting daily that what had seemed at first to be a perfect marriage was apparently winding down to an inevitable end, it seemed foolish to recall. Nothing could really be gained by trying to put those same pleasant memories in mothballs for another ten years, as she'd done with the maillot, she assured herself and, putting a short terry cloth robe over the bathing suit and carrying a towel over her arm, Rebecca took the elevator to the ground floor.

When she looked out at the pool, she saw that the group from the Dolphin Lounge had pre-empted it now and were engaged in a furious game of water polo. Going back to the elevator, she pushed the button for the penthouse floor but, when the elevator stopped, decided to go on up to the rooftop lounge instead, in the hope that the air would be cooler at that height.

A number of lounge chairs and potted palms had been placed on the flat, gravel-studded roof to give the illusion of a garden for those who might want to sun-bathe there by day or make love by night. At this height a light sea breeze was blowing and the wash of the wavelets breaking against the bulkhead was easily audible.

Across the bay the hotels and apartments along the beach formed a pattern of lighted rectangles, while the flowing streams of automobile headlights along the causeways and bridges reminded Rebecca of the swift currents of blood cells through capillaries in the webbed foot of a frog during an experiment she and Ken had conducted long ago in the Physiology Laboratory as medical students.

She'd thought she was alone, until the tiny glowing arc of a cigarette flipped out into space to fall like a tiny shooting star told her someone else had come up here tonight, too, seeking solitude to think. Not wanting to intrude, she started toward the fire stairway to the lower floors but stopped when a familiar voice spoke from the darkness beyond the potted palm.

"Is that you, Reb?" It was Ken.

"Yes. I didn't know—"

"I'm glad you came up, we need to talk."

Rebecca moved to the front parapet where he was standing, a tall shadow against the backdrop of the city across the bay. Like her, she saw, he was in swim trunks and a robe.

"I was going for a swim," he explained, "until that crowd of young people pre-empted the pool."

"So was I. At least it's cool up here. You've lost weight," said Rebecca. "Where have you been eating?"

He laughed a little self-consciously. "Tonight I had two beers and a bowl of pretzels with Kevin."

"I know. He's worried about you—and so am I."

He turned to face her then, three or four feet away, but made no move to shorten the distance between them.

"Afraid I'll start hitting the bottle?"

"That—among other things. Jeffry Toler was looking for you earlier—to apologize for what Ross McKenzie said."

"McKenzie was right, you know."

"He was nothing of the sort," she flared. "Every surgeon loses patients— if he dares to operate and tries to save lives."

"But not every case—you know Kevin's having some trouble again, don't you?"

Rebecca wasn't surprised at the acuity of his clinical instinct. This ability to anticipate trouble, even before it could be discovered by machines and laboratories and other technical adjuncts to diagnosis, was one of the things that made him the great surgeon he was.

"I'm not sure," she hedged. "He's coming to the lab day after tomorrow for a checkup."

"You'll find signs of another developing rejection crisis. Kevin's been trying to hide them by not reporting for checkups. I suspected it, but I was discouraged enough not to insist that he come in—and afraid of what your tests would show, if the truth were told."

"It can't be very far developed yet."

"I'll agree there, you'll probably be able to pull him through this time. But there'll be others, each a little worse than the one before, until the end."

"They're still doing heart transplants in California, and saving them. Not that I'm critical," she added, when she saw him wince.

"You have a right to be," he said. "My guess is that the California results are produced by careful selection and attention to detail. If I'd gone more slowly and taken the time to try to find a way to overcome rejection, the story might have been different here too. But I had to have more cases than DeBakey, Cooley, or even Shumway in California. We used to say surgeons who always wanted to be operating were seized by the *furor operativus,* but I never thought it would happen to me."

"Is that any reason to be moaning about your failures all the time?" Rebecca was half crying herself. "The man I married wasn't a crybaby— just because he had a run of bad luck. I used to sneak into the gallery of the operating room when you were operating. And when I watched the way your hands moved, I felt like they were moving on my own body."

She shivered, although the night was warm. "What happened to us, Ken? Why did what we had go away?"

He took a step toward her and she caught her breath, waiting for him to take the second step and knowing she would throw herself into his arms if he did, begging him to hold her as he had held her so many times—but she didn't.

"You're a success and I'm a failure, Reb. It all adds up to that and nothing else." The agony in his voice tore at her heart, erasing her anger, erasing everything save the urge to take him in her arms and comfort him in the way lovers have comforted each other in times of stress since time immemorial. Yet from somewhere in the depths of the wisdom her love for him had given her, she knew that if she were the aggressor now, everything would be lost. Only one possible way remained, one hope alone—that of shaming him to anger.

"Did you ever ask yourself which role you began to fail at first, Ken— surgeon or lover?"

"God damn you!" She knew a sudden surge of hope at the anger in his voice and her heart sang a wild keening note when she felt his hands upon her body, ripping away the fabric of the blue maillot, exposing lovely taut breasts and tearing at her body in the desperate urgency of shared passion.

CHAPTER EIGHT

I

It was ten o'clock before Mike Raburn could break free from Emergency and come to the main ICU nursing station. Helga was punching the eleven-to-seven medication orders into the small, hand-held control keyboard by which it was possible to communicate directly with the main computer bank, as well as with the smaller mini-computers used within the unit itself for less complicated operations.

Once the medication schedule was programed, the needed doses would be delivered exactly on time during the next shift from the central dispensing pharmacy by way of the hospital-wide pneumatic carrier system. The nurses on duty would also be warned by blinking lights on the main control panel, until the medication was given and a record of its administration punched into the computer's memory bank and printed on the patient's record.

Helga looked up when Mike Raburn stopped at the nursing station.

"Give me a minute to finish these orders and I'll make rounds with you," she said.

"How is Carmelita tonight?"

"Her temperature's going up again, in spite of the blanket. Could you take a look at Joey Gates first? His ECG skitters a little on the monitor every now and then. I suspect the end of that catheter may be touching the atrium."

"You're probably right, I had to adjust it while we were in the tank. Did they get the portable chest film I asked for?"

"A couple of hours ago. The report may be in the data bank by now."

Helga punched in the code number from Joey Gates's chart and immediately three lines of printed words appeared on the storage scope controlled by the computer to display data from the clinical record.

PORTABLE AP AND LATERAL FILMS OF CHEST SHOW TIP OF IV CATHETER AT EDGE OF CARDIAC ATRIAL SHADOW, POSSIBLY TOUCHING IT. LUNGS CLEAR. HEART SHADOW NORMAL.

"There's your ESP again," said Mike.

Helga had finished punching the medication orders into the computer and they were leaving the station. The printed record of the chest X-ray report had disappeared from the screen into the memory bank from which it could be recalled in approximately a millionth of a second if the need arose.

"You almost have to, if you're going to stay ahead of that gadget," she said.

Joey Gates was sleeping and didn't even waken when Mike very gently withdrew the catheter about an inch.

"We'll have a good report for Big Joe when he gets here in the morning," he said. "Let's take a look at the preemie Dr. Dalton delivered this afternoon."

In NICU, Helga filled a syringe with the rich mixture of milk, protein concentrate, and vitamins used to feed premature babies and injected it into the tiny stomach through a small tube that ran through one nostril. As she did so, her body touched Mike's, but neither of them made any effort to break the contact, until Helga moved to the head of the bassinet and flicked a switch to display the reading from the blood oxygen tension electrode inside the catheter that ran through the baby's umbilical stump into the aorta.

"Ninety millimeters," she said. "Looks like this little fellow will make it."

"Marcia Weston wants to do a story on Baby Hornsby," said Mike. "Do you know whether Social Service has anything yet on the mother?"

"She was a college student but dropped out in the second year. Worked up from grass to heroin. Her boy friend was a pusher; they've got him in jail for beating her up but he claims any one of a dozen men could be the father of the child."

"Meanwhile a girl is dead and a premature baby starts life cold turkey with HMD into the bargain. It's a cruel world."

"No crueler than the people who inhabit the globe make it," said the blonde nurse. "Whenever I have to sweat another of these addict babies through withdrawal, I feel like going out and tying one on—and sometimes do."

"No wonder Emergency and ICU have the highest ulcer rate among hospital personnel," said Mike as they left the NICU and moved to Cubicle Four. "If we didn't blow off steam every now and then, we'd explode."

"You don't get rid of that sort of tension at a church social, either."

Mike grinned. "Bayside Terrace seems to provide pretty good facilities for group therapy—not that I get in on much of it."

"I've often wondered why. All work and no play—"

"Makes jack—but doesn't let Jack make much else, I know. But when I'm off duty in the ER, there always seems to be something I need to know more about."

"Like that needle-catheter technique?"

"You were the one who used it."

"I wouldn't have known how if you hadn't spent an evening reading medical journals, when you could have been making out with a willing nurse."

"Between us we saved a life and, according to an oriental tradition, that makes us responsible for it."

Helga laughed. "If you had to be responsible forever for all the people you save, you'd never get much else accomplished."

"Nor you." He was looking at her with the same expression of seeing her for the first time that she'd seen in his eyes earlier that afternoon, when he'd almost had to carry her to his office in the Emergency Department. And she was startled by the sudden warmth it created inside her.

"When I last studied math, two things equal to a third were equal to each other," said Mike.

"I don't think that law has changed."

"Then it looks like we're going to have to be responsible for each other. Right?"

"If you want it that way—in spite of—"

"I said as of now, remember? The past doesn't exist."

"And the future?"

"We'll play that as it happens," he said firmly. "And break clean, if it comes to that. Okay?"

She nodded then looked down at the sleeping Cuban girl. "Half the hospital believes you're in love with her. What are you going to do if she wakes up and decides you're Prince Charming?"

"With this mug of mine?" Mike laughed. "*That* would be a miracle."

"Women patients are always falling in love with their doctors."

"Her fiancé is on the way to becoming a doctor—and a fine young man into the bargain." He looked down at Carmelita. "I've always had a weakness for sick kittens, and this one's the sickest because she reminds me of Juliet. You probably remember the lines:

> "Death, that hath sucked the honey of thy breath,
> Hath had no power yet upon thy beauty.
> Thou art not conquer'd. Beauty's ensign yet
> Is crimson in thy lips and in thy cheeks,
> And death's pale flag is not advancèd there."

"Stop it!" Helga's voice was husky. "I think I'm going to cry, and my reputation as hard-boiled Helga will be ruined."

"I'll guard your secret," he promised.

"If only there were some way to wash the poisons of jaundice from her bloodstream. And the virus with them."

Mike turned to her quickly. "What did you say?"

"When?"

"Just now."

"If only there were some way to wash the poisons of jaundice from her bloodstream—and the virus with them."

"That's what I've been trying to remember!" he said excitedly. "I saw a reference not long ago to a method of exchange transfusion that substitutes a fresh supply of blood for practically the whole volume of the circulation." He started for the door, then turned back. "If anybody wants me, I'll be in the library—maybe all night."

II

A splattering of rain, sweeping across the rooftop lounge, awakened Rebecca Dalton. Shivering, she quickly put her arms into the terry cloth robe she'd pulled across her body on the wheeled couch after the explosive bout of lovemaking. The torn remnants of the blue maillot lay on the floor beside the stairway leading down to the penthouse floor of Bayside Terrace.

In her apartment, Rebecca stepped into the shower and turned on the water. The body she saw in the full-length mirror on the bathroom door as she toweled herself dry was glowing with life and she felt a shiver of delight at the memory of Ken's hands upon it. As she was dropping a sheer nightgown over her head, the telephone rang and, moving to the bed, she picked it up.

"Reb?"

"Yes, Ken."

"Are you all right? I called ten minutes ago."

"I fell asleep on the roof. You remember how I always did, after—"

"I remember."

"I'll be black and blue tomorrow—but fortunately the bruises won't show."

"That was a low-down trick you pulled on me tonight, Reb."

"I know," she said happily. "But it worked."

"And it doesn't change anything."

"Except that now I know you still love me as much as ever."

There was a silence at the other end of the line, then he spoke again: "It *was* like old times, but the fact remains that you're a success and I'm a failure."

"You're not, darling, either as a surgeon or as a lover. What matters now is the knowledge that you still love me."

"Good night then."

"Good night, darling." She was cradling the telephone when she heard his voice again in the receiver and lifted it to her ear.

"What were you saying, Ken?"

"I almost forgot. Karen Fletcher says she thinks Dale Tyndall is having more dyspnea and cyanosis. Maybe—"

"When did Karen see him?"

"This afternoon, after her daily swim. She asked me to stop by the laboratory and proved to me with some toxicological tests that the Hornsby girl really died from heroin poisoning. We went up to the Executive Committee meeting together."

"That was nice of her." Rebecca's voice had cooled sharply.

"Wasn't it?" Ken didn't seem to have noticed the change. "You'll check on Dale, won't you?"

"I'll set up an appointment tomorrow. I guess it *has* been almost six months since we had him in the laboratory. Good night."

The receiver clicked and she put down the phone. It was a long time before she went to sleep, however, for Jeffry Toler's words that afternoon kept repeating themselves in her brain:

"That might just start to happen, you know. This place teems with attractive single women, divorcees, and wives looking to better themselves."

And of all of those at Biscayne General, Karen Fletcher was easily one of the most attractive.

III

Carolyn Payson was sitting propped up in bed, reading, about eleven-thirty when Helga Sundberg came into the apartment they shared in Bayside Terrace. The blonde nurse started shedding her uniform on the way to the closet.

"Heavy date?" Carolyn asked.

"No such luck. The guy I'd be dating, if I were going out, just told me he'd be in the medical library most of the night."

"Who was that?"

"Mike Raburn."

"Mike?" Carolyn put down her magazine. "How long has this been going on?"

"Since five minutes to three this afternoon."

Carolyn started to laugh, until she realized her roommate was quite serious. "That sudden, eh?"

"I don't know how it happened myself."

"Maybe if you told me about it—"

"There isn't much to tell. The whole thing has been so fast, I can still hardly believe it isn't a dream. But here goes."

When Helga finished the account, Carolyn shook her head.

"I don't understand it," she admitted.

"Real love isn't supposed to be understandable, is it?" Helga asked. "How was it with you and Gus?"

A shadow passed over the other nurse's face. "That's different; I'm just seizing what measure of happiness I can take now, knowing it can't last. When Father dies, I'll have to break it off in all fairness to Gus. No man with the career he has ahead of him should be saddled with a wife who might be a millstone around his neck by the time she's thirty-five, and unable to give him children into the bargain."

"There's always the fifty-fifty chance that it won't happen that way."

"I love Gus too much to take that risk."

"Any idea what you're going to do?"

"When the time comes, I'll probably go back to Brazil. I enjoyed working in the mission hospital that year after we graduated."

"So did I," Helga agreed. "Until I made the mistake of letting myself fall in love—with a man who had a wife back in the States."

"But you didn't know that," Carolyn reminded her. "And you broke clean and came back as soon as you found out."

"With a few shards of pride intact and a resolve not to let it happen again—but it has. Only this time it's ten times worse."

"Worse—or better?"

Helga smiled. "So much better that it scares me. How could I be around that big lug for almost two years, knowing he's one doctor in a thousand, but not feeling the least bit like falling in love with him?"

"Maybe 'cause you were seeing him only as a doctor."

"Could be. Then one day he looks down at a dying girl, quotes a verse from *Romeo and Juliet,* and bingo, it hits me between the eyes that he's something special—"

"Mike is that all right. But it really started eight hours earlier, from what you told me, with the asphyxiated child."

"What's eight hours—when they make you feel like you're going to die if you don't spend the rest of your life looking after the big lug?"

"I know that feeling," said Carolyn soberly. "So what are you going to do?"

"There's one way to make sure. If I wake up in bed with Mike one morning, listen to him snore, see a day's growth of beard on his cheeks, realize he needs a deodorant—and still want him to make love to me then and there, it's bound to be the real thing."

"Mike doesn't have a reputation for playing around much, which puts him in a class by himself," said Carolyn. "So how are you going to put him to this acid test?"

"I'll make him take me some place where there'll be just the two of us together, no matter how many other people are around," said Helga as she finished buttoning tailored silk pajamas.

"Sounds like the Garden of Eden."

"Could be, I'll know for sure when I give him the apple," Helga laughed suddenly. "And the damndest thing of all is that right now I wish more than anything else it could be a cherry—mine."

IV

In Apartment 5A, Valerie LeMoyne switched off the television at which she had been looking for the past hour with no memory of what the program had been—and stubbed out a cigarette in the ashtray on the end table. She hadn't really expected, when she came into the doctors' lounge of the surgical suite that afternoon, that the brief conversation with Jerry Singleton and his invitation for the weekend would stir within her such a tangible surge of longing for the embrace of a man, almost any man, once again.

Val knew very well what yielding to the fire burning constantly within her body, demanding the quenching every new affair promised but rarely fulfilled, could mean. That same fire had sent her fleeing in panic from France, lest its demands put her at the mercy of Marcel Thibaut, who had been perfectly willing to share her with others for his own advancement in his chosen career with the French Foreign Office.

She'd been lucky in finding a promising appointment here in the United States and later in Miami, with its constant inundation by successive hordes of conventioneers, anxious for a fling before they returned to their split-level homes all across the country and the wives who strove, but without the skill of women like Valerie LeMoyne, to keep them happy and contented—and usually failed, as the herd instinct of male conventioneering in places like Miami Beach amply proved. But that, too, had become too risky, with the constant danger of publicity from the occasional police raid designed to assure the public that the law, in its majesty, was zealously guarding the morality of the community.

That Jerry Singleton was the answer to her own particular problem Val had tried to convince herself since his divorce but had held back instinctively until today. Then the craving, stronger than ever in springtime, when all of nature was seized by the reproductive instinct, had sent her to the doctors' lounge, ostensibly for a cigarette, but really because she knew Jerry would be showering there after his last operation. She'd known, too, that he would invite her to spend the weekend with him, just as surely as she knew now that she would accept—and that the affair would almost certainly end as the others had ended, when his prowess as a lover proved inadequate to the demands of her body.

To her credit she usually resisted until resistance was no longer possible, just as she was resisting now. But the very thought of yielding, and what would follow, set Valerie LeMoyne trembling and, moving quickly, she went to the medicine cabinet to count out first one, then two Nembutal capsules. Swallowing them with water, she undressed for the bed whose emptiness the potent barbiturate would shortly assuage with the dreamless sleep of a chemically induced narcosis.

V

Ed Vogel was on call for the ICU and the Cardiology Section, when the telephone rang shortly after midnight in the small room off the Intensive Care Section where the night resident still slept. He'd just come in from a final check of the ward and still wore the short white coat that distinguished the Fellows from the faculty.

"Dr. Vogel," he said.

"There's an outside call for Dr. Desmond, but he's out of the city, Dr. Vogel," said the operator. "The woman is pretty hysterical and asked for Dr. Rebecca Dalton when I told her Dr. Desmond wasn't available."

"I'll take it," said Ed. "Put her on."

"Dr. Dalton?" the voice of the woman on the other end of the line did indeed sound disturbed.

"This is Dr. Vogel, Dr. Rebecca Dalton's assistant. Can I help you?"

"Just a minute."

Ed could hear a man's voice in the background during a brief interchange, then the woman came back on.

"This is Mr. Ross McKenzie's housekeeper," she said. "Mr. McKenzie thinks he's had a heart attack and wants to know if you can make a house call."

"Was the attack brought on by exertion?"

There was a brief hesitation, then she said, "You could say that, yes."

"I'll send a Rescue Squad ambulance to bring him to the hospital."

"B-but—"

"If it's a real heart attack, we can't waste time," said the cardiologist firmly. "The ambulance will be there in five minutes. Don't let him move until they get there."

"Yes, Doctor." Even over the telephone, there was no mistaking the relief in the woman's voice, or the fact that she must be considerably younger than McKenzie.

As soon as he had called the Fire Department Rescue Squad dispatcher and ordered a specially equipped cardiac ambulance with a crew trained in cardiac evaluation and resuscitation sent to Ross McKenzie's house in Coral Gables, Ed rang Rebecca Dalton's apartment. She answered sleepily on the third ring.

"Mr. Ross McKenzie's on the way to the hospital, probably with a heart attack," he told her. "I sent a cardiac ambulance for him."

The telephone was silent for a moment, then Rebecca asked, "Did Mr. McKenzie ask for me?"

"The call was for Dr. Desmond, it came from McKenzie's housekeeper. But when the operator told her Dr. Desmond left the city right after the Executive Committee meeting this afternoon for a convention, she asked for you."

"I'll come right over," said Rebecca. "But Mr. McKenzie voted against my promotion this afternoon, so he may not want me to be in charge of his case."

"Sort of poetic justice for him to have a heart attack tonight, wouldn't you say?"

"I don't have the time to ponder the philosophical aspects of the case," said Rebecca. "When the patient gets there, admit him directly to CICU, Ed, and get an ECG. I'll dress and be there in ten minutes. You'd better start heparinizing him too, just in case this is a coronary."

Ross McKenzie had just been put to bed in the Coronary Intensive Care Unit of the hospital when Rebecca came into the cubicle where he was lying, pale and gasping for breath. One of the night laboratory technicians was connecting him to an electrocardiographic machine. Since it could take more leads than the sensors that fed information into the small monitor screen beside the bed and the larger display scope at the nursing station, the conventional ECG tracing gave a more detailed picture of what was happening to his heart.

Ed Vogel was starting an intravenous into which the blood-thinning agent, heparin, had been mixed, in order to cut down the likelihood of the clot spreading, if one or more of his coronary vessels had been blocked by a thrombosis. The tiny pulse indicator light just below the small screen of the monitor located beside the bed—but opposite the head where it could not be seen by the patient if he were conscious—was blinking so rapidly that the individual flashes could hardly be distinguished from each other. McKenzie himself appeared to be semiconscious.

"How is he, Ed?" Rebecca asked as she came up beside the special bed.

"Pulse volume seems to be good in spite of the rate. I gave him some Demerol but I haven't had time to take his blood pressure yet. From the ECG monitor it looks like an atrial paroxysm."

Rebecca took a stethoscope from a pocket and, putting the tips in her ears, placed the round flat diaphragm on the patient's chest over his heart. She didn't have to explain to either the other doctor or to Mary Pearson, the night ICU supervisor, the danger represented by such a paroxysmal attack. The nurses in the CICU unit were trained to recognize the significance of such complications and to take action quickly when necessary.

Otherwise normal people occasionally developed exceedingly rapid heartbeats, with no permanent damage to the heart if it was controlled soon enough. But in the case of an already damaged heart, this complication could presage a rapid lowering of cardiac output when the heart itself became unco-ordinated as it struggled to keep up with the barrage of stimuli to contract coming from its own stimulus center in the upper chamber.

The heavily muscled ventricles, the main pumping chambers, would then not be able to keep up with the demand and an irreversible loss of co-ordination between the upper chambers—the atria, which received blood from the large veins, and the ventricles, which pumped it out into the lungs and the aorta—could quickly follow. With the heart no longer able to cope with the blood being poured into the right side from the rest of the body and into the left side from the lungs, back pressures could develop quickly. The valves would then be unable to function properly and, when contraction occurred, some of the blood would be forced back through them, setting up a reverse pressure condition, particularly in the lungs, that could quickly lead to serious trouble.

Ed Vogel had been studying the conventional electrocardiogram produced by a metal stylus vibrating against a moving paper strip, as electrical impulses from the heart flowed into the machine from several connections—leads—on Ross McKenzie's chest, arms, and legs.

"The ECG is typical of atrial paroxysm," he said as the two doctors moved from the cubicle to discuss the case where Ross McKenzie couldn't hear. "P waves at the beginning of the heart contractions are sometimes getting in the way of the Ts at the end of the cycle."

"The QRS complexes are intact, so function is still holding up well," Rebecca observed.

"But for how long?" Ed voiced the question that was uppermost in both their minds.

Moving back to the patient's side, Rebecca leaned down until her mouth was near the sick man's ear.

"I'm Dr. Rebecca Dalton, Mr. McKenzie," she said. "How much pain are you having?"

The grower opened his eyes drowsily. "Not much," he said. "But my heart's trying to jump out of my throat."

"We'll control that in a little while," she promised. "The problem is to determine what is behind this attack. Do you object to my treating you?"

"Is anyone else available?"

"Only Dr. Vogel and myself."

"Looks like I'm in your hands." The grower closed his eyes again and a puffing snore escaped from his lips.

"Our best course is carotid sinus massage," said Rebecca. "He appears to have lapsed into coma already so we can't waste time with anything less certain."

"It's hazardous," said Vogel a bit doubtfully.

"So is *that.*" Rebecca indicated the rapidly blinking light marking the pulse rate. "If we're dealing with a heart that's not getting enough oxygen by way of the coronary arteries, it can't keep beating very long at this rate without starting to fail."

"I wasn't objecting," said Ed Vogel. "But I'm damn glad you're here to do it."

He didn't need to explain his meaning. The carotid bodies, tiny nodes of very highly specialized tissue, were located on each side of the neck within the forks formed by the division of the two carotid arteries carrying blood to the head, including the brain. Just below the angle of the jaw each carotid divided into two channels, an external branch supplying the face, scalp, and most of one side of the head, plus an internal branch which, penetrating into the skull, brought the major blood supply to each side of the brain.

Known since antiquity, not so much for their presence as for their effect, the tiny nodes of tissue called the carotid bodies—or sinuses—were very susceptible to external force. When pressed upon, they exerted an effect upon the rest of the body so profound that assassins had long ago discovered how, by pressing deeply and quickly upon each side of a victim's neck, to produce unconsciousness and death in seconds.

"We'll need to keep monitoring the heart action while I carry out the massage, so it's best to do it here in the cubicle." Rebecca turned to the nursing supervisor. "Can we move the bed out a little from the wall, Mrs. Pearson? Just enough so I can get behind it?"

"Certainly, Doctor."

The bed was narrow and on wheels, so the nurse and Ed Vogel were able to move it far enough for Rebecca to slip around the end and stand there. Steadying Ross McKenzie's head with her left hand, she felt along the neck just below the angle of the jaw with her right hand, seeking to locate the pulsation of the main carotid artery there.

"I have the vessel under my fingers," Rebecca reported after a moment. "Watch the screen, Ed, and tell me immediately if there's any change."

"Right."

"Give me four seconds from when I say, 'Now,' please, Mrs. Pearson."

The nurse shifted the watch on her left wrist so she could easily see the sweep second hand.

"Now!" said Rebecca, as she pressed the artery backward and toward the midline, rolling it with her thumb against the bodies of the neck vertebrae. Holding it there, she moved her thumb in a slightly rotary motion that massaged the pea-sized carotid body beneath.

"Four seconds," Mrs. Pearson reported, and Rebecca released the pressure of her right thumb.

"No change," Ed Vogel reported.

"I'll try once more on this side, then shift to the other," said Rebecca. "Ready again when I say, 'Now'?"

The others nodded and she moved her thumb slightly again until she could feel once more the heavy pulsation of the carotid beneath it.

"Now!" she said, and began the massaging movement once again. But when the nurse called time after four seconds, there was still no change.

The others looked at Rebecca questioningly, but she was already seeking the pulsation of the carotid artery on the left side, moving her left thumb about as she felt for it.

"Do you ever do both sides at once, Dr. Dalton?" Mary Pearson asked.

"Not unless you want to murder someone in a hurry," Rebecca said cryptically. "And while you're worrying, you can pray the other artery hasn't been closed up by an atheromatous plaque. In such a case, we could shut down the major part of the brain circulation and create the same effect as a massive stroke."

"Like I said, Dr. Dalton." Ed Vogel spoke again. "I'm glad you're here."

"Ready?" Rebecca asked quietly, when her thumb found the artery pulsation, and the others nodded.

"Now!"

"The heart's asystolic!" Ed Vogel's voice was suddenly tense, for the dancing line on the small monitor screen marking the heart currents had flattened out, indicating that the heart had stopped beating.

The tension in the room was palpable but there was no panic. Both doctors and the nurse were trained to cope with such an emergency and kept their eyes on their jobs, Ed Vogel and Mary Pearson concentrating upon the screen and Rebecca upon the now stilled artery beneath her left thumb, since she couldn't see the monitor. When she spoke, her voice was loud in the suddenly silent room.

"Get ready to start CPR, Ed," she said as the seconds ticked off with no sign of a resumption of the heartbeat.

Ed Vogel leaned across the bed and placed the heel of his left hand over the lower half of Ross McKenzie's breastbone, ready to push down and jolt the heart itself by pressing it between the sternum in front and the spine at the back. This time, however, the dramatic maneuver of cardiopulmonary resuscitation wasn't needed.

"There's a contraction!" Mrs. Pearson reported suddenly. "And another."

Ed Vogel quickly moved to where he could see the small monitor clearly and the flashing pattern of the electrocardiographic tracing that was now appearing.

"Those are ventricular ectopic beats," he said, but even as he was speaking, the irregular line on the monitor suddenly shaped itself, as if by magic, into a normal pattern.

"By God, you've done it!" Vogel exclaimed. "The rhythm is normal again."

"Print the ECG pattern for me at the central console, Mrs. Pearson," said Rebecca as she moved around the bed. "I'd like to study it a little more closely before I decide what else to do."

As the nurse moved out of the cubicle, Ed Vogel wiped the sweat from his forehead with a handkerchief. At the same moment Ross McKenzie opened his eyes and a look of pleased surprise appeared on his face.

"I don't feel my heart beating in my throat any more," he exclaimed. "What did you do?"

"Dr. Dalton stopped your heart," Ed Vogel told him.

"And started it again?"

"*You* did that, Mr. McKenzie," said Rebecca. "But we were ready, if you hadn't saved us the trouble. You see, women doctors have their moments, too, in spite of what their critics say."

"Somebody call me a taxi," McKenzie started to push himself up into a sitting position. "I'm going home."

"You'll do nothing of the sort," said Rebecca sharply. "The attack of arrhythmia you just had is a warning, which is more of a break than most heart cases get. But it still didn't just happen and the next one could be really serious, so I'm going to keep you here a few days and find out why these things are happening. And I'm also going to put you on digitalis."

"What could be wrong?"

"At your age a reduction of blood flow to the heart muscle, rheumatic heart disease, high blood pressure, unusual exertion—almost anything." Rebecca picked up his chart and started from the cubicle.

VI

Ed Vogel was on his way back to the Emergency Room quarters of the night-duty Fellows about 3:00 A.M. after examining an oldster on the fourth floor who'd been given phenobarbital to sleep on and had promptly started seeing small animals crawling over the walls. Certain that he would be eaten alive, the patient had left his bed and padded down the hall to the chart desk, dragging a urine bag, an IV setup, and a tube in his common bile duct behind him, before collapsing in the doorway at the feet of a startled charge nurse.

Since any patient leaving his bed without permission under such circumstances had to be examined by a doctor to see how much damage he had done—in this case mercifully none—Ed had been called. As he was passing the door to the medical library, he noticed a light burning and went inside to turn it off, only to find Mike Raburn slumped over an open medical journal on the table before him, fast asleep.

"Wake up!" Ed shook the broad-shouldered surgeon.

Mike raised his head and blinked. "What time is it?"

"Three o'clock. You been in here long?"

"Since about ten-thirty. The last thing I remember, it was one o'clock and I'd just found what I was looking for."

"Which was?"

"How much do you know about exchange transfusion for serum hepatitis with hepatic coma, Ed?"

"You mean that business about using a baboon's liver to extract toxins from the blood? I thought it hadn't proved feasible."

"It didn't, there were too many bugs. This is a new method that's been worked out in an Air Force hospital in the Middle West. The patient's body is cooled to where it's almost in a state of suspended animation, while practically all the blood is pumped out and the entire circulatory system washed out with buffered Ringer's lactate solution, before it's filled again with fresh donor blood."

"You thinking of using it on the Cuban girl?"

"I'm *going* to use it on her, if I can convince the family that it's her only chance."

"That suspended animation business sounds pretty dangerous."

"Of course it is, but the risk seems to be justified." Mike picked up the journal he had been reading and followed Vogel to the door. "The guy who worked this out figured that you have nine minutes to get the whole procedure completed before permanent brain damage is likely from the cold and the lack of oxygen."

"Nine minutes from death? In addition to being a good title for a suspense novel, that's cutting it pretty close, my friend."

"The whole business has to go off without a hitch," Mike admitted. "But Dr. Dalton's had a lot of experience with open heart surgery on patients in hypothermia and on the pump oxygenator. This procedure shouldn't be any harder to bring off than that."

"I read a book once called *Seven Minutes*, but that had to do with making love. Good luck, Mike, I've got a hunch you're going to need it. And if you fail, just don't let the girl's death knock you the way losing those transplant cases did Ken Dalton."

CHAPTER NINE

I

Carolyn Payson hadn't slept well and it was a relief when dawn finally came. Getting out of bed as quietly as possible so as not to disturb Helga, who was fast asleep like the healthy and completely uninhibited female animal she was, Carolyn left the old hotel and walked along the bay front for a half hour before entering the hospital. It was a beautiful morning, particularly for one deeply in love who knew she was loved in return, but the knowledge only made the pain from the predicament in which Carolyn found herself all the more severe.

She arrived at the hospital cafeteria at half past six and ate a leisurely breakfast before going on duty and taking the morning report from Mary Pearson.

"The Cuban girl's temperature is still creeping up," Mary reported. "Mike Raburn was in here early to see her. He's talking about some new treatment, but if you ask me, he'll never save her."

"What about the baby Dr. Dalton delivered by section?"

"Since Dr. Henderson put Baby Hornsby on CPAP late yesterday afternoon, it's been responding well even in the middle of cold turkey, but I feel so sorry for it I could cry. Mr. Ross McKenzie was admitted about midnight—a heart case." Mary Pearson went on with the report. "Dr. Rebecca Dalton did a carotid body massage on him and slowed it down."

"Looks like you had a busy night."

"Just routine for the ICU. Well, I'll be going. See you in the morning."

"Not tomorrow. I'm off duty, Thursdays."

"Well, have fun." Mary was at the door, when she turned and came back. "Could I ask you something, Carolyn?"

"Of course."

"Is it true that you've asked the God Committee to consider your father's case? One of the girls told me during the coffee break last night that you had."

"I asked Chaplain Hagan to arrange it."

"It's none of my business, but I want you to know I think you're being very brave."

"Brave? Why?"

"You know how people talk. But I don't care what they say, I think you're doing the right thing." Mary Pearson turned and hurried from the ward.

Carolyn sat for a long moment, staring at the door through which the other nurse had just disappeared. Mary's concern—and her avowal of support—could only mean that the hospital staff was already taking sides. Which could make it even harder for the Moriturus Committee to be strictly impartial in their deliberations, as well as for Carolyn herself to live with her own conscience, which had been troubling her ever since she'd begged the chaplain to request a meeting of the God Committee.

After a moment she called one of the other nurses to take her place at the nursing station which, as the very heart of the ICU, was never left unattended, and went to the cubicle where her father was lying. Both side frames of the bed were raised, in case his constantly twitching muscles shifted his body sufficiently to make him fall out of the bed.

Richard Payson's eyes were open and, as on other occasions, Carolyn could almost convince herself that a light of recognition showed in them. As usual, too, the muscles of his lips and jaw were moving but whether without purpose, like the other contractions throughout his body, or in an attempt to speak, she couldn't be sure. Overcome by the surge of pity she always felt, when she saw her father thus and remembered how strong and happy he'd been only months before, Carolyn was turning away from the bed when a harsh croak came from Richard Payson's lips. She couldn't distinguish the words for certain but, as she moved closer to listen, they came again.

"Let me die." This time there was no doubting their meaning; it was the same refrain she'd heard so many times before, the cry of a soul tormented beyond bearing by its own deterioration and begging for the end that could bring peace.

"I promise," she whispered, putting her hand upon his. "Only a little while longer and you can be free."

She couldn't really be sure the spasmodic grasping of her hand by his fingers, a movement lasting only an instant, was not as purposeless as were the movements in the rest of his body. But it didn't really matter any more, for all her doubts about what must be done had been removed.

Gus Henderson was standing just outside the cubicle when Carolyn left it. Absorbed in trying to listen to her father and understand the words she was convinced he had spoken, she hadn't realized Gus was there. But at the sight of the craggy face with its unruly mop of reddish hair and the blue eyes that were always warm when he looked at her, she reached out instinctively to him for support.

Taking her hands, Gus held them between his own large-knuckled ones that looked awkward, as did the rest of him for that matter, yet could be as tender as a mother's when handling a baby or, as Carolyn very well knew, the body of a woman.

"Morning," said Gus. "Are you okay?"

Carolyn nodded. "Seeing him like this always breaks me up for a minute or two."

"I know. That little preemie we've got on cold turkey damn near tears my heart out every time I look at him, too, jerking and twisting all the time."

"But the baby will be all right one day, while my father—"

"Are you still determined to bring him before the God Committee?"

"Yes."

"It will take a lot of courage—"

"Compassion, Gus, the same sort of compassion you feel for Baby Hornsby. And I'm only carrying out my father's wishes after all. If you could have heard him speak just now."

"I did hear," he said with an odd note in his voice. "Would it help any if I testify to that before the committee?"

"You'd do that, even if you're not convinced you heard him?" They were so close in their love that she could read his thoughts.

"I heard sounds that could have been 'Let me die.' If you tell me that's what it was, that's what I heard."

"No wonder I love you so much." She gave his hands a quick squeeze. "But he really did speak the words this morning, Gus, you can take my word for it."

"That's good enough for me—do you know yet when the committee will meet?"

"No. But I hope it's today."

They had been walking through the ward toward the nursing station while they were talking. Now Gus stopped beside the main console, whose battery of monitors, dials, and flashing lights made it look like a surrealist's dream of a machine for controlling life—and death.

"Don't expect too much from the God Committee, Carolyn," he warned. "After all, it's new and I doubt if the lay members on it understand what it means for a doctor to deliberately let go of a life that's been placed in his hands."

"It's what Father wants, Gus. Even if I wasn't sure of what's best for him, I'd have to consider it seriously."

"Then promise you won't let it break you up if things don't go your way when the committee meets. They're only human too."

He shook his head, in frustration, she sensed, at not quite being able to put his thoughts into exactly the words he needed to express them.

"We call it the 'God Committee' facetiously," he added finally. "But I'm not sure anybody is cut out to be God. Will I see you tonight?"

"I don't know," said Carolyn. "At least not until I find out when the committee will meet. But I'm off duty tomorrow."

"I'll keep in touch," Gus promised, and reached out to give her hand a squeeze once again.

"Dr. Henderson, 131," the paging operator said. "Dr. Augustus Henderson, 131. Dr. Henderson, 131."

"That must be Professor McHale getting ready to make rounds," said Gus. "See you."

II

Mike Raburn was lucky enough to corral both Rebecca and Ken Dalton shortly after he left the Coffee Shop from breakfast for a conference about Carmelita Sanchez. They met in the physicians' office of the ICU, which was also equipped with a large monitor screen and a multiterminal switching unit. With it the essential parameters of information on any patient in the unit could be instantly studied without leaving the room, as well as the entire hospital record stored in the data bank. When Mike switched on the closed television circuit, a picture of the cubicle where Carmelita lay, with one of the ICU nurses watching over her, appeared on the screen.

"Obviously you didn't ask me to see her because any surgery is indicated, Mike," said Ken Dalton. "What's on your mind?"

"I hope to do an 'asanguineous hypothermic total body perfusion,' otherwise known as TBW—'total body washout.'"

"Pretty new, isn't it?"

"So far I know of only about three successful cases. A TBW involves cooling the body to as low as 25 degrees Centigrade and a disappearance of all parameters."

"That's clinical death." The surgeon's tone was sober.

"I know. But it has been maintained for as long as nine minutes, with the patient's heartbeat returning spontaneously at the end of that period."

"Suppose you need more than nine minutes to complete the washout?" Rebecca asked.

"We don't know what will happen, of course, but I don't think it will take longer. One case—in Connecticut, I believe—was completed in seven minutes."

"Successfully?"

"Yes. TBW seeks to remove practically all the blood from the body and wash most of the hepatitis toxin from the circulation with a special Ringer's solution plus albumin precooled to a temperature of 5 to 10 degrees Centigrade."

Ken Dalton whistled softly. "No wonder you get such rapid body cooling and a total suppression of all clinical signs of life."

"When the washout is completed," Mike continued, "the only Au antigen left in the body should be what's in the intercellular spaces and the cells themselves, a fraction of what was there before. At that point, the heart-lung pump is filled with blood and plasma to which packed red cells have been added. The mixture is then warmed as it's forced through the circulation by the heart-lung pump until the patient's temperature reaches 35 degrees Centigrade. In both reported cases, heart action began spontaneously by the time that temperature was reached and recovery of consciousness was rapid."

"It sounded like too much of a gadget job to me when I first read the report," said Rebecca. "But I don't think so now, especially in your hands, Mike."

"Seems like you've got it worked out very well," Ken agreed. "But you're quite capable of putting in all the cannulae needed in the procedure, Mike. Just where do I come in?"

"You've had far more experience working with the heart-lung pump and hypothermia in your open heart surgery than anyone in the hospital, Dr.

Dalton. I'm hoping you'll work beside me and give me the benefit of your experience."

"That hasn't been too sanguine lately."

"You still did fifteen transplants without a surgical death—and innumerable open heart cases. I'd be very grateful if you'd help me."

"Have you talked to the girl's family?"

"They're due here at ten. They know we've exhausted all other means of treatment, so I don't think they'll object."

"Do you approve, Reb?" Ken asked.

She nodded. "Maybe not in anyone's hands except yours and Mike's, but I have confidence in both of you."

"When do you want to schedule it, Mike?" Ken asked.

"Tomorrow morning if the parents agree."

"Use the main vascular surgery operating room and the first team," Ken told him. "With a major new procedure like this, you'll need all the technical help you can get."

III

Shortly before ten o'clock Mike Raburn heard himself being paged and went to the telephone.

"Mr. Joe Gates is waiting to see you in the ICU waiting room, Dr. Raburn," said the operator.

In the small waiting room, Mike found the Miami Snappers star forward pacing up and down. As they shook hands he could see that the black athlete was considerably disturbed.

"Your boy's out of danger, Joe," Mike reassured him.

"I'd like to talk to you alone, Mike." The two men were old friends from college days and, besides, Mike had filled in a number of times as team physician for the Snappers.

"We'll go to my office in the Emergency Department," said Mike. "I think we can both get into it, even as big as we are."

Mike led the way to the office, strategically placed between the Emergency Room and the adjoining small Observation Ward, where patients could be watched for brief periods without actually admitting them to the hospital.

"Tell me what happened to Joey," said Gates when they were seated and Mike had closed the door.

"Shortly after noon yesterday, he went into a serious crisis with sickle cell anemia."

"Rachel told me that much and Joey's obviously coming out of it okay. But what about the future?"

"We believe we can prevent more trouble with small daily doses of a new drug. You really don't have to worry—"

"I didn't, as soon as Dr. Henderson told me you were looking after him."

"Then what's bothering you?"

"Myself. Oh, don't get me wrong. I'm not really afraid of sickle cell anemia, even though I know enough about it to realize that it's almost entirely confined to the black race."

"Something like ninety-nine per cent," Mike confirmed. "But all we need to do is test your blood to know whether you transmitted the inherited tendency to Joey."

"Maybe I'd better explain," said Gates. "You see, my contract with the Snappers has two more years to run and can't be broken by either the owners or myself—unless I'm found to have some chronic physical disturbance that wouldn't permit me to play."

"That puts a different light on things," Mike admitted. "But surely the Snapper management wouldn't want to bench you unless your physical condition didn't allow you to play."

"If I were found to have the sickling trait, would you advise me to play?"

"Maybe not. We could only decide that after a thorough medical study. But not everybody with the sickling trait develops symptoms, so it's quite possible that even if you have the trait you could still play basketball. We have experts on sickle disease on the faculty here and I could easily get an opinion for you."

"If the time comes, we'll do that," said Gates. "But what's involved right now goes deeper than whether or not I'm physically able to play. In San Francisco I was backstopping a group of athletes trying to form a professional players' union that can deal with the owners from strength."

"Surely *you* don't need—"

"*I* don't. But a lot of players who are not much in demand *do* need expert representation to negotiate the best possible terms, something they don't get now by bargaining piecemeal. I'm known to be working with the group on the West Coast, so the owners have ganged up on me."

"A blacklist?"

Joe Gates smiled wryly.

"No pun intended, of course," Mike assured the big athlete.

"I guess you could still call it that, since I'm at the top of the list," Gates conceded. "The owners can't do anything to me the way things are now. I've got a contract and they have to pay me so they're going to let me play. But if they could pin a physical disability like sickle cell disease on me and get a panel of doctors to testify that I'm physically disqualified, they could break my contract. And with it would go the best chance professional players in all sports have ever had to form a union."

"It's a dilemma, all right."

"So you see why it's vitally necessary that I not be diagnosed as having the sickling trait, at least not until after the last postseason exhibition game tomorrow night."

"*I'll* certainly not give out any information on you," Mike promised. "But I would like to test Rachel. If she should turn out to be positive, we'll have presumptive evidence that Joey got the sickling tendency from her side and not yours."

"Can you be sure?"

"Not absolutely. But if the trait came from both of you, I would guess that Joey would have developed severe symptoms much earlier."

Gates stood up. "I can't tell you how grateful Rachel and I are, Mike. She's pretty nervous right now, though, and I'd appreciate your waiting a few days before testing her."

"Certainly. We can always do it just before Joey is ready to be discharged."

"I'll send you a pair of ducats for the final exhibition game tomorrow night," Gates promised. "You and the chick of your choice will have box seats."

IV

Señor and Señora Rodrigo Sanchez were well known to Mike Raburn; he'd seen them many times when they were visiting their daughter. And as always with a very ill patient for whose recovery he could give the family little hope, he had felt genuine sympathy for them. They had once been in the upper levels of Havana's intellectual society, he knew. And like so many upper-class Cubans, who had fled rather than submit to Castro's regime, Rodrigo Sanchez had become an important business leader in the teeming section of Miami called Little Havana.

They looked up hopefully when Mike came over to the corner of the main hospital lobby where they were waiting.

"Sorry I'm late," he told them. "But I've found a new treatment that may help Carmelita and I wanted to discuss it with two other doctors before I spoke of it to you."

The sudden look of hope in their eyes was one of the most moving things Mike had ever experienced.

"This treatment, Doctor," said Señora Sanchez. "You say it is something new?"

"Very new," said Mike. And then, because he was fundamentally honest, he added, "And also very dangerous. I'll try to explain why."

As simply as he could Mike described how he proposed to wash the toxin of serum hepatitis out of Carmelita's body. When he finished, Señora Sanchez particularly looked very concerned.

"Did I understand you to say that for nine minutes Carmelita will be dead?" she asked.

"Not dead—in the sense that you mean. But it is true that none of the instruments by which we measure life will show any signs of it."

"If Carmelita's heart does not beat and she does not breathe how can you say she will not be dead?"

Mike sought a way to explain what was actually unexplainable, and found it in one of the classic stories from the Bible.

"Do you remember in the Old Testament where Joshua was leading the Israelites into Canaan and the sun stood still?"

"Yes, but—"

"It will be like that with Carmelita."

"Do you mean that for nine minutes her life processes will stand still?" Señor Sanchez asked.

"I have every confidence that they will," Mike assured them. "And that she will regain consciousness and be well."

"For always?"

"We think that once the poisons threatening her life are washed from her body, she will be able to overcome the infection."

"It would be like a miracle," said Señora Sanchez.

"Not *like* a miracle, but truly a miracle," said her husband. "We must go at once and make a novena for Carmelita." He stopped suddenly, and when he spoke again, his voice was troubled.

"Since our daughter will be so close to death, Dr. Raburn, would it disturb you if we asked our priest to administer the last rites?"

"Of course not."

"It would not be from any lack of confidence in you, Doctor," Señora Sanchez added.

"I understand. We will start tomorrow morning at nine o'clock."

V

At exactly eleven-fifteen Wednesday morning a red warning light flicked on at the CICU control panel before which Carolyn Payson was sitting,

checking charts. The warning buzzer accompanying the panel light
attracted her attention to it immediately and, with her left hand, she flipped
the switch that kept Ross McKenzie's room in direct closed circuit television
connection with the panel and the master screen before her.

Immediately a picture appeared upon it of the room where McKenzie was
lying in bed. The nurse who was specialing him was bending over listening
to his heart with a stethoscope and looking at her watch, quite unconscious
of the remote observer.

"What's wrong, June?" Carolyn asked, by way of the small speaker on
the wall, and saw the nurse jump, then turn and look at the camera with
startled eyes.

"How did you know anything was wrong?" she asked, speaking into the
two-way communication intercom set in the wall beside the bed.

"The computer just upstaged you again."

One of the sensors attached to Ross McKenzie's body after his admission
last night to watch his blood pressure had been set to give a warning when it
fell below a hundred millimeters of mercury in the higher, systolic phase,
measuring the maximum force applied to the blood leaving the heart by the
thick-walled muscular lower chamber called the left ventricle. The systolic
reading was a sensitive indicator of heart function, second only perhaps to
the pressure in the veins, also being faithfully recorded by the highly
sophisticated monitoring system of the Coronary Intensive Care Unit.

Reaching for the Patient Selector switch, Carolyn pressed it, concentrating the tremendously intricate monitoring system upon Ross McKenzie's
body. The Elapsed Time Indicator immediately began to record the number
of seconds that had passed since the warning buzzer sounded and the Signal
Delay started an endless-loop magnetic tape device, automatically recording
the blood pressure for forty seconds, beginning ten seconds before the alarm,
for playback when a doctor reached the CICU. Thus the cardiologist could
tell whether the change was a sudden one, as in an acute disaster of some
kind, or gradual.

At the same time, by depressing another switch among the battery facing
Carolyn on the elaborate panel before her, she started the electrocardiographic printer, and a strip of paper tape, with a running account of the
heart's electrical action recorded upon it by a moving stylus, began to spew
slowly from the side of the instrument. CICU nurses were trained to
interpret ECG tracings and, picking up the paper tape, Carolyn pulled it
through her fingers, studied the pattern being printed there briefly, then
picked up the direct line telephone to the paging operator and spoke into it
tersely.

"Dr. Rebecca Dalton, CODE FOUR, CICU." The calm voice poured from
loudspeakers all over the hospital. "Dr. Edward Vogel, CODE FOUR,
CICU."

CODE FOUR indicated the need for the designated doctor at the indicated
point immediately, but was less of an emergency than CODE FIVE, which sent
the CPR team assigned to a particular area rushing to the spot.

Putting down the phone, Carolyn turned again to the battery of monitors
and began to assay the information being reported there on Ross
McKenzie's condition—blood pressure, both systolic and diastolic; venous
pressure; ECG; pulse, respiration, and other data. The quick study of the
ECG tracing had already told her that, in spite of the falling blood pressure,
McKenzie's heart seemed to be following a normal pattern of action, as far
as the various electrical components characterizing the individual beats
were concerned. Most important of all, too, there was no irregularity of the
beats, a sign which might have presaged a rapid disintegration of his
cardiac condition.

Moving quickly, Carolyn covered the twenty feet or so from the nursing station to McKenzie's bedside. The patient, she noted, was snoring softly, which was fortunate. CICU patients were usually apprehensive in times of crisis and the arrival of several doctors, plus the inevitable flurry of activity in the restricted area of the glass-walled cubicle, sometimes frightened them into a severe setback.

"Take over the station," she told the nurse who had been specialing McKenzie. "Did you notice anything else before the BP began to drop?"

"The change came all at once, Miss Payson. You can see the pressure curve on the graphic chart there."

Carolyn was already studying the record printed out by a pen against the slowly moving strip of graph paper. It gave little information, however, except what the sensitive electronic instrument had already observed, that the grower's blood pressure had suddenly started falling—for no reason that was immediately discernible.

"Do you have any idea what happened?" The student nurse was still at the foot of the bed, concerned whether she might have overlooked any sign that would have warned of the impending change earlier.

"Looks like cardiogenic shock." Carolyn was opening the stopcock of the intravenous drip so the fluid would flow more rapidly into McKenzie's veins. "His skin's beginning to turn pale, which means the peripheral vessels are contracting in order to send blood to the heart and the brain. Get to the nursing station and ask the operator whether she's located Dr. Vogel or Dr. Dalton. If not, tell her to call Dr. Raburn."

Picking up an ampule marked "Isoproterenol, one milligram" from a tray on a table beside the bed, Carolyn snapped off the blue needle cover protecting from contamination the needle attached to a sterile plastic syringe. Inserting the metal needle into the ampule, she drew the contents up into the syringe. Then holding the plastic tubing, through which the contents of a bottle of five per cent dextrose and water had been dripping slowly into Ross McKenzie's circulation through a tiny catheter in a hand vein, she injected the single dose of the powerful blood-vessel-constricting drug through the wall of the IV tube so it would flow directly into his circulation.

Ross McKenzie stirred and opened his eyes. "What the hell's going on?" he mumbled.

"Just giving you some medicine," said Carolyn cheerfully—one of the first characteristics of a good CICU nurse was that she didn't panic.

McKenzie closed his eyes and his lips puffed again in a faint snore.

On the graphic chart being traced by the indicator pen, the systolic blood pressure had started to rise as soon as the powerful drug began to exert its effect upon the tiniest blood vessels throughout the body. A vast network of circulatory channels, their opening or closing could markedly affect the blood pressure, literally allowing a patient in severe shock to bleed to death by loss of vital plasma from the bloodstream into the millions of tiny capillary blood vessels lying between the arterial system taking blood from the heart to the tissues and the venous system by which it was returned to the central pump.

Ed Vogel appeared at the other side of the bed, his eyes moving swiftly from the small monitor screen to the graphic chart of the blood pressure.

"Looks like cardiogenic shock," said Carolyn. "I put a milligram of Isoproterenol into the IV and stepped up the flow."

The cardiologist laid the diaphragm on McKenzie's chest, listened carefully for a moment, then moved it an inch or so and listened again. Repeating this process several times, he finally came back to the original position to the left and below the nipple, and listened awhile longer. Then, holding the diaphragm of the stethoscope in place, he took the rubber tips from his ears and handed that portion of the instrument to Carolyn.

She listened briefly to the sound, then handed him back the stethoscope.

"What do you hear?" Ed Vogel asked.

"A systolic apical murmur—pretty loud, and rather rough."

"Go to the head of the class."

"What could cause it?" Carolyn asked as they moved outside the cubicle.

"That kind of murmur means the mitral valve isn't closing completely and some blood is spurting back into the left atrium with every heartbeat. If I wanted to go way out on a limb, I'd say one or two of the *chordae tendinae*—do you remember what they are?"

"Fibrous cords attaching the cusps of the heart valves to the inner wall of the heart itself?"

"Right. If those cords—or the valves attached to them—are diseased, the valve cusps no longer close completely at the beginning of ventricular contraction and a backflow of blood occurs, hence the murmur."

"And beginning failure, as the heart tries to cope, causes the blood pressure drop?"

"Yes."

The telephone at the nursing station rang softly and the nurse on duty picked it up, listened a moment, then called to the cardiologist.

"Dr. Dalton for you, Dr. Vogel."

Ed Vogel spoke briefly with Rebecca Dalton, then came back to the cubicle where Carolyn was watching the patient and the various instruments recording important facts about McKenzie's general condition—especially the function of his heart.

"Dr. Dalton's busy arranging a meeting of a special committee for this afternoon," he said.

"The 'God Committee'?" Carolyn asked quickly.

"She didn't say. But it must be important, or she would have come here right away."

"Are you sure Dr. Dalton didn't say more about the committee meeting?" Carolyn asked.

"I'm sure." Vogel gave her an appraising look. "Your father?"

"Yes."

"You know some people will condemn you for it, don't you?"

"It's already started. But Helga says I'm doing the right thing."

"Our Helga's a pragmatist—about nearly everything. And also a very smart girl. By the way, Dr. Dalton said tell you she would like to see you in her office for a few minutes when you go off at three. If you can't make it, you can call her."

"I'll make it. What do we do about Mr. McKenzie."

"You seem to have taken care of him, for the moment at least. She asked me to request a surgical consultation stat with Dr. Kenneth Dalton."

"Does that mean Mr. McKenzie is liable to come to surgery?"

"What happens to his mitral valve and the left side of his heart in the next twenty-four hours or so should decide that question," said Vogel. "If they can adjust to that leak you heard in the stethoscope just now, he'll probably be okay, as long as he behaves himself. If not, somebody will have to go in and put a new valve in place of the defective one."

"Could he stand the operation? That change just now was pretty sudden."

"And pretty drastic," Ed Vogel agreed. "If McKenzie is going to need surgery eventually, it's better not to wait too long. But if he doesn't need it, anybody who operates would be subjecting him to a risk that wasn't necessary. I'm damned glad I don't have to make the decision."

CHAPTER TEN

I

As chief of the two-technician team charged with operating the heart-lung pump—correctly labeled a pump oxygenator—that substituted for both heart and lungs during open heart surgery, Peggy Tyndall was a vital part of the highly skilled group who had contributed much to Ken Dalton's reputation in the field of cardiovascular surgery. When Mike Raburn came into the Cardiac Research Laboratory about ten-thirty Wednesday morning, Peggy looked up from the colorimeter she had been using to check blood gas determinations for a pulmonary function test.

"Dr. Rebecca Dalton called awhile ago and told me to drop everything and work with you, Dr. Raburn," she said. "What's up?"

"This."

On a table under a brilliant droplight, Mike opened the medical journal he was carrying and showed the diminutive physician's assistant the diagrams of the apparatus needed for performing Total Body Washout. Peggy studied it a moment and, when she looked up, her eyes were bright with interest.

"Looks like the kind of pump oxygenator Rube Goldberg might have designed. The word's out that you're going to try something new to medical science tomorrow. Is this part of it?"

"This is the heart of it. Can you make one for me?"

Peggy looked at the diagrams again for a moment, then nodded. "Essentially it's a Travenol-type bag oxygenator with a roller pump and side vents in some pretty odd places."

"Don't forget the heat exchanger. When the time comes, we'll be needing that in a hurry."

"You mean *if* the time comes, don't you?" Peggy had been scanning the article. "What I'm reading here scares the hell out of me."

"Me too," Mike admitted. "But it has to work."

"I'll start right away," said Peggy. "Where shall I work?"

"Dr. LeMoyne's turning over a workroom in the OR suite to us. She'll spend as much time with you as she can and I plan to be there most of the day too."

"I'll load a cart with whatever it looks like I may need from here and go right up to surgery," said Peggy. "The pump oxygenators are up there already and I'll start taking one apart."

"Dr. Raburn, 175," said the paging operator over the loudspeaker system. "Dr. Michael Raburn, 175. Dr. Raburn, 175."

Mike frowned. "That's Dr. Toler's extension. I wonder what he could want?"

"Whatever it is, you'd better answer," said Peggy. "See you upstairs."

II

"Mike," said Jeffry Toler over the telephone. "Can you come up here?"

"Certainly," said the Surgical Fellow. "Be there in a minute."

On the way up in the elevator, Mike couldn't help wondering what the administrator of the medical center could possibly want with him and was afraid it might be what he half expected it would. With the hospital already in the news because of the controversy with the Finance Committee of the County Commission over the budget, there was the possibility that Toler might wish to avoid possible public criticism over the use of such a largely untried and admittedly hazardous procedure as TBW. Nevertheless Mike was determined not to give in to pressure—should it be exerted.

"I want to talk to you about the Sanchez girl, Mike." Characteristically, Toler came directly to the point. "What are her chances?"

"Without Total Body Washout—none."

"And with it?"

"I know of about five cases with detailed reports in the literature; two of those died but the rest are apparently cured. Admittedly, Carmelita Sanchez is in worse condition than I'd like to see her, but if it were any better, we might hesitate to use such a dramatic procedure. Are you worried about what losing her will do to the reputation of the hospital, sir?"

"Lord, no, Mike! I wouldn't think of imposing my professional judgment on that of the staff, when I haven't practiced medicine for fifteen years. I had a call this morning from Marcia Weston, a reporter for one of the local TV stations—"

"I know her. She covered Joe Gates's boy and also Baby Hornsby yesterday."

"And gave us a nice plug," said Toler. "Miss Weston has been after me for several weeks to let her do a TV profile on Rebecca Dalton—you know, the standard fem lib approach."

"I doubt that Dr. Dalton would like to be identified with that movement, but her work certainly deserves recognition."

"Especially since yesterday, when she was made chief of the Cardiology Section and a full professor of medicine," Toler agreed. "When Miss Weston called this morning, I was sure that was what she wanted and was wondering how I could put her off with things the way they are between the Daltons."

"She couldn't have chosen a worse time, I'm sure."

"This time we're lucky. What Marcia Weston wants to do is a story on you—a day in the life of a dedicated doctor."

"Gus Henderson is taking care of both the cases she saw yesterday—"

"We're in a different ball game, Mike, plus a knock-down, drag-out fight with the County Commission on medical center finances. Right now we can use all the good will we can get."

"At least Mr. McKenzie will be out of action for a while. Ed Vogel just told me he may have to come to surgery."

"Lord, I hope not! But Ross McKenzie wouldn't let the way he's treated as a patient influence him, as far as knocking this hospital is concerned. No matter what happens to McKenzie, though, we'll still have to fight our battle before the County Commission."

"What do you have in mind, sir?"

"If it won't bother you during what is bound to be a delicate procedure, I'd like to let Miss Weston and a camera crew from her TV station film the—what did you call it?"

"Total Body Washout."

"The Cuban girl's father is one of the most important men in Little Havana. If we have to put a proposal for a separate medical center millage on the ballot in the fall elections, the Cuban vote could help us win."

"Suppose I fail tomorrow?"

"Everybody knows this is a last-ditch fight, but you could brief the

Weston girl before you start the procedure, so she would emphasize that aspect of it in her commentary. You're already a medical hero for saving Joey Gates, Mike. And, if you succeed tomorrow morning, you'll be the doctor of the hour."

"Tell Miss Weston to be here with her crew at eight-thirty, then," said Mike. "We're starting at nine but I don't want them walking in and messing up an operating room during the most important nine minutes in that girl's life."

III

Rebecca Dalton came into the cubicle in the CICU where Ross McKenzie was lying just as Ken finished examining the patient. The surgeon put the stethoscope he had been using back into the pocket of his long white coat and his expression was grave as he stepped outside the cubicle. Rebecca and Ed Vogel followed.

"Was the systolic murmur there when he was admitted?" Ken asked.

"Ed heard it for the first time this morning, when the pressure suddenly dropped," said Rebecca. "What do you think?"

"My guess would be that we're dealing with some changes in the mitral valve area, perhaps some involvement of the *chordae tendineae.*"

"I agree," said Rebecca. "The echocardiogram might help us determine exactly what's happening but our instrument is out of order at the moment."

Even newer than tomorrow's space shuttle, echocardiography was a technique of bouncing ultrasonic sound waves off the heart and other organs and photographing the resulting wave pattern with a Polaroid camera. It achieved a degree of accuracy that could allow measuring even the thickness of the heart wall, but with the instrument not functioning they were deprived of a valuable diagnostic tool.

"He went into shock very suddenly about an hour ago," said Vogel. "I'm sure it would have been much more marked, if Miss Payson hadn't been right on the ball and given him Isoproterenol."

"The shock was probably a warning of the change in mitral valve function," Rebecca suggested.

"I'll buy that," Ken agreed.

Rebecca hesitated momentarily, then asked the question that was uppermost in her mind: "Do you think any surgical intervention is indicated, Ken?"

"Not at the moment, but what happened here is a definite warning. I'd like to see a record of at least three main physiologic correlates over the next six or eight hours: the level of heart muscle function, the tone of the blood vessels themselves, and an index of how much blood is being shunted because of the shock effect on the arteriovenous network in the lungs."

"Berggren's Equation should help us obtain that index," said Rebecca. "Ed can put in the necessary catheters and let us have the computer read-out when he gets it."

"Right," said Vogel. "Anything else?"

"I'd like to see what that mitral valve looks like," said Ken. "But we won't put him through a left heart catheterization unless there's more of an indication than we have now."

Rebecca asked the question that was foremost in her mind. "Do you think it's safe to wait as long as six hours?"

"I hope so," said Ken. "Trying to repair ruptured *chordae tendineae* is a pretty hopeless job; the tissues are usually so friable that sutures don't hold well. Of course if McKenzie does come to open heart surgery in order to put in an artificial mitral valve, it would be a lot better to do it before his left ventricle and the valve ring become stretched and thinned out from an acute dilation. But I'm not convinced yet that surgery is inevitable."

"Would you have any qualms about operating on McKenzie?" Rebecca asked after the two had left the cubicle and were beyond earshot of Ed Vogel.

"Qualms?" Ken frowned. "Why?"

"After what he said about you yesterday."

"Are you worried that it might affect my decision to recommend surgery, Reb? Or my operative technique?"

"Neither. I just wanted to be sure *you* weren't."

"The way you women manage men constantly amazes me." Ken shook his head a bit ruefully. "Most of the time we don't even realize we're being manipulated, until we've done what you want us to do—like last night."

"Maybe I did start out that way, but things sort of got away from me."

"From both of us." He lowered his voice. "Did I hurt you?"

She shook her head, her eyes warm with memory. "Only the way a woman likes to be hurt by the man she loves."

He changed the subject abruptly. "Congratulations on your promotion, it's well deserved."

"I didn't ask for it."

"You wouldn't, and we both know the reason—because you don't want to put yourself before me. But holding back on your own professional advancement when you've earned it wouldn't change anything, Reb. We're both doctors and both naturally competitive, so our professional life is an important part of our existence, together or separate."

"I've always felt the same way," Rebecca agreed. "You've been successful with other transplants besides the heart and just because we haven't licked the problem of rejection yet doesn't mean you can't go on with your work in transplanting other organs, Ken. In fact, what you'd learn transplanting kidneys, the pancreas in severe diabetes, even the lungs, might one day help solve the heart problem."

"You're right, as usual," he admitted wryly. "I'd been up on the roof nearly an hour before you came up last night, thinking things out. When I failed to save the Hornsby girl yesterday afternoon, I was ready to call it quits—for good. Then Karen proved to me that she had been beyond saving—"

Rebecca stiffened at his words. "It was lucky for you that she ran the tests so soon after the patient's death," she said tersely.

"Yes, it was." He appeared not to have noted the change in Rebecca's voice, which had suddenly become harsh. "Actually the State Attorney's office had asked Karen for a quick report, so they'd know whether to arrest the man the Hornsby girl was living with for murder. It was a tactical mistake for me to let Ross McKenzie goad me into leaving the Executive Committee meeting yesterday afternoon, I knew that as soon as I was outside and had a chance to think about it. I also realized that McKenzie's accusations had been just what I needed to make me face up to the truth that I had almost reached the point of no return. Anyway, up there on the roof, I finally admitted to myself that, since you have already gone well past me in our professional careers, I have to catch up if we're ever to solve our own problems. If Karen hadn't—"

Rebecca's control suddenly snapped. "You're really saying that none of this talk about our remaining professional equals is the truth," she said harshly.

Ken looked at her in startled surprise. "What brought that on?" he asked.

"The real trouble between us hinges on the male ego," Rebecca continued on the same furious note. "You'll only be satisfied when you restore me to the same inferior professional status I occupied when you were a surgical god here, the same position most men insist on their women occupying."

She stopped for breath, color high and eyes hot with anger.

"That's absurd, Reb—"

"Is it? I've gone as far as I can, Ken." She knew she was being unreasonable and didn't care, though she would hardly have admitted that the real reason for the outburst was the fact that he appeared to be crediting Karen Fletcher with being more responsible than she for his decision to turn and fight at last.

"Go on, if you insist, and destroy your reputation as a surgeon, and as a man, over a shibboleth," Rebecca flung at him as she was leaving. "I can't hold back any longer, waiting for you to catch up."

She was gone, head high, cheeks flaming, her body stiff with indignation—and, he thought, more lovely, more utterly desirable, than ever before. But she had put her finger upon the tenderest spot of all, he couldn't help admitting—the simple fact that, until he had once more proved himself by gaining a lead, however small, in the professional world where they both moved and occupied responsible positions, he couldn't drop back to run beside her. All of which meant, he admitted somewhat ruefully, that she'd been correct in her evaluation of the real thorn in their relationship. And what was more, proving once again, if it needed proof, that women invariably understood the men they loved better than the men understood themselves.

When Ken came in, Ed Vogel looked up from the desk in the ICU doctors' office, where he was making some notes on a chart. The young doctor had seen Rebecca leave and realized she was in a huff, but he made no comment.

"Peggy Tyndall's tied up in the OR putting together a special pump oxygenator for Mike Raburn," he said. "But Miss Sundberg is putting a catheter tray together and we'll take Mr. McKenzie to the ICU treatment room when it's ready. You'll want them in both the subclavian vein and femoral artery, as usual, won't you, so we can determine the stroke work index?"

"I was just thinking that this would be an ideal case for that fiberoptic catheter I brought back from Boston a few months ago," said Ken. "The one they've been using at Peter Bent Brigham Hospital in the Harvard Medical School complex."

"It isn't sterile." Ed Vogel's tone was doubtful. "As I remember it, those fiberoptics are supposed to be sterilized in ethylene oxide at 60 degrees Centigrade and that will take a couple of hours at least."

"I'd still rather use it," said Ken firmly. "In Boston they say the information the fiberoptics give will let you predict which way a heart is going as much as twelve hours in advance."

"That's what we need," said Ed Vogel. "I'll get to work sterilizing the catheter right away and put it in as soon as it's ready."

IV

Mike Raburn was working with Val LeMoyne and Peggy Tyndall in the OR suite setting up the necessary special apparatus for the TBW procedure in the morning, when the voice of the paging operator sounded from the loudspeaker in the corridor outside.

"Dr. Raburn, 161. Dr. Michael Raburn, 161. Dr. Raburn, 161."

"That's the Information Desk," said Mike. "What could they want with me?"

"Probably Marcia Weston wanting you to go over plans tonight for the TBW at her apartment," said Val. "That's what you get for pandering to famous people."

"Don't go away," Mike said as he left the workroom to pick up the wall telephone in a corridor outside. "We've still got a lot to do."

"Mr. Sanchez wants to talk to you about his daughter, Dr. Raburn," said the Gray Lady volunteer at the main desk in the lobby.

"Tell them I'll try to make it in ten minutes," said Mike. "I'm tied up right now."

"Carmelita's father is downstairs," Mike told Val and Peggy when he went back into the workroom. "He wants to talk to me."

"Think they're backing out?" Val asked. "The noon edition carried a story about what you're going to try tomorrow—emphasizing the danger element."

"I haven't had time to look at a paper for days. Dr. Toler is handling the publicity for this case himself, trying to put the screws on the Finance Committee of the commission. Maybe I'd better go down, though, and see what Sanchez wants."

"Peggy and I will check out the heat exchanger unit while you're gone," said Val. "It's got to work perfectly, or you'll never get that circulation refill of fresh warm blood and packed red cells into her in time to keep from damaging some of the brain cells from anoxia."

"Aren't you the encouraging one?" Mike said with a grunt. "I'll be right back."

Downstairs he found Señor Sanchez and his wife in one corner of the waiting room. With them was a tall, stern-looking man wearing the cassock of a Catholic priest.

"This is Father Junípero Cortez, Dr. Raburn," said Señora Sanchez. "He wants to talk to you."

"Would you like to come to my office, Father? It's on this floor."

"I think Carmelita's parents should hear our discussion, Doctor." Mike was a bit puzzled by the distinctly antagonistic note in the priest's voice, but couldn't imagine the reason.

"Perhaps we should all go to my office," he agreed. "It's more private than the lobby here."

The office was small but, with a couple of extra chairs, accommodated everybody. Father Junípero preferred to stand.

"Señor Sanchez has asked me to render last rites to his daughter, Dr. Raburn," said the priest. "Do I understand that you intend to perform an operation on her tomorrow from which you do not expect her to recover?"

"Of course not," said Mike. "I tried to explain what is involved to them—"

"Señora Sanchez tells me that for nine minutes during this procedure Carmelita will not be alive. The newspaper accounts this afternoon intimate the same thing."

"I haven't seen the papers, Father, but I assure you that she will be alive and that I have every expectation of her recovery. Else I wouldn't undertake an exchange transfusion."

"I am familiar with the use of exchange transfusions for jaundice in the newborn," said the priest. "Do you propose to do the same thing?"

"Not quite, but the difference is only in degree. Total Body Washout involves removing practically all blood from the circulatory system, washing out the antigen and resultant toxins of serum hepatitis from the circulation, and replacement with fresh blood."

"The entire volume of the circulation?" the priest asked.

"As nearly as we can."

"Is that compatible with life?"

"In order to reduce the needs of the body tissues for oxygen to the point where they can survive for the nine minutes the procedure may take, we must chill them, particularly the brain, to a point where no sign of life actually exists because all body processes have been reduced to the absolute minimum degree of metabolism compatible with life."

"Then she will be clinically dead?"

"I suppose she could be declared so according to the now generally accepted final criterion calling for absence of all physiological evidence of brain activity," Mike admitted. "But I don't regard the state of suspended animation we obtain as representing clinical death."

"Can you be sure of it?" the priest insisted.

"No, I cannot." Mike was beginning to understand what was troubling the priest and from a theological point of view he could sympathize with Father Junípero's dilemma.

"Simply put, Dr. Raburn, if Carmelita will be physiologically dead for nine minutes tomorrow morning, what will be happening to her soul during that period?"

"I'm afraid that question is in your sphere, not mine, Father."

"Unfortunately, theology has no precedent by which to make a decision— just as this appears to be a medical procedure for which there is no precedent."

"Except that it has already been performed successfully several times."

"With full recovery?"

"As far as can be told at present, in three out of five cases. But now that you've brought up the subject, Father, a corollary question might also be argued that may be at the base of your difficulty in understanding. Before I decided to subject Carmelita to anything this new and potentially dangerous, I asked myself whether as a doctor I had the right to reduce a patient to a condition so near to actual death that it cannot be distinguished from death."

"I think it would help all of us if you could put into words just what led you to assume such a responsibility," said the priest.

"Frankly it never occurred to me that a metaphysical aspect of what I propose to do existed," Mike admitted. "But I can see an answer."

"Please let us have it."

"No one can tell exactly how a particular person's body is going to react to any medical or surgical procedure, Father. Instant death under anesthesia doesn't occur very often, but it is a hazard; sometimes life ceases before the operation is even begun and medically we have no way of predicting it. Which means that every time I order the anesthetic started on a patient in preparation for surgery, I am in essence taking the responsibility for that life. The same goes for surgical procedures where occasionally, in spite of every precaution I take, my technique may fail to control hemorrhage or maintain life."

"I can understand that," Father Junípero admitted.

"What I plan to do for Carmelita tomorrow is certainly an extreme case, but it belongs in the same category, Father. The difference is only a matter of extent."

"Looked at that way, I can see your rationale."

"And you accept its necessity in Carmelita's case?"

"Yes."

"Then we are, to a degree, in partnership. By ministering to her spiritual welfare and giving her extreme unction, you are as I understand it, preparing her for death according to the tenets of your religious belief and hers, as well as insuring a continuation of life in heaven after death. In a different way, but with the same purpose, I am seeking to continue her life here on earth."

The Catholic priest smiled. "You are very persuasive, Dr. Raburn—and also very eloquent. If you will forgive my saying so, your profession produces rather fewer real philosophers than it should, but I am glad to meet one."

"Then you agree that, in Carmelita's case, the possible physical benefits justify the theological risks?"

"I'm sure they do, Doctor, although I was far from certain when I asked to speak to you. I shall be praying for you tomorrow. To use Señor Sanchez' and my native tongue, *vaya con Dios.*"

"The whole apparatus checks out to a very handsome setup; Peggy here is a real expert," said Val LeMoyne when Mike came back to the room where they had been working on the TBW apparatus. "Is the family still willing?"

"Believe it or not, I've just been discussing theology with a very smart Catholic priest."

"Who came out ahead?" Peggy asked.

"I think it was a draw. He was troubled by the fact that Carmelita will be physiologically dead for nine minutes tomorrow, but fortunately we all agree that it has to be done. I've been looking at the whole question through someone else's eyes for the past fifteen or twenty minutes and it was an interesting experience."

"The priest didn't raise any doubts in your mind, did he?" Val asked.

"No," said Mike. "Every good surgeon learns early that he has to be two people: one is the guy who handles the scalpel in the sterile world of the operating room, the other is the one who on occasion has to withstand the buffetings of outrageous fortune."

Peggy Tyndall stood up and pushed the stool on which she had been sitting back from the worktable. "Miss Sundberg called a little while ago about sterilizing a fiberoptic catheter Dr. Ken Dalton wants put into Mr. McKenzie," she said. "If you'll excuse me for a few minutes, I'll run down to CICU to check on it."

"Sure, Peg," said Mike. "You and Dr. LeMoyne have done a fine job with the new pump."

"Not many women go into anesthesia for open heart surgery," said Mike as he was leaving the OR suite with Val LeMoyne. "I should think watching a patient for an hour or more on a pump oxygenator, with the heart and lungs not working at all, and knowing all the time that whether you win out or are credited with an anesthesia death depends solely on something as vulnerable as an electric motor or a mechanical valve inside the machine, must be pretty rough. How do you manage to stand up so well under it?"

"Because I long ago divided my life into two separate compartments, almost two separate existences," said Val. "When I walk through the front door into the hospital every morning, I'm stepping into the world of medicine, as a doctor. Just before I walk through it in the other direction in the evening, I shed my medical life, when I shed my hospital gown, and until the next morning I'm responsible to no one but myself. I think I'm the better anesthesiologist for it."

"I guess you are. At least I've never met a better one."

"Coming from a perfectionist like you, Mike, that's a real accolade."

"Maybe if I could separate my two lives I'd be better off, but so far I don't seem to be able to have but one."

"Stay just like you are, Mike. All of us need someone to cling to when one of our two worlds suddenly blows apart and it's nice to know there's at least one rock named Mike Raburn around."

V

"I hope you haven't had your lunch," said Jeffry Toler when Rebecca came into his office shortly after noon.

"I was on my way to the cafeteria for a bite when I got your call. Ken has just seen Ross McKenzie with Ed Vogel and myself in consultation."

"How is the old curmudgeon?"

"Sleeping most of the time. Ed Vogel is putting in some catheters to measure cardiac output."

"Has McKenzie accepted you as his doctor?"

"Apparently. Like he said last night, he doesn't have much choice."

"Just how severe a coronary attack did he have?"

"As far as we can tell, it isn't a coronary at all—unless there's a small infarct involving the area around the mitral valve. It looks more like he was already getting degenerative changes in the *chordae tendineae* that control the valve, and under strain some of them broke, letting the valve flap a little and causing enough mitral insufficiency to produce a fairly loud systolic murmur. If our echocardiograph was working we could get a clear picture of the valve and the rest of that part of the heart with ultrasonic waves. But the transmitter had to be sent back to the factory so we're deprived of one of our most important diagnostic tools."

"What's the prognosis?"

"Nobody can tell at this stage. If the valve breaks loose entirely, all the blood in the left side of the heart will be shoved back into the atrium and the pulmonary veins with each contraction of the ventricle, so the effect on the hemodynamics of the circulation could be pretty drastic. Fortunately Carolyn Payson, the ICU nursing supervisor for the morning shift, acted quickly this morning when McKenzie started going into cardiac shock. We pulled him out of it before things went too far, but it could happen again at any time."

"Why not operate now?"

"If Mr. McKenzie does have an infarct from a blocked coronary, surgery would put a considerable strain on the heart. Besides, there's some chance that he may stabilize with partial function of the heart, at least until we can get him in better shape. Ken appears to be counting on that."

"And you don't agree?" Toler had not missed the change in her voice.

"Let's say I hope he's right—for Mr. McKenzie's sake and Ken's."

"I take it that the decision is a pretty ticklish one to have to make."

Rebecca nodded. "I don't envy Ken the responsibility, but no one else can assume it for him. Ed Vogel and I can get all the facts he needs but he has to make the decision."

"Do you think his emotional state is such that he's qualified to make it?" He saw her hesitate and was immediately concerned.

"I—I'm not sure, Jeffry," she admitted.

"Yesterday you seemed much more optimistic. What happened to change your mind?"

"I think he should operate but he doesn't want to. And I'm afraid I just blew my top over it, which doesn't help any." She didn't mention Karen Fletcher, whose name had triggered her sudden explosion.

A white-uniformed waitress from the staff cafeteria came in just then with two trays.

"Put them on the coffee table over there in the corner," Toler instructed the waitress, then turned back to Rebecca.

"I hope you like ham sandwiches and coffee," he said. "I thought we could both save time by talking while we have a snack."

"Sandwiches will be fine."

He served her two sandwiches on a paper plate while she poured coffee for them from a Thermos flask.

"So what's the prognosis?" Toler asked as he put a spoonful of a non-dairy creamer into his coffee and emptied a small packet of artificial sweetener into it.

"I've already told you—"

"I mean about you and Ken."

"I don't know, Jeff; last night I shamed him into almost raping me." Her color heightened a little. "The first sign of a break between us was when our sex life practically disappeared, but last night he was as successful a lover as he was on our honeymoon."

"So he's not impotent, but surely you don't think going to bed with you once will cure his feeling of playing second fiddle to you professionally."

"Of course not. I was hoping Ross McKenzie would do that."

Jeffry Toler looked surprised. "Come again."

"As soon as Ken studied the information Ed Vogel and I were able to give him from our medical studies of McKenzie's heart, he made a diagnosis."

"The right one?"

"I'm sure of it. Right now we're using every tool at our command to stabilize Mr. McKenzie medically, but I think we're going to fail. If Ken has to operate, it will mean I have failed as a cardiologist, but if Mr. McKenzie lives, our marriage just may be saved."

"Suppose he does operate and Ross McKenzie dies?"

"I'm woman enough to believe Ken will succeed, Jeffry; in fact, I was staking my chance at happiness on it. But I'm afraid I pushed Ken too far this morning by intimating that I was convinced Mr. McKenzie would need surgery and that Ken is playing for time because he doesn't want to assume the responsibility for another serious open heart operation. He didn't agree—and I'm afraid my temper got the best of me."

Toler smiled. "Natural redheads aren't particularly noted for their even dispositions."

"I'm afraid I blew my cool just now."

"You took a long chance, Reb, in trying to run a squeeze play on Ken. But then I suppose a desperate situation can only be handled by desperate measures. Good luck."

"Thank you, Jeffry. Was that why you sent for me?"

"Good Lord! I was so worried about you two that I almost forgot," said the administrator. "Father Hagan tells me you're going to be the devil's advocate when the Moriturus Committee meets this afternoon, so I thought I should warn you that Judge Robie had to go out of town. He asked Anthony Broadhurst to take his place on the committee."

Rebecca didn't need to be told the reason for Jeffry Toler's concern. One of the trickiest aspects of the God Committee's activities was the fact that it had no legal status. In fact, according to existing law in most states, acceding to the request of relatives that the patient in question be allowed to die could make committee members technically accessories to murder.

Anthony Broadhurst was a brilliant and ambitious county prosecutor who was locally famous for holding accused and accusers to the strict letter of the law. So far Judge Robie's presence on the committee had given it quasi-legal status, but nobody could predict how Broadhurst would act in a God Committee situation—except the certainty that he would bring to the deliberations very little of the broad understanding and humanity that characterized Judge Robie.

"Do you want me to postpone the hearing?" Toler asked.

"I can't answer that until I talk to Carolyn Payson," said Rebecca. "I've asked her to come to my office as soon as the shift changes at three."

"Will you let me know at once what she decides? The hearing is scheduled for six o'clock in the Board Room, so we don't have much time."

"I'll get a decision from Carolyn as quickly as I can," Rebecca promised. "Thanks for the lunch, Jeffry."

CHAPTER ELEVEN

I

At 1:30 P.M. Wednesday afternoon the warning bell on the Regional Medical Program Network teletype in the Cardiac Research Laboratory at Biscayne General started ringing. Peggy Tyndall moved quickly to the network teletype printer as the message was typed out swiftly by flying keys:

"Dr. Harvey Boldt at the Veterans' Memorial Hospital in Marathon, Florida, requests ECG consultation with Dr. Rebecca Dalton re condition of a patient, Mr. Kevin McCartney. Please expedite. Will start transmitting at 1:45 P.M."

Peggy was reaching for the telephone before the teletype keys stopped chattering. The fact that Kevin McCartney was in trouble could hardly mean anything except another rejection crisis, quite likely his last. Nor could it bode less than ill for the developing reconciliation between the Daltons, for both of whom Peggy felt a genuine fondness.

"Page Dr. Rebecca Dalton, please," she told the operator.

"What is it, Peggy?" Rebecca Dalton's voice sounded in the technician's ear a few minutes later.

"A teletype on the network, Doctor. Marathon wants to transmit an ECG at one forty-five. Dr. Boldt."

"I know Dr. Boldt. He's a capable general practitioner."

"The patient is Kevin McCartney. What do you suppose he was doing down in the Keys?"

"Fishing. He told me last night in the Dolphin Lounge that he wanted to go and I gave him permission, after he promised to report to you tomorrow morning for an ECG and blood work."

"I've got the requisition," said Peggy. "Can you make it in fifteen minutes, or shall I teletype Dr. Boldt to make it later?"

"I'll be there right away," said Rebecca. "You'd better ask Dr. Vogel to join us, too."

"Do you want anyone else?" Both of them knew very well whom Peggy meant.

"Not yet," said Rebecca. "Kevin's situation may not be too bad but make sure the ECG printer is in order. We want to get a clear picture."

The Cardiology Section of the South Florida Regional Medical Program had been organized by Rebecca herself a couple of years before. Joining eight smaller hospitals in a heart-monitoring network covering most of South Florida, the federally financed program gave doctors outside the medical center the benefit of expert help in diagnosing heart disease and in following patients, once the condition was fully diagnosed.

In the outlying hospitals, an electrocardiographic amplifier and oscilloscope recorded the electrical picture of the heartbeat as an electrocardiogram. This was transmitted over a leased telephone wire to the medical school, where the ECG was recorded on what was usually called a "slave" monitor equipped with another writer-recorder. In this way the pattern of the electrocardiographic tracing was reproduced at Biscayne General and could be visualized as well as recorded on moving paper strips by a conventional printer for permanent record. Simultaneous voice transmission was possible, too, all at a considerably lower cost and far more quickly than by transporting a trained cardiologist to the outlying hospital for consultation.

Promptly at one forty-five Rebecca sat down before the network monitor, with Ed Vogel looking over her shoulder. At one side was a conventional telephone amplifier. When a small light on the amplifier started blinking, Rebecca pressed the button beside it.

"This is Dr. Rebecca Dalton in Miami."

"Dr. Boldt in Marathon, Dr. Dalton. A patient of yours named Kevin McCartney was brought here about an hour ago after he collapsed while fishing near the reef. His ECG worries us somewhat."

"I'm ready whenever you want to transmit, Dr. Boldt. How is Mr. McCartney's general condition?"

"He says he's having a rejection crisis."

"He ought to know. We've pulled him through four of them."

"He also insists that this one is his last. My technician tells me she's ready to transmit now, so I'll sign off for the moment."

A jumble of lines appeared upon the ground-glass screen and Peggy Tyndall fiddled with the controls of the oscilloscope until the picture cleared. When it did, Rebecca leaned forward to study the pattern of electric waves from Kevin McCartney's heart, roughly a hundred miles away across water, the Florida Keys in between and part of the Everglades.

Although the peaks of the tracing were low, indicating a decreased voltage of the current produced by the heart muscle, the beats were still fairly strong. The pattern at first seemed normal, although the rate was somewhat rapid, close to a hundred and twenty a minute when seventy or eighty would have been a more normal figure. But as Rebecca and Ed Vogel watched, subtle changes, discernible only to an expert eye, began to be noticeable.

"Print a ten-second strip for me, Peggy," said the cardiologist when the first abnormal beat appeared.

The technician pressed a button on the direct writer-recorder and the moving stylus that was the heart of the instrument began to trace out upon a paper strip the picture appearing upon the monitor screen. Picking up the tape as it came from the recorder, Rebecca studied it briefly.

"Dr. Boldt?" She spoke into the telephone beside her.

"Yes?" The other doctor's voice came back to her across the watery expanse of Florida Bay.

"How soon after Mr. McCartney was admitted did you start monitoring the ECG?"

"As soon as he told me he had received a transplant. Do you think those T-wave changes are significant?"

"I believe so," said Rebecca. "They're usually part of the rejection pattern."

"We took an X ray of his chest. The cardiac shadow appears to be considerably enlarged."

"That could be an accumulation of fluid around the heart inside the pericardium; it's part of the rejection picture too." Rebecca was dreading the task of breaking the news to Ken that his last transplant case was probably dying.

"Look at that!" Ed Vogel's voice broke into her reverie and she glanced quickly at the screen.

"What was it?" she asked, for the pattern seemed the same.

"Looked like a burst of atrial fibrillation, as if the left atrium had gone berserk for a moment."

"Dr. Boldt," Rebecca said quickly into the telephone, "have you noticed any disorders of rhythm?"

"That's another reason why I called you." The distant voice of the doctor in Marathon sounded disturbed. "There have been bursts of atrial fibrillation."

"There it is again," said Ed Vogel, and Rebecca reached for the button that started the writer-recorder printing a graphic record of the heart's action.

An irritable heart was, at least potentially, a diseased heart, vulnerable to any unusual strain or circumstance, and Rebecca's face showed her concern as she studied the ECG tape. The disorderly action phase lasted only about twenty seconds, however, then the normal rhythm was regained.

"I don't like the looks of these changes, Dr. Boldt," said Rebecca concisely.

"What do you suggest?"

"Have you injected Lidocaine?"

"No."

"I would suggest fifty milligrams intravenously and a hundred and fifty milligrams intramuscularly."

"That can be done immediately," said Dr. Boldt. "We have an IV drip going."

"We can monitor Mr. McCartney's cardiac condition continuously for you on the Regional Medical Program Network if you like," Rebecca offered.

"I'd feel a lot better if he was in Biscayne General with you watching his heart," said Dr. Boldt.

"We'll be glad to have him of course—if you think his general condition doesn't preclude moving him."

"It would have to be by helicopter. Do you think you can persuade the Department of Public Safety to send out of the county for him?"

"Give me a moment to check with them," said Rebecca. "Hang on, please.

"A specially equipped helicopter ambulance will be there in about an hour," she reported after conferring with the central Rescue Squad dispatcher. "We'll be able to monitor Mr. McCartney's heart while he's in transit and will be in constant communication with the firemen in the copter, so tell him not to worry. And thank you for getting in touch with me so quickly, Dr. Boldt. I'll keep you posted.

"Make arrangements to take Kevin directly from the landing pad on the rooftop to X ray for a six-foot film, Ed," Rebecca directed her assistant when the network lines were switched off. "This time I suspect we're going to have the fight of our lives."

"And Kevin's."

Neither of them added the postscript in both their minds—that the surgical career of the brilliant man who had given Kevin McCartney a new heart nearly two years ago might well come to a halt, too, if that heart stopped beating forever.

II

"Why don't you go home and take a nap?" It was ten after three and Helga Sundberg had finished taking Carolyn Payson's report on the previous eight hours in the Intensive Care Unit.

"I couldn't sleep." Carolyn was haggard from worry.

"Take a Valium or something."

"I might oversleep then and miss the God Committee meeting."

"I'll call you at five o'clock, if that will help you relax. Even with Dr. Dalton pleading your case, you need to be on your toes. They're liable to ask a lot of questions—"

"What troubles me most is whether I can make them understand that I'm not just trying to get rid of the burden of my father's care—or the finances."

"Anybody who knows you would understand that."

"But some of these people are laymen, Helga. Besides, if I can't convince Gus that it's the thing to do, how can I convince a total stranger?"

"Gus has only had to deal with babies, mostly mongoloids. They're enough to tear the heart of even a tough pro like me."

"Pull for me anyway, Helga. I'm going to see Dr. Dalton now. She wants to go over the strategy or something."

"Good luck," said Helga. "Now scat."

"Everything's ready for the catheterization on Mr. McKenzie," said Carolyn as she was leaving. "Ed Vogel wanted to do it an hour ago but we had to be sure the new catheter he's going to use was sterile."

Carolyn had to wait almost fifteen minutes in Rebecca Dalton's office before the cardiologist came in. The nurse could see at once that something was disturbing her.

"I'm sorry you had to wait, Carolyn," said Rebecca. "A helicopter is flying Kevin McCartney in from Marathon—"

"Another rejection crisis?" Carolyn asked quickly.

"A bad one from the looks of things. We'll know for sure when Kevin gets here."

"That's too bad."

"In more ways than one," said Rebecca crisply. "Now about the Moriturus Committee meeting this afternoon. It's scheduled for six o'clock but Dr. Toler wanted me to warn you that Judge Robie can't be here. The judge asked Mr. Anthony Broadhurst to substitute—"

"The State's Attorney?"

"Yes. And I might as well tell you that neither Dr. Toler nor I think it's a good omen for approval of your request that all treatment of any kind be stopped in your father's case."

"It isn't just that," said Carolyn. "I'm asking for positive action by medical authority to end his life."

"I understand that, but I don't know how Mr. Broadhurst and the other members of the committee will look at it. Dr. Toler felt you should be warned so you can withdraw the request if you wish."

"For submission later?"

"Possibly."

"Wouldn't that imply that my own convictions about the rightness of what I'm asking aren't very strong?"

"It could—yes." Rebecca gave her a quick, inquiring look. "Are you sure in your own mind that they are?"

"I'm absolutely sure," said Carolyn. "What's *your* advice, Dr. Dalton? After all, you're my law—my representative."

"If you're absolutely convinced that what you're asking is what your father wants, or would want if he were able to analyze the situation, I would go on as planned. If you aren't, I would wait and rethink the whole question."

"I have no doubts about what Father wants," said Carolyn firmly. "Or that I owe it to him to carry out his wishes any way I can."

"Then we'll go ahead. I have worked out a simple plan for presenting your case before the committee, but we'd better go over it before the hearing begins."

"I'll do whatever you say, except withdraw the request."

III

In the spotless tiled CICU treatment room, into which Ross McKenzie's bed had been pushed, Ed Vogel was just starting the catheterization of the grower's heart when Helga came in. Peggy Tyndall, who would normally have helped him, was making some last-minute changes in the TBW heart-lung pump before it was sterilized for tomorrow's attempt to bring Carmelita Sanchez back from the very edge of the grave. Ross McKenzie was sleeping quietly from an injection of Demerol a half hour earlier.

"I'll stand by here, Miss Smith," Helga told the nurse who had been specialing McKenzie. "You can watch the nursing station."

"Welcome aboard," said Ed Vogel.

He had finished injecting novocaine into the skin at the front of the grower's elbow, where a fairly large vein could be seen. Picking up a scalpel from the sterile tray beside the bed, he made a small incision and, with a forceps, dissected out roughly an inch of the vein, slipping a small probe beneath it to make it more easily accessible.

Helga waited with a sterile pair of ring forceps in her hand, ready to hand the cardiologist anything he needed from a reserve table next to the wall. Upon it lay a somewhat larger instrument that was ordinarily used in vein catheterizations of the right heart, a procedure that had become almost standard in evaluating the status of seriously ill heart patients.

"That's quite a gadget," she said, looking down at the catheter.

"Would you believe that inside the woven outer covering on that fancy piece of tubing there are about a hundred cladded glass fibers?"

"The label on the package said it's a fiberoptic system, but you'll never make me believe you're going to look inside the heart with that little thing."

Ed Vogel laughed. "Not quite. Actually the catheter contains three individual systems, each with a different purpose. One is a wire electrode for recording ECG impulses from inside the heart or stimulating it with a pacemaker if it decides to quit."

"That we can do without."

"Another is a simple catheter for measuring venous pressure, injecting medications, taking blood specimens, or what have you. The third, and most complicated, part is really a pair of fiberoptic strands, one for sending pulses of light into the heart and the main pulmonary artery to the lungs, the other for returning the pulses of light picked up on reflection from the red blood cells, after injecting a green dye, and transmitting them through the glass fibers to register on a detector."

"Sounds complicated."

"It really isn't. Using this gadget in conjunction with a second ordinary catheter beside it, we can measure right-sided heart pressure, record dye dilution studies for cardiac performance, determine oxygen saturation, cardiac output, and a few other things."

Ed Vogel had been working steadily while he was talking. Threading the fiberoptic catheter carefully through a small opening in the wall of the vein he had exposed, he worked it up the arm toward the heart through ever larger venous channels, by way of the connecting subclavian vein, where it entered the chest, and then on into the superior vena cava just outside the right atrium of the heart itself. When, from the height of the ECG pattern being recorded from the electric impulses of the heart itself by means of the wire terminal inside the catheter, he judged that the tip should be in the right atrium, he covered the small skin incision with a sterile towel.

"We'll check with an X ray now," he said.

The technician who had been waiting outside with the portable X-ray machine, wheeled it into the room and positioned the tube over Ross McKenzie's chest. Only seconds were required to expose the film placed beneath his body, after which the machine was wheeled out again. While they waited for the result, Ed carefully positioned a smaller conventional catheter in the superior vena cava by inserting it through the same arm vein.

"When did Dr. Rebecca get the idea for this gadget?" Helga asked as they were waiting for the film to be developed.

"Oddly enough, it wasn't hers," said the cardiologist. "Dr. Ken brought a couple of these fiberoptic catheters back from Boston when he was up there months ago; they've been using them at Peter Bent Brigham Hospital in the Harvard Medical School complex. But he hasn't been doing much in the heart lately and she's a little more conservative, so until today the catheter's lain in its box unused."

"If it does half the things you mentioned, it will make monitoring serious heart cases a lot simpler," said Helga. "Do you think this means Dr. Ken is getting a grip on things again?"

"Your guess is as good as mine," said the Research Fellow. "I'm pretty sure she thinks he's trying to avoid having to operate and I'd bet they quarreled over just that."

"You mean she favors surgery?"

Vogel nodded. "It's a tough decision for everybody."

"Why?"

"If she has to give her opinion, as the chief cardiologist for the hospital, that surgery is needed, and he refuses, this will be the final showdown."

"But he always left the decision of who should receive transplants up to her."

"And now he's blaming her, maybe unconsciously, but blaming her just the same, for the way things turned out."

"There's a man for you. When Eve gave Adam the apple, he didn't have to be persuaded to eat it. But when the Lord came around and caught him, after he did, the first thing he said was: 'The woman whom thou gavest to be with me, she gave me of the tree, and I did eat.'"

Ed Vogel shook his head admiringly. "You constantly amaze me, Helga. Where did you ever study the Bible?"

"When I was growing up, we had to go to Sunday school and church twice every Sunday, plus Wednesday night prayer meeting. In a way, it was fun though, especially once a year when we all went to what was called the Association. That was when a lot of the churches got together and held a preaching marathon under a bush arbor to protect people from the sun."

"Doesn't sound very exciting to me."

"That's what you think. You see, everybody camped out and, while the older people were being preached at, the young ones were making out in the bushes."

"Not much different from around here, would you say?"

Helga shrugged. "Maybe not but there was something about making love with pine needles and sandspurs pricking your backside that seemed to give sex a different flavor then."

The arrival of the X-ray film put an end to the conversation and Helga held it up against the light for Ed Vogel to study without contaminating the sterile gloves he still wore.

"The tip of the main catheter's in the right atrium," he said. "The question now is whether to go any farther."

"Let me study that a moment, please, Miss Sundberg." Neither of them had heard Ken Dalton approach the door of the treatment room. When Helga handed him the still wet film in the metal frame that had held it for developing, he examined it briefly, then gave it back to her.

"Was there any change in the ECG while you were putting the catheter in, Ed?" he asked.

"None at all."

"I'd like to get the tip through the right heart and into the pulmonary artery if we can. It could tell us how much pressure is developing in the lung circulation because of leakage through the mitral valve."

"I don't think I'll have any difficulty in putting it through into the artery, Dr. Dalton."

"Go ahead then. I'll stay around in case there's any trouble."

The procedure so far had been simple, but the next step involved threading the rather large catheter down through the right atrium and past the tricuspid valve separating the upper chamber from the ventricle below. From there it had to pass through the ventricle and the pulmonary valve leading into the main artery to the lungs, where it could be positioned in the midst of the stream of blood forced into the lung circulation with each stroke of the right heart. All went well here, too, however, and the chest X-ray film showed the tip of the catheter in excellent position.

"Nice going, Ed," said Ken Dalton. "They told me in Boston that with a catheter like this danger signs will ordinarily show up fully twenty-four hours before any significant clinical warning can be detected. I want you to plot curves of the oxygen saturation, the pulmonary artery pressure and dye clearance rate every hour. With the information this type of catheter can give us, we can chart the cardiac output and the stroke work index, so it ought to be safe to watch McKenzie for a while longer. I'll be checking the first results on the computer as soon as you can connect the fiberoptic catheter to the bedside monitor unit."

"He knows exactly what he's doing," said Helga when Ken Dalton left the treatment room. "It could be that you and Dr. Rebecca have been selling him short."

"And the risk he's taking," Ed agreed.

"He wouldn't be the great surgeon he is if he didn't," said the blonde nurse cryptically. "I'd better get back to the console in case he needs any help."

"Tell him I've got the catheters connected here. He can start recording the data when he's ready."

Into the keyboard of the computer, Ken had already punched the figures representing the different values being fed to the main console from the bedside unit, while Ed Vogel checked the various new parameters made available by the sensitive fiberoptic catheter and the pulses of light flowing through it in both directions. Since Ken Dalton had first inserted into the computer circuits the fixed information about body surface, heartbeat, and other nomograms—normal values—the computer was able to calculate and display almost immediately the values for cardiac index, stroke volume, and stroke index. All of which were accurate indications of heart function which, prior to the development of the amazingly efficient single fiberoptic catheter, had required a number of separate and time-consuming measurements and analyses.

The surgeon studied the results, then compared them with previous estimates of Ross McKenzie's cardiac function made by more conventional methods.

"I don't see much change yet," he told Ed Vogel when the younger man came to the nursing station. "But the next six or eight hours ought to settle the question of whether to intervene surgically."

"I was hoping the new catheter would tell us something definite," said Ed.

"So was I. All of which goes to prove that, when you're working with the human heart, either physically or emotionally, you can never be entirely sure about anything."

CHAPTER TWELVE

I

Strengthened by one of the late afternoon thunderstorms making up to the south almost daily this time of the year, the normal sea breeze sweeping across the narrow island of Miami Beach from the ocean to the east was whipping the surface of Biscayne Bay into low whitecaps when Rebecca Dalton and Ed Vogel stepped out of the elevator that had brought them to the helicopter landing pad on the roof of the central hospital tower. They moved to a corner of the elevator housing upon the roof for protection against the wind and the additional blast from the helicopter rotors, when it settled upon the landing pad.

It had cost more than an extra hundred thousand dollars over the original estimated cost of the hospital tower to put the landing pad there with a special high-speed elevator to the ground-floor Emergency Room. But a half dozen lives had already been saved by the speed with which the two rescue helicopters of the Metro Fire Department had been able to shuttle serious accident and other emergencies to the hospital in the some six months they had been in operation.

With the quickened breeze, the helicopter was forced to make a second pass at the landing pad before it settled down smoothly, the whirling blades of its rotors adding to the wind sweeping across the roof of one of the two or three loftiest buildings in Miami. As the rotating blades came to a halt, a young man in a blue denim jumpsuit swung out of the cockpit and down to the pad.

"His ECG was skittering around constantly when we radioed you a little while ago, Dr. Dalton," he said. "But it settled down again."

"Looks like we taught you something, Sanders."

The young man, freshly returned from a two-year stint as medical corpsman with the Army and enrolled mornings in the new physician's assistant course operated jointly by the university and the medical school, was one of a new breed of paramedical personnel that was already increasing the efficiency of overworked doctors in many parts of the country.

The pilot came around to the side of the helicopter fuselage and the two men opened the wide doors that made entrance and exit easy with the basket stretcher used to handle patients.

"Hello, Dr. Dalton." Kevin McCartney could still smile, although his face was drawn from pain and his skin a sickly pallor in hue. "I'm sorry I couldn't bring you a fish."

"You brought one," Rebecca assured him. "Right now it looks like it's been out of the water too long, but we'll have you swimming again in no time."

The two men swung the basket litter down skillfully and transferred Kevin to a wheeled stretcher waiting beside the pad.

"We would have gotten here sooner," said the pilot, "but we had to fly around that storm."

"Thanks for making the trip," said Rebecca. "Kevin here is the only bartender in the world with a girl's heart inside his chest. We keep him around just as a curiosity."

Her fingers had moved to Kevin's wrist as he was being placed on the wheeled stretcher. His pulse was full, almost bounding in character, but regular and fairly strong, with none of the arrhythmia—at least for the moment—that had made Dr. Boldt put his electrocardiographic tracing on the remote monitoring network.

"Travel seems to be good for you, Kevin," said Rebecca as she released his wrist. "Your heart's behaving better than it was before you left Marathon."

"The Lidocaine did that, I've had it enough times to recognize the effects. But a lot of my other equipment is running pretty rough." He grimaced with pain. "I never could understand why one of the first signs of heart rejection is a knot in your gut."

"Dr. Vogel is going to take you by X ray for a six-foot chest film," Rebecca told him. "But I'll ask Miss Sundberg to send a hypo for you from CICU."

Taken with the target of the X-ray tube six feet distant from the patient's chest, the film allowed exact measurements of heart size upon the film itself, giving a far more accurate picture than was possible from physical examination or an ordinary chest film.

"Peggy will take some blood and do an ECG, too, before we put you to bed on Intensive Care," Rebecca added. "Okay?"

"Whatever you say, Doc," said Kevin. "I never could resist a pretty woman—particularly one in white."

"Will you sign for him, Dr. Dalton?" The pilot had been eying the thunderstorm that was moving perceptibly nearer the landing pad. "I'd like to get off this tower before we're blown into the bay."

Rebecca scribbled her name at the bottom of the routing sheet on the small clipboard.

"Thank Chief Bates for me," she said as she handed back the board.

"He'll probably ask you to testify before the Commission Finance Committee," said the pilot as he swung himself up into the helicopter cabin. "The Fire Department budget is coming up for approval soon just like yours. Is it true that you've got old man Ross McKenzie in the hospital with a heart attack?"

"He's a patient," said Rebecca. "But we're not quite sure of the diagnosis yet."

"Do us all a favor and smother him before he can do any more damage," said the pilot. "He's already got the salaries and the morale of the Fire Department so low that we're having trouble getting recruits."

Stepping into the elevator behind the stretcher, Rebecca pressed the button for "1" and the doors of the elevator closed smoothly, shutting away the roar of the engine, as the helicopter pilot gunned his motor to lift this latest and most sophisticated "Angel of Mercy" into the air once more.

II

Helga Sundberg had finished making rounds on the entire ICU section, after helping Ed Vogel with Ross McKenzie, when Mike Raburn appeared at the nursing station. She looked up from using the storage recall scope to check the orders Carolyn had punched into the computer data bank before going off duty.

"I didn't see you come in through the ER just now," said Mike.

"Don't tell me you were looking for me."

"I shouldn't admit it to a designing female, but I was. You assured me yesterday that you weren't interested in marriage for a long time, so I felt safe."

"A lot can happen in twenty-four hours."

"A lot happened between three and eleven yesterday, though I'm still not quite certain what it was."

"Neither am I," said Helga. "But maybe I should warn you that I plan to find out."

"We might make that a joint project starting, say, this weekend?"

"Why not, unless you get a swelled head from performing for television tomorrow morning. The grapevine has it that you'll be hitting the networks."

"Lord, I hope not," said Mike. "If I have as much trouble tomorrow as I've been having today, the program will be canceled."

"What's wrong?"

"Mainly blood. We'll be needing quarts of it tomorrow morning at the crucial point in the TBW, and unfortunately Carmelita's a Type A-negative. I've had to line up the A-negative resources of every blood bank in town and it looks like we'll just make it even then."

"I'm sorry I'm an O," said Helga.

"Me too," said Mike. "Which would appear to be something else that we have in common."

"Do you really only have nine minutes to complete the washout?" Helga asked. "That seems terribly short and you're bound to be under considerable strain."

"Nobody has taken any longer than that so far, that I know of. And I certainly don't want to push my luck with my first case."

"You'll make it," she assured him.

"I wish I had your confidence. The more I think of all the things that could happen during those nine minutes, the more leery I get."

"Any surgeon who can quote Shakespeare at 11:00 P.M. after a long day's work must be something special. I've never seen you fail at anything yet that you had set your heart to."

"I was clobbered plenty of times on the football field—Joe Gates could vouch for that. And there always has to be a first time. Look at what happened to Ken Dalton; a year ago you would have said he couldn't even lose a patient, and now he is practically out of operative surgery entirely."

"Will you let it knock you tomorrow, if you fail to save Carmelita?"

"I don't know," Mike admitted gravely. "I'm way out on a limb this time, with a lot more than a girl's life, important though that is, at stake. Besides, if I make a mistake in the operating room tomorrow, everybody will know it, with those cameras grinding away."

"It's not too late to call off the broadcast."

Mike shook his head. "I can't let Dr. Toler and the hospital down; he's depending on this affair to be the finest public relations stunt anyone has ever brought off."

"I'm still betting on you." Helga's voice had a warm note which Mike didn't miss.

"Enough to help me celebrate this weekend, if everything turns out all right?"

"If you'll let me name the place and the time."

"Name it," he said promptly, and waited for an answer, but Helga shook her head.

"I won't tell you before tomorrow night, when you're sure you've won."

"And if I lose?"

"I'll let you cry on my shoulder as a consolation prize."

"Fair enough," he said. "Win or lose, I'll have a lot to look forward to."

III

Kevin McCartney had been taken directly from the X-ray room to the Cardiac Research Laboratory, on the special cardiac stretcher that allowed his condition to be monitored all the while by remote telemetry, the picture being received on the master screen of the ICU. He flinched a little as Peggy Tyndall stuck him with a rather large needle, so she could take enough blood for the tests Rebecca Dalton wanted to run in addition to the regular CS-11 group, so called because the eleven tests could be run automatically by a fantastic machine that had taken over the work of several technicians.

After dividing into several test tubes the blood she had taken, Peggy taped a small dressing over the puncture wound on Kevin's arm and began to attach the leads used for a conventional ECG to his wrists, ankles, and the front of his chest.

"Dr. Fletcher says both you and she think Dale's getting more short of breath," said Peggy, as she started the machine. "I guess that's sort of a reflection on me as a mother."

"Did she say that?" Kevin demanded indignantly.

"Not in so many words. It was more like she was criticizing Dr. Rebecca for not watching Dale more closely."

"What's she trying to do? Cause trouble between Dr. Rebecca and Dr. Ken?"

"There's enough of that already," said Peggy. "But if anybody's to blame where Dale is concerned, it's me. When I get to the apartment at night, I'm usually tired, so I guess I don't pay as much attention to him as I should."

"Dr. Fletcher and I could both be wrong," said Kevin. "When Dale comes to the lounge in the afternoon for his root beer, he's always panting from having run most of the way from Bayside Arms—"

"I've tried to slow him down," said Peggy, "but Dr. Rebecca says it's best to let him set his own pace, so he won't feel different from the other children. Dr. Rebecca's going to see him next week when the echocardio-scope is fixed. By using it, she hopes he won't have to go through having a catheter put into his heart again."

"You can trust her to do what's best," Kevin assured the petite technician. "By the way, how is the work on the artificial heart coming?"

"The whole project has sort of stopped, since Dr. Ken and Dr. Rebecca aren't working together any more."

"Six months ago he told me he was about ready to implant an artificial heart run by atomic power in the chest of a calf. Every time I went to Mass, I said a prayer that Dr. Ken would get it perfected before the damn lymphocytes in my blood managed to kill me off. Now I'm half dead and you tell me it's a lost cause."

"I'm not any happier about it than you are, Kevin," said the technician. "After all, I've got a son with a heart that's all screwed up inside and he might need that pump one day too."

"Couldn't anybody else go on with the work?"

"Dr. Raburn could, I suppose. But Dr. Rebecca is still carrying the torch for her husband, and Mike's the busiest surgeon in the hospital."

"Meanwhile the one thing that might keep me going for another ten years or so is kaput. If you ask me, it's a hell of a way to treat a patient who depends on you."

Peggy gave him a quick, appraising look. "Have you told Dr. Ken that?"

"No. I figure he's got troubles enough of his own."

Peggy moved the sensor on Kevin's chest to another position and a motor hummed while the ECG tape flowed smoothly from the machine.

"It could just be that you'd be doing him a favor by reminding him he owes you that much," she said.

"You might have something there, beautiful," said Kevin. "How does that ticker seem to be working?"

"I've seen worse. You'll probably outlast me, especially since you're not drinking the product you sell."

"When do I get a report?"

"When Dr. Dalton and Dr. Vogel finish examining you and the lab work is done, which means several hours." She disconnected him from the machine. "Meanwhile, I'll leave you to the tender mercies of your friend Miss Sundberg."

Picking up the telephone, Peggy called for an attendant to take Kevin and the stretcher to the CICU.

"And don't forget what I said about reminding Dr. Ken that you're waiting for him to perfect the artificial heart," she told Kevin in parting.

IV

It was almost four o'clock when Ed Vogel and Helga Sundberg finished connecting Kevin McCartney to the various monitoring instruments that would give a continuous picture of his vital signs. The narcotic administered by hypodermic before he was taken to the X-ray room and the Cardiac Research Laboratory had eased the pain that so often accompanied the rejection phenomenon and Kevin was dozing. But his breathing was rather shallow and the tracings of the ECG on the monitor screen at the head of his bed, as well as on the larger screen at the main nursing station console, were noticeably narrowed by the decreased voltage of the heart's electrical system.

At the storage data computer keyboard, Ed Vogel had completed punching in the standing orders and was dictating the findings of his physical examination into the red telephone of the CICU doctors' office that communicated directly with the typing pool.

"This is the worst rejection crisis Kevin's had, isn't it?" Helga asked through the opening between the nursing station and the doctors' office adjoining it.

"So far. Actually each one is usually worse than the last until—"

"When you look at the ECG tracing, it's almost as if his heart were being squeezed."

"That's really what's happening," said the young cardiologist. "With lymphocytes attacking the conduction system and the heart muscle itself from the inside, his heart really doesn't have much of a chance."

"Since we're monitoring all possible parameters on both Kevin and Mr. McKenzie, I'm going to need all the visual channels available," said Helga. "The monitors on Mr. Payson don't tell us anything we didn't already know and, if you discontinue them, I'll have two more channels for Kevin and Mr. McKenzie."

"Write the order, I'll sign it."

Rebecca Dalton came into the CICU as Vogel was about to leave.

"Did you find anything new with Kevin, Ed?" she asked.

"His spleen is larger than it was on the last admission and there's some fluid in the abdomen, besides what's in the pericardium."

"I just glanced at the X rays. The cardiac shadow is considerably enlarged too, but much of that could be fluid in the pericardium."

"Shall I aspirate it?"

"He's been subjected to enough diagnostic procedures for today. We can wait until tomorrow to remove the fluid."

"I've doubled the dosage of methyl prednisolone and ALG," said Vogel. "And also started heparin and Actinomycin D."

"Good," said Rebecca. "I'm going to be tied up from about five-thirty to six-thirty or seven with a committee meeting, but you can call me out of the Board Room if you need me. How's Mr. McKenzie?"

"The computer print-out on his stroke work index just came through." Ed Vogel handed Rebecca a sheet of figures. "It seems to be holding up pretty well."

"Unless there's another sudden change." Rebecca had voiced the reservation that was in both their minds.

"Is Dr. Dalton coming up to see Kevin?" Ed Vogel asked on a casual note.

"This is one of his three afternoons on duty in the PDC," she said. "I sent word to him that Kevin was being admitted, so I imagine he'll stop by when he's free."

"I'll call his attention to the fact that Mr. McKenzie's index doesn't seem to be improving," said Ed. "The phonocardiogram appears to verify that, too."

He passed to Rebecca a strip of tracing paper upon which a continuous pattern of peaks and depressions somewhat resembling an ECG was recorded. A method of reproducing the heart sounds by photographing the conversion of sound waves into electronic impulses, the phonocardiogram was far more efficient than the conventional stethoscope. Even more important, it produced a graphic record which became part of the clinical data bank accumulated on the patient.

"The split in the second sound does seem to be wider than normal," said Rebecca thoughtfully. "The height of that apical third indicates an abnormally rapid left ventricular filling, too."

"Which means a larger stroke volume is needed to compensate for the amount of backflow into the atrium, when the ventricle contracts," said Ed. "So the amount of blood pumped out into his aorta with each heartbeat may actually be declining."

"Doesn't that mean his heart is failing at a faster rate than the clinical signs seem to indicate?" Helga asked.

"Possibly," said Rebecca soberly.

None of the three voiced the thought uppermost in all their minds: that if Ross McKenzie's heart function was actually declining, every hour that passed made surgical correction of the damaged mitral valve—the operation of choice, should surgery become necessary—more difficult and a successful outcome less certain. Or the fact that, by making the official request for surgery that Rebecca's position as chief medical consultant to the cardiovascular service might require of her, she could be driving a final wedge between herself and Ken.

V

"I didn't see you come in, Carolyn." Helga Sundberg spoke from the door to the cubicle where Richard Payson lay, with Carolyn bending over him to smooth the hair back from his forehead.

"You were busy with Dr. Dalton and Dr. Vogel. I just wanted to spend a little while with Father before I go to the God Committee meeting."

"The whole hospital is waiting to see what the decision will be."

"No more than I am," said the other nurse. "Even though I'm pretty sure I already know."

Helga changed the subject, somewhat abruptly. "Dr. Rebecca and Ed Vogel were going over Mr. McKenzie's record just now. She seems to think surgery can't be postponed much longer without cutting down sharply his chances of coming through it. I guess it's a case of Hobson's choice for her, too."

Carolyn looked up. "Is that a reminder to me that I'm not the only one in Biscayne General with problems?"

"Everybody's got 'em," said Helga with a shrug. "Mike Raburn is risking the blame for Carmelita Sanchez' death tomorrow with a hazardous procedure he doesn't have to undertake."

"Mike wouldn't do the TBW if he weren't convinced that's the only chance she has."

"I know," said Helga. "That's the sort of guy he is. But he's still taking a large risk."

Carolyn gave her roommate an appraising look. "Do you still feel the same way about him—after a night to sleep on the question?"

"More than ever," said Helga. "What's more, I'm going to test him this weekend—with the apple."

"His idea—or yours?"

"His, of course." Helga gave a creditable burlesque of outraged virtue. "What do you think I am anyway—a pushover? By the way, I asked Ed Vogel just now to write an order taking your father off the monitors when he's brought back later from the meeting upstairs."

"Why?" Carolyn asked.

"We need the extra channels for Kevin and Mr. McKenzie and your father's heart condition doesn't change anyway so there's no reason to keep detailed records." Helga's tone was casual. "His urinary output dropped some in the past twenty-four hours, too, so Ed ordered a continuous IV drip started later—also at my suggestion. That way we can be sure he's getting a full dose of chlorpromazine all the time to keep him relaxed. Besides, with the IV catheter in place, anything else he needs can be given quickly, too."

Carolyn didn't miss the change of emphasis Helga had given her last observation—or the reason.

"Thanks, Helga," she said. "I'm sorry if I was sharp with you just now."

"Forget it. What's a roommate for anyway except to lean on?"

"With everybody waiting to learn how the hearing will turn out, I wonder what the staff is saying about me for making the request."

"Who cares? You're doing what you think is right for your father and that's the only thing that really matters. Seen Gus lately?"

"No. I was pretty depressed when I finished talking to Dr. Dalton this afternoon, so I dodged him."

"He's in the NICU now, checking on the Hornsby baby and the Gates boy."

"They were both doing fine when I went off duty."

"They still are, but Dr. Desmond read an article last night about the incidence of small lung emboli from clots forming around the ends of catheters left in blood vessels. He wants them taken out as early as possible, so Gus is trying to decide whether to let the catheters in Baby Hornsby's umbilical stump go another twenty-four hours, or risk taking them out now."

Carolyn managed to smile. "Around here it's nothing but decisions, decisions—all day long."

"Whatever the God Committee decides, just remember it isn't the end of everything for you," Helga urged. "Go on out with Gus this evening and forget everything else. Tell you what," she added. "I'll bunk with Magda Gatton tonight; her roommate's in the hospital with an acute mono."

"That's sweet of you, Helga, but—"

"There's a time when a woman needs a lover to hold her in his arms all through the black hours of the night and this is it for you. Be my guest."

"All right," said Carolyn. "Maybe tomorrow things will look different."

Gus Henderson was standing beside the crib, looking down at Baby Hornsby, when Carolyn came into the NICU.

"Take a look at our prize patient," he said, "sleeping like a cherub."

"No cherub ever had that much plumbing attached to it," said Maria Alvarez, who was specialing the baby. "Except maybe the Mannikin Pis."

"It's not even quivering," said Carolyn. "What happened?"

"Somebody used his head," said Gus. "Oh, it wasn't me. I was still set enough in my ways to believe cold turkey had to be cold turkey, instead of thinking of a simple thing like slipping enough methadone into the IV to take the edge off withdrawal."

"Who *did* think of it?"

"Some pediatricians in New York and another group in Philadelphia; one of the internes abstracted a medical journal article on their work at the weekly pediatric luncheon confab today. They found that babies born to addicted mothers on methadone did a lot better if they were breast-fed for a while because they kept on getting a small amount of methadone in the milk. So, I put one and one together and got the idea of adding a very small dose to Baby Hornsby's feedings."

"That was brilliant, Gus."

"The interesting part is that Baby Hornsby has not only stopped shaking like a leaf in a hurricane but his pO_2 has gone up sharply. If it keeps on like this for another twenty-four hours, we can take it off CPAP." He lowered his voice to a more intimate note as they moved to the door, beyond earshot of Mrs. Alvarez. "Are you okay? About the committee, I mean?"

"I'll cope. Helga just reminded me that the world won't stop, even if the decision goes against me."

"That's my girl. You're going out with me tonight, aren't you?"

"If you want me."

"Don't you know I'll never stop wanting you?"

"That's nice to hear but I promise not to hold you to it." Her voice was a little husky. "See you about seven-thirty. Helga's spending the night in Magda Gatton's apartment—"

Gus's eyes lit up. "Say! That's great."

"I'll even cook your breakfast," she promised. "But I'd better run now. Dr. Rebecca Dalton asked me to meet her in her office at five-fifteen so we can go up to the Board Room together."

Gus Henderson was thoughtful as he dictated a note for insertion into Baby Hornsby's record. When he finished, he stopped by the nursing station where Helga Sundberg was working on clinical charts with her ear always tuned to the frequency of the alarm buzzer that would signal any sudden change in the vital parameters of the half dozen patients being measured continuously on the monitors before her.

"I'd like to talk to you a minute, Helga," he said. "Can I buy you a cup of coffee?"

"And start tongues wagging from here to the helicopter landing pad on the roof? Let's have it in the lounge, nobody's in there right now."

In the small lounge provided for nurses and doctors who must stay within range of the monitor alarm buzzer, Helga poured two cups from the urn that kept a supply of coffee steaming twenty-four hours a day. Giving one to Gus, she spooned sugar into her own and stirred it vigorously.

"Do you ever worry about weight?" he asked.

"Never," said Helga. "It takes a lot of calories to keep this machine humming."

"I've never seen you worried either. What's your secret?"

"Whatever I'm doing, I give it everything I've got. That means I get everything there is to get out of it, too. So what's to worry about?"

"In my case, it's Carolyn," Gus admitted. "She said something strange to me just now. I'd asked her to go out with me tonight and she said she would if I wanted her."

"And you do?"

"Of course. But when I answered, 'I'll never stop wanting you,' she said, 'I won't hold you to it!' What do you suppose she meant?"

"Carolyn can't help wondering whether she's really doing the right thing in asking the God Committee to end her father's life, Gus. She's bound to be concerned that some people may feel she's wrong and turn away from her."

"But not me. Surely she knows that."

"Whatever happens up there in the Board Room this afternoon, she's going to need all the understanding and love you can give her. The best thing both of you can do tonight is to really hang on and try to forget the outside world."

CHAPTER THIRTEEN

I

The monthly Tissue Conference for the surgical service met on Wednesday afternoon in the Pathology Amphitheater in the basement of the main hospital tower. Regarded as one of the most important teaching activities in the entire medical school, it was also rightly feared by the surgeons. During the hour, they were forced to watch while final evidence proving whether their diagnoses had been correct or incorrect was presented to a jury of their peers, either the results of autopsies performed on patients they had lost, or the diagnosis of microscopic slides from tissues removed.

Today the rows of seats were filled, for this was to be the first conference with Karen Fletcher presiding as acting head of pathology since Dr. Adrian Cooper, the ailing professor of pathology, had been felled by a stroke. The largely male audience was waiting to see how well she would be able to handle herself in the inevitable controversies that resulted, when the fat cats of the surgical staff were faced with the bald evidence of their failures.

At exactly four o'clock Karen Fletcher entered the open tiled space before the curving rows of seats, each row a little higher than the one below, so all might look down upon the specimens being exhibited. Behind her was Dr. Sam Toyota, resident in pathology, who was pushing a cart on which were several enameled trays covered with towels. A spattering of applause, mainly from the younger and brasher members of the house staff, greeted Karen's entrance but she ignored it coolly. Placing a hospital record upon the lectern, she looked up at the crowd through dark horn-rimmed glasses she affected as part of her rather severe workaday uniform and waited for the brief flurry created by her entrance to subside.

"The case to be presented for discussion this afternoon," Karen announced, "is from the Department of Obstetrics and Gynecology, the service of Dr. Jeremiah Singleton."

Jerry Singleton was sitting in the front row of seats, not more than six feet from where Karen was standing. At her words, he suddenly sat up straight.

"I received no notice that a case of mine would be discussed," he said stiffly.

"I was not aware that it had been Dr. Cooper's custom to notify the surgeons when their cases were to be presented," said Karen.

"Well, it wasn't," Jerry conceded.

"Of course, if you would like to put it to a vote, Dr. Singleton—"

"Never mind," said Jerry tartly.

"The case we are presenting is typical of many—except for the outcome," said Karen. "The patient was a thirty-eight-year-old housewife from an upper-income group and the mother of four. At the birth of her last child six months ago, she was instructed by Dr. Singleton to, in her own words, 'come into the hospital in six months for my birthday hysterectomy.'"

A round of laughter from the audience greeted this familiar phrase and Jerry flushed angrily.

"In all fairness to Dr. Singleton," Karen continued, "I must concede that this custom has been becoming more and more frequent with gynecologists in recent years. In fact the number of vaginal hysterectomies in non-pregnant women with minimal or no indications for surgery, except to achieve sterilization, rose by 742 per cent in one Western medical center between July 1968 and December 31, 1970."

A murmur of astonishment from the onlookers interrupted Karen's presentation for a moment and she patiently waited for it to subside.

"The patient was operated upon the day after admission," Karen continued. "A conventional vaginal hysterectomy was performed, taking thirty minutes from start to finish, with the entire uterus, tubes, and ovaries being removed and some repair being made of the outlet."

Looking up from the summary, Karen added dryly: "I think most of you will admit that this feat is not only a tribute to Dr. Singleton's extraordinary skill but also proves that the uterus was not enlarged."

In his seat, Jerry Singleton was slowly turning a light shade of purple.

"The patient's recovery was complicated by a urinary infection," Karen continued, "but this seems to be almost a rule. In fact vaginal hysterectomy carries with it a morbidity rate of close to 22 per cent, most of it because of urinary complications. She was leaving the hospital on the sixth postoperative day, when she suddenly gasped and collapsed in her room. Attempts at resuscitation were futile and she came to autopsy with a clinical diagnosis of pulmonary embolism."

Slipping on a pair of rubber gloves, Karen removed the towel from a tray on the cart Dr. Toyota had wheeled into the room, revealing a human lung. Lifting it in her gloved hands, she separated the two halves of a bisected lobe to reveal a blood clot filling a large section of the pulmonary artery.

"I think all of you can see the embolus, even from the back row," she said. "It was large and, as with such clots, instantly fatal. The slides, please, Dr. Toyota."

Sam Toyota switched on the projection microscope and doused the room lights with the same motion. Instantly, a much-enlarged section of lung tissue appeared on the screen behind where Karen was standing. Picking up a pointer, she moved up to the screen and began to indicate the significant findings.

"All of you can see the clots that fill the branches of the pulmonary artery," she said. "They form the classic picture of pulmonary embolism."

Dr. Toyota placed another slide beneath the microscope and a section of uterine wall appeared on the screen.

"You can also see," Karen said, "that the uterine muscle is quite normal in appearance and we found no significant changes in it. The pathological diagnosis, then, is a normal uterus and postoperative pulmonary embolism causing death.

"As both a pathologist and a woman," she continued as the lights went up and she peeled off the rubber gloves, before moving back to the lectern, "I can only deplore the tremendous increase in major surgery, particularly hysterectomy, simply as a means of insuring that the patient shall be freed from further childbearing. And lest I be influenced by a personal prejudice, I have made a study of cases in such a category here at Biscayne General, plus many other reports throughout the country. The results are, to say the least, shocking.

"Leaving out, for the moment, the question of how much a human life is worth, the fact remains that, in the average case of simple hysterectomy, the hospital bill amounts to almost fifteen hundred dollars, to say nothing of the surgeon's fee. Balance this, if you will, against the use of laparoscopy—visualization of the interior of the abdomen with a fiberoptic instrument somewhat resembling a cystoscope—and occlusion of the Fallopian tubes with metal clips, a procedure that costs less than two hundred dollars. Or far less costly, the inter-uterine device known as an IUD which can be inserted into the cavity of the uterus as an office procedure, largely preventing pregnancy, at the cost of only one office visit to the gynecologist per year.

"Even more important, however, is the psychological shock when a woman loses an organ many of them consider the fountain of their own femininity, weeping as it does every twenty-eight days to remind them of it. In addition psychiatry has determined that, in a distressingly large number of cases, women unconsciously look upon hysterectomy as a castration procedure, naturally a profound shock."

"Excuse me, Dr. Fletcher," said Jerry Singleton, his tone heavy with sarcasm, "but aren't you gilding the lily a bit with all these horror stories?"

"I think not, Dr. Singleton," said Karen in the same even tone. "After all, less than 5 percent of the surgery performed today can be called emergency in nature, nor can more than 7 per cent be considered urgent. Twice as many operations are performed in the average American city as in an English city of comparable size, so the conclusion would seem to be inescapable that almost half of the operations performed in the United States today are probably unnecessary. This means, of course, that a comparable number of deaths occur—some estimates run as high as thirty thousand a year—which could have been avoided if surgery had not been done. And high on the list must be the 'birthday hysterectomy' which resulted in the death of this patient from an embolus to the lungs. The case is now open for general discussion."

Jerry Singleton shot to his feet, spluttering with anger.

"Never, in this amphitheater or any other," he snapped, "have I heard a more biased presentation of a pathological report. You have heard in the case history that this patient recovered from surgery and was ready to go home when the embolism occurred. And I don't have to tell an audience of surgeons that pulmonary embolism is a recognized complication of surgery which no amount of research so far has learned to prevent."

"Don't forget the bladder infection, Jerry," said a urologist in the front row. "You fellows drag a uterus out through an opening perhaps an inch and a half in diameter normally. But when the bladder becomes infected because you traumatized it, you turn the patient over to us."

"It's not my fault, Doctor, that God chose to put the birth canal between the waterworks and the sewer," said the gynecologist. "Besides, this opening you describe as an inch and a half in diameter is also capable of dilating to admit the passage of a baby's head. Infections of the urinary tract do occur after any kind of vaginal surgery, of course. But with adequate preoperative preparation and prophylactic doses of urinary antiseptics afterward, the number of such cases is considerably smaller than has been intimated."

"Getting back to Dr. Fletcher's shotgun accusations," Jerry Singleton continued, "more and more gynecologists today are convinced that halfway measures like laparoscopy to block the tubes and even tying them off immediately after delivery are a poor substitute for the full benefits to be obtained by a hysterectomy, particularly by the vaginal route."

"You refer, I believe, Dr. Singleton," said Karen dryly, "to what is rapidly becoming known as 'hysterilization.'"

"Call it what you like, hysterectomy after the child-bearing period has ended protects the patient from the uncertain menstrual future of the menopause and removes the possibility of cancer of the cervix or the fundus, among the most frequent sites of malignancy in women. And if the ovaries are removed, too, the danger of ovarian cancer is also eliminated."

"Leaving the psychological trauma of an early menopause."

"Which can be completely relieved with hormones by mouth."

"You will still find competent gynecologic opinion," Karen retorted coolly, "stating that it doesn't make sense to remove the baby carriage, leave the playpen intact, and think that everything is going to be all right."

The double-barbed sally drew delighted laughter from the audience. But even though Jerry Singleton had recognized by now that he was in retreat, he continued to fight back.

"With women today seeking to remove every aspect of femininity in favor of full equality, Dr. Fletcher, it would seem that the only completely liberated woman would be one who has had her uterus out."

Karen smiled tolerantly as if she were listening to a child. "I can only answer you, Dr. Singleton, with a quotation from *Planned Parenthood*. While devoted to the very principle you advocate of freeing women from the specter of childbearing at will, the organization still says regarding hysterilization: 'Preventive lobotomies for young people statistically at risk of developing violent psychoses, or ophthalmectomy for those populations found most likely to get cancer of the eye at some future time, have not been suggested by physicians writing in psychiatric or opthalmologic journals.' To which I might add that the widespread use of bilateral prophylactic mammectomy simply because the female breast is a frequent site of cancer would certainly detract considerably from what one might call the contour of society."

Another roar of laughter greeted Karen's retort and Jerry Singleton subsided in his seat, knowing he was beaten.

"I see that it is five o'clock," said Karen, "and since quitting time takes precedence over even the most learned discussions, this session of the surgical Tissue Conference is adjourned."

As she was leaving the amphitheater, Jerry Singleton loomed up beside her, causing her to look oddly fragile and defenseless against his height.

"What the hell were you trying to do, Karen?" he demanded angrily. "Crucify me?"

"Not at all, Jerry," she said. "I was merely doing what I considered to be my duty, as acting head of the department." Then she added, but in a lower tone, "But perhaps we should discuss it later—under more friendly circumstances."

And with the smile of a cat who has enjoyed its cream she left the room while, temporarily speechless, Jerry Singleton could find no words with which to answer her.

II

A sober group of people had gathered around the long gleaming table in the Board Room on the top floor of the hospital tower, when Dr. Jeffry Toler gaveled the meeting of the Moriturus Committee to order exactly at five-thirty. Moments earlier, an orderly and a nurse from the ICU had pushed into the room the narrow hospital bed upon which Richard Payson lay. An extra dose of chlorpromazine had been injected into his veins about a half hour earlier and under the influence of the powerful tranquilizer, the writhing of his muscles was not quite so pronounced as usual. He still did not appear, however, to be conscious of his surroundings.

Next to Jeffry Toler, who sat at the head of the table, was the State's Attorney who was substituting for Judge Robie that afternoon. Anthony Broadhurst was a stocky man of about forty-five, with a square jaw and a no-nonsense look about him. Watching him go into the Board Room as she sat outside alone, Carolyn Payson had felt her hopes for a favorable decision, never very high, start to fade even more.

Seated next to the attorney was Dr. Manning Desmond, chief of medical services, and beyond him, Dr. Angus McHale from pediatrics. Surgery was represented by Dr. James Karnes, associate professor of urology. On the other side of the table, Helen Gaynor, secretary of the medical center Board of Directors, sat at Jeffry Toler's elbow with the stenotype machine, upon which she would keep a running account of the proceedings, in front of her. Beyond her was Dr. Lewis Katz from psychiatry, Father Hagan, the hospital chaplain, and a guest expert, Professor Cecil Thorne from the Genetics Department of Biscayne University. At the end sat Dr. Peter Gross, the neurologist in charge of Richard Payson's case, and Rebecca Dalton, representing Carolyn Payson.

"I call this meeting of the Moriturus Committee to order," said Jeffry

Toler. "Miss Gaynor will make a record of everything as usual.

"For the benefit of Mr. Broadhurst, who is here for the first time," he continued, "I might say that this committee came into being because of intense public interest in providing a way whereby patients who are hopelessly ill, with no prospect of a cure, may petition medical authority, as represented by this committee, either in person or through their closest relative, if the subjects are unable to speak for themselves, to allow life to be ended.

"One of the cases that brought this problem to something of a focus was decided some time ago here in the Miami area, when a woman patient in a local hospital with a terminal illness requested the physicians in charge of her case not to take measures to keep her alive any longer. In order to protect themselves against possible suits for negligence and malpractice, if they acceded to her request, the physicians and the hospital involved undertook legal action against this patient, seeking a final court opinion on the question of a person's right to make the decision not to be treated further and to be allowed to die.

"The judge in this case ruled that the patient's wishes could be obeyed by the physicians and the hospital without prejudice or danger of their being blamed for the consequences. The woman then received no more treatment for an advanced malignant condition and shortly died.

"I don't have to tell you, of course, that the very name we have chosen for this committee is a statement of the basic principle to which it seeks to adhere. *Moriturus* in Latin is part of the well-known salute of the gladiators before entering the arena: 'We who are about to die salute you.'" Jeffry Toler looked around the table. "Are there any questions?"

Only one member spoke, Anthony Broadhurst.

"Am I to understand that all patients brought before this committee are about to die?" he asked.

"That is a major criterion," Jeffry Toler conceded. "I might add that the appearance of similar committees in hospitals all over the country first came about largely as a result of the development of techniques for transplantation of the heart from one individual to another. Successful heart transplants require methods of keeping the body of a possible donor in what might be called a state of automatic functioning, even when death is inevitable and—"

"But has medical science reached the point where you can predict death absolutely?" Anthony Broadhurst inquired.

"That depends upon what you call death," said Dr. Katz. "From the philosophic point of view, physicians have always regarded death as occurring when the heart stops beating, the lungs stop breathing, and the patient no longer responds to any stimulus. More recently the determination of 'brain death' by means of the electroencephalograph has been added as the ultimate criterion."

"Exactly what is determined by that test, Doctor?" the attorney asked.

"Merely the cessation in brain tissue of the action currents which characterize all life," said the psychiatrist. "It must be said, however, that many investigators now believe real life ceases essentially with the ending of a person's ability to think, feel, reason for himself and maintain body functions consciously—in other words the end of consciousness permanently is the end of life."

"But can you measure the end of consciousness, as you describe it, any better than you can measure the brain's action currents?"

"Not as well," Dr. Katz admitted. "Which brings us back to the real dilemma—just what is death?"

"A court in Richmond recently heard a suit for malpractice against a group of physicians who carried out a heart transplant," said Toler. "The judge ruled there that death occurs when brain function ends, even though the heart still beats and the patient breathes."

"And a suit that ended yesterday against Dr. Kenneth Dalton came to practically the same conclusion," Dr. Katz reminded the committee.

"All of which brings us down to the basic truth," said Dr. Manning Desmond, "that the physician has to be the judge of what is best for his patient. With so many factors governing life or death decisions, no set formula is going to fit all cases. The ultimate criterion has to be based on common sense and common humanity, just as it has always been."

"That may have been true before malpractice suits became so popular," Dr. James Karnes demurred. "But however much I may agree with Dr. Desmond, as a surgeon I must always bear in mind that, unless I take every possible measure to keep a patient alive as long as I can, and then use the most accurate method of determining death at my disposal, I am liable under present law. And with due respect to your profession, Mr. Broad-hurst, some lawyer is usually waiting in the wings to take over and do everything he can to wreck my career."

"Gentlemen," said Jeffry Toler firmly, "I believe this discussion has reached the non-productive point. Our committee, like those in most large centers today, was set up to remove from the individual physician the burden of responsibility for deciding whether a patient shall go on living under intolerable conditions or be let to die. The patient before us today would appear to be a prime example of this purpose: he is Mr. Richard Payson, who has been on the neurological service for the past month under the care of Dr. Peter Gross, professor of neurology in the Department of Medicine. Dr. Gross, you have the floor."

The pudgy neurologist got to his feet and motioned for the orderly and nurse accompanying the movable bed on which Richard Payson lay to push it near the table so all could see him.

"The patient is fifty years old," he began. "Until the onset of the present illness, he was a successful architect. I have known the family for many years but the nature of his illness was only diagnosed about six months ago when he first consulted me, although some symptoms of Huntington's disease had been present for almost five years."

"Do you feel that there is any question of his having Huntington's?" Jeffry Toler asked.

"None at all," said Dr. Gross. "The case was discussed at a staff meeting last week and everyone there agreed."

Turning to the attorney, the neurologist continued: "Dr. Cecil Thorne is a world authority on genetic conditions, Mr. Broadhurst. I asked him to come here today and explain some of the pertinent facts about Huntington's disease, so I will defer at this point to superior knowledge."

"Huntington's disease," said the geneticist, "is a degenerative condition of the brain and nervous system transmitted solely by heredity. The gene for Huntington's apparently arrived in this country about the time of the American Revolution when several members of a single family—some reports say six, others only three—emigrated to America."

"You mean those few people have been responsible for every case that has happened in the United States since?" Anthony Broadhurst inquired.

"That is the general consensus," said the geneticist. "The Huntington gene is a Mendelian dominant characteristic transmitted without relation-ship to sex, so a fifty-fifty chance exists that a parent who has the gene will pass it on to the offspring. Other hereditary conditions follow a similar pattern, but what makes Huntington's such a deadly condition is the fact that every individual possessing the gene will eventually develop symptoms of the disease, if he or she lives long enough."

"But don't inherited diseases manifest themselves in childhood?" Broadhurst asked.

"Most of them do," Professor Thorne conceded. "With H-D, however, the symptoms of deterioration almost never begin before age thirty-five and usually later. By that time a person who does not know he possesses the possibility of having inherited H-D from a gene-bearing parent has probably already married and had children."

"With half of them certain to develop the disease?"

"Yes."

"My God!" the lawyer exclaimed. "Then this man's offspring have had to go through life with the sword of Damocles suspended over their heads."

"Mr. Payson has only one daughter," said Rebecca Dalton. "The one who is bringing him before this committee."

"Did she know. . . ?"

"Not until a few months ago," said Dr. Gross. "Her father lived in Atlanta and managed to hide his real condition from Carolyn."

"She is determined never to have children," Rebecca added, "in order that this particular gene shall die in her father's body and in her own."

"Is there no possibility of a cure, Dr. Thorne?" the lawyer asked.

"Inherited conditions are never cured," said the geneticist. "All we can do is try to recognize them early, so they won't be passed on to succeeding generations. Fortunately a method of doing that has recently been discovered, but too late to help either father or daughter."

"Richard Payson kew what would happen to him," said Dr. Gross. "That's why he willed his body to the medical school here."

"Does anyone wish to question Professor Thorne further?" Dr. Toler asked and, when there was no answer, nodded to Dr. Gross. "Go on, Pete."

"There isn't much more except to show you the patient." The neurologist lifted Richard Payson's arm so all could see the continuous squirming and purposeless movements of the muscles, in spite of the heavy sedation that had been given to him. "He appears to be conscious at times but we cannot even be sure of that any more."

"Can you be certain that he doesn't know what's happening, Doctor?" the chaplain asked quietly.

"His daughter is convinced he still does at times," said Gross, "but I'm not at all sure I agree."

"What does she base that conviction on?" the attorney asked.

"Occasionally, but never except when she is with him, the patient makes sounds that could be construed to be words. In her opinion, they're always the same—begging her to let him die."

When there were no further questions, Dr. Gross helped the nurse and orderly push the bed from the room and called to Carolyn, who was sitting outside.

"Would you come in, please, Carolyn," he said. "The committee would like to hear you now."

III

At ten minutes before six o'clock the Patient Distress Alarm at the CICU nursing station sounded its two-second-interval beep and the small red bulb on the face of the alarm boxes in a half dozen spots scattered over the ICU floor suddenly began to glow. A glance at the master monitor screen told Helga the nature of the emergency, for the flashing pattern of the ECG tracing from Kevin McCartney's heart had suddenly become a flat line, indicating cessation of the heartbeat.

In one swift movement, Helga punched the red call button on the panel before her. But even before the taped call of "CODE FIVE—CICU" started sounding from loudspeakers throughout the hospital, she was across the main passageway separating the control panel from the glass-fronted cubicles in which the patients lay and into the one occupied by Kevin McCartney.

"Load a syringe with one cc. of adrenalin and attach a long needle," she told the nurse who had been watching beside Kevin's bed.

"His heart just stopped, Miss Sundberg." This was the nurse's first day on CICU and her voice had a slightly hysterical note.

"I know. Get the adrenalin!"

Pulling down the sheet that covered Kevin's chest and jerking up his hospital shirt, Helga leaned over and started pounding with her fist upon the long scar of the transplant operation that bisected the skin over his breastbone, timing the blows to a one-second interval by an instinct generated by long practice. From a distance she could hear the monotonous taped voice calling: "CODE FIVE—CICU" over and over and knew that the nearest doctor on the CICU Cardiopulmonary Resuscitation team would be there at any moment. She didn't, however, wait for him to arrive.

"Strap a respirator mask on and start the oxygen going," she directed the nurse who was placing a syringe with a long needle and a cubic centimeter of adrenalin in the barrel on a sterile towel atop the bedside table. If a doctor did not appear in a few seconds, Helga would jab the long needle through Kevin's chest wall and into the now stilled heart, pumping the powerful stimulant adrenalin into the heart muscle.

At the sixth pounding stroke upon Kevin's chest—the skin was already taking on the dusky hue of cyanosis—a flicker showed up on the small ECG monitor beside the bed, revealing at least a tentative attempt by his heart to restart itself under the stimulus of the hammer blows. Meanwhile the other nurse, her slight touch of hysteria expelled by Helga's swift and skillful action in the routine of CPR, had strapped a mask tightly over his face.

When the respirator sighed into action, Kevin's lungs were inflated with pure oxygen for a moment, then allowed to collapse, when the pressure was released through the rhythmic action of the valve that was the very heart of the machine. Two more blows to the pallid chest and the faint pattern of an entire ECG tracing appeared upon the monitor screen, hesitating between beats, as if not yet certain that it really wanted to continue, but not quite ceasing again.

"Was there any warning, Miss Sundberg?" Ken Dalton, the first to arrive, spoke at her elbow.

"No, sir. The tracing just flattened out suddenly into a straight line."

Picking up the syringe containing the adrenalin, Ken plunged the long needle downward between the ribs until it was buried to the shank where it was connected to a plastic disposable syringe, the only kind used for injections in the hospital. When Ken pulled back on the plunger, dark blood spurted into the chamber of the syringe, telling him he was inside the heart, and he injected part of the contents directly into the heart. Then drawing the needle part way out, until blood could no longer be drawn into it— indicating that the point was now in the muscle of the heart wall—he injected about a third of the remaining dose before removing the needle.

On the monitor screen, the heart tracing leaped like a skittish horse under the powerful stimulus of the adrenalin. The height of the peak showing ventricular contraction had almost doubled, and the pallid hue to the skin was lessening rapidly too. When Ken Dalton pinched Kevin's cheek, a pink flush showed for a moment, the simple maneuver telling the surgeon that the oxygen flowing into the air sacs of Kevin's lungs, under the rhythmic pressure of the respirator, was already passing through the walls of the tiny capillaries surrounding those air sacs and streaming toward the brain and the other vital organs, which had been deprived of the vital gas for perhaps a minute by the sudden cessation of the heartbeat.

By now the corridor outside the cubicle was filled with people, but all was order and purposeful action, as each person went about the assigned activity with a skill born of repeated practice.

Ed Vogel pushed a pacemaker cart, ready to shock the heart into contraction if it was needed. The ICU interne carried a sterile cut-down tray, in case it was necessary to expose a vein through a small incision in front of the ankle and insert a catheter to start a second intravenous injection. And Val LeMoyne quietly moved into the cubicle to take over the respirator operation from the student nurse.

"Chalk up another victory for Miss Sundberg," said the surgeon. "We've got to do better, gentlemen. As I remember it, the nursing staff has beaten the CPR teams to the last four cessations."

"I got the first flicker of contraction with the sixth sock to his chest," said Helga proudly, then laughed. "I guess it's a good thing I'm a big girl."

"And an intelligent one," said Ken crisply. "Someday one of these little circuses is going to give me a heart attack, so remind me to ask for you to special me, Miss Sundberg."

He watched the small monitor screen for a full minute and, when the ECG pattern showed no sign of failing, nodded to Ed Vogel.

"Release the team, Ed, but stick around," he said. "We're going to have to take some measures to keep this from happening again."

IV

"Please come up to the end of the table, Miss Payson, so the court reporter can hear you," said Jeffry Toler, when the door had closed behind Richard Payson's bed. "I believe you know everyone here, except perhaps Mr. Broadhurst and Professor Thorne."

"I consulted Professor Thorne at Dr. Gross's suggestion, after he told me Father's diagnosis," said Carolyn. "How do you do, Mr. Broadhurst?"

"I'm fine, thank you," said the attorney.

"Suppose you tell us just why you have brought your father before the Moriturus Committee, Miss Payson," said Toler.

When she first saw the sober-faced group around the long polished mahogany table and the secretary with her stenotype machine that gave the committee much the air of a courtroom, if not the reality, Carolyn had been intimidated for a moment. But she had herself fully under control now.

"I felt that I had no choice, Dr. Toler," she answered.

"Why do you feel that way, Miss Payson?" Anthony Broadhurst inquired.

"Because almost every time I see my father now, he begs me to let him die."

"Are you certain that he really knows what's happening?"

"Only at times, sir. The last few days, I've barely been able to make out the words because the deterioration in his muscular control seems to be involving the speech mechanism more and more."

"This is the usual course with Huntington's," Dr. Gross volunteered.

"But are you *sure* he wants to die?" Broadhurst persevered.

"Wouldn't you, if you were like he is, Mr. Broadhurst?"

"We're not here to question what anyone else would do under similar circumstances, Miss Payson, but to inquire into your own reasons. Is your father a financial burden upon you or other members of your family?"

"There are no other members of my family—and there never will be."

"Then he *is* a burden upon you?"

"Not yet, Mr. Broadhurst." Carolyn could see the trend the questioning was taking and also its possible implications, at least in the mind of the lawyer, but had no intention of denying the truth.

"My father's funds will last perhaps another week," she added. "But I have saved a few thousand dollars and that will be used as long as it lasts."

"And afterward?"

"If the committee does not choose to free him from what you can surely see is at best a hell on earth, I shall borrow what I can."

"May I ask whether you have considered transferring him to a state institution?"

"I brought Father here from Atlanta, where he had gone to a nursing home, Mr. Broadhurst, because I wanted him to be as comfortable as possible during whatever time he has left to live. And because I wish to be near him."

"In his present condition he could be committed to a state institution and the financial burden would be lifted from you," the attorney insisted. "My office would be glad to help with the details."

"Perhaps the financial burden but not the ethical one," Carolyn said quietly.

"Ethical?"

"As a little girl I was taught in Sunday school to honor my parents. My mother died when I was a very little girl and Father brought me up. He is a very proud man and I know what having people—even me—see him as he is now must be doing to him."

"If he is conscious of it."

"He must realize it. Why else would he beg me to let him die?"

"You have a point there—if he is conscious of the state he's in," the lawyer concluded. "But as I understand it, mental degeneration is as much a part of this disease as are the obvious physical changes. Which means that, even if your father does know what is happening now, which I personally doubt, he probably will not know much longer."

"Have you visited a state mental institution recently, Mr. Broadhurst?"

"No."

"When I was a student getting my degree in nursing at the University of Florida in Gainesville, I spent several weeks at a large state mental hospital as part of my training. On the basis of what I saw there I have resolved that my father shall never have to be left in such a place."

"I can understand your emotional reaction, Miss Payson," Broadhurst conceded, not unkindly, "but I can't help believing a more pragmatic approach would be best for you."

"And for my father?"

"It could hardly hurt him—when he doesn't know what is happening."

"I want you to know that we all feel great sympathy for you, Miss Payson," said Dr. Jeffry Toler gently. "But I wonder if you really understand what you are asking of us?"

"I am asking the committee to take measures to end my father's life as quickly and as painlessly as possible."

"By starvation, Miss Payson?" Dr. McHale asked. "I'm sure you have seen some of the mongoloids with pyloric stenosis and meningoceles that have been let die."

"I have, Dr. McHale. That is why I would never approve of starvation."

"Just a minute." Anthony Broadhurst frowned. "I don't exactly understand what is involved in this question of starvation."

"Because of his muscular condition, Mr. Payson cannot swallow without danger of aspiration—what you call strangulation—Mr. Broadhurst," Rebecca Dalton explained. "He is fed only through the tube you probably noticed running through one nostril."

"But starvation would be even more cruel than letting him live," the lawyer protested.

"I'm sure we all agree with that," said Rebecca. "Which really leaves us only two alternatives."

"What are they, Doctor?"

"A drug is probably the first choice, in a large enough dose to produce death. That would be painless, although several hours might be required before death occurred."

"And the other?"

"Air embolism."

"I'm afraid I don't understand."

"Air injected directly into the circulation through a vein blocks the flow of blood to the lungs and the brain and causes death rather quickly."

"Then it's true that a drop of air injected with a hypodermic can cause death?"

"Not a drop, Mr. Broadhurst. But a fairly large syringeful would do it."

"Either way involves what is technically murder," said the attorney bluntly.

"In a legal sense, I suppose you could only call it that," Rebecca agreed. "I prefer to think of it the way Miss Payson does, as an act of mercy."

"I can see that pulling the plug and stopping a respirator when the patient is not really alive might be defensible," Broadhurst conceded. "But euthanasia with the committee actually usurping a right possessed only by God is quite another matter."

"That's why the students call us the God Committee," Jeffry Toler said dryly. "Does anyone else wish to question Miss Payson? I'm sure all this is very painful to her.

"Thank you, Miss Payson," said Toler when there were no more questions of her. "Dr. Dalton will answer any other questions we may have about the case and will give you the decision of the committee. You may go."

Carolyn left the room, but there was no spring to her step. She hadn't really expected the God Committee to agree to her request and now she was convinced that it would be denied.

Even bringing her father before them had been futile, she was convinced. But it was a last and desperate legal resort, which had to be exhausted before anything else could be done.

CHAPTER FOURTEEN

I

"I'm going to try something different, Ed," said Ken Dalton after the CPR team had left the CICU. "The presence of so much fluid inside the pericardium means the heart is probably being squeezed down, just as it would be by blood escaping through the wall in a stab wound of the heart itself."

"We can remove it," said Vogel. "But do you think that will have any lasting effect?"

"Not simply removing the fluid. We must remember that what's happening here is an invasion of the lymphocytes triggered by the body's own protective mechanism against what it considers to be the threat of a foreign invader, in this case the proteins in the transplanted heart. But we do know that, when a cancer metastasizes to the heart area and effusion occurs, certain cell-destroying drugs can be injected into the pericardium with good effect."

"And lymphocytes in a rejection crisis could be considered a metastasis from the spleen and bone marrow?"

"Something like that."

"It might work," Vogel conceded. "And even if it doesn't, it's worth trying."

"Worth trying if for no other reason than because it's probably the only weapon we have left," Ken agreed soberly.

"What chemical agent will you use?"

"For a start, Thiotepa and Prednisone; with metastatic malignancy these chemotherapeutic agents sometimes produce remissions that last several months or longer. We have to remove the fluid anyway and by putting a heavy dose right into the space around Kevin's heart, we ought to get the best possible effect."

"Shall I get the aspiration tray, Dr. Dalton?" Helga had been listening to the discussion with considerable interest.

"Please," said Ken. "Have the pharmacy send up a single sixty-milligram dose of Thiotepa in two percent procaine hydrochloride, as well as some Prednisone ampules. I'll want to inject the drugs as soon as I get most of the fluid out of the pericardium."

"I'll get the tray and order the medication." Helga vanished from the cubicle and Ken turned back to study the monitor screen beside the bed.

"There's not too much T-wave change, so I doubt if the heart itself has been badly damaged yet by the rejection," he said. "I'm gambling on much of this crisis being connected with the large effusion in the pericardium."

"At least we can hope," said Vogel.

"Any report on the blood work yet?"

"None on the record. I'll call Peggy Tyndall in the lab and see what she has for us."

At the nursing station, Ed rang the laboratory and Peggy answered almost immediately.

"I was just going to bring up the report," she said. "Anything new?"

"Kevin McCartney had a cessation, but Miss Sundberg got his heart started again."

"That was the CODE FIVE, wasn't it?"

"Yes. Have you found anything?"

"The enzymes are not significantly elevated, not even LDH-1."

"At least that's a good sign."

One of the first indicators of heart damage, whether by coronary thrombosis or by rejection, is an increase in certain biochemical agents in the blood, as the body seeks to absorb the damaged muscle. One in particular called LDH-1 is elevated in severe rejection crises, when the patient's heart muscle itself is literally cannibalized by the patient's own lymphocytes.

"Anything else?" Peggy asked.

"Dr. Dalton is going to put some Thiotepa and a slug of Prednisone right into the pericardium, but the pharmacy can supply that."

"At least he's doing *something* at last," said Peggy. "Is Dr. Rebecca there?"

"She had an important committee meeting."

"It's the God Committee about Carolyn Payson's father, but she's losing that battle."

"How in the hell would you know about that, if the committee is still meeting?"

"The attendant who took Mr. Payson to the Board Room was just in here with a cart of supplies. He says the D.A. who's sitting on the God Committee today in place of Judge Robie is giving everybody up there the third degree. And he isn't liking the answers he's getting."

"I've often wondered how the grapevine is able to find out things before they happen," said Vogel. "Now I know."

II

"Do you wish to make a statement before we vote on Miss Payson's request, Dr. Dalton?" Jeffry Toler asked, after Carolyn had left the room.

"I would like to put the philosophical aspects of this particular case into some sort of perspective, if I may," said Rebecca. "Admittedly as much for my own benefit as for anything else."

"Please do," said Toler. "I'm sure we can all benefit from your analysis."

"As I see it, the question here is one thoughtful people have asked themselves since the beginning of medical science: to what degree is a physician justified in assuming full responsibility for the life or death of a patient? I haven't studied the Aphorisms of Hippocrates lately, but I am sure we could find much in them that would help guide us in cases like this. Certainly we are all familiar with the profound principles of ethics set down for us in the Oath of Hippocrates most of us swore when we graduated from medical school. Largely because medicine is a challenge to overcome death by using our technical knowledge to prevent it, doctors naturally tend to regard the loss of a patient as a personal defeat. Thus we tend to elevate the principle of biological continuance of the individual to the status of an absolute, even to a point where we ignore what we may be doing to the dignity of that individual."

"Are you saying that physicians tend to take the view that their efforts are always helpful to the patient?" Anthony Broadhurst asked.

"Not only the view, Mr. Broadhurst; we must also be certain at all times that our efforts do not harm those under our care. It is a basic principle of medical ethics that *nolle nocere*—to do no harm—takes precedence even over doing good through treatment. And with that view in mind, we must ask ourselves whether we will not in fact be doing harm to Richard Payson's status as an individual, his personal dignity, by letting him live longer in the condition he is in now."

"I admire your eloquence and grant at least part of your logic, Doctor," said the lawyer. "But I am not sure they apply to the case in point."

"I was just coming to that."

"Please forgive the interruption, then."

"The first successful transplantation of the human heart occurred less than ten years ago, in December 1967, to be exact. As you may know, my husband has been severely criticized for continuing to perform heart transplants after it became evident that in most cases the process of rejection severely limits the chances of success with the operation. As Dr. Toler said, a long and painful case of alleged malpractice in one transplant case ended day before yesterday with exoneration of my husband."

"During which, I believe, he did not defend himself?"

"Yes," she conceded, "the reason being a matter of conscience on his part. My husband and I worked as a team during the transplant program and, as a cardiologist, I was largely responsible for selecting the cases. Few, if any, of the patients he operated on would have lived more than a few months without surgery, most of them as cardiac invalids and all in great pain. Yet after transplantation of another heart, some lived as long as eighteen months in relative comfort, and don't forget that some of them had previously even begged for death."

"Euthanasia?"

"That's the technical term; 'mercy killing' has caught the public interest even more. But there can be two forms of euthanasia. In the 'active form' the patient is given an agent that produces death painlessly and as quickly as possible, for example the air injection mentioned earlier. In 'passive euthanasia,' however, the patient is given sufficient medicine to relieve pain, even if his life is shortened. Or, as is more usually the case, where pain is intractable or brain damage irreversible, supportive measures such as the use of a respirator or cardiopulmonary resuscitation are simply stopped with the same result. Did you know a magazine survey recently showed that ninety-one per cent of the readers responding to a questionnaire felt that a terminal patient should be permitted to refuse treatment which would prolong life artificially?"

"I am familiar with the survey, Doctor," said Broadhurst. "And also the fact that a similar survey among parents of severely handicapped children overwhelmingly rejected euthanasia. Obviously the passive form has to be rejected in Mr. Payson's case, since it could only be accomplished by slow starvation. As his daughter's representative before this committee, do you recommend the active form?"

"That is what his daughter is asking," said Rebecca.

"And yourself?"

"I don't know. If I had seen several of the patients my husband operated upon successfully before heart transplantation was a fact, I would have been strongly tempted to recommend stopping their medication. But, as I said, some of them lived fairly comfortably for as much as a year and a half after surgery. One is still alive."

"Aren't you saying, Dr. Dalton, that in a sense you and your husband performed mercy killing in the end—by recommending them for surgery?"

"My conscience is clear on that score, Mr. Broadhurst."

"But not your husband's? His failure to defend himself at the trial would seem to prove that."

"I think you can begin to see some of the ethical questions a doctor must ask himself, Mr. Broadhurst," Manning Desmond interposed. "Particularly when treating people who are seriously, perhaps even hopelessly, ill. But in justification of Dr. Dalton and her husband, even their failures have helped immeasurably in our understanding of how to combat rejection in the case of other organs."

"Such as?"

"Specifically kidneys, which are far easier to transplant than hearts. And we hope with other organs as well."

"Surely you don't argue that Mr. Payson's death can contribute anything to science?"

"I am not at all certain that it will not, Mr. Broadhurst," said Professor Thorne. "Huntington's is relatively rare and the opportunity to study cells from the patient's tissues could be valuable. Knowing the importance of post-mortem examinations in the study of medicine, I'm sure Miss Payson would agree—"

"If Mr. Payson should die under anything resembling suspicious circumstances, Professor Thorne," Broadhurst interrupted, "be assured that my position as attorney for the state would require me to order a post-mortem, whether his relatives permitted it or not."

"I've already reported that the patient has willed his body to this medical school," said Dr. Gross. "So the question of its disposition after death is academic."

"The point I am making," Rebecca said firmly, "is that in Mr. Payson's case we are dealing with an absolutely incurable disease, one that proceeds inexorably from the beginning of symptoms to the death of the individual."

"Over what period, Doctor?"

"Dr. Gross can answer that better than I."

"In most cases death occurs in a few years. But some have lived as much as ten years after the major symptoms of H-D appeared and a few even longer."

"With no possibility of a cure?" the attorney asked.

"Absolutely none," said Professor Thorne.

"So if there ever was a case where active euthanasia is justified, this is it," said Rebecca.

"And yet you have just refused to advocate it, Dr. Dalton," said Broadhurst.

"We seem to have come to an impasse," Jeffry Toler said firmly. "Do you have any other points to make, Rebecca?"

"Only to remind the committee that Carolyn Payson is making what seems to her a reasonable request and that she is perfectly sincere in her belief that, by arranging her father's death, she will be carrying out his wishes."

"Does anyone doubt that statement?" Toler asked.

"I am convinced that Miss Payson firmly believes what she is asking is best for her father," said the attorney. "Nevertheless one court case, in which a patient who was in command of her faculties insisted that no further treatment be carried out for what was a terminal condition, does not constitute a precedent for euthanasia, especially the deliberate killing of a patient by a doctor or a hospital. Therefore I must warn you that, if I am outvoted here today and you approve the death of this patient, you will be opening a Pandora's box that can only damage the reputation of this hospital and yourselves as physicians and teachers, at a time when the institution is already under fire by certain forces in the community."

"Thank you, Mr. Broadhurst," said Jeffry Toler. "I think we might hear from Father Hagan before we take a final vote."

"I am greatly in sympathy with both Miss Payson and her father and, as you all know, I initiated proceedings before the committee at her request," said the old priest. "But I agree with Mr. Broadhurst that we have no right to give official approval to what can hardly be called by any other name except euthanasia."

"Or murder," said the attorney bluntly.

"I think we are ready to vote," said Jeffry Toler. "If you approve Miss Payson's request that her father's life be ended, please write 'Yes' on the small writing pad before you. If you do not approve, write 'No.' Dr. Dalton and Professor Thorne are not members of the Moriturus Committee and cannot vote. Please do not sign your ballot and be sure to fold it so no one else can see your vote. They will be tabulated by Mrs. Gaynor."

The secretary collected the ballots and examined them at one side of the room.

"There was one vote of 'Yes,' Dr. Toler," she reported. "The rest were all 'No.'"

"The request is denied and the ballot slips will be destroyed," said Jeffry Toler. "I need not remind the committee members that everything done or said here this afternoon is strictly confidential and must not be divulged to anyone, except that Dr. Dalton is authorized to inform Miss Carolyn Payson of this decision."

He tapped the polished block of wood upon which the gavel lay. "The meeting is adjourned."

III

Helga Sundberg pushed the small table containing the aspiration tray into the cubicle where Kevin McCartney lay and Ed Vogel helped her move the bed to one side. While Ken Dalton was putting on a pair of sterile gloves, Helga opened the tray, folding back the sterile covers to reveal its contents.

Upon it was a fifty-cubic-centimeter syringe, needles, and a metal stopcock by which the fluid being aspirated could be drawn up into the syringe, then, simply by turning the handle of the cock, expelled through a section of plastic tubing into the large basin she placed on the bed beside Kevin's chest.

With quick, skilled movements, Helga painted the still somewhat pallid skin of Kevin's chest with a crimson-colored antiseptic, then stepped back so Ken could place a sheet about two feet square, with a small window cut into it, over the bartender's chest. Feeling through the sterile drape, the surgeon counted ribs by pressing upon them, then centered the window on a spot in the lower chest, a little to the left of the surgical scar that extended from the top of the sternum to the bottom.

"I'm going in low so as to drain the entire pericardium if I can," he explained. "Please watch the monitor, Ed, and speak out if there is any change."

Watching the syringe in Ken Dalton's hand, Ed Vogel saw the slight perceptible hesitation as the point of the needle touched the crimson skin. It was only momentary, however, before the needle was thrust firmly between the ribs and into the chest. Drawing back on the barrel of the syringe, he removed about twenty cc. of fluid before pushing the needle deeper, so it would remain inside the pericardium while the tough membranous sac itself was being emptied.

The fluid was thin and cloudy, but flowed easily through the needle. As the process of emptying the pericardial sac continued, the level of the cloudy fluid in the basin Helga was holding to collect it grew steadily higher.

"Must be close to a liter," Ed Vogel observed. "No wonder his heart had trouble beating."

"I guess our concern for Kevin and our assumption that this might be his last bout of rejection made us fail to realize that this amount of fluid could have crippled the heart enough to produce the picture he showed," said Ken. "All of which should teach us not to jump to conclusions too easily."

The aspiration completed, Ken injected the two drugs carefully into the sac around the heart, taking longer with the Thiotepa, which could have an irritating action.

"No change in the ECG," Ed Vogel reported from his observation of the small monitor.

Ken stepped back after removing the needle and Helga strapped a small dressing over the puncture wound.

"Let's hope the medication will slow down the attack of the lymphocytes upon his heart," he said. "If it does, we could have won this skirmish."

"Maybe it will buy time enough to help win the battle, too," said Helga. "This place somehow wouldn't be the same without Kevin behind the bar of the Dolphin Lounge."

IV

Carolyn Payson was sitting patiently in the small alcove just off the Board Room when Rebecca Dalton came out. One look at Rebecca's face told Carolyn her mission had failed.

"I'm sorry," said the cardiologist. "The decision went against us."

"I knew it would, the moment I walked into the room and saw Mr. Broadhurst."

"You mustn't blame him entirely, Carolyn," said Rebecca. "As State's Attorney, he must view something like this differently from the way we would." She hesitated, then added: "The real stumbling block was the fact that we weren't asking simply that your father be given the right to die in peace, but that someone be the active agent in what can hardly be called anything but euthanasia. I'm afraid neither the medical profession nor the public are ready for that, so under the circumstances we could hardly expect any other decision."

"I don't feel any resentment, Dr. Dalton," said Carolyn. "Not against the committee, or anybody."

"It's not the end of the world, you know," said Rebecca gently. "Dr. Gross thinks your father can't live more than a few more months."

"Thank you for pleading my case, Dr. Dalton. It wasn't really fair of me to ask you."

"I'm sorry I wasn't able to do a better job," said Rebecca. "Dr. Toler has asked that the decision of the committee not be made public, and I assured him that he could rely on our discretion."

"You can be sure of that. Thanks again—and good-by."

Rebecca stood in the hall outside the Board Room, watching the lithe, erect figure of the girl as she marched to the elevator and into it without so much as a backward look.

"How did she take it, Reb?" Dr. Peter Gross came out of the Board Room and stopped beside Rebecca.

"Very determined. You know, Pete, I believe she was sure from the start that it would turn out this way but felt she had to bring it up, if for no other reason than to convince herself she had done everything she could."

"That's a reasonable enough thought—under the circumstances."

"But somehow I can't help believing it's not the whole thought. And I'm not even sure I want to know what the rest is."

"When you spoke in the Board Room just now about the philosophy and ethics of this situation, I couldn't help remembering some phrases from the Hippocratic Oath we all swore as a part of the medical school graduation ceremony," he said, "particularly the part that goes:

> "So far as power and discernment shall be mine, I will carry out regimen for the benefit of the sick and will keep them from harm and wrong. To none will I give a deadly drug, even if solicited, nor offer counsel to such an end.

"It's pretty sobering, when you think of it," Gross added. "Doctors have been swearing that oath for more than two thousand years and it has been the guiding principle of our profession. But when we start deciding not only who can exercise the right to choose when to die, which conceivably might fall within our province where the patient himself initiates the action, but also undertake to bring about the death of another human, the whole thing begins to get to you."

"It got to me just now, and I don't mind telling you I was happy not to have a vote. The single 'Yes' vote just now was yours, wasn't it, Pete?"

"Yes."

"Mind telling me why?"

"I'm not quite sure myself. When I looked at Richard Payson I thought, 'There but for the lack of one single gene go I.' And I knew that, if I were in the same fix, I'd want somebody to shoot a gram or so of morphine into my veins."

"Or that you would have the courage to do it yourself?"

"There I think I would chicken out. How about you?"

"When Ken and I first separated, I was so depressed that I would have welcomed the decision of someone to intervene in my life—"

"You're too young and there's too much ahead for you to even think of that, Reb. The kind of knowledge you possess and your skill in helping other people isn't something you can willfully destroy, just because you're only thinking of yourself."

"I finally saw that," said Rebecca. "But I can't help wondering whether an oath I swore ten years ago can have much real meaning for me, now that I know what it is to want to die."

V

When she left the Board Room floor, Rebecca Dalton was strongly tempted to visit the CICU to see what decisions Ken had made about Kevin and Ross McKenzie, but resisted the urge. She had already done everything she could medically for Kevin except perhaps to remove the fluid from his pericardium and she was planning to do that tomorrow. Or rather to suggest that it be done, since Kevin was technically Ken's patient, as the surgeon who had operated upon him.

Ross McKenzie, however, was in an entirely different category. As the doctor in charge from the beginning, she was responsible for the politician until he was transferred to the Cardiovascular Surgery Section. And if she became convinced that Ken was unduly delaying surgery and thereby seriously endangering Ross McKenzie's already sharply decreasing chances, she would have no alternative except to make an official demand from the medical service for action by the surgical service.

Such a demand would either require Ken to act or lead to the case being assigned to another surgeon from the faculty, perhaps to Mike Raburn, whose skill in the field of heart and blood vessel surgery was not far behind Ken's own. Mike, however, was quite preoccupied with preparations for the TBW on Carmelita Sanchez and it wasn't fair to involve him in the inevitable controversy such a move on her part would cause—unless she became convinced that McKenzie's life was being endangered greatly by further delaying a mitral valve replacement.

Soberly evaluating the consequences of such a last resort as she rode down to the cafeteria floor on the elevator, Rebecca faced up to the fact that a demand for surgical intervention by her could only mean the end of her marriage to Ken. And after last night, she knew that in spite of her brief flare-up that morning she must avoid that eventuality, unless she was faced with a possible choice between the life of her marriage and that of a patient who had entrusted himself to her care, leaving her no alternative. Bemused with the thought, she almost ran into Ed Vogel, who was hurrying from the cafeteria.

"Well, I got it in and it's working," he said jubilantly.

"I thought you'd inserted the brachial and femoral catheters for determining Mr. McKenzie's cardiac function long ago."

"Then you didn't know?"

"Is Mr. McKenzie being prepared for surgery?" she asked quickly—even hopefully.

Ed looked puzzled. "Didn't you and Dr. Dalton decide to use the fiberoptic catheter right after you left the CICU? I saw you talking in the corridor and right afterward he came back and told me to get the fiberoptic catheter ready. But it had to be sterilized in a special way with ethylene oxide and that took a couple of hours. I just finished putting it in a little while ago."

"He must have thought about it after I left him." Rebecca covered up her irritation as best she could but she was sure Ed Vogel realized it was there. "How's the catheter working?"

"Like a Swiss watch," said the younger cardiologist. "You can calculate the stroke work index in less than half the time it took with catheters in both an arm vein and the groin. They've been using it at Peter Bent."

"I read the journals," Rebecca said, a little tartly. "But thanks for telling me."

She marched into the cafeteria, leaving Ed Vogel staring at her rigid back. Then, shaking his head, he turned toward the elevators.

Angry, both at Ken for not mentioning the special instrument, and at herself for being irritated when she knew perfectly well that she had been tied up with the God Committee and therefore not available for him to notify her of the change in Ross McKenzie's program, Rebecca hardly noticed the dishes she chose as she passed through the busy cafeteria line, until Jerry Singleton called to her from his place back of her in the line.

"May I join you, Rebecca?" he asked.

"Certainly, Jerry."

"Go ahead and pick a table," he said as she was leaving the cash register and, choosing one in the corner somewhat separated from the rest of the large room with its din of conversation, Rebecca put down her tray.

"Congratulations on your promotion," said the gynecologist as he brought his own tray to the table and pulled out a chair. "I had to call a special meeting of the Faculty Personnel Committee Monday afternoon so we could approve it for action by the Hospital Board. Ken's on the committee, too, but I managed to keep him in the dark."

"I'd forgotten you were the chairman; thanks for taking the trouble," she said. "But how does it happen that you're dining with the hoi polloi? I thought your evening routine always included beautiful women and *coq au vin*."

"Right now I feel more like a plucked chicken," the surgeon admitted wryly.

"What's happened?"

"For one thing, I've got to wait a couple of hours here for the daughter of a rich casino owner who's being flown over from Nassau with a suspected ruptured ovarian follicle that may turn out to be only a premenstrual bellyache. I told him over the phone that any surgeon in the Bahamas could operate on her, but I took care of his wife some years ago and he won't let anybody else touch her.''

"That should make you feel good.''

"Sic transit gloria.'' Jerry Singleton shrugged. "You mean you haven't heard how Karen Fletcher raked me over the coals at the Tissue Conference this afternoon before the entire surgical service? And all because I lost an elective hysterectomy last week from a pulmonary embolism nobody could have foreseen.''

"The Moriturus Committee met this afternoon and I was tied up with a case I was presenting until after six. But why did Karen pick on you?''

"I'm asking myself the same question—and not getting any answer,'' Jerry admitted. "Most gyn. specialists are doing a lot more elective hysterectomies on women who've had as many children as they'd planned and don't want to be bothered with taking the pill or putting in a diaphragm whenever hubby—or the boy friend—starts getting romantic.''

"Maybe I'm prejudiced because I seem to be sterile—''

"I've never been able to find a reason for that either.''

"Go on, Jerry. I'm sorry I interrupted.''

"The point I'm making is that this whole question was thrashed out a few years ago at a meeting of the American College of Obstetrics and Gynecology—with the consensus overwhelmingly in favor of elective hysterectomy, particularly by the vaginal route, in such cases. Then I lost a simple case last week, for no reason I could be blamed for, and Karen Fletcher chooses to rake me over the coals before a jury of my peers. Don't get me wrong, I'm in favor of peer review. But the way she put it, I was practically a murderer.''

"Karen can be very effective when she wants to be, and she's as smart as a whip.'' Rebecca gave Jerry a quick sidelong glance. "You haven't been ignoring her lately, have you?''

"Ignoring?'' he spluttered. "She always looks so unapproachable that I've never even made a pass at her.''

"Did it ever occur to you that you may have just put your finger on the reason she cut you down this afternoon?''

"You mean . . . ? Hell, Rebecca! Doctors don't mix sex and love with medicine; it would be unethical.''

Rebecca laughed. "For a medical Don Juan, you're really very naïve, Jerry. Women doctors are still women.'' Then she sobered. "I know because I've found myself doing something like that lately.''

"Really, Rebecca,'' he protested, "I find that very hard to believe— maybe of Karen because, come to think of it, there have been times when I couldn't be certain I wasn't receiving signals but didn't believe it at the time.''

"I don't know why. You're very attractive.''

"Then why would she deliberately cut me down, knowing it would make me mad as hell?''

"Aren't you more conscious of Karen right now than you were three hours ago?''

"Conscious of her! I'd like nothing better than to wring her neck.''

"It's a very lovely neck—or hadn't you noticed?''

"Of course I've noticed. What man on the faculty hasn't?''

"One, I hope.'' Rebecca's voice was suddenly sober. "But I'm afraid I'm wrong there too.''

Jerry looked at her in surprise. "Ken—and Karen? You're talking through your hat.''

"Maybe. But she went to the trouble yesterday of running a special test right after the patient Ken did the Caesarean on died to prove that heroin killed her. And she called him down to her private laboratory to show him the results."

"What was wrong with that?"

"Those lab reports don't usually come through for several days, Jerry. Pathology is one department that takes its time."

The surgeon shook his head unbelievingly. "If anybody else but you had told me women doctors would mix sex and medicine, I wouldn't have believed it. But come to think of it, maybe you're right. And I guess it's inevitable, with women taking over so much of the medical field these days."

He glanced around the dining room, which was largely filled with women, most of them in white uniforms. "When I was in medical school they hadn't moved into very much, but from the looks of this cafeteria, there must be a half dozen of 'em for every doctor in the place."

"Anybody connected with medicine knows women in white just about rule the medical world these days, in numbers at least," Rebecca agreed. "I guess it's not surprising that so many emotional relationships develop and so many marriages go on the rocks."

"Like mine," Jerry agreed. "But surely not yours, Rebecca?"

"Ken and I are on a collision course, Jerry. And I don't know what to do."

"You could try telling me about it. I was headed for a career in psychiatry a long time ago, until I figured out that I could straighten out the female world about as effectively as a gynecologist as I could being a shrink."

"Suppose you were married to a woman doctor who tried to force you into an operation you were afraid to do, Jerry?"

"Afraid, Reb?" His tone was grave now. "That's a serious charge to make."

"Especially against someone you love."

"I think you'd better tell me more about it. You and Ken are fellow members of the faculty, besides being my friends. If it comes to a controversy between you, people will start taking sides and that could easily tear the school apart."

In a few terse sentences, Rebecca gave him a summary of the course of Ross McKenzie's illness since his admission to the hospital around midnight.

"How certain can you be that McKenzie is losing ground?" he asked.

"He's not gaining—the stroke work index Ken seems to be depending on indicates that."

"How much of your conviction that the patient is failing because of an incompetent mitral valve could be attributed to the fact that you don't trust this new catheter Ken is using?"

She gave him a startled look. "What makes you think that?"

"I could hear it in your voice just now, when you spoke of the fiberoptic instrument. My guess would be that you unconsciously resent Ken's decision to use it without consulting you. Isn't that true?"

"I don't know, Jerry. I've been so concerned with what might happen to Ken if I put him on the spot by demanding that he operate, I haven't stopped to analyze my motives."

"I suspect a certain amount of ambivalence."

"Ambivalence?"

"It's only natural for you to be concerned for Ken's career and for your marriage, but you're tops in your field, too. If this new gadget should turn out to be more accurate in determining heart function than the traditional methods you've been using, with a catheter threaded through an arm vein into the right side of the heart and another directed upward from the groin through the femoral artery into the left, it's bound to reflect a little on your skill as a cardiologist."

"I can't accept that argument." Her tone was somewhat cool now.

"I read the medical journals—particularly the *JAMA*. The article on the catheter Ken is using first appeared there, and quite a number of cardiologists are also becoming disenchanted lately with the femoral route. You'll have to admit that the incidence of complications like clot formation and embolism has been found to be much higher when that route is used."

"That is true," she conceded.

"Then if this fiberoptic catheter inserted through an arm vein really accomplishes the same thing with much less danger, it will end up being the procedure of choice."

"Do you expect me to stand by and watch the optimum time for replacing the mitral valve pass without saying anything, and then have McKenzie's death on my conscience?"

"You can always withdraw from the case."

"Would that make me any less guilty of a patient's death?"

"Perhaps not, being you."

"What does that mean?"

"Simply that both you and Ken are too conscientious for your own good, so naturally you blame yourselves for the failure of the transplants."

"Ken blames me, I'm sure of that."

"Perhaps he does—unconsciously," Jerry agreed. "When we get in trouble we always hunt for a scapegoat."

"And he *did* take over the McKenzie case."

"So we're back where we started." Jerry shook his head sadly. "And it looks like I've only made the situation worse by trying to help two people I like very much. Maybe next time I'll keep my fool mouth shut, but at the risk of making the same mistake twice, I'll give you one last piece of advice, Reb."

"What's that?"

"Be patient. In spite of all our sophisticated monitoring gadgets, surgeons sometimes have to depend on instinct alone in making a decision, particularly when they're not sure of themselves. And in a surprising number of cases, a well-trained instinct turns out to be more reliable than a computer." He stood up. "Excuse me, please. I've got a job to do before that case from the Bahamas gets here."

VI

Mike Raburn had decided to stop by the ICU to check on Carmelita Sanchez before going to dinner. The local six o'clock news was on the color TV set in the small ICU staff lounge and he stopped briefly to watch.

Sports came on last and he'd started to leave when he heard Big Joe Gates's name mentioned and turned back. The station sports director was delivering a television editorial. And as soon as Mike heard the first words, he knew the campaign Joe Gates was expecting to be launched against him had already begun:

> "Local backers of the Miami Snappers professional basket-
> ball team are asking themselves whether their star forward,
> Big Joe Gates, has been entirely candid with them. While Joe
> was busy in San Francisco, helping promote a players' union
> for all participants in professional sports, his son, Joe, Jr.,

barely missed dying at Biscayne General Hospital from a crisis associated with sickle cell anemia.

"It's no secret, of course, that sickle cell disease is hereditary, and limited mostly to the black race. So the question this reporter feels hasn't been answered is: Did Joe Gates know of this tendency in his family before the crisis that threatened to take the life of his son? If so, there is a strong question whether Joe has played fair with backers and fans, or with the betting public, in not warning them that he, too, might be incapacitated at any time and not be able to play.

"In question, too, is whether Big Joe has the right to help organize a union of professional players without prior permission by the group of sportsmen who have spent large amounts of money to bring big-time professional basketball to Miami. In the opinion of this reporter, Joe Gates owes both the owners and the public an answer to one question: *Are you or aren't you a possible victim of sickle cell anemia, Joe? Your followers have a right to know!*"

"The dirty sonsabitches," Mike muttered as he turned down the sound on the color set.

Helga Sundberg had appeared in the door of the lounge in time to hear his last words. She was supporting Rachel Gates, who was weeping softly.

"Are you cussing somebody or just muttering to yourself?" Helga asked.

"Anything wrong, Rachel?" Mike asked in quick concern.

"One of those people you were just talking about was in the ICU waiting room and upset her by saying something nasty about her husband," said Helga. "I'm busy getting a cardiac stroke work index reading on Mr. McKenzie, Dr. Raburn. Could you take care of her?"

"Sure." Mike took Rachel Gates's arm and led her to a chair. "Wait here, I'll get you something—"

"A cup of coffee will be enough, Mike. It was foolish of me to get so upset."

"You're under a double strain—with Joey in here and the big guns opening up on Big Joe," Mike assured her. "Didn't Joe tell you he was expecting this sort of thing?"

"No." She accepted the coffee he gave her. "Joe's been pretty nervous since he got in from San Francisco. What does all this mean, Mike?"

"The owners don't like the idea of a players' union and they know how much your husband's supporting the players who want to organize one can mean. So they're trying to shut him up."

"Could Joey have really gotten the sickle cell thing from Joe?"

"Possibly. How old is Big Joe by the way?"

"Thirty his last birthday. Why?"

"If he had the sickling tendency, I'd have expected him to develop symptoms earlier."

"Like Joey's?"

"Maybe not as bad, but much the same thing. Before we learned the new treatments we're using with your son, not many black males with an inherited sickling tendency got beyond twenty without showing the disease. And a lot of them didn't live much longer."

Rachel Gates shuddered. "I'm just beginning to understand how much I owe to you and Dr. Henderson for—"

"Forget it," said Mike. "We were just doing our jobs. Besides, you and Joe and Joey are friends and, if you can't help friends, who can you help? But I hope you won't let this TV campaign worry you too much. Once Joe went into labor politics, it was inevitable that he would be attacked. The newspapers will be on him next."

"I can take it, as long as I know what it's all about, Mike. But I wish Joe wasn't so nervous. He's playing tomorrow night in the last postseason game, then we were going across the country in our Winnebago. But now—"

"Joey's going to be all right," he assured her.

"Are you sure?"

"Sickle cell disease is really a medical condition and Joey's a pediatric patient, but Dr. Henderson tells me all the signs are good. My only role was in getting oxygen to him fast in the hyperbaric chamber."

"And saving his life."

"I doubt that it was in quite that much danger."

"You kept his brain from being damaged by lack of oxygen. Dr. Henderson and Professor McHale both told me that."

"Will you do me a favor, Rachel?" Mike asked.

"Of course."

"I'd like to take a blood specimen from your finger."

"To look for sickling?"

"Yes."

"Joe told me if any of you asked me, not to let you take it."

"I'll only have to prick your finger and that won't show, so Joe doesn't have to know anything about it. Then if you show the sickling trait, it will tell me how to handle this campaign against your husband, when it comes to a showdown."

"Please do it then."

"The ICU lab is across the hall," he told her. "We won't even make an official record of this, until the right time comes."

In the laboratory, Mike pricked Rachel's finger and touched the blood on it with the surface of a glass slide, dropping a thin cover slip upon it in what was known as a "fresh preparation." Placing this under a microscope, he focused the controls until the biscuit-shaped red blood cells of the preparation sprang into sharp focus.

It took him several minutes to find what he was looking for, several cells whose outlines were ragged and a few that were even shaped like a quarter moon. Their shape was practically diagnostic of a carrier of the sickling trait or tendency, though not necessarily the disease itself, which depended upon the formation of masses of elongated cells large enough to block important small blood vessels.

"You have the trait," he told Rachel. "We'll double-check it with Sickledex, of course, but there's no doubt as far as I'm concerned."

"Then Joey inherited it from me?"

"Almost certainly. Of course, Big Joe could have the trait too. But if both of you possessed the tendency, I doubt that Joey would have lived through more than the first two or three years of life."

"Shouldn't I call Big Joe now and tell him?"

"I don't think so," said Mike. "Joe's determined to play this thing his way, and part of his chance of success depends on how much the owners attack him. My guess, judging from the way the TV station went after him tonight, is that he'll be under heavy attack in the newspapers tomorrow. But that's what he wants."

"I still can't see why."

"Joe's giving the owners a lot of rope, Rachel, in the hope that they'll hang themselves, so to speak. First he'll let the heat build up for a day or so, long enough to show how vicious some people can be to gain their own ends. Then he'll cut the rug from beneath them by letting himself be tested for sickle cell anemia. When it turns out that he doesn't have the sickling tendency at all, he can show up the owners' attack for what it is, an attempt to keep lesser-known players under their thumbs. The public is almost certain to react unfavorably to such tactics so the owners will be over a barrel as far as the players' union is concerned."

"But Joe isn't absolutely certain that he doesn't have sickle cell anemia, Mike."

"Are you sure?"

She nodded. "He doesn't tell me much but I know when Joe's worried about something. And from what little he does say, I can tell that he's troubled by the possibility that he's positive too."

"Then he really is taking a long chance by letting this campaign against him go as far as it already has," said Mike.

"But what can you—or anybody—do?"

"Play it by ear, I guess."

Rachel shook her head. "This is all too complicated for me to understand, but thank you for taking so much trouble with us." She reached for her handbag. "Goodness! I almost forgot that Joe told me to give you this."

She handed him an envelope; inside were two box seats for the final exhibition game between the Snappers and the Lakers Thursday night.

CHAPTER FIFTEEN

I

Karen Fletcher finished her daily thirty laps of the Bayside Terrace swimming pool and, climbing from the water, put on the short terry cloth robe draped over a beach chair. Slipping her feet into a pair of fiber scuffs, she rubbed her hair dry with a towel as she crossed the grassy plot to the back door of the terrace. By the time she took the elevator to her floor and pushed open the door of her apartment, the silver pile of hair about her shoulders was beginning to dry. Moving into the apartment, she closed the door and started across the small living room, dropping the terry robe on a chair as she passed and leaving her only garment the black nylon tank suit that failed to hide even the taut thrust of her nipples through the thin fabric.

"Very lovely," said a masculine voice from across the room where Jerry Singleton was sitting in a wing chair, smoking a filter-tip cigarette.

At his voice, Karen turned quickly but did not reach for the robe. In fact, to a really close observer, it would have appeared that she was hardly surprised to find him there, but Jerry seemed not to have realized it.

"How did you get in?" she asked, crossing to a mirror and starting to brush her still slightly damp hair with long, practiced strokes.

"Walked in, the door was open."

"I ran down for a quick swim."

"You could get into trouble that way. A man could be waiting for you—"

Brush in hand, she turned to face him and laughed. "It seems that one is."

"You could be attacked."

Karen moved across the room and took a cigarette from the small table beside the chair where he was sitting, but when he reached out to touch her thigh, she moved away casually.

"I'm an athlete, Jerry. And I also hold the black belt in karate."

"Is that a warning?"

"I only use karate on enemies, not on friends. Which, by the way, are you?"

"Until you came in just now, I felt like an enemy. But now—"

"There's no reason for us to be enemies, Jerry. Just because I did my duty as head of the Pathology Department and presented a case of embolism at the Tissue Conference—"

"But did it have to be mine?" His voice had taken on a slight edge.

"It was the only death from pulmonary embolism we've had in the past six months. And the younger members of the surgical staff need reminding periodically that embolism can complicate even the simplest surgical operations."

"Rebecca Dalton thinks you may have chosen me as the target because I haven't paid much attention to you—"

"Really? It would seem that I have underestimated Rebecca."

"I haven't heard you deny the allegation."

"Perhaps because I don't." She shrugged, a highly stimulating action in the thin tank suit.

"Then?"

"You're a very attractive man, Jerry—with quite a reputation as a woman chaser." She surveyed him coolly but he didn't miss the glint in her eye nevertheless. "As such you're legitimate prey for every attractive unattached woman around."

"Mind telling me why you deliberately chose to attack me?"

"When you know me better, Jerry"—she was back brushing her hair again—"you'll know that everything I do is deliberate."

"I still don't see why it had to be today."

"I just told you. The case I presented was the first fatal embolism at Biscayne General in six months and the only one I can remember happening to one of your patients. It was ideal for my purpose."

"Which was?"

"Don't you know?" She laughed and the throaty tone in her voice made the short hairs along his spine rise in a reflex as old as life itself, as well as set his heart to pounding. "If you don't, you're really not as sharp as I credited you with being, Jerry."

He was halfway across the room toward her when a thought stopped him dead.

"You planned all this, didn't you? Even to leaving the door open."

"Really, Jerry." Now her tone was purely sensual. "Do you have to use so many words? I'm beginning to think what I've been hearing about you as a lover was exaggerated."

The sarcasm in her words released him, even though he knew the answer to his question without her having to speak it. But before he could touch her body she moved back.

"Just a minute," she said. "These tank suits are hard to find—and expensive."

With a sinuous movement that somehow reminded him of the graceful rhythmic sway of a cobra to its master's flute, she slipped down the straps of the tank suit and, peeling the damp fabric swiftly down over her breasts, hips, and thighs, stepped out of it, leaving a small pile of black nylon on the thick white pile of the rug. Jerry's eyes bugged at the perfection of the lovely nude body facing him, a perfection so complete that he was reminded of an alabaster statue of a Grecian goddess—except for the sudden glow of fire in her eyes.

II

Carolyn Payson opened the door of the apartment she shared with Helga at Gus Henderson's first ring. She was fully dressed, even to make-up, which, he noticed, was heavier than she usually wore.

"Could we have a drink in the Dolphin Lounge before we go out to dinner?" she asked. "I've had a pretty rough day."

"I heard about some of it. Sorry things didn't go your way."

"Let's not talk about that. Helga said the best thing we could do tonight is to hang one on and for once I feel like drowning my sorrows."

At the long highly polished bar in the Dolphin Lounge, they had bourbon highballs. Gus was surprised when Carolyn asked for another; she usually didn't go beyond a limit of one drink, but he sensed that tonight she was in a different mood. Both were feeling fine when they came out of the lounge and went to his car.

"The place doesn't seem to be the same without Kevin McCartney," said Gus. "No matter how low you were feeling, you could come in there and tell yourself how much better off you were than somebody with a time bomb ticking away inside his chest."

"Do you know how Kevin is tonight?"

"Not too good. He had a cessation a couple of hours ago but Helga got him started before Ed or Dr. Ken could get there."

"Helga's been like the Rock of Ages these last few days to me. I don't know what I'll do without her."

"You always have me," Gus assured her. "Have you decided where you want to go to dinner?"

"Any place that's gay, and bright. And where we can dance, too."

"There's a Polynesian restaurant on the North Bay Causeway. We might try it."

III

Ken Dalton was having a hamburger and coffee in a booth at the far end of the nearly deserted Coffee Shop when Rebecca stopped at the cashier's desk to get change for the newspaper vending machine outside. When he beckoned to her, she came over to the booth and slid into the seat across from him.

"How about a piece of strawberry pie and a cup of coffee?" he asked. "I was just about to order it."

"I've already had dinner—with Jerry Singleton."

"So?" Ken's eyebrows rose. "I've been wondering when he would go on the make for you."

"Jerry's lonely, Ken."

"About as lonely as a single bull in a pasture of young heifers. He's having a ball."

"You could, too, if you wanted to."

"Not a chance." His voice was suddenly sober. "Once you've had a glimpse of heaven, Reb, you don't settle even for paradise. And I had a good look at both down in Florida Bay."

"Stop it! You'll have me bawling."

"You didn't have dessert with your dinner, did you?"

"No."

"Two strawberry pies and some coffee for Dr. Dalton, Maggie," he called. "And some more coffee for me, too."

"Comin' right up, Doctors," said the waitress.

"You'll ruin my figure," Rebecca protested.

"As I remember, it can stand a pound or two more."

"I hear you were busy while I was tied up with the God Committee meeting," said Rebecca.

"You mean the fiberoptic catheter?"

"That." With an effort Rebecca kept her voice even. "And other things."

"Kevin almost went out on us, but Helga got his heart going again before the CPR team arrived. That girl's a real tower of strength in this hospital."

"She's absolutely unflappable."

"You've taught her a lot since she came here. I used to think you were the only completely self-sustained individual I ever saw, Reb, but our Helga has you beaten."

"Did you know she and Carolyn Payson spent a year nursing at a hospital in northeast Brazil, just after they got their nursing degrees at Gainesville?"

"Helga a missionary? She's better equipped to play the part of Sadie Thompson."

Maggie brought their pie and filled the coffee cups.

"By the way, what was the verdict of the God Committee?" Ken asked.

"It's not supposed to be broadcast, but Carolyn and I lost."

"What now?"

"She'll just have to make the best of it and hope her father doesn't last long. She was terribly tense before but I somehow got the feeling afterward that the committee meeting only crystallized something for her. She thanked me—and told me good-by."

"The girl was and is under a terrible strain. I wouldn't try to read anything special into what she does or says under these circumstances."

"Jerry just read me a lecture on trying to pressure people into doing what I think they should," Rebecca admitted. "But nobody would know that better than you do."

"I don't think many people resent the pressure, Reb." Ken's voice was entirely sober now. "It's just that you're always so infernally right. Take this business of trying to get me to go on with heart transplants—"

"I've sworn off that." Rebecca raised her right hand. "Scout's honor."

"Maybe so, but you got under my skin the other night."

She smiled. "I'm still reminded of it occasionally."

"I was lashing out at you, so I guess I did treat you pretty rough. But it started me thinking about the way you've been pressuring me to go back into research on that plastic heart pump I was working on, so I started looking up the literature and right off I found some things I didn't know. Do you realize that a Frenchman has been living nearly five years with a transplanted heart?"

"Where did you find that?"

"A publisher in Paris has brought out a book about him. If you want to read it, you can find it in the medical school library, the title is *C'est pour ce soir*. My French is pretty lousy, but I understood enough to know the patient is doing very well."

"Did you find any concrete reason why?"

Ken shook his head. "My own idea is that he belongs to a class of people who might be called hyporeactive—the unflappables like Helga Sundberg. They can stand almost anything and bounce right back, because something inside them, maybe the endocrine system, doesn't go pumping a lot of stress-produced hormones into their bloodstreams at the slightest excuse."

"But you can't select only that kind of person for major surgery."

"Which is why surgeons are always going to have failures," he agreed. "What we can do, though, is pay more attention to the emotional make-up of our patients, knowing that the hyperreactives, like you and me, are going to develop all the complications possible—and take measures accordingly."

"It's an interesting theory."

"And worth exploring."

"Then you're going back into research?"

"Maybe. I won't know until I've studied other people's results."

"Meanwhile, there's no reason why you can't do other types of surgery, like Ross McKenzie, for example."

"Have you already decided he's going to need it?"

"Everything looks that way, doesn't it?"

"Not to me."

"What more evidence do you need with his mitral valve flapping like a sail in the wind?" Rebecca tried to curb her instinctive irritation at what she considered to be his stubbornness. "If you replace it with an artificial one now, the chance of his coming through the operation okay should be almost certain."

"Nothing is certain when you're doing open heart surgery on a man who's sixty-five years old, Reb. Besides, I examined the arteries in his eye grounds, and they're considerably more tortuous and sclerotic than his age seems to indicate."

"B-but—"

"How many congenital floppy mitral valves have you diagnosed in the past couple of years, since you've had the echocardiograph to work with?"

"More than we ever knew existed." Rebecca had the strange feeling that she was being backed into a corner, and it wasn't pleasant for one whose judgment, in matters concerning the function of the heart, was rarely challenged.

"Every one of them leaks a little blood back through into the atrium each time the left ventricle contracts," he said. "Yet most of those hearts aren't even noticeably enlarged, although some of them have been leaking since the patient was born. Isn't that true?"

"Y-yes. But I thought—"

"I couldn't have lived with you ten years without knowing something about your thought processes, Reb. Plus the fact that you have your share of an essentially feminine psychological quirk that allows you to convince yourself without much argument that, in dealing even with someone as close to you as a husband, the end justifies the means."

"I didn't know you had a degree in psychiatry." She was stung at last into tartness and Ken's slightly mocking grin only made it worse, just as Jerry Singleton's analysis of her emotions had done a little earlier.

"When Ross McKenzie was brought in here last night with the story of some sort of heart attack after pretty strenuous exertion, you found a dysfunction of the mitral valve and made a brilliant diagnosis of ruptured *chordae tendineae* attached to the valve, keeping it from closing completely."

"You agreed. Remember?"

"Of course, I agree. Because you were, and are, right."

"And he *did* go into cardiogenic shock."

"No doubt about that, either. Unless I miss my guess, the first thought that popped into your mind was that, if you could persuade me to operate on McKenzie and replace the damaged mitral successfully with an artificial one, you'd be giving me back my confidence."

"Was anything wrong with that?"

"Only one thing, it just could be that you weren't doing what was best for the patient. And when a doctor loses sight of that, the seeds of real trouble are being sown."

"Have you thought of the possibility that you're emphasizing the hazards of cardiac surgery on Ross McKenzie because you're not sure of your own ability to perform it successfully any more?"

When she saw him wince as the angry words went home, she knew she hadn't been fair to him—but it was too late now to recall them.

"*Et tu, Brute?*" he said wryly, rising to his feet.

"Ken, I—"

"I guess all along I've been telling myself you didn't really feel that way, Reb, and ignoring an obvious truth. If it's your medical decision that Ross McKenzie can only be saved by replacing that mitral valve, you have an obligation to put in an official request that someone else be assigned to do it. I have no intention of operating on him until I'm convinced there's no other alternative."

"Nobody ever accused me of letting my own wishes interfere with a medical decision before."

"And I know you couldn't be charged with it this time, if your desire to help me wasn't so strong. But have you studied the incidence of cerebral artery block lately from clots forming on artificial heart valves and then breaking loose?"

"No."

"It's far more frequent than any of us ever thought would happen, just as we're seeing a lot of failures we didn't expect after coronary by-pass surgery. It was a nice try, Reb, and I appreciate the thought behind it. But I'll have to work myself out of this the only way I know how—by being stubborn."

He moved toward the cash register. "Are you going to request surgical intervention?"

"I don't know," said Rebecca soberly, conscious that they had come at last to the very brink of disaster in their marriage. "The only thing I can do now is go over the case again in detail, then do what I have to do."

IV

Mike Raburn was on the way to the cafeteria for a belated dinner when the paging operator called his name. Stepping into his office in the Emergency Department, he picked up the telephone from the desk.

"This is Dr. Raburn. Did you want me?"

"You have an outside call, Doctor. Mr. Joe Gates."

"Put him on, please. . . . Looks like you called the shots right, Joe," said Mike. "That sports editorial on TV really slammed into you."

"Tomorrow morning's paper will be worse; one of the sports writers just called to warn me."

"That figures."

"They think they've got me over a barrel because of Joey."

"Dr. Henderson has taken the catheter out of Joey's arm vein. He's taking his medicine by mouth, now, and asking when he can go home."

"That's good. Did Rachel give you the tickets?"

"She did but I'm not going to be able to use them. I'll be watching a special patient all day tomorrow and we won't know which way it will go for her much before midnight."

"That's too bad," said Joe. "The team physician came down with a strep throat this afternoon and we don't have a doctor for the game tomorrow night. I was hoping you'd come and bring a medical bag."

"Come to think of it, Ed Vogel has tomorrow night off. You want to hold the phone while I find out whether he can go? Or shall I call you back?"

"I'd better hold. I'm supposed to go out on the court again in five minutes to practice."

On the wall beside the door to the Emergency Department, Mike took an inside phone off the hook and asked the paging operator to ring Ed Vogel. The cardiologist answered almost immediately.

"I've got a couple of box seat tickets for the Snappers-Lakers game tomorrow night, but I can't go," said Mike. "Joe Gates is on the telephone now wanting to know if someone from here can bring a medical bag. The team doctor has a strep throat."

"I'll use 'em," said Ed Vogel promptly. "I've got a date but the game will be over before eleven, leaving the shank of the evening."

At the other phone, Mike found Joe Gates still on the line.

"Dr. Vogel will be glad to go tomorrow night, Joe; he's a cardiologist and will bring his own medical bag. By the way, Rachel was pretty upset over that six o'clock broadcast but I told her it wasn't nearly as bad as it sounded."

"I'm not used to this sort of thing either and it's given me a bad case of the jitters," the athlete admitted. "If I don't play any better tomorrow night than I did in the first half hour of practice tonight, the Snappers will probably trade me to Slippery Rock."

"Want me to phone you a prescription for a sedative?"

"Doc Moriarity gave us all some pills for emergencies like this during the season. If I'm still shook up tomorrow night, I'll take one or two of 'em."

V

The moon was shining brightly when Carolyn and Gus Henderson took the causeway toward North Bay Village and Normandy Shores, turning the surface of the bay into a vast sheet of rippling molten silver. At the restaurant Gus surrendered the car to a parking attendant wearing a colorful pareu and they went inside through a somewhat garishly decorated passageway of bamboo framing interlaced with palm fronds.

The décor was authentic enough to allow the diners, especially after several tall drinks called Tahiti Trips, to imagine they were in the South Seas. The food was exotic and the floor show exciting, with hula dancing, in which the guests joined, and a fire walk by the parking attendant doubling in brass—in which they didn't.

Carolyn seemed to be enjoying herself, with a hectic, almost fervid gaiety Gus had never seen in her before. He was happy to see it, however, because it seemed to mean she had decided she could do nothing about her father's condition, now that the final termination of life had been refused by the God Committee, and should live her own life to the full with no thought of the horror later years might bring.

VI

Kevin McCartney opened his eyes and tried to focus them on the shadowy white-clad figure standing beside the bed but the oxygen mask got in the way. He could hear the rush of gas as it bubbled through the water bottle that gave an index of its flow and also added moisture to keep from drying out the mucous membrane lining of his lungs.

"What happened?" he mumbled.

Helga Sundberg moved around the bed and shut off the flow of gas before removing the mask.

"Think you can breathe on your own?" she asked. "Or are you still too lazy?"

"Hello, beautiful, I thought for a while I was in heaven and you were an angel."

Helga chuckled. "That's sweet, Kevin, but not very practical, I'm afraid."

"Mind telling me what happened?"

"You tried to quit this life and I had to knock you around a bit with CPR."

"So that's why my chest feels like it's been stepped on by an elephant?"

"I got your pump started up again and Dr. Dalton took about a quart of fluid out of your pericardium."

"Is that why I don't feel like my heart's being squeezed to death any longer?"

"That, plus some drugs he left in there to discourage any more fluid from forming, plus the stuff we've been shooting into your veins to overcome the rejection."

"So I'm going to make it this time?"

"If you don't you'll have to answer to me," Helga promised him. "Now do you think you can keep functioning on your own while a student sits with you so I can get back to where I'm supposed to be?"

"I promise," said Kevin. "Do you suppose Dr. Ken will be back tonight?"

"I'm not sure. Why?"

"I want to talk to him, something important."

"We're watching another patient of his pretty closely, so he'll probably be in later."

"In that case I think I'll take another nap. Be sure to wake me when he comes around."

"Will do," said Helga. "And just to be sure you don't get lazy again, I'll be watching you on the big screen. One cessation a night is about all my nervous system can stand."

VII

In Apartment 1011 at Bayside Arms, Peggy Tyndall finished giving Dale his bath and rolled him dry in a nubby towel, before helping him into his pajamas. Was the dusky hue of cyanosis his skin had shown since birth really more marked than before as Dr. Karen Fletcher thought? she asked herself—and couldn't be sure of the answer. Mrs. Taylor, the baby sitter who watched the boy, thought so too, but she hadn't counted the times Dale was forced to squat for a moment each day to get his breath, though she had promised to do so from now on.

Warm, tired, and sleepy, Dale reached up to hug Peggy when she bent down to kiss him in his youth bed. Then, gathering the Teddy bear he always slept with in his arms, he turned on his side as she pulled up the small blanket he, like so many small children, insisted on having around him when he slept. Gently Peggy lifted the small hand and examined the fingers but, aside from the clubbing tendency that characterized children with congenital hearts, she couldn't be sure of any change.

"Honey," she said, "are you having any more trouble keeping up with the other children than you used to?"

"Maybe. Jack Peters can run faster'n me—but he's bigger." Dale squirmed farther under the small blanket. "Nighty-night."

"Good night, darling." Peggy leaned down to kiss him again but he was already asleep and she smoothed the dark hair from his forehead instead, gently squeezing his ear lobes, where the telltale bluish tint from the cyanosis of oxygen lack was most apparent.

A full checkup meant catheterization of the heart again to study it with the X ray and she was reluctant to put this small reminder of the husband who had died in Vietnam in a chopper accident to even that not entirely innocuous procedure. Meanwhile, there was the alternative of waiting for the echocardioscope, with its amazing ability to explore the interior of the heart with reflected sound waves, to be repaired. Dr. Rebecca Dalton felt that it was safe to wait and that was almost enough to reassure Peggy— almost but not quite.

VIII

The bedside clock said ten minutes before eight when the electronic pager in Jerry Singleton's coat pocket emitted its sharp, high-pitched "beep," awakening him. Beside him in the bedroom of the apartment, Karen Fletcher stirred beneath the sheet that partly covered her but left an arm, a shoulder, and one lovely breast bare. She did not awaken when Jerry got out of bed and moved to the chair over which he had draped his coat. The electronic pager, capable of transmitting its signal for ten miles or more, was carried by all the staff while on call outside the hospital and inside as well after nine o'clock, when the loudspeaker call system was turned off so as not to disturb the sleep of patients. When Jerry pressed the switch on the side of the cigarette-pack-sized instrument, telling the operator he had answered, her voice came to him, somewhat tinny from the electronic transmission, but perfectly distinguishable.

"Mrs. Valenti was just admitted to Private Gyn, Dr. Singleton," she said.

Jerry switched off the pager, letting the operator know he had received the message without, however, betraying his whereabouts. As he dressed hurriedly, he glanced toward the bed, where Karen still lay, her face flushed from their love-making and her hair tousled upon the pillow. For a moment Jerry Singleton debated awakening her to tell her he would be back, then put the idea from him.

If the patient flown as an emergency to Biscayne General from the Bahamas was indeed hemorrhaging internally from a ruptured ovarian follicle, where an ovum had burst from its nest on the surface of an ovary, after undergoing maturation to the point where it was ready for fertilization should a live spermatozoön be encountered on its way down the reproductive tract, he might be busy for the next couple of hours. And remembering, with a stir of his own pulse, how the lovely perfect body beneath the silken sheet had responded to his own, like the highly tuned instrument for love-making it was, he knew he could no more resist coming to her again than he could have stopped the progress of the blood clot she had demonstrated that afternoon. Loosened from its source in a leg vein and floating free in the rush of blood through ever larger veins until it was swept through the right side and into the lung circulation, where it had shortly blocked a large branch of the pulmonary artery, the clot had caused instant death, giving

Karen Fletcher the lure that had drawn him here as surely as if it had been foreordained.

What difference did it make that Karen had actually been the aggressor, from the moment she had attacked him before the surgical Tissue Conference? The important thing was that she had been attracted to him strongly enough to execute such a clever plan for bringing him to her bed. It was a heady thought, almost as heady as the prospect of their next coming together. And with that in mind, he finished dressing and left the apartment.

The click of the lock released Karen from the enforced rigidity she had maintained since she, too, had been awakened by the sharp beeping tone of the pager. Throwing back the sheet, she moved to the door and made certain that it was locked. Then, still nude, she moved across the living room to a bookcase and, pulling down a copy of the Biscayne University Medical School Directory, leafed through the pages until she came to the listings for the Faculty and Administrative committees. Running her finger down the page, she stopped at the Personnel Committee and, beneath it, the Subcommittee on Faculty Promotion.

"Dr. Jeremiah Singleton, Chairman," she read silently.

Picking up a pencil from the desk beside her, she carefully made a ring around the name. Then, moving down the Personnel Committee list, she came upon the name of Ken Dalton and, after a moment of hesitancy, carefully penciled a ring around it, too, confident that her move in performing an immediate test for heroin yesterday and demonstrating the result to Ken had put him in her debt.

The next two names were faculty nonentities who could be counted on to vote with the majority. The bottom name on the list of five was that of Val LeMoyne and Karen chewed on the eraser while her mind moved rapidly, deciding upon the course of action that would insure her the third vote needed when Jerry Singleton presented her name for promotion to full professor. After a moment she nodded and closed the directory.

Everything was working out fine, she told herself as she put the book back into the bookcase and moved to the bath for her shower. She had no intention of suggesting to Jerry, even obliquely, that she should be promoted, until the retirement of Dr. Adrian Cooper was a fact. The important thing there was that, when her promotion to the rank of full professor was approved, her appointment as chief of the Pathology Department should accompany it. Jerry might need some softening up before he would go that far out on a limb in one action but Karen was in no hurry. And in the meantime there was the prospect, not at all unexciting in itself, of future evenings like this one, evenings in which Jerry would no doubt be fully as adequate as he had been tonight.

As for Val LeMoyne, Karen had already decided upon a simpler, less devious way. But one that would be equally effective—for her purpose.

CHAPTER SIXTEEN

I

Shortly after nine o'clock Rebecca Dalton called Ed Vogel from her office on the medical floor. "Can you meet me on the CICU right away, Ed?" she asked.

"Certainly, Dr. Dalton, I was just up there. Is anything wrong?"

"I'm considering requesting immediate surgery on Mr. McKenzie."

When there was silence at the other end of the line, Rebecca spoke again, impatiently. "Did you hear me, Ed?"

"Yes. Will Dr. Kenneth Dalton be there?"

"I presume not. He told me about an hour ago that he refuses to operate on the patient." Rebecca's voice became more brusque. "You can see, of course, that his refusal leaves me no alternative except to request that another surgeon be assigned to the case. We can't let a patient die because the Cardiovascular Surgery Section refuses to operate."

"I'll go to CICU right away."

"If you get there before I do, you can be getting together the data I need to call an emergency meeting of the executive staff."

"You'll have it," Ed promised. "Are you going to call them first?"

"What difference does that make?" Rebecca's patience at what seemed to be the Cardiology Fellow's reluctance to support her decision broke through the grip she was maintaining upon her emotions.

"None, Dr. Dalton." Ed Vogel spoke hurriedly. "I'll get going right away."

At the CICU nursing station, the younger cardiologist studied the curve of the stroke work index being recorded every half hour as an indication of Ross McKenzie's condition; the line was moving upward slowly, but definitely. In McKenzie's cubicle, he checked once again, too, the findings being reported by the fiberoptic catheter in his pulmonary artery, the smaller conventional tube in the vena cava just outside the heart, and the various other parameters being constantly measured. All showed slight, but definite, improvement over the patient's condition some six hours before, when Ed had started inserting the special catheter.

Ross McKenzie opened his eyes while the young doctor was fiddling with the bedside unit that transformed the information furnished by pulsations of light through the fiberoptic catheter into electric voltages which could be assimilated and reported upon by the control console for the master information center at the main nursing station.

"When are you going to take that damned tube out of my arm?" the politician demanded. "You've got me tied to so many boards I might as well be crucified."

"Keep on the way you're going and it won't be much longer," Ed promised. "Are you feeling better?"

"How could anyone feel better with all these gadgets hanging from him? No wonder it costs so much to run this damned hospital."

"I'm glad you've had a chance to see where the money goes, Mr. McKenzie."

"What about that fellow McCartney? I heard one of the nurses say he almost died this afternoon."

"Kevin had a close shave, but he's a lot better now," said Vogel. "His heart stopped but Miss Sundberg got it started again."

"If you ask me, the nurses around here know more than the doctors."

"That could be, Mr. McKenzie. That could be."

II

When Rebecca Dalton came on the ward about ten minutes later, Helga was working at the control panel and Ed Vogel was in the doctors' office adjoining it, with the entire monitor bank visible through the large counter-topped opening between the two.

"Your hus—Dr. Kenneth Dalton ordered hourly calculations of the stroke work index," Helga told Rebecca. "I just finished plotting the most recent one on the chart."

She handed Rebecca the graph but the woman doctor didn't pause to study it.

"I want to make my own examination," she said brusquely.

"Certainly, Doctor." Helga was not flustered in the least by the terse note in Rebecca's voice. "I'll get the examining basket."

On every ward, the instruments for physical examination not ordinarily carried by doctors in making rounds were kept in a basket. They included a combined ophthalmoscope-otoscope for examining eyes, ears, and nasal passages, an extra stethoscope, a blood pressure manometer, reflex hammer, and other paraphernalia for a neurological examination, plus a few special instruments used only on the ward in question. Picking up the basket on the way to Ross McKenzie's cubicle, Helga stepped inside and drew down the sheet, exposing the grower's chest, with the cardiac sensors attached to the skin.

Using the personal stethoscope she always carried in the pocket of her long white coat, Rebecca listened carefully over Ross McKenzie's chest. Then, moving around the electrodes attached to his skin, she tapped on his chest to percuss the outlines of his heart, marking them with a wax pencil upon the patient's skin. This finished, she carefully located the edges of his liver and his spleen below the lowest ribs on either side, marking them, too, with the wax pencil. Finally she took the ophthalmoscope from the basket and switched on its tiny light.

"Look at the ceiling, please," she told the patient. "I'm going to examine your eyes."

The inner lining of the eyeballs showed bright pink as Rebecca studied the pattern of the retinal arteries. They were tortuous from arteriosclerosis, as Ken had said, which didn't improve her temper any more than the fact, obvious even from her clinical examination, that Ross McKenzie was unquestionably holding his own and probably gaining as well.

Helga pulled the sheet back up over the grower's chest when Rebecca finished. He'd been silent during the examination. Now he spoke and his words startled them all.

"Twelve hours ago, I would have said you'd be pulling that sheet up over my face for good before now," said the grower. "Think I can go home tomorrow, Doctor?"

"Not unless you want to commit suicide," said Rebecca dryly, but much of the brusqueness that had been in her voice when she came on the ward was gone. "You had a pretty close shave, Mr. McKenzie."

And so did I, she said—but not aloud.

"Don't you think I know that?" said McKenzie. "If that day-time nurse hadn't been on the ball this morning, I wouldn't be here."

"I'll see you in the morning," said Rebecca. "Good night, Mr. McKenzie."

"Good night, Doctor."

Kevin McCartney was sleeping soundly and a glance at the ECG tracing being recorded on the small bedside monitor told Rebecca all she needed to know about him. At the nursing station, she carefully studied the records Helga gave her on Ross McKenzie's progress, then turned to face the other two.

"You've just witnessed something that I hope never happens again," she said. "A woman doctor who almost allowed the woman in her to make a fool of the doctor."

Neither Helga nor Ed Vogel spoke, for there was nothing really to say.

"Are you going to tell him that?" Helga asked finally with a twinkle in her eye.

Rebecca smiled. "Not if you two don't."

"We women have to stand together," said Helga promptly, and two pairs of eyes were turned on Ed Vogel.

"You gave me my job, Dr. Dalton, and you could take it away," he said with a shrug. "What sort of a fool would I be to buck you?"

III

Ken Dalton came on the CICU about a half hour after Rebecca and Ed Vogel left. Helga was working at the nursing station as usual, when no critical emergency existed with any of the patients.

"How's Kevin?" he asked.

She answered by flicking a switch on the master console so the tracing of Kevin's heartbeat would appear on the large monitor screen.

"The voltage is holding up well," the surgeon observed. "Have you noticed any T-wave changes or arrhythmias lately?"

"Only very occasionally and then it's barely noticeable. He's been sleeping most of the evening."

"No point in bothering him then." When he hesitated, Helga answered the question which, she sensed, was foremost in his mind.

"Your wife left not over a half hour ago," she said.

"I suppose she examined Mr. McKenzie."

"She went over the whole case with Dr. Vogel—and Mr. McKenzie."

"He was awake then?"

"And asking to go home."

Ken Dalton laughed. "He's a tough one—thank God. Did she leave any further orders?"

"No, Doctor. But she made a note for the record. I punched it into the data storage bank right after she left."

Reaching across to the end of the console, Helga pressed the keys on the portable keyboard. The printed words appeared immediately on the data storage monitor screen, extracted from the infinitely complicated electronic channels of the main computer.

PATIENT IMPROVING, CONTINUATION OF PRESENT EXPEC-
TANT MEDICAL TREATMENT INDICATED. R.D.

"Looks like you made a first down, Dr. Dalton," said the statuesque blonde nurse. "And I think you're going to win the game."

IV

Helga was busy with the small, hand-held keyboard that could both feed data into the storage computer and retrieve it at the rate of one million operations a second, when Mike Raburn came into the main ICU about ten-thirty.

"I'm getting jealous of that thing," he said. "Every time I come in here, you're holding hands with it."

"I'll be through in a minute, just have to key in the special orders for the eleven-to-seven shift."

She finished the job quickly and, reaching over to the control panel, switched on the retrieving circuits to display the orders on Carmelita Sanchez.

"Dr. LeMoyne was here earlier and ordered a pre-op medication for tomorrow morning, a hypo of atropine. Do you want to add anything?"

"No. Just came by to see if there'd been any change in her condition."

"None at all."

"The family been in?"

"They were here until about nine o'clock, but left and took Miguel Quintera with them. He'd been here all day and was bushed."

"Miguel's beginning to get on my nerves," Mike admitted. "He sits there by Carmelita's bed and looks at me when I come by like he blames me for not being able to save her."

"Do you know that's the first time I ever heard you admit something could get to you?"

"You haven't been watching me—"

"Only since yesterday afternoon at three, but it's beginning to seem like I've been close to you all my life."

Mike chuckled, but his eyes were warm and his hand lingered when he touched the orlon fabric of her sleeve.

"Don't get sloppy, Sundberg," he said softly. "But for your information, that goes double for me."

"Are you really worried about tomorrow morning, Mike? You certainly don't look it."

"Maybe not outside, but inside I'm as jittery as an interne doing his first appendectomy. When I think of how many things could go wrong in those nine minutes—"

"Everything's ready, isn't it?"

"As near as Val LeMoyne, Peggy Tyndall, and I can make them. But it would help if I'd had a chance to see one of the TBW's being performed and even more if I could have scrubbed on it."

"Father Junípero was here just after Carmelita's family left," said Helga. "He gave her last rites, but of course she didn't know anything about what was happening."

"That's part of what's bugging me, I guess," Mike admitted. "As a theologian, Father Junípero is troubled about what will be happening to Carmelita's soul during those nine minutes tomorrow morning, when she'll be clinically dead. But he's able to hedge by giving her extreme unction and making sure she's ready to enter heaven, at least the way he sees it, while all I've got to depend on are these two hands." He held them up. "And right now they look pretty big and awkward to me."

"Don't you believe it," said Helga. "I've seen them work too many times. Will it trouble you if I watch from the gallery tomorrow?"

"I was hoping you would; having you around doesn't bother me at all. In fact, since yesterday afternoon at three o'clock, I've been more and more convinced that I'd like to make such an arrangement permanent."

Helga looked away quickly. "Don't rush me, Mike. I had my life all worked out—"

"So you told me—and we'll leave it that way, for the time being at least. But I'm still counting on you to be in the cheering section tomorrow. Want me to give you a ring at the apartment about eight-thirty to make sure you don't oversleep?"

"I'll be in the gallery," Helga promised. "Besides, I'm staying with Magda Gatton over in Bayside Arms tonight. Gus and Carolyn have the apartment."

"You shouldn't be walking around outside the hospital at that time of night, with all the muggings and rapings we've been having," he said in quick concern. "I'll meet you in the lobby about eleven-fifteen and see you to the Arms."

"You need your sleep, Mike—for tomorrow."

"Then promise me you'll ask one of the security guards to walk over to the Arms with you."

"All right. But I still don't—"

"I've got a whole weekend invested in you, woman—the most important weekend of my life."

"Go to bed, you big lug." Helga's voice was husky. "Before I start a hospital scandal by swooning in your arms like a love-sick schoolgirl—with that damned computer watching every move and recording it for posterity."

At the door, he paused. "The word's out that the God Committee turned your roommate down. Is she okay?"

"I haven't seen Carolyn since around five o'clock but she really didn't expect them to agree to her request. It was just something she had to get out of the way first."

"I can understand how she would feel the way she does," he said soberly. "But whatever she has decided, you're not going to be involved, are you?"

"Some things people have to do for themselves, Mike. I guess this is one of them."

V

The clock over the central switchboard showed five minutes to eleven and all through the tightly organized city-within-a-city women in white were busy with last-minute chores before going off duty. Except for the supervisors, who were giving reports to their night-shift counterparts, most of those going off were busy in the ward nurses' lounges, applying lipstick, combing hair, smoothing uniforms rumpled from bedside sitting or more active nursing care, quite conscious that, outside, husbands, sweethearts, and just hopeful male admirers waited for the exodus of dozens of young and old, a nylon brigade in retreat to mark the end of the afternoon shift.

At the main nursing station of the ICU unit, Mary Pearson, buxom, gray-haired and wise from long experience in the eleven-to-seven activities characterizing the vertical city that was Biscayne General, listened while Helga recited the salient occurrences of the past eight hours.

"There goes the night!" she exclaimed when Helga told of Kevin McCartney's cessation.

"He seems to be a lot better. And so does Mr. McKenzie."

"Any time there's been a crisis like a cessation during the day, we're certain to have a bad night," said Mary. "Hearts will be skipping all over the place."

"I've noticed that too. Dr. Rebecca says she thinks it's because in the daytime, when they're fully conscious or even dozing, heart patients and other really sick people are subconsciously controlling the rate of their heartbeats."

"But when they go to sleep the control is lifted? Could be."

"I see a lot more heart rhythm changes on the monitors while people are sleeping than when they're awake," Helga added. "Sometimes it looks like all the tracings get St. Vitus' Dance and Dr. Rebecca says a lot of the people who die in the hospital for no apparent reason are killed by their nervous systems."

"Scared to death?"

"When they're asleep, they can't keep their circulations under conscious control. The result is a skittering heartbeat, followed by collapse of the circulation, and before we can get to 'em and start beating their chests, Bingo! They're gone."

Mary Pearson's eyes swept the bank of smaller monitor screens on which the ECG tracings of nearly a dozen critically ill patients were being constantly recorded.

"Who's tonight's candidate, would you say?" she asked.

"Nobody, I hope. If there's anything that bugs me, it's coming on duty and finding an empty bed that housed somebody I thought was making it okay the night before."

Mary Pearson glanced at the small monitor screen where Carmelita Sanchez' heart and temperature patterns were being recorded electronically.

"If what Mike Raburn is going to try is as chancy as it sounds, you might just do that," she said. "Is it true that they're going to have TV cameras in the OR tomorrow watching the whole TBW?"

"That's the plan. If all goes well, you and your husband can watch on the six o'clock news."

"If it doesn't come on, I'll know Mike lost—and that's going to upset me a lot. I love that boy like I would my own son, if I had one."

"So do a lot of people around here," said Helga. "And not all of 'em as a son."

Mary Pearson gave the tall nurse a surprised look. "How long has this been going on?"

"Since yesterday afternoon at three o'clock. And don't tell me the real thing couldn't happen that fast, because I can hardly believe it myself."

VI

Kevin McCartney was awake when Mary Pearson made rounds about eleven-thirty.

"Where's Dr. Ken?" he asked. "I told Helga I wanted to see him tonight."

"You were asleep when Dr. Dalton made rounds. What did you want to see him for?"

"I'm getting over this crisis, ain't I?"

"Every sign we're monitoring says you are."

"Then I'm going to lay it on the line with him. He gave me a new lease on life by putting that girl's heart inside my chest. Now it's up to him to see that I keep going—if necessary with one of them plastic pumps he was working on for a while."

"I thought he'd stopped the artificial heart project."

"I'm going to insist that he start it again. He can't just operate on me once and save my life a second time, like he did this afternoon with that needle, then throw me aside like I was an old shoe. It's not ethical."

"Go back to sleep now," said Mary. "Dr. Dalton is helping Dr. Raburn with the Sanchez girl tomorrow morning but he's sure to make rounds after that's finished. You can tell him then."

"All right, slave driver. But be sure the alarm is set on that monitor. I don't want my pulse to stop beating and nobody discover it until Carolyn

Payson comes on duty in the morning."

"Don't look for her. She has the day off."

"And Helga's off for the weekend. Who's going to look after me the next few days?"

"You just finished telling me you're getting well."

"Turn the little monitor around then, so I can see it and call you, if my heart quits. It's too much trouble trying to watch the reflection in that glass pane over the door."

"You mean you've been watching all the time?"

"I discovered I could see it right after I was admitted. When I saw the line flatten out with that cessation this afternoon, I only had time before I blacked out entirely to pray that somebody at the main panel would see it right away—or wait so long it couldn't be started again. The last thing I want is to be one of them human vegetables with a brain that's been cut off from oxygen too long. The next time I see that line flatten out, I'm going to use all the strength I've got left calling somebody before I go out. But between God hearing me in time to do something about it and Helga Sundberg, I'd rather take my chances with Helga."

VII

"Let's go back the long way, Gus, I haven't seen Miami Beach in ages." They had left the Polynesian restaurant and were waiting for the car to be brought from the parking lot.

"Sure, darling. This is your night."

Carolyn hardly spoke as they negotiated the miles of brilliantly lighted Collins Avenue southward to the MacArthur Causeway, but he couldn't fail to notice that she was scanning the luxurious shops and hotels along the famous thoroughfare almost, it occurred to him, as if she were seeing them for the last time.

"I want to go home now," she said, settling back in the seat as he turned westward on the causeway toward Miami itself.

In the small apartment in Bayside Terrace, Carolyn came into Gus's arms as soon as the door was closed. The desperate urgency with which she made love stirred an answering passion within him that demanded an explosive relief. When the first need had been sated, they lay close together in the half-darkness of the room, her body pressed against him as if she couldn't bear a moment's separation.

"You made love that time like you thought Congress was going to make it illegal, darling," he said.

"Did I shock you?"

"Surprised is a better word, like a child expecting one present who gets two."

"That's how much I love you."

She reached up to pull his head down so their lips could meet once more. And almost as soon as they touched, he felt her mouth grow avid beneath his own and her body start to move against him with the onset of passionate demand. It was after two when, exhausted, they finally drifted off to sleep, still in each other's arms.

Sometime during the night the whine of an ambulance siren pulling into the emergency entrance to the hospital, plus the pain where her head pressed against his arm, woke Gus. Carolyn didn't awaken when he moved slightly to ease the pain, but he could feel the dampness of her tears against his cheek where her face had been pressed.

He put her strangeness tonight down as an emotional reaction to the ordeal before the God Committee the previous afternoon and wished he could help her in some way other than the sharing of their bodies. But he couldn't—for even in her passion tonight he'd sensed that she'd been seeking something he hadn't been able to bring her.

CHAPTER SEVENTEEN

I

When the alarm clock jangled its strident summons a little before seven, Carolyn got out of bed at once.

"Snooze a few minutes more while I get a shower," she told Gus. "Then I'm going to fix you some breakfast."

"My cup runneth over," he said. "Are you all right?"

"Sure." She was opening the venetian blinds at the window that looked toward the hospital tower. "Why?"

"You cried sometime during the night."

"See you in a minute," she said, stepping into the bathroom.

Gus didn't obey her suggestion and go back to sleep, however. She'd given no explanation for weeping and obviously didn't intend to, but that didn't stop him from worrying.

She spent only a few minutes in the shower and, when she came out, pink and glowing, Gus thought he'd never seen anyone so beautiful. But as he started to get out of bed she quickly moved to a closet and pulled down a negligee.

"Wait till I get something on," she said.

"Leave it off and I'll go without breakfast."

"No, you don't. I've got a lot of running around to do today while I'm off duty, and you have early morning rounds with Dr. McHale on Thursdays. Go shave and shower while I get your breakfast."

It was ready by the time he finished dressing: orange juice, bacon, eggs, toast, and coffee, arranged on a small table before the window through which the sun was streaming. They sat at the table like any married couple, he thought with a sense of pleasure that left a lump in his throat, eating breakfast and watching the seven-thirty news.

"Will I see you today?" he asked as he was leaving about ten minutes to eight.

"I doubt it, I've got some things to do."

When she kissed him good-by, she held onto him for an instant with a grip that actually brought pain to his arm.

"Go to work now," she said, shoving him out the door. "We've got eternity before us."

Going quickly to the window, she stood watching until she saw his tall form cross from the apartment building to the hospital, stopping for a moment to get the morning paper from a vending machine, and turning to wave just before the automatic doors opening into the lobby moved apart for him.

As she waved back, Carolyn felt the tears she'd managed to control until then begin to flow. Nor did she make any attempt to stop them for a long time.

II

Ed Vogel was already on the CICU when Kenneth Dalton stopped by there about eight-fifteen, on the way from the staff cafeteria, where he'd had breakfast, to the operating room.

"You look bushed, Ed," he said. "Night off?"

"Night on, which is sometimes worse," said the Cardiology Fellow. "With that TBW coming up this morning, I figured Mike needed all the sleep he could get, so I took emergency calls."

"Rough, eh?"

"Mary Pearson told me once that, whenever there's a crisis during the day in any part of the ICU, hell is sure to break loose here at night. Now I know she's right."

"Any trouble with Kevin or Mr. McKenzie?"

"The really sick ones have been okay. McKenzie's stroke work index curve has been moving up steadily. Kevin's having soft diet for breakfast and griping because it isn't steak."

"That's good."

"But there have been arrhythmias all over the place, plus a coronary admitted at 3:00 A.M. that I had to start on heparin. By the way, Kevin's awfully anxious to see you about something."

Ken looked at his watch. "I've got about a half hour before I start scrubbing. Might as well see him now."

Kevin McCartney was sitting up in bed, eating soft-boiled eggs—with obvious distaste.

"What the hell have they got me on soft diet for, Dr. Dalton?" he asked. "I need a breakfast steak to combat all them cell-destroying drugs you're piping into me."

"Yesterday you were settling for five per cent glucose intravenously, and liking it."

"That was before you pulled me out of the grave and injected that Thiotepa around my heart."

"How did you learn about that?"

"Helga said if you hadn't gone to bat for me in a hurry yesterday afternoon I wouldn't be here."

"Did she tell you she started your heart before the CPR team could get here?"

"I figured that, when she said she was the one that pounded on my chest." Kevin put down the spoon with which he had been eating the eggs. "I told Helga to wake me if you came around last night, so I could pick a bone with you. But she was pretty busy, with that new catheter in Mr. McKenzie and all, so she probably forgot it."

"Do you want to tell me what's bothering you in five minutes right now? Or would you rather wait until I have more time? I have to scrub—"

"I know—with Mike Raburn for that Sanchez girl. Everybody's excited about it."

"Nothing's secret in a hospital."

"Including the fact that you psyched out your wife with that new catheter Dr. Vogel put into Mr. McKenzie and Dr. Reb was a bit miffed about it."

"You're using up time with hospital gossip, Kevin."

"I'll give it to you straight then, Doc. You've saved my life twice already so you probably don't have over one more chance left. I just want you to know that, the way I figure it, you've been layin' down on the job of looking after my future by not keeping on with that research you were doing on a plastic heart before everything started going to pot."

"I hadn't really proved anything, Kevin."

"Peggy Tyndall told me you were just about ready to put an atomic-powered artificial heart into a calf when you stopped the research about six months ago. What I want to know is when are you going to get back to work on that thing?"

"I've been thinking—"

"Thinking isn't enough; I've lost six months and maybe my third chance at living, while you were out of action. How about going to work again before it's too late?"

Ken gave Kevin an appraising look. "Did my wife ask you to put the bite on me, Kevin?"

"Absolutely not. I swear it."

"You may well be right about the artificial heart program. I'll see what I can do."

"You don't resent my saying it?"

"Nobody should resent hearing the truth, Kevin, even about himself. I guess in a way I *have* been pretty selfish, thinking only of my own feelings." Ken glanced at his watch. "I'll have to run. We'll talk about this again another time."

"Maybe over a bottle of Cold Duck soon—with Dr. Rebecca? I remember just how you like it and the way I feel now, I'll be back tending bar in a few days."

"You might be right—on both counts," Ken told him. "Who can tell?"

III

Peggy Tyndall was in Operating Room Two by eight-thirty, in a green scrub tunic and wearing cap and mask. She was fussing over the elaborate pump oxygenator setup when Hans Brokaw, the other pump technician, came in.

"Damnedest-looking gadget I ever saw." Hans was a German male nurse who had married an Army nurse during her tour of duty and emigrated to the United States when she returned. Trained by the manufacturer of the pump oxygenator they were using, Hans was wholly without imagination and inclined to regard any modification of the basic machine as heresy. "Think it will work?" he added.

"Of course it will work," said Peggy. "Get busy and help me cool this Ringer's solution."

Hans helped her pour crushed ice into a small tub and pile it around a large flask containing the solution that would take the place of Carmelita Sanchez' blood for the brief period during which the toxins of hepatitis would, hopefully, be washed out of her circulation.

"That Ringer's looks a little opalescent to me," he observed. "Are you sure you're using the right solution?"

"Dr. Raburn decided to add some albumin and heparin to it. We had to make up a fresh solution and sterilize it while you were off yesterday afternoon."

Hans Brokaw studied her for a moment, then shook his head in bafflement. "The way you're jumping around, you'd think you were performing this operation instead of Dr. Raburn, Peg. What have you got the ants about?"

"Guess you're right." Peggy controlled herself with a visible effort. "After

I finished making the changes in the pump oxygenator yesterday afternoon, with Dr. LeMoyne and Dr. Raburn, I took some journal articles home with me last night to read up on TBW. And I discovered that this same method of inducing deep hypothermia is being used a lot in operating on children with congenital hearts while they're very small."

"Dale having more trouble?"

"I can't be sure. But from what I read last night, it's possible to correct some of these mixed-up hearts in kids during the first weeks of life, by cooling their bodies the way Mike Raburn's going to do with this girl and operating on a stilled heart."

The other technician dumped more ice into the tub and piled it around the flask of Ringer's solution.

"You know what you're saying, don't you?" he asked.

"It's not Dr. Ken's faul—" Peggy said quickly. She stopped, then burst out, "Damn you, Hans. You trapped me."

He shrugged and went on with his work.

"One thing I did learn, though," she continued. "They're not real sure the technique works too well with tetralogy of Fallot, so maybe Dr. Ken is only playing it safe by trying to carry Dale until he's old enough to do the complete job with an open heart operation."

"You'll be better able to decide whether to ask for another consultation after you see how this case goes." Hans voiced the thought that was uppermost in Peg's mind. "I'd better check the temperature of the blood Dr. Raburn will be putting back into the patient's circulation—if she lasts that long."

IV

Mike Raburn had almost finished scrubbing when Ken Dalton came into the scrubroom adjoining Operating Room Two. The older surgeon was wearing operating pajamas and a cap and held a mask in his hand.

Operating Room Two was especially equipped with a full range of monitoring instruments, as well as a small adjoining laboratory where rapid blood gas and other tests could be performed. The very last word in operating theaters, the room was used for all heart and blood vessel surgery at Biscayne General. Tying on his mask, Ken moved to the door leading into the surgery itself.

"Looks more like a TV studio than an operating room, Mike," he observed.

"I don't particularly like it," Mike admitted. "But Dr. Toler is very anxious for this procedure to be publicized as widely as possible."

"If you bring this off, it should certainly improve the hospital's image—as well as yours."

"The first part I can see a reason for, the second makes no difference," said Mike. "Fortunately we'll be making only two incisions, neither of them very large or very deep, so we should be able to avoid infection, even with the increased possibility from the cameras and the extra people around."

"I wasn't being critical, Mike. It takes a lot of guts, as well as ingenuity, to try something as new as this. Good luck."

"Shall I go ahead and make the incisions while you're scrubbing?" Mike asked.

"This is your show. I'm just assisting."

"It's still a lot of comfort to me that we'll be working together, Dr. Dalton."

"Just how are you handling the TV side?" Picking up a sterile brush from a bowl filled with them on a shelf above the long sink that ran almost the length of the scrubroom, Ken started scrubbing his hands and forearms.

"The TV crew positioned the two cameras you see at the back of the OR on platforms. I wouldn't let them come any closer to the actual field. The highest one will be focused on the patient so the technique of the washout will be photographed at all times. The second camera is centered on the bank of monitors against the wall. Both of them of course will record on videotape."

"It's quite a setup."

"I added a timer, too—at Miss Weston's suggestion."

"Like the ones the TV cameras always show during a launch?"

"Yes. NASA flew one down here from the Kennedy Space Center yesterday afternoon."

"Then all you need now is Walter Cronkite." Ken's smile robbed the words of any sarcastic intent.

"I'm afraid I'll be a poor substitute." Noting Mike's tone, Ken gave him a sharp glance.

"All of us are a bit jittery the first time we have to do an entirely new operation, especially when it's liable to be touch and go," he said. "It's like the stage fright all good actors feel just before a performance; I've had them tell me that if they don't experience it they usually louse up the show. You'll be okay by the time the pump starts humming."

"I'd better be," said the younger surgeon. "Else you'll be doing the first TBW in the history of Biscayne General."

Through the open door to the operating theater, Ken glanced up at the packed gallery that allowed as many as two dozen observers to watch an operation closely, with no danger of contaminating the wound, while the action was described by the surgeon over the closed circuit sound and TV system with a microphone hanging around his neck beneath the gown. The closed circuit TV cameras also enabled the operation to be watched on large screens in the teaching amphitheater across the hall.

"Miss Weston will be in the gallery," said Mike. "I dictated sort of a script for her, so she'll know what's happening as we go along. She can fill in from time to time in addition to my own description—all on tape, of course. The sound will be recorded separately from the taped television picture and dubbed in this afternoon."

"Sounds complicated to me."

"Me too," said Mike. "But Miss Weston thinks there's a good chance that part of the procedure, at least, will go to the network—if everything turns out all right, of course."

Lifting his hands so the antiseptic ran down his forearms and dripped from his elbows, thereby removing the possibility of contaminating his scrubbed forearms from the unscrubbed area of his elbows and arms, Mike moved into the OR. Accepting a sterile towel from a waiting scrub nurse, he dried his hands and forearms carefully, then dropped the towel into a waste container before donning a sterile gown. Only moments longer were required to put on sterile gloves, while a circulating nurse was tying the strings of the pale green garment.

As Mike moved to the center of the room, where Carmelita lay with at least a dozen wires connecting the bank of monitor screens to the sensors Val LeMoyne had applied to her body, a "dirty" nurse, so named because she was not scrubbed, picked up the wire trailing behind him from the throat microphone he wore and plugged it into a jack on the floor connecting him to the gallery and amphitheater PA systems, as well as to the tape recorder brought by the TV crew.

Val LeMoyne sat at the head of the table, an anesthetic machine beside her. The hose from it ran to an intratracheal tube she had inserted through Carmelita's larynx into her windpipe to attain a closed system between her lungs and the breathing bag of the anesthetic machine. The bag was emptying and filling in a regular, though somewhat hastened, rhythm and the respiratory rate was also being indicated by a small flashing light on one of the monitors.

"Did you have any trouble with the tracheal tube, Dr. LeMoyne?" Mike asked as he took the long forceps the nurse waiting at her small sterile instrument table handed him and dipped it into a sterile bowl of light brown antiseptic solution.

"The pharyngeal reflex was slightly active but a local anesthetic spray took care of that," said Val. "I don't want to give her any anesthetic unless I have to, so I'm carrying her on oxygen alone."

"I don't believe we'll need a general anesthetic," said Mike. "I'll infiltrate the skin with xylocaine before I make the incisions to put in the artery and vein catheters, just to make sure."

Across Carmelita's body Mike could see the heart-lung pump, with Peggy and Hans Brokaw, whose responsibility it was to operate the machine, busy making final adjustments. Unlike open heart surgery, where the pump must act as both heart and lungs for the patient while the heart was open and was therefore charged with donor blood, the pump reservoir now contained a solution that was almost as clear as water, except for the hint of opalescence caused by the small amount of albumin which had been added. A mixture of blood and packed red cells—obtained when the plasma was separated from donor blood—waited at one side, warmed and ready for the moment when the Total Body Washout was completed and replacement of the circulatory volume could be started.

As he began the familiar task of painting an area on Carmelita's groin with antiseptic in preparation for inserting two of the three cannulas that would connect her to the heart-lung machine. Mike lifted his eyes to the gallery. And he felt his tense nerves steady when he saw Helga, in the front row of seats across the glass-fronted gallery, lift her hand with thumb and forefinger joined in a salute of victory.

"The patient is a twenty-two-year-old laboratory technician who contracted Australian antigen hepatitis, ordinarily called serum hepatitis, while taking blood from a patient with this disease," he told the onlookers by way of the PA system. "She has become progressively worse during the past two weeks with a marked degree of jaundice, which the television audience may be able to see in the color picture as a deep ocher tint to her skin.

"Serum hepatitis is a far more serious illness than ordinary contagious hepatitis, which runs a predictable course, usually with complete, or near complete, recovery and the prognosis is consistently poor. We therefore advised this patient's family that an asanguineous hypothermic total body perfusion—more easily pronounced as Total Body Washout and further shortened usually to TBW—should be performed.

"Until recently TBW was an experimental procedure and only a small number of human cases have yet been treated with this method. It involves, as you will shortly see, the reduction of body temperature to a point where the ordinary life processes cease to be recorded on our monitoring systems, plus the removal of as much blood as possible from the entire circulation.

"With the toxin-containing blood removed, the circulatory system is then washed out with previously refrigerated Ringer's lactate solution containing sodium, potassium, calcium, chloride, and lactate ions in approximately the same concentrations that occur in the liquid portion of the blood called plasma, plus small amounts of heparin and albumin to prevent clotting.

During the TBW Ringer's solution will actually substitute for the patient's blood—a medical procedure known as perfusion—so you will hear us refer to the solution as the perfusate.

"The purpose of the entire procedure, of course, is to wash out of her blood vessels as much of the hepatitis antigen as possible, after which the circulation will be replenished with blood and packed red blood cells and the body warmed.

"The longest period so far recorded during which a living human body has been kept in what is essentially a state of suspended animation during TBW is nine minutes. Four minutes is generally considered to be the longest period that brain cells can ordinarily live without oxygen, but by dropping the entire body temperature, including the brain, to a very low level, the need for oxygen by all body cells is very much reduced. We still don't know whether it is safe to maintain a state of suspended animation longer than nine minutes, even with refrigeration, but we hope, of course, to accomplish our purpose in less than that time.

"Since the patient's heart will not be beating during that period and she will not be breathing, the heart-lung pump you see on Dr. LeMoyne's left will take over as soon as removal of the blood and lowering of body temperature begins. Needless to say, we will be watching the patient by every available sensor to observe her condition. But once the procedure is begun, it must be carried to completion as swiftly as possible, preferably in less than the nine-minute period already established, but certainly not more.

"You will note that Dr. LeMoyne has already inserted several small catheters into the patient's arm veins to measure blood gases and pressure, while we proceed with the TBW," Mike continued. "If you glance at the monitors on the wall, you will see representations of these parameters, along with the more familiar electrocardiographic and electroencephalographic tracings measuring the activity of the heart and the brain respectively.

"Prior to surgery, Dr. LeMoyne passed an electronic thermometer into the patient's esophagus and with it a tiny microphone that can pick up the heart sounds without interfering with our work. You can hear those sounds when she increases the volume on what is called the phonocardioscope."

Valerie LeMoyne moved a rheostat control on the panel beside her and the steady, though hurried, "lup-dup, lup-dup" of a normal heartbeat echoed from the speakers.

Dropping the ring forceps he had been using into a basin, Mike carefully placed sterile towels around the groin area where he planned to make the incision. Then taking the windowed sheet handed him by the instrument nurse, he gave one end to the interne across the table from him, who had scrubbed earlier. When they opened the sheet, the rectangular window in its center fitted neatly over the area of skin left bare by the covering towels, while the drape covered the lower half of Carmelita's body.

Moving then to her neck, he painted an area just above the collarbone with antiseptic and draped it to make a small area there available for surgery, the two sterile sheets now covering her body completely. While the scrub nurse was moving the table containing the instruments and dressings into place across Carmelita's sheet-covered form, Mike spoke again to the listeners in the gallery and the nearby surgical auditorium:

"Another electronic thermometer has been inserted into the lower part of the digestive tract, allowing us to watch very accurately the temperature inside the body itself, sometimes called the core temperature. When you hear the parameters being reported and see the temperature readings on the monitors, please remember that they are being registered on the Centigrade scale, where 0 degrees is freezing, 100 degrees is the boiling point of water, and the normal body temperature is roughly 37 degrees. When you consider that the temperature of the solution we will use to wash out the patient's circulation will be as near 5 degrees Centigrade as we can keep it, you will understand how rapidly her body temperature will be lowered during TBW."

While he talked, Mike had been injecting areas of skin in both the groin and lower neck with a local anesthetic solution. The injections completed, he handed the syringe to the scrub nurse and took the scalpel she gave him.

The bright lights of the operating theater were reflected from the thin, sharp blade, giving it almost the appearance of a flash of light as it moved swiftly across the groin for a distance of about four inches, laying open the skin and subcutaneous tissue down to the glistening white fibrous layer of the fascia enveloping the deeper muscles. Dropping into a basin the scalpel he had used for the incision, Mike began to clamp small bleeders in the fatty layer beneath the skin. Only the larger ones were tied off with fine catgut ligatures by the interne who was assisting him; the rest would be closed by the pressure of the hemostatic forceps used to seal their mouths.

Into the incision Mike now inserted a self-retaining retractor, two rakelike arms separated by a ratchet device, spreading the edges open so he could get at the deeper structures. With curved scissors, he split the fascia downward from a round opening through which a fairly large vein emerged.

"The vessel you see is the great saphenous vein," he told the watching audience. "It will guide us to the femoral, which it joins at a deeper level."

Dissecting carefully now, he uncovered the femoral vein, a dark blue tube in the depths of the muscles. Slipping a curved hemostat beneath the vein, he gripped the end of a piece of narrow cloth tape the interne placed between its jaws and pulled the tape through, isolating the vein where it could easily be lifted up. A similar maneuver isolated the femoral artery, a whitish firm-walled tube about the size of his little finger lying beside the vein.

By the time Ken Dalton, now gowned and gloved as Mike was, moved into the position vacated by the interne at his approach, Mike was ready to insert the catheters through which Carmelita's blood would be removed. When they were in place inside the femoral artery and vein, Ken allowed the backflow of blood to fill them until it dripped from them, then clamped the outer ends. Meanwhile Mike had moved to the neck, exposing the jugular vein through a smaller incision, and placed a catheter inside it, clamping it off too, like the others.

Only a few moments were required to attach the outer ends of the three catheters to tubes leading to and from the heart-lung pump where Peggy Tyndall and Hans Brokaw were waiting. When it was finished, only the clamps shutting off the ends of the vein and artery catheters separated the girl's circulation from the heart-lung pump and the five-degrees-above-freezing Ringer's solution that would substitute for her blood during the long minutes of Total Body Washout.

"We have just finished connecting the patient to a standard heart-lung pump unit, such as is used in open heart surgery," Mike explained to the watchers. "You will note, however, that a side vent has been placed in the circuit from the femoral and jugular veins so the body can be drained of blood through it, while refrigerated Ringer's solution is pumped into the circulation through the femoral artery catheter. When the circulatory system is empty of blood, it will be flushed with Ringer's, then refilled with warmed blood. The heat exchanger you see between the roller-head pump that substitutes for the heart and the femoral artery catheter leading back into the circulation will further warm the replacement blood and with it increase body temperature."

He paused and glanced around the table, checking each item as he described it, then spoke to Val LeMoyne.

"Give us the preperfusion parameters, please."

On the monitor TV screen behind Val LeMoyne, a picture of the bank of dials and controls appeared.

"Hematocrit, 29 per cent," she read them off. "Esophageal temperature, 37 degrees Centigrade. Rectal temperature 37.4 degrees. Blood pressure, 120 over 75. Arterial pO_2, 150. pH, 7.34. Blood urea nitrogen, 70. Alkaline phosphate, 72. SGOT, 237. Perfusate temperature, 5 degrees Centigrade. Flow rate, 0."

"The patient's general condition is satisfactory," Mike summarized the findings. "The blood chemistry changes are what you would expect with an advanced case of impending hepatic failure."

He looked at Ken Dalton, who nodded without taking his eyes from the heart-lung pump. Moving swiftly then, Mike unclamped the three catheters.

"Open the side vent," he said.

Peggy quickly turned the stopcocks shutting off the tubes connected to the catheters and blood immediately began to flow from the open end into a container placed beneath it.

"Start the pump, please."

Hans Brokaw, whose duty it was to watch the vital machine at all times, pressed a switch and the roller-head pump hummed into action.

"Rate of flow, 3000 millileters per minute." Mike's voice was even and controlled but the listeners could sense the underlying tension in it as, under the force of the pump, the flow of blood from the open side vent suddenly spurted and the pattern of the blood pressure tracing on one of the monitor screens began to trend downward.

The removal of poisoned blood from Carmelita's veins and arteries had begun.

CHAPTER EIGHTEEN

I

Ed Vogel hadn't missed Helga Sundberg's victory signal to Mike, as he slipped into a seat beside her in the front row of the gallery. Wearing slacks and a soft woolen sweater with a turtleneck, Helga was attracting almost as much attention from the largely male audience as the drama whose first act was just beginning on the stage of Operating Room Two below them.

"How long has this been going on?" he asked in a whisper.

"What?"

"You're as tense as a bride. Is it over Mike?"

She nodded but did not look up.

"Does he know it?"

She nodded again.

"Well I'll be damned," said the young cardiologist.

Mike's voice filled the gallery as he began to explain what he proposed to do, shutting off any answer Helga might have given.

"I never saw you dewy-eyed before," said Vogel in a tone of wonder. "It's positively nauseating."

"Shut up," Helga told him, without taking her eyes from the stocky form of the surgeon.

"You still didn't tell me how long this has been going on," Ed reminded her.

"Forty-two and a half hours, give or take a few minutes."

"I still don't believe it." Ed looked down at Mike, then back at the lovely blonde girl beside him. "Yeah, I guess I do," he admitted. "Does Mike know how lucky he is?"

"Not quite," said Helga. "But he will."

"Just be sure this time." The cardiologist's tone was dead serious. "Mike's not the kind that can take something special like you—or leave it. He's big but in a lot of ways he's like a little child—inclined to trust people and easily hurt when they turn out to be something less than he expects."

"Don't you think I'm as worried about that as you are?" said Helga.

"If you lead him on—and then drop him, I'll wring that beautiful neck with my own two hands."

"You won't have to. If this doesn't work out, I'll wring it myself." Helga looked up from the scene below and, as her eyes swept the gallery, stiffened suddenly.

"Miguel Quintera's in the back row, Ed," she said.

"The girl's fiancé?"

"Yes. He's only a first-year med student at the University of Madrid and, from the way he looks, this may be too much for him."

"Want me to take him out?"

"Not right now. But you can be ready in case he passes out."

II

Maria Alvarez, subbing for Carolyn Payson on the morning shift, was at the main ICU nursing station when Rebecca Dalton came into the ward shortly after nine-thirty to make rounds.

"Is this Miss Payson's day off?" Rebecca asked when she saw the plump Cuban nurse at the control station for the ward.

"Yes, and she really needed it," said Maria Alvarez. "I saw her right after the God Committee refused her request yesterday afternoon; she looked like she was taking it pretty hard."

"The committee decisions are supposed to be secret."

"If you can find a secret around here that isn't on the grapevine before it stops happening, I'll be surprised," said the nurse. "Sometimes everybody even knows what's going to happen before it really does. Would you believe there's a pool going right now on how long it will be before Carmelita wakes up?"

"But the TBW just began."

"Like I was saying, Dr. Dalton, the grapevine is like the Shadow used to be on the radio a long time ago, it knows everything. But this time it's in the bag. Around here, Mike—Dr. Raburn—can do no wrong."

"I know," said Rebecca, but did not add that sometimes she couldn't help wishing she could say the same thing about herself. . . . "Could I have the chart on Mr. McKenzie?" she asked.

"Right here." The nurse handed Rebecca a bulky chart. On the front was the graph sheet upon which the night's readings of the cardiac stroke index calculations by the computer had been plotted earlier by Ed Vogel in preparation for Rebecca's morning visit. "He was asking for breakfast this morning."

In Ross McKenzie's cubicle, Rebecca listened to the grower's heart carefully, then percussed out its size. The measurements were somewhat smaller than the day before, when the heart had appeared to be dilating to accommodate the extra blood spurting through the incompetent mitral valve with each ventricular contraction. Nor was there any doubting that McKenzie had shown steady improvement in the some eighteen hours since Ed Vogel had inserted the remarkably versatile fiberoptic catheter into the right side of his heart and on into the pulmonary artery on Ken's orders.

"How much longer do I have to keep this damn tube in my arm, Dr. Dalton?" McKenzie demanded when Rebecca finished examining him.

"Probably another twenty-four hours. Dr. Kenneth Dalton will have to decide that."

"What the hell has he got to do with deciding how I'm to be treated? I'm your patient, not his."

"For your information, Mr. McKenzie," Rebecca said evenly, "I was ready yesterday at noon to demand that you have open heart surgery, but Dr. Dalton didn't agree and had this special catheter put into your circulation instead. As late as last evening, I was still inclined toward surgery, but the new catheter is telling us more about your heart than we could possibly have learned in any other way."

"I could have told you I was better," McKenzie grumbled. "But nobody took the trouble to ask me."

"You could hardly have predicted twelve hours in advance what your heart action would be like. That's what this new instrument did."

"How much extra are these gadgets you're using going to cost me?"

"I don't have the least idea, Mr. McKenzie. But I can tell you it's a lot less than surgery would cost, and a lot safer."

"Just how much trouble am I going to have when I get out of here?" McKenzie asked.

"You'll be able to live a normal life—for a man of your age."

"Hell! I might as well be dead."

Rebecca laughed. "Maybe if you didn't stay mad all the time you wouldn't put such a strain on your heart, Mr. McKenzie. My assistant will get another ECG later this morning and I'll see you again this evening. Maybe tomorrow we can talk about taking the catheter out."

"Are you going to give me something to eat besides pap?"

"That's another area where you'll have to practice a little more moderation. The arteries in your eye grounds show quite a lot of hardening, so those of the heart have probably undergone much the same changes too. I'll give you detailed instructions about diet and several other things before you leave the hospital. We're going to want to check up on you about every three months, too."

"Damn nuisance," McKenzie muttered.

"I'll put you on a light diet for the time being," she promised. "But animal fat for you is a thing of the past."

Kevin McCartney was watching television, an old Humphrey Bogart movie. He flicked it off with the remote control switch when Rebecca came into the room.

"Hi, Dr. Reb," he said. "How about me getting out of here?"

"All at once, everybody wants to leave. First Mr. McKenzie and now you."

"Don't let him go unless he agrees not to cut down the hospital budget. The fact that you just saved his life doesn't make any difference to that old goat."

"That would be blackmail—or something."

"I'm still glad he's had a chance to see what the taxpayers' money is spent for around here. Think it will change him any?"

"I doubt it," said Rebecca. "Besides, I almost flubbed his case. And we almost lost you, too, because I failed to realize how much the fluid in your pericardium was crippling your heart. Actually, you have Miss Sundberg to thank for your being here at all."

"I've already thanked her, me 'n' Helga are buddies. And I read the riot act to Dr. Ken, too, when he was in here early this morning."

"Why?"

"Because he almost let me down."

"You've been through enough rejection crises to know the only reason why you're coming out of this one so fast is because he injected antilymphocyte drugs into your pericardium yesterday after he removed the fluid."

"I give him credit for that," said Kevin. "But I told him I wasn't going to stand for him laying down on the job no more with that plastic heart project he used to work on. One of these days I may need that gimmick and I want him to have one ready by the time I do."

"I can understand that."

"I also told him he took on the job of keeping me alive when he put that girl's heart into my chest, so it's up to him to stay on the job."

Rebecca didn't ask the question that was foremost in her mind, because she was afraid of what the answer might be.

"He didn't promise me anything, just said he'd have to see about it," Kevin continued. "But I think he's going to start back on his research. And you know what that means, Dr. Reb?"

"Yes, Kevin." Rebecca's eyes were warm with appreciation—and with hope. "I do know."

III

"Increase the pump rate to 3500 millileters a minute, please."

Mike Raburn's voice sounded loud in the stillness gripping those in the operating room and the observers in the gallery, as they watched the blood pouring out of Carmelita Sanchez' jugular and femoral veins and the flow of Ringer's solution into her body through the femoral artery. Already the blood spurting from the side vent draining the joint circuit of the two venous catheters was noticeably paler, as the Ringer's solution mixed with the remainder of the blood still inside the vessels.

"Parameters, please, Dr. LeMoyne?"

"Esophageal temperature, 30 degrees. Rectal, 32 degrees." Val Le-Moyne's voice was calm. "Respiration, 20. Blood pressure, 100 over 70. Arterial pO_2, 100. Perfusate temp, 10 degrees."

"Everything seems to be going well," said Mike.

"Couldn't be better," Val agreed.

On the monitor screens the height of the ECG tracing was already sharply diminished and the voltage represented by the waves from the brain's action currents was also noticeably less than before the side vent had been opened and the blood tainted by the Au antigen of hepatitis allowed to leave her body.

"Time since pump activation, five minutes," Peggy Tyndall reported from her station at the pump oxygenator.

"You will notice that, as the toxin-containing blood is removed and replaced with the refrigerated perfusate, the indices of body metabolism represented by the ECG and EEG tracings are decreasing steadily," Mike said for the benefit of the television and gallery audience. "These indicate that our intended purpose of reducing metabolism and oxygen use by the body cells to as near zero as possible is being rapidly attained."

"Pulse, 160. Blood pressure, 90 over 60," Val LeMoyne reported. "Arterial pO_2, 70."

"The human body is a remarkably well-balanced machine," Mike continued, as if he were lecturing an audience of students. "When not enough oxygen is being received by the red blood cells, the heart rate increases in order to pump the blood through the circulation more rapidly. This accounts for the steadily increasing pulse rate, as the blood inside the vessels of the body is thinned by mixture with the perfusate solution."

On the monitor screens, the ECG had become so rapid in the past several minutes that the separate heartbeats could hardly be distinguished from each other and the tracing was now little more than a rapidly vibrating pinpoint of light. On the EEG tracing, too, the waves were so low that they could hardly be seen.

"As you can see from the monitors, the heart is now beating so rapidly and with such a low voltage in the action currents registered by the ECG tracing that it can almost be considered to have stopped," Mike continued. "The same is true of the brain's action currents recorded by the EEG on the monitor screen."

"Esophageal temperature 25 degrees. Rectal, 26 degrees. Arterial pO_2 no longer measurable," Val LeMoyne reported. "Blood pressure cannot be obtained. Pulse cannot be counted."

"We are now approaching cardiac standstill known in medical terms as asystole." Mike's voice had taken on a somewhat strained note as the crucial period approached swiftly. "Since our time limit is nine minutes, time will be counted in half minutes from my signal. Those of you who can see the patient's face will note that it is quite pallid, indicating that almost no blood remains in her circulation. We will continue pumping the perfusate solution through the circulatory system after asystole, however, in an attempt to wash out the largest possible amount of the hepatitis antigen before replenishing the circulation with blood."

"Esophageal temperature, 20 degrees. Rectal, 22 degrees." The voice of the anesthesiologist was still calm, the only such in the room. "Patient is asystolic."

"Now!" said Mike tersely, and the counter began to tick off the seconds, while one camera watched it. "Pump speed, 4000."

The hum of the pump as the rate was increased and the click of the timer were almost the only sounds in the room. The breathing bag on the machine through which Val had been administering oxygen had long since stopped its motion, since the heart-lung pump had taken over not only the heart's function of pumping blood through the arteries and veins but also the task of oxygenating what blood remained in Carmelita's body by exposing it to an atmosphere with a high concentration of the gas before it was pumped back into the body. At the moment, however, the almost clear Ringer's solution substituting for blood could carry no oxygen.

"One half minute since asystole." The voice of the nurse watching the counter was high-pitched with tension.

"You will note now that there is practically no color to the perfusate being drained from the jugular and femoral veins," Mike pointed out to the audience, "indicating that we have already removed as much of the circulating blood as it is possible for us to remove. We will continue to pump the perfusate through the vessels a little while longer, however, in order to wash out all the toxins we can."

"One minute since asystole," the nurse announced.

"Parameters, please, Dr. LeMoyne?" Mike's tone was also tense.

"Esophageal temperature still 20 degrees. Rectal, 21 degrees." Val's voice was calm. "Arterial pO_2 and all other parameters not obtainable. This patient is clinically without metabolism. Early resuscitation advised."

IV

In the observation gallery looking down upon Operating Room Two only the low voice of Marcia Weston, the television reporter, intruded upon the tense silence, as she spoke into the microphone of a small tape recorder describing the scene below, while the TV cameras in the operating theater recorded the event on videotape:

"This is surely one of the most remarkable, and moving, moments this reporter has ever experienced," she was saying. "The patient upon the operating table now shows no signs of life and you just heard the anesthetist announce that metabolism is absent, the same thing as saying she is clinically dead. Actually the only thing about the patient even simulating life at this moment is the roller-pump of the heart-lung machine forcing a clear frigid solution through her blood vessels to wash the greatest possible amount of the hepatitis toxin from her body.

"As I watch, I cannot help asking myself whether any procedure that so remarkably simulates death isn't too dangerous to justify its use? And whether a clinically dead person can be resurrected, the only name that can rightly be given to what will happen here, if Carmelita Sanchez does indeed live again?"

At the back of the gallery, Miguel Quintera had been watching the scene below with growing apprehension and horror. Now a sudden sob of anguish drowned out the voice of the reporter as, stumbling to his feet, the young Cuban lurched from the gallery, the sound of his sobbing suddenly cut short when the door slammed behind him.

"Poor devil," said Ed Vogel. "Looks like it was too much for him."

"It's almost too much for me." Helga's voice was shaky. "Can you imagine what Mike is going through down there now, wondering where he can draw the line between possibly saving her from a liver death and damaging her brain cells beyond any return of consciousness, even if the hepatitis is cured?"

"I hope I never have to make such a choice." Ed Vogel's words were more of a prayer than a statement.

V

Miguel Quintera staggered through the door of the first-floor Coffee Shop and into an empty booth.

"Coffee!" he managed to gasp.

Seeing how pale he was, Maggie McCloud, who was working the morning shift for another waitress, quickly drew a cup, picking up a glass of ice water as she passed the tap on the way to the booth.

"Drink this," she commanded, and he gulped the scalding brew obediently.

"What happened?" she asked.

"Carmelita's dead!"

"On the operating table?"

"Yes. I was watching, but I had to leave."

"We've all been pulling for her," said Maggie sadly. "I'm so sorry. And Dr. Raburn worked so hard."

"He killed her." The Cuban's voice was shrill with hysteria from strain. "He drained all the blood from her body! Then he just stood there and watched her die."

Quintera buried his head in his arms and started sobbing again. But when Maggie tried to pat him on the shoulder in an instinctive gesture of sympathy, he shook off her hand angrily. Pushing his way out of the booth, he knocked over the glass of water and almost spilled what remained of the coffee.

"Dr. Raburn killed Carmelita!" he shouted as he lurched through the door that gave access to the garden outside.

A business office clerk, coming to the Coffee Shop for her morning break, heard the words and saw Miguel Quintera lurch from the shop.

"What's wrong with him, Maggie?" she asked.

"The Sanchez girl just died on the operating table. They're engaged and he was watching."

"My God! What a tough break!"

Death in one or another of its myriad forms was a constant dweller in a hospital, but none of its masks was so dreaded, so fraught with utter defeat, as death on the operating table. In the surgical theater, more even than on the Intensive Care Units, all the forces with which death could be fought were available, all needed expert help immediately at hand.

A highly trained anesthesiologist like Valerie LeMoyne was the ultimate expert in resuscitation. Surgeons with the experience of Mike Raburn and Ken Dalton were highly qualified to carry out such a dramatic procedure as opening the chest to massage the heart, although more recent techniques of resuscitation had made this desperate measure rarely necessary any more. And so the triumph of death over all the forces arrayed against it represented the ultimate defeat, particularly in one so young and so beautiful as Carmelita Sanchez.

Moving across the lobby, the clerk paused beside the desk of the hospital receptionist.

"Did you hear, Mrs. Peters?" she asked. "Carmelita Sanchez just died on the operating table."

"How do you know?"

"Her fiancé saw the whole thing. He just ran outside shouting that Dr. Raburn killed Carmelita."

"Poor things." The receptionist was gray-haired and a grandmother. "They're both so young."

The telephone on the receptionist's desk rang and she picked it up.

"Biscayne General—Patient Information, can I help you? Oh, it's you, Evelyn. No, I can't take my break yet. The Sanchez girl just died—on the operating table."

Dr. Jeffry Toler's secretary knocked softly on the door of the administrator's office before going in.

"The Sanchez girl just died on the operating table, Dr. Toler," she said when he looked up inquiringly from his desk. "I thought you'd want to know."

"When did it happen?" Jeffry Toler's shock at the news showed on his face.

"Just now, apparently. Mrs. Peters called from downstairs to tell me. The girl's fiancé just came down from the OR."

Toler reached for the telephone, then drew his hand away. "No use bothering Dr. Raburn and Dr. Dalton now. They'll be busy breaking the news to the relatives."

In the lobby downstairs, Mrs. Peters dialed an outside number and spoke into the phone softly, so she couldn't be heard in the rest of the room.

"I thought you could use the news, John," she said, "maybe between records. You know the Sanchez case, the one that's been on TV and in the newspapers the last day or two. Well, Dr. Raburn was doing a very dangerous operation on her, draining all her blood and replacing it and she just died on the operating table. No, I don't have any details, but I thought this would be a real scoop for you—son."

From the radio station Mrs. Peters had just called where her son was a disc jockey, the excited voice of the announcer broke into the music:

"We interrupt this program to bring you an exclusive bulletin. Most of Miami and much of the country have been waiting to hear the outcome of the daring surgical procedure being carried out this morning on Carmelita Sanchez, the Sleeping Beauty of Biscayne General Hospital. She has been in coma for several weeks with a severe form of hepatitis, and this morning doctors at the hospital resorted to a desperate measure in an attempt to save her, involving a new and largely untried surgical operation designed to wash the poisons of hepatitis from her body. Key to success was to be the critical period of nine minutes in which the patient was clinically dead, after which she would be revived by replacement of her blood volume with a fresh transfusion.

"What was hoped to be a gift of life for Carmelita Sanchez this morning turned out to be the grim stroke of death, however. Word has just come from a reliable source inside the hospital that she died a few moments ago on the operating table, while the desperate surgical operation was being attempted."

On the CICU, Maria Alvarez had answered the telephone moments before. Now she hung it up and looked bleakly at the console before her.

"Poor Carmelita," she said. "And poor Miguel. I guess I'd better wait for Dr. Raburn to tell the family."

No more than five minutes had elapsed since Miguel Quintera lurched from the observation gallery of Operating Room Two. Yet in that time the news had raced through the twenty floors of the hospital by the elaborate communications network known as the grapevine, from Dr. Jeffry Toler's office on the twentieth floor to the Pathology Laboratory in the basement, alerted there by a technician who had brought coffee for the morning break to Dr. Karen Fletcher and Dr. Sam Toyota and picked up the information from Maggie in the Coffee Shop en route.

Rebecca Dalton heard the news when she called the main laboratory to request a multi-lead ECG tracing on Ross McKenzie. Putting down the phone, she stared unseeingly at the framed certificate on the wall indicating that she was fully qualified as a specialist in cardiology. Ken had merely been backstopping Mike Raburn that morning, she knew, but he was present in the operating room during the TBW and must therefore accept some of the onus for the girl's death—in his own mind at least. And just when she had dared to hope he was on the point of regaining the confidence in himself he must possess if he were ever to go back into cardiac surgery and research.

"I'm going to OR Two, Ellen," she told her secretary.

"It's tough luck for Dr. Dalton and Mike—Dr. Raburn," said the secretary.

Rebecca stopped short. "Were you listening to my telephone conversation, Ellen?"

"Oh no, Doctor," said the secretary, somewhat intimidated by the note of coolness in Rebecca's voice. "I got it about two minutes ago, when the record librarian brought up some charts for you to sign."

"And you didn't tell me?"

"I guess I did wrong, Dr. Dalton," said the girl. "But it *was* bad news and I thought—"

"I know what you thought, Ellen—and why. But I would have heard about it soon anyway."

When she came into the observation gallery above OR Two and looked down upon the scene below her, Rebecca frowned. Carmelita certainly could be dead, judging from the pallor that marked the skin of her face, the only part of her body Rebecca could see. But none of the activity in the operating theater faintly resembled the sort of frenzied order that usually characterized a last-ditch attempt to bring life back to a seemingly dead body.

Moving down the steps to where Ed Vogel and Helga Sundberg sat watching the scene below intently, Rebecca took a seat in the row behind them made available by a student who recognized her.

"What's happening?" she asked in a whisper.

"They're getting ready to recharge the pump with blood and packed red cells," said Ed Vogel. "Want to come down here?"

"No. I'm fine here. Is everything going okay?"

"Like a Swiss watch." Ed turned and, seeing Rebecca's face, asked quickly, "Is anything wrong?"

"Somebody started a rumor that the girl died on the operating table. I even heard it on a patient's radio set on the way here."

"Miguel!" Helga exclaimed.

"Who's that?"

"Carmelita's fiancé—a first-year medical student at the University of Madrid. He was here at the beginning of the TBW, and I could see that he was quite disturbed. When Mike—Dr. Raburn—drained out all the blood just now and Miguel saw only the Ringer's solution going through the heart-lung pump, with no heartbeat and no other sign of life, I guess he panicked. Anyway, he ran out."

"You never saw anything like the way the story that she died on the table has traveled," said Rebecca. "It's all over town by now, from the radio broadcast."

"Excuse me, Dr. Dalton." It was Marcia Weston, the TV reporter. "Did you say you heard a broadcast on the radio saying Carmelita was dead?"

"Just a few moments ago."

"Do you know what station?"

"No. I was passing a patient's room on the way here and the radio was on."

The reporter looked anxiously at her watch, then down at the scene in the operating room.

"This is the climax of the TBW," she said. "I'd give anything to be able to warn my own newsroom, but I can't leave here now."

"Neither can I," said Rebecca. "Give me a rundown on what's happened so far, Ed."

CHAPTER NINETEEN

I

"Five minutes since asystole." The nurse's voice was a little unsteady as she read the figures on the steadily ticking clock.

"Esophageal temperature, 20 degrees. Rectal, 21 degrees." Val Le-Moyne's voice was still calm as that of a highly trained anesthesiologist should be in a grave emergency. "No other parameters obtainable."

"Perfusate clear, pump rate, 4000 millileters per minute." Peggy Tyndall looked at Mike and had all she could do to keep from urging him to start returning blood to Carmelita's circulation.

"Blood and packed red cells ready?" Mike asked quietly.

"Yes, Doctor," said the operating supervisor, a tall nurse whose nerves were like steel from weathering many crises.

"Oxygenation tank—"

"Ready. Oxygen, 95 percent. CO_2, 5 per cent."

"Five and one half minutes since asystole," the nurse reported.

"Don't push your luck, Mike," Ken Dalton said softly, and the younger surgeon nodded.

"Clamp the femoral artery catheter, please, Dr. Dalton," he said, and Ken quickly closed off the catheter through which the almost freezing-cold Ringer's solution had been pumped into Carmelita's circulation.

"Open side vent to drain system," said Mike.

Peggy moved quickly to obey and, with the pump still running but no more of the perfusate being forced into Carmelita's circulatory system, an almost clear stream began to spurt from the side vent of the system. The level of perfusate in the pump reservoir diminished rapidly as it was emptied through the vent and in a few seconds the flow of Ringer's solution from it became a mere trickle, indicating that the pump reservoir had been emptied.

"Pump off!" said Mike.

"Pump off," Peggy verified as Hans Brokaw threw the switch.

"Recharge system with blood and packed cell mixture."

Peggy and Hans Brokaw worked rapidly and efficiently together, as a highly trained team should, pouring the warm mixture of two parts transfused blood to one part of packed cells in plasma into the pump reservoir.

"Start pump, 3000 millileters," said Mike. "Leave side vent open."

"Seven minutes since asystole," the nurse watching the timer reported, as the pump started humming and blood started flowing from the open side vent. Mike did not order it closed immediately, however, for bubbles could be seen in the stream of flow.

"We are allowing oxygen and CO_2 to be removed from the tubing in order to prevent embolism," he explained to the audience, watching the flow from the side vent closely as he spoke.

"Unclamp the femoral catheter," he ordered when the flow of blood had cleared and no more bubbles could be seen.

"We are now starting to refill the patient's circulatory system with a fresh mixture of blood and red cells," he told the audience as the color visible through the walls of the catheter in the femoral artery darkened, indicating that blood was flowing through it.

"Heat exchanger on," Mike ordered before speaking again to the audience:

"The rate of oxygenation of this blood will be kept as high as possible, so as to provide an oxygen-rich supply to the body tissues which have been without oxygen now for about nine minutes," he said to them. "With luck, most of the Au antigen of viral hepatitis was removed with the blood drained from her circulation plus the further washing out of the entire circulatory system with refrigerated Ringer's solution. The rapidity with which she awakens from coma, possibly as early as twelve hours from now, will tell us how successful we have been.

"You will note, too, that with the blood being warmed as it flows into the body, the technicians are now adjusting the rate of flow through the pump about 2500 milliliters per minute. This level will be maintained during the rest of the procedure, since it closely approximates the normal output of the human heart."

"Esophageal temperature, 30 degrees. Rectal, 31 degrees," Val LeMoyne reported. "Arterial pO_2, 50 and rising."

There was silence as the pump hummed, sending blood circulating through Carmelita's body, then Mike spoke again:

"By adding 5 per cent CO_2 to the 95 per cent oxygen concentration in the pump chamber, we hope to stimulate spontaneous respiration and, of course, a beginning of heart function as quickly as possible."

"Esophageal temperature, 32 degrees. Rectal, 33 degrees," said Val. "pO_2, 68."

"Flow rate, 2900," the technician at the pump reported.

"Step up the heat exchange rate a little, please," said Mike.

"Nine minutes since asystole," the nurse at the clock reported.

All eyes in the room and the gallery were now centered upon the ECG monitor. Only a moving pinpoint of light traveled across the ground glass of the screen, but the watchers knew the entire success of the procedure depended upon whether or not the heart would resume its spontaneous beat under the influence of the warming of the blood and the steadily rising oxygen tension in the arteries.

"pO_2, 90 millimeters," Val reported. "Urine excretion resumed."

"That's the best sign we've had so far," said Mike in a tone of deep satisfaction. "It means that the kidneys withstood the lowered temperature. Now if the ECG and the EEG come through on time, we'll be okay."

The electroencephalographic tracing had shown no sign yet of brain waves. But as those gathered around the operating table and in the gallery watched—plus the crowded surgical auditorium where everything that happened was being reproduced upon the teaching monitors of the closed circuit TV receivers—the spot of light indicating heart action suddenly darted upward in an attempt to form the QRS complex that was the center of every heartbeat pictured on the screen.

"It's trying to start," said Val.

"We may have to use the pacemaker, sir," Mike told Ken Dalton. "Would you drop out and take charge of it?"

"Certainly." Moving to the other side of the patient, Ken picked up the electrodes used to apply an electrical stimulation to a balky heart or, by switching to the defibrillator current, still an unruly one.

"Spontaneous respiration established," said Val LeMoyne as the light on the small screen monitoring respiration started to blink. At the same instant a corresponding wave appeared upon the ground-glass face of the screen in the respiratory channel.

"Say when," said Ken. "We're ready."

"Hold a second more, please. The pump seems to be handling heart function very well."

As if to corroborate his words, Val reported: "Arterial pO_2, 90 millimeters and rising."

The dancing pinpoint of light suddenly darted up, down, and up, forming a QRS pattern. On the heels of that contraction came another, this time preceded by the small P-wave signifying contraction of the auricles and the beginning of a full heartbeat cycle.

"Cardiac function resumed." Nobody could mistake the joyous note in Val LeMoyne's voice now and a somewhat shaky laugh ran through both the operating room and the gallery.

"Congratulations, Mike," said Ken. "You made it."

"We all made it," said the younger surgeon. "If there ever was a team play, this was it."

II

In the gallery, Marcia Weston moved toward the door.

"Can anybody tell me where's the nearest outside phone?" she asked.

"Tell the nurse in charge of the floor nursing station just outside that I said you could use the inside phones, Miss Weston," Rebecca Dalton answered. "Dial 9 for outside."

"Thank you, Doctor." The TV reporter disappeared through the door.

"Mike's over the first hurdle," said Ed Vogel as he, Helga and Rebecca were leaving the gallery. "The next will be to see whether the girl regains consciousness."

Rebecca stopped at the ward nursing station to make sure Marcia Weston had been able to get an outside line.

Ed Vogel looked at his watch and whistled. "Can you believe it's only nine-thirty? I could have sworn that TBW took an hour instead of nine minutes."

"It was the longest nine minutes in my life," said Helga. "And I'm sure in Mike's."

III

From the operating room, Ken Dalton took the elevator down to the CICU. Maria Alvarez was at the central console.

"Kevin's SGOT is still elevated some, Dr. Dalton," she reported. "But Mr. McKenzie's is almost back to normal. Here are the latest lab reports."

Ken studied the laboratory report sheets and the last multi-lead ECGs that reported on the heart from several angles, registering a picture of its action in sections, so to speak.

"Looks like they're both pretty close to being out of the woods," he agreed. "Has my wife seen these?"

Maria noted the absence of hesitation when he spoke the word "wife"; it was the first time in many months that he'd failed to stumble over the word when he happened to mention it.

"Not yet," she said. "It's a shame about Carmelita, isn't it?"

"What do you mean?"

"It's been all over the hospital that she died on the table about ten minutes ago."

Ken stared at her blankly. "Whatever gave you that idea?"

"Maggie was in the Coffee Shop when the girl's fiancé told her. He was there." A look of horror came over the nurse's face. "You mean she didn't . . . ?"

"The patient was doing very well when I left the operating room less than ten minutes ago."

"Oh, my God! Mrs. Peters at the reception desk is telling it all over the hospital. And it's on the radio, too."

"How could that happen?"

"Mrs. Peters told me once that her son's a disc jockey on a local radio station."

"I'd better warn Mike." Ken Dalton reached for the telephone. "He'll want to talk to the family immediately and assure them the girl's okay."

Valerie LeMoyne answered the telephone in the operating room. "Mike's gone down to the first floor to talk to the girl's parents, Ken," she said.

"How is she?"

"Fine. All the parameters are returning to normal, some more slowly than others, of course."

"Did you know that for the past ten minutes or so the whole hospital and half of Miami has believed the girl was dead?"

"What?"

"It was even broadcast over the radio."

"That's the weirdest thing I ever heard of."

"Well, if Mike's talking to the family he probably knows about it too, by now. Thanks, Val."

IV

"Where's Carmelita's family?" Mike asked Maria Alvarez.

"They're not in the ICU waiting room?"

"No."

"They must have gone to the main waiting room. Or maybe out in the garden. They were pretty up—"

Mike was already through the door leading to the main lobby and the gardens so he didn't hear the last two words. He had no trouble finding the Sanchez family, however. The furious babble of Spanish and the sound of sobbing coming from the center of the garden told him where they were.

He was halfway across the open space around the fish pool when Miguel Quintera saw him. Leaving the others, Miguel ran toward Mike, who just had time to throw up a hand and set himself against the unexpected attack, when the younger man piled into him, flailing with his fists and sobbing.

"Murderer!" the Cuban shouted. "You killed Carmelita."

Mike held the slight Cuban off as best he could without actually striking him, for Quintera was much lighter and shorter than he, while he looked for the familiar face of Mr. Sanchez to bring some order out of the melee. Then he saw the priest sitting on a bench talking to Mrs. Sanchez, whose head was bowed.

"Father Junípero!" he called. "Get this madman away from me."

The priest moved then and Mr. Sanchez, too, appeared, accompanied by a gray-haired man with a clipped mustache. Together they pulled the young Cuban away, still shouting, "Murderer!"

"Will somebody tell me what's going on here?" Mike snapped.

"Dr. Raburn!" Father Junípero's voice was sharp. "You have no reason to speak like that to grieving relatives."

"Grieving?" Mike was thoroughly irritated now. "What kind of people are you anyway?"

"It would be more appropriate for me to ask you that, Doctor." The priest's voice was icy.

Mike shook his head, baffled and angered by behavior he couldn't understand.

"The minute I could leave the operating room, Father, I came down to tell Carmelita's family she came through the procedure in excellent condition. And I get attacked by this young man—"

"You mean she's still alive?" The priest's tone was incredulous.

"I just finished telling you Carmelita came through in excellent condition. Of course she won't be conscious for—" Mike stopped, a partial comprehension of what had happened starting to dawn upon him. "You mean you thought . . . ?"

"The family were told Carmelita died on the operating table. It was even broadcast—"

"Nobody but the doctor in charge has the authority to tell a patient's family that. Who did it?"

For a moment there was silence.

"It was I," Miguel said brokenly. Then he broke into a torrent of Spanish Mike couldn't understand.

Señor Sanchez translated.

"Miguel says he saw you drain the blood from Carmelita's body," Sanchez explained, "and when her heart and her breathing stopped, she was dead."

"Where did he see all this?" Mike demanded.

"I am a student of medicine at the University of Madrid." Miguel Quintera was speaking English again. "One of the internes at the hospital directed me to the gallery of the operating room."

"Mr. Sanchez," said Mike, "I explained to you yesterday how we would drain the blood from your daughter's circulation and wash out her heart and blood vessels with saline before putting in fresh blood. I thought you understood."

"It seems we have all done you an injustice, Dr. Raburn," said Father Junípero. "I hope you will be charitable and forgive us."

"It was on the radio," said Señor Sanchez. "Are you sure Carmelita will get well now, Dr. Raburn?"

"Her chances are at least a hundred times better than they were two hours ago."

"When can I see her?" young Quintera asked.

"I'm going to keep her in the recovery room on the operating-room floor for several hours, so Dr. LeMoyne can watch her," said Mike. "But she should be back in her room on the Intensive Care Section by midafternoon."

"Thank you, Dr. Raburn, for saving my daughter's life," said Mr. Sanchez. "I'm sorry we caused you so much trouble. It was all a mistake, thank God."

"*You* suffered because of it, not me," said Mike. "Why don't you all have some coffee or something in the Coffee Shop? Just keep the receptionist informed as to where you'll be."

V

Peggy Tyndall and Ed Vogel were busy when Rebecca Dalton came into the Cardiac Research Laboratory shortly before noon. Spread out on a long laboratory table was an assortment of odd-looking pieces of apparatus, much of it plastic in various shapes.

"Looks like you've been cleaning out the storage closet," said Rebecca. "Why all the sudden activity?"

"Dr. Dalton called me right after the Sanchez operation," Ed explained. "He wants us to start working right away on that plastic heart."

"The one he thought of implanting in a calf?" Rebecca felt a sudden surge of excitement and hope.

"He's stopped thinking about it and is going ahead. Wants the first one ready next week so he can put it in before he leaves for Paris." Vogel looked at her questioningly. "When did he decide that?"

"There's a transplant patient in France who's still living five years after the operation." Rebecca was careful to keep the exultation she felt out of her voice, not wanting the others to know Ken's sudden decision was as much of a surprise to her as it had been to them.

Or was it? she asked herself. She'd never admit—to him—that Ken was right, of course, about the way she had been gently nudging him toward a renewal of his very promising experimental work. And his decision to resume it could actually be a result of Kevin's bald reminder that Ken was now responsible for his life, a final stimulus that had carried him over the barrier represented by the failure of the other transplants. But whatever the cause, he seemed on the point of going back to work again, the first and most important step toward the resumption of their marriage.

"Dr. Rebecca Dalton, 275." The voice of the paging operator poured from a loudspeaker. "Dr. Rebecca Dalton, 275."

"That's his number," said Peggy. "I forgot to tell you he said he would call you as soon as he could."

Rebecca dialed the extension and Ken himself answered.

"I'm in the Research Lab," she said.

"That's what I wanted to talk to you about, Reb. Would you have time to look over that last experimental work we did and give me an opinion on its present status?"

"Certainly. I remember most of it, Peggy and Ed can fill me in on the rest."

"I've got to work in the PDC this afternoon and Jeffry has called a meeting of the Executive Committee for five o'clock. I could meet you in the cafeteria at six, though, unless you have other plans."

"I don't have any other plans," said Rebecca. "I hear you're going to be traveling."

"I want to talk to you about that, too. Six o'clock?"

"Right. 'By."

As she was hanging up the telephone, Rebecca saw Peggy looking at her with a speculative light in her eyes. But when she turned back to the table where the tiny physician's assistant and Ed Vogel were working, their attention was once more directed to the apparatus scattered before them.

"Get me the data on that last experiment we did with the plastic pump, Peggy," said Rebecca. "Dr. Dalton wants me to look over it and give him an opinion tonight at dinner."

"Right," said Peggy happily. "I can tell you one person who'll be glad to hear about this, too—Kevin McCartney."

"He may be responsible for its getting started again."

"I know," said Peggy. "I practically had to break Kevin's arm to make him tell Dr. Ken that it was up to him now to keep him living, but he must have come through."

"Kevin told me about it this morning but not that you had put him up to it."

"Never underestimate the power of women when they put their heads together." Ed Vogel chuckled. "Especially women in white—God bless their conniving little souls."

VI

By one o'clock that afternoon all parameters being recorded on Carmelita Sanchez were approaching the normal range and Val LeMoyne allowed her to be wheeled from the recovery room on the surgical floor to her own cubicle on the ICU. Val was still busy with the heavy OR schedule so Mike came up from Emergency, where he had been busy since completing the TBW, to watch the transition.

"It's hard to believe she's the same person," said Maria Alvarez, as they were attaching the sensors to the girl's body. "If there ever was a medical miracle, this is one."

"The bilirubin level in her blood has dropped from 31 to 3 since early this morning," said Mike.

"You can almost see the jaundice decreasing," the nurse agreed. "Did Miguel Quintera really attack you, Dr. Raburn?"

"He tried, but I suppose it was a natural mistake for anyone as worked up as he was. I don't mind admitting I was pretty tight inside myself during those nine minutes."

"I was talking to Helga at lunch. She said it was the most exciting thing she ever saw."

"If Helga was excited, it must have been something." Mike straightened up from attaching a sensor and pulled the sheet up across Carmelita's breast. "I don't think we can expect her to become conscious in much less than twelve hours, but please make a note that I'm to be called if Carmelita shows the slightest sign. I'm going through PICU to see about Joey Gates and after that I'll be in the Emergency Department all afternoon."

Rachel Gates was sitting in Joey's cubicle. The boy was sleeping quietly but she looked haggard and rather worn.

"You look like you could use a shot of Java," said Mike. "Shall I get it, or will you be my guest?"

When she looked hesitantly at the boy, he added, "Joey's doing fine, I just checked his record."

"Okay," said Rachel. "If you don't mind having coffee with a member of an oppressed minority."

"You're the wife of one of the finest athletes this country has ever produced," he said. "I'm the one who's honored."

"You wouldn't think so if you read the morning paper."

"I missed it this morning." Mike waited for her to slide into an empty booth in the Coffee Shop, then took the opposite seat himself. "Had other things on my mind."

"So I heard. They're after Joe again, Mike—in full cry."

"He asked for it, you know—by taking up the cause of less famous athletes."

"But I'm sure Joe never thought the owners and the media would be this vicious."

"Nothing is more vicious than a man with money who thinks somebody else is trying to take it away from him. But if somebody doesn't stand up for the rights of the little man, the way Joe is standing up for the other players, the guys with the monopolies will have everything their way."

"That's what Joe says. I guess he could have stood that all right, too, if Joey hadn't gotten sick."

"Joey's out of the woods as far as this attack is concerned, Rachel. And from all the evidence we have now about sickle cell anemia, Joey may never have another crisis, if you keep up the medication Dr. Henderson will prescribe."

"It's not just that, Mike. Joe's scared stiff that he has the sickling trait, too."

"I can settle that question quickly enough. Have him come by and I'll take some blood."

"He isn't going to do it, at least not now."

"Why not?"

"You know how it is when people develop a fear of something, Mike; they don't think rationally any more. Joe knows that if he does have the sickling trait no basketball team in the country would hire him, for fear he'd have one of those cramps in the legs like I—"

She stopped but not before Mike was alerted by something in her voice.

"How bad are the ones you're having, Rachel?"

"What's the use of trying to fool you?" She shrugged. "I've had them for a long time, but I didn't have any idea what it was, until you did the test the other night and found sickling. I'm not worried about myself, though; it's that guy I'm married to that's driving me crazy."

"You still can't afford to take a chance, Rachel. I'll get Gus Henderson to figure out the dosage of potassium cyanate you need for your weight and you can start on it tonight. Did you tell Joe your test was positive?"

She nodded. "I thought it might help him but it only made things worse. I tell you, Mike, Joe's scared absolutely stiff over this thing. He knows ninety-nine per cent of the people with sickle cell anemia are black, so he won't have the test because he's sure it will be positive and that will be the end of his career."

"Don't sweat this so much." Mike put his hand over hers and gently uncurled her fingers, which were clenched. "The important thing is that Joey's safe and you'll be too, as soon as we get the medication started. How much do you weigh?"

"A hundred and thirty-four."

"I'll get the prescription filled for you and bring it up to Joey's cubicle. We'll get the blood for Big Joe's test somehow, too, if I have to slug him and take it while he's unconscious."

"That will be the day, even for somebody as big as you." But she could laugh, which was what he wanted.

VII

Gus Henderson came to the main ICU nursing station as soon as Helga Sundberg finished taking the afternoon shift report from Maria Alvarez; it was five minutes past three.

"Seen Carolyn today?" he asked.

"Just for a few minutes when I went to the apartment about eight-thirty to dress before I came to watch Mike do the TBW." Helga's tone was casual. "She said she had some errands to run. Why?"

"I figured she would probably come by to see her father and left word with Mrs. Alvarez to call me," said the pediatrician.

"Carolyn's probably shopping. With only one day off a week, plus the time she spends with her father, a lot can accumulate that needs to be done."

"I'm worried about her, Helga. She didn't seem to be herself when I left her this morning."

"The God Committee meeting yesterday afternoon was bound to upset her. Give her time, Gus."

"Do you think she'll come to the hospital for dinner?"

"Would you eat in a hospital cafeteria if you had a chance to eat out somewhere?"

"I guess not, but I can't help being worried about Carolyn. If she does come over to see her father, be sure to call me."

"Of course," said Helga soothingly. "And don't worry."

When Gus Henderson left the section, Helga started on her rounds. Her first stop was the cubicle where Carmelita Sanchez lay sleeping. Miguel Quintera was sitting beside the bed, but rose when the tall nurse came into the small room.

"This morning I made a fool of myself, Miss Sundberg," he said. "Dr. Raburn should have slugged me."

"He's a very gentle man, Miguel, and a very fine surgeon."

"I know that. But when I saw Carmelita lying there, with no life, I guess I went—"

"Berserk?"

He nodded. "I felt so helpless that I was like a child who flails out at those who would help."

"You must love her very much," Helga said gently.

The anxiety and embarrassment were suddenly erased from the young Cuban's face by a warm smile. "You cannot know—"

"I think I do." Helga's voice was soft for an instant, then once again became conversational. "Have you two been engaged very long?"

"Since we were children. I wanted us to be married before I left for medical school in Spain. But Carmelita said I would need to think only of my studies so I would make high grades and do well on the examinations I will have to take before coming back to the United States as a doctor."

"I've seen a lot of fine doctors who were trained in foreign medical schools. And I understand that the University of Madrid is one of the best."

"It is rated so. But I'm not going to leave Carmelita behind when I go back this time."

"It may be months before she'll be well enough to travel."

"Then I will stay out of medical school a year and work here, perhaps as an attendant."

"Even then, she may not be entirely well for a long time."

"I will look after her. I almost lost her this time and I will never let us be separated again."

"You are both very young, and very much in love." Helga's voice was warm. "Don't let anything—or anyone—ever take that from you."

CHAPTER TWENTY

I

Shortly after four o'clock the telephone rang in Val LeMoyne's office in the surgical suite. It was Karen Fletcher.

"Do you have a few minutes, Val?" the pathologist asked.

"Sure. What's on your mind?"

"I'll tell you when I get there. Five minutes?"

"Whenever you say. I'm through for the day—with luck."

Karen arrived in four minutes, and shut the door of the office behind her when she came in.

"I hear you and Mike Raburn covered yourselves with glory this morning," she said.

"It was a team effort, Mike said so himself."

"I guess I've missed something by going into pathology. Nobody in a morgue ever talks back."

"Have you ever regretted the choice?"

Karen shook her head. "There aren't many women pathologists in the country."

"And even fewer who are board-certified in forensic pathology," Val observed, and Karen gave her a startled look.

"How did you know that?"

"I'm on the Faculty Personnel Committee as well as the Subcommittee on Faculty Promotions—or didn't you know?"

"As a matter of fact, I did." Karen decided to come directly to the point. "Which is why I came to see you."

"If you knew I was on the subcommittee, you must have known that Jerry Singleton is the chairman."

"I did."

"Then was it a good idea to tear into Jerry the way you did at the surgical Tissue Conference yesterday?"

"It must have been." Karen smiled. "He came to see me last night."

Val studied her for a moment, then nodded slowly and somewhat admiringly.

"In other words, you took a calculated risk and it paid off."

"It will, I think. Do you blame me?"

"No. I guess when you come down to it we're somewhat alike, Karen. We both know our business and what we're worth—"

"And we intend to get everything we're entitled to out of it," Karen completed the sentence. "Except, I think, that you have principles and I don't."

"I suspect you have more than you've admitted—at least where medicine is concerned."

"I don't mix my personal life with my professional life any more than you do," Karen said with a shrug. "Except, of course, where the two seem to coincide, as they do now. You've already gotten where you want to be,

Val—a full professorship and head of your own department."

"I saw Adrian Cooper in Rebecca Dalton's PDC clinic the other day," said Val. "He'll never be able to come back to work and Jerry has already spoken to Ken Dalton and myself about putting him up for early retirement. Which means you'll head the Department of Pathology eventually, with the rank of full professor."

"If eventually, why not now? After Adrian is retired, of course." Karen leaned forward intently. "With you a full professor and department head and Rebecca in a similar status, I'm the only woman associate professor who's eligible for promotion. And I intend to get it."

"You'll have my support," Val assured her. "We'd have a hard job finding anyone else in your field as capable as you are—male or female."

"Thanks, Val. I was sure I could depend on you."

"But after yesterday afternoon, can you depend on Jerry?"

"When the Tissue Conference ended, he wouldn't have approved anything less than my being fired," Karen admitted. "But I think I convinced him differently later. He's quite a man, Val—everything you've heard he is, and more."

Val had been studying the other woman thoughtfully while she was talking. "Are you saying Jerry's enough for both of us?"

Karen laughed. "I'm glad we understand each other. But there's no need to tell Jerry that, is there?"

"None at all," Val agreed. "You might say this is just between us girls."

Karen got to her feet. "Thanks for saving me the trouble of beating around the bush. I always prefer the direct route. You're off this weekend, aren't you?"

"Yes. Jerry has invited me to go to the Keys with him—for scuba diving."

"Go by all means, Val. I'm sure you'll enjoy yourself. 'By."

"What about the post of medical director that will be vacant when Adrian Cooper is retired?" Valerie asked as Karen was reaching for the doorknob. "Are you going for that too?"

"Of course. As you said, only a few women in the country are certified in forensic pathology—a *very, very* few."

"And I suppose you already have plans for getting that post too?"

"Tentative plans, yes. I'll have to play that one by ear, though, so it may take more time."

When the door closed behind Karen Fletcher, Val lit a cigarette and sat smoking it thoughtfully for a while. Then, picking up the telephone on her desk, she dialed an inside number.

"Jerry," she said when a familiar male voice answered, "I've decided to take you up on that weekend offer. Shall I bring my own scuba gear?"

"Just bring yourself, Val." She heard his delighted, and triumphant, laugh over the wires. "I'll supply everything else."

As she hung up the telephone, Val LeMoyne didn't need to put a finger to the artery at her temple where anesthetists were trained to take the pulse, to know hers was beating much more rapidly than usual. Karen Fletcher was obviously experienced when it came to judging the capability of a lover. So it just might be that in Jerry Singleton's arms she would find relief from the steady build-up lately in a craving she'd learned to fear, even while another part of her welcomed the excitement it always brought.

The very thought was so stirring that her hands were trembling as she unlocked the top drawer of her desk and shook a yellow Valium tablet from the bottle there, before going to the adjoining lavatory for a cup of water with which to wash it down.

II

Six o'clock was a slack period on all the wards. The dinner trays had come and gone, and the regular chores of evening care for the patients wouldn't start for another thirty minutes. As many of the ICU nurses and attendants as could be spared had been released for dinner: in the cafeteria, the Coffee Shop, or from the bank of vending machines just off the main lobby, where everything from hot coffee to submarine sandwiches were available to possessors of a sufficient store of dimes and quarters. One machine would even take dollar bills but was usually out of order.

Helga Sundberg glanced up momentarily when she saw Carolyn Payson enter the ward, then looked down again at the chart she was updating. Nor did she lift her eyes when Carolyn passed the nursing station though she could have almost touched her.

Only one nurse was working in the general section and she was watching Carmelita Sanchez, so no one besides Helga noticed Carolyn enter the cubicle where her father lay, with the glucose solution from a bottle hanging upside down from a tall stand beside the bed dripping slowly through the glass chamber of the intravenous setup, as the fluid nutrient flowed into his veins.

The relatively heavy sedation Dr. Gross had ordered before Richard Payson was taken to the Board Room for the meeting of the God Committee yesterday had been continued by orders of the pudgy neurologist and the patient was fairly quiet. He opened his eyes when Carolyn reached down to smooth back the hair from his forehead and a travesty of a smile—although perhaps no one else could have interpreted it as such—showed briefly on his face, tearing at her heart.

The large syringe used to inject liquid food every four hours through the nasal tube leading to Richard Payson's stomach lay on the table beside the bed. The metal adapter by which its glass tip was decreased in diameter, so it could slip easily into the end of the nasal tube, was still on the syringe, as it had been when Helga injected his liquid dinner into the nasal tube shortly before six. A fairly large needle lay beside it but, looking at the syringe, Carolyn thought with a surge of sudden panic how small it appeared to be, considering the purpose she had been steeling herself over the past twenty-four hours to accomplish with it.

Nobody knew for sure just how much air would have to be injected into a vein to bring about the merciful instant death by air embolism that was the last duty she could perform for her father. But more would be required, she was certain now, than the few bubbles most people considered sufficient to act as the lethal agent of air embolism, a sudden blockage of blood to the lungs as air flowed through the veins to the right side of the heart and thence into the pulmonary circulation. Or, if it got through the lungs and into the left heart, blocking the circulation to the vital centers in the brain.

The intravenous drip afforded an easy route by which the air could reach her father's veins; she had only to inject it through the plastic wall of the tubing between the glucose bottle hanging from its stand and the catheter in an arm vein, using the syringe and the needle beside it. But, whether the amount she could inject in the time available would be sufficient to cause death, or merely turn Richard Payson into more of an inert vegetable than he already was, she had no way of knowing. Nor was there time to waste for, although she had not missed Helga's studiedly ignoring her presence, another nurse might appear at any moment and see her there.

Then Carolyn's eyes fell upon the oxygen tube hanging in a coil from a hook on the panel attached to the wall at the head of the bed and she suddenly remembered Helga describing in detail just how she had connected an oxygen tube to a needle-catheter setup and used the central supply piped throughout the hospital to save the child in the Emergency Room only a little more than forty-eight hours ago. And remembering Helga's graphic description of the technique, she also knew the answer to her own immediate problem.

Picking up the needle from the bedside table, she quickly worked the end of the oxygen tubing over the flanged coupling for receiving the top of a syringe. The tubing fitted snugly over the large end of the needle and, when she reached up and opened the valve that shut off the main system until oxygen was needed, the gas hissed through the smaller shaft of the needle.

Glancing outside, she saw only Helga's blonde head still bent over the desk at the nursing station. And, picking up the intravenous tubing below the drip chamber that measured its flow, she thrust the point of the needle through it, then shut off the tubing above the needle puncture with the thumb and forefinger of her left hand, to keep the oxygen stream from flowing back up into the glucose bottle, and sent the gas pouring through the small tubing.

It made a faint bubbling sound as it cleared out the glucose solution ahead of it in the lower part of the IV setup, then surged under pressure directly into Richard Payson's arm vein. Watching for some sign of a leak or blowout of the needle connection from the pressure of the gas, Carolyn saw the vein into which a small nylon catheter had been inserted, when the intravenous was started last night, suddenly swell. At the same moment the transparent plastic catheter lost its normal bluish tint, as the blood that had filled it seconds before was pushed ahead of the column of oxygen flowing rapidly into Richard Payson's bloodstream.

A sudden gasping sound made Carolyn look quickly at her father's face. She half expected it to be convulsed with agony, for the stream of gas had certainly reached his lungs through the pulmonary artery by now, driven there by contraction of the right ventricle of the heart. But instead, his eyes were open and a smile of utter peace had settled upon his features. It remained, too, even when he no longer breathed and she could feel no pulse in his wrist.

Only when she was sure his heart and respiration had stopped did Carolyn shut off the oxygen valve and remove the needle from the plastic tubing wall, noting with satisfaction that, even though the needle was larger than was ordinarily used to inject medications through the wall of intravenous tubing, there was no leakage.

In her haste to remove all signs of how death had come to Richard Payson, Carolyn accidentally dropped the needle to the floor as she disconnected it. She wasted no time looking for the needle, however; at the moment it was more important to replace the oxygen source so no one would realize it had been used.

Looping the oxygen supply tubing expertly into its previous position, she hung it on the hook in the panel at the head of the bed. Only a few additional seconds were required to milk the gas still inside the IV setup back into the glucose flask, removing the last external evidence of how his death had been accomplished. Except that Richard Payson's body no longer writhed in the tortured movements of H-D and his features were more peaceful than Carolyn remembered seeing them in years, nothing about either him or the room appeared to have changed.

Only the probing scalpel of the pathologist at autopsy would reveal the fact that the blood vessels of his lungs were filled with oxygen, as were many of the vessels of the brain. And unless the post-mortem was done reasonably soon, even that evidence might dissolve during the interim into his body tissues where it could never be discovered.

Although intent only upon an act of mercy, Carolyn Payson had also discovered the perfect agent for murder.

III

Helga's head was still bent over the desk when Carolyn passed it on her way out of the ward. Only when she heard the door to the ICU waiting room outside sigh shut did Helga look up. Going to a window that looked out upon the circular drive in front of the hospital, she watched until she saw Carolyn come out and step into one of the taxis that were almost always waiting at the stand halfway around the circular drive from the marquee. Nor did she need to hear Carolyn's voice tell the driver, "International Airport," to know the other girl's destination, more than two thousand miles to the south. Returning to the nursing station by way of Richard Payson's cubicle, Helga glanced inside just long enough to note that his chest no longer moved in respiration and that the intravenous had stopped running.

"I noticed that Mr. Payson's intravenous has stopped, Miss Garth," Helga told the student nurse who was the first to return from dinner some ten minutes later. "He seems to be quiet, though, so why don't you give him evening care last tonight? I'll restart the IV then."

"Yes, Miss Sundberg," the young nurse said. "I guess it's not going to make much difference to him whether he's first or last."

"No difference at all now—or ever," Helga could have assured her, but lowered her eyes to the chart on which she had been working instead. Nor was she surprised to find that she had been writing gibberish.

Helga waited until another of the regular ICU nurses came back from dinner, then picked up her handbag from the shelf beside her desk, where she had placed it when she came back from an early dinner in the cafeteria.

"Watch the station for me, please, Helen," she said. "I've got to make a private outside call. Mr. Payson's IV has stopped but he's quiet, so I wouldn't bother him until Miss Garth finishes his evening care. I'll restart the IV later."

"Sure, Helga," said the other nurse. "See if your friend's got a friend."

In one of the telephone booths off the main lobby of the hospital, Helga dropped in a dime and dialed a number she had looked up in one of the directories outside.

"International Airport Information," said a pleasant voice with just a hint of an accent. "Can I help you?"

"Could you tell me when the next flight to Brazil leaves? And by what airline?"

"What day, please?"

"Today."

"That would be Varig Flight 803, leaving for Rio at 8:00 P.M. Anything else?"

"No, thank you."

Outside, Helga glanced up at the clock above the receptionist's desk. It said six-thirty and an hour and a half was a long time to keep hidden the fact that a patient on ICU was already dead. But she had to string it out long enough to keep the State's Attorney from learning of it much before 8:00 P.M. and starting to wonder just what had been the cause.

IV

Mike Raburn had been tied up in the Emergency Room with a fracture case from the daily six o'clock traffic jam on the Miami Expressway system so it was six-thirty before he received a note to call Marcia Weston at her home.

"Oh, Lord!" he said when he was handed the call slip. "She's going to ask what I thought of the way she handled the TBW on the news tonight and I'll have to admit that I didn't even see it."

"Neither did anybody else," said the three-to-eleven Emergency Room supervisor. "We had a portable TV on in the office but they barely mentioned the most exciting thing that's happened around here in a month of Sundays."

Marcia Weston herself answered the telephone. "I called to apologize," she said, "but you know the worst by now."

"I got tied up with a case and didn't even see the news."

"I'm glad you didn't have a chance to be disappointed then. We had trouble editing the tape, there was so much material that the station manager decided to use just a flash of it on the evening news."

"Then it came out all right?"

"It's beautiful, just beautiful. We're going to show a bit more at eleven— the part the 'Today' show will use in the morning—and the rest will be edited into a half-hour special. I don't know when we'll show that but I'll give you a ring well beforehand. Thanks again for all that suspense."

Mike laughed. "One thing you can be sure of, it wasn't contrived. I was sweating all the way."

"So what happened?" the ER head nurse asked when he hung up the phone.

"You'll never believe this," Mike told her, "but I'm so big they couldn't squeeze me into the small screens everybody watches the six o'clock news on while they eat dinner. They're going to make it a half-hour special—for big screens only."

"I should have known I'd never get a straight answer out of you," said the veteran nurse. "But at least they won't be drafting you for 'Emergency Hospital.' And that's something to be thankful for."

"They're going to remake 'Medic' instead. I'm playing Richard Boone."

V

Rebecca Dalton was ten minutes late getting to the cafeteria. Ken was waiting outside the entrance when she arrived, breathless, flushed and, he thought, lovelier every day.

"You should have gone on and gotten your dinner before the best dishes are gone," she said as they took their places in the single line that was serving late-comers. "Peggy Tyndall stopped me to ask whether I knew when the echocardioscope would be back from the factory. We're going to check Dale with it as soon as it comes; Peggy is pretty sure the boy is getting more cyanotic lately."

"That could mean an early operation."

She looked at him quickly, wondering instinctively whether his failure to identify himself with the operation had any meaning.

"If the echoscope isn't ready by the last of next week, I suppose we'll have to bring Dale in and study him with conventional catheterization of the heart," she said. "But I was hoping we could spare him the discomfort."

"And the danger. Even in the hands of an expert like Ed Vogel, there's always a chance of cessation. I hope the machine gets back in time."

"What was the big deal with the Executive Committee?" she asked.

"Jeffry Toler is working out the problems connected with putting a separate millage for the medical center on the ballot in a referendum at the next election. But not everybody is satisfied that it's a wise thing to do."

"Couldn't the Hospital Board budget more effectively if a probable veto by the Commission Finance Committee wasn't hanging over it?"

"Yes. But if we go to the people with a referendum and lose, the Finance Committee and Ross McKenzie will have been handed a big stick. And the first order of business will be to clobber the Hospital Board."

"Is there much doubt about how the vote would go in a referendum?"

"Andrew Graves thinks so. It's going to be interesting to see whether Ross McKenzie keeps after us, now that he's had a chance to see why it costs so much to run a hospital."

"He already knows how close a call he had, I laid that on the line," said Rebecca. "Also the fact that, if you had gone on and operated when I wanted to, he'd be on the surgical ICU right now and a lot sicker than he is."

"It's not that simple, Reb. When you first asked me to see McKenzie, I was just as certain he was going to need surgery as you were—and scared to death into the bargain that I would have to be the surgeon and lose him. My happening to remember their telling me at Peter Bent that, by using the fiberoptic catheter, you could anticipate a major change in cardiac function as much as twenty-four hours before it happened was really an act of desperation."

"There you go, low-rating yourself again."

"It's true, Reb. When I had Ed put in the fiberoptic catheter without telling you, I was afraid I'd have to fight you—and not at all sure I'd be right."

"And I almost made a fool of myself by getting my back up because you went ahead and put it in without consulting me."

"I guess that's part of where we get into trouble," he admitted. "We were unconsciously competing with each other—"

"Not entirely unconsciously," Rebecca corrected him. "At least not on my part."

"Or mine, which means we've each got to give a little. But you're already ahead of me there."

"I don't see—"

"When you admitted to Ross McKenzie that you misjudged his case."

"That was the truth."

"Truth is sometimes the hardest thing to face—as I've discovered twice today."

"I don't understand."

"The first time was when Kevin told me early this morning that I was responsible for his life from now on and he expected me to keep him going a long time. He wasn't kidding, either."

"I know. Peggy confessed that she put him up to it."

"I'll have to thank her," he said. "But the real crisis for me came when I stood across that Cuban girl from Mike Raburn and watched him drain all the blood from her body and then let Ringer's solution wash through her circulation, when every half minute was a lifetime. I'm telling you, Reb, that took guts—"

"The same kind of guts you showed when you did those fifteen transplants without losing one."

"And then lost, when my courage failed and I turned yellow because you held your head up, while they were dying one by one, and I couldn't face the fact that you were a better doctor than I was."

"But I'm not. You proved that."

"Let's say I was lucky. Both with Kevin and in realizing that, if I didn't start scratching again, Mike Raburn was going to show me up for a failure by being a better surgeon than I am—if he isn't already."

"As much as I like Mike, I doubt that," said Rebecca. They had finished the meal and Ken went back to the coffee urn and filled their cups again.

"Nothing's really settled completely until I prove that the emotional turmoil of the past six months hasn't dulled my surgical skill," he admitted. "Writers run dry, you know, and I've already proved that something like it can happen to surgeons."

"But you're cured."

"Perhaps—but I still can't risk a patient's life to prove it. That's why I asked you to look over that plastic heart experiment I was working on before I developed the acute attack of what you might call 'surgeon's slump.' Did you have time this afternoon?"

"That's another reason why I was late for dinner," she confessed. "I spent an hour in the Research Lab going over the whole thing with Peggy and Ed and didn't get to the PDC until almost three o'clock."

"What do you think?"

"I'm not sure the model you stopped work on over six months ago is going to be the one that makes history. But by putting what you already have in a calf—" She stopped suddenly. "That's the way you're going to prove you've regained your skill, isn't it?"

He nodded. "If I can successfully replace a calf's heart with an artificial one, I'll know I'm cured."

"Dr. Rebecca Dalton—Operator, please. Dr. Dalton—Operator, please. Dr. Rebecca Dalton," the loudspeaker at the corner of the large room intoned, interrupting Ken's final word.

Rebecca pushed back her chair and moved quickly to a telephone in a corner booth. When she came back not much more than a minute later, however, her expression was grave.

"That was Peggy," she said. "Dale has disappeared and the security guards have started a search of the grounds."

VI

June afternoons in South Florida are extra long, thanks to Daylight Saving Time, and little boys playing in the hot Florida sun become very thirsty. Dale Tyndall often went to meet Peggy when she came home from her work in the Cardiac Research Laboratory. He was almost to the hospital entrance when he remembered that Kevin McCartney should be on duty at this time of day and would have a cold root beer in the refrigerator for him. Detouring to the lounge, he climbed up on a stool but was so winded that he had to lean his head on his arms against the polished surface of the bar for several minutes to get his breath. Finally the bartender—a man he didn't recognize—came to the end where he was sitting.

"What do you want, little boy?" he asked, not unkindly.

"Beer?" Dale managed to gasp.

"What?" Then the bartender laughed. "You must be the one Kevin told me about—that drinks the root beer."

"That's me. Where's Kevin?"

The bartender opened a bottle of root beer from the refrigerator and poured it into a frosted mug, sliding the mug along the bar to where Dale was sitting.

"Kevin's sick. They had to put him in the hospital yesterday."

"Kevin's got heart trouble, like me." Dale put down the mug and wiped his mouth on his arm. "I was a blue baby."

"Well, what do ya know?" The bartender put his elbows on the bar. "You're still blue, ain't you?"

"A little," said Dale. "But when I'm old enough, Dr. Dalton is going to operate on me and then I won't be so blue any more. And I can run and play like the other children."

"That's nice. When will this be?"

"Mommy says when I'm eight or ten. I start to school next year."

"You're a smart little fellow," said the bartender as Dale finished his beer. "Come in any time."

"Maybe tomorrow?" said Dale hopefully.

"Sure."

"Good-by, Mr. Bartender. You're almost as nice as Kevin is."

"Thanks, kid. That's saying a lot."

The bartender stood watching the little boy as he left the lounge, then shook his head as he lifted the empty mug and wiped the polished surface.

"That's a smart kid, but he sure is blue," he told a customer who came up to pay his tab just then. "Says he has heart trouble, and I can certainly believe it."

Outside in the sunlight, Dale walked a dozen steps, then suddenly squatted. He had no way of knowing, of course, that filling his small stomach with an ice-cold drink, when his heart was already laboring to keep up with the demands for oxygen from the body tissues, had placed a heavier burden on it than the structurally disarranged organ was capable of bearing very long.

Getting up again, he took a short cut behind a huge bougainvillea that fanned out between several ficus trees. They made a natural screen, hiding him from immediate view, and thus no one saw him when he tumbled into a flower bed.

There, a hospital security guard taking part in the search found him almost an hour later—unconscious.

VII

Rebecca Dalton started to turn right as they left the elevator that had taken them to the first floor but Ken caught her by the arm.

"Where are you going?" he asked.

"To help search for Dale Tyndall. What else?"

"The hospital security force can take care of that," he said. "You and I need to be in the Emergency Room when they bring him in—"

"You're right, of course," she said. "He must be unconscious somewhere from not getting enough oxygen through to his blood—"

"It's more like not getting enough blood to his oxygen," said Ken. "With the pulmonary artery almost closed, as it is in most tetralogy of Fallot cases, the boy could die of asphyxiation in a crisis, simply because not enough oxygen from the air he breathes is absorbed by the hemoglobin in his blood and gets to the brain. On second thought, I'll go to the Emergency Room and backstop Mike. You'd better get Val LeMoyne. If Dale is in a cardiorespiratory crisis, Val can intubate him and start pressurized oxygen."

Rebecca nodded and turned toward the elevator. But neither of them voiced the thought that was foremost in both their minds—that Ken might very well have to start operating again and considerably sooner than either of them had expected.

VIII

"Miss Sundberg!" Miss Garth, the student nurse who had been giving evening care to the patients not ill enough to require constant specialing, was standing just inside Richard Payson's cubicle. "Come here, please!"

Helga glanced at the clock on the control panel. It said seven and, if the Lord was in His heaven and all was right with the world, Varig Flight 803 would soon be moving up to the loading tunnel preparing to take on passengers for Rio.

"No wonder Mr. Payson's intravenous stopped and he was so quiet," the student nurse added, a little shakily. "He's dead."

"Help me get the pacemaker that's outside Mr. McCartney's door into Mr. Payson's room." Helga spoke quickly. "Then call the operator and ask her to sound CODE FIVE on the PA system. And on the way back you can bring a Mark VII respirator."

"Right," said Miss Garth as she followed Helga to where the pacemaker, on its mobile cart, had been standing beside Kevin McCartney's door since he'd had the cessation the day before.

"Hey! What's up?" Kevin asked when he saw the cart moving.

"Mr. Payson. And don't try to help," Helga called over her shoulder. "A CPR team will come through here like the thundering herd in a minute or two and I don't want you to be run over."

In Richard Payson's cubicle, Helga moved quickly, attaching the terminals from the pacemaker to the skin of the dead man's chest with rubber suction cups. Plugging the power cord into a baseboard socket, she set the controls and switched on the machine. Immediately, as rhythmic jolts of the shocking current surged through circuits thus formed between Payson's body and the machine, his chest muscles jerked. The pulse at his temple took up a visible regular beat, too, indicating that the heart was being stimulated to contract, sending blood surging through his arteries and veins. While Helga was working she could hear the call from the loudspeaker outside, muted somewhat here where the usual strident summons might disturb already apprehensive patients:

"CODE FIVE—CICU. CODE FIVE—CICU."

Working quickly and protected against electric shock from the pacemaker by the rubber-soled shoes she wore, Helga disconnected the nylon catheter in Richard Payson's arm vein from the IV set, noting that blood still flowed from the open end of the catheter. Lifting the glucose bottle from the stand attached to the bed, she dropped tubing, drip chamber, and partially filled bottle into a wastebasket. Meanwhile, the student nurse—only seniors worked in the ICU—had slipped a curved plastic airway into Richard Payson's mouth to hold his tongue back and connected him to the respirator kept on the floor for just such an emergency.

Since the catheter was still patent, Helga quickly injected an ampule of Isoproterenol through it, completing the routine of CPR.

Mike Raburn was the first doctor to appear. He took in the scene with one glance, as well as the fact that, between the pacemaker, the Isoproterenol Helga had just finished injecting into the venous catheter, and the click of the respirator valve as Richard Payson's lungs were being rhythmically inflated with oxygen and then allowed to deflate, the situation was well under control.

"Any sign of spontaneous resumption?" Mike asked, his voice somewhat muffled as he reached down, apparently tying a shoe.

"No," said Helga.

"Why the pacemaker and not routine CPR?"

"Miss Garth thinks he may have been dead awhile and this looked like a standstill arrest, so I thought electric stimulation seemed to offer more hope."

"You're probably a better cardiologist than I am," he said. "Where's Carolyn?"

"I haven't talked to her since early this morning." The statement was literally true.

The rest of the CPR team had arrived by now but there was nothing to be done at the moment except watch the pacemaker stimulate the heart and the respirator inflate the lungs.

"Cut the current, please," Mike said after some five minutes with no visible result. Reaching for Richard Payson's wrist, he held it for ten seconds while listening over the chest with a stethoscope, then dropped it.

"You can start the respirator again," he said as he put the stethoscope back into his pocket. "But I think it's too late even for heroic measures."

"Shouldn't I continue pacemaker stimulation for a while longer, just in case?" Helga asked.

"It can't do any harm, since you've already chosen this method of resuscitation."

"No need to hang around," he told the rest of the CPR team.

The others left, but Mike stayed at his post near the foot of the bed watching the rhythmic contraction of the patient's chest muscles, the pulse in the temple artery that followed each time, and the inflation cycle of the respirator breathing bag.

"Interesting thing about blood," he said casually. "It's still liquid enough for an hour after death, maybe even longer, to be pumped around the body, if the heart can be made to contract. Different parts of the body die at different times, too, depending on whether they get oxygen through the circulation."

At his words, Helga glanced quickly at the oxygen tubing hanging from the panel on the wall at the head of the bed. When the tubing came from Central Supply, it had been coiled, with a strip of transparent tape holding the coils together so it could be hung out of the way from a hook beside the oxygen valve on the wall but still instantly available, merely by jerking it down and pulling the coils apart to loosen one end of the tape.

"Somebody down in Central Supply didn't check this." Mike reached up and pinched the coil together, so the short strip of transparent tape could easily encompass it again, and Helga suddenly understood the method Carolyn had used to bring instant death to her father. More than that, she knew Mike Raburn had also figured it out—except that he probably attributed the final act of mercy to Helga herself.

"I don't think we can accomplish anything more with this," he said after some ten minutes had passed.

Reaching past Helga to the switch, he turned off the current to the pacemaker and pulled the plug to the respirator. Returning, his hand brushed against the side pocket of Helga's white nylon uniform. But that it wasn't simply the kind of exploring pass so many men tried she knew at once when she felt something drop into the pocket.

"I'll certify Mr. Payson while I'm up here," said Mike. "What time did you say death occurred?"

"I looked in about six forty-five and saw that his IV had stopped. But he was quiet like he is—was—when asleep, so I thought I wouldn't disturb him by starting the IV again until after Miss Garth had given him evening care."

"Could he have been dead then?"

"I guess so," Helga confessed. "I just glanced at the drip chamber of the IV the way I do all of them whenever I pass the door of a cubicle, but didn't go inside. Looks like I goofed, doesn't it?"

"Nothing you could have done would have mattered, I suspect, but I'll put the time of death down as seven. And I'm glad to see you goof occasionally. It proves you're not perfect."

"Is that supposed to be a compliment?"

"Very much so. You haven't had time to notify Carolyn, have you?"

"No."

"She'd rather hear it from you, I'm sure. Why don't you call her while I fill in the front of the chart?"

He went into the small doctors' office adjoining the nursing station and Helga sat down before the desk phone. She let the telephone in the apartment ring for at least a minute, then hung up.

"Carolyn's not there," she called through the opening between the control station and the office. "She probably went out to dinner somewhere, she's been off all day."

"You can get her later, she knew this would happen before long." Mike handed Helga the chart with the front sheet filled in. "While I'm here I'll stop by and see Joey Gates and Carmelita."

"Carmelita's been moving her arms and legs spontaneously. I put some water on her tongue just now and she made swallowing movements, too."

"That's good news." He glanced up at the screen that displayed the parameters being monitored continuously on the sleeping girl. "The way her pulse has slowed certainly looks good and the pO_2 is close to normal."

"I'm betting she'll regain consciousness before I go off at eleven."

"Then we'll have to celebrate." His eyes hadn't left hers. "Have you decided where?"

"I'm betting she'll regain consciousness before I go off tonight."

"Fair enough," he said. "When you've waited for something all your life, a few hours more can't be too bad."

"Dr. Raburn—Emergency Room," said the paging operator, and Mike started for the door. "They must have found Dale Tyndall," he called over his shoulder as he left the ICU, a stocky figure that possessed, Helga knew, the solidity of Gibraltar in spite of the almost delicate grace with which his hands moved, when encased in surgeon's gloves.

Then Helga's hand went to her pocket. And when she found there the large intravenous needle Mike had dropped into it, she understood fully just what she had come to mean to him in some fifty-two hours—and he to her. In the desperate need to get the blood moving in a dead man's circulation and thus dissipate in the body tissues the oxygen that had brought about his death, where Carolyn had no doubt dropped it when she pulled off the tubing. But Mike had seen it and, although he had almost certainly decided already that Helga herself had accomplished Richard Payson's death, he had still picked it up so no one else would know, taking that measure to protect her even though he must have thought she had violated one of the basic obligations of their profession, to save life with every means at her disposal.

If there had been any doubt in her mind—and there had not—she knew now that what had happened to both of them in an incredibly short period of time was something they must hold onto for the rest of their lives—at all cost.

CHAPTER TWENTY-ONE

I

The security guard who found Dale Tyndall in the flower bed hadn't waited to call for help. Lifting the small form in his arms, he carried the boy directly to the Emergency Room, where Mrs. Connor placed him on the examining table in the specially equipped cubicle. Noting the dangerously deep cyanosis of Dale's skin, the veteran nurse began to administer oxygen with a face mask, while the student nurse on duty called Mike and Dr. Valerie LeMoyne, who was also on emergency call for cases of apparent respiratory failure.

Word that the child had been found spread quickly. Peggy Tyndall, who had been helping with the search, came into the Emergency Room just as Mike and Val LeMoyne arrived, followed quickly by Ken and Rebecca Dalton, who had been standing by.

"I think we'd better intubate Dale and put him on oxygen under pressure, Dr. LeMoyne," said Mike.

Val had brought emergency equipment with her and wasted no time in discussion. Opening the case, she removed a small laryngoscope and intratracheal tube, while Mike was sliding Dale's head off the end of the examining table in order to facilitate direct visualization of his larynx.

With the child in deep coma from oxygen lack, his pharyngeal reflexes were already gone and Val had no trouble inserting the tube. Connecting the outer end to the hose from an anesthetic machine with a metal adapter, she began to administer oxygen under pressure to the gasping patient. Meanwhile Rebecca Dalton started percussing out the outline of his heart on the small chest. When she looked up, her face was grave.

"It's starting to dilate," she said, speaking directly to Ken, who was standing by, and her words confirmed what everyone there already knew, that the case was now in his hands—or Mike Raburn's.

"Gus Henderson used a new gold-tipped electrode inserted into the umbilical artery on Baby Hornsby the other day to measure oxygen tension continuously, Dr. Dalton," said Mike, speaking to Ken. "It worked beautifully and gives the readings much more quickly than the laboratory can do with routine blood gas determinations."

"Is it still in the Hornsby baby?"

"No. Gus told me he took it out yesterday, but it was sterilized in case he needed to use it again."

"You'd better expose the radial artery then and slip the electrode into it," said Ken. "We're going to need all the help we can get."

Rebecca had lifted the stethoscope, with which she had been listening to Dale's chest, in time to hear the last words. "The picture hasn't changed, except for the enlargement of the heart," she reported. "And that could be because it's trying to pump more blood and step up the tissue oxygenation rate."

She didn't have to explain further to any of those present the significance of the enlarging heart, or the danger of failure if it was not able to stand up under the demands upon it. At five, Dale was small for his age, his growth slowed by the lowered concentration of oxygen in his body tissues due to the congenital heart defect called the tetralogy of Fallot. The most common abnormal heart condition found in children at birth, its greatest danger to life lay in an extra opening between the right and left ventricles, the main pumping chambers of the heart, allowing blood from the right side to pass directly to the left without going through the lungs and thus not receiving its quota of oxygen.

Second in importance was a marked narrowing of the pulmonary artery itself, by which the right heart normally pumped blood directly through the lungs. This obstruction served to increase the pressure in that ventricle and to force more blood through the abnormal opening between it and the left side. With these two defects also went an enlargement of the right ventricle and, in most cases, a displacement of the aorta, the large artery carrying blood from the left heart to most of the body. Normally arching to the left as it leaves the heart, the aorta in tetrad cases often arches to the right.

A not uncommon congenital abnormality, the tetralogy of Fallot is usually recognized quite easily from the loud murmur heard over the heart as blood rushes back and forth between the two ventricles, and the marked decrease in the blood oxygen concentration, the pO_2. Moreover, it is one of the most successfully correctible congenital abnormalities by surgery, in most cases after age six when the heart and vessels are larger than at birth and more amenable to suturing.

Mike Raburn had put on a pair of sterile gloves while Mrs. Connor was opening one of the surgical trays kept at all times in the ER supply closet for any emergency. Through a small incision on the thumb side of Dale's wrist, he now quickly exposed the radial artery there, easily identifiable by its palpable pulsation. Meanwhile, Mrs. Connor had ordered the gold-tipped electrode sent down from the operating suite supply room and, when it came, removed the sterile cover and dropped the slender electronic sensor on the tray where Mike could easily reach it.

"The electrode will be inside the artery in a few minutes," Mike promised as he began to slide it into the small opening he had made in the wall of the rapidly pulsating radial artery. "With it we should be able to determine pretty quickly whether pressure breathing is getting any more O_2 into his blood."

"I don't think it is," said Val LeMoyne quietly. "The degree of cyanosis hasn't lessened."

Ken moved over to the corner of the room where Peggy Tyndall was sitting on a stool, watching the scene of hurried, though purposeful, activity with eyes that were bleak from pain and worry.

"Feel like telling me what happened, Peg?" he asked gently.

"The sitter usually stays until I get home, Dr. Dalton," she said, "but today she had to leave at five-thirty. Dale likes to play with the other children and I let him because I don't want him to feel that he's different. Usually, if his breath gets short, he just squats, like most children with congenital hearts do, but sometimes, unless somebody stops him, he plays until he drops. I wasn't there to stop him at the usual time because I worked late getting out that plastic artificial heart you're interested in—"

She broke off speaking, with a look of horror in her eyes as she realized she had implied that Ken had been responsible for her working late, then added quickly: "I don't mean that you—"

"It's all right, Peggy, I understand." He reached out to touch her shoulder reassuringly, but she seized his hand and held it between her two smaller ones, while her shoulders shook in a sob.

Mike had finished inserting the oxygen electrode and closed the small skin wound with two Teflon sutures. He applied the surface electrode to Dale Tyndall's skin, completing the circuit, and connected both to the accompanying meter and continuous strip recorder on a bedside cart.

"Blood oxygen tension is 40 millimeters of mercury, Dr. Dalton," he reported as the reading was recorded on the moving paper strip.

"He's been getting 100 per cent oxygen for ten minutes," Val LeMoyne added. "So it looks like no more is being absorbed by the hemoglobin in his RBC than before we put him on positive pressure breathing."

"Watch him, please, Val," said Ken. "We'll be in Dr. Raburn's office close by."

When the others, including Peggy, were in the small office adjacent to the nursing station, Ken pressed the keys of the portable keyboard connection and began to retrieve the salient facts of Dale Tyndall's medical history from the data storage bank deep in the heart of the main computer in the basement. Line by line, the story of the boy's birth, clinic record, and two previous admissions flashed upon the ground-glass screen as rapidly as the words could be read, including the notes Rebecca had made after her last examination of him in the Private Diagnostic Clinic. When the screen was blank, Ken switched off the computer connection and put down the small hand retriever.

"I'm afraid we have no choice except to operate right away, Peggy," he said. "I don't have to tell you how serious this is, either. Or that I feel personally responsible for its happening."

"Please, Dr. Dalton. I didn't mean—"

"All of us knew Dale would one day come to surgery. If the circumstances were different, we would have chosen a more auspicious time, but they aren't."

Peggy voiced another question that had been in all their minds: "You'll operate yourself, won't you, Dr. Dalton?"

"If you want me to."

"Oh, I do."

"I'll talk to Dr. LeMoyne," said Ken. "It isn't safe to wait, with the pO_2 as low as it is."

Val LeMoyne didn't question the wisdom of immediate surgery either. Trained to evaluate the condition of a patient and, weighing the chances of life or death, act swiftly and effectively, she was able to recognize the gravity of the emergency.

"Hold this mask, Mike," she said. "I'll call the OR and get things started.

"OR Two is clear," Val reported when she came back from the nursing station a few minutes later. "I know you like to use it because of the monitors, Ken, so we'll do the boy there, starting thirty minutes from now. You understand, of course, that I'll have to carry him as light as possible; he may even squirm when you make the incision but he won't remember it."

"You're the boss in that area, Val." Ken turned to Mike. "Can anyone cover Emergency for you?"

"Ed Vogel's off and so is Nolan Gaither, so I think I'd better stay available. But Ned Green is in his room, he can assist you." As chief surgical resident, Green was just below Mike himself in the non-faculty surgical hierarchy.

"Ned will be fine," said Ken. "Let's get Dale up to surgery."

II

Rebecca Dalton didn't follow the others when Dale Tyndall was moved to the operating suite on the special cardiac stretcher that had its own oxygen supply, allowing the vital gas to be given under pressure without interruption. Even greater than her desire to watch Ken while he operated was the fear that her presence there, and the knowledge of how much depended upon his having retained all his skills during the months of relative surgical inactivity, might put him under additional tension when he needed every faculty for the task at hand.

To occupy herself meanwhile, Rebecca decided to make evening rounds in the CICU. She stopped by the nursing station just as Helga was gathering up the records that were to go to the morgue with Richard Payson's body.

"I was tied up when the CODE FIVE sounded a little while ago," Rebecca told Helga. "It was for Mr. Payson, wasn't it?"

Helga nodded. "You couldn't have done anything, Dr. Dalton. All the monitor channels were being used, so we didn't even realize he was dead for a while."

"When the operator told me Dr. Raburn was with the CPR team that responded, I figured I'd just be in the way," said Rebecca. "Not that he's so big, of course."

"I guess there are more ways of being big than just in size." Helga's voice was soft and Rebecca looked at the nurse in surprise.

"Mike is most of them," she agreed.

"I'll remember that," said Helga. "Are you sure you don't need me on the floor, Dr. Dalton? I can stay but Miss Garth is helping and I always hate to send a student to the morgue."

"Don't start now, please," said Rebecca. "I remember well my first day in anatomy. Do you have any idea what happened to Mr. Payson?"

"Apparently a standstill arrest."

"With so many varied stimuli reaching his muscles from a disordered brain, it's not surprising that those going to the heart would get involved enough to literally tie it into a knot and bring about arrest. Was Carolyn much upset?"

"We haven't been able to get her," Helga admitted. "She was off duty today."

"She couldn't have done anything anyway. And it will be a greater relief to her when she finds it's all over."

"I'm sure it will," said Helga.

"Go ahead and take Mr. Payson's body down to the morgue," Rebecca told the blonde nurse. "I want to see Kevin and Mr. McKenzie but if I need any help I'll call one of the other nurses."

Ross McKenzie didn't speak while Rebecca checked his heart, had him cough so she could listen over his lungs for the fine râles of congestion, and checked his ankles for any sign of edema, the swelling that would perhaps have signaled the beginning of a failing heart.

"Do you feel like talking a little, Mr. McKenzie?" she asked him when she had finished the examination.

"I feel like getting out of here, if I could get rid of some of this plumbing and electric wiring you've got attached to me."

"We will probably remove the catheter from your arm tomorrow. It did its job by telling my husband about twenty hours in advance that your heart was adjusting and surgery would probably not be necessary, at a time when I felt certain that it would be."

"Where did he learn about this gadget?"

"Doctors attend medical conventions and visit other clinics regularly to keep themselves informed on new things. He's going to Paris soon to try and discover why a heart transplant case in France is still living, five years after his operation."

"Does that mean Dr. Dalton's going to start transplanting hearts again?"

"That's possible. We know a lot more about rejection than we did a year ago."

"I suppose you learned from the ones who died."

"Partly, but work in that area is being done in a lot of laboratories besides ours."

McKenzie studied her for a moment. "Do you love your husband that much? To assume responsibility for his mistakes?"

Rebecca flushed. "To keep fifteen people alive for as much as two years longer than they would have lived otherwise can hardly be called a mistake, Mr. McKenzie."

"That cute little technician of yours—"

"Peggy Tyndall?"

"Yes."

"She's a physician's assistant, not just a technician."

"What's the difference?"

"Medical schools that train PA candidates usually require them to have had around two thousand hours' experience in some aspect of the medical field before acceptance. Most of those we have trained as PAs here are former corpsmen and technicians from the armed services. Peggy had three years as a *Wave* corpsman in one of the largest naval medical centers in the country. After her husband was killed in Vietnam, leaving her with a newborn baby, she put herself through the PA course under the GI Bill. She deserves a lot of credit, Mr. McKenzie."

"She tells me Dr. Dalton has started to work again on an artificial heart."

"He has—but I don't know how far he'll be able to go, if you succeed in cutting the appropriation for the hospital."

McKenzie shrugged. "That was a low blow, Doctor."

"No lower than your accusing him of contributing to the death rate of other people in the hospital, Mr. McKenzie. Right now he's getting ready to operate on Peggy's little boy for a serious heart abnormality."

"And she's letting him?"

"She asked him to do the operation."

He shook his head, as if baffled. "I'll never understand women. You have admitted you were ready to demand that I be operated on by your husband, when I didn't need it."

"Would you have agreed?"

"Of course, if you had said it was necessary. And incidentally, your husband passed up a fine chance to perform a brilliant operation on me that would have made all the local newspapers at least, proving he wasn't all washed up. Even if it had failed, he could always have claimed you had made a mistake in diagnosis, so why didn't he operate?"

"Because he's a dedicated doctor and not an opportunist," said Rebecca. "Now I'd like to ask you a question, Mr. McKenzie."

"Fire away, then."

"You've said you would have submitted to surgery yesterday if I had told you it was necessary to save your life. Suppose I had recommended a transplant and a donor had become available. Would you have let my husband operate?"

"Of course."

"You trust us that much?"

"I didn't." Ross McKenzie smiled and Rebecca realized that she was seeing a side of him she—nor anyone else, she suspected, except perhaps someone very close to him—had never seen before. "But that was before I was brainwashed—by an honest female doctor and a bartender named Kevin McCartney."

III

Helga herself went down to the morgue with Richard Payson's body, remembering very well the time when, a timorous probationer, she had accompanied the first corpse she had ever been close to—drumming up her courage as best she could while half expecting to feel icy fingers close around her throat at every corner.

"Miss Sundberg!" Dr. Sam Toyota, the resident in pathology, looked up from the desk where he had been dictating an autopsy report, his eyes beaming behind thick lenses. "We don't see much of you down here, worse luck."

"This is my roommate's father, Mr. Richard Payson."

"The Huntington's disease case?"

"Yes."

Toyota came over to the stretcher and pulled back the sheet that covered Richard Payson's face.

"There's something you hardly ever see," he remarked.

"What's that, Doctor?"

"Somebody who looks like he welcomed death. There's even a smile on his face, but I guess he had reason to smile at that. H-D is a pretty horrible fate. His cheeks are pink, too."

"Anything significant in that?"

"Death was sudden, probably a cessation. Didn't your monitors show it?"

"Our channels were tied up with two severe heart cases, so Dr. Vogel took him off the monitors yesterday."

Dr. Toyota shrugged. "It was just as well, he couldn't have had anything to live for."

"I guess not," said Helga. "Will you let me know if you find anything?"

"Sure. Come to think of it, I've got a note from Dr. Fletcher on him somewhere here." He rummaged through some papers on the desk. "Here it is: '*Autopsy to be performed immediately after death.*' Hmm!" He looked up. "By request of the State's Attorney."

"Mr. Broadhurst?" Helga hoped the Japanese pathologist didn't notice the apprehensive note in her voice.

"Yes. I wonder why?" He reached for the telephone. "I'd better call Dr. Fletcher."

"I haven't been able to get in touch with Mr. Payson's daughter; she's off duty today and must have gone out for the evening." Helga was playing for time. "You'll need her permission for the post, won't you?"

"Not for a coroner's case." Dr. Toyota glanced down at the note again. "Besides, it says here that Mr. Payson willed his body to the medical school."

Defeated, Helga was turning toward the door when she heard the pathologist say into the telephone: "Mr. Payson just died, Dr. Fletcher. Want me to get started with him—drugs? Sure, I'll be on the watch. See you later."

In the corridor outside the Pathology Laboratory, Helga stopped beside a cooler and filled a cup with cold water, drinking it down without even feeling the chill. She'd been counting on Richard Payson's body being treated like any other routine autopsy on a patient who died during the night. Usually they were put into one of the long refrigerator drawers to await post-mortem in the morning. But Anthony Broadhurst was apparently as thorough as she'd heard he was and had anticipated the possibility that, after the God Committee refused to take the responsibility for ending her father's life from Carolyn, she would undertake it herself.

There was one ray of sunlight, however. If the medical examiner looked for a drug as the possible death agent, he'd find nothing but chlorpromazine. And the hospital record would show that the powerful tranquilizing agent had been given regularly for most of the time Richard Payson had been in the hospital.

Helga's watch showed eight o'clock and Carolyn's plane was presumably just taking off, so she'd be safe. But seeing a pay telephone on the wall of the empty corridor, Helga stopped and searched in her purse until she found a dime.

"International Airport—Information," a bored voice said in her ear.

Helga looked quickly up and down the corridor but could see no one near enough to hear. Nor did she hear any footfalls on the steps.

"International Airport—Information," the voice repeated. "Can I help you?"

"Could you tell me whether Varig Flight 803 has departed?"

"One moment, puh-lease. Yes, Varig Flight 803 departed Miami on schedule at 8:00 P.M."

"Thank you." Helga started to hang up the phone, but froze beside it with the receiver still in her hand when an angry voice said in her ear:

"Now tell me what the hell this is all about, Helga."

It was Gus Henderson.

IV

Ned Green had finished scrubbing and was soaking his hands and arms in antiseptic, when Ken Dalton came into the scrubroom, adjoining Operating Room Two, where final preparations for surgery were going on rapidly.

"Hope we didn't interfere with any other plans you had for the evening, Ned," said Ken. "I was hoping not to have to operate on this boy for another few years, when we could do a complete repair, but it looks like we were a bit too conservative."

"I was just brushing up on anatomy for the American Board exam, Dr. Dalton," said the resident. "I notice that his hematocrit is pretty high."

"Too high—for comfort," said Ken. "These Fallot children compensate for not getting enough oxygen into the red blood cells by making more cells—which is all right if the RBC count and the blood viscosity, as measured by the hematocrit, don't go too high. When Dale was examined in the Cardiac Research Laboratory six months ago, the hematocrit was 50 per cent, but just now it was up to 80, which explains why he had the severe attack of anoxia."

"Shall I drape the operative field?" Ned Green asked as he lifted his hands and arms from the antiseptic basin.

"Please. The catheterization we did, when Dale first started having the spells of anoxia, shows that the aortic arch is to the left, instead of reversed like it is with so many of these children. We'll go in through the third right interspace."

"Right," said the resident, and moved into the operating theater.

When Ken came in some five minutes later and began to remove the antiseptic from his hands and forearms with a sterile towel handed him by the scrub nurse, Dale Tyndall's small body was already covered by a voluminous sterile sheet leaving only a rectangle of skin, bright red from the antiseptic, exposed on his upper chest.

"How is he, Val?" Ken asked as the circulating nurse was tying the strings at the back of his gown.

"The pO_2 is a little better since the blood's been diluted by the IV."

"I considered bleeding him to reduce the number of red cells in his circulation and lower the hematocrit a little. Maybe I should have."

"Benjamin Rush would approve, at least. According to the history books, he must have bled practically everybody in Philadelphia about the time of the Revolution. I'm still carrying Dale very light, mostly oxygen."

"Good." Ken moved to the table. "I'm hoping this won't take very long."

Watching from the gallery, Mike Raburn wasn't even sure he detected an instant of hesitation before the surgeon made a fairly long incision outward in the space between the third and fourth ribs on the right. But if there had been any hesitation, it was only before that first cut through the skin, for Ken Dalton's movements as he opened the chest cavity through the muscle layer between the ribs were as sure and as skilled as ever.

No more than fifteen minutes after the first cut, a rib spreader was in the wound, opening it wide to expose the small heart beating rapidly but regularly in its protective sac, which in some instances—as it had yesterday with Kevin McCartney—could also be a threat to life itself.

The picture that presented itself in the almost square frame of the incision maintained by the rib spreader was one Ken Dalton—and Mike—had seen many times: the right ventricle thickened in an attempt to raise pressure in the right heart and supply the lungs adequately with blood; the purring vibration called a "thrill"—easily felt when the heart itself was touched as blood rushed through the opening between the ventricles which had failed to close as it should by birth; the markedly constricted pulmonary artery, literally exerting the effect of a tourniquet upon the flow of blood to the lungs—all were part of a classic picture of congenital heart disease.

Lifting his eyes to the gallery, Ken spoke over the surgical suite PA system.

"Except for the fact that the aorta is not reversed, this is a classic case," he said. "We can feel the thrill as the blood moves from the right ventricle to the left and you may even be able to see the small size of the pulmonary artery compared to what it should be. If the patient's hematocrit wasn't so high and this wasn't an emergency, I'd choose to put him on the pump. Then I could open the left ventricle, repair the opening, and enlarge the strictured portion of the pulmonary artery by means of a Teflon patch. But everything considered, I'm going to do a simple Blalock-Taussig shunt between the subclavian artery and the pulmonary."

In the gallery, where about a dozen of the hospital staff and students were watching, Mike Raburn nodded agreement. Communication with the theater was only one way, but he understood that Ken's words had been a message for him to transmit to Rebecca Dalton and Peggy that the relatively simple operation of shunting blood from a major artery, the subclavian, which also supplied the arm, into the lungs where it could be adequately supplied with oxygen, was almost certain to be a success.

Leaving the gallery, Mike stopped at the OR suite nursing station and dialed the hospital operator. "Do you know where Dr. Rebecca Dalton is?" he asked.

"She was on CICU a few minutes ago, Dr. Raburn," said the operator. "Shall I call her?"

"Don't bother," he said. "I'm going to the first floor, so I'll stop by there."

V

Ed Vogel was enjoying himself immensely, and the evening had hardly begun. The two seats at the Coliseum for the final postseason basketball game between the Miami Snappers and the league-leading Lakers were in the owner's box right at mid-court. And the redhead beside him, a teacher from Vero Beach attending summer school at the University of Miami, was gorgeous—and probably impressed.

"I've never been to a real professional game before," she confided. "Imagine sitting in the owner's box. I could love you to death, Ed."

"I'm liable to hold you to that, Beautiful," said Vogel happily. "Now just pray nobody gets injured and I have to make a house call."

"Can I go, if you do? Anything about medicine excites me."

"I wouldn't leave you behind for the world," he assured her, allowing the arm he had casually placed across the back of the adjoining seat to drop, so his hand touched the warm pink skin of a lovely shoulder left bare by a sleeveless dress.

"Umm!" She shivered and moved closer to him. "I'm so excited from all this, I must have goose pimples."

"I haven't found any but I'll be glad to—"

"Oh! Oh!" The girl stood up suddenly, along with practically everybody watching the game, almost tumbling Ed, who hadn't been watching the game at all, out of his seat.

"Wha—what happened?" he asked.

"It's Big Joe Gates. He's down."

"Hell!" said Ed in disgust. "Now I'll probably have to be a doctor. And just when I was—"

"Dr. Vogel!" It was the Snappers' coach, calling up from the bench. "We need you on the floor—right away."

VI

Joey Gates was watching TV on one of the small portable sets allowed in the ICU when Mike stopped by the room, after giving Peggy and Rebecca, who were sitting together in the ICU waiting room, the good news about Dale.

"How's the game going, Joey?" he asked.

"Great, Dr. Mike! Just great! Dad's shooting more baskets than the rest of the Snappers put together. And guess what?"

"I give up."

"We saw Dr. Vogel just now—in the owner's box."

"I know. Your dad sent me the tickets but I couldn't go. Dr. Vogel's substituting for the team doctor."

"He's also enjoying the company of a stunning redhead," said Rachel.

"Ed knows how to pick 'em."

"Daddy just shot another basket," Joey exclaimed.

"My husband is showing off, Mike. He's been saying all day that he was going to make the owners realize they can't write him off, so he's really putting on the heat tonight."

"Nobody can do it better."

"Let's go outside," she said. "I want to talk to you, but I can't hear myself think with Joey jumping around."

"Maybe turning on the heat tonight will be good for Joe," said Mike as he followed her out into the corridor. "It might even help him get the worry out of his system."

"By getting hopped up on Dex?"

"Joe?" Mike stared at her unbelievingly. "He's got better sense than that."

"Ordinarily, yes. But when you're scared to death that you have an incurable disease, and at the same time afraid the owners are going to discover it and dump you"—she shrugged—"you're liable to do anything."

"At least he seems to be getting away with it. And the way he's going, he'll burn up a lot of amphetamine before the game's over."

"Mommy!" Joey's voice, anxious and afraid, drew them back into the room.

"What is it?" Rachel asked but they needed only to look at the TV set to see.

"It's Daddy! He's down! And he must be hurt bad, 'cause he ain't moving."

"Oh, my God! That big fool has gone and killed himself."

CHAPTER TWENTY-TWO

I

"Dammit, Gus!" said Helga. "You scared me half to death. Where did you come from anyway?"

"Miss Garth told me you had brought Mr. Payson's body down here. I just got out of the elevator but you were so busy phoning the airport, you didn't hear me."

"Don't talk so loud, or *everybody* will hear you. Come on. I know a place where we won't be overheard."

She led the way to the end of the corridor, turned right, and opened a door at the end of a side passage. The room was small with a cot, a chair, a small table, and a half bath attached.

"What's this?" Gus demanded as she pushed him in and shut the door. "I didn't even know it was here."

"Quarters for the night pathology technician. But they don't have one just now."

"What happened tonight?"

"Mr. Payson died about seven-thirty."

"Where was Carolyn?"

"I don't know. I've called but she doesn't answer."

"Maybe because she's on Varig Flight 803?"

"Could be."

"Going where?"

"The first stop that flight makes is Rio. And Brazil doesn't have an extradition treaty with the United States."

"Then it's true? She did kill him?" The tall pediatrician sank into the chair before the small table, the stricken look on his face that of one who has just seen a nightmare become reality.

"I haven't spoken to Carolyn since early this morning," said Helga.

"But how could she do anything so foolish?"

"It was an act of love—"

He shot to his feet, his face flushed with anger. "Was it an act of love to risk shattering our whole life together—and my career—by having a charge of murder brought against her?"

"If it's all right for a man to kill a dog he loves, when the dog's in pain and can't recover, Gus, why isn't it right for a daughter to help a parent she loves by putting *him* out of his misery?"

"It's not the same thing, and you know it," Gus snapped. "You put her up to it, Carolyn never would have had the courage to do it alone." He wheeled suddenly. "How do I know you didn't do it yourself?"

"Because then I'd be flying to Brazil tonight instead of Carolyn."

"God, what a mess!" He threw up his hands in a gesture which, Helga suddenly realized, was more exasperation than grief or despair. "She'll be charged with murder now for sure."

"You're probably right. I didn't know it until I brought the body down, but Mr. Broadhurst—"

"The State's Attorney?"

"Yes. He had left a note with the medical examiner that, if Mr. Payson died, his body was to be posted immediately. I think he expected Carolyn to use a narcotic. Sam Toyota's going to start the autopsy in a few minutes and he'll be looking for evidence of a narcotic overdose."

"What will he find?"

"Nothing, I hope. Mike Raburn put down the cause of death as 'Cardiac Arrest, Cause Undetermined.'"

"How did she do—no, don't tell me. Then if they subpoena me I'll have to admit that I know."

Helga studied the tall doctor for a moment thoughtfully.

"What are *you* going to do, Gus?" she asked. "About Carolyn, I mean?"

"How do I know? She deliberately ran away—"

"From a charge of murder. Not from you."

"She couldn't have been thinking much about me to risk—"

"Carolyn didn't really care very much what happened to her, Gus. The way she looked at it, she was doomed from the day she was conceived. The thing that did concern her was that, if she stayed here and faced the charge of murder Anthony Broadhurst would probably bring against her, you might still be loyal to her and become involved, with all the damage that could do to your career."

She was looking at him speculatively as she spoke, waiting for the indignant explosion her deliberate use of the words "you might still be loyal" should have elicited. And when it didn't come, she let out her breath in a sigh, though whether of relief or disappointment, she wasn't quite certain.

"*Your* choice now," Helga added, "is between accepting her sacrifice or deciding that the fifteen or so years you and Carolyn could have together, even if she does develop H-D later, plus your natural wish to stand beside someone you love in a time of trouble, are worth giving up your immediate plans for the future."

"How could that be?" She could hardly have missed the note of wariness in his voice.

"Brazil's a big country. I'm still not going to tell you where Carolyn will be by tomorrow or the next day, depending on flight schedules, until I'm sure you're going there too."

"You want me to bring her back? When you just said Broadhurst is likely to place charges against her?"

"Not bring her back, Gus. Stay with her."

"You're out of your mind, Helga."

"I guess I am," she said wearily. "But I owed it to Carolyn to give you at least a glimpse of what you two can have together down there, if you go to her the first of July instead of joining the faculty here."

"I already know—professional suicide."

"That's where you're wrong, Gus. You'd be working in a modern hospital that serves an area of over a million people, with only one doctor for every eighteen thousand. The infant mortality is over a hundred and fifty per thousand live births, where the U.S. is around twenty."

"Twenty-two."

"Children under five account for more than half the deaths in the area, so if there ever was a place needing a fine pediatrician, that's it. And even if Anthony Broadhurst is politically ambitious enough to bring charges against Carolyn, the whole thing will be forgotten in three to five years, with public opinion on the 'right to die' question changing the way it is. Then you two could come back to the United States. Or you could stay in Brazil and have a very rewarding life together."

"For God's sake, Helga," he exploded. "You know I can't make a decision like that on a moment's notice."

"No, Gus, I guess you couldn't. But I doubt that you felt any hesitation in sleeping with Carolyn the first time you had a chance."

"When did you get to be such a damned moralist?"

"Touché." Helga looked at her watch. "I go off duty at eleven. If you decide to go to Carolyn, let me know by then and I'll tell you where she'll be. If not, I'll expect you to forget that this conversation ever occurred. Excuse me, please. I've got a ward to watch upstairs."

II

Joe Gates had been hot, hotter than he ever remembered being, even when he'd played forward for the Lakers in '70 and handled more rebounds than anyone else in the league that year. As the ball left his hands from his favorite position in the corner of the court, he'd sensed that it would arch in a curve as beautiful as anything ever revealed by a bikini, right through the basket without touching metal.

It had, too. But even before the ball cleared the fringes of the net Joe was already halfway down the court, legs pumping, heart pounding until it threatened to come out of his throat, moving fast to be ahead of the tall black Laker forward with the goatee who was the season's high scorer.

With the Snappers ahead by ten points before the quarter was over, Joe knew he was the hottest thing on the court—and so, he hoped, did the owners. Convinced that tonight could be crucial, he'd taken no chances on being anything less than at the top of his form—plus a little more. And from the very first tip at center, he'd been maintaining a pace far more taxing than even a veteran like Joe Gates should try to maintain.

And so, when the ball came into play on a long pass intended for the tall Laker waiting for it under the enemy basket, Joe had to beat it to the man for whom it was intended. Straining every muscle of those famous legs to the utmost of its strength, Joe went up, up, until his outstretched fingers touched the ball just before the Laker forward, tipping it to a Snapper player racing down the court.

Even as his body started downward, Joe had felt the blackout coming and fought to keep a hold upon his senses. But the effort had sent so much blood to his legs, leaving so little for his brain, that something had to give—in this case the brain.

The blackout lasted only an instant, but the Snappers' coach called time even as one of his own players caught the tipped ball. When Big Joe regained consciousness moments later, shaking his head to clear his vision and trying to sit up, a young doctor whose face was vaguely familiar pushed him back without much effort.

"Lie still." The doctor's finger reached for Joe's wrist, and when he felt the pulse, a startled expression came over his face.

"What is it, Doc?" It was the coach, anxious—both about Joe and about maintaining that ten-point lead. "It looked to me like he was tripped."

"Tripped over his own heart most likely," said Ed Vogel. "I can't even count his pulse and it's skittering all over the place. Let's get him off the court and into the locker room."

Joe tried to rise again but Ed Vogel pushed him down once more.

"Get some help and carry him," he told the trainer who was kneeling beside them. "This man's in no shape to walk."

Willing hands lifted Joe and carried him to the locker room, but he didn't hear the burst of applause that accompanied his departure from the court, having blacked out once again. When he came to, he was lying on a rubbing table and the trainer was waving a crushed ample of ammonia beneath his nostrils. The young doctor had ripped open his jersey and was attaching something that grabbed the skin over his chest.

"What's that thing, Doctor?" Joe heard the trainer ask.

"It's called a ventricular impulse detector; you can transmit an electrocardiogram to a central monitoring station by telephone with it. Besides, it's got a built-in alarm and its own computer."

A faint but perfectly audible sound came from the small unit, interrupting the speaker. It continued for perhaps eight seconds before shutting off.

"That's the alarm," Vogel explained. "It means his pulse is either a little below fifty, above a hundred and fifty beats per minute, or that he's having more than seven abnormal ventricular contractions per minute."

Glancing at his watch, the cardiologist picked up Joe Gates's wrist again.

"The rate's about one-forty now," he said at the end of a half minute. "That's not high enough to set the alarm off, so he must be having enough ventricular contractions to do it."

"What does that mean, Doc?" Joe was able to ask, as Ed Vogel was inserting the tips of a stethoscope into his ears.

"It means you're damn lucky you didn't drop dead out there on the court."

"But I was hot—"

"That you were. That you were."

"I can go back in the second half, can't I?" Joe asked, but somehow didn't seem to have enough breath to say any more.

"Not in the second half of *this* game," said Ed Vogel crisply. "You're going to the hospital."

The tiny buzzer sounded its warning again.

"Call the Rescue Squad," the young cardiologist told the trainer, as he applied the flat diaphragm of the instrument to Joe's chest over the heart. "And tell them to be sure to bring a cardiac ambulance.

"All right, Joe," said Vogel when the trainer disappeared into the adjoining office where the telephone was located and the two of them were alone. "What did you take?"

"I don't know what—"

"Don't try to con me, I've seen too many kids high on bennies not to recognize what they can do even to an athlete's heart. How much?"

"Seventy-five milligrams of Dexedrine."

"Jesus Christ! Were you trying to commit suicide?"

"This is an important game, Doc. My whole career could depend on it."

"You chose one helluva way to save it then. God only knows what you've done to your heart."

"A lot of fellows take the pills before the game, even the hard stuff," Joe protested. "They say it gives them a lift."

"If you'd taken any more, it would have given you a lift—right through the Pearly Gates or wherever it is you're trying to go."

"The ambulance is on the way, Doc," the trainer reported when he came back. "The dispatcher said it ought not to be more'n five minutes."

"Good." Ed Vogel opened his medical bag and took out a plastic syringe and a small sterile pack. Opening the pack swiftly with skilled fingers, he reached in and pulled out two ampules, swabbed them with an alcohol sponge, knocked the tops off, and drew the contents of both up into the syringe. Pulling up the hem of Joe's shorts, he rubbed the skin with alcohol and jammed the needle deep into the muscle, pumping in the contents of the syringe. Moving then to the adjoining office, he dialed Biscayne General and was immediately connected with Mike Raburn.

"I'm sending Joe Gates in with a heart that's spraying premature beats all over the place," Ed reported.

"I was outside Joey's door talking to Rachel when the boy saw him fall on TV. He says Joe was tripped."

"Seventy-five milligrams of Dexedrine tripped him, when his heart rate got past 150. I put a VIDA on him and it sounded like a fire alarm. He'll be there in a few minutes but you'd better have Dr. Rebecca see him, Mike. This guy could go into acute dilatation any minute."

"I'll get her. Things are sort of humming around here, too. Peggy Tyndall's little boy, Dale, overexerted and went into acute oxygen insufficiency. Ken Dalton is just starting to do a shunt on him."

"Is Dr. Dalton operating himself?"

"Yes. Ned Green is assisting."

"I hate to think what losing Dale would do to Peggy."

"Or Dr. Dalton," said Mike, "but it looks like the kid will be okay. The worst part is that, if Peggy hadn't been working late in the laboratory on that plastic heart project, she'd have been home and this might not have happened."

"I hear the ambulance siren outside," said Vogel. "Unless you need me, I won't come in."

"We saw that redhead on TV, too," said Mike. "Good luck, fellow."

III

In the teaching theater of the Pathology Department located in the basement of the Biscayne General tower, the glaring lights shone down upon the nude body of Richard Payson, laid out on the marble top of the autopsy table. Dr. Sam Toyota stood beside it, a razor-sharp knife in his gloved hand, his body protected from accidental spattering by a large rubber apron.

"Ready to go, Sam?" Karen Fletcher had just come into the room, wearing a long white coat over beige slacks and shirt, and a matching bandeau restraining the silver-tinted hair.

"All set, Dr. Fletcher."

"You might as well begin. I got in touch with Mr. Broadhurst, and he'll be here by the time you get to the internal organs."

Karen moved nearer to the table as the Japanese pathologist made his initial incision, a sweeping curve that began under one armpit, swung down to about four inches above the navel, then up to the opposite armpit.

"That blood look overoxygenated to you, Sam?" she asked.

"It's certainly oxygen-rich, but then he'd only been dead a little over an hour. He died very suddenly, too, from cardiac arrest and the hospital record says he was on a pacemaker and a respirator for fifteen minutes or so."

"I guess that explains it, though I've never seen blood that highly oxygenated before. We'll check the pO_2 on the blood itself, so be sure and save enough for that and all the other tests Mr. Broadhurst is going to insist that we make."

"That will be no trouble, the blood's still pretty liquid."

Dr. Toyota dissected up the large flap he had made, exposing the rib cage and the upper part of the abdomen. When he finished, he casually turned up the flap, covering the dead man's face.

"It's really remarkable how much variation there is in blood liquidity after death," Karen observed. "An embalmer for a large mortuary once told me he sometimes finds it liquid as much as four or five hours afterward."

Reaching for a pair of rib shears, Sam Toyota began to cut through the rib cage on either side of the chest, exposing the organs of the thorax.

"Why is it I always seem to come in when you're doing that?" Anthony Broadhurst spoke from the doorway. "Even though I've heard that blade crunch ribs at least fifty times, it still gives me the willies."

"Wait in my office, if you'd rather," said Karen. "We'll call you if anything significant turns up."

"Unh! Unh! I'd just come back about the time Sam starts in on the skull with that damned saw, and it gets to me worse than the rib shears. Find anything yet?"

"No," said Dr. Toyota. "Mind telling us what you suspect?"

"During that God Committee meeting yesterday afternoon, I got the distinct impression that, if the committee didn't allow her father's life to be ended, Payson's daughter would do it herself."

"So all you're going on is a hunch?" Karen asked.

"Being a nurse and on the same ward where her father was, that girl could easily have given him a massive injection of morphine."

"That's pretty flimsy circumstantial evidence. Besides, the nurses have to account strictly for all narcotic drugs."

"Come now, Dr. Fletcher. We all know that an addict has been employed as a nurse more than once, either because she's worked out a clever trick or because she's a bona fide nursing graduate. Some of them even manage to supply themselves with morphine from the hospital supply for months."

"Not with a computer keeping watch, the way it does here," said Karen.

"At the committee meeting yesterday," said Broadhurst, "it was suggested that a quick method of euthanasia would be the injection of a large amount of air into a vein."

"Air embolism can easily be fatal," Karen conceded. "How about it in this case, Sam?"

"I think not, but we can certainly find out." Picking up a lung he had just removed, the Japanese pathologist sliced the organ open and examined the cut surface carefully.

"No air bubbles in the larger vessels," he reported, then squeezed the soft spongy lung, forcing bright red blood out of the cut surface. "This blood is highly oxygenated, too, and it wouldn't be if enough air had been injected to drive much of it out of the lung vessels."

"Can you be absolutely sure he didn't get a large dose of morphine?" Broadhurst insisted.

Karen had been studying intently the cut surface of the lung Sam Toyota had exposed and the blood he had squeezed out of it. Now she looked up.

"If Carolyn Payson had managed to give her father a lethal dose of a narcotic, his respirations would have failed gradually from the effect of the drug on the respiratory center of the brain," she said. "The proximate cause of death would then have been a decrease in the oxygen supply to the brain cells below their life tolerance and the blood would be dark from cyanosis, not red the way it is here."

"How about a heart drug?"

"Did you have any particular one in mind?"

"I read a novel last year about a pharmacist who killed a man by putting a powerful poison in beer and paralyzing his heart."

"I read the same story," said Karen. "The drug was aconite."

"If that made the heart stop suddenly, wouldn't the blood show oxygen?" Broadhurst asked.

"Yes. But aconite is easy to detect chemically in body fluids and even in tissues."

"She could still have given him something like that, couldn't she?"

"It's a possibility, except that aconite is hard to come by," said Karen. "We almost never use it in medicine and it wouldn't be in the hospital pharmacy—or any other one I can think of offhand."

"Could she have used another drug?"

Karen smiled. "I can see why you win so many cases, Mr. Broadhurst. Be sure and take plenty of blood for testing, Sam. And sample all the major organs, too. We don't want to let the DA catch us napping."

"Another thing," said Broadhurst. "Before I came over here, I tried to call Carolyn Payson at the hospital and the operator gave me her apartment number but nobody answered. I wanted to warn her to stay put, until you could determine the cause of death. I also questioned the security man at the front door when I came in just now. He remembers seeing her go into the hospital around dinnertime and Payson died not long after that."

"Are you going to put out an APB?" Sam Toyota asked.

"Not unless you can find a cause of death tonight that could involve her," said the attorney. "With all this public agitation and discussion over the 'right to die,' I'd be a fool to arrest and charge the nurse unless you can nail down the cause of death. That's why I asked that Payson be posted immediately, in case he died soon after the Moriturus Committee meeting yesterday afternoon."

"It's going to take awhile to finish the autopsy," Karen told the attorney as she picked up the bulky hospital record. "Why don't we wait in my office? That way you won't have to listen to the saw, and Sam can call us if he finds anything suspicious."

In Karen's office, Broadhurst lit a cigarette and relaxed in a comfortable chair while she took the one behind the desk.

"Anything new in Dr. Cooper's condition?" he asked.

"Dr. Desmond is going to recommend retirement for him soon. There's been no improvement in the paralysis since the last major stroke, so it's not likely that he will ever be able to work again."

"If you don't mind my asking, where does that leave you?"

"Dr. Jacob Barrows' retirement from the medical service because of angina was approved by the Hospital Board Tuesday afternoon. Dr. Rebecca Dalton was promoted to full professor and made chief of the section at the same time."

"So why not you as head of Pathology?"

"And professor," said Karen. "I'm pretty sure both will happen after Dr. Cooper's retirement. Or don't you approve?"

"I have nothing against women lawyers," said Broadhurst. "Some of the smartest ones I know are women. So why should I object to women doctors?"

"Thanks for the vote of confidence." Karen swiveled her chair so she could look directly into his eyes. "Now what about a woman as county medical examiner?"

Broadhurst looked surprised. "So that's the way the wind blows?"

"Any reason why it shouldn't?" Karen's eyes had never left his.

"Probably not, I just hadn't thought about it." He put down his cigarette. "It can be a pretty messy job sometimes."

"So can this one," said Karen. "I'm the only board-certified forensic pathologist in the county besides Dr. Cooper. And I've been his deputy for the past year."

"You want that post pretty badly, don't you?"

"I've set my heart on it. And what I set my heart on, I usually get."

Anthony Broadhurst's eyes had begun to glow with a light Karen recognized and quite understood. "Does the fact that you will probably be the only woman medical examiner in the country have anything to do with that ambition?"

"Of course—for the same reason you expect one day to be governor of Florida. Or do you deny that?"

Anthony Broadhurst shook his head and Karen decided that now was the time to make her real play, the clincher so to speak.

"If there's any doubt in your mind about my being fitted for the job of medical examiner," she said, "I'll tell you how the death of Richard Payson was almost certainly accomplished—for a price."

He leaned forward eagerly. "How was it done?"

"I said for a price—remember?"

"My support of you when the question of Dr. Cooper's successor comes up?"

"Yes."

"How do you know I wouldn't have given you that anyway?" he asked, and Karen knew with a surge of exultation that victory was only one step away—a step she was quite prepared, even eager, to take.

"I think you would have," she admitted. "But it never hurts to be certain and I rarely leave anything to chance."

"We're in agreement there. Now give—"

"You noticed how red Richard Payson's blood was out there just now, didn't you?"

"Yes. But then—"

"You can take my word for it that the redness was abnormal."

"So what does that prove?"

"That he was killed with an embolism—"

"But Dr. Toyota said not."

"Sam said there was no sign of *air* embolism. But that doesn't mean it couldn't have been *oxygen* embolism."

"What is this, anyway? Some Perry Mason type of trick?"

"It's clever enough to be worthy of one of Mason's best cases," Karen conceded. "Let me explain the sequence of events, as I believe they happened."

"Please do."

"Every room in this hospital has an oxygen supply of its own connected to a central source. Payson was getting an intravenous, too." She picked up the chart and turned up the top sheet of the nurses' record. "It was started yesterday."

"What has that got to do with—"

"Let me finish, please. With a catheter used for continuous intravenous injection of glucose already in place in an arm vein, it would have been a simple matter to connect the end of the oxygen tube hanging on the wall of every room to the outer end of the catheter. Or simpler still to put a needle on it and inject the oxygen through the intravenous tubing. A lot of medication is given that way to patients getting intravenous injection."

"But Sam Toyota said just now that air in the veins would have been detectable. Why not oxygen?"

"For a very simple reason. Oxygen is absorbed by the hemoglobin in the red blood cells all the time, but air is four fifths nitrogen, which is inert, though some is dissolved in the blood. The record shows that the patient was put on a pacemaker and his heart kept beating for at least fifteen minutes after there was no sign of respiration or heartbeat."

"Surely the Payson girl couldn't have—"

"She didn't need to," said Karen. "In an ultramodern hospital like this, with respirators and external pacemakers on every floor, nobody gets to die in peace. They're pumped and shocked until the CPR team gives out. While Payson was on a respirator, oxygen was going in and out of his lungs in simulated breathing. And with the heart beating, blood was circulating in his arteries, veins, and the capillaries in his body tissues, so the oxygen injected into his circulation was quickly absorbed by the hemoglobin in his red cells."

"But he was dead."

"Was he really? We don't know just how long different tissues live after what we call death, for lack of a better word. Actually his brain tissues may have been alive all the time, along with some others. But whether he was dead or alive, blood was circulating in his arteries, veins, and capillaries and some chemical changes were going on."

"It's an interesting theory," said Broadhurst. "And a clever one. If it all happened the way you say, you've just discovered the perfect way to accomplish a murder without detection." His tone changed suddenly. "But can you prove it happened that way?"

"Not a chance," said Karen. "If you put me on the stand and I tried to explain how a person could be killed by an element that not only passes freely into the body in one form and out of it as CO_2 in the next breath, a lay jury would be lost before I got started. And a defense lawyer wouldn't even have to be clever to tear the whole thing down with one question."

"I can figure that one out, at least," said the attorney. "'Do you mean to tell me, Doctor, that something as vital to life as oxygen would also kill?'"

"Exactly," said Karen.

"So Dr. Toyota isn't going to find anything that would let me bring a charge of murder against Carolyn Payson?"

"Not a thing."

The telephone on Karen's desk rang and she picked it up, listened a moment, then handed it to Anthony Broadhurst.

"It's Police Headquarters. They want you."

Broadhurst listened for a short time, asked several terse questions, and then hung up.

"Seems like you called the shots," he said. "The Payson girl left for Brazil tonight on Varig Flight 803—first stop Rio. And Brazil has no extradition treaty with the United States."

"You weren't going to indict her anyway."

"I might try—now that she ran away." He shrugged. "But it wouldn't do any good, unless she tried to come back."

"I'm not an attorney," said Karen, "but I don't think you could make that bit of circumstantial evidence stick either."

"By now, I'm sure you're right," said Broadhurst. "But I'd like to know how you arrived at that conclusion."

"You're a very positive man, Tony, that's what I particularly like about you." Karen's voice had taken on a warm, throaty note that set the lawyer's hackles stirring. "According to the scuttlebutt, you threatened to investigate if Richard Payson died soon after the meeting, so Carolyn Payson knew—"

"But she wasn't there when I warned the Board."

"Rebecca Dalton was the girl's representative, wasn't she?"

"Yes."

"Rebecca's very conscientious and would consider it her duty to warn Carolyn Payson about what might happen. Carolyn must have been fairly certain the method she used to kill her father wouldn't be discovered, but she couldn't afford to take any chances and left the country."

"Proving she was guilty."

"Not necessarily. You see, she must have realized that even if you were able to bring her back she could claim that, when her father died, she was so afraid of what you might do that she left the country. So she has you buffaloed either way."

"I'm damned glad you chose medicine instead of law," said Broadhurst on a note of pure admiration. "The best defense lawyers I know couldn't hold a candle to you."

"It's nice to be appreciated," said Karen. "Are you going back on our bargain because I can't prove what happened and Carolyn Payson got away?"

"Not at all," said the attorney. "I'm beginning to think tonight marks the beginning of a profitable—and I hope pleasant—relationship between the State's Attorney and the soon-to-be new county medical examiner. If you're free for a while, we might cement that beginning with a drink."

"It might be best if we weren't seen together in public until after my actual appointment," said Karen as they left the office. "But I have some excellent Wild Turkey bourbon, if you'd care to drop by my apartment."

Anthony Broadhurst chuckled delightedly. "You're not only beautiful and smart, Karen, you also have ESP."

IV

Surrounded by the scientific paraphernalia of the Coronary Intensive Care Unit, Big Joe Gates was beginning to be alarmed. The effects of the massive dose of Dexedrine he'd taken before the game were beginning to subside, too, bringing on the inevitable reaction of depression.

"How am I, Doctor?" he asked when Rebecca Dalton and Mike Raburn finished examining him.

"It appears that you escaped without serious effects, Mr. Gates—"

"I told Dr. Vogel I was all right, but he—"

"Dr. Vogel is one of the finest young heart specialists we have ever trained here, Mr. Gates." Rebecca's voice was sharp. "You may well have escaped severe heart damage because he recognized your condition and took action immediately to counteract the effects of the drug you took."

"But, Doctor—"

"If you want to wreck your heart, that's your privilege. But don't expect me to praise you for being a fool."

Joe looked at her and knew she meant every word of it.

"All right, Doctor," he said. "I apologize to you and I'll apologize to Dr. Vogel. What do I do now?"

"We'll keep you here a day or two and make a complete study of your heart function. By the way, how often have you been taking amphetamines?"

"Tonight was the first time in years, not many professional athletes take 'em. Team doctors are usually pretty strict about drugs. But the coaches and trainers see that they're available if you want 'em. It's the amateurs who really go for stimulants, from the Olympics right down to the Little League. Doctors sometimes even give bennies to their sons, when they're trying out for high school teams."

"I've seen several of those," said Mike. "Every time there's a tight series, we can count on having high school athletes and some college ones, too, in the Emergency Department half the night. We try to calm 'em down so they can go home and sleep it off but the really bad part comes when some football hero wins the game while he's high and takes his girl home—by way of the Florida Turnpike and West Palm Beach, at a hundred miles an hour. If the two of 'em are lucky, I spend a couple of hours later that night putting them back together, after the car hits a tree or another automobile. But a lot of 'em end up in the basement—under refrigeration."

"An athlete that takes drugs is only doing what's expected of him—so he figures why not?" said Joe Gates. "Take me, tonight: if I hadn't taken that last jump to try to get the ball, I might have finished out the game and been a hero. But now what do I have to look forward to?"

"A good night's rest from the hypo Miss Sundberg is waiting to give you," said Mike Raburn. "Turn over."

The needle was barely out before Joe Gates began to relax from the powerful dose of Demerol Mike had ordered. About thirty minutes later he roused up in the half-darkness when he felt the prick of a needle in his arm.

"Hey!" he mumbled. "Whatcha doin'?"

"Just a routine test, Mr. Gates." The technician was a vague figure in white. "You can go back to sleep now."

CHAPTER TWENTY-THREE

I

An hour after the initial incision, Ken Dalton stepped back from the table and washed his gloves in the sterile basin of water beside the operating table. During that hour Dale Tyndall's subclavian artery, by which blood was normally channeled to the right arm, had first been severed and the farther end tied off. Next the cut end nearest the heart had been connected to an opening Ken had made into the side of the pulmonary artery, the main blood supply to the lungs, above the constriction that had almost closed the artery even before Dale was born. Fortunately the body provided its own collateral arterial supply almost everywhere like backup circuits on a space capsule, so blood in an adequate amount still flowed to the arm, even though the main artery was no longer open.

Moving back to the table, Ken examined the rows of delicate sutures surrounding the new opening, and felt a warm sense of pride and satisfaction at the realization that they were as neatly placed and tied as any he'd ever done.

"I'm going to remove the clamps and test the suture line," he told Val LeMoyne.

"Good. He can use the extra oxygen."

Two clamps had blocked the arteries while Ken had been suturing the shunt. As he prepared to remove them, Ned Green's gloved left hand was poised above the operative field with a gauze sponge between his fingers, ready to stop any sudden geyser of blood that would have indicated a leak in the suture line. Ned's right hand held a lighted plastic spatula that had not only helped expose the small blood vessels Ken had been working on but also flooded the area with light.

Gingerly, Ken loosened the clamp that had occluded the channel of the cut subclavian artery. It slipped away easily and, when not even a drop of blood appeared along the suture line, he drew a deep sigh of relief. Dropping the forceps to the instrument table, he loosened the second clamp that had blocked the pulmonary artery and removed it, too. As he did, he could feel the rush of blood into a vessel that had never known an adequate flow before, while above the anastomosis the walls of the artery swelled with the surge of blood into the lungs and began to pulsate in rhythm with the beat of the small heart visible in the depths of the operative wound.

"There's no sign of leakage." No one could mistake the thrill of satisfaction in Ken's voice.

"The pO_2 has already started to rise and his color is distinctly better." Val LeMoyne looked around the small tent of draperies that separated her from the operative field. "May I say that it's nice to have the not-so-old master back on the job again? Welcome home, Doctor."

II

When Mike Raburn came into the ICU laboratory about nine-thirty, the night technician looked up from the microscope, where she had been studying a preparation of the blood she had removed from Joe Gates's veins on Mike's instructions.

"The preliminary Sickledex test is somewhat equivocal, Dr. Raburn," she reported. "It's positive in some forms of non-S hemoglobin besides the regular S-compound of sickle cell disease. Just to make sure I added some three-molar urea to one sample and ran two through the autoanalyzer simultaneously in order to measure the difference in light transmission between urea and non-urea Sickledex solutions."

"What's the verdict?" he asked.

"There's no question about it; Mr. Gates does *not* have either sickle cell disease or the trait."

In the doctors' office adjacent to the nursing station of the central ICU, Mike took a slip of paper from his pocket and dialed the number he'd written on it when he talked to Marcia Weston earlier. She answered, but sounded sleepy.

"I hope you hadn't gone to bed," he said.

"I usually get in bed by eight-thirty, when I'm not going out, and read or look at TV until after the eleven o'clock news, but that show you put on this morning was so exciting I was worn out. If you hadn't called I would probably have slept right through the eleven o'clock news and missed your segment."

"Joe Gates was brought to the hospital this evening—"

"I saw his accident on TV before I fell asleep. Was he injured badly?"

"It wasn't an injury. Joe's been under quite a strain lately, what with the owners in full cry after him and his son's close shave with a sickle cell crisis. He overexerted and had a spell of arrhythmia."

"That's tough."

"It may have been the best thing that could have happened for him and his family. Since the newspapers and other media started insinuating that he's the carrier of the sickling trait that almost got Joey, he's been convinced he has it and that his career is over. I hadn't even been able to get him to let me test his blood for sickle cell disease, but tonight I got a specimen under the guise of a routine admission test."

"That's interesting. What did you find?"

"The test proved absolutely that Joe has neither the sickling trait nor the disease."

"Then how did his son get it? Isn't sickle cell anemia hereditary?"

"Rachel, Joe's wife, is the carrier. I've already started prophylactic treatment and she shouldn't have any trouble—"

"You never fail to amaze me, Dr. Raburn. I think I'll ask the station to let me title the half-hour show we'll be putting together from those tapes we made this morning 'Superdoctor.'"

"I look more like King Kong," Mike chuckled. "But right now I'm more concerned about getting the truth that Joe absolutely does not have the sickle trait publicized as rapidly as possible, along with the fact that he's going to be okay. Is there any newsman on the eleven o'clock news I could depend on to broadcast that information?"

"Jim Long is sports director. He called the Snapper game tonight, so he'll also be doing the sports segment at eleven. I know he hasn't approved of this campaign that's been going on against Joe Gates and our station hasn't carried any of those editorials the owners of the team have been planting. The game's over by now, so you can call Jim at the station."

She gave him the telephone number and Mike jotted it down. When he hung up the telephone, he saw Helga looking at him across the counter separating the nursing station from the adjoining doctors' office.

"Sounds like you and the willowy Marcia have a thing going," she said. "Should I be jealous?"

"She wants to call me Superdoctor in the special they're doing on the TBW. How could I help loving her?"

"With those shoulders of yours, it's going to be awful close quarters changing into tights in phone booths."

Mike had been dialing the number Marcia Weston gave him. When he asked for Jim Long, a man with a deep voice he recognized from TV newscasts answered.

"This is Dr. Mike Raburn from Biscayne General."

"*The* Dr. Raburn? Superdoctor?"

"That's Marcia Weston's idea, not mine. If she goes through with it, the Medical Association will blacklist me for unethical publicity."

"From the little I saw of the tape Marcia and her crew made at the hospital this morning, you deserve the title, Dr. Raburn. What can I do for you?"

"I admitted Joe Gates earlier this evening—"

"One of our young floor reporters interviewed Dr. Vogel at the game. He said Joe should be all right with a day or two of rest and some sedation. We're going to run the interview with Dr. Vogel again on the eleven o'clock news. By the way, how is Joe?"

"Fine. Like Dr. Vogel told you, it was just a case of anxiety over Joey's illness and overexertion—"

"I think we can stop there, Doctor. I've seen enough of what happens to kids who get hopped up before high school games to know what really sent Joe's pulse skittering. But I'm pretty sure this was his first offense—"

"It was, at least since high school."

"So we'll not condemn him. But thanks for the information that Joe is okay—"

"If you'll help me, I'm sure we can settle this business the media have been pushing about Joe's having sickle cell disease," said Mike. "He wouldn't let me have the blood for a test before, because he was convinced that he's responsible for Joey's having it. But I sneaked up on him tonight and got a specimen. The test is absolutely negative, Joe Gates doesn't have a trace of the sickle cell trait—"

"Which means he couldn't have given it to his son or have it himself?" Jim Long sounded excited.

"There is absolutely no possibility that Joe Gates could ever have the disease or pass the trait to anyone."

"Do you mind if I quote you, Dr. Raburn?"

"If you think it's best."

"It's not only best, it's the best time in the world to lay to rest this ghost that's been haunting one of the finest athletes America has ever produced. Hold the phone while I get us connected to a tape recorder. We'll run your statement right after the segment on the miraculous operation you did on that girl this morning. If the public doesn't believe you after that, they won't believe anything."

"Isn't that featuring me a little too heavily?"

"You might as well face the fact that, as of this morning, you're the hottest news item in the medical sphere. With your authority behind it, a statement that Joe Gates is free of the sickle trait will have twice the punch it would otherwise have."

III

Ken Dalton telephoned Rebecca at her apartment just after ten o'clock. She'd gone there after Dale Tyndall, recovering rapidly from surgery and already conscious, had been taken to PICU by Val LeMoyne.

"I'm sorry to be late," he said.

"I hear you did a beautiful job on Dale."

"Dr. Alfred Blalock and Dr. Helen Taussig deserve the praise for working out that shunt idea at Johns Hopkins a long time ago. Can you meet me in the Dolphin Lounge in fifteen minutes, Reb? I want to ask you a couple of questions."

"Certainly, I didn't undress because you said you would call. Besides, I was busy with Joe Gates."

"See you there," he said. "Whichever of us is first can hold a table."

IV

Rebecca sat for a moment on the bed after cradling up the telephone, which was on a bedside table. She could feel the pulse beating more rapidly in her throat at the thought of what Ken's questions could mean, and wondered if she should let herself hope she already knew the answers. Then suddenly realizing that she was still wearing the sweater and skirt she customarily wore under the long white coat that was the working uniform of the medical school faculty—except the surgeons, who often wore operating suits, and the house staff in stiff white duck—she stood up and quickly peeled them off.

There was no time for a shower, so perfume and an anti-perspirant would have to suffice. But she did select a canary-yellow dress with a swing skirt she remembered he'd always particularly liked. Brushing her hair, putting on fresh make-up, and heightening the color of her lips a little more than the shade she customarily wore on duty, she took the elevator from the penthouse down to the ground floor of Bayside Terrace.

Ken was sitting at a table in the corner of the Dolphin Lounge when she came in. He got up and came across the room to take her hands.

"I'm glad you remembered that I always liked that dress," he told her. "You look lovely in it."

"Careful, or you'll turn my head with all this flattery. Don't forget that we're a couple of hard-working unemotional doctors."

"Maybe that was part of our trouble, Reb," he said as he seated her and took the chair across the small table from her. "We worked too hard and had too little time for emotion—among other things."

"There *were* other things. And I was just as guilty of them as you were, Ken, maybe more. I suppose when a husband and wife are pursuing careers in fields as closely related as our are, there's bound to be competition between them and I'm willing to admit that at times I carried it too far."

The waitress appeared with a bottle of Cold Duck surrounded with ice in a silver bucket and placed it on a corner of the table, with a pair of wineglasses.

"Shall I open the wine now, Dr. Dalton?" she asked.

"Just leave it and the opener, Evelyn," said Ken. "We'll have it a little later."

When the waitress was gone he turned back to Rebecca.

"I decided definitely tonight that I'm going to take that trip to San Francisco and Paris I've been thinking about," he said. "And I want you to go with me."

The suddenness of his words made her catch her breath, although this was what she had been hoping for. And for a moment, the tension in her throat kept her from speaking.

"I don't blame you for hesitating about resuming a relationship that brought you a lot of pain and unhappiness," he continued. "This probably isn't the right way to tell you I want us back together again either, and I know there's a long list of omissions and some commissions I should plead guilty to at the same time. But you can be sure of one thing, Reb: since I first fell in love with you that day, when you insisted on doing your own dissection in Anatomy I, there's never been anyone else."

"If there's anything in the world I'm sure of, darling, it's that." Rebecca found her voice at last. "And I guess when the two lists of misdeeds are totted up, mine is as long as yours."

"Then you'll go?"

"If Jeffry will give me the time off. How about you?"

"I've been a fixture around here for so many months, hardly anybody will miss me. By next week we ought to have a version of that plastic heart I stopped work on six months ago developed to a point where I can implant it in a calf out at the university's Animal Husbandry Department. Ed and Peggy can be checking it while we're gone; as I remember it, our passports are still in order, so we should be able to leave in ten days at the latest."

"I'll need clothes—"

"You can buy them in Paris. Maybe we can even spend a few days on a houseboat on the Seine."

Rebecca laughed. "Not dressed like we were most of the time in Florida Bay, I'm sure."

"This calls for a personal celebration," he said. "Shall I open the wine?"

Rebecca looked around the room, which was almost filled with people.

"Let's take it with us, darling," she said. "We've got a lovely penthouse that's certainly a lot more appropriate place than this for a private celebration."

V

At twenty minutes to eleven, Helga Sundberg was punching the orders for the eleven-to-seven shift into the computer data bank with the small hand-held keyboard when a light beside the monitor screen reporting the information coming into the main nursing station from the sensors on Carmelita Sanchez' body started flashing.

A quick glance at the screen itself told Helga none of the parameters being reported by light tracings across the ground-glass surface of the screen, or upon the recording meters at one side of the monitor, were abnormal. Pressing the communications switch, she spoke into the microphone beside her.

"Anything wrong, Helen?" she asked the nurse who was specialing Carmelita.

"Nothing wrong, Miss Sundberg. I think she's about to regain consciousness."

"I'll be right there."

Inside the narrow cubicle where Carmelita lay, Helga turned up the light and leaned over to lift an eyelid. The girl's skin was already perceptibly lighter in color than it had been that morning, further proof of the sharp decrease in the concentration of bile pigments in her blood achieved during the nine climactic minutes of the TBW.

The pupil of the lovely dark eye contracted immediately from the light and Carmelita tried to move her head to escape the stimulus upon her retina. One arm was held down by the intravenous catheter through which fluid and glucose were dripping into her body, but with the other she reached up and tried to push Helga's hand away.

When the blonde nurse pressed upon one temple with her thumb, causing a mild pain stimulus, the sleeping girl opened her eyes and grimaced, frowning slightly as she stared at Helga. Her lips moved too, but the sound was so faint that neither Helga nor the younger nurse could distinguish the word she spoke, until she tried a second time—and whispered, "Miguel."

"Do you know where her fiancé is?" Helga asked.

"He was in here ten minutes or so ago. Said he was going down to the Coffee Shop."

"I'll call Dr. Raburn and see if I can get Miguel too. They'll both want to be here for this.

"Please page Dr. Raburn and have him call the ICU," Helga told the telephone operator when she returned to the nursing station.

Mike called back in a few minutes. "What's up?" he asked.

"Carmelita seems to be coming out of coma. I thought you'd want to know."

"You'd better alert the family, if any of them are there."

"Miguel Quintera's in the Coffee Shop. The rest of them went home."

"I'm on the ground floor," said Mike. "I'll bring Miguel up with me."

As Helga hung up the telephone, she heard the door of the ward open and saw the shadow of someone going into the ICU waiting room. Moving to the door she saw Miguel Quintera in the act of picking up a magazine.

"Carmelita seems to be regaining consciousness," she told him. "I thought you'd want to be with her when she awakens."

The young Cuban's dark-skinned face lit up like that of a pilgrim who has just witnessed a miracle. "I—I" Words failed him.

"Go on into the cubicle," Helga told him. "She spoke your name just now, so she may awaken at any moment. I'll wait for Dr. Raburn."

Helga had just finished punching the orders for the eleven-to-seven shift into the computer when Mike Raburn came into the main ICU and stopped at the nursing station.

"You bet me she'd regain consciousness before you went off duty," he said. "What did you do? Give her a shot of psychic energizer?"

"I live right—and usually win my bets."

Miguel Quintera started to his feet when Mike came into the small cubicle, but the broad-shouldered doctor waved him to his chair.

"Any more signs of consciousness?" Mike asked the student nurse, but she shook her head.

"Not yet, Doctor," she said. "At least nothing we could be sure of."

"Maybe a little oxygen would help bring her out. Hand me the mask and breathing bag, please."

Taking the oxygen mask and bag from the hook where it was hanging, Helga opened the valve to the main oxygen system and the bubbles started flowing in the water bottle that allowed the flow to be visualized and measured. Mike let the bag fill, then put the mask over Carmelita's mouth and nose and opened the small valve that let the stream of gas flow from the bag into her lungs.

For perhaps a dozen breaths nothing happened, then the Cuban girl opened her eyes and reached up with her free hand to push the mask away. Closing the valve between mask and breathing bag, Mike removed the mask from her face and nodded to Helga to shut off the main supply.

Carmelita looked around dazedly but did not close her eyes again.

"Why don't you stand on the other side of the bed?" Mike said to Miguel Quintera. "She can see you better there."

When the young Cuban came within the girl's range of vision, the response was immediate. A happy smile broke over Carmelita's face. Her lips moved too and this time they had no trouble distinguishing the words they spoke.

"Miguel!" she cried. *"Querido mio!"*

"This is Dr. Raburn, Carmelita," Miguel managed to say. "He saved your life."

The girl seemed not to hear, however; all her senses were tuned to the single fact of her fiancé's presence and her happiness because of it. She reached out her hand and, when Miguel took it, pulled him down to kiss her. And when she released him, tears were streaming from Quintera's eyes.

"God will surely bless you, Dr. Raburn," he said brokenly. "You have given her back to me."

Turning without speaking, Mike left the room and Helga followed. But when he started to leave the ward, she touched his arm.

"Why don't you watch the eleven o'clock news on the TV in the staff lounge?" she said. "Maybe I can finish the report in time to watch your part of it with you."

"I'd forgotten all about it," he admitted, but turned into the small lounge. "I guess I'm just a sentimental slob after all," he admitted as he poured a cup of coffee for himself from the urn there. "The way those two love each other sort of got to me."

"It should happen to me that way." Helga's voice was a little husky as she left the small lounge for the nursing station.

And she could just as well have added: "I'm quite sure it has."

VI

"You're just in time to see the debut of 'Superdoctor,'" said Mike when Helga came back into the lounge. "If you laugh, I'll slug you."

"I still think you ought to wear tights." She settled down on a hassock beside him and, when his hand groped for hers, wasn't at all surprised to discover how comfortable her slender fingers felt with his much larger ones around them. The brief scenes from the morning's drama had been well chosen; they covered most of the climactic minutes while the blood was being washed from Carmelita's veins and replaced with a fresh supply.

"I'll call Marcia Weston at the station tomorrow morning and tell her they can come out any time and tape the wrap-up, now that Carmelita is conscious," said Mike.

"With her fiancé beside her, it will go over big in Little Havana, when it's time to vote on the Hospital Authority referendum."

"They make a handsome pair."

"Miguel's going to take Carmelita back to Spain with him," she said. "He told me about it this afternoon."

"She may not be ready to go very soon."

"I told him that. He says if she isn't he's going to skip a year and work in the hospital."

The news closed with Jim Long's story about Joe Gates and Mike's taped statement exploding the accusations that Joe was a carrier of the sickling trait. As the closing commercial was coming on, Mary Pearson came to the door of the lounge.

"A flash just came over the grapevine from the Dolphin Lounge," she said. "Dr. Ken and Dr. Rebecca have taken the elevator to her penthouse."

"*Their* penthouse," said Helga.

"I guess you're right at that, they were carrying a bottle of Cold Duck in a silver bucket."

Helga looked at her watch. "It's eleven-thirty. Looks like Gus Henderson isn't going to make the deadline I gave him, so I might as well go home."

"I'll make sure you get there safely," Mike told her. "Besides, you haven't told me how we're going to celebrate the success of the TBW."

At the front door to the hospital, they took the walk heading to Bayside Terrace and the Dolphin Lounge. But where the graveled walk debouched toward the apartment hotel, Mike took Helga's arm and guided her along a winding side path that ended on the bulkhead marking the bay.

"Did you really think Gus would come?" They were standing on the bulkhead but neither was looking at the bright wall of lights marking the Miami Beach hotels across the bay.

"Not after he didn't jump at the knowledge that I could tell him how to join Carolyn." Helga looked up at the sky where an airplane, homing in from the sea for the airport almost directly west of the hospital tower, angled downward, its running lights blinking rhythmically. "Poor Carolyn," she said. "She's going to be lonely in Brazil."

Mike looked at her quickly. "Then it really was Carolyn—not you?"

Helga nodded. "I thought I would die those five minutes or so she was in her father's room, wondering whether one of the other nurses would come back early from dinner and find Carolyn there."

"I saw Sam Toyota just before you called me for Carmelita," said Mike. "He told me they weren't able to find a thing to justify any charge against Carolyn."

"Does that mean there won't be any prosecution?"

"To prosecute for murder, you need a *corpus delicti*, with medical proof of the cause of death. Broadhurst has the body, but not the proof, so he can't do anything."

"I wonder what the verdict will be here in the hospital."

"I'd say most people will believe Carolyn engineered her father's death, but I doubt if many who knew her well will hold it against her. Do you think she'll come back?"

"I hope she doesn't—not for quite a while," said Helga. "With Gus feeling as resentful as he does, what was between them has to be at an end and she'll get over it a lot quicker with two thousand-odd miles between them. Besides, Carolyn is the sort of girl who needs to be needed and down there she will be. Promise me something, darling—that someday we'll fly down to see her. It's a lovely place."

"Of course we will," he assured her. "Now tell me how her father's death was really accomplished."

"I can't, Mike."

"Why?"

"That would make you an access—" She broke off as he reached into her pocket and took out the large needle he'd picked up from the floor of Richard Payson's cubicle when he stooped down several hours before, ostensibly to tie his shoe. The rays of a floodlight shining through the fronds of a palm near where they were standing were reflected from the metal as he threw it far out into the bay where it struck the water with the faintest of plops and disappeared.

"Now I *am* an accessory," he told her. "So give.

"I thought that must be the way it was done," he said when she finished.

"Mr. Broadhurst would have had a case, wouldn't he, if I hadn't made the mistake of using the pacemaker and driving the heart to contract immediately and disperse all the oxygen throughout the body, where it would be absorbed into the tissues?"

"Mistake, hell!" Mike chuckled. "The minute I saw it, I told myself Helga wouldn't choose a pacemaker instead of the CPR that's SOP in a standstill arrest—unless there was a reason. And when I really looked for it, there was the presumptive proof—at least—in a poorly coiled oxygen tube."

"Which you promptly fixed so no one could tell it had been used," said Helga softly. "Why?"

"I couldn't let you go to jail as an accessory." He pretended indignation. "Have you forgotten that you're committed to helping me celebrate a successful TBW this weekend?"

"I hadn't forgotten. But—"

"You also promised to tell me what we're going to do."

"I had in mind a weekend on Grand Bahama; there's a plane out at five o'clock every Friday afternoon and we could have been there in time for dinner." She turned and put her hands on his arms in a pleading gesture. "Would you believe I've got cold feet?"

"I believe it," he said. "Because I was getting them myself."

"I can't come to you a virgin, Mike; they're pretty scarce nowadays. But I don't want us to start our life together as if it were a casual affair."

"There's an answer," he said, and his voice assured her that everything was going to be all right.

"Tell me, Mike—"

"A boat leaves Palm Beach late every afternoon for Grand Bahama; if we drive up tomorrow afternoon, we can make it. The ship crosses international waters, too, even though the trip only takes a few hours, so the captain could marry us. Are you game?"

"Thank you, darling." She slipped her arms around him and kissed him. "And since we're being so square, let's spend our two-day honeymoon at the Holiday Inn. There's a big one on Grand Bahama."

Sword and Scalpel

THE PRESIDIO

I

Larry Kirk was having trouble with his lead. For the first time in years the ace television commentator faced his typewriter with a mind empty as a cave whence even the bats had fled.

In the past hour he had tried all his pump primers; he had even resorted to automatic writing, a leftover from his last analysis. (*Face it Kirk whoever taught you to type should be drawn and quartered you cautious timeserver why not do something useful with those fat white hands besides coaxing half-truths out of these too-facile keys.*) The flash of self-contempt had been easily conquered. Ten minutes ago he had used the oldest of his self-starters—the summary, the reduction of an unanswered question to its essence.

He read that summary over now, while the wall clock in his Radio City office ticked on, reminding him that he had just thirty-five minutes to air time. It made a neat block of type in the center of an empty page:

> Tomorrow, in San Francisco's Presidio, Captain Paul
> Scott of the Army Medical Corps, fresh from two
> years in a Chinese prisoner-of-war camp, faces court-
> martial for treason. *How* it happened is a question all
> too easily answered: everyone is familiar with the
> techniques of the enemy brainwashers. The burning
> question is *why*.

Why, this fall of 1953, when thousands of American prisoners in North Korea had come back untouched by the Communist evil, had Captain Paul Scott yielded? Why, after what seemed only routine persuasion, had he signed another of those grotesque statements accusing the United Nations forces of germ warfare? A copy of the statement, with Scott's signature, was in the possession of the judge advocate. Why, then, did Scott refuse to plead guilty, to make a coherent statement for the press—even to produce a single witness in his behalf?

Who, what, when and *where,* reflected Larry, had always been easy to handle: life had been far less demanding when he had been only a simple newspaperman. *Why* was a harder nut to crack. Tonight (while maintaining the fair-minded pose for which his program was famous), it was essential that he give some valid cause for Scott's defection—just as it was essential that he make some estimate of the court-martial's outcome. His public would expect as much.

Larry did not doubt for a moment that this quixotic young doctor in uniform would be found guilty—or that the Army court would exact the maximum punishment. The *why* persisted, irritating as a cocklebur on the surface of his brain. Until he had banished the irritant, Larry knew that a well-disciplined talent (which usually ground out these daily TV broadcasts with ease) would continue to stumble in the dark.

He ripped the summary from his typewriter and ran in a fresh sheet. Overhead the clock ticked on in tune with his frightened heart. What would happen if he faced the network cameras tonight (and an audience estimated at forty million Americans) without a script?

For once, he told himself, you're the victim of your own pride, your insistence that you be given your head each weekday at nine. *The program that you are about to hear is unrehearsed and unedited. The opinions of international newshawk Larry Kirk are his own, exactly as they have emerged from Larry's battered old portable.* For the past year, thanks to his whopping Trendex rating, the boast of Larry's sponsors had been almost literally true. . . . Of course, there was no way of shutting off the sponsor's occasional phone call.

Earlier that evening, when Larry had talked long distance to old Herman Bowers (the president of Bowers Brewery), his backer had foamed as industriously as his product.

"What are you saying about Scott?"

"I haven't quite decided, H.B."

"Hit that Commie, Larry. Give him hell. He should go to the gas chamber."

"I can't condemn him before his trial."

"Why not? Men like Scott are America's number-one menace; exterminating them is our number-one problem. Help your listeners to see that. You always have."

"H.B., the whole country is howling for his head. Are you suggesting I make it unanimous?"

"Larry, when *you* say a man is dead he stays dead. I want you to bury this traitor."

"I'm sorry, H.B.—but I've no idea what I'll say at this moment. I will promise you to say something." ·

"You had better. Why else are we flying you to Frisco tomorrow?"

Larry Kirk had hung up then. He could still applaud his own courage. . . .

Glancing at the wall clock one more time, he spread his notes. There was no reason for panic. After all (as a world traveler), he had a personal image of Captain Paul Scott to offer his public. Even at their first meeting in Korea he had noticed something queer about the fellow—a quality of strain, a brooding intentness that defied such catchall labels as battle fatigue. In his way the young doctor with the haunted eyes had seemed as much an offhorse as his battalion chaplain, the mystic the GIs called Father Tim. . . . At the time, Larry had sensed that the two men shared a credo they could never reveal to ordinary mortals—least of all to a famous figure from the television world.

> Two years ago I interviewed Dr. Paul Scott in his surgical-aid station on the Korean front only a short time before his capture. I found him brilliant, overwrought—and profoundly dubious as to his own future or the future of humanity. I also interviewed Father Timothy O'Fallon, the chaplain of the battalion—who said little to enlighten me on the cause of Scott's mental turmoil. Later, in Seoul, I talked to Kay Storey, the USO entertainer who planned to marry him. To her, he was also an enigma—and, in her own words, an enigma even to himself.

> Today the enigma remains. Why would a Johns Hopkins alumnus, a surgeon with a brilliant record and a clear-cut future before him, prefer capture by the North Korean forces to a dash for liberty with his own outfit? Why did he begin to collaborate with

those captors almost from the first moment? How, in
short, could he commit this outrage against his
conscience, his country, and his God?

The surface facts (as Colonel Jasper Hardin, the
battalion commander relates them) are simple.

Captain Scott's defection began when he elected to
remain behind in the medical bunker on Hill 1049, a
position which Colonel Hardin was forced to evacuate
under enemy pressure. The colonel ordered Captain
Scott to join the retreat: the medical officer refused to
obey. Others who refused to obey the order were two
medics under Scott's command, Kay Storey, the above-
mentioned USO entertainer (who had been trapped
there while on a front-line tour), and Chaplain
O'Fallon.

Despite their attempt to fight their way to freedom,
Colonel Hardin and those of his men who survived
were pinned on the slopes of Hill 1049 and forced to
join the march of other prisoners to the North
Korean rear. Their destination was a concentration
camp near Pyongyang. En route, the colonel states, he
encountered Scott and his group—in the courtyard of
a farm outside the town of Sinmak. Though Dr. Scott
and his party had the status of prisoners, says
Colonel Hardin, they were well fed and specially
favored. That night Scott's group slept on dry beds in
the barn. The colonel and his officers were forced to
bivouac in the open in a driving rainstorm.

Larry Kirk paused long enough to note the time on the wall clock: already
that malignant timepiece seemed to tick at a faster tempo. His fingers
resumed their dance on the typewriter keyboard:

In the prison compound at Pyongyang, as Colonel
Hardin relates it, Dr. Scott took over the camp
hospital, where he ministered to guards and
prisoners alike, and received the same food as the
Chinese doctors, who were soon taking his orders.
Later when he put down an epidemic of meningitis
his favors increased. During the last months of the
war he saved the life of the camp commandant in a
daring operation. Dr. Scott's signing of a (quote)
confession (unquote) that his country had waged
bacterial warfare in Korea, said Colonel Hardin, was
the logical climax of a long collaboration.

That, Larry reflected, was only half the wrap-up. Scott's court-martial
would be on every front page tomorrow and stay there for its course. His
broadcast needed something beyond the surface facts—a sinister chord or

two that would make a natural carry-over to his next TV appearance, in San Francisco, after the opening of the trial.

> The part that Father Timothy O'Fallon, the battalion chaplain, played in Dr. Scott's surrender to the evil we call world Communism must remain a puzzling mystery. Father Tim lies in a cemetery outside Pyongyang: he cannot appear at the Presidio tomorrow as a witness.

> Once again, the facts are simple. When the war ended this July, Father Tim was ill in the prison-camp hospital: when Colonel Hardin prepared to lead the others to their repatriation Captain Scott insisted on remaining at the chaplain's bedside. Weeks later, long after Father O'Fallon's death, this lonely and controversial doctor was finally sent to an exchange point in the neutral zone.

> A final element of mystery remains, the role of the USO entertainer Kay Storey, famous as "The Girl Next Door," a singing part that took her into Army camps all over South Korea. As we have said, Miss Storey was captured on Hill 1049 and went with the others to Pyongyang; she was a prisoner there until July when she departed under the protection of Colonel Hardin.

> Until then it was rumored that she and Scott would marry at the war's end: neither will confirm that story today. Miss Storey will soon begin work on a motion picture, an Eric Lindman production, highlighting her own adventures as a prisoner and as "The Girl Next Door." Since she will not be called as a witness for her alleged fiance, so far as we could learn tonight, it would seem that a romance, if one existed, is now a thing of yesterday.

> When the court-martial opens tomorrow Colonel Hardin will be the chief witness for the prosecution. Technicians, aides and noncoms who were fellow prisoners will also testify. Hilary Saunders, the well-known Hollywood lawyer and a former artillery captain in Korea, will undertake Dr. Scott's defense. Mr. Saunders plans to call no witnesses besides the defendant himself, since none are available.

Larry Kirk lifted his fingers from the keys. Perhaps the package is wrapped too neatly, he thought. It's quite likely that you've stretched your reputation for fairness to the breaking point. Tonight you'll be telling forty million patriots what they want to hear.

II

A continent away, Hilary Saunders glared at the rented television in his hotel parlor, then rose to kill the program. It was a gesture that destroyed commentator Larry Kirk's statesmanlike profile and Larry's resonant baritone in the same satisfying flash.

Because of the time lag between New York and San Francisco it was still daylight on Nob Hill—but Hi Saunders had been working behind drawn blinds since early afternoon, when the day had begun to boil with fog. It had always been his custom to closet himself thus the day before he took a vital case to court. The hotel desk was cluttered with the weapons of the successful trial lawyer—lawbooks and ancient briefs, a much-marked copy of the Army *Manual of Courts-Martial*, the toy donkey he kept for luck because the face reminded him of a long-dead judge who had almost, but not quite, disbarred him years ago. The air was blue with the cheap cigars Hi smoked when he was really working and had no one to impress but himself.

His suite was high in the Mark Hopkins: merely by opening the blinds of his picture window, he could have inhaled some of the finest ozone in the western world. . . . God knows the brain could stand airing, he reflected— though he made no move to relax his feline crouch above his work. It was a greater relief to glare back at the vacant eye of the TV and curse Larry Kirk as he deserved.

Not that Hi was surprised by the broadcast; like other ex-liberals he had known at Harvard, Larry had simply grown more cautious as his age, and his income, increased. Nowadays, Hi realized, his former classmate usually bayed with the wolf pack whenever a new victim appeared. Paul Scott, in short, had been tried and convicted by his fellow countrymen well in advance of his formal court-martial. As unofficial foreman of that vast jury, Larry Kirk had just summed up the reasons for the verdict.

Though he was not under formal arrest, Paul had been confined to the Presidio for his trial. Yielding to impulse, Hi picked up his phone and rang the Bachelor Officers' Quarters.

Paul was a long time coming to the phone.

"Don't tell me you were *asleep?*" the lawyer barked.

"Sorry, Hi. Tonight I thought I'd turn in early."

"Didn't I tell you to watch Kirk's broadcast?"

"I'm afraid it slipped my mind."

"I'll give you odds the judge advocate tuned in. The whole country was waiting to see which way Kirk would jump."

"You'll have to forgive me, Hi. Today I figured I'd done my good deed."

Hi Saunders scowled at the phone: he had expected this. "You've seen Kay?"

"We've just had dinner. She's promised to stay clear."

Weeks ago when Kay Storey had begged him to put her on the stand Hi had refused—because Paul had expected his refusal. There had been some point to Paul's attitude. Major James MacArdle (the able lawyer whom the judge advocate had appointed as trial counsel) would have welcomed Kay's appearance as a defense witness—and would have proceeded to tear her apart. Yet Hi had not expected Paul to take her withdrawal this calmly.

"Won't you feel a bit lonely when court opens?"

"Loneliness is a cross we must all bear, Hi; it's one of the first things Father Tim taught me."

"What does it take to get you really mad, Paul?"

"Kay deserves her career. Lindman has one ready-made for her. It would ruin her chances if she stood up for me in court. Why should she be tarred with the same brush, when it won't help win my acquittal?"

"Someone's got to stand up for you, Paul."

"Say what you mean, Hi. Do you think I'm guilty?"

The lawyer dodged the question neatly. "Tomorrow that seven-man court will sit with its collective mind made up. Our job is to change it. My work would be easier if I had one witness beside yourself."

"We can't call Father Tim." Paul's voice had the same baffling note of calm. "From the start we agreed to keep Kay out of it."

"We'd have a stronger case if your girl went to bat. Even if she only struck out."

"Sorry, Hi—I've just sent her back to Lindman."

"What about your marriage plans?"

"We can hardly think of marriage if I draw ten years in Leavenworth."

Paul Scott's voice had never risen above an easy monotone. When he hung up the phone Hi reflected that his friend had seemed remote as an anchorite in his cell. Remembering the Paul he had known in the lines at Korea, he could wonder once again at the spell Father Tim had cast—if that was what really had happened.

True, Paul's reason for keeping Kay out of the witness box was excellent—for Kay. In Korea, as "The Girl Next Door," she had been the USO's prime drawing card. Her chance to star in pictures now seemed made to order—especially with a self-confessed genius like Eric Lindman to direct her. There was no denying the wisdom of her withdrawal—Paul had been downright noble to suggest it.

As Paul's lawyer, Hi could wish that his client had been a trifle less unselfish. Not that the omission was fatal, not that there wasn't time to rectify it if things went against them tomorrow. Hi, who knew his man all too well, had demanded carte blanche before he had agreed to undertake Paul's defense: he could summon Kay to the stand on his own if her presence there seemed vital.

So far—aside from their shared ordeal at the concentration camp—Hi had not tried to plumb the relationship of Kay Storey and his client. Unraveling the emotional life of Paul Scott was outside his province; fighting for his acquittal would be chore enough. The lawyer sighed and returned to the mass of notes before him.

Cross-examinations tomorrow would be routine, he told himself; it would be wiser to forego an opening statement unless Jim MacArdle indulged in his usual rhetoric. Paul's own strategy would be impossible to plan in detail until Major MacArdle showed his hand. His reason for each act at the prison camp had its own logic, including the farce of the confession. It was unfortunate that these reasons would have a hollow ring when spoken by the defendant himself. Or that—item by item—he could do no more than match Paul's word against the sworn indictment of Colonel Jasper Hardin, his commanding officer.

In the moment before his mind meshed with the task before him, Hi wondered if Captain Paul Scott had foreseen the depths of his peril—if he meant to stand (or fall) on his own testimony. Was it possible that he was courting martyrdom, for a reason that had meaning to him alone?

III

Ten stories above Hi Saunders' suite, at a window table in the Top of the Mark, Kay Storey faced Eric Lindman with a look that almost—but not quite—approached trust.

"I suppose I've lost the argument," she said.

"You can still admit it gracefully," the man in dark glasses murmured softly.

"So you're suggesting I come back to you—just like that?"

"Just like that," said Eric Lindman. "With Scott out of your life—for keeps."

"Only he isn't out. He'll never be."

"At least he's being sensible—where you're concerned."

"Let's be clear on one thing, Eric. Tonight I told Paul I'd stay away from the trial—because he *wanted* it that way. If things go against him I can still change my mind."

"Suppose I won't let you change it?"

Kay studied her escort under half-lowered lids. Save for the conventional glasses and a certain imperial air there was little of the Hollywood wonder boy in Eric Lindman. His white dinner coat came from the best tailor on Savile Row, and his accent, like his table manners, was a thing of beauty. At first glance he could have passed for a distinguished bird of prey in any field. What's more, the concern in his tone was quite genuine.

"So my career comes first," she said.

"I said as much the day you shipped overseas. It's time you believed me."

"Suppose I'd flopped on that USO tour, Eric. Would we be sitting here tonight?"

"Of course not," said Lindman cheerfully. "The point is, you succeeded."

I *have* succeeded, the girl thought; I found myself in Korea, in a way you'll never understand. "Aren't you being kinder than I deserve?" she asked.

"I've never been kind in my life," said Eric. "You should know by now that I use people and expect to be used in return. Right now opportunity is knocking for us both—providing you watch your step."

"And stay clear of Paul Scott's court-martial?"

"Scott knows he's guilty. That's why he's kept you out of it."

"He isn't pleading guilty."

"He's guilty as charged, darling. So far, you haven't said a word to change my mind."

"I haven't tried, Eric. I promised Hi Saunders not to discuss the case."

"What defense does he have? The facts speak for themselves."

Kay listened in silence while Eric went over his version of the Paul Scott case. It was the judgment the country had long since made—from the moment the story broke with Colonel Jasper Hardin's famous (and completely damning) interview. Kay admitted that Eric was presenting it brilliantly—but then, everything that Eric Lindman did was brilliant.

An opportunist from the word go, she thought. And yet, Eric was an authentic genius, as the word is used in pictures. A creator who could smell a trend before it had taken shape and dramatize its essence with the touch of the born showman. Why else would he plan to star her in a movie called *The Girl Next Door?*

"This court-martial will be Scott's funeral, and he's stuck with it," said

Eric. "The fact that your paths crossed in Korea is a coincidence we'll both ignore."

"We can't ignore Paul."

"We already have—at his own request. You aren't being disloyal, Kay— you're just being yourself. *The Girl Next Door.* Even the title was made to order."

The Girl Next Door. It was true that she stood on the threshold of a dream tonight—a dream that could easily become a shining reality tomorrow, thanks to Eric's magic. She felt the tears start behind her eyelids as she admitted how little that dream meant now. Nothing really mattered tonight but the fact that Paul Scott needed her help and had refused it.

"I'm still going to marry him," Kay said defiantly, "the minute this trial is over."

Eric shook his head. "Scott isn't buying that, darling. He told me as much this afternoon—by phone."

"You asked Paul—about us?" Kay wondered why she was not more indignant.

"Certainly. I had to know—for sure—before I put your picture in work."

"Are there *any* facts about me you don't have on file, Eric?"

"An hour ago," said the producer, "you went to the Presidio, full of self-sacrifice. But you met your match in Dr. Paul Scott. Believe me, *he* knows the score. There's no room for wives in an Army stockade."

The voice was gentle, with no hint of Eric's usual mockery. The fingers that closed on her hand were gentle too—but there was a reminder in their pressure that Eric (no less than Paul) had certain claims on her future. . . . Kay took up her glass and stared down at the pattern of San Francisco.

"You're giving a good imitation of Satan," she said. "The Top of the Mark will do nicely for a mountain. There's even an excuse to salve my pride. After all, why shouldn't I come back to the studio—if the man I love won't have me?"

"I knew you'd see the point, darling. All you needed was time."

"Hi may still put me on the stand."

"Show your face in that courthouse, Kay, and you're a dead pigeon in Hollywood."

"Suppose I don't care?"

"You've got to care. Day after tomorrow I'll make you a star. And you're going to jump at the chance. It would be un-American not to."

"Maybe I'm more than just an American. Father Tim taught us to be citizens of the world in that prison camp."

"Darling," said Lindman, "sometimes you baffle even me. And I know you better than most."

"You *knew* me, Eric—before I went to Korea."

"Who was this Father Tim really? Some kind of archangel in khaki?"

"He was as lonely—and as frightened—as the greenest soldier in that camp." Kay shook her head slowly—there was really no way to make Eric understand, but she tried, regardless. "You see, he taught us a lesson we'll never forget—that men must help one another, even when they are enemies."

"Is that why Scott operated on the camp commandant?"

"It was one of the reasons. I *said* I can't discuss the case, Eric."

He shrugged. "Fair enough. Now we've agreed on that much—when are you coming to the studio for your tests? We can't start rolling too soon. . . ."

Letting the producer's voice go on, vaguely soothed by the sincerity of his praise, Kay let her mind go back to the moment of farewell in the lounge of the Bachelor Officers' Quarters. She had stood eye-to-eye with Paul as they went through the solemn farce of good-by; she could hear his quiet pleading before she had promised to put him from her mind forever. . . . Of course she had no intention of keeping that promise. Even so, the tears had blinded her when she stumbled into a taxi and drove to this date with Eric. The selflessness that Paul had shown tonight, she thought, is not of this world.

"Are you listening, darling?"

She came back painlessly to what Eric was saying. After all, it was Hi Saunders, not his client, who would have the last word in the conduct of this trial.

"Of course I heard you, Eric. I quite agree that you can't wait to start shooting—"

If she seemed to accept the wonder boy with those ambiguous words, no real harm was done. Once more Kay Storey leaned back in her chair and let her eyes rove across San Francisco Bay: Eric's voice had enveloped her in a soothing cocoon, and she was reluctant to stir.

And yet, curiously enough, it was not the image of stardom that formed in her mind's eye. Nor was it the memory of Paul, now that her tears for his obstinacy were behind her . . . it was Father Tim she saw tonight, exactly as she remembered him from that hell-camp outside Pyongyang—and the image on the screen of memory was indeed an archangel in khaki.

IV

Colonel Jasper Hardin had been leaving the Presidio at the moment when Kay summoned a taxi at the gate. He recognized her purely by accident; as a good strategist should, he jumped into a second cab and ordered the driver to keep her in view; the fact that their destinations were the same tonight had seemed a happy stroke of fate.

Now, seated with his own companion in a wall divan at the Top of the Mark, Hardin could rejoice again at his good fortune. It was a pleasure he had not mentioned to the pretty, rather sharp-faced girl who shared his table. Nonetheless he found himself rumbling with laughter as he downed his fourth highball of the evening.

"What's so funny, Jasper?"

"Sorry, Gloria—it wouldn't interest you."

"Try me. You've been dreadfully silent tonight."

"That's because I've things to mull over. It isn't easy, being Nemesis."

"Nemesis?"

"Exactly—even when the victim deserves extermination."

"Doesn't it help to unburden yourself?"

"Naturally—in the right company. That's why I asked you out tonight." He gave his drinking companion an appraising glance, pleased to note that she had colored just a bit under his proprietary eyes. "Switch on your TV tomorrow if you want the details."

"I *hoped* you'd tell me just a little tonight," she pouted. "After all, you're the one with the inside story."

Hardin's eye roved again toward Lindman's table: he saw that the producer had just covered Kay Storey's hand a second time. He felt all the thrill of a Peeping Tom on his first mission. Lindman's after her again, he gloated. For once, the gossip columns are right.

"Can't you tell me the joke, Bunny?"

He looked sternly at Gloria. "I've asked you not to call me that, my dear. Especially in public."

"Tonight, you have your line-officer look," said Gloria. "You pulled the

same face when they took that photo in Tokyo. You know, right after you
escaped from Korea—"

"I didn't *escape*, damn it. I was repatriated—after the armistice."

"Don't use such big words, Jasper. You still looked mighty pleased with
yourself. I wondered why."

"Can't a man rejoice when he finds there's justice in the world?"

Kay Storey was Scott's last prop, he told himself. If she had remained
loyal, it's possible the court would ponder its verdict; a man with a friend at
the judge's bench is always more important than a man alone. Now, Hardin
knew, he didn't have to worry any more. Lindman would never spend an
evening with Kay Storey (in the most famous of Frisco night spots) if she
had not already agreed to abandon Scott to his fate.

"He can't escape us now," said Hardin. "We've dead-ended him at last."

"What did Captain Scott do, Jasper? And try not to shout."

"Don't you read the papers?"

"Why should I—when you explain them so beautifully?"

That pouting smile had entranced Hardin before; tonight he had the
obscure conviction that Gloria (who was not half so stupid as she
pretended) was baiting him. Yet she was an audience—and, as such,
deserved an answer.

"I'll tell you what I can't forgive Scott for," he said. "He made me
afraid."

"I can't imagine *you* afraid of anything."

The mirror above the facing wall booth assured Hardin that Gloria's
compliment was sincere. Tonight in his dress pinks he was every inch the
soldier—and the row of ribbons on his breast had been earned to the last
combat star.

"I know it's hard to picture," he said. "But the ordeal of battle isn't the
worst thing we fellows must suffer. The fear a scoundrel like Scott inspires is
far worse—"

"*Why*, Bunny?"

"Because it goes deeper. Beyond good and evil as we can grasp them. Into
the night of the soul, where Communism is bred—" Hardin paused and
wondered what editorial he was quoting. "So far, the firing squad is our
only defense against Scott—or the court-martial, if we're not at war. Yet
what can death accomplish, or a prison stockade, if the poison's done its
work?"

"But what did he *do?*"

"That, my dear, is the sort of ignorance that makes the poison potent.
Didn't you read how he refused to leave his bunker on Hill 1049 when I
gave him a direct order? Or how I slept in the rain at Sinmak while he
wallowed in a dry billet?"

"Yes, Jasper. Is that all?"

"It's only the beginning. At the concentration camp he saved a hundred
Commie lives—my master sergeant kept the score. He operated on Colonel
Pak—the prison commander—when the whole camp wanted Pak to die. He
swore that our troops used bacteria bombs. When the repatriation order
came he wouldn't budge. In God's name, girl, what does it take to rouse
you?"

"Can you prove that Captain Scott was a Communist? Suppose he tells a
different story at the trial?"

"He will—rely on that. I know the shyster who's defending him. It
wouldn't surprise me if they were two of a kind."

"Don't they hear both sides at a court-martial?"

Gloria, thought Hardin, could be infuriating at times. As he felt his
temper boil up he considered walking out on her—until he reminded himself

that she had already proved an expensive luxury and he would be a fool not to enjoy his investment fully.

"Of course they'll hear both sides," he said. "Traitors get a fair trial here—that's where we differ from our enemies."

"I'm glad of that, Jasper."

"Stop acting like a fool," he snapped. "Scott's confession is on the record—and I've witnesses to back up every point I just made. Men who *saw* him behave like a turncoat—and a mutineer. No matter what he's cooked up with Saunders, it's his word against ours. The chaplain's dead. As you can see right now, Scott's girl has walked out on him—"

"Are you sure?"

"Would Lindman touch her with a ten-foot pole if she hadn't?"

"Have it your way, Bunny. I was only trying to get your story straight."

"It'll be clear enough tomorrow. The judge advocate expects a verdict in two days—" Hardin bit the prophecy short (he had been given that estimate in secret). "I've said too much now," he grumbled. "Let's get out of here."

"Anything you say, Bunny."

Hardin lurched just a little when he rose, but the mirrored walls gave back a dozen hero images, creating the illusion that he was larger than life. He forced steadiness into his gait and stared with a cold martial aloofness at each face he encountered in the treacherous march to the elevator. The slight testiness he had felt at the table melted rapidly as he continued to pick up envious looks from other tables. Now that he had forced Gloria to follow his timetable his sense of well-being was complete.

Ten years at Leavenworth was the minimum sentence Scott would draw: Major MacArdle had said as much this afternoon at the final briefing. If they played each card well, he could be jailed for life. . . . Hardin wondered what the Red-lover was doing at this moment. Quaking in his boots, no doubt, and praying frantically to his strange new gods. It was incredible that this sang-froid could last into the eve of his humiliation.

V

After his lawyer's phone call Paul had been unable to sleep again.

Not that the call had upset him too badly; not that he was really fearful of the morrow. Captain Paul Scott had learned to put most fears behind him, along with anger and such unpredictable emotions as regret. Still, he had hoped to go to his court-martial with a clear head; after the parting with Kay Storey he felt that he had earned that much respite.

In the Korean lines it had been easy to fold his mind in black velvet whenever he could snatch a few hours' rest. In the prison compound his brain, like his muscles, had relaxed without pain as he sank into the well of oblivion. Here, in the Spartan comfort of his room at the Bachelor Officers' Quarters, he rose from his cot at last and admitted that repose had eluded him.

Wrapping himself in a bathrobe, he opened the single window his room boasted and stared across the lawns of the Presidio at the distant glimmer of the Pacific. Fog had crept in with the approach of dawn; it had blotted the lights of the Golden Gate Bridge and would soon move on to obscure the Oakland shore line. . . . Somewhere in that fog was the building that would house his trial.

Paul breathed deep of the chill air and felt a familiar tumult invade his heart. His insulation from fear was not yet perfect; anger and regret could still enter his thoughts, on crafty tiptoe. Father Tim's lessons had been well learned—but the flesh is always weaker than the spirit.

He had gone into the Korean War as one man—and had emerged as another. He was still not quite sure how the change had come about. Father Tim could have explained it, but the battalion chaplain was beyond earthly questioning. Would the padre have understood—and pardoned—his present lonely anguish, the wild need to call Kay back, to beg her to stand beside him?

At least he had found the strength to send her away tonight; in the lounge of the BOQ he had managed to seem calm enough—to say good-by in words that had but one meaning. If Kay were beside him now, he knew he would take her in his arms and cling to her through eternity.

Yet he must learn to bear his lot—if he was destined to spend the rest of his life in a stockade on some sun-bitten prairie. Kay could never follow him to Leavenworth should the verdict go against him. But she could still have a brilliant career, with Lindman's help; she could find fulfillment without him. . . .

Or so he had reasoned when he had put her from him in the drab lounge of the BOQ. He had chosen the setting deliberately—and he had needed all his control to turn away, to focus his eyes on the painting above the mantel when Kay had left him at last. He would always remember that canvas— the Battle of Buena Vista, complete with charging cavalry, fleeing Mexicans, and Winfield Scott like a blue eagle in the rocket bursts.

A strangled sob escaped him now as he continued to stand at the fog-drenched window. At this hour (when man's will to survive is at its lowest ebb) his need for Kay Storey was tangible as hunger. It was not the last time her ghost would visit him with might-have-beens—but even now, on the eve of his trial, he knew that he could not have acted otherwise.

The ordeal at Pyongyang had made such a surrender possible: rather than involve Kay in his troubles, he was prepared to go down to defeat alone. It was a decision he could not explain (Hi Saunders had only stared at him this afternoon when he had tried to put it into words). So be it, he thought sadly. Let them brand you a Communist: you could have behaved no differently.

Father Tim could have cleared him, of course. Even Kay might have helped. As things stood, there was no voice to defend him but his own. And, though he spoke with the tongues of angels, his failure seemed foreordained.

It was three-thirty by his wrist watch, seven hours before his court-martial opened. Perhaps it would ease the pain of waiting if he collected his memories one more time—if he returned to the beginning, to the moment when his path had first crossed Kay Storey's. . . . Captain Paul Scott stood at the sill of the open window and closed his eyes in a silent prayer. The fog had filled both earth and sea when he looked out, but the image of the past was crystal clear.

HOLLYWOOD

I

A California fog, Dr. Paul Scott reflected, can be both friend and menace, depending on one's mood. On the waterfront at San Pedro that winter evening in 1951, he had begun by welcoming its almost feline approach across the vast, oil-slick harbor. Even now, after a year as resident surgeon at the Holt Clinic in Pasadena, he had not quite adjusted to the endless brassy sunshine: the fog, he told himself, was nature's antidote for that unrelenting flood of light. It was also a protection of sorts, a haven where a man could hide the smallness of his thoughts. And yet, as the gray blanket thickened, the very isolation had made it hard for Paul to hide that smallness from himself.

With San Pedro blotted almost completely from view and its inhabitants no more than shadows, his own world had shrunk to the space his body occupied; thanks to the toxin of rage that boiled through his blood stream, he found himself poor company in that prison. Little by little he had retreated to the infinitely smaller refuge of the soul—the fortress without walls that is man's last haven when reality seems too burdensome to endure.

Tonight the haven was cramped indeed. Never before had he surrendered so completely to the bludgeonings of fate; never had the resources within himself been so meager.

II

That afternoon in Pasadena (when Paul had left the Holt Clinic for the last time) righteous anger had carried him as far west as the Hollywood Hotel, where he had deposited his Val-Pak. Obeying the instinct that was forcing him toward a basic reappraisal of his future, he had driven at once to the great staging area of San Pedro. Long before his taxi had dropped him at his first waterfront bar he could name his compulsion accurately. Today he was facing his impending tour of duty in Korea head on—reminding himself (with the presence of those troop transports at the pier's end) that an unwanted war had robbed him of the first real opportunity he had ever known.

He had worked almost a quarter century for that chance.

Even as a boy he had felt there was a special skill in his fingers: the first dollar he had earned (in the slate pit of a West Virginia mining town) had been set aside to help finance a career in medicine. Years of self-denial had brought him to a university campus; a scholarship had seen him through pre-med, where his grades had proved that he had chosen wisely. . . . World War II had been only a romantic interruption. Like thousands of other young Americans, he had ridden the white charger of idealism into the ETO, served as a pharmacist's mate from D-Day to Aachen (where he had earned a Purple Heart), returned to his university in '46 to barrel through to a degree.

With the GI Bill to finance him, he had entered Johns Hopkins. . . . Until day before yesterday (he told himself grimly) yours was a standard boy-makes-good story, complete with heiress. Is it Daphne Holt's fault, or yours, that you failed to achieve the happy ending?

Dr. Paul Scott (who was now Lieutenant Paul Scott, MC, USAR) continued to stare through the foggy windows of the bar at the cluster of troopships along the quay—and resisted the impulse to order his fifth drink in less than an hour: the fact that he was counting proved that a measure of sanity remained.

Life at Johns Hopkins, he reflected, had been a simple struggle to exist— and the reward seemed, at times, more distant than the stars. The government bounty had paid for essentials, enough for the lab fees, for an occasional flyer in research that is the medic's *sine qua non*. But there had been nights when he had served as a substitute orderly because his funds for the month were exhausted. For days on end he had eaten but a single meal, because the pennies saved brought him a step nearer the coveted M.D.

At graduation he had qualified automatically as a Johns Hopkins intern—a wonderful opportunity with practically no pay. In those final years of training a pack of cigarettes had been a luxury beyond his means, a gift of bourbon from a grateful patient a true bonanza. But his skill had kept pace with his ambition; rumors had gone abroad from the operating rooms in Baltimore, opening the way to the achievement of his dream.

Daphne Holt had brought the dream alive with a special sleight of hand that only the rich can produce.

Proving his worth had always been second nature with young Dr. Scott. Each day in medical school, in hospital work, had been a trial of strength—and he had refused to settle for second best. Daphne Holt had been something else again; not even in his wildest fantasies had he believed that she would find an orphan from a West Virginia slag heap appealing. Daphne had dominated the Johns Hopkins dances as only the daughter of a famous alumnus could: if he had cut in occasionally from the stag line, it had been only from bravado. Girls like the honey-haired Miss Holt, Paul Scott had told himself, were for well-heeled Princetonians from the Pithotomy Club who drove their own cars and swanked on their fathers' expense accounts at the Lord Baltimore.

His love life, so far, had been decidedly on the impromptu side. The night of a fraternity hop when Daphne had invited him to go driving in her canary-yellow Jaguar he had just escaped gaping. When she had kissed him, with lingering finesse, the moment she had found a convenient spot to park he had been almost too flabbergasted to respond.

The whole night had had the same Scheherazade quality. Looking back on it now, from his present plateau of experience, Paul realized that he had been a novelty to her, a bear from the hill country she had enjoyed taming—but the novelty had lasted, all through his senior spring. When the time came to join the scramble for a job Daphne had suggested he apply for the post as resident at her father's clinic in Pasadena—an opportunity that any young surgeon would have given his eyeteeth to win.

Once he had written to Dr. Lucius Holt, Paul had never visioned the possibility of failure. When his name had been posted at the head of his class on graduation day he had taken the accolade in his stride—scholastic honors, after all, were but one element in the dynamics of success. The same had been true of his hospital training. Confident of his own ability—which he had proved again and again—it had been easy to accept Daphne's co-operation as his due. When Dr. Holt—that paragon among California physicians—had offered him the residency he had merely shrugged a second time and wired a calm acceptance.

Since he was now the quasi fiancé of his employer's daughter, he had been white-haired boy at the Holt Clinic. True, he had gagged a bit at the pastel luxury; he had lifted a cynic's eyebrow when he scanned the financial report and learned what the wealthy will pay to keep their livers and their libidos in order. But the surgery had absorbed him from the first day. A month after his arrival word of his skill had spread beyond the horizons of Pasadena and the film world—and his future seemed assured. Even his enemies (who had circulated the usual gossip) now admitted that he was the Old Man's most likely successor whenever Dr. Lucius Holt dropped the mantle from his still-vigorous shoulders.

As the summer of 1950 opened, the end of the journey had been in clear view for Dr. Paul Scott—a surgical reputation that would soon be nationwide, a position at the clinic that was unassailable. As added insurance there was a rich wife for the asking (he had never quite proposed to Daphne but he could guess her answer).

Best of all, he could honestly say that he had earned his success. As eventual chairman of the clinic he would do an outstanding job. In his hands that medical juggernaut would roll on to still greater glory—and continue to flatten most opponents en route. The rich could always afford the best in medicine, and Dr. Paul Scott was fast mastering the technique of giving the rich just what they wanted.

III

The blow, when it came, had been stunning in its impact.

Since most of Paul's World War II duty had been in combat areas, his discharge points had piled up rapidly: after twenty-two months of service he had been granted his terminal leave. Unfortunately those twenty-two months did not keep his name from the Korean draft list. Like other veterans, he had refused to believe that he would be asked to serve when the doctors' draft was announced—but the long arm of selection (moving swiftly to answer what few Americans realized was a national emergency) had already come up with his name. Less than four months after the outbreak of war in Asia, Dr. Paul Scott (only yesterday heir apparent at the Holt Clinic) had become Lieutenant Paul Scott of the Army Medical Corps.

Dr. Holt had been furious. He had lavished much care on Paul; he had opened every door; now he cried out that his assistant's failure to mention his draft status had been just short of treasonable. The scene had grown explosive when Paul—failing to yield to the great man's scolding—had shouted back just as loudly. Finally he had added a few sharp criticisms of the clinic's built-in pampering.

As a result he had been suspended until his position had clarified: he had been dropped entirely when it was evident that he would stay in the Army's clutches. Daphne—who had been abroad at the time—had sided coolly with her father, making it abundantly clear that Paul's status as her chief fiancé had vanished as mysteriously as his position on the staff. Daphne was waiting for no hero to return from a distant war without glory that no one really wanted.

This initial blow had fallen two months ago, and hectic months they had been. Indoctrination had not been too wearing. With his memories of World War II training still green, Paul had mastered his new rituals with solemn efficiency: he had been careful to drop no hint of the burning resentment against a country that had rewarded his previous service so cavalierly. At least, he told himself, he was now a surgeon of note. As such, he would probably be assigned to a stateside hospital service: with luck he could keep up his connections, perhaps even salvage something from the collapse of his career.

The crowning blow had descended in the past fortnight, when orders had come through attaching Lieutenant Scott to a heavy-weapons outfit about to go overseas, with the rank of battalion surgeon. The group was already alerted. Only yesterday it had been assigned to the transport *Millard Fillmore* moored at San Pedro.

In Europe Paul had observed battalion surgeons in action; so far, the reality had been no more dismal than the remembrance. During his brief service with his outfit he had discharged his duties with a thoroughness that gave no hint of the abyss of boredom beneath. But nothing had prepared him for Lieutenant Colonel Jasper Hardin, his commanding officer. Though he had heard of such men at second hand, he had never quite believed in their existence.

To call Hardin a throwback, Paul told himself, was a gross understatement: the mold in which his C.O. was cast (though it had been useful once) had long since been relegated to the lumber room. Sun-baked posts from Cuba to Shanghai had hardened the mold; the last global war had confirmed its pattern beyond all change. If a man existed behind that glazed shell, Paul had yet to discover him. If Hardin possessed a spark of human warmth under the maze of protocol that ruled his slightest action, it was a boon he shared with no one. . . .

There was a fresh drink on the bar, though Paul had no memory of ordering it. He took it at a swallow and walked out into the fog. In another moment he was on the pier, skirting the ghostly shapes of the transports. The *Millard Fillmore* was the third vessel from the end: he paused at the gangway, with the vague notion of inspecting his quarters. Save for the light above the watch officer's desk, the ship was completely obscured: the hooded gangway lifting at a sharp angle from the pier seemed to open into a void as mysterious as the portal to another world.

It took no effort at all to ignore the guard's tentative salute and continue down the pier. All that long day the thought of boarding that transport had been more than he could endure: now that he had put himself to the test and turned aside, he wondered if he would ever go abroad. Holding the thought at arm's length, he could feel his heart beat faster with a vague fear he had yet to name.

At the *Millard Fillmore*'s bow he steadied himself with a hand on a bollard. Above him a mooring hawser snaked away into grayness; beyond, he heard the pulse of the tide, though the fog hid the water. For the first time in his twenty-eight years on earth Paul Scott could pause in his tracks and ask himself, quite seriously, what it was like to die.

Freud, he remembered, had isolated the death wish that dwells in every man; he had explained the constant battle it wages for the soul. The battle is often fought in unlikely places (at a cliff's edge, on a railway trestle, beside a rushing stream). Paul knew that men had cast their lives away at such times—as carelessly as a child might discard a toy—when every rule of nature urged them to draw back. As an intern he had gone out on such ambulance calls—most of them dead-on-arrival, mute evidence that the irrational urge to self-destruction can be stronger than the ego.

Letting his hand trail along the hawser, he took a step toward the water, and another. He, of course, would never make that final move; it was absurd to let the possibility cross his mind. Yet he continued to approach the edge of the quay; it was an exciting—because deadly—game to see how far he could go and still outface the nameless demon within him.

Fear stabbed at his vitals and the fear was real now. The discovery he had just made was a paralyzing one—the fact that he *could* face the thought of self-extinction and know he might be powerless to conquer it. He took yet another step toward the oil-slick water. Somewhere, he told himself frantically, you've a reserve of strength to draw on—but did it exist at the moment? Or had it been devoured long since by the poison of hate?

Another step brought him to the very edge of the pier—and here he paused at last, with one foot on the stringpiece, to measure the distance to the water below. At that moment a voice spoke his name in the fog.

"Going my way, Dr. Scott?"

IV

It was a familiar voice, though Paul could not place it at once; for all its gentle timbre it had cut through the skein of his madness like a surgeon's scalpel. He stood on the stringpiece a moment more, pretending to inspect the bow moorings of the transport. Then he turned to lift a hand in greeting as the battalion chaplain emerged from the murk.

"Good evening, Padre." He spoke coldly; Father Timothy O'Fallon had never been among his intimates. "What brings you into the fog?"

"God, I hope."

"Yours, or mine?" He had long since informed the chaplain that he was not a practicing Christian—so the response had come naturally enough. In another moment, Paul promised himself, he would recover his sang-froid.

"We all worship the same God, Doctor," said the priest. "Even though we give Him different titles."

"I'm afraid I've none at all, Father."

"But you have—you've just said as much. Give yourself time; you'll learn His name."

The priest joined him on the stringpiece; once again Paul noticed how puny he seemed, a mere wisp of khaki in the mist.

"Did you follow me here, Padre?" he asked, a little contemptuously.

"Yes, Dr. Scott."

"To discuss theology in the fog?"

"No, Doctor—to ask if you were going aboard the transport. I wanted to look at her myself."

"Sorry if I misunderstood. Shall we go exploring?"

The chaplain gave a nervous laugh. "Only if you insist. Now that I'm standing at the gangway I'd prefer to go back. To tell the truth I've a mortal terror of fog."

The man's eyes brushed Paul's as he spoke: he seemed to grow shyer with each word he uttered—yet he continued to stand on the stringpiece. There was a sturdiness in his manner that contrasted oddly with his almost timid utterance: Paul wondered how much he had guessed about his real reason for visiting the pier. He put down the wonder and took refuge in brusqueness.

"You're right to turn back. This old tub may be taking us both to immortality. Why should we go aboard before our time?"

"Yet we were both drawn to this pier tonight," said the priest quietly. "I wonder why."

"You said that God sent you."

"It's quite true, Doctor. An hour ago I was dozing in my billet at Port Headquarters. Some force outside myself brought me to the gangway of the *Millard Fillmore*. Don't ask me to give it a name. God will do, for now."

Paul was glad that the yellow-white mist continued to swirl between them: he could only hope that it had softened the mocking laughter he had just choked down. "You really mean that, don't you?" he managed at last. The words were lame enough, but he felt that some retort was needed.

"Of course I do, Doctor. May I ask your reason for being here?"

"Perhaps I'm a masochist at heart."

"My guess is that you're the truest patriot of all. One who can lock his fear of death away and still serve his country. To say nothing of his creator."

That, thought Paul swiftly, is quite enough offbeat for one evening. He decided to end this jabberwocky with no further thought of manners. "I *have* served my country, Padre. For twenty months of combat in Europe. I brought back a broken tibia to prove it, and a good many shattered ideals. Right now I'm not in the least afraid. Just regretful that another doctor isn't taking my place on that transport."

"Forgive me, Dr. Scott. I didn't mean to offend."

"I'm sure you didn't." To his astonishment Paul found that his resentment had left him, now that he had put this little bumbler in his place. Perhaps it was the guileless look the priest offered him: when he smiled the quiet radiance in his face seemed out of place in the world. For no reason that made sense Paul was suddenly reminded of a shell-blasted church in St. Lô—and a head of St. Francis that had rolled, unbidden, into the corner where he was setting up a field hospital.

Again he took refuge in a shrug. "Since we aren't tempting fate by going aboard—shall we guide each other to dry land?"

"We can try, Doctor."

They walked down the pier together in a silence that was oddly without strain. "Why do you fear the fog, Padre?" he asked.

"It's not easy to say. Perhaps because it is a symbol of the forces of darkness. Is that too mystical for a man of science?"

"A bit, I'm afraid. Didn't it take courage to come this far?"

"You made it, Dr. Scott. I felt that I could follow."

In another moment their heels rang on the cobbles of the waterfront. Here, because of a dozen brightly lighted bars, the universe seemed in perspective again—including the Army jeep parked at the curb. The driver (whom Paul recognized as one of the battalion runners) saluted briskly.

"Where to, Chaplain?"

"I'll settle for the USO canteen, Corporal," said Father O'Fallon. "Why don't you join me, Doctor? They've a special show tonight—a unit that's about to go overseas."

"Whatever you say, Padre."

It was almost a relief to step into the jeep, to let his unwanted companion take over for a while. Only later did Paul wonder at the presence of the jeep at that particular corner in San Pedro—and the fact that the driver seemed to take his appearance for granted, no less than the chaplain's. The age of miracles, like the age of saints, belonged to the more credulous past. He could hardly thank Father O'Fallon for saving his life—when that humorless neophyte was clearly unaware of the service.

V

Long before he had settled into the empty wall booth at the USO center Paul realized that it had been a mistake to come here.

He made no protest when Father O'Fallon hurried to the row of vending machines: for the moment he was too busy making himself small in the booth. There was no rule against his presence at a servicemen's canteen (several ensigns and their girls were in the crowd tonight, as well as a few juniors like himself). Still it was felt that officers were paid enough to provide their own diversions. . . . He would only stay a moment, Paul promised himself, just long enough to make this over-zealous cleric happy. Then he'd take refuge in his hotel room: there was enough nembutal in his Val-Pak to insure oblivion until morning.

"You'll like this place, Dr. Scott."

Paul accepted a Coca-Cola from the chaplain. "I can't stay long—"

"The girl who's singing is a friend of mine. I'll invite her over when this number ends."

For the first time Paul turned his attention to the bandbox stage above the dance floor. The singer who was belting out "Night and Day" at the microphone seemed like a hundred other synthetic blondes—not bad, though she was certainly no Doris Day. He pulled his eyes away from the spotlight with no effort and gave Father O'Fallon what he hoped was a disarming grin.

"She's working too hard," he said.

"Exactly what I've always told her," said the chaplain. "She could be a sensation if she'd only sing naturally. Her voice was made for chamber music. Folk songs—or perhaps the *lieder* of Schumann."

Paul cocked an ironic eye at the priest, who had cupped both hands beneath his chin and was listening entranced. He did not speak again until the girl paused for an intermezzo and looked out over the audience with one of those show-business smiles that might have been painted on her too-bright lips.

"She's a nice person, Doctor, even nicer than her voice."

"I'm sure of that, Padre." This obviously was not the moment to enlighten the priest on one of life's fundamentals. Paul was still admiring his own forbearance when the song ended and the singer bowed to rather tepid applause. The master of ceremonies, a bald young man in a sharp tuxedo, bustled to the microphone, clapping just a bit louder than the audience.

"That was Kay Storey, fellows. A little lady who's going places fast. Let's give her another big hand."

The GIs (who packed every table around the dance floor) stepped up the tempo of their applause a trifle, and the girl took a second bow. She was on her way to the dressing room when Father O'Fallon bustled out of the booth.

"Miss Storey!"

Even in the depths of his apathy Paul noticed that the girl's face had brightened at the sound of the padre's voice.

"This is a surprise, Father O'Fallon."

"Tonight I'm here with deliberate intent. There's someone I'd like you to meet."

The smile on the girl's overpainted lips was still quite genuine as she permitted the chaplain to lead her toward the booth: Paul saw her face go blank when he rose in response to the padre's introductions. Not that he could blame her too much: he could imagine how dour his own face must seem at the moment.

"Won't you join us, my dear?"

For a split second, Paul saw, the blonde singer contemplated a refusal. Then, just as mechanically, she put down the urge. That, too, he could understand. The metal crosses on Father O'Fallon's tunic were insurance against most rebuffs.

"I was just going to have a Coke in my dressing room—"

"Have one here instead." By some private legerdemain the padre had already produced a third bottle; he pressed it into the girl's hand and ushered her into the booth. "Dr. Scott, will you entertain this young lady a moment while I visit with our outfit?"

A duenna out of Dickens, thought Paul, would have been less gauche. He watched the padre bustle into the crowd—and felt the emptiness of the night invade his heart again, the void to which he had all but yielded on the pier. . . . Detached as he was, he could admire Kay Storey's poise as she settled beside him and lifted the Coca-Cola in a parody of a toast.

"I won't keep you," he said quickly. "Not if you'd rather rest awhile.

Father O'Fallon has yet to learn the facts of the theater."

"I've a few minutes, Doctor." Her voice, like her aplomb, was disarming—and much friendlier than he deserved, Paul added gloomily. "Would you be surprised if I said I'd seen you before?"

Now that they were side by side he noted that Kay Storey was much smaller than she had seemed in the spotlight's glare: her voice was pitched low, with a deeper resonance than the microphone had revealed. A voice for folk songs, or Schumann *lieder:* could Father O'Fallon's ear be keener than his own? Paul found himself looking into her smoky green eyes with genuine appraisal.

"Forgive my poor memory. Where did we meet?"

"We didn't. I was singing at the Kit-Kat last summer, in Altadena. My car was sideswiped and they brought me to the Holt Clinic."

"Nothing serious, I hope."

"Just a cut scalp. They were taking the last stitches when you came through the emergency room."

"I'd pretend to remember if I dared," he said politely. "Apparently I didn't officiate."

"Hardly. You were in a tail coat, and looked as though you owned the world." Kay Storey's generous lips widened in a smile that held no hint of mockery. "I could guess why: I'd seen your picture in the *Examiner* that morning, with Daphne Holt."

"I'm afraid tail coats belong to the past," he said. "May I compliment you on your song?"

"Don't bother. You've heard better singers—and you needn't deny it."

"Are you really going overseas?"

"Not quite so soon as the 141st Battalion."

"Has our chaplain been talking *that* freely?"

She gave him a level look. "Is it tomorrow, Lieutenant—or the day after?"

"The day after, I'm afraid. You aren't a North Korean spy, by any chance?"

Kay Storey laughed lightly, but her eyes were still serious as she continued to study him with that same disarming interest. "Father Tim will endorse me, I'm sure. And you mustn't blame him for talking out of turn. The first night we met here we told each other our life stories. Isn't that what a chaplain's for?"

"I don't blame him at all," said Paul—and this time, he almost meant it. "In fact, I'm hoping we'll meet in Korea."

"Shall we make a tentative date for April?"

"April in Seoul," said Paul. "It hasn't the lilt of April in Paris."

"Did you win those service ribbons in France? You've a lot for a lieutenant."

He saw that she was keeping a standard USO conversation moving. It was hardly her fault that she had touched him on a sore spot. "Most of them were earned in combat," he said evenly. "Right now, I'm a casualty of the doctors' draft."

"Has it made you as unhappy as you sound?"

"Need you ask?"

"At least you'll have prospects when you get out. Don't forget I've seen both the Holt Clinic and your fiancée."

"Daphne Holt was never my fiancée," he said. "And I'm no longer employed by the clinic. Dr. Holt felt that he couldn't wait for my discharge in *this* war." It was incredible that he could speak so calmly of Daphne and her father. The sensation was remarkably pleasant. So pleasant that he decided to prolong it. "Odd as it sounds, the Holt Clinic doesn't seem too important—now."

"What I saw of it that night looked pretty important. So, for that matter, did you."

"Let's say I was on my way up—and took a fast tumble."

"Would you believe me, Doctor, if I say I'm sorry?"

"Of course, if you'll prove it."

The green eyes did not flicker. "What's your idea of proof?"

"Shall we say dinner—after your last number?"

"Do you have your chaplain's approval for this invitation?"

"By no means. And I'm not asking him to make a third."

"I'll weigh your proposition," said Kay Storey. "How well do you know Father Tim?"

"I don't know him at all. In fact, I've rather avoided him since I joined his outfit."

"Why, Doctor?"

"What do you make of him? Don't stop and think—answer straight off."

"I think he's sweet."

"Sweet—and a bit too naïve?"

"Not nearly so naïve as he seems."

"Surely he's a little nosy."

"Isn't that part of his job?"

"Don't think I'm complaining," said Paul. "Shall we dine at Chasen's— or Romanoff's?"

"You needn't be so grand," said the girl. "I suppose you've already labeled me a Hollywood siren, but I live on the wrong side of Pico Boulevard."

"You'll accept, then?"

"I'm still not sure, Doctor. Why do you dislike Father Tim?"

"How can I dislike him? He's brought us together."

"*Together,* Dr. Scott?"

"For dinner, at least, if you'll trust me that far."

"I might—if you'll answer me. What don't you like about your chaplain? What has he done to hurt you?"

A trifle nettled by her perception, Paul withdrew his hand, which had been on the point of covering hers. "Is Father O'Fallon by any chance your confessor?"

"I'm a backsliding Methodist," said the girl. "What are you?"

"How did you guess I wasn't a Catholic?"

"No good Catholic would use his priest to help along a conquest."

"Isn't that rather a strong word?"

"I don't think so, Doctor. If anything, it's an understatement."

Their eyes held. When he dropped his glance it was only to lift her hand and kiss one finger tip gently. "Can you blame me?"

Kay Storey took back her hand with no appearance of haste. "The answer is no, Dr. Scott."

"You mean, you *don't* blame me?"

"I'm refusing your dinner invitation—politely but firmly." She got up as she spoke, taking a cigarette from his pack and accepting a light.

"Any particular reason for the refusal?"

"Just one. It seems only fair to save your time." She left him on that to vanish briefly through the curtained entrance to the dressing rooms.

He was still pondering that exit when he spied Father Tim approaching the booth. Not that he had been too startled by Kay Storey's abrupt departure: in fact, their brief passage at arms had been stimulating—almost elating. He just missed laughing aloud as he grasped the reason for that lift.

However briefly, the girl *had* teased him out of his own selfishness. Her refusal to dine with him had given him a problem outside himself—and the challenge had made him want life again. . . . He was still chuckling over the discovery when the chaplain slipped into the booth.

"I'm afraid the lady has left us, Father."

"She'll be out directly, Doctor. She has to change for the next number."

"That isn't what I meant. I drove her away."

"I'm sorry to hear that, Dr. Scott. When I introduced you I was sure you could help each other."

"Father O'Fallon," he said a little testily, "did it ever occur to you that most foot-loose men and women are interested only in helping themselves?"

The priest smiled across the table—another of those gentle smiles that began and ended in the eyes. "I refuse to believe that about either you or Kay, Paul. May I call you that, since you've opened your heart to me?"

"How could I when I've said nothing of myself?"

"You've told me that you have a grudge against the world. So, I fear, does Kay Storey—though hers doesn't show quite so plainly. I was hoping you'd both have a go at solving those grudges. It's been done before, you know."

"Are you suggesting I try again?"

"Believe me, Paul, she's a fine girl. Give her a chance to prove it."

Paul shrugged. "If you wish, Father Tim, I'll give her every chance."

"She's going on for the last time now. It won't be long before she can join us again—"

"Apparently she's run into heavy weather."

Both of them turned to the bandstand: as Paul had just said, Kay Storey had become the focal point of one of those sudden brawls so characteristic of wartime canteens. At first glance he could not identify the reason for the fracas, though it had already involved most of the dance floor.

"Do you have this sort of blowup often?"

"Almost nightly, I'm afraid. I'm sure she can handle it."

Standing on his chair for a better view, Paul saw that the troublemaker was a large, rather beefy officer who was evidently determined to join the musicians. Several noncoms were doing their best to dissuade him. Kay, with one foot on the dance floor, was working hard at her role of peacemaker. While Paul watched, the intruder shoved the noncoms aside and climbed to the stage; with a bellow of triumph he snatched a saxophone from one of the musicians and turned to face the dance floor. Paul felt a prickle of unholy rage along his spine when he recognized Colonel Jasper Hardin, his battalion commander. Despite Kay's persuasions Hardin had already launched into a rendition of the dance tune—a braying travesty that suggested he had studied music via the mail-order school.

"What's our C.O. doing here?"

Father Tim sighed. "He's visited us before, Paul. You see, he usually dines—and drinks—at the officers' club."

The officers' club stood only a few doors from the canteen. More than once Paul had observed Hardin's antics at the bar; tonight it was evident that his libations had been more prolonged than usual. "Isn't there some legal way to keep him out?"

"I'm afraid not. Usually he pretends he's sober until he reaches the bandstand. Then he *always* wants to lead the orchestra."

Hardin had kept his footing: when Kay attempted to deprive him of the saxophone he prisoned her with one arm and planted a highly inaccurate kiss on her cheek. The hall rang with booing now. And yet, intimidated by the silver eagles on Hardin's shoulders, no one had ventured to approach the bandstand. Paul got to his feet, feeling the worst of his rage dissolve in action.

"I'm going to break this up, Padre."

"Believe me, Paul, she can manage. It's happened before."

He shook off the chaplain's hand and reached the bandstand in a dozen long strides. The enlisted men on the crowded floor outdid each other to let him pass; the colonel, his arm still about Kay's waist, gave him a glassy stare of nonrecognition when he stepped up to the stage.

"The lady promised me this dance, sir."

Hardin's answer was a prolonged bray on the horn. Confident that his whim was law, he had already turned his back on the intruder and made a second attempt to kiss Kay Storey.

"If the colonel pleases—"

"As y'were, shavetail!"

The parade-ground bellow had struck terror to hearts from Fort Dix to Manila: tonight it only translated resentment into action. Paul's elbow, smashed into Hardin's midriff, was all the help Kay needed to free herself. Deprived of that support, the colonel sat down heavily on the platform, missing the snare drum by inches. The hall shook with cheers as Paul handed Kay down to the floor and spun her into a waltz turn with the sudden revival of the orchestra.

"Thanks, Doctor," she whispered.

"It was a pleasure."

"I could have handled him, you know—"

"It was still a pleasure."

There was no time for more. Because of the crowd Paul had been able to dance Kay only a few steps from the bandstand. Too late, he realized that Hardin was on his feet again with the saxophone raised.

A sergeant tried to bar the way, but the drunken officer flailed him from his path: there was barely time to push Kay aside before the blow descended. For a split second the horn seemed to hang in mid-air, a grotesque, golden bludgeon. . . . Paul saw that Hardin was glaring at him insanely: the red hate that glowed in those eyes assured him the C.O. had recognized him. He heard Father O'Fallon's cry of protest from a great distance as the saxophone connected solidly with his head.

VI

When Paul opened his eyes he was in a strange bed; the flawless California sunlight patterning the carpet told him that some time had elapsed since his brush in the canteen.

He tested his reflexes cautiously and was gratified by the result. Whatever their other faults his forebears had bequeathed him a solid skull; save for a decided headache and a tenderness in the area of the left temple, he was feeling fit enough. A second glance assured him that this was not his room at the Hollywood Hotel—nor were the somewhat flamboyant pajamas his own; the bed (though it was made up with hospital precision) was a living-room divan. The room itself, he surmised, belonged to a person of taste and little present means.

Kay Storey's humming reached him through one of the two closed doors; the situation fell into perspective before she could enter with a coffee service. In slacks and a powder-blue pullover, she looked much younger than he remembered—and her smile was part of the sunny morning.

"Sleep well, Dr. Scott?"

Paul sat up in bed and rechecked the lump behind his temple. "Is sleep the proper word?"

"Indeed it is. I gave you a rather strong sedative before I tucked you in— three grains of seconal. Don't look alarmed, please: I was an R.N. before I decided to have a career." Kay Storey settled on a leather-covered cushion beside the divan and hugged her knees. "You look wonderfully rested."

Paul sipped his coffee gratefully. What she had said was true enough: even the headache was dissolving rapidly in the fragrant steam from his cup. "It would help if I knew just what you've done for me," he ventured. "Whatever it is, Miss Storey—"

"If I call you Paul, will you return the compliment?"

"Do I deserve it, Kay?"

"I think so, after your bout with Colonel Hardin."

They surveyed each other, across the counterpane of the day bed. "Is it proper to ask how I got here?"

"It seemed the best place to bring you. Father Tim wasn't sure of your hotel—"

"Don't tell me I arrived under my own power?"

"Partly. Two enlisted men helped you to my car."

"And afterward?"

"Don't you even remember climbing my stairs?"

"My last clear image is a tenor saxophone connecting with my ear."

"Your colonel was a mad dog last night," said Kay. "There's no other name for him."

"What became of *him* afterward?"

"The noncoms spirited him out ahead of the Shore Patrol." Kay smiled as she took Paul's empty cup. "He's still sleeping it off."

"How come you're so well informed?"

"Father Tim phoned an hour ago. He's dropping around later."

"*Here*, Kay?"

"I'd promised to show him Hollywood: he hasn't had time to make the tour—and today's his last chance. Care to join us?"

She left him before he could frame an answer and took the cup into her tiny kitchen. On her return with fresh coffee, she opened the second door and went in to tidy the bedroom where she had obviously slept. Kay Storey, Paul gathered, was not a girl to waste words. Only the pajamas he was wearing remained unexplained.

"Perhaps I should apologize for the trouble I've caused," he said, when she had settled again on the cushion. "Obviously I behaved like a knight-errant with delusions of grandeur. Still, I couldn't stand by and let that drunken goat maul you."

"Do you think he recognized you?"

"For just a moment, I'm afraid. Probably the liquor washed out the memory."

"You've made a lifetime enemy if it hasn't."

He shrugged. "Hardin has hated me from the moment I reported for duty."

"Any special reason?"

"People like him *need* someone to hate. As his newest officer, I'm a natural victim."

"Are you sure he doesn't hate himself most of all?"

"What's this, Kay? Freud in reverse?"

"You must see what I mean, Paul. Father Tim told me the colonel's been passed over twice on the promotion lists. That's slow death to a West Pointer."

"Don't tell me you're *sorry* for Hardin?"

"A little. Can you imagine feeding on hate to nourish your own self-esteem?"

"You wouldn't make such excuses if you were in his command."

"I can still pity him because he's failed so badly. Maybe that's because I'm on the edge myself."

Remembering Father Tim's words in the canteen last night, Paul sat up in the day bed. He was pleased to note that he was not dizzy, proving that the slugging last night had left no permanent effects.

"Move over then while I join you," he said quietly.

"*You* haven't failed, Paul."

He studied himself in the glass of a wardrobe door. The pajamas, he noted, were of white silk decorated with a pattern of crossed scimitars. He wondered why he did not feel more awkward wearing them.

"I failed to make a date with you last night," he reminded her.

"Yet here you are."

"Only because I stopped that horn with my skull. And the chaplain's arriving any moment now to keep us respectable—even if I am wearing your husband's pajamas."

"I have no husband, Paul."

"Then you're making your point the hard way."

"Perhaps I am." She got up from the cushion. "You'd better dress before Father Tim *does* arrive. The bath's in there—and so are your clothes. If you like you can finish your life story through the kitchen door while I wash up."

He found his uniform on the shower rail, neatly folded on a hanger. The sting of cold water banished the last of his hangover: he was himself again when he walked into the living room and stood at the wardrobe mirror to knot his service tie. Kay was busy in the kitchen: he wondered if she had taken that refuge deliberately, and was careful to keep clear of the open door.

"I told you my life story at the canteen," he said. "In a way I'm a worse failure than Hardin: only mine has come in a single installment."

"How can you call yourself a failure? You've always had what you wanted."

"Only by fighting every step of the way."

"Why stop fighting now?"

The question seemed preposterous in the clear light of morning: Paul spoke mechanically to gain time. "So I'm to accept Korea—*and* Hardin—and make the best of both?"

Kay emerged from the kitchen, dropping an apron en route. "Is it too much to ask?"

"Must I keep a stiff upper lip, too?"

"You'll finish this job, Paul—the way you finished the others. What's more, you'll be the better for it; your satisfaction will come in a way you least expect. Once you've seen it's the work that matters, not the reward, you may even discover you're a happy man."

"Are you quoting the chaplain, by any chance?"

"Word for word," she said. "You see, he's given me the same advice."

Kay was leaning against the doorjamb as she spoke. He moved toward her slowly, giving her time to avoid him before he lifted her chin and kissed her gently. It was not a lover's kiss. Yet he sensed that it had set off (as definitely as a comma) a second clause in their relationship.

"Thanks, Kay."

"What have I done now?"

"You may not realize it but you've set me on my feet again. Can I do as much for you?"

"Is this my cue to identify the pajamas?"

"Only if it will help."

She moved a little away from him. "They belonged to Eric Lindman."

"Lindman? The director with all the Oscars?"

"At one time he was a visitor here."

Now that she had surmounted the first hurdle, her story was both honest and matter-of-fact. She told it without hesitation, as though speaking of a stranger. A girl who had come to Hollywood all of three years ago via the beauty-contest trail. A too-eager, too-credulous girl whose talent had been submerged in the tidal wave that inundates the film capital. . . .

"Maybe it's symbolic, Paul—but I was born in McPherson, Kansas. It's the geographical center of the United States. When you're dead center you have to break free—"

"I was dead center too," he said. "So far, we're two of a kind."

"Last year they gave me a bit in *Sirocco*—Eric's best picture. A street scene in Cairo—I was a bazaar dancer. It was a fill-in scene: one of his assistants directed it. But Eric saw the rushes. That night he rang my doorbell. He—offered to help me. If I'd accept his help."

"Help you—with your acting?"

"With my acting," she said firmly. "That's all I ever took from him. When he came here—which wasn't often—it was only to get away. Do you believe me so far?"

"Of course. When did you fall in love with him?"

"I—respected Eric's genius. There's no one like him."

"Even his worst critics admit that."

"I was grateful for his help, Paul, and he *did* help. He made me believe in myself as an actress. But I wasn't in love with him. Not even at the beginning."

"Are you sure?" He wondered a little at the relief in his voice.

"Absolutely."

"Where is he now?"

"On location in Africa. He's been gone for six months but he writes steadily. He says he'll have a part for me—whenever I feel I'm ready."

"Meanwhile you're to sink or swim on your own?"

"Isn't that what makes an actress? Eric has helped me all he can. I've got to prove I can make it from there."

"Have you worked regularly?"

"Enough to have my own apartment and be independent. I've done the small night-club circuit and kept my voice in training. And when there were no bookings I could always find other jobs. I've sold real estate in Beverly Hills and I've been a barker on a tourist bus. I've been a car-hop at a drive-in more than once—" She gave him a smile that was only a trifle strained. "Don't feel sorry for me, Paul. I've my own prescription for survival."

"Does it include naming yourself a failure? That's a dangerous ingredient."

"I *am* a failure by all reasonable standards. Be honest: what did you think of my singing last night—really?" Her fingers closed briefly on his before he could answer. "No—I won't embarrass you. Perhaps I'm exactly what you saw. A platinum blonde with no assets but her youth. Another contest winner who's too stubborn to take the Hollywood brush-off. On the other hand there's Eric and his faith in me. He *will* give me a chance if I ask for it—"

"Of course he will." To his astonishment, Paul found that he meant it.

"Only I won't ask until I'm ready. Until my talent really comes through. And I *do* have talent: that's one thing I'm sure of."

"You've made your point, Kay. Where does your R.N. degree fit in?"

"I went into training to get away from McPherson. One of my aunts paid my way through Barnes Hospital in St. Louis. It seemed only fair to *be* a nurse until I'd paid her back. I was good at it, too—"

"You'd be good at anything you do, Kay."

She gave him a grateful smile. "Like you, Paul. I guess we're a couple of mavericks, cut from the same pattern." This time it was she who bent forward to kiss him—and this time, he knew, there was an invitation in the kiss she could not quite bring herself to utter.

"Thanks for putting me in your class," he said. "It's an honor I'll try to deserve."

"Still like to tour Hollywood with Father Tim and me?"

"There's nothing I'd like more—if you'll both promise to dine with me at Romanoff's."

"Father Tim has a six o'clock service at Port Headquarters."

"The two of us, then?"

There was a flush at her cheeks when she answered: he felt his heart leap at the knowledge that she understood him perfectly. "It's your last evening here, Paul. Are you sure you want to spend it with me?"

"There's no one I'd rather spend it with."

"It's a date then," she said quietly. "*After* we've shown your chaplain Hollywood." Her color was still high—but she did not avoid his eye as she moved to answer the buzzer downstairs. A discreet ring that could be only Father Timothy O'Fallon.

VII

When Paul wakened the next morning he had no need to ask his whereabouts: his mind rang out the news as joyfully as a carillon.

After they had put the chaplain on the San Pedro bus Kay and Paul had gone hand in hand to their tour of the Hollywood fleshpots. They had dined royally at Romanoff's and danced at Mocambo and Ciro's, secure in the knowledge that they had earned these hours together. Afterward they had gone back to the apartment on Pico Boulevard: there had been no hidden tensions when the lock of her apartment door had clicked shut behind them. . . . Now, rousing in earnest, he knew that he had never been happier, never more deeply content.

"Where are you, Kay?"

There was no answer to his shout: he roamed the tiny apartment twice before admitting that he was alone there. On the second tour he saw that the coffee service was ready on the range. A note was propped against the percolator: like Kay herself, it was to the point:

> Leaving for an early rehearsal call. (Our final workout before we join forces with the Korean unit.)
>
> I'll be at the pier—if they let me out in time. If not, it's April in Seoul. Remember—we're *both* seeing this war through.

He wrote his own hurried farewell while the coffee boiled over: a glance at the clock had reminded him of the tyranny of time. At the Hollywood Hotel he collected his Val-Pak and paid two nights' rent on an unused room. While hailing a taxi he remembered Daphne Holt: in another hour she would be stepping off a plane from New York. It was good to remember, beyond all doubting, that his bondage to Daphne's world was ended.

There was hardly a moment to spare before he boarded the transport. It was only when he ascended the gangway with his surgical unit that he realized he had neglected to write down the address of the apartment on Pico Boulevard. Father Tim would have it, of course: he would send Kay his APO later. . . .

He needed a half hour to check in at quarters, to assure himself that the enlisted men under his command were well billeted. A post band was blaring at the pierhead when he returned to the deck, and the transport had begun to back ponderously into the harbor.

Somehow the gala air was forced, though there were sweethearts and wives by the dozens on the pier, and the band's rendition of "Aloha" could not have been more spirited. Paul found the chaplain at last, in the press of uniforms at the bow. A glance told him why Father Tim was waving so wildly: Kay Storey's runabout had just nosed into the crowd and she was running to the stringpiece of the pier with all the skill of a halfback determined on a touchdown.

Already the strip of water between ship and shore was too wide to shout across. Evidently she had realized she might be unable to wish him the usual good-by; when she reached the stringpiece the placard she lifted told its own story in foot-high block letters.

CARRYING THE TORCH TO SEOUL.
HAPPY LANDINGS!

All over the transport voices roared an answer to that message, on the assumption that it was a general tribute. Crushed among the windmilling arms in the coaming, Paul felt his throat tighten at the energy of that response. Thanks to Kay Storey, the tepid ceremony of leave-taking (which the blaring of the post band had only underlined) was now transformed into a genuine farewell, a blend of tears and wholehearted cheering.

Now that these vigorous young voices had taken over he was reminded once again that youth is eternal, that the young will always live down the evils devised by their elders. . . . America's wars, he added solemnly, will always be won—so long as there is a Kay Storey waiting at the war's end.

"The girl next door," said Father Tim. "That's what I called her the day we met. D'you understand why, Paul?"

"Yes, Father Tim. I understand perfectly."

He cupped his hands to add his farewell shout to the others, knowing in advance that she could not pick out his voice. But he was sure that she had found him in that cheering multitude, that she was waving to him alone. And he knew that he loved her beyond reason—even though he had not yet put his love in words.

THE PRESIDIO

I

The image of the troopship dimmed, though he could half hear the wail of the siren. Alone in his room at the Bachelor Officers' Quarters, Captain Paul Scott saw that dawn was waiting behind the fogbound eastern sky.

The silent prayer had helped; so had his familiar communion with the past. He was glad that he had gone back to the beginning with Kay—and happier still that he could face that beginning with no regrets. Until their meeting he had not quite realized that he was a member (in reasonable standing) of the family of man. The lesson had taken a deal of learning; he had passed his last exam in the hell of the prison camp at Pyongyang. But he had learned to forget the demands of self with Kay. For the first time he had discovered that being in love was only a short cut to the admission that it is more blessed to give than to receive.

Only a few hours ago, in the lounge of the BOQ, he had tried to thank Kay for the part she had played in his education. There had been no words to convey his thanks—not even to the woman he loved. . . . Paul turned to his Spartan cot now with a sigh. Wondering if sleep would elude him again, he found himself dropping into oblivion as his head touched the pillow.

II

"Will you read the charges—or shall I?"

"Fire away, Hi. You can explain as we go along."

Hilary Saunders glanced up sharply while he emptied the contents of his brief case on the rumpled blanket covering Paul's cot. The question was deliberately prodding, in the hope of shattering his friend's inattention.

"I stopped counting clients years ago," said Hi, "but you win the blue ribbon for sang-froid."

Paul was seated in the window frame, breathing deep of the flawless morning. The fog had burned away with the sunrise and San Francisco was as clean-washed as its sky. Maybe it's a hangover from two years behind barbed wire, thought Hi. Maybe freedom has made him a little balmy. So balmy that he doesn't realize he may be facing another prison stockade tomorrow. . . .

"Is it wrong to enjoy a little sunshine?"

"You know what I mean," said Hi. "No one can be so cool. Not when he's fighting for his life. Is it something you learned from Confucius?" (He regretted the fumble at humor instantly. Paul's captors had been largely Chinese: for all Hi knew, a perverted Confucianism had been part of the brain-washing.)

"My only credo comes from a more recent teacher," said Paul. "An unsung philosopher named Father Timothy O'Fallon. Remember *him?*"

Hi nodded. "A runty priest with his nose in everyone's troubles—and a line of malarky that might have been funny, if it had been less crude. Of course, I never really *knew* him. That might make a difference?"

"It would," said Paul. "I can remember when my reaction was identical with yours."

"Shall we skip the padre for now? We'll be walking into your court-martial in just twenty minutes. It might help to remind you of the charges."

"We've been over them, Hi."

"Let's repeat them again—in the ineffable prose of the Army." The lawyer picked up a blue-bound dossier that lay among the notes on the blanket. "Charges and Specifications," he intoned, in a bailiff's voice—enunciating each word clearly, but dwelling on none:

"CHARGE 1: Violation of the Uniform Code of Military Justice, Article 105. .

"*Specification 1:* In that Captain Paul R. Scott, U.S. Army, 141st Battalion, while a prisoner at Pyongyang, North Korea, on or about

September 1, 1951, without proper authority and for the purpose of seeking favorable treatment from his captors, did offer and give medical treatment to enemy personnel in a prison camp maintained by North Korean and Chinese military forces near the said city of Pyongyang.

"*Specification 2:* In that Captain Paul R. Scott did use captured medical and other supplies in the treatment of enemy personnel for the selfsame purpose.

"*Specification 3:* In that the same Captain Paul R. Scott did freely confess and sign a statement that he had personally helped to load bombs with bacteria to be dropped upon the enemy—said confession being, to the accused's own knowledge, false and without basis and made solely to obtain favorable treatment for himself.

"*Specification 4:* In that Captain Paul R. Scott, having been offered release from prison, following the signing of an armistice, did refuse repatriation and chose, at the time, to remain with the enemy though later, and of his own accord, he did seek and receive repatriation.

"CHARGE 2: Violation of the Uniform Code of Military Justice, Article 133.

"*Specification:* In that Captain Paul R. Scott did, while a prisoner at Pyongyang, act in a manner unbecoming to an officer of the United States Army and did directly because of such conduct, give aid to the enemy through the publication of propaganda material.

"CHARGE 3: Violation of the Uniform Code of Military Justice, Article 134.

"*Specification:* In that Captain Paul R. Scott did, while a prisoner at Pyongyang, conduct himself in such a manner as to bring about the prejudice of good order and discipline in the armed forces and in such a manner as to bring discredit upon the armed forces of the United States."

The lawyer was silent for a moment after he had intoned the last syllable. A smile of sorts played about his lips. "Shall we plead guilty to the lot?" he asked finally.

"Do you believe a word of that jargon?"

"Your prosecutor does—and Jim MacArdle's a smooth lawyer. If he gets your scalp he'll probably win his eagles—so he'll use every trick in the book. First trick, the grapevine tells me, will be to move for dismissal of some of the charges. Probably the first two items in Charge One. Maybe the Army won't accuse you of aiding the enemy sick, or using captured medicine—"

"Why not?"

"Because it will look better in the headlines if Jim can nail you as a Grade-A collaborator—and skip the fact that you're also a Grade-A doctor. There's no point in saying that you stopped a few epidemics with captured U.N. supplies. It might make you seem a shade too human."

"Shouldn't we insist on keeping the charges as they stand?"

"We can try. It probably won't stick—but I can hold Mac's feet in the fire until I've made the point." Hi took a list of names from his brief case. "We've just time to go over your judges."

"Is that cricket?"

"Once we're in that star chamber, pal, *anything* is cricket that doesn't land us in clink." The lawyer checked a name on the list. "I've told you that Colonel Sellers will preside. Old regime, but fair as they come. So's Major Duggan: as second officer he'll sit on Sellers' right. He's a Korean veteran and he knows the score." Hi checked a third name, with a visible pucker. "I can't say the same for Captain Carter—he's bucking for a permanent place in the judge advocate's office. The rest are run-of-the-mine Army boys— remote from reality as monks. All but Major Betts, the law officer—*he's* a walking encyclopedia of protocol and as full of crotchets as a National League umpire. You can forget him. He's my headache—"

Hi let his voice trail and marveled again at his friend's apparent unconcern. Had they been about to attend a routine classroom lecture, Paul could hardly have seemed more relaxed. An unwanted phantom rose in the lawyer's mind—the suspicion that his client might really be guilty as charged. He dropped his eyes before Paul could notice his distress, and closed the clasps of his brief case.

"We can walk over now," he said. "It'll be better if we're early— wouldn't look well to make an entrance."

"Lead the way, counselor," said Paul. "From now on, I'm taking orders."

"No more questions?"

"Just one. Do we have a chance?"

"We could use a few witnesses," said Hi carefully. "I'll do what I can to make MacArdle's boys work for our side but I'm afraid they've been too well coached." He looked hard at Paul. "I won't say this again—but it might be easier if you'd plead guilty—throw yourself on the court's mercy—"

"I'm not guilty, Hi."

"Have it your way. Want to say a prayer before we go?"

"I said it last night. This is your show now."

III

Early as they were, they found the courtroom jammed. Marching in behind a wedge of white-helmeted military police, Paul had an impression of hot, glaring lamps, of Brobdingnagian cameras, of clustering faces blank as dinner plates. In a corner someone was chanting a litany in a tongue that was not quite English—he would learn later that this was a network technician, checking his monitors to make sure that the nationwide television coverage was complete.

Paul recognized several of the men at the press table, writers from the wire services and the great dailies of the East; most of them had pounced on him in Tokyo after his repatriation and he felt himself bridle under their staring. Larry Kirk, throned in their midst and doodling on a scratch-pad, had not lifted his eyes: there was something in the famous commentator's boredom that was more damning than the newsmen's X-ray appraisals.

Since they had entered by a side door, Paul had only a distant look at the audience—and audience, he reflected, was the proper term.

People were seated in the aisles, and there was a dense mass of standees behind the last row of benches. Outside, at the gateway of the Presidio, he could hear loud-speakers urging the crowd to disperse. Since it had been the decision of the Secretary of the Army to admit both spectators and television, Paul could understand the interest in the court-martial. Just the same, it had shocked him to learn that people had waited outside the court since early morning and that thousands had been turned away for lack of space.

There was no sign of Kay Storey; after their last meeting he had not expected to find her here. Instinct told him that she was nearby—waiting, like the unseen audience that could be counted by the millions, to follow the trial on radio or television.

The courtroom itself was drab enough: the only spot of color was the flag between the two tall windows that let in a blaze of sunlight. The railed enclosure, with its chocolate-brown dado and plain wooden tables, could have been duplicated in a dozen dusty Army posts. So could the half-moon of desks on the dais, and the seven chairs where the court would sit. (The dais, Paul noted, was placed between the two casements, so that the sun glare would fall on the witness box, a lonely eminence facing the president's chair.)

Major James MacArdle and the lieutenant who was his assistant were sorting papers at the prosecutor's table; Paul gave the trial counsel a cautious glance before he settled in his own chair. MacArdle was hardly forty: his face gleamed with the special ferretlike intelligence that is the hallmark of the successful lawyer. The fact that such a man could be content with the rewards of a judge advocate's office was an endorsement of his zeal. So was the spark that illumined his pale eyes. (They were a trifle protuberant in a too-thin face, and seemed equipped with invisible magnifiers.) Torquemada himself, thought Paul, could not have enjoyed his work more. . . . He dismissed the comparison as unworthy and snapped to attention with the others as a master sergeant bawled the order from the doorway.

With Colonel Sellers at its head, the seven-man court took its place on the dais. Studying each face with care, Paul felt his heart sink. Reason though he might, he was certain that these solemn martinets had already sealed his fate.

Sellers was a head taller than the others, a handsome saturnine man with deep-set brooding eyes. Major Duggan, a mahogany-dark campaigner, needed no service ribbons to advertise his veteran's status. The others, Paul admitted, were unmilitary by contrast, despite their beautifully tailored uniforms and ramrod airs; stripped of their insignia, the lesser members of the court could have passed for lodge brothers ready to officiate at a weekend ritual. Sellers and Duggan, he realized, would be his real judges—with an assist from the overeager captain at the president's left, a buoyant young man with all the gusto of a college football manager.

For an instant the court remained frozen behind the seven chairs while a small, tubby man arrived at a special table beside the dais. The late-comer, Paul gathered, was Major Betts, the legal light who would interpret the Army code for those court members who were not lawyers.

Colonel Sellers lifted his hand for silence and spoke in a voice that seemed, to Paul's anxious ears, incredibly mild.

"At ease!"

Army and spectators settled in their chairs. Only MacArdle remained standing, his chin lifting a trifle when he saw that the TV cameras were turning. Sellers gave him a curt nod and opened the file on his blotter.

"The court will come to order."

Paul, watching the television go into gear and the scribblers at the press tables, held his breath in the expectation of shattering drama. Not even Shakespeare, he reflected, had commanded a fraction of MacArdle's present audience. Actually the proceedings of the next half hour were freighted with boredom.

There was a long recital of names, the swearing-in of court reporters, a statement of the qualifications of the Honorable Hilary Saunders (the only civilian present within the railed enclosure). Members of the court were sworn, including Betts, the trial counsel, and his assistant. Thanks to last night's insomnia, Paul was half dozing in his chair when the president announced that the court was now in session.

MacArdle rose and stated the source of the charges. There was a final hiatus while he offered Hi the right to challenge any of the judges. When this privilege was waived a subtle change in the prosecutor's manner told Paul that this, at last, was the first true attack.

Striding to the clear space between the lawyers' tables, MacArdle faced the bench with his eyes half closed and a notebook seemingly forgotten in his hand. He spoke diffidently—and so rapidly that the stenotype operators seemed hard put to catch the words.

"By direction of the convening authority, the prosecution withdraws the first and second specifications of Charge One, and will not pursue the same further in this trial."

"Objection!"

Hi Saunders' voice had stopped the prosecutor's half-audible drone. Colonel Sellers opened his eyes wide for the first time. Paul noted that they were a clear light blue: they seemed completely innocent in their careworn setting.

"Does defense counsel *object* to withdrawal of charges against the accused?"

"I do, sir. Charges and specifications, in their entirety, are general in nature. Later I intend to move their dismissal *in toto*. To withdraw any part of them now will prejudice the prepared defense of the accused."

MacArdle kept his poise. "If the court please, this is irregular to the extreme."

"The handling of this whole case has been irregular," said Hi. "I repeat that withdrawal of any part of the formal charge will deprive Captain Scott of a full opportunity to clear himself."

The president leaned forward: his eyes were magnets now, drawing both lawyers to the bench. After Major Betts had joined the whispered huddle the court rose as a body and filed from the room to deliberate the objection.

"Don't look so puzzled," said Hi, when he had returned to the defense table. "All I said was that you're ready to take your punishment—and mean to fight back. It registered on TV—that's all we care about."

"What will happen?"

"Nothing. A distress call will go to the convening authority, and they'll rule for MacArdle."

True to Hi's prediction, the court returned in a few moments to uphold the withdrawal of the first two specifications of Charge One. When Hi had protested (and the protest had been recorded), copies of the revised charges were passed to each member of the court and to the press tables. After this solemn obeisance to justice the court-martial ground into motion again.

"With the consent of the accused," said MacArdle, "I will omit the reading of the charges. As the court knows, they are sworn to by Colonel Jasper Hardin, who is thereby subject to the military code as the accuser. Charges and specifications, the name and description of the accused, his affidavit, and the reference for trial will be copied verbatim into the record."

"The accused consents," said Hi.

"On September twentieth last," said MacArdle, "the charges were served by me on the accused. How does he plead?"

"The defense moves for a dismissal of all charges and specifications," said Hi.

"On what grounds?" asked the president.

"On the grounds that the accuser publicized the charges at a time when Captain Scott was still in Korea. On the grounds that copies of an alleged confession, signed by Captain Scott in the enemy prison at Pyongyang, have long since found their way into the newspapers—with the result that this case has been tried by headline before the accused could prepare a defense. On the further ground that these charges are false in their entirety and were made solely for the purpose of discrediting Captain Scott—the aim being to prevent him from making known the truth about his conduct in Korea."

Colonel Sellers' gavel enforced silence. "Mr. Saunders, the accuser in this case is an officer of the United States Army. He has sworn to the charges. Are you implying he committed perjury?"

"It is our intention, sir, to prove that the charges *do* constitute perjury."

"The court will withdraw to discuss the motion and vote on it."

Hi assumed a grave face for the television as he stood at attention and watched the seven judges leave the room. But his eyes twinkled when he settled beside Paul.

"I'm improvising," he admitted. "But it was too good a chance to miss. In any case, we'll want these protests on the record in case we appeal."

It was a suffocating thought, but Paul could see it made sense. With the charges as grave as they were, conviction at the present court-martial was all too likely. Hi was already laying the groundwork for a possible second trial before the Court of Military Appeals. Composed of civilians, it was a final resort in such cases, short only of the Supreme Court itself.

This time, Paul's seven judges filed back after the briefest of recesses.

"The motion is denied," said Sellers. "Proceed, Major MacArdle."

"How does the accused plead?" the trial counsel asked.

"The accused pleads not guilty to all specifications and charges," Hi Saunders announced.

MacArdle addressed the court. "The prosecution states at this time that it will introduce in evidence a confession by the accused."

Hi barked an instant objection. "The accused will deny making any confession that would prove valid in a court of law. The statement by the prosecution at this point tends to indicate that a valid document of such nature exists, which the accused denies."

"The objection is sustained, subject to objection by any member of the court," said the president. "The reporter will strike from the record all reference to a confession. Has trial counsel any further statement?"

MacArdle's eyes were modestly lowered before Sellers' glare, but his lips were tight with anger. "None, sir."

"Are you ready to call your first witness?"

"I am. The prosecution calls as witness Corporal Harold Jackson."

IV

Corporal Jackson marched stiffly into court: a rangy, horsefaced regular who had once seemed as familiar to Paul as a foster brother. He felt the expected pang at his heart when Harry favored him with a totally blank stare. He had guessed that Jackson would be the first to testify against him. In his way, the corporal's reactions summed up the case from the prosecution's point of view.

After the witness had been duly sworn MacArdle handled him with friendly competence, establishing the fact that he had served in Korea with the 141st Battalion, and that he had been captured after the surrender of Hill 1049, in the summer of 1951.

"You were, I believe, a member of the medical detail under Captain Scott?"

"Yes, sir, I was."

"Did he ever say or do anything while in the front line that suggested he was thinking of co-operating with the enemy?"

"Well, I heard him say once 'I'm going to make the best of this that I can.'"

There was a stir of interest among the spectators; the prosecutor let it run its course. "You're sure that Captain Scott used those precise words?"

"Yes, sir. I heard him."

"What did you think?"

"Nothing at the time; I figured it was just a front-line gripe. But I remembered it later—when we were prisoners at Pyongyang. When Captain Scott began to co-operate with the Chinese—".

"Objection," said Hi. "Prosecution has offered no proof of co-operation."

"I intend to do so through this witness," said MacArdle.

"Any reference to co-operation will be struck from the record," said Sellers. "Proceed, Major."

"Think carefully, Corporal. Did you notice anything different in Captain Scott's conduct after you reached the prison camp?"

"He was running the camp hospital."

"Was there anything unusual in that?"

"Well, they had Chinese doctors there before."

"Were you ever admitted as a patient?"

"Yes, sir."

"How would you describe Captain Scott's position at the time?"

"He was head man; they all did what he said."

"You would say, then, that he was co-operating with the enemy?"

"I would, sir."

"Did other prisoners share your belief?"

"Everyone in my barracks called him a canary."

"Canary?"

"A progressive. Someone who's gone over to the Commie side."

"No further questions."

There was an edge to Hi Saunders' voice when he rose to cross-examine. "Corporal, what were your duties on Hill 1049?"

"I was a first-aid technician." The deference had gone from Jackson's manner; it was evident that he resented the presence of a civilian lawyer. Remembering the months they had shared in the lines (when Hi had also been in uniform) and how friendly the lawyer had been with the members of his surgical team, Paul wondered if Jackson had put that camaraderie from his thoughts deliberately.

"Did you assist Captain Scott with operations?"

"Yes, sir."

You did indeed, thought Paul; not too long ago, you helped to save your questioner's life on Hill 1049. A great sense of frustration claimed him as Jackson's surly voice went on. Already the monstrous blackening of his past was underway. Could he keep his mask of unconcern unbroken while the lie took shape and depth until it was a living thing?

Paul felt his eyelids droop as a familiar alembic began to function in his brain; it was a trick of disassociation that had saved his sanity in Korea, and it seemed only fair to use it now. In another moment the drone of the corporal's testimony had grown fainter, along with Hi's sharp efforts to break down his veracity. . . . There would be time enough later to measure the success of those efforts. For the present it was simpler to let his mind go back—to the very scene that Harry Jackson was distorting so fatally.

Hill 1049 had been the place where his faith in his fellows had had its first real testing. It was worth a visit in memory—now that Major MacArdle's trap had begun to close about him. The prosecutor need never know that his victim (thanks to that knack of immersion in the past) could escape the trap at will.

HILL 1049

I

The crest of Hill 1049 dominated the long funnel of the valley below it. For this reason a series of observation posts had been scooped in its spine the last time it had changed hands. After the United Nations lines had been pushed down the northern slope the posts had been largely abandoned by the lookouts, who could now spy out enemy maneuvers at closer range. This afternoon the lone observer who squatted in one of these two-man foxholes was lost in his own musings—though he was alert enough to keep his head down. The crest of Hill 1049 was still within sniper range. Not ten minutes ago (when Captain Paul Scott had scrambled in from the far side of the ridge) a bullet had whined across the sandbags.

It had become Paul's custom to watch the sunset from this vantage point, whenever his presence was not required at the aid station. The communion with death that he shared down below was a burden no man could discard for long—a surgeon least of all. For that reason he had begun to prize these rare moments of solitude—and today, after all, was a milestone of sorts. Just six months ago (he could almost name the hour) the 141st Battalion had first set foot in Korea. In that interval, he felt, he had earned these brief retirements from his job.

Six months to the day, he added, with a trace of bitter pride. Add three weeks for the crossing and yet another month for final indoctrination in Japan: it's more than half a year since Kay Storey waved good-by to you from a pier in San Pedro.

II

His fingers touched the packet of air-mail envelopes in the upper pocket of his shirt; he always reread Kay's letters at this hour, though he could have recited their contents verbatim. Going through them one more time, he felt the familiar tug at his heart; the need for her living presence was as real as it had been on the deck of the *Millard Fillmore*—and the chances of reunion seemed remote as ever.

The troupe for which Kay had qualified (thanks to one of the last-minute switches so dear to the Army) had not sailed after all. Instead, it had gone on a nationwide tour to boost morale in the cantonments. Paul's letters (which he had somehow managed to keep cheerful) had followed Kay all over the United States; they had been answered promptly from such unlikely addresses as Key West and Pocatello and Seattle. His last, however, mailed a good six weeks ago, was still unanswered. So far, he could not even assure himself that this was a hopeful sign and that she had really embarked at last. . . .

There had been no word of love in their correspondence, no sentiment beyond a playful tenderness; by unspoken agreement they had both avoided serious topics. After all—and he had reasoned this out a hundred times—he had no right to assume that his desire, which had grown so steadily in their long separation, would find an answering chord in Kay. A night of shared rapture (he reminded himself wryly of this obvious fact) is a common thing in wartime. In granting him that boon, Kay had remained herself: perhaps, in her mind, it had been only a patriotic duty. Certainly it did not prove that she had felt more than a friendly interest in him.

He put the chilling possibility aside and looked through the observer's slit at the scarred landscape below. As always he was stirred by the sinister beauty of this mountain terrain. It was a beauty that transcended such man-made artifacts as bunkers, gun mounts, slit trenches, the black slashes on a northern hill where aircraft had loosed napalm fires at low-level range. Even there, new grass had already begun to clothe the ravaged earth. . . . Perhaps it was a fact that the truce talks (begun a few weeks ago, after the war had ground into a second year of stalemate) would bring results. At least it was comforting to note that nature was already working to erase the thumbprints of Mars.

So far, Paul told himself, you've kept your head and survived. You've earned a captain's bars and a firm place as battalion surgeon. Never mind what that promotion's worth in a foxhole—or the psychotic ragings of Colonel Jasper Hardin. The C.O.'s enmity is a thing you've learned to take in stride. . . . His nerve ends sprang alive as a pebble rolled into the observation post—and eased again when he saw that it was one of his technicians. The friendly horse-face of Corporal Harry Jackson restored Paul to the problems of the everyday. Thanks to willing helpers such as Jackson, most of those problems had solved themselves.

"Litter case comin' in, sir. Figured I should warn you."

"This is too fine a day for casualties, Harry. Why couldn't you tell me they've declared a truce at Kaesong?"

"Cap'n, if there's a truce comin' up, this sector ain't been alerted. Or maybe the gooks across the way just can't read."

"The front's been quiet as a church since dawn."

"Easy Company don't think so. They just had a killed-in-action—guy stepped on a mine coming back from patrol. The fellow with him got some iron in his tail: they're sending him to us for repairs."

Paul jammed his helmet over his ears and lifted himself carefully until his head was level with the sandbagged rim of the post. Behind him, Jackson followed the move without orders: Jackson was a regular who had been in this war from the beginning.

"No snipers when you came in, Harry?"

"Nary one, sir. Maybe they *can* read, after all." They exchanged a grin when a bullet sang across the crest, near enough to pull their heads down together, like puppets in some Punch and Judy booth.

"Maybe they don't believe their own propaganda," said Paul. He was glad that Jackson had come here to fetch him when he might easily have sent a runner: he had always liked the corporal and felt that the liking was returned. Both Sergeant Furness (his senior NCO in the medical detail) and Jackson had welcomed him from the start. So, for that matter, had the other medics, the battalion aid men and the stretcher-bearers—mere boys, for the most part, who risked their lives daily in his behalf. Perhaps it was because of this shared danger (and the will to ignore it) that the aid station was a close-knit unit, a striking contrast to the battalion it served.

He repeated the conviction solemnly while he crawled out of the post in Jackson's wake and scrambled down the ridge. Friendships such as these (when the stakes of the game were life and death) could never be valued too highly. Without them, he would have long since broken under Hardin's goading.

III

Well down the southern slope, protected by the walls of a deep ravine, the aid station occupied a roomy bunker the Chinese had dug there months before. Compared to the usual station in the lines, Paul had found these quarters almost luxurious. Even in the nightly barrages the surgical bunker had never been shelled too heavily. This, obviously, was an ominous proof that the enemy intended to bag Hill 1049 in his next push and wished to keep the shelter intact for his own use. Meanwhile it permitted the medics to catch up on sleep.

Two litter-bearers were approaching when Paul dropped into the ravine. The casualty, a rawboned boy still in his teens, was dozing comfortably under the morphine administered by the company aid man, and there was a clean dressing over his wounds. At Paul's direction the stretcher was placed on two empty oil drums outside the bunker entrance. The boy's pulse, he noted, was strong and his color good; the medical tag indicated that the wound itself was scarcely a half-hour old.

One look at the injuries completed the clinical pattern: Paul had treated scores of these cases during his long months in the bunker. The mine boxes the Chinese used were always hard to spot—but this soldier had been lucky. Both thighs were badly chewed (there was no better way to describe the gnawing cruelty of the wounds). Bits of muscle hung from the jagged lacerations, showing that part of that burst of scrap metal had buried itself beneath the fascia. But this, after all, was only a minor mishap. Given prompt surgery and a few weeks in a rest area, Private Ewell Hansen would live to fight again.

"How'd he get off so lightly, Harry?"

"The other guy stepped on the box. They're scrapin' *him* off the rock."

The boy's eyelids had flickered at the sound of voices: he stared up at them sleepily from morphine-tight pupils.

"Is it bad, Doc?"

"You've some iron in your legs," said Paul. "It's nothing serious, Hansen. You've bought a rest ticket at a bargain."

Sergeant Furness had already heaved up from the bunker like an outsize mole emerging from its burrow. The chief technician, a tireless, grizzled veteran whose build had always reminded Paul of a Japanese wrestler, carried an extra blanket: his hands were surprisingly gentle as he swathed the casualty.

"We're ready when you are, Cap'n."

"Keep him warm, Tom," said Paul. "I'll see if we can get him back to MASH." The Mobile Army Surgical Hospital was ten miles to the rear, and chances of transport at this hour were slight. Still, it was an inflexible rule that a call must go through in such a situation.

"I've set up to operate here," said Furness.

"He must go back, if they'll take him."

"Cap'n, you're better than those jokers at Regiment."

Paul spoke for the benefit of the stretcher-bearers: this, too, was a routine that seldom varied. "As you were, Furness. The colonel doesn't approve of front-line surgery."

"If you ask me, sir, the colonel can—" The rest was lost when Furness popped back into his bunker. Paul closed his ears to the burst of profanity the walls could not quite muffle: during these months in the lines, Colonel Jasper Hardin had been cursed in many tongues.

Battalion headquarters was located well down the slope, in a steel-and-concrete bunker—another legacy from the Chinese, which Hardin had spared no pains to make even safer. Paul had always found the place a trifle grotesque after a tour of the lines, and the dress-parade manners that the C.O. insisted on there were, to him, just short of macabre. From the first day he had established himself in this heavily sandbagged retreat, Hardin had insisted that his officers report to him in person, no matter how small the request. The colonel himself rarely ventured outside. When the shelling began the steel door slammed—and orders were transmitted to the forward posts by telephone.

This afternoon the door was open wide, and a spruce sentry gave Paul a model present-arms as he moved into its shadow. (The soldiers on the far slope of this same hill might resemble sullen mud turtles—but Hardin's own quarters were always spotless.) The room where the colonel worked was at the far end of the bunker, a compact nest piled high with maps and heavy with field phones. Hardin did not look up when Paul came to attention before the desk. The corner of the comic book he had been reading still showed under the map he had pushed foward to conceal it: comic books (of the gorier sort) were the C.O.'s one relaxation besides the bottle. . . . Sniffing the lifeless air of the bunker, Paul concluded that Hardin was sober. After all, it had been a quiet day on Hill 1049.

"You may speak, Captain."

"Easy Company just sent in a casualty, sir. A land-mine burst."

"The fool got what he deserved. Every member of this battalion has gone through a course in mine detection."

"The man who stepped on this one was KIA," said Paul. "The boy they brought in was the innocent bystander."

"Will he live?"

"His wounds aren't dangerous if he undergoes surgery promptly. I'd like to call for an ambulance to take him to MASH."

"Request is denied, Captain. Our MSR is under fire again."

The main supply route to the rear, though it had been bombed sporadically, was usually navigable. The fact that it was now under steady fire was bad news indeed—the probable overture to an all-out attack on their position.

"May I order a 'copter, sir?"

"The word is *helicopter*, Captain. You're supposed to be an educated man. Don't speak like a juvenile delinquent in my presence."

Since he had been given no order to stand at ease, Paul's shoulders were still painfully braced, his arms rigid at his sides. Feeling his fingers curl, he kept his voice level. "Sorry, sir. Request permission to call helicopter evacuation unit."

"Permission granted, Captain. Dismissed."

Paul gave the colonel a model salute, which the other acknowledged with a flick of his hand: the about-face that took him from the C.O.'s presence would not have disgraced a West Pointer. The communications center was in the room behind Hardin's sanctum; in a few moments the enlisted operator had put through a call to regimental headquarters. The chief surgeon at the mobile hospital unit, a friend of long standing, informed Paul that all available helicopters were busy elsewhere.

"It sounds like a routine casualty. Can't you operate there?"

"Certainly, Major; I'd prefer it that way if he can be evacuated later."

"Go ahead, then. I'll send an egg beater to the hill tomorrow."

What Paul had said was no vain boast. As soon as the divisional surgeon had learned of his qualifications he had sent up enough special equipment to the battalion station to transform it into a small but highly efficient hospital. Somewhat to his surprise, Paul had learned that this was routine practice in the Korean War, when large groups of infantry were often cut off for days from communication with headquarters and unable to evacuate wounded. Because of this early and adequate surgery, fatalities on Hill 1049 had been held to a minimum.

He had never quite understood why Hardin should object so strongly to his using the battalion aid station as a hospital: perhaps it was involved with the dark suspicions that gnawed at the C.O.'s brain whenever he was forced to accept a deviation from standard operational procedure. Like all small-souled men, Hardin was a slavish follower of the book, and any threat to S.O.P. (those hallowed initials, Paul suspected, had been burned into his psyche at West Point) was a threat to his own shaky pride. Then too, it was a reminder that Paul took orders—as well as help—from higher authorities, particularly the regimental and division surgeons—and was therefore not always responsible to battalion headquarters for his actions.

In any event, Hardin had fought furiously to keep his chief medical officer from functioning as a surgeon. As he knocked for a second time on the C.O.'s door Paul knew that he was girding himself for the inevitable battle—and prayed that his badly frayed temper would not betray him.

This time there was an appreciable pause before the shouted permission to enter. The stale air of the bunker room held a tangible reek of whiskey now. Sunset (which brought the first gun flashes from the north) was usually the time of Hardin's first potation.

"You may speak, Captain."

"Efforts to evacuate the casualty have been negative, sir. All helicopters are absent on other missions."

"Hold him overnight, then. We can't ask for an ambulance with the MSR under fire."

"Waiting doesn't help wounds of this kind, sir. Bits of clothing are always driven in by the mine fragments. It's a prime spot for a gas-bacillus infection to develop." Paul had mentioned the threat deliberately, hoping that it would rouse an echo of Hardin's own experiences in World War II. Actually those vicious germs had been largely conquered in the present conflict, due largely to front-line surgery.

"Would you like to be a hero, Captain, and take out an ambulance yourself?"

"That won't be necessary, sir. The regimental surgeon has ordered me to operate here."

"Since when does Major Williams exercise command over troops? His is a staff function only."

"Part of his staff function, Colonel, is to be responsible for the medical welfare of the troops—just as mine is here."

"Your function is to obey my orders, Scott." Hardin was really shouting now. "Do you understand that much, you conceited fool?"

"I understand, sir," said Paul quietly. "I'll make the notation on the man's medical tag. I hope that higher commands will realize why I did not carry out my duty."

It was a calculated risk, but the implied threat struck home. (Actually he had no intention of letting Private Hansen pass the night without surgery. If the official record had gone forward tomorrow with such a notation, his head would have rolled, rather than Hardin's.) When the C.O. did not answer at once Paul knew that he had won. This time, at least, Hardin had been shrewd enough to yield, though his reply was bellowed in a voice that shook the casements.

"Very well, Scott. Stick out your neck again if you must. D'you take full responsibility?"

"Of course, sir."

"Then operate—and be sure you know what you're doing. It's against all regulations to give surgical aid in the front lines."

"Not in this war, Colonel."

"Dismissed, damn it, *dismissed!* Get out of my sight!"

Another dress-parade salute and a precise about-face took Paul through the door: as ordeals went with Hardin, this one had been mild enough. As he turned to the incline heading to the outer world, the technician at the battalion switchboard gave him a wink of pure sympathy. There was no impertinence in the gesture: it was simply Sergeant Luppino's way of telling a friend that he, too, was bearing his burden as best he could.

Outside, an ominous purple light had invaded the sky; an alien burst of flame had just violated these dregs of sunset. The explosion that followed was strong enough to shake dust from the bunker roof.

"Concert's early tonight, sir," said the technician.

"You ought to sleep through it here, Angelo."

"After six months in these hills," said Luppino, "I could sleep anywhere. Wish I could say as much for the old man."

They exchanged another wordless look as they heard the unmistakable *wheet* of a cork from the colonel's sanctum. There was no other sound to advertise a human presence, save for the whisper of the chair leg that Hardin had just propped against the already locked door.

"You're a doctor, sir," said Luppino. "Tell me what a man does when he's scared—and still can't sleep?"

IV

On his return to the aid station, Paul was pleased to find Father Tim standing above Hansen's stretcher. A stole lay across the chaplain's shoulder and there was an open Bible in his hand—but Paul knew that the phrases pouring from his lips were recited from memory. The battalion surgeon had heard that prayer for the recovery of the wounded a hundred times and knew better than to interrupt. The few minutes that Father Tim needed to minister to Hansen would make no difference in his treatment— and he had profound respect for the balm that litany could bring to war-torn nerves.

When the priest had closed his Bible and folded the narrow stole inside the cover, Paul saw that the boy on the stretcher had quieted visibly: as always, he was grateful for this mysterious therapy, without attempting to diagnose its cause.

"You'll be all right now, Hansen," said Father Tim. "You may not realize it, but the surgeon who's operating on you tonight is the finest in the whole Eighth Army."

Paul stepped aside to give Sergeant Furness a path to the stretcher. "Thanks for the vote of confidence, Padre," he said. "Who told you we were operating?"

A faint smile lit Father Tim's tired countenance. "Colonel Hardin's voice carries when he's really roused. I won't keep you from your work, Paul:

we'll be meeting again tonight before the concert's over."

"Seems they're tuning up now, Father," said Sergeant Furness. The three men lifted their eyes to the brow of the hill, where a series of garish orange flares continued to violate the afterglow of the sunset. With each burst the earth rumbled faintly, as though an unseen colossus were stamping in anger, far down the valley.

"Is the table ready, Tom?"

"Ready and waiting, Cap'n."

"Take him in, and get your anesthetic started. I'll be with you in a moment."

Paul linked an arm with Father Tim's and walked the priest down the ravine to the door of the officers' shelter. It was a custom he followed whenever possible, for the frail young padre's nerves were none too steady when these bombardments opened. Yet unlike Hardin—who merely burrowed for cover when danger threatened—Father Tim seemed to risk exposure deliberately. On occasion Paul had been forced to speak sharply, lest the chaplain stop a bullet in his haste to reach a dying soldier's side. Had it been feasible he would have insisted that he administer last rites in the safety of the aid station.

"Get what rest you can, Padre," he said. "So far, they're only feeling each other out."

Experience had told Paul that the present "concert" (as Hill 1049 had dubbed the nighttime bombardments) was only a prelude for another of those senseless head-on charges that had proved nothing, so far, but the enemy's disregard for his own man power. In a few moments more the stepped-up tempo of the salvos confirmed his guess. Far back in the American bastions the 240's and 155 Long Toms were barking steadily: a symphony filled with dissonants, counterpointed by individual bursts from M-1s on the northern slope. . . . It was music from hell—and although he had memorized every note in the infernal cadence, it could still rattle the teeth in his head.

And yet, when he had gone back to the aid station and finished scrubbing, Paul felt his panic slip away. On the flanks of Hill 1049 men might go on slaughtering each other until dawn. Here, at least, he was above the din. His job was clearcut, and a life depended on his skill.

Hansen was on the table now; Furness had begun to inject the ampoule of sodium pentothal. Jackson, who would serve as Paul's assistant tonight, stood waiting at the instrument table. Doctor and medics had stripped to the waist: they would work thus through the summer night, when the artillery duel brought its harvest to their door.

"Ready to go to sleep for a while, soldier?"

"Sure thing, Doc. Reckon they'll evacuate me tomorrow?"

In a few seconds more the boy was snoring peacefully. Above the table the gasoline lamp hissed faintly, bathing the dugout in a white glare. Paul had dropped the blanket flap over the entrance when he came in, shutting the world of healing from the world of war. . . . The business of probing the wounds was a ticklish affair: he approached it carefully, with a hemostat in his free hand, wary for signs of hemorrhage. It was a tedious process as well, but a vital one. The smallest scrap of cloth, hidden in those gaping lacerations, could set up a focus for later infection that would mean untold trouble. Minutes spent now in removing such fragments might save months of hospitalization later.

Now and then the forceps grated loudly in the quiet of the bunker; the gleaming jaws lifted from the wound to drop splinters of steel into the basin that stood beside the table. Furness, the syringe of pentothal cradled in his palm, steadied the patient with easy competence. With each dart of the forceps, Jackson was ready with a swab, sponging away the bright ooze of blood that inundated the wound with each removal.

"That makes thirteen, Cap'n. This guy owes the Russkis something—hope our fellows pay it back."

Hansen moaned under the anesthesia, and the sergeant pressed gently on the plunger of the syringe: the injection, flooding the blood stream with its soothing contents, quieted the movement almost instantly. Once again Paul rejoiced in the easy magic of sodium pentothal: in cases like these he liked the patient to be carried as lightly as possible.

"'Bout through, sir?"

Paul glanced at Furness in mild astonishment. So intense was his concentration, he had been unaware of the passage of time. A whole half hour had slipped by unnoticed while he proceeded with his meticulous cleansing of the wounds.

"Almost. Retractor, please, Harry. We'll make a final exploration and call it a day."

Jackson slapped the metal strip into his palm and stood ready with fresh sponges. Enlarging each wound with care, Paul swabbed it from end to end and studied the exposed fascia minutely. There was no trace of cloth or metal: the last possible focus of infection now lay in the basin.

"I'll bandage him, Sergeant. You can let him out."

Furness eased the needle from the vein and stood by to assist in taping the long spiral bandage that Paul had begun to wind around the patient's leg. The activating dose of tetanus toxoid had already been injected: by tomorrow Hansen's resistance to the once-dread lockjaw would have risen to a point where he would be amply protected. When he had bandaged the other leg Paul injected a heavy dose of penicillin as an added precaution—and stood back while his two assistants transferred the boy to the far side of the bunker where a half dozen cots always stood ready.

Hansen's pulse was only a trifle faster than before the operation, but Paul decided to take no chances. A unit of plasma was opened at his order: so skilled were his technicians in this routine, it took only a moment before the dark brown iquid was flowing into a vein. Not even a base hospital, Paul reflected, could have provided more complete assurance of recovery. Yet the operation had been performed only a stone's toss from enemy trenches.

There had been no more casualties while they worked: the battalion had grown adept at taking cover during these nightly assaults. However, though losses would be held to a minimum, Paul knew that he could expect a dozen wounded before morning. At least he could use his own initiative at this time, with Hardin safely under cover. Frequently he had operated from dusk to dawn, here in the harsh glare of the gas lamp.

"Better chow up while you can, sir," said Jackson. "Me and Tom had ours early."

Paul nodded and turned to the door. As always, he felt a warm glow of satisfaction in the knowledge that his two medics (thanks to their months of teamwork) could solve most post-operative problems without him.

"Take a breather yourselves," he said. "You know where to find me."

This, too, was part of the nighttime ritual. On the step of the dugout he paused to slip into his shirt (there was no chance of an encounter with Hardin, but the precaution was automatic). Furness had already cut off the gas lamp above the operating table: with only a small oil lantern to illumine it, the bunker had a curiously homelike air. Paul put down the impulse to linger and forced himself to step over the sill. It was always a slight wrench to break free of this little world.

V

Outside, Paul found that the artillery duel had rumbled into silence, though heavier pieces still quarreled far down the valley. Evidently the attack on Hill 1049 had been a feint, to hide a thrust elsewhere. Only a few whispers broke the eerie silence while he groped toward the mess. It was hard to believe that the slope was thick with men, still waiting behind their guns to repel an advance that had already recoiled on the northern slope.

Hearing the chatter of static from the portable radio inside, he paused for an instant on the sill of the headquarters bunker. A wiry form, disengaging from the blackout curtain, spoke his name as he was about to move on.

"Evenin', Cap'n. Operation over?"

"Wrapped up for delivery in the morning" said Paul shortly. He had never liked Master Sergeant Bates, the chief figure in the camarilla that insulated Hardin from his battalion. There was nothing on which he could base his dislike, unless it was the man's carefully controlled impudence. Bates, did his job efficiently. True, the battalion had a special (and unprintable) label for the Sergeant Major and his genius for currying favor with the colonel—but that, too, was only inevitable.

"Enjoy tonight's concert, sir?"

"I was too busy to listen."

"Didn't care for the selections myself," said Bates. "Not that they hit us too hard. It's another story on the MSR."

"Is that why the colonel is using the radio?"

"Phones went out an hour ago. The gooks are behind us, all right."

The surgeon shrugged off the news and moved on. In this queer war of thrust and counterthrust Hill 1049 had been isolated before: the main supply route had always been reopened in time, after determined regimental action. He could hear Hardin on the radiophone, bellowing for a relief column. Even at the distance he could catch the man's strident note of panic—and understood all too well why Bates was standing guard. . . . Paul shrugged off Colonel Jasper Hardin in turn. Bates had his uses after all. At least the fears that churned in Hardin's brain would not infect the men who stood guard beyond.

In the warm, Spam-flavored haven of the battalion mess Paul felt his nerve ends unwind as a cook ladled stew into his mess kit. "Better eat hearty, Captain. I hear we might have fried gook for breakfast."

It was an old joke and a stale one, but he found that he could laugh at it nonetheless. The chance that the hill might be swept before morning had never disturbed this stolen half hour of rest.

"Mind if I join you, Scott?"

Paul smiled up into the soot-blackened face of Major Hilary Saunders—a liaison officer from the battery on the next hill. Like himself, Saunders looked tired but happy as he dropped into the place beside him: the face was slack with fatigue, but the eyes in the coal-black mask were sparkling with good humor. Save for the trench knife and the .45 attached to the webbing of his belt, Hi could have passed for an end man in a minstrel show, about to unburden himself of a sure-fire joke.

"What brings you here tonight, my friend?"

"Who but your C.O.? Ever since sundown he's been shouting for artillery support. As a result I've been giving an imitation of a blacksnake to get here. I can assure you it's rough going in the country between your hill and mine. Grenades all the way: some of those Chinese noncoms can pitch like big-leaguers."

"Why come over in person?"

"Colonel Hardin insisted. Wanted a gunnery officer whole on the hoof." Saunders glanced at the drowsy cooks and lowered his voice. "How can you stand him on a round-the-clock basis?"

"I sometimes wonder, Hi."

"The man's a psychotic. You can't deny that."

"I've known it from our first interview."

"Back home he might be bearable: discipline and the old Army routine could keep him in line. Out here he must be hell on wheels."

"I'm hoping he'll sweat it out."

"Sure he will—if he can dissolve his fear in booze. If he can hold this hill he may even emerge a hero. The fact remains he can't stay in that bunker forever." Hi Saunders yawned and rubbed the worst of the soot from his forehead. "Not if the enemy *really* means to smash our present line. Ever wonder what might happen if Hardin really blew his top?"

"I've tried not to dwell on it," said Paul.

"Funny, isn't it, how death gets to be a commonplace here? Most of us discover we can bear it—so long as *we* aren't the ones to die. Hardin is a different breed of cat. He would sacrifice the lot of you without turning a hair."

"What are you suggesting? A round robin, asking for his removal? You know how higher authority would react."

Saunders nodded soberly. "It's no picnic, watching the wheels of tradition turn and measuring the waste with a civilian's brain. The irony of it is, Hardin might have been a success if he'd been born the same year as Napoleon—"

"When wars were fought by the book?"

"Exactly—when a man could exist by the code, without thinking at all."

Paul found that he was chuckling at Hi's low, earnest whisper. He knew that he should stop this flow of words, that such relaxation bordered on mutiny. But it was a profound relief to hear an analysis that matched his own.

"The colonel himself has a standard lecture on that subject," he said. "From his viewpoint the trouble began after Pearl Harbor. World War II was the show that really fouled up the Army—putting a lot of civilians in officers' uniforms, with jobs they couldn't handle. Today even the dogfaces are given comforts the *old* Army couldn't spell—recreation centers, education, psychiatric help—"

It was Hi Saunders' turn to chuckle. "You were in the last big one, Paul. *All* old-school officers aren't like Hardin."

"Far from it. Call him the eternal throwback every profession is cursed with."

"In another minute you'll say he's more to be pitied than blamed."

"Oddly enough, I *do* think he's to be pitied."

"So does the chaplain," said Hi. "Of course, he has a perspective that's denied us."

"Father Tim would forgive Mao himself if he could get within hailing distance," said Paul.

Hi Saunders looked at him keenly. "Are you picking up his viewpoint?"

"Not quite. I'm in this business to get what I can out of it—particularly a whole skin." Anger had lifted Paul's voice: he broke off when he saw that Corporal Jackson had come into the mess for coffee. "Let's secure this patter," he said. "You aren't being paid to hear my gripes."

"You hear mine," said Hi. "So it's fifty-fifty. Speaking of angels, here's your chaplain now."

Father Tim, who had paused at the cook's counter for a word with Jackson, dropped into a seat beside them when the corporal left the mess. Watching Hi's offhand welcome, Paul could envy the artillery officer his aplomb. Harvard had helped, he reflected, as well as the silver spoon. Still and all, his friend had made his own life: a born lawyer, with a vast practice in Los Angeles, it was ironic that he should have been chosen for heavy-weapons duty in Korea—simply because he had served with the ordnance department in the last world war.

"You've arrived just in time, Chaplain," said Hi. "Paul is insisting that all men are brothers—including your C.O. I was about to enter a minority opinion."

Father Tim stirred his coffee. "Give me time to collect myself," he said.

Paul spoke as severely as he could; it was always hard to bear down too heavily on the padre. "Were you listening to the concert out of doors?"

"Yes, Paul. On the brow of the hill."

"I've warned you before to stay under cover until you're needed."

"If I'm in the open I can follow the stretcher-bearers."

"You could do as well if you'd stay in the first-aid bunker. The men will call you whenever you're needed."

Father Tim smiled. "If tonight's show had gone on another ten minutes I'd have scuttled for this burrow like a rabbit."

"Fear is man's oldest emotion, Father," said Hi. "There's no cause to feel ashamed if you yield to it."

"You and Paul have never yielded."

"Tonight we've nowhere to run," said Paul. "Or hadn't you heard that we're surrounded?"

The priest knotted his fingers. There was something touching in the fact that he made no effort to hide their trembling.

"What's to become of us?"

"We'll hold the position—I hope. Tomorrow a regimental combat team will clear our supply route."

"I believe you, Paul, but I'm still afraid. I'm the one who comforts the dying and speaks of life after death. Yet I'm afraid of dying myself."

"Maybe it isn't *dying* you're afraid of, Padre," said Hi Saunders. "Could be your anger kicking back."

"I've long since put anger behind me, Major Saunders."

"Twentieth-century man has every reason to curse the history that's been forced upon him," said Paul. "Suppose we die here, with no chance whatever to write our names on the honor roll. Haven't you ever dreamed of being a cardinal someday? Or another Albert Schweitzer?"

"My only desire is to serve my fellow man, to outlive the demands of self." The priest looked up at the step that had just sounded outside the dugout. Paul had guessed Sergeant Furness' errand before he could put in his head.

"Call from Able Company, sir. Infiltrator just knifed a sentry."

"Can they bring him in?"

"Afraid not. He's too badly hurt."

"I'll come at once," said Paul. "Sorry to end this metaphysical discussion, gentlemen, but duty calls. Did you bring my pack, Sergeant?"

"It's right outside, sir. I'll show you the way down."

"The company aid man will be with the casualty. I can go alone."

"Not with Fu Manchu on the loose: you'll need a pair of eyes looking backward."

"You're to stay in the aid station, Tom. We're sure to have other cases."

"But, Captain—"

"That's an order, Sergeant. Help me with the pack."

Absorbed in the business at hand, they had moved outside the dugout: Furness bent to lift the pack containing the equipment a surgeon would need for an emergency dressing in the field. It was a familiar summons if a risky one: Paul had ministered to dozens of wounded on the spot, when expert care was needed.

"Let me take the sergeant's place, Paul."

Looking into the chaplain's troubled eyes, Paul saw that they were blank with terror. "Thanks, Padre," he said. "I can find my way alone."

"The sentry may need a priest."

"Wait at the aid station: I'll bring him back."

"What if you can't move him? Besides, I *want* to go."

"In God's name, why?"

"Because I *am* here in God's name."

Their glances locked—and the padre's eyes won, for all the panic that lurked in their depths. It was not the first time Paul had yielded to similar pleas.

"Are you trying to prove I'm wrong, Father?"

"About forgetting self, Paul—or about dying?"

"Never mind. Just hang on to my pack strap and keep your head down."

VI

They whispered the first password where headquarters company guarded the approaches to the bunkers. From that point a ditch snaked toward the lines on the lower slope, a furrow so deep that it was possible to move downhill at a slight crouch, without exposure. Below, a foxhole-pitted slope led in turn to the outposts: they traversed it at a swift crabwise gait, repeating the password a dozen times in response to whispers in the dark. Twice they froze to the earth when illumination shells spouted up from the enemy lines, bathing the slope in a greenish glare. On each occasion there was a spatter of machine-gun fire from the nests that commanded this terrain by daylight.

"Easy does it, Padre—we're almost there."

Paul had worked on the slope so often he could have found every outpost blindfolded. Five minutes later, he dropped into a rifle pit and exchanged the password one more time. He had not yet dared to glance back at Father Tim, who had labored in his wake, with a death grip on the pack.

Together they bent over the wounded sentry, who lay on his back in the pit. The company aid man (distinguishable in the starlight because of his white brassard) lifted a plasma bottle against the night and gave the surgeon room.

"Knife wound, sir—severe. Doesn't seem to gain—"

Paul felt for the man's pulse: as he had feared, it was hard to time the rapid, fluttering beats. His flash lamp showed the red crater of the knife wound. Blood bubbled at the sentry's lips with each anguished breath, a sure sign that the knife point had found a vessel inside the lung. The miracle was that he had lived so long.

"*Mother of God—I want a priest!*"

"I am here, my son."

Paul moved to one side as the chaplain knelt beside the dying boy. Father Tim was no longer the white-faced, trembling misfit he had led down the hillside: in his stead was a man of God, whose command was absolute. The mortally wounded sentry felt the priest's power instantly, and the sense of communion was transferred to his pulse beat, which slowed even as it became stronger.

Hearing the chaplain's voice as he whispered the prayers for the dying, Paul marveled anew at a phenomenon that was almost unbelievable even as the proof was translated by his finger ends. He was aware that the chaplain's effect on the dying man was purely psychological. Deep in the victim's chest, the collapse of the soft, spongy lung (caused by the pressure of air sucked in with each breath) was slowing the hemorrhage; it was barely possible that the plasma dripping into the blood stream would step up the circulation rate in time. . . . Unemotionally the surgeon's part of his brain rejected the thought in advance: the puncture had been far too severe to justify such wild hopes. Yet the sentry clung to life with all his senses as the prayer continued.

In another moment the pulse had resumed its ominous flutter: the hoarse gasp of the sentry's breathing slowed and finally ceased. Paul disengaged the plasma needle from the collapsed vein and rose to his feet. The company aid man, packing his equipment with a few quick motions, spoke in an angry whisper.

"Didn't have a chance—did he, sir?"

"Not a chance. The diagnosis for his tag is *wound, penetrating, thorax*. If we can we'll send him back for burial in the morning."

"I'll stand by until his relief comes through," said the aid man. "Better watch yourself going back, Captain Scott. That infiltrator is still on the loose."

The exchange restored Paul's sense of proportion, which Father Tim's transfiguration had jolted badly. Concentrating on the business of reaching the hilltop alive, he gave little heed to the slight figure stumbling in his wake: he needed no second glance to tell him the priest, now that he had fulfilled his God-given function, was only a badly frightened man again.

"We've over the top, Padre. You can stand up again."

They were in the headquarters area once more, with the spine of the ridge behind them. Paul could see the battalion aid station clearly, and the silhouette of Sergeant Furness moving about some routine task within. At the same moment he was conscious of the newcomer approaching the dugout from another angle, via one of the many short gullies that led down from the ridge.

The man wore an American uniform: even by starlight he could see that much clearly. But there was no mistaking his unfamiliarity with the terrain or his hesitation as he drew abreast of the ravine that opened to the aid station.

Perhaps he was a runner from another company, fumbling his way to the headquarters area for the first time—but Paul was taking no chances.

"You there—give the password."

The newcomer, marking their position by the muttered challenge, did not answer. Instead, arm and body described a sweeping arc: the object that cannoned toward them was a grenade, the kind that GIs called an ink bottle.

"Down, Father!"

Paul had spread-eagled to earth with his own warning, conscious that the priest had blundered a few steps nearer the ravine and that the grenade had already landed at his feet. Exploding in that area, it could kill them both instantly—to say nothing of guards from headquarters company whose shallow foxholes were within range.

Had he been a stride closer Paul would have caught the priest in a flying tackle, hoping to fall into the ravine, where the rocky outcrop offered cover of a sort. As things stood he was too far away to intercept Father Tim when he charged the lethal missile, like a shortstop fielding a slow-rolling grounder. Rizzuto in his prime could not have set up a double play more accurately. The padre's snatch at the grenade and the sweeping underhand pitch that sent it winging were part of the same fluent motion.

Paul was still on his feet with seconds to spare: his tackle sent the priest sprawling. Dropping at Father Tim's side, he was in time to see the North Korean (still in sharp silhouette against the stars) in the act of dodging to avoid the expected destruction below. The thud of the grenade striking the man's chest at the moment of detonation sounded clearly in the night, before the thunder of the explosion blotted out the world.

Fragments of metal screamed overhead, to send rock splinters flying; the shock of the concussion smashed Paul into the earth with giant fists. Deafened as he was by the blast, he scarcely heard the machine-gun bursts as a dozen nests enfiladed the hill in the belief that a sneak attack had been launched against the line.

"Fire one round illumination!" The voice seemed to rise from the earth at Paul's elbow. He saw now that he had plowed down the slope as he tackled Father Tim, so that they were sprawled at the doorframe of the communications shack.

The exploding shell, bathing the whole hill in its glare, gave convincing proof that the attack (a strictly one-man affair) was over before it began. Brief though the illumination was, it gave Paul a ghastly glimpse of the infiltrator. Lifted by the force of the blast, his body had been literally demolished. The pulpy-red pelt of some freshly skinned animal, plastered to a barn door by a not-too-skillful taxidermist.

Father Tim was unconscious: there was a dark bruise at his temple but no other sign of injury. Furness and Jackson (who had come out on the double) eased the priest onto a litter. In another moment they were safely within the bunker, where Paul could examine him thoroughly.

The chaplain's body showed no sign of a wound, but there was no mistaking the depth of his coma. Meeting the sergeant's eyes above the cot, Paul shook his head in silent disbelief. It was an astonishment that both Jackson and Furness echoed after he had told his story.

"Now that you mention it, Doc," said Jackson, "he *did* play shortstop at the seminary. A good glove man, he told me. But he could never hit in the clutch."

"He proved it tonight," said Paul.

"What's he got? Concussion?"

Paul shook his head. Concussion could destroy a man without leaving a mark on the victim—but he, too, had been close to the explosion and had escaped unharmed.

"Bed rest until morning may bring him out of it. I'll stand by until my trick is over."

Father Tim still slept as soundly as before when a bleary-eyed Furness stumbled in to relieve Paul. He sent the sergeant for coffee while he pondered the case—and asked himself if he might use a novel therapy to help his diagnosis. When Hi Saunders (who had passed the night in the officers' bunker) looked in to say good-by he ventured to bring his idea into the open.

"He'll get a bronze star for that throw," said Hi. "But you'll have to rouse him somehow before they pin it on."

"Has it occurred to you that he may not *want* to waken?"

"Psychic block, eh?"

"For a lawyer turned artilleryman," said Paul, "that's a good snap diagnosis. Tell me, Hi, have you ever killed a man?"

"Dozens. Why?"

"How did it feel the first time?"

"Bad, Paul: the stuff nightmares are made of. Happened last year on the big push for the Yalu. I was leading a patrol and fresh as new paint. We must have overreached our mission, because I'm sure this fellow didn't think there was a Yank in miles. There he was at a crossroad, bigger than life and a perfect target. And yet, when I got him in my sights, I couldn't pull the trigger."

"A lot of men have had combat paralysis," said Paul. "Nothing could be more natural."

"Two seconds later he started shooting at *me*. I blew his head off then."

"Something of the sort happened to Father Tim, I'm sure. When that grenade came rolling down the slope he used a set of reflexes he'd buried years ago. I never saw a sharper fielding play. If that Chinaman had been wearing a baseball uniform he'd have been hit letter-high."

"Then Father Tim knows he's killed a man?"

"His instinct for self-preservation made him aim the toss. The discovery must have cut through his soul. The result is identical with your experience. Only you got your paralysis before you dropped your enemy. Father Tim got his afterwards."

"Are you a surgeon or a psychoanalyst?"

"Working this close to death, I'm a bit of both. Besides, I must get the padre on his feet before Hardin sleeps off his hangover. You know what he'd make of it if I gave Father Tim a rest ticket. Hardin hates his chaplain as much as he does his medical officer—for the same reasons."

"How *can* you start him ticking again?"

"He seems in good shape physically," said Paul. "My problem is to break through his mental trauma—if that's the proper term. I'm going to try a little experiment and keep my fingers crossed."

Five minutes after Hi Saunders had reluctantly taken his leave Paul reached for a tourniquet and the sodium pentothal. Mixing the yellowish solution with sterile water and drawing a light injection into a syringe, he pondered his chances. The technique (called narcosynthesis) had been used frequently in World War II with excellent results: even if it failed today it could not harm the priest.

Narcosynthesis, he reminded himself, was based on the fact that the conscious mind could not always be controlled by the will. In cases like Father Tim's its withdrawal from reality could be complete, often for an extended interval. In France Paul had seen soldiers rigid with paralysis on the eve of battle. Others had gone temporarily blind. Still others had dropped in their tracks, like zombies. . . . These men were not malingerers. Theirs was a profound wound of the mind as definitely as a bullet through the leg was a crippling wound of the body. Rest and quiet usually cured them in time. On occasion special drugs had been used to hasten the process—and one of the most effective of these was sodium pentothal.

Normally a small dose of this anesthetic put the conscious mind to sleep, relieving the brain from the psychic block it had established and permitting the deeper subconscious portion to reveal itself. Usually this release took the form of a monologue in which the patient poured out the problems that had brought on the attack. Often the victim himself was unaware of the cause of his paralysis—and the mere voicing of that cause was enough to free him of its spell.

Now as he injected the pentothal slowly into a vein Paul began to speak to the priest in an even voice. At first there was no response. Then, as the drug took hold, Father Tim opened his eyes and stared up at Paul with a smile of recognition. This, too, was part of the clinical picture: Paul had seen many patients go into stupors during which they seemed oblivious of externals. At a later date (when they chose, for reasons of their own, to become conscious), they could recall everything that had gone on around them.

"Why am I here, Paul?"

"A grenade exploded, Padre. The concussion knocked you out."

"A grenade? I remember now. It came rolling down the slope—"

"Fortunately you fielded it in time."

"Fielded it, you say?"

"Like Rizzuto making a play at second."

"Like a play at second. Yes, Paul: it's much clearer now."

"Why didn't you tell me you were once a star shortstop?"

"It was only softball—at the seminary. I haven't played in years."

"The fact remains, I never saw a finer underhand toss."

"Where did I throw the grenade? I can't quite remember—"

"You tossed it over the hill," said Paul quietly. He was careful not to mention the North Korean soldier. "It had just landed in the middle of headquarters company. A dozen men owe their lives to that play at second."

"I wish I could remember more. I *do* have a picture of scooping up a grenade. Then my mind blacks out."

Paul had continued to inject the drug slowly. He stopped now, lest it pile up in the padre's blood stream and bring genuine unconsciousness. So far, Father Tim was responding favorably.

"What sort of grenade was it, Paul?"

"An ink bottle, I think. It banged off at the crest of the hill. You were lucky you weren't hit."

"I remember that you pulled me down beside you." Father Tim had been staring at the bunker wall; now he turned his head and looked into Paul's eyes. "What's this you're giving me? Plasma?"

"You don't need plasma, Father. You weren't even scratched and you've slept the night through. This is sodium pentothal."

"Isn't that an anesthetic?"

"You've been unconscious ever since the grenade went off. I'm trying to find out why."

The priest closed his eyes and his slight body trembled. "If my memory won't function, I must have sinned grievously."

"I've said you saved a dozen men from death. That's hardly a sin."

"What *really* happened, Paul?"

He had hoped that Father Tim would answer that question of his own accord. But he could hardly hesitate now. "An infiltrator threw a grenade at us, Padre."

"A man in an American uniform. I remember. Did I—toss it back at him? *Like a play at second?"*

"Like a play at second. You put him out—for keeps."

The priest's face was drawn now, and there was hell in his eyes. "I *wanted* to hit him, Paul. It's a dreadful thought but it's true."

"What you did was pure instinct. He meant to kill us both, but you hit him first."

"You can take out the needle, Paul," said Father Tim quietly. "I'm all right now."

"Most facts can be faced, once they're put into words," said Paul, as he removed the needle and strapped a pad on the slender arm.

"Only yesterday I'd have said the confessional was my task, rather than yours." The priest managed a wan smile. "Still, it's good of you to take over my office."

"You mustn't blame yourself. Self-preservation is the first law of nature."

"*Thou shalt not kill* is a law of God."

"Which is older, Padre? Nature or God?"

"If my religion means anything it means that God is the beginning. Hate may be older than love—but love must conquer if the world is to endure."

"I wish I could share that hope."

"You'll share it some day, Paul, I promise you. If you can't, then your chaplain has failed."

"Right now it's enough we're both alive. Can't you thank God for that?"

"First I must ask God to forgive me for killing another human creature."

"Doesn't the Bible say *For a man's blood shall a man's blood be shed?*"

"*Whoso sheddeth man's blood, by man shall his blood be shed,*" the priest corrected gently. "Perhaps that will be my atonement before this war is ended."

"You mustn't say such things, Padre. Remember, that's the Old Testament God we've been quoting."

"The *lex talionis*," said the chaplain with another smile. "For an unbeliever, you do know your Bible."

"Jesus taught another way, Padre. Wouldn't He forgive what you did last night?"

There was a long silence in the bunker: Father Tim had not ceased his trembling. "I can see the man so clearly now," he said at last. "His arms were spread wide: the grenade must have struck his chest. The explosion silhouetted him for a second—then there was nothing."

"You took an enemy's life to save your friends. How often must I tell you that?"

"A man of God can have no enemies, Paul. It was hate that made me throw back the grenade—that made me choose *him* for my target. I could have tossed it aside as easily."

"I've told you there was no time to think."

"That's just the point. Hate had taken over: when hate rules the mind it leaves no room for God."

"Have it your way, Padre," said Paul resignedly. "We'll still make sure you're awarded the bronze star."

"You mustn't, Paul. I couldn't accept it."

"Not even for heroism above the call of duty?"

"Soldiers have the right to be heroes, I suppose. And the right to kill when they're ordered to kill. *My* orders are to save souls, including my own. What I did last night was the most grievous of sins. I must pray for absolution before I can do my work again."

"Sleep on it, Padre. You'll feel differently when you awaken."

"I'll feel the same—now you've helped me to face the facts. Still, I *would* like to sleep awhile."

"You're going under now," said Paul soothingly. "That's another reason for the syringe."

"I wanted to record my confession. I suppose it can wait until I've rested."

"We're still cut off, Father. They can hardly bring another priest to the hill."

Father Tim smiled drowsily. "I don't need a *human* confessor, Paul. Surely you've seen me writing in the diary I keep in my duffel bag?"

Like his brother officers, Paul knew it was the chaplain's custom to make copious entries in a notebook with a special lock, which he kept hidden in his quarters: he had often wondered what the padre was writing there. Usually Father Tim made his entries at the day's end when he had time to himself. But he was not above writing in the diary at odd moments in a kind of frowning concentration that discouraged questions.

"I won't pretend I wasn't curious," Paul admitted.

"That diary is my confession book."

"Confession book?"

"It's a dispensation my bishop allows me when no priest is available; God can read what I write there, even with the covers closed. I try to put something down each day—when I have sinned or been found wanting. If anything happens, I'll be ready."

"Nothing will happen to you now, if you'll stay inside this bunker," said Paul. "At least I can rely on the pentothal to keep you quiet for a while."

"It's a true wonder drug, Paul. Thank you again for using it—and saving me from being a coward."

VII

. . . in the first world war, I'm told, the address was "somewhere in France." For now, I've had to settle on "somewhere in Korea" to describe my present whereabouts— though it isn't half so romantic. (Or was it *you* who said that first, Paul? Bits and pieces of our talk keep coming back to me. They're a help in making you stay real.)

Do I have to say I'm eager to see you again? And hoping against hope that you'll have some leave coming up, so you can watch our unit perform?

I can't tell you where we'll be when you receive this. Only that we have come overseas at last—and that the show (after a fairly rugged start) has succeeded beyond all my dreams.

Don't try to answer this until you've seen a special messenger I'm sending with the latest news. Again I can't mention dates or names. But he'll be with you in a few days' time—rely on that.

How have you been making out with the promise you gave me? I've been making out right well with mine.

The letter had reached Hill 1049 ten days ago, and Paul had read it through a hundred times. He read it once more now, between chores in the aid station, by the light of the hissing gasoline lamp. Like Kay Storey's other letters, it was short and to the point—but this time he could feel her affection in every line, her solid belief that he would fulfill his promise.

With a little effort he could even put that promise into words. . . . It was quite true that he had done his job here with all his heart and soul. From what Larry Kirk had just told him, Kay had done hers too, even more brilliantly.

The visit of the famous television commentator to the front lines had not been entirely unheralded. Kirk had arrived only yesterday, preceded by a helicopter loaded with cameras and nervous public-relations officers who had taken over the headquarters bunker on orders from above. Kirk (spruce in brand-new suntans, with the green crescents of a war correspondent shining at each shoulder) had proved far more regular than his build-up had suggested. Within an hour Paul found that he was chatting with the journalist like an old friend.

Even Colonel Hardin (a far calmer C.O., now that the enemy had ceased punching at his sector for a while) had been on his best behavior. Kirk, as Paul now perceived, had the knack of penetration, of seeing beneath mud and resentments to the essentials. If he had slipped a bit on Hardin, it could be put down to the colonel's protective coloration—a defense in depth so massive that it was sometimes hard to decide where officer ended and man began. (Now that Kirk had flown out with his film and his notes, Paul could only hope that he himself had not spoken too freely.)

As for Kay Storey, the news Kirk brought was both amazing and heartening.

The show that had taken its brassy routines across the United States had been completely revamped after its first performance in Pusan. Now, with Kay as its focal point, it had perfected a special technique for making the audience part of the performance—with the accent on nostalgia. Kirk had been purposely indefinite on this point: he had informed Paul that it would only spoil his pleasure if he divulged the plot of *The Girl Next Door* in advance. Not that an hour of genuine home-grown entertainment, combining the best features of *commedia dell' arte* and an old-fashioned American picnic, could be said to have a plot. . . .

"Even up here we've heard of 'The Girl Next Door,'" Paul admitted.

"You should have," said the journalist. "She's the best thing to hit Seoul since the liberation."

"Why couldn't Kay write sooner?"

"I can answer that with a direct quote," said Kirk. "Miss Storey didn't want to build your hopes up in advance—if there was no chance of your getting leave."

"Couldn't they have billed her by name?"

"The fact they haven't is part of the show's charm. Headline entertainers give the boys one sort of lift. Kay Storey is each man's sweetheart when she sings—because she *is* anonymous."

Kirk had broken off abruptly on that, with the all-American grin that had warmed millions of living rooms. "I won't say another word—except I wish someone was looking forward to seeing me as she is you."

"Apparently she's hit her stride at last," said Paul. "I couldn't be happier."

"You can say that twice," said Larry Kirk, and departed in a whirl of helicopter blades and glory two days before the enemy had begun to probe lazily at Hill 1049 again, with all the offhand assurance of a tiger teasing an exhausted mouse.

VIII

The battalion surgeon had meant every word at the time. He meant them today as he folded the letter away and began to check the setup for an emergency call that had reached him from the next hill. Kay's summons still upset him a little; he could put his confusion down to the accumulated fatigue of these months in the lines.

The fact that orders for a week's leave in Seoul had just been cut at regimental headquarters—and the still more amazing fact that Hardin had approved—seemed only appropriate nods from fate, now that Kay was in Korea. He hardly minded the fact that her arrival in Seoul and his long-overdue leave were strangely coincidental. Nor did it matter if "The Girl Next Door," with Larry Kirk's help, had expedited the orders in high places.

What really mattered at this moment was the fact that his own desperate need might betray him. . . . For six long months, he told himself, he had fulfilled her belief in him: he had done his job on Hill 1049 and done it well. Thanks to Father Tim (and friends like Hi Saunders), he had kept his sanity, after a fashion. But the thing that had really sustained him had been the memory of Kay Storey and the hours they had shared in Hollywood. How could he be sure that love and that brief encounter were synonyms in Kay's dictionary?

Perhaps he could find the strength and the wisdom to keep things in proportion when they met. To realize that "The Girl Next Door" was not his special sweetheart—until she made the first move of her own accord. . . . He was reaching for Kay's letter again to search for hidden meanings, when he heard the litter-bearers in the ravine.

Paul was not too surprised when he saw that the man on the stretcher was Major Hilary Saunders—Hi's group on the next hill had been beating off a flanking thrust for the past two days, and its casualty list had been heavy. What disturbed him immediately was the artillery officer's chalk-white face and the way his hands compressed his abdomen: he had observed these ominous portents far too often.

"What happened, Sergeant?"

"Seems he stopped a tank with a bazooka," said Furness. "A whole gook company was tailing it. Major took a ticket home before the M-1s could wipe 'em out."

Harry Jackson, who had hurried ahead of the litter-bearers, had already set up a plasma unit in the bunker: between them, the two medics transferred Hi to the operating table. A runner was waiting in the doorframe for Paul's report. He gave it quickly, knowing that Hardin would not dare object to frontline surgery on an emergency case: the C.O. had been almost co-operative since Larry Kirk's visit and the journalist's evident interest in Paul.

The morphine Saunders had received in the field had blunted his perceptions: when Paul sank a second needle in his arm, he stared up at the surgeon from a deep well of sedation, with eyes that barely took in his surroundings.

Jackson had slashed away the uniform to permit an evaluation of the wound, an innocent red pucker just below the rib cage. Closer inspection revealed a somewhat larger wound of exit, lower down the right side.

"Think it missed the spleen, sir?" asked Furness. He had already begun to sponge the evident area of operation while Jackson swung the instrument table under the lights.

"Let's hope so; the exit was low enough to skip the liver too, if we're lucky." Paul had not paused to complete the clinical picture that was forming with such merciless clarity. Between those two vital organs lay the whole coiled length of the small intestine, with the U-shaped larger colon arching above it. Inevitably this area had been damaged as the bullet passed through, probably by multiple perforations. The boardlike rigidity of the abdominal wall could only come from irritation of the peritoneum when the contents of the intestine (acid, base, digestive juices, and, if the colon was injured, teeming malignant bacteria) were suddenly sprayed against it.

Part of the shock that had turned Hi's skin an ashen white was due to this grave insult to the sensitive peritoneal lining. But there must be internal hemorrhage too—and this would continue until the injury was corrected. Nor would the inflammation cease until the contamination was sponged away and the perforations sutured.

"Will you do a laparotomy, Captain?"

"I'm afraid we'll have to, Sergeant."

"No chance of sending him back to MASH?"

Paul glanced at the emergency cots in the bunker annex where a BAR man was snoring peacefully under a booster shot of morphine. An hour ago they had saved his life by tying off an artery in the groin. With the main supply route closed, and the 'copters busy with even more urgent evacuations, Paul had fallen into the habit of operating at once on cases such as these. The fact that Hardin no longer opposed such judgments was, of course, only a temporary windfall, but he meant to reap its benefits tonight.

"Put through a call to division," he said. "They'll understand this case can't wait till morning."

While Furness relayed the message to another headquarters runner, Jackson started the pentothal; one of the aid men, who had volunteered for emergencies of this sort, came forward at Paul's nod to inject a double dose of penicillin and set up a second plasma unit. Some of the color had returned to Hi Saunders' cheeks by the time Furness had painted the operative area with two layers of bright red antiseptic and draped it with towels. Despite the fact that the operation he was about to perform was surgery whittled to its essentials, Paul saw with satisfaction that the patient's response was encouraging.

"You can discontinue the pentothal, Harry," he said. "It's time to start the ether: we want this one deep under."

"Ether coming up, sir."

Paul watched narrowly as Jackson placed the cone above Major Saunders' face and began to drip in the pungent liquid—and saw at once that the man's technique was adequate. There would be no time later to correct the mistakes of a fumbling anesthetist. In a few moments Hi's profound snore at the end of each respiration advertised a depth of anesthesia sufficient to relax the muscles of the pharynx, an absolute necessity in abdominal surgery.

"About right for now, sir?"

"Just about, Harry. We may need more when we get inside."

Furness had drawn on a fresh set of gloves; now he slapped a scalpel into Paul's hand and arranged several forceps and a strand of catgut on a towel spread across the patient's thighs. From chest to knees, Hi was blanketed in sterile linen, with only the operative area exposed, a rectangle of cherry red that glowed in the lamplight as intensely as freshly spread lacquer.

"Ready, everyone?"

Three heads nodded in unison as the knife described a lateral slash across the rectangle. "Since there can be perforations anywhere along the track of the bullet," said Paul, "I'm making a transverse incision. I'll make it only large enough to explore—and enlarge later as needed."

The knife cut deeper; as the skin parted, droplets of blood appeared where the superficial vessels of the abdominal wall had been severed. Paul and Furness worked rapidly, sponging the incision clean and tying off the open mouths of the vessels with catgut after they had been clamped. Then, using a second scalpel, the surgeon cut through the tough whitish layer that surrounded the mid-muscles of the abdomen and severed the red fibers themselves whenever they appeared in the depths of the rapidly widening wound.

Here, as was to be expected, the bleeding was more severe. In a few moments the incision was thick with forceps. The muscle barrier had not been penetrated completely, and only the glistening membrane of the peritoneum showed in the nest of clamps.

"Step up the ether a little, Harry," said Paul. "I'll need full relaxation before I go in."

When Saunders was completely relaxed under the anesthetic Paul tented the peritoneal membrane with a slender forcep and nicked it with a sharp tap of the knife. The sergeant held the forcep while Paul inserted a second clamp. Surgical scissors were used to slit the membrane, a precise technique that opened it for a distance only a little smaller than the dimensions of the wound itself—perhaps twelve inches in all. As Paul had expected, the incision was promptly inundated with a whitish fluid mixed with blood. It was an ominous advertisement of the damage he would find within the abdomen itself.

"Too bad we haven't a suction machine," he said. "Towel, please."

Three sterile towels were needed to sponge the incision clean. For the first time he dared to peer into the abdomen through the formidable window he had opened in its wall. The whole complex of the alimentary tract was clearly visible—the pinkish, tight-packed loops of the small intestine, the fanning mesentery which supplied blood vessels in this area, the descending curve of the colon itself. To the layman's eye these vital organs might have seemed undamaged; yet somewhere in that convoluted mass were perforations that could be Hi Saunders' death warrant.

Paul slipped a gloved hand into the abdomen, reaching under the left end of the transverse incision. "I can feel the wound of entry," he said. "It's clean and closed tight by muscle contraction. The spleen is undamaged and so is the kidney on this side. Hold him just as he is, Harry, while I check the colon."

The three-man operating team hung motionless above the table as the surgeon continued to explore organs he could feel but not see. "The left side of the colon appears uninjured," he said, letting some of his relief come through with the announcement. With this organ unpunctured, the task ahead was simpler.

"I'm now following the transverse colon, across and down the right side. There is no injury there, nor in the right kidney." With each word he spoke he could feel Hi Saunders' life expectancy rise. "The bullet was too far forward to injure the spinal cord. I'll check the small intestine now."

This check was made by direct vision, starting at the lower end of the small bowel where it joined the massive dilatation of the colon called the cecum, with the appendix hanging from it like a small, forgotten finger. Paul's hands moved swiftly, lifting the intestine loop by loop, then dropping it into the abdominal cavity. Over six feet were stripped in this way before he found what he was seeking—a reddish nick that seemed superficial until he discovered the telltale pout of the inner lining.

"Perforation number one," he said. "Not large, but definite." A gauze pad soaked in water came into his hand; taking the loop gently between thumb and forefinger, he showed the sergeant how to hold it clear of the wound.

"Sutures, sir?"

"Not yet. We can't close this one until we see what else is damaged."

Another foot of intestine, delivered from the cavity with the same testing, revealed the first severe injury. Here the bowel had been cut entirely across—and there were five separate punctures just beyond. Paul covered this section with a moistened, sterile towel. A painstaking exploration of the remaining convolutions failed to reveal another injury.

"How's he bearing up, Harry?"

"Pulse is a hundred, Doctor," said the corporal. "He's breathing well."

"What about the plasma?" With his whole being concentrated on the ruptured organ, Paul did not even lift his head to examine the bottle above the table: until those ruptures had been mended they represented the boundaries of his world.

"On the last third of the second flask, sir."

"Good: he should continue to hold up. I'm going to resect this portion of the intestine: it's too badly damaged for separate repairs."

No one spoke around the table: there was nothing for the assistants to contribute. Since this was a command decision, the responsibility would rest on the surgeon alone.

"I'll need extra forceps, Sergeant," said Paul, as he took the length of damaged bowel from Furness' hands. "Just drop them on the towel with the sutures." He had already slit the fanlike mesentery; now he took a loop of catgut and pulled it through the opening. Several inches farther along he pushed the forcep through again—and, lifting one end of the catgut, placed a loop around that section of the mesentery. Tightly knotted, the catgut constricted the dangerous vessels in this area; across this captive portion he clamped a forcep on the side toward the intestine and cut cleanly, freeing the bowel completely from the tissue that nourished it.

With the extra forceps that Furness had placed within his reach it was a simple matter for Paul to repeat this maneuver; the section of intestine he intended to remove was now completely free and was easily lifted into the incision. Extra-large clamps were fastened firmly at each end of the damage area. Placed in pairs, they enabled him to cut between them, severing the intestine cleanly but retaining its contents. Several feet of injured bowel, still gleaming pinkly, and flaccid as a torpid snake, was lifted free of the wound and dropped in the basin beside the table.

Moving his fingers gently, Paul brought the two clamped ends together, so that they were resting side by side in the wound, like the two barrels of a shotgun with the muzzle down. A catgut-bearing needle came into his hand: the point bit firmly into the intestinal wall (first on one side, then on the other) in the area just behind the forceps. It was a delicate technique, but a vital one: working at the side away from the forceps, and holding the two severed sections firmly together, Paul continued the joining until the needle reached the twin forceps themselves.

Now, taking his time to make sure that he had fashioned the joining accurately, he turned the forceps completely in the wound, until the matched ends of the bowel projected upward. A few more stitches, and the resection began to take on a definite pattern: when the steel clamps were almost hidden he freed them gently. There remained only two more bites of the needle to cover the spot where they had disengaged their grip.

The suturing was now virtually complete: Paul permitted himself a shrug as he felt the admiration in Corporal Jackson's eyes. "It's a technique you learn early in surgery," he explained. "Actually, it's as simple as a housewife's darning. But I'll place another row of sutures, just to be sure."

The reserve stitches were quickly placed: two complete rows of sutures now encircled the junction point—one of them the absorbable catgut, the other black silk that would fix this area permanently. One minor manipulation remained, and it was pure pleasure to perform it. Using the gentlest of pressures, Paul pushed his finger through the opening—now completely concealed within the intestinal wall. As though it possessed a separate life, the bowel assumed its normal shape, as naturally as a toe might invert a sock.

IX

The operation had succeeded with that final probe of the surgeon's finger: Hi Saunders would survive, with luck on his side and the therapies of modern war to sustain him.

The business of closing the incision was a tedious anticlimax, but Paul took pleasure in every stitch: it was only when he had stripped off his gloves that he realized how tired he was—and how wonderfully relaxed. Hi would pass a quiet night, he hoped, along with the bandaged automatic-rifle man: they could both be delivered to the collecting station tomorrow—and would probably sleep in a Tokyo hospital before the day's end. It was a heady triumph to take into the night.

On the dugout step he breathed deeply of the late-summer air. For once, the night above Hill 1049 was silent: the clean stars that studded the Korean sky were shining brightly, unclouded by the smoke of the usual bombardment. For an instant Paul paused above the headquarters bunker and put down the impulse to report the operation to Hardin: even in his present mood, it would not do to press the C.O. too far. (In time, of course, there would be a showdown with Hardin: this was not the moment.)

The sense of quiet gladness persisted—tinged but faintly with panic—as he thought of his impending meeting with Kay Storey. The achievement of tonight was definite, and no tomorrow could spoil it. Hill 1049 had been a synonym for hell in the months that he had labored there—but he had worked hard at his chosen calling and he had found a new dedication there. Come what may, he told himself, you've earned a week's leave in Seoul.

THE PRESIDIO

I

The screen of memory faded, and he was back in the crowded courtroom in San Francisco—dimly conscious that the court had risen to vote on another question of law. Captain Paul Scott summoned a grin for his counsel—and admitted privately that the experience had been a refreshing one. At least he had been spared the preliminaries.

"How's it going, Hi?"

The defense lawyer returned the grin. "I saw you woolgathering, pal. Can't say that I blame you. To the lay mind, it's been damned dull so far."

"I wasn't exactly woolgathering," said Paul. "It's a trick you learn in Communist prison camps. You might call it shutting off the present—when the present begins to drive you nuts."

"You haven't missed a great deal. So far, MacArdle and I have been rolling with each others' punches. I got Jackson to admit that he and Sergeant Major Bates were cronies in prison—and that he joined Hardin's group because the food was better. He still insisted the real reason for the switch was because you operated on the camp commander. So does Bates, of course—"

Paul glanced at the master sergeant, lolling at ease in the witness chair while he awaited the return of the court. Bates returned his stare with heavy-lidded insolence; the surgeon was glad indeed that he had missed the first part of that born conniver's testimony.

"I gather you made no headway there?"

Hi shook his head. "MacArdle has rehearsed him like a straight man in a Broadway play."

"When will they introduce the confession?"

"My guess is that Hardin himself will read it from the stand. MacArdle knows I'll keep it off the record as long as I can. He's too smart to muff *that* big scene."

"Why let Hardin read it?"

"The colonel brought it out of Korea, remember? It's his big stick: obviously, he plans to use it for your *coup de grâce*."

"What about Kay? Will they try to drag her in?"

Again Hi shook his head. "Not MacArdle—things are going the way he wants them so far, except for a few tricks I've pulled on the witnesses to show a selfish motive in the food. If I leave it to *him*, he'll hardly mention her—except as a prisoner who shared your captivity."

"And Father Tim?"

"They've dodged him too, pretty successfully. So far as the court knows, they both went along for the ride because they couldn't help themselves. The fact that they were also your friends has gone unmentioned."

"Isn't it time you brought it out, Hi?"

"I'm saving that element for the afternoon session," said the lawyer calmly. "Mac will probably put Hardin on the stand after lunch as the final witness for the prosecution. Don't bite my head off, Paul—but I've got to open our own case with Kay."

"You said we could keep her out."

"Only because you wanted her out. Now that I've seen MacArdle in action I'm afraid she's essential."

Paul stirred uneasily. He had foreseen this change of front on Hi's part and, since he had given the defense lawyer a free hand on strategy, he knew he was powerless to combat it. "MacArdle will only crucify her," he said quickly.

"She won't mind if it'll help our case," said Hi. "Don't be such an exclusive martyr."

"How can she help?"

"By getting to the root of this court-martial. By telling the court that Hardin's persecution of you goes back to his cowardice on Hill 1049 and even further."

"Can't you bring that out another way?"

"Maybe you *should* have listened," said Hi. "All morning long I've tried to break that very barrier. It's been a struggle even to get Hill 1049 on the court record: MacArdle keeps insisting you're being tried for what happened *after* your group was captured there." He stared unhappily at the seven empty seats on the bench. "That's why they've recessed now—to decide how far they'll limit my questioning."

"Surely I can go into Hardin's past when I testify?"

"To a point, if we move fast. I can't let you go too far: we mustn't seem to be matching your word against his. That's another reason we need Kay up there. *She* can speak her mind. With luck we can even make them listen."

"Can't you forget Kay?"

"I'll forget her for now," said Hi cheerfully, "but I'm calling her this afternoon. On your feet, boy—here come Sellers and company. And I can read their ruling in advance."

II

Hi's prediction was confirmed: in a tone that seemed even frostier than usual, Colonel Sellers announced that the last objection of trial counsel had been sustained by a vote of the court. Henceforth, Hi was instructed to confine his questions to matters pertaining directly to the charges and specifications. On this note he resumed his cross-examination of Master Sergeant Bates.

"Before the court retired, Sergeant, we were discussing your arrival as a prisoner of war at Pyongyang. When was Colonel Hardin appointed commander of prisoners in the compound?"

"Straight off, sir. He was senior officer."

"And when was Captain Scott put in charge of the prison hospital?"

"Maybe two or three weeks later. It was a few days after he joined us."

"Then he did not travel with Colonel Hardin's group?"

"No, sir. We were captured separately. The two groups came together for just one night—at Sinmak. Next morning, the Chinese gave the colonel truck transport."

"Captain Scott did not ride in the truck?"

"There wasn't room."

"So he was forced to march from Sinmak to Pyongyang?"

"So I'm told."

"Who marched with him?"

"Three people from his group. I think they were Miss Storey, Sergeant Furness, and Corporal Jackson. And one from ours—Lieutenant Crosby."

"Will you identify Lieutenant Crosby for the court?"

"He was a recent replacement on Colonel Hardin's staff. We'd been under heavy pressure on Hill 1049 and lost several of our officer personnel. Lieutenant Crosby was second in command when we made our withdrawal."

Paul, studying Bates narrowly, marveled at the precision of the man's coaching. Though he had described Crosby accurately, he had naturally failed to mention that the lieutenant had been in command on Hill 1049 for almost twenty-four hours before the mad scramble that he had called a withdrawal—or that Hardin himself, for most of that interval, had been too drunk to stand. . . .

Hi had taken the witness quietly, so far—permitting his description of Crosby to register with the court before he attacked from a new angle. "Isn't it unusual for a staff officer to be parted from his C.O., even when they're prisoners of war?"

"Not in this case, sir."

"Say what you mean, Sergeant. You must know that Lieutenant Crosby gave up his place at Sinmak so that Chaplain O'Fallon could ride in the truck?"

"I believe he did, sir."

"Because the chaplain was ill?"

"That may have been the reason."

"After Colonel Hardin had refused to make room for him?"

MacArdle, sensing the trap, was on his feet now. "If it please the court— what is the purpose of this random questioning?"

"Charges and specifications make much of an alleged confession which Captain Scott signed at Pyongyang," said Hi. "Defense will establish the fact that he signed this document for just one reason—to obtain the release of both Miss Storey and Chaplain O'Fallon from solitary confinement, where they were in grave danger of death. Surely it is germane to prove that Father O'Fallon's health was already failing on the prisoners' march to Sinmak."

"Trial counsel's objection is overruled," said Sellers.

"Now, Sergeant," said Hi, in a tone that was deceptively mild, "isn't it true that Captain Scott had already requested a place on the truck for the chaplain, because of his illness?"

"I believe he did, sir."

"And did not Colonel Hardin refuse the request?"

"The colonel was riled that morning at Sinmak. Dr. Scott had taken the best billets; he'd made the colonel sleep in the barnyard—"

"He relented, then, only because Lieutenant Crosby gave up his place to the chaplain?"

"That is correct, sir."

"Do you know where Lieutenant Crosby is today?"

"He died a few weeks later at Pyongyang. In the meningitis epidemic."

"The same epidemic that Dr. Scott treated?"

"Yes, sir. The lieutenant was one of the first to go."

"But the epidemic was checked?"

"It was in time."

"Because Captain Scott administered a drug, sulfadiazine, to everyone in camp. Didn't you take a dose of that drug yourself?"

Bates' voice rose a trifle: he spoke rapidly as though to forestall interruption. "Colonel Pak had put the doc in charge. He was dosing everyone—gooks and prisoners both. We had to follow orders."

"What were the sanitary conditions in the camp, Sergeant, when you arrived with Colonel Hardin's group?"

"Bad, sir."

"You have said that Colonel Hardin was put in immediate charge of all prisoner discipline. Did he take steps to improve these conditions?"

"Objection!" said MacArdle. "Colonel Hardin is not on trial."

He faced the court. "Defense considers it vital to show that Captain Scott, and none other, was responsible for the good health record of this prison camp. His forthright action in controlling epidemics and improving sanitary conditions—"

MacArdle was shouting now. "If the court please!"

"*Quiet!*" Sellers had barely raised his voice, but the murmurs among the spectators died out, along with the contending voices of counsel. "Objection overruled, subject to review by any member of the court. You may answer the question, Sergeant."

Bates swallowed hard but kept his composure. "There was nothing the colonel could do. It wasn't his line."

"But there *was* an improvement in the health of the prisoners after Captain Scott arrived."

"I believe so."

"Wasn't there a marked improvement—with a lowered sickness and death rate?"

"For a while. Things got worse later."

"Because the captured medical supplies were exhausted. Isn't that correct?"

"I believe that was the case."

"Then United Nations prisoners did benefit from Captain Scott's medical skill, regardless of whether he received preferential treatment at the camp hospital?"

"I think you could say that."

"Thank you, Sergeant. Speaking of preferential treatment, you have already testified that Captain Scott received favors from the Chinese commander, Colonel Pak. Just where was the captain quartered?"

"I'm not sure, sir."

"You were Colonel Hardin's assistant. Didn't your duties include constant camp inspections?"

"Of course, sir."

"Then you must know that Captain Scott slept in Barracks Four with the other prisoners and had his meals there."

"So it seemed."

"*Seemed*, Sergeant Bates?"

"Everyone said he got extra food at the hospital and took long rests there."

"But you've no personal knowledge that he did?"

"No, sir. How could I?"

"Let us move on to the moment when the camp was evacuated after the armistice. Did you hear Captain Scott state that he did not wish repatriation?"

"No, sir."

"Isn't it true that your only knowledge of his wishes is based on Colonel Hardin's report?"

"That's correct, sir." Bates was still intact under pressure: he seemed the picture of innocence, buffeted by waves of protocol beyond his ken.

"Didn't you know that Chaplain O'Fallon was gravely ill at the time?"

"I'd heard he was sick."

"Wasn't he in the last extremity? And was that not Captain Scott's true reason for remaining in Pyongyang?"

"I can't say I thought of it that way, sir. Speaking for myself, I was too anxious to get home again. So was every Joe in the compound."

"That is all."

MacArdle rose for his rebuttal. "Did you have personal knowledge of the chaplain's illness, Sergeant?"

"No, sir."

"Not even when Captain Scott refused to be repatriated?"

Hi objected vigorously. "Nothing in the testimony had proved a refusal."

"I'll rephrase the question," said MacArdle, with a side glance at the court. "You have testified that you saw a report made by Colonel Hardin in which Captain Scott declined repatriation?"

"Yes, sir. It was part of my duty to file those reports."

"Does the file exist today?"

"It may. Colonel Pak confiscated it when we were sent to Panmunjom."

"Do you recall the notation?"

"Not exactly. It said something like 'Captain Scott refused repatriation in my presence, and in the presence of Colonel Pak. Reasons undisclosed.'"

"Did Colonel Hardin comment on this at the time?"

"He did, sir. He said, 'I hope that son-of-a-bitch never goes home, except to face a court-martial.'"

"No more questions."

III

A perfect witness to the end, Master Sergeant Bates walked out on a ripple of amusement from the spectators. There was something in that undercurrent that ran like ice water down Paul's spine. Nor did it help when Sellers made no immediate move to restore order.

"I'm sure no such report existed," he whispered to Hi. "Why didn't you challenge it?"

"It's too early to start calling Hardin a liar," said the lawyer. "Wait till he's on the stand himself. We've planted a reasonable doubt. As of now, we can hardly hope for more."

"Still think I've a chance, Hi?"

The lawyer took the question in stride. "An outside chance—when I bring in Kay. Already we're proving this isn't the open-and-shut case the papers are calling it. One good rooter for your side could make all the difference."

"Are you sure that Kay would be such a witness?"

"If we move fast, she can brand Hardin as a drunken poltroon. She can surely tell the court why you signed that phony confession, and made it stick. All *we* can do between us is make you look too self-sacrificing to be true."

"MacArdle will ruin her chances for a picture career. You must see that."

"Kay's quite a girl, pal. I don't think she'll mind ruin in the slightest if it saves our case." Hi gave a wry grimace as Sergeant Furness marched toward the witness chair. "Maybe you're *both* too good to be true. I've suspected it for some time."

Sergeant Furness took the stand with only a stony stare for Paul. (Like the other witnesses, it was obvious that his indoctrination had been complete.) Under MacArdle's guidance he repeated most of Bates' story. Unlike Bates, Paul could see that his belief in each statement was absolute.

"While you were a prisoner, Sergeant," said MacArdle, "were you closely associated with Captain Scott?"

"I was a member of his medical team."

"For how long?"

"Over a year. Until I asked the C.O. to reassign me."

"Why did you make that request?"

"It was after Captain Scott operated on Colonel Pak."

"What was the nature of the operation?"

"Closure of a perforated ulcer."

"Was the operation a success?"

"It was."

"What were your feelings after Colonel Pak recovered?"

"I thought he deserved to die. I couldn't take it—standing by and watching Captain Scott keep him alive."

"So you went to Sergeant Bates and asked for a transfer."

"That's it, sir."

"No more questions."

Hi Saunders rose. "About that transfer, Sergeant. You say you couldn't take the fact that the commandant recovered. Did you mention your unhappiness to Captain Scott?"

"No, I didn't. We'd stopped speaking."

"Did the captain ever treat you badly?"

"No, sir. We were good friends before—"

"Before what?"

"Before he started handling gook patients like they were *human!*"

Hi shrugged off the outburst. "Did it occur to you that you were making his job much harder by leaving?"

"I couldn't go on helping *them*."

"Was that your only reason, Sergeant? Corporal Jackson has already said that he was tempted by the better food served in Colonel Hardin's quarters. Did you yield to a similar temptation?"

"Maybe I did eat better afterward. That wasn't the reason at the time."

"Did Sergeant Bates suggest that you request the transfer? Or was it your own idea?"

For the first time Furness looked uncomfortable. "It was his idea too—in a way."

"Cast your mind back, Sergeant. At the time of your transfer how many prisoners from Hill 1049 were alive in the Pyongyang compound?"

"Well, there was the colonel and Sergeant Bates. Corporal Jackson and

myself. And a Sergeant Luppino, on the C.O.'s staff: he died early in '53, as
I remember."

"That was the colonel's group, I take it. Can you name the others?"

Furness looked faintly aggrieved. "Of course. There were three others—
the chaplain, Miss Storey, and Captain Scott."

"The chaplain and Miss Storey were in solitary confinement when you
transferred, weren't they?"

"Yes, sir."

"In other words, Captain Scott had two sure friends at the time—both of
whom were expected to die—and four against him?"

For once MacArdle was caught napping. His objection, when it came,
was stentorian. "Counsel had no right to use the word *against.*"

"Surely it describes the situation."

Colonel Sellers leaned forward from the bench. "I must warn defense
counsel against making reckless allegations."

"If my allegations are reckless," said Hi, "the court has my apology. The
fact remains that the witnesses for the prosecution are Colonel Hardin,
Sergeants Bates and Furness, and Corporal Jackson. At the moment the
only witness for the defense is Captain Scott himself."

"The court will retire to vote on the propriety of your last question, Mr.
Saunders."

Hi settled at the defense table while the seven uniformed backs vanished
through the door. "I think we've shaken them a bit," he said. "Not that
we've established collusion—but they do realize that Hardin has snake-
charmed your technicians. Which means *everyone* who could help you—
except Kay. You must see why I'll have to use her."

Paul covered his eyes for a moment. "You're a good lawyer, Hi," he said.
"I wish you wouldn't play psychiatrist too."

"Every good lawyer's a bit of a head-shrinker," said Hi. "What are you
trying to prove here, after all? That all men are brothers, regardless of who's
shooting who?"

"You might call it that."

"Then why are *you* alone in court?"

Paul let his hand fall: with the gesture, he knew that he had yielded.
Despite his fears for Kay, he could not keep down a surge of gratitude. Hi
was right, of course: no man (not even Father Tim) could fight the whole
world singlehanded.

"Have it your way," he said. "Just spare her all you can."

IV

Hi Saunders had studied Paul narrowly while he spoke. Now he was both
startled and pleased at his friend's capitulation. *At least it's something to know
you're lonely,* he told Paul silently. *Lonely and frightened enough to forget that
martyr's mask. Human enough to be less than perfect, when the chips are down.*

When he had agreed to take the case Hi had seen clearly that Paul's
chances were slim indeed, so long as he continued to stand alone against the
juggernaut of the Army's legal code. If he had seemed to agree, at first, to
the exclusion of Kay, it was only because he had sensed that Paul would
yield in time. . . . Ever since it had come by messenger that morning, Kay's
note had burned his pocket. For an instant he considered showing it to Paul,
but restrained the impulse. A mystic is always difficult, he told himself
soberly. When he's fresh from the hell of a Chinese prison camp, he needs
kid-glove treatment.

Hi got briskly to his feet as the court returned. Clearly that was not the moment to inform Paul that the girl he loved was waiting to see him at this very moment. Or that her eagerness to testify in this trial was no less intense than Hi's need of that testimony. . . .

As he had expected, Sellers upheld the objection of trial counsel and his last question was stricken from the record.

"Let us return to Colonel Pak, Sergeant," he said. "Do you think Captain Scott should have refused to operate?"

"I can't blame him for operating," said Furness. "They'd have shot him if he hadn't. He could still have let something happen."

"D'you realize what you are saying, Sergeant?"

"It's what they said all over camp."

"That Captain Scott should have used his surgical training to commit murder?"

"We didn't call it that."

"What did you call it?"

Furness did not budge. "We figured gooks like Pak were better off dead."

"I believe you gave the anesthetic at the operation. If anyone could have caused Colonel Pak's death and gotten away with it, weren't you the one?"

"I couldn't do it. Captain Scott was too smart to let me."

"But you expected *him* to kill a patient on the table?"

"We all expected it."

"Sergeant, are you familiar with the Hippocratic oath?"

"I know most of it."

"Can you say, from your own personal knowledge, that Captain Scott has ever broken that oath?"

"No, sir, he hasn't."

"Thank you, Sergeant. I have only two more questions. Did you see Miss Storey and Chaplain O'Fallon when they were brought from solitary confinement?"

"I did, sir."

"What was your opinion of their condition?"

"They both seemed to be dying."

"That is all."

Hi smiled inwardly as he watched MacArdle charge up for rebuttal. The violence of the trial counsel's attack told him that he had scored this time.

"Sergeant, from what medical school did you graduate?"

"None, sir. I'm just an MC technician. You have my service record."

"Never mind your service record. By what authority do you give a medical diagnosis?"

"Objection," said Hi. "The witness *thought* the two prisoners were dying. He gave no diagnosis—nor was he asked to do so."

From the bench, Sellers upheld the objection with asperity. MacArdle resumed, with a stain of red at each jowl.

"Sergeant, do you consider yourself competent to make a diagnosis?"

"Objection," said Hi. "Trial counsel is badgering his own witness."

Sellers leaned forward. His brows were knitted and he resembled an outraged eagle more than ever. Hi masked his elation when he observed that Major Duggan (the Korean veteran on the president's right) was frowning just as darkly.

"Trial counsel is warned against such outbursts."

But MacArdle had already recovered his poise. "Sergeant, could you decide, beyond a doubt, if a person were dying?"

"No, sir."

"No further questions."

"We are about to recess for lunch," said the president. "Does any member of this court wish to query the witness?"

Major Duggan thrust forward in his chair. "Sergeant, you and Corporal Jackson were the only members of your barracks who transferred to Colonel Hardin's quarters—is that correct?"

"Yes, sir."

"Then you can compare the food in both places. Was it better in the colonel's quarters?"

"Yes, sir."

"In quality or quantity?"

"In—both."

"I'll give you three choices, Sergeant. Was it simply better, much better, or very much better?"

There was a gleam of sweat on the sergeant's forehead, and he answered in a voice that was just above a whisper. "Very much better, sir."

"No further questions."

MacArdle, with a line between his brows, dismissed the witness at the president's nod. There was a great scraping of chairs as the court rose.

"Call that our inning, Paul," said Hi. "Not that it means the game, of course: the enemy's just warming up. But that major could be our entering wedge. *He* was captured too, four months before the war ended: he knows what passed for food in North Korea."

"Speaking of food, will you lunch with me?"

"I've a date at Tarrantino's," lied Hi glibly. "Take my advice, and have a tray sent to your room at the BOQ. This afternoon promises to be rough going."

"What about Kay?"

"Kay's my headache now; forget about her. You've done your damnedest to keep her out of this: you can rest your conscience."

Hi delayed a little longer at the defense table while the familiar wedge of MPs shepherded Paul down the aisle. His friend moved easily in that cordon: he seemed unaware of the flash bulbs, the jab of the reporters' questions. Shaking his head in pure wonder, Hi stole a glance at Kay's note:

> I'll be in a maroon convertible, parked at the ocean end of Highland Avenue, Sausalito, waiting for the court's luncheon break. Will you meet me there alone—and tell me the quickest way to get into this fight?

Paul had just gone through the side door with his head high: a prince of the blood en route to the guillotine could not have seemed calmer. Whatever brand of salvation Father Tim was selling in Korea, Hi thought, Paul has absorbed the essence. His need for Kay Storey is still the chink in his armor.

V

Kay had written to Hi Saunders an hour before dawn, when sleep was clearly impossible: she had not paused to weigh the words. Once the note was in a messenger's hands, she had felt a strange peace descend upon her, the fatalism of a warrior committed to a battle she could not vision clearly.

Even when she was breakfasting with Eric Lindman (just before his plane left for Hollywood) it gave her a perverse satisfaction to keep her own counsel. Eric would surely have jumped out of his skin had she confessed that she was determined to testify in Paul's behalf, no matter what the cost; but she was in no mood for the wonder boy's glib arguments—and she had no excess strength to combat them.

Now, parked in Sausalito, with the car radio purring out its version of the trial at the Presidio, she was profoundly glad to be alone. When she had driven across the Golden Gate Bridge her eyelids had been heavy with wariness, but her mind had never been more wide-awake; she could even rejoice in the spot she had chosen for her meeting with Hi. Sausalito, a San Francisco suburb clinging to the peninsula across the Golden Gate, was a perfect backdrop for her mood. The wheels of her convertible (cramped at the curb where Highland Avenue ended at the sheer drop above the Pacific) were set at a precarious angle: had she released the hand brake, the car would have plunged for the spouting waves below her. . . . The sense of danger gave an added fillip to her pulse beat.

The euphoria had not endured. She had reckoned without her own impatience—which had forced her to arrive here a good hour before Hi could join her. Nor could she pin her mind to the radio and the long wrangles of the lawyers—though she had understood perfectly when the court had refused to permit questions on events prior to the surrender of Hill 1049.

Her anger had subsided when she realized that no questions from Hi could bring out the true story. The fact that a line officer of the Army could be a fool and a coward was a possibility this court would never admit, even in the abstract.

Somehow (she told herself bitterly) there must be a way to break the tissue of half-truth that MacArdle was weaving. *Between us, Hi Saunders and I must turn the hard, white light of reality on this case, or Paul is lost. . . .* Perhaps the true story of Hill 1049 would never be told. Yet her mind returned persistently to that battle-scarred ridge and the terror she had met and conquered on its slope. Of course she had been mad to venture there: she had deserved every aftermath of that visit. Yet she could not regret the impulse that had brought about her reunion with Paul and Father Tim, in the very shadow of catastrophe.

Her eye moved for the tenth time to the dashboard clock, and her hand darted forward impatiently to twist the dial of the car radio. Back in San Francisco the court-martial seemed on the point of adjourning—but it would be some time before Hi could cross the bridge to join her. The lawyer would want the details of her Korean adventure exactly as she remembered them. There was still time to rehearse that story once again—beginning with the night in Pusan that had witnessed the creation of "The Girl Next Door."

That strange, hybrid dream girl had been her special triumph; as "The Girl Next Door," she had felt that she could do no wrong. There had been no sense of trespass when she had pulled wires deliberately to bring Paul to Seoul on leave—or, later, to arrange a visit at his surgical bunker on Hill 1049. . . .

On the car radio the court-martial at the Presidio had been replaced by a disk jockey who was retailing the star dust of yesterday. Appropriately enough, the record he was playing now was "Night and Day." Kay found that she was murmuring the words of the lyric as "The Girl Next Door" had murmured them—speaking rather than singing, as she had done at that ancient piano in the cantonment at Pusan. Her eyelids drooped, shutting out the stark, bright colors of Sausalito. She was deep in the past again, with every sinister overtone as clear as it had been halfway across the world.

THE GIRL NEXT DOOR

I

It was a song she had shouted from a hundred platforms, in barracks from Governors Island to San Diego. She had sung it in theaters as well equipped as any Broadway show shop—and in unlighted, unheated barns. Tonight's theater in Pusan was somewhere in between—a drafty cave that boasted nearly a thousand seats, a switchboard of sorts, and acoustics that could almost be described as adequate. . . . She had expected the house to be packed: audiences were ready-made in a staging area and presumably eager to be entertained. The fact that the present audience was not even mildly amused had baffled the troupe of which Kay Storey was a featured, if not a vital, unit.

Whirling into the final chorus (in a serpentine dance step that lifted her flaring sequin gown to thigh level), Kay wondered numbly at the lack of response from those tiers of khaki beyond the footlight trough. The song was a Hit Parade favorite; the special lyrics she was using were knowing and naughty: they had raised gales of laughter in stateside cantonments. Tonight the risqué rhymes fell like wet pennies in the mud. Even the glimpse of her legs, in black opera-length nylons, had produced only a few wolf whistles.

Kay had played to tough audiences before; she could gauge her applause expertly, long before the number ended—and braced herself for the scolding that would await her in the wings. As she had expected, Danny Dietz was at the prompt table—but the fox-faced director (who doubled as a stage manager and a straight man for the comic) gave her no more than a harassed grimace. Danny's own number had fared just as badly as her song: the director's gloomy visage hardly suited his checkerboard zoot suit and bright scarlet tie. Off stage, behind the plywood door of a dressing cubicle, Kay could hear the cursing of the star. Bugs Jordan was a comedian who took his art seriously, and his drinking even more so.

Regardless of its lack of applause, the show rolled smoothly on. Kay stood back to let the six-girl chorus line scamper on stage for its burlesque of "The Easter Parade," a strip-tease routine that had delighted a California air base three weeks ago. Waiting for the laughs that did not come, she shivered just a little, despite the thick bathrobe Dietz had tossed over her shoulders.

"What are we doing wrong, Danny?"

"Nothing," said the director. "You were in there punching."

"Did I punch too hard?"

"Don't try to take it apart, Kay. Last week they had Bob Hope—and they howled their heads off. Does anyone work harder?"

"Maybe they've had too much Hope," said Kay. "Maybe these unit shows are too alike. If we had a change of pace—"

"Don't *you* worry about our pace, darling. That's my department—and I'm stuck with it."

"We can't lay eggs all over Korea, Danny."

"Starting tomorrow," said the director, "we're cutting down to size. You for looks, me for laughs—and the quartet for background. The rest fly back to Tokyo: maybe they'll sound better with cherry blossoms."

"What about Bugs?"

"*He's* going back for sure. I always figured Bugs Jordan was a Lambs' Club actor. Now I'm sure of it." Dietz bit off the words as the comic (exuding a mixture of despair and bourbon) stalked from his dressing room, like Hamlet on a rainy Monday, and moved to the wings to await his cue.

"Shall I go cheer him up, Danny?"

Dietz shrugged. "What can you say to an actor who's just fallen on his face? So swear a bit yourself if you like—you deserve it."

"I don't feel in the least like swearing," said Kay. "I think I'll write a letter to Paul."

II

But no words would emerge on paper when she switched on the naked bulb in her own dressing cubicle and opened her writing kit. She had looked forward to surprising Paul with the news that she was in Korea at last. Now that she had set foot on the perimeter of his war, the space that divided them seemed wider than ever. It was absurd to imagine (even for a sentimental moment) that the divinity that watches over lovers would miraculously arrange their meeting.

The divinity that watches over lovers. Had they really been in love, those two days in Hollywood? Was she guilty of the sin of pride when she hoped he loved her still?

In fairness to Paul, she had not put that love into words. She would wait (she told herself) until she had looked into his eyes and seen if her love was returned. For that reason she had kept her letters brief and gay, with no overtone of the emotion that gripped her. . . . Tonight she could ask herself if the show's failure was a portent. Had it been presumptuous of her to force her way into this world of fighting men, a gray existence she could never share?

Puzzling over her failure, she continued to stare down at the empty page in her writing kit. Somewhere, she perused, there must be an antidote for that grayness, for the boredom of those boys in khaki (most of them were really no more than that). A reminder, however fleeting, of a happiness they had left behind them—a universe of football rallies, midnight sodas, love-making in jalopies. . . . A universe, in short, where they had been themselves.

Tonight's show had forgotten to bring back the color and shape of that universe. The clowning of Bugs Jordan and company had merely repeated the ennui of other evenings when these GIs has watched other Broadway maestros go through their imitations of Hope and Berle and Jolson. Since she had been only an assistant in that routine, she could hardly blame her audience for its polite parody of applause.

Now that she had failed to prove herself, had she been wrong to take the job? Her voice was unsuited to torch singing: she had done far better in the smaller night clubs, where she could work in the midst of her audience. With a more compact troupe, it might be possible to perform at canteen level. . . . Or was this, too, only another hopeless fancy—since USO entertainment, by its very nature, was geared to a vast audience?

If Korea was the end of the road, she would return to Hollywood and accept what jobs were available. If Eric Lindman had overestimated her small but steady talent, she would take the defeat in stride. With that resolve to steady her, Kay closed her writing desk and prepared to leave the theater.

Outside, a raw rain was lashing the cantonment. She turned up the collar of her trench coat and followed a boardwalk that led to the guest wing housing the female members of the troupe. In America there had usually been rehearsal pianos available in such quarters: it had been her custom to strum idly for an hour after the last show—a kind of busman's holiday that had brought its special relaxation. Tonight a glance told her that her billet was only a segment of an officers' wing. There was not even a sitting room for the convenience of weary Thespians, and the heavy breathing that reached her ears suggested that the ladies of the chorus had long since called quits on the evening. Knowing that she could not sleep, Kay followed a second boardwalk and a sign pointing to the canteen.

The recreation center was a pair of converted loading sheds joined by a tin corridor that served as a sounding board for the rain; the nearer of the two held a half dozen chairs and a battered piano. Beyond, in the larger room, a half hundred GIs were at checkers or flipping the pages of ancient magazines. Most of the loungers seemed lost in apathy—a basic emptiness that isolated each man from his neighbor; to the girl's appraising eyes, it seemed a sloth more paralyzing than despair.

Daring to enter the smaller room, she found that there was a droplight above the piano. The keyboard of the instrument was yellowed with age, scarred by a hundred cigarette burns; but the strings were true when she struck her first lazy chord. Thanks to her high collar and overseas cap, she might pass for another of those weary boys, provided she could keep her distance. If she glided into her first tune more emphatically than usual, it was only to underline the fact that she (no less than these sullen young effigies) was lonely enough to scream.

> "As I walked out in the streets of Laredo
> As I walked out in Laredo one day. . . ."

Why had she picked a cowboy's lament out of her endless repertoire? And when had she begun to hum in the husky contralto that had always been her natural singing style? It hardly surprised her when several voices (not all of them Texan) picked up the words: in the female barracks she had shared so often, it was customary to join in during the last half hour before bedtime. . . . Kay let her fingers slip into a long arpeggio, not too different from the riff of a cowboy's guitar, and went to the next verse without conscious thought.

> "I see by your outfit that you are a cowboy.
> These words I did say as I boldly walked by. . . ."

A score of voices had picked up the melody now—and most of the singers had begun to converge on the piano. So far, the group was neither an audience nor a crowd of rebellious young men who might, conceivably, get out of hand. The sharing of the tune was all that mattered.

"What's your name, sister?"

"I'm not your sister," said Kay. "I'm the girl next door."

"D'you know 'Sometimes I'm Happy?'"

"I know them all."

She had been a natural by-ear pianist since childhood, with nearly total recall. Gliding into the old musical-comedy favorite, she could bless her easy gift and the boon it had brought to this plywood haven. Her audience was with her this time—though it was not an audience at all, in the usual sense, and she felt none of the nervous tension of a performance. When she finished the first request number GIs were banked ten-deep around the keyboard and the requests were coming too fast to sort.

"'Night and Day,' sister!"

"She isn't your sister, yardbird—and *we* want 'Star Dust!'"

"'St. Louis Blues!'"

"'Melancholy Baby!'"

"D'you know 'As Time Goes By,' lady?"

"D'you know 'The Missouri Waltz?'"

For an interval that could have been a night or an hour Kay ceased to measure time while she ranged through the whole rich field of the American folk song. Scores of forgotten musicals came back to her, entire. Together they sang the songs of Romberg and Kern and Gershwin, of Porter and Rodgers and Coward; they explored the melodies of Hoagy Carmichael and Irving Berlin. For the most part, she played with her eyes half closed, sure that the vigorous young voices would sustain her; between numbers she talked to them as easily as she had once chatted with friends on her porch in Kansas. . . . As the improvisation continued, she could pretend she was singing to Paul alone (the dim lights helped, and a tall noncom who stood a trifle apart from the others made a fair stand-in). The nonsense she spoke was for his ears. The jokes she traded were part of the fun they might have shared, had fate dealt different cards.

This, she told herself, was entertainment in its purest form—the element of make-believe that lifted them all outside their drab surroundings; this was a family party where she had become, quite by accident, the guiding spirit. As the song fest continued, she found that she had answered every request— and, in response to the clamor, repeated a score of favorites. She sang "Margie" and "Let Me Call You Sweetheart" as happily as she gave them "Someday I'll Find You" and "Tiger Rag." She sang "The Foggy Foggy Dew" to a basso-profundo counterpoint, and "Night and Day" as it was meant to be sung—a sentimental threnody rather than a torch song.

Toward the end she was aware of Danny's presence in the front rank of the singers and realized that the male quartet had mingled with the crowd to set the pitch for the more difficult numbers. Aside from these gentle assists, it was her show alone. When the lights went up at last and she left the canteen with Danny's arm in hers she was genuinely startled by the thunder of the applause—and touched, no less poignantly, when none of her listeners pressed forward to meet her in person. The illusion she had created, she saw, was too precious to spoil by contact with an actual performer.

It was only when she paused in the portal of her billet that the magnitude of her success struck home. Oblivious of the teeming rain, she faced Dietz with shining eyes.

"What happened, Danny?"

"Shall we say a star was born, darling?"

"Don't talk nonsense. That wasn't *me.*"

"So you were singing off the cuff," said Danny. "All really great acting is spontaneous—and don't contradict your director."

"Can we try it again?"

"We can and will, right up to the Thirty-Eighth Parallel—if the brass will give us clearance."

"Promise to let my ad libs ride, and never rehearse me?"

"After tonight, Kay, you've got a deal."

"What shall we call it?"

"You've named your act, darling. Can you think of a better label than *The Girl Next Door?*"

"I didn't invent it," said Kay soberly. "The first man to call me that was a chaplain in San Pedro. Funny, isn't it, that *he* should see where my talent lay?"

III

The pride of achievement lasted in the busy weeks that followed, while the reorganized unit (with Kay as its focal point) repeated the success of that first impromptu song fest in canteens from Pusan to the edge of the combat zone. Riding a wave of self-esteem no less heady than the wine of success, she was strangely content to hold the thought of Paul at arm's length—now that she could name the time and place for their reunion. She could even put off the summons deliberately: it gave her an odd thrill to realize that the growing fame of "The Girl Next Door" must reach him in time, though the girl herself was anonymous.

She had made that stipulation from the beginning, in spite of Danny Dietz's protests.

"Give me another month—I'll make you the toast of the whole Eighth Army," said Danny. "Think what *that'll* be worth to Kay Storey in Hollywood."

"It isn't *me* they love," Kay had insisted. "I'm not that vain, Heaven knows. It's the memories I bring back. If I had a name, it might spoil everything."

"You've turned your torch down low, darling—all you've used so far is the back burner—but the kids always catch fire. Won't you take some of the credit?"

"Be smart for once, Danny. Let 'The Girl Next Door' call the tune. Don't bring show business into the act."

Dietz had capitulated, of course—and the show moved north on the note Kay had established in Pusan. As he had done on the memorable first performance, Danny mingled with the crowd in each canteen, getting things under way with a few adroit impromptus. The male quartet (inconspicuous in ODs) was also part of each group, helping to set pitch and tempo. Otherwise it was Kay's night—and the Army's. The Army continued to enjoy it to the hilt.

Playing to one-night stands (with extra performances when a barracks boasted more than one canteen) the troupe had used no press agent or other formal drum beater to advertise its coming: the word of mouth that preceded it was enough to assure packed houses.

"Larry Kirk's at the PRO," Danny told Kay at the end of their first thundering success in a camp outside Seoul. "So's the AP man, and a feature writer from the King syndicate. You've *got* to give those boys some time. It's in the cards."

"I don't mind—if you'll keep my name under wraps."

"They may recognize you from your pictures."

"I wasn't *that* famous in Hollywood, Danny."

She was still enjoying her anonymity when she arrived in the Army public-relations headquarters and submitted to mass questioning from a group of newsmen that had swollen to the proportions of a mob. Afterward Larry Kirk had insisted that Dietz bring her to the Hotel Chosun for a drink—and a more exclusive interview. Despite the artful pumping of that famous television commentator, Kay had refused to give an inch—until he had mentioned his impending tour of the lines.

"The boys will be wondering how soon you're coming north. What can I tell them?"

"I'm ready to sing anywhere," said Kay. "The Army knows that." She had thought of Paul then—and yielded to impulse before she could quite arrange her thoughts. "Could you find time to visit the 141st Battalion?"

"With the friends I have on staff," said Larry Kirk, "I can go anywhere short of the Yalu. Is there someone special in the 141st you'd like to flag down?"

"Will you deliver a note to the battalion surgeon—a Captain Paul Scott?"

"If you like, I'll ship him back in person."

"Things can't be that easy, Mr. Kirk. Not even for you."

"Just put me to the test, young woman," said Kirk. "You've given this man's Army a great deal. It's time they reciprocated."

IV

Her mass interview in Seoul made the front pages in America. A few weeks later word reached Kay that there were features in more than one magazine—and a front cover on *Life* (a candid-camera shot) that showed her singing out her heart. She found that she could take such publicity in stride. Korea, after all, was far from the bustle of the home front. Regardless of this civilian hubbub, "The Girl Next Door" would continue to serve her purpose.

She could hardly keep her cloak of mystery now. Her first real shock was a cable from Eric Lindman. It addressed her as casually as though they had parted yesterday:

ALWAYS KNEW YOUD HIT YOUR STRIDE WHEN ARE YOU COMING HOME TO BE FAMOUS?

Such a wire would once have opened the gates of paradise. Today (with a show to give in ten minutes) it was only a tribute, to be pasted in her memory book. She did not even show the cable to Danny—though the USO director was bustling with plans for her future. So long as the war continued she would stay on in Korea—moved by a compulsion far more complex than the need to share the same continent with Paul Scott.

A few nights later, when she was singing in a camp just north of Seoul, it seemed quite natural to look up from the keyboard and find herself looking into his eyes at last.

Apparently he had entered the hall after the song fest began; now, he stood on a table top that made a natural vantage point. Two bulky enlisted men shared the perch with him, and the three had linked arms for balance. It gave her an odd sense of her importance (if that was the proper word) when Paul made no immediate attempt to catch her attention. Even when he called a request of his own, toward the concert's end, he did not quite meet her eyes.

She pretended to misunderstand, though she had heard perfectly. "What was that again, Captain?"

"'Night and Day,' please."

The night they first met in San Pedro she had sung the Cole Porter classic with all the brass of the orchestra behind her; here in Korea she sang it simply—and if the song was addressed to Paul alone, no soldier in the jam-packed room was aware of the exclusion. When it was over at last, she permitted Danny to fold her trench coat about her and whisk her out as he always did—with only a finger-tossed kiss for her farewell. Nor was she disturbed when Paul (obeying the unwritten law that had surrounded her with a magic circle no man had crossed) let her depart with no outward sign of recognition.

It was after midnight, and she had given two more shows in the interval, before she returned to her hotel to find him waiting in the lobby. This time, when he held out his arms she came into them as naturally as though she had never been away. He held her for a moment before their kiss—and the kiss was worth all her months of waiting.

"It's been so long, Paul—"

"It's been an eternity," he said. "I wonder how we've survived—but we have."

"Now you're here, it seems as though you've never been away."

He smiled down at her as she tossed aside her trench coat and settled before the fireplace, on the sofa with the broken spring. It was a smile she remembered well—but there was an added depth she did not recognize. It was like looking again at the painting of a loved one, she told herself. Each feature was in place—yet there was a difference she could not define.

"You've changed, haven't you, Paul? I think it's for the better, war or no war."

"*You* haven't," he told her, "except to grow more beautiful."

"After the day I've put in I must look a fright."

"Don't talk nonsense—you understand me perfectly. *This* beauty is something from within. If Father Tim were here, he'd call it an added richness of spirit—"

She savored the phrase for a moment: after all, it was an exact description of the light in Paul's own eyes when she had walked into the lobby. As lovers will, she wondered if this empathy was a special magic—which she, alone among mortals, was privileged to share.

"How is the padre?"

"Much the same," said Paul. "A little more frail, I'm afraid—and a great deal wiser. Or so it seems, now I know him better." He looked at her with a rather sheepish grin. "Perhaps I'm the one who has grown up."

"*Must* we talk of Father Tim?"

"Of course not. I'm using him as a shield, to avoid mentioning 'The Girl Next Door.'"

"We can forget her for tonight: she won't give her next show until tomorrow."

"Doesn't fame make a difference?"

"Not if you'll promise never to confuse me with that girl at the piano."

"Come off it, Kay. Dietz showed me a copy of *Life*. We both know what's waiting for you in Hollywood. So does Eric Lindman."

"Hollywood's a whole world away—and I haven't changed a bit. That's one observation you can't withdraw."

"You're sure of that? When people like Larry Kirk run errands for you? I realize that you arranged my leave between you—"

"Didn't you deserve a leave?"

"That's beside the point. Not that I don't thank you for separating me from Colonel Hardin, however briefly—"

"Has it been bad, Paul?"

"Not too bad to endure. I'm prepared to stick it out."

"And so am I, darling. 'The Girl Next Door' is signed on for the duration—and she's happy that she's needed. Her happiness would be complete—if you need Kay Storey too."

With only a glance to make sure the lobby was deserted, he took her in his arms with all the hunger she had awaited from their first kiss. It was a savage embrace—but she did not cry out at the hurt. This, after all, was the answer she had sought across half a world.

V

If the week that followed was a blissful one, it was not because of physical passion; the new, warm relationship between them was sufficient in itself. At San Pedro their coming together had been an inevitable end product of their frantic searching for shelter in the midst of chaos. Here in Seoul, while Paul's leave ran its course, they discovered that liking could be as precious as love.

At nightfall Paul was forced to share her with the thousands who thronged to her song fests. Usually (so great was the demand for *The Girl Next Door*) the performances overlapped the official lights-out—and it was a weary, happy Kay who returned to the Hotel Chosun in the dawn. But the days were theirs alone—and they made the most of the hours she could steal from her work.

Twice in that week there were cables from California—a second teaser from Lindman, an outright offer from Barney Gould, the head man at Eric's studio. Kay had left both of them unanswered with hardly a pang. It was true that Paul had said no word of marriage. But she knew, quite without words, that they were already wedded, that the final, legal seal must come when this business was ended.

On their last afternoon together they borrowed a jeep from the motor pool and drove into the country for an outing, complete with a picnic hamper (procured from the officers' mess) and a bottle of contraband champagne. It had taken searching, but they had found a green hillside, with a grove of pine trees and a meadow at its foot. For a time they rested quietly in the shadow pattern of the pines, half afraid to spoil the perfect afternoon.

"When will I see you again, Paul?"

"I'd give a great deal to answer accurately."

"Everyone says the war may end at any moment."

"Perhaps it will, Kay. But I won't mind serving my time, with no more favors. It's something I'm not sure I can explain."

"Won't you even try?"

He drew her close. "This will sound pompous, I'm sure. Like a one-worlder praising the brotherhood of man. But I've learned to call myself a member of the human race on Hill 1049. Here with you I'm enjoying a happiness I haven't paid for. It's like buying something on the installment plan. Maybe I *have* made the down payment—but there's a lot of earning ahead."

"Darling, do you *want* to go back?"

"Only to make those other payments, Kay. Now we've had this week together, I can endure anything."

She lifted her head from his shoulder and met his eyes. "Including the fact that I might do a picture for Eric someday?"

"Of course—if it's what you want."

"I do want it," she said quietly. "You see, it's the one challenge I haven't met—and I've won all my battles so far. I've even made you love me; you'll admit *that* took doing."

"Did you think I'd stand in the way?"

"I don't want a *career*, Paul; just to prove to Eric that I am an actress. Once that's behind me, I'll rest on my laurels. I could belong to you forever—if you still wanted me."

"I'll always want you, Kay—"

The argument (if she could call it that) had ended without words, as most of their discussions had ended, so far. Marriage was still unmentioned when he kissed her good-by that night and vaulted to the tail gate of a convoy truck going north. Kay had wept at their second parting—but not too bitterly. After all, she had just completed her plans for a tour of the front (though she had been careful to keep this surprise from Paul). The certainty that they would meet again blunted the pain of farewell.

Now that the fighting was in a genuine lull, the public-relations office at Seoul had been overjoyed at her offer to sing just behind the lines. For the next week she performed in mobile hospitals, in mountain caves made to serve as rest areas, in amphitheaters pocked by old shell holes. Dietz had been left in the Korean capital, since he was busy with a projected tour in Japan. When she told her current liaison officer (an applecheeked boy from GHQ) that she was eager to visit her old friend Chaplain O'Fallon, and hoped she could give her next song fest on Hill 1049, it had been quickly arranged.

That noon she had sung to wild applause at a regimental collecting station less than ten miles from the hill. An hour later, perched like a truant schoolboy on a box of supplies destined for Paul's surgery, with the pilot as her only companion, she was riding a helicopter to her destination.

VI

Her first view of the front was a pure anticlimax. She had seen foxholes before, and battery mounts; she had explored the strange burrows that passed for men's homes in this wilderness. So far, Korea had resembled the massif of the Sierra Madre behind the Sunset Strip in Hollywood: from the whirlybird, the resemblance seemed even more marked today—nor was the actual battle line (which the pilot sketched with a vague gesture) a jot different from the regimental base she had just quitted.

Then, as the helicopter settled upon its improvised field on the slope of Hill 1049, she saw that the earth here was more brown than green, that the battle scars were alarmingly fresh when contrasted with the grassy craters at the rear. The officers who greeted her when she stepped from the plane was a wizened, old-young lieutenant. His eyes were red from lack of sleep; his voice, at first, was peevish as his manner.

"Lieutenant Crosby, Miss Storey. Colonel's in the sack. As of now, we're badly understaffed: I'm all the welcome committee we could spare."

Paul's name was on her lips, but she suppressed it. She had told regimental headquarters that she wished to see the chaplain—and her reason was genuine.

"I'm sure I'm a nuisance, Lieutenant. But I flew in early to visit with Father O'Fallon before I perform."

"He's in the surgical bunker, ma'am." Crosby's peevishness had vanished, now that he had been granted a close look at the visitor. "Don't mind if I'm staring—but we seldom get entertainers this far north. Maybe never is the right word."

When she recalled it later, that conversation with Crosby seemed as inappropriate as her presence here. Her mind, like her nerve ends, felt strangely detached when she stepped over a sandbagged incline that tunneled down to Dr. Paul Scott's domain. She had pictured a clammy dugout, a welter of blood and groans: she had feared that she might surprise Paul in the midst of an operation. But this spacious cave resembled nothing more than a windowless bedroom in some university fraternity house— complete with neat cots, its walls thick with pinups. Only the sterilizer in the alcove, the precise geometry of a dozen field-instrument cases, and the bare operating table identified the bunker for what it really was.

Father Tim was seated in a corner, writing busily in a leather-bound book by the light of a portable gas lamp: he could not have seemed more at ease in his own rectory, nor did he notice her presence at once. Hesitating before she spoke, she marveled at the maturity that had settled on the young priest's shoulders—if *maturity* was the exact word for a change that seemed far more profound. There was a visible comfort in this man's presence, a strength that defied all labels. Even before she addressed him she was certain that he could explain the compulsion which had brought her here.

The priest lifted his eyes from his writing, and she saw that this was no philosopher in khaki, but a tired man who needed a definite effort to adjust to her presence. She drew back a little: she had not expected Father Tim to make her feel like an intruder.

"Call me any name you like," she said. "From *femme fatale* to plain busybody. I deserve them all."

"You do indeed, my dear," said Father Tim, rising to greet her with a warm smile that banished all her doubts. "But you're welcome just the same."

"I shouldn't have come, Padre. I knew as much when I stepped from that helicopter."

"I'm glad you did, Kay—really glad."

"At least it's a legitimate visit," she said lightly. "I'll be singing for the battalion later."

"Come into the light where I can see your face. It's wonderful how success has fulfilled you."

"I hope it hasn't spoiled me too."

"Nothing could spoil you, my dear."

"It was you I came to see, not Paul. Will you believe that?"

"Of course, Kay."

She had spoken in an outburst: it was much easier now to go on. "I came to tell you everything, Padre—about Paul and me. I want your advice for the future."

"Are you sure it's wise to ask me?"

"If I were of your faith, you'd take my confession."

"I hardly think you've anything serious to confess, my dear."

"What about the sin of pride, Father? Proving I can have anything I like these days—including this visit?"

The chaplain's smile forgave her in advance. "Now that you're here, let's make the best of it," he said quietly. "The enlisted technicians are checking supplies in headquarters. Paul's on the next hill for an emergency. So you chose a perfect time."

As though by common consent, they left the bunker to follow a path that snaked up the ravine to the distant spine of the hill. As they walked, Father Tim pointed out items of defense that Kay already knew by heart from similar tours: the machine-gun nests that flanked the headquarters bunker, the gun mounts on adjacent slopes that had held Hill 1049 against all comers, so far. She accepted the information gratefully, knowing that he was only talking thus to put her at her ease. . . . It pleased her to note that she had drawn few glances from the men who worked like patient, mud-brown moles along the slope. Thanks to her OD fatigues and the trench helmet that concealed her hair, she hoped that she was passing for the chaplain's assistant, absorbing a first lesson in salvation under enemy guns.

The actual enemy was nonexistent today. Even when they had climbed to the summit of the hill and entered an observation post that commanded the whole topsy-turvy landscape to the north, the mountains that faced them seemed empty of life.

"Why did you bring me up here, Father?"

"Two reasons, Kay. First, I wanted you to see the front as it really is: the whole sector is before you now."

"Don't tell me the North Korean Army is on that next ridge."

"A few weeks ago this post was in rifle range. Since then, we've pushed our outposts to the edge of the valley and forced their snipers to pull back—"

"You said we had *two* reasons for being here."

"The second is more important. Paul usually climbs to this spot for a breather at the day's end. I thought you might wish to meet him here—in a foxhole, between two hostile worlds. It would be something to tell your grandchildren."

"Will we have them, Padre? Grandchildren, I mean?"

"Isn't that the topic you came to discuss with me?"

She told him everything then—as calmly as though they were discussing the emotional impasse of a friend they both knew intimately. She described her night with Paul in Hollywood, the love that had crept in, unheralded, to flower after his departure. She told of their reunion in Seoul and the communion it had brought them both. Finally she confessed to the folly of her front-line visit, the need for advice that was its only real justification.

Father Tim heard her in silence. When she had finished her recital he did not speak at once, though the pressure of his fingers on her arm told her that he understood her dilemma perfectly.

"What has the war done to Paul, Padre? Can you tell me?"

"Shall we say it has given him a reason for being—a reason he lacked before?"

"It's more than that."

"Call it a dedication, if you like, Kay. It's a word we all use: few of us could define it accurately. I think, however, that Paul's own case sums up for us both. After all, you and I are responsible for his success here."

Kay forced a smile. "Do you plead guilty too?"

"I wouldn't say this to another soul, my dear, but I'm sure I saved him from a suicide attempt back in San Pedro. It happened just before I introduced you at the canteen."

"Was Paul that desperate?"

"I'm afraid so—for that moment. Remember, it takes only a moment to snuff life out, and a whole lifetime to earn the right to call oneself a man."

"You saved him from dying?"

The priest nodded. "From a sickness of our times, Kay; from the despair we all feel when we discover that there is no security in our century, that our little world can crumble overnight. It was a small service and a negative one. *You* gave him the urge to fight back, when you gave him your love. I can guess how precious that gift has been."

"You don't blame me, then, for what happened in Hollywood?"

"As a man of the cloth, I must censure you most severely. If you were a Catholic, I'd prescribe the worst penance I could devise." The priest moved to the parapet of the observation post and stared down at the valley. "Not that it's my place to speak of atonement. God, in His wisdom, has already given you your special burden. I think you'll learn to bear it gallantly."

"Does that mean Paul can never belong to me?"

"No human being really belongs to another; the fact is more apparent when a man is truly dedicated. I'd say it was the first lesson Paul's wife must learn."

"I'm sure he wants to marry me, Father."

"There is nothing he wants more. As of now, he might even persuade himself to return to practice in Hollywood—while you have the success there that you so richly deserve. But I'm afraid he's outgrown that pattern, Kay: his destiny lies elsewhere now."

"Don't you feel that he should marry?"

"Of course he should."

"But I'm not the best wife he could choose?"

"Emotionally, you are perfectly suited. But it takes more than love to sustain a true marriage. One needs a shared achievement too."

"Surely 'The Girl Next Door' has her value."

"Her value is above rubies. She heals the wounds of the soul no less surely than Paul heals the body. Perhaps she should continue doing that—even after the war; perhaps she has already found her destiny."

"Can't two destinies be combined?"

"I hope and pray they can; fond as I am of you both, I couldn't do less."

"What would you have Paul do if you had charge of his future?"

The priest smiled. "Now you're asking me to presume upon the rights of God. Only He can give orders to His army."

"You and Paul must have talked things over."

"We've talked more than once. I think he should go wherever man is oppressed by man. Only last night he was speaking of the miners in West Virginia, the miseries he knows there at first hand. They could use a man like Dr. Scott in those hills. Perhaps he'll settle there eventually and open the clinic of tomorrow."

Kay suppressed a faint sense of loss as the priest's quiet voice flowed on: already his wisdom had penetrated to the roots of her being. What he had just told her was unassailable: the true healer must dwell in a special world, and the impulses that drive him are inviolate. Come what may, she warned herself solemnly, I will never interfere. . . .

"The first lesson we must learn is the hardest, Kay. It has nothing to do with you or Paul as people. We must see this struggle in Korea for what it really is, in the framework of a godless culture. Even the enemy has his place in history when he is judged in perspective—"

"I thought you had no enemies, Father."

"The devil is my eternal enemy. If the Korean War proves nothing else, it will go down in the books as a symbol. Here in these mountains the free world drew a line, beyond which the devil could not pass. Not even when he was wearing his most ancient disguise, the armor of Mars."

"Do you think we'll win here, Padre?"

"The fact that we made a stand is what really matters. It will be remembered always—even if the present stalemate ends in a truce. Even if the truce is broken—"

"Why are you telling me this?"

"Because you must realize that we are all part of that struggle. You with your music, Paul with his scalpel, and I with the teachings of the Man I serve. If the naked force of the enemy falls in Korea, it will be only our first victory. The war with evil will go on. With other weapons on other battlegrounds."

The priest stood with both hands spread on the sandbags of the parapet— as though the foxhole were his special pulpit and Kay a congregation of one. Now he turned and lifted her gently to his side. With that simple motion he was Father Tim again, a rather tired Army chaplain in dirt-stained fatigues.

"Don't stop, Padre—"

"I've said all that matters, Kay. Enough to make you see that Paul and I are in *this* war for the duration, because this war is never-ending." Father Tim crossed the observation post and looked down the southern slope of

Hill 1049. "The sermon is over just in time. Paul is coming up the ravine now, and I can see the men gathering at the headquarters bunker for your song fest. I'll go down and tell Corporal Jackson to tune his guitar."

VII

She had expected her performance (in a spacious, man-made cave beyond the headquarters bunker) to be something of an ordeal. Actually it was one of her greatest triumphs—thanks, in no small measure, to the easy authority of Jackson's guitar, which blended perfectly with her own ad-lib style. From his first lazy chords, she had sensed that the lanky corporal was a born musician. Once the jammed bunker had thundered into the chorus of "Oklahoma!," she felt she was among friends and enjoyed each note as thoroughly as her audience.

News had reached her, via field telephone, that her helicopter had suffered a breakdown on a nearby hill and would not be repaired before morning. She had taken the information without missing a beat, so complete was her identity with the singing voices that surrounded her. . . . At first, Colonel Hardin and his camarilla had been a puzzle: until the audience had warmed up, the antagonisms dividing the GIs and the battalion brass were as vivid as though a trench had bisected the cave where she was performing. But even that line had melted as song followed song. In the end the colonel was bellowing choruses as heartily as his newest replacement. Master Sergeant Bates (a shifty-eyed regular Kay had disliked on sight) had straddled the line of demarcation, to lend a deceptively pure tenor to each song he knew. . . .

She had feared the moment when Paul faced her in the observation post. Fortunately he had been warned of her arrival. After their first wild embrace he had seemed almost calm while he explained the pattern of survival they followed here—and the tensions that had kept Hill 1049 in constant, undercover turmoil. She had led him on with further questions deliberately, if only to escape the scolding she knew she deserved.

"Why is it so different here, Paul? Why is it more dangerous? I've sung under the guns before."

"Not *these* guns, I'm afraid. Helicopters and parachutes are the only means of transport, for one thing. The main supply route is one long shell hole."

"Does that matter, if the front is quiet?"

"It's been quiet too long, Kay. That, in itself, could mean trouble—like living in Maine for ten days in January without a blizzard."

"Must you sound so ominous, darling?"

He grinned at that question, for the first time. "Sorry: I realize you're here to keep up morale—I mustn't break *yours* down. But I'll be happier when you've boarded the first 'copter that stops here tomorrow."

"Does that mean I get off without a scolding?"

"How can a mere battalion surgeon scold 'The Girl Next Door,' when she arrives through channels?"

"I meant to surprise you, Paul. I *hoped* you'd be pleased."

"Of course I'm pleased. Just promise not to surprise me this way again."

"I'll go quietly in the morning," she promised. "My mission's accomplished now."

After Paul's warning Kay had expected to find the whole battalion crawling with neuroses. When she was presented to Colonel Hardin (as solemnly as though they had never met in San Pedro) she had needed her self-control to avoid staring, to uncover the mad bull beneath the florid soldier's mask. . . . The colonel had been the soul of courtesy, so far as manners went. Only the puffs beneath his bloodshot eyes and his care with three-syllable words betrayed the fact that he was balanced on the fine edge of inebriation.

The single jarring note had come at the end of the song fest. She was still accepting the thunder of applause when a deeper thunder rumbled out of the night, somewhere beyond the blackout curtains. Even her untrained ears had recognized the *crump* of an artillery salvo—and it had pleased her mightily to find that she could hear that rumble without fear.

The second round of shells had dropped nearer, but she felt no threat in the sound: the fact that a dozen GIs had darted into the night without a word of command was part of the bizarre pattern of the evening. So, for that matter, was the greenish hue that invaded Colonel Hardin's cheeks and the muttered excuse that took him from the cave, on the double. Paul had prepared her for that withdrawal.

In a matter of minutes, it seemed, the song fest had dissolved. A noncom escorted her to the spot prepared for her night's rest—a storeroom deep in the headquarters bunker, complete with a folding cot and a hastily carpentered door. It was only when she had settled there that she remembered Paul had disappeared (no less hastily than Colonel Hardin), that Corporal Jackson, his guitar forgotten, had been on the battalion surgeon's heels. Later, of course, she would realize that both men had hurried to the aid station to prepare for expected casualties.

Exhausted as she was, she dropped into a deep and untroubled slumber. She wakened with a start, aware of the chink of daylight gleaming through a crack in that improvised door. Until she could regain her senses she was positive that she had dropped off in a boiler factory.

Overhead, the air was a sheet of iron, shaken continually in the hands of a maniac with designs on her own sanity. The blanket on her cot was deep in silt that had fallen from the beams above her, and her hair was thickly powdered with the same brownish dirt as she shook the drowsiness from her eyelids. . . . When she had scrambled from the bed and donned her trench helmet the floor seemed to tremble too—and, for the first time, she was aware of a roaring quarrel in the orderly room outside.

The crack in the doorframe made an adequate peephole. Paul and Hardin were pacing the floor outside—and she had already identified the surgeon's voice, raised, for the moment, above Hardin's taurine bellow. The third figure in the churning group was strange at first—until the man turned on his heel, and she recognized Lieutenant Crosby's hatchet-sharp profile.

The C.O.'s bellow, when it rose again, all but drowned the artillery duel outside. "Damn it to *hell*, Scott! *I won't have it!*"

"Sorry, sir. The deed's done."

"You've gone to division headquarters, over my head? Yes or no?"

"It was imperative, sir. We needed helicopters on the strip at dawn."

"Did you endorse the call, Crosby?"

"I did, sir." The lieutenant had managed to stand his ground, though he had not met the blaze of hatred in the colonel's eye.

"Why couldn't you waken me, man?"

"We tried, Colonel."

"We?"

"Chaplain O'Fallon and myself. You were—sleeping too soundly."

Hardin whirled on Paul, with one trembling finger extended. "Did you send that sky pilot to my quarters, Scott?"

"If you must put it that way, sir." To her amazement, Kay noticed that

Paul had grown progressively calmer as the colonel's shouting increased in volume. "I wanted a witness when I reported you unfit for duty."

"Unfit for duty? *Me?*"

"For various reasons, Colonel. Shall I spell them out in my report?"

There was no time for more. A concussion that seemed to expand inside Kay's brain had sent every timber in the bunker into a crazy dance. While the blast endured she was certain that the walls had collapsed above their heads. Then, as the breath returned to her body, the dance of the timbers subsided: while the thunder died outside, she heard someone shouting for litter-bearers.

Colonel Hardin had pancaked to the floor with the first impact; now, on hands and knees, he scuttled for his quarters like a homing crab. Neither officer stirred until the door had slammed behind him. After the burst outside, the dugout was strangely quiet; when Paul spoke his voice was emotionless and a little tired.

"Easy does it, Crosby. We've been cut off before."

"Not with *this* fire power against us."

"We can handle things—if he'll stay under wraps."

"He always did when Major Prescott was here," said the lieutenant miserably. "The major could manage him—with help from Bates."

"From your last report I'd say the perimeter defense is still intact." Even in her bewilderment it seemed odd to Kay that the battalion surgeon, not the lieutenant, seemed to be issuing the orders. "If our lines hold until afternoon, the division can send an armored column through. That should peel them back—"

"It isn't a question of holding the perimeter, Doctor—it's the C.O. Remember how he screamed for a general retreat last time—until Prescott quieted him?" Crosby's face, at the moment, had a greenish tinge that recalled the complexion of his commander all too graphically. Yet Kay could sense that this terror, at least, was normal, the near-panic of a boy who had assumed a burden too big for his shoulders.

"I remember that last collapse all too well," said Paul. "This time, *you're* acting C.O. Try to behave like one."

Crosby's teeth closed on his upper lip. When he spoke, his tone was almost formal. "Just as you say, Doctor. Do I put Colonel Hardin on the morning report?"

"Sick in quarters," Paul ordered. "I'll sign it later." He stood back as Crosby half ran, half stumbled from the bunker in response to a shouted question outside. Then he turned to Kay's door and opened it. "I knew you were listening," he said quietly—and there was something in his voice that eased her thudding heart. "Apparently your tour of Hill 1049 is now complete."

"What happened, Paul?"

"With luck," he said, "we can still get you out."

"What *happened?*"

He took her hand and led her toward the bunker exit. "Tell you on the way," he said crisply. "Keep your head down. It's safe enough—for now. That last shell was looking for the ammo dump and fell short."

She permitted him to lead her up the bunker steps and into the glow of a flawless summer morning. Expecting death to menace her from every side, Kay was confused by the smiling face of nature. Paul's grip tightened on her hand as he noted her bewilderment.

"We'll make a run for it," he said. "Straight to the aid station. Up there you'll be nearer the landing strip."

"What *happened*, Paul?"

"The hill's surrounded. Run, Kay. Don't waste your breath."

VIII

Despite his warning, Paul himself continued to speak in snatches while they dashed up the ravine.

"Sorry, Kay, meant to come sooner. Couldn't. Been operating since midnight."

"You needn't explain, Paul—"

"Want you to know the worst. Better that way." He paused to gauge the approach of a shell. "We've had just one 'copter since dawn. Needed that for two shock cases—"

"I understand."

"This is the fourth time they've surrounded us. Each time we've smashed through from the division area and restored the supply route. We'll do it again if things don't get too hot—" He had held her against a solid outcrop of rock while he counted the shell bursts in the rear; now he flattened abruptly to earth, pulling her down beside him. The last shell from the distant enemy battery filled the air with a long, querulous whining as it passed overhead. The detonation, when it came, was too far off to seem real. Long before the sound could reach her, Paul had yanked Kay to her feet again and resumed their dash up the ravine.

"Taking no chances," he said. "Keep you under cover until things slacken off." They were on the last long slope now, with the haven of the surgical bunker just above them. Paul eased his pace for the first time and offered her the exhausted travesty of a smile. "'Copters will be coming in all morning, to take away casualties. They'll get you aboard somehow—" Again they flattened to the dirt while the shell whined in and struck, close enough to send a geyser of mud into the ravine.

"They fall short, now and then," he said, as though apologizing for the enemy gunners. "In you go, Kay. On the double!"

This time the battalion aid station was all she had imagined. Sergeant Furness and Corporal Jackson, stripped to the waist and glistening with sweat, were working quietly among the cots—and each cot groaned with its load of misery. A file of walking wounded awaited the surgeon in the sandbagged entrance; a windrow of litter cases had backed up outside during his brief absence. Some of the stretchers were already draped in blankets, grim evidence that these men, at least, were beyond help.

"Sit in the dispensary," Paul directed. "You won't be underfoot there." He had already turned to the operating table as the sergeant came up from the opposite side with an ampoule of pentothal. The case that awaited him, Kay saw, was a relatively minor one, the spraying type of wound that comes from a shrapnel burst. A quick debridement (she groped for the word in her R.N. lore and came up with it promptly) would take care of this one and make room for another.

Watching Paul work, she sensed the nicety of judgment that was essential here—and, in its way, as important as operative skill. Even at the height of the shelling a certain proportion of these cases would be ticketed for a base hospital and flown there: Paul's job was to decide who should go now and who could stay longer, to benefit from what surgery he could give under pressure. The routine crises were no less vital—the constant giving of plasma, the insertion of a tube in a shattered windpipe, a quick needle tap to relieve a collapsing lung. . . .

As the hours passed and the press of casualties continued, Kay grew tired of waiting in the dispensary. Long before the fury of the attack had eased outside the bunker, she found herself helping the hard-pressed medics—in small ways at first, then as a full-fledged partner. Once they saw that she was not afraid of the blood they accepted her gratefully. From that moment it was only a question of time before she was assisting the surgeon too.

Steadying the head of a brain-wound (Paul had paused over it just long enough to clear the approach and cover the wound itself with a dressing, before giving it top priority on the next helicopter), she knew he was aware of her presence, that he was grateful for another pair of hands that remembered their former skill.

He gave her no overt sign of recognition while he worked: this was a Paul she had never seen before, a technician whose concentration was absolute. Even when she had helped with several cases she did not cease to marvel at his easy competence, at the command decisions that made order of this blood-drenched chaos.

From her rough count Kay estimated that five of each six cases that reached the table had been selected for evacuation to MASH. Most of them would have a chance for survival, thanks to those tireless surgeon's hands and the roaring efficiency of the hospital 'copters on the strip outside. Working at top speed beside him, she had lost track of time—though she realized vaguely that it was already afternoon when he pushed back his mask at last and recognized her presence out of startled eyes.

"Why are you still here, Kay? Furness could have put you aboard a plane."

"He didn't dare," she said. "He needed me here too badly. So, I trust, did you."

"You're leaving the moment there's a place."

"If the place isn't needed." It was Kay's turn to look around her: she realized that the flow of new cases had stopped, though the din outside seemed more intense than ever. "Is every morning like this, Paul?"

"Only when the pressure's really on," he said. "We can all breathe for a moment now. I'll get coffee."

"That's *my* job, Doctor: I remember that much from my nursing."

She was still filling cups for the medics when Father Tim came down the bunker steps. The priest's slender body was sagging with weariness. He accepted the canvas chair that Kay offered, and the steaming cup, with a smile of gratitude: all that long morning they had worked side by side among the wounded—but there had been no chance to speak before.

"Will you tell Paul he mustn't have me on his conscience, Padre?" she said—as much for Paul's benefit as the chaplain's. Somewhat to her chagrin, she saw that the surgeon had already crossed to the far side of the bunker to check the evacuation-priority list with Sergeant Furness.

"I'm sorry you had to see this, Kay—"

"Believe me, Father Tim, I'm *glad* I stayed. I needed to watch Paul at work. It's helped me to see just what you meant yesterday."

The priest put down his cup and leaned back in the chair, pressing his fingers to his eyes. "Be that as it may, my dear, we'll breathe easier when you're back at the base."

"Are things really bad outside?"

"We're hard pressed, I'm afraid. It's never been quite like this."

"Isn't help on the way?"

"It may come—in time; we've always been reinforced before. The helicopters are doing a fine job in the meantime."

Kay lowered her voice. "Tell me about Colonel Hardin, Padre. Is he always drunk during an attack?"

The chaplain nodded soberly. "It's an open secret in the headquarters bunker. So far, he's brazened it out—and his staff has covered him. What the Colonel can't endure is that Paul understands his fear and covers him too. He will this time, unless Hardin really goes berserk."

"If you've taught him to forgive Hardin, you've accomplished wonders."

"The forgiveness came from his own heart, Kay. He's a doctor first of all, and the colonel is a sick man."

"But should Hardin be in command?"

"Frankly, no—though it's something we'd never explain on the record. So far, he *has* held his position, and his tactics have been above reproach, to the outside world. Paul is hoping that he'll let himself be certified as unable to carry on for medical reasons—particularly after today's show. That's why he listed him on the morning report as sick in quarters: if it goes on long enough, he can certify him for evacuation too."

Lieutenant Crosby came into the bunker a bit later, mud-daubed to the eyes. A glance told Kay that the temporary commander was harried to the breaking point when he addressed Paul. Once again she was conscious of the strange reversal of their roles in the battalion: an outside observer, unaware of the two men's status, would have sworn that Crosby was reporting here for instructions.

Trying not to seem an eavesdropper, she heard their conversation only in snatches. Crosby was fresh from a tour of the command posts and brought back a tale of rising unrest among the men. Clearly he felt that Hill 1049 was already untenable—but the division commander had just telephoned an order to hold his position.

"The colonel would countermand that order if he was on his feet, Doctor."

"How is he now?"

"Sergeant Bates is working on him, with coffee and amphetamine. Can't you give him some kind of shot to bring him round?"

"A shot strong enough to bring the C.O. out of that bender would kill him."

"Suppose we *could* begin a general withdrawal, while it's still light?"

"You say you've lost contact with Hill 1056; it'd be suicide, without flank support."

"Not if we followed the ravines," said Crosby eagerly. "Easy Company brought in a gook weapons-carrier that ran out of gas. We could use that as cover—"

"Cover for whom—the headquarters command and a few wounded? It'd still be suicide for the men." Paul had spoken sharply: Kay realized that the whole bunker was listening now.

"But, Doctor—"

"Go back to headquarters, Lieutenant," said Paul, in a gentler tone. "Stay with your phones until the divisional commander changes our orders. It's all you can do."

Despite her best resolve, Kay could not keep herself from joining Paul after the lieutenant had made his unhappy exit. The surgeon was supervising the transfer of a splint-wound from table to helicopter: at his nod, she stayed beside the litter until the man was aboard the waiting plane.

"I wish we could send you out on this one, Kay. But it's been the same story since dawn."

"The wounded come first. We both know that."

Paul turned slowly and looked at her with admiration. "You're willing to stay—after what Crosby just said?"

"Will headquarters order a withdrawal?"

"Of course not. But it's beginning to look as though Crosby isn't experienced enough for his job."

Standing at Paul's side in the dugout entrance, she needed all her self-control to keep her fingers from closing on his hand. The pressure might have given him the answer he needed, the assurance that she refused to be afraid, so long as they could share the danger. They watched in silence while the medics transferred other cases to the helicopter. In another moment the ungainly craft had lifted from the slope, seeming to balance precariously between earth and heaven until it gained altitude and spun south toward the distant base.

"Don't be a heroine forever," he said. "It isn't healthy."

"I'm where I want to be, Paul. Won't you believe me now?"

IX

Within the next hour the last of the seriously wounded were evacuated, though there was still no room for Kay in the overloaded helicopters. In that interval there had been no fresh casualties and the throb of the guns had stilled somewhat, for no reason she could fathom. The answer came at dusk, when Sergeant Furness (who had been sent to headquarters bunker with a report on the wounded) came scrambling up the ravine, all but incoherent with news.

"Better see the colonel, sir. We're shipping out!"

Kay would always remember the babble of voices that followed, and the sudden, decisive motion of Paul's arm that froze the others into silence.

"Who gave the order—Lieutenant Crosby?"

"No, Cap'n. It was the C.O. himself."

"Is he on his feet?"

"Sergeant Bates finally brought him round."

"Did he contact division headquarters?"

"So they say. All companies are ready to move. They're loading the battalion records in the weapons-carrier. The C.O. wants us in the formation—pronto."

Paul addressed the four other occupants of the bunker. "It's suicide. The enemy's watching those southern ravines—*hoping* for a general withdrawal. It'll be far easier to cut the battalion down in the open than to root us out of these bunkers. The colonel *must* know that."

The words fell into a void of agreement, a silence which Kay broke when Paul moved toward the bunker steps. "Can you stop them, Paul?"

"I certified Colonel Hardin as unfit for duty on the morning report." Again Paul seemed to address all of them. "This time he *stays* unfit, if I have to use handcuffs." He went up the bunker steps with the words, running with long, loping strides down the ravine. Ignoring Father Tim's warning, Kay ran out on his heels.

The path to the headquarters bunker, which had been so long that morning, seemed much shorter in that downhill rush. She made out the weapons-carrier in the thickening dusk—a monstrous shape with caterpillar treads and bulging armor. Dust roiled thickly at its flanks, and several gnomelike figures swarmed around it: even in the bad light she could recognize the members of Hardin's camarilla. It was only when she had tumbled down the last slope that she saw the platoons of the battalion, drawn up in close order and bristling with bayonets.

Each eye in that double column was fixed on the weapons-carrier. Kay could sense the uneasiness, the awareness that something had gone amiss at command level. Here, an almost indecent haste to cut and run was nakedly apparent. Sergeant Bates, popping from the bunker, seemed intent on no one's survival but his own. Lieutenant Crosby, already inside the carrier, was cursing frantically as he jabbed at the balky ignition.

Kay paused on the slope to watch Paul stride into the melee of crisscrossing orders. There was still no sign of Colonel Hardin: because of her vantage point, Kay was the first to observe his fuddled emergence from the bunker. The C.O. was in battle dress; he wore a heavy automatic strapped to one leg, and a crash helmet was pulled level with his eyes. At first glance he seemed furiously competent as he barked a command to close ranks and scrambled for a foothold on his transport.

Sergeant Bates, who had been busy elsewhere, hurried up a second too late: the colonel had already missed his footing and dropped to his knees in the dust. His crash helmet was knocked off in the fall. When he got to his feet again and faced Paul, his eyeballs were rolling wildly: without the master sergeant's support, he would have fallen a second time.

"What's this mean, Colonel?"

The C.O.'s voice, when it emerged, was oddly crisp—an incredible contrast to the sagging body that produced it. "Fall in, Captain Scott! You have your orders!"

"You're a sick man, sir. Go to your quarters."

"Fall in, I said!"

"Did HQ order a retreat, Colonel?"

"D'you question a direct command?"

"May I verify that order on the battalion phone?"

"Scott, are you calling me a liar?"

"With your permission, Colonel—"

The exchange in the shelter of the towering flank of the weapons-carrier had been short and venomous—with Kay and Master Sergeant Bates as the only witnesses. Now, as Paul turned on his heel, no other eyes saw Hardin's fist close on the pistol and lift it, butt-first, from its holster. Kay's cry of warning choked in her throat while the steel bludgeon descended in a vicious arc, to connect with the base of the surgeon's skull.

For a crazy instant she was back in time, moving too late to stop a similar blow delivered by the same hand in a San Pedro canteen. Watching Paul's knees buckle, she flung herself forward to save him from further harm—but the move was needless. Colonel Hardin, bellowing a final order, had already tumbled over the side of the unwieldy vehicle.

The command, repeated by a dozen voices, put the columns in motion before Kay could kneel beside Paul and cradle his head in her arms. Master Sergeant Bates, climbing into the carrier, gave her a brief, incurious glance before he, too, disappeared behind the armor plate.

In the cloud of dust set up by the caterpillar treads of the carrier and the fast-closing darkness, the marchers seemed oblivious of their surgeon's presence. Bemused as she was, Kay could not even summon a call for help. Instead, she continued to stare in silence while the battalion took the path to the southern ravines and fanned into open order. Here and there a splinter of dying sunlight picked out a bayonet before the last squad vanished in the murk.

Paul stirred in her arms and opened his eyes. "I should know by this time," he said. "Don't turn your back on a madman."

"Did he hurt you badly, darling?"

"Stunned me, that's all. I've a hard skull, as you should remember."

"I'll call the medics."

"Give me a minute longer to rest. After all, there's nothing we can do now. Hardin has resumed command." Paul's eyelids had dropped again, as though that flash of irony had exhausted him. "Call it a retreat against overwhelming force. It'll read that way in the records."

"Can't we *do* something?"

"Nothing but wait—and keep our heads."

Kay looked up as a step sounded in the loose rubble of the slope. In another moment Father Tim was kneeling beside them.

"Is he wounded, Kay?"

"I'm not hurt at all, Padre," said Paul—and proved it, after a fashion, by getting shakily to his feet, with the chaplain's aid. "Let's see if we can reach division headquarters by radio."

In the orderly room of the bunker the wall lamps burned brightly above a scene of the wildest disorder. The headquarters detail had emptied the battalion files helter-skelter, snatching what records they could carry in their dash for freedom. A glance at the radiophones told Kay that it was too late to report their plight. Someone (she could guess that it was Sergeant Bates) had smashed the tubes.

Paul sank to a stool and rocked his head in his hands. Without protest, he accepted a half tumbler of whiskey Kay fetched from the colonel's quarters, and downed it in a swallow.

"At least Hardin left a bottle behind," he said. "It was more than I hoped for."

"Shall we try to overtake the column?"

"We'd only walk into enfilading fire. Any moment now, you'll hear them open up."

"Do you think he really called division headquarters, Paul?"

"He may have gone through the motions, to hoodwink Crosby."

A long roll of rifle fire swept up from the south, to be followed by a second fusillade and a third. Between the bursts, an angry chatter of M-1s responded as the 141st Battalion (discovering, too late, that it had blundered into enemy cross fire) did its frantic best to fight back. The protest, blotted out in a final, roaring volley, was short-lived—a spine-chilling demonstration of a basic fact of war. The battalion, its escape cut off, had evidently dispersed into the darkness in a last desperate scramble for survival.

Hysteria was building rapidly inside Kay's mind: she fought down that surge of panic with a great effort, grateful for the soothing pressure of Father Tim's hand on her arm. Paul's voice, when he spoke again, seemed very small in the quiet bunker.

"Who is left, Padre?"

"Just the five of us. You, Kay, the two medics, and myself."

"No walking wounded?"

"There were only a few," said the priest. "They got aboard the weapons-carrier before it moved out."

"You're sure that Furness and Jackson stayed?"

"Of course, Paul. They take orders from you."

"If Hardin had dug in until morning, we might have held our position." Paul's voice was a whisper: it was a statement of fact, made without bitterness. "Maybe the weapons-carrier got through the enfilade. If it did, they'll be lucky to lead a platoon to safety."

Already that quiet voice had done a great deal to restore Kay's courage. "Won't the colonel be court-martialed for leaving without orders?" she asked.

Paul shrugged. "He was in command when the withdrawal began— thanks to Bates and his amphetamine. He gave coherent orders to everyone—including me. It isn't his fault that I was the turncoat who refused to obey."

"*Turncoat,* Paul?"

"It's an insult he's flung at me before, when I've operated on North Korean prisoners. Give him time, Kay. If he gets through tonight he'll swear I deserted under fire."

"You've two witnesses who'll expose him."

"For what? A C.O. who pulled out to save his command? Battalion officers have a right to ignore divisional instructions when they consider a position untenable."

"Surely we'll get a chance to tell the truth?"

"Don't bank on it, Kay. Truth is the first casualty of war."

"Are we trapped, Paul? Tell me what you think: I can take it."

"There's no use pretending. By morning we'll either be dead or prisoners."

"We've still a chance," said Father Tim. "Don't forget our status under the Geneva Convention."

"So far, there's little evidence that the Chinese honor its provisions."

"All of us are noncombatants. There's a supply of brassards in the aid station and a few banners—white flags with a cross. They'll establish our status."

"Let us help you back to the surgery, Paul," said Kay. "We mustn't be captured here."

The mere acts of helping Paul climb the ravine, of rummaging in the medical stores, did much to improve Kay's morale. In the half hour following the retreat, each member of the oddly-assorted quintet had been provided with an arm band. Four of the square white banners (prominently displayed at each approach to the aid station) identified their haven beyond question. . . . Paul, resting on a cot while these precautions went forward, seemed himself again when Kay finally settled at his side, bearing a mug of coffee.

"What comes next, Paul?"

Her eyes followed his as he glanced around the surgery. The medics, their last chore behind them, had sprawled on a blanket for a game of acey-deucy, as calmly as though their world had not just collapsed outside. Father Tim had already taken his favorite perch on the dugout steps, where he could watch the slow wheeling of the stars. Paul's smile widened—and the grip of his fingers tightened.

"What comes next," he said, "is the greatest test of war—the waiting. At least I'm in good company."

X

Hours later, she roused from an uneasy doze in the first gray promise of dawn, aware that she had dropped off while she sat beside Paul's cot. A glance told her that he was relaxed in slumber, and she marveled again at the training that had permitted him a full night's rest, though death itself might prowl outside the bunker door.

Father Tim was dozing on the steps, his frail figure outlined clearly against the pale sky. There was no sign of the medics: when she joined the chaplain on the steps, Kay saw that they were scouting the ridge. The padre had a leather-bound book on his knee. She recognized the diary he had been writing in when they had met in the surgery—and put out her hand to close the book before it could slip to the ground. At that moment the priest opened his eyes: with something that resembled a guilty start, he dropped the diary into the pocket of his trench coat.

"Forgive me, Kay," he said. "I'm seldom caught with my confession book open."

"Confession book, Father?"

"Since I've no confessional at the front, this diary takes its place. Eventually it will go back to my archbishop in San Francisco—as a record of my failure with Colonel Hardin."

"How did you fail with him?"

"At one time, I'm ashamed to admit, I hated him—almost as much as Paul did. Now, of course, we've both learned to accept his weakness. Still, I should have tried much harder to help him overcome it. His flight is proof of my failure."

"Some people are beyond redemption, Father Tim."

"No one is beyond redemption, my dear."

"The colonel is all evil. You couldn't have changed him in a thousand years."

"I would have been a better man for trying. More than once I've seen Paul operate on hopeless cases. Sometimes he saved them."

"Medicine is different. There's always an outside chance you'll succeed when you're dealing with something as complex as the human body."

"The soul is even more complex, Kay. I should have taken the outside chance." Father Tim touched the book in his pocket. "Pray God I'll be able to atone someday."

"Is that hope in your confession book, Padre?"

"Of course." The priest smiled gently, with his eyes on the hilltop and the two soldiers moving cautiously among the empty command posts. "It's a strange thing, Kay. Here we sit, facing possible death—or hardships that may make us cry out for the release that death brings. And yet, now it's morning and I've written down my shortcomings, I have no fear at all."

"How do you explain that, Padre?"

"I'm not sure, my dear. Perhaps confession is really good for the soul."

Kay moved softly into the dugout and stood above the cot where Paul was still relaxed in slumber. "You've watched him save lives here," she whispered. "Can he save *us* from the trap we're in now?"

"Paul—and God: don't forget they are both on our side. Perhaps we're more fortunate than we realize." The priest rose from his place in the shadow of the bunker entrance. With the morning light on his face, Kay could see the fatigue lines around his fine eyes. "Suppose we get some supplies together. Perhaps we'll be allowed to keep them later."

When they started rummaging in the dugout they found that the medics had anticipated them. Four packs were waiting in a corner, each containing a robust load of coffee, cigarettes, and canned rations.

"I'll make a pack for myself," said Kay. "They mustn't leave me out."

She was still working at this task, with the help of Father Tim, when Paul wakened and sat up with a long yawn. One glance at his face told her that the tensions of the night were left behind him—that he was ready (thanks to an alchemy she could only half understand) for whatever the day might bring.

"How's the head, darling?" She managed to keep her voice light and hoped that she had not betrayed the sick hopelessness that gripped her.

"Clear as a bell," he said cheerfully. "Apparently I've the sort of brain that thrives on hard knocks." He moved quickly to the dugout steps and studied the terrain beyond the ridge. "Did you notice that the firing has stopped?"

"I haven't heard a shot since midnight," said Father Tim.

Kay, strapping her impromptu food pack, managed to force a smile. "Could it be the war is over?"

Paul shook his head. "The enemy is waiting too—just as we've been doing here. Probably they can't believe that Hill 1049 is theirs at last."

The estimate was confirmed when the two enlisted men returned from their scout. "We worked down the ridge, sir," said Furness, "and we had a look in all the gullies. If I didn't know better I'd swear they'd gone home."

"Any sign of casualties to the south?"

Furness crossed himself before he spoke. "Counted a hundred dead on the first slope, sir. And the weapons-carrier was *kaput.*"

So Hardin's dash for the rear had met its just reward. Kay could not keep down a savage thrill of pleasure at the news.

"Was he killed or captured?"

"Captured's my guess, ma'am," the sergeant said. "A line officer would be quite a prize."

Jackson, squatting on the bottom step of the dugout, straightened up with a bray of laughter. "No offense, Cap'n—but isn't it a victory for us—if the *gooks* have the colonel?"

"Don't sound off too soon, Harry," said the sergeant. "We may still meet in Pyongyang—"

The strained banter died as Kay gave a sharp gasp. *"Someone's outside, Paul!"*

Paul lifted his hand for silence as Jackson moved toward the door. "Shall I have a look sir?"

"Keep your places—everyone. Remember, this is an aid station. It establishes our identity if we're found here as a group."

This time Kay discovered that emotion was stronger than self-control and gripped Paul's arm for assurance. In the silence that followed his order there was no mistaking the clatter of feet outside or the identity of the shadow that fell across the dugout door. Clinging to Paul with all her strength, Kay felt her heart skip a beat while the shadow changed into a man—a dwarf soldier in a blue-gray quilted uniform.

There was no need to translate the one-word command, barked in a strange tongue: like the burp gun on the man's arm, the meaning was unmistakable. Kay felt her grip on Paul relax. She raised her hands with the others in mute admission of her new status as a prisoner of war.

THE PRESIDIO

I

Before they could leave Sausalito the bright promise of noon had blurred: fog warnings were lighted on the Golden Gate Bridge when the maroon convertible sped down the last ramp. Kay had passed the bridge entrance to the Presidio by instinct—turning instead to enter the bustle of downtown San Francisco. It had seemed only logical to grant Hi Saunders an extra quarter hour to state his case. Now, as the car sighed to a stop at a traffic light, she gave him a sidelong smile.

"Don't tell me I can still back out," she said. "We both know I'm in this for the duration."

"Bringing you in like this is a gamble, pure and simple," said the lawyer. "Have I made that clear?"

"Perfectly: you've said Paul can't win without me. What else matters?"

"Maybe nothing can save Paul. If this gamble fails, you may find yourself minus a career—and a reputation."

"Stop talking nonsense. Tell me what to do."

"I refuse to rehearse you, Kay. You're being smuggled into court today as a surprise package for MacArdle. We'd ruin the effect if we wrote the dialogue in advance."

"Suppose he asks questions I can't answer?"

"There's no question that can't be answered, once it gets past the presiding judge. That's the risk you'll be taking, Kay. Still game?"

The girl reached over to squeeze the lawyer's hand and jumped the car through the changing light. "I liked you better in Sausalito," she said. "When you were being completely ruthless. Can't you stay ruthless—for Paul's sake?"

"I guess that makes you our girl Friday," said Hi, much more cheerfully. "In fact, it was your final test."

"You'd put Father Tim on the stand if he were alive, wouldn't you?"

"Like a shot. This trial could use a saint or two."

"What about a sinner—if she has a good story to tell?"

"For the last time, Kay, we can't bring up Hill 1049. Sellers will only nail me for contempt."

"Surely there's some way to expose Hardin for what he is."

"When he's on the stand I'll get in every rabbit punch I can. With luck, a few of them may bruise him. But your story must begin with the meeting at Sinmak, when you were all P.O.W.s."

They fell silent on that gloomy note, while the car climbed the high ground to the Presidio. Kay spoke just once more, after Hi had shown his pass at the gate.

"Must I be in the same room with Hardin?"

"No, Kay—that's one thing you're spared in a court-martial. The witnesses come in separately. I'll closet you in a special room with Les Pearson. He's my junior partner—a Harvard man with a sense of humor and a sharp game of gin."

"You think of everything, don't you, Hi? Can I see Paul for a moment?"

"Better not—it might spoil everything."

II

Paul was already waiting at the defendant's table when Hi entered the courtroom. A glance at the lawyer's bland countenance answered his question in advance.

"Enjoy your lunch at Tarrantino's?"

"Enormously," said Hi. "Did you take the rest I prescribed?"

Paul continued to study the lawyer narrowly. "You're going to call Kay, aren't you?"

"Of course I am."

"Where is she now?"

"Down the hall, trimming my junior partner at gin rummy. What's more, you're to leave her strictly alone."

Paul subsided with a small groan that was not altogether despairing. Much as he feared the outcome of Hi's strategy, he could not keep down a feeling of release. With Kay outside the courtroom door he no longer felt alone.

"Will she go on the stand today?"

"Probably—if Hardin's been as well coached as MacArdle's other boys. Once your old C.O. has recited, I'm sure the prosecution will rest its case. He's waiting to make his entrance: I saw him in the corridor just now, strutting for the photographers."

Lawyer and client rose while the court filed in to take its seats. Paul kept his eyes down when he heard Major MacArdle's crisp voice order a military policeman to bring in the next witness—but he was still amazed by the oblique glimpse of Colonel Jasper Hardin.

At Pyongyang the colonel had fared better than most—but he had resembled a scarecrow more than a line officer when he had led his troops from the compound for repatriation. Today it was incredible that the bandbox officer in the witness chair and the prisoner Paul last remembered were one and the same. Hardin's manner was as sharp as the creases of his beautifully tailored uniform; even the snow-white hair and mustache added, in some queer fashion, to the impression of solidity. If those white hairs were dramatic proofs of the ordeal this man had suffered, the man himself had obviously emerged with colors flying.

The witness showed no awareness of Paul's presence at the defense table while he answered the first routine questions. His voice was both stern and relaxed: judging by the hush in the courtroom, he had made a good impression on his audience. At the press tables a score of pencils were dancing busily. Paul glanced at Larry Kirk—impassive as a totem in the midst of the fourth estate—and felt he could write the commentator's next broadcast in advance.

MacArdle asked his first significant question with deceptive gentleness. "Colonel, I believe you were the signer of the charges against Captain Scott?"

"I was."

"For your information, Specifications One and Two of Charge One have been withdrawn by ruling of the convening authority."

"I bow to orders, as always."

Paul, listening to every inflection, gave an inward sigh: Hardin, it seemed, was an actor of parts. Despite the correctness of his response, he had conveyed the impression that he disapproved thoroughly of the convening authority's action.

"Colonel, other witnesses have covered most of the period of your imprisonment. There has been testimony that you and Captain Scott did not get on well together. Can you tell us why?"

"Captain Scott was always resentful of military authority—particularly mine."

"Can you give some details?"

"He was lax in preparing his reports."

"Did you warn him of this specifically?"

"On several occasions. I explained, as kindly as I could, where he was in error. I gave him every chance to rectify his mistakes."

"Did he?"

"Eventually—and with obvious reluctance."

"Colonel Hardin, other witnesses have stated that there was a clash between you and Captain Scott near the Korean town of Sinmak shortly after your capture by the enemy."

"That is true."

"Can you recall the date?"

"My memory is hazy there. Scott's group and mine were taken separately. It happened the first moment we joined forces."

"Do you remember the cause?"

"Distinctly. According to military law I was in command of all personnel in the two merged groups, since I was the senior officer present. There was room for a few of us to sleep inside a covered area—I believe it was a cow shed. Captain Scott stated that he had already bribed the guards to open the shed. He used cigarettes from a pack of Army rations. As commanding officer, it was clearly my right to assign billets as I saw fit. When I attempted to do so Captain Scott was insolent and refused to let me make the assignments."

"Did he give a reason?"

"He said the cigarettes were his—and that the billets were already occupied by his own group."

"What did you do?"

Hardin shrugged—and the gesture was as tolerant as his voice. "I did not make an issue of it, though it was my clear duty to check the misuse of supplies by Army personnel."

"Colonel, was this your first major clash with Captain Scott?"

"Frankly I wouldn't call it a major clash. All of us were pretty tired: tempers are apt to flare at such a time."

"You say you were captured in two separate groups. How did that separation occur?"

Hardin hesitated so artfully that Paul could have sworn the reluctance was genuine. "When we withdrew from Hill 1049 Captain Scott refused to join us. He stayed in the first-aid bunker, and kept his detail with him."

"Did you order him to join the retreat?"

"I did."

"Wouldn't you say *that* was a major clash—if he refused to obey an order under fire?"

"It was a pretty tight corner for a civilian soldier. Perhaps he felt there was less risk in being captured than in joining a withdrawing action."

Paul leaned toward Hi across the defense table. "The court wouldn't let *us* cover what happened before the capture."

"Easy does it, boy—and don't ask me to object just yet. I'm giving them rope."

MacArdle fired the next question point-blank. "Why didn't you include this in the charges against Captain Scott?"

Again Hardin's slight hesitation could not have seemed more genuine. "The tension was great. I didn't wish to accuse a man of cowardice—"

"*Objection!*" barked Hi.

Sellers leaned down from the bench. "On what grounds?"

It was Hi's turn to rise and face the cameras—and the attentive courtroom. "I would much prefer to let this line of questioning continue," he said. "The court must realize that I was not allowed to question witnesses concerning events prior to Captain Scott's capture. Trial counsel has now introduced just such an incident. I must warn the court that the defense intends to probe this matter thoroughly during cross-questioning. If need be, we will recall all witnesses—until the true facts about the surrender of Hill 1049 are brought out."

For the first time Paul noted a spasm of uneasiness in the witness. Caught off balance, MacArdle did not counter Hi's statement at once, and it was necessary for Sellers to gavel the onlookers into silence before the trial counsel could speak.

"With the permission of the court," he said, "I move that all questions and answers beginning with *You were captured in two separate groups. How did that separation occur?* be stricken from the record, and that the members of the court be instructed by the president to disregard them."

"Defense objects to this motion," said Hi. "It is designed to prevent defense from bringing out points favorable to the accused."

Again the president's gavel enforced quiet. "The motion is approved," he said. "The reporter will strike from the record all references to events before the capture." He leaned forward again—and this time his glare transfixed the unfortunate MacArdle. "Trial counsel is warned against further introduction of extraneous matter. You may proceed with the witness."

The prosecutor's voice had regained its timbre: only the receding flush at his collar line betrayed his awareness of a narrow escape. "Other witnesses, Colonel, have said they felt that Captain Scott was co-operating with the enemy when he was placed in charge of the prison hospital at Pyongyang. Was that your impression?"

"Not at the time."

Paul turned startled eyes on Hardin. Aware though he was of MacArdle's expert coaching, he had not expected this.

"When you began your prison term you had no doubts as to Captain Scott's loyalty?"

"None whatever. In fact it was I who recommended that he be put in charge of cleaning up the camp and improving conditions at the hospital."

"Why did you recommend him?"

"Dr. Scott was the best physician available; no one can deny that."

"Did later events justify the recommendation?"

"So far as the disease rate at camp was concerned. Both prisoners and guards were better for the change. But I can see now it was a serious error— so far as Captain Scott himself was concerned."

"Why do you say that?"

"Well—by putting him in close contact with the Chinese, I'm afraid I made it easier for him to—"

"To collaborate?"

"Objection!" snapped Hi. "Trial counsel is coaching the witness."

"I will rephrase the query," said MacArdle. "Colonel, what evidence did you have of Captain Scott's alleged co-operation with the Chinese prison authorities?"

"First of all, there was the matter of interrogations—"

"Interrogations?"

"All of us were badgered incessantly by the enemy security officers. Some of us were tortured when we—refused to give the right answers." Hardin studied his beautifully-manicured nails. "Captain Scott was almost never questioned, from the moment he took over the hospital."

"Was his lot made easier in other ways?"

"In many ways. For one thing, he used the hospital as a personal asylum—"

"More than his duties demanded?"

"In my opinion, much more."

"Was he quartered there?"

"He was not. I'd given orders that he should share a barracks with the other prisoners. I could hardly object to his spending time with the hospital personnel, and with Miss Storey."

"Was Miss Storey quartered in the hospital?"

"Permanently—after she volunteered to serve as a nurse."

"What were Captain Scott's relations with her?"

"They were very close."

"Closer than is usual with a doctor and his nurse?"

"I'd prefer not to answer that."

"I request that you answer, sir—however reluctant you may be to do so."

"Objection," said Hi. "Trial counsel is attempting to imply something improper in Miss Storey's relationship to Dr. Scott. It is no secret that they contemplated marriage at the time."

"Trial counsel will keep to the charges," said the president.

MacArdle bowed to the court. "It was your impression, Colonel, that Captain Scott was collaborating with the enemy. When did you become certain?"

"When he operated on Colonel Pak, the camp commandant."

"You were Captain Scott's commanding officer. Did he discuss the operation with you?"

"He did not. He knew I would object."

"On what grounds?"

"If Pak had died during the operation, there would have been reprisals against us all."

"Then, in your opinion, Captain Scott risked your lives by operating?"

"There's no question about it."

"Could not the opposite have been true, sir? Surely Captain Scott would have been punished had he refused to operate."

"He was the only competent doctor in the camp. Had he said it was not an operative case, none of his Chinese colleagues would have disputed the diagnosis."

"You believe, then, that Captain Scott seized this chance to ingratiate himself with the prison head—by making it appear that he had saved his life?"

"That is my opinion. It was shared by the whole camp. Scott was ostracized afterward."

"Let us proceed to the time of the armistice, Colonel. It has been stated that Captain Scott refused repatriation because he wished to remain with Chaplain O'Fallon. Defense counsel has alleged that the chaplain was desperately ill from a lung hemorrhage. To your knowledge, had Chaplain O'Fallon suffered this complication?"

"Not to my knowledge."

"Did Captain Scott, in your hearing, give this as a reason for his remaining behind?"

"No, he did not."

Paul could not trust himself to protest aloud. What Hardin had just said was outright perjury—yet an objection at this time would only have forced a question of credibility which could not possibly be resolved in his favor. Bottling his helpless anger, he contented himself with a glance at Hi—whose shrug told him that the lawyer was also aware of the impasse.

MacArdle, pretending to consult his assistant, had given Hardin's last reply a good ten seconds to register. Subsiding in his chair, Paul admitted that the prosecutor's timing had been perfect. The faces of the seven officers on the bench, which had seemed calmly judicial when the afternoon session began, now loomed above him like avenging Fates.

"What reason, if any, did Captain Scott give for remaining at Pyongyang?"

"He gave none in my presence."

"Did he request that you notify the American truce authorities?"

"I had no such request," said Hardin.

"Why, in your opinion, did he choose to remain?"

"I judged that he had chosen to cast his lot with the enemy."

"Did you attempt to dissuade him, Colonel?"

"No. I felt that it was quite useless. We had been over two years at Pyongyang. For most of that time I had observed his leanings toward Communism—"

"Objection," said Hi. "No such leanings have been proved."

"Denied," snapped the president. "Subject to objection by any member of the court."

So far, this coda to the president's ruling had been a mere formality. This time, however, Major Duggan leaned forward. "I object to this denial," he said quietly. "I request a vote by the court on the question."

For the first time in the trial the judges did not rise to discuss the point at issue—and this reluctance to leave the courtroom was, in itself, an ominous portent. After a moment of whispers and note taking, Duggan leaned back in his chair with a chastened look.

"Objection is overruled by vote of the court," said Colonel Sellers. "Proceed, Major MacArdle."

"You may complete your answer, Colonel."

"I had seen Captain Scott leaning toward Communism for a long time. I was hardly surprised at his decision to remain behind and felt it would be pointless to discuss the matter further."

"Did you make any comment on his decision?"

"I may have."

"Your sergeant major has testified that you said *I don't care if the son-of-a-bitch never goes back home—except to face a court-martial.* Did you make such a statement?"

"I believe it was to that effect."

MacArdle turned to the prosecutor's table and returned with a much-creased sheet of paper. "I now introduce this paper as evidence," he said solemnly. "I request that the reporter mark it exhibit for identification."

The paper went from hand to hand and was duly recorded.

"Have you seen this paper before, Colonel?"

"I have. It is a copy of a confession made by Captain Scott at Pyongyang."

"Objection," said Hi. "It has not been proved that such a confession was ever made."

"The prosecution is in the process of proving that very thing."

"Objection overruled," said Colonel Sellers, "subject to objection by any member of the court." He glanced at Duggan, but the major's face was a stone mask.

"When did you first see the paper you now hold in your hand, Colonel?"

"Last fall at Pyongyang. It was one of two copies."

"Were the copies identical?"

"They were."

"Who asked you to examine them?"

"Colonel Pak."

"Were both copies signed?"

"Yes—by Captain Scott."

"Did you recognize his signature?"

"I did."

"Would you certify that this is one of the originals?"

"I would. In fact I have done so on this sheet."

"Please read the entire document, Colonel."

Hardin opened the paper on his knee and read slowly and deliberately—a schoolboy rendition by a man unused to reading aloud. For that very reason the impact of the words was even more damning:

"I, Captain Paul R. Scott, a medical officer in the United States Army, make this confession of my own free will and without torture or coercion.

"I confess that I helped to prepare bombs containing bacteria and other disease-producing agents, to be dropped on defenseless towns and cities of North Korea.

"I have been shown one of these bombs that was

dropped on the city of Pyongyang, and I have
identified it as being exactly similar to bombs which I
myself helped to load.

"I make this confession so that the world may
know how I and my fellow Americans have used
inhuman methods of warfare against the North
Korean people and the Volunteers from the Chinese
People's Republic.

"I am sorry for my part in this inhuman action and
state that the punishment I have received is a just
one for my crimes.

Signed, *Paul R. Scott.*
Captain, Medical Corps.
United States Army."

I, Captain Paul Scott, a medical officer in the United
States Army, make this confession of my own free
will and without torture . . .

III

Hi Saunders got to his feet. Before he began his cross-examination he
stared hard at the witness. "That was a most effective reading," he said.
"Obviously you are quite familiar with this document."

"Naturally I am. I brought it from Korea."

"For the express purpose of persecuting Captain Scott?"

"Objection," said MacArdle: he had not troubled to raise his voice—and
barely smiled when the court sustained him.

"Colonel, why were you so careful to bring this document from Korea?"

"I felt the authorities should see it without delay."

"You have testified that this was one of two original copies—both of them
signed by Captain Scott. How did you manage to obtain it?"

"Colonel Pak gave it to me the day it was signed," said Hardin. "I felt it
should be preserved as part of the camp records."

"The newspapers have stated that other prisoners made similar confessions in that same compound. Did you also preserve copies of their
confessions?"

"They were not given to me by the Chinese."

"But the document you are holding was?"

The witness passed the paper to the court reporter. With the gesture, he
seemed to wash his hands of a distasteful contact. "I have so stated."

"Colonel, doesn't it seem strange that only this alleged confession was
handed to you—out of several others broadcast by the Chinese?"

"Not at all. Colonel Pak valued it more highly than the others."

"Isn't it true, Colonel, that you *asked* for this original document so that
reproductions could be made?"

"It is not."

"How do you account for the fact that the whole camp was flooded with
copies?"

"I can't account for it."

"Weren't they mimeographed and distributed by members of your staff?"

"Not on my order."

"Very well, Colonel. You have testified that, as ranking officer in the compound, you were in charge of prisoners?"

"I was—subject to the authority of the Chinese commander."

"Did you know that Chaplain O'Fallon and Miss Storey were placed in solitary confinement?"

"I had heard that they were."

"Did Captain Scott tell you that they had become dangerously ill?"

"He did."

"What action did you take—if any?"

"I spoke to Colonel Pak; he refused to release them."

"You're positive you intervened, Colonel? You did not refuse aid and order Captain Scott from your quarters?"

"I did not."

"And you did not realize, months later, that Captain Scott signed what he knew was a bogus confession—in order to save Miss Storey and Chaplain O'Fallon from dying?"

"I realized no such thing."

"Very well, Colonel. Let us now proceed to the operation on Colonel Pak. You have said that you think Captain Scott endangered the safety of the prisoners by rushing the operation?"

"That is correct."

"You have also stated, I believe, that Captain Scott is a competent surgeon."

"I said he was the best available."

"Would you expect a competent surgeon to let a man die—after he had diagnosed a condition which surgery could cure?"

"Perhaps not—if he had the patient in a modern hospital. With the equipment in the prison, a major operation was obviously hazardous."

"More hazardous, for example, than one performed in a front-line surgical bunker?"

"Circumstances alter cases."

"Do they? For your information Captain Scott operated on me in the front lines when the whole salient was under heavy enemy pressure. The operation he performed on me was an intestinal resection—far more dangerous than Colonel Pak's. Yet, had he not taken that risk I would be dead today—and so would Pak. Do you still feel that he should have let the patient die?"

"I think he should not have operated," said Hardin firmly. "Whether or not Pak would have died is a question I cannot decide."

"Colonel Hardin, have you ever heard of medical ethics?"

"Of course."

"Didn't Dr. Scott's code force him to operate if he thought there was a chance of saving a life? Isn't it immaterial if the patient was friend or enemy?"

"Perhaps. But I repeat that his decision was influenced by his desire to curry favor with the Chinese. It is my opinion that he needlessly risked the lives of others in the camp by aiding the enemy."

Hi faced the television cameras for a moment of thought. "Let us proceed to another topic," he said. "Other witnesses have testified that you operated a special prison mess for your headquarters. Will you tell the court whether or not your staff had better food than the other prisoners?"

"We may have. The Geneva Convention says that differences in treatment among prisoners is lawful and is based on rank."

"Did Captain Scott receive preferential treatment?"

"He spent much time at the hospital, as I've already said. Food was better there."

"Is it your belief he ate at the hospital?"

Hardin shrugged and glanced at the court. "It was his own fault if he didn't."

"Then it is your opinion that if Captain Scott did not get enough to eat, it was his own fault?"

"Something like that. Prison conditions at Pyongyang were unspeakably bad."

"Were they hard for you, Colonel?"

"Extremely. I was very low for the first fortnight of my imprisonment—"

"May I ask the nature of your illness?"

"It wasn't an illness. It was exhaustion, following the march to Pyongyang."

"Who made that diagnosis?"

"Dr. Scott."

"Did he treat you thereafter?"

"I recovered on my own. All I really needed was rest and nourishment— such as it was."

"But Dr. Scott prescribed a regimen that hastened your recovery?"

"Not as I recall—beyond standard medication."

"Colonel Hardin, isn't it true that you were suffering from the aftereffects of alcoholism?"

Major MacArdle was on his feet with an instant shout of fury. "Counsel for the defense is trying to blacken the witness' character, for obvious motives." He was still sputtering when Colonel Sellers' gavel fell.

"Court desires to address the witness," he said. "Colonel Hardin, you need not answer the last question—"

"I've no objection," said Hardin. "The answer is no."

"If the court please," said Hi, "we are prepared to prove the contrary."

"How?"

"By the testimony of two witnesses—Miss Storey and the accused."

"Do you have medical records to back this assertion?"

"No, sir. No records were brought from the prison camp at Pyongyang other than Colonel Hardin's file."

"Objection sustained," said Colonel Sellers. "The honor of an American officer is involved here, Mr. Saunders. Further questions in this vein may force me to lodge a contempt charge against you."

Hi stood with bowed head while the whispers died in the courtroom.

"Disregarding the nature of your indisposition, Colonel," Hi said, "did you recover promptly?"

"In about two weeks—yes." During the exchange, Hardin's plumage had remained unruffled. He seemed to preen himself now as he pulled down the waistband of his perfectly cut tunic, the left breast heavy with its sunburst of campaign ribbons.

"Colonel, I have here two reports of physical examinations that I am about to introduce into the record. I will read paragraphs from each report, describing the general condition of the person examined—"

The president frowned down from the bench while the court reporter was tagging the exhibits for the defense. "Mr. Saunders, can any possible purpose be served by this expenditure of time?"

"The court has my assurance that a considerable purpose will be served."

"You may proceed."

"Colonel Hardin, here is a general description of one prisoner returned after the armistice; he was examined by Major Strauss of the Army Medical Department at the exchange point in Korea. I will read from the record, as signed by Major Strauss:"

> This officer is markedly emaciated. Practically all the subcutaneous fat is absent. Lips and mucous membranes quite pale, indicating advanced secondary anemia. Moderate night blindness. Advanced skin irritation of the pellagric type. Exquisite tenderness along the peripheral nerves. Marked inflammation of the gums suggestive of scurvy. Whole picture indicates chronic advanced starvation and vitamin lack. Hospitalization was suggested but refused by the patient.

Hi put down the first sheet of the exhibit and picked up the second. "Now, Colonel, I'll read from an examination made by the same medical officer on another returning prisoner":

> This officer's skin is tanned and smooth. Color of lips and mucous membranes good. Some evidence of loss of weight, but general state of nutrition excellent. Reflexes normal. No tenderness along the peripheral nerves. State of teeth and gums sound. No disturbance of vision to gross tests.

The defense lawyer returned both sheets to the reporter. "I don't think one needs to be a physician to see a marked difference between these two prisoners—do you, Colonel?"

"Obviously not."

"The first officer has certainly suffered a starvation regimen—as did most of the inmates at the camp in Pyongyang?"

"It seems logical from the evidence," said Hardin.

"I read these reports into the record, Colonel, because the first describes the condition of Captain Paul Scott on his repatriation. The second report is your own. No further questions."

No one stirred in the court when Hi returned to his table; even MacArdle (whose mouth had opened to shout an objection) had restrained the impulse in time and sat with sagging jaw. It was only when Sellers glanced in his direction that he rose for his rebuttal.

"He'll make this short," Hi whispered to Paul. "That *was* a rabbit punch—and I intended it to be."

The prosecutor had accepted a glass of water from his assistant before he snatched up his notes. He seemed to address his first question to the court rather than Hardin—who was staring glassily into space out of a face that had turned into a turkey-red mask.

"Colonel Hardin, did you at any time ask for special favors from the Chinese commander at the Pyongyang prison camp?"

"Never."

"So if your treatment *was* better than others, it was through no request of yours?"

"It was not."

"No further questions. The prosecution rests."

IV

There was no visible reaction from the spectators while Hardin passed down the aisle, walking with his familiar marionette strut. Only the slight sag between his shoulder blades told Paul that he had felt Hi's last blow: the military mold had weathered the impact, no matter how the man within might be cringing.

When Kay entered the courtroom behind the sergeant at arms her color was high: Paul surmised uneasily that her path had crossed Hardin's in the anteroom. Hoping that she would offer him a passing glance, he knew that she would be too wise to risk it. This, after all, was an ordeal she had sought against his pleading.

Hi took his time in the preliminary questioning, building the background picture with a few strokes, and permitting Kay to tell her story in her own words. This testimony included her arrival in Korea and the impulse that had brought her to Hill 1049.

"Will you describe your capture, Miss Storey?"

"The five of us were alone in the bunker when the firing stopped. All at once there was a Chinese soldier in the doorway. Then a half dozen. Then a swarm—"

"Were you harmed in any way?"

"No, Mr. Saunders. We were—herded with other prisoners and marched to the rear—"

Hearing the clear, quiet voice go on, Paul remembered his own astonishment at that matter-of-fact capture. Somehow the ordeal would have been less dreadful had there been overt abuse—but their captors had simply taken them for granted. Accustomed as they were to bagging prisoners in wholesale lots, they had handled that day's batch like cattle—feeding them enough to keep their feet in motion, letting them pant a few moments at the roadside when exhaustion overtook them. . . .

"Let us proceed to your reunion with Colonel Hardin's group, Miss Storey. How long had you been marching when you reached Sinmak?"

"I'm not sure. I'm afraid I'd lost track of time."

Time had really stood still that day, thought Paul—time had become a waking dream with no visible boundaries, broken only by those halts in the open field, the occasional feedings. But he could remember the farmyard outside Sinmak clearly—the whitewashed command post that dominated the crossroads, the guards with fixed bayonets and identical stares, the sudden, grateful pelting of the rain on his dust-caked body. When they had tumbled into the straw of the cow shed that formed one wall of the farmyard they had been too exhausted to think. No one had troubled to ask why this small group of five had been detached from the marching column. . . .

"Did your captors explain the reason for the halt at Sinmak, Miss Storey?"

"Not at the time. We learned the reason later. They'd found our records on Hill 1049. Enough, at any rate, to learn that we were a medical unit attached to the 141st Battalion."

The mills of the law grind slowly, thought Paul: he could truly admire Kay's poise and the precision of her answers. The fact that Colonel Jasper Hardin and the members of his staff had been held captive in a compound nearby to await their arrival here was only a coincidence of war. The fact that a truck had rolled into their bivouac that night, dumping Hardin into the courtyard before it rumbled on, seemed a grotesque joke—though all of them were too tired for laughter. . . .

"Can you recall when your two groups made contact, Miss Storey?"

"Perhaps a half hour after sunset."

"You had already taken possession of the cow shed?"

"Only Captain Scott and I were awake. The others had collapsed in the straw."

"And the newcomers?"

"None of the guards spoke English. They simply pushed Hardin and his group into the courtyard and locked the gates."

"Leaving them to shift for themselves?"

"You might put it that way, Mr. Saunders."

"Were you carrying rations at the time?"

"All of us had packs."

"Did you offer to share them with the others?"

"Yes, we did. One of the men had been slightly wounded. Captain Scott put on a new dressing with my help and gave him some tablets."

"When and how did the clash between Captain Scott and Colonel Hardin occur?"

"When they began searching for billets and found we'd taken the shed."

"Why, in your opinion, did Captain Scott refuse to surrender his shelter?"

"We'd been marching for days; they had ridden all that afternoon by truck. Captain Scott felt we should keep up our strength. Besides, Chaplain O'Fallon was suffering from a persistent cough. Both of us refused to waken him. When Colonel Hardin attempted to force an entrance, we barred the door. Unfortunately we forgot to close the hay chute as well—"

"Why do you say unfortunately?"

"Sometime that night an attempt was made on Captain Scott's life—"

"By whom, Miss Storey?"

"We'll never be sure now. But I think it was Colonel Hardin."

This time the surge of voices in the courtroom went unrebuked, while Sellers glared down at the witness as though he could not quite believe his ears.

"Mr. Saunders, I've already warned you—"

Hi stood his ground and his voice was as harsh as the president's. "If it please the court, Miss Storey's opinions are her own."

"The court will question the witness."

Silence clamped down on the room as the president fixed his eye on Kay. "Miss Storey, the insinuation you are making is of the utmost seriousness. Think well before you answer. Why did you mention Colonel Hardin's name?"

"For two reasons." Kay's voice was clear and cold. "Father O'Fallon was a light sleeper. He wakened around midnight and saw the colonel's face at the hay chute. Captain Scott himself wakened later and heard an intruder moving about the shed. They wrestled for a moment. Then the—visitor left the way he had entered—"

"By the hay chute?"

"Yes. This time Captain Scott closed the trap door and slept until morning. That's when he discovered the weapon."

"What weapon?"

"A *sake* bottle. Or rather the neck, and a broken edge."

"What does this have to do with Colonel Hardin?"

"The night before, he was drunk when he got down from the truck. Drunk on *sake*—we smelled it on his breath."

"Miss Storey, did you see this bottle with your own eyes?"

"I saw it in the morning."

"Did *you* see anyone enter the cow shed?"

"I'm afraid I slept through it all."

"Are you aware that hearsay is not evidence in a court of law?"

"Mr. Saunders said I could express an opinion. Someone tried to take Captain Scott's life that night—"

"Your opinion cannot be accepted," said the president. "Not without eyewitness proof. The reporter will strike this whole interchange from the record." Sellers turned back to Hi. "Defense counsel is excused in this instance—the witness is obviously unrehearsed. But a similar allegation, if unsupported by prima-facie evidence, will earn a citation for contempt. This is your final warning."

Hi acknowledged the rebuke with a curt nod. "With all due respect to the court," he said, "I must point out that a threat upon the life of the accused is most pertinent."

"Miss Storey was asleep. So, it seems, were Sergeant Furness and Corporal Jackson. Father O'Fallon is in the grave. Produce an eyewitness, Mr. Saunders, or take another line."

Hi turned back to Kay. "Let us move on, Miss Storey. You say that Colonel Hardin and his group arrived by truck. Did they use the same means of departure?"

"They left by truck early the next morning."

"Did the colonel offer you transport?"

"He did, but I refused—after he said he couldn't take Chaplain O'Fallon as well."

"How did Colonel Hardin react to your refusal?"

"He told me that on second thought there was no room for either of us in the truck."

"Was it then that Lieutenant Crosby volunteered to walk with your group—so that the chaplain could ride?"

"It was. Even then the colonel was reluctant to take Father Tim."

"Can you give any valid reason?"

"There were two: the chaplain and Captain Scott were good friends."

"And the other?"

"Am I forbidden to say that the colonel was suffering from hangover and had run out of *sake?*"

Hi turned to Sellers with a wordless apology, while the president gaveled for silence.

"In your judgment, Miss Storey, was there room in the truck for both you and Chaplain O'Fallon?"

"There was room for us all."

"Let us move on to the prison camp at Pyongyang. When did you reach it?"

"About two weeks after Colonel Hardin."

"Did you march the whole distance?"

"We marched as long as we could. Eventually we collapsed by the roadside. We were taken the rest of the way in carts."

"How do you account for your assignment to the prison hospital as a nurse?"

"It was Captain Scott's suggestion. He knew I'd had nursing training and felt I'd recover my strength there."

"Was your recovery complete?"

"Yes—except for an attack of amebiasis. I was in good health until I was placed in solitary confinement."

"When was that?"

"In the spring of 1952. Solitary was a special discipline at the camp, to punish prisoners who wouldn't co-operate. We were put on a starvation diet—"

At the defense table Paul closed his eyes as the voice went on. He could still remember the skeleton-thin body that had emerged from the detention pen: had Kay been the phantom she resembled, she would have seemed heavier in his arms. . . . Somehow, he told himself, her story *must* reach the hearts of the court. But there was no change in those seven masks as the recital went on.

"Toward the last," said Kay, "I was too delirious to remember what really happened—until I wakened in a hospital bed."

"Did anyone explain why you were confined?"

"They wanted to make Captain Scott sign the confession."

"Did you expect him to sign it?"

"I prayed that he wouldn't."

"Even if it meant your death?"

"I knew that Colonel Hardin would use the confession to wreck Paul's career."

"You loved Captain Scott enough to die rather than let that happen?"

"I hoped I'd have the courage to endure. When I was out of my head I was afraid I'd send for him. But I didn't. I'm sure of that much."

"We now come to the repatriation of the prisoners, Miss Storey. Did Captain Scott tell you why he stayed behind?"

"He did. Chaplain O'Fallon had suffered a severe hemorrhage after his own confinement in solitary. He would have died if Captain Scott hadn't given him a transfusion. When the exchange of prisoners was arranged the chaplain was too weak to move: Captain Scott was almost sure he'd die eventually—but he felt he should remain."

"Did he tell anyone else of his decision?"

"He informed Colonel Pak—in Colonel Hardin's hearing."

Paul saw that the president had glanced up sharply at this contradiction of Hardin's testimony. The look he fastened on Kay was far from benign.

"The court will question the witness, Mr. Saunders. Remember, Miss Storey, you are under oath. Were you present at the meeting you describe?"

"I was not: I was ill myself at the time. Captain Scott told me about it later."

"The reporter will strike the witness' last reply from the record as hearsay. Proceed, Mr. Saunders—and try to keep to your point."

"Did Captain Scott send any message to the United States Army authorities?"

"Yes—via Colonel Hardin."

Again the court cut in sharply, forcing Kay to admit that this, too, was hearsay—and again the reply was erased.

"Did you also wish to remain and nurse the chaplain?" asked Hi, with weary patience.

"Very much—but I was too ill. Captain Scott insisted I leave at once so that I could be flown to Japan."

"Were you surprised when you learned that Colonel Hardin had accused Captain Scott of collaboration?"

"I was more shocked than surprised. I knew it was inevitable."

"No further questions."

V

MacArdle came forward with a cat-and-canary smile.

"Miss Storey, what is your profession?"

"I am an actress."

"Am I correct in assuming that you plan to star in a forthcoming motion picture—based on your experiences in the Korean War?"

"Such a picture is in preparation. So far, no contracts have been signed."

"It is true that you attained wide popularity among the enlisted men in an act called *The Girl Next Door?*"

"It was a song fest in which the men participated—not an act."

"Did you also entertain the prison inmates?"

"Yes, on the few occasions the Chinese allowed us to sing."

"Now, Miss Storey, a statement has been made in court—by the defense, I believe—that you and the accused were very close during your imprisonment. Is it not true that there has been intimacy between you?"

"At one time we planned to marry—"

"Answer my question, Miss Storey. Have you ever had intimate relations with Captain Scott?"

Hi was already roaring toward the bench. "You need not answer, Miss Storey—"

The president's gavel banged. "The court will rule on all answers, Mr. Saunders."

"Colonel Sellers, I must object, in the strongest terms. This line of questioning is beneath the dignity of the uniform the trial counsel wears. It is an insult to the witness and to the court."

"This witness," MacArdle countered, "has practically accused Colonel Hardin of perjury and assault with intent to murder. In the face of such monstrous charges, it is my right to attack her credibility."

"Objection denied," rapped out Sellers, "subject to objection by any member of the court."

Major Duggan leaned forward, thought better of the interruption, and settled in his seat again. MacArdle's eyes swiveled to each face on the seven-man court: apparently he liked what he read there. "The reporter will read the question," he said quietly.

The corporal at the stenotype read tonelessly: *Answer my question, Miss Storey. Have you ever had intimate relations with Captain Scott?*

Kay did not speak at once; the flush that had stained her cheeks was gone now. "Yes—I have."

There was a scramble at the press table as reporters for afternoon papers dove for the hallway and the phones. Glancing at MacArdle, Paul guessed that he had been prepared for a negative response, which he would have been forced to twist to create the effect he desired. For once, he seemed at a loss for words.

"I—appreciate your frankness, Miss Storey," he said at last. "Let us go on to the encounter in the farmyard outside Sinmak. You have already told the court that you did not see Captain Scott's alleged attacker—"

"I know he was attacked."

"How can you know?"

"I believe what Captain Scott told me."

"Naturally, considering the intimacy between you."

"*Objection!*"

"Sustained," barked Sellers—and glared down the bench, as though daring anyone to dispute the ruling. "Clerk will strike the prosecutor's statement from the record as immaterial."

MacArdle rolled easily with the punch. "Now, Miss Storey, about your hospital work. Didn't you fare better there than you would have in barracks?"

"Yes, I did. It was something I worked for."

"That I can believe," said MacArdle.

"Proceed, Major," said the president. "We'll dispense with dramatic asides."

"Miss Storey, were you permitted to live in the hospital because Captain Scott specially recommended you?"

"I wasn't specially recommended. Captain Scott said only that I was a former nurse—and that I might be useful. There were no women's barracks: it solved the problem of my billeting."

"After you'd established yourself at the hospital, Miss Storey, did Captain Scott put in a good word for you then?"

"I am sure he did not."

"On what grounds?"

"He said often that he could never bring himself to ask for favors—either for himself or for me."

"But he did intervene to obtain your release from solitary?"

"Only because he knew both Chaplain O'Fallon and I were dying there."

"We come now to the time of your repatriation. Did you see Chaplain O'Fallon after his alleged hemorrhage?"

"He was under treatment at the hospital. No visitors were allowed."

"So you have no personal knowledge that a hemorrhage occurred?"

"Captain Scott told—"

"To your own knowledge?"

"No."

"So this illness of the chaplain's *could* have been used by Captain Scott as an excuse to refuse repatriation?"

"That is impossible."

"How do you know?"

"I know Captain Scott."

"I am nearly finished, Miss Storey: forgive me if this has proved trying. On your journey to Panmunjom and afterward—how did Colonel Hardin treat you?"

"With courtesy."

"Did he not insist upon hospitalization in Tokyo and arrange plane priority?"

"He did—because Captain Scott asked him."

"Not because he, too, was genuinely concerned?"

"I thought so at the time. Now I see he was anxious to get me in a hospital bed before I could be interviewed."

"Why, Miss Storey?"

"Because he feared that I might refute the charges he intended to make against Captain Scott."

"If you felt this so strongly, why didn't you deny his statements at once?"

"I was desperately ill for weeks and didn't see a newspaper. When I did the damage was done. I made denials then, but it was too late—"

"That is all, Miss Storey."

MacArdle settled in his chair with the air of a school principal dismissing an unruly sophomore. Sellers glanced at Hi, who got to his feet.

"The defense has no further questions."

"Does any member of the court?"

When there was no answer the president rose and bowed to the witness with an odd old-world courtesy. It was, Paul felt sure, the salute of one fighter to another, the acknowledgment of a lost cause that had been contested gallantly.

"The court stands adjourned until ten tomorrow. You may step down, Miss Storey."

VI

Kay walked out of the courtroom with her eyes straight ahead. Though she did not risk a glance at the defense table she knew that Hi had laid a restraining hand on Paul's arm, lest he rush out after her. Despite the tumult in her brain, she could be grateful for that small mercy. Convinced, as she was, that she had just dealt Paul his deathblow, she could not face him now.

At the press table the staring moonface of Larry Kirk loomed up at her briefly: she could have sworn that he had nodded before he plunged into his notes. Then she was in the open air, blinking down the tears—and fighting the photographers.

"Just one more, Miss Storey!"

"Got a statement?"

"Will you marry him?"

"Still making that movie for Lindman?"

She got through, in time, with an assist from the MPs. When the gate of the parking lot clanged shut on the wolf pack, she knew privacy of a sort. It was a heaven-sent relief to be alone, to fumble at details—the car ticket in her purse, the ignition key that unlocked the door of her convertible. In a moment more she was roaring out of the Presidio. Through the racing motor she heard someone call her name and feared that it was Paul. She knew better than to look back.

Kay remembered little of the long, careening drive through the afternoon traffic. The room clerk at the Mark Hopkins brought her back to reality when she asked for the keys to her suite.

"Mr. Lindman took them, Miss Storey. He's been waiting for you since noon."

At least she was prepared for Eric: she was even grateful that he had come in person to release her from her agreement with the studio. At her foyer door she drew a deep breath before she tiptoed into the suite. Eric (magnificent in a white linen suit and a Liberty silk neckcloth) was stretched on a divan before the dead TV. A telephone was cradled on his shoulder; evidently he was in the midst of a long-distance call—a standard activity for the wonder boy, who was always giving his opinions to people at the ends of the earth. . . . This time, Kay gathered, long-distance was no farther than Hollywood, and the recipient of Eric's lecture was his studio head. What was really astounding was the fact that Barney Gould had been charmed into silence.

"I've told you this once, Barney," said Eric, "and I'll tell you again. Not even *I* can guess which way the public will jump. . . . All right! Eighty-one per cent of the messages came from women. Who else sets the fashion at the box office? . . . *Of course* you did right to tune in, Barney—you never did a smarter thing. . . . Yep, the press release is out: I phoned it in myself. . . . It'll hit the street in the late editions—"

Listening to the confident cadences of Eric's voice, Kay told herself that he might have spared her this—even though he could hardly know that she was an unwilling eavesdropper. A moment later, when he had replaced the phone, she squared her shoulders and made a brisk second entrance.

"*Eric!* I thought you were in Hollywood."

"I was, darling," said the wonder boy. "Until I heard you meant to testify. You've cost the studio a pretty penny in plane fares."

"You didn't have to fly back."

"I figured you'd need me afterward. Now I can see how right I was."

Kay stripped off her gloves, and flung her hat aside. "The picture's dead, Eric. You've already said as much."

"On the contrary. The picture was never more alive."

Kay settled in the nearest armchair—just before she felt her knees give way. "Wasn't that Barney Gould on the phone?"

"It was Barney."

"Does he *still* want to sign me?"

"I've already initialed the contract in your name."

"But you *said* I'd dig my own grave if I testified—"

"Sometimes I'm appalled by my own ignorance." The wonder boy rose from his chair, circled the television warily, then gave it a punishing blow with one fist. "I've always insisted that this squawk box would ruin Hollywood—but it does have its uses."

"It does indeed," said Kay bitterly. "Today it helped to drive the last nail in Paul Scott's coffin."

"It also gave us the last big scene for *The Girl Next Door*. The *scène à faire*, as the French say—"

"Will you make sense, Eric?"

"Wake up, darling. Forty million females were glued to that box today, watching you go to bat for your man. And there's nothing the average female loves more than sacrifice."

"Will you make sense?"

"The moment you left the witness stand the studio was jammed with calls demanding that you get the part. It's been the same at the network. Your public has spoken, Kay—you can't ignore its voice."

Her first impulse was to knock the highball from Eric's hand, if only to crack that smiling mask. And then, as the impact of his words reached her mind, Kay realized that he, too, was applauding her courage in his own strange fashion. Incredible as it might seem, Eric Lindman could be human at times. . . . If he had prolonged the suspense deliberately, it was only to drive his message home.

"Don't tell me the public is backing Paul?"

"On the contrary. So far, they've voted him guilty as charged. Those who were intelligent enough to express an opinion think that you were tragically misled—and they're cheering you all the more for it. In case you've forgotten, it's an old American custom to stand by the man you love. Never mind if he's hero or villain."

Kay covered her eyes with her hands. Her temples were throbbing madly: she needed all her strength to keep down a shout of idiot laughter. "So the picture goes before the cameras—if I still want the part?"

"You can't refuse it, Kay, I've just phoned your acceptance to the afternoon papers: it'll make the late editions."

"Eric, do you enjoy the role of *deus ex machina?*"

"As I've said, my part in this business has been anything but intelligent. I'm doing my best to make amends."

"Suppose I do say yes—will you promise me one thing?"

"Anything at all, darling. Even if it isn't in reason."

"Don't let me see Paul again until the trial's over. I've harmed him enough."

VII

Paul, pacing his room at the BOQ, looked up for the tenth time at the step in the hall. Some of his tension vanished when Hi Saunders came in briskly, an evening paper folded under his arm.

"Did you find her?"

"I got Lindman on the phone. Kay refuses to see you—or anyone." Hi slapped the newspaper face down on the table. "Don't look so blank, pal. What else did you expect?"

"She must have realized that I'd want to talk to her."

"With or without reporters?"

"Don't make jokes, Hi. I *had* to tell her—"

"What? That we're sorry Kay behaved like Kay on the witness stand? We both knew she did her damnedest to clear you: it isn't her fault she failed. MacArdle just happens to be a smarter lawyer than I figured—and a good deal less of a gentleman."

"Did you expect her to perjure herself—like Hardin?"

"Not for a minute, and I still say we were smart to put her on." Hi turned the paper over so that Paul could see the headlines. "This front page bears me out. Never mind what cynics like Lindman are saying—"

Paul stared down at the fresh-faced likeness of Kay Storey that smiled up at him from the paper, in the glossy perfection of a USO release. "So she's making her picture, regardless."

"By public demand," said Hi. "Any good lawyer could have told Lindman that."

"Thank God we didn't spoil her career, Hi. She'll have that now—no matter what becomes of me."

"Don't let that headline throw you," said Hi. "It's true a few million readers think you're guilty. So will your judge, I'm afraid—if we can't rip Hardin open and show what makes him tick. Just the same, your girl stood up for you in court. Win or lose, you've a potential movie star on your side. It'll help when the chips are down."

"Isn't there some way I can see her?"

"You've nothing to say to each other now," said Hi. "Meanwhile, you take the stand tomorrow. The final witness in the case of Paul Scott versus American public opinion. Any notion of what you're going to say?"

"Must we go over *that* again?"

Hi glanced at his watch—and the night that had begun to invade the immaculate green parade outside. "It's the last toss of the dice, boy. This time we've got to roll a seven."

"We can't hit Hardin—and we can't change my story."

"Brood on it awhile: I'll come back after dinner for a real huddle. Maybe there's still a gimmick we can use."

"What if there isn't?"

"Face it, Paul. So far, Sellers and company assume we've been shadowboxing to cover you. If you repeat the same story on the stand, they'll think you're lying to save yourself. We need a new angle or we're sunk."

"Isn't the truth enough?"

"It isn't that simple, Paul. The law aims at certainty: it must test one witness against another. So far, in this case I've been a bricklayer without straw."

"Don't blame yourself, Hi. No one could have fought harder."

"I'm blaming no one," said Hi. "Not even the climate of suspicion we live in today. Don't start me on *that*, or I'll begin preaching a sermon—and I must let you collect your thoughts." He turned to the door and paused with one hand on the knob. "Have a tray sent up—and this time try to rest afterward. I'll be back around nine for your final briefing."

When Hi had gone Paul saw that his first problem was to stay clear of the phone. Three times in the next quarter hour of pacing he yielded to its magnet and lifted the receiver at the first ring, knowing that only Lindman would answer. He could be thankful, in a way, that the Army had confined him to the Presidio. Otherwise he might have roamed Nob Hill until morning, hoping that he might catch a glimpse of Kay. . . .

Instead, he told himself, you must marshal your strength for the final duel with MacArdle; you must rehearse your story from beginning to end. You must keep to the truth—only the truth will make you free.

Where did his story really begin—and how (if he meant to save his good name) could he end it? *Keep to the truth, for the truth will make you free.* Had that ancient maxim outlived its usefulness? Had the Hardins of his century, riding down all men who opposed them, changed truth into falsehood, good into evil?

Thanks to MacArdle's smoke screen, he could not begin at the beginning. The truth about Hill 1049 would never emerge at this court-martial. Nor would the truth about the events at Sinmak—Hardin's insane assault in the cow shed, with intent to kill, the brutal refusal to share his transport on that hell-march to Pyongyang. Perhaps, if he insisted, the court would permit him to speak of the incredible hardships of that two-week trek. From the court's viewpoint it would seem only an exercise in self-pity.

Could he describe his first glimpse of the prison compound? Merely by closing his eyes he could bring back that thirty acres of sun-cracked earth again—the barricades at the gate (as real as the mouth of hell made visible), the tar-paper barracks, the walking cadavers that dwelt there. It was a picture he could never share—unless the listener had endured the same trial and learned to rise above it. . . .

The misery in which so much of the world dwelt today (he repeated the conviction with a sinking heart) was actual only to the dwellers. Here at home, sufferings in far places had been overdramatized in a hundred books, overpreached by a thousand do-gooders—until they had become a crashing bore. Once again he would only be accused of bidding for the court's pity.

Of course, he might use Pyongyang as a point of departure for his own achievement. He could tell how he had fought with Colonel Pak to obtain proper rations, heat for the shacks in their first winter, elementary relief from the filth and vermin that had claimed lives by the score. He could describe the horror of the meningitis epidemic that had killed Lieutenant Crosby, and the steps he had followed to conquer it. . . . But even here, he would only be laboring a point that MacArdle had conceded at the beginning—the fact that he was a dedicated doctor, willing to heal friend and foe alike.

What of Hardin—a sodden wreck when he had finally reached Pyongyang, a near-maniac trembling on the brink of delirium tremens, now that even the solace of *sake* was denied him? Would it help his chances if he told how he had pulled the colonel back from madness—or would he be accused once again of lying? Knowing that answer in advance, Paul let his mind slide over the long first year of his imprisonment, without a pause. After all, it was the *second* year that mattered, the time when the deep comradeship he had shared with his fellow inmates had changed to black hatred—the months of compromise for the sake of those he loved, of betrayal and forgiveness.

Forgiveness? He weighed the word and knew it was well chosen. He *could* forgive Hardin, now that he saw the man's pitiable weakness clearly. Still, he could not go down before Hardin's savage onslaught without a fight—however feeble the weapons he might summon in his defense.

Take it from there, he told his rebellious memory. Tell a straight story tomorrow. Make it sound real, no matter how incredible it seems in retrospect. . . . Probably they won't believe a word. Men who have lived on the earth's abundance have a way of closing their ears to harsh reality. . . . Yet you must tell the story of that second year at Pyongyang if only to convince yourself that you did right.

Once he had made that decision, he could feel his mind settle painlessly into the groove of memory. Kay, at least, had been rewarded for her unselfishness: no matter what the court's verdict, her career was safe. . . . As for Captain Paul Scott, he would face the future without fear. Father Tim had endorsed his conduct at the prison camp. He would endorse it tonight, were he still among the living.

PYONGYANG

I

The snow nightmare had come again, just before dawn. Now, sitting bolt upright on his pallet in Barracks Number Four, Paul blinked for a long and frightening moment before his eyes could focus clearly on the summer light outside the lattice. It was a comfort of sorts to note that the day promised to be fair and warm: for a time, at least, the horror of window-high drifts outside was only a visitation from the past.

He was glad that he had wakened ahead of the others. As doctor to the whole prison camp, he was entitled to leave the barracks when he wished. Since he had put down the meningitis epidemic, he had found it simpler to shun his fellow inmates whenever he could do so naturally. . . . He glanced at the boy who lay curled in slumber on the next pallet: a new prisoner, he thought dully, is a novelty here. Now that Colonel Pak had stepped up the food ration at his urging (enough, at any rate, to hold death by starvation to a minimum), there had been no vacancies for over a month.

The newcomer was an Air Force navigator, picked up from the wreck of an American bomber: his gray-green battle uniform was still spotless, a glaring contrast to the ragged sleepers beyond. It was significant, thought Paul, that the navigator should have taken the pallet next to his own— unaware that the others now slept apart from him, so far as these cramped quarters permitted.

Wondering what would be said when his back was turned, Paul put the question aside. It was enough to know in his own heart that he had acted for the general good when he had treated guards and prisoners alike in that last-ditch fight to stop a deadly epidemic. He could hardly blame the camp for calling it his first long step down the road to collaboration. How could they think differently—when his hospital duties claimed him from dawn to dark? How could he convince them that his endless meetings with Colonel Pak were all that had ransomed many of them from the grave?

II

In the doorway he returned the salute of the guard and paused to stare back at the fetid rookery he was quitting after a few hours of exhausted stupor.

The hundred-odd prisoners who shared Barracks Four were still deep in oblivion. In repose they seemed oddly defenseless and heartbreakingly young. True, there were exceptions—Dalton, the squadron leader who was rounding out his second year as a prisoner (and resembled a gnome from some nameless inferno), and Pierce, the grizzled sergeant who had been shot down in the same strike. Both of these men were moaning in their sleep as they continued to battle their own special demons: both would require forcible detention in the near future. . . . For the rest, he thought, there was still hope of salvage—if Pak kept his promise and held the rations to the minimum necessary to sustain life.

Since there were less than fifty pallets, the sleepers took turns on the bare floor: save for the inevitable rice bowls along one wall, there was no other furniture whatever. The garb of each prisoner was identical—OD blouses in various stages of ruin, and nankeen pantaloons thrust into laceless boondockers (a bootlace made an excellent garrote if a man planned to strangle a guard or take his own life).

Thanks to the guards' habit of boarding up each window, the air above the pallets seemed almost too heavy to breathe. The only light fell in chinks through the lattice of the single doorway: it was easy to imagine phantoms from the past, stirring restlessly in this mongrel time between night and day. . . . Last winter (when the snow nightmare had been all too real) a dozen men had died of the numbing cold; three others had gone via the suicide route, before the guards had stripped them of their last means of self-destruction. Others had died—just as deliberately—in a crazy rush for the gateway after the third day without food, a punishment for some breach of discipline Paul had long since forgotten.

Their first year of prison, he reflected, had separated the weak from the strong. Today the survivors of Barracks Four were united in a common will to endure—and a common hatred for their captors that passed the bounds of reason. Naturally the fact that he served as prison doctor (and stood with a foot in both camps) had made him suspect. Even Furness and Jackson, who had once given him unquestioning loyalty, had begun to whisper with the others, to turn their backs when he risked a greeting in the compound. . . . He shook off the impasse with a sigh of pure frustration and stepped into the clean morning air.

Seen in the light of the September dawn, the camp was even more forlorn than usual. For a reason that Paul could not define, he had always found the huddle of tar-paper shacks more bearable in bad weather. Pressed down in the midst of a treeless plain, this huddle of roofs seemed more deserted than usual today, a ghost town forgotten in the glow of the flawless sunrise. For the hundredth time he thought how much his prison resembled the set for a third-rate Western, months after the last cowboy had moved on to another acting chore. . . . Only the ditch beyond the barbed wire and the floodlights on the four watchtowers brought the picture into focus. It would be real enough in the next half hour when the prisoners had turned out for morning roll call and the dismal routines of the day began.

The hospital stood on a low rise, between the commandant's quarters and the cabin that had been assigned to Colonel Jasper Hardin. Following the path to the dispensary, Paul forced his eyes to dwell for a moment on the colonel's billet and the plume of smoke that rose from its special cookshack. Master Sergeant Bates, busily dismembering a chicken on the chopping block outside, waved a greeting which Paul ignored: he had been long aware of Bates' campaign to discredit him in his barracks, and the man's hypocrisy today was more than he could endure.

As senior officer in the compound it was logical that Hardin should have separate quarters. By the same token he had the right to his own rations: no one knew what skulduggery Bates used to obtain such unheard-of items as fresh poultry. . . . At least Hardin had been deprived of his bottle for almost a year: Paul had seen to that, just as he had supervised the colonel's drying-out. Now that the C.O.'s abstinence was a *fait accompli*, his delirium tremens was only an ironic note in the hospital log.

Bates had been Paul's wholehearted ally in that drying-out: the little weasel was shrewd enough to see that Hardin must be deprived of alcohol during his imprisonment, or go screaming mad. . . . The shutters that still masked the cabin windows were a reminder of the measures they had taken to keep his condition under wraps. Later (after Hardin had ceased his doglike baying for *sake*) Bates had treated the episode as a figment of Paul's imagination. When the colonel was well enough to resume his daily musters, the sergeant major had simply donned his armor of insolence again.

Paul had expected no gratitude from Hardin himself: if anything, the C.O.'s hatred had been strengthened by the therapies which had saved him. More surprising (because of the Spartan regime of the camp and the food that Bates procured in such quantities), he seemed healthier than he had been in years—but this, too, was a fact for which Hardin assumed sole credit. The near-fatal thirst of yesteryear, like the cowardice that had driven him from Hill 1049, had suffered the same blackout.

Putting the colonel and his psychosis firmly out of mind, Paul crossed the hospital porch and entered the sanctuary of his own domain. Part of the building had once been a Buddhist shrine, in the days before Marxism had invaded North Korea: the gilded statue of the god looked down at Paul from a lacquered niche. (Each morning he found solace in the inscrutable smile, pitiless though it seemed to Western eyes.) With the acceptance of the night charts from the Chinese orderly in the foyer, he began his day as camp surgeon.

Because of Paul's insistence on a better diet for the prisoners (even though that diet was at the rice-and-vegetable level, for the most part), the disease rate in the camp had dropped sharply during the spring. In the summer months fevers had once more plagued the inmates; after a recent reduction in the shipment of vitamins and other essential drugs the wards had begun to fill again. Today he needed a full two hours to make his rounds: faint though he was from hunger, he did not dare to pause, for fear he would be unable to continue. . . . Food that could keep an idle prisoner almost healthy was not sufficient for this exacting routine—yet he had consistently refused to supplement the barracks rations from the hospital larder. Even at the best, there was little enough to divide among those crowded beds.

He had long since learned that it was essential to check each case. Dr. Chang, the ex-intern who had been in charge here before his arrival, could follow direct instructions (though he was apt to fly into a hissing torrent of excuses if confronted with something really serious). The four male nurses who served the ward were competent enough in their sullen fashion—and Kay had been a tower of strength from the start. Paul still found it impossible to leave the hospital with a clear conscience until he visited every bed and verified each notation on the charts.

When his morning inspection was behind him he managed to steal a few moments' rest in the doubtful privacy of the consulting room he had set up just off the surgery. There was a splinter of mirror on the wall: he glanced at his image before he settled in the single broken-back chair and closed his eyes. His face, like the body beneath the tattered uniform blouse, was skeleton-thin: the cords of his neck seemed taut as violin strings tuned beyond their pitch. Obviously, he told himself, you can't go on like this forever. . . .

Hardin had recommended him for this post because he had had no choice. Once Paul had proved his worth, the C.O. had been prudent enough to keep clear of all hospital matters—and contented himself with an occasional dressing down, for which Paul could have supplied the words in advance. Recently the colonel's attack had been mounted on another front—the whispering campaign that had begun to fasten the dread label of "progressive" on the camp doctor. So far, with the solid achievement of the hospital to sustain him, Paul had managed to endure the goading.

Resting his head on a desk top for a stolen nap, he remembered last night's emergency operation, the elevation of a skull fracture. He had managed it with Chang's inexpert help: Sergeant Furness had been the unwilling anesthetist, and Kay had served as instrument passer. The patient had been one of the guards, the wound an aftermath of a break from Barracks Two, which had resulted in the merciless machine-gunning of seven prisoners. He had performed the same operation often: the present case was a routine one. But this time it was an enemy's life he had salvaged: once the story had spread through the camp, the gulf that divided him from the others would be even wider than before.

At the moment, however, it was not his ostracism that bemused him. He was remembering an ominous incident while the operation was at its most ticklish stage. For a second of animal terror, he was positive that the lights above the table had dimmed to mere coals. His hand (fastened on the Hudson burr he had been using for his trephine) had trembled so violently he had needed all his will power to hold his ground. The attack had passed and he had finished the operation. But his emotional exhaustion had been complete when he groped his way into the consulting room.

Kay, following him at once, had knelt by his side and put her arms around him. It was one of the few moments of tenderness they had allowed themselves here.

"What happened, Paul? I was sure you'd faint at the table."

"I'm afraid it was night blindness."

"Doesn't that mean a lack of vitamin A?"

"That's the usual cause."

"We have some vitamins here. Why haven't you been taking them?"

"For the same reason I eat barracks food and sleep there with the others. Just because they're sure I have special privileges here, I feel I must refuse them."

"You've the right to a few tablets, darling."

"The supply is limited. We'll need all we have for our pellagra patients— and the berberi cases."

"Paul, how can you call yourself a doctor—and be such a stubborn fool? Suppose *you* come down with pellagra—or have another blackout?"

He had yielded then and obediently swallowed several of the precious tablets, which Kay brought from the padlocked medicine chest. "Keep this our secret," he warned. "Otherwise, they'll be calling me a progressive to my face."

"They won't dare. Not after you've saved them all, ten times over."

"All I've really done here is hold a few bodies and souls together."

"If you'd *explain* why you acted as you did in the epidemic—"

"They'll never forgive me for treating the guards, too. You see, Kay, hate's about the only luxury a prisoner of war can afford. They wanted to see a few Chinese die in agony—the way poor Crosby died."

"All right, darling. We'll admit that this existence brings out the worst in some of us. Father Tim knows you did right—and so do I. Is that a large enough jury for now?"

He took her in his arms then—and kissed her for the first time in months. Her lips were warm and alive as she clung to him fiercely. In her embrace, the wretched world about them had seemed to dissolve, to lose its meaning.

III

Paul lifted his head from the desk and shook off his treacherous brooding. Reverie of this kind was a thing he could afford only in snatches; with a great effort he forced himself to return to the foyer and the makeshift admissions desk he had placed there. No new cases had been recorded in the daybook. He was almost sorry to find himself faced with an hour of idleness; at the moment he would have welcomed some task to blunt the sharp edge of his thoughts.

Kay would still be sleeping after last night's emergency duty. He decided to look in on Father Tim—who had recently (and much against his will) been admitted here as a patient. He needed such a pause to collect himself before he faced the compound again, swarming with life at the moment, while a thousand prisoners shuffled through the dusty routine of noonday exercise.

The chaplain's cot had been placed in a special cubicle, apart from the crowded ward: Father Tim was deep in slumber when Paul picked up his chart. Thirteen months behind barbed wire had taken their toll of his vitality: on his admission to the hospital he had been cadaverous rather than merely thin, and the racking cough that had troubled him on the march to Sinmak had returned, despite the fine weather. Even more disturbed by the red stain in the priest's cheeks, Paul had insisted on a week of bed rest.

Father Tim had been entered in the admission book with a diagnosis of acute bronchitis and dysentery—a disease that was all but universal in the compound. Later, Paul had X-rayed his chest, using the inferior equipment at his disposal, which did little more than distinguish the lungs from the rib cage. There had been no evidence of the thing he feared—a budding case of tuberculosis. In the past few days Father Tim's rapid improvement had done much to dissipate his fears.

Now, as he looked down at the slender figure in the cot, Paul could not help reflecting that the priest's appearance had become more saintlike with each passing day. The prisoner's beard helped, of course (it was strange that it should be so luxuriant a red). So did the faint nimbus of sunlight that fell through a skylight overhead. Yet there was something in the padre's appearance that brought its own aura of peace, a strength that transcended the frail body. Even in this short, wordless communion with the sleeping man, Paul had discovered the refreshment he sought. . . .

He found that he stood in need of refreshment when he stepped out to the hospital porch and met Sergeant Luppino, one of the less offensive members of Hardin's camarilla.

"C.O. wants you at headquarters pronto, Cap'n."

"We've nothing else but time here, Sergeant. Why must it always be pronto?"

"Search me, sir. Guess the old man figures it's important to keep up our morale."

"Apparently it suits you, Angelo," said Paul: he was already following Luppino's cocky progress through the compound. In a suit of freshly washed suntans, with his cap at a rakish angle, the sergeant might have stepped from a regimental PX: his boots shone like chestnuts, and even the cigarette between his lips was tailor-made. The stare he bestowed on the ragged hulks he shouldered from his path was the hallmark of Hardin's staff. Luppino (whom Paul remembered as a thoroughly decent noncom) had finally assumed the protective coloration of his group.

For all its ramshackle exterior, the C.O.'s quarters were comfortable enough—a fact that Hardin was careful to keep guarded. Colonel Pak had long since granted him virtual autonomy in his sphere, and Hardin had taken full advantage of that privilege. To say that the compound was run with all the efficiency of a marine boot camp (as Hardin boasted) was highly inaccurate—most of the prisoners were too feeble for that. Yet the C.O. was a stern moral policeman, insisting on daily formations, rigorous barrack policing, and more saluting than seemed humanly possible under such conditions.

From the start Hardin had exacted fines for the smallest lapse—and the noncoms were merciless in their enforcement. True, there was little to fine these days: the usual routine was to farm out offenders for road mending and the repair of bomb damage in Pyongyang. This strictly illegal labor was dispatched through Colonel Pak's office, and his guards herded the prisoners to and from their tasks. But Paul had long since guessed that Hardin was paid for their work—usually in food, soap, and other items beyond price here. It helped to explain the glow of health that filled the cabin, as tangible as the odor of roasting chicken that still hung in the shuttered air. . . .

Hardin, as was his invariable custom, kept the camp doctor waiting a quarter hour before he strode in portentously from the kitchen. He was wolfing the last of a drumstick and ignored his visitor completely while he settled at his improvised desk. Glancing at his crude worktable, Paul saw that the documents the C.O. was fingering were copies of his own medical reports, run off on the mimeographing machine which Bates had recently procured in Pyongyang. It was not the first time that Hardin had prepared his sermon beforehand, complete with notes.

"Why is this sick list padded, Scott?"

The question, spat out with the drumstick, stabbed at Paul's mind with a familiar, dull pain. As always in Hardin's presence, he had the sensation of a noose tightening, though the rope was still invisible.

"I'd call it only normal, sir—for a bad week." He had long since abandoned hope of a *modus vivendi* with the colonel. At Sinmak he had wrestled with the man when Hardin was too drunk to stand, and knocked a potential murder weapon from his fist; in this same room he had seen him roll on the floor like a sick animal and beg for a drink with tear-filled eyes. . . . The fact that he had pardoned the C.O. for an attempt on his life (and rescued him from the alcoholism that had nearly destroyed him) was something Hardin would never forget—or forgive.

"What d'you mean, a *bad* week? One's as bad as another in this hog-pen."

"We've managed to survive, sir—thanks to the deal I made with Colonel Pak." Paul regretted the words instantly—knowing that Master Sergeant Bates was behind the door with a notebook. "I promised to keep his guard room well if he'd do as much for us."

"It isn't your province to make agreements here, Scott. You take orders from me."

"Granted, sir. I was only trying to get what food and medication I could—for the whole camp."

"It seems your deal miscarried. Your ward is filled to the last bed."

"I've admitted only the worst cases of malnutrition and avitaminosis."

"Skip the medical jargon, man. Explain this deal with the commandant."

"The details are common knowledge, sir."

"So they are, Captain. And what I hear is hardly to your credit."

Paul stood his ground patiently. "Am I accused of collaboration, Colonel? If so, I'd like to face my accusers."

"No accusations have been made—so far. I'm still wondering why you spend so much time in Colonel Pak's office."

"I've reported those meetings, sir, as fast as they occurred. So far, they've been standard interrogations—"

"Until you made your deal?"

"It was the commandant's suggestion, not mine. He was impressed by the lives we saved during the meningitis epidemic."

"There were still twenty deaths, as I recall." Hardin glanced meaningly at a paper on the desk. "Four of them were barracks officers. The epidemic raged through the whole camp, but not a single guard was taken sick. How d'you explain that?"

"The disease began in Barracks Two, when Lieutenant Crosby died there. Others were infected before I was allowed to begin treatment with sulfadiazine. Naturally Colonel Pak insisted that his own personnel receive treatment first—"

"Excuses of that sort will get you nowhere, Scott."

"The facts will stand, sir, before any medical board: so will my agreement with Colonel Pak. I've promised to do my utmost to keep his guards in health. In return, he's granted a ration for each prisoner sufficient to sustain life. Vitamins to cover all normal breakdowns—" Paul could hear his voice trail off in the face of Hardin's apathetic stare: he had seen the colonel's eyes glaze over before, in these meaningless interviews.

"So *that's* your reason for filling your hospital with goldbrickers?"

"These men are badly ill, sir. Despite the improved diet, most of them were too weak to stand when I admitted them—"

"This is a prison camp, and I'm responsible for its discipline. I can't maintain morale if you turn your ward into a rest home."

For an instant only, as he faced that sneering, too-healthy stare, Paul let his resentment rip to the surface. It was sheer luxury to snatch the paper from Hardin's hand and circle a single item. "Speaking of rest homes, will you match the calorie count in your kitchen with my own figures for the barracks diet list?"

The shot rang a bell. For an instant Hardin's full-fleshed visage went white to the eyes. "Is that a threat, Scott? he roared.

"I'm only reminding you that not a man on your staff has appeared on sick call since the epidemic. Your own health has been excellent since you recovered from your—battle fatigue." Paul stressed the word lightly, feeling an unholy joy as Hardin's eyes dropped. "As I say, I'd like to know your secret. Since you won't share it, I must keep down our disease rate as best as I can."

But Hardin had already recovered his aplomb. "You're here to answer questions, Captain, not to ask them. I won't remind you that rank has its privileges. Even you must realize that elementary fact—"

While Hardin launched into a long and rambling diatribe against what he termed the coddling of hospital patients, Paul listened without really hearing. Already he regretted his jab at the older man's pride. At the moment Hardin's number-one project was, obviously, the destruction of his battalion surgeon. He was shrewd enough to realize that Paul had saved the camp from wholesale decimation—and thus had a certain value. But this was only a temporary protection for the victim. When the war ended and the prison gates opened at last, Hardin would be sure to strike—and the blow would be a crippling one.

"These cases you call avitaminosis, Scott, I say these men are only in the hospital to get extra food, which means there'll be less for the others—"

"Believe me, sir, there was no other way to save them." Since the interview began, Paul had stood rigidly at attention: he could feel the ache of his resentment seep into his bones. *You* haven't missed night latrine because you were half blind and afraid of falling in the ditch, he added silently. You wouldn't know how it feels to rot with scurvy or wake up howling with the pain of beriberi. . . .

"I see you've got Chaplain O'Fallon on the sick list. Is *he* turning goldbrick too?"

"The chaplain is under observation for tuberculosis of the lungs."

"Have you made such a diagnosis?"

"Not definitely, so far. The X-ray was inconclusive."

"Then why keep him on bed rest?"

"He was badly run down, sir. No one in this camp has lived on less—or given more."

"That's a matter of opinion," Hardin snapped. "I want O'Fallon discharged the moment he's fit—along with the others you've been mollycoddling. There will be no special cases, Captain, and no favoritism. Is that clear?"

"Quite, sir."

"That will be all—except for this. In the past year, you've done an adequate job of organizing our sanitation. Because of it, you've been given a certain freedom. But no one is indispensable. Now that your work has been done, others can carry on. Keep this in mind before you make your next deal with Pak."

IV

Once he stood in the noon sunshine again, Paul felt his head clear. As ordeals went, his collision with Hardin had been standard brand. He could spell out his daily interview with Colonel Pak just as accurately and he was overdue for that appointment now. Squaring his shoulders (and ignoring the scornful stares of the prisoners he encountered en route), he forced himself to march briskly across the compound of the high-stilted office that housed the prison commandant.

Pak's quarters had been strategically placed, a wide-windowed room that commanded a panorama of the entire camp. Beside it, across a boarded passageway, was a matching building that served the needs of the Security Police. A boarded passageway between the two (known among the barracks as "pneumonia alley") was also used for interrogations. In the winter months prisoners were stripped to the skin there and forced to stand at attention by the hour, while questions were dinned into both ears with the persistence of a trip hammer. . . . So far, for reasons he could not fathom, Paul had not been questioned in either of these star chambers, save for an occasional short workout: that task had been assumed by the commandant himself.

Today, when the camp doctor paused in the doorway, Colonel Pak was seated alone at his worktable, examing what appeared to be a fragment of shell casing. His smile could not have been friendlier had they been brother officers sharing the comforts of the same club.

"Sit down, Doctor. Tell me what you make of this souvenir."

Save for a sibilant or two, the commandant's English was perfect. Paul settled unwillingly in the comfortable visitor's chair. No one, he reflected, could look less the tyrant than Colonel Pak—or more the humorous philosopher. Even the colonel's appearance belied his calling: he was far taller than most members of his race and a good deal plumper. His full-lipped moonface would not have disgraced one of those United Nations posters that insist all men are brothers.

One need a second, wiser look to realize that the man was neither as robust nor as relaxed as he seemed. The bottle of anti-acid pills on the table (which Paul had prescribed for a persistent stomach ailment) was proof enough that the Chinese suffered from a peptic ulcer. The febrile dart of his hands, as he continued to fondle the shell casing, was a further reminder that he had not been given this sensitive post by accident. Colonel Pak (and Paul had sensed it from their first encounter) was an efficient instrument of propaganda, eager for victims.

"Surely, Captain Scott, you recognize the unpleasant object in my hands?"

"I'm a doctor, Colonel, not an artilleryman."

"It was dropped on a suburb of Pyongyang," said Pak. "You might even have helped load it."

"Battalion surgeons in America do not load shells, Colonel. The armies of the United Nations are not that short-handed." Paul spoke the conventional rebuttal a little wearily. Knowing what was coming, he had made the counter as automatically as a chess player responding to an opening gambit.

"This weapon was not prepared by ordnance, Doctor. It contained a far deadlier charge—bacteria."

"It looks like an ordinary bomb to me."

"I wish I could agree. For sometime now, we've been trying to obtain one of your germ-warfare bombs intact. Fortunately we've been able to reconstruct the apparatus from fragments such as this." Pak put the shell casing aside and picked up a blueprint. "Here is a scale model which should convince you that our engineering experts are as alert as yours. As we understand it, the device is simple enough—a light bomb of the incendiary type, with just enough war head to fragment the casing and spray the contents widely."

Paul took the blueprint and studied it carefully. The drawing was flamboyant, with a flourish that bespoke the Oriental artist with more imagination than background. It was in two parts—the first showing the bomb in flight, the second after its impact. The winged menaces released by the explosion suggested the opening of a Pandora's box.

"Is the re-creation accurate, Dr. Scott?"

"In my country, Colonel," said Paul, "a high-school student could have made this drawing in an hour. You'll have to do better if you expect to convince anyone but your own people."

"We have already convinced them, Doctor—but not with this evidence alone. We have a number of statements from your fellow prisoners as to how the bombs are handled—"

"I know," Paul said grimly. "I've helped to doctor them after their interviews."

"Let us not confuse the issue with details: a confession obtained by any means is still valid, in our eyes. At present we need only a statement as to how the bomb is loaded, and with what bacteria, to make our proof complete."

"Are you suggesting I supply that misinformation?"

The commandant looked up sharply: it was evident that he had not expected this riposte. "Surely you can see the wisdom of doing so."

"We both know that this is an absurd fake. Can you ask me to perpetrate a lie?"

"Captain Scott. We have been at great pains to assemble this bomb; as you already know. I regard you as a man of intelligence. Surely you'd oblige me in this matter to save your own life."

"If I were concerned with my own welfare," said Paul wearily, "I'd have come to you long ago."

"I must say I expected that answer. Despite your intelligence, you are also a born romantic."

"Put that another way: I'll have myself to live with when I get out of here."

"If you get out, you mean."

"*Touché*, Colonel. The fact remains."

"Surely there must be a way to persuade you. Proof that you Americans originated germ warfare is vital to us. We will go to any lengths to obtain it."

"Including the abandonment of all principles of civilized warfare?"

"War has never been civilized. And you mustn't accuse me of lack of principles, Dr. Scott. I have extremely strong principles—though they happen to be the reverse of yours."

"I can believe that, Colonel."

"One of them is that the end always justifies the means. Perhaps we will not win a clear-cut decision on our present try in Korea. The thrust may be made elsewhere. Or we may choose the same battleground later, with a force that is really invincible. Meanwhile, we're determined to convince Asia that the United States is not the great white hope of mankind—"

"Aren't you having delusions of grandeur, Colonel?"

"By no means. Once we accomplish this end, we will have neutralized your influence on this continent. Make no mistake, it is in Asia—and in Africa—that we must prove our philosophy will rule the world."

"Even if you won such a victory—could you take pride in it?"

"Dr. Scott, let us not waste time on trifles. I intend to persuade you to sign a confession stating that you helped to load bacterial bombs. Since you are a medical officer, such a statement will carry great weight. It will also contribute to my pride in my own dialectic."

Paul drew a deep breath as the Chinese pushed the shell casing aside, opened a desk drawer, and tossed two typewritten sheets on the blotter. So the test has come at last, he thought. He forced himself to answer calmly.

"I'll never sign such a document, Colonel."

"Never is an ambitious word, and one that idealists use at their peril. It is my unpleasant duty to tell you that Major Sung of our Security Police is waiting now in the room across the way. I promised him that this confession would be signed on his next visit. You'll find him a far less gentle persuader than I."

The commandant touched a buzzer on his desk: two guards appeared instantly in the doorway. Paul was seized by the elbows and hustled from the office with no need of a formal command. Pneumonia alley, even in summer, had a special chill of its own. Before the guards could thrust him into the interrogation room beyond, he could feel goose flesh prick his skin and knew that his heart was pounding.

He had stood in the star chamber for routine inquiries, so he was prepared for the lights that glared down from the ceiling, the folding table and its facing stools that were the only furniture the windowless room boasted. The man seated at the table was a slender North Korean officer with the lidless stare of a dacoit thug. His uniform, with the green tabs of the Security Police at the shoulders, was faultlessly tailored. His cold glance bored into Paul before he spoke. The eyes were large and seemed unpigmented as the eyes of a fish.

"I am Major Sung," he said, in a voice that was so high as to seem almost feminine. "You will face me, please."

Paul glanced at the second stool: a prod from the guard's rifle brought him to attention. Apparently the purpose of that other seat would be explained later.

"Your name, rank, and serial number?"

"Paul R. Scott, Captain Medical Corps, United States Army Reserve; serial number 0-270106."

"Organization?"

"We are not required to give that information under the rules of warfare."

The security officer stared at him haughtily. Why did the man remind him of Hardin? Was it because each word he had spoken today seemed part of the same futile pattern?

"I have been warned that you might prove unco-operative, Doctor. It will be better if you cause no trouble for yourself."

So far, the probing had been standard. "The United Nations forces are instructed to give their name, rank, and serial number when captured," said Paul. "I am only obeying orders."

"I give orders here, Captain. What is your organization?"

"I am not at liberty to say."

The interrogator snapped an order to the guard, who gave Paul a backhanded slap that sent him sprawling. As he got to his feet (and braced for the next blow) Paul told himself that this was only the beginning.

"Attention!"

Once again Paul squared his aching shoulders, his torso rigid, his hands at his trouser seams. It was a perfect brace, and he took a certain perverse pride in it. Somehow it lessened the sting of the guard's blow, though his head ached from the impact.

"That is better, Doctor. For a medical officer, you are well trained. Now tell me what organization you served before your capture."

"I am not at liberty to say."

This time the guard used his fist to tumble Paul to the floor; since his body had been rigid, he could not roll with the punch. For an instant he lay there, too stunned to move: a second command brought both guards to his side. He was kicked without mercy—just hard enough to drive the breath from his body, without cracking the rib cage.

"Get up, Doctor. You may be seated."

He did not quite remember how he reached the stool, though he feared it was on hands and knees. His pride returned, after a fashion, and he snapped again to attention as he sat facing Major Sung, with only the field table between them.

The interrogator smiled affably: Paul had long since noted the same change of front in Colonel Pak. Apparently it was part of the oriental technique of questioning—a crude assault to stir anger, then a sudden show of sympathy to catch the prisoner off guard.

"You can see how useless it is to oppose us, Captain Scott. Naturally I have your organization in my notes—the 141st Battalion."

"Why ask me then?"

"To see for myself if you were as stubborn as your reputation. Tell me, where do you get the bacteria that your airplanes drop on innocent North Korean civilians?"

"We dropped no bacteria."

"What about flies, mosquitoes, and the mites that cause fever?"

"We dropped no insects. It would have been like carrying coals to Newcastle."

The major's smile vanished instantly, in favor of a suspicious frown. "What are coals to Newcastle?"

"With the flies and mosquitoes you now have, a few more would make little difference."

"Then you admit your planes did drop them?"

"I admit nothing. The rules of war require me to give you my name, rank, and serial number. You have that—so you'll get nothing else from me."

"Have you observed our methods of torture, Doctor?"

"Only the end product, in my hospital."

"As a scientist, you will be interested in our techniques. Permit me to offer an elementary demonstration. Will you give me your hand?"

The major took a small case from his pocket. Grasping Paul's wrist firmly, he opened the case and extracted a sliver of bamboo no larger than a toothpick. His free fingers had the tensile strength of steel as he anchored Paul's thumb to the desk and began to work the sliver through the nail bed, between it and the nail itself. The insertion was accomplished with great skill, as though Sung had performed the act many times before. A tongue of flame lanced at the nerves in Paul's forearm: he drew back instinctively, but his hand and wrist were solidly anchored.

"Are you beginning to see, Doctor, why it is simpler to confess your misdeeds and those of your comrades?"

The bamboo sliver was now deeply embedded: Paul felt the sweat pearl his forehead and wondered how long he could endure that lance of pain without screaming. Major Sung, he gathered, had barely started. He braced himself as the interrogator extracted a tiny mallet from the case and began to tap gently at the end of the bamboo, driving it still deeper.

Each tap was deliberate, as though Sung was husbanding the torture he could inflict. Meeting the man's unwinking stare, forcing himself to keep from flinching, Paul could feel his stomach knot under the agony. And yet, despite the pain, there was a strange comfort in the discovery that fear had left him. Now that the enemy's method was nakedly apparent, he could put his strength into a wordless defiance—and pray that that strength would endure.

"Of course this is just a sample, Doctor. Sometimes we set fire to the bamboo. You've no idea how long these slivers will continue to smolder before they burn out beneath your nail. I'm told the sensation is exquisite—"

Was he swooning at last, or had his brain moved into an area beyond pain? Paul's face was drenched with sweat, but there was no coolness there: rather, each rivulet felt like a stream of fire upon his skin. Yet he knew that he would not yield so long as he could keep that strange gulf between mind and flesh. It was as though an unseen hand had cut the current that pulsed normally from finger end to skull—permitting him to watch his torture from a distance.

"Why did you load bombs with bacteria, Doctor? Why did your planes drop them?"

"We dropped no germs—"

The interrogator plucked the bloody splinter from the nail and ground it under his heel. Despite the strange emancipation of his brain, Paul could feel his nerve ends respond to that unexpected relief so violently that he just escaped tumbling to the floor.

A double buffet from the guards' gun butts restored him to the stool, and he understood why Sung had abandoned the torment. This was a surgeon's hand—and as such it could hardly be mutilated beyond repair. After all, those fingers had saved a guard's life in the surgery last midnight.

"We have other tortures, Doctor. I will describe them for you."

Paul listened with that same fixed smile as the major's toneless voice recited the litany of man's barbarities to man, a list of torments as old as the Neanderthals and as new as a haunted tomorrow. He did not flinch when the guards' fists belabored him, though he was now bruised from head to toe. Nor did he cry out when he was restored to the stool and Sung repeated the bamboo torture on the opposite thumbnail.

By then he had lost track of time: when his tired body slumped on the stool, a jab of the guards' rifles restored him to a rigid attention, until the flesh of his legs and thighs seemed inert as frozen jelly and just as helpless under the next rain of blows. But he knew that his victory was certain, the sundering of mind and body complete. What was better, he saw that Sung knew it too, and continued his techniques more from desperation than any hope of success.

Twice in the next few hours he must have fainted briefly, for he felt the sting of water on his face as the guards worked to revive him. Finally, with no real sense of shock, he could feel himself lifted from the floor and realized that he was being carried into the commandant's office and placed on a cot. A rolled coat was thrust beneath his head and water was dashed into his face before the guards withdrew. Half blinded as he was by exhaustion, he could still glimpse Pak's silhouette, relaxed in a chair nearby.

"I warned you, Colonel—" It was an effort to speak, but he forced out the words. "You are wasting your time."

"So it seems, Dr. Scott." Pak poured a stiff shot of brandy and held it to the camp doctor's lips: the gesture seemed part of the cat-and-mouse battle from which he had just emerged. "Of course I suspected as much from the start—but Major Sung was most insistent. It is usually wise to let the Security Police have their way."

"Will you tell him his methods are useless?"

"At the moment that is impossible. Your interrogation has prostrated him: he will sleep until morning, at least."

Paul managed a glance at the wall clock. The torture had lasted a little over six hours. It had seemed far longer.

"Wouldn't it be simpler, Colonel, if you killed me out of hand?"

"Don't talk nonsense, Doctor. You're too valuable a man to lose."

"I'll die before I sign your confession."

"Don't say that, please. I have other means of persuading you."

"What are they?"

"Today, you gave us ample proof that you do not fear death—for yourself. But what if death should threaten those you love? The chaplain, say—or Miss Storey? Or both?"

V

Colonel Pak did not speak again, and Paul could find no answer in his whirling brain. When he dared to glance toward the chair that stood across the room, it was vacant. Perhaps he had dreamed the last words, he thought drowsily, from the black pit where he lay. Perhaps, if he closed his eyes again, the commandant's phantom would give him peace. . . .

When he wakened bright sunlight glowed at the wide office windows. He was still sprawled on the cot. A glance at his battered body told him that someone had dressed his wounded hands and poulticed the worst of his bruises. Dr. Chang, he thought sleepily: Pak would never admit Kay to his office. . . . The thought of Kay brought back the commandant's threat. He got shakily to his feet just as the door opened and Pak strolled in—debonair as ever in a fresh uniform. The commandant was polishing his glasses on a snow-white handkerchief: save for the military dress, he could have passed for a benign exchange professor, fresh from a summer-school forum and still relishing the meeting of minds.

"Where are they?"

The commandant shook off Paul's hands with his familiar, urbane smile: the gesture was almost gentle. "If you are referring to your friends, Dr. Scott—I sent them to solitary confinement yesterday."

So the threat had been real; the shock was no less intense as the man's words fell into the stillness. Paul sank into the nearest chair and groaned aloud. The pain of Major Sung's torture was as nothing when measured against this discovery.

"Somehow, Colonel," he said, "I didn't think you'd dare go that far."

The commandant's eyebrows lifted. *"Dare,* my dear Captain, is a strong expression for a man in your present plight."

"This is a fight between you and me. The chaplain and Miss Storey have no part of it."

"If they can bring you to your senses they have a vital part."

Paul continued to rock his head between his hands: the full import of the news had penetrated slowly. "You put them in solitary *yesterday?*"

"Yes, Dr. Scott. While you were still defying the Security Police."

"Have I been dead to the world since then?"

"Major Sung put a severe strain on your constitution. I'm afraid he was carried away by his zeal. I had Dr. Chang give you an opiate by injection."

"What happens to my friends—if I won't play your game?"

"Nothing, really."

"Nothing?"

"They'll gradually be forgotten, Doctor. You've seen it happen to other prisoners."

Paul needed no blueprint to complete the enemy strategy. More than once he had been granted permission to enter the building that housed the solitary cells, to give the wretched inmates what aid he could. For the most part the cells were used to discipline recent arrivals at the camp, usually with the hope of extracting military information. The building itself was a converted storage barn on the edge of the compound. Most of it (as was usual in Korea) had been sunk below ground level. Here, with an ingenuity typical of his calling, the commandant had built a series of minuscule cells that were, in reality, no more than pens. Some of these individual jails were mere upended coffins, just large enough for a man to stand upright or crouch in twisted slumber. Others resembled Pullman berths cast in concrete. . . . The camp doctor had seen many prisoners enter that converted storage barn. A few had emerged in time, ready to babble the information Pak sought. Other more stubborn inmates had gone straight to the camp cemetery, with no detour to the hospital.

"Well, Captain Scott? Need I tell you more?"

He came back to the commandant's office, and Pak's ever-tranquil smile. A single blow of his fist would spoil that feline grin beyond repair: he resisted the impulse in time. "You've said quite enough, Colonel."

"At last we understand each other. I have played my trump card, Doctor. As you can see, it takes the trick."

"May I see my friends?"

"Of course—if you feel up to it. Believe me, I'm trying to be reasonable."

In the compound the prisoners were clustered thickly around the barracks. Paul caught the knowing glances of his own group and realized that they had drawn the worst conclusions from his long sojourn in the commandant's quarters. Reason told him to approach his former friends and exhibit his wounds. A perverse impulse made him thrust both hands into his pockets and continue in silence to the warehouse as though he were bound on a routine medical check.

As always, two guards stood at the doorway. The manner in which they saluted, before they stepped back to admit him, struck a jarring note: had he worn the enemy uniform, the two blue-quilted marionettes could not have seemed more deferential. Paul closed his ears to the hostile murmur in the compound and plunged down the stairway leading to the detention cells.

A turnkey with a bull's-eye lantern beside him had been dozing on a stool at the near end of the slimy corridor; he sprang instantly to his feet, another indication that Pak had already set the stage for his visit. Paul followed the man in silence as the bobbing lantern led the way through utter blackness; there was a low, constant moaning that was almost but not quite human, a stench that seemed older than the Stone Age. . . . Kay's cell was at the far end of the corridor, a box bare of furniture save for a little straw, lightless and without ventilation. There was a grating flush with the low ceiling.

The turnkey put the lantern into Paul's hand and drew back a deferential pace. A full half minute elapsed before he could force himself to lift the bull's-eye and peer inside.

It was hard to believe that the figure in dungarees, hunched between the stone walls like a broken jack-in-the-box, was Kay Storey. She did not lift her eyes at once, though the lantern was trained directly upon her bowed head. This in itself was chilling evidence that she had been under constant scrutiny since the steel door had clanged shut.

"It's Paul, Kay."

"Paul?"

He had spoken in a husky whisper, half afraid to disturb her numb repose when he had no solace to offer. Her reply was dreamlike, almost inaudible. The sudden, incredulous widening of her eyes when she lifted her head at last stabbed him to the heart.

"I thought you'd never come," she said quietly. It was a simple statement, with no hint of reproach.

"Pak only told me a moment ago—"

"What have I done, darling?"

"Nothing, Kay. Nothing at all—"

"Then why would he put me here? He knows I have no military information."

Paul glanced at the guard, who stood above him with folded arms and the familiar, unblinking stare that seemed an extension of his uniform. Uncertain of the man's English, he wondered if he could risk the truth. It was surely a needless cruelty to hold back the reason for Kay's confinement in this modern oubliette. Anything was better than the nameless terrors that surrounded her.

"Have you seen Father Tim?" he asked—if only to gain time.

"We were brought here together. Does *he* know why?"

"I haven't talked to him," Paul admitted. "I'm not even sure I can tell you—"

"Then it *is* something we've done?"

"No, darling. Pak is using you both—in a game he's playing with me." Once the basic fact was out, he found he could tell her everything, omitting only the worst details of his treatment in the hands of Major Sung.

Kay heard him out in silence—with only a gasp of pity at his mention of Sung. Watching her chin lift at the end, he saw that she had taken the news with far more courage than he had mustered. "Now that I'm here," she said slowly, "I wonder why he didn't think of it sooner."

"Strange as it sounds, Pak is something of a scholar. He believes the doctrine he preaches—and he takes pride in his skill as a debater. I think he hopes to win me over—even now."

"Are you sure they won't torture you again?"

"Reasonably. As a doctor, I'm too valuable to damage."

"Then don't worry a moment about *us*. Pak won't let us die. If he did, he'd lose the only weapon he has."

"Just because I've refused to give in so far, I can't let you and the padre suffer. I'm going back now—and tell Pak he's won."

"But you can't, darling. I won't let you."

He could not help smiling, despite the pity that twisted his heart. "How can you stop me?"

"You'll stop yourself, Paul—when you think it over. Pak hasn't won. He

couldn't break you with torture. Why should we break, just because we're
locked up underground?"

"It's worse than that. You've seen what a few weeks in these cells can do
to a man."

"You mean the ones that gave in—and the punishment cases? The
Chinese didn't care if they lived or died. Father Tim and I are here for
another reason. Pak's counting on you to give in right away. When he sees
you won't he'll probably release us."

He hated to argue with her, to drive home the hopeless truth that Pak
would stop at nothing. "You could be right," he said. "I doubt it."

"Talk to the padre. I'm sure he'll say the same."

He had known she would answer thus, from the moment he peered into
the cell: he had come down the corridor determined to counter all her
arguments, to insist on saving her. He had not expected that her own
strength would weaken his decision.

"You'd endure this for my sake, Kay?"

"For all our sakes. Prison life hasn't been too hard on me, so far. I can
thank you for that, Paul. I'll feel that I've paid you back if I can keep you
from signing that confession. Besides, the armistice may come at any
moment—"

"We've lived on that hope for a year."

"Let's live with it a bit longer. Promise you won't give in, darling?"

"I'll promise—for now."

He left her on that, with only a whispered endearment. The turnkey
took the lantern and led the way down a second corridor to the chaplain's
cell.

This detention pen, by way of contrast, was one of the horizontal type, a
concrete shelf with bars down its length: there was just room enough for the
occupant to turn from side to side. Father Tim lay there serenely with his
hands crossed upon his breast. It was an attitude of repose suggesting (all
too graphically) the effigy of a crusader on some medieval tomb. But the
priest's smile of recognition was both warm and untroubled when Paul
thrust an arm through the gratings and pressed the thin hand.

"It was good of you to come, Paul."

"I'd have come sooner—if they'd let me."

The chaplain nodded. "You needn't explain: I've learned a good deal of
Chinese this past year. Apparently you made Major Sung lose face: the
guards are betting he'll be transferred."

"I'm afraid my refusal to give in has helped nobody, Father. It's the
reason you and Kay are here."

"I know that, Paul. And I know you won't change your mind."

"Frankly I came here to tell you I'd already changed it."

"Until you talked to Kay?"

Paul glanced sharply at the priest, but Father Tim's expression of serene
acceptance was unchanged: it was not the first time he had anticipated a
thought. "I'm not sure, Padre. Tell me what to do."

"Leave us."

"Here?"

"Don't deprive us of our little moment of resistance. We'll not yield to the
godless the first time we're tested."

"Maybe that's what I'm afraid of. That you'll never ask for mercy until
it's too late."

"Did you ask the commandant for mercy, Paul? Or Major Sung?"

"Pak has a dozen germ-warfare confessions. Can one more make that
much difference?"

"It must, Paul. Remember, the best brains in Asia will ask for real evidence before they'll accept so monstrous a charge."

"Padre, the girl I love is being left to die in darkness. How can I condemn her to that?"

"The girl you love will be the first to cheer when you stand up to Pak." A spasm of coughing shook the priest's frail body, and he turned his head away. "You'd better go, Paul Seeing us like this has only distressed you needlessly."

"How long will *you* last here—with that cough?"

The coughing had subsided and the chaplain could speak again. "I've given no thought to dying, Paul. And I have refused to let myself suffer. The mind can rise above most pain, if the heart has faith. It's a lesson you'll learn in time."

"Perhaps I'm learning it now," said Paul slowly. He was remembering the agony of the bamboo torture—and the strange release that had lifted him, however briefly, above the anguish of his body. It was only natural that the cough-racked figure before him should recall that experience and its aftermath. At this moment—when the priest seemed to totter on the edge of extinction and could still ignore the void—he felt the stirring of their greatest kinship.

"Go back to the compound," said Father Tim. "Take up your duties again as though nothing had happened. Tonight, before you sleep, say a prayer—for all of us. You'll find the strength to go on tomorrow. I'd stake my life on that."

"You already have, Padre."

The priest smiled. "Only faith is eternal, Paul. And even that can get a bit tarnished if it isn't reaffirmed."

VI

A few moments later, when he knocked on Colonel Hardin's door, Paul knew it was the counsel of desperation that brought him there. He had spoken his last coherent word to Hardin months ago (so far as the colonel himself was concerned). The present visit was solely for the record.

To his surprise, the C.O. received him at once. His manner was nearly affable as he accepted Paul's stiff-armed salute and waved him to a chair.

"You may sit down, Captain Scott. I gather you're somewhat done in."

"I'm afraid I am, Colonel," Paul said grimly. "Until an hour ago I was unable to walk."

"Did you spend the last day in Pak's office?"

"When I wasn't in the interrogation room. Dr. Chang gave me an injection of morphine after that was over." Hardin's apparent solicitude had already thrown Paul off balance. Knowing the C.O.'s power, he was positive that the man had reconstructed his acts to the last detail. Nevertheless, as a junior officer it was necessary that he make his report. He told his story from the beginning with no special pleading—including his visit to solitary.

"So you couldn't wait to see how the chaplain and Miss Storey had fared."

"I hope I did right, sir." Paul continued to watch Hardin warily—wondering when this teasing technique would end.

"Your courage does you credit," Hardin admitted. "So does your concern for your friends. Unfortunately your fellow prisoners won't understand too well."

"Nobody could believe I *enjoyed* a night in Pak's office?"

"I've heard a dozen accounts of that stay, Captain. The least damaging rumor states that you were drinking with the commandant and trying to curry favor by losing to him at chess."

"Do *you* think I'm a progressive, Colonel?"

"At the moment," said Hardin, "I'm not sure what to think. It might help if you'd explain the next deal you have in mind."

"Isn't the next move yours, sir? Obviously I've done all I can."

"So far—if your story is true—you've done nothing."

"Colonel, will you intercede?"

"As a protest for your treatment?"

"Never mind me. For the chaplain—and Miss Storey."

"How can I intercede in a matter outside my province?"

"You have influence with the commandant, sir: he's put you in charge of all prisoners. With armistice talks proceeding, you can say he's committed a grave error—"

"How has he erred? By sending two prisoners to solitary, as a disciplinary measure?"

"I've explained what's behind the move."

"Suppose your story is true, Scott—in every particular. The threat is to you, not to the camp as a whole."

"Does that mean you'll do nothing?"

"I am responsible only for the administration of the barracks. This is a propaganda matter instigated by the Security Police. How can I interfere?"

"Surely you could go to Colonel Pak. As a matter of common humanity—"

"Since when has a gook been human?"

Paul tried one more time, though he was all but choking with rage and despair. "Chaplain O'Fallon and Miss Storey are the two best-loved people in the compound. When the news gets out that they're in solitary—"

"A few of the prisoners will be distressed, of course. But at times like these the average soldier thinks only of himself. Things would be worse if I meddled. It could have repercussions on *everyone's* welfare."

Paul bowed his head in silent admission of defeat: he got up slowly, feeling the pain of last night's beatings run down his legs in a rocket burst of nerves. "As you wish, sir. If you'll excuse me—"

"A moment, Captain. You aren't dismissed."

"I'm sorry, sir. After last night—"

"Come to attention, dammit!"

Paul clenched his teeth and flung his body into the straining brace the order demanded. It was sheer torment to hold the pose: as a matter of pride he knew that he would not budge until Hardin gave his dismissal—and that his level eyes would force the other to turn aside.

"Yes, Colonel?"

"As I said, the next deal is yours, not mine. I'll wait for you to show your hand."

"Are you suggesting I sign that confession?"

"Far from it; in your place I'd know my duty to my country. However the whole camp is convinced you've some kind of understanding with the Chinese. Where there's smoke there must be fire."

"Will that be all, Colonel?"

"Go, by all means. I see you're about to commune with your conscience. Far be it from me to interfere."

"I'll ask one question first," said Paul. "Outside of your own group, just three people know the true story of Hill 1049—and are prepared to tell it after the armistice. Are you planning to destroy two of them here? And if you succeed, how will you dispose of me?"

Hardin's grin widened as he jerked a thumb toward the door. "Don't put ideas in my head, Scott. It could be dangerous."

Stumbling down the path to the hospital, Paul found it necessary to pause for a few long breaths before his sick frustration could spend itself. When he had assumed his daytime mask again he strode into the hospital without returning the curious glances that followed him.

Let them think the worst, he told himself, let them take Hardin's story as gospel. At least there would be work piled up in the wards. He would need the numbing pressure of that work to ease the battle he would now be fighting alone.

VII

In the weeks that followed, Paul could almost welcome a series of epidemics that raged through the barracks in defiance of all medical logic.

The first was a mysterious pyrexia that menaced prisoners and guards alike, which he finally diagnosed as acute hemorrhagic fever spread by mites. A thorough dusting with DDT powder stopped that menace before it could take a single life. Next came a bout with the scourge of all concentration camps—dysentery in its most virulent form. This time the ancient plague swept to the door of Hardin's own quarters, killing Sergeant Luppino and driving the C.O. into a state of complete isolation. Last and most vexing was a prolonged bout of virus hepatitis that he could only let burn itself out for lack of any specific treatment.

Weeks grew into months, another savage winter smote the camp—and Paul was, quite literally, too busy to think beyond the problems of the moment. Each night, as Father Tim had directed, he prayed for the chaplain and for Kay—and, by some alchemy he dared not explore, the prayer sustained him through the morrow. . . . Again and again, when he could spare a little time from his duties, he made desperate attempts to penetrate the catacombs of solitary, but on each occasion entry was barred.

Bribery of a guard whose ills Paul had treated produced bits of meager information. At least he could tell himself that Kay and the padre were alive and in reasonable health. Fighting a rear-guard action with his deepest instincts, insisting that he must find the strength to reject Pak's bargain, he made no attempt to seek another interview with the commandant. . . . He was hardly surprised when a message reached him one icy December evening, stating that Pak had just been admitted to the hospital and required his services immediately. The new patient's ulcer had kicked up before: Paul had always realized that someday more than anti-acid pills would be needed to control it.

When he entered the emergency room of the hospital he found Pak stretched on the couch, his face drawn with pain. Dr. Chang, in the act of releasing a syringe of morphine in the commandant's arm, drew back to allow an examination. Between them they had diagnosed the nature of Pak's ailment long ago: both had agreed that the appearance of real complications was only a matter of time.

A quick check on the patient's abdominal muscles (rigid as boards and exquisitely tender to pressure) was all the confirmation Paul needed. He had already sent for Sergeant Furness when Chang returned with the X-ray plate. As they had expected, the film showed a bubble inside the peritoneal cavity, beneath the diaphragm. It was proof positive of an opening in the stomach or duodenum from which air had escaped, along with the scalding acid contents of those organs.

The sergeant was in the operating room when Paul appeared there to check on the preparations Dr. Chang had made. Sometime in the past month (time had a way of blurring, these days) Corporal Jackson had left his hospital duties entirely and moved into Hardin's quarters after a long and adroit wooing by Master Sergeant Bates. In the interval the sergeant had developed into an adequate anesthetist. Now, as the two men moved about their task of readying the instruments, Paul could sense a reluctance in Furness' movements—a slowdown that had grown familiar of late when they aided camp personnel.

"Aren't you well, Sergeant?"

"I'm fine, Doc."

Paul gave his anesthetist a covert glance. Over the past week—as he was too well aware—Furness had been dropping into Hardin's cabin for an occasional meal: he could guess that the sergeant had dined there tonight, if only from the air of well-being that surrounded him.

"What's with Mr. Big, sir?"

"Mr. Big?"

"The gook in the consulting room."

"My diagnosis is perforated duodenal ulcer."

"You mean you're goin' to *operate?*"

"Of course."

"Cap'n, d'you mind if I bow out?"

"Of course I mind. Who else is competent to give the anesthetic?"

"What about Chang?"

"Dr. Chang will pass instruments. I'm afraid that's all he's good for."

"I'd still like to bow out, sir."

"You'll stay where you are, Sergeant. That's a direct order."

For an instant doctor and medic matched glares across the sterile gleam of the operating table. Watching Furness' eyes go blank with fury, Paul braced himself for the sergeant's departure: Hardin, he was sure, would sustain any act of insubordination. Then, with a profound sense of relief, he watched discipline reassert itself.

"Very good, sir."

"You can get ready, Sergeant. I'll have another look at the patient."

In the emergency room he found the commandant relaxed under the opiate and talking in whispers with the Chinese intern. There was no fear in Pak's eyes as he bent above the couch.

"Chang has prepared me for the worst, Dr. Scott," he said. "Am I about to die?"

"Not at all. An operation of this kind is simple if it's performed by a capable surgeon. I need hardly add that there is only one surgeon in this camp—myself."

Pak waved Dr. Chang from the room. "Is this by any chance an attempt to bargain?"

"Precisely. Your life—for two others."

"So the chaplain and Miss Storey have been on your mind of late. I was beginning to fear you had spurned my offer."

"I'm not interested in your offer. For once, Colonel, I hold the trump card. You are in no real danger at the moment, thanks to our prompt diagnosis. But you will probably die by morning if I don't correct your condition."

"Chang has explained that much, Dr. Scott. The question is—will you really refuse to operate, if I do not free Miss Storey and the chaplain?"

"You'd refuse in my place, wouldn't you?"

"I am not in your place, Captain Scott. And you are not Colonel Pak. If you were, life might be simpler for us both."

Paul did not speak for a long moment. The Chinese, of course, had put his finger on the single weakness in an otherwise perfect plan. "Are you sure you know me that well, Colonel?" he finally asked.

"Well enough, certainly, to put my life in your hands."

"You must realize there is a point beyond which you cannot push the strongest man."

Pak smiled cryptically, out of the relaxation of the morphia. "Eventually I'm sure that even you will reach that point," he said. "Tonight you are still an American surgeon and a Christian. As such, you can never bargain with lives."

Paul turned on his enemy with a curse on his lips—but the commandant had already drifted into limbo with the same relaxed smile. Shouting for Chang to prepare the patient, he went to his consulting room and buried his face in his hands: tonight, the tears that filled his eyelids rose from a well of pure despair. . . .

As he had expected, the operation was a textbook affair: there was no real element of danger, once he had subjected Sergeant Furness to a narrow-eyed check and assured himself that the anesthesia was flowing smoothly. Chang, as usual, was a bungler with the instruments—but the surgery was elementary, and Paul had long since learned to manage his own retractors. A suction pump cleared the area in short order, once the incision was established: the perforation was a classic one, in the duodenum, just beyond its juncture with the stomach wall.

The perforation—it was in the duodenum, and easily accessible—was no larger than a match head. Paul closed it with a catgut suture. Then, reaching for a tab of omentum (the fatty sheet that draped the abdominal organs like an apron), he secured a small patch of this tissue over the area for re-enforcement. When he had closed the incision he gave the patient an injection from the small store of penicillin that remained in the medicine chest and made his entry in the record. The job had been done in a trifle over twenty minutes. Par for the course, he thought grimly, and stood back to permit two male nurses to wheel out the patient.

Five minutes later, when he returned from the scrub room, he saw that Sergeant Furness had thrown his mask and gown on the floor and departed without a word of good night.

VII

Colonel Pak's convalescence was a prolonged one. Because of the severe winter weather (which twined icy fingers through the whole camp, including the jerry-built hospital), the patient was threatened for a time with pneumonia, and special drugs were flown from Mukden to assure his recovery. It was not until the first signs of spring were apparent beyond the barbed wire that the commandant was able to transfer to his regular quarters again and resume his work—after a fashion—from an easy chair.

Once his patient was off the critical list, Paul had held aloof, permitting Chang to handle the medications. Three days after Pak's departure from the hospital he received the expected summons to his office.

In a dressing gown and mandarin cap the Chinese looked oddly unmilitary—and resigned as a philosopher who has put most earthly lures behind him. The hands that rested on the arms of the chair trembled just a little, belying the man's air of repose; the eyes he fixed on the camp doctor had all their remembered fire.

"I've wanted to thank you for some time, Dr. Scott," he said in a tired voice. "You'll forgive me if my gratitude is expressed so tardily?"

"You've no reason for thanks, Colonel Pak. I did no more than my duty; as I told you, the operation was a simple one."

"Be that as it may, I feel a great obligation toward you. Will you accept living quarters here in the future?"

"My accommodations are adequate now."

"A pallet in a barracks where you've been ostracized for months?"

Paul shrugged. It was true that he had been shunned by the entire camp since the operation, but no one could change that. "You know I've just one thing to ask of you," he said. "Release the chaplain and Miss Storey."

"Sorry—my price for their release is unchanged." Pak turned the chair toward the desk and took two sheets of paper from a drawer. "Here is your confession, Captain—typed in duplicate. You need only sign both copies— and your friends will be under your care at once."

"You must realize they both advised me to resist you to the end."

The commandant's eyebrows lifted. "Captain Scott, the *end,* as you call it, may be nearer than you think."

Paul felt his heart constrict. From the start, he'd had reports from the guards assuring him that both captives were surviving their ordeal. Still, in the hell of that underground dungeon, death could strike quickly.

"Are you telling me they're dead, Colonel?"

Pak shook his head. "Not yet, Doctor. But I'm afraid that things went somewhat further than I intended, due to my own long illness." He held up a detaining hand as the camp doctor turned instinctively toward the door. "Patience—you may see them both in a moment. There is still time if you'll co-operate—"

"What have you done to them?"

"Not I, Captain Scott—solitary confinement. Dr. Chang tells me that Miss Storey is suffering again from a condition which you treated last year."

"Amebiasis?"

"That is the word. I understand that it can be dangerous unless treated properly."

"And Father O'Fallon?"

"He has a definite tuberculosis of the lungs, with small hemorrhages." The commandant was speaking calmly, in a dry-as-dust tone, as though he were disposing of a boring detail of camp routine. "I am surprised by your astonishment, Captain. You must have realized that their health would break in time, if not their spirits. After all, that was the reason I confined them."

Paul could not trust himself to speak again. While he fought for control he deliberately reviewed the illness for which he had treated Kay almost a year ago. The amebic infection had been mild then, but he could well imagine the ravages of a relapse that had gone unchecked. In Father Tim's case, he was not surprised. He had expected something like this for months—and the time spent on that damp stone shelf had merely hastened the crisis.

"Why did you wait so long to tell me?" It was an effort to force out the question, but his voice was steady now.

"My illness confused the timetable, Doctor. If you'll permit me, I'm prepared to atone for the lapse."

"How can you?"

"Would you care to examine the patients—here and now?"

"Here?"

The commandant tapped a bell on his desk. "I took the liberty of having them brought over. Time, as you will see, is now of the essence."

The outer door had already swung open to admit four litter-bearers and their dreadful burdens. Paul could not quite choke down the cry of revulsion that rose in his throat at the first sight of Kay. Emaciated as she was, he would hardly have known her had he discovered her in an anonymous hospital bed. There was no recognition in the fever-hot eyes that brushed him, then closed again in sockets that were no more than skin-covered bone. Only his medical training saved him from a complete breakdown as he knelt by the litter to examine her.

Desperate though her condition was, he saw at once that she was not in the last extremity. The pulse, for all its galloping rhythm, was still strong— and the skin (burning and loose from the dehydration that was a symptom of her illness) retained some of its former resilience. But Pak was right: his timetable of destruction had gone awry. Had Kay been left in solitary a few more days, it would have been too late.

"I'll save you, darling. With God's help, I'll save you." Paul had addressed the promise to no one in particular. Certainly there was no way of reaching the wasted human being on the litter; Kay had long since fallen into delirium too deeply to react to speech.

"Don't sign the confession, Paul!"

The voice startled him, and he turned—with a guilty flush—to Father Tim. At first glance Paul had the bizarre certainty that time was a dream: the priest seemed exactly as he remembered him from his visit to solitary. Even the air of repose was identical—the hands crossed on the breast; the prophet's beard like a flaming banner above them. . . . Once again, the compulsion of his call saved Paul from tumbling into madness. It took an effort to leave Kay's side even for a moment, but he forced himself to move to the second litter. The color burning in the padre's cheeks was ominous confirmation of Chang's report; so was the familiar cough that seized him when he tried to speak again.

"Not another word, Father. You're in your doctor's hands now."

"Don't sign, Paul."

"I'm afraid I've no choice."

"Don't yield to the godless!" This time the effort proved too much, and the spasm of coughing seemed never-ending. The padre closed his eyes as he fought for breath: he made no further objection when Paul signaled to the bearers to lift the stretcher.

"Will you send them to the hospital, Colonel?"

"Of course, Doctor."

Paul did not meet the commandant's eyes as he snatched up the two sheets of paper that lay on the desk, and forced his mind to take in the neatly typed words:

> I, Captain Paul Scott, a medical officer in the United
> States Army, make this confession of my own free
> will and without torture . . .

There was more, but he did not read further before he slashed a signature across both copies, flung the sheets at Pak, and hurried out on the trail of the stretcher-bearers.

THE PRESIDIO

I

Colonel Sellers' gavel, breaking Paul's recital, seemed unusually loud in the quiet of the courtroom. Meeting the president's cold but impartial stare, Paul was grateful for the interruption. The wall clock announced that he had been only an hour on the stand—but he felt he had been talking forever.

"The court will question the witness, Mr. Saunders."

Watching Hi step back, Paul saw that his relief was shared. The defense lawyer had permitted his client to use his own words, with a minimum of direct questions: from Hi's viewpoint the intervention of the court might be a hopeful sign. . . . One of the most ominous aspects of Paul's testimony had been the aloofness of both bench and prosecution. Throughout, MacArdle had doodled on a scratch-pad without a single objection. Sellers' own withdrawal had seemed just as definite.

"You say that Miss Storey's recovery was a *miracle,* Captain?"

"There's no other word to describe it."

"What of your own skills as a doctor? Weren't they of help, too?"

"I'd reached the limit of my skill. And she was still sinking."

It was true enough, Paul thought—with a familiar ache at the memory. Even after the chloroquine phosphate and the plasma units had done their work, the fever had continued to rage in Kay's blood stream. Indeed (as is so often the case with a patient whose condition is desperately poor), the treatment itself had seemed to cause an actual flare-up of the infection. For two long days he had done his poor best to save her. During that time he had stayed at her bedside, holding her in his arms when she cried out in her delirium—hoping, at least, that she would realize he was there while the flame of her life force wavered.

"When the crisis came," he said, "I could do nothing else but pray."

It had happened as simply as that, and as incredibly. Since it was so incredible, how could he make Sellers accept it?

After two days of alternate chills and fever Kay's body had seemed frail as a feather, the lips and ear lobes blue from deadly oxygen lack. It was then that the prayer had come unbidden to his lips. The words had poured out in a torrent—not for himself, this time, not for any desire of his own, but for this woman he loved so greatly. . . . When had the voice answered him, assuring him that his terrors were groundless? When had he found his own strength again, in the knowledge that Kay would live?

"On the dawn of the third day," he said, "her fever broke. After that I was sure of her recovery. But it wasn't *my* doing."

The president of the court continued to stare down from the dais. "You may resume examination, Mr. Saunders," he said at last. The small shrug that accompanied the words was more emphatic than any formal dismissal.

Paul closed his eyes as Hi took up his questioning: he could feel his voice droop with defeat as he made the first mechanical response. Miracles, it seemed, are not the stuff on which court-martials are won: he was positive that his whole story had fallen on deaf ears.

Nonetheless he forced himself to tell that story to the end. His hopeless struggle to save Father Tim. Kay's long but steady convalescence. His insistence that she leave with Colonel Hardin's group when the armistice was a reality. . . . Finally he told of the padre's need of his presence, the fact that he had informed Hardin that he must remain, his belief that Hardin would take the truth to Panmunjom. He spoke briefly of Father Tim's death, of his own repatriation, and of the salvo of flash bulbs that had greeted him when he crossed the truce line.

Waiting for MacArdle to assemble his notes, he was glad that he had done no more than mention Father Tim's last hours on earth. Like Kay's return from death, that was sacred ground. Why, when the court had refused to accept a miracle, would they believe the priest could die with a smile on his lips and his faith unshaken?

The soul of Father Timothy O'Fallon (Paul told himself solemnly) had been at peace when he wrote the last entry in his confession book. His mind (divorced from the ills of the flesh) had remained sunny to the end. But he could never put that resignation into words. It was enough to know that Father Tim had absolved him of all guilt when he closed his eyes. Whatever the verdict of this court, he would treasure that absolution always.

II

Major James MacArdle approached the stand with his notes neatly folded, his expression almost benign. "Captain Scott, you are aware that you're under oath?"

"I am."

The prosecutor launched his attack on Paul's testimony with quiet good humor; by his very underplaying, he suggested that he was performing an elementary task, with all the dispatch at his command. He covered Paul's defiance of Hardin at Sinmak, his appointment as medical officer at the prison camp, his operation on Colonel Pak. The duplicate of the confession was brought to the box and offered to the witness.

"Do you acknowledge that this is your signature, Captain?"

"I do."

"You persist in the statement that you signed this document to save Miss Storey and Chaplain O'Fallon?"

"That was my only reason."

"You did not sign to obtain favors for yourself? Or to help the cause of Communism?"

"I signed to preserve two lives."

"Aren't you ascribing a great deal to yourself, Captain? First, you assert that you saved the whole prison camp in a meningitis epidemic. Next, you magnanimously save the life of the prison commandant. Now you tell me that you saved the lives of Miss Storey and Chaplain O'Fallon."

"Not Chaplain O'Fallon. In my own opinion I was the cause of his death."

"Then you're not infallible after all, Captain?"

"I have never claimed to be. Chaplain O'Fallon died because I originally withheld my signature—after months of pressure."

"You still maintain, in the face of Colonel Hardin's statements, that you signed only to save two people from death?"

"I do."

"Let us move up to the time of repatriation, Captain. You have heard Colonel Hardin say that he knew nothing of the chaplain's alleged hemorrhage. Do you still assert that such a thing did happen?"

"It happened as I have described it."

"Isn't it true that both you and the chaplain preferred to remain with the Communists?"

MacArdle's expression of patient industry remained unchanged when the court had sustained Hi's instant objection. "Captain, you have testified that you notified both the prison commandant and Colonel Hardin of your intention to remain."

"I did so notify them both."

"You didn't, by any chance, invent this story to protect yourself—*after* you decided to renounce Communism?"

"The facts are as I have stated."

The prosecutor tossed up his hands. "Since you persist in evading the truth, there is little point in my detaining you. No further questions at this time."

Hi Saunders came forward to re-examine. "Captain, I wish to establish one point with the court. When you decided to remain with the chaplain did you know of any authority that justified your action?"

"Yes—Article Fourteen of Title Three in the provision of the Geneva Convention."

MacArdle sat up in his chair for the first time that day: Paul noted the hard worry wrinkle that had suddenly defaced his forehead. At the defense table Hi had already opened the book that lay there.

"I will read Article Fourteen into the record: *It shall be lawful for belligerents reciprocally to authorize, by means of private arrangements, the retention in the camp of physicians and attendants to care for prisoners of their own country.* The defense contends that Captain Scott, through his notifications—to both the prison commandant and to Colonel Hardin, his own commanding officer—has completely fulfilled this provision. Therefore the defense moves at this time that, as to Specifications Three and Four of Charge One, a finding of not guilty be entered on the grounds that they have not been proven."

The courtroom stirred before the president's gavel fell. "You may state your reasons for this motion, Mr. Saunders."

"First, on the matter of Specification Three. It alleges that Captain Scott signed a confession for the purpose of obtaining preferential treatment. Testimony has shown that the defendant branded the so-called confession as a lie at the time of signing, and that the signing itself was a formality, performed to save lives. Specification Four alleges that Captain Scott refused repatriation for personal reasons. He has just testified that he remained at Pyongyang to care for another prisoner of war, who was too ill to travel, and such conduct is justified by the Geneva Convention."

MacArdle was on his feet. "This is a preposterous request," he said—he was really shouting now, his pose of tolerance forgotten. "No such thing has been proved. Colonel Hardin's testimony is in direct contradiction to that of Captain Scott's."

"The court is aware of that fact, Major MacArdle," said the president drily. "Mr. Saunders, is it your intention to imply that Colonel Hardin's testimony regarding these specifications of Charge One constitutes perjury?"

"The defense so contends," said Hi. "Were it not for the court's ruling—which prohibits testimony on events occurring before the capture of Hill 1049—the reason for this perjury could be shown clearly."

"This is a grave charge, Mr. Saunders."

"So are the charges against the accused, sir."

"Do you wish to re-examine the witness further?"

"Not at this time."

"You may step down, Captain Scott. The court will withdraw to consider defense counsel's motion."